THE

WAVERLEY NOVELS

BY

SIR WALTER SCOTT, BART.

Old Mortality
The Heart of Midlothian

NEW YORK
THOMAS Y. CROWELL & COMPANY
PUBLISHERS

OLD MORTALITY.

TALES OF MY LANDLORD

First Series

Hear, Land o' Cakes and brither Scots,
Frae Maidenkirk to Johnny Groat's,
If there's a hole in a' your coats,
       I rede ye tent it ;
A chiel's amang you takin' notes,
       An' faith he'll prent it !
BURNS

Ahora bien, dixo il Cura, traedme, senor huésped, aquesos libros, que los quiero ver. Que me place, respondió el, y entrando en su aposento, sacó dél una maletilla vieja cerrada con una cadenilla, y abriéndola halló en ella tres libros grandes y unos papeles de muy buena letra escritos de mano.—DON QUIXOTE, Parte I., Capitulo xxxii.

It is mighty well, said the priest; pray, landlord, bring me those books, for I have a mind to see them. With all my heart, answered the host; and going to his chamber, he brought out a little old cloke-bag, with a padlock and chain to it, and opening it, he took out three large volumes, and some manuscript papers written in a fine character.—JARVIS's *Translation.*

INTRODUCTION TO OLD MORTALITY

THE remarkable person called by the title of Old Mortality was well known in Scotland about the end of the last century. His real name was Robert Paterson. He was a native, it is said, of the parish of Closeburn, in Dumfriesshire, and probably a mason by profession—at least educated to the use of the chisel. Whether family dissensions, or the deep and enthusiastic feeling of supposed duty, drove him to leave his dwelling, and adopt the singular mode of life in which he wandered, like a palmer, through Scotland, is not known. It could not be poverty, however, which prompted his journeys, for he never accepted anything beyond the hospitality which was willingly rendered him, and when that was not proffered, he always had money enough to provide for his own humble wants. His personal appearance, and favorite, or rather sole, occupation, are accurately described in the preliminary chapter of the following work.

It is about thirty years since, or more, that the Author met this singular person in the churchyard of Dunnottar, when spending a day or two with the late learned and excellent clergyman, Mr. Walker, the minister of that parish, for the purpose of a close examination of the ruins of the Castle of Dunnottar, and other subjects of antiquarian research in that neighborhood. Old Mortality chanced to be at the same place, on the usual business of his pilgrimage ; for the Castle of Dunnottar, though lying in the anti-covenanting district of the Mearns, was, with the parish churchyard, celebrated for the oppressions sustained there by the Cameronians in the time of James II.

It was in 1685, when Argyle was threatening a descent upon Scotland, and Monmouth was preparing to invade the west of England, that the privy council of Scotland, with cruel precaution, made a general arrest of more than a hundred persons in the southern and western provinces, supposed, from their religious principles, to be inimical to government, together with many women and children. These captives were driven northward like a flock of bullocks, but with less precaution to provide for their wants, and finally penned up in a subterranean dungeon in the Castle of Dunnottar, having a window opening to the front of a precipice which overhangs the German Ocean. They had suffered not a little on the journey, and were much hurt both at the scoffs of the northern Prelatists, and the mocks, gibes, and contemptuous tunes played by the fiddlers and pipers who had come from every quarter as they passed, to triumph over the revilers of their calling. The repose which the melancholy dungeon afforded them was anything but undisturbed. The guards made them pay for every indulgence, even that of water; and when some of the prisoners resisted a demand so unreasonable, and insisted on their right to have this necessary of life untaxed, their keepers emptied the water on the prison floor, saying, "If they were obliged to bring water for the canting Whigs, they were not bound to afford them the use of bowls or pitchers gratis."

In this prison, which is still termed the Whigs' Vault, several died of the diseases incidental to such a situation; and others broke their limbs, and incurred fatal injury, in desperate attempts to escape from their stern prison-house. Over the graves of these unhappy persons, their friends, after the Revolution, erected a monument with a suitable inscription.

This peculiar shrine of the Whig martyrs is very much honored by their descendants, though residing at a great distance from the land of their captivity and death. My friend, the Rev. Mr. Walker, told me that, being once upon a tour in the south of Scotland, probably about forty years since, he had the bad luck to involve himself in the labyrinth of passages and tracks which cross, in every direction, the extensive waste called Lochar Moss, near Dumfries, out of which it is scarcely possible for a stranger to extricate himself; and there was no small difficulty in procuring a guide, since such people as he saw were engaged in digging their peats—a work of paramount necessity, which will hardly brook interruption. Mr. Walker could, therefore, only procure unintelligible directions in the southern brogue, which differs widely from that of the Mearns. He was beginning to think himself in a serious dilemma, when he stated his case to a farmer of rather the better class, who was employed, as the others, in digging his winter fuel. The old man at first made the same excuse with those who had already declined acting as the traveller's guide; but perceiving him in great perplexity, and paying the respect due to his profession, "You are a clergyman, sir?" he said. Mr. Walker assented. "And I observe from your speech that you are from the north?" "You are right, my good friend," was the reply. "And may I ask if you have ever heard of a place called Dunnottar?" "I ought to know something about it, my friend," said Mr. Walker, "since I have been several years the minister of the parish." "I am glad to hear it," said the Dumfriesian, "for one of my near relations lies buried there, and there is, I believe, a monument over his grave. I would give half of what I am aught to know if it is still in existence." "He was one of those who perished in the Whigs' Vault at the castle?" said the minister; "for there are few southlanders besides lying in our churchyard, and none, I think, having monuments." "Even sae—even sae," said the old Cameronian, for such was the farmer. He then laid down his spade, cast on his coat, and heartily offered to see the minister out of the moss, if he should lose the rest of the *day's dargue*. Mr. Walker was able to requite him amply, in his opinion, by reciting the epitaph, which he remembered by heart. The old man was enchanted with finding the memory of his grandfather or great-grandfather faithfully recorded among the names of brother sufferers; and rejecting all other offers of recompense, only requested, after he had guided Mr. Walker to a safe and dry road, that he would let him have a written copy of the inscription.

It was while I was listening to this story, and looking at the monument referred to, that I saw Old Mortality engaged in his daily task of cleaning and repairing the ornaments and epitaphs upon the tomb. His appearance and equipment were exactly as described in the Novel. I was very desirous to see something of a person so singular, and expected to have done so, as he took up his quarters with the hospitable and liberal-spirited minister. But though Mr. Walker invited him up after dinner to partake of a glass of spirits and water, to which he was supposed not to be very averse, yet he would not speak frankly upon the subject of his occupation. He was in bad humor, and had, according to his phrase, no freedom for conversation with us.

His spirit had been sorely vexed by hearing, in a certain Aberdonian kirk, the psalmody directed by a pitch-pipe, or some similar instrument, which was to Old Mortality the abomination of abominations. Perhaps, after all, he did not feel himself at ease with his company; he might suspect the questions asked by a north-country minister and a young barrister to savor more of idle curiosity than profit. At any rate, in the phrase of John Bunyan, Old Mortality went on his way, and I saw him no more.

The remarkable figure and occupation of this ancient pilgrim was recalled to my memory by an account transmitted by my friend, Mr. Joseph Train, supervisor of excise at Dumfries, to whom I owe many obligations of a similar nature. From this, besides some other circumstances, among which are those of the old man's death, I learned the particulars described in the text. I am also informed that the old palmer's family, in the third generation, survives, and is highly respected both for talents and worth.

While these sheets were passing through the press, I received the following communication from Mr. Train, whose undeviating kindness had, during the intervals of laborious duty, collected its materials from an indubitable source:

"In the course of my periodical visits to the Glenkens, I have become intimately acquainted with Robert Paterson, a son of Old Mortality, who lives in the little village of Balmaclellan; and although he is now in the seventieth year of his age, preserves all the vivacity of youth—has a most retentive memory, and a mind stored with information far above what could be expected from a person in his station of life. To him I am indebted for the following particulars relative to his father and his descendants down to the present time.

"Robert Paterson, *alias* Old Mortality, was the son of Walter Paterson and Margaret Scott, who occupied the farm of Haggisha, in the parish of Hawick, during nearly the first half of the 18th century. Here Robert was born, in the memorable year 1715.

"Being the youngest son of a numerous family, he, at an early age, went to serve with an elder brother, named Francis, who rented, from Sir John Jardine of Applegarth, a small tract in Corncockle Moor, near Lochmaben. During his residence there he became acquainted with Elizabeth Gray, daughter of Robert Gray, gardener to Sir John Jardine, whom he afterwards married. His wife had been for a considerable time a cook-maid to Sir Thomas Kirkpatrick of Closeburn, who procured for her husband, from the Duke of Queensberry, an advantageous lease of the freestone quarry of Gatelowbrigg, in the parish of Morton. Here he built a house, and had as much land as kept a horse and cow. My informant cannot say with certainty the year in which his father took up his residence at Gatelowbrigg, but he is sure it must have been only a short time prior to the year 1746, as, during the memorable frost in 1740, he says his mother still resided in the service of Sir Thomas Kirkpatrick. When the Highlanders were returning from England on their route to Glasgow, in the year 1745-46, they plundered Mr. Paterson's

house at Gatelowbrigg, and carried him a prisoner as far as
Glenbuck, merely because he said to one of the straggling
army that their retreat might have been easily foreseen, as the
strong arm of the Lord was evidently raised, not only against
the bloody and wicked house of Stewart, but against all who
attempted to support the abominable heresies of the Church
of Rome.   From this circumstance it appears that Old Mortality had, even at that early period of his life, imbibed the
religious enthusiasm by which he afterwards became so much
distinguished.

"The religious sect called Hill-men, or Cameronians, was
at that time much noted for austerity and devotion, in imitation of Cameron, their founder, of whose tenets Old Mortality became a most strenuous supporter.   He made frequent
journeys into Galloway to attend their conventicles, and
occasionally carried with him gravestones from his quarry at
Gatelowbrigg, to keep in remembrance the righteous whose
dust had been gathered to their fathers.   Old Mortality was
not one of those religious devotees who, although one eye is
seemingly turned towards heaven, keep the other steadfastly
fixed on some sublunary object.   As his enthusiasm increased,
his journeys into Galloway became more frequent; and he
gradually neglected even the common prudential duty of providing for his offspring.   From about the year 1758, he neglected wholly to return from Galloway to his wife and five
children at Gatelowbrigg, which induced her to send her
eldest son Walter, then only twelve years of age, to Galloway
in search of his father.   After traversing nearly the whole of
that extensive district, from the Nick of Benncorie to the
Fell of Barhullion, he found him at last working on the
Cameronian monuments, in the old kirkyard of Kirkchrist,
on the west side of the Dee, opposite the town of Kirkcud-
bright.   The little wanderer used all the influence in his
power to induce his father to return to his family; but in
vain.   Mrs. Paterson sent even some of her female children
into Galloway in search of their father, for the same purpose
of persuading him to return home; but without any success.
At last, in the summer of 1768, she removed to the little up-
land village of Balmaclellan, in the Glenkens of Galloway,
where, upon the small pittance derived from keeping a little
school, she supported her numerous family in a respectable
manner.

"There is a small monumental stone in the farm of the
Caldon, near the House of the Hill, in Wigtonshire, which is
highly venerated as being the first erected, by Old Mortality,

to the memory of several persons who fell at that place in defence of their religious tenets in the civil war, in the reign of Charles Second.*

"From the Caldon, the labors of Old Mortality, in the course of time, spread over nearly all the Lowlands of Scotland. There are few churchyards in Ayrshire, Galloway, or Dumfriesshire, where the work of his chisel is not yet to be seen. It is easily distinguished from the work of any other artist by the primitive rudeness of the emblems of death, and of the inscriptions which adorn the ill-formed blocks of his erection. This task of repairing and erecting gravestones, practised without fee or reward, was the only ostensible employment of this singular person for upwards of forty years. The door of every Cameronian's house was indeed open to him at all times when he chose to enter, and he was gladly received as an inmate of the family ; but he did not invariably accept of these civilities, as may be seen by the following account of his frugal expenses, found, among other little papers (some of which I have likewise in my possession), in his pocket-book after his death :

Gatehouse of Fleet, 4th February 1796.

ROBERT PATERSON *debtor to* MARGARET CHRYSTALE

	£	s	d
To drye Lodginge for seven weeks	£0	4	1
To Four Auchlets of Ait Meal	0	3	4
To 6 Lippies of Potatoes	0	1	8
To Lend Money at the time of Mr. Reid's Sacrament	0	6	0
To 3 Chappins of Yell with Sandy the Keelman † .	0	0	9
	£0	15	5
Received in part . . .	0	10	0
Unpaid . . .	£0	5	5

"This statement shows the religious wanderer to have been very poor in his old age ; but he was so more by choice than through necessity, as at the period here alluded to his children were all comfortably situated, and were most anxious to keep their father at home, but no entreaty could induce him to alter his erratic way of life. He travelled from one churchyard to another, mounted on his old white pony, till the last day of his existence, and died, as you have described, at Bankhill, near Lockerby, on the 14th February 1801, in the eighty-

* The house was stormed by a Captain Orchard or Urquhart, who was shot in the attack.

† A well-known humorist, still alive, popularly called by the name of Old Keely-bags, who deals in the keel or chalk with which farmers mark their flocks.

sixth year of his age. As soon as his body was found, intimation was sent to his sons at Balmaclellan ; but, from the great depth of the snow at that time, the letter communicating the particulars of his death was so long detained by the way that the remains of the pilgrim were interred before any of his relations could arrive at Bankhill.

" The following is an exact copy of the account of his funeral expenses, the original of which I have in my possession :

Memorandum of the Funral Charges of Robert Paterson, who dyed at Bankhill on the 14th day of February 1801

	£	s.	d.
To a Coffon	£0	12	0
To Munting for do	0	2	8
To a Shirt for him	0	5	0
To a pair of Cotton Stockings	0	2	0
To Bread at the Founral	0	2	6
To Chise at ditto	0	3	0
To 1 pint Rume	0	4	6
To 1 pint Whiskie	0	4	6
To a man going to Annan	0	2	0
To the grave diger	0	1	0
To Linnen for a sheet to him	0	2	8
	£2	1	10
Taken off him when dead	1	7	6
	£0	14	4

"The above account is authenticated by the son of the deceased.

" My friend was prevented by indisposition from even going to Bankhill to attend the funeral of his father, which I regret very much, as he is not aware in what churchyard he was interred.

" For the purpose of erecting a small monument to his memory, I have made every possible inquiry, wherever 1 thought there was the least chance of finding out where Old Mortality was laid ; but I have done so in vain, as his death is not registered in the session-book of any of the neighboring parishes.* I am sorry to think that in all probability this singular person, who spent so many years of his lengthened

---

* This good intention was, however, carried out. A headstone was erected November, 1869, to the memory of Old Mortality in the churchyard of Caerlavrock, where there is satisfactory proof of his having been interred in the month of February, 1801. Mr. Train seems to have been misled in his information respecting the name of the village where Robert Paterson died. There is now strong evidence that not Bankhill, but Bankend, about fifteen miles from Bankhill, was the place where Old Mortality breathed his last (*Laing*).

existence in striving with his chisel and mallet to perpetuate the memory of many less deserving than himself, must remain even without a single stone to mark out the resting-place of his mortal remains.

"Old Mortality had three sons, Robert, Walter, and John; the former, as has been already mentioned, lives in the village of Balmaclellan, in comfortable circumstances, and is much respected by his neighbors. Walter died several years ago, leaving behind him a family now respectably situated in this point. John went to America in the year 1776, and, after various turns of fortune, settled at Baltimore."

Old Nol himself is said to have loved an innocent jest (see Captain Hodgson's *Memoirs*). Old Mortality somewhat resembled the Protector in this turn to festivity. Like Master Silence, he had been merry twice and thrice in his time; but even his jests were of a melancholy and sepulchral nature, and sometimes attended with inconvenience to himself, as will appear from the following anecdote:

The old man was at one time following his wonted occupation of repairing the tombs of the martyrs, in the churchyard of Girthon, and the sexton of the parish was plying his kindred task at no small distance. Some roguish urchins were sporting near them, and by their noisy gambols disturbing the old men in their serious occupation. The most petulant of the juvenile party were two or three boys, grandchildren of a person well known by the name of Cooper Climent. This artist enjoyed almost a monopoly in Girthon and the neighboring parishes for making and selling ladles, caups, bickers, bowls, spoons, cogues, and trenchers, formed of wood, for the use of the country people. It must be noticed that, notwithstanding the excellence of the cooper's vessels, they were apt, when new, to impart a reddish tinge to whatever liquor was put into them, a circumstance not uncommon in like cases.

The grandchildren of this dealer in wooden work took it into their head to ask the sexton what use he could possibly make of the numerous fragments of old coffins which were thrown up in opening new graves. "Do you not know," said Old Mortality, "that he sells them to your grandfather, who makes them into spoons, trenchers, bickers, bowies, and so forth?" At this assertion, the youthful group broke up in great confusion and disgust, on reflecting how many meals they had eaten out of dishes which, by Old Mortality's account, were only fit to be used at a banquet of witches or of ghouls. They carried the tidings home, when many a dinner was spoiled by the loathing which the intelligence imparted;

for the account of the materials was supposed to explain the reddish tinge which, even in the days of the cooper's fame, had·seemed somewhat suspicious.   The ware of Cooper Climent was rejected in horror, much to the benefit of his rivals the muggers, who dealt in earthenware.   The man of cutty-spoon and ladle saw his trade interrupted, and learned the reason, by his quondam customers coming upon him in wrath to return the goods which were composed of such unhallowed materials, and demand repayment of their money.   In this disagreeable predicament, the forlorn artist cited Old Mortality into a court of justice, where he proved that the wood he used in his trade was that of the staves of old wine-pipes bought from smugglers, with whom the country then abounded, a circumstance which fully accounted for their imparting a color to their contents.   Old Mortality himself made the fullest declaration that he had no other purpose in making the assertion than to check the petulance of the children.   But it is easier to take away a good name than to restore it. Cooper Climent's business continued to languish, and he died in a state of poverty.

OLD MORTALITY

CHAPTER I

PRELIMINARY

Why seeks he with unwearied toil
  Through death's dim walks to urge his way,
Reclaim his long-asserted spoil,
  And lead oblivion into day ?

LANGHORNE.

"Most readers," says the Manuscript of Mr. Pattieson, "must have witnessed with delight the joyous burst which attends the dismissing of a village school on a fine summer evening. The buoyant spirit of childhood, repressed with so much difficulty during the tedious hours of discipline, may then be seen to explode, as it were, in shout, and song, and frolic, as the little urchins join in groups on their playground, and arrange their matches of sport for the evening. But there is one individual who partakes of the relief afforded by the moment of dismission, whose feelings are not so obvious to the eye of the spectator, or so apt to receive his sympathy. I mean the teacher himself, who, stunned with the hum, and suffocated with the closeness of his schoolroom, has spent the whole day (himself against a host) in controlling petulance, exciting indifference to action, striving to enlighten stupidity, and laboring to soften obstinacy ; and whose very powers of intellect have been confounded by hearing the same dull lesson repeated a hundred times by rote, and only varied by the various blunders of the reciters. Even the flowers of classic genius, with which his solitary fancy is most gratified, have been rendered degraded in his imagination by their connection with tears, with errors, and with punishment; so that the *Eclogues* of Virgil and *Odes* of Horace are each inseparably allied in association with the sullen figure and monotonous recitation of some blubbering schoolboy. If to these mental

distresses are added a delicate frame of body, and a mind ambitious of some higher distinction than that of being the tyrant of childhood, the reader may have some slight conception
of the relief which a solitary walk in the cool of a fine summer
evening affords to the head which has ached, and the nerves
which have been shattered, for so many hours in plying the
irksome task of public instruction.

"To me these evening strolls have been the happiest hours
of an unhappy life ; and if any gentle reader shall hereafter
find pleasure in perusing these lucubrations, I am not unwilling
he should know that the plan of them has been usually traced
in those moments when relief from toil and clamor, combined
with the quiet scenery around me, has disposed my mind to
the task of composition.

"My chief haunt, in these hours of golden leisure, is the
banks of the small stream which, winding through a 'lone vale
of green bracken,' passes in front of the village school-house
of Gandercleugh.   For the first quarter of a mile, perhaps, I
may be disturbed from my meditations in order to return the
scrape or doffed bonnet of such stragglers among my pupils
as fish for trouts or minnows in the little brook, or seek rushes
and wild flowers by its margin.   But beyond the space I have
mentioned the juvenile anglers do not after sunset voluntarily
extend their excursions.   The cause is, that further up the
narrow valley, and in a recess which seems scooped out of the
side of the steep heathy bank, there is a deserted burial-ground,
which the little cowards are fearful of approaching in the
twilight.   To me, however, the place has an inexpressible
charm.   It has been long the favorite termination of my walks,
and, if my kind patron forgets not his promise, will (and probably at no very distant day) be my final resting-place after my
mortal pilgrimage.*

"It is a spot which possesses all the solemnity of feeling
attached to a burial-ground, without exciting those of a more
unpleasing description.   Having been very little used for many
years, the few hillocks which rise above the level plain are
covered with the same short velvet turf.   The monuments, of
which there are not above seven or eight, are half sunk in the
ground and overgrown with moss.   No newly erected tomb
disturbs the sober serenity of our reflections by reminding us
of recent calamity, and no rank-springing grass forces upon
our imagination the recollection, that it owes its dark luxuriance to the foul and festering remnants of mortality which
ferment beneath.   The daisy which sprinkles the sod, and

* See Peter Pattieson's Grave. Note 1.

the harebell which hangs over it, derive their pure nourishment from the dew of heaven, and their growth impresses us with no degrading or disgusting recollections. Death has indeed been here, and its traces are before us; but they are softened and deprived of their horror by our distance from the period when they have been first impressed. Those who sleep beneath are only connected with us by the reflection, that they have once been what we now are, and that, as their relics are now identified with their mother earth, ours shall at some future period undergo the same transformation.

"Yet, although the moss has been collected on the most modern of these humble tombs during four generations of mankind, the memory of some of those who sleep beneath them is still held in reverent remembrance. It is true that, upon the largest, and, to an antiquary, the most interesting monument of the group, which bears the effigies of a doughty knight in his hood of mail, with his shield hanging on his breast, the armorial bearings are defaced by time, and a few worn-out letters may be read at the pleasure of the decipherer, *Dns. Johan de Hamel*, or *Johan de Lamel*. And it is also true that of another tomb, richly sculptured with an ornamental cross, mitre, and pastoral staff, tradition can only aver that a certain nameless bishop lies interred there. But upon other two stones which lie beside may still be read in rude prose and ruder rhyme the history of those who sleep beneath them. They belong, we are assured by the epitaph, to the class of persecuted Presbyterians who afforded a melancholy subject for history in the times of Charles II. and his successor.* In returning from the battle of Pentland Hills, a party of the insurgents had been attacked in this glen by a small detachment of the king's troops, and three or four either killed in the skirmish, or shot after being made prisoners, as rebels taken with arms in their hands. The peasantry continued to attach to the tombs of those victims of prelacy an honor which they do not render to more splendid mausoleums; and, when they point them out to their sons, and narrate the fate of the sufferers, usually conclude by exhorting them to be ready, should times call for it, to resist to the death in the cause of civil and religious liberty, like their brave forefathers.

"Although I am far from venerating the peculiar tenets asserted by those who call themselves the followers of those men, and whose intolerance and narrow-minded bigotry are at least as conspicuous as their devotional zeal, yet it is with-

---

* James, Seventh King of Scotland of that name, and Second according to the numeration of the Kings of England.—J. C.

out depreciating the memory of those sufferers, many of whom united the independent sentiments of a Hampden with the suffering zeal of a Hooper or Latimer.   On the other hand, it would be unjust to forget that many even of those who had been most active in crushing what they conceived the rebellious and seditious spirit of those unhappy wanderers, displayed themselves, when called upon to suffer for their political and religious opinions, the same daring and devoted zeal, tinctured, in their case, with chivalrous loyalty, as in the former with republican enthusiasm.   It has often been remarked of the Scottish character, that the stubbornness with which it is moulded shows most to advantage in adversity, when it seems akin to the native sycamore of their hills, which scorns to be biassed in its mode of growth even by the influence of the prevailing wind, but, shooting its branches with equal boldness in every direction, shows no weather-side to the storm, and may be broken, but can never be bended.   It must be understood that I speak of my countrymen as they fall under my own observation.   When in foreign countries, I have been informed that they are more docile.   But it is time to return from this digression.

"One summer evening as, in a stroll such as I have described, I approached this deserted mansion of the dead, I was somewhat surprised to hear sounds distinct from those which usually soothe its solitude, the gentle chiding, namely, of the brook, and the sighing of the wind in the boughs of three gigantic ash-trees, which mark the cemetery.   The clink of a hammer was on this occasion distinctly heard; and I entertained some alarm that a march dike, long meditated by the two proprietors whose estates were divided by my favorite brook, was about to be drawn up the glen, in order to substitute its rectilinear deformity for the graceful winding of the natural boundary.*   As I approached I was agreeably undeceived. An old man was seated upon the monument of the slaughtered Presbyterians, and busily employed in deepening with his chisel the letters of the inscription which, announcing in Scriptural language the promised blessings of futurity to be the lot of the slain, anathematized the murderers with corresponding violence.   A blue bonnet of unusual dimensions covered the gray hairs of the pious workman.   His dress was a large old-fashioned coat of the coarse cloth called 'hodden-gray,' usually worn by the elder peasants, with waistcoat and breeches of the same ; and the whole suit, though still in decent repair, had obviously seen a train of long service.

* See A March-Dike Boundary.   Note 2.

Strong clouted shoes, studded with hob-nails and 'gramashes' or 'leggins,' made of thick black cloth, completed his equipment. Beside him, fed among the graves a pony, the companion of his journey, whose extreme whiteness, as well as its projecting bones and hollow eyes, indicated its antiquity. It was harnessed in the most simple manner, with a pair of branks, a hair tether, or halter, and a 'sunk,' or cushion of straw, instead of bridle and saddle. A canvas pouch hung around the neck of the animal, for the purpose, probably, of containing the rider's tools, and anything else he might have occasion to carry with him. Although I had never seen the old man before, yet from the singularity of his employment and the style of his equipage, I had no difficulty in recognizing a religious itinerant whom I had often heard talked of, and who was known in various parts of Scotland by the title of Old Mortality.

"Where this man was born, or what was his real name, I have never been able to learn; nor are the motives which made him desert his home and adopt the erratic mode of life which he pursued known to me except very generally. According to the belief of most people, he was a native of either the county of Dumfries or Galloway, and lineally descended from some of those champions of the Covenant whose deeds and sufferings were his favorite theme. He is said to have held, at one period of his life, a small moorland farm; but. whether from pecuniary losses or domestic misfortune, he had long renounced that and every other gainful calling. In the language of Scripture, he left his house, his home, and his kindred, and wandered about until the day of his death, a period of nearly thirty years.

"During this long pilgrimage, the pious enthusiast regulated his circuit so as annually to visit the graves of the unfortunate Covenanters who suffered by the sword, or by the executioner, during the reigns of the two last monarchs of the Stewart line. These are most numerous in the western districts of Ayr, Galloway, and Dumfries; but they are also to be found in other parts of Scotland, wherever the fugitives had fought, or fallen, or suffered by military or civil execution. Their tombs are often apart from all human habitation, in the remote moors and wilds to which the wanderers had fled for concealment. But wherever they existed, Old Mortality was sure to visit them when his annual round brought them within his reach. In the most lonely recesses of the mountains the moor-fowl shooter has been often surprised to find him busied in cleaning the moss from the gray stones, renewing with his chisel the half-defaced inscriptions, and repairing the emblems of death with which these simple monuments are usually adorned. Motives of the most sincere, though fanciful, devotion induced the old man to dedicate so many years of existence to perform this tribute to the memory of the deceased warriors of the church. He considered himself as fulfilling a sacred duty, while renewing to the eyes of posterity the decaying emblems of the zeal and sufferings of their forefathers, and thereby trimming, as it were, the beacon-light which was to warn future generations to defend their religion even unto blood.

"In all his wanderings the old pilgrim never seemed to need, or was known to accept, pecuniary assistance. It is true, his wants were very few; for wherever he went, he found ready quarters in the house of some Cameronian of his own sect, or of some other religious person. The hospitality which was reverentially paid to him he always acknowledged by repairing the grave-stones (if there existed any) belonging to the family or ancestors of his host. As the wanderer was usually to be seen bent on this pious task within the precincts of some country churchyard, or reclined on the solitary tombstone among the heath, disturbing the plover and the blackcock with the clink of his chisel and mallet, with his old white pony grazing by his side, he acquired, from his converse among the dead, the popular appellation of Old Mortality.

"The character of such a man could have in it little connection even with innocent gayety. Yet among those of his own religious persuasion, he is reported to have been cheerful. The descendants of persecutors, or those whom he supposed guilty of entertaining similar tenets, and the scoffers at religion by whom he was sometimes assailed, he usually termed the generation of vipers. Conversing with others, he was grave and sententious, not without a cast of severity. But he is said never to have been observed to give way to violent passion, excepting upon one occasion, when a mischievous truant-boy defaced with a stone the nose of a cherub's face which the old man was engaged in retouching. I am in general a sparer of the rod, notwithstanding the maxim of Solomon, for which schoolboys have little reason to thank his memory; but on this occasion I deemed it proper to show that I did not hate the child. But I must return to the circumstances attending my first interview with this interesting enthusiast.

"In accosting Old Mortality, I did not fail to pay respect to his years and his principles, beginning my address by a respectful apology for interrupting his labors. The old man intermitted the operation of the chisel, took off his spectacles and wiped them, then, replacing them on his nose, acknowledged my courtesy by a suitable return. Encouraged by his affability, I intruded upon him some questions concerning the sufferers on whose monument he was now employed. To talk of the exploits of the Covenanters was the delight, as to repair their monuments was the business, of his life. He was profuse in the communication of all the minute information which he had collected concerning them, their wars, and their wanderings. One would almost have supposed he must have been their contemporary, and have actually beheld the passages which he related, so much had he identified his feelings and opinions with theirs, and so much had his narratives the circumstantiality of an eye-witness.

" 'We,' he said, in a tone of exultation—'*we* are the only true Whigs. Carnal men have assumed that triumphant appellation, following him whose kingdom is of this world. Which of them would sit six hours on a wet hillside to hear a godly sermon ? I trow an hour o't wad staw them. They are ne'er a hair better than them that shamena to take upon themsells the persecuting name of bluidthirsty Tories. Self-seekers all of them, strivers after wealth, power, and worldly ambition, and forgetters alike of what has been dree'd and done by the mighty men who stood in the gap in the great day of wrath. Nae wonder they dread the accomplishment of what was spoken by the mouth of the worthy Mr. Peden—that precious servant of the Lord, none of whose words fell to the ground—that the French monzies sall rise as fast in the glens of Ayr and the Kens of Galloway as ever the Highlandmen did in 1677. And now they are gripping to the bow and to the spear, when they suld be mourning for a sinfu' land and a broken Covenant.'

" Soothing the old man by letting his peculiar opinions pass without contradiction, and anxious to prolong conversation with so singular a character, I prevailed upon him to accept that hospitality which Mr. Cleishbotham is always willing to extend to those who need it. In our way to the schoolmaster's house we called at the Wallace Inn, where I was pretty certain I should find my patron about that hour of the evening. After a courteous interchange of civilities, Old Mortality was, with difficulty, prevailed upon to join his host in a single glass of liquor, and that on condition that he should be permitted to name the pledge, which he prefaced with a grace of about five minutes, and then, with bonnet doffed and eyes uplifted, drank to the memory of those heroes of the Kirk who had first uplifted her banner upon the mountains. As no persuasion could prevail on him to extend his conviviality to a second cup, my patron accompanied him home, and accommodated him in the ' prophet's chamber,' * as it is his pleasure to call the closet which holds a spare bed, and which is frequently a place of retreat for the poor traveller.

" The next day I took leave of Old Mortality, who seemed affected by the unusual attention with which I had cultivated his acquaintance and listened to his conversation. After he had mounted, not without difficulty, the old white pony, he took me by the hand, and said, ' The blessing of our Master be with you, young man ! My hours are like the ears of the latter harvest, and your days are yet in the spring ; and yet you may be gathered into the garner of mortality before me, for the sickle of death cuts down the green as oft as the ripe, and there is a color in your cheek that, like the bud of the rose, serveth oft to hide the worm of corruption. Wherefore labor as one who knoweth not when his Master calleth. And if it be my lot to return to this village after ye are gane hame to your ain place, these auld withered hands will frame a stane of memorial, that your name may not perish from among the people.'

" I thanked Old Mortality for his kind intentions in my behalf, and heaved a sigh, not, I think, of regret so much as of resignation, to think of the chance that I might soon require his good offices. But though, in all human probability, he did not err in supposing that my span of life may be abridged in youth, he had overestimated the period of his own pilgrimage on earth. It is now some years since he has been missed in all his usual haunts, while moss, lichen, and deer-hair are fast covering those stones to cleanse which had been the business of his life. About the beginning of this century he closed his mortal toils, being found on the highway near Lockerbie, in Dumfriesshire, exhausted and just expiring. The old white pony, the companion of all his wanderings, was standing by the side of his dying master. There was found about his person a sum of money sufficient for his decent interment, which serves to show that his death was in no ways hastened by violence or by want. The common people still regard his memory with great respect ; and many are of opinion that the stones which he repaired will not again require the assistance of the chisel. They even assert that on the tombs where the manner of the martyrs' murder is recorded, their names have remained in-

* See Note 3.

delibly legible since the death of Old Mortality, while those
of the persecutors, sculptured on the same monuments, have
been entirely defaced. It is hardly necessary to say that this
is a fond imagination, and that, since the time of the pious
pilgrim, the monuments which were the objects of his care are
hastening, like all earthly memorials, into ruin or decay.

"My readers will of course understand that in embodying
into one compressed narrative many of the anecdotes which I
had the advantage of deriving from Old Mortality, I have
been far from adopting either his style, his opinions, or even
his facts, so far as they appear to have been distorted by party
prejudice. I have endeavored to correct or verify them from
the most authentic sources of tradition, afforded by the representatives of either party.

"On the part of the Presbyterians, I have consulted such
moorland farmers from the western districts as, by the kindness of their landlords, or otherwise, have been able, during
the late general change of property, to retain possession of
the grazings on which their grandsires fed their flocks and
herds. I must own, that of late days, I have found this a
limited source of information. I have, therefore, called in
the supplementary aid of those modest itinerants whom the
scrupulous civility of our ancestors denominated travelling
merchants, but whom, of late, accommodating ourselves in
this as in more material particulars to the feelings and sentiments of our more wealthy neighbors, we have learned to
call packmen or peddlers. To country weavers travelling in
hopes to get rid of their winter web, but more especially to
tailors, who, from their sedentary profession, and the necessity in our country of exercising it by temporary residence in
the families by whom they are employed, may be considered
as possessing a complete register of rural traditions, I have
been indebted for many illustrations of the narratives of Old
Mortality, much in the taste and spirit of the original.

"I had more difficulty in finding materials for correcting
the tone of partiality which evidently pervaded those stores
of traditional learning, in order that I might be enabled to
present an unbiassed picture of the manners of that unhappy
period, and at the same time to do justice to the merits of
both parties. But I have been enabled to qualify the narratives of Old Mortality and his Cameronian friends by the reports of more than one descendant of ancient and honorable
families, who, themselves decayed into the humble vale of
life, yet look proudly back on the period when their ancestors
fought and fell in behalf of the exiled house of Stewart. I

may even boast right reverend authority on the same score ;
for more than one nonjuring bishop, whose authority and income were upon as apostolical a scale as the greatest abomina-
tor of Episcopacy could well desire, have deigned, while partaking of the humble cheer of the Wallace Inn, to furnish me
with information corrective of the facts which I learned from
others.   There are also here and there a laird or two who,
though they shrug their shoulders, profess no great shame in
their fathers having served in the persecuting squadrons of
Earlshall and Claverhouse.   From the gamekeepers of these
gentlemen, an office the most apt of any other to become
hereditary in such families, I have also contrived to collect
much valuable information.

" Upon the whole, I can hardly fear that at this time, in
describing the operation which their opposite principles produced upon the good and bad men of both parties, I can be
suspected of meaning insult or injustice to either.   If recollection of former injuries, extra-loyalty, and contempt and
hatred of their adversaries, produced rigor and tyranny in
the one party, it will hardly be denied, on the other hand,
that, if the zeal for God's house did not eat up the Conventi-
clers, it devoured at least, to imitate the phrase of Dryden,
no small portion of their loyalty, sober sense, and good breeding.   We may safely hope that the souls of the brave and
sincere on either side have long looked down with surprise and
pity upon the ill-appreciated motives which caused their
mutual hatred and hostility while in this valley of darkness,
blood, and tears.   Peace to their memory !   Let us think of
them as the heroine of our only Scottish tragedy entreats her
lord to think of her departed sire :

> "O rake not up the ashes of our fathers !
> Implacable resentment was their crime,
> And grievous has the expiation been."

CHAPTER II

Summon an hundred horse by break of day,
To wait our pleasure at the castle gates.
Douglas.

UNDER the reign of the last Stewarts there was an anxious
wish on the part of government to counteract, by every
means in their power, the strict or puritanical spirit which
had been the chief characteristic of the republican government, and to revive those feudal institutions which united the
vassal to the liege lord, and both to the crown. Frequent
musters and assemblies of the people, both for military
exercise and for sports and pastimes, were appointed by authority. The interference in the latter case was impolitic,
to say the least ; for, as usual on such occasions, the consciences which were at first only scrupulous became confirmed in their opinions, instead of giving way to the terrors
of authority ; and the youth of both sexes, to whom the pipe
and tabor in England, or the bagpipe in Scotland, would
have been in themselves an irresistible temptation, were enabled to set them at defiance from the proud consciousness
that they were at the same time resisting an act of council.
To compel men to dance and be merry by authority has rarely
succeeded even on board of slave-ships, where it was formerly
sometimes attempted by way of inducing the wretched captives to agitate their limbs and restore the circulation during
the few minutes they were permitted to enjoy the fresh air
upon deck. The rigor of the strict Calvinists increased in
proportion to the wishes of the government that it should be
relaxed ; a Judaical observance of the Sabbath, a supercilious
condemnation of all manly pastimes and harmless recreations,
as well as of the profane custom of promiscuous dancing—
that is, of men and women dancing together in the same
party, for I believe they admitted that the exercise might be
inoffensive if practised by the parties separately—distinguishing those who professed a more than ordinary share of sanctity.
They discouraged, as far as lay in their power, even the
ancient " wappenschaws," as they were termed, when the

feudal array of the county was called out, and each crown-vassal was required to appear with such muster of men and armor as he was bound to make by his fief, and that under high statutory penalties. The Covenanters were the more jealous of those assemblies, as the lord-lieutenants and sheriffs under whom they were held had instructions from the government to spare no pains which might render them agreeable to the young men who were thus summoned together, upon whom the military exercise of the morning, and the sports which usually closed the evening, might naturally be supposed to have a seductive effect.

The preachers and proselytes of the more rigid Presbyterians labored, therefore, by caution, remonstrance, and authority, to diminish the attendance upon these summonses, conscious that in doing so they lessened not only the apparent, but the actual, strength of the government, by impeding the extension of that *esprit de corps* which soon unites young men who are in the habit of meeting together for manly sport, or military exercise. They, therefore, exerted themselves earnestly to prevent attendance on these occasions by those who could find any possible excuse for absence, and were especially severe upon such of their hearers as mere curiosity led to be spectators, or love of exercise to be partakers, of the array and the sports which took place. Such of the gentry as acceded to these doctrines were not always, however, in a situation to be ruled by them. The commands of the law were imperative ; and the privy council, who administered the executive power in Scotland, were severe in enforcing the statutory penalties against the crown-vassals who did not appear at the periodical wappenschaw. The landholders were compelled, therefore, to send their sons, tenants, and vassals to the rendezvous, to the number of horses, men, and spears at which they were rated ; and it frequently happened that, notwithstanding the strict charge of their elders to return as soon as the formal inspection was over, the young men-at-arms were unable to resist the temptation of sharing in the sports which succeeded the muster, or to avoid listening to the prayers read in the churches on these occasions, and thus, in the opinion of their repining parents, meddling with the accursed thing which is an abomination in the sight of the Lord.

The sheriff of the county of Lanark was holding the wappenschaw of a wild district, called the Upper Ward of Clydesdale, on a haugh or level plain near to a royal borough, the name of which is no way essential to my story, on the morning of the 5th of May, 1679, when our narrative commences.

When the musters had been made and duly reported, the
young men, as was usual, were to mix in various sports, of
which the chief was to shoot at the popinjay,* an ancient game
formerly practised with archery, but at this period with firearms. This was the figure of a bird decked with party-col-
ored feathers, so as to resemble a popinjay or parrot. It was
suspended to a pole, and served for a mark, at which the competitors discharged their fusees and carabines in rotation,
at the distance of sixty or seventy paces. He whose ball
brought down the mark held the proud title of Captain of the
Popinjay for the remainder of the day, and was usually escorted in triumph to the most reputable change-house in the
neighborhood, where the evening was closed with conviviality,
conducted under his auspices, and, if he was able to sustain
it, at his expense.

It will, of course, be supposed that the ladies of the country
assembled to witness this gallant strife, those excepted who
held the stricter tenets of Puritanism, and would therefore
have deemed it criminal to afford countenance to the profane
gambols of the malignants. Landaus, barouches, or tilburies,
there were none in those simple days. The lord-lieutenant of
the county (a personage of ducal rank) alone pretended to the
magnificence of a wheel-carriage, a thing covered with tarnished
gilding and sculpture, in shape like the vulgar picture of Noah's
ark, dragged by eight long-tailed Flanders mares, bearing eight
" insides " and six " outsides." The insides were their Graces
in person, two maids of honor, two children, a chaplain stuffed
into a sort of lateral recess, formed by a projection at the door
of the vehicle, and called, from its appearance, the boot, and
an equerry to his Grace ensconced in the corresponding convenience on the opposite side. A coachman and three postilions, who wore short swords and tie-wigs with three tails,
had blunderbusses slung behind them, and pistols at their
saddle-bow, conducted the equipage. On the foot-board, behind this moving mansion-house, stood, or rather hung, in
triple file, six lackeys in rich liveries, armed up to the teeth.
The rest of the gentry, men and women, old and young, were
on horseback, followed by their servants ; but the company, for
the reasons already assigned, was rather select than numerous.

Near to the enormous leathern vehicle which we have attempted to describe, vindicating her title to precedence over
the untitled gentry of the country, might be seen the sober palfrey of Lady Margaret Bellenden, bearing the erect and primitive form of Lady Margaret herself, decked in those widow's

<hr>

* See Note 4.

weeds which the good lady had never laid aside since the execution of her husband for his adherence to Montrose.

Her granddaughter, and only earthly care, the fair-haired Edith, who was generally allowed to be the prettiest lass in the Upper Ward, appeared beside her aged relative like Spring placed close to Winter. Her black Spanish jennet, which she managed with much grace, her gay riding-dress, and laced side-saddle, had been anxiously prepared to set her forth to the best alvantage. But the clustering profusion of ringlets, which, escaping from under her cap, were only confined by a green ribbon from wantoning over her shoulders ; her cast of features, soft and feminine, yet not without a certain expression of playful archness, which redeemed their sweetness from the charge of insipidity sometimes brought against blondes and blue-eyed beauties—these attracted more admiration from the western youth than either the splendor of her equipments or the figure of her palfrey.

The attendance of these distinguished ladies was rather inferior to their birth and fashion in those times, as it consisted only of two servants on horseback. The truth was, that the good old lady had been obliged to make all her domestic servants turn out to complete the quota which her barony ought to furnish for the muster, and in which she would not for the universe have been found deficient. The old steward, who, in steel cap and jack-boots, led forth her array, had, as he said, sweated blood and water in his efforts to overcome the scruples and evasions of the moorland farmers, who ought to have furnished men, horse, and harness on these occasions. At last their dispute came near to an open declaration of hostilities, the incensed Episcopalian bestowing on the recusants the whole thunders of the commination, and receiving from them in return the denunciations of a Calvinistic excommunication. What was to be done ? To punish the refractory tenants would have been easy enough. The privy council would readily have imposed fines, and sent a troop of horse to collect them. But this would have been calling the huntsman and hounds into the garden to kill the hare.

" For," said Harrison to himself, " the carles have little eneugh gear at ony rate, and if I call in the redcoats and take away what little they have, how is my worshipful lady to get her rents paid at Candlemas, which is but a difficult matter to bring round even in the best of times ? "

So he armed the fowler and falconer, the footman and the ploughman, at the home farm, with an old drunken

Cavaliering butler, who had served with the late Sir Richard under Montrose, and stunned the family nightly with his exploits at Kilsyth and Tippermuir, and who was the only man in the party that had the smallest zeal for the work in hand. In this manner, and by recruiting one or two latitudinarian poachers and black-fishers, Mr. Harrison completed the quota of men which fell to the share of Lady Margaret Bellenden, as life-rentrix of the barony of Tillietudlem and others. But when the steward, on the morning of the eventful day, had mustered his *troupe dorée* before the iron gate of the Tower, the mother of Cuddie Headrigg, the ploughman, appeared, loaded with the jack-boots, buff coat, and other accoutrements which had been issued forth for the service of the day, and laid them before the steward, demurely assuring him that, "whether it were the colic, or a qualm of conscience, she couldna tak upon her to decide, but sure it was Cuddie had been in sair straits a' night, and she couldna say he was muckle better this morning. The finger of Heaven," she said, "was in it, and her bairn should gang on nae sic errands." Pains, penalties, and threats of dismission were denounced in vain : the mother was obstinate, and Cuddie, who underwent a domiciliary visitation for the purpose of verifying his state of body, could, or would, answer only by deep groans. Mause, who had been an ancient domestic in the family, was a sort of favorite with Lady Margaret and presumed accordingly. Lady Margaret had herself set forth, and her authority could not be appealed to. In this dilemma, the good genius of the old butler suggested an expedient.

"He had seen mony a braw callant, far less than Guse Gibbie, fight brawly under Montrose. What for no tak Guse Gibbie ?"

This was a half-witted lad, of very small stature, who had a kind of charge of the poultry under the old henwife ; for in a Scottish family of that day there was a wonderful substitution of labor. This urchin, being sent for from the stubble-field, was hastily muffled in the buff coat, and girded rather *to* than *with* the sword of a full-grown man, his little legs plunged into jack-boots, and a steel cap put upon his head, which seemed, from its size, as if it had been intended to extinguish him. Thus accoutred he was hoisted, at his own earnest request, upon the quietest horse of the party ; and prompted and supported by old Gudyill the butler as his front file he passed muster tolerably enough, the sheriff not caring to examine too closely the recruits of so well-affected a person as Lady Margaret Bellenden.

To the above cause it was owing that the personal retinue of Lady Margaret, on this eventful day, amounted only to two lackeys, with which diminished train she would on any other occasion have been much ashamed to appear in public. But for the cause of royalty she was ready at any time to have made the most unreserved personal sacrifices. She had lost her husband and two promising sons in the civil wars of that unhappy period ; but she had received her reward, for, on his route through the west of Scotland to meet Cromwell in the unfortunate field of Worcester, Charles the Second had actually breakfasted at the Tower of Tillietudlem ; an incident which formed from that moment an important era in the life of Lady Margaret, who seldom afterwards partook of that meal, either at home or abroad, without detailing the whole circumstances of the royal visit, not forgetting the salutation which his Majesty conferred on each side of her face, though she sometimes omitted to notice that he bestowed the same favor on two buxom serving-wenches who appeared at her back, elevated for the day into the capacity of waiting gentlewomen.

These instances of royal favor were decisive ; and if Lady Margaret had not been a confirmed Royalist already, from sense of high birth, influence of education, and hatred to the opposite party, through whom she had suffered such domestic calamity, the having given a breakfast to majesty, and received the royal salute in return, were honors enough of themselves to unite her exclusively to the fortunes of the Stewarts. These were now, in all appearance, triumphant ; but Lady Margaret's zeal had adhered to them through the worst of times, and was ready to sustain the same severities of fortune should their scale once more kick the beam. At present she enjoyed, in full extent, the military display of the force which stood ready to support the crown, and stifled as well as she could the mortification she felt at the unworthy desertion of her own retainers.

Many civilities passed between her ladyship and the representatives of sundry ancient loyal families who were upon the ground, by whom she was held in high reverence ; and not a young man of rank passed by them in the course of the muster but he carried his body more erect in the saddle, and threw his horse upon its haunches, to display his own horsemanship and the perfect bitting of his steed to the best advantage in the eyes of Miss Edith Bellenden. But the young Cavaliers, distinguished by high descent and undoubted loyalty, attracted no more attention from Edith than the laws

of courtesy peremptorily demanded ; and she turned an indifferent ear to the compliments with which she was addressed,
most of which were little the worse for the wear, though
borrowed for the nonce from the laborious and long-winded
romances of Calprenede and Scuderi, the mirrors in which
the youth of that age delighted to dress themselves, ere Folly
had thrown her ballast overboard, and cut down her vessels
of the first-rate, such as the romances of *Cyrus, Cleopatra,*
and others, into small craft, drawing as little water, or, to
speak more plainly, consuming as little time, as the little
cock-boat in which the gentle reader has deigned to embark.
It was, however, the decree of fate that Miss Bellenden should
not continue to evince the same equanimity till the conclusion
of the day.

CHAPTER III

Horseman and horse confess'd the bitter pang,
And arms and warrior fell with heavy clang.
Pleasures of Hope.

WHEN the military evolutions had been gone through toler‧
ably well, allowing for the awkwardness of men and of horses,
a loud shout announced that the competitors were about to
step forth for the game of the popinjay already described. The
mast, or pole, having a yard extended across it, from which
the mark was displayed, was raised amid the acclamations of
the assembly ; and even those who had eyed the evolutions of
the feudal militia with a sort of malignant and sarcastic sneer,
from disinclination to the royal cause in which they were pro-
fessedly embodied, could not refrain from taking considerable
interest in the strife which was now approaching. They
crowded towards the goal, and criticised the appearance of
each competitor, as they advanced in succession, discharged
their pieces at the mark, and had their good or bad address
rewarded by the laughter or applause of the spectators. But
when a slender young man, dressed with great simplicity, yet
not without a certain air of pretension to elegance and gentil-
ity, approached the station with his fusee in his hand, his
dark green cloak thrown back over his shoulder, his laced ruff
and feathered cap indicating a superior rank to the vulgar,
there was a murmur of interest among the spectators, whether
altogether favorable to the young adventurer it was difficult
to discover.

"Ewhow, sirs, to see his father's son at the like o' thae
fearless follies !" was the ejaculation of the elder and more
rigid Puritans, whose curiosity had so far overcome their bigotry as to bring them to the playground. But the generality
viewed the strife less morosely, and were contented to wish
success to the son of a deceased Presbyterian leader, without
strictly examining the propriety of his being a competitor for
the prize.

Their wishes were gratified. At the first discharge of his
piece the green adventurer struck the popinjay, being the

first palpable hit of the day, though several balls had passed very near the mark. A loud shout of applause ensued. But the success was not decisive, it being necessary that each who followed should have his chance, and that those who succeeded in hitting the mark should renew the strife among themselves, till one displayed a decided superiority over the others. Two only of those who followed in order succeeded in hitting the popinjay. The first was a young man of low rank, heavily built, and who kept his face muffled in his gray cloak ; the second, a gallant young cavalier, remarkable for a handsome exterior, sedulously decorated for the day. He had been since the muster in close attendance on Lady Margaret and Miss Bellenden, and had left them with an air of indifference when Lady Margaret had asked whether there was no young man of family and loyal principles who would dispute the prize with the two lads who had been successful. In half a minute young Lord Evandale threw himself from his horse, borrowed a gun from a servant, and, as we have already noticed, hit the mark. Great was the interest excited by the renewal of the contest between the three candidates who had been hitherto successful. The state equipage of the Duke was, with some difficulty, put in motion, and approached more near to the scene of action. The riders, both male and female, turned their horses' heads in the same direction, and all eyes were bent upon the issue of the trial of skill.

It was the etiquette in the second contest, that the competitors should take their turn of firing after drawing lots. The first fell upon the young plebeian, who, as he took his stand, half uncloaked his rustic countenance, and said to the gallant in green, " Ye see, Mr. Henry, if it were ony other day, I could hae wished to miss for your sake ; but Jenny Dennison is looking at us, sae I maun do my best."

He took his aim, and his bullet whistled past the mark so nearly that the pendulous object at which it was directed was seen to shiver. Still, however, he had not hit it, and, with a downcast look, he withdrew himself from further competition, and hastened to disappear from the assembly, as if fearful of being recognized. The green *chasseur* next advanced, and his ball a second time struck the popinjay. All shouted; and from the outskirts of the assembly arose a cry of, " The good old cause forever ! "

While the dignitaries bent their brows at these exulting shouts of the disaffected, the young Lord Evandale advanced again to the hazard, and again was successful. The shouts and congratulations of the well-affected and aristocratical part of the audience attended his success, but still a subsequent trial of skill remained.

The green marksman, as if determined to bring the affair to a decision, took his horse from a person who held him, having previously looked carefully to the security of his girths and the fitting of his saddle, vaulted on his back, and motioning with his hand for the bystanders to make way, set spurs, passed the place from which he was to fire at a gallop, and, as he passed, threw up the reins, turned sideways upon his saddle, discharged his carabine, and brought down the popinjay. Lord Evandale imitated his example, although many around him said it was an innovation on the established practice which he was not obliged to follow. But his skill was not so perfect, or his horse was not so well trained. The animal swerved at the moment his master fired, and the ball missed the popinjay. Those who had been surprised by the address of the green marksman were now equally pleased by his courtesy. He disclaimed all merit from the last shot, and proposed to his antagonist that it should not be counted as a hit, and that they should renew the contest on foot.

"I would prefer horseback, if I had a horse as well bitted, and, probably, as well broken to the exercise, as yours," said the young Lord, addressing his antagonist.

"Will you do me the honor to use him for the next trial, on condition you will lend me yours?" said the young gentleman.

Lord Evandale was ashamed to accept this courtesy, as conscious how much it would diminish the value of victory; and yet, unable to suppress his wish to redeem his reputation as a marksman, he added, "that although he renounced all pretensions to the honor of the day (which he said somewhat scornfully), yet, if the victor had no particular objection, he would willingly embrace his obliging offer, and change horses with him for the purpose of trying a shot for love."

As he said so, he looked boldly towards Miss Bellenden, and tradition says, that the eyes of the young *tirailleur* travelled, though more covertly, in the same direction. The young Lord's last trial was as unsuccessful as the former, and it was with difficulty that he preserved the tone of scornful indifference which he had hitherto assumed. But, conscious of the ridicule which attaches itself to the resentment of a losing party, he returned to his antagonist the horse on which he had made his last unsuccessful attempt, and received back his own; giving at the same time, thanks to his competitor,

Shooting the popinjay.

who, he said, had re-established his favorite horse in his good opinion, for he had been in great danger of transferring to the poor nag the blame of an inferiority, which every one, as well as himself, must now be satisfied remained with the rider. Having made this speech in a tone in which mortification assumed the veil of indifference, he mounted his horse and rode off the ground.

As is the usual way of the world, the applause and attention even of those whose wishes had favored Lord Evandale were, upon his decisive discomfiture, transferred to his triumphant rival.

"Who is he? what is his name?" ran from mouth to mouth among the gentry who were present, to few of whom he was personally known. His style and title having soon transpired, and being within that class whom a great man might notice without derogation, four of the Duke's friends, with the obedient start which poor Malvolio ascribes to his imaginary retinue, made out to lead the victor to his presence. As they conducted him in triumph through the crowd of spectators, and stunned him at the same time with their compliments on his success, he chanced to pass, or rather to be led, immediately in front of Lady Margaret and her granddaughter. The Captain of the Popinjay and Miss Bellenden colored like crimson, as the latter returned, with embarrassed courtesy, the low inclination which the victor made, even to the saddle-bow, in passing her.

"Do you know that young person?" said Lady Margaret.

"I—I—have seen him, madam, at my uncle's, and—and elsewhere occasionally," stammered Miss Edith Bellenden.

"I hear them say around me," said Lady Margaret, "that the young spark is the nephew of old Milnwood."

"The son of the late Colonel Morton of Milnwood, who commanded a regiment of horse with great courage at Dunbar and Inverkeithing," said a gentleman who sat on horseback beside Lady Margaret.

"Ay, and who, before that, fought for the Covenanters both at Marston Moor and Philiphaugh," said Lady Margaret, sighing as she pronounced the last fatal words, which her husband's death gave her such sad reason to remember.

"Your ladyship's memory is just," said the gentleman, smiling, "but it were well all that were forgot now."

"*He* ought to remember it, Gilbertscleugh," returned Lady Margaret, "and dispense with intruding himself into the company of those to whom his name must bring unpleasing recollections."

"You forget, my dear lady," said her nomenclator, "that

the young gentleman comes nere to discharge suit and service in name of his uncle. I would every estate in the country sent out as pretty a fellow."

"His uncle, as well as his umquhile father, is a Roundhead, I presume," said Lady Margaret.

"He is an old miser," said Gilbertscleugh, "with whom a broad piece would at any time weigh down political opinions, and, therefore, although probably somewhat against the grain, he sends the young gentleman to attend the muster to save pecuniary pains and penalties. As for the rest, I suppose the youngster is happy enough to escape here for a day from the dulness of the old house at Milnwood, where he sees nobody but his hypochondriac uncle and the favorite housekeeper."

"Do you know how many men and horse the lands of Milnwood are rated at?" said the old lady, continuing her inquiry.

"Two horsemen with complete harness," answered Gilbertscleugh.

"Our land," said Lady Margaret, drawing herself up with dignity, "has always furnished to the muster eight men, cousin Gilbertscleugh, and often a voluntary aid of thrice the number. I remember his sacred Majesty King Charles, when he took his disjune at Tillietudlem, was particular in inquiring——"

"I see the Duke's carriage in motion," said Gilbertscleugh, partaking at the moment an alarm common to all Lady Margaret's friends, when she touched upon the topic of the royal visit at the family mansion—"I see the Duke's carriage in motion; I presume your ladyship will take your right of rank in leaving the field. May I be permitted to convoy your ladyship and Miss Bellenden home? Parties of the wild Whigs have been abroad, and are said to insult and disarm the well-affected who travel in small numbers."

"We thank you, cousin Gilbertscleugh," said Lady Margaret; "but as we shall have the escort of my own people, I trust we have less need than others to be troublesome to our friends. Will you have the goodness to order Harrison to bring up our people somewhat more briskly; he rides them towards us as if he were leading a funeral procession."

The gentleman in attendance communicated his lady's orders to the trusty steward.

Honest Harrison had his own reasons for doubting the prudence of this command; but, once issued and received, there was a necessity for obeying it. He set off, therefore, at a hand-gallop, followed by the butler, in such a military attitude as became one who had served under Montrose, and with a look of defiance, rendered sterner and fiercer by the inspiring fumes of a gill of brandy, which he had snatched a moment to bolt to the king's health and confusion to the Covenant, during the intervals of military duty. Unhappily this potent refreshment wiped away from the tablets of his memory the necessity of paying some attention to the distresses and difficulties of his rear-file, Goose Gibbie. No sooner had the horses struck a canter than Gibbie's jack-boots, which the poor boy's legs were incapable of steadying, began to play alternately against the horse's flanks, and, being armed with long-rowelled spurs, overcame the patience of the animal, which bounced and plunged, while poor Gibbie's entreaties for aid never reached the ears of the too heedless butler, being drowned partly in the concave of the steel cap in which his head was immersed, and partly in the martial tune of the "Gallant Græmes," which Mr. Gudyill whistled with all his power of lungs.

The upshot was that the steed speedily took the matter into his own hands, and having gambolled hither and thither to the great amusement of all spectators, set off at full speed towards the huge family coach already described. Gibbie's pike, escaping from its sling, had fallen to a level direction across his hands, which, I grieve to say, were seeking dishonorable safety in as strong a grasp of the mane as their muscles could manage. His casque, too, had slipped completely over his face, so that he saw as little in front as he did in rear. Indeed, if he could, it would have availed him little in the circumstances; for his horse, as if in league with the disaffected, ran full tilt towards the solemn equipage of the Duke, which the projecting lance threatened to perforate from window to window, at the risk of transfixing as many in its passage as the celebrated thrust of Orlando, which, according to the Italian epic poet, broached as many Moors as a Frenchman spits frogs.

On beholding the bent of this misdirected career, a panic shout of mingled terror and wrath was set up by the whole equipage, insides and outsides at once, which had the happy effect of averting the threatened misfortune. The capricious horse of Goose Gibbie was terrified by the noise, and stumbling as he turned short round, kicked and plunged violently as soon as he recovered. The jack-boots, the original cause of the disaster, maintaining the reputation they had acquired when worn by better cavaliers, answered every plunge by a fresh prick of the spurs, and by their ponderous weight kept their place in the stirrups. Not so Goose Gibbie, who was fairly spurned out of those wide and weighty greaves, and precipitated over the horse's head, to the infinite amusement of all the spectators. His lance and helmet had forsaken him in his fall, and, for the completion of his disgrace, Lady Margaret Bellenden, not perfectly aware that it was one of her own warriors who was furnishing so much entertainment, came up in time to see her diminutive man-at-arms stripped of his lion's hide—of the buff coat, that is, in which he was muffled.

As she had not been made acquainted with this metamorphosis, and could not even guess its cause, her surprise and resentment were extreme, nor were they much modified by the excuses and explanations of her steward and butler. She made a hasty retreat homeward, extremely indignant at the shouts and laughter of the company, and much disposed to vent her displeasure on the refractory agriculturist whose place Goose Gibbie had so unhappily supplied. The greater part of the gentry now dispersed, the whimsical misfortune which had befallen the *gensdarmerie* of Tillietudlem furnishing them with huge entertainment on their road homeward. The horsemen also, in little parties, as their road lay together, diverged from the place of rendezvous, excepting such as, having tried their dexterity at the popinjay, were, by ancient custom, obliged to partake of a grace-cup with their captain before their departure.

CHAPTER IV

At fairs he play'd before the spearmen,
And gaily graithed in their gear then,
Steel bonnets, pikes, and swords shone clear then
    As ony bead ;
Now wha sall play before sic weir-men,
    Since Habbie's dead?
      Elegy on Habbie Simpson.

THE cavalcade of horsemen on their road to the little borough-town were preceded by Niel Blane, the town-piper, mounted on his white galloway, armed with his dirk and broadsword, and bearing a chanter streaming with as many ribbons as would deck out six country belles for a fair or preaching. Niel, a clean, tight, well-timbered, long-winded fellow, had gained the official situation of town-piper of —— by his merit, with all the emoluments thereof ; namely, the piper's croft, as it is still called, a field of about an acre in extent, five merks, and a new livery-coat of the town's colors, yearly ; some hopes of a dollar upon the day of the election of magistrates, providing the provost were able and willing to afford such a gratuity ; and the privilege of paying, at all the respectable houses in the neighborhood, an annual visit at spring-time, to rejoice their hearts with his music, to comfort his own with their ale and brandy, and to beg from each a modicum of seed-corn.

In addition to these inestimable advantages, Niel's personal or professional accomplishments won the heart of a jolly widow who then kept the principal change-house in the borough. Her former husband having been a strict Presbyterian, of such note that he usually went among his sect by the name of Gaius the Publican, many of the more rigid were scandalized by the profession of the successor whom his relict had chosen for a second helpmate. As the " browst " or brewing of the Howff retained, nevertheless, its unrivalled reputation, most of the old customers continued to give it a preference. The character of the new landlord, indeed, was of that accommodating kind which enabled him, by close attention to the helm, to keep his little vessel pretty steady amid the contending tides of faction. He was a good-humored, shrewd, selfish sort of fellow, indifferent alike to the disputes about church and state, and only anxious to secure the good-will of customers of every description. But his character, as well as the state of the country, will be best understood by giving the reader an account of the instructions which he issued to his daughter, a girl about eighteen, whom he was initiating in those cares which had been faithfully discharged by his wife, until about six months before our story commences, when the honest woman had been carried to the kirkyard.

"Jenny," said Niel Blane, as the girl assisted to disencumber him of his bagpipes, "this is the first day that ye are to take the place of your worthy mother in attending to the public ; a douce woman she was, civil to the customers, and had a good name wi' Whig and Tory, baith up the street and down the street. It will be hard for you to fill her place, especially on sic a thrang day as this ; but Heaven's will maun be obeyed. Jenny, whatever Milnwood ca's for, be sure he maun hae't, for he's the Captain o' the Popinjay, and auld customs maun be supported ; if he canna pay the lawing himsell, as I ken he's keepit unco short by the head, I'll find a way to shame it out o' his uncle. The curate is playing at dice wi' Cornet Grahame. Be eident and civil to them baith ; clergy and captains can gie an unco deal o' fash in thae times, where they take an ill-will. The dragoons will be crying for ale, and they wunna want it, and maunna want it ; they are unruly chields, but they pay ane some gate or other. I gat the humlie-cow, that's the best in the byre, frae black Frank Inglis and Sergeant Bothwell for ten pund Scots, and they drank out the price at ae downsitting."

"But, father," interrupted Jenny, "they say the twa reiving loons drave the cow frae the gudewife o' Bell's Moor, just because she gaed to hear a field-preaching ae Sabbath afternoon."

"Whisht ! ye silly tawpie," said her father, "we have naething to do how they come by the bestial they sell ; be that atween them and their consciences. Aweel, take notice, Jenny, of that dour, stour-looking carle that sits by the cheek o' the ingle and turns his back on a' men. He looks like ane o' the hill-folk, for I saw him start a wee when he saw the redcoats, and I jalouse he wad hae liked to hae ridden by, but his horse —it's a gude gelding—was ower sair travailed ; he behoved to stop whether he wad or no. Serve him cannily, Jenny, and wi' little din, and dinna bring the sodgers on hir speering ony questions at him ; but let na him hae a room to himsell, they wad say we were hiding him. For yoursell, Jenny,

ye'll be civil to a' the folk, and take nae heed o' ony nonsense
and daffing the young lads may say t'ye. Folk in the hostler
line maun pit up wi' muckle. Your mither, rest her saul,
could pit up wi' as muckle as maist women, but aff hands is
fair play ; and if onybody be uncivil ye may gie me a cry.
Aweel, when the malt begins to get aboon the meal, they'll
begin to speak about government in kirk and state, and then,
Jenny, they are like to quarrel. Let them be doing : anger's
a drouthy passion, and the mair they dispute, the mair ale
they'll drink ; but ye were best serve them wi' a pint o' the sma'
browst, it will heat them less, and they'll never ken the difference."

"But, father," said Jenny, "if they come to lounder ilk
ither, as they did the last time, suldna I cry on you ? "

"At no hand, Jenny ; the redder gets aye the warst lick
in the fray. If the sodgers draw their swords, ye'll cry on the
corporal and the guard. If the country folk tak the tangs
and poker, ye'll cry on the bailie and town-officers. But in
nae event cry on me, for I am wearied wi' doudling the bag o'
wind a' day, and I am gaun to eat my dinner quietly in the
spence. And now I think on't, the Laird of Lickitup—that's
him that was the laird—was speering for sma' drink and a
saut herring. Gie him a pu' be the sleeve, and round into his
lug I wad be blithe o' his company to dine wi' me ; he was a
gude customer anes in a day, and wants naething but means
to be a gude ane again : he likes drink as weel as e'er he did.
And if ye ken ony puir body o' our acquaintance that's blate
for want o' siller, and has far to gang hame, ye needna stick
to gie them a waught o'. drink and a bannock ; we'll ne'er
miss't, and it looks creditable in a house like ours. And now,
hinny, gang awa' and serve the folk ; but first bring me my
dinner, and twa chappins o' yill and the mutchkin stoup o'
brandy."

Having thus devolved his whole cares on Jenny as prime
minister, Niel Blane and the *ci-devant* laird, once his patron,
but now glad to be his trencher-companion, sat down to en·
joy themselves for the remainder of the evening, remote from
the bustle of the public room.

All in Jenny's department was in full activity. The knights
of the popinjay received and requited the hospitable entertainment of their captain, who, though he spared the cup
himself, took care it should go round with due celerity among
the rest, who might not have otherwise deemed· themselves
handsomely treated. Their numbers melted away by degrees,
and were at length diminished to four or five, who began to

talk of breaking up their party. At another table, at some distance, sat two of the dragoons whom Niel Blane had mentioned, a sergeant and a private in the celebrated John Grahame of Claverhouse's regiment of Life Guards. Even the non-commissioned officers and privates in these corps were not considered as ordinary mercenaries, but rather approached to the rank of the French mousquetaires, being regarded in the light of cadets, who performed the duties of rank and file with the prospect of obtaining commissions in case of distinguishing themselves.

Many young men of good families were to be found in the ranks, a circumstance which added to the pride and self-consequence of these troops. A remarkable instance of this occurred in the person of the non-commissioned officer in question. His real name was Francis Stewart; but he was universally known by the appellation of Bothwell, being lineally descended from the last earl of that name, not the infamous lover of the unfortunate Queen Mary, but Francis Stewart, Earl of Bothwell, whose turbulence and repeated conspiracies embarrassed the early part of James Sixth's reign, and who at length died in exile in great poverty. The son of this earl had sued to Charles I. for the restitution of part of his father's forfeited estates ; but the grasp of the nobles to whom they had been allotted was too tenacious to be unclinched. The breaking out of the civil wars utterly ruined him, by intercepting a small pension which Charles I. had allowed him, and he died in the utmost indigence. His son, who, after having served as a soldier abroad and in Britain, had passed through several vicissitudes of fortune, was fain to content himself with the situation of a non-commissioned officer in the Life Guards, although lineally descended from the royal family, the father of the forfeited Earl of Bothwell having been a natural son of James V.* Great personal strength, and dexterity in the use of his arms, as well as the remarkable circumstances of his descent, had recommended this man to the attention of his officers. But he partook in a great degree of the licentiousness and oppressive disposition which the habit of acting as agents for government in levying fines, exacting free quarters, and otherwise oppressing the Presbyterian recusants, had rendered too general among these soldiers. They were so much accustomed to such missions, that they conceived themselves at liberty to commit all manner of license with impunity, as if totally exempted from all law and authority, excepting the command of their offi-

* See Sergeant Bothwell. Note 5.

cers. On such occasions Bothwell was usually the most forward.

It is probable that Bothwell and his companions would not so long have remained quiet but for respect to the presence of their cornet, who commanded the small party quartered in the borough, and who was engaged in a game at dice with the curate of the place. But both of these being suddenly called from their amusement to speak with the chief magistrate upon some urgent business, Bothwell was not long of evincing his contempt for the rest of the company.

" Is it not a strange thing, Halliday," he said to his comrade, " to see a set of bumpkins sit carousing here this whole evening without having drunk the king's health ? "

" They have drank the king's health," said Halliday. "I heard that green kail-worm of a lad name his Majesty's health."

" Did he ? " said Bothwell. " Then, Tom, we'll have them drink the Archbishop of St. Andrews' health, and do it on their knees too."

" So we will, by G—," said Halliday; " and he that refuses it, we'll have him to the guard-house, and teach him to ride the colt foaled of an acorn, with a brace of carabines at each foot to keep him steady."

" Right, Tom," continued Bothwell; " and, to do all things in order, I'll begin with that sulky blue-bonnet in the ingle-nook."

He rose accordingly, and taking his sheathed broadsword under his arm to support the insolence which he meditated, placed himself in front of the stranger noticed by Niel Blane, in his admonitions to his daughter, as being, in all probability, one of the hill-folk, or refractory Presbyterians.

" I make so bold as to request of your precision, beloved," said the trooper, in a tone of affected solemnity, and assuming the snuffle of a country preacher, "that you will arise from your seat, beloved, and, having bent your hams until your knees do rest upon the floor, beloved, that you will turn over this measure, called by the profane a gill, of the comfortable creature, which the carnal denominate brandy, to the health and glorification of his Grace the Archbishop of St. Andrews, the worthy primate of all Scotland."

All waited for the stranger's answer. His features, austere even to ferocity, with a cast of eye which, without being actually oblique, approached nearly to a squint, and which gave a very sinister expression to his countenance, joined to a frame, square, strong, and muscular, though something under the middle size, seemed to announce a man unlikely to understand rude jesting, or to receive insults with impunity.

"And what is the consequence," said he, "if I should not be disposed to comply with your uncivil request ?"

"The consequence thereof, beloved," said Bothwell, in the same tone of raillery, " will be, firstly, that I will tweak thy proboscis or nose.   Secondly, beloved, that I will administer my fist to thy distorted visual optics ; and will conclude, beloved, with a practical application of the flat of my sword to the shoulders of the recusant."

"Is it even so ?" said the stranger; "then give me the cup ;" and, taking it in his hand, he said, with a peculiar expression of voice and manner, "The Archbishop of St. Andrews, and the place he now worthily holds ; may each prelate in Scotland soon be as the Right Reverend James Sharp !"

"He has taken the test," said Halliday, exultingly.

"But with a qualification," said Bothwell; "I don't understand what the devil the crop-eared Whig means."

"Come, gentlemen," said Morton, who became impatient of their insolence, "we are here met as good subjects, and on a merry occasion ; and we have a right to expect we shall not be troubled with this sort of discussion."

Bothwell was about to make a surly answer, but Halliday reminded him in a whisper that there were strict injunctions that the soldiers should give no offence to the men who were sent out to the musters agreeably to the council's orders. So, after honoring Morton with a broad and fierce stare, he said, " Well, Mr. Popinjay, I shall not disturb your reign ; I reckon it will be out by twelve at night. Is it not an odd thing, Halliday," he continued, addressing his companion, "that they should make such a fuss about cracking off their birding-pieces at a mark which any woman or boy could hit at a day's practice ? If Captain Popinjay now, or any of his troop, would try a bout, either with the broadsword, backsword, single rapier, or rapier and dagger, for a gold noble, the first-drawn blood, there would be some soul in it ; or, zounds, would the bumpkins but wrestle, or pitch the bar, or put the stone, or throw the axletree, if (touching the end of Morton's sword scornfully with his toe) they carry things about them that they are afraid to draw."

Morton's patience and prudence now gave way entirely, and he was about to make a very angry answer to Bothwell's insolent observations when the stranger stepped forward.

"This is my quarrel," he said, "and in the name of the good cause I will see it out myself. Hark thee, friend (to Bothwell) wilt thou wrestle a fall with me?"

"With my whole spirit, beloved," answered Bothwell; "yea, I will strive with thee, to the downfall of one or both."

"Then, as my trust is in Him that can help," retorted his antagonist, "I will forthwith make thee an example to all such railing Rabshakehs."

With that he dropped his coarse gray horseman's coat from his shoulders, and extending his strong brawny arms with a look of determined resolution, he offered himself to the contest. The soldier was nothing abashed by the muscular frame, broad chest, square shoulders, and hardy look of his antagonist, but whistling with great composure, unbuckled his belt, and laid aside his military coat. The company stood round them, anxious for the event.

In the first struggle the trooper seemed to have some advantage, and also in the second, though neither could be considered as decisive. But it was plain he had put his whole strength too suddenly forth against an antagonist possessed of great endurance, skill, vigor, and length of wind. In the third close the countryman lifted his opponent fairly from the floor and hurled him to the ground with such violence that he lay for an instant stunned and motionless. His comrade Halliday immediately drew his sword: "You have killed my sergeant," he exclaimed to the victorious wrestler; "and by all that is sacred you shall answer it!"

"Stand back!" cried Morton and his companions. "It was all fair play; your comrade sought a fall, and he has got it."

"That is true enough," said Bothwell, as he slowly rose; "put up your bilbo, Tom. I did not think there was a crop-ear of them all could have laid the best cap and feather in the King's Life Guards on the floor of a rascally change-house. Hark ye, friend, give me your hand." The stranger held out his hand. "I promise you," said Bothwell, squeezing his hand very hard, "that the time will come when we shall meet again and try this game over in a more earnest manner."

"And I'll promise you," said the stranger, returning the grasp with equal firmness, "that when we next meet I will lay your head as low as it lay even now, when you shall lack the power to lift it up again."

"Well, beloved," answered Bothwell, "if thou be'st a

Whig, thou art a stout and a brave one, and so good even to thee. Hadst best take thy nag before the Cornet makes the round; for I promise thee he has stay'd less suspicious-looking persons."

The stranger seemed to think that the hint was not to be neglected; he flung down his reckoning, and going into the stable, saddled and brought out a powerful black horse, now recruited by rest and forage, and turning to Morton, observed, "I ride towards Milnwood, which I hear is your home; will you give me the advantage and protection of your company?"

"Certainly," said Morton, although there was something of gloomy and relentless severity in the man's manner from which his mind recoiled. His companions, after a courteous good-night, broke up and went off in different directions, some keeping them company for about a mile, until they dropped off one by one, and the travellers were left alone.

The company had not long left the Howff, as Blane's public-house was called, when the trumpets and kettle-drums sounded. The troopers got under arms in the market-place at this unexpected summons, while, with faces of anxiety and earnestness, Cornet Grahame, a kinsman of Claverhouse, and the provost of the borough, followed by half a dozen soldiers and town-officers with halberts, entered the apartment of Niel Blane.

"Guard the doors!" were the first words which the Cornet spoke; "let no man leave the house. So, Bothwell, how comes this? Did you not hear them sound boot and saddle?"

"He was just going to quarters, sir," said his comrade; "he has had a bad fall."

"In a fray, I suppose?" said Grahame. "If you neglect duty in this way, your royal blood will hardly protect you."

"How have I neglected duty?" said Bothwell, sulkily.

"You should have been at quarters, Sergeant Bothwell," replied the officer; "you have lost a golden opportunity. Here are news come that the Archbishop of St. Andrews has been strangely and foully assassinated by a body of the rebel Whigs, who pursued and stopped his carriage on Magus Muir, near the town of St. Andrews, dragged him out, and despatched him with their swords and daggers."*

All stood aghast at the intelligence.

"Here are their descriptions," continued the Cornet, pulling out a proclamation; "the reward of a thousand merks is on each of their heads."

"The test, the test, and the qualification!" said Both-

* See Assassination of Archbishop Sharp. Note 6.

well to Halliday ; " I know the meaning now.   Zounds, that we should not have stopped him ! Go, saddle our horses, Halliday.   Was there one of the men, Cornet, very stout and square-made, double-chested, thin in the flanks, hawk-nosed ? "

" Stay, stay," said Cornet Grahame, " let me look at the paper.   Hackston of Rathillet, tall, thin, black-haired."

" That is not my man," said Bothwell.

" John Balfour, called Burley, aquiline nose, red-haired, five feet eight inches in height——"

" It is he—it is the very man ! " said Bothwell ; " skellies fearfully with one eye ? "

" Right," continued Grahame ; " rode a strong black horse, taken from the primate at the time of the murder."

" The very man," exclaimed Bothwell, " and the very horse !   He was in this room not a quarter of an hour since."

A few hasty inquiries tended still more to confirm the opinion that the reserved and stern stranger was Balfour of Burley, the actual commander of the band of assassins who, in the fury of misguided zeal, had murdered the primate whom they accidently met as they were searching for another person against whom they bore enmity.*   In their excited imagination the casual rencounter had the appearance of a providential interference, and they put to death the archbishop, with circumstances of great and cold-blooded cruelty, under the belief that the Lord, as they expressed it, had delivered him into their hands.†

" Horse, horse, and pursue, my lads ! " exclaimed Cornet Grahame ; " the murdering dog's head is worth its weight in gold."

* See Sheriff-Depute Carmichael. Note 7.
† See Murderers of Archbishop Sharp. Note 8.

CHAPTER V

Arouse thee, youth !   It is no human call :
God's church is leaguer'd, haste to man the wall;
Haste where the red-cross banners wave on high,
Signal of honour'd death or victory !

JAMES DUFF.

MORTON and his companion had attained some distance from
the town before either of them addressed the other.   There
was something, as we have observed, repulsive in the manner
of the stranger which prevented Morton from opening the conversation, and he himself seemed to have no desire to talk,
until, on a sudden, he abruptly demanded, "What has your
father's son to do with such profane mummeries as I find you
this day engaged in ?"

"I do my duty as a subject, and pursue my harmless recreations according to my own pleasure," replied Morton, somewhat offended.

"Is it your duty, think you, or that of any Christian young
man, to bear arms in their cause who have poured out the
blood of God's saints in the wilderness as if it had been water ?
Or is it a lawful recreation to waste time in shooting at a
bunch of feathers, and close your evening with wine-bibbing
in public-houses and market-towns, when He that is mighty
is come into the land with His fan in His hand, to purge the
wheat from the chaff ?"

"I suppose from your style of conversation," said Morton,
"that you are one of those who have thought proper to stand
out against the government.   I must remind you that you are
unnecessarily using dangerous language in the presence of a
mere stranger, and that the times do not render it safe for me
to listen to it."

"Thou canst not help it, Henry Morton," said his companion ; "thy Master has His uses for thee, and when He
calls, thou must obey.   Well wot I thou hast not heard the
call of a true preacher, or thou hadst ere now been what thou
wilt assuredly one day become."

"We are of the Presbyterian persuasion, like yourself,"
said Morton ; for his uncle's family attended the ministry of

one of those numerous Presbyterian clergymen, who, complying with certain regulations, were licensed to preach without interruption from the government. This "indulgence," as it was called, made a great schism among the Presbyterians, and those who accepted of it were severely censured by the more rigid sectaries, who refused the proffered terms.

The stranger, therefore, answered with great disdain to Morton's profession of faith. "That is but an equivocation —a poor equivocation. Ye listen on the Sabbath to a cold, wordly, time-serving discourse from one who forgets his high commission so much as to hold his apostleship by the favor of the courtiers and the false prelates, and ye call that hearing the Word ! Of all the baits with which the devil has fished for souls in these days of blood and darkness, that Black Indulgence has been the most destructive. An awful dispensation it has been, a smiting of the shepherd and a scattering of the sheep upon the mountains, an uplifting of one Christian banner against another, and a fighting of the wars of darkness with the swords of the children of light !"

"My uncle," said Morton, "is of opinion that we enjoy a reasonable freedom of conscience under the indulged clergymen, and I must necessarily be guided by his sentiments respecting the choice of a place of worship for his family."

"Your uncle," said the horseman, "is one of those to whom the least lamb in his own folds at Milnwood is dearer than the whole Christian flock. He is one that could willingly bend down to the golden calf of Bethel, and would have fished for the dust thereof when it was ground to powder and cast upon the waters. Thy father was a man of another stamp."

"My father," replied Morton, "was indeed a brave and gallant man. And you may have heard, sir, that he fought for that royal family in whose name I was this day carrying arms."

"Ay, and had he lived to see these days, he would have cursed the hour he ever drew sword in their cause ; but more of this hereafter. I promise thee full surely that thy hour will come, and then the words thou hast now heard will stick in thy bosom like barbed arrows. My road lies there."

He pointed towards a pass leading up into a wild extent of dreary and desolate hills ; but as he was about to turn his horse's head into the rugged path which led from the high-road in that direction, an old woman wrapped in a red cloak, who was sitting by the cross-way, arose, and approaching him said, in a mysterious tone of voice, "If ye be of our ain folk, gangna up the pass the night for your lives. There is a lion in the path that is there.   The curate of Brotherstane ana ten soldiers hae beset the pass to hae the lives of ony of our puir wanderers that venture that gate to join wi' Hamilton and Dingwall."

"Have the persecuted folk drawn to any head among themselves?" demanded the stranger.

"About sixty or seventy horse and foot," said the old dame; "but, ewhow! they are puirly armed, and warse fended wi' victual."

"God will help His own," said the horseman.   "Which way shall I take to join them?"

"It's a mere impossibility this night," said the woman, "the troopers keep sae strict a guard; and they say there's strange news come frae the east that makes them rage in their cruelty mair fierce than ever.   Ye maun take shelter somegate for the night before ye get to the muirs, and keep yoursell in hiding till the gray o' the morning, and then you may find your way through the Drake Moss.   When I heard the awfu' threatenings o' the oppressors, I e'en took my cloak about me and sat down by the wayside to warn ony of our puir scattered remnant that chanced to come this gate, before they fell into the nets of the spoilers."

"Have you a house near this?" said the stranger; "and can you give me hiding there?"

"I have," said the old woman, "a hut by the wayside, it may be a mile from hence; but four men of Belial, called dragoons, are lodged therein, to spoil my household goods at their pleasure, because I will not wait upon the thowless, thriftless, fissenless ministry of that carnal man, John Halftext, the curate."

"Good-night, good woman, and thanks for thy counsel," said the stranger as he rode away.

"The blessings of the promise upon you," returned the old dame; "may He keep you that can keep you."

"Amen!" said the traveller; "for where to hide my head this night mortal skill cannot direct me."

"I am very sorry for your distress," said Morton; "and had I a house or place of shelter that could be called my own, I almost think I would risk the utmost rigor of the law rather than leave you in such a strait.   But my uncle is so alarmed at the pains and penalties denounced by the laws against such as comfort, receive, or consort with intercommuned persons, that he has strictly forbidden all of us to hold any intercourse with them."

"It is no less than I expected," said the stranger; "nevertheless, I might be received without his knowledge.   A barn, a hay-loft, a cart-shed, any place where I could stretch me down, would be to my habits like a tabernacle of silver set about with planks of cedar."

" I assure you," said Morton, much embarrassed, " that I have not the means of receiving you at Milnwood without my uncle's consent and knowledge ; nor, if I could do so, would I think myself justifiable in engaging him unconsciously in a danger which, most of all others, he fears and deprecates."

" Well," said the traveller, " I have but one word to say. Did you ever hear your father mention John Balfour of Burley ?"

" His ancient friend and comrade who saved his life, with almost the loss of his own, in the battle of Long Marston Moor ? Often, very often."

" I am that Balfour," said his companion. "Yonder stands thy uncle's house ; I see the light among the trees. The avenger of blood is behind me, and my death certain unless I have refuge there. Now, make thy choice, young man ; to shrink from the side of thy father's friend like a thief in the night, and to leave him exposed to the bloody death from which he rescued thy father, or to expose thine uncle's worldly goods to such peril as in this perverse generation attends those who give a morsel of bread or a draught of cold water to a Christian man when perishing for lack of refreshment !"

A thousand recollections thronged on the mind of Morton at once. His father, whose memory he idolized, had often enlarged upon his obligations to this man, and regretted that after having been long comrades, they had parted in some unkindness at the time when the kingdom of Scotland was divided into Resolutioners and Protesters ; the former of whom adhered to Charles II., after his father's death upon the scaffold, while the Protesters inclined rather to a union with the triumphant republicans. The stern fanaticism of Burley had attached him to this latter party, and the comrades had parted in displeasure, never, as it happened, to meet again. These circumstances the deceased Colonel Morton had often mentioned to his son, and always with an expression of deep regret that he had never, in any manner, been enabled to repay the assistance which on more than one occasion he had received from Burley.

To hasten Morton's decision, the night-wind, as it swept along, brought from a distance the sullen sound of a kettle-drum, which, seeming to approach nearer, intimated that a body of horse were upon their march towards them.

"It must be Claverhouse with the rest of his regiment. What can have occasioned this night-march ? If you go on you fall into their hands ; if you turn back towards the borough-town you are in no less danger from Cornet Grahame's party.   The path to the hill is beset.   I must shelter you at Milnwood, or expose you to instant death ; but the punishment of the law shall fall upon myself, as in justice it should, not upon my uncle.   Follow me."

Burley, who had awaited his resolution with great composure, now followed him in silence.

The house of Milnwood, built by the father of the present proprietor, was a decent mansion, suitable to the size of the estate, but since the accession of this owner, it had been suffered to go considerably into disrepair.   At some little distance from the house stood the court of offices.   Here Morton paused.

"I must leave you here for a little while," he whispered, "until I can provide a bed for you in the house."

"I care little for such delicacy," said Burley ; "for thirty years this head has rested oftener on the turf, or on the next gray stone, than upon either wool or down.   A draught of ale, a morsel of bread, to say my prayers, and to stretch me upon dry hay, were to me as good as a painted chamber and a prince's table."

It occurred to Morton at the same moment that to attempt to introduce the fugitive within the house would materially increase the danger of detection.   Accordingly, having struck a light with implements left in the stable for that purpose, and having fastened up their horses, he assigned Burley for his place of repose a wooden bed, placed in a loft half full of hay, which an out-of-door domestic had occupied until dismissed by his uncle in one of those fits of parsimony which became more rigid from day to day.   In this untenanted loft Morton left his companion, with a caution so to shade his light that no reflection might be seen from the window, and a promise that he would presently return with such refreshments as he might be able to procure at that late hour.   This last, indeed, was a subject on which he felt by no means confident, for the power of obtaining even the most ordinary provisions depended entirely upon the humor in which he might happen to find his uncle's sole confidante, the old housekeeper.   If she chanced to be abed, which was very likely, or out of humor, which was not less so, Morton well knew the case to be at least problematical.

Cursing in his heart the sordid parsimony which pervaded

every part of his uncle's establishment, he gave the usual
gentle knock at the bolted door, by which he was accustomed
to seek admittance when accident had detained him abroad
beyond the early and established hours of rest at the house of
Milnwood. It was a sort of hesitating tap, which carried an
acknowledgment of transgression in its very sound, and seemed
rather to solicit than command attention. After it had been
repeated again and again, the housekeeper, grumbling betwixt
her teeth as she rose from the chimney-corner in the hall, and
wrapping her checked handkerchief round her head to secure
her from the cold air, paced across the stone passage, and repeated a careful "Wha's there at this time o' night?" more
than once before she undid the bolts and bars and cautiously
opened the door.

"This is a fine time o' night, Mr. Henry," said the old
dame, with the tyrannic insolence of a spoiled and favorite
domestic; "a braw time o' night and a bonny to disturb a
peaceful house in, and to keep quiet folk out o' their beds
waiting for you. Your uncle's been in his maist three hours
syne, and Robin's ill o' the rheumatize, and he's to his bed too,
and sae I had to sit up for ye mysell, for as sair a hoast as I hae."

Here she coughed once or twice in further evidence of the
egregious inconvenience which she had sustained.

"Much obliged to you, Alison, and many kind thanks."

"Hegh, sirs, sae fair-fashioned as we are! Mony folk ca'
me Mistress Wilson, and Milnwood himsell is the only ane
about this town thinks o' ca'ing me Alison, and indeed he as
often says Mrs. Alison as ony other thing."

"Well, then, Mistress Alison," said Morton, "I really
am sorry to have kept you up waiting till I came in."

"And now that you are come in, Mr. Henry," said the cross
old woman, "what for do you no tak up your candle and gang to
your bed? and mind ye dinna let the candle sweal as ye gang
alang the wainscot parlor, and haud a' the house scouring to
get out the grease again."

"But, Alison, I really must have something to eat, and
a draught of ale, before I go to bed."

"Eat! and ale, Mr. Henry! My certie, ye're ill to serve.
Do ye think we havena heard o' your grand popinjay wark
yonder, and how ye bleezed away as muckle pouther as wad
hae shot a' the wild-fowl that we'll want atween this and
Candlemas; and then ganging majoring to the piper's Howff
wi' a' the idle loons in the country, and sitting there birling
at your poor uncle's cost, nae doubt, wi' a' the scaff and raff o'

the water-side till sundown, and then coming hame and crying for ale as if ye were maister and mair!"

Extremely vexed, yet anxious, on account of his guest, to procure refreshments if possible, Morton suppressed his resentment, and good-humoredly assured Mrs. Wilson that he was really both hungry and thirsty; "and as for the shooting at the popinjay, I have heard you say you have been there yourself, Mrs. Wilson. I wish you had come to look at us."

"Ah, Maister Henry," said the old dame, "I wish ye binna beginning to learn the way of blawing in a woman's lug wi' a' your whilly-wha's! Aweel, sae ye dinna practise them but on auld wives like me the less matter. But tak heed o' the young queans, lad. Popinjay—ye think yoursell a braw fellow enow; and troth! [surveying him with the candle] there's nae fault to find wi' the outside, if the inside be conforming. But I mind when I was a gilpy of a lassock seeing the Duke—that was him that lost his head at London; folks said it wasna a very gude ane, but it was aye a sair loss to him, puir gentleman. Aweel, he wan the popinjay, for few cared to win it ower his Grace's head. Weel, he had a comely presence, and when a' the gentles mounted to show their capers, his Grace was as near to me as I am to you, and he said to me, 'Tak tent o' yoursell, my bonny lassie'—these were his very words—'for my horse is not very chancy.' And now, as ye say ye had sae little to eat or drink, I'll let you see that I havena been sae unmindfu' o' you; for I dinna think it's safe for young folk to gang to their bed on an empty stamach."

To do Mrs. Wilson justice, her nocturnal harangues upon such occasions not unfrequently terminated with this sage apothegm, which always prefaced the producing of some provision a little better than ordinary, such as she now placed before him. In fact, the principal object of her "maundering" was to display her consequence and love of power; for Mrs. Wilson was not at the bottom an ill-tempered woman, and certainly loved her old and young master (both of whom she tormented extremely) better than any one else in the world. She now eyed Mr. Henry, as she called him, with great complacency as he partook of her good cheer.

"Muckle gude may it do ye, my bonny man. I trow ye dinna get sic a skirl-in-the-pan as that at Niel Blane's. His wife was a canny body, and could dress things very weel for ane in her line o' business, but no like a gentleman's housekeeper, to be sure. But I doubt the daughter's a silly thing; an unco cockernony she had busked on her head at the kirk last

Sunday. I am doubting that there will be news o' a' thae braws. But my auld e'en's drawing thegither; dinna hurry yoursell, my bonny man. Tak mind about the putting out the candle, and there's a horn of ale and a glass of clow-gillie-flower water. I dinna gie ilka body that; I keep it for a pain I hae whiles in my ain stamach, and it's better for your young blood than brandy. Sae gude-night to ye, Mr. Henry, and see that ye tak gude care o' the candle."

Morton promised to attend punctually to her caution, and requested her not to be alarmed if she heard the door opened, as she knew he must again, as usual, look to his horse and arrange him for the night. Mrs. Wilson then retreated, and Morton, folding up his provisions, was about to hasten to his guest when the nodding head of the old housekeeper was again thrust in at the door with an admonition to remember to take an account of his ways before he laid himself down to rest, and to pray for protection during the hours of darkness.

Such were the manners of a certain class of domestics,* once common in Scotland, and perhaps still to be found in some old manor-houses in its remote counties. They were fixtures in the family they belonged to; and, as they never conceived the possibility of such a thing as dismissal to be within the chances of their lives, they were, of course, sincerely attached to every member of it. On the other hand, when spoiled by the indulgence or indolence of their superiors, they were very apt to become ill-tempered, self-sufficient, and tyrannical; so much so that a mistress or master would sometimes almost have wished to exchange their cross-grained fidelity for the smooth and accommodating duplicity of a modern menial.

* See Old Family Servants. Note 9.

CHAPTER VI

Yea, this man's brow, like to a tragic leaf,
Foretells the nature of a tragic volume.

SHAKESPEARE.

BEING at length rid of the housekeeper's presence, Morton made a collection of what he had reserved from the provisions set before him and prepared to carry them to his concealed guest. He did not think it necessary to take a light, being perfectly acquainted with every turn of the road ; and it was lucky he did not do so, for he had hardly stepped beyond the threshold ere a heavy tramping of horses announced that the body of cavalry, whose kettle-drums* they had before heard, were in the act of passing along the high-road which winds round the foot of the bank on which the house of Milnwood was placed. He heard the commanding officer distinctly give the word "Halt." A pause of silence followed, interrupted only by the occasional neighing or pawing of an impatient charger.

"Whose house is this ?" said a voice in a tone of authority and command.

"Milnwood, if it like your honor," was the reply.

"Is the owner well affected ?" said the inquirer.

"He complies with the orders of government, and frequents an indulged minister," was the response.

"Hum ! ay ! indulged ! A mere mask for treason, very impolitically allowed to those who are too great cowards to wear their principles barefaced. Had we not better send up a party and search the house in case some of the bloody villains concerned in this heathenish butchery may be concealed in it ?"

Ere Morton could recover from the alarm into which this proposal had thrown him a third speaker rejoined, "I cannot think it at all necessary ; Milnwood is an infirm, hypochondriac old man, who never meddles with politics, and loves his money-bags and bonds better than anything else in the world. His nephew, I hear, was at the wappenschaw to-day, and

* See Military Music at Night. Note 10.

42

gained the popinjay, which does not look like a fanatic. I should think they are all gone to bed long since, and an alarm ᴄ. this time of night might kill the poor old man."

"Well," rejoined the leader, "if that be so, to search the house would be lost time, of which we have but little to throw away. Gentlemen of the Life Guards, forward. March!"

A few notes on the trumpet, mingled with the occasional boom of the kettle-drum to mark the cadence, joined with the tramp of hoofs and the clash of arms, announced that the troop had resumed its march. The moon broke out as the leading files of the column attained a hill up which the road winded and showed indistinctly the glittering of the steel caps; and the dark figures of the horses and riders might be imperfectly traced through the gloom. They continued to advance up the hill and sweep over the top of it in such long succession as intimated a considerable numerical force.

When the last of them had disappeared young Morton resumed his purpose of visiting his guest. Upon entering the place of refuge he found him seated on his humble couch with a pocket Bible open in his hand, which he seemed to study with intense meditation. His broadsword, which he had unsheathed in the first alarm at the arrival of the dragoons, lay naked across his knees, and the little taper that stood beside him upon the old chest, which served the purpose of a table, threw a partial and imperfect light upon those stern and harsh features, in which ferocity was rendered more solemn and dignified by a wild cast of tragic enthusiasm. His brow was that of one in whom some strong o'ermastering principle has overwhelmed all other passions and feelings, like the swell of a high spring-tide, when the usual cliffs and breakers vanish from the eye, and their existence is only indicated by the chafing foam of the waves that burst and wheel over them. He raised his head after Morton had contemplated him for about a minute.

"I perceive," said Morton, looking at his sword, "that you heard the horsemen ride by; their passage delayed me for some minutes."

"I scarcely heeded them," said Balfour; "my hour is not yet come. That I shall one day fall into their hands and be honorably associated with the saints whom they have slaughtered, I am full well aware. And I would, young man, that the hour were come; it should be as welcome to me as ever wedding to bridegroom. But if my Master has more work for me on earth I must not do His labor grudgingly."

"Eat and refresh yourself," said Morton; "to-morrow your safety requires you should leave this place in order to gain the hills so soon as you can see to distinguish the track through the morasses."

"Young man," returned Balfour, "you are already weary of me, and would be yet more so, perchance, did you know the task upon which I have been lately put. And I wonder not that it should be so, for there are times when I am weary of myself. Think you not it is a sore trial for flesh and blood to be called upon to execute the righteous judgments of Heaven while we are yet in the body, and continue to retain that blinded sense and sympathy for carnal suffering which makes our own flesh thrill when we strike a gash upon the body of another? And think you that when some prime tyrant has been removed from his place, that the instruments of his punishment can at all times look back on their share in his downfall with firm and unshaken nerves? Must they not sometimes even question the truth of that inspiration which they have felt and acted under? Must they not sometimes doubt the origin of that strong impulse with which their prayers for heavenly direction under difficulties have been inwardly answered and confirmed, and confuse, in their disturbed apprehensions, the responses of Truth itself with some strong delusion of the enemy?"

"These are subjects, Mr. Balfour, on which I am ill-qualified to converse with you," answered Morton; "but I own I should strongly doubt the origin of any inspiration which seemed to dictate a line of conduct contrary to those feelings of natural humanity which Heaven has assigned to us as the general law of our conduct."

Balfour seemed somewhat disturbed, and drew himself hastily up, but immediately composed himself and answered coolly, "It is natural you should think so; you are yet in the dungeon-house of the law, a pit darker than that into which Jeremiah was plunged, even the dungeon of Malcaiah the son of Hamelmelech, where there was no water but mire. Yet is the seal of the covenant upon your forehead, and the son of the righteous who resisted to blood, where the banner was spread on the mountains, shall not be utterly lost as one of the children of darkness. Trow ye that in this day of bitterness and calamity nothing is required at our hands but to keep the moral law as far as our carnal frailty will permit? Think ye our conquests must be only over our corrupt and evil affections and passions? No; we are called upon, when we have girded up our loins, to run the race boldly, and when we have drawn the sword we are enjoined to smite the ungodly though he be our neighbor, and the man of power and cruelty though he were of our own kindred and the friend of our own bosom.''

"These are the sentiments," said Morton, "that your enemies impute to you, and which palliate, if they do not vindicate, the cruel measures which the council have directed against you. They affirm that you pretend to derive your rule of action from what you call an inward light, rejecting the restraints of legal magistracy, of national law, and even of common humanity, when in opposition to what you call the spirit within you.''

"They do us wrong," answered the Covenanter; "it is they, perjured as they are, who have rejected all law, both divine and civil, and who now persecute us for adherence to the Solemn League and Covenant between God and the kingdom of Scotland, to which all of them, save a few Popish malignants, have sworn in former days, yet which they now burn in the market-places, and tread under foot in derision. When this Charles Stewart returned to these kingdoms, did the malignants bring him back? They had tried it with strong hand, but they failed, I trow. Could James Grahame of Montrose and his Highland caterans have put him again in the place of his father? I think their heads on the Westport told another tale for many a long day. It was the workers of the glorious work, the reformers of the beauty of the tabernacle that called him again to the high place from which his father fell. And what has been our reward? In the words of the prophet, ' We looked for peace, but no good came ; and for a time of health, and behold trouble. The snorting of his horses was heard from Dan ; the whole land trembled at the sound of the neighing of his strong ones ; for they are come, and have devoured the land and all that is in it.' ''

"Mr. Balfour," answered Morton, "I neither undertake to subscribe to or refute your complaints against the government. I have endeavored to repay a debt due to the comrade of my father by giving you shelter in your distress, but you will excuse me from engaging myself either in your cause or in controversy. I will leave you to repose, and heartily wish it were in my power to render your condition more comfortable.''

"But I shall see you, I trust, in the morning ere I depart? I am not a man whose bowels yearn after kindred and friends of this world. When I put my hand to the plough I entered into a covenant with my worldly affections that I should not look back on the things I left behind me.

Yet the son of mine ancient comrade is to me as mine own, and I cannot behold him without the deep and firm belief that I shall one day see him gird on his sword in the dear and precious cause for which his father fought and bled."

With a promise on Morton's part that he would call the refugee when it was time for him to pursue his journey, they parted for the night.

Morton retired to a few hours' rest ; but his imagination, disturbed by the events of the day, did not permit him to enjoy sound repose. There was a blended vision of horror before him, in which his new friend seemed to be a principal actor. The fair form of Edith Bellenden also mingled in his dream, weeping, and with dishevelled hair, and appearing to call on him for comfort and assistance which he had not in his power to render. He awoke from these unrefreshing slumbers with a feverish impulse and a heart which foreboded disaster. There was already a tinge of dazzling lustre on the verge of the distant hills, and the dawn was abroad in all the freshness of a summer morning.

" I have slept too long," he exclaimed to himself, "and must now hasten to forward the journey of this unfortunate fugitive."

He dressed himself as fast as possible, opened the door of the house with as little noise as he could, and hastened to the place of refuge occupied by the Covenanter. Morton entered on tiptoe, for the determined tone and manner, as well as the unusual language and sentiments of this singular individual, had struck him with a sensation approaching to awe. Balfour was still asleep. A ray of light streamed on his uncurtained couch, and showed to Morton the working of his harsh features, which seemed agitated by some strong internal cause of disturbance. He had not undressed. Both his arms were above the bed-cover, the right hand strongly clinched, and occasionally making that abortive attempt to strike which usually attends dreams of violence ; the left was extended, and agitated from time to time by a movement as if repulsing some one. The perspiration stood on his brow "like bubbles in a late disturbed stream," and these marks of emotion were accompanied with broken words which escaped from him at intervals—"Thou art taken, Judas—thou art taken. Cling not to my knees—cling not to my knees ; hew him down ! A priest ! Ay, a priest of Baal, to be bound and slain, even at the brook Kishon. Firearms will not prevail against him. Strike—thrust with the cold iron—put him out of pain—put him out of pain, were it but for the sake of his gray hairs."

Much alarmed at the import of these expressions, which seemed to burst from him even in sleep with the stern energy accompanying the perpetration of some act of violence, Morton shook his guest by the shoulder in order to awake him. The first words he uttered were, "Bear me where ye will, I will avouch the deed!"

His glance around having then fully awakened him, he at once assumed all the stern and gloomy composure of his ordinary manner, and throwing himself on his knees before speaking to Morton poured forth an ejaculatory prayer for the suffering Church of Scotland, entreating that the blood of her murdered saints and martyrs might be precious in the sight of Heaven, and that the shield of the Almighty might be spread over the scattered remnant, who, for His name's sake, were abiders in the wilderness. Vengeance, speedy and ample vengeance on the oppressors, was the concluding petition of his devotions, which he expressed aloud in strong and emphatic language, rendered more impressive by the Orientalism of Scripture.

When he had finished his prayer he arose, and taking Morton by the arm, they descended together to the stable, where the Wanderer (to give Burley a title which was often conferred on his sect) began to make his horse ready to pursue his journey. When the animal was saddled and bridled, Burley requested Morton to walk with him a gun-shot into the wood and direct him to the right road for gaining the moors. Morton readily complied, and they walked for some time in silence under the shade of some fine old trees, pursuing a sort of natural path, which, after passing through woodland for about half a mile, led into the bare and wild country which extends to the foot of the hills.

There was little conversation between them, until at length Burley suddenly asked Morton, "Whether the words he had spoken over-night had borne fruit in his mind?"

Morton answered, "That he remained of the same opinion which he had formerly held, and was determined, at least as far and as long as possible, to unite the duties of a good Christian with those of a peaceful subject."

"In other words," replied Burley, "you are desirous to serve both God and Mammon—to be one day professing the truth with your lips, and the next day in arms, at the command of carnal and tyrannic authority, to shed the blood of those who for the truth have forsaken all things? Think ye," he continued, "to touch pitch and remain undefiled ? to mix in the ranks of malignants, papists, papa-prelatists, latitudinarians, and scoffers ; to partake of their sports, which are like the meat offered unto idols ; to hold intercourse, perchance, with their daughters, as the sons of God with the daughters of men in the world before the flood. Think you, I say, to do all these things and yet remain free from pollution ? I say unto you that all communication with the enemies of the church is the accursed thing which God hateth ! Touch not, taste not, handle not! And grieve not, young man, as if you alone were called upon to subdue your carnal affections, and renounce the pleasures which are a snare to your feet. I say to you, that the son of David hath denounced no better lot on the whole generation of mankind."

He then mounted his horse, and, turning to Morton, repeated the text of Scripture, "An heavy yoke was ordained for the sons of Adam from the day they go out of their mother's womb till the day that they return to the mother of all things, from him who is clothed in blue silk and weareth a crown even to him who weareth simple linen—wrath, envy, trouble, and unquietness, rigor, strife, and fear of death in the time of rest."

Having uttered these words he set his horse in motion, and soon disappeared among the boughs of the forest.

"Farewell, stern enthusiast," said Morton, looking after him ; "in some moods of my mind how dangerous would be the society of such a companion ! If I am unmoved by his zeal for abstract doctrines of faith, or rather for a peculiar mode of worship [such was the purport of his reflections], can I be a man and a Scotchman, and look with indifference on that persecution which has made wise men mad ? Was not the cause of freedom, civil and religious, that for which my father fought ; and shall I do well to remain inactive or to take the part of an oppressive government if there should appear any rational prospect of redressing the insufferable wrongs to which my miserable countrymen are subjected ? And yet, who shall warrant me that these people, rendered wild by persecution, would not, in the hour of victory, be as cruel and as intolerant as those by whom they are now hunted down ? What degree of moderation or of mercy can be expected from this Burley, so distinguished as one of their principal champions, and who seems even now to be reeking from some recent deed of violence, and to feel stings of remorse which even his enthusiasm cannot altogether stifle ? I am weary of seeing nothing but violence and fury around me—now assuming the mask of lawful authority, now taking that of religious zeal. I am sick of my country, of myself, of my dependent situation, of my repressed feelings, of these woods, of that river, of that house, of all but Edith, and she can never be mine ! Why should I haunt her walks? Why encourage my own delusion, and perhaps hers? She can never be mine. Her grandmother's pride, the opposite principles of our families, my wretched state of dependence—a poor miserable slave, for I have not even the wages of a servant ; all circumstances give the lie to the vain hope that we can ever be united. Why then protract a delusion so painful ?

"But I am no slave," he said aloud, and drawing himself up to his full stature—"no slave in one respect surely. I can change my abode, my father's sword is mine, and Europe lies open before me as before him and hundreds besides of my countrymen who have filled it with the fame of their exploits. Perhaps some lucky chance may raise me to a rank with our Ruthvens, our Lesleys, our Monros, the chosen leaders of the famous Protestant champion, Gustavus Adolphus, or if not, a soldier's life or a soldier's grave."

When he had formed this determination he found himself near the door of his uncle's house, and resolved to lose no time in making him acquainted with it.

"Another glance of Edith's eye, another walk by Edith's side, and my resolution would melt away. I will take an irrevocable step, therefore, and then see her for the last time."

In this mood he entered the wainscotted parlor, in which his uncle was already placed at his morning's refreshment, a huge plate of oatmeal porridge, with a corresponding allowance of buttermilk. The favorite housekeeper was in attendance, half standing, half resting on the back of a chair, in a posture betwixt freedom and respect. The old gentleman had been remarkably tall in his earlier days, an advantage which he now lost by stooping to such a degree that at a meeting, where there was some dispute concerning the sort of arch which should be thrown over a considerable brook, a facetious neighbor proposed to offer Milnwood a handsome sum for his curved backbone, alleging that he would sell anything that belonged to him. Splay feet of unusual size, long thin hands garnished with nails which seldom felt the steel, a wrinkled and puckered visage, the length of which corresponded with that of his person, together with a pair of little sharp bargain-making gray eyes that seemed eternally looking out for their advantage, completed the highly unpromising exterior of Mr. Morton of Milnwood. As it would have been very injudicious to have lodged a liberal or benevolent disposition in such an unworthy cabinet, nature had suited his person with a mind exactly in conformity with it—that is to say, mean, selfish, and covetous.

When this amiable personage was aware of the presence of his nephew he hastened, before addressing him, to swallow the spoonful of porridge which he was in the act of conveying to his mouth, and as it chanced to be scalding hot, the pain occasioned by its descent down his throat and into his stomach inflamed the ill-humor with which he was already prepared to meet his kinsman.

"The deil take them that made them!" was his first ejaculation, apostrophizing his mess of porridge.

"They're gude parritch eneugh," said Mrs. Wilson, "if ye wad but take time to sup them. I made them mysell; but if folk winna hae patience they should get their thrapples causewayed."

"Haud your peace, Alison! I was speaking to my nevoy. How is this, sir? And what sort o' scampering gates are these o' going on? Ye were not at hame last night till near midnight."

"Thereabouts, sir, I believe," answered Morton, in an indifferent tone.

"Thereabouts, sir! What sort of an answer is that, sir? Why came ye na hame when other folk left the grund?"

"I suppose you know the reason very well, sir," said Morton: "I had the fortune to be the best marksman of the day, and remained, as is usual, to give some little entertainment to the other young men."

"The deevil ye did, sir! And ye come to tell me that to my face? *You* pretend to gie entertainments that canna come by a dinner except by sorning on a carefu' man like me? But if ye put me to charges I'se work it out o' ye. I seena why ye shouldna haud the pleugh now that the pleughman has left us; it wad set ye better than wearing thae green duds and wasting your siller on powther and lead; it wad put ye in an honest calling, and wad keep ye in bread without being behadden to ony ane."

"I am very ambitious of learning such a calling, sir, but I don't understand driving the plough."

"And what for no? It's easier than your gunning and archery that ye like sae weel. Auld Davie is ca'ing it e'en now, and ye may be goadsman for the first twa or three days; and tak tent ye dinna o'erdrive the owsen, and then ye will

be fit to gang between the stilts.   Ye'll ne'er learn younger,
I'll be your caution.   Haggie Holm is heavy land, and Davie
is ower auld to keep the coulter down now."

"I beg pardon for interrupting you, sir, but I have formed
a scheme for myself which will have the same effect of relieving you of the burden and charge attending my company."

"Ay!   Indeed! a scheme o' yours! that must be a denty
ane!" said the uncle, with a very peculiar sneer.   "Let's hear
about it, lad."

"It is said in two words, sir.   I intend to leave this country and serve abroad as my father did before these unhappy
troubles broke out at home.   His name will not be so entirely
forgotten in the countries where he served but that it will
procure his son at least the opportunity of trying his fortune
as a soldier."

"Gude be gracious to us!" exclaimed the housekeeper;
"our young Mr. Harry gang abroad?   Na, na! eh, na! that
maun never be."

Milnwood, entertaining no thought or purpose of parting
with his nephew, who was, moreover, very useful to him in
many respects, was thunderstruck at this abrupt declaration
of independence from a person whose deference to him had
hitherto been unlimited.   He recovered himself, however, immediately.

"And wha do you think is to give you the means, young
man, for such a wild-goose chase?   Not I, I am sure.   I can
hardly support you at hame.   And ye wad be marrying, I'se
warrant, as your father did afore ye, too, and sending your uncle
hame a pack o' weans to be fighting and skirling through the
house in my auld days, and to take wing and flee aff like
yoursell whenever they were asked to serve a turn about the
town?"

"I have no thoughts of ever marrying," answered Henry.

"Hear till him now!" said the housekeeper.   "It's a
shame to hear a douce young lad speak in that way, since a'
the warld kens that they maun either marry or do waur."

"Haud your peace, Alison," said her master; "and you,
Harry (he added more mildly), put this nonsense out o' your
head.   This comes o' letting ye gang a-sodgering for a day;
mind, ye hae nae siller, lad, for ony sic nonsense plans."

"I beg you pardon, sir, my wants shall be very few; and
would you please to give me the gold chain which the margrave gave to my father after the battle of Lutzen——"

"Mercy on us! the gowd chain!" exclaimed his uncle.

"The chain of gowd!" re-echoed the housekeeper—both aghast with astonishment at the audacity of the proposal.

"I will keep a few links, to remind me of him by whom it was won, and the place where he won it," continued Morton; "the rest shall furnish me the means of following the same career in which my father obtained that mark of distinction."

"Mercifu' powers!" exclaimed the governante, "my master wears it every Sunday."

"Sunday and Saturday," added old Milnwood, "whenever I put on my black velvet coat; and Wylie Mactrickit is partly of opinion it's a kind of heirloom that rather belangs to the head of the house than to the immediate descendant. It has three thousand links; I have counted them a thousand times. It's worth three hundred pounds sterling."

"That is more than I want, sir; if you choose to give me the third part of the money and five links of the chain it will amply serve my purpose, and the rest will be some slight atonement for the expense and trouble I have put you to."

"The laddie's in a creel!" exclaimed his uncle. "O, sirs, what will become o' the rigs o' Milnwood when I am dead and gane! He would fling the crown of Scotland awa if he had it."

"Hout, sir," said the old housekeeper, "I maun e'en say it's partly your ain faut. Ye maunna curb his head ower sair in neither; and, to be sure, since he *has* gane doun to the Howff, ye maun just e'en pay the lawing."

"If it be not abune twa dollars, Alison," said the old gentleman, very reluctantly.

"I'll settle it mysell wi' Niel Blane the first time I gang down to the clachan," said Alison, "cheaper than your honor or Mr. Harry can do;" and then whispered to Henry, "Dinna vex him ony mair; I'll pay the lave out o' the butter siller, and nae mair words about it." Then proceeding aloud, "And ye maunna speak o' the young gentleman hauding the pleugh; there's puir distressed Whigs enow about the country will be glad to do that for a bite and a soup; it sets them far better than the like o' him."

"And then we'll hae the dragoons on us," said Milnwood, "for comforting and entertaining intercommuned rebels; a bonny strait ye wad put us in! But take your breakfast, Harry, and then lay by your new green coat and put on your raploch-gray, it's a mair mensfu' and thrifty dress, and a mair seemly sight than thae dangling slops and ribbands."

Morton left the room, perceiving plainly that he had at

present no chance of gaining his purpose, and perhaps not altogether displeased at the obstacles which seemed to present themselves to his leaving the neighborhood of Tillietudlem. The housekeeper followed him into the next room, patting him on the back and bidding him "be a gude bairn and pit by his braw things."

"And I'll loop doun your hat and lay by the band and ribband," said the officious dame; "and ye maun never at no hand speak o' leaving the land or of selling the gowd chain, for your uncle has an unco pleasure in looking on you, and in counting the links of the chainzie; and ye ken auld folk canna last forever, sae the chain and the lands and a' will be your ain ae day; and ye may marry ony leddy in the country-side ye like, and keep a braw house at Milnwood, for there's enow o' means; and is not that worth waiting for, my dow?"

There was something in the latter part of the prognostic which sounded so agreeably in the ears of Morton that he shook the old dame cordially by the hand, and assured her he was much obliged by her good advice, and would weigh it carefully before he proceeded to act upon his former resolution.

CHAPTER VII

From seventeen years till now, almost fourscore,
Here lived I, but now live here no more.
At seventeen years many their fortunes seek,
But at fourscore it is too late a week.
As You Like It.

WE must conduct our readers to the Tower of Tillietudlem,
to which Lady Margaret Bellenden had returned, in romantic
phrase, malcontent and full of heaviness at the unexpected,
and, as she deemed it, indelible affront which had been brought
upon her dignity by the public miscarriage of Goose Gibbie.
That unfortunate man-at-arms was forthwith commanded to
drive his feathered charge to the most remote parts of the
common moor, and on no account to awaken the grief or resentment of his lady by appearing in her presence while the
sense of the affront was yet recent.

The next proceeding of Lady Margaret was to hold a
solemn court of justice, to which Harrison and the butler were
admitted, partly on the footing of witnesses, partly as assess-
ors, to inquire into the recusancy of Cuddie Headrigg the
ploughman, and the abetment which he had received from
his mother—these being regarded as the original causes of the
disaster which had befallen the chivalry of Tillietudlem.
The charge being fully made out and substantiated, Lady Margaret resolved to reprimand the culprits in person, and, if she
found them impenitent, to extend the censure into a sentence
of expulsion from the barony. Miss Bellenden alone ventured to say anything in behalf of the accused; but her
countenance did not profit them, as it might have done on any
other occasion. For so soon as Edith had heard it ascertained
that the unfortunate cavalier had not suffered in his person,
his disaster had affected her with an irresistible disposition
to laugh, which, in spite of Lady Margaret's indignation, or
rather irritated, as usual, by restraint, had broken out repeatedly on her return homeward, until her grandmother, in no
shape imposed upon by the several fictitious causes which the
young lady assigned for her ill-timed risibility, upbraided her
in very bitter terms with being insensible to the honor of her

family. Miss Bellenden's intercession, therefore, had on this occasion little or no chance to be listened to.

As if to evince the rigor of her disposition, Lady Margaret on this solemn occasion exchanged the ivory-headed cane with which she commonly walked for an immense gold-headed staff which had belonged to her father, the deceased Earl of Torwood, and which, like a sort of mace of office, she only made use of on occasions of special solemnity. Supported by this awful baton of command, Lady Margaret Bellenden entered the cottage of the delinquents.

There was an air of consciousness about old Mause as she rose from her wicker chair in the chimney-nook, not with the cordial alertness of visage which used on other occasions to express the honor she felt in the visit of her lady, but with a certain solemnity and embarrassment, like an accused party on his first appearance in presence of his judge, before whom he is nevertheless determined to assert his innocence. Her arms were folded, her mouth primmed into an expression of respect mingled with obstinacy, her whole mind apparently bent up to the solemn interview. With her best courtesy to the ground, and a mute motion of reverence, Mause pointed to the chair which on former occasions Lady Margaret (for the good lady was somewhat of a gossip) had deigned to occupy for half an hour sometimes at a time, hearing the news of the county and of the borough.

But at present her mistress was far too indignant for such condescension. She rejected the mute invitation with a haughty wave of her hand, and, drawing herself up as she spoke, she uttered the following interrogatory in a tone calculated to overwhelm the culprit. "Is it true, Mause, as I am informed by Harrison, Gudyill, and others of my people, that you hae taen it upon you, contrary to the faith you owe to God and the king and to me, your natural lady and mistress, to keep back your son frae the wappenschaw, held by the order of the sheriff, and to return his armor and abulyiements at a moment when it was impossible to find a suitable delegate in his stead, whereby the barony of Tillietudlem, baith in the person of its mistress and indwellers, has incurred sic a disgrace and dishonor as hasna befa'en the family since the days of Malcolm Canmore?"

Mause's habitual respect for her mistress was extreme; she hesitated, and one or two short coughs expressed the difficulty she had in defending herself. "I am sure, my leddy —hem, hem! I am sure I am sorry, very sorry, that ony cause of displeasure should hae occurred ; but my son's illness——"

"Dinna tell me of your son's illness, Mause ! Had he been sincerely unweel, ye would hae been at the Tower by daylight to get something that wad do him gude ; there are few ailments that I havena medical recipes for, and that ye ken fu' weel."

"O ay, my leddy ! I am sure ye hae wrought wonderful cures ; the last thing ye sent Cuddie, when he had the batts, e'en wrought like a charm."

"Why, then, woman, did ye not apply to me, if there was ony real need ? But there was none, ye fause-hearted vassal that ye are ! "

"Your leddyship never ca'd me sic a word as that before. Ohon ! that I suld live to be ca'd sae," she continued, bursting into tears, "and me a born servant o' the house o' Tillietudlem! I am sure they belie baith Cuddie and me sair, if they said he wadna fight ower the boots in bluid for your leddyship and Miss Edith and the auld Tower—ay suld he, and I would rather see him buried beneath it than he suld gie way ; but thir ridings and wappenschawings, my leddy, I hae nae broo o' them ava. I can find nae warrant for them whatsoever."

"Nae warrant for them ! " cried the high-born dame. "Do ye na ken, woman, that ye are bound to be liege vassals in all hunting, hosting, watching and warding, when lawfully summoned thereto in my name ? Your service is not gratuitous. I trow ye hae land for it. Ye're kindly tenants, hae a cothouse, a kale-yard, and a cow's grass on the common. Few hae been brought farther ben, and ye grudge your son suld gie me a day's service in the field ? "

"Na, my leddy—na, my leddy, it's no that ! " exclaimed Mause, greatly embarrassed, "but ane canna serve twa maisters; and, if the truth maun e'en come out, there's Ane abune whase commands I maun obey before your leddyship's. I am sure I would put neither king's nor kaisar's nor ony earthly creature's afore them."

"How mean ye by that, ye auld fule woman ? D'ye think that I order onything against conscience ?"

"I dinna pretend to say that, my leddy, in regard o' your leddyship's conscience, which has been brought up, as it were, wi' prelatic principles ; but ilka ane maun walk by the light o' their ain, and mine," said Mause, waxing bolder as the conference became animated, "tells me that I suld leave a'— cot, kale-yard, and cow's grass—and suffer a', rather than that I or mine should put on harness in an unlawfu' cause."

"Unlawfu'!" exclaimed her mistress; "the cause to which you are called by your lawful leddy and mistress, by the command of the king, by the writ of the privy council, by the order of the lord-lieutenant, by the warrant of the sheriff!"

"Ay, my leddy, nae doubt; but, no to displeasure your leddyship, ye'll mind that there was ance a king in Scripture they ca'd Nebuchadnezzar, and he set up a golden image in the plain o' Dura, as it might be in the haugh yonder by the water-side, where the array were warned to meet yesterday, and the princes, and the governors, and the captains, and the judges themsells, forbye the treasurers, the counsellors, and the sheriffs, were warned to the dedication thereof, and commanded to fall down and worship at the sound of the cornet, flute, harp, sackbut, psaltery, and all kinds of music."

"And what o' a' this, ye fule wife? Or what had Nebuchadnezzar to do with the wappenschaw of the Upper Ward of Clydesdale?"

"Only just thus far, my leddy," continued Mause, firmly, "that prelacy is like the great golden image in the plain of Dura, and that as Shadrach, Meshach, and Abednego were borne out in refusing to bow down and worship, so neither shall Cuddie Headrigg, your leddyship's poor pleughman, at least wi' his auld mither's consent, make murgeons or jenny-flections, as they ca' them, in the house of the prelates and curates, nor gird him wi' armor to fight in their cause, either at the sound of kettle-drums, organs, bagpipes, or ony other kind of music whatever."

Lady Margaret Bellenden heard this exposition of Scripture with the greatest possible indignation as well as surprise.

"I see which way the wind blaws," she exclaimed, after a pause of astonishment; "the vile spirit of the year 1642 is at wark again as merrily as ever, and ilka auld wife in the chimley-neuk will be for knapping doctrine wi' doctors o' divinity and the godly fathers o' the church."

"If your leddyship means the bishops and curates, I'm sure they hae been but stepfathers to the Kirk o' Scotland. And since your leddyship is pleased to speak o' parting wi' us, I am free to tell you a piece o' my mind in another article. Your leddyship and the steward hae been pleased to propose that my son Cuddie suld work in the barn wi' a newfangled machine* for dighting the corn frae the chaff, thus impiously thwarting the will of Divine Providence by raising wind for your leddyship's ain particular use by human art, instead of soliciting it by prayer, or waiting patiently for whatever dis-

* See Winnowing Machine. Note 11.

pensation of wind Providence was pleased to send upon the sheeling-hill. Now, my leddy——"

"The woman would drive ony reasonable being daft!" said Lady Margaret; then resuming her tone of authority and indifference, she concluded, "Weel, Mause, I'll just end where I suld hae begun. Ye're ower learned and ower godly for me to dispute wi'; sae I have just this to say—either Cuddie must attend musters when he's lawfully warned by the ground-officer, or the sooner he and you flit and quit my bounds the better. There's nae scarcity o' auld wives or ploughmen; but if there were, I had rather that the rigs of Tillietudlem bare naething but windlestraes and sandy lavrocks than that they were ploughed by rebels to the king."

"Aweel, my leddy," said Mause, "I was born here, and thought to die where my father died; and your leddyship has been a kind mistress, I'll ne'er deny that, and I'se ne'er cease to pray for you and for Miss Edith, and that ye may be brought to see the error of your ways. But still——"

"The error of my ways!" interrupted Lady Margaret, much incensed—"the error of *my* ways, ye uncivil woman!"

"Ou, ay, my leddy, we are blinded that live in this valley of tears and darkness, and hae a' ower mony errors, grit folks as weel as sma'; but, as I said, my puir bennison will rest wi' you and yours wherever I am. I will be wae to hear o' your affliction and blithe to hear o' your prosperity, temporal and spiritual. But I canna prefer the commands of an earthly mistress to those of a Heavenly Master, and sae I am e'en ready to suffer for righteousness' sake."

"It is very well," said Lady Margaret, turning her back in great displeasure; "ye ken my will, Mause, in the matter. I'll hae nae Whiggery in the barony of Tillietudlem; the next thing wad be to set up a conventicle in my very withdrawing-room."

Having said this she departed with an air of great dignity; and Mause, giving way to feelings which she had suppressed during the interview—for she, like her mistress, had her own feeling of pride—now lifted up her voice and wept aloud.

Cuddie, whose malady, real or pretended, still detained him in bed, lay perdue during all this conference, snugly ensconced within his boarded bedstead, and terrified to death lest Lady Margaret, whom he held in hereditary reverence, should have detected his presence and bestowed on him personally some of those bitter reproaches with which she loaded his mother. But as soon as he thought her ladyship fairly out of hearing he bounced up in his nest.

"The foul fa' ye, that I suld say sae," he cried out to his mother, "for a lang-tongued clavering wife, as my father, honest man, aye ca'd ye ! Couldna ye let the leddy alane wi' your Whiggery ? And I was e'en as great a gomeral to let ye persuade me to lie up here amang the blankets like a hurcheon instead o' gaun to the wappenschaw like other folk. Odd, but I put a trick on ye, for I was out at the window-bole when your auld back was turned, and awa down by to hae a baff at the popinjay, and I shot within twa on't. I cheated the leddy for your clavers, but I wasna gaun to cheat my jo. But she may marry whae she likes now, for I'm clean dung ower. This is a waur dirdum than we got frae Mr. Gudyill when ye garr'd me refuse to eat the plum-porridge on Yule Eve, as if it were ony matter to God or man whether a pleughman had suppit on minched pies or sour sowens."

"O, whisht, my bairn, whisht," replied Mause ; "thou kensna about thae things. It was forbidden meat, things dedicated to set days and holidays, which are inhibited to the use of Protestant Christians."

"And now," continued her son, "ye hae brought the leddy hersell on our hands ! An I could but hae gotten some decent claes in, I wad hae spanged out o' bed and tauld her I wad ride where she liked, night or day, an she wad but leave us the free house and the yaird, that grew the best early kale in the haill country, and the cow's grass."

"O wow ! my winsome bairn, Cuddie," continued the old dame, "murmur not at the dispensation ; never grudge suffering in the gude cause."

"But what ken I if the cause is gude or no, mither," rejoined Cuddie, "for a' ye bleeze out sae muckle doctrine about it ? It's clean beyond my comprehension a'thegither. I see nae sae muckle difference atween the twa ways o't as a' the folk pretend. It's very true the curates read aye the same words ower again ; and if they be right words, what for no ? A gude tale's no the waur o' being twice tauld, I trow ; and a body has aye the better chance to understand it. Everybody's no sae gleg at the uptake as ye are yoursell, mither."

"O, my dear Cuddie, this is the sairest distress of a'," said the anxious mother. "O, how aften have I shown ye the difference between a pure evangelical doctrine and ane that's corrupt wi' human inventions ? O, my bairn, if no for your ain saul's sake, yet for my gray hairs——"

"Weel, mither," said Cuddie, interrupting her, "what need ye mak sae muckle din about it ? I hae aye dune whate'er ye bade me, and gaed to kirk whare'er ye likit on the

Sundays, and fended weel for ye in the ilka days besides. And that's what vexes me mair than a' the rest, when I think how I am to fend for ye now in thae brickle times. I am no clear if I can pleugh ony place but the mains and Mucklewhame, at least I never tried ony other grund, and it wadna come natural to me. And nae neighboring heritors will daur to take us after being turned aff thae bounds for non-enormity."

"Non-conformity, hinnie," sighed Mause, "is the name that thae warldly men gie us."

"Weel, aweel, we'll hae to gang to a far country, maybe twall or fifteen miles aff. I could be a dragoon, nae doubt, for I can ride and play wi' the broadsword a bit, but ye wad be roaring about your blessing and your gray hairs." Here Mause's exclamations became extreme. "Weel, weel, I but spoke o't; besides, ye're ower auld to be sitting cocked up on a baggage-wagon wi' Eppie Dumblane, the corporal's wife. Sae what's to come o' us I canna weel see. I doubt I'll hae to tak the hills wi' the wild Whigs, as they ca' them, and then it will be my lot to be shot down like a mawkin at some dike-side, or to be sent to heaven wi' a Saint Johnstone's tippit about my hause."

"O, my bonnie Cuddie," said the zealous Mause, "forbear sic carnal, self-seeking language, whilk is just a misdoubting o' Providence. I have not seen the son of the righteous begging his bread, sae says the text; and your father was a douce, honest man, though somewhat warldly in his dealings, and cumbered about earthly things, e'en like yoursell, my jo!"

"Aweel," said Cuddie, after a little consideration, "I see but ae gate for't, and that's a cauld coal to blaw at, mither. Howsomever, mither, ye hae some guess o' a wee bit kindness that's atween Miss Edith and young Mr. Henry Morton, that suld be ca'd young Milnwood, and that I hae whiles carried a bit book, or maybe a bit letter, quietly atween them, and made believe never to ken wha it cam frae, though I kenn'd brawly. There's whiles convenience in a body looking a wee stupid; and I have aften seen them walking at e'en on the little path by Dinglewood burn; but naebody ever kenn'd a word about it frae Cuddie. I ken I'm gay thick in the head; but I'm as honest as our auld fore-hand ox, puir fallow, that I'll ne'er work ony mair. I hope they'll be as kind to him that come ahint me as I hae been. But, as I was saying, we'll awa down to Milnwood and tell Mr. Harry our distress. They want a pleughman, and the grund's no unlike our ain. I am sure Mr.

Harry will stand my part, for he's a kind-hearted gentleman. I'll get but little penny-fee, for his uncle, auld Nippie Milnwood, has as close a grip as the deil himsell. But we'll aye win a bit bread and a drap kale, and a fireside and theeking ower our heads, and that's a' we'll want for a season. Sae get up, mither, and sort your things to gang away; for since sae it is that gang we maun, I wad like ill to wait till Mr. Harrison and auld Gudyill cam to pu' us out by the lug and the horn."

CHAPTER VIII

The devil a puritan, or anything else he is, but a time-server.
Twelfth Night.

IT was evening when Mr. Henry Morton perceived an old woman wrapped in her tartan plaid, supported by a stout, stupid-looking fellow in hodden-gray, approach the house of Milnwood. Old Mause made her courtesy, but Cuddie took the lead in addressing Morton. Indeed, he had previously stipulated with his mother that he was to manage matters his own way ; for though he readily allowed his general inferiority of understanding, and filially submitted to the guidance of his mother on most ordinary occasions, yet he said, " For getting a service or getting forward in the warld he could somegate gar the wee pickle sense he had gang muckle farther than hers, though she could crack like ony minister o' them a'."

Accordingly, he thus opened the conversation with young Morton . " A braw night this for the rye, your honor ; the west park will be breering bravely this e'en."

"I do not doubt it, Cuddie ; but what can have brought your mother—this is your mother, is it not ? [Cuddie nodded]—what can have brought your mother and you down the water so late ? "

"Troth, stir, just what gars the auld wives trot—neshessity, stir. I'm seeking for service, stir."

" For service, Cuddie, and at this time of the year ? how comes that ? "

Mause could forbear no longer. Proud alike of her cause and her sufferings, she commenced with an affected humility of tone, " It has pleased Heaven, an it like your honor, to distinguish us by a visitation——"

" Deil's in the wife and nae gude ! " whispered Cuddie to his mother, " an ye come out wi' your Whiggery they'll no daur open a door to us through the haill country ! " Then aloud and addressing Morton, " My mother's auld, stir, and she has rather forgotten hersell in speaking to my leddy, that

canna weel bide to be contradickit—as I ken naebody likes it
if they could help themsells—especially by her ain folk ; and
Mr. Harrison the steward, and Gudyill the butler, they're no
very fond o' us, and it's ill sitting at Rome and striving wi'
the Pope. Sae I thought it best to flit before ill came to
waur ; and here's a wee bit line to your honor frae a friend
will maybe say some mair about it."

Morton took the billet, and, crimsoning up to the ears between joy and surprise, read these words : " If you can serve
these poor helpless people, you will oblige E. B."

It was a few instants before he could attain composure
enough to ask, " And what is your object, Cuddie ? and how
can I be of use to you ?"

" Wark, stir, wark and a service is my object, a bit beild
for my mither and mysell ; we hae gude plenishing o' our ain,
if we had the cast o' a cart to bring it down, and milk and
meal and greens enow, for I'm gay gleg at meal-time, and sae
is my mither, lang may it be sae ! And for the penny-fee and
a' that I'll just leave it to the laird and you. I ken ye'll no
see a poor lad wranged if ye can help it."

Morton shook his head. " For the meat and lodging,
Cuddie, I think I can promise something ; but the penny-fee
will be a hard chapter, I doubt."

" I'll take my chance o't, stir," replied the candidate for
service, " rather than gang down about Hamilton or ony sic
far country."

" Well, step into the kitchen, Cuddie, and I'll do what I
can for you."

The negotiation was not without difficulties. Morton had
first to bring over the housekeeper, who made a thousand
objections, as usual, in order to have the pleasure of being besought and entreated ; but when she was gained over, it was
comparatively easy to induce old Milnwood to accept of a
servant whose wages were to be in his own option. An outhouse was therefore assigned to Mause and her son for their
habitation, and it was settled that they were for the time to
be admitted to eat of the frugal fare provided for the family,
until their own establishment should be completed. As for
Morton, he exhausted his own very slender stock of money in
order to make Cuddie such a present, under the name of
"arles," as might show his sense of the value of the recommendation delivered to him.

" And now we're settled ance mair," said Cuddie to his
mother, " and if we're no sae bien and comfortable as we were
up yonder, yet life's life ony gate, and we're wi' decent kirk-

ganging **folk** o' your ain persuasion, mither ; there will be nae quarrelling about that."

" Of *my* persuasion, hinnie !" said the too-enlightened Mause ; " wae's me for thy blindness and theirs. O, Cuddie, they are but in the court of the Gentiles, and will ne'er win farther ben, I doubt ; they are but little better than the Prelatists themsells. They wait on the ministry of that blinded man, Peter Poundtext, ance a precious teacher of the Word, but now a backsliding pastor that has, for the sake of stipend and family maintenance, forsaken the strict path and gane astray after the Black Indulgence. O, my son, had ye but profited by the gospel doctrines ye hae heard in the Glen of Bengonnar frae the dear Richard Rumbleberry, that sweet youth who suffered martyrdom in the Grassmarket afore Candlemas ! Didna ye hear him say that Erastianism was as bad as Prelacy, and that the Indulgence was as bad as Erastianism ? "

" Heard ever onybody the like o' this !" interrupted Cuddie. " We'll be driven out o' house and ha' again afore we ken where to turn oursells. Weel, mither, I hae just ae word mair. An I hear ony mair o' your din—afore folk, that is, for I dinna mind your clavers mysell, they aye set me sleeping—but if I hear ony mair din afore folk, as I was saying, about Poundtexts and Rumbleberries, and doctrines and malignants, I'se e'en turn a single sodger mysell, or maybe a sergeant or a captain, if ye plague me the mair, and let Rumbleberry and you gang to the deil thegither. I ne'er gat ony gude by his doctrine, as ye ca't, but a sour fit o' the batts wi' sitting amang the wat moss-hags for four hours at a yoking, and the leddy cured me wi' some hickery-pickery ; mair by token, an she had kenn'd how I came by the disorder, she wadna hae been in sic a hurry to mend it."

Although groaning in spirit over the obdurate and impenitent state, as she thought it, of her son Cuddie, Mause durst neither urge him further on the topic, nor altogether neglect the warning he had given her. She knew the disposition of her deceased helpmate, whom this surviving pledge of their union greatly resembled, and remembered that, although submitting implicitly in most things to her boast of superior acuteness, he used on certain occasions, when driven to extremity, to be seized with fits of obstinacy, which neither remonstrance, flattery, nor threats were capable of overpowering. Trembling, therefore, at the very possibility of Cuddie's fulfilling his threat, she put a guard over her tongue, and even when Poundtext was commended in her presence as an able and fructifying preacher, she had the good sense to suppress the contradiction which thrilled upon her tongue, and to express her sentiments no otherwise than by deep groans, which the hearers charitably construed to flow from a vivid recollection of the more pathetic parts of his homilies. How long she could have repressed her feelings it is difficult to say. An unexpected accident relieved her from the necessity.

The Laird of Milnwood kept up all old fashions which were connected with economy. It was therefore still the custom in his house, as it had been universal in Scotland about fifty years before, that the domestics, after having placed the dinner on the table, sat down at the lower end of the board and partook of the share which was assigned to them in company with their masters. On the day, therefore, after Cuddie's arrival, being the third from the opening of this narrative, old Robin, who was butler, *valet-de-chambre*, footman, gardener, and what not, in the house of Milnwood, placed on the table an immense charger of broth thickened with oatmeal and colewort, in which ocean of liquid were indistinctly discovered by close observers two or three short ribs of lean mutton sailing to and fro. Two huge baskets, one of bread made of barley and pease and one of oat-cakes, flanked this standing dish. A large boiled salmon would nowadays have indicated more liberal housekeeping; but at that period salmon was caught in such plenty in the considerable rivers in Scotland that, instead of being accounted a delicacy, it was generally applied to feed the servants, who are said sometimes to have stipulated that they should not be required to eat a food so luscious and surfeiting in its quality above five times a week. The large black-jack, filled with very small beer of Milnwood's own brewing, was allowed to the company at discretion, as were the bannocks, cakes, and broth ; but the mutton was reserved for the heads of the family, Mrs. Wilson included ; and a measure of ale, somewhat deserving the name, was set apart in a silver tankard for their exclusive use. A huge kebbock—a cheese, that is, made with ewe-milk mixed with cow's milk—and a jar of salt butter were in common to the company.

To enjoy this exquisite cheer was placed at the head of the table the old Laird himself, with his nephew on the one side and the favorite housekeeper on the other. At a long interval, and beneath the salt, of course, sat old Robin, a meagre, half-starved serving-man, rendered cross and cripple by rheumatism, and a dirty drab of a housemaid, whom use had rendered callous to the daily exercitations which her temper underwent at the hands of her master and Mrs. Wilson. A barnsman, a white-headed cowherd boy, with Cuddie the new ploughman and his mother, completed the party. The other laborers belonging to the property resided in their own houses, happy at least in this, that if their cheer was not more delicate than that which we have described, they could eat their fill unwatched by the sharp, envious gray eyes of Milnwood, which seemed to measure the quantity that each of his dependants swallowed as closely as if their glances attended each mouthful in its progress from the lips to the stomach. This close inspection was unfavorable to Cuddie, who sustained much prejudice in his new master's opinion by the silent celerity with which he caused the victuals to disappear before him. And ever and anon Milnwood turned his eyes from the huge feeder to cast indignant glances upon his nephew, whose repugnance to rustic labor was the principal cause of his needing a ploughman, and who had been the direct means of his hiring this very cormorant.

"Pay thee wages, quotha!" said Milnwood to himself. "Thou wilt eat in a week the value of mair than thou canst work for in a month."

These disagreeable ruminations were interrupted by a loud knocking at the outer gate. It was a universal custom in Scotland that, when the family was at dinner, the outer gate of the courtyard, if there was one, and if not, the door of the house itself, was always shut and locked, and only guests of importance, or persons upon urgent business, sought or received admittance at that time.* The family of Milnwood were therefore surprised and, in the unsettled state of the times, something alarmed at the earnest and repeated knocking with which the gate was now assailed. Mrs. Wilson ran in person to the door, and having reconnoitred those who were so clamorous for admittance, through some secret aperture with which most Scottish doorways were furnished for the express purpose, she returned wringing her hands in great dismay, exclaiming, "The redcoats! the redcoats!"

"Robin—ploughman, what ca' they ye?—barnsman— nevoy Harry—open the door—open the door!" exclaimed old Milnwood, snatching up and slipping into his pocket the two or three silver spoons with which the upper end of the table was garnished, those beneath the salt being of goodly horn. "Speak them fair, sirs—Lord love ye, speak them fair;

* See Locking the Door during Dinner. Note 12.

they winna bide thrawing ; we're a' harried—we're a' harried ! ''

While the servants admitted the troopers, whose oaths and threats already indicated resentment at the delay they had been put to, Cuddie took the opportunity to whisper to his mother, '' Now, ye daft auld carline, mak yoursell deaf—ye hae made us a' deaf ere now—and let me speak for ye.   I wad like ill to get my neck raxed for an auld wife's clashes, though ye be our mither.''

'' O hinny, ay ; I'se be silent or thou sall come to ill,'' was the corresponding whisper of Mause ; '' but bethink ye, my dear, them that deny the Word, the Word will deny——''

Her admonition was cut short by the entrance of the Life Guardsmen, a party of four troopers commanded by Bothwell.

In they tramped, making a tremendous clatter upon the stone floor with the iron-shod heels of their large jack-boots and the clash and clang of their long, heavy, basket-hilted broadswords.   Milnwood and his housekeeper trembled from well-grounded apprehensions of the system of exaction and plunder carried on during these domiciliary visits.   Henry Morton was discomposed with more special cause, for he remembered that he stood answerable to the laws for having harbored Burley.   The widow, Mause Headrigg, between fear for her son's life and an overstrained and enthusiastic zeal which reproached her for consenting even tacitly to belie her religious sentiments, was in a strange quandary.   The other servants quaked for they knew not well what.   Cuddie alone, with the look of supreme indifference and stupidity which a Scottish peasant can at times assume as a mask for considerable shrewdness and craft, continued to swallow large spoonfuls of his broth, to command which he had drawn within his sphere the large vessel that contained it, and helped himself amid the confusion to a sevenfold portion.

'' What is your pleasure here, gentlemen ? '' said Milnwood, humbling himself before the satellites of power.

'' We come in behalf of the King,'' answered Bothwell. '' Why the devil did you keep us so long standing at the door ? ''

'' We were at dinner,'' answered Milnwood, '' and the door was locked, as is usual in landwart towns* in this country.   I am sure, gentlemen, if I had kenn'd ony servants of our gude King had stood at the door—— But wad ye please to drink some ale—or some brandy—or a cup of canary sack, or claret

* See Landward Town. Note 13.

wine ?" making a pause between each offer as long as a stingy bidder at an auction, who is loath to advance his offer for a favorite lot.

" Claret for me," said one fellow.

" I like ale better," said another, "provided it is right juice of John Barleycorn."

" Better never was malted," said Milnwood. " I can hardly say sae muckle for the claret; it's thin and cauld, gentlemen."

" Brandy will cure that," said a third fellow ; " a glass of brandy to three glasses of wine prevents the curmurring in the stomach."

" Brandy, ale, sack, and claret—we'll try them all," said Bothwell, " and stick to that which is best. There's good sense in that if the damn'dest Whig in Scotland had said it."

Hastily, yet with a reluctant quiver of his muscles, Milnwood lugged out two ponderous keys, and delivered them to the governante.

" The housekeeper," said Bothwell, taking a seat and throwing himself upon it, " is neither so young nor so handsome as to tempt a man to follow her to the gauntrees, and devil a one here is there worth sending in her place. What's this ? meat ?" searching with a fork among the broth, and fishing up a cutlet of mutton. " I think I could eat a bit ; why, it's as tough as if the devil's dam had hatched it."

"If there is anything better in the house, sir," said Milnwood, alarmed at these symptoms of disapprobation——

"No, no," said Bothwell, "it's not worth while; I must proceed to business. You attend Poundtext, the Presbyterian parson, I understand, Mr. Morton ?"

Mr. Morton hastened to slide in a confession and apology.

" By the indulgence of his gracious Majesty and the government, for I wad do nothing out of law. I hae nae objection whatever to the establishment of a moderate episcopacy, but only that I am a country-bred man and the ministers are a hamelier kind of folk, and I can follow their doctrine better ; and, with reverence, sir, it's a mair frugal establishment for the country."

" Well, I care nothing about that," said Bothwell ; "they are indulged, and there's an end of it ; but, for my part, if I were to give the law, never a crop-ear'd cur of the whole pack should bark in a Scotch pulpit. However, I am to obey commands. There comes the liquor ; put it down, my good old lady."

He decanted about one-half of a quart bottle of claret into a wooden quaigh or bicker, and took it off at a draught.

"You did your good wine injustice, my friend ; it's better than your brandy, though that's good too. Will you pledge me to the King's health ?"

"With pleasure," said Milnwood, "in ale; but I never drink claret, and keep only a very little for some honored friends."

"Like me, I suppose," said Bothwell ; and then pushing the bottle to Henry, he said, "Here, young man, pledge you the King's health."

Henry filled a moderate glass in silence, regardless of the hints and pushes of his uncle, which seemed to indicate that he ought to have followed his example in preferring beer to wine.

"Well," said Bothwell, "have ye all drank the toast ? What is that old wife about ? Give her a glass of brandy ; she shall drink the King's health, by——"

"If your honor pleases," said Cuddie, with great stolidity of aspect, "this is my mither, stir ; and she's as deaf as Corra Linn. We canna mak her hear day nor door ; but if your honor pleases, I am ready to drink the King's health for her in as mony glasses of brandy as ye think neshessary."

"I dare swear you are," answered Bothwell ; "you look like a fellow that would stick to brandy. Help thyself, man ; all's free where'er I come. Tom, help the maid to a comfortable cup, though she's but a dirty jilt neither. Fill round once more. Here's to our noble commander, Colonel Grahame of Claverhouse ! What the devil is the old woman groaning for ? She looks as very a Whig as ever sat on a hillside. Do you renounce the Covenant, good woman ?"

"Whilk Covenant is your honor meaning ? Is it the Covenant of Works or the Covenant of Grace ?" said Cuddie, interposing.

"Any covenant ; all covenants that ever were hatched," answered the trooper.

"Mither," cried Cuddie, affecting to speak as to a deaf person, "the gentleman wants to ken if ye will renunce the Covenant of Works ?"

"With all my heart, Cuddie," said Mause, "and pray that my feet may be delivered from the snare thereof."

"Come," said Bothwell, "the old dame has come more frankly off than I expected. Another cup round, and then we'll proceed to business. You have all heard, I suppose, of the horrid and barbarous murder committed upon the person of the Archbishop of St. Andrews, by ten or eleven armed fanatics ?"

All started and looked at each other ; at length Milnwood himself answered, " They had heard of some such misfortune, but were in hopes it had not been true."

"There is the relation published by government, old gentleman ; what do you think of it ?"

"Think, sir ? Wh—wh—whatever the council please to think of it," stammered Milnwood.

"I desire to have your opinion more explicitly, my friend," said the dragoon, authoritatively.

Milnwood's eyes hastily glanced through the paper to pick out the strongest expressions of censure with which it abounded, in gleaning which he was greatly aided by their being printed in italics. "I think it a—bloody and execrable —murder and parricide—devised by hellish and implacable cruelty—utterly abominable, and a scandal to the land."

"Well said, old gentleman !" said the querist. "Here's to thee, and I wish you joy of your good principles. You owe me a cup of thanks for having taught you them ; nay, thou shalt pledge me in thine own sack, sour ale sits ill upon a loyal stomach. Now comes your turn, young man ; what think you of the matter in hand ?"

"I should have little objection to answer you," said Henry, "if I knew what right you had to put the question."

"The Lord preserve us !" said the old housekeeper, "to ask the like o' that at a trooper, when a' folk ken they do whatever they like through the haill country wi' man and woman, beast and body."

The old gentleman exclaimed in the same horror at his nephew's audacity, "Hold your peace, sir, or answer the gentleman discreetly. Do you mean to affront the King's authority in the person of a sergeant of the Life Guards ?"

"Silence, all of you !" exclaimed Bothwell, striking his hand fiercely on the table—"silence, every one of you, and hear me ! You ask me for my right to examine you, sir (to Henry). My cockade and my broadsword are my commission, and a better one than ever Old Nol gave to his Roundheads ; and if you want to know more about it you may look at the act of council empowering his Majesty's officers and soldiers to search for, examine, and apprehend suspicious persons ; and therefore once more I ask you your opinion of the death of Archbishop Sharp. It's a new touchstone we have got for trying people's metal."

Henry had by this time reflected upon the useless risk to

which he would expose the family by resisting the tyrannical
power which was delegated to such rude hands ; he therefore
read the narrative over, and replied composedly, " I have no
hesitation to say that the perpetrators of this assassination
have committed, in my opinion, a rash and wicked action,
which I regret the more as I foresee it will be made the cause
of proceedings against many who are both innocent of the
deed and as far from approving it as myself."

While Henry thus expressed himself, Bothwell, who bent
his eyes keenly upon him, seemed suddenly to recollect his
features. " Aha ! my friend, Captain Popinjay, I think I
have seen you before, and in very suspicious company."

" I saw you once," answered Henry, " in the public-house
of the town of——"

" And with whom did you leave that public-house, youngster ? Was it not with John Balfour of Burley, one of the
murderers of the Archbishop ? "

" I did leave the house with the person you have named,"
answered Henry, " I scorn to deny it ; but so far from knowing him to be a murderer of the primate, I did not even know
at the time that such a crime had been committed."

" Lord have mercy on me, I am ruined !—utterly ruined and
undone !" exclaimed Milnwood. " That callant's tongue will
rin the head aff his ain shoulders, and waste my gudes to the
very gray cloak on my back !"

" But you knew Burley," continued Bothwell, still addressing Henry, and regardless of his uncle's interruption,
" to be an intercommuned rebel and traitor, and you knew the
prohibition to deal with such persons. You knew that as a
loyal subject you were prohibited to reset, supply, or inter-
commune with this attainted traitor, to correspond with him
by word, writ, or message, or to supply him with meat, drink,
house, harbor, or victual, under the highest pains—you knew
all this, and yet you broke the law. [Henry was silent.]
Where did you part from him ?" continued Bothwell ; " was
it in the highway, or did you give him harborage in this very
house ?"

" In this house !" said his uncle ; " he dared not for his
neck bring ony traitor into a house of mine."

" Dare he deny that he did so ?" said Bothwell.

" As you charge it to me as a crime," said Henry,
" you will excuse my saying anything that will criminate
myself."

" O, the lands of Milnwood ! the bonny lands of Milnwood,
that have been in the name of Morton twa hundred years !"

exclaimed his uncle. "They are barking and fleeing, outfield and infield, haugh and holme!"

"No, sir," said Henry, "you shall not suffer on my account. I own," he continued, addressing Bothwell, "I did give this man a night's lodging, as to an old military comrade of my father. But it was not only without my uncle's knowledge, but contrary to his express general orders. I trust, if my evidence is considered as good against myself, it will have some weight in proving my uncle's innocence."

"Come, young man," said the soldier, in a somewhat milder tone, "you're a smart spark enough, and I am sorry for you; and your uncle here is a fine old Trojan, kinder, I see, to his guests than himself, for he gives us wine and drinks his own thin ale. Tell me all you know about this Burley, what he said when you parted from him, where he went, and where he is likely now to be found; and, d—n it, I'll wink as hard on your share of the business as my duty will permit. There's a thousand merks on the murdering Whigamore's head an I could but light on it. Come, out with it; where did you part with him?"

"You will excuse my answering that question, sir," said Morton. "The same cogent reasons which induced me to afford him hospitality at considerable risk to myself and my friends would command me to respect his secret, if indeed he had trusted me with any."

"So you refuse to give me an answer?" said Bothwell.

"I have none to give," returned Henry.

"Perhaps I could teach you to find one by tying a piece of lighted match betwixt your fingers," answered Bothwell.

"O, for pity's sake, sir," said old Alison apart to her master, "gie them siller; it's siller they're seeking. They'll murder Mr. Henry, and yoursell next!"

Milnwood groaned in perplexity and bitterness of spirit, and, with a tone as if he was giving up the ghost, exclaimed, "If twenty p—p—punds would make up this unhappy mat-ter——"

"My master," insinuated Alison to the sergeant, "would gie twenty punds sterling——"

"Punds Scotch, ye b—h!" interrupted Milnwood; for the agony of his avarice overcame alike his Puritanic precision and the habitual respect he entertained for his housekeeper.

"Punds sterling," insisted the housekeeper, "if ye wad hae the gudeness to look ower the lad's misconduct. He's that dour ye might tear him to pieces and ye wad ne'er get a word out o' him ; and it wad do ye little gude, I'm sure, to burn his bonny finger-ends."

"Why," said Bothwell, hesitating, "I don't know. Most of my cloth would have the money, and take off the prisoner too ; but I bear a conscience, and if your master will stand to your offer, and enter into a bond to produce his nephew, and if all in the house will take the test-oath, I do not know but——"

"O ay, ay, sir," cried Mrs. Wilson, "ony test, ony oaths ye please !" And then aside to her master, "Haste ye away, sir, and get the siller, or they will burn the house about our lugs."

Old Milnwood cast a rueful look upon his adviser, and moved off like a piece of Dutch clockwork to set at liberty his imprisoned angels in this dire emergency. Meanwhile Sergeant Bothwell began to put the test-oath with such a degree of solemn reverence as might have been expected, being just about the same which is used to this day in his Majesty's custom-house.

"You—what's your name, woman ?"

"Alison Wilson, sir."

"You, Alison Wilson, solemnly swear, certify, and declare that you judge it unlawful for subjects, under pretext of reformation or any other pretext whatsoever, to enter into Leagues and Covenants——"

Here the ceremony was interrupted by a strife between Cuddie and his mother, which, long conducted in whispers, now became audible.

"Oh, whisht, mither, whisht ! they're upon a communing. Oh ! whisht, and they'll agree weel eneugh e'enow."

"I will not whisht, Cuddie," replied his mother ; "I will uplift my voice and spare not. I will confound the man of sin, even the scarlet man, and through my voice shall Mr. Henry be freed from the net of the fowler."

"She has her leg ower the harrows now," said Cuddie, "stop her wha can. I see her cocked up behint a dragoon on her way to the tolbooth. I find my ain legs tied below a horse's belly. Ay, she has just mustered up her sermon, and there, wi' that grane, out it comes, and we are a' ruined, horse and foot !"

"And div ye think to come here," said Mause, her withered hand shaking in concert with her keen though wrinkled visage, animated by zealous wrath, and emancipated, by the very mention of the test, from the restraints of her own prudence and Cuddie's admonition—"div ye think to come here wi' your soul-killing, saint-seducing, conscience-confounding oaths and tests and bands, your snares and your traps and your gins ? Surely it is in vain that a net is spread in the sight of any bird."

"Eh ! what, good dame ?" said the soldier. "Here's a Whig miracle, egad ! the old wife has got both her ears and tongue, and we are like to be driven deaf in our turn. Go to, hold your peace, and remember whom you talk to, you old idiot."

"Whae do I talk to ! Eh, sirs, ower weel may the sorrowing land ken what ye are. Malignant adherents ye are to the prelates, foul props to a feeble and filthy cause, bloody beasts of prey and burdens to the earth."

"Upon my soul," said Bothwell, astonished as a mastiff dog might be should a hen-partridge fly at him in defence of her young, "this is the finest language I ever heard ! Can't you give us some more of it ?"

"Gie ye some mair o't ?" said Mause, clearing her voice with a preliminary cough. "I will take up my testimony against you ance and again. Philistines ye are, and Edomites ; leopards are ye, and foxes ; evening wolves that gnaw not the bones till the morrow ; wicked dogs that compass about the chosen ; thrusting kine, and pushing bulls of Bashan ; piercing serpents ye are, and allied baith in name and nature with the great Red Dragon—Revelations, twalfth chapter, third and fourth verses."

Here the old lady stopped, apparently much more from lack of breath than of matter.

"Curse the old hag !" said one of the dragoons ; "gag her and take her to headquarters."

"For shame, Andrews !" said Bothwell ; "remember the good lady belongs to the fair sex, and uses only the privilege of her tongue. But hark ye, good woman, every bull of Bashan and Red Dragon will not be so civil as I am, or be contented to leave you to the charge of the constable and ducking-stool. In the meantime I must necessarily carry off this young man to headquarters. I cannot answer to my commanding officer to leave him in a house where I have heard so much treason and fanaticism."

"See now, mither, what ye hae dune," whispered Cuddie ; "there's the Philistines, as ye ca' them, are gaun to whirry awa' Mr. Henry, and a' wi' your nash-gab, deil be on't !"

"Haud yere tongue, ye cowardly loon," said the mother, "and layna the wyte on me ; if you and thae thowless gluttons, that are sitting staring like cows bursting on clover, wad testify wi' your hands as I have testified wi' my tongue, they should never harle the precious young lad awa' to captivity."

While this dialogue passed the soldiers had already bound and secured their prisoner. Milnwood returned at this instant, and, alarmed at the preparations he beheld, hastened to proffer to Bothwell, though with many a grievous groan, the purse of gold which he had been obliged to rummage out as ransom for his nephew. The trooper took the purse with an air of indifference, weighed it in his hand, chucked it up into the air, and caught it as it fell, then shook his head and said, "There's many a merry night in this nest of yellow, boys, but d—n me if I dare venture for them; that old woman has spoken too loud, and before all the men too. Hark ye, old gentleman," to Milnwood, "I must take your nephew to headquarters, so I cannot in conscience keep more than is my due as civility-money;" then opening the purse he gave a gold piece to each of the soldiers and took three to himself. "Now," said he, "you have the comfort to know that your kinsman, young Captain Popinjay, will be carefully looked after and civilly used; and the rest of the money I return to you."

Milnwood eagerly extended his hand.

"Only you know," said Bothwell, still playing with the purse, "that every landholder is answerable for the conformity and loyalty of his household, and that these fellows of mine are not obliged to be silent on the subject of the fine sermon we have had from that old Puritan in the tartan plaid there; and I presume you are aware that the consequences of delation will be a heavy fine before the council."

"Good sergeant! worthy captain!" exclaimed the terrified miser, "I am sure there is no person in my house, to my knowledge, would give cause of offence."

"Nay," answered Bothwell, "you shall hear her give her testimony, as she calls it, herself. You, fellow [to Cuddie], stand back and let your mother speak her mind. I see she's primed and loaded again since her first discharge."

"Lord! noble sir," said Cuddie, "an auld wife's tongue's but a feckless matter to mak sic a fash about. Neither my father nor me ever minded muckle what our mither said."

"Hold your peace, my lad, while you are well," said Bothwell; "I promise you I think you are slyer than you would like to be supposed. Come, good dame, you see your master will not believe that you can give us so bright a testimony."

Mause's zeal did not require this spur to set her again on full career. "Woe to the compilers and carnal self-seekers," she said, "that daub over and drown their consciences by complying with wicked exactions, and giving mammon of unrighteousness to the sons of Belial that it may make their peace with them! It is a sinful compliance, a base confederacy with the Enemy. It is the evil that Menahan did in the sight of the Lord when he gave a thousand talents to Peel, King of Assyria, that his hand might be with him—Second Kings, feifteen chapter, nineteen verse. It is the evil deed of Ahab when he sent money to Tiglath-Peleser—see the saame Second Kings, saxteen and aught. And if it was accounted a backsliding even in godly Hezekiah that he complied with Sennacherib, giving him money and offering to bear that which was put upon him—see the saame Second Kings, aughteen chapter, fourteen and feifteen verses—even so it is with them that in this contumacious and backsliding generation pays localities and fees, and cess and fines, to greedy and unrighteous publicans, and extortions and stipends to hireling curates—dumb dogs which bark not, sleeping, lying down, loving to slumber—and gives gifts to be helps and hires to our oppressors and destroyers. They are all like the casters of a lot with them, like the preparing of a table for the troop and the furnishing a drink-offering to the number."

"There's a fine sound of doctrine for you, Mr. Morton! How like you that?" said Bothwell; " or how do you think the council will like it? I think we can carry the greatest part of it in our heads without a keelyvine pen and a pair of tablets, such as you bring to conventicles. She denies paying cess, I think, Andrews?"

"Yes, by G—," said Andrews; "and she swore it was a sin to give a trooper a pot of ale, or ask him to sit down to a table."

"You hear," said Bothwell, addressing Milnwood; "but it's your own affair;" and he proffered back the purse with its diminished contents with an air of indifference.

Milnwood, whose head seemed stunned by the accumulation of his misfortunes, extended his hand mechanically to take the purse.

"Are ye mad?" said his housekeeper, in a whisper. "Tell them to keep it; they *will* keep it either by fair means or foul, and it's our only chance to make them quiet."

"I canna do it, Ailie—I canna do it," said Milnwood, in the bitterness of his heart. " I canna part wi' the siller I hae counted sae often ower to thae blackguards."

"Then I maun do it mysell, Milnwood," said the house-keeper, "or see a' gang wrang thegither. My master, sir," she said, addressing Bothwell, "canna think o' taking back onything at the hand of an honorable gentleman like you ; he implores ye to pit up the siller and be as kind to his nephew as ye can, and be favorable in reporting our dispositions to government, and let us tak nae wrang for the daft speeches of an auld jaud [here she turned fiercely upon Mause, to indulge herself for the effort which it cost her to assume a mild demeanor to the soldiers], a daft auld Whig randy, that ne'er was in the house, foul fa' her ! till yesterday afternoon, and that sall ne'er cross the door-stane again an anes I had her out o't."

"Ay, ay," whispered Cuddie to his parent, "e'en sae ! I kenn'd we wad be put to our travels again whene'er ye suld get three words spoken to an end. I was sure that wad be the upshot o't, mither."

"Whisht, my bairn," said she, "and dinna murmur at the cross. Cross their door-stane ! weel I wot I'll ne'er cross their door-stane. There's nae mark on their threshold for a signal that the destroying angel should pass by. They'll get a back-cast o' his hand yet that think sae muckle o' the creature and sae little o' the Creator ; sae muckle o' warld's gear and sae little o' a broken Covenant ; sae muckle about thae wheen pieces o' yellow muck and sae little about the pure gold o' the Scripture ; sae muckle about their ain friend and kinsman and sae little about the elect that are tried wi' hornings, harassings, huntings, searchings, chasings, catchings, imprisonments, torturings, banishments, headings, hangings, dismemberings, and quarterings quick, forbye the hundreds forced from their ain habitations to the deserts, mountains, muirs, mosses, moss-flows, and peat-hags, there to hear the Word like bread eaten in secret."

"She's at the Covenant now, sergeant, shall we not have her away ?" said one of the soldiers.

"You be d—d !" said Bothwell aside to him ; "cannot you see she's better where she is, so long as there is a respectable, sponsible, money-broking heritor like Mr. Morton of Milnwood, who has the means of atoning her trespasses ? Let the old mother fly to raise another brood, she's too tough to be made anything of herself. Here," he cried, "one other round to Milnwood and his roof-tree, and to our next merry meeting with him, which I think will not be far distant if he keeps such a fanatical family."

He then ordered the party to take their horses, and pressed

the best in Milnwood's stable into the king's service to carry the prisoner. Mrs. Wilson, with weeping eyes, made up a small parcel of necessaries for Henry's compelled journey, and as she bustled about, took an opportunity, unseen by the party, to slip into his hand a small sum of money. Bothwell and his troopers in other respects kept their promise and were civil. They did not bind their prisoner, but contented themselves with leading his horse between a file of men. They then mounted and marched off with much mirth and laughter among themselves, leaving the Milnwood family in great confusion. The old Laird himself, overpowered by the loss of his nephew, and the unavailing outlay of twenty pounds sterling, did nothing the whole evening but rock himself backwards and forwards in his great leathern easy-chair, repeating the same lamentation of "Ruined on a' sides—ruined on a' sides; harried and undone—harried and undone, body and gudes—body and gudes!"

Mrs. Alison Wilson's grief was partly indulged and partly relieved by the torrent of invectives with which she accompanied Mause and Cuddie's expulsion from Milnwood. "Ill luck be in the graning corse o' thee! The prettiest lad in Clydesdale this day maun be a sufferer, and a' for you and your daft Whiggery!"

"Gae wa'," replied Mause; "I trow ye are yet in the bonds of sin and in the gall of iniquity, to grudge your bonniest and best in the cause of Him that gave ye a' ye hae. I promise I hae dune as muckle for Mr. Harry as I wad do for my ain; for if Cuddie was found worthy to bear testimony in the Grassmarket——"

"And there's gude hope o't," said Alison, "unless you and he change your courses."

"And if," continued Mause, disregarding the interruption, "the bloody Doegs and the flattering Ziphites were to seek to ensnare me with a proffer of his remission upon sinful compliances, I wad persevere, natheless, in lifting my testimony against Popery, Prelacy, Antinomianism, Erastianism, Lapsarianism, Sublapsarianism, and the sins and snares of the times; I wad cry as a woman in labor against the Black Indulgence that has been a stumbling-block to professors; I wad uplift my voice as a powerful preacher."

"Hout tout, mither," cried Cuddie, interfering and dragging her off forcibly, "dinna deave the gentlewoman wi' your testimony! ye hae preached eneugh for sax days. Ye preached us out o' our canny free-house and gude kale-yard, and out o' this new city o' refuge afore our hinder end was

weel hafted in it ; and ye hae preached Mr. Harry awa' to the
prison ; and ye hae preached twenty punds out o' the Laird's
pocket that he likes as ill to quit wi' ; and sae ye may haud
sae for ae wee while, without preaching me up a ladder and
down a tow. Sae come awa'—come awa'; the family hae had
eneugh o' your testimony to mind it for ae while."

So saying he dragged off Mause, the words "Testimony,
Covenant, malignants, indulgence" still thrilling upon her
tongue, to make preparations for instantly renewing their
travels in quest of an asylum.

"Ill-faur'd, crazy, crack-brained gowk that she is!" exclaimed the housekeeper, as she saw them depart, "to set up
to be sae muckle better than ither folk, the auld besom, and
to bring sae muckle distress on a douce quiet family! If it
hadna been that I am mair than half a gentlewoman by my
station, I wad hae tried my ten nails in the wizen'd hide o'
her !"

CHAPTER IX

I am a son of Mars, who have been in many wars,
And show my cuts and scars wherever I come ;
This here was for a wench, and that other in a trench,
When welcoming the French at the sound of the drum.
BURNS.

"DON'T be too much cast down," said Sergeant Bothwell to
his prisoner as they journeyed on towards the headquarters ;
"you are a smart pretty lad, and well connected ; the worst
that will happen will be strapping up for it, and that is many
an honest fellow's lot.   I tell you fairly your life's within the
compass of the law, unless you make submission and get off
by a round fine upon your uncle's estate ; he can well afford it."

"That vexes me more than the rest," said Henry.   "He
parts with his money with regret ; and, as he had no concern
whatever with my having given this person shelter for a night,
I wish to Heaven, if I escape a capital punishment, that the
penalty may be of a kind I could bear in my own person."

"Why, perhaps," said Bothwell, "they will propose to
you to go into one of the Scotch regiments that are serving
abroad.   It's no bad line of service ; if your friends are active,
and there are any knocks going, you may soon get a commission."

"I am by no means sure," answered Morton, "that such
a sentence is not the best thing that can happen to me."

"Why, then, you are no real Whig after all ?" said the
sergeant.

"I have hitherto meddled with no party in the state," said
Henry, "but have remained quietly at home ; and sometimes
I have had serious thoughts of joining one of our foreign regi-
ments."

"Have you ?" replied Bothwell.   "Why, I honor you for
it ; I have served in the Scotch French guards myself many
a long day ; it's the place for learning discipline, d—n me.
They never mind what you do when you are off duty ; but
miss you the roll-call, and see how they'll arrange you.   D—n
me, if old Captain Montgomery didn't make me mount guard
upon the arsenal in my steel back and breast, plate-sleeves and

head-piece, for six hours at once, under so burning a sun that gad I was baked like a turtle at Port Royal. I swore never to miss answering to Francis Stewart again, though I should leave my hand of cards upon the drum-head. Ah ! discipline is a capital thing."

"In other respects you liked the service ?" said Morton.

"*Par excellence*," said Bothwell ; "women, wine, and wassail, all to be had for little but the asking ; and if you find it in your conscience to let a fat priest think he has some chance to convert you, gad he'll help you to these comforts himself, just to gain a little ground in your good affection. Where will you find a crop-eared Whig parson will be so civil ?"

"Why, nowhere, I agree with you," said Henry ; "but what was your chief duty ?"

"To guard the king's person," said Bothwell, " to look after the safety of Louis le Grand, my boy, and now and then to take a turn among the Huguenots—Protestants, that is. And there we had fine scope ; it brought my hand pretty well in for the service in this country. But, come, as you are to be a *bon camerado*, as the Spaniards say, I must put you in cash with some of your old uncle's broad-pieces. This is cutter's law : we must not see a pretty fellow want if we have cash ourselves."

Thus speaking, he pulled out his purse, took out some of the contents, and offered them to Henry without counting them. Young Morton declined the favor ; and not judging it prudent to acquaint the sergeant, notwithstanding his apparent generosity, that he was actually in possession of some money, he assured him he should have no difficulty in getting a supply from his uncle.

"Well," said Bothwell, " in that case these yellow rascals must serve to ballast my purse a little longer. I always make it a rule never to quit the tavern—unless ordered on duty— while my purse is so weighty that I can chuck it over the sign-post.* When it is so light that the wind blows it back, then, boot and saddle, we must fall on some way of replenishing. But what tower is that before us, rising so high upon the steep bank out of the woods that surround it on every side ?"

"It is the Tower of Tillietudlem," said one of the soldiers. "Old Lady Margaret Bellenden lives there. She's one of the best affected women in the country, and one that's a soldier's friend. When I was hurt by one of the d—d Whig

* See Throwing the Purse over the Gate. Note 14.

dogs that shot at me from behind a fauld-dike, I lay a month there, and would stand such another wound to be in as good quarters again."

"If that be the case," said Bothwell, "I will pay my respects to her as we pass, and request some refreshment for men and horses ; I am as thirsty already as if I had drunk nothing at Milnwood. But it is a good thing in these times," he continued, addressing himself to Henry, "that the King's soldier cannot pass a house without getting a refreshment. In such houses as Tillie—— what d'ye call it ? you are served for love ; in the houses of the avowed fanatics you help yourself by force ; and among the moderate Presbyterians and other suspicious persons you are well treated from fear ; so your thirst is always quenched on some terms or other."

"And you propose," said Henry, anxiously, "to go upon that errand up to the Tower yonder ? "

"To be sure I do," answered Bothwell. "How should I be able to report favorably to my officers of the worthy lady's sound principles unless I know the taste of her sack, for sack she will produce, that I take for granted ; it is the favorite consoler of your old dowager of quality, as small claret is the potation of your country laird."

"Then, for Heaven's sake," said Henry, "if you are determined to go there, do not mention my name, or expose me to a family that I am acquainted with. Let me be muffled up for the time in one of your soldier's cloaks, and only mention me generally as a prisoner under your charge."

"With all my heart," said Bothwell ; "I promised to use you civilly, and I scorn to break my word. Here, Andrews, wrap a cloak round the prisoner, and do not mention his name nor where we caught him, unless you would have a trot on a horse of wood." *

They were at this moment at an arched gateway, battlemented and flanked with turrets, one whereof was totally ruinous, excepting the lower story, which served as a cow-house to the peasant whose family inhabited the turret that remained entire. The gate had been broken down by Monk's soldiers during the Civil War, and had never been replaced, therefore presented no obstacle to Bothwell and his party. The avenue, very steep and narrow, and causewayed with large round stones, ascended the side of the precipitous bank in an oblique and zigzag course, now showing, now hiding, a view of the tower and its exterior bulwarks, which seemed to rise almost perpendicularly above their heads. The frag-

* See Wooden Mare. Note 15.

ments of Gothic defences which it exhibited were upon such a scale of strength as induced Bothwell to exclaim, "It s well this place is in honest and loyal hands. Egad, if the enemy had it, a dozen of old Whigamore wives with their dis-taffs might keep it against a troop of dragoons, at least if they had half the spunk of the old girl we left at Milnwood. Upon my life," he continued, as they came in front of the large double tower and its surrounding defences and flankers, "it is a superb place, founded, says the worn inscription over the gate—unless the remnant of my Latin has given me the slip —by Sir Ralph de Bellenden in 1350, a respectable antiquity. I must greet the old lady with due honor, though it should put me to the labor of recalling some of the compliments that I used to dabble in when I was wont to keep that sort of com-pany."

As he thus communed with himself, the butler, who had reconnoitred the soldiers from an arrow-slit in the wall, an-nounced to his lady that a commanded party of dragoons, or, as he thought, Life Guardsmen, waited at the gate with a prisoner under their charge.

"I am certain," said Gudyill, "and positive, that the sixth man is a prisoner; for his horse is led, and the two dragoons that are before have their carabines out of their budgets, and rested upon their thighs. It was aye the way we guarded pris-oners in the days of the Great Marquis."

"King's soldiers!" said the lady; "probably in want of refreshment. Go, Gudyill, make them welcome, and let them be accommodated with what provision and forage the Tower can afford. And stay, tell my gentlewoman to bring my black scarf and manteau. I will go down myself to receive them; one cannot show the King's Life Guards too much respect in times when they are doing so much for royal authority. And d'ye hear, Gudyill, let Jenny Dennison slip on her pearlings to walk before my niece and me, and the three women to walk behind; and bid my niece attend me instantly."

Fully accoutred, and attended according to her directions, Lady Margaret now sailed out into the courtyard of her tower with great courtesy and dignity. Sergeant Bothwell saluted the grave and reverend lady of the manor with an assurance which had something of the light and careless address of the dissipated men of fashion in Charles the Second's time, and did not at all savor of the awkward or rude manners of a non-commissioned officer of dragoons. His language, as well as his manners, seemed also to be refined for the time and occasion; though the truth was that, in the fluctuations of an adventurous and profligate life, Bothwell had sometimes kept company much better suited to his ancestry than to his present situation of life.   To the lady's request to know whether she could be of service to them he answered, with a suitable bow, "That as they had to march some miles farther that night, they would be much accommodated by permission to rest their horses for an hour before continuing their journey."

"With the greatest pleasure," answered Lady Margaret; "and I trust that my people will see that neither horse nor men want suitable refreshment."

"We are well aware, madam," continued Bothwell, "that such has always been the reception, within the walls of Tillie-tudlem, of those who served the king."

"We have studied to discharge our duty faithfully and loyally on all occasions, sir," answered Lady Margaret, pleased with the compliment, "both to our monarchs and to their followers, particularly to their faithful soldiers.   It is not long ago, and it probably has not escaped the recollection of his sacred Majesty now on the throne, since he himself hon-ored my poor house with his presence, and breakfasted in a room in this castle, Mr. Sergeant, which my waiting-gentle-woman shall show you ; we still call it the King's room."

Bothwell had by this time dismounted his party and com-mitted the horses to the charge of one file and the prisoner to that of another ; so that he himself was at liberty to con-tinue the conversation which the lady had so condescendingly opened.

"Since the King, my master, had the honor to experience your hospitality, I cannot wonder that it is extended to those that serve him, and whose principal merit is doing it with fidelity.   And yet I have a nearer relation to his Majesty than this coarse red coat would seem to indicate."

"Indeed, sir ? Probably," said Lady Margaret, " you have belonged to his household ?"

"Not exactly, madam, to his household, but rather to his *house ;* a connection through which I may claim kindred with most of the best families in Scotland, not, I believe, exclusive of that of Tillietudlem."

"Sir !" said the old lady, drawing herself up with dignity at hearing what she conceived an impertinent jest, " I do not understand you."

"It's but a foolish subject for one in my situation to talk of, madam," answered the trooper ; "but you must have heard of the history and misfortunes of my grandfather Francis Stewart, to whom James I., his cousin-german, gave the title of Bothwell, as my comrades give me the nickname. It was not in the long-run more advantageous to him than it is to me."

"Indeed!" said Lady Margaret, with much sympathy and surprise. "I have indeed always understood that the grandson of the last earl was in necessitous circumstances, but I should never have expected to see him so low in the service. With such connections, what ill fortune could have reduced you——"

"Nothing much out of the ordinary course, I believe, madam," said Bothwell, interrupting and anticipating the question. "I have had my moments of good luck like my neighbors, have drunk my bottle with Rochester, thrown a merry main with Buckingham, and fought at Tangiers side by side with Sheffield. But my luck never lasted; I could not make useful friends out of my jolly companions. Perhaps I was not sufficiently aware," he continued, with some bitterness, "how much the descendant of the Scottish Stewarts was honored by being admitted into the convivialities of Wilmot and Villiers."

"But your Scottish friends, Mr. Stewart, your relations here, so numerous and so powerful?"

"Why, ay, my lady," replied the sergeant, "I believe some of them might have made me their gamekeeper, for I am a tolerable shot; some of them would have entertained me as their bravo, for I can use my sword well; and here and there was one who, when better company was not to be had, would have made me his companion, since I can drink my three bottles of wine. But I don't know how it is, between service and service among my kinsmen, I prefer that of my cousin Charles as the most creditable of them all, although the pay is but poor and the livery far from splendid."

"It is a shame, it is a burning scandal!" said Lady Margaret. "Why do you not apply to his most sacred Majesty? He cannot but be surprised to hear that a scion of his august family——"

"I beg your pardon, madam," interrupted the sergeant, "I am but a blunt soldier, and I trust you will excuse me when I say, his most sacred Majesty is more busy in grafting scions of his own than with nourishing those which were planted by his grandfather's grandfather."

"Well, Mr. Stewart," said Lady Margaret, "one thing you must promise me, remain at Tillietudlem to-night; to-morrow I expect your commanding officer, the gallant Claverhouse, to whom king and country are so much obliged for his exertions against those who would turn the world upside down. I will speak to him on the subject of your speedy promotion ; and I am certain he feels too much both what is due to the blood which is in your veins, and to the request of a lady so highly distinguished as myself by his most sacred Majesty, not to make better provision for you than you have yet received."

"I am much obliged to your ladyship, and I certainly will remain here with my prisoner since you request it, especially as it will be the earliest way of presenting him to Colonel Grahame and obtaining his ultimate orders about the young spark."

"Who is your prisoner, pray you ?" said Lady Margaret.

"A young fellow of rather the better class in this neighborhood, who has been so incautious as to give countenance to one of the murderers of the primate, and to facilitate the dog's escape."

"O, fie upon him !" said Lady Margaret ; "I am but too apt to forgive the injuries I have received at the hands of these rogues, though some of them, Mr. Stewart, are of a kind not like to be forgotten ; but those who would abet the perpetrators of so cruel and deliberate a homicide on a single man, an old man, and a man of the Archbishop's sacred profession—O, fie upon him ! If you wish to make him secure with little trouble to your people, I will cause Harrison or Gudyill look for the key of our pit, or principal dungeon. It has not been open since the week after the victory of Kilsyth, when my poor Sir Arthur Bellenden put twenty Whigs into it ; but it is not more than two stories beneath ground, so it cannot be unwholesome, especially as I rather believe there is somewhere an opening to the outer air."

"I beg your pardon, madam," answered the sergeant ; "I dare say the dungeon is a most admirable one ; but I have promised to be civil to the lad, and I will take care he is watched so as to render escape impossible. I'll set those to look after him shall keep him as fast as if his legs were in the boots, or his fingers in the thumbikins."

"Well, Mr. Stewart," rejoined the lady, "you best know your own duty. I heartily wish you good evening, and commit you to the care of my steward, Harrison. I would ask you to keep ourselves company, but a—a—a——"

"O, madam, it requires no apology ; I am sensible the coarse red coat of King Charles II. does and ought to annihilate the privileges of the red blood of King James V."

"Not with me, I do assure you, Mr. Stewart ; you do me

injustice if you think so.   I will speak to your officer to-morrow ; and I trust you shall soon find yourself in a rank where there shall be no anomalies to be reconciled."

"I believe, madam," said Bothwell, "your goodness will find itself deceived ; but I am obliged to you for your intention, and, at all events, I will have a merry night with Mr. Harrison."

Lady Margaret took a ceremonious leave, with all the respect which she owed to royal blood, even when flowing in the veins of a sergeant of the Life Guards, again assuring Mr. Stewart that whatever was in the Tower of Tillietudlem was heartily at his service and that of his attendants.

Sergeant Bothwell did not fail to take the lady at her word, and readily forgot the height from which his family had descended in a joyous carousal, during which Mr. Harrison exerted himself to produce the best wine in the cellar, and to excite his guest to be merry by that seducing example which, in matters of conviviality, goes further than precept.   Old Gudyill associated himself with a party so much to his taste, pretty much as Davy, in the Second Part of *Henry the Fourth*, mingles in the revels of his master, Justice Shallow.   He ran down to the cellar at the risk of breaking his neck to ransack some private catacomb known, as he boasted, only to himself, and which never either had or should, during his superintendence, render forth a bottle of its contents to any one but a real king's friend.

"When the Duke dined here," said the butler, seating himself at a distance from the table, being somewhat overawed by Bothwell's genealogy, but yet hitching his seat half a yard nearer at every clause of his speech, "my leddy was importunate to have a bottle of that Burgundy [here he advanced his seat a little] ; but I dinna ken how it was, Mr. Stewart, I misdoubted him.   I jaloused him, sir, no to be the friend to government he pretends : the family are not to lippen to.   That auld Duke James lost his heart before he lost his head ; and the Worcester man was but wersh parritch, neither gude to fry, boil, nor sup cauld."   With this witty observation, he completed his first parallel, and commenced a zigzag after the manner of an experienced engineer, in order to continue his approaches to the table.   "Sae, sir, the faster my leddy cried, 'Burgundy to his Grace—the auld Burgundy—the choice Burgundy—the Burgundy that came ower in the thirty-nine,' the mair did I say to mysell, 'Deil a drap gangs down his hause unless I was mair sensible o' his principles : sack and claret may serve him.'   Na, na, gentlemen, as lang as I hae the trust o' butler in this house o' Tillietudlem, I'll tak it upon me to see that nae disloyal or doubtfu' person is the better o' our binns.   But when I can find a true friend to the king and his cause, and a moderate episcopacy ; when I find a man, as I say, that will stand by Church and Crown as I did mysell in my master's life, and all through Montrose's time, I think there's naething in the cellar ower gude to be spared on him."

By this time he had completed a lodgement in the body of the place, or, in other words, advanced his seat close to the table.

"And now, Mr. Francis Stewart of Bothwell, I have the honor to drink your gude health and a commission t'ye, and much luck may ye have in raking this country clear o' Whigs and Roundheads, fanatics and Covenanters."

Bothwell, who, it may well be believed, had long ceased to be very scrupulous in point of society, which he regulated more by his convenience and station in life than his ancestry, readily answered the butler's pledge, acknowledging, at the same time, the excellence of the wine ; and Mr. Gudyill, thus adopted a regular member of the company, continued to furnish them with the means of mirth until an early hour in the next morning.

CHAPTER X

Did I but purpose to embark with thee
On the smooth surface of a summer sea,
And would forsake the skiff and make the shore
When the winds whistle and the tempests roar?
PRIOR.

WHILE Lady Margaret held, with the high-descended sergeant
of dragoons, the conference which we have detailed in the
preceding pages, her granddaughter, partaking in a less degree her ladyship's enthusiasm for all who were sprung of the
blood royal, did not honor Sergeant Bothwell with more attention than a single glance, which showed her a tall powerful
person and a set of hardy weather-beaten features, to which
pride and dissipation had given an air where discontent mingled with the reckless gayety of desperation. The other
soldiers offered still less to detach her consideration ; but from
the prisoner, muffled and disguised as he was, she found it
impossible to withdraw her eyes. Yet she blamed herself for
indulging a curiosity which seemed obviously to give pain to
him who was its object.

"I wish," she said to Jenny Dennison, who was the immediate attendant on her person—" I wish we knew who that
poor fellow is."

"I was just thinking sae mysell, Miss Edith," said the
waiting woman ; " but it canna be Cuddie Headrigg, because
he's taller and no sae stout."

"Yet," continued Miss Bellenden, " it may be some poor
neighbor for whom we might have cause to interest ourselves."

" I can sune learn wha he is," said the enterprising Jenny,
" if the sodgers were anes settled and at leisure, for I ken ane
o' them very weel—the best-looking and the youngest o' them."

" I think you know all the idle young fellows about the
country," answered her mistress.

" Na, Miss Edith, I am no sae free o' my acquaintance as
that," answered the *fille-de-chambre*. " To be sure, folk canna
help kenning the folk by head-mark that they see aye glowring and looking at them at kirk and market ; but I ken few
lads to speak to unless it be them o' the family, and the three

Steinsons, and Tam Rand, and the young miller, and the five
Howisons in Nethersheils, and lang Tam Gilry, and——”

“Pray cut short a list of exceptions which threatens to be
a long one, and tell me how you come to know this young
soldier,” said Miss Bellenden.

“Lord, Miss Edith, it’s Tam Halliday, Trooper Tam, as
they ca’ him, that was wounded by the hill-folk at the conventicle at Outerside Muir, and lay here while he was under
cure. I can ask him onything, and Tam will no refuse to
answer me, I’ll be caution for him.”

“Try, then,” said Miss Edith, “if you can find an opportunity to ask him the name of his prisoner, and come to my
room and tell me what he says.”

Jenny Dennison proceeded on her errand, but soon returned
with such a face of surprise and dismay as evinced a deep interest in the fate of the prisoner.

“What is the matter?” said Edith, anxiously; “does it
prove to be Cuddie, after all, poor fellow?”

“Cuddie, Miss Edith! Na! na! it’s nae Cuddie,” blubbered out the faithful *fille-de-chambre*, sensible of the pain
which her news were about to inflict on her young mistress.
“O dear, Miss Edith, it’s young Milnwood himsell!”

“Young Milnwood!” exclaimed Edith, aghast in her turn;
“it is impossible—totally impossible! His uncle attends the
clergyman indulged by law, and has no connection whatever
with the refractory people; and he himself has never interfered in this unhappy dissension. He must be totally innocent, unless he has been standing up for some invaded right.”

“O, my dear Miss Edith,” said her attendant, “these are
not days to ask what’s right or what’s wrang; if he were as
innocent as the new-born infant, they would find some way
of making him guilty if they liked; but Tam Halliday says it
will touch his life, for he has been resetting ane o’ the Fife
gentlemen that killed that auld carle of an archbishop.”

“His life!” exclaimed Edith, starting hastily up, and
speaking with a hurried and tremulous accent; “they cannot, they shall not; I will speak for him; they shall not hurt
him!”

“O, my dear young leddy, think on your grandmother;
think on the danger and the difficulty,” added Jenny; “for
he’s kept under close confinement till Claverhouse comes up
in the morning, and if he doesna gie him full satisfaction,
Tam Halliday says there will be brief wark wi’ him. Kneel
down—mak ready—present—fire—just as they did wi’ auld

deaf John Macbriar that never understood a single question they pat till him, and sae lost his life for lack o' hearing."

"Jenny," said the young lady, "if he should die I will die with him. There is no time to talk of danger or difficulty; I will put on a plaid and slip down with you to the place where they have kept him; I will throw myself at the feet of the sentinel and entreat him, as he has a soul to be saved——"

"Eh, guide us!" interrupted the maid, "our young leddy at the feet o' Trooper Tam, and speaking to him about his soul, when the puir chield hardly kens whether he has ane or no, unless that he whiles swears by it! That will never do; but what maun be maun be, and I'll never desert a true-love cause. And sae if ye maun see young Milnwood, though I ken nae gude it will do but to make baith your hearts the sairer, I'll e'en tak the risk o't, and try to manage Tam Halliday. But ye maun let me hae my ain gate and no speak ae word; he's keeping guard o'er Milnwood in the easter round of the Tower."

"Go, go, fetch me a plaid," said Edith. "Let me but see him, and I will find some remedy for his danger. Haste ye, Jenny, as ever ye hope to have good at my hands."

Jenny hastened, and soon returned with a plaid, in which Edith muffled herself so as completely to screen her face, and in part to disguise her person. This was a mode of arranging the plaid very common among the ladies of that century and the earlier part of the succeeding one; so much so, indeed, that the venerable sages of the Kirk, conceiving that the mode gave tempting facilities for intrigue, directed more than one act of Assembly against this use of the mantle. But fashion, as usual, proved too strong for authority, and while plaids continued to be worn, women of all ranks occasionally employed them as a sort of muffler or veil.* Her face and figure thus concealed, Edith, holding by her attendant's arm, hastened with trembling steps to the place of Morton's confinement.

This was a small study or closet in one of the turrets, opening upon a gallery in which the sentinel was pacing to and fro; for Sergeant Bothwell, scrupulous in observing his word, and perhaps touched with some compassion for the prisoner's youth and genteel demeanor, had waived the indignity of putting his guard into the same apartment with him. Halliday, therefore, with his carabine on his arm, walked up and down the gallery, occasionally solacing him-

* See Concealing the Face. Note 16.

self with a draught of ale, a huge flagon of which stood upon the table at one end of the apartment, and at other times humming the lively Scottish air—

> " Between Saint Johnstone and Bonny Dundee,
> I'll gar ye be fain to follow me."

Jenny Dennison cautioned her mistress once more to let her take her own way.

" I can manage the trooper weel eneugh," she said, " for as rough as he is ; I ken their nature weel ; but ye maunna say a single word."

She accordingly opened the door of the gallery just as the sentinel had turned his back from it, and taking up the tune which he hummed, she sung in a coquettish tone of rustic raillery—

> " If I were to follow a poor sodger lad,
> My friends wad be angry, my minnie be mad ;
> A laird, or a lord, they were fitter for me,
> Sae I'll never be fain to follow thee."

" A fair challenge, by Jove," cried the sentinel, turning round, " and from two at once. But it's not easy to bang the soldier with his bandoleers ; " then taking up the song where the damsel had stopped—

> " To follow me ye weel may be glad,
> A share of my supper, a share of my bed,
> To the sound of the drum to range fearless and free,
> I'll gar ye be fain to follow me.

Come, my pretty lass, and kiss me for my song."

" I should not have thought of that, Mr. Halliday," answered Jenny, with a look and tone expressing just the necessary degree of contempt at the proposal, " and I'se assure ye, ye'll hae but little o' my company unless ye show gentler havings. It wasna to hear that sort o' nonsense that brought me here wi' my friend, and ye should think shame o' yoursell, 'at should ye."

" Umph ! and what sort of nonsense did bring you here, then, Mrs. Dennison ? "

" My kinswoman has some particular business with your prisoner, young Mr. Harry Morton, and I am come wi' her to speak till him."

" The devil you are !" answered the sentinel ; " and pray, Mrs. Dennison, how do your kinswoman and you propose to get in ? You are rather too plump to whisk through a key-hole, and opening the door is a thing not to be spoke of."

"It's no a thing to be spoken o', but a thing to be dune," replied the persevering damsel.

"We'll see about that, my bonny Jenny;" and the soldier resumed his march, humming as he walked to and fro along the gallery—

> "Keek into the draw-well,
>   Janet, Janet,
> Then ye'll see your bonny sell,
>   My jo Janet."

"So ye're no thinking to let us in, Mr. Halliday ? Weel, weel; gude e'en to you; ye hae seen the last o' me, and o' this bonny die too," said Jenny, holding between her finger and thumb a splendid silver dollar.

"Give him gold, give him gold," whispered the agitated young lady.

"Silver's e'en ower gude for the like o' him," replied Jenny, "that disna care for the blink o' a bonny lassie's ee; and what's waur, he wad think there was something mair in't than a kinswoman o' mine. My certy! siller's no sae plenty wi' us, let alane gowd." Having addressed this advice aside to her mistress, she raised her voice, and said, "My cousin winna stay ony langer, Mr. Halliday; sae, if ye please, gude e'en t'ye."

"Halt a bit—halt a bit," said the trooper; "rein up and parley, Jenny. If I let your kinswoman in to speak to my prisoner, you must stay here and keep me company till she come out again, and then we'll all be well pleased, you know."

"The fiend be in my feet, then," said Jenny; "d'ye think my kinswoman and me are gaun to lose our gude name wi' cracking clavers wi' the like o' you or your prisoner either, without somebody by to see fair play ? Hegh, hegh, sirs, to see sic a difference between folks' promises and performance ! Ye were aye willing to slight puir Cuddie; but an I had asked him to oblige me in a thing, though it had been to cost his hanging, he wadna hae stude twice about it."

"D—n Cuddie ! " retorted the dragoon, " he'll be hanged in good earnest, I hope. I saw him to-day at Milnwood with his old Puritanical b—— of a mother, and if I had thought I was to have had him cast in my dish, I would have brought him up at my horse's tail ; we had law enough to bear us out."

"Very weel—very weel. See if Cuddie winna hae a lang shot at you ane o' thae days, if ye gar him tak the muir wi' sae many honest folk. He can hit a mark brawly ; he was third at the popinjay ; and he's as true of his promise as of ee and hand, though he disna mak sic a phrase about it as some acquaintance o' yours. But it's a' ane to me. Come, cousin, we'll awa'."

"Stay, Jenny ; d—n me if I hang fire more than another when I have said a thing," said the soldier, in a hesitating tone. "Where is the sergeant ?"

"Drinking and driving ower," quoth Jenny, "wi' the steward and John Gudyill."

"So, so, he's safe enough ; and where are my comrades ?" asked Halliday.

"Birling the brown bowl wi' the fowler and the falconer and some o' the serving folk."

"Have they plenty of ale ?"

"Sax gallons as gude as e'er was masked," said the maid.

"Well, then, my pretty Jenny," said the relenting senti-nel, "they are fast till the hour of relieving guard, and per-haps something later ; and so if you will promise to come alone the next time——"

"Maybe I will and maybe I winna," said Jenny ; "but if ye get the dollar, ye'll like that just as weel."

"I'll be d—d if I do," said Halliday, taking the money, however ; "but it's always something for my risk, for if Claverhouse hears what I have done he will build me a horse as high as the Tower of Tillietudlem. But every one in the regiment takes what they can come by ; I am sure Bothwell and his blood royal shows us a good example. And if I were trusting to you, you little jilting devil, I should lose both pains and powder ; whereas this fellow," looking at the piece, "will be good as far as he goes. So, come, there is the door open for you ; do not stay groaning and praying with the young Whig now, but be ready, when I call at the door, to start as if they were sounding ' Horse and away.'"

So speaking, Halliday unlocked the door of the closet, ad-mitted Jenny and her pretended kinswoman, locked it behind them, and hastily reassumed the indifferent measured step and time-killing whistle of a sentinel upon his regular duty.

The door, which slowly opened, discovered Morton with both arms reclined upon a table, and his head resting upon them in a posture of deep dejection. He raised his face as the door opened, and perceiving the female figures which it ad-mitted, started up in great surprise. Edith, as if modesty had quelled the courage which despair had bestowed, stood about a yard from the door without having either the power to speak or to advance. All the plans of aid, relief, or comfort which she had proposed to lay before her lover seemed at once to have vanished from her recollection, and left only a painful chaos of ideas, with which was mingled a fear that she had degraded herself in the eyes of Morton by a step which might appear precipitate and unfeminine. She hung motionless and almost powerless upon the arm of her attendant, who in vain endeavored to reassure and inspire her with courage by whispering, "We are in now, madam, and we maun mak the best o' our time; for doubtless the corporal or the sergeant will gang the rounds, and it wad be a pity to hae the poor lad Halliday punished for his civility."

Morton in the meantime was timidly advancing, suspecting the truth; for what other female in the house excepting Edith herself was likely to take an interest in his misfortunes? and yet afraid, owing to the doubtful twilight and the muffled dress, of making some mistake which might be prejudicial to the object of his affections.

Jenny, whose ready wit and forward manners well qualified her for such an office, hastened to break the ice. "Mr. Morton, Miss Edith's very sorry for your present situation, and——"

It was needless to say more; he was at her side, almost at her feet, pressing her unresisting hands and loading her with a profusion of thanks and gratitude which would be hardly intelligible from the mere broken words, unless we could describe the tone, the gesture, the impassioned and hurried indications of deep and tumultuous feeling with which they were accompanied.

For two or three minutes Edith stood as motionless as the statue of a saint which receives the adoration of a worshipper; and when she recovered herself sufficiently to withdraw her hands from Henry's grasp she could at first only faintly articulate, "I have taken a strange step, Mr. Morton—a step," she continued, with more coherence, as her ideas arranged themselves in consequence of a strong effort, "that perhaps may expose me to censure in your eyes. But I have long permitted you to use the language of friendship—perhaps I might say more—too long to leave you when the world seems to have left you. How or why is this imprisonment? what can be done? Can my uncle, who thinks so highly of you—can your own kinsman, Milnwood, be of no use? are there no means? and what is likely to be the event?"

"Be what it will," answered Henry, contriving to make himself master of the hand that had escaped from him, but which was now again abandoned to his clasp—" be what it will, it is to me from this moment the most welcome incident of a weary life. To you, dearest Edith—forgive me, I should have said Miss Bellenden, but misfortune claims strange privileges—to you I have owed the few happy moments which have gilded a gloomy existence; and if I am now to lay it down, the recollection of this honor will be my happiness in the last hour of suffering."

"But is it even thus, Mr. Morton ? " said Miss Bellenden. " Have you, who used to mix so little in these unhappy feuds, become so suddenly and deeply implicated that nothing short of——" She paused, unable to bring out the word which should have come next.

" Nothing short of my life, you would say ? " replied Morton, in a calm but melancholy tone ; " I believe that will be entirely in the bosoms of my judges. My guards spoke of a possibility of exchanging the penalty for entry into foreign service. I thought I could have embraced the alternative; and yet, Miss Bellenden, since I have seen you once more I feel that exile would be more galling than death."

" And it is then true," said Edith, " that you have been so desperately rash as to entertain communication with any of those cruel wretches who assassinated the primate ? "

" I knew not even that such a crime had been committed," replied Morton, " when I gave unhappily a night's lodging and concealment to one of those rash and cruel men, the ancient friend and comrade of my father. But my ignorance will avail me little ; for who, Miss Bellenden, save you will believe it ? And what is worse, I am at least uncertain whether, even if I had known the crime, I could have brought my mind, under all the circumstances, to refuse a temporary refuge to the fugitive."

" And by whom," said Edith, anxiously, " or under what authority will the investigation of your conduct take place ? "

" Under that of Colonel Grahame of Claverhouse, I am given to understand," said Morton ; " one of the military commission, to whom it has pleased our king, our privy council, and our parliament, that used to be more tenacious of our liberties, to commit the sole charge of our goods and of our lives."

" To Claverhouse ? " said Edith, faintly ; " merciful Heaven, you are lost ere you are tried ! He wrote to my grandmother that he was to be here to-morrow morning on his road to the head of the county, where some desperate man, animated by the presence of two or three of the actors in the primate's murder, are said to have assembled for the purpose of making a stand against the government. His expressions made me shudder even when I could not guess that —that—a friend——"

"Do not be too much alarmed on my account, my dearest Edith," said Henry, as he supported her in his arms; "Claverhouse, though stern and relentless, is, by all accounts, brave, fair, and honorable. I am a soldier's son, and will plead my cause like a soldier. He will perhaps listen more favorably to a blunt and unvarnished defence than a truckling and time-serving judge might do. And, indeed, in a time when justice is in all its branches so completely corrupted, I would rather lose my life by open military violence than be conjured out of it by the hocus-pocus of some arbitrary lawyer, who lends the knowledge he has of the statutes, made for our protection, to wrest them to our destruction."

"You are lost—you are lost, if you are to plead your cause with Claverhouse!" sighed Edith; "root and branch-work is the mildest of his expressions. The unhappy primate was his intimate friend and early patron. 'No excuse, no subterfuge,' said his letter, 'shall save either those connected with the deed, or such as have given them countenance and shelter, from the ample and bitter penalty of the law, until I shall have taken as many lives in vengeance of this atrocious murder as the old man had gray hairs upon his venerable head.' There is neither ruth nor favor to be found with him."

Jenny Dennison, who had hitherto remained silent, now ventured, in the extremity of distress which the lovers felt, but for which they were unable to devise a remedy, to offer her own advice.

"Wi' your leddyship's pardon, Miss Edith, and young Mr. Morton's, we maunna waste time. Let Milnwood take my plaid and gown; I'll slip them aff in the dark corner if he'll promise no to look about, and he may walk past Tam Halliday, who is half blind with his ale, and I can tell him a canny way to get out o' the Tower, and your leddyship will gang quietly to your ain room, and I'll row mysell in his gray cloak and pit on his hat, and play the prisoner till the coast's clear, and then I'll cry in Tam Halliday and gar him let me out."

"Let you out!" said Morton; "they'll make your life answer it."

"Ne'er a bit," replied Jenny. "Tam daurna tell he let onybody in, for his ain sake; and I'll gar him find some other gate to account for the escape."

"Will you, by G—?" said the sentinel, suddenly opening the door of the apartment; "if I am half blind I am not deaf, and you should not plan an escape quite so loud if you expect to go through with it. Come, come, Mrs. Janet— march, troop—quick time—trot, d—n me! And you, madam kinswoman; I won't ask your real name, though you were going to play me so rascally a trick, but I must make a clear garrison; so beat a retreat, unless you would have me turn out the guard."

"I hope," said Morton, very anxiously, "you will not mention this circumstance, my good friend, and trust to my honor to acknowledge your civility in keeping the secret. If you overheard our conversation, you must have observed that we did not accept of, or enter into, the hasty proposal made by this good-natured girl."

"Oh, devilish good-natured to be sure," said Halliday. "As for the rest, I guess how it is, and I scorn to bear malice or tell tales as much as another; but no thanks to that little jilting devil Jenny Dennison, who deserves a tight skelping for trying to lead an honest lad into a scrape, just because he was so silly as to like her good-for-little chit face."

Jenny had no better means of justification than the last apology to which her sex trust, and usually not in vain: she pressed her handkerchief to her face, sobbed with great vehemence, and either wept or managed, as Halliday might have said, to go through the motions wonderfully well.

"And now," continued the soldier, somewhat mollified, "if you have anything to say, say it in two minutes, and let me see your backs turned; for, if Bothwell take it into his drunken head to make the rounds half an hour too soon, it will be a black business to us all."

"Farewell, Edith," whispered Morton, assuming a firmness he was far from possessing; "do not remain here; leave me to my fate; it cannot be beyond endurance since you are interested in it. Good-night—good-night! Do not remain here till you are discovered."

Thus saying, he resigned her to her attendant, by whom she was partly led and partly supported out of the apartment.

"Every one has his taste, to be sure," said Halliday; "but d—n me if I would have vexed so sweet a girl as that is for all the Whigs that ever swore the Covenant."

When Edith had regained her apartment she gave way to a burst of grief which alarmed Jenny Dennison, who hastened to administer such scraps of consolation as occurred to her.

"Dinna vex yoursell sae muckle, Miss Edith," said that faithful attendant; "wha kens what may happen to help young Milnwood?   He's a brave lad and a bonny, and a gentleman of a good fortune, and they winna string the like o' him up as they do the puir Whig bodies that they catch in the muirs like straps o' onions.   Maybe his uncle will bring him aff, or maybe your ain grand-uncle will speak a gude word for him; he's weel acquent wi' a' the redcoat gentlemen."

"You are right, Jenny—you are right," said Edith, recovering herself from the stupor into which she had sunk; "this is no time for despair, but for exertion.   You must find some one to ride this very night to my uncle's with a letter."

"To Charnwood, madam?   It's unco late, and it's sax miles an' a bittock doun the water; I doubt if we can find man and horse the night, mair especially as they hae mounted a sentinel before the gate.   Puir Cuddie! he's gane, puir fallow, that wad hae dune aught in the warld I bade him, and ne'er asked a reason; an' I've had nae time to draw up wi' the new pleugh-lad yet; forbye that, they say he's gaun to be married to Meg Murdieson, ill-faur'd cuttie as she is."

"You *must* find some one to go, Jenny; life and death depend upon it."

"I wad gang mysell, my leddy, for I could creep out at the window o' the pantry, and speel down by the auld yew-tree weel eneugh; I hae played that trick ere now.   But the road's unco wild, and sae mony redcoats about, forbye the Whigs, that are no muckle better—the young lads o' them—if they meet a fraim body their lane in the muirs.   I wadna stand for the walk; I can walk ten miles by moonlight weel eneugh."

"Is there no one you can think of that, for money or favor, would serve me so far?" asked Edith, in great anxiety.

"I dinna ken," said Jenny, after a moment's consideration, "unless it be Guse Gibbie; and he'll maybe no ken the way, though it's no sae difficult to hit if he keep the horse-road and mind the turn at the Cappercleugh, and dinna drown himsell in the Whomlekirn pule, or fa' ower the scaur at the Deil's Loaning, or miss ony o' the kittle steps at the Pass o' Walkwary, or be carried to the hills by the Whigs, or be taen to the tolbooth by the redcoats."

"All ventures must be run," said Edith, cutting short the list of chances against Goose Gibbie's safe arrival at the end of his pilgrimage—"all risks must be run, unless you can find a better messenger.   Go, bid the boy get ready, and get him out of the Tower as secretly as you can.   If he meets any one, let him say he is carrying a letter to Major Bellenden of Charnwood, but without mentioning any names."

"I understand, madam," said Jenny Dennison. "I warrant the callant will do weel eneugh, and Tib the hen-wife will tak care o' the geese for a word o' my mouth; and I'll tell Gibbie your leddyship will mak his peace wi' Lady Margaret, and we'll gie him a dollar."

"Two if he does his errand well," said Edith.

Jenny departed to rouse Goose Gibbie out of his slumbers, to which he was usually consigned at sundown or shortly after, he keeping the hours of the birds under his charge. During her absence Edith took her writing materials and prepared against her return the following letter, superscribed—

For the hands of Major Bellenden of Charnwood, my much honored uncle, These :

"MY DEAR UNCLE—This will serve to inform you I am desirous to know how your gout is, as we did not see you at the wappenschaw, which made both my grandmother and myself very uneasy. And if it will permit you to travel, we shall be happy to see you at our poor house to-morrow at the hour of breakfast, as Colonel Grahame of Claverhouse is to pass this way on his march, and we would willingly have your assistance to receive and entertain a military man of such distinction, who probably will not be much delighted with the company of women. Also, my dear uncle, I pray you to let Mrs. Carefor't, your housekeeper, send me my doubletrimmed paduasoy with the hanging sleeves, which she will find in the third drawer of the walnut press in the green room, which you are so kind as to call mine. Also, my dear uncle, I pray you to send me the second volume of the *Grand Cyrus*, as I have only read as far as the imprisonment of Philidaspes upon the seven hundredth and thirty-third page; but, above all, I entreat you to come to us to-morrow before eight of the clock, which, as your pacing nag is so good, you may well do without rising before your usual hour. So praying to God to preserve your health, I rest your dutiful and loving niece,

"EDITH BELLENDEN.

"*Postscriptum.*—A party of soldiers have last night brought your friend, young Mr. Henry Morton of Milnwood, hither as a prisoner. I conclude you will be sorry for the young gentleman, and, therefore, let you know this in case you may think of speaking to Colonel Grahame in his behalf. I have not mentioned his name to my grandmother, knowing her prejudice against the family."

This epistle being duly sealed and delivered to Jenny, that faithful confidante hastened to put the same in the charge of Goose Gibbie, whom she found in readiness to start from the castle. She then gave him various instructions touching the road, which she apprehended he was likely to mistake, not having travelled it above five or six times, and possessing only the same slender proportion of memory as of judgment. Lastly, she smuggled him out of the garrison through the pantry window into the branchy yew-tree which grew close beside it, and had the satisfaction to see him reach the bottom in safety and take the right turn at the commencement of his journey. She then returned to persuade her young mistress to go to bed, and to lull her to rest, if possible, with assurances of Gibbie's success in his embassy, only qualified by a passing regret that the trusty Cuddie, with whom the commission might have been more safely reposed, was no longer within reach of serving her.

More fortunate as a messenger than as a cavalier, it was Gibbie's good hap rather than his good management which, after he had gone astray not oftener than nine times, and given his garments a taste of the variation of each bog, brook, and slough between Tillietudlem and Charnwood, placed him about daybreak before the gate of Major Bellenden's mansion, having completed a walk of ten miles—for the bittock, as usual, amounted to four—in little more than the same number of hours.

CHAPTER XI

At last comes the troop, by the word of command
Drawn up in our court, where the Captain cries, Stand !
SWIFT.

MAJOR BELLENDEN'S ancient valet, Gideon Pike, as he adjusted his master's clothes by his bedside, preparatory to the worthy veteran's toilet, acquainted him, as an apology for disturbing him an hour earlier than his usual time of rising, that there was an express from Tillietudlem.

"From Tillietudlem ?" said the old gentleman, rising hastily in his bed and sitting bolt upright. "Open the shutters, Pike. I hope my sister-in-law is well ; furl up the bed-curtain. What have we all here ? [glancing at Edith's note]. The gout ! why, she knows I have not had a fit since Candlemas. The wappenschaw ! I told her a month since I was not to be there. Paduasoy and hanging sleeves ! why, hang the gypsy herself ! *Grand Cyrus* and Philipdastus ! Philip Devil ! is the wench gone crazy all at once ? was it worth while to send an express and wake me at five in the morning for all this trash ? But what says her postscriptum ? Mercy on us !" he exclaimed, on perusing it. "Pike, saddle old Kilsyth instantly, and another horse for yourself."

"I hope nae ill news frae the Tower, sir ?" said Pike, astonished at his master's sudden emotion.

"Yes—no—yes—that is, I must meet Claverhouse there on some express business ; so boot and saddle, Pike, as fast as you can. O Lord ! what times are these ! The poor lad, my old cronie's son ! and the silly wench sticks it into her postscriptum, as she calls it, at the tail of all this trumpery about old gowns and new romances !"

In a few minutes the good old officer was fully equipped ; and, having mounted upon his arm-gaunt charger as soberly as Mark Antony himself could have done, he paced forth his way to the Tower of Tillietudlem.

On the road he formed the prudent resolution to say nothing to the old lady (whose dislike to Presbyterians of all kinds he knew to be inveterate) of the quality and rank of the prisoner detained within her walls, but to try his own influence with Claverhouse to obtain Morton's liberation.

"Being so loyal as he is, he must do something for so old a Cavalier as I am," said the veteran to himself; "and if he is so good a soldier as the world speaks of, why, he will be glad to serve an old soldier's son. I never knew a real soldier that was not a frank-hearted, honest fellow; and I think the execution of the laws—though it's a pity they find it necessary to make them so severe—may be a thousand times better intrusted with them than with peddling lawyers and thick-skulled country gentlemen."

Such were the ruminations of Major Miles Bellenden, which were terminated by John Gudyill (not more than half drunk) taking hold of his bridle, and assisting him to dismount in the rough-paved court of Tillietudlem.

"Why, John," said the veteran, "what devil of a discipline is this you have been keeping? You have been reading Geneva print * this morning already."

"I have been reading the Litany," said John, shaking his head with a look of drunken gravity, and having only caught one word of the Major's address to him. "Life is short, sir; we are flowers of the field, sir—hiccup—and lilies of the valley."

"Flowers and lilies! Why, man, such carles as thou and I can hardly be called better than old hemlocks, decayed nettles, or withered ragweed; but I suppose you think that we are still worth watering."

"I am an old soldier, sir, I thank Heaven—hiccup——"

"An old skinker, you mean, John. But come, never mind, show me the way to your mistress, old lad."

John Gudyill led the way to the stone hall, where Lady Margaret was fidgeting about, superintending, arranging, and re-forming the preparations made for the reception of the celebrated Claverhouse, whom one party honored and extolled as a hero, and another execrated as a bloodthirsty oppressor.

"Did I not tell you," said Lady Margaret to her principal female attendant—"did I not tell you, Mysie, that it was my especial pleasure on this occasion to have everything in the precise order wherein it was upon that famous morning when his most sacred Majesty partook of his disjune at Tillietudlem?"

"Doubtless such were your leddyship's commands, and to the best of my remembrance——" was Mysie answering, when her ladyship broke in with, "Then wherefore is the

* The Geneva *Book of Discipline*, adopted by the Scottish Presbyterians (*Laing*).

venison pasty placed on the left side of the throne, and the stoup of claret upon the right, when ye may right weel remember, Mysie, that his most sacred Majesty with his ain hand shifted the pasty to the same side with the flagon, and said they were too good friends to be parted ?"

"I mind that weel, madam," said Mysie; "and if I had forgot, I have heard your leddyship often speak about that grand morning sin' syne; but I thought everything was to be placed just as it was when his Majesty, God bless him ! came into this room, looking mair like an angel than a man if he hadna been sae black-a-vised."

"Then ye thought nonsense, Mysie ; for in whatever way his most sacred Majesty ordered the position of the trenchers and flagons, that, as weel as his royal pleasure in greater matters, should be a law to his subjects, and shall ever be to those of the house of Tillietudlem."

" Weel, madam," said Mysie, making the alterations required, "it's easy mending the error ; but if everything is just to be as his Majesty left it there should be an unco hole in the venison pasty."

At this moment the door opened.

"Who is that, John Gudyill ?" exclaimed the old lady. " I can speak to no one just now. Is it you, my dear brother ?" she continued, in some surprise, as the Major entered; " this is a right early visit."

"Not more early than welcome, I hope," replied Major Bellenden, as he saluted the widow of his deceased brother; " but I heard by a note which Edith sent to Charnwood about some of her equipage and books that you were to have Claver'se here this morning, so I thought, like an old firelock as I am, that I should like to have a chat with this rising soldier. I caused Pike saddle Kilsyth, and here we both are."

" And most kindly welcome you are," said the old lady ; "it is just what I should have prayed you to do if I had thought there was time. You see I am busy in preparation. All is to be in the same order as when——"

" The King breakfasted at Tillietudlem," said the Major, who, like all Lady Margaret's friends, dreaded the commencement of that narrative, and was desirous to cut it short. "I remember it well , you know I was waiting on his Majesty."

" You were, brother," said Lady Margaret ; " and perhaps you can help me to remember the order of the entertain · ment."

"Nay, good sooth, ' said the Major, " the damnable dinner that Nol gave us at Worcester a few days afterwards drove

all your good cheer out of my memory.   But how's this ? you
have even the great Turkey-leather elbow-chair with the tapestry cushions placed in state."

"The throne, brother, if you please," said Lady Margaret,
gravely.

"Well, the throne be it, then," continued the Major.
"Is that to be Claver'se's post in the attack upon the pasty ?"

"No, brother," said the lady ; "as these cushions have
been once honored by accommodating the person of our most
sacred monarch, they shall never, please Heaven, during my
lifetime, be pressed by any less dignified weight."

"You should not, then," said the old soldier, "put them
in the way of an honest old Cavalier who has ridden ten miles
before breakfast ; for, to confess the truth, they look very in-
viting.   But where is Edith ?"

"On the battlements of the warder's turret," answered the
old lady, "looking out for the approach of our guests."

"Why, I'll go there too ; and so should you, Lady Margaret, as soon as you have your line of battle properly formed
in the hall here.   It's a pretty thing, I can tell you, to see a
regiment of horse upon the march."

Thus speaking, he offered his arm with an air of old-fashioned gallantry, which Lady Margaret accepted with such a
courtesy of acknowledgment as ladies were wont to make in
Holyrood House before the year 1642, which, for one while,
drove both courtesies and courts out of fashion.

Upon the bartizan of the turret, to which they ascended
by many a winding passage and uncouth staircase, they found
Edith, not in the attitude of a young lady who watches with
fluttering curiosity the approach of a smart regiment of
dragoons, but pale, downcast, and evincing by her countenance that sleep had not during the preceding night been the
companion of her pillow.   The good old veteran was hurt
at her appearance, which, in the hurry of preparation, her
grandmother had omitted to notice.

"What is come over you, you silly girl ?" he said ; "why,
you look like an officer's wife when she opens the news-letter
after an action and expects to find her husband among the
killed and wounded.   But I know the reason : you will persist in reading these nonsensical romances day and night, and
whimpering for distresses that never existed.   Why, how the
devil can you believe that Artamines, or what d'ye call him,
fought single-handed with a whole battalion ?   One to three
is as great odds as ever fought and won, and I never knew anybody that cared to take that except old Corporal Raddlebanes

But these d—d books put all pretty men's actions out of countenance.   I dare say you would think very little of Raddlebanes
if he were alongside of Artamines.   I would have the fellows
that write such nonsense brought to the picquet for leasing-
making." *

Lady Margaret, herself somewhat attached to the perusal
of romances, took up the cudgels.

"Monsieur Scuderi," she said, "is a soldier, brother ; and,
as I have heard, a complete one, and so is the Sieur d'Urfé."

"More shame for them ; they should have known better
what they were writing about.   For my part, I have not read
a book these twenty years, except my Bible, *The Whole Duty
of Man*, and of late days, Turner's *Pallas Armata, or Treatise
on the Ordering of the Pike Exercise*,† and I don't like *his*
discipline much neither.   He wants to draw up the cavalry in
front of a stand of pikes, instead of being upon the wings.
Sure am I, if we had done so at Kilsyth, instead of having our
handful of horse on the flanks, the first discharge would have
sent them back among our Highlanders.   But I hear the kettle-drums."

All heads were now bent from the battlements of the turret which commanded a distant prospect down the vale of the
river.   The Tower of Tillietudlem stood, or perhaps yet
stands, upon the angle of a very precipitous bank, formed by
the junction of a considerable brook with the Clyde.‡   There
was a narrow bridge of one steep arch across the brook near
its mouth, over which, and along the foot of the high and
broken bank, winded the public road ; and the fortalice, thus
commanding both bridge and pass, had been in times of war
a post of considerable importance, the possession of which was
necessary to secure the communication of the upper and wilder
districts of the country with those beneath, where the valley
expands and is more capable of cultivation.   The view downwards is of a grand woodland character ; but the level ground
and gentle slopes near the river form cultivated fields of an
irregular shape, interspersed with hedgerow trees and copses,
the enclosures seeming to have been individually cleared out
of the forest which surrounds them, and which occupies in
unbroken masses the steeper declivities and more distant
banks.   The stream, in color a clear and sparkling brown,
like the hue of the Cairngorm pebbles, rushes through this
romantic region in bold sweeps and curves, partly visible and

* See Romances of the Seventeenth Century. Note 17.
† See Sir James Turner.   Note 18.
‡ See Tillietudlem Castle.   Note 19.

partly concealed by the trees which clothe its banks. With a providence unknown in other parts of Scotland, the peasants have in most places planted orchards around their cottages, and the general blossom of the apple-trees at this season of the year gave all the lower part of the view the appearance of a flower-garden.

Looking up the river, the character of the scene was varied considerably for the worse. A hilly, waste, and uncultivated country approached close to the banks; the trees were few and limited to the neighborhood of the stream, and the rude moors swelled at a little distance into shapeless and heavy hills, which were again surmounted in their turn by a range of lofty mountains dimly seen on the horizon. Thus the tower commanded two prospects, the one richly cultivated and highly adorned, the other exhibiting the monotonous and dreary character of a wild and inhospitable moorland.

The eyes of the spectators on the present occasion were attracted to the downward view, not alone by its superior beauty, but because the distant sounds of military music began to be heard from the public high-road which winded up the vale and announced the approach of the expected body of cavalry. Their glimmering ranks were shortly afterwards seen in the distance, appearing and disappearing as the trees and the windings of the road permitted them to be visible, and distinguished chiefly by the flashes of light which their arms occasionally reflected against the sun. The train was long and imposing, for there were about two hundred and fifty horse upon the march, and the glancing of the swords and waving of their banners, joined to the clang of their trumpets and kettle-drums, had at once a lively and awful effect upon the imagination. As they advanced still nearer and nearer, they could distinctly see the files of those chosen troops following each other in long succession, completely equipped and superbly mounted.

"It's a sight that makes me thirty years younger," said the old cavalier; "and yet I do not much like the service that these poor fellows are to be engaged in. Although I had my share of the civil war, I cannot say I had ever so much real pleasure in that sort of service as when I was employed on the Continent, and we were hacking at fellows with foreign faces and outlandish dialect. It's a hard thing to hear a hamely Scotch tongue cry 'Quarter,' and be obliged to cut him down just the same as if he called out '*Miséricorde.*' So there they come through the Netherwood haugh; upon my word, fine-looking fellows and capitally mounted. He that is galloping from the rear of the column must be Claver'se himself ; ay, he gets into the front as they cross the bridge, and now they will be with us in less than five minutes."

At the bridge beneath the tower the cavalry divided, and the greater part, moving up the left bank of the brook and crossing at a ford a little above, took the road of the Grange, as it was called, a large set of farm-offices belonging to the Tower, where Lady Margaret had ordered preparation to be made for their reception and suitable entertainment. The officers alone, with their colors and an escort to guard them, were seen to take the steep road up to the gate of the Tower, appearing by intervals as they gained the ascent, and again hidden by projections of the bank and of the huge old trees with which it is covered. When they emerged from this narrow path they found themselves in front of the old Tower, the gates of which were hospitably open for their reception. Lady Margaret, with Edith and her brother-in-law, having hastily descended from their post of observation, appeared to meet and to welcome their guests, with a retinue of domestics in as good order as the orgies of the preceding evening permitted. The gallant young cornet (a relation as well as namesake of Claverhouse, with whom the reader has been already made acquainted) lowered the standard, amid the fanfare of the trumpets, in homage to the rank of Lady Margaret and the charms of her granddaughter, and the old walls echoed to the flourish of the instruments and the stamp and neigh of the chargers.

Claverhouse * himself alighted from a black horse, the most beautiful, perhaps, in Scotland. He had not a single white hair upon his whole body, a circumstance which, joined to his spirit and fleetness, and to his being so frequently employed in pursuit of the Presbyterian recusants, caused an opinion to prevail among them that the steed had been presented to his rider by the great Enemy of Mankind in order to assist him in persecuting the fugitive wanderers. When Claverhouse had paid his respects to the ladies with military politeness, had apologized for the trouble to which he was putting Lady Margaret's family, and had received the corresponding assurances that she could not think anything an inconvenience which brought within the walls of Tillietudlem so distinguished a soldier and so loyal a servant of his sacred Majesty , when, in short, all forms of hospitable and polite ritual had been duly complied with, the Colonel requested permission to receive the report of Bothwell, who was now in

* See John Grahame of Claverhouse. Note 20.

attendance, and with whom he spoke apart for a few minutes. Major Bellenden took that opportunity to say to his niece, without the hearing of her grandmother, " What a trifling foolish girl you are, Edith, to send me by express a letter crammed with nonsense about books and gowns, and to slide the only thing I cared a marvedi about into the postscript !"

"I did not know," said Edith, hesitating very much, " whether it would be quite—quite proper for me to——"

" I know what you would say—whether it would be right to take any interest in a Presbyterian. But I knew this lad's father well. He was a brave soldier; and if he was once wrong, he was once right too. I must commend your caution, Edith, for having said nothing of this young gentleman's affair to your grandmother; you may rely on it I shall not. I will take an opportunity to speak to Claver'se. Come, my love, they are going to breakfast. Let us follow them."

CHAPTER XII

Their breakfast so warm to be sure they did eat,
A custom in travellers mighty discreet.

PRIOR.

THE breakfast of Lady Margaret Bellenden no more resembled a modern dejeune than the great stone hall at Tillietudlem could brook comparison with a modern drawing-room. No tea, no coffee, no variety of rolls, but solid and substantial viands—the priestly ham, the knightly sirloin, the noble baron of beef, the princely venison pasty ; while silver flagons, saved with difficulty from the claws of the Covenanters, now mantled, some with ale, some with mead, and some with generous wine of various qualities and descriptions. The appetites of the guests were in correspondence to the magnificence and solidity of the preparation—no piddling, no boy's play, but that steady and persevering exercise of the jaws which is best learned by early morning hours and by occasional hard commons.

Lady Margaret beheld with delight the cates which she had provided descending with such alacrity into the persons of her honored guests, and had little occasion to exercise, with respect to any of the company, saving Claverhouse himself, the compulsory urgency of pressing to eat, to which, as to the *peine forte et dure*, the ladies of that period were in the custom of subjecting their guests.

But the leader himself, more anxious to pay courtesy to Miss Bellenden, next whom he was placed, than to gratify his appetite, appeared somewhat negligent of the good cheer set before him. Edith heard without reply many courtly speeches addressed to her in a tone of voice of that happy modulation which could alike melt in the low tones of interesting conversation and rise amid the din of battle "loud as a trumpet with a silver sound." The sense that she was in the presence of the dreadful chief upon whose fiat the fate of Henry Morton must depend, the recollection of the terror and awe which were attached to the very name of the commander, deprived her for some time, not only of the courage to answer, but even of the power of looking upon him. But when, emboldened by the soothing tones of his voice, she lifted her eyes to frame some reply, the person on whom she looked bore, in his appearance at least, none of the terrible attributes in which her apprehensions had arrayed him.

Grahame of Claverhouse was in the prime of life, rather low of stature, and slightly, though elegantly, formed; his gesture, language, and manners were those of one whose life had been spent among the noble and the gay. His features exhibited even feminine regularity. An oval face, a straight and well-formed nose, dark hazel eyes, a complexion just sufficiently tinged with brown to save it from the charge of effeminacy, a short upper lip, curved upward like that of a Grecian statue, and slightly shaded by small mustachios of light brown, joined to a profusion of long curled locks of the same color, which fell down on each side of his face, contributed to form such a countenance as limners love to paint and ladies to look upon.

The severity of his character, as well as the higher attributes of undaunted and enterprising valor, which even his enemies were compelled to admit, lay concealed under an exterior which seemed adapted to the court or the saloon rather than to the field. The same gentleness and gayety of expression which reigned in his features seemed to inspire his actions and gestures ; and, on the whole, he was generally esteemed at first sight rather qualified to be the votary of pleasure than of ambition. But under this soft exterior was hidden a spirit unbounded in daring and in aspiring, yet cautious and prudent as that of Machiavel himself. Profound in politics, and imbued, of course, with that disregard for individual rights which its intrigues usually generate, this leader was cool and collected in danger, fierce and ardent in pursuing success, careless of facing death himself, and ruthless in inflicting it upon others. Such are the characters formed in times of civil discord, when the highest qualities, perverted by party spirit and inflamed by habitual opposition, are too often combined with vices and excesses which deprive them at once of their merit and of their lustre.

In endeavoring to reply to the polite trifles with which Claverhouse accosted her, Edith showed so much confusion that her grandmother thought it necessary to come to her relief.

"Edith Bellenden," said the old lady, "has, from my retired mode of living, seen so little of those of her own sphere that truly she can hardly frame her speech to suitable answers.

A soldier is so rare a sight with us, Colonel Grahame, that, unless it be my young Lord Evandale, we have hardly had an opportunity of receiving a gentleman in uniform.   And now I talk of that excellent young nobleman, may I inquire if I was not to have had the honor of seeing him this morning with the regiment?"

"Lord Evandale, madam, was on his march with us," answered the leader, "but I was obliged to detach him with a small party to disperse a conventicle of those troublesome scoundrels, who have had the impudence to assemble within five miles of my headquarters."

"Indeed!" said the old lady; "that is a height of presumption to which I would have thought no rebellious fanatics would have ventured to aspire.   But these are strange times! There is an evil spirit in the land, Colonel Grahame, that ex cites the vassals of persons of rank to rebel against the very house that holds and feeds them.   There was one of my ablebodied men the other day who plainly refused to attend the wappenschaw at my bidding.   Is there no law for such recusancy, Colonel Grahame?"

"I think I could find one," said Claverhouse, with great composure, "if your ladyship will inform me of the name and residence of the culprit."

"His name," said Lady Margaret, "is Cuthbert Headrigg; I can say nothing of his domicile, for ye may weel believe, Colonel Grahame, he did not dwell long in Tillietudlem, but was speedily expelled for his contumacy.   I wish the lad no severe bodily injury; but incarceration, or even a few stripes, would be a good example in this neighborhood.   His mother, under whose influence I doubt he acted, is an ancient domestic of this family, which makes me incline to mercy; although," continued the old lady, looking towards the pictures of her husband and her sons, with which the wall was hung, and heaving at the same time a deep sigh, "I, Colonel Grahame, have in my ain person but little right to compassionate that stubborn and rebellious generation.   They have made me a childless widow, and, but for the protection of our sacred Sovereign and his gallant soldiers, they would soon deprive me of lands and goods, of hearth and altar.   Seven of my tenants, whose joint rent-mail may mount to well-nigh a hundred merks, have already refused to pay either cess or rent, and had the assurance to tell my steward that they would acknowledge neither king nor landlord but who should have taken the Covenant."

"I will take a course with them—that is, with your ladyship's permission," answered Claverhouse; "it would ill become me to neglect the support of lawful authority when it is lodged in such worthy hands as those of Lady Margaret Bellenden.   But I must needs say, this country grows worse and worse daily, and reduces me to the necessity of taking measures with the recusants that are much more consonant with my duty than with my inclinations.   And speaking of this, I must not forget that I have to thank your ladyship for the hospitality you have been pleased to extend to a party of mine who have brought in a prisoner charged with having resetted the murdering villain, Balfour of Burley."

"The house of Tillietudlem," answered the lady, "hath ever been open to the servants of his Majesty, and I hope that the stones of it will no longer rest on each other when it surceases to be as much at their command as at ours.   And this reminds me, Colonel Grahame, that the gentleman who commands the party can hardly be said to be in his proper place in the army, considering whose blood flows in his veins; and if I might flatter myself that anything would be granted to my request, I would presume to entreat that he might be promoted on some favorable opportunity."

"Your ladyship means Sergeant Francis Stewart, whom we call Bothwell?" said Claverhouse, smiling. "The truth is, he. is a little too rough in the country, and has not been uniformly so amenable to discipline as the rules of the service require. But to instruct me how to oblige Lady Margaret Bellenden is to lay down the law to me.   Bothwell," he continued, addressing the sergeant, who just then appeared at the door, "go kiss Lady Margaret Bellenden's hand, who interests herself in your promotion, and you shall have a commission the first vacancy."

Bothwell went through the salutation in the manner prescribed, but not without evident marks of haughty reluctance, and when he had done so, said aloud, "To kiss a lady's hand can never disgrace a gentleman; but I would not kiss a man's, save the king's, to be made a general."

"You hear him," said Claverhouse, smiling, "there's the rock he splits upon: he cannot forget his pedigree."

"I know, my noble colonel," said Bothwell, in the same tone, "that *you* will not forget your promise; and then perhaps you may permit *Cornet* Stewart to have some recollection of his grandfather, though the *Sergeant* must forget him."

"Enough of this, sir," said Claverhouse, in the tone of

command which was familiar to him, "and let me know what
you came to report to me just now."

"My Lord Evandale and his party have halted on the high-
road with some prisoners," said Bothwell.

"My Lord Evandale?" said Lady Margaret. "Surely,
Colonel Grahame, you will permit him to honor me with his
society, and to take his poor disjune here, especially considering that even his most sacred Majesty did not pass the Tower
of Tillietudlem without halting to partake of some refreshment."

As this was the third time in the course of the conversation
that Lady Margaret had adverted to this distinguished event,
Colonel Grahame, as speedily as politeness would permit, took
advantage of the first pause to interrupt the further progress
of the narrative, by saying, "We are already too numerous a
party of guests; but as I know what Lord Evandale will suffer
[looking towards Edith] if deprived of the pleasure which we
enjoy, I will run the risk of overburdening your ladyship's
hospitality. Bothwell, let Lord Evandale know that Lady
Margaret Bellenden requests the honor of his company."

"And let Harrison take care," added Lady Margaret,
"that the people and their horses are suitably seen to."

Edith's heart sprung to her lips during this conversation;
for it instantly occurred to her that, through her influence over
Lord Evandale, she might find some means of releasing Morton
from his present state of danger, in case her uncle's intercession
with Claverhouse should prove ineffectual. At any other time
she would have been much averse to exert this influence; for,
however inexperienced in the world, her native delicacy taught
her the advantage which a beautiful young woman gives to a
young man when she permits him to lay her under an obligation. And she would have been the further disinclined to request any favor of Lord Evandale, because the voice of the
gossips in Clydesdale had, for reasons hereafter to be made
known, assigned him to her as a suitor, and because she could
not disguise from herself that very little encouragement was
necessary to realize conjectures which had hitherto no foundation. This was the more to be dreaded that, in the case of
Lord Evandale's making a formal declaration, he had every
chance of being supported by the influence of Lady Margaret
and her other friends, and that she would have nothing to oppose
to their solicitations and authority, except a predilection, to
avow which she knew would be equally dangerous and unavailing. She determined, therefore, to wait the issue of her uncle's intercession, and should it fail, which she conjectured she

Graham of Claverhouse.

should soon learn, either from the looks or language of the open-hearted veteran, she would then, as a last effort, make use in Morton's favor of her interest with Lord Evandale. Her mind did not long remain in suspense on the subject of her uncle's application.

Major Bellenden, who had done the honors of the table, laughing and chatting with the military guests who were at that end of the board, was now, by the conclusion of the repast, at liberty to leave his station, and accordingly took an opportunity to approach Claverhouse, requesting from his niece, at the same time, the honor of a particular introduction. As his name and character were well known, the two military men met with expressions of mutual regard ; and Edith, with a beating heart, saw her aged relative withdraw from the company, together with his new acquaintance, into a recess formed by one of the arched windows of the hall. She watched their conference with eyes almost dazzled by the eagerness of suspense, and, with observation rendered more acute by the internal agony of her mind, could guess from the pantomimic gestures which accompanied the conversation the progress and fate of the intercession in behalf of Henry Morton.

The first expression of the countenance of Claverhouse betokened that open and willing courtesy which, ere it requires to know the nature of the favor asked, seems to say, how happy the party will be to confer an obligation on the suppliant. But as the conversation proceeded the brow of that officer became darker and more severe, and his features, though still retaining the expression of the most perfect politeness, assumed, at least to Edith's terrified imagination, a harsh and inexorable character. His lip was now compressed as if with impatience, now curled slightly upward, as if in civil contempt of the arguments urged by Major Bellenden. The language of her uncle, as far as expressed in his manner, appeared to be that of earnest intercession, urged with all the affectionate simplicity of his character, as well as with the weight which his age and reputation entitled him to use. But it seemed .to have little impression upon Colonel Grahame, who soon changed his posture, as if about to cut short the Major's importunity, and to break up their conference with a courtly expression of regret, calculated to accompany a positive refusal of the request solicited. This movement brought them so near Edith that she could distinctly hear Claverhouse say, "It cannot be, Major Bellenden ; lenity, in his case, is altogether beyond the bounds of my commission, though in anything else I am heartily desirous to oblige you. And here comes Evandale with news, as I think. What tidings do you bring us, Evandale?" he continued, addressing the young lord, who now entered in complete uniform, but with his dress disordered and his boots spattered, as if by riding hard.

"Unpleasant news, sir," was his reply. "A large body of Whigs are in arms among the hills, and have broken out into actual rebellion. They have publicly burnt the Act of Supremacy, that which established episcopacy, that for observing the martyrdom of Charles I., and some others, and have declared their intention to remain together in arms for furthering the covenanted work of reformation."

This unexpected intelligence struck a sudden and painful surprise into the minds of all who heard it, excepting Claverhouse.

"Unpleasant news call you them?" replied Colonel Grahame, his dark eyes flashing fire; "they are the best I have heard these six months. Now that the scoundrels are drawn into a body, we will make short work with them. When the adder crawls into daylight," he added, striking the heel of his boot upon the floor, as if in the act of crushing a noxious reptile, "I can trample him to death; he is only safe when he remains lurking in his den or morass. Where are these knaves?" he continued, addressing Lord Evandale.

"About ten miles off among the mountains, at a place called Loudon Hill," was the young nobleman's reply. "I dispersed the conventicle against which you sent me, and made prisoner an old trumpeter of rebellion—an intercommuned minister, that is to say—who was in the act of exhorting his hearers to rise and be doing in the good cause, as well as one or two of his hearers who seemed to be particularly insolent; and from some country people and scouts I learned what I now tell you."

"What may be their strength?" asked his commander.

"Probably a thousand men; but accounts differ widely."

"Then," said Claverhouse, "it is time for us to be up and be doing also. Bothwell, bid them sound to horse."

Bothwell, who, like the war-horse of Scripture, snuffed the battle afar off, hastened to give orders to six negroes in white dresses richly laced, and having massive silver collars and armlets. These sable functionaries acted as trumpeters, and speedily made the castle and the woods around it ring with their summons.

"Must you then leave us?" said Lady Margaret, her heart sinking under recollection of former unhappy times; "had ye not better send to learn the force of the rebels?

O, how many a fair face hae I heard these fearfu' sounds call away frae the Tower of Tillietudlem that my auld een were ne'er to see return to it!"

"It is impossible for me to stop," said Claverhouse; "there are rogues enough in this country to make the rebels five times their strength if they are not checked at once."

"Many," said Evandale, "are flocking to them already, and they give out that they expect a strong body of the indulged Presbyterians, headed by young Milnwood, as they call him, the son of the famous old Roundhead, Colonel Silas Morton."

This speech produced a very different effect upon the hearers. Edith almost sunk from her seat with terror, while Claverhouse darted a glance of sarcastic triumph at Major Bellenden, which seemed to imply, "You see what are the principles of the young man you are pleading for."

"It's a lie—it's a d—d lie of these rascally fanatics," said the Major, hastily. "I will answer for Henry Morton as I would for my own son. He is a lad of as good church principles as any gentleman in the Life Guards. I mean no offence to any one. He has gone to church service with me fifty times, and I never heard him miss one of the responses in my life. Edith Bellenden can bear witness to it as well as I. He always read on the same Prayer Book with her, and could look out the lessons as well as the curate himself. Call him up; let him be heard for himself."

"There can be no harm in that," said Claverhouse, "whether he be innocent or guilty. Major Allan," he said, turning to the officer next in command, "take a guide, and lead the regiment forward to Loudon Hill by the best and shortest road. Move steadily, and do not let the men blow the horses; Lord Evandale and I will overtake you in a quarter of an hour. Leave Bothwell with a party to bring up the prisoners."

Allan bowed and left the apartment with all the officers, excepting Claverhouse and the young nobleman. In a few minutes the sound of the military music and the clashing of hoofs announced that the horsemen were leaving the castle. The sounds were presently heard only at intervals, and soon died away entirely.

While Claverhouse endeavored to soothe the terrors of Lady Margaret, and to reconcile the veteran Major to his opinion of Morton, Evandale, getting the better of that conscious shyness which renders an ingenuous youth diffident in approaching the object of his affections, drew near to Miss

Bellenden and accosted her in a tone of mingled respect and interest.

"We are to leave you," he said, taking her hand, which he pressed with much emotion—"to leave you for a scene which is not without its dangers. Farewell, dear Miss Bellenden; let me say for the first and perhaps the last time, dear Edith! We part in circumstances so singular as may excuse some solemnity in bidding farewell to one whom I have known so long and whom I—respect so highly."

The manner, differing from the words, seemed to express a feeling much deeper and more agitating than was conveyed in the phrase he made use of. It was not in woman to be utterly insensible to his modest and deep-felt expression of tenderness. Although borne down by the misfortunes and imminent danger of the man she loved, Edith was touched by the hopeless and reverential passion of the gallant youth who now took leave of her to rush into dangers of no ordinary description.

"I hope—I sincerely trust," she said, "there is no danger. I hope there is no occasion for this solemn ceremonial; that these hasty insurgents will be dispersed rather by fear than force, and that Lord Evandale will speedily return to be what he must always be, the dear and valued friend of all in this castle."

"Of *all?*" he repeated, with a melancholy emphasis upon the word. "But be it so; whatever is near you is dear and valued to me, and I value their approbation accordingly. Of our success I am not sanguine. Our numbers are so few that I dare not hope for so speedy, so bloodless, or so safe an end of this unhappy disturbance. These men are enthusiastic, resolute, and desperate, and have leaders not altogether unskilled in military matters. I cannot help thinking that the impetuosity of our Colonel is hurrying us against them rather prematurely. But there are few that have less reason to shun danger than I have."

Edith had now the opportunity she wished to bespeak the young nobleman's intercession and protection for Henry Morton, and it seemed the only remaining channel of interest by which he could be rescued from impending destruction. Yet she felt at that moment as if, in doing so, she was abusing the partiality and confidence of the lover whose heart was as open before her as if his tongue had made an express declaration. Could she with honor engage Lord Evandale in the service of a rival? or could she with prudence make him any request, or lay herself under any obligation to him, without affording ground for hopes which she could never realize? But the moment was too urgent for hesitation, or even for those explanations with which her request might otherwise have been qualified.

"I will but dispose of this young fellow," said Claverhouse from the other side of the hall, "and then, Lord Evandale— I am sorry to interrupt again your conversation—but then we must mount. Bothwell, why do not you bring up the prisoner? and, hark ye, let two files load their carabines."

In these words Edith conceived she heard the death-warrant of her lover. She instantly broke through the restraint which had hitherto kept her silent.

"My Lord Evandale," she said, "this young gentleman is a particular friend of my uncle's; your interest must be great with your Colonel; let me request your intercession in his favor; it will confer on my uncle a lasting obligation."

"You overrate my interest, Miss Bellenden," said Lord Evandale; "I have been often unsuccessful in such applications when I have made them on the mere score of humanity."

"Yet try once again for my uncle's sake."

"And why not for your own?" said Lord Evandale. "Will you not allow me to think I am obliging *you* personally in this matter? Are you so diffident of an old friend that you will not allow him even the satisfaction of thinking that he is gratifying your wishes?"

"Surely, surely," replied Edith; "you will oblige me infinitely. I am interested in the young gentleman on my uncle's account. Lose no time for God's sake!"

She became bolder and more urgent in her entreaties, for she heard the steps of the soldiers who were entering with their prisoner.

"By heaven! then," said Evandale, "he shall not die if I should die in his place! But will not you," he said, resuming the hand which in the hurry of her spirits she had not courage to withdraw—"will not you grant me one suit in return for my zeal in your service?"

"Anything you can ask, my Lord Evandale, that sisterly affection can give."

"And is this all," he continued—"all you can grant to my affection living, or my memory when dead?"

"Do not speak thus, my lord," said Edith, "you distress me, and do injustice to yourself. There is no friend I esteem more highly, or to whom I would more readily grant every mark of regard—providing—but——"

A deep sigh made her turn her head suddenly ere she had

well uttered the last word; and as she hesitated how to frame the exception with which she meant to close the sentence, she became instantly aware she had been overheard by Morton, who, heavily ironed and guarded by soldiers, was now passing behind her in order to be presented to Claverhouse. As their eyes met each other, the sad and reproachful expression of Morton's glance seemed to imply that he had partially heard and altogether misinterpreted the conversation which had just passed. There wanted but this to complete Edith's distress and confusion. Her blood, which rushed to her brow, made a sudden revulsion to her heart, and left her as pale as death. This change did not escape the attention of Evandale, whose quick glance easily discovered that there was between the prisoner and the object of his own attachment some singular and uncommon connection. He resigned the hand of Miss Bellenden, again surveyed the prisoner with more attention, again looked at Edith, and plainly observed the confusion which she could no longer conceal.

"This," he said, after a moment's gloomy silence, "is, I believe, the young gentleman who gained the prize at the shooting match."

"I am not sure," hesitated Edith; "yet—I rather think not," scarce knowing what she replied.

"It *is* he," said Evandale, decidedly; "I know him well. A victor," he continued, somewhat haughtily, "ought to have interested a fair spectator more deeply."

He then turned from Edith, and advancing towards the table at which Claverhouse now placed himself, stood at a little distance, resting on his sheathed broadsword, a silent, but not an unconcerned, spectator of that which passed.

CHAPTER XIII

To explain the deep effect which the few broken passages of the conversation we have detailed made upon the unfortunate prisoner by whom they were overheard, it is necessary to say something of his previous state of mind, and of the origin of his acquaintance with Edith.

Henry Morton was one of those gifted characters which possess a force of talent unsuspected by the owner himself. He had inherited from his father an undaunted courage and a firm and uncompromising detestation of oppression, whether in politics or religion. But his enthusiasm was unsullied by fanatic zeal and unleavened by the sourness of the Puritanical spirit. From these his mind had been freed, partly by the active exertions of his own excellent understanding, partly by frequent and long visits at Major Bellenden's, where he had an opportunity of meeting with many guests whose conversation taught him that goodness and worth were not limited to those of any single form of religious observance.

The base parsimony of his uncle had thrown many obstacles in the way of his education ; but he had so far improved the opportunities which offered themselves, that his instructors as well as his friends were surprised at his progress under such disadvantages. Still, however, the current of his soul was frozen by a sense of dependence, of poverty, above all, of an imperfect and limited education. These feelings impressed him with a diffidence and reserve which effectually concealed from all but very intimate friends the extent of talent and the firmness of character which we have stated him to be possessed of. The circumstances of the times had added to this reserve an air of indecision and of indifference ; for, being attached to neither of the factions which divided the kingdom, he passed for dull, insensible, and uninfluenced by the feeling of religion or of patriotism. No conclusion, however, could be more unjust ; and the reasons of the neutrality which he had hitherto professed had root in very different and most praiseworthy motives. He had formed few congenial ties

with those who were the objects of persecution, and was disgusted alike by their narrow-minded and selfish party spirit,
their gloomy fanaticism, their abhorrent condemnation of all
elegant studies or innocent exercises, and the envenomed
rancor of their political hatred.   But his mind was still more
revolted by the tyrannical and oppressive conduct of the government, the misrule, license, and brutality of the soldiery, the
executions on the scaffold, the slaughters in the open field,
the free quarters and exactions imposed by military law,
which placed the lives and fortunes of a free people on a level
with Asiatic slaves.   Condemning, therefore, each party as
its excesses fell under his eyes, disgusted with the sight of
evils which he had no means of alleviating, and hearing
alternate complaints and exultations with which he could not
sympathize, he would long ere this have left Scotland had it
not been for his attachment to Edith Bellenden.

The earlier meetings of these young people had been at
Charnwood, when Major Bellenden, who was as free from suspicion on such occasions as Uncle Toby himself, had encouraged their keeping each other constant company without
entertaining any apprehension of the natural consequences.
Love, as usual in such cases, borrowed the name of friendship, used her language, and claimed her privileges.   When
Edith Bellenden was recalled to her [grand] mother's castle, it
was astonishing by what singular and recurring accidents she
often met young Morton in her sequestered walks, especially
considering the distance of their places of abode. Yet it somehow happened that she never expressed the surprise which the
frequency of these *rencontres* ought naturally to have excited,
and that their intercourse assumed gradually a more delicate
character, and their meetings began to wear the air of appointments. Books, drawings, letters, were exchanged between
them, and every trifling commission given or executed gave
rise to a new correspondence.   Love indeed was not yet mentioned between them by name, but each knew the situation
of their own bosom, and could not but guess at that of the
other.   Unable to desist from an intercourse which possessed
such charms for both, yet trembling for its too probable consequences, it had been continued without specific explanation
until now, when fate appeared to have taken the conclusion
into its own hands.

It followed, as a consequence of this state of things, as well
as of the diffidence of Morton's disposition at this period, that
his confidence in Edith's return of his affection had its occasional cold fits.   Her situation was in every respect so su-

perior to his own, her worth so eminent, her accomplishments so many, her face so beautiful, and her manners so bewitching, that he could not but entertain fears that some suitor more favored than himself by fortune, and more acceptable to Edith's family than he durst hope to be, might step in between him and the object of his affections. Common rumor had raised up such a rival in Lord Evandale, whom birth, fortune, connections, and political principles, as well as his frequent visits at Tillietudlem, and his attendance upon Lady Bellenden and her niece at all public places, naturally pointed out as a candidate for her favor. It frequently and inevitably happened that engagements to which Lord Evandale was a party interfered with the meeting of the lovers, and Henry could not but mark that Edith either studiously avoided speaking of the young nobleman, or did so with obvious reserve and hesitation.

These symptoms, which in fact arose from the delicacy of her own feelings towards Morton himself, were misconstrued by his diffident temper, and the jealousy which they excited was fermented by the occasional observations of Jenny Dennison. This true-bred serving-damsel was, in her own person, a complete country coquette, and when she had no opportunity of teasing her own lovers, used to take some occasional opportunity to torment her young lady's. This arose from no ill-will to Henry Morton, who, both on her mistress's account and his own handsome form and countenance, stood high in her esteem. But then Lord Evandale was also handsome ; he was liberal far beyond what Morton's means could afford, and he was a lord, moreover, and if Miss Edith Bellenden should accept his hand she would become a baron's lady, and, what was more, little Jenny Dennison, whom the awful housekeeper at Tillietudlem huffed about at her pleasure, would be then Mrs. Dennison, Lady Evandale's own woman, or perhaps her ladyship's lady-in-waiting. The impartiality of Jenny Dennison, therefore, did not, like that of Mrs. Quickly, extend to a wish that both the handsome suitors could wed her young lady ; for it must be owned that the scale of her regard was depressed in favor of Lord Evandale, and her wishes in his favor took many shapes extremely tormenting to Morton ; being now expressed as a friendly caution, now as an article of intelligence, and anon as a merry jest, but always tending to confirm the idea that sooner or later his romantic intercourse with her young mistress must have a close, and that Edith Bellenden would, in spite of summer walks beneath the greenwood tree, exchange of verses, of drawings, and of books, end in becoming Lady Evandale.

These hints coincided so exactly with the very point of his own suspicions and fears, that Morton was not long of feeling that jealousy which every one has felt who has truly loved, but to which those are most liable whose love is crossed by the want of friends' consent, or some other envious impediment of fortune.   Edith herself unwittingly, and in the generosity of her own frank nature, contributed to the error into which her lover was in danger of falling.   Their conversation once chanced to turn upon some late excesses committed by the soldiery on an occasion when it was said (inaccurately, however) that the party was commanded by Lord Evandale.   Edith, as true in friendship, as in love, was somewhat hurt at the severe strictures which escaped from Morton on this occasion, and which, perhaps, were not the less strongly expressed on account of their supposed rivalry.   She entered into Lord Evandale's defence with such spirit as hurt Morton to the very soul, and afforded no small delight to Jenny Dennison, the usual companion of their walks.   Edith perceived her error, and endeavored to remedy it ; but the impression was not so easily erased, and it had no small effect in inducing her lover to form that resolution of going abroad which was disappointed in the manner we have already mentioned.

The visit which he received from Edith during his confinement, the deep and devoted interest which she had expressed in his fate, ought of themselves to have dispelled his suspicions ; yet, ingenious in tormenting himself, even this he thought might be imputed to anxious friendship, or at most to a temporary partiality, which would probably soon give way to circumstances, the entreaties of her friends, the authority of Lady Margaret, and the assiduities of Lord Evandale.

"And to what do I owe it," he said, "that I cannot stand up like a man and plead my interest in her ere I am thus cheated out of it ? to what but to the all-pervading and accursed tyranny which afflicts at once our bodies, souls, estates, and affections ?   And is it to one of the pensioned cutthroats of this oppressive government that I must yield my pretensions to Edith Bellenden ?   I will not, by Heaven !   It is a just punishment on me for being dead to public wrongs that they have visited me with their injuries in a point where they can be least brooked or borne."

As these stormy resolutions boiled in his bosom, and while he ran over the various kinds of insult and injury which he had sustained in his own cause and in that of his country, Bothwell entered the tower, followed by two dragoons, one of whom carried handcuffs.

"You must follow me, young man," said he, "but first we must put you in trim."

"In trim !" said Morton. "What do you mean ?"

"Why, we must put on these rough bracelets. I durst not —nay, d—n it, I *durst* do anything—but I *would* not for three hours' plunder of a stormed town bring a Whig before my Colonel without his being ironed. Come, come, young man, don't look sulky about it."

He advanced to put on the irons ; but, seizing the oaken seat upon which he had rested, Morton threatened to dash out the brains of the first who should approach him.

"I could manage you in a moment, my youngster," said Bothwell, " but I had rather you would strike sail quietly."

Here indeed he spoke the truth, not from either fear or reluctance to adopt force, but because he dreaded the consequences of a noisy scuffle, through which it might probably be discovered that he had, contrary to express orders, suffered his prisoner to pass the night without being properly secured.

" You had better be prudent," he continued, in a tone which he meant to be conciliatory, " and don't spoil your own sports. They say here in the castle that Lady Margaret's niece is immediately to marry our young captain, Lord Evandale. I saw them close together in the hall yonder, and I heard her ask him to intercede for your pardon. She looked so devilish handsome and kind upon him that on my soul—— But what the devil's the matter with you ? You are as pale as a sheet. Will you have some brandy ?"

" Miss Bellenden ask my life of Lord Evandale !" said the prisoner, faintly.

" Ay, ay ; there's no friend like the women ; their interest carries all in court and camp. Come, you are reasonable now. Ay, I thought you would come round."

Here he employed himself in putting on the fetters, against which Morton, thunderstruck by this intelligence, no longer offered the least resistance.

" My life begged of him, and by her ! Ay, ay, put on the irons ; my limbs shall not refuse to bear what has entered into my very soul. My life begged by Edith, and begged of Evandale !"

" Ay, and he has power to grant it too," said Bothwell. " He can do more with the Colonel than any man in the regiment."

And as he spoke he and his party led their prisoner towards the hall. In passing behind the seat of Edith the unfortunate prisoner heard enough, as he conceived, of the broken expressions which passed between Edith and Lord Evandale to confirm all that the soldier had told him. That moment made a singular and instantaneous revolution in his character. The depth of despair to which his love and fortunes were reduced, the peril in which his life appeared to stand, the transference of Edith's affections, her intercession in his favor, which rendered her fickleness yet more galling, seemed to destroy every feeling for which he had hitherto lived, but at the same time awakened those which had hitherto been smothered by passions more gentle though more selfish. Desperate himself, he determined to support the rights of his country insulted in his person. His character was for the moment as effectually changed as the appearance of a villa which, from being the abode of domestic quiet and happiness, is, by the sudden intrusion of an armed force, converted into a formidable post of defence.

We have already said that he cast upon Edith one glance in which reproach was mingled with sorrow, as if to bid her farewell forever; his next motion was to walk firmly to the table at which Colonel Grahame was seated.

"By what right is it, sir," said he, firmly, and without waiting till he was questioned—"by what right is it that these soldiers have dragged me from my family and put fetters on the limbs of a free man?"

"By my commands," answered Claverhouse; "and I now lay my commands on you to be silent and hear my questions."

"I will not," replied Morton, in a determined tone, while his boldness seemed to electrify all around him. "I will know whether I am in lawful custody, and before a civil magistrate, ere the charter of my country shall be forfeited in my person."

"A pretty springald this, upon my honor!" said Claverhouse.

"Are you mad?" said Major Bellenden to his young friend. "For God's sake, Henry Morton," he continued, in a tone between rebuke and entreaty, "remember you are speaking to one of his Majesty's officers high in the service."

"It is for that very reason, sir," returned Henry, firmly, "that I desire to know what right he has to detain me without a legal warrant. Were he a civil officer of the law, I should know my duty was submission."

"Your friend here," said Claverhouse to the veteran,

coolly, "is one of those scrupulous gentlemen who, like the madman in the play, will not tie his cravat without the warrant of Mr. Justice Overdo; but I will let him see before we part that my shoulder-knot is as legal a badge of authority as the mace of the Justiciary. So, waving this discussion, you will be pleased, young man, to tell me directly when you saw Balfour of Burley."

"As I know no right you have to ask such a question," replied Morton, "I decline replying to it."

"You confessed to my sergeant," said Claverhouse, "that you saw and entertained him, knowing him to be an intercommuned traitor; why are you not so frank with me?"

"Because," replied the prisoner, "I presume you are from education taught to understand the rights upon which you seem disposed to trample; and I am willing you should be aware there are yet Scotsmen who can assert the liberties of Scotland."

"And these supposed rights you would vindicate with your sword, I presume?" said Colonel Grahame.

"Were I armed as you are, and we were alone upon a hillside, you should not ask me the question twice."

"It is quite enough," answered Claverhouse, calmly; "your language corresponds with all I have heard of you; but you are the son of a soldier, though a rebellious one, and you shall not die the death of a dog; I will save you that indignity."

"Die in what manner I may," replied Morton, "I will die like the son of a brave man; and the ignominy you mention shall remain with those who shed innocent blood."

"Make your peace, then, with Heaven in five minutes' space. Bothwell, lead him down to the courtyard and draw up your party."

The appalling nature of this conversation, and of its result, struck the silence of horror into all but the speakers. But now those who stood round broke forth into clamor and expostulation. Old Lady Margaret, who, with all the prejudices of rank and party, had not laid aside the feelings of her sex, was loud in her intercession.

"O, Colonel Grahame," she exclaimed, "spare his young blood! Leave him to the law; do not repay my hospitality by shedding men's blood on the threshold of my doors!"

"Colonel Grahame," said Major Bellenden, "you must answer this violence. Don't think, though I am old and feckless, that my friend's son shall be murdered before my eyes with impunity. I can find friends that shall make you answer it."

"Be satisfied, Major Bellenden, I *will* answer it," replied Claverhouse, totally unmoved; "and you, madam, might spare me the pain of resisting this passionate intercession for a traitor, when you consider the noble blood your own house has lost by such as he is."

"Colonel Grahame," answered the lady, her aged frame trembling with anxiety, "I leave vengeance to God, who calls it His own. The shedding of this young man's blood will not call back the lives that were dear to me ; and how can it comfort me to think that there has maybe been another widowed mother made childless, like mysell, by a deed done at my very door-stane !"

"This is stark madness," said Claverhouse ; "I *must* do my duty to church and state. Here are a thousand villains hard by in open rebellion, and you ask me to pardon a young fanatic who is enough of himself to set a whole kingdom in a blaze ! It cannot be. Remove him, Bothwell."

She who was most interested in this dreadful decision had twice strove to speak, but her voice had totally failed her ; her mind refused to suggest words, and her tongue to utter them. She now sprang up and attempted to rush forward ; but her strength gave way and she would have fallen flat upon the pavement had she not been caught by her attendant.

"Help !" cried Jenny—"help, for God's sake ! my young lady is dying."

At this exclamation, Evandale, who, during the preceding part of the scene, had stood motionless, leaning upon his sword, now stepped forward, and said to his commanding officer, "Colonel Grahame, before proceeding in this matter, will you speak a word with me in private ?"

Claverhouse looked surprised, but instantly rose and withdrew with the young nobleman into a recess, where the following brief dialogue passed between them :

"I think I need not remind you, Colonel, that, when our family interest was of service to you last year in that affair in the privy council, you considered yourself as laid under some obligation to us ?"

"Certainly, my dear Evandale," answered Claverhouse, "I am not a man who forgets such debts ; you will delight me by showing how I can evince my gratitude."

"I will hold the debt cancelled," said Lord Evandale, "if you will spare this young man's life."

"Evandale," replied Grahame, in great surprise, "you are mad—absolutely mad; what interest can you have in this young spawn of an old Roundhead? His father was positively the most dangerous man in all Scotland—cool, resolute, soldierly, and inflexible in his cursed principles. His son seems his very model; you cannot conceive the mischief he may do. I know mankind, Evandale; were he an insignificant, fanatical, country booby, do you think I would have refused such a trifle as his life to Lady Margaret and this family? But this is a lad of fire, zeal, and education; and these knaves want but such a leader to direct their blind enthusiastic hardiness. I mention this, not as refusing your request, but to make you fully aware of the possible consequences. I will never evade a promise, or refuse to return an obligation; if you ask his life he shall have it."

"Keep him close prisoner," answered Evandale, "but do not be surprised if I persist in requesting you will not put him to death. I have most urgent reasons for what I ask."

"Be it so, then," replied Grahame; "but, young man, should you wish in your future life to rise to eminence in the service of your king and country, let it be your first task to subject to the public interest and to the discharge of your duty your private passions, affections, and feelings. These are not times to sacrifice to the dotage of graybeards or the tears of silly women the measures of salutary severity which the dangers around compel us to adopt. And remember that, if I now yield this point in compliance with your urgency, my present concession must exempt me from future solicitations of the same nature."

He then stepped forward to the table and bent his eyes keenly on Morton, as if to observe what effect the pause of awful suspense between death and life, which seemed to freeze the bystanders with horror, would produce upon the prisoner himself. Morton maintained a degree of firmness which nothing but a mind that had nothing left upon earth to love or to hope could have supported at such a crisis.

"You see him?" said Claverhouse, in a half whisper, to Lord Evandale. "He is tottering on the verge between time and eternity, a situation more appalling than the most hideous certainty; yet his is the only cheek unblanched, the only eye that is calm, the only heart that keeps its usual time, the only nerves that are not quivering. Look at him well, Evandale. If that man shall ever come to head an army of rebels, you will have much to answer for on account of this morning's work." He then said aloud, "Young man, your life is for the present safe, through the intercession of your friends. Remove him, Bothwell, and let him be properly guarded and brought along with the other prisoners."

"If my life," said Morton, stung with the idea that he owed his respite to the intercession of a favored rival—"if my life be granted at Lord Evandale's request——"

"Take the prisoner away, Bothwell," said Colonel Grahame, interrupting him; "I have neither time to make nor to hear fine speeches."

Bothwell forced off Morton, saying, as he conducted him into the courtyard, "Have you three lives in your pocket, besides the one in your body, my lad, that you can afford to let your tongue run away with them at this rate? Come, come, I'll take care to keep you out of the Colonel's way; for, egad, you will not be five minutes with him before the next tree or the next ditch will be the word. So come along to your companions in bondage."

Thus speaking, the sergeant, who in his rude manner did not altogether want sympathy for a gallant young man, hurried Morton down to the courtyard, where three other prisoners, two men and a woman, who had been taken by Lord Evandale, remained under an escort of dragoons.

Meantime Claverhouse took his leave of Lady Margaret. But it was difficult for the good lady to forgive his neglect of her intercession.

"I have thought till now," she said, "that the Tower of Tillietudlem might have been a place of succor to those that are ready to perish, even if they werena sae deserving as they should have been ; but I see auld fruit has little savor ; our suffering and our services have been of an ancient date."

"They are never to be forgotten by me, let me assure your ladyship," said Claverhouse. "Nothing but what seemed my sacred duty could make me hesitate to grant a favor requested by you and the Major. Come, my good lady, let me hear you say you have forgiven me, and as I return to-night I will bring a drove of two hundred Whigs with me, and pardon fifty head of them for your sake."

"I shall be happy to hear of your success, Colonel," said Major Bellenden ; "but take an old soldier's advice, and spare blood when battle's over ; and once more let me request to enter bail for young Morton."

"We will settle that when I return," said Claverhouse. "Meanwhile, be assured his life shall be safe."

During this conversation Evandale looked anxiously around for Edith ; but the precaution of Jenny Dennison had occasioned her mistress being transported to her own apartment.

Slowly and heavily he obeyed the impatient summons of Claverhouse, who, after taking a courteous leave of Lady Margaret and the Major, had hastened to the courtyard. The prisoners with their guard were already on their march, and the officers with their escort mounted and followed. All pressed forward to overtake the main body, as it was supposed they would come in sight of the enemy in little more than two hours.

CHAPTER XIV

My hounds may a' rin masterless,
  My hawks may fly frae tree to tree,
My lord may grip my vassal lands,
  For there again maun I never be !

Old Ballad.

WE left Morton, along with three companions in captivity, travelling in the custody of a small body of soldiers, who formed the rear-guard of the column under the command of Claverhouse, and were immediately under the charge of Sergeant Bothwell. Their route lay towards the hills in which the insurgent Presbyterians were reported to be in arms. They had not prosecuted their march a quarter of a mile ere Claverhouse and Evandale galloped past them, followed by their orderly-men, in order to take their proper places in the column which preceded them. No sooner were they past than Bothwell halted the body which he commanded, and disencumbered Morton of his irons.

" King's blood must keep word," said the dragoon. " I promised you should be civilly treated as far as rested with me. Here, Corporal Inglis, let this gentleman ride alongside of the other young fellow who is prisoner ; and you may permit them to converse together at their pleasure, under their breath, but take care they are guarded by two files with loaded carabines. If they attempt an escape, blow their brains out. You cannot call that using you uncivilly," he continued, addressing himself to Morton ; " it's the rules of war, you know. And, Inglis, couple up the parson and the old woman ; they are fittest company for each other, d—n me ; a single file may guard them well enough. If they speak a word of cant or fanatical nonsense, let them have a strapping with a shoulder-bolt. There's some hope of choking a silenced parson ; if he is not allowed to hold forth, his own treason will burst him."

Having made this arrangement, Bothwell placed himself at the head of the party, and Inglis, with six dragoons, brought up the rear.   The whole then set forward at a trot, with the purpose of overtaking the main body of the regiment.

Morton, overwhelmed with a complication of feelings, was totally indifferent to the various arrangements made for his secure custody, and even to the relief afforded him by his release from the fetters.   He experienced that blank and waste of the heart which follows the hurricane of passion, and, no longer supported by the pride and conscious rectitude which dictated his answers to Claverhouse, he surveyed with deep dejection the glades through which he travelled, each turning of which had something to remind him of past happiness and disappointed love.   The eminence which they now ascended was that from which he used first and last to behold the ancient tower when approaching or retiring from it; and it is needless to add that there he was wont to pause and gaze with a lover's delight on the battlements which, rising at a distance out of the lofty wood, indicated the dwelling of her whom he either hoped soon to meet or had recently parted from.   Instinctively he turned his head back to take a last look of a scene formerly so dear to him, and no less instinctively he heaved a deep sigh.   It was echoed by a loud groan from his companion in misfortune, whose eyes, moved, perchance, by similar reflections, had taken the same direction. This indication of sympathy on the part of the captive was uttered in a tone more coarse than sentimental; it was, however, the expression of a grieved spirit, and so far corresponded with the sigh of Morton.   In turning their heads their eyes met, and Morton recognized the stolid countenance of Cuddie Headrigg, bearing a rueful expression, in which sorrow for his own lot was mixed with sympathy for the situation of his companion.

"Hegh, sirs!" was the expression of the *ci-devant* ploughman of the mains of Tillietudlem; "it's an unco thing that decent folk should be harled through the country this gate as if they were a warld's wonder."

"I am sorry to see you here, Cuddie," said Morton, who, even in his own distress, did not lose feeling for that of others.

"And sae am I, Mr. Henry," answered Cuddie, "baith for mysell and you; but neither of our sorrows will do muckle gude that I can see.   To be sure, for me," continued the captive agriculturist, relieving his heart by talking, though he well knew it was to little purpose—"to be sure, for my part, I hae nae right to be here ava', for I never did nor said a word against either king or curate; but my mither, puir body, couldna haud the auld tongue o' her, and we maun baith pay for't, it's like."

"Your mother is their prisoner likewise?" said Morton, hardly knowing what he said.

"In troth is she, riding ahint ye there like a bride, wi' that auld carle o' a minister that they ca' Gabriel Kettle-drummle.   Deil that he had been in the inside of a drum or a kettle either, for my share o' him!   Ye see, we were nae sooner chased out o' the doors o' Milnwood, and your uncle and the housekeeper banging them to and barring them ahint us as if we had had the plague on our bodies, than I says to my mither, 'What are we to do neist? for every hole and bore in the country will be steekit against us; now that ye hae affronted my auld leddy, and gar't the troopers tak up young Milnwood.'   Sae she says to me, 'Binna cast doun, but gird yoursell up to the great task o' the day, and gie your testimony like a man upon the mount o' the Covenant.'"

"And so I suppose you went to a conventicle?" said Morton.

"Ye sall hear," continued Cuddie.   "Aweel, I kendna muckle better what to do, sae I e'en gaed wi' her to an auld daft carline like hersell, and we got some water-broo and bannocks; and mony a weary grace they said, and mony a psalm they sang, or they wad let me win to, for I was amaist famished wi' vexation.   Aweel, they had me up in the gray o' the morning, and I behoved to whig awa' wi' them, reason or nane, to a great gathering o' their folk at the Miry Sikes; and there this chield, Gabriel Kettledrummle, was blasting awa' to them on the hillside about lifting up their testimony, nae doubt, and ganging down to the battle of Roman Gilead, or some sic place.   Eh, Mr. Henry, but the carle gae them a screed o' doctrine!   Ye might hae heard him a mile down the wind.   He routed like a cow in a fremd loaning.   'Weel,' thinks I, 'there's nae place in this country they ca' Roman Gilead; it will be some gate in the west muirlands; and or we win there I'll see to slip awa' wi' this mither o' mine, for I winna rin my neck into a tether for ony Kettledrummle in the country-side.'   Aweel," continued Cuddie, relieving himself by detailing his misfortunes, without being scrupulous concerning the degree of attention which his companion bestowed on his narrative, "just as I was wearying for the tail of the preaching, cam word that the dragoons were upon us. Some ran, and some cried, 'Stand!' and some cried, 'Down wi' the Philistines!'   I was at my mither to get her awa' sting and ling or the redcoats cam up, but I might as weel

hae tried to drive our auld fore-a-hand ox without the goad—
deil a step wad she budge.   Weel, after a', the cleugh we were
in was strait, and the mist cam thick, and there was good
hope the dragoons wad hae missed us if we could hae held our
tongues ; but, as if auld Kettledrummle himsell hadna made
din eneugh to waken the very dead, they behoved a' to skirl
up a psalm that ye wad hae heard as far as Lanrick !   Aweel,
to mak a lang tale short, up cam my young Lord Evandale,
skelping as fast as his horse could trot, and twenty redcoats
at his back.   Twa or three chields wad needs fight wi' the
pistol and the whinger in the tae hand and the Bible in the
tother, and they got their crouns weel cloured ; but there
wasna muckle skaith dune, for Evandale aye cried to scatter
us, but to spare life."

"And did you not resist ?" said Morton, who probably
felt that at that moment he himself would have encountered
Lord Evandale on much slighter grounds.

"Na, truly," answered Cuddie, "I keepit aye before the
auld woman, and cried for mercy to life and limb ; but twa
o' the redcoats cam up, and ane o' them was gaun to strike
my mither wi' the side o' his broadsword.   So I got up my
kebbie at them, and said I wad gie them as gude.   Weel,
they turned on me, and clinked at me wi' their swords, and I
garr'd my hand keep my head as weel as I could till Lord
Evandale came up, and then I cried out I was a servant at
Tillietudlem—ye ken yoursell he was aye judged to hae a look
after the young leddy—and he bade me fling down my kent ;
and sae me and my mither yielded oursells prisoners.   I'm
thinking we wad hae been letten slip awa' ; but Kettledrummle
was taen near us, for Andrew Wilson's naig that he was riding on had been a dragooner lang syne, and the sairer Kettledrummle spurred to win awa', the readier the dour beast ran
to the dragoons when he saw them draw up.   Aweel, when
my mither and him forgathered they set till the sodgers, and
I think they gae them their kale through the reek !   Bastards
o' the hure o' Babylon was the best words in their wame.
Sae then the kiln was in a bleeze again, and they brought us
a' three on wi' them to mak us an example, as they ca't."

"It is most infamous and intolerable oppression !" said
Morton, half speaking to himself.   "Here is a poor peaceable fellow, whose only motive for joining the conventicle
was a sense of filial piety, and he is chained up like a thief
or murderer, and likely to die the death of one, but without
the privilege of a formal trial, which our laws indulge to the
worst malefactor.   Even to witness such tyranny, and still

more to suffer under it, is enough to make the blood of the tamest slave boil within him."

"To be sure," said Cuddie, hearing, and partly understanding, what had broken from Morton in resentment of his injuries, "it is no right to speak evil o' dignities. My auld leddy aye said that, as nae doubt she had a gude right to do, being in a place o' dignity hersell; and troth I listened to her very patiently, for she aye ordered a dram, or a soup-kale, or something to us, after she had gien us a hearing on our duties. But diel a dram, or kale, or onything else, no sae muckle as a cup o' cauld water, do thae lords at Edinburgh gie us; and yet they are heading and hanging amang us, and trailing us after thae blackguard troopers, and taking our goods and gear as if we were outlaws. I canna say I tak it kind at their hands."

"It would be very strange if you did," answered Morton, with suppressed emotion.

"And what I like warst o' a'," continued poor Cuddie, "is thae ranting redcoats coming amang the lasses and taking awa' our joes. I had a sair heart o' my ain when I passed the mains down at Tillietudlem this morning about parritch-time, and saw the reek comin' out at my ain lum-head, and kenn'd there was some ither body than my auld mither sitting by the ingle-side. But I think my heart was e'en sairer when I saw that hellicat trooper, Tam Halliday, kissing Jenny Dennison afore my face. I wonder women can hae the impudence to do sic things; but they are a' for the redcoats. Whiles I hae thought o' being a trooper mysell, when I thought naething else wad gae down wi' Jenny; and yet I'll no blame her ower muckle neither, for maybe it was a' for my sake that she loot Tam touzle her tap-knots that gate."

"For your sake?" said Morton, unable to refrain from taking some interest in a story which seemed to bear a singular coincidence with his own.

"E'en sae, Milnwood," replied Cuddie; "for the puir quean gat leave to come near me wi' speaking the loon fair— d—n him, that I suld say sae!—and sae she bade me Godspeed, and she wanted to stap siller into my hand; I'se warrant it was the tae half o' her fee and bountith, for she wared the ither half on pinners and pearlings to gang to see us shoot yon day at the popinjay."

"And did you take it, Cuddie?" said Morton.

"Troth did I no, Milnwood; I was sic a fule as to fling it back to her; my heart was ower grit to be behadden to her when I had seen that loon slavering and kissing at her. But

I was a great fule for my pains; it wad hae dune my mither and me some gude, and she'll ware't a' on duds and nonsense."

There was here a deep and long pause. Cuddie was probably engaged in regretting the rejection of his mistress's bounty, and Henry Morton in considering from what motives, or upon what conditions, Miss Bellenden had succeeded in procuring the interference of Lord Evandale in his favor.

Was it not possible, suggested his awakening hopes, that he had construed her influence over Lord Evandale hastily and unjustly? Ought he to censure her severely if, submitting to dissimulation for his sake, she had permitted the young nobleman to entertain hopes which she had no intention to realize? Or what if she had appealed to the generosity which Lord Evandale was supposed to possess, and had engaged his honor to protect the person of a favored rival?

Still, however, the words which he had overheard recurred ever and anon to his remembrance with a pang which resembled the sting of an adder.

"Nothing that she could refuse him! Was it possible to make a more unlimited declaration of predilection? The language of affection has not, within the limits of maidenly delicacy, a stronger expression. She is lost to me wholly and forever, and nothing remains for me now but vengeance for my own wrongs and for those which are hourly inflicted on my country."

Apparently Cuddie, though with less refinement, was following out a similar train of ideas, for he suddenly asked Morton in a low whisper, "Wad there be ony ill in getting out o' thae chields' hands an ane could compass it?"

"None in the world," said Morton; "and if an opportunity occurs of doing so, depend on it I for one will not let it slip."

"I'm blithe to hear ye say sae," answered Cuddie. "I'm but a puir silly fallow, but I canna think there wad be muckle ill in breaking out by strength o' hand if ye could mak it onything feasible. I am the lad that will ne'er fear to lay on, if it were come to that; but our auld leddy wad hae ca'd that a resisting o' the king's authority."

"I will resist any authority on earth," said Morton, "that invades tyrannically my chartered rights as a freeman; and I am determined I will not be unjustly dragged to a jail, or perhaps a gibbet, if I can possibly make my escape from these men either by address or force."

"Weel, that's just my mind too, aye supposing we hae a feasible opportunity o' breaking loose. But then ye speak o' a charter; now these are things that only belang to the like o' you that are a gentleman, and it mightna bear me through that am but a husbandman."

"The charter that I speak of," said Morton, "is common to the meanest Scotchman. It is that freedom from stripes and bondage which was claimed, as you may read in Scripture, by the Apostle Paul himself, and which every man who is free born is called upon to defend for his own sake and that of his countrymen."

"Hegh, sirs!" replied Cuddie, "it wad hae been lang or my Leddy Margaret, or my mither either, wad hae fund out sic a wise-like doctrine in the Bible! The tane was aye graning about giving tribute to Cæsar, and the tither is as daft wi' her Whiggery. I hae been clean spoilt, just wi' listening to twa blethering auld wives; but if I could get a gentleman that wad let me tak on to be his servant, I am confident I wad be a clean contrary creature; and I hope your honor will think on what I am saying if ye were ance fairly delivered out o' this house of bondage, and just take me to be your ain wally-de-shamble."

"My valet, Cuddie!" answered Morton. "Alas! that would be sorry preferment, even if we were at liberty."

"I ken what ye're thinking—that because I am landward-bred I wad be bringing ye to disgrace afore folk; but ye maun ken I'm gay gleg at the uptak: there was never onything dune wi' hand but I learned gay readily, 'septing reading, writing, and ciphering; but there's no the like o' me at the fitba', and I can play wi' the broadsword as weel as Corporal Inglis there. I hae broken his head or now, for as massy as he's riding ahint us. And then ye'll no be gaun to stay in this country?" said he, stopping and interrupting himself.

"Probably not," replied Morton.

"Weel, I carena a boddle. Ye see I wad get my mither bestowed wi' her auld graning tittie, Auntie Meg, in the Gallowgate o' Glasgow, and then I trust they wad neither burn her for a witch, or let her fail for fau't o' fude, or hang her up for an auld Whig wife; for the provost, they say, is very regardfu' o' sic puir bodies. And then you and me wad gang and pouss our fortunes like the folk i' the daft auld tales about Jock the Giant-killer and Valentine and Orson; and we wad come back to merry Scotland, as the sang says, and I wad tak to the stilts again, and turn sic furs on the bonny rigs o' Milnwood holmes that it wad be worth a pint but to look at them."

"I fear," said Morton, "there is very little chance, my

good friend Cuddie, of our getting back to our old occupation."

"Hout, stir—hout, stir," replied Cuddie, "it's aye gude to keep up a hardy heart, as broken a ship's come to land. But what's that I hear? Never stir, if my auld mither isna at the preaching again! I ken the sough o' her texts, that sound just like the wind blawing through the spence; and there's Kettledrummle setting to wark too. Lordsake, if the sodgers anes get angry they'll murder them baith, and us for company!"

Their further conversation was in fact interrupted by a blatant noise which rose behind them, in which the voice of the preacher emitted, in unison with that of the old woman, tones like the grumble of a bassoon combined with the screaking of a cracked fiddle. At first the aged pair of sufferers had been contented to condole with each other in smothered expressions of complaint and indignation; but the sense of their injuries became more pungently aggravated as they communicated with each other, and they became at length unable to suppress their ire.

"Woe, woe, and a threefold woe unto you, ye bloody and violent persecutors!" exclaimed the Reverend Gabriel Kettledrummle. "Woe, and threefold woe unto you, even to the breaking of seals, the blowing of trumpets, and the pouring forth of vials!"

"Ay, ay; a black cast to a' their ill-faur'd faces, and the outside o' the loof to them at the last day!" echoed the shrill counter-tenor of Mause, falling in like the second part of a catch.

"I tell you," continued the divine, "that your rankings and your ridings, your neighings and your prancings, your bloody, barbarous, and inhuman cruelties, your benumbing, deadening, and debauching the conscience of poor creatures by oaths, soul-damning and self-contradictory, have arisen from earth to Heaven like a foul and hideous outcry of perjury for hastening the wrath to come——hugh! hugh! hugh!"

"And I say," cried Mause, in the same tune, and nearly at the same time, "that wi' this auld breath o' mine, and it's sair taen down wi' the asthmatics and this rough trot——"

"Deil gin they would gallop," said Cuddie, "wad it but gar her haud her tongue!"

"—Wi' this auld and brief breath," continued Mause, "will I testify against the backslidings, defections, defalcations, and declinings of the land—against the grievances and the causes of wrath !"

"Peace, I pr'ythee—peace, good woman," said the preacher, who had just recovered from a violent fit of coughing, and found his own anathema borne down by Mause's better wind— "peace, and take not the word out of the mouth of a servant of the altar. I say, I uplift my voice and tell you, that before the play is played out—ay, before this very sun gaes down—ye sall learn that neither a desperate Judas, like your prelate Sharp that's gane to his place ; nor a sanctuary-breaking Holofernes, like bloody-minded Claverhouse ; nor an ambitious Diotrephes, like the lad Evandale ; nor a covetous and warld-following Demas, like him they ca' Sergeant Bothwell, that makes every wife's plack and her meal-ark his ain ; neither your carabines, nor your pistols, nor your broadswords, nor your horses, nor your saddles, bridles, surcingles, nose-bags, nor martingales, shall resist the arrows that are whetted and the bow that is bent against you !"

"That shall they never, I trow," echoed Mause. "Castaways are they ilk ane o' them ; besoms of destruction, fit only to be flung into the fire when they have sweepit the filth out o' the Temple ; whips of small cords, knotted for the chastisement of those wha like their warldly gudes and gear better than the Cross or the Covenant, but when that wark's done, only meet to mak latchets to the deil's brogues."

"Fiend hae me," said Cuddie, addressing himself to Morton, "if I dinna think our mither preaches as weel as the minister ! But it's a sair pity o' his hoast, for it aye comes on just when he's at the best o't, and that lang routing he made air this morning is sair again him too. Deil an I care if he wad roar her dumb, and then he wad hae't a' to answer for himsell. It's lucky the road's rough, and the troopers are no taking muckle tent to what they say wi' the rattling o' the horses' feet ; but an we were anes on saft grund we'll hear news o' a' this."

Cuddie's conjectures were but too true. The words of the prisoners had not been much attended to while drowned by the clang of horses' hoofs on a rough and stony road ; but they now entered upon the moorlands, where the testimony of the two zealous captives lacked this saving accompaniment. And, accordingly, no sooner had their steeds begun to tread heath and greensward, and Gabriel Kettledrummle had again raised his voice with, "Also, I uplift my voice like that of a pelican in the wilderness——"

"And I mine," had issued from Mause, "like a sparrow on the housetops——"

When "Hollo, ho !" cried the corporal from the rear; "rein up your tongues; the devil blister them, or I'll clap a martingale on them."

"I will not peace at the commands of the profane," said Gabriel.

"Nor I neither," said Mause, "for the bidding of no earthly potsherd, though it be painted as red as a brick from the Tower of Babel, and ca' itsell a corporal."

"Halliday," cried the corporal, "hast got never a gag about thee, man ? We must stop their mouths before they talk us all dead."

Ere any answer could be made, or any measure taken in consequence of the corporal's motion, a dragoon galloped towards Sergeant Bothwell, who was considerably ahead of the party he commanded. On hearing the orders which he brought, Bothwell instantly rode back to the head of his party, ordered them to close their files, to mend their pace, and to move with silence and precaution, as they would soon be in presence of the enemy.

CHAPTER XV

Quantum in nobis, we've thought good
To save the expense of Christian blood,
And try if we, by mediation
Of treaty, and accommodation,
Can end the quarrel, and compose
This bloody duel without blows.

                                        BUTLER.

THE increased pace of the party of horsemen soon took away
from their zealous captives the breath, if not the inclination,
necessary for holding forth. They had now for more than a
mile got free of the woodlands, whose broken glades had for
some time accompanied them after they had left the woods
of Tillietudlem. A few birches and oaks still feathered the
narrow ravines, or occupied in dwarf clusters the hollow plains
of the moor. But these were gradually disappearing, and a
wide and waste country lay before them, swelling into bare
hills of dark heath, intersected by deep gullies, being the passages by which torrents forced their course in winter, and
during summer the disproportioned channels for diminutive
rivulets that winded their puny way among heaps of stones
and gravel, the effects and tokens of their winter fury, like
so many spendthrifts dwindled down by the consequences of
former excesses and extravagance. This desolate region
seemed to extend further than the eye could reach, without
grandeur, without even the dignity of mountain wildness,
yet striking, from the huge proportion which it seemed to
bear to such more favored spots of the country as were
adapted to cultivation and fitted for the support of man, and
thereby impressing irresistibly the mind of the spectator with
a sense of the omnipotence of nature and the comparative
inefficacy of the boasted means of amelioration which man is
capable of opposing to the disadvantages of climate and soil.

It is a remarkable effect of such extensive wastes that they
impose an idea of solitude even upon those who travel through
them in considerable numbers, so much is the imagination
affected by the disproportion between the desert around and
the party who are traversing it. Thus the members of a car-

avan of a thousand souls may feel, in the deserts of Africa or
Arabia, a sense of loneliness, unknown to the individual traveller whose solitary course is through a thriving and cultivated country.

It was not, therefore, without a peculiar feeling of emotion
that Morton beheld, at the distance of about half a mile, the
body of the cavalry to which his escort belonged creeping up
a steep and winding path which ascended from the more
level moor into the hills. Their numbers, which appeared
formidable when they crowded through narrow roads, and
seemed multiplied by appearing partially and at different
points among the trees, were now apparently diminished by
being exposed at once to view, and in a landscape whose extent bore such immense proportion to the columns of horses
and men, which, showing more like a drove of black cattle
than a body of soldiers, crawled slowly along the face of the
hill, their force and their numbers seeming trifling and contemptible.

"Surely," said Morton to himself, "a handful of resolute
men may defend any defile in these mountains against such
a small force as this is, providing that their bravery is equal
to their enthusiasm."

While he made these reflections, the rapid movement of
the horsemen who guarded him soon traversed the space
which divided them from their companions; and ere the front
of Claverhouse's column had gained the brow of the hill
which they had been seen ascending, Bothwell, with his rear-
guard and prisoners, had united himself, or nearly so, with
the main body led by his commander. The extreme difficulty of the road, which was in some places steep and in
others boggy, retarded the progress of the column, especially
in the rear; for the passage of the main body in many instances poached up the swamps through which they passed,
and rendered them so deep that the last of their followers were
forced to leave the beaten path and find safer passage where
they could.

On these occasions the distresses of the Reverend Gabriel
Kettledrummle and of Mause Headrigg were considerably
augmented, as the brutal troopers by whom they were guarded
compelled them, at all risks which such inexperienced riders
were likely to incur, to leap their horses over drains and gullies, or to push them through morasses and swamps.

"Through the help of the Lord I have luppen ower a
wall," cried poor Mause, as her horse was by her rude attendants brought up to leap the turf enclosure of a deserted fold,

in which feat her curch flew off, leaving her gray hairs uncovered.

"I am sunk in deep mire where there is no standing; I
am come into deep waters where the floods overflow me!"
exclaimed Kettledrummle, as the charger on which he was
mounted plunged up to the saddle-girths in a "well-head," as
the springs are called which supply the marshes, the sable
streams beneath spouting over the face and person of the captive preacher.

These exclamations excited shouts of laughter among their
military attendants; but events soon occurred which rendered
them all sufficiently serious.

The leading files of the regiment had nearly attained the
brow of the steep hill we have mentioned when two or three
horsemen, speedily discovered to be a part of their own advanced guard who had acted as a patrol, appeared returning
at full gallop, their horses much blown and the men apparently in a disordered flight. They were followed upon the spur
by five or six riders, well armed with sword and pistol, who
halted upon the top of the hill on observing the approach of
the Life Guards. One or two who had carabines dismounted,
and taking a leisurely and deliberate aim at the foremost rank
of the regiment, discharged their pieces, by which two troopers
were wounded, one severely. They then mounted their horses
and disappeared over the ridge of the hill, retreating with so
much coolness as evidently showed that, on the one hand, they
were undismayed by the approach of so considerable a force
as was moving against them, and conscious, on the other, that
they were supported by numbers sufficient for their protection. This incident occasioned a halt through the whole body
of cavalry; and while Claverhouse himself received the report
of his advanced guard, which had been thus driven back upon
the main body, Lord Evandale advanced to the top of the
ridge over which the enemy's horsemen had retired, and Major
Allan, Cornet Grahame, and the other officers employed
themselves in extricating the regiment from the broken ground
and drawing them up on the side of the hill in two lines, the
one to support the other.

The word was then given to advance; and in a few minutes the first lines stood on the brow and commanded the
prospect on the other side. The second line closed upon them,
and also the rear-guard with the prisoners; so that Morton
and his companions in captivity could in like manner see the
form of opposition which was now offered to the further progress of their captors.

The brow of the hill, on which the Royal Life Guards were now drawn up, sloped downwards (on the side opposite to that which they had ascended) with a gentle declivity for more than a quarter of a mile, and presented ground which, though unequal in some places, was not altogether unfavorable for the manœuvres of cavalry, until near the bottom, when the slope terminated in a marshy level, traversed through its whole length by what seemed either a natural gully or a deep artificial drain, the sides of which were broken by springs, trenches filled with water, out of which peats and turf had been dug, and here and there by some straggling thickets of alders, which loved the moistness so well that they continued to live as bushes, although too much dwarfed by the sour soil and the stagnant bog-water to ascend into trees. Beyond this ditch or gully the ground arose into a second heathy swell, or rather hill, near to the foot of which, and as if with the object of defending the broken ground and ditch that covered their front, the body of insurgents appeared to be drawn up with the purpose of abiding battle.

Their infantry was divided into three lines. The first, tolerably provided with firearms, were advanced almost close to the verge of the bog, so that their fire must necessarily annoy the royal cavalry as they descended the opposite hill, the whole front of which was exposed, and would probably be yet more fatal if they attempted to cross the morass. Behind this first line was a body of pikemen, designed for their support in case the dragoons should force the passage of the marsh. In their rear was their third line, consisting of countrymen armed with scythes set straight on poles, hay-forks, spits, clubs, goads, fish-spears, and such other rustic implements as hasty resentment had converted into instruments of war. On each flank of the infantry, but a little backward from the bog, as if to allow themselves dry and sound ground whereon to act in case their enemies should force the pass, there was drawn up a small body of cavalry, who were in general but indifferently armed and worse mounted, but full of zeal for the cause, being chiefly either landholders of small property or farmers of the better class, whose means enabled them to serve on horseback. A few of those who had been engaged in driving back the advanced guard of the Royalists might now be seen returning slowly towards their own squadrons. These were the only individuals of the insurgent army which seemed to be in motion. All the others stood firm and motionless as the gray stones that lay scattered on the heath around them.

The total number of the insurgents might amount to about a thousand men; but of these there were scarce a hundred cavalry, nor were the half of them even tolerably armed. The strength of their position, however, the sense of their having taken a desperate step, the superiority of their numbers, but, above all, the ardor of their enthusiasm, were the means on which their leaders reckoned for supplying the want of arms, equipage, and military discipline.

On the side of the hill that rose above the array of battle which they had adopted were seen the women, and even the children, whom zeal, opposed to persecution, had driven into the wilderness. They seemed stationed there to be spectators of the engagement, by which their own fate, as well as that of their parents, husbands, and sons, was to be decided. Like the females of the ancient German tribes, the shrill cries which they raised when they beheld the glittering ranks of their enemy appear on the brow of the opposing eminence acted as an incentive to their relatives to fight to the last in defence of that which was dearest to them. Such exhortations seemed to have their full and emphatic effect; for a wild halloo, which went from rank to rank on the appearance of the soldiers, intimated the resolution of the insurgents to fight to the uttermost.

As the horsemen halted their lines on the ridge of the hill their trumpets and kettle-drums sounded a bold and warlike flourish of menace and defiance, that rang along the waste like the shrill summons of a destroying angel. The Wanderers, in answer, united their voices and sent forth in solemn modulation the two first verses of the seventy-sixth Psalm, according to the metrical version of the Scottish Kirk—

> In Judah's land God is well known,
>   His name's in Isr'el great:
> In Salem is his tabernacle,
>   In Sion is his seat.
> There arrows of the bow he brake,
>   The shield, the sword, the war.
> More glorious thou than hills of prev
>   More excellent art far.

A shout, or rather a solemn acclamation, attended the close of the stanza; and after a dead pause the second verse was resumed by the insurgents, who applied the destruction of the Assyrians as prophetical of the issue of their own impending contest—

> Those that were stout of heart are spoil'd,
>   They slept their sleep outright;
> And none of those their hands did find,
>   That were the men of might.
> When thy rebuke, O Jacob's God,
>   Had forth against them past,
> Their horses and their chariots both
>   Were in a deep sleep cast.

There was another acclamation, which was followed by the most profound silence.

While these solemn sounds, accented by a thousand voices, were prolonged among the waste hills, Claverhouse looked with great attention on the ground and on the order of battle which the Wanderers had adopted, and in which they determined to await the assault.

"The churls," he said, "must have some old soldiers with them; it was no rustic that made choice of that ground."

"Burley is said to be with them for certain," answered Lord Evandale, "and also Hackston of Rathillet, Paton of Meadowhead, Cleland, and some other men of military skill."

"I judged as much," said Claverhouse, "from the style in which these detached horsemen leaped their horses over the ditch as they returned to their position. It was easy to see that there were a few Roundhead troopers among them, the true spawn of the old Covenant. We must manage this matter warily as well as boldly. Evandale, let the officers come to this knoll."

He moved to a small moss-grown cairn, probably the resting-place of some Celtic chief of other times, and the call of "Officers to the front" soon brought them around their commander.

"I do not call you around me, gentlemen," said Claverhouse, "in the formal capacity of a council of war, for I will never turn over on others the responsibility which my rank imposes on myself. I only want the benefit of your opinions, reserving to myself, as most men do when they ask advice, the liberty of following my own. What say you, Cornet Grahame? Shall we attack these fellows who are bellowing yonder? You are youngest and hottest, and therefore will speak first whether I will or no."

"Then," said Cornet Grahame, "while I have the honor to carry the standard of the Life Guards it shall never, with my will, retreat before rebels. I say, charge, in God's name and the king's!"

"And what say you, Allan?" continued Claverhouse,

"for Evandale is so modest we shall never get him to speak till you have said what you have to say."

"These fellows," said Major Allan, an old Cavalier officer of experience, "are three or four to one; I should not mind that much upon a fair field, but they are posted in a very formidable strength, and show no inclination to quit it. I therefore think, with deference to Cornet Grahame's opinion, that we should draw back to Tillietudlem, occupy the pass between the hills and the open country, and send for reinforcements to my Lord Ross, who is lying at Glasgow with a regiment of infantry. In this way we should cut them off from the Strath of Clyde, and either compel them to come out of their stronghold and give us battle on fair terms, or if they remain here we will attack them so soon as our infantry has joined us and enabled us to act with effect among these ditches, bogs, and quagmires."

"Pshaw!" said the young Cornet, "what signifies strong ground when it is only held by a crew of canting, psalm-singing old women?"

"A man may fight never the worse," retorted Major Allan, "for honoring both his Bible and Psalter. These fellows will prove as stubborn as steel; I know them of old."

"Their nasal psalmody," said the Cornet, "reminds our Major of the race of Dunbar."

"Had you been at that race, young man," retorted Allan, "you would have wanted nothing to remind you of it for the longest day you have to live."

"Hush, hush, gentlemen," said Claverhouse, "these are untimely repartees. I should like your advice well, Major Allan, had our rascally patrols—whom I will see duly punished —brought us timely notice of the enemy's numbers and position. But having once presented ourselves before them in line, the retreat of the Life Guards would argue gross timidity and be the general signal for insurrection throughout the west; in which case, so far from obtaining any assistance from my Lord Ross, I promise you I should have great apprehensions of his being cut off before we can join him, or he us. A retreat would have quite the same fatal effect upon the king's cause as the loss of a battle; and as to the difference of risk or of safety it might make with respect to ourselves, that, I am sure, no gentleman thinks a moment about. There must be some gorges or passes in the morass through which we can force our way; and were we once on firm ground, I trust there is no man in the Life Guards who supposes our squadrons, though so weak in numbers, are unable to trample into dust twice the number of these unpractised clowns.   What say you, my Lord Evandale ?"

"I humbly think," said Lord Evandale, "that go the day how it will it must be a bloody one ; and that we shall lose many brave fellows, and probably be obliged to slaughter a great number of these misguided men, who, after all, are Scotchmen and subjects of King Charles as well as we are."

"Rebels ! rebels ! and undeserving the name either of Scotchmen or of subjects," said Claverhouse ; "but come, my lord, what does your opinion point at ?"

"To enter into a treaty with these ignorant and misled men," said the young nobleman.

"A treaty ! and with rebels having arms in their hands ! Never while I live," answered his commander.

"At least send a trumpet and flag of truce summoning them to lay down their weapons and disperse," said Lord Evandale, "upon promise of a free pardon.   I have always heard that had that been done before the battle of Pentland Hills much blood might have been saved. "

"Well," said Claverhouse, "and who the devil do you think would carry a summons to these headstrong and desperate fanatics?   They acknowledge no laws of war.   Their leaders, who have been all most active in the murder of the Archbishop of St. Andrews, fight with a rope round their necks, and are likely to kill the messenger, were it but to dip their followers in loyal blood, and to make them as desperate of pardon as themselves."

"I will go myself," said Evandale, "if you will permit me. I have often risked my blood to spill that of others ; let me do so now in order to save human lives."

"You shall not go on such an errand, my lord," said Claverhouse ; "your rank and situation render your safety of too much consequence to the country in an age when good principles are so rare.   Here's my brother's son, Dick Grahame, who fears shot or steel as little as if the devil had given him armor of proof against it, as the fanatics say he has given to his uncle.   He shall take a flag of truce and a trumpet, and ride down to the edge of the morass to summon them to lay down their arms and disperse."

"With all my soul, Colonel," answered the Cornet ; "and I'll tie my cravat on a pike to serve for a white flag ; the rascals never saw such a pennon of Flanders lace in their lives before."

"Colonel Grahame," said Evandale, while the young officer prepared for his expedition, "this young gentleman is your nephew and your apparent heir ; for God's sake, permit me to go.   It was my counsel, and I ought to stand the risk."

"Were he my only son," said Claverhouse, "this is no cause and no time to spare him.   I hope my private affections will never interfere with my public duty.   If Dick Grahame falls, the loss is chiefly mine ; were your lordship to die, the king and country would be the sufferers.   Come, gentlemen, each to his post.   If our summons is unfavorably received we will instantly attack ; and, as the old Scottish blazon has it, 'God shaw the right !'"

CHAPTER XVI

CORNET RICHARD GRAHAME aescended the hill, bearing in
his hand the extempore flag of truce, and making his managed
horse keep time by bounds and curvets to the tune which he
whistled. The trumpeter followed. Five or six horsemen,
having something the appearance of officers, detached themselves from each flank of the Presbyterian army, and meeting
in the centre, approached the ditch which divided the hollow
as near as the morass would permit. Towards this group,
but keeping the opposite side of the swamp, Cornet Grahame
directed his horse, his motions being now the conspicuous
object of attention to both armies; and, without disparagement to the courage of either, it is probable there was a
general wish on both sides that this embassy might save the
risks and bloodshed of the impending conflict.

When he had arrived right opposite to those who, by their
advancing to receive his message, seemed to take upon themselves as the leaders of the enemy, Cornet Grahame commanded his trumpeter to sound a parley. The insurgents
having no instrument of martial music wherewith to make
the appropriate reply, one of their number called out with a
loud, strong voice, demanding to know why he approached
their leaguer.

"To summon you in the king's name and in that of Colonel John Grahame of Claverhouse, specially commissioned
by the right honorable Privy Council of Scotland," answered
the Cornet, "to lay down your arms and dismiss the followers
whom ye have led into rebellion, contrary to the laws of God,
of the king, and of the country."

"Return to them that sent thee," said the insurgent
leader, "and tell them that we are this day in arms for a
broken Covenant and a persecuted Kirk; tell them that we
renounce the licentious and perjured Charles Stewart, whom
you call king, even as he renounced the Covenant after hav-

ing once and again sworn to prosecute to the utmost of his power all the ends thereof, really, constantly, and sincerely all the days of his life, having no enemies but the enemies of the Covenant, and no friends but its friends.   Whereas, far from keeping the oath he had called God and angels to witness, his first step, after his incoming into these kingdoms, was the fearful grasping at the prerogative of the Almighty by that hideous Act of Supremacy, together with his expulsing, without summons, libel, or process of law, hundreds of famous, faithful preachers, thereby wringing the bread of life out of the mouth of hungry, poor creatures, and forcibly cramming their throats with the lifeless, saltless, foisonless, lukewarm drammock of the fourteen false prelates and their sycophantic, formal, carnal, scandalous creature-curates.”

“ I did not come to hear you preach,” answered the officer, “ but to know in one word if you will disperse yourselves, on condition of a free pardon to all but the murderers of the late Archbishop of St. Andrews, or whether you will abide the attack of his Majesty’s forces, which will instantly advance upon you.”

“ In one word, then,” answered the spokesman, “we are here with our swords on our thighs, as men that watch in the night.   We will take one part and portion together as brethren in righteousness.   Whosoever assails us in our good cause, his blood be on his own head.   So return to them that sent thee, and God give them and thee a sight of the evil of your ways !”

“ Is not your name,” said the Cornet, who began to recollect having seen the person whom he was now speaking with, “ John Balfour of Burley ?”

“ And if it be,” said the spokesman, “ hast thou aught to say against it ?”

“ Only,” said the Cornet, “ that, as you are excluded from pardon in the name of the king and of my commanding officer, it is to these country people, and not to you, that I offer it ; and it is not with you, or such as you, that I am sent to treat.”

“ Thou art a young soldier, friend,” said Burley, “ and scant well learned in thy trade, or thou wouldst know that the bearer of a flag of truce cannot treat with the army, but through their officers ; and that if he presume to do otherwise, he forfeits his safe-conduct.”

While speaking these words, Burley unslung his carabine and held it in readiness.

“ I am not to be intimidated from the discharge of my duty by the menaces of a murderer,” said Cornet Grahame.

"Hear me, good people ; I proclaim, in the name of the king and of my commanding officer, full and free pardon to all, excepting——"

"I give thee fair warning," said Burley, presenting his piece.

"A free pardon to all," continued the young officer, still addressing the body of the insurgents—"to all but——"

"Then the Lord grant grace to thy soul. Amen !" said Burley.

With these words he fired, and Cornet Richard Grahame dropped from his horse. The shot was mortal. The unfortunate young gentleman had only strength to turn himself on the ground and mutter forth, "My poor mother !" when life forsook him in the effort. His startled horse fled back to the regiment at the gallop, as did his scarce less affrighted attendant.

"What have you done ?" said one of Balfour's brother officers.

"My duty," said Balfour, firmly. "Is it not written, 'Thou shalt be zealous even to slaying ?' Let those who dare NOW venture to speak of truce or pardon !" *

Claverhouse saw his nephew fall. He turned his eye on Evandale, while a transitory glance of indescribable emotion disturbed for a second's space the serenity of his features, and briefly said, "You see the event."

"I will avenge him, or die !" exclaimed Evandale ; and, putting his horse into motion, rode furiously down the hill, followed by his own troop and that of the deceased Cornet, which broke down without orders ; and, each striving to be the foremost to revenge their young officer, their ranks soon fell into confusion. These forces formed the first line of the Royalists. It was in vain that Claverhouse exclaimed, "Halt ! halt ! this rashness will undo us." It was all that he could accomplish by galloping along the second line, entreating, commanding, and even menacing the men with his sword, that he could restrain them from following an example so contagious.

"Allan," he said, as soon as he had rendered the men in some degree more steady, "lead them slowly down the hill to support Lord Evandale, who is about to need it very much. Bothwell, thou art a cool and a daring fellow——"

"Ay," muttered Bothwell, "you can remember that in a moment like this."

"Lead ten file up the hollow to the right," continued his commanding officer, "and try every means to get through the

* See Cornet Grahame. Note 21.

bog ; then form and charge the rebels in flank and rear while they are engaged with us in front."

Bothwell made a signal of intelligence and obedience, and moved off with his party at a rapid pace.

Meantime the disaster which Claverhouse had apprehended did not fail to take place. The troopers who, with Lord Evandale, had rushed down upon the enemy, soon found their disorderly career interrupted by the impracticable character of the ground. Some stuck fast in the morass as they attempted to struggle through, some recoiled from the attempt and remained on the brink, others dispersed to seek a more favorable place to pass the swamp. In the midst of this confusion the first line of the enemy, of which the foremost rank knelt, the second stooped, and the third stood upright, poured in a close and destructive fire that emptied at least a score of saddles, and increased tenfold the disorder into which the horsemen had fallen. Lord Evandale in the meantime, at the head of a very few well-mounted men, had been able to clear the ditch, but was no sooner across than he was charged by the left body of the enemy's cavalry, who, encouraged by the small number of opponents that had made their way through the broken ground, set upon them with the utmost fury, crying, "Woe, woe to the uncircumcised Philistines ! down with Dagon and all his adherents !"

The young nobleman fought like a lion ; but most of his followers were killed, and he himself could not have escaped the same fate but for a heavy fire of carabines which Claverhouse, who had now advanced with the second line near to the ditch, poured so effectually upon the enemy that both horse and foot for a moment began to shrink, and Lord Evandale, disengaged from his unequal combat, and finding himself nearly alone, took the opportunity to effect his retreat through the morass. But, notwithstanding the loss they had sustained by Claverhouse's first fire, the insurgents became soon aware that the advantage of numbers and of position were so decidedly theirs that, if they could but persist in making a brief but resolute defence, the Life Guards must necessarily be defeated. Their leaders flew through their ranks exhorting them to stand firm, and pointing out how efficacious their fire must be where both men and horse were exposed to it ; for the troopers, according to custom, fired without having dismounted. Claverhouse more than once, when he perceived his best men dropping by a fire which they could not effectually return, made desperate efforts to pass the bog at various points and renew the battle on firm ground and fiercer terms. But the close fire of the insurgents, joined to the natural difficulties of the pass, foiled his attempts in every point.

"We must retreat," he said to Evandale, "unless Bothwell can effect a diversion in our favor. In the meantime draw the men out of fire and leave skirmishers behind these patches of alder-bushes to keep the enemy in check."

These directions being accomplished, the appearance of Bothwell with his party was earnestly expected. But Bothwell had his own disadvantages to struggle with. His detour to the right had not escaped the penetrating observation of Burley, who made a corresponding movement with the left wing of the mounted insurgents, so that when Bothwell, after riding a considerable way up the valley, found a place at which the bog could be passed, though with some difficulty, he perceived he was still in front of a superior enemy. His daring character was in no degree checked by this unexpected opposition.

"Follow me, my lads!" he called to his men; "never let it be said that we turned our backs before these canting Roundheads!"

With that, as if inspired by the spirit of his ancestors, he shouted, "Bothwell! Bothwell!" and throwing himself into the morass, he struggled through it at the head of his party, and attacked that of Burley with such fury that he drove them back above a pistol-shot, killing three men with his own hand. Burley, perceiving the consequences of a defeat on this point, and that his men, though more numerous, were unequal to the regulars in using their arms and managing their horses, threw himself across Bothwell's way and attacked him hand to hand. Each of the combatants was considered as the champion of his respective party, and a result ensued more usual in romance than in real story. Their followers on either side instantly paused and looked on as if the fate of the day were to be decided by the event of the combat between these two redoubted swordsmen. The combatants themselves seemed of the same opinion; for, after two or three eager cuts and pushes had been exchanged, they paused, as if by joint consent, to recover the breath which preceding exertions had exhausted, and to prepare for a duel in which each seemed conscious he had met his match.

"You are the murdering villain, Burley," said Bothwell, griping his sword firmly, and setting his teeth close; "you escaped me once, but [he swore an oath too tremendous to be written down] thy head is worth its weight of silver, and it shall go home at my saddle-bow, or my saddle shall go home empty for me."

"Yes," replied Burley, with stern and gloomy deliberation, "I am that John Balfour who promised to lay thy head where thou shouldst never lift it again; and God do so unto me, and more also, if I do not redeem my word!"

"Then a bed of heather or a thousand merks!" said Bothwell, striking at Burley with his full force.

"The sword of the Lord and of Gideon!" answered Balfour, as he parried and returned the blow.

There have seldom met two combatants more equally matched in strength of body, skill in the management of their weapons and horses, determined courage, and unrelenting hostility. After exchanging many desperate blows, each receiving and inflicting several wounds, though of no great consequence, they grappled together as if with the desperate impatience of mortal hate, and Bothwell, seizing his enemy by the shoulder-belt, while the grasp of Balfour was upon his own collar, they came headlong to the ground. The companions of Burley hastened to his assistance, but were repelled by the dragoons, and the battle became again general. But nothing could withdraw the attention of the combatants from each other, or induce them to unclose the deadly clasp in which they rolled together on the ground, tearing, struggling, and foaming with the inveteracy of thoroughbred bull-dogs.

Several horses passed over them in the *mêlée* without their quitting hold of each other, until the sword-arm of Bothwell was broken by the kick of a charger. He then relinquished his grasp with a deep and suppressed groan, and both combatants started to their feet. Bothwell's right hand dropped helpless by his side, but his left griped to the place where his dagger hung; it had escaped from the sheath in the struggle, and, with a look of mingled rage and despair, he stood totally defenceless as Balfour, with a laugh of savage joy, flourished his sword aloft, and then passed it through his adversary's body. Bothwell received the thrust without falling; it had only grazed on his ribs. He attempted no further defence, but, looking at Burley with a grin of deadly hatred, exclaimed, "Base peasant churl, thou hast spilt the blood of a line of kings!"

"Die, wretch! die!" said Balfour, redoubling the thrust with better aim; and, setting his foot on Bothwell's body as he fell, he a third time transfixed him with his sword. "Die, bloodthirsty dog! die as thou hast lived! die like the beasts that perish, hoping nothing, believing nothing——"

"And FEARING nothing!" said Bothwell, collecting the

last effort of respiration to utter these desperate words, and expiring as soon as they were spoken.

To catch a stray horse by the bridle, throw himself upon it, and rush to the assistance of his followers, was with Burley the affair of a moment. And as the fall of Bothwell had given to the insurgents all the courage of which it had deprived his comrades, the issue of this partial contest did not remain long undecided. Several soldiers were slain, the rest driven back over the morass and dispersed, and the victorious Burley, with his party, crossed it in their turn, to direct against Claverhouse the very manœuvre which he had instructed Bothwell to execute. He now put his troop in order with the view of attacking the right wing of the Royalists; and, sending news of his success to the main body, exhorted them, in the name of Heaven, to cross the marsh and work out the glorious work of the Lord by a general attack upon the enemy.

Meanwhile Claverhouse, who had in some degree remedied the confusion occasioned by the first irregular and unsuccessful attack, and reduced the combat in front to a distant skirmish with firearms, chiefly maintained by some dismounted troopers whom he had posted behind the cover of the shrubby copses of alders, which in some places covered the edge of the morass, and whose close, cool, and well-aimed fire greatly annoyed the enemy, and concealed their own deficiency of numbers—Claverhouse, while he maintained the contest in this manner, still expecting that a diversion by Bothwell and his party might facilitate a general attack, was accosted by one of the dragoons, whose bloody face and jaded horse bore witness he was come from hard service.

" What is the matter, Halliday ? " said Claverhouse, for he knew every man in his regiment by name. " Where is Bothwell ? "

" Bothwell is down," replied Halliday, " and many a pretty fellow with him."

"Then the king," said Claverhouse, with his usual composure, " has lost a stout soldier. The enemy have passed the marsh, I suppose ? "

" With a strong body of horse, commanded by the devil incarnate that killed Bothwell," answered the terrified soldier.

"Hush ! hush !" said Claverhouse, putting his finger on his lips, " not a word to any one but me. Lord Evandale, we must retreat. The fates will have it so. Draw together the men that are dispersed in the skirmishing work. Let Allan form the regiment, and do you two retreat up the hill in two bodies, each halting alternately as the other falls back. I'll keep the rogues in check with the rear-guard, making a stand and facing from time to time. They will be over the ditch presently, for I see their whole line in motion and preparing to cross; therefore lose no time."

"Where is Bothwell with his party?" said Lord Evandale, astonished at the coolness of his commander.

"Fairly disposed of," said Claverhouse, in his ear; "the king has lost a servant and the devil has got one. But away to business, Evandale; ply your spurs and get the men together. Allan and you must keep them steady. This retreating is new work for us all; but our turn will come round another day."

Evandale and Allan betook themselves to their task; but ere they had arranged the regiment for the purpose of retreating in two alternate bodies, a considerable number of the enemy had crossed the marsh. Claverhouse, who had retained immediately around his person a few of his most active and tried men, charged those who had crossed in person while they were yet disordered by the broken ground. Some they killed, others they repulsed into the morass, and checked the whole so as to enable the main body, now greatly diminished, as well as disheartened by the loss they had sustained, to commence their retreat up the hill.

But the enemy's van, being soon reinforced and supported, compelled Claverhouse to follow his troops. Never did man, however, better maintain the character of a soldier than he did that day. Conspicuous by his black horse and white feather, he was first in the repeated charges which he made at every favorable opportunity to arrest the progress of the pursuers and to cover the retreat of his regiment. The object of aim to every one, he seemed as if he were impassive to their shot. The superstitious fanatics, who looked upon him as a man gifted by the Evil Spirit with supernatural means of defence, averred that they saw the bullets recoil from his jackboots and buff-coat like hailstones from a rock of granite, as he galloped to and fro amid the storm of the battle. Many a Whig that day loaded his musket with a dollar cut into slugs, in order that a silver bullet (such was their belief) might bring down the persecutor of the holy kirk, on whom lead had no power.

"Try him with the cold steel," was the cry at every renewed charge; "powder is wasted on him. Ye might as weel shoot at the Auld Enemy himsell."*

* See Proof against Shot given by Satan. Note 22.

But though this was loudly shouted, yet the awe on the insurgents' minds was such that they gave way before Claverhouse as before a supernatural being, and few men ventured to cross swords with him. Still, however, he was fighting in retreat, and with all the disadvantages attending that movement. The soldiers behind him, as they beheld the increasing number of enemies who poured over the morass, became unsteady ; and at every successive movement Major Allan and Lord Evandale found it more and more difficult to bring them to halt and form line regularly ; while, on the other hand, their motions in the act of retreating became by degrees much more rapid than was consistent with good order. As the retiring soldiers approached nearer to the top of the ridge, from which in so luckless an hour they had descended, the panic began to increase. Every one became impatient to place the brow of the hill between him and the continued fire of the pursuers ; nor could any individual think it reasonable that he should be the last in the retreat, and thus sacrifice his own safety for that of others. In this mood several troopers set spurs to their horses and fled outright, and the others became so unsteady in their movements and formations that their officers every moment feared they would follow the same example.

Amid this scene of blood and confusion, the trampling of the horses, the groans of the wounded, the continued fire of the enemy, which fell in a succession of unintermitted musketry, while loud shouts accompanied each bullet which the fall of a trooper showed to have been successfully aimed—amid all the terrors and disorders of such a scene, and when it was dubious how soon they might be totally deserted by their dispirited soldiery, Evandale could not forbear remarking the composure of his commanding officer. Not at Lady Margaret's breakfast-table that morning did his eye appear more lively, or his demeanor more composed. He had closed up to Evandale for the purpose of giving some orders and picking out a few men to reinforce his rear-guard.

" If this bout lasts five minutes longer," he said in a whisper, " our rogues will leave you, my lord, old Allan, and myself the honor of fighting this battle with our own hands. I must do something to disperse the musketeers who annoy them so hard, or we shall be all shamed. Don't attempt to succor me if you see me go down, but keep at the head of your men ; get off as you can, in God's name, and tell the king and the council I died in my duty ! "

So saying, and commanding about twenty stout men to

follow him, he gave, with this small body, a charge so desperate and unexpected that he drove the foremost of the pursuers back to some distance. In the confusion of the assault he singled out Burley, and, desirous to strike terror into his followers, he dealt him so severe a blow on the head as cut through his steel headpiece and threw him from his horse, stunned for the moment, though unwounded. A wonderful thing, it was afterwards thought, that one so powerful as Balfour should have sunk under the blow of a man to appearance so slightly made as Claverhouse ; and the vulgar, of course, set down to supernatural aid the effect of that energy which a determined spirit can give to a feebler arm. Claverhouse had in this last charge, however, involved himself too deeply among the insurgents, and was fairly surrounded.

Lord Evandale saw the danger of his commander, his body of dragoons being then halted, while that commanded by Allan was in the act of retreating. Regardless of Claverhouse's disinterested command to the contrary, he ordered the party which he headed to charge down hill and extricate their Colonel. Some advanced with him, most halted and stood uncertain, many ran away. With those who followed Evandale, he disengaged Claverhouse. His assistance just came in time, for a rustic had wounded his horse in a most ghastly manner by the blow of a scythe, and was about to repeat the stroke when Lord Evandale cut him down. As they got out of the press they looked round them. Allan's division had ridden clear over the hill, that officer's authority having proved altogether unequal to halt them. Evandale's troop was scattered and in total confusion.

"What is to be done, Colonel ?" said Lord Evandale.

"We are the last men in the field, I think," said Claverhouse ; "and when men fight as long as they can there is no shame in flying. Hector himself would say, 'Devil take the hindmost,' when there are but twenty against a thousand. Save yourselves, my lads, and rally as soon as you can. Come, my lord, we must e'en ride for it."

So saying, he put spurs to his wounded horse ; and the generous animal, as if conscious that the life of his rider depended on his exertions, pressed forward with speed unabated either by pain or loss of blood.* A few officers and soldiers followed him, but in a very irregular and tumultuary manner. The flight of Claverhouse was the signal for all the stragglers who yet offered desultory resistance to fly as fast as they could, and yield up the field of battle to the victorious insurgents.

* See Claverhouse's Charger. Note 23.

CHAPTER XVII

DURING the severe skirmish of which we have given the details, Morton, together with Cuddie and his mother and the Reverend Gabriel Kettledrummle, remained on the brow of the hill, near to the small cairn or barrow, beside which Claverhouse had held his preliminary council of war, so that they had a commanding view of the action which took place in the bottom. They were guarded by Corporal Inglis and four soldiers, who, as may readily be supposed, were much more intent on watching the fluctuating fortunes of the battle than in attending to what passed among the prisoners.

"If yon lads stand to their tackle," said Cuddie, "we'll hae some chance o' getting our necks out o' the brecham again ; but I misdoubt them ; they hae little skeel o' arms."

"Much is not necessary, Cuddie," answered Morton ; "they have a strong position, and weapons in their hands, and are more than three times the number of their assailants. If they cannot fight for their freedom now, they and theirs deserve to lose it forever."

"O, sirs," exclaimed Mause, "here's a goodly spectacle, indeed ! My spirit is like that of the blessed Elihu : it burns within me ; my bowels are as wine which lacketh vent, they are ready to burst like new bottles. O that He may look after His ain people in this day of judgment and deliverance ! And now, what ailest thou, precious Mr. Gabriel Kettledrummle ? I say, what ailest thou that wert a Nazarite purer than snow, whiter than milk, more ruddy than sulphur [meaning, perhaps, sapphires]—I say, what ails thee now, that thou art blacker than a coal, that thy beauty is departed, and thy loveliness withered like a dry potsherd ? Surely it is time to be up and be doing, to cry loudly and to spare not, and to wrestle for the puir lads that are yonder testifying with their ain bluid and that of their enemies."

This expostulation implied a reproach on Mr. Kettledrummle, who, though an absolute Boanerges or son of thunder in the pulpit, when the enemy were afar, and indeed sufficiently contumacious, as we have seen, when in their power, had been struck dumb by the firing, shouts, and shrieks which now arose from the valley, and—as many an honest man might have been, in a situation where he could neither fight nor fly—was too much dismayed to take so favorable an opportunity to preach the terrors of Presbytery, as the courageous Mause had expected at his hand, or even to pray for the successful event of the battle. His presence of mind was not, however, entirely lost any more than his jealous respect for his reputation as a pure and powerful preacher of the Word.

"Hold your peace, woman!" he said, "and do not perturb my inward meditations and the wrestlings wherewith I wrestle. But of a verity the shooting of the foemen doth begin to increase; peradventure some pellet may attain unto us even here. Lo! I will ensconce me behind the cairn, as behind a strong wall of defence."

"He's but a coward body after a'," said Cuddie, who was himself by no means deficient in that sort of courage which consists in insensibility to danger; "he's but a daidling coward body. He'll never fill Rumbleberry's bonnet. Odd! Rumbleberry fought and flyted like a fleeing dragon. It was a great pity, puir man, he couldna cheat the woodie. But they say he gaed singing and rejoicing till't, just as I wad gang to a bicker o' brose, supposing me hungry, as I stand a gude chance to be. Eh, sirs! yon's an awfu' sight, and yet ane canna keep their een aff frae it!"

Accordingly, strong curiosity on the part of Morton and Cuddie, together with the heated enthusiasm of old Mause, detained them on the spot from which they could best hear and see the issue of the action, leaving to Kettledrummle to occupy alone his place of security. The vicissitudes of combat, which we have already described, were witnessed by our spectators from the top of the eminence, but without their being able positively to determine to what they tended. That the Presbyterians defended themselves stoutly was evident from the heavy smoke, which, illumined by frequent flashes of fire, now eddied along the valley and hid the contending parties in its sulphureous shade. On the other hand, the continued firing from the nearest side of the morass indicated that the enemy persevered in their attack, that the affair was fiercely disputed, and that everything was to be apprehended from a continued contest in which undisciplined rustics had to repel the assaults of regular troops, so completely officered and armed.

At length horses, whose caparisons showed that they belonged to the Life Guards, began to fly masterless out of the confusion. Dismounted soldiers next appeared, forsaking the conflict and straggling over the side of the hill in order to escape from the scene of action. As the numbers of these fugitives increased, the fate of the day seemed no longer doubtful. A large body was then seen emerging from the smoke, forming irregularly on the hillside, and with difficulty kept stationary by their officers, until Evandale's corps also appeared in full retreat. The result of the conflict was then apparent, and the joy of the prisoners was corresponding to their approaching deliverance.

"They hae dune the job for anes," said Cuddie, "an they ne'er do't again."

"They flee! they flee!" exclaimed Mause, in ecstasy. "O, the truculent tyrants! they are riding now as they never rode before. O, the false Egyptians, the proud Assyrians, the Philistines, the Moabites, the Edomites, the Ishmaelites ! The Lord has brought sharp swords upon them to make them food for the fowls of heaven and the beasts of the field. See how the clouds roll and the fire flashes ahint them, and goes forth before the chosen of the Covenant, e'en like the pillar o' cloud and the pillar o' flame that led the people of Israel out o' the land of Egypt ! This is indeed a day of deliverance to the righteous, a day of pouring out of wrath to the persecutors and the ungodly !"

"Lord save us, mither," said Cuddie, "haud the clavering tongue o' ye, and lie down ahint the cairn, like Kettledrummle, honest man ! The Whigamore bullets ken unco little discretion, and will just as sune knock out the harns o' a psalm-singing auld wife as a swearing dragoon."

"Fear naething for me, Cuddie," said the old dame, transported to ecstasy by the success of her party; "fear naething for me ! I will stand, like Deborah, on the tap o' the cairn, and tak up my sang o' reproach against these men of Harosheth of the Gentiles, whose horse-hoofs are broken by their prancing."

The enthusiastic old woman would, in fact, have accomplished her purpose of mounting on the cairn and becoming, as she said, a sign and a banner to the people, had not Cuddie, with more filial tenderness than respect, detained her by such force as his shackled arms would permit him to exert.

"Eh, sirs !" he said, having accomplished this task, "look

out yonder, Milnwood ; saw ye ever mortal fight like the deevil Claver'se ? Yonder he's been thrice doun amang them, and thrice cam free aff. But I think we'll soon be free oursells, Milnwood. Inglis and his troopers look ower their shouthers very aften, as if they liked the road ahint them better than the road afore."

Cuddie was not mistaken ; for, when the main tide of fugitives passed at a little distance from the spot where they were stationed, the corporal and his party fired their carabines at random upon the advancing insurgents, and, abandoning all charge of their prisoners, joined the retreat of their comrades. Morton and the old woman, whose hands were at liberty, lost no time in undoing the bonds of Cuddie and of the clergyman, both of whom had been secured by a cord tied round their arms above the elbows. By the time this was accomplished, the rear-guard of the dragoons, which still preserved some order, passed beneath the hillock or rising ground which was surmounted by the cairn already repeatedly mentioned. They exhibited all the hurry and confusion incident to a forced retreat, but still continued in a body. Claverhouse led the van, his naked sword deeply dyed with blood, as were his face and clothes. His horse was all covered with gore, and now reeled with weakness. Lord Evandale, in not much better plight, brought up the rear, still exhorting the soldiers to keep together and fear nothing. Several of the men were wounded, and one or two dropped from their horses as they surmounted the hill.

Mause's zeal broke forth once more at this spectacle, while she stood on the heath with her head uncovered and her gray hairs streaming in the wind, no bad representation of a superannuated bacchante, or Thessalian witch in the agonies of incantation. She soon discovered Claverhouse at the head of the fugitive party, and exclaimed with bitter irony, " Tarry, tarry, ye wha were aye sae blithe to be at the meetings of the saints, and wad ride every muir in Scotland to find a conventicle. Wilt thou not tarry now thou hast found ane ? Wilt thou not stay for one word mair ? Wilt thou na bide the afternoon preaching ? Wae betide ye !" she said, suddenly changing her tone, " and cut the houghs of the creature whase fleetness ye trust in ! Sheugh, sheugh ! awa' wi' ye that hae spilled sae muckle bluid, and now wad save your ain—awa' wi' ye for a railing Rabshakeh, a cursing Shimei, a bloodthirsty Doeg ! The sword's drawn now that winna be lang o' o'ertaking ye, ride as fast as ye will."

Claverhouse, it may be easily supposed, was too busy to attend to her reproaches, but hastened over the hill, anxious to get the remnant of his men out of gun-shot, in hopes of again collecting the fugitives round his standard. But as the rear of his followers rode over the ridge a shot struck Lord Evandale's horse, which instantly sunk down dead beneath him. Two of the Whig horsemen who were the foremost in the pursuit hastened up with the purpose of killing him, for hitherto there had been no quarter given. Morton, on the other hand, rushed forward to save his life, if possible, in order at once to indulge his natural generosity, and to requite the obligation which Lord Evandale had conferred on him that morning, and under which circumstances had made him wince so acutely. Just as he had assisted Evandale, who was much wounded, to extricate himself from his dying horse and to gain his feet, the two horsemen came up, and one of them, exclaiming, "Have at the red-coated tyrant!" made a blow at the young nobleman, which Morton parried with difficulty, exclaiming to the rider, who was no other than Burley himself, "Give quarter to this gentleman, for my sake—for the sake," he added, observing that Burley did not immediately recognize him, "of Henry Morton, who so lately sheltered you."

"Henry Morton!" replied Burley, wiping his bloody brow with his bloodier hand; "did I not say that the son of Silas Morton would come forth out of the land of bondage, nor be long an indweller in the tents of Ham? Thou art a brand snatched out of the burning. But for this booted apostle of Prelacy, he shall die the death! We must smite them hip and thigh, even from the rising to the going down of the sun. It is our commission to slay them like Amalek, and utterly destroy all they have, and spare neither man nor woman, infant nor suckling; therefore hinder me not," he continued, endeavoring again to cut down Lord Evandale, "for this work must not be wrought negligently."

"You must not, and you shall not, slay him, more especially while incapable of defence," said Morton, planting himself before Lord Evandale so as to intercept any blow that should be aimed at him. "I owed my life to him this morning—my life, which was endangered solely by my having sheltered you; and to shed his blood when he can offer no effectual resistance were not only a cruelty abhorrent to God and man, but detestable ingratitude both to him and to me."

Burley paused. "Thou art yet," he said, "in the court of the Gentiles, and I compassionate thy human blindness and frailty. Strong meat is not fit for babes, nor the mighty and grinding dispensation under which I draw my sword for those whose hearts are yet dwe...ing in huts of clay, whose footsteps are tangled in the mesh of mortal sympathies, and who clothe themselves in the righteousness that is as filthy rags. But to gain a soul to the truth is better than to send one to Tophet; therefore I give quarter to this youth, providing the grant is confirmed by the general council of God's army, whom He hath this day blessed with so signal a deliverance. Thou art unarmed. Abide my return here. I must yet pursue these sinners, the Amalekites, and destroy them till they be utterly consumed from the face of the land, even from Havilah unto Shur."

So saying, he set spurs to his horse and continued to pursue the chase.

"Cuddie," said Morton, "for God's sake catch a horse as quickly as you can. I will not trust Lord Evandale's life with these obdurate men. You are wounded, my lord. Are you able to continue your retreat?" he continued, addressing himself to his prisoner, who, half stunned by the fall, was but beginning to recover himself.

"I think so," replied Lord Evandale. "But is it possible? Do I owe my life to Mr. Morton?"

"My interference would have been the same from common humanity," replied Morton; "to your lordship it was a sacred debt of gratitude."

Cuddie at this instant returned with a horse.

"God-sake, munt—munt and ride like a fleeing hawk, my lord," said the good-natured fellow, "for ne'er be in me if they arena killing every ane o' the wounded and prisoners!"

Lord Evandale mounted the horse, while Cuddie officiously held the stirrup.

"Stand off, good fellow, thy courtesy may cost thy life. Mr. Morton," he continued, addressing Henry, "this makes us more than even; rely on it, I will never forget your generosity. Farewell."

He turned his horse, and rode swiftly away in the direction which seemed least exposed to pursuit.

Lord Evandale had just rode off, when several of the insurgents, who were in the front of the pursuit, came up denouncing vengeance on Henry Morton and Cuddie for having aided the escape of a Philistine, as they called the young nobleman.

"What wad ye hae had us to do!" cried Cuddie. "Had we aught to stop a man wi' that had twa pistols and a sword? Sudna ye hae come faster up yoursells, instead of flyting at huz?"

This excuse would hardly have passed current ; but Kettledrummle, who now awoke from his trance of terror, and was known to, and reverenced by, most of the Wanderers, together with Mause, who possessed their appropriate language as well as the preacher himself, proved active and effectual intercessors.

"Touch them not, harm them not," exclaimed Kettledrummle, in his very best double-bass tones ; "this is the son of the famous Silas Morton, by whom the Lord wrought great things in this land at the breaking forth of the reformation from Prelacy, when there was a plentiful pouring forth of the Word and a renewing of the Covenant ; a hero and champion of those blessed days when there was power and efficacy, and convincing and converting of sinners, and heart-exercises, and fellowships of saints, and a plentiful flowing forth of the spices of the garden of Eden."

"And this is my son Cuddie," exclaimed Mause, in her turn, "the son of his father, Judden Headrigg, wha was a douce honest man, and of me, Mause Middlemas, an unworthy professor and follower of the pure gospel, and ane o' your ain folk. Is it not written, 'Cut ye not off the tribe of the families of the Kohathites from among the Levites ?' Numbers fourth and aughteenth. O, sirs ! dinna be standing here prattling wi' honest folk when ye suld be following forth your victory with which Providence has blessed ye."

This party having passed on, they were immediately beset by another, to whom it was necessary to give the same explanation. Kettledrummle, whose fear was much dissipated since the firing had ceased, again took upon him to be intercessor, and grown bold, as he felt his good word necessary for the protection of his late fellow-captives, he laid claim to no small share of the merit of the victory, appealing to Morton and Cuddie whether the tide of battle had not turned while he prayed on the Mount of Jehovah-Nissi, like Moses, that Israel might prevail over Amalek ; but granting them, at the same time, the credit of holding up his hands when they waxed heavy, as those of the prophet were supported by Aaron and Hur. It seems probable that Kettledrummle allotted this part in the success to his companions in adversity lest they should be tempted to disclose his carnal self-seeking and falling away, in regarding too closely his own personal safety.

These strong testimonies in favor of the liberated captives quickly flew abroad, with many exaggerations, among the victorious army. The reports on the subject were various ; but it was universally agreed that young Morton of Milnwood,

the son of the stout soldier of the Covenant, Silas Morton,
together with the precious Gabriel Kettledrummle, and a singular devout Christian woman, whom many thought as good
as himself at extracting a doctrine or a use, whether of terror or consolation, had arrived to support the good old cause,
with a reinforcement of a hundred well-armed men from the
Middle Ward.*

* See Skirmish at Drumclog.   Note 24.

CHAPTER XVIII

When pulpit, drum ecclesiastic,
Was beat with fists instead of a stick.
Hudibras.

IN the meantime, the insurgent cavalry returned from the pursuit, jaded and worn out with their unwonted efforts, and the infantry assembled on the ground which they had won, fatigued with toil and hunger. Their success, however, was a cordial to every bosom, and seemed even to serve in the stead of food and refreshment. It was, indeed, much more brilliant than they durst have ventured to anticipate ; for, with no great loss on their part, they had totally routed a regiment of picked men, commanded by the first officer in Scotland, and one whose very name had long been a terror to them. Their success seemed even to have upon their spirits the effect of a sudden and violent surprise, so much had their taking up arms been a measure of desperation rather than of hope. Their meeting was also casual, and they had hastily arranged themselves under such commanders as were remarkable for zeal and courage, without much respect to any other qualities. It followed from this state of disorganization that the whole army appeared at once to resolve itself into a general committee for considering what steps were to be taken in consequence of their success, and no opinion could be started so wild that it had not some favorers and advocates. Some proposed they should march to Glasgow, some to Hamilton, some to Edinburgh, some to London. Some were for sending a deputation of their number to London to convert Charles II. to a sense of the error of his ways ; and others, less charitable, proposed either to call a new successor to the crown, or to declare Scotland a free republic. A free parliament of the nation, and a free assembly of the Kirk, were the objects of the more sensible and moderate of the party. In the meanwhile, a clamor arose among the soldiers for bread and other necessaries ; and while all complained of hardship and hunger, none took the necessary measures to procure supplies. In short, the camp of the Covenanters, even in the very moment of success, seemed about to dissolve like a rope of sand, from want of the original principles of combination and union.

Burley, who had now returned from the pursuit, found his followers in this distracted state. With the ready talent of one accustomed to encounter exigencies, he proposed that one hundred of the freshest men should be drawn out for duty; that a small number of those who had hitherto acted as leaders should constitute a committee of direction until officers should be regularly chosen; and that, to crown the victory, Gabriel Kettledrummle should be called upon to improve the providential success which they had obtained by a word in season addressed to the army. He reckoned very much, and not without reason, on this last expedient as a means of engaging the attention of the bulk of the insurgents, while he himself and two or three of their leaders held a private council of war, undisturbed by the discordant opinions or senseless clamor of the general body.

Kettledrummle more than answered the expectations of Burley. Two mortal hours did he preach at a breathing; and certainly no lungs or doctrine excepting his own could have kept up, for so long a time, the attention of men in such precarious circumstances. But he possessed in perfection a sort of rude and familiar eloquence peculiar to the preachers of that period, which, though it would have been fastidiously rejected by an audience which possessed any portion of taste, was a cake of the right leaven for the palates of those whom he now addressed. His text was from the forty-ninth chapter of Isaiah, "Even the captives of the mighty shall be taken away, and the prey of the terrible shall be delivered: for I will contend with him that contendeth with thee, and I will save thy children. And I will feed them that oppress thee with their own flesh; and they shall be drunken with their own blood, as with sweet wine: and all flesh shall know that I the Lord am thy Saviour and thy Redeemer, the Mighty One of Jacob."

The discourse which he pronounced upon this subject was divided into fifteen heads, each of which was garnished with seven uses of application, two of consolation, two of terror, two declaring the causes of backsliding and of wrath, and one announcing the promised and expected deliverance. The first part of his text he applied to his own deliverance and that of his companions; and took occasion to speak a few words in praise of young Milnwood, of whom, as of a champion of the Covenant, he augured great things. The second part he applied to the punishments which were about to fall upon the persecuting government. At times he was familiar and colloquial ; now he was loud, energetic, and boisterous ; some parts of his discourse might be called sublime, and others sunk below burlesque. Occasionally he vindicated with great animation the right of every freeman to worship God according to his own conscience ; and presently he charged the guilt and misery of the people on the awful negligence of their rulers, who had not only failed to establish Presbytery as the national religion, but had tolerated sectaries of various descriptions, Papists, Prelatists, Erastians assuming the name of Presbyterians, Independents, Socinians, and Quakers ; all of whom Kettledrummle proposed, by one sweeping act, to expel from the land, and thus re-edify in its integrity the beauty of the sanctuary. He next handled very pithily the doctrine of defensive arms and of resistance to Charles II., observing that, instead of a nursing father to the Kirk, that monarch had been a nursing father to none but his own bastards. He went at some length through the life and conversation of that joyous prince, few parts of which, it must be owned, were qualified to stand the rough handling of so uncourtly an orator, who conferred on him the hard names of Jeroboam, Omri, Ahab, Shallum, Pekah, and every other evil monarch recorded in the Chronicles, and concluded with a round application of the Scripture, "Tophet is ordained of old ; yea, for the KING it is provided : he hath made it deep and large ; the pile thereof is fire and much wood : the breath of the Lord, like a stream of brimstone, doth kindle it."

Kettledrummle had no sooner ended his sermon and descended from the huge rock which had served him for a pulpit than his post was occupied by a pastor of a very different description. The Reverend Gabriel was advanced in years, somewhat corpulent, with a loud voice, a square face, and a set of stupid and unanimated features, in which the body seemed more to predominate over the spirit than was seemly in a sound divine. The youth who succeeded him in exhorting this extraordinary convocation, Ephraim Macbriar by name, was hardly twenty years old ; yet his thin features already indicated that a constitution, naturally hectic, was worn out by vigils, by fasts, by the rigor of imprisonment, and the fatigues incident to a fugitive life. Young as he was he had been twice imprisoned for several months, and suffered many severities, which gave him great influence with those of his own sect. He threw his faded eyes over the multitude and over the scene of battle ; and a light of triumph arose in his glance, his pale yet striking features were colored with a transient and

hectic blush of joy. He folded his hands, raised his face
to heaven, and seemed lost in mental prayer and thanksgiving
ere he addressed the people. When he spoke, his faint and
broken voice seemed at first inadequate to express his concep-
tions. But the deep silence of the assembly, the eagerness
with which the ear gathered every word, as the famished Israelites collected the heavenly manna, had a corresponding
effect upon the preacher himself. His words became more
distinct, his manner more earnest and energetic ; it seemed as
if religious zeal was triumphing over bodily weakness and infirmity. His natural eloquence was not altogether untainted
with the coarseness of his sect ; and yet, by the influence of
a good natural taste, it was freed from the grosser and more
ludicrous errors of his contemporaries ; and the language of
Scripture, which in their mouths was sometimes degraded
by misapplication, gave, in Macbriar's exhortation, a rich and
solemn effect, like that which is produced by the beams of the
sun streaming through the storied representation of saints
and martyrs on the Gothic window of some ancient cathedral.

He painted the desolation of the church, during the late
period of her distresses, in the most affecting colors. He described her, like Hagar watching the waning life of her infant
amid the fountainless desert ; like Judah, under her palm-
tree, mourning for the devastation of her temple ; like Rachel,
weeping for her children and refusing comfort. But he
chiefly rose into rough sublimity when addressing the men yet
reeking from battle. He called on them to remember the
great things which God had done for them, and to persevere
in the career which their victory had opened.

"Your garments are dyed, but not with the juice of the
wine-press ; your swords are filled with blood," he exclaimed,
"but not with the blood of goats or lambs ; the dust of the
desert on which ye stand is made fat with gore, but not with
the blood of bullocks, for the Lord hath a sacrifice in Bozrah,
and a great slaughter in the land of Idumea. These were not
the firstlings of the flock, the small cattle of burnt-offerings,
whose bodies lie like dung on the ploughed field of the husbandman ; this is not the savor of myrrh, of frankincense, or of
sweet herbs that is steaming in your nostrils ; but these
bloody trunks are the carcasses of those who held the bow and
the lance, who were cruel and would show no mercy, whose
voice roared like the sea, who rode upon horses, every man in
array as if to battle ; they are the carcasses even of the mighty
men of war that came against Jacob in the day of his deliver-

ance, and the smoke is that of the devouring fires that have consumed them. And those wild hills that surround you are not a sanctuary planked with cedar and plated with silver; nor are ye ministering priests at the altar with censers and with torches; but ye hold in your hands the sword and the bow and the weapons of death. And yet verily, I say unto you, that not when the ancient temple was in its first glory was there offered sacrifice more acceptable than that which you have this day presented, giving to the slaughter the tyrant and the oppressor, with the rocks for your altars, and the sky for your vaulted sanctuary, and your own good swords for the instruments of sacrifice. Leave not, therefore, the plough in the furrow; turn not back from the path in which you have entered like the famous worthies of old, whom God raised up for the glorifying of His name and the deliverance of His afflicted people; halt not in the race you are running, lest the latter end should be worse than the beginning. Wherefore, set up a standard in the land; blow a trumpet upon the mountains; let not the shepherd tarry by his sheepfold, or the seedsman continue in the ploughed field; but make the watch strong, sharpen the arrows, burnish the shields, name ye the captains of thousands, and captains of hundreds, of fifties, and of tens; call the footmen like the rushing of winds, and cause the horsemen to come up like the sound of many waters; for the passages of the destroyers are stopped, their rods are burned, and the face of their men of battle hath been turned to flight. Heaven has been with you and has broken the bow of the mighty; then let every man's heart be as the heart of the valiant Maccabeus, every man's hand as the hand of the mighty Samson, every man's sword as that of Gideon, which turned not back from the slaughter; for the banner of reformation is spread abroad on the mountains in its first loveliness, and the gates of hell shall not prevail against it.

"Well is he this day that shall barter his house for a helmet, and sell his garment for a sword, and cast in his lot with the children of the Covenant, even to the fulfilling of the promise; and woe, woe unto him who, for carnal ends and self-seeking, shall withhold himself from the great work, for the curse shall abide with him, even the bitter curse of Meroz, because he came not to the help of the Lord against the mighty. Up, then, and be doing; the blood of martyrs, reeking upon scaffolds, is crying for vengeance; the bones of saints, which lie whitening in the highways, are pleading for retribution; the groans of innocent captives, from desolate isles of the sea, and from the dungeons of the tyrants' high places, cry for deliverance ; the prayers of persecuted Christians, sheltering themselves in dens and deserts from the sword of their persecutors, famished with hunger, starving with cold, lacking fire, food, shelter, and clothing, because they serve God rather than man—all are with you, pleading, watching, knocking, storming the gates of heaven in your behalf. Heaven itself shall fight for you, as the stars in their courses fought against Sisera. Then whoso will deserve immortal fame in this world, and eternal happiness in that which is to come, let them enter into God's service, and take arles at the hand of His servant—a blessing, namely, upon him and his household, and his children, to the ninth generation, even the blessing of the promise, forever and ever ! Amen."

The eloquence of the preacher was rewarded by the deep hum of stern approbation which resounded through the armed assemblage at the conclusion of an exhortation so well suited to that which they had done, and that which remained for them to do. The wounded forgot their pain, the faint and hungry their fatigues and privations, as they listened to doctrines which elevated them alike above the wants and calamities of the world, and identified their cause with that of the Deity. Many crowded around the preacher as he descended from the eminence on which he stood, and, clasping him with hands on which the gore was not yet hardened, pledged their sacred vow that they would play the part of Heaven's true soldiers. Exhausted by his own enthusiasm, and by the animated fervor which he had exerted in his discourse, the preacher could only reply in broken accents, " God bless you, my brethren—it is His cause. Stand strongly up and play the men ; the worst that can befall us is but a brief and bloody passage to heaven."

Balfour and the other leaders had not lost the time which was employed in these spiritual exercises. Watch-fires were lighted, sentinels were posted, and arrangements were made to refresh the army with such provisions as had been hastily collected from the nearest farm-houses and villages. The present necessity thus provided for, they turned their thoughts to the future. They had despatched parties to spread the news of their victory, and to obtain, either by force or favor, supplies of what they stood most in need of. In this they had succeeded beyond their hopes, having at one village seized a small magazine of provisions, forage, and ammunition which had been provided for the royal forces. This success not only gave them relief at the time, but such hopes for the future, that, whereas formerly some of their number had begun to slacken in their zeal, they now unanimously resolved to abide together in arms, and commit themselves and their cause to the event of war.

And whatever may be thought of the extravagance or narrow-minded bigotry of many of their tenets, it is impossible to deny the praise of devoted courage to a few hundred peasants, who, without leaders, without money, without magazines, without any fixed plan of action, and almost without arms, borne out only by their innate zeal and a detestation of the oppression of their rulers, ventured to declare open war against an established government, supported by a regular army and the whole force of three kingdoms.

CHAPTER XIX

Why, then, say an old man can do somewhat.
                                   Henry IV., Part II.

WE must now return to the Tower of Tillietudlem, which the march of the Life Guards on the morning of this eventful day had left to silence and anxiety. The assurances of Lord Evandale had not succeeded in quelling the apprehensions of Edith. She knew him generous, and faithful to his word ; but it seemed too plain that he suspected the object of her intercession to be a successful rival ; and was it not expecting from him an effort above human nature to suppose that he was to watch over Morton's safety, and rescue him from all the dangers to which his state of imprisonment, and the suspicions which he had incurred, must repeatedly expose him ? She therefore resigned herself to the most heartrending apprehensions, without admitting, and indeed almost without listening to, the multifarious grounds of consolation which Jenny Dennison brought forward, one after another, like a skilful general who charges with the several divisions of his troops in regular succession.

First, Jenny was morally positive that young Milnwood would come to no harm ; then, if he did, there was consolation in the reflection that Lord Evandale was the better and more appropriate match of the two ; then, there was every chance of a battle in which the said Lord Evandale might be killed, and there wad be nae mair fash about that job ; then, if the Whigs gat the better, Milnwood and Cuddie might come to the Castle, and carry off the beloved of their hearts by the strong hand. "For I forgot to tell ye, madam," continued the damsel, putting her handkerchief to her eyes, "that puir Cuddie's in the hands of the Philistines as weel as young Milnwood, and he was brought here a prisoner this morning, and I was fain to speak Tam Halliday fair, and fleech him, to let me near the puir creature ; but Cuddie wasna sae thankfu' as he needed till hae been neither," she added, and at the same time changed her tone, and briskly withdrew the handkerchief from her face ; "so I will ne'er waste my een wi' greeting about the matter. There wad be aye enow o' young men left, if they were to hang the tae half o' them."

The other inhabitants of the Castle were also in a state of dissatisfaction and anxiety. Lady Margaret thought that Colonel Grahame, in commanding an execution at the door of her house, and refusing to grant a reprieve at her request, had fallen short of the deference due to her rank, and had even encroached on her seigniorial rights.

"The Colonel," she said, "ought to have remembered, brother, that the barony of Tillietudlem has the baronial privilege of pit and gallows ; and therefore, if the lad was to be executed on my estate—which I consider as an unhandsome thing, seeing it is in the possession of females, to whom such tragedies cannot be acceptable—he ought, at common law, to have been delivered up to my bailie, and justified at his sight."

"Martial law, sister," answered Major Bellenden, "super-sedes every other. But I must own I think Colonel Grahame rather deficient in attention to you ; and I am not over and above pre-eminently flattered by his granting to young Evandale—I suppose because he is a lord, and has interest with the privy council—a request which he refused to so old a servant of the king as I am. But so long as the poor young fellow's life is saved, I can comfort myself with the fag-end of a ditty as old as myself." And therewithal he hummed a stanza :

> " And what though winter will pinch severe
>   Through locks of gray and a cloak that's old ?
> Yet keep up thy heart, bold cavalier,
>   For a cup of sack shall fence the cold.

I must be your guest here to-day, sister. I wish to hear the issue of this gathering on Loudon Hill, though I cannot conceive their standing a body of horse appointed like our guests this morning. Woe's me, the time has been that I would have liked ill to have sat in biggit wa's waiting for the news of a skirmish to be fought within ten miles of me ! But, as the old song goes,

> " For time will rust the brightest blade,
>   And years will break the strongest bow ;
> Was ever wight so starkly made,
>   But time and years would overthrow ? "

"We are well pleased you will stay, brother," said Lady Margaret ; "I will take my old privilege to look after my household, whom this collation has thrown into some disorder, although it is uncivil to leave you alone."

" O, I hate ceremony as I hate a stumbling horse," replied the Major. " Besides, your person would be with me, and your mind with the cold meat and reversionary pasties. Where is Edith ? "

" Gone to her room a little evil-disposed, I am informed, and laid down in her bed for a gliff," said her grandmother ; " as soon as she wakes, she shall take some drops."

" Pooh ! pooh ! she's only sick of the soldiers," answered Major Bellenden. " She's not accustomed to see one acquaintance led out to be shot, and another marching off to actual service, with some chance of not finding his way back again. She would soon be used to it, if the Civil War were to break out again."

" God forbid, brother !" said Lady Margaret.

" Ay, Heaven forbid, as you say ; and, in the meantime, I'll take a hit at trick track with Harrison."

" He has ridden out, sir," said Gudyill, " to try if he can hear any tidings of the battle."

" D—n the battle," said the Major ; " it puts this family as much out of order as if there had never been such a thing in the country before ; and yet there was such a place as Kilsyth, John."

" Ay, and as Tippermuir, your honor," replied Gudyill, " where I was his honor my late master's rear-rank man."

" And Alford, John," pursued the Major, " where I commanded the horse ; and Innerlochy, where I was the Great Marquis's aide-de-camp ; and Auld Earn, and Brig o' Dee."

" And Philiphaugh, your honor," said John.

"Umph !" replied the Major ; " the less, John, we say about that matter, the better."

However, being once fairly embarked on the subject of Montrose's campaigns, the Major and John Gudyill carried on the war so stoutly as for a considerable time to keep at bay the formidable enemy called Time, with whom retired veterans, during the quiet close of a bustling life, usually wage an unceasing hostility.

It has been frequently remarked that the tidings of important events fly with a celerity almost beyond the power of credibility, and that reports, correct in the general point, though inaccurate in details, precede the certain intelligence, as if carried by the birds of the air. Such rumors anticipate the reality, not unlike to the "shadows of coming events," which occupy the imagination of the Highland seer. Harrison, in his ride, encountered some such report concerning the event of the battle, and turned his horse back to Tillietudlem in great dismay. He made it his first business to seek out the Major, and interrupted him in the midst of a prolix account of the siege and storm of Dundee with the ejaculation, "Heaven send, Major, that we do not see a siege of Tillietudlem before we are many days older!"

"How is that, Harrison? what the devil do you mean?" exclaimed the astonished veteran.

"Troth, sir, there is strong and increasing belief that Claver'se is clean broken, some say killed; that the soldiers are all dispersed; and that the rebels are hastening this way, threatening death and devastation to a' that will not take the Covenant."

"I will never believe that," said the Major, starting on his feet—"I will never believe that the Life Guards would retreat before rebels; and yet why need I say that," he continued, checking himself, "when I have seen such sights myself? Send out Pike and one or two of the servants for intelligence, and let all the men in the Castle and in the village that can be trusted take up arms. This old tower may hold them play a bit if it were but victualled and garrisoned, and it commands the pass between the high and low countries. It's lucky I chanced to be here. Go, muster men, Harrison. You, Gudyill, look what provisions you have, or can get brought in, and be ready, if the news be confirmed, to knock down as many bullocks as you have salt for. The well never goes dry. There are some old-fashioned guns on the battlements; if we had but ammunition we should do well enough."

"The soldiers left some casks of ammunition at the Grange this morning, to bide their return," said Harrison.

"Hasten, then," said the Major, "and bring it into the Castle, with every pike, sword, pistol, or gun that is within our reach; don't leave so much as a bodkin. Lucky that I was here! I will speak to my sister instantly."

Lady Margaret Bellenden was astounded at intelligence so unexpected and so alarming. It had seemed to her that the imposing force which had that morning left her walls was sufficient to have routed all the disaffected in Scotland, if collected in a body; and now her first reflection was upon the inadequacy of their own means of resistance to an army strong enough to have defeated Claverhouse and such select troops. "Woe's me! woe's me!" said she; "what will all that we can do avail us, brother? What will resistance do but bring

sure destruction on the house and on the bairn Edith ! for,
God knows, I thinkna on my ain auld life."

"Come, sister," said the Major, "you must not be cast
down. The place is strong, the rebels ignorant and ill provided ; my brother's house shall not be made a den of thieves
and rebels while old Miles Bellenden is in it. My hand is
weaker than it was, but I thank my old gray hairs that I have
some knowledge of war yet. Here comes Pike with intelligence. What news, Pike ? Another Philiphaugh job, eh ?"

"Ay, ay," said Pike, composedly ; "a total scattering. I
thought this morning little gude would come of their newfangled gate of slinging their carabines."

"Whom did you see ? Who gave you the news ?" asked
the Major.

"O, mair than half a dozen dragoon fellows that are a' on
the spur whilk to get first to Hamilton. They'll win the
race, I warrant them, win the battle wha like."

"Continue your preparations, Harrison," said the alert
veteran ; "get your ammunition in, and the cattle killed.
Send down to the borough-town for what meal you can gather.
We must not lose an instant. Had not Edith and you, sister,
better return to Charnwood, while we have the means of sending you there ?"

"No, brother," said Lady Margaret, looking very pale,
but speaking with the greatest composure; "since the auld
house is to be held out, I will take my chance in it. I have
fled twice from it in my days, and I have aye found it desolate of its bravest and its bonniest when I returned ; sae that
I will e'en abide now, and end my pilgrimage in it."

"It may, on the whole, be the safest course both for Edith
and you," said the Major ; "for the Whigs will rise all the way
between this and Glasgow, and make your travelling there, or
your dwelling at Charnwood, very unsafe."

"So be it, then," said Lady Margaret ; "and, dear brother,
as the nearest blood relation of my deceased husband, I deliver to you by this symbol [here she gave into his hand the
venerable gold-headed staff of the deceased Earl of Torwood]
the keeping and government and seneschalship of my Tower
of Tillietudlem, and the appurtenances thereof, with full
power to kill, slay, and damage those who shall assail the
same, as freely as I might do myself. And I trust you will
so defend it as becomes a house in which his most sacred
Majesty has not disdained——"

"Pshaw ! sister," interrupted the Major, "we have no time
to speak about the king and his breakfast just now."

And hastily leaving the room he hurried, with all the alertness of a young man of twenty-five, to examine the state of his garrison, and superintend the measures which were necessary for defending the place.

The Tower of Tillietudlem, having very thick walls and very narrow windows, having also a very strong courtyard wall, with flanking turrets on the only accessible side, and rising on the other from the very verge of a precipice, was fully capable of defence against anything but a train of heavy artillery.

Famine or escalade was what the garrison had chiefly to fear. For artillery, the top of the Tower was mounted with some antiquated wall-pieces, and small cannons, which bore the old-fashioned names of culverins, sakers, demi-sakers, falcons, and falconets. These the Major, with the assistance of John Gudyill, caused to be scaled and loaded, and pointed them so as to command the road over the brow of the opposite hill, by which the rebels must advance, causing, at the same time, two or three trees to be cut down, which would have impeded the effect of the artillery when it should be necessary to use it. With the trunks of these trees, and other materials, he directed barricades to be constructed upon the winding avenue which rose to the Tower along the high-road, taking care that each should command the other. The large gate of the courtyard he barricaded yet more strongly, leaving only a wicket open for the convenience of passage. What he had most to apprehend was the slenderness of his garrison ; for all the efforts of the steward were unable to get more than nine men under arms, himself and Gudyill included, so much more popular was the cause of the insurgents than that of the government. Major Bellenden and his trusty servant Pike made the garrison eleven in number, of whom one-half were old men. The round dozen might indeed have been made up, would Lady Margaret have consented that Goose Gibbie should again take up arms. But she recoiled from the proposal, when moved by Gudyill, with such abhorrent recollection of the former achievements of that luckless cavalier that she declared she would rather the Castle were lost than that he were to be enrolled in the defence of it. With eleven men, however, himself included, Major Bellenden determined to hold out the place to the uttermost.

The arrangements for defence were not made without the degree of fracas incidental to such occasions. Women shrieked, cattle bellowed, dogs howled, men ran to and fro, cursing and swearing without intermission ; the lumbering of the old guns backwards and forwards shook the battlements, the courts resounded with the hasty gallop of messengers who went and returned upon errands of importance, and the din of warlike preparation was mingled with the sound of female laments.

Such a Babel of discord might have awakened the slumbers of the very dead, and, therefore, was not long ere it dispelled the abstracted reveries of Edith Bellenden. She sent out Jenny to bring her the cause of the tumult which shook the Castle to its very basis; but Jenny, once engaged in the bustling tide, found so much to ask and to hear that she forgot the state of anxious uncertainty in which she had left her young mistress. Having no pigeon to dismiss in pursuit of information when her raven messenger had failed to return with it, Edith was compelled to venture in quest of it out of the ark of her own chamber into the deluge of confusion which overflowed the rest of the Castle. Six voices speaking at once informed her, in reply to her first inquiry, that Claver'se and all his men were killed, and that ten thousand Whigs were marching to besiege the Castle, headed by John Balfour of Burley, young Milnwood, and Cuddie Headrigg. This strange association of persons seemed to infer the falsehood of the whole story, and yet the general bustle in the Castle intimated that danger was certainly apprehended.

"Where is Lady Margaret?" was Edith's second question.

"In her oratory," was the reply—a cell adjoining to the chapel, in which the good old lady was wont to spend the greater part of the days destined by the rules of the Episcopal Church to devotional observances, as also the anniversaries of those on which she had lost her husband and her children, and, finally, those hours in which a deeper and more solemn address to Heaven was called for by national or domestic calamity.

"Where, then," said Edith, much alarmed, "is Major Bellenden?"

"On the battlements of the Tower, madam, pointing the cannon," was the reply.

To the battlements, therefore, she made her way, impeded by a thousand obstacles, and found the old gentleman in the midst of his natural military element, commanding, rebuking, encouraging, instructing, and exercising all the numerous duties of a good governor.

"In the name of God, what is the matter, uncle?" exclaimed Edith.

"The matter, my love!" answered the Major, coolly, as, with spectacles on his nose, he examined the position of a gun. "The matter! Why—raise her breech a thought more, John

Gudyill—the matter! Why, Claver'se is routed, my dear, and the Whigs are coming down upon us in force, that's all the matter."

"Gracious powers!" said Edith, whose eye at that instant caught a glance of the road which ran up the river, "and yonder they come!"

"Yonder! where?" said the veteran; and, his eyes taking the same direction, he beheld a large body of horsemen coming down the path. "Stand to your guns, my lads!" was the first exclamation; "we'll make them pay toll as they pass the heugh. But stay, stay, these are certainly the Life Guards."

"O no, uncle, no," replied Edith; "see how disorderly they ride, and how ill they keep their ranks; these cannot be the fine soldiers who left us this morning."

"Ah, my dear girl!" answered the Major, "you do not know the difference between men before a battle and after a defeat; but the Life Guards it is, for I see the red and blue and the king's colors. I am glad they have brought them off, however."

His opinion was confirmed as the troopers approached nearer, and finally halted on the road beneath the Tower; while their commanding officer, leaving them to breathe and refresh their horses, hastily rode up the hill.

"It is Claverhouse, sure enough," said the Major; "I am glad he has escaped, but he has lost his famous black horse. Let Lady Margaret know, John Gudyill; order some refreshments; get oats for the soldiers' horses; and let us to the hall, Edith, to meet him. I surmise we shall hear but indifferent news."

CHAPTER XX

COLONEL GRAHAME of Claverhouse met the family, assembled
in the hall of the Tower, with the same serenity and the same
courtesy which had graced his manners in the morning.   He
had even had the composure to rectify in part the derangement
of his dress, to wash the signs of battle from his face and
hands, and did not appear more disordered in his exterior
than if returned from a morning ride.

"I am grieved, Colonel Grahame," said the reverend old
lady, the tears trickling down her face—"deeply grieved."

"And I am grieved, my dear Lady Margaret," replied
Claverhouse, "that this misfortune may render your remaining at Tillietudlem dangerous for you, especially considering your recent hospitality to the king's troops, and your
well-known loyalty.   And I came here chiefly to request Miss
Bellenden and you to accept my escort—if you will not scorn
that of a poor runaway—to Glasgow, from whence I will see
you safely sent either to Edinburgh or to Dumbarton Castle,
as you shall think best."

"I am much obliged to you, Colonel Grahame," replied
Lady Margaret; "but my brother, Major Bellenden, has
taken on him the responsibility of holding out this house
against the rebels; and, please God, they shall never drive
Margaret Bellenden from her ain hearth-stane while there's
a brave man that says he can defend it."

"And will Major Bellenden undertake this?" said Claverhouse, hastily, a joyful light glancing from his dark eye as he
turned it on the veteran.   "Yet why should I question it?
it is of a piece with the rest of his life.   But have you the
means, Major?"

"All but men and provisions, with which we are ill supplied," answered the Major.

" As for men," said Claverhouse, " I will leave you a dozen or twenty fellows who will make good a breach against the devil. It will be of the utmost service if you can defend the place but a week, and by that time you must surely be relieved."

" I will make it good for that space, Colonel," replied the Major, " with twenty-five good men and store of ammunition, if we should gnaw the soles of our shoes for hunger ; but I trust we shall get in provisions from the country."

" And, Colonel Grahame, if I might presume a request," said Lady Margaret, " I would entreat that Sergeant Francis Stewart might command the auxiliaries whom you are so good as to add to the garrison of our people ; it may serve to legitimate his promotion, and I have a prejudice in favor of his noble birth."

" The sergeant's wars are ended, madam," said Grahame, in an unaltered tone, " and he now needs no promotion that an earthly master can give."

" Pardon me," said Major Bellenden, taking Claverhouse by the arm, and turning him away from the ladies, " but I am anxious for my friends ; I fear you have other and more important loss. I observe another officer carries your nephew's standard."

" You are right, Major Bellenden," answered Claverhouse, firmly ; " my nephew is no more. He has died in his duty, as became him."

" Great God !" exclaimed the Major, " how unhappy ! The handsome, gallant, high-spirited youth !"

" He was indeed all you say," answered Claverhouse ; " poor Richard was to me as an eldest son, the apple of my eye, and my destined heir ; but he died in his duty, and I—I —Major Bellenden [he wrung the Major's hand hard as he spoke], I live to avenge him."

" Colonel Grahame," said the affectionate veteran, his eyes filling with tears, " I am glad to see you bear this misfortune with such fortitude."

" I am not a selfish man," replied Claverhouse, " though the world will tell you otherwise—I am not selfish either in my hopes or fears, my joys or sorrows. I have not been severe for myself, or grasping for myself, or ambitious for myself. The service of my master and the good of the country are what I have tried to aim at. I may, perhaps, have driven severity into cruelty, but I acted for the best ; and now I will not yield to my own feelings a deeper sympathy than I have given to those of others."

"I am astonished at your fortitude under all the unpleasant circumstances of this affair," pursued the Major.

"Yes," replied Claverhouse, "my enemies in the council will lay this misfortune to my charge; I despise their accusations. They will calumniate me to my sovereign; I can repel their charge. The public enemy will exult in my flight; I shall find a time to show them that they exult too early. This youth that has fallen stood betwixt a grasping kinsman and my inheritance, for you know that my marriage-bed is barren; yet, peace be with him! the country can better spare him than your friend Lord Evandale, who, after behaving very gallantly, has, I fear, also fallen."

"What a fatal day!" ejaculated the Major. "I heard a report of this, but it was again contradicted; it was added that the poor young nobleman's impetuosity had occasioned the loss of this unhappy field."

"Not so, Major," said Grahame; "let the living officers bear the blame, if there be any; and let the laurels flourish untarnished on the grave of the fallen. I do not, however, speak of Lord Evandale's death as certain; but killed or prisoner I fear he must be. Yet he was extricated from the tumult the last time we spoke together. We were then on the point of leaving the field with a rear-guard of scarce twenty men; the rest of the regiment were almost dispersed."

"They have rallied again soon," said the Major, looking from the window on the dragoons, who were feeding their horses and refreshing themselves beside the brook.

"Yes," answered Claverhouse, "my blackguards had little temptation either to desert or to straggle farther than they were driven by their first panic. There is small friendship and scant courtesy between them and the boors of this country; every village they pass is likely to rise on them, and so the scoundrels are driven back to their colors by a wholesome terror of spits, pike-staves, hay-forks, and broomsticks. But now let us talk about your plans and wants, and the means of corresponding with you. To tell you the truth, I doubt being able to make a long stand at Glasgow, even when I have joined my Lord Ross; for this transient and accidental success of the fanatics will raise the devil through all the western counties."

They then discussed Major Bellenden's means of defence, and settled a plan of correspondence, in case a general insurrection took place, as was to be expected. Claverhouse renewed his offer to escort the ladies to a place of safety; but, all things considered, Major Bellenden thought they would be in equal safety at Tillietudlem

The Colonel then took a polite leave of Lady Margaret and Miss Bellenden, assuring them that though he was reluctantly obliged to leave them for the present in dangerous circumstances, yet his earliest means should be turned to the redemption of his character as a good knight and true, and that they might speedily rely on hearing from or seeing him.

Full of doubt and apprehension, Lady Margaret was little able to reply to a speech so much in unison with her usual expressions and feelings, but contented herself with bidding Claverhouse farewell, and thanking him for the succors which he had promised to leave them. Edith longed to inquire the fate of Henry Morton, but could find no pretext for doing so, and could only hope that it had made a subject of some part of the long private communication which her uncle had held with Claverhouse. On this subject, however, she was disappointed ; for the old Cavalier was so deeply immersed in the duties of his own office that he had scarce said a single word to Claverhouse, excepting upon military matters, and most probably would have been equally forgetful had the fate of his own son, instead of his friend's, lain in the balance.

Claverhouse now descended the bank on which the Castle is founded, in order to put his troops again in motion, and Major Bellenden accompanied him to receive the detachment who were to be left in the tower.

"I shall leave Inglis with you," said Claverhouse, "for, as I am situated, I cannot spare an officer of rank ; it is all we can do, by our joint efforts, to keep the men together. But should any of our missing officers make their appearance I authorize you to detain them ; for my fellows can with difficulty be subjected to any other authority."

His troops being now drawn up, he picked out sixteen men by name, and committed them to the command of Corporal Inglis, whom he promoted to the rank of sergeant on the spot.

"And hark ye, gentlemen," was his concluding harangue, "I leave you to defend the house of a lady, and under the command of her brother, Major Bellenden, a faithful servant to the king. You are to behave bravely, soberly, regularly, and obediently, and each of you shall be handsomely rewarded on my return to relieve the garrison. In case of mutiny, cowardice, neglect of duty, or the slightest excess in the family, the provost-marshal and cord ; you know I keep my word for good and evil."

He touched his hat as he bade them farewell, and shook hands cordially with Major Bellenden.

"Adieu," he said, "my stout-hearted old friend ! Good luck be with you, and better times to us both."

The horsemen whom he commanded had been once more reduced to tolerable order by the exertions of Major Allan ; and, though shorn of their splendor, and with their gilding all besmirched, made a much more regular and military appearance on leaving, for the second time, the Tower of Tillietudlem than when they returned to it after their rout.

Major Bellenden, now left to his own resources, sent out several videttes, both to obtain supplies of provisions, and especially of meal, and to get knowledge of the motions of the enemy. All the news he could collect on the second subject tended to prove that the insurgents meant to remain on the field of battle for that night. But they also had abroad their detachments and advanced guards to collect supplies, and great was the doubt and distress of those who received contrary orders, in the name of the king and in that of the kirk ; the one commanding them to send provisions to victual the Castle of Tillietudlem, and the other enjoining them to forward supplies to the camp of the godly professors of true religion, now in arms for the cause of covenanted reformation, presently pitched at Drumclog, nigh to Loudon Hill. Each summons closed with a denunciation of fire and sword if it was neglected ; for neither party could confide so far in the loyalty or zeal of those whom they addressed as to hope they would part with their property upon other terms. So that the poor people knew not what hand to turn themselves to ; and, to say truth, there were some who turned themselves to more than one.

"Thir kittle times will drive the wisest o' us daft," said Niel Blane, the prudent host of the Howff ; "but I'se aye keep a calm sough. Jenny, what meal is in the girnel ?"

" Four bows o' aitmeal, twa bows o' bear, and twa bows o' pease," was Jenny's reply.

"Aweel, hinny," continued Niel Blane, sighing deeply, " let Bauldy drive the pease and bear meal to the camp at Drumclog ; he's a Whig, and was the auld gudewife's pleughman ; the mashlum bannocks will suit their muirland stamachs weel. He maun say it's the last unce o' meal in the house, or, if he scruples to tell a lie—as it's no likely he will when it's for the gude o' the house—he may wait till Duncan Glen, the auld drucken trooper, drives up the aitmeal to Tillietudlem, wi' my dutifu' service to my Leddy and the Major, and I haena as muckle left as will mak my parritch ; and if Duncan manage right, I'll gie him a tass o' whiskey shall mak the blue low come out at his mouth."

"And what are we to eat oursells, then, father," asked Jenny, "when we hae sent awa' the haill meal in the ark and the girnel ?"

"We maun gar wheat-flour serve us for a blink," said Niel, in a tone of resignation; "it's no that ill food, though far frae being sae hearty or kindly to a Scotchman's stamach as the curney aitmeal is. The Englishers live amaist upon't; but to be sure, the pock-puddings ken nae better."

While the prudent and peaceful endeavored, like Neil Blane, to make fair weather with both parties, those who had more public (or party) spirit began to take arms on all sides. The Royalists in the country were not numerous, but were respectable from their fortune and influence, being chiefly landed proprietors of ancient descent, who, with their brothers, cousins, and dependants to the ninth generation, as well as their domestic servants, formed a sort of militia capable of defending their own peel-houses against detached bodies of the insurgents, of resisting their demand of supplies, and intercepting those which were sent to the Presbyterian camp by others. The news that the Tower of Tillietudlem was to be defended against the insurgents afforded great courage and support to these feudal volunteers, who considered it as a stronghold to which they might retreat, in case it should become impossible for them to maintain the desultory war they were now about to wage.

On the other hand, the towns, the villages, the farm-houses, the properties of the small heritors, sent forth numerous recruits to the Presbyterian interest. These men had been the principal sufferers during the oppression of the time. Their minds were fretted, soured, and driven to desperation by the various exactions and cruelties to which they had been subjected ; and although by no means united among themselves either concerning the purpose of this formidable insurrection, or the means by which that purpose was to be obtained, most of them considered it as a door opened by Providence to obtain the liberty of conscience of which they had been long deprived, and to shake themselves free of a tyranny directed both against body and soul. Numbers of these men, therefore, took up arms ; and, in the phrase of their time and party, prepared to cast in their lot with the victors of Loudon Hill.

CHAPTER XXI

Ananias. I do not like the man. He is a heathen,
And speaks the language of Canaan truly.
   Tribulation. You must await his calling, and the coming
Of the good spirit. You did ill to upbraid him.

The Alchemist.

WE return to Henry Morton, whom we left on the field of battle. He was eating by one of the watch-fires his portion of the provisions which had been distributed to the army, and musing deeply on the path which he was next to pursue, when Burley suddenly came up to him, accompanied by the young minister, whose exhortation after the victory had produced such a powerful effect.

"Henry Morton," said Balfour, abruptly, "the council of the army of the Covenant, confiding that the son of Silas Morton can never prove a lukewarm Laodicean, or an indifferent Gallio in this great day, have nominated you to be a captain of their host, with the right of a vote in their council, and all authority fitting for an officer who is to command Christian men."

"Mr. Balfour," replied Morton, without hesitation, "I feel this mark of confidence, and it is not surprising that a natural sense of the injuries of my country, not to mention those I have sustained in my own person, should make me sufficiently willing to draw my sword for liberty and freedom of conscience. But I will own to you, that I must be better satisfied concerning the principles on which you bottom your cause ere I can agree to take a command among you."

"And can you doubt of our principles," answered Burley, "since we have stated them to be the reformation both of church and state, the rebuilding of the decayed sanctuary, the gathering of the dispersed saints, and the destruction of the man of sin?"

"I will own frankly, Mr. Balfour," replied Morton, "much of this sort of language, which I observe is so powerful with others, is entirely lost on me. It is proper you should be aware of this before we commune further together." The young clergyman here groaned deeply. "I distress you, sir," said

190

Morton; "but perhaps it is because you will not hear me out. I revere the Scriptures as deeply as you or any Christian can do. I look into them with humble hope of extracting a rule of conduct and a law of salvation. But I expect to find this by an examination of their general tenor, and of the spirit which they uniformly breathe, and not by wresting particular passages from their context, or by the application of Scriptural phrases to circumstances and events with which they have often very slender relation."

The young divine seemed shocked and thunderstruck with this declaration, and was about to remonstrate.

"Hush, Ephraim!" said Burley, "remember he is but as a babe in swaddling-clothes. Listen to me, Morton. I will speak to thee in the worldly language of that carnal reason which is for the present thy blind and imperfect guide. What is the object for which thou art content to draw thy sword? Is it not that the church and state should be reformed by the free voice of a free parliament, with such laws as shall hereafter prevent the executive government from spilling the blood, torturing and imprisoning the persons, exhausting the estates, and trampling upon the consciences of men at their own wicked pleasure?"

"Most certainly," said Morton; "such I esteem legitimate causes of warfare, and for such I will fight while I can wield a sword."

"Nay, but," said Macbriar, "ye handle this matter too tenderly; nor will my conscience permit me to fard or daub over the causes of divine wrath——"

"Peace, Ephraim Macbriar!" again interrupted Burley.

"I will not peace," said the young man. "Is it not the cause of my Master who hath sent me? Is it not a profane and Erastian destroying of His authority, usurpation of His power, denial of His name, to place either King or Parliament in His place as the master and governor of His household, the adulterous husband of His spouse?"

"You speak well," said Burley, dragging him aside, "but not wisely; your own ears have heard this night in council how this scattered remnant are broken and divided, and would ye now make a veil of separation between them? Would ye build a wall with unslaked mortar? If a fox go up, it will breach it."

"I know," said the young clergyman, in reply, "that thou art faithful, honest, and zealous, even unto slaying; but, believe me, this worldly craft, this temporizing with sin and with infirmity, is in itself a falling away; and I fear me Heaven

will not honor us to do much more for His glory, when we
seek to carnal cunning and to a fleshly arm.   The sanctified
end must be wrought by sanctified means."

"I tell thee," answered Balfour, "thy zeal is too rigid in
this matter ; we cannot yet do without the help of the Lao-
diceans and the Erastians ; we must endure for a space the
indulged in the midst of the council ; the sons of Zeruiah
are yet too strong for us."

"I tell thee I like it not," said Macbriar ; "God can work
deliverance by a few as well as by a multitude.   The host of
the faithful that was broken upon Pentland Hills paid but
the fitting penalty of acknowledging the carnal interest of
that tyrant and oppressor, Charles Stewart."

"Well, then," said Balfour, "thou knowest the healing
resolution that the council have adopted—to make a comprehending declaration that may suit the tender consciences of
all who groan under the yoke of our present oppressors.
Return to the council if thou wilt, and get them to recall it,
and send forth one upon narrower grounds ; but abide not here
to hinder my gaining over this youth, whom my soul travails
for ; his name alone will call forth hundreds to our banners."

"Do as thou wilt, then," said Macbriar ; "but I will not
assist to mislead the youth, nor bring him into jeopardy of life,
unless upon such grounds as will insure his eternal reward."

The more artful Balfour then dismissed the impatient
preacher and returned to his proselyte.

That we may be enabled to dispense with detailing at
length the arguments by which he urged Morton to join the
insurgents, we shall take this opportunity to give a brief sketch
of the person by whom they were used, and the motives which
he had for interesting himself so deeply in the conversion of
young Morton to his cause.

John Balfour of Kinloch, or Burley, for he is designated
both ways in the histories and proclamations of that melancholy period, was a gentleman of some fortune, and of good
family, in the county of Fife, and had been a soldier from
his youth upwards.   In the younger part of his life he had
been wild and licentious, but had early laid aside open profligacy and embraced the strictest tenets of Calvinism.   Unfortunately, habits of excess and intemperance were more
easily rooted out of his dark, saturnine, and enterprising
spirit than the vices of revenge and ambition, which continued,
notwithstanding his religious professions, to exercise no small
sway over his mind.   Daring in design, precipitate and violent in execution, and going to the very extremity of the

most rigid recusancy, it was his ambition to place himself at the head of the Presbyterian interest.

To attain this eminence among the Whigs, he had been active in attending their conventicles, and more than once had commanded them when they appeared in arms, and beaten off the forces sent to disperse them. At length the gratification of his own fierce enthusiasm, joined, as some say, with motives of private revenge, placed him at the head of that party who assassinated the Primate of Scotland as the author of the sufferings of the Presbyterians. The violent measures adopted by government to revenge this deed, not on the perpetrators only, but on the whole professors of the religion to which they belonged, together with long previous sufferings without any prospect of deliverance, except by force of arms, occasioned the insurrection which, as we have already seen, commenced by the defeat of Claverhouse in the bloody skirmish of Loudon Hill.

But Burley, notwithstanding the share he had in the victory, was far from finding himself at the summit which his ambition aimed at. This was partly owing to the various opinions entertained among the insurgents concerning the murder of Archbishop Sharp. The more violent among them did indeed approve of this act as a deed of justice executed upon a persecutor of God's church through the immediate inspiration of the Deity ; but the greater part of the Presbyterians disowned the deed as a crime highly culpable, although they admitted that the Archbishop's punishment had by no means exceeded his deserts. The insurgents differed in another main point, which has been already touched upon. The more warm and extravagant fanatics condemned, as guilty of a pusillanimous abandonment of the rights of the church, those preachers and congregations who were contented, in any manner, to exercise their religion through the permission of the ruling government. This, they said, was absolute Erastianism, or subjection of the church of God to the regulations of an earthly government, and therefore but one degree better than Prelacy or Popery. Again, the more moderate party were content to allow the king's title to the throne, and in secular affairs to acknowledge his authority, so long as it was exercised with due regard to the liberties of the subject, and in conformity to the laws of the realm. But the tenets of the wilder sect, called, from their leader, Richard Cameron, by the name of Cameronians, went the length of disowning the reigning monarch, and every one of his successors who should not acknowledge the Solemn

League and Covenant. The seeds of disunion were therefore thickly sown in this ill-fated party ; and Balfour, however enthusiastic, and however much attached to the most violent of those tenets which we have noticed, saw nothing but ruin to the general cause if they were insisted on during this crisis, when unity was of so much consequence. Hence he disapproved, as we have seen, of the honest, downright, and ardent zeal of Macbriar, and was extremely desirous to receive the assistance of the moderate party of Presbyterians in the immediate overthrow of the government, with the hope of being hereafter able to dictate to them what should be substituted in its place.

He was on this account particularly anxious to secure the accession of Henry Morton to the cause of the insurgents. The memory of his father was generally esteemed among the Presbyterians ; and as few persons of any decent quality had joined the insurgents, this young man's family and prospects were such as almost insured his being chosen a leader. Through Morton's means, as being the son of his ancient comrade, Burley conceived he might exercise some influence over the more liberal part of the army, and ultimately perhaps ingratiate himself so far with them as to be chosen commander-in-chief, which was the mark at which his ambition aimed. He had therefore, without waiting till any other person took up the subject, exalted to the council the talents and disposition of Morton, and easily obtained his elevation to the painful rank of a leader in this disunited and undisciplined army.

The arguments by which Balfour pressed Morton to accept of this dangerous promotion, as soon as he had gotten rid of his less wary and uncompromising companion, Macbriar, were sufficiently artful and urgent. He did not affect either to deny or to disguise that the sentiments which he himself entertained concerning church government went as far as those of the preacher who had just left them ; but he argued that when the affairs of the nation were at such a desperate crisis, minute difference of opinion should not prevent those who, in general, wished well to their oppressed country from drawing their swords in its behalf. Many of the subjects of division, as, for example, that concerning the Indulgence itself, arose, he observed, out of circumstances which would cease to exist, provided their attempt to free the country should be successful, seeing that the Presbytery, being in that case triumphant, would need to make no such compromise with the government, and, consequently, with the abolition of the Indulgence all discussion of its legality would be at once ended. He insisted much and strongly upon the necessity of taking advantage of this favorable crisis, upon the certainty of their being joined by the force of the whole western shires, and upon the gross guilt which those would incur who, seeing the distress of the country and the increasing tyranny with which it was governed, should, from fear or indifference, withhold their active aid from the good cause.

Morton wanted not these arguments to induce him to join in any insurrection which might appear to have a feasible prospect of freedom to the country. He doubted, indeed, greatly whether the present attempt was likely to be supported by the strength sufficient to insure success, or by the wisdom and liberality of spirit necessary to make a good use of the advantages that might be gained. Upon the whole, however, considering the wrongs he had personally endured, and those which he had seen daily inflicted on his fellow-subjects, meditating also upon the precarious and dangerous situation in which he already stood with relation to the government, he conceived himself, in every point of view, called upon to join the body of Presbyterians already in arms.

But while he expressed to Burley his acquiescence in the vote which had named him a leader among the insurgents, and a member of their council of war, it was not without a qualification.

"I am willing," he said, "to contribute everything within my limited power to effect the emancipation of my country. But do not mistake me. I disapprove, in the utmost degree, of the action in which this rising seems to have originated; and no arguments should induce me to join it, if it is to be carried on by such measures as that with which it has commenced."

Burley's blood rushed to his face, giving a ruddy and dark glow to his swarthy brow.

"You mean," he said, in a voice which he designed should not betray any emotion—"you mean the death of James Sharp?"

"Frankly," answered Morton, "such is my meaning."

"You imagine, then," said Burley, "that the Almighty in times of difficulty does not raise up instruments to deliver His church from her oppressors? You are of opinion that the justice of an execution consists, not in the extent of the sufferer's crime, or in his having merited punishment, or in the wholesome and salutary effect which that example is likely to produce upon other evil-doers, but hold that it rests solely in

the robe of the judge, the height of the bench, and the voice
of the doomster ? Is not just punishment justly inflicted,
whether on the scaffold or the moor ? And where constituted
judges, from cowardice, or from having cast in their lot with
transgressors, suffer them not only to pass at liberty through
the land, but to sit in the high places and dye their garments
in the blood of the saints, is it not well done in any brave
spirits who shall draw their private swords in the public
cause ?"

"I have no wish to judge this individual action," replied
Morton, "further than is necessary to make you fully aware
of my principles. I therefore repeat that the case you have
supposed does not satisfy my judgment. That the Almighty,
in His mysterious providence, may bring a bloody man to an
end deservedly bloody does not vindicate those who, without
authority of any kind, take upon themselves to be the instruments of execution, and presume to call them the executors
of divine vengeance."

"And were we not so ?" said Burley, in a tone of fierce
enthusiasm. "Were not we—was not every one who owned
the interest of the Covenanted Church of Scotland—bound
by that covenant to cut off the Judas who had sold the cause
of God for fifty thousand merks a year ? Had we met him by
the way as he came down from London, and there smitten
him with the edge of the sword, we had done but the duty of
men faithful to our cause and to our oaths recorded in heaven.
Was not the execution itself a proof of our warrant ? Did not
the Lord deliver him into our hands when we looked out but
for one of His inferior tools of persecution ? Did we not
pray to be resolved how we should act, and was it not borne in
on our hearts as if it had been written on them with the point
of a diamond, 'Ye shall surely take him and slay him ?'
Was not the tragedy full half an hour in acting ere the sacrifice was completed, and that in an open heath, and within the
patrols of their garrisons ; and yet who interrupted the great
work ? What dog so much as bayed us during the pursuit,
the taking, the slaying, and the dispersing ? Then, who will
say—who dare say, that a mightier arm than ours was not
herein revealed ?"

"You deceive yourself, Mr. Balfour," said Morton ;
"such circumstances of facility of execution and escape have
often attended the commission of the most enormous crimes.
But it is not mine to judge you. I have not forgotten that
the way was opened to the former liberation of Scotland by
an act of violence which no man can justify—the slaughter

of Cumming by the hand of Robert Bruce; and therefore condemning this action, as I do and must, I am not unwilling to suppose that you may have motives vindicating it in your own eyes, though not in mine or in those of sober reason. I only now mention it because I desire you to understand that I join a cause supported by men engaged in open war, which it is proposed to carry on according to the rules of civilized nations, without in any respect approving of the act of violence which gave immediate rise to it."

Balfour bit his lip, and with difficulty suppressed a violent answer. He perceived with disappointment that, upon points of principle, his young brother-in-arms possessed a clearness of judgment and a firmness of mind which afforded but little hope of his being able to exert that degree of influence over him which he had expected to possess. After a moment's pause, however, he said, with coolness, " My conduct is open to men and angels. The deed was not done in a corner; I am here in arms to avow it, and care not where or by whom I am called on to do so, whether in the council, the field of battle, the place of execution, or the day of the last great trial. I will not now discuss it further with one who is yet on the other side of the veil. But if you will cast in your lot with us as a brother, come with me to the council, who are still sitting to arrange the future march of the army and the means of improving our victory."

. Morton arose and followed him in silence, not greatly delighted with his associate, and better satisfied with the general justice of the cause which he had espoused than either with the measures or the motives of many of those who were embarked in it.

CHAPTER XXII

And look how many Grecian tents do stand
Hollow upon this plain—so many hollow factions.
                    Troilus and Cressida.

IN a hollow of the hill, about a quarter of a mile from the field
of battle, was a shepherd's hut—a miserable cottage, which, as
the only enclosed spot within a moderate distance, the leaders
of the Presbyterian army had chosen for their council-house.
Towards this spot Burley guided Morton, who was surprised,
as he approached it, at the multifarious confusion of sounds
which issued from its precincts. The calm and anxious gravity
which it might be supposed would have presided in councils
held on such important subjects, and at a period so critical,
seemed to have given place to discord, wild and loud uproar,
which fell on the ear of their new ally as an evil augury of
their future measures. As they approached the door, they
found it open, indeed, but choked up with the bodies and
heads of countrymen, who, though no members of the council,
felt no scruple in intruding themselves upon deliberations in
which they were so deeply interested. By expostulation, by
threats, and even by some degree of violence, Burley, the
sternness of whose character maintained a sort of superiority
over these disorderly forces, compelled the intruders to retire,
and introducing Morton into the cottage, secured the door
behind them against impertinent curiosity. At a less agitating moment the young man might have been entertained with
the singular scene of which he now found himself an auditor
and a spectator.

The precincts of the gloomy and ruinous hut were enlightened partly by some furze which blazed on the hearth, the
smoke whereof, having no legal vent, eddied around, and
formed over the heads of the assembled council a clouded
canopy as opaque as their metaphysical theology, through
which, like stars through mist, were dimly seen to twinkle a
few blinking candles, or rather rushes dipped in tallow, the
property of the poor owner of the cottage, which were stuck
to the walls by patches of wet clay. This broken and dusky

light showed many a countenance elated with spiritual pride, or rendered dark by fierce enthusiasm ; and some whose anxious, wandering, and uncertain looks showed they felt themselves rashly embarked in a cause which they had neither courage nor conduct to bring to a good issue, yet knew not how to abandon for very shame. They were, indeed, a doubtful and disunited body. The most active of their number were those concerned with Burley in the death of the Primate, four or five of whom had found their way to Loudon Hill, together with other men of the same relentless and uncompromising zeal, who had in various ways given desperate and unpardonable offence to the government.

With them were mingled their preachers, men who had spurned at the Indulgence offered by government, and preferred assembling their flocks in the wilderness to worshipping in temples built by human hands, if their doing the latter should be construed to admit any right on the part of their rulers to interfere with the supremacy of the kirk. The other class of counsellors were such gentlemen of small fortune, and substantial farmers, as a sense of intolerable oppression had induced to take arms and join the insurgents. These also had their clergymen with them ; and such divines, having many of them taken advantage of the Indulgence, were prepared to resist the measures of their more violent brethren, who proposed a declaration in which they should give testimony against the warrants and instructions for indulgence as sinful and unlawful acts. This delicate question had been passed over in silence in the first draught of the manifestoes which they intended to publish of the reasons of their gathering in arms ; but it had been stirred anew during Balfour's absence, and to his great vexation he now found that both parties had opened upon it in full cry, Macbriar, Kettledrummle, and other teachers of the Wanderers being at the very spring-tide of polemical discussion with Peter Poundtext, the indulged pastor of Milnwood's parish, who, it seems, had e'en girded himself with a broadsword, but, ere he was called upon to fight for the good cause of Presbytery in the field, was manfully defending his own dogmata in the council. It was the din of this conflict, maintained chiefly between Poundtext and Kettledrummle, together with the clamor of their adherents, which had saluted Morton's ears upon approaching the cottage. Indeed, as both the divines were men well gifted with words and lungs, and each fierce, ardent, and intolerant in defence of his own doctrine, prompt in the recollection of texts wherewith they battered each other without mercy, and deeply impressed with the importance of the subject of discussion, the noise of the debate betwixt them fell little short of that which might have attended an actual bodily conflict.

Burley, scandalized at the disunion implied in this virulent strife of tongues, interposed between the disputants, and, by some general remarks on the unseasonableness of discord, a soothing address to the vanity of each party, and the exertion of the authority which his services in that day's victory entitled him to assume, at length succeeded in prevailing upon them to adjourn further discussion of the controversy. But although Kettledrummle and Poundtext were thus for the time silenced, they continued to eye each other like two dogs, who, having been separated by the authority of their masters while fighting, have retreated, each beneath the chair of his owner, still watching each other's motions, and indicating, by occasional growls, by the erected bristles of the back and ears, and by the red glance of the eye, that their discord is unappeased, and that they only wait the first opportunity afforded by any general movement or commotion in the company to fly once more at each other's throats.

Balfour took advantage of the momentary pause to present to the council Mr. Henry Morton of Milnwood, as one touched with a sense of the evils of the times, and willing to peril goods and life in the precious cause for which his father, the renowned Silas Morton, had given in his time a soul-stirring testimony. Morton was instantly received with the right hand of fellowship by his ancient pastor, Poundtext, and by those among the insurgents who supported the more moderate principles. The others muttered something about Erastianism, and reminded each other in whispers that Silas Morton, once a stout and worthy servant of the Covenant, had been a backslider in the day when the Resolutioners had led the way in owning the authority of Charles Stewart, thereby making a gap whereat the present tyrant was afterwards brought in to the oppression both of kirk and country. They added, however, that on this great day of calling they would not refuse society with any who should put hand to the plough ; and so Morton was installed in his office of leader and counsellor, if not with the full approbation of his colleagues, at least without any formal or avowed dissent. They proceeded, on Burley's motion, to divide among themselves the command of the men who had assembled, and whose numbers were daily increasing. In this partition the insurgents of Poundtext's parish and congregation were naturally placed under the command of Morton ; an arrangement mutually agreeable to both parties, as he was recommended to their confidence as well by his personal qualities as his having been born among them.

When this task was accomplished, it became necessary to determine what use was to be made of their victory. Morton's heart throbbed high when he heard the Tower of Tillietudlem named as one of the most important positions to be seized upon. It commanded, as we have often noticed, the pass between the more wild and the more fertile country, and must furnish, it was plausibly urged, a stronghold and place of rendezvous to the Cavaliers and Malignants of the district, supposing the insurgents were to march onward and leave it uninvested. This measure was particularly urged as necessary by Poundtext and those of his immediate followers whose habitations and families might be exposed to great severities if this strong place were permitted to remain in possession of the Royalists.

"I opine," said Poundtext, for, like the other divines of the period, he had no hesitation in offering his advice upon military matters, of which he was profoundly ignorant—"I opine that we should take in and raze that stronghold of the woman Lady Margaret Bellenden, even though we should build a fort and raise a mount against it; for the race is a rebellious and a bloody race, and their hand has been heavy on the children of the Covenant, both in the former and the latter times. Their hook hath been in our noses, and their bridle betwixt our jaws."

"What are their means and men of defence?" said Burley. "The place is strong; but I cannot conceive that two women can make it good against a host."

"There is also," said Poundtext, "Harrison the steward, and John Gudyill, even the lady's chief butler, who boasteth himself a man of war from his youth upward, and who spread the banner against the good cause with that man of Belial, James Grahame of Montrose."

"Pshaw!" returned Burley, scornfully, "a butler!"

"Also, there is that ancient Malignant," replied Poundtext, "Miles Bellenden of Charnwood, whose hands have been dipped in the blood of the saints."

"If that," said Burley, "be Miles Bellenden, the brother of Sir Arthur, he is one whose sword will not turn back from battle; but he must now be stricken in years."

"There was word in the country as I rode along," said another of the council, "that so soon as they heard of the victory which has been given to us, they caused shut the gates of the Tower, and called in men, and collected ammunition. They were ever a fierce and a malignant house."

"We will not, with my consent," said Burley, "engage in a siege which may consume time. We must rush forward and follow our advantage by occupying Glasgow ; for I do not fear that the troops we have this day beaten, even with the assistance of my Lord Ross's regiment, will judge it safe to await our coming."

"Howbeit," said Poundtext, "we may display a banner before the Tower, and blow a trumpet and summon them to come forth. It may be that they will give over the place into our mercy though they be a rebellious people. And we will summon the women to come forth of their stronghold— that is, Lady Margaret Bellenden and her granddaughter, and Jenny Dennison, which is a girl of an ensnaring eye, and the other maids, and we will give them a safe-conduct, and send them in peace to the city, even to the town of Edinburgh. But John Gudyill, and Hugh Harrison, and Miles Bellenden, we will restrain with fetters of iron, even as they in times by-past have done to the martyred saints."

"Who talks of safe-conduct and of peace ?" said a shrill, broken, and overstrained voice from the crowd.

"Peace, brother Habakkuk," said Macbriar, in a soothing tone to the speaker.

"I will not hold my peace," reiterated the strange and unnatural voice ; "is this a time to speak of peace, when the earth quakes, and the mountains are rent, and the rivers are changed into blood, and the two-edged sword is drawn from the sheath to drink gore as if it were water, and devour flesh as the fire devours dry stubble ?"

While he spoke thus, the orator struggled forward to the inner part of the circle, and presented to Morton's wondering eyes a figure worthy of such a voice and such language. The rags of a dress which had once been black, added to the tattered fragments of a shepherd's plaid, composed a covering scarce fit for the purposes of decency, much less for those of warmth or comfort. A long beard, as white as snow, hung down on his breast, and mingled with bushy, uncombed, grizzled hair, which hung in elf-locks around his wild and staring visage. The features seemed to be extenuated by penury and famine, until they hardly retained the likeness of a human aspect. The eyes, gray, wild, and wandering, evidently betokened a bewildered imagination. He held in his hand a rusty sword, clotted with blood, as were his long lean hands, which were garnished at the extremity with nails like eagle's claws.

"In the name of Heaven! who is he?" said Morton, in a whisper to Poundtext, surprised, shocked, and even startled at this ghastly apparition, which looked more like the resurrection of some cannibal priest, or Druid red from his human sacrifice, than like an earthly mortal.

"It is Habakkuk Mucklewrath," answered Poundtext, in the same tone, "whom the enemy have long detained in captivity in forts and castles, until his understanding hath departed from him, and, as I fear, an evil demon hath possessed him. Nevertheless, our violent brethren will have it that he speaketh of the spirit, and that they fructify by his pouring forth."

Here he was interrupted by Mucklewrath, who cried in a voice that made the very beams of the roof quiver—"Who talks of peace and safe-conduct? who speaks of mercy to the bloody house of the Malignants? I say take the infants and dash them against the stones; take the daughters and the mothers of the house and hurl them from the battlements of their trust, that the dogs may fatten on their blood as they did on that of Jezabel, the spouse of Ahab, and that their carcasses may be dung to the face of the field even in the portion of their fathers!"

"He speaks right," said more than one sullen voice from behind; "we will be honored with little service in the great cause if we already make fair weather with Heaven's enemies."

"This is utter abomination and daring impiety," said Morton, unable to contain his indignation. "What blessing can you expect in a cause in which you listen to the mingled ravings of madness and atrocity?"

"Hush, young man!" said Kettledrummle, "and reserve thy censure for that for which thou canst render a reason. It is not for thee to judge into what vessels the spirit may be poured."

"We judge of the tree by the fruit," said Poundtext, "and allow not that to be of divine inspiration that contradicts the divine laws."

"You forget, brother Poundtext," said Macbriar, "that these are the latter days when signs and wonders shall be multiplied."

Poundtext stood forward to reply; but ere he could articulate a word, the insane preacher broke in with a scream that drowned all competition. "Who talks of signs and wonders? Am not I Habakkuk Mucklewrath, whose name is changed to Magor-Missabib, because I am made a terror unto myself and unto all that are around me ? I heard it. When did I hear it ? Was it not in the Tower of the Bass, that overhangeth the wide wild sea ? And it howled in the winds, and it roared in the billows, and it screamed, and it whistled, and it clanged, with the screams and the clang and the whistle of the sea-birds, as they floated, and flew, and dropped, and dived, on the bosom of the waters. I saw it. Where did I see it ? Was it not from the high peaks of Dunbarton, when I looked westward upon the fertile land, and northward on the wild Highland hills ; when the clouds gathered and the tempest came, and the lightnings of heaven flashed in sheets as wide as the banners of an host ? What did I see ? Dead corpses and wounded horses, the rushing together of battle, and garments rolled in blood. What heard I ? The voice that cried, 'Slay, slay, smite, slay utterly, let not your eye have pity ! slay utterly, old and young, the maiden, the child, and the woman whose head is gray. Defile the house and fill the courts with the slain ! ' "

"We receive the command," exclaimed more than one of the company. "Six days he hath not spoken nor broken bread, and now his tongue is unloosed. We receive the command ; as he hath said, so will we do."

Astonished, disgusted, and horror-struck at what he had seen and heard, Morton turned away from the circle and left the cottage. He was followed by Burley, who had his eye on his motions.

"Whither are you going ? " said the latter, taking him by the arm.

"Anywhere, I care not whither ; but here I will abide no longer."

"Art thou so soon weary, young man ? " answered Burley. "Thy hand is but now put to the plough, and wouldst thou already abandon it ? Is this thy adherence to the cause of thy father ?"

"No cause," replied Morton, indignantly—"no cause can prosper so conducted. One party declares for the ravings of a bloodthirsty madman ; another leader is an old scholastic pedant ; a third "—he stopped, and his companion continued the sentence—"Is a desperate homicide, thou wouldst say, like John Balfour of Burley ? I can bear thy misconstruction without resentment. Thou dost not consider that it is not men of sober and self-seeking minds who arise in these days of wrath to execute judgment and to accomplish deliverance. Hadst thou but seen the armies of England during her Parliament of 1640, whose ranks were filled with sectaries and enthusiasts wilder than the Anabaptists of Munster, thou wouldst have had more cause to marvel; and yet these men were unconquered on the field, and their hands wrought marvellous things for the liberties of the land."

"But their affairs," replied Morton, "were wisely conducted, and the violence of their zeal expended itself in their exhortations and sermons, without bringing divisions into their counsels, or cruelty into their conduct. I have often heard my father say so, and protest that he wondered at nothing so much as the contrast between the extravagance of their religious tenets and the wisdom and moderation with which they conducted their civil and military affairs. But *our* councils seem all one wild chaos of confusion."

"Thou must have patience, Henry Morton," answered Balfour; "thou must not leave the cause of thy religion and country either for one wild word or one extravagant action. Hear me. I have already persuaded the wiser of our friends that the counsellors are too numerous, and that we cannot expect that the Midianites shall, by so large a number, be delivered into our hands. They have hearkened to my voice, and our assemblies will be shortly reduced within such a number as can consult and act together; and in them thou shalt have a free voice, as well as in ordering our affairs of war and protecting those to whom mercy should be shown. Art thou now satisfied?"

"It will give me pleasure, doubtless," answered Morton, "to be the means of softening the horrors of civil war; and I will not leave the post I have taken unless I see measures adopted at which my conscience revolts. But to no bloody executions after quarter asked, or slaughter without trial, will I lend countenance or sanction; and you may depend on my opposing them, with both heart and hand, as constantly and resolutely, if attempted by our own followers, as when they are the work of the enemy."

Balfour waved his hand impatiently.

"Thou wilt find," he said, "that the stubborn and hardhearted generation with whom we deal must be chastised with scorpions ere their hearts be humbled, and ere they accept the punishment of their iniquity. The word is gone forth against them, 'I will bring a sword upon you that shall avenge the quarrel of my Covenant.' But what is done shall be done gravely, and with discretion, like that of the worthy James Melvin, who executed judgment on the tyrant and oppressor, Cardinal Beaton."

" I own to you," replied Morton, " that I feel still more abhorrent at cold-blooded and premeditated cruelty than at that which is practised in the heat of zeal and resentment."

" Thou art yet but a youth," replied Balfour, " and hast not learned how light in the balance are a few drops of blood in comparison to the weight and importance of this great national testimony. But be not afraid ; thyself shall vote and judge in these matters ; it may be we shall see little cause to strive together anent them."

With this concession Morton was compelled to be satisfied for the present ; and Burley left him, advising him to lie down and get some rest, as the host would probably move in the morning.

" And you," answered Morton, " do not you go to rest also ? "

" No," said Burley ; " my eyes must not yet know slumber. This is no work to be done lightly ; I have yet to perfect the choosing of the committee of leaders, and I will call you by times in the morning to be present at their consultation."

He turned away, and left Morton to his repose.

The place in which he found himself was not ill adapted for the purpose, being a sheltered nook, beneath a large rock, well protected from the prevailing wind. A quantity of moss with which the ground was overspread made a couch soft enough for one who had suffered so much hardship and anxiety. Morton wrapped himself in the horseman's cloak which he had still retained, stretched himself on the ground, and had not long indulged in melancholy reflections on the state of the country, and upon his own condition, ere he was relieved from them by deep and sound slumber.

The rest of the army slept on the ground, dispersed in groups, which chose their beds on the fields as they could best find shelter and convenience. A few of the principal leaders held wakeful conference with Burley on the state of their affairs, and some watchmen were appointed who kept themselves on the alert by chanting psalms, or listening to the exercises of the more gifted of their number.

CHAPTER XXIII

Got with much ease—now merrily to horse.
                                     Henry IV., Part I

WITH the first peep of day Henry awoke and found the
faithful Cuddie standing beside him with a portmanteau in
his hand.

"I hae been just putting your honor's things in readiness
again ye were waking," said Cuddie, "as is my duty, seeing
ye hae been sae gude as to tak me into your service."

"I take you into my service, Cuddie?" said Morton;
"you must be dreaming."

"Na, na, stir," answered Cuddie; "didna I say when I
was tied on the horse yonder, that if ever ye gat loose I would
be your servant, and ye didna say no? and if that isna hiring, I kenna what is. Ye gae me nae arles, indeed, but ye
had gien me eneugh before at Milnwood."

"Well, Cuddie, if you insist on taking the chance of my
unprosperous fortunes——"

"Ou, ay, I'se warrant us a' prosper weel eneugh," answered Cuddie, cheeringly, "an anes my auld mither was
weel putten up. I hae begun the campaigning trade at an
end that is easy eneugh to learn."

"Pillaging, I suppose?" said Morton, "for how else
could you come by that portmanteau?"

"I wotna if it's pillaging, or how ye ca't," said Cuddie,
"but it comes natural to a body, and it's a profitable trade.
Our folk had tirled the dead dragoons as bare as bawbees
before we were loose amaist. But when I saw the Whigs a' weel
yokit by the lugs to Kettledrummle and the other chield, I
set off at the lang trot on my ain errand and your honor's.
Sae I took up the syke a wee bit, away to the right, where I
saw the marks o' mony a horse-foot; and sure eneugh I cam
to a place where there had been some clean leatherin', and a'
the puir chields were lying there buskit wi' their claes just
as they had put them on that morning—naebody had found
out that pose o' carcages; and wha suld be in the midst
thereof, as my mither says, but our auld acquaintance, Sergeant Bothwell?"

"Ay, has that man fallen?" said Morton.

"Troth has he," answered Cuddie; "and his een were open and his brow brent, and his teeth clinched thegither, like the jaws of a trap for foumarts when the spring's doun. I was amaist feared to look at him; however, I thought to hae turn about wi' him, and sae I e'en riped his pouches, as he had dune mony an honester man's; and here's your ain siller again—or your uncle's, which is the same—that he got at Milnwood that unlucky night that made us a' sodgers thegither."

"There can be no harm, Cuddie," said Morton, "in making use of this money, since we know how he came by it; but you must divide with me."

"Bide a wee—bide a wee," said Cuddie. "Weel, and there's a bit ring he had hinging in a black ribbon doun on his breast—I am thinking it has been a love-token, puir fallow, there's naebody sae rough but they hae aye a kind heart to the lasses—and there's a book wi' a wheen papers, and I got twa or three odd things, that I'll keep to mysell, forbye."

"Upon my word, you have made a very successful foray for a beginner," said his new master.

"Haena I e'en now?" said Cuddie, with great exultation. "I tauld ye I wasna that dooms stupid, if it cam to lifting things. And forbye, I hae gotten twa gude horse. A feckless loon of a Straven weaver, that has left his loom and his bien house to sit skirling on a cauld hillside, had catched twa dragoon naigs, and he could neither gar them hup nor wind, sae he took a gowd noble for them baith. I suld hae tried him wi' half the siller, but it's an unco ill place to get change in. Ye'll find the siller's missing out o' Bothwell's purse."

"You have made a most excellent and useful purchase, Cuddie; but what is that portmanteau?"

"The pockmantle?" answered Cuddie. "It was Lord Evandale's yesterday, and it's yours the day. I fand it ahint the bush o' broom yonder; ilka dog has its day. Ye ken what the auld sang says,

"Take turn about, mither, quo' Tam o' the Linn.

And speaking o' that, I maun gang and see about my mither, puir auld body, if your honor hasna ony immediate commands."

"But, Cuddie," said Morton, "I really cannot take these things from you without some recompense."

"Hout fie, stir," answered Cuddie, "ye suld aye be taking; for recompense, ye may think about that some other time; I hae seen gay weel to mysell wi' some things that fit me better. What could I do wi' Lord Evandale's braw claes? Sergeant Bothwell's will serve me weel eneugh."

Not being able to prevail on the self-constituted and disinterested follower to accept of anything for himself out of these warlike spoils, Morton resolved to take the first opportunity of returning Lord Evandale's property, supposing him yet to be alive; and in the meanwhile, did not hesitate to avail himself of Cuddie's prize, so far as to appropriate some changes of linen and other trifling articles among those of more value which the portmanteau contained.

He then hastily looked over the papers which were found in Bothwell's pocketbook. These were of a miscellaneous description. The roll of his troop, with the names of those absent on furlough, memorandums of tavern bills, and lists of delinquents who might be made subjects of fine and persecution, first presented themselves, along with a copy of a warrant from the privy council to arrest certain persons of distinction therein named. In another pocket of the book were one or two commissions which Bothwell had held at different times, and certificates of his services abroad, in which his courage and military talents were highly praised. But the most remarkable paper was an accurate account of his genealogy, with reference to many documents for establishment of its authenticity; subjoined was a list of the ample possessions of the forfeited Earls of Bothwell, and a particular account of the proportions in which King James VI. had bestowed them on the courtiers and nobility by whose descendants they were at present actually possessed; beneath this list was written, in red letters, in the hand of the deceased, *Haud Immemor*, F. S. E. B., the initials probably intimating Francis Stewart, Earl of Bothwell. To these documents, which strongly painted the character and feelings of their deceased proprietor, were added some which showed him in a light greatly different from that in which we have hitherto presented him to the reader.

In a secret pocket of the book, which Morton did not discover without some trouble, were one or two letters, written in a beautiful female hand. They were dated about twenty years back, bore no address, and were subscribed only by initials. Without having time to peruse them accurately, Morton perceived that they contained the elegant yet fond expressions of female affection directed towards an object whose jealousy they endeavored to soothe, and of whose hasty, suspicious, and impatient temper the writer seemed gently to complain. The ink of these manuscripts had faded by time, and, notwithstanding the great care which had obviously been taken for their preservation, they were in one or two places chafed so as to be illegible.

" It matters not," these words were written on the envelope of that which had suffered most, " I have them by heart."

With these letters was a lock of hair wrapped in a copy of verses, written obviously with a feeling which atoned, in Morton's opinion, for the roughness of the poetry, and the conceits with which it abounded, according to the taste of the period :

> Thy hue, dear pledge, is pure and bright,
> As in that well-remember'd night,
> When first thy mystic braid was wove,
> And first my Agnes whisper'd love.
>   Since then, how often hast thou press'd
> The torrid zone of this wild breast,
> Whose wrath and hate have sworn to dwell
> With the first sin which peopled hell ;
> A breast whose blood's a troubled ocean,
> Each throb the earthquake's wild commotion !
> O, if such clime thou canst endure,
> Yet keep thy hue unstain'd and pure.
> What conquest o'er each erring thought
> Of that fierce realm had Agnes wrought!
> I had not wander'd wild and wide,
> With such an angel for my guide ;
> Nor heaven nor earth could then reprove me,
> If she had lived, and lived to love me.
>   Not then this world's wild joys had been
> To me one savage hunting-scene,
> My sole delight the headlong race,
> And frantic hurry of the chase,
> To start, pursue, and bring to bay,
> Rush in, drag down, and rend my prey,
> Then from the carcass turn away ;
> Mine ireful mood had sweetness tamed,
> And soothed each wound which pride inflamed ;—
> Yes, God and man might now approve me,
> If thou hadst lived, and lived to love me !

As he finished reading these lines, Morton could not forbear reflecting with compassion on the fate of this singular and most unhappy being, who, it appeared, while in the lowest state of degradation, and almost of contempt, had his recollections continually fixed on the high station to which his birth seemed to entitle him ; and, while plunged in gross licentiousness, was in secret looking back with bitter remorse to the period of his youth, during which he had nourished a virtuous, though unfortunate, attachment.

"Alas! what are we," said Morton, "that our best and most praiseworthy feelings can be thus debased and depraved; that honorable pride can sink into haughty and desperate indifference for general opinion, and the sorrow of blighted affection inhabit the same bosom which license, revenge, and rapine have chosen for their citadel? But it is the same throughout; the liberal principles of one man sink into cold and unfeeling indifference, the religious zeal of another hurries him into frantic and savage enthusiasm. Our resolutions, our passions, are like the waves of the sea, and, without the aid of Him who formed the human breast, we cannot say to its tides, 'Thus far shall ye come, and no farther.'"

While he thus moralized, he raised his eyes, and observed that Burley stood before him.

"Already awake?" said that leader. "It is well, and shows zeal to tread the path before you. What papers are these?" he continued.

Morton gave him some brief account of Cuddie's successful marauding party, and handed him the pocketbook of Bothwell, with its contents. The Cameronian leader looked with some attention on such of the papers as related to military affairs or public business; but when he came to the verses he threw them from him with contempt.

"I little thought," he said, "when, by the blessing of God, I passed my sword three times through the body of that arch tool of cruelty and persecution, that a character so desperate and so dangerous could have stooped to an art as trifling as it is profane. But I see that Satan can blend the most different qualities in his well-beloved and chosen agents, and that the same hand which can wield a club or a slaughter-weapon against the godly in the valley of destruction can touch a tinkling lute or a gittern, to soothe the ears of the dancing daughters of perdition in their Vanity Fair."

"Your ideas of duty, then," said Morton, "exclude love of the fine arts, which have been supposed in general to purify and to elevate the mind?"

"To me, young man," answered Burley, "and to those who think as I do, the pleasures of this world, under whatever name disguised, are vanity, as its grandeur and power are a snare. We have but one object on earth, and that is to build up the temple of the Lord."

"I have heard my father observe," replied Morton, "that many who assumed power in the name of Heaven were as severe in its exercise, and as unwilling to part with it, as if they had been solely moved by the motives of worldly ambition,—

but of this another time.   Have you succeeded in obtaining a committee of the council to be nominated ?"

"I have," answered Burley.   "The number is limited to six, of which you are one, and I come to call you to their deliberations."

Morton accompanied him to a sequestered grass-plot, where their colleagues awaited them.   In this delegation of authority, the two principal factions which divided the tumultuary army had each taken care to send three of their own number. On the part of the Cameronians were Burley, Macbriar, and Kettledrummle ; and on that of the Moderate party Poundtext, Henry Morton, and a small proprietor, called the Laird of Langcale.   Thus the two parties were equally balanced by their representatives in the committee of management, although it seemed likely that those of the most violent opinions were, as is usual in such cases, to possess and exert the greater degree of energy.   Their debate, however, was conducted more like men of this world than could have been expected from their conduct on the preceding evening.   After maturely considering their means and situation, and the probable increase of their numbers, they agreed that they would keep their position for that day, in order to refresh their men, and give time to reinforcements to join them, and that, on the next morning, they would direct their march towards Tillietudlem, and summon that stronghold, as they expressed it, of Malignancy.   If it was not surrendered to their summons, they resolved to try the effect of a brisk assault ; and should that miscarry, it was settled that they should leave a part of their number to blockade the place, and reduce it, if possible, by famine, while their main body should march forward to drive Claverhouse and Lord Ross from the town of Glasgow.   Such was the determination of the council of management ; and thus Morton's first enterprise in active life was likely to be the attack of a castle belonging to the parent of his mistress, and defended by her relative, Major Bellenden, to whom he personally owed many obligations !   He felt fully the embarrassment of his situation, yet consoled himself with the reflection that his newly acquired power in the insurgent army would give him, at all events, the means of extending to the inmates of Tillietudlem a protection which no other circumstance could have afforded them ; and he was not without hope that he might be able to mediate such an accommodation betwixt them and the Presbyterian army as should secure them a safe neutrality during the war which was about to ensue.

CHAPTER XXIV

There came a knight from the field of slain,
His steed was drench'd in blood and rain.
FINLAY.

WE must now return to the fortress of Tillietudlem and its
inhabitants. The morning, being the first after the battle of
Loudon Hill, had dawned upon its battlements, and the defenders had already resumed the labors by which they proposed to render the place tenable, when the watchman, who
was placed in a high turret, called the Warder's Tower, gave
the signal that a horseman was approaching. As he came
nearer, his dress indicated an officer of the Life Guards; and
the slowness of his horse's pace, as well as the manner in
which the rider stooped on the saddle-bow, plainly showed
that he was sick or wounded. The wicket was instantly
opened to receive him, and Lord Evandale rode into the courtyard, so reduced by loss of blood that he was unable to dismount without assistance. As he entered the hall, leaning
upon a servant, the ladies shrieked with surprise and terror;
for, pale as death, stained with blood, his regimentals soiled
and torn, and his hair matted and disordered, he resembled
rather a spectre than a human being. But their next exclamation was that of joy at his escape.

"Thank God!" exclaimed Lady Margaret, "that you are
here, and have escaped the hands of the bloodthirsty murderers who have cut off so many of the king's loyal servants!"

"Thank God!" added Edith, "that you are here and in
safety! We have dreaded the worst. But you are wounded,
and I fear we have little the means of assisting you."

"My wounds are only sword-cuts," answered the young
nobleman, as he reposed himself on a seat; "the pain is not
worth mentioning, and I should not even feel exhausted but
for the loss of blood. But it was not my purpose to bring
my weakness to add to your danger and distress, but to relieve them, if possible. What can I do for you? Permit
me," he added, addressing Lady Margaret—"permit me to
think and act as your son, my dear madam—as your brother,
Edith!"

213

He pronounced the last part of the sentence with some emphasis, as if he feared that the apprehension of his pretensions as a suitor might render his proffered services unacceptable to Miss Bellenden. She was not insensible to his delicacy, but there was no time for exchange of sentiments.

"We are preparing for our defence," said the old lady, with great dignity; "my brother has taken charge of our garrison, and, by the grace of God, we will give the rebels such a reception as they deserve."

"How gladly," said Evandale, "would I share in the defence of the Castle! But in my present state I should be but a burden to you; nay, something worse, for the knowledge that an officer of the Life Guards was in the Castle would be sufficient to make these rogues more desperately earnest to possess themselves of it. If they find it defended only by the family, they may possibly march on to Glasgow rather than hazard an assault."

"And can you think so meanly of us, my lord," said Edith, with the generous burst of feeling which woman so often evinces, and which becomes her so well, her voice faltering through eagerness, and her brow coloring with the noble warmth which dictated her language—"can you think so meanly of your friends, as that they would permit such considerations to interfere with their sheltering and protecting you at a moment when you are unable to defend yourself, and when the whole country is filled with the enemy? Is there a cottage in Scotland whose owners would permit a valued friend to leave it in such circumstances? And can you think we will allow you to go from a castle which we hold to be strong enough for our own defence?"

"Lord Evandale need never think of it," said Lady Margaret. "I will dress his wounds myself; it is all an old wife is fit for in war time; but to quit the Castle of Tillietudlem when the sword of the enemy is drawn to slay him—the meanest trooper that ever wore the king's coat on his back should not do so, much less my young Lord Evandale. Ours is not a house that ought to brook such dishonor. The Tower of Tillietudlem has been too much distinguished by the visit of his most sacred——"

Here she was interrupted by the entrance of the Major.

"We have taken a prisoner, my dear uncle," said Edith—"a wounded prisoner, and he wants to escape from us. You must help us to keep him by force."

"Lord Evandale!" exclaimed the veteran. "I am as

much pleased as when I got my first commission. Claverhouse reported you were killed, or missing at least."

"I should have been slain but for a friend of yours," said
Lord Evandale, speaking with some emotion, and bending his
eyes on the ground, as if he wished to avoid seeing the impression that what he was about to say would make upon Miss
Bellenden. "I was unhorsed and defenceless, and the sword
raised to despatch me, when young Mr. Morton, the prisoner
for whom you interested yourself yesterday morning, interposed in the most generous manner, preserved my life, and
furnished me with the means of escaping."

As he ended the sentence, a painful curiosity overcame his
first resolution ; he raised his eyes to Edith's face, and imagined he could read, in the glow of her cheek and the sparkle
of her eye, joy at hearing of her lover's safety and freedom,
and triumph at his not having been left last in the race of
generosity. Such, indeed, were her feelings ; but they were
also mingled with admiration of the ready frankness with which
Lord Evandale had hastened to bear witness to the merit of a
favored rival, and to acknowledge an obligation which, in all
probability, he would rather have owed to any other individual
in the world.

Major Bellenden, who would never have observed the emotions of either party, even had they been much more mark-
edly expressed, contented himself with saying, "Since Henry
Morton has influence with these rascals, I am glad he has so
exerted it ; but I hope he will get clear of them as soon as he
can. Indeed, I cannot doubt it. I know his principles, and
that he detests their cant and hypocrisy. I have heard him
laugh a thousand times at the pedantry of that old Presbyterian scoundrel, Poundtext, who, after enjoying the Indulgence of the government for so many years, has now, upon the
very first ruffle, shown himself in his own proper colors, and
set off, with three parts of his crop-eared congregation, to join
the host of the fanatics. But how did you escape after leaving the field, my lord ?"

"I rode for my life, as a recreant knight must," answered
Lord Evandale, smiling. "I took the route where I thought
I had least chance of meeting with any of the enemy, and I
found shelter for several hours—you will hardly guess where."

"At Castle Bracklan, perhaps," said Lady Margaret, "or
in the house of some other loyal gentleman ?"

"No, madam. I was repulsed, under one mean pretext or
another, from more than one house of that description, for
fear of the enemy following my traces ; but I found refuge in

the cottage of a poor widow whose husband had been shot within these three months by a party of our corps, and whose two sons are at this very moment with the insurgents."

"Indeed!" said Lady Margaret Bellenden; "and was a fanatic woman capable of such generosity? But she disapproved, I suppose, of the tenets of her family?"

"Far from it, madam," continued the young nobleman; "she was in principle a rigid recusant, but she saw my danger and distress, considered me as a fellow-creature, and forgot that I was a Cavalier and a soldier. She bound my wounds, and permitted me to rest upon her bed, concealed me from a party of the insurgents who were seeking for stragglers, supplied me with food, and did not suffer me to leave my place of refuge until she had learned that I had every chance of getting to this tower without danger."

"It was nobly done," said Miss Bellenden; "and I trust you will have an opportunity of rewarding her generosity."

"I am running up an arrear of obligation on all sides, Miss Bellenden, during these unfortunate occurrences," replied Lord Evandale; "but when I can attain the means of showing my gratitude, the will shall not be wanting."

All now joined in pressing Lord Evandale to relinquish his intention of leaving the Castle; but the argument of Major Bellenden proved the most effectual.

"Your presence in the Castle will be most useful, if not absolutely necessary, my lord, in order to maintain, by your authority, proper discipline among the fellows whom Claverhouse has left in garrison here, and who do not prove to be of the most orderly description of inmates; and, indeed, we have the Colonel's authority, for that very purpose, to detain any officer of his regiment who might pass this way."

"That," said Lord Evandale, "is an unanswerable argument, since it shows me that my residence here may be useful, even in my present disabled state."

"For your wounds, my lord," said the Major, "if my sister, Lady Bellenden, will undertake to give battle to any feverish symptom, if such should appear, I will answer that my old campaigner, Gideon Pike, shall dress a flesh-wound with any of the incorporation of barber-surgeons. He had enough of practice in Montrose's time, for we had few regularly bred army chirurgeons, as you may well suppose. You agree to stay with us, then?"

"My reasons for leaving the Castle," said Lord Evandale, glancing a look towards Edith, "though they evidently seemed weighty, must needs give way to those which infer the power of serving you.   May I presume, Major, to inquire into the means and plan of defence which you have prepared ? or can I attend you to examine the works ?"

It did not escape Miss Bellenden that Lord Evandale seemed much exhausted both in body and mind.   "I think, sir," she said, addressing the Major, "that since Lord Evandale condescends to become an officer of our garrison, you should begin by rendering him amenable to your authority, and ordering him to his apartment, that he may take some refreshment ere he enters on military discussions."

"Edith is right," said the old lady; "you must go instantly to bed, my lord, and take some febrifuge, which I will prepare with my own hand ; and my lady-in-waiting, Mistress Martha Weddell, shall make some friar's chicken, or something very light.   I would not advise wine.   John Gudyill, let the housekeeper make ready the chamber of dais.   Lord Evandale must lie down instantly.   Pike will take off the dressings and examine the state of the wounds."

"These are melancholy preparations, madam," said Lord Evandale, as he returned thanks to Lady Margaret, and was about to leave the hall ; " but I must submit to your ladyship's directions, and I trust that your skill will soon make me a more able defender of your castle than I am at present.   You must render my body serviceable as soon as you can, for you have no use for my head while you have Major Bellenden."

With these words he left the apartment.

"An excellent young man, and a modest," said the Major.

"None of that conceit," said Lady Margaret, "that often makes young folk suppose they know better how their complaints should be treated than people that have had experience."

"And so generous and handsome a young nobleman," said Jenny Dennison, who had entered during the latter part of this conversation, and was now left alone with her mistress in the hall, the Major returning to his military cares, and Lady Margaret to her medical preparations.

Edith only answered these encomiums with a sigh ; but, although silent, she felt and knew better than any one how much they were merited by the person on whom they were bestowed.

Jenny, however, failed not to follow up her blow.   " After a', it's true that my leddy says, there's nae trusting a Presbyterian ; they are a' faithless man sworn louns.   Wha wad hae thought that young Milnwood and Cuddie Headrigg wad hae taen on wi' thae rebel blackguards ? "

"What do you mean by such improbable nonsense, Jenny?" said her young mistress, very much displeased.

"I ken it's no pleasing for you to hear, madam," answered Jenny, hardily, "and it's as little pleasant for me to tell; but as gude ye suld ken a' about it sune as syne, for the haill Castle's ringing wi't."

"Ringing with what, Jenny? Have you a mind to drive me mad?" answered Edith, impatiently.

"Just that Henry Morton of Milnwood is out wi' the rebels, and ane o' their chief leaders."

"It is a falsehood!" said Edith—"a most base calumny! and you are very bold to dare to repeat it to me. Henry Morton is incapable of such treachery to his king and country, such cruelty to me—to—to all the innocent and defenceless victims, I mean—who must suffer in a civil war; I tell you he is utterly incapable of it, in every sense."

"Dear! dear! Miss Edith," replied Jenny, still constant to her text, "they maun be better acquainted wi' young men than I am, or ever wish to be, that can tell preceesely what they're capable or no capable o'. But there has been Trooper Tam and another chield out in bonnets and gray plaids, like countrymen, to recon—reconnoitre, I think John Gudyill ca'd it; and they hae been amang the rebels, and brought back word that they had seen young Milnwood mounted on ane o' the dragoon horses that was taen at Loudon Hill, armed wi' swords and pistols, like wha but him, and hand and glove wi' the foremost o' them, and dreeling and commanding the men; and Cuddie at the heels o' him, in ane o' Sergeant Bothwell's laced waistcoats, and a cockit hat with a bab o' blue ribbands at it for the auld cause o' the Covenant—but Cuddie aye liked a blue ribband—and a ruffled sark, like ony lord o' the land; it sets the like o' him, indeed!"

"Jenny," said her young mistress, hastily, "it is impossible these men's report can be true; my uncle has heard nothing of it at this instant."

"Because Tam Halliday," answered the handmaiden, "came in just five minutes after Lord Evandale; and when he heard his lordship was in the Castle, he swore—the profane loon!—he would be d—d ere he would make the report, as he ca'd it, of his news to Major Bellenden, since there was an officer of his ain regiment in the garrison. Sae he wad have said naething till Lord Evandale wakened the next morning; only he tauld me about it [here Jenny looked a little down], just to vex me about Cuddie."

"Poh, you silly girl," said Edith, assuming some courage, "it is all a trick of that fellow to teaze you."

"Na, madam, it canna be that, for John Gudyill took the other dragoon—he's an auld hard-favored man, I wotna his name—into the cellar, and gae him a tass o' brandy to get the news out o' him, and he said just the same as Tam Halliday, word for word; and Mr. Gudyill was in sic a rage that he tauld it a' ower again to us, and says the haill rebellion is owing to the nonsense o' my leddy and the Major, and Lord Evandale, that begged off young Milnwood and Cuddie yesterday morning, for that, if they had suffered, the country wad hae been quiet; and troth I am muckle o' that opinion mysell."

This last commentary Jenny added to her tale, in resentment of her mistress's extreme and obstinate incredulity. She was instantly alarmed, however, by the effect which her news produced upon her young lady, an effect rendered doubly violent by the High Church principles and prejudices in which Miss Bellenden had been educated. Her complexion became as pale as a corpse, her respiration so difficult that it was on the point of altogether failing her, and her limbs so incapable of supporting her that she sunk, rather than sat, down upon one of the seats in the hall, and seemed on the eve of fainting. Jenny tried cold water, burnt feathers, cutting of laces, and all other remedies usual in hysterical cases, but without any immediate effect.

"God forgie me! what hae I done?" said the repentant *fille-de-chambre*. "I wish my tongue had been cuttit out! Wha wad hae thought o' her taking on that way, and a' for a young lad? O, Miss Edith—dear Miss Edith, haud your heart up about it; it's maybe no true for a' that I hae said. O, I wish my mouth had been blistered! A'body tells me my tongue will do me a mischief some day. What if my leddy comes? or the Major? and she's sitting in the throne, too, that naebody has sat in since that weary morning the King was here! O, what will I do? O, what will become o' us?"

While Jenny Dennison thus lamented herself and her mistress, Edith slowly returned from the paroxysm into which she had been thrown by this unexpected intelligence.

"If he had been unfortunate," she said, "I never would have deserted him. I never did so, even when there was danger and disgrace in pleading his cause. If he had died, I would have mourned him; if he had been unfaithful, I would have forgiven him; but a rebel to his king, a traitor to his country, the associate and colleague of cutthroats and common stabbers, the persecutor of all that is noble, the professed and blasphemous enemy of all that is sacred,—I will tear him from my heart, if my life-blood should ebb in the effort!"

She wiped her eyes and rose hastily from the great chair (or throne, as Lady Margaret used to call it), while the terrified damsel hastened to shake up the cushion, and efface the appearance of any one having occupied that sacred seat; although King Charles himself, considering the youth and beauty as well as the affliction of the momentary usurper of his hallowed chair, would probably have thought very little of the profanation. She then hastened officiously to press her support on Edith, as she paced the hall apparently in deep meditation.

"Tak my arm, madam—better just tak my arm; sorrow maun hae its vent, and doubtless——"

"No, Jenny," said Edith, with firmness, "you have seen my weakness, and you shall see my strength."

"But ye leaned on me the other morning, Miss Edith, when ye were sae sair grieved."

"Misplaced and erring affection may require support, Jenny; duty can support itself,—yet I will do nothing rashly. I will be aware of the reasons of his conduct, and then—cast him off forever," was the firm and determined answer of her young lady.

Overawed by a manner of which she could neither conceive the motive nor estimate the merit, Jenny muttered between her teeth, "Odd, when the first flight's ower, Miss Edith taks it as easy as I do, and muckle easier, and I'm sure I ne'er cared half sae muckle about Cuddie Headrigg as she did about young Milnwood. Forbye that, it's maybe as weel to hae a friend on baith sides; for, if the Whigs suld come to tak the Castle, as it's like they may, when there's sae little victual, and the dragoons wasting what's o't, ou, in that case, Milnwood and Cuddie wad hae the upper hand, and their freendship wad be worth siller; I was thinking sae this morning or I heard the news."

With this consolatory reflection the damsel went about her usual occupations, leaving her mistress to school her mind as she best might, for eradicating the sentiments which she had hitherto entertained towards Henry Morton.

CHAPTER XXV

Once more into the breach, dear friends, once more !
Henry V.

On the evening of this day, all the information which they
could procure led them to expect that the insurgent army
would be with early dawn on their march against Tillietudlem.   Lord Evandale's wounds had been examined by Pike,
who reported them in a very promising state.   They were
numerous, but none of any consequence ; and the loss of
blood, as much perhaps as the boasted specific of Lady Margaret, had prevented any tendency to fever ; so that, notwithstanding he felt some pain and great weakness, the patient maintained that he was able to creep about with the
assistance of a stick. In these circumstances, he refused to be
confined to his apartment, both that he might encourage the
soldiers by his presence, and suggest any necessary addition
to the plan of defence, which the Major might be supposed to
have arranged upon something of an antiquated fashion of
warfare.   Lord Evandale was well qualified to give advice on
such subjects, having served, during his early youth, both in
France and in the Low Countries.   There was little or no occasion, however, for altering the preparations already made ;
and, excepting on the article of provisions, there seemed no
reason to fear for the defence of so strong a place against such
assailants as those by whom it was threatened.

With the peep of day, Lord Evandale and Major Bellenden
were on the battlements again, viewing and re-viewing the state
of their preparations, and anxiously expecting the approach
of the enemy.   I ought to observe, that the report of the spies
had now been regularly made and received ; but the Major
treated the report that Morton was in arms against the government with the most scornful incredulity.

"I know the lad better," was the only reply he deigned to
make ; "the fellows have not dared to venture near enough,
and have been deceived by some fanciful resemblance, or have
picked up some story."

"I differ from you, Major," answered Lord Evandale ; " I

think you will see that young gentleman at the head of the insurgents ; and, though I shall be heartily sorry for it, I shall not be greatly surprised."

" You are as bad as Claverhouse," said the Major, " who contended yesterday morning down my very throat that this young fellow, who is as high-spirited and gentlemanlike a boy as I have ever known, wanted but an opportunity to place himself at the head of the rebels."

" And considering the usage which he has received, and the suspicions under which he lies," said Lord Evandale, " what other course is open to him ? For my own part, I should hardly know whether he deserved most blame or pity."

" Blame, my lord ! pity ? " echoed the Major, astonished at hearing such sentiments. " He would deserve to be hanged, that's all ; and were he my own son, I should see him strung up with pleasure. Blame, indeed ! But your lordship cannot think as you are pleased to speak ? "

" I give you my honor, Major Bellenden, that I have been for some time of opinion that our politicians and prelates have driven matters to a painful extremity in this country, and have alienated, by violence of various kinds, not only the lower classes, but all those in the upper ranks whom strong party feeling or a desire of court interest does not attach to their standard."

" I am no politician," answered the Major, " and I do not understand nice distinctions. My sword is the king's, and when he commands, I draw it in his cause."

" I trust," replied the young lord, " you will not find me more backward than yourself, though I heartily wish that the enemy were foreigners. It is, however, no time to debate that matter, for yonder they come, and we must defend ourselves as well as we can."

As Lord Evandale spoke, the van of the insurgents began to make their appearance on the road which crossed the top of the hill, and thence descended opposite to the Tower. They did not, however, move downwards, as if aware that, in doing so, their columns would be exposed to the fire of the artillery of the place. But their numbers, which at first seemed few, appeared presently so to deepen and concentrate themselves that, judging of the masses which occupied the road behind the hill from the closeness of the front which they presented on the top of it, their force appeared very considerable. There was a pause of anxiety on both sides ; and, while the unsteady ranks of the Covenanters were agitated, as if by pressure behind or uncertainty as to their next movement, their arms, picturesque from their variety, glanced in the morning sun, whose beams were reflected from a grove of pikes, muskets, halberds, and battle-axes. The armed mass occupied, for a few minutes, this fluctuating position, until three or four horsemen, who seemed to be leaders, advanced from the front, and occupied the height a little nearer to the Castle. John Gudyill, who was not without some skill as an artilleryman, brought a gun to bear on this detached group.

"I'll flee the falcon [so the small cannon was called]—I'll flee the falcon whene'er your honor gies command; my certie, she'll ruffle their feathers for them!"

The Major looked at Lord Evandale.

"Stay a moment," said the young nobleman, "they send us a flag of truce."

In fact, one of the horsemen at that moment dismounted, and, displaying a white cloth on a pike, moved forward towards the Tower, while the Major and Lord Evandale, descending from the battlement of the main fortress, advanced to meet him as far as the barricade, judging it unwise to admit him within the precincts which they designed to defend. At the same time that the ambassador set forth, the group of horsemen, as if they had anticipated the preparations of John Gudyill for their annoyance, withdrew from the advanced station which they had occupied, and fell back to the main body.

The envoy of the Covenanters, to judge by his mien and manner, seemed fully imbued with that spiritual pride which distinguished his sect. His features were drawn up to a contemptuous primness, and his half-shut eyes seemed to scorn to look upon the terrestrial objects around, while, at every solemn stride, his toes were pointed outwards with an air that appeared to despise the ground on which they trod.

Lord Evandale could not suppress a smile at this singular figure. "Did you ever," said he to Major Bellenden, "see such an absurd automaton? One would swear it moves upon springs. Can it speak, think you?"

"O, ay," said the Major; "that seems to be one of my old acquaintance, a genuine Puritan of the right pharisaical leaven. Stay, he coughs and hems; he is about to summon the Castle with the butt-end of a sermon instead of a parley on the trumpet."

The veteran, who in his day had had many an opportunity to become acquainted with the manners of these religionists, was not far mistaken in his conjecture; only that instead of a prose exordium, the Laird of Langcale—for it was no less a personage—uplifted, with a stentorian voice, a verse of the twenty-fourth Psalm :

> " Ye gates lift up your heads ! ye doors,
> Doors that do last for aye,
> Be lifted up——"

"I told you so," said the Major to Evandale, and then presented himself at the entrance of the barricade, demanding to know for what purpose or intent he made that doleful noise, like a hog in a high wind, beneath the gates of the Castle.

" I come," replied the ambassador, in a high and shrill voice, and without any of the usual salutations or deferences —" I come from the godly army of the Solemn League and Covenant, to speak with two carnal Malignants, William Maxwell, called Lord Evandale, and Miles Bellenden of Charnwood."

" And what have you to say to Miles Bellenden and Lord Evandale ? " answered the Major.

" Are you the parties ? " said the Laird of Langcale, in the same sharp, conceited, disrespectful tone of voice.

" Even so, for fault of better," said the Major.

" Then there is the public summons," said the envoy, putting a paper into Lord Evandale's hand, " and there is a private letter for Miles Bellenden from a godly youth, who is honored with leading a part of our host.   Read them quickly, and God give you grace to fructify by the contents, though it is muckle to be doubted."

The summons ran thus : " We, the named and constituted leaders of the gentlemen, ministers, and others presently in arms for the cause of liberty and true religion, do warn and summon William Lord Evandale and Miles Bellenden of Charnwood, and others presently in arms, and keeping garrison in the Tower of Tillietudlem, to surrender the said Tower upon fair conditions of quarter, and license to depart with bag and baggage, otherwise to suffer such extremity of fire and sword as belong by the laws of war to those who hold out an untenable post.   And so may God defend His own good cause ! "

This summons was signed by John Balfour of Burley, as quartermaster-general of the army of the Covenant, for himself, and in name of the other leaders.

The letter to Major Bellenden was from Henry Morton. It was couched in the following language :

"I have taken a step, my venerable friend, which, among many painful consequences, will, I am afraid, incur your very decided disapprobation. But I have taken my resolution in honor and good faith, and with the full approval of my own conscience. I can no longer submit to have my own rights and those of my fellow-subjects trampled upon, our freedom violated, our persons insulted, and our blood spilled, without just cause or legal trial. Providence, through the violence of the oppressors themselves, seems now to have opened a way of deliverance from this intolerable tyranny, and I do not hold him deserving of the name and rights of a freeman who, thinking as I do, shall withhold his arm from the cause of his country. But God, who knows my heart, be my witness that I do not share the angry or violent passions of the oppressed and harassed sufferers with whom I am now acting. My most earnest and anxious desire is to see this unnatural war brought to a speedy end by the union of the good, wise, and moderate of all parties, and a peace restored which, without injury to the King's constitutional rights, may substitute the authority of equal laws for that of military violence, and, permitting to all men to worship God according to their own consciences, may subdue fanatical enthusiasm by reason and mildness, instead of driving it to frenzy by persecution and intolerance.

"With these sentiments, you may conceive with what pain I appear in arms before the house of your venerable relative, which we understand you propose to hold out against us. Permit me to press upon you the assurance that such a measure will only lead to the effusion of blood; that, if repulsed in the assault, we are yet strong enough to invest the place, and reduce it by hunger, being aware of your indifferent preparations to sustain a protracted siege. It would grieve me to the heart to think what would be the sufferings in such a case, and upon whom they would chiefly fall.

"Do not suppose, my respected friend, that I would propose to you any terms which could compromise the high and honorable character which you have so deservedly won, and so long borne. If the regular soldiers, to whom I will insure a safe retreat, are dismissed from the place, I trust no more will be required than your parole to remain neuter during this unhappy contest; and I will take care that Lady Margaret's property, as well as yours, shall be duly respected, and no garrison intruded upon you. I could say much in favor of this proposal; but I fear, as I must in the present instance appear criminal in your eyes, good arguments would lose their influence when coming from an unwelcome quarter. I will, therefore, break off with assuring you that, whatever your sentiments may be hereafter towards me, my sense of gratitude to you can never be diminished or erased ; and it would be the happiest moment of my life that should give me more effectual means than mere words to assure you of it.   Therefore, although in the first moment of resentment you may reject the proposal I make to you, let not that prevent you from resuming the topic, if future events should render it more acceptable ; for whenever, or howsoever, I can be of service to you, it will always afford the greatest satisfaction to

"HENRY MORTON."

Having read this long letter with the most marked indignation, Major Bellenden put it into the hands of Lord Evandale.

"I would not have believed this," he said, "of Henry Morton, if half mankind had sworn it !   The ungrateful, rebellious traitor ! rebellious in cold blood, and without even the pretext of enthusiasm, that warms the liver of such a crack-brained fop as our friend the envoy there.   But I should have remembered he was a Presbyterian ; I ought to have been aware that I was nursing a wolf-cub, whose diabolical nature would make him tear and snatch at me on the first opportunity.   Were Saint Paul on earth again, and a Presbyterian, he would be a rebel in three months ; it is in the very blood of them."

"Well," said Lord Evandale, "I will be the last to recommend surrender ; but, if our provisions fail, and we receive no relief from Edinburgh or Glasgow, I think we ought to avail ourselves of this opening to get the ladies, at least, safe out of the Castle."

"They will endure all, ere they would accept the protection of such a smooth-tongued hypocrite," answered the Major, indignantly ; "I would renounce them for relatives were it otherwise.   But let us dismiss the worthy ambassador.   My friend," he said, turning to Langcale, "tell your leaders, and the mob they have gathered yonder, that, if they have not a particular opinion of the hardness of their own skulls, I would advise them to beware how they knock them against these old walls.   And let them send no more flags of truce, or we will hang up the messenger in retaliation of the murder of Cornet Grahame."

With this answer the ambassador returned to those by whom he had been sent.   He had no sooner reached the main body than a murmur was heard among the multitude, and there was raised in front of their ranks an ample red flag, the borders of which were edged with blue. As the signal of war and defiance spread out its large folds upon the morning wind, the ancient banner of Lady Margaret's family, together with the royal ensign, was immediately hoisted on the walls of the Tower, and at the same time a round of artillery was discharged against the foremost ranks of the insurgents, by which they sustained some loss. Their leaders instantly withdrew them to the shelter of the brow of the hill.

"I think," said John Gudyill, while he busied himself in recharging his guns, "they hae fund the falcon's neb a bit ower hard for them. It's no for naught that the hawk whistles."

But as he uttered these words the ridge was once more crowded with the ranks of the enemy. A general discharge of their firearms was directed against the defenders upon the battlements. Under cover of the smoke, a column of picked men rushed down the road with determined courage, and, sustaining with firmness a heavy fire from the garrison, they forced their way, in spite of opposition, to the first barricade by which the avenue was defended. They were led on by Balfour in person, who displayed courage equal to his enthusiasm ; and, in spite of every opposition, forced the barricade, killing and wounding several of the defenders, and compelling the rest to retreat to their second position. The precautions, however, of Major Bellenden rendered this success unavailing ; for no sooner were the Covenanters in possession of the post than a close and destructive fire was poured into it from the Castle, and from those stations which commanded it in the rear. Having no means of protecting themselves from this fire, or of returning it with effect against men who were under cover of their barricades and defences, the Covenanters were obliged to retreat ; but not until they had, with their axes, destroyed the stockade, so as to render it impossible for the defenders to reoccupy it.

Balfour was the last man that retired. He even remained for a short space almost alone, with an axe in his hand, laboring like a pioneer amid the storm of balls, many of which were specially aimed against him. The retreat of the party he commanded was not effected without heavy loss, and served as a severe lesson concerning the local advantages possessed by the garrison.

The next attack of the Covenanters was made with more caution. A strong party of marksmen, many of them competitors at the game of the popinjay, under the command of

Henry Morton, glided through the woods where they afforded them the best shelter, and, avoiding the open road, endeavored, by forcing their way through the bushes and trees, and up the rocks which surrounded it on either side, to gain a position from which, without being exposed in an intolerable degree, they might annoy the flank of the second barricade, while it was menaced in front by a second attack from Burley. The besieged saw the danger of this movement, and endeavored to impede the approach of the marksmen by firing upon them at every point where they showed themselves. The assailants, on the other hand, displayed great coolness, spirit, and judgment in the manner in which they approached the defences. This was in a great measure to be ascribed to the steady and adroit manner in which they were conducted by their youthful leader, who showed as much skill in protecting his own followers as spirit in annoying the enemy.

He repeatedly enjoined his marksmen to direct their aim chiefly upon the redcoats, and to save the others engaged in the defence of the Castle ; and, above all, to spare the life of the old Major, whose anxiety made him more than once expose himself in a manner that, without such generosity on the part of the enemy, might have proved fatal. A dropping fire of musketry now glanced from every part of the precipitous mount on which the Castle was founded. From bush to bush, from crag to crag, from tree to tree, the marksmen continued to advance, availing themselves of branches and roots to assist their ascent, and contending at once with the disadvantages of the ground and the fire of the enemy. At length they got so high on the ascent that several of them possessed an opportunity of firing into the barricade against the defenders, who then lay exposed to their aim, and Burley, profiting by the confusion of the moment, moved forward to the attack in front. His onset was made with the same desperation and fury as before, and met with less resistance, the defenders being alarmed at the progress which the sharpshooters had made in turning the flank of their position. Determined to improve his advantage, Burley, with his axe in his hand, pursued the party whom he had dislodged even to the third and last barricade, and entered it along with them.

" Kill, kill ! down with the enemies of God and His people ! No quarter ! The Castle is ours !" were the cries by which he animated his friends, the most undaunted of whom followed him close, while the others, with axes, spades, and other implements, threw up earth, cut down trees, hastily laboring to establish such a defensive cover in the rear of the second barricade as might enable them to retain possession of it, in case the Castle was not carried by this *coup-de-main*.

Lord Evandale could no longer restrain his impatience. He charged with a few soldiers who had been kept in reserve in the courtyard of the Castle ; and, although his arm was in a sling, encouraged them, by voice and gesture, to assist their companions who were engaged with Burley. The combat now assumed an air of desperation. The narrow road was crowded with the followers of Burley, who pressed forward to support their companions. The soldiers, animated by the voice and presence of Lord Evandale, fought with fury, their small numbers being in some measure compensated by their greater skill, and by their possessing the upper ground, which they defended desperately with pikes and halberds, as well as with the butt of the carabines and their broadswords. Those within the Castle endeavored to assist their companions, whenever they could so level their guns as to fire upon the enemy without endangering their friends. The sharpshooters, dispersed around, were firing incessantly on each object that was exposed upon the battlement. The Castle was enveloped with smoke, and the rocks rang to the cries of the combatants. In the midst of this scene of confusion, a singular accident had nearly given the besiegers possession of the fortress.

Cuddie Headrigg, who had advanced among the marksmen, being well acquainted with every rock and bush in the vicinity of the Castle, where he had so often gathered nuts with Jenny Dennison, was enabled, by such local knowledge, to advance further, and with less danger, than most of his companions, excepting some three or four who had followed him close. Now Cuddie, though a brave enough fellow upon the whole, was by no means fond of danger, either for its own sake or for that of the glory which attends it. In his advance, therefore, he had not, as the phrase goes, taken the bull by the horns, or advanced in front of the enemy's fire. On the contrary, he had edged gradually away from the scene of action, and, turning his line of ascent rather to the left, had pursued it until it brought him under a front of the Castle different from that before which the parties were engaged, and to which the defenders had given no attention, trusting to the steepness of the precipice. There was, however, on this point, a certain window belonging to a certain pantry, and communicating with a certain yew-tree, which grew out of a steep cleft of the rock, being the very pass through which Goose Gibbie was smuggled out of the Castle in order to carry Edith's express to Charnwood, and which had probably, in its day, been used for other contraband purposes. Cuddie, resting upon the butt of his gun, and looking up at this window, observed to one of his companions, "There's a place I ken weel; mony a time I hae helped Jenny Dennison out o' the winnock, forbye creeping in whiles mysell to get some daffin' at e'en after the pleugh was loosed."

"And what's to hinder us to creep in just now?" said the other, who was a smart enterprising young fellow.

"There's no muckle to hinder us, an that were a'," answered Cuddie; "but what were we to do neist?"

"We'll take the Castle," cried the other; "here are five or six o' us, and a' the sodgers are engaged at the gate."

"Come awa' wi' you, then," said Cuddie; "but mind, deil a finger ye maun lay on Lady Margaret, or Miss Edith, or the auld Major, or, aboon a', on Jenny Dennison, or onybody but the sodgers; cut and quarter amang them as ye like, I carena."

"Ay, ay," said the other, "let us once in, and we will make our ain terms with them a'."

Gingerly, and as if treading upon eggs, Cuddie began to ascend the well-known pass, not very willingly; for, besides that he was something apprehensive of the reception he might meet with in the inside, his conscience insisted that he was making but a shabby requital for Lady Margaret's former favors and protection. He got up, however, into the yew-tree, followed by his companions, one after another. The window was small, and had been secured by stanchions of iron; but these had been long worn away by time, or forced out by the domestics to possess a free passage for their own occasional convenience. Entrance was therefore easy, providing there was no one in the pantry, a point which Cuddie endeavored to discover before he made the final and perilous step. While his companions, therefore, were urging and threatening him behind, and he was hesitating and stretching his neck to look into the apartment, his head became visible to Jenny Dennison, who had ensconced herself in said pantry as the safest place in which to wait the issue of the assault. So soon as this object of terror caught her eye, she set up an hysteric scream, flew to the adjacent kitchen, and, in the desperate agony of fear, seized on a pot of kail-brose which she herself had hung on the fire before the combat began, having promised to Tam Halliday to prepare his breakfast for him. Thus burdened, she returned to the window of the pantry, and still exclaiming, "Murder! murder!—we are a' harried and ravished—the Castle's taen—tak it amang ye!" she discharged the whole scalding contents of the pot, accompanied with a dismal yell, upon the person of the unfortunate Cuddie. However welcome the mess might have been, if Cuddie and it had become acquainted in a regular manner, the effects, as administered by Jenny, would probably have cured him of soldiering forever, had he been looking upwards when it was thrown upon him. But, fortunately for our man of war, he had taken the alarm upon Jenny's first scream, and was in the act of looking down, expostulating with his comrades, who impeded the retreat which he was anxious to commence; so that the steel cap and buff coat which formerly belonged to Sergeant Bothwell, being garments of an excellent endurance, protected his person against the greater part of the scalding brose. Enough, however, reached him to annoy him severely, so that in the pain and surprise he jumped hastily out of the tree, oversetting his followers, to the manifest danger of their limbs, and, without listening to arguments, entreaties, or authority, made the best of his way by the most safe road to the main body of the army whereunto he belonged, and could neither by threats nor persuasion be prevailed upon to return to the attack.

As for Jenny, when she had thus conferred upon one admirer's outward man the viands which her fair hands had so lately been in the act of preparing for the stomach of another, she continued her song of alarm, running a screaming division upon all those crimes which the lawyers call the four pleas of the crown, namely, murder, fire, rape, and robbery. These hideous exclamations gave so much alarm, and created such confusion within the Castle, that Major Bellenden and Lord Evandale judged it best to draw off from the conflict without the gates, and, abandoning to the enemy all the exterior defences of the avenue, confine themselves to the Castle itself, for fear of its being surprised on some unguarded point. Their retreat was unmolested; for the panic of Cuddie and his companions had occasioned nearly as much confusion on the side of the besiegers as the screams of Jenny had caused to the defenders.

There was no attempt on either side to renew the action that day. The insurgents had suffered most severely; and, from the difficulty which they had experienced in carrying the barricaded positions without the precincts of the Castle, they could have but little hope of storming the place itself. On the other hand, the situation of the besieged was disspiriting and gloomy. In the skirmishing they had lost two or three men, and had several wounded; and though their loss was in proportion greatly less than that of the enemy, who had left twenty men dead on the place, yet their small number could much worse spare it, while the desperate attacks of the opposite party plainly showed how serious the leaders were in the purpose of reducing the place, and how well seconded by the zeal of their followers. But, especially, the garrison had to fear for hunger, in case blockade should be resorted to as the means of reducing them. The Major's directions had been imperfectly obeyed in regard to laying in provisions ; and the dragoons, in spite of all warning and authority, were likely to be wasteful in using them. It was, therefore, with a heavy heart that Major Bellenden gave directions for guarding the window through which the Castle had so nearly been surprised, as well as all others which offered the most remote facility for such an enterprise.

CHAPTER XXVI

The King hath drawn
The special head of all the land together.
Henry IV., Part II.

THE leaders of the Presbyterian army had a serious consultation upon the evening of the day in which they had made the attack on Tillietudlem. They could not but observe that their followers were disheartened by the loss which they nad sustained, and which, as usual in such cases, had fallen upon the bravest and most forward. It was to be feared that, if they were suffered to exhaust their zeal and efforts in an object so secondary as the capture of this petty fort, their numbers would melt away by degrees, and they would lose all the advantages arising out of the present unprepared state of the government. Moved by these arguments, it was agreed that the main body of the army should march against Glasgow, and dislodge the soldiers who were lying in that town. The council nominated Henry Morton, with others, to this last service, and appointed Burley to the command of a chosen body of five hundred men, who were to remain behind for the purpose of blockading the Tower of Tillietudlem. Morton testified the greatest repugnance to this arrangement.

"He had the strongest personal motives," he said, "for desiring to remain near Tillietudlem ; and if the management of the siege were committed to him, he had little doubt but that he would bring it to such an accommodation as, without being rigorous to the besieged, would fully answer the purpose of the besiegers."

Burley readily guessed the cause of his young colleague's reluctance to move with the army ; for, interested as he was in appreciating the characters with whom he had to deal, he had contrived, through the simplicity of Cuddie and the enthusiasm of old Mause, to get much information concerning Morton's relations with the family of Tillietudlem. He therefore took the advantage of Poundtext's arising to speak to business, as he said, for some short space of time (which

Burley rightly interpreted to mean an hour at the very least),
and seized that moment to withdraw Morton from the hearing of their colleagues, and to hold the following argument
with him :

"Thou art unwise, Henry Morton, to desire to sacrifice
this holy cause to thy friendship for an uncircumcised Philistine, or thy lust for a Moabitish woman."

"I neither understand your meaning, Mr. Balfour, nor
relish your allusions," replied Morton, indignantly ; "and I
know no reason you have to bring so gross a charge or to use
such uncivil language."

"Confess, however, the truth," said Balfour, "and own
that there are those within yon dark Tower over whom thou
wouldst rather be watching like a mother over her little ones,
than thou wouldst bear the banner of the Church of Scotland over the necks of her enemies."

"If you mean that I would willingly terminate this war
without any bloody victory, and that I am more anxious to
do this than to acquire any personal fame or power, you may
be," replied Morton, "perfectly right."

"And not wholly wrong," answered Burley, "in deeming
that thou wouldst not exclude from so general a pacification
thy friends in the garrison of Tillietudlem."

"Certainly," replied Morton ; "I am too much obliged
to Major Bellenden not to wish to be of service to him, as
far as the interest of the cause I have espoused will permit.
I never made a secret of my regard for him."

"I am aware of that," said Burley ; "but if thou hadst
concealed it, I should, nevertheless, have found out thy riddle. Now, hearken to my words. This Miles Bellenden hath
means to subsist his garrison for a month."

"This is not the case," answered Morton ; "we know his
stores are hardly equal to a week's consumption."

"Ay, but," continued Burley, "I have since had proof,
of the strongest nature, that such a report was spread in the
garrison by that wily and gray-headed Malignant, partly to
prevail on the soldiers to submit to a diminution of their
daily food, partly to detain us before the walls of his fortress
until the sword should be whetted to smite and destroy us."

"And why was not the evidence of this laid before the
council of war ? " said Morton.

"To what purpose ? " said Balfour. "Why need we undeceive Kettledrummle, Macbriar, Poundtext, and Langcale
upon such a point ? Thyself must own, that whatever is
told to them escapes to the host out of the mouth of the

preachers at their next holding-forth. They are already discouraged by the thoughts of lying before the fort a week.
What would be the consequence were they ordered to prepare
for the leaguer of a month ?"

"But why conceal it, then, from me ? or why tell it me
now ? and, above all, what proofs have you got of the fact ?"
continued Morton.

"There are many proofs," replied Burley ; and he put into
his hands a number of requisitions sent forth by Major Bellenden, with receipts on the back to various proprietors, for
cattle, corn, meal, etc., to such an amount that the sum total
seemed to exclude the possibility of the garrison being soon
distressed for provisions. But Burley did not inform Morton
of a fact which he himself knew full well, namely, that most
of these provisions never reached the garrison, owing to the
rapacity of the dragoons sent to collect them, who readily sold
to one man what they took from another, and abused the
Major's press for stores pretty much as Sir John Falstaff did
that of the king for men.

"And now," continued Balfour, observing that he had
made the desired impression, "I have only to say that I concealed this from thee no longer than it was concealed from
myself, for I have only received these papers this morning ;
and I tell it unto thee now, that thou mayest go on thy way
rejoicing, and work the great work willingly at Glasgow, being
assured that no evil can befall thy friends in the Malignant
party, since their fort is abundantly victualled, and I possess
not numbers sufficient to do more against them than to prevent their sallying forth."

"And why," continued Morton, who felt an inexpressible
reluctance to acquiesce in Balfour's reasoning—"why not
permit me to remain in the command of this smaller party,
and march forward yourself to Glasgow ? It is the more honorable charge."

"And therefore, young man," answered Burley, "have I
labored that it should be committed to the son of Silas Morton. I am waxing old, and this gray head has had enough of
honor where it could be gathered by danger. I speak not of
the frothy bubble which men call earthly fame, but the honor
belonging to him that doth not the work negligently. But
thy career is yet to run. Thou hast to vindicate the high
trust which has been bestowed on thee through my assurance
that it was dearly well-merited. At Loudon Hill thou wert
a captive, and at the last assault it was thy part to fight under
cover, while I led the more open and dangerous attack ; and,

shouldst thou now remain before these walls when there is active service elsewhere, trust me, that men will say that the son of Silas Morton hath fallen away from the paths of his father."

Stung by this last observation, to which, as a gentleman and soldier, he could offer no suitable reply, Morton hastily acquiesced in the proposed arrangement. Yet he was unable to divest himself of certain feelings of distrust which he involuntarily attached to the quarter from which he received this information.

" Mr. Balfour," he said, " let us distinctly understand each other. You have thought it worth your while to bestow particular attention upon my private affairs and personal attachments ; be so good as to understand that I am as constant to them as to my political principles. It is possible that, during my absence, you may possess the power of soothing or of wounding those feelings. Be assured that, whatever may be the consequences to the issue of our present adventure, my eternal gratitude or my persevering resentment will attend the line of conduct you may adopt on such an occasion ; and however young and inexperienced I am, l have no doubt of finding friends to assist me in expressing my sentiments in either case."

" If there be a threat implied in that denunciation," replied Burley, coldly and haughtily, " it had better have been spared. I know how to value the regard of my friends, and despise, from my soul, the threats of my enemies. But I will not take occasion of offence. Whatever happens here in your absence shall be managed with as much deference to your wishes as the duty I owe to a higher power can possibly permit."

With this qualified promise Morton was obliged to rest satisfied.

" Our defeat will relieve the garrison," said he, internally, " ere they can be reduced to surrender at discretion ; and, in case of victory, I already see, from the numbers of the Moderate party, that I shall have a voice as powerful as Burley's in determining the use which shall be made of it."

He therefore followed Balfour to the council, where they found Kettledrummle [Poundtext] adding to his *lastly* a few words of practical application. When these were expended, Morton testified his willingness to accompany the main body of the army, which was destined to drive the regular troops from Glasgow. His companions in command were named, and the whole received a strengthening exhortation from the preachers who were present. Next morning, at break of day, the insurgent army broke up from their encampment and marched towards Glasgow.

It is not our intention to detail at length incidents which may be found in the history of the period. It is sufficient to say that Claverhouse and Lord Ross, learning the superior force which was directed against them, intrenched, or rather barricaded, themselves in the centre of the city, where the town-house and old jail were situated, with the determination to stand the assault of the insurgents rather than to abandon the capital of the west of Scotland. The Presbyterians made their attack in two bodies, one of which penetrated into the city in the line of the college and cathedral church, while the other marched up the Gallowgate or principal access from the south-east. Both divisions were led by men of resolution, and behaved with great spirit. But the advantages of military skill and situation were too great for their undisciplined valor.

Ross and Claverhouse had carefully disposed parties of their soldiers in houses, at the heads of the streets, and in the entrances of closes, as they are called, or lanes, besides those who were intrenched behind breastworks which reached across the streets. The assailants found their ranks thinned by a fire from invisible opponents, which they had no means of returning with effect. It was in vain that Morton and other leaders exposed their persons with the utmost gallantry, and endeavored to bring their antagonists to a close action ; their followers shrank from them in every direction. And yet, though Henry Morton was one of the very last to retire, and exerted himself in bringing up the rear, maintaining order in the retreat, and checking every attempt which the enemy made to improve the advantage they had gained by the repulse, he had still the mortification to hear many of those in his ranks muttering to each other, that " this came of trusting to latitudinarian boys ; and that, had honest, faithful Burley led the attack, as he did that of the barricades of Tillietudlem, the issue would have been as different as might be."

It was with burning resentment that Morton heard these reflections thrown out by the very men who had soonest exhibited signs of discouragement. The unjust reproach, however, had the effect of firing his emulation, and making him sensible that, engaged as he was in a perilous cause, it was absolutely necessary that he should conquer or die.

"I have no retreat," he said to himself. "All shall allow—even Major Bellenden—even Edith—that in courage. at least, the rebel Morton was not inferior to his father."

The condition of the army after the repulse wa⁀ so undisciplined, and in such disorganization, that the leaders thought it prudent to draw off some miles from the city to gain time for reducing them once more into such order as they were capable of adopting. Recruits, in the meanwhile, came fast in, more moved by the extreme hardships of their own condition, and encouraged by the advantage obtained at Loudon Hill, than deterred by the last unfortunate enterprise. Many of these attached themselves particularly to Morton's division. He had, however, the mortification to see that his unpopularity among the more intolerant part of the Covenanters increased rapidly. The prudence beyond his years which he exhibited in improving the discipline and arrangement of his followers, they termed a trusting in the arm of flesh, and his avowed tolerance for those of religious sentiments and observances different from his own obtained him, most unjustly, the nickname of Gallio, "who cared for none of those things." What was worse than these misconceptions, the mob of the insurgents, always loudest in applause of those who push political or religious opinions to extremity, and disgusted with such as endeavor to reduce them to the yoke of discipline, preferred avowedly the more zealous leaders, in whose ranks enthusiasm in the cause supplied the want of good order and military subjection, to the restraints which Morton endeavored to bring them under. In short, while bearing the principal burden of command—for his colleagues willingly relinquished in his favor everything that was troublesome and obnoxious in the office of general—Morton found himself without that authority which alone could render his regulations effectual.*

Yet, notwithstanding these obstacles, he had, during the course of a few days, labored so hard to introduce some degree of discipline into the army, that he thought he might hazard a second attack upon Glasgow with every prospect of success.

It cannot be doubted that Morton's anxiety to measure himself with Colonel Grahame of Claverhouse, at whose hands he had sustained such injury, had its share in giving motive to his uncommon exertions. But Claverhouse disappointed his hopes; for, satisfied with having the advantage in repulsing the first attack upon Glasgow, he determined that he would not, with the handful of troops under his command, await a second assault from the insurgents, with more numerous and better disciplined forces than had supported their

* See Dissensions among the Covenanters. Note 25.

first enterprise. He therefore evacuated the place, and marched at the head of his troops towards Edinburgh. The insurgents of course entered Glasgow without resistance and without Morton having the opportunity, which he so deeply coveted, of again encountering Claverhouse personally. But, although he had not an opportunity of wiping away the disgrace which had befallen his division of the army of the Covenant, the retreat of Claverhouse, and the possession of Glasgow, tended greatly to animate the insurgent army, and to increase its numbers. The necessity of appointing new otficers, of organizing new regiments and squadrons, of making them acquainted with at least the most necessary points of military discipline, were labors which, by universal consent, seemed to be devolved upon Henry Morton, and which he the more readily undertook, because his father had made him acquainted with the theory of the military art, and because he plainly saw that, unless he took this ungracious but absolutely necessary labor, it was vain to expect any other to engage in it.

In the meanwhile, fortune appeared to favor the enterprise of the insurgents more than the most sanguine durst have expected. The privy council of Scotland, astonished at the extent of resistance which their arbitrary measures had provoked, seemed stupefied with terror, and incapable of taking active steps to subdue the resentment which these measures had excited. There were but very few troops in Scotland, and these they drew towards Edinburgh, as if to form an army for protection of the metropolis. The feudal array of the crown vassals in the various counties was ordered to take the field, and render to the king the military service due for their fiefs. But the summons was very slackly obeyed. The quarrel was not generally popular among the gentry; and even those who were not unwilling themselves to have taken arms were deterred by the repugnance of their wives, mothers, and sisters to their engaging in such a cause.

Meanwhile, the inadequacy of the Scottish government to provide for their own defence, or to put down a rebellion of which the commencement seemed so trifling, excited at the English court doubts at once of their capacity and of the prudence of the severities they had exerted against the oppressed Presbyterians. It was, therefore, resolved to nominate to the command of the army of Scotland the unfortunate Duke of Monmouth, who had by marriage a great interest, large estate, and a numerous following, as it was called, in the southern parts of that kingdom. The military skill which he had displayed on different occasions abroad was supposed more than adequate to subdue the insurgents in the field; while it was expected that his mild temper, and the favorable disposition which he showed to Presbyterians in general, might soften men's minds and tend to reconcile them to the government. The Duke was, therefore, invested with a commission, containing high powers for settling the distracted affairs of Scotland, and despatched from London with strong succors to take the principal military command in that country.

CHAPTER XXVII

THERE was now a pause in the military movements on both sides. The government seemed contented to prevent the rebels advancing towards the capital, while the insurgents were intent upon augmenting and strengthening their forces. For this purpose they established a sort of encampment in the park belonging to the ducal residence at Hamilton, a centrical situation for receiving their recruits, and where they were secured from any sudden attack by having the Clyde, a deep and rapid river, in front of their position, which is only passable by a long and narrow bridge, near the castle and village of Bothwell.

Morton remained here for about a fortnight after the attack on Glasgow, actively engaged in his military duties. He had received more than one communication from Burley; but they only stated, in general, that the Castle of Tillietudlem continued to hold out. Impatient of suspense upon this most interesting subject, he at length intimated to his colleagues in command his desire, or rather his intention—for he saw no reason why he should not assume a license which was taken by every one else in this disorderly army—to go to Milnwood for a day or two to arrange some private affairs of consequence. The proposal was by no means approved of; for the military council of the insurgents were sufficiently sensible of the value of his services to fear to lose them, and felt somewhat conscious of their own inability to supply his place. They could not, however, pretend to dictate to him laws more rigid than they submitted to themselves, and he was suffered to depart on his journey without any direct objection being stated. The Reverend Mr. Poundtext took the same opportunity to pay a visit to his own residence in the neighborhood of Milnwood, and favored Morton with his company on the journey. As the country was chiefly friendly to their cause, and in possession of their detached parties, excepting here and there the stronghold of some old Cavaliering baron, they travelled without any other attendant than the faithful Cuddie.

It was near sunset when they reached Milnwood, where Poundtext bid adieu to his companions, and travelled forward alone to his own manse, which was situated half a mile's march beyond Tillietudlem. When Morton was left alone to his own reflections, with what a complication of feelings did he review the woods, banks, and fields that had been familiar to him! His character, as well as his habits, thoughts, and occupations, had been entirely changed within the space of little more than a fortnight, and twenty days seemed to have done upon him the work of as many years. A mild, romantic, gentle-tempered youth, bred up in dependence, and stooping patiently to the control of a sordid and tyrannical relation, had suddenly, by the rod of oppression and the spur of injured feeling, been compelled to stand forth a leader of armed men, was earnestly engaged in affairs of a public nature, had friends to animate and enemies to contend with, and felt his individual fate bound up in that of a national insurrection and revolution. It seemed as if he had at once experienced a transition from the romantic dreams of youth to the labors and cares of active manhood. All that had formerly interested him was obliterated from his memory, excepting only his attachment to Edith; and even his love seemed to have assumed a character more manly and disinterested, as it had become mingled and contrasted with other duties and feelings. As he revolved the particulars of this sudden change, the circumstances in which it originated, and the possible consequences of his present career, the thrill of natural anxiety which passed along his mind was immediately banished by a glow of generous and high-spirited confidence.

"I shall fall young," he said, "if fall I must, my motives misconstrued and my actions condemned by those whose approbation is dearest to me. But the sword of liberty and patriotism is in my hand, and I will neither fall meanly nor unavenged. They may expose my body and gibbet my limbs; but other days will come, when the sentence of infamy will recoil against those who may pronounce it. And that Heaven whose name is so often profaned during this unnatural war will bear witness to the purity of the motives by which I have been guided."

Upon approaching Milnwood, Henry's knock upon the gate no longer intimated the conscious timidity of a stripling who has been out of bounds, but the confidence of a man in full possession of his own rights, and master of his own actions—bold, free, and decided. The door was cautiously opened by his old acquaintance, Mrs. Alison Wilson, who started back when she saw the steel cap and nodding plume of the martial visitor.

"Where is my uncle, Alison ?" said Morton, smiling at her alarm.

"Lordsake, Mr. Harry ! is this you ?" returned the old lady. "In troth, ye garr'd my heart loup to my very mouth. But it canna be your ainsell, for ye look taller and mair manly-like than ye used to do."

"It is, however, my own self," said Henry, sighing and smiling at the same time. "I believe this dress may make me look taller, and these times, Ailie, make men out of boys."

"Sad times indeed !" echoed the old woman ; "and O that you suld been dangered wi' them ! But wha can help it ? ye were ill eneugh guided, and, as I tell your uncle, if ye tread on a worm it will turn."

"You were always my advocate, Ailie," said he, and the housekeeper no longer resented the familiar epithet, "and would let no one blame me but yourself, I am aware of that. Where is my uncle ?"

"In Edinburgh," replied Alison ; "the honest man thought it was best to gang and sit by the chimley when the reek rase. A vex'd man he's been and a feared—but ye ken the Laird as weel as I do."

"I hope he has suffered nothing in health ?" said Henry.

"Naething to speak of," answered the housekeeper, "nor in gudes neither ; we fended as weel as we could ; and, though the troopers of Tillietudlem took the red cow and auld Hackie—ye'll mind them weel—yet they sauld us a gude bargain o' four they were driving to the Castle."

"Sold you a bargain ?" said Morton ; "how do you mean ?"

"Ou, they cam out to gather marts for the garrison," answered the housekeeper ; "but they just fell to their auld trade, and rade through the country couping and selling a' that they gat, like sae mony west-country drovers. My certie, Major Bellenden was laird o' the least share o' what they lifted, though it was taen in his name."

"Then," said Morton, hastily, "the garrison must be straitened for provisions ?"

"Stressed eneugh," replied Ailie, "there's little doubt·o' that."

A light instantly glanced on Morton's mind.

"Burley must have deceived me; craft as well as cruelty is permitted by his creed." Such was his inward thought ; he said aloud, "I cannot stay, Mrs. Wilson ; I must go forward directly."

" But, oh ! bide to eat a mouthfu'," entreated the affectionate housekeeper, "and I'll mak it ready for you as I used to do afore thae sad days."

" It is impossible," answered Morton.   " Cuddie, get our horses ready."

" They're just eating their corn," answered the attendant.

" Cuddie !" exclaimed Ailie; " what garr'd ye bring that ill-faur'd, unlucky loon alang wi' ye ?   It was him and his randie mother began a' the mischief in this house."

" Tut, tut," replied Cuddie, " ye should forget and forgie, mistress.   Mither's in Glasgow wi' her tittie, and sall plague ye nae mair ; and I'm the Captain's wallie now, and I keep him tighter in thack and rape than ever ye did ; saw ye him ever sae weel put on as he is now ? "

"In troth and that's true," said the old housekeeper, looking with great complacency at her young master, whose mien she thought much improved by his dress.   " I'm sure ye ne'er had a laced cravat like that when ye were at Milnwood ; that's nane o' my sewing."

" Na, na, mistress," replied Cuddie, " that's a cast o' my hand ; that's ane o' Lord Evandale's braws."

" Lord Evandale !" answered the old lady, " that's him that the Whigs are gaun to hang the morn, as I hear say."

" The Whigs about to hang Lord Evandale ?" said Morton, in the greatest surprise.

" Ay, troth are they," said the housekeeper.   " Yesterday night he made a sally, as they ca't—my mother's name was Sally ; I wonder they gie Christian folks' names to sic unchristian doings—but he made an outbreak to get provisions, and his men were driven back and he was taen, an' the Whig Captain Balfour garr'd set up a gallows, and swore—or said upon his conscience, for they winna swear—that if the garrison was not gien ower the morn by daybreak, he would hing up the young lord, poor thing, as high as Haman.   These are sair times ! but folk canna help them, sae do ye sit down and tak bread and cheese until better meat's made ready.   Ye suldna hae kenn'd a word about it, an I had thought it was to spoil your dinner, hinny."

" Fed or unfed," exclaimed Morton, " saddle the horses instantly, Cuddie.   We must not rest until we get before the Castle."

And, resisting all Ailie's entreaties, they instantly resumed their journey.

Morton failed not to halt at the dwelling of Poundtext and summon him to attend him to the camp. That honest divine had just resumed for an instant his pacific habits, and was perusing an ancient theological treatise, with a pipe in his mouth and a small jug of ale beside him, to assist his digestion of the argument. It was with bitter ill-will that he relinquished these comforts, which he called his studies, in order to recommence a hard ride upon a high-trotting horse. However, when he knew the matter in hand, he gave up, with a deep groan, the prospect of spending a quiet evening in his own little parlor ; for he entirely agreed with Morton that, whatever interest Burley might have in rendering the breach between the Presbyterians and the government irreconcilable, by putting the young nobleman to death, it was by no means that of the Moderate party to permit such an act of atrocity. And it is but doing justice to Mr. Poundtext to add that, like most of his own persuasion, he was decidedly adverse to any such acts of unnecessary violence ; besides, that his own present feelings induced him to listen with much complacence to the probability held out by Morton of Lord Evandale's becoming a mediator for the establishment of peace upon fair and moderate terms. With this similarity of views, they hastened their journey, and arrived about eleven o'clock at night at a small hamlet adjacent to the Castle of Tillietudlem, where Burley had established his headquarters.

They were challenged by the sentinel, who made his melancholy walk at the entrance of the hamlet, and admitted upon declaring their names and authority in the army. Another soldier kept watch before a house, which they conjectured to be the place of Lord Evandale's confinement, for a gibbet * of such great height as to be visible from the battlements of the Castle was erected before it, in melancholy confirmation of the truth of Mrs. Wilson's report. Morton instantly demanded to speak with Burley, and was directed to his quarters. They found him reading the Scriptures, with his arms lying beside him, as if ready for any sudden alarm. He started upon the entrance of his colleagues in office.

"What has brought ye hither?" said Burley, hastily. "Is there bad news from the army?"

"No," replied Morton ; "but we understand that there are measures adopted here in which the safety of the army is deeply concerned. Lord Evandale is your prisoner?"

"The Lord," replied Burley, "hath delivered him into our hands."

* See The Cameronians' Gibbet. Note 26.

"And you will avail yourself of that advantage, granted you by Heaven, to dishonor our cause in the eyes of all the world, by putting a prisoner to an ignominious death ?"

"If the house of Tillietudlem be not surrendered by daybreak," replied Burley, "God do so to me and more also, if he shall not die that death to which his leader and patron, John Grahame of Claverhouse, hath put so many of God's saints."

"We are in arms," replied Morton, "to put down such cruelties, and not to imitate them, far less to avenge upon the innocent the acts of the guilty. By what law can you justify the atrocity you would commit ?"

"If thou art ignorant of it," replied Burley, "thy companion is well aware of the law which gave the men of Jericho to the sword of Joshua, the son of Nun."

"But we," answered the divine, "live under a better dispensation, which instructeth us to return good for evil, and to pray for those who despitefully use us and persecute us."

"That is to say," said Burley, "that thou wilt join thy gray hairs to his green youth to controvert me in this matter ?"

"We are," rejoined Poundtext, "two of those to whom, jointly with thyself, authority is delegated over this host, and we will not permit thee to hurt a hair of the prisoner's head. It may please God to make him a means of healing these unhappy breaches in our Israel."

"I judged it would come to this," answered Burley, "when such as thou wert called into the council of the elders."

"Such as I !" answered Poundtext. "And who am I, that you should name me with such scorn ? Have I not kept the flock of this sheepfold from the wolves for thirty years ? Ay, even while thou, John Balfour, wert fighting in the ranks of uncircumcision, a Philistine of hardened brow and bloody hand. Who am I, say'st thou ?"

"I will tell thee what thou art, since thou wouldst so fain know," said Burley. "Thou art one of those who would reap where thou hast not sowed, and divide the spoil while others fight the battle ; thou art one of those that follow the Gospel for the loaves and for the fishes, that love their own manse better than the church of God, and that would rather draw their stipends under Prelatists or heathens than be a partaker with those noble spirits who have cast all behind them for the sake of the Covenant."

"And I will tell thee, John Balfour," returned Poundtext, deservedly incensed—"I will tell thee what *thou* art. Thou art one of those for whose bloody and merciless disposition a reproach is flung upon the whole church of this suffering kingdom, and for whose violence and blood-guiltiness, it is to be feared, this fair attempt to recover our civil and religious rights will never be honored by Providence with the desired success."

"Gentlemen," said Morton, "cease this irritating and unavailing recrimination ; and do you, Mr. Balfour, inform us whether it is your purpose to oppose the liberation of Lord Evandale, which appears to us a profitable measure in the present position of our affairs ?"

"You are here," answered Burley, "as two voices against one, but you will not refuse to tarry until the united council shall decide upon this matter ?"

"This," said Morton, "we would not decline if we could trust the hands in whom we are to leave the prisoner. But you know well," he added, looking sternly at Burley, "that you have already deceived me in this matter."

"Go to," said Burley, disdainfully, "thou art an idle, inconsiderate boy, who, for the black eyebrows of a silly girl, would barter thy own faith and honor, and the cause of God and of thy country."

"Mr. Balfour," said Morton, laying his hand on his sword, "this language requires satisfaction."

"And thou shalt have it, stripling, when and where thou darest," said Burley ; "I plight thee my good word on it."

Poundtext, in his turn, interfered to remind them of the madness of quarrelling, and effected with difficulty a sort of sullen reconciliation.

"Concerning the prisoner," said Burley, "deal with him as ye think fit.   I wash my hands free from all consequences. He is my prisoner, made by my sword and spear, while you, Mr. Morton, were playing the adjutant at drills and parades, and you, Mr. Poundtext, were warping the Scriptures into Erastianism.   Take him unto you, nevertheless, and dispose of him as ye think meet.   Dingwall," he continued, calling a sort of aide-de-camp who slept in the next apartment, "let the guard posted on the Malignant Evandale give up their post to those whom Captain Morton shall appoint to relieve them.   The prisoner," he said, again addressing Poundtext and Morton, "is now at your disposal, gentlemen.   But remember that for all these things there will one day come a term of heavy accounting."

So saying, he turned abruptly into an inner apartment without bidding them good evening.   His two visitors, after a moment's consideration, agreed it would be prudent to insure the prisoner's personal safety by placing over him an additional guard, chosen from their own parishioners. A band of them happened to be stationed in the hamlet, having been attached for the time to Burley's command, in order that the men might be gratified by remaining as long as possible near to their own homes. They were, in general, smart, active young fellows, and were usually called by their companions the Marksmen of Milnwood. By Morton's desire, four of these lads readily undertook the task of sentinels, and he left with them Headrigg, on whose fidelity he could depend, with instructions to call him if anything remarkable happened.

This arrangement being made, Morton and his colleague took possession for the night of such quarters as the over-crowded and miserable hamlet could afford them. They did not, however, separate for repose till they had drawn up a memorial of the grievances of the Moderate Presbyterians, which was summed up with a request of free toleration for their religion in future, and that they should be permitted to attend Gospel ordinances as dispensed by their own clergymen, without oppression or molestation. Their petition proceeded to require that a free parliament should be called for settling the affairs of Church and State, and for redressing the injuries sustained by the subject ; and that all those who either now were or had been in arms for obtaining these ends should be indemnified. Morton could not but strongly hope that these terms, which comprehended all that was wanted, or wished · for, by the Moderate party among the insurgents, might, when thus cleared of the violence of fanaticism, find advocates even among the Royalists, as claiming only the ordinary rights of Scottish freemen.

He had the more confidence of a favorable reception, that the Duke of Monmouth, to whom Charles had intrusted the charge of subduing this rebellion, was a man of gentle, moderate, and accessible disposition, well known to be favorable to the Presbyterians, and invested by the king with full powers to take measures for quieting the disturbances in Scotland. It seemed to Morton that all that was necessary for influencing him in their favor was to find a fit and sufficiently respectable channel of communication, and such seemed to be opened through the medium of Lord Evandale. He resolved, therefore, to visit the prisoner early in the morning, in order to sound his dispositions to undertake the task of mediator ; but an accident happened which led him to anticipate his purpose.

CHAPTER XXVIII

Gie ower your house, lady, he said,—
Gie ower your house to me.
                    Edom of Gordon.

MORTON had finished the revisal and the making out of a fair
copy of the paper on which he and Poundtext had agreed to
rest as a full statement of the grievances of their party, and
the conditions on which the greater part of the insurgents
would be contented to lay down their arms ; and he was about
to betake himself to repose, when there was a knocking at the
door of his apartment.

"Enter," said Morton ; and the round bullet-head of
Cuddie Headrigg was thrust into the room. "Come in," said
Morton, "and tell me what you want.   Is there any alarm ?"

"Na, stir ; but I hae brought ane to speak wi' you."

"Who is that, Cuddie ?" inquired Morton.

"Ane o' your auld acquaintance," said Cuddie ; and opening the door more fully, he half led, half dragged in a woman,
whose face was muffled in her plaid. "Come, come, ye needna
be sae bashfu' before auld acquaintance, Jenny," said Cuddie,
pulling down the veil, and discovering to his master the well-
remembered countenance of Jenny Dennison. "Tell his
honor, now, there's a braw lass—tell him what ye were wanting to say to Lord Evandale, mistress."

"What was I wanting to say," answered Jenny, "to his
honor himsell the other morning, when I visited him in captivity, ye muckle hash ?   D'ye think that folk dinna want to
see their friends in adversity, ye dour crowdy-eater ?"

This reply was made with Jenny's usual volubility ; but
her voice quivered, her cheek was thin and pale, the tears
stood in her eyes, her hand trembled, her manner was fluttered, and her whole presence bore marks of recent suffering
and privation, as well as nervous and hysterical agitation.

"What is the matter, Jenny ?" said Morton, kindly.
"You know how much I owe you in many respects, and can
hardly make a request that I will not grant, if in my power."

"Many thanks, Milnwood," said the weeping damsel ;

"but ye were aye a kind gentleman, though folk say ye hae become sair changed now."

"What do they say of me?" answered Morton.

"A'body says," replied Jenny, "that you and the Whigs hae made a vow to ding King Charles aff the throne, and that neither he, nor his posteriors from generation to generation, shall sit upon it ony mair; and John Gudyill threeps ye're to gie a' the church organs to the pipers, and burn the Book o' Common Prayer by the hands of the common hangman, in revenge of the Covenant that was burnt when the King cam hame."

"My friends at Tillietudlem judge too hastily and too ill of me," answered Morton. "I wish to have free exercise of my own religion, without insulting any other; and as to your family, I only desire an opportunity to show them I have the same friendship and kindness as ever."

"Bless your kind heart for saying sae," said Jenny, bursting into a flood of tears; "and they never needed kindness or friendship mair, for they are famished for lack o' food."

"Good God!" replied Morton, "I have heard of scarcity, but not of famine. Is it possible? Have the ladies and the Major——"

"They hae suffered like the lave o' us," replied Jenny; "for they shared every bit and sup wi' the whole folk in the Castle. I'm sure my poor een see fifty colors wi' faintness, and my head's sae dizzy wi' the mirligoes that I canna stand my lane."

The thinness of the poor girl's cheek, and the sharpness of her features, bore witness to the truth of what she said. Morton was greatly shocked.

"Sit down," he said, "for God's sake!" forcing her into the only chair the apartment afforded, while he himself strode up and down the room in horror and impatience. "I knew not of this," he exclaimed, in broken ejaculations—"I could not know of it. Cold-blooded, iron-hearted fanatic—deceitful villain! Cuddie, fetch refreshments—food—wine, if possible—whatever you can find."

"Whiskey is gude eneugh for her," muttered Cuddie; "ane wadna hae thought that gude meal was sae scant amang them, when the quean threw sae muckle gude kail-brose scalding het about my lugs."

Faint and miserable as Jenny seemed to be, she could not hear the allusion to her exploit during the storm of the Castle without bursting into a laugh, which weakness soon converted into an hysterical giggle. Confounded at her state, and reflecting with horror on the distress which must have been in the Castle, Morton repeated his commands to Headrigg in a peremptory manner; and when he had departed, endeavored to soothe his visitor.

"You come, I suppose, by the orders of your mistress, to visit Lord Evandale? Tell me what she desires; her orders shall be my law."

Jenny appeared to reflect a moment, and then said, "Your honor is sae auld a friend, I must needs trust to you, and tell the truth."

"Be assured, Jenny," said Morton, observing that she hesitated, "that you will best serve your mistress by dealing sincerely with me."

"Weel, then, ye maun ken we're starving, as I said before, and have been mair days than ane; and the Major has sworn that he expects relief daily, and that he will not gie ower the house to the enemy till we have eaten up his auld boots—and they are unco thick in the soles, as ye may weel mind, forbye being teugh in the upper-leather. The dragoons, again, they think they will be forced to gie up at last, and they canna bide hunger weel, after the life they led at free quarters for this while bypast; and since Lord Evandale's taen, there's nae guiding them; and Inglis says he'll gie up the garrison to the Whigs, and the Major and the leddies into the bargain, if they will but let the troopers gang free themsells."

"Scoundrels!" said Morton; "why do they not make terms for all in the Castle?"

"They are fear'd for denial o' quarter to themsells, having dune sae muckle mischief through the country; and Burley has hanged ane or twa o' them already; sae they want to draw their ain necks out o' the collar at hazard o' honest folks'."

"And you were sent," continued Morton, "to carry to Lord Evandale the unpleasant news of the men's mutiny?"

"Just e'en sae," said Jenny; "Tam Halliday took the rue, and tauld me a' about it, and gat me out o' the Castle to tell Lord Evandale, if possibly I could win at him."

"But how can he help you?" said Morton; "he is a prisoner."

"Well-a-day, ay," answered the afflicted damsel; "but maybe he could mak fair terms for us; or maybe he could gie us some good advice; or maybe he might send his orders to the dragoons to be civil; or——"

"Or maybe," said Morton, "you were to try if it were possible to set him at liberty?"

"If it were sae," answered Jenny, with spirit, "it wadna be the first time I hae done my best to serve a friend in captivity."

"True, Jenny," replied Morton, "I were most ungrateful to forget it. But here comes Cuddie with refreshments; I will go and do your errand to Lord Evandale while you take some food and wine."

"It willna be amiss ye should ken," said Cuddie to his master, "that this Jenny—this Mrs. Dennison—was trying to cuittle favor wi' Tam Rand, the miller's man, to win into Lord Evandale's room without onybody kennin'. She wasna thinking, the gypsy, that I was at her elbow."

"And an unco fright ye gae me when ye cam ahint and took a grip o' me," said Jenny, giving him a sly twitch with her finger and her thumb; "if ye hadna been an auld acquaintance, ye daft gomeril——"

Cuddie, somewhat relenting, grinned a smile on his artful mistress, while Morton wrapped himself up in his cloak, took his sword under his arm, and went straight to the place of the young nobleman's confinement. He asked the sentinels if anything extraordinary had occurred."

"Nothing worth notice," they said, "excepting the lass that Cuddie took up, and two couriers that Captain Balfour had despatched, one to the Reverend Ephraim Macbriar, another to Kettledrummle," both of whom were beating the drum ecclesiastic in different towns between the position of Burley and the headquarters of the main army near Hamilton.

"The purpose, I presume," said Morton, with an affectation of indifference, "was to call them hither."

"So I understand," answered the sentinel, who had spoke with the messengers.

"He is summoning a triumphant majority of the council," thought Morton to himself, "for the purpose of sanctioning whatever action of atrocity he may determine upon, and thwarting opposition by authority. I must be speedy, or I shall lose my opportunity."

When he entered the place of Lord Evandale's confinement, he found him ironed, and reclining on a flock bed in the wretched garret of a miserable cottage. He was either in a slumber or in deep meditation when Morton entered, and turned on him, when aroused, a countenance so much reduced by loss of blood, want of sleep, and scarcity of food, that no one could have recognized in it the gallant soldier who had behaved with so much spirit at the skirmish of Loudon Hill. He displayed some surprise at the sudden entrance of Morton.

"I am sorry to see you thus, my lord," said that youthful leader.

"I have heard you are an admirer of poetry," answered the prisoner; "in that case, Mr. Morton, you may remember these lines—

> "Stone walls do not a prison make,
>   Or iron bars a cage;
> A free and quiet mind can take
>   These for a hermitage.

But were my imprisonment less endurable, I am given to expect to-morrow a total enfranchisement."

"By death?" said Morton.

"Surely," answered Lord Evandale; "I have no other prospect. Your comrade, Burley, has already dipped his hand in the blood of men whose meanness of rank and obscurity of extraction might have saved them. I cannot boast such a shield from his vengeance, and I expect to meet its extremity."

"But Major Bellenden," said Morton, "may surrender in order to preserve your life."

"Never, while there is one man to defend the battlement, and that man has one crust to eat. I know his gallant resolution, and grieved should I be if he changed it for my sake."

Morton hastened to acquaint him with the mutiny among the dragoons, and their resolution to surrender the Castle, and put the ladies of the family, as well as the Major, into the hands of the enemy. Lord Evandale seemed at first surprised and something incredulous, but immediately afterwards deeply affected.

"What is to be done?" he said. "How is this misfortune to be averted?"

"Hear me, my lord," said Morton. "I believe you may not be unwilling to bear the olive branch between our master the King and that part of his subjects which is now in arms, not from choice but necessity."

"You construe me but justly," said Lord Evandale; "but to what does this tend?"

"Permit me, my lord——" continued Morton. "I will set you at liberty upon parole; nay, you may return to the Castle, and shall have a safe-conduct for the ladies, the Major, and all who leave it, on condition of its instant surrender. In contributing to bring this about you will only submit to circumstances ; for, with a mutiny in the garrison, and without provisions, it will be found impossible to defend the place twenty-four hours longer. Those, therefore, who refuse to accompany your lordship must take their fate. You and your followers shall have a free pass to Edinburgh, or wherever the Duke of Monmouth may be. In return for your liberty, we hope that you will recommend to the notice of his Grace, as Lieutenant-General of Scotland, this humble petition and remonstrance, containing the grievances which have occasioned this insurrection, a redress of which being granted, I will answer with my head that the great body of the insurgents will lay down their arms."

Lord Evandale read over the paper with attention.

"Mr. Morton," he said, "in my simple judgment I see little objection that can be made to the measures here recommended ; nay, further, I believe, in many respects, they may meet the private sentiments of the Duke of Monmouth ; and yet, to deal frankly with you, I have no hopes of their being granted, unless, in the first place, you were to lay down your arms."

" The doing so," answered Morton, "would be virtually conceding that we had no right to take them up ; and that, for one, I will never agree to."

" Perhaps it is hardly to be expected you should," said Lord Evandale ; " and yet on that point I am certain the negotiations will be wrecked. I am willing, however, having frankly told you my opinion, to do all in my power to bring about a reconciliation."

" It is all we can wish or expect," replied Morton ; " the issue is in God's hands, who disposes the hearts of princes. You accept, then, the safe-conduct ? "

" Certainly," answered Lord Evandale ; " and if I do not enlarge upon the obligation incurred by your having saved my life a second time, believe that I do not feel it the less."

" And the garrison of Tillietudlem ? " said Morton.

" Shall be withdrawn as you propose," answered the young nobleman. " I am sensible the Major will be unable to bring the mutineers to reason ; and I tremble to think of the consequences, should the ladies and the brave old man be delivered up to this bloodthirsty ruffian, Burley."

" You are in that case free," said Morton. " Prepare to mount on horseback ; a few men whom I can trust shall attend you till you are in safety from our parties."

Leaving Lord Evandale in great surprise and joy at this unexpected deliverance, Morton hastened to get a few chosen

men under arms and on horseback, each rider holding the
rein of a spare horse. Jenny, who, while she partook of her
refreshment, had contrived to make up her breach with Cuddie, rode on the left hand of that valiant cavalier. The tramp
of their horses was soon heard under the window of Lord
Evandale's prison. Two men whom he did not know entered
the apartment, disencumbered him of his fetters, and, conducting him downstairs, mounted him in the centre of the
detachment. They set out at a round trot towards Tillietudlem.

The moonlight was giving way to the dawn when they
approached that ancient fortress, and its dark massive tower
had just received the first pale coloring of the morning. The
party halted at the Tower barrier, not venturing to approach
nearer for fear of the fire of the place. Lord Evandale alone
rode up to the gate, followed at a distance by Jenny Dennison. As they approached the gate, there was heard to arise
in the courtyard a tumult which accorded ill with the quiet
serenity of a summer dawn. Cries and oaths were heard, a
pistol-shot or two were discharged, and everything announced
that the mutiny had broken out. At this crisis Lord Evandale arrived at the gate where Halliday was sentinel. On
hearing Lord Evandale's voice he instantly and gladly admitted him, and that nobleman arrived among the mutinous
troopers like a man dropped from the clouds. They were in
the act of putting their design into execution, of seizing the
place into their own hands, and were about to disarm and
overpower Major Bellenden and Harrison, and others of the
Castle, who were offering the best resistance in their power.

The appearance of Lord Evandale changed the scene. He
seized Inglis by the collar, and, upbraiding him with his villany, ordered two of his comrades to seize and bind him,
assuring the others that their only chance of impunity consisted in instant submission. He then ordered the men into
their ranks. They obeyed. He commanded them to ground
their arms. They hesitated ; but the instinct of discipline,
joined to their persuasion that the authority of their officer, so
boldly exerted, must be supported by some forces without the
gate, induced them to submit.

"Take away those arms," said Lord Evandale to the people of the Castle ; "they shall not be restored until these
men know better the use for which they are intrusted with
them. And now," he continued, addressing the mutineers,
"begone ! Make the best use of your time, and of a truce of
three hours, which the enemy are contented to allow you,

Take the road to Edinburgh, and meet me at the House of
Muir.   I need not bid you beware of committing violence by
the way ; you will not, in your present condition, provoke resentment for your own sakes.   Let your punctuality show
that you mean to atone for this morning's business."

The disarmed soldiers shrank in silence from the presence
of their officer, and, leaving the Castle, took the road to the
place of rendezvous, making such haste as was inspired by the
fear of meeting with some detached party of the insurgents,
whom their present defenceless condition, and their former
violence, might inspire with thoughts of revenge.   Inglis,
whom Evandale destined for punishment, remained in custody.
Halliday was praised for his conduct, and assured of succeeding to the rank of the culprit.   These arrangements being
hastily made, Lord Evandale accosted the Major, before
whose eyes the scene had seemed to pass like the change of a
dream.

"My dear Major, we must give up the place."

"Is it even so ?" said Major Bellenden.   "I was in hopes
you had brought reinforcements and supplies."

"Not a man—not a pound of meal," answered Lord Evandale.

"Yet I am blithe to see you," returned the honest Major ;
"we were informed yesterday that these psalm-singing rascals
had a plot on your life, and I had mustered the scoundrelly
dragoons ten minutes ago in order to beat up Burley's quarters
and get you out of limbo, when the dog Inglis, instead of
obeying me, broke out into open mutiny.   But what is to be
done now ?"

"I have myself no choice," said Lord Evandale ; "I am a
prisoner, released on parole, and bound for Edinburgh.   You
and the ladies must take the same route.   I have, by the
favor of a friend, a safe-conduct and horses for you and your
retinue.   For God's sake make haste ; you cannot propose to
hold out with seven or eight men, and without provisions.
Enough has been done for honor, and enough to render the
defence of the highest consequence to government.   More were
needless, as well as desperate.   The English troops are arrived
at Edinburgh, and will speedily move upon Hamilton.   The
possession of Tillietudlem by the rebels will be but temporary."

"If you think so, my lord," said the veteran, with a reluctant
sigh—"I know you only advise what is honorable—if, then,
you really think the case inevitable, I must submit ; for, the
mutiny of these scoundrels would render it impossible to man
the walls   Gudyill, let the women call up their mistresses,

and all be ready to march.   But if I could believe that my remaining in these old walls, till I was starved to a mummy, could do the king's cause the least service, old Miles Bellenden would not leave them while there was a spark of life in his body!"

The ladies, already alarmed by the mutiny, now heard the determination of the Major, in which they readily acquiesced, though not without some groans and sighs on the part of Lady Margaret, which referred, as usual, to the disjune of his most sacred Majesty in the halls which were now to be abandoned to rebels.   Hasty preparations were made for evacuating the Castle ; and long ere the dawn was distinct enough for discovering objects with precision, the ladies, with Major Bellenden, Harrison, Gudyill, and the other domestics, were mounted on the led horses, and others which had been provided in the neighborhood, and proceeded towards the north, still escorted by four of the insurgent horsemen.   The rest of the party who had accompanied Lord Evandale from the hamlet took possession of the deserted Castle, carefully forbearing all outrage or acts of plunder.   And when the sun arose the scarlet and blue colors of the Scottish Covenant floated from the Keep of Tillietudlem.

CHAPTER XXIX

And, to my breast, a bodkin in her hand
Were worth a thousand daggers.

MARLOW.

THE cavalcade which left the Castle of Tillietudlem halted for a few minutes at the small town of Bothwell, after passing the outposts of the insurgents, to take some slight refreshments which their attendants had provided, and which were really necessary to persons who had suffered considerably by want of proper nourishment. They then pressed forward upon the road towards Edinburgh, amid the lights of dawn which were now rising on the horizon. It might have been expected, during the course of the journey, that Lord Evandale would have been frequently by the side of Miss Edith Bellenden. Yet, after his first salutations had been exchanged, and every precaution solicitously adopted which could serve for her accommodation, he rode in the van of the party with Major Bellenden, and seemed to abandon the charge of immediate attendance upon his lovely niece to one of the insurgent cavaliers, whose dark military cloak, with the large flapped hat and feather, which drooped over his face, concealed at once his figure and his features.

They rode side by side in silence for more than two miles, when the stranger addressed Miss Bellenden in a tremulous and suppressed voice. "Miss Bellenden," he said, "must have friends wherever she is known, even among those whose conduct she now disapproves. Is there anything that such can do to show their respect for her, and their regret for her sufferings ?"

"Let them learn for their own sakes," replied Edith, "to venerate the laws and to spare innocent blood. Let them return to their allegiance, and I can forgive them all that I have suffered, were it ten times more."

"You think it impossible, then," rejoined the cavalier, "for any one to serve in our ranks, having the weal of his country sincerely at heart, and conceiving himself in the discharge of a patriotic duty ?"

"It might be imprudent, while so absolutely in your power," replied Miss Bellenden, "to answer that question."

"Not in the present instance, I plight you the word of a soldier," replied the horseman.

"I have been taught candor from my birth," said Edith; "and, if I am to speak at all, I must utter my real sentiments. God only can judge the heart; men must estimate intentions by actions. Treason, murder by the sword and by gibbet, the oppression of a private family such as ours, who were only in arms for the defence of the established government and of our own property, are actions which must needs sully all that have accession to them, by whatever specious terms they may be gilded over."

"The guilt of civil war," rejoined the horseman, "the miseries which it brings in its train, lie at the door of those who provoked it by illegal oppression, rather than of such as are driven to arms in order to assert their natural rights as freemen."

"That is assuming the question," replied Edith, "which ought to be proved. Each party contends that they are right in point of principle, and therefore the guilt must lie with them who first drew the sword; as, in an affray, law holds those to be the criminals who are the first to have recourse to violence."

"Alas!" said the horseman, "were our vindication to rest there, how easy would it be to show that we have suffered with a patience which almost seemed beyond the power of humanity, ere we were driven by oppression into open resistance! But I perceive," he continued, sighing deeply, "that it is vain to plead before Miss Bellenden a cause which she has already prejudged, perhaps as much from her dislike of the persons as of the principles of those engaged in it."

"Pardon me," answered Edith; "I have stated with freedom my opinion of the principles of the insurgents; of their persons I know nothing—excepting in one solitary instance."

"And that instance," said the horseman, "has influenced your opinion of the whole body?"

"Far from it," said Edith; "he is—at least I once thought him—one in whose scale few were fit to be weighed; he is— or he seemed—one of early talent, high faith, pure morality, and warm affections. Can I approve of a rebellion which has made such a man, formed to ornament, to enlighten, and to defend his country, the companion of gloomy and ignorant fanatics or canting hypocrites, the leader of brutal clowns, the brother-in-arms to banditti and highway murderers?

Should you meet such an one in your camp, tell him that Edith Bellenden has wept more over his fallen character, blighted prospects, and dishonored name than over the distresses of her own house ; and that she has better endured that famine which has wasted her cheek and dimmed her eye than the pang of heart which attended the reflection by and through whom these calamities were inflicted."

As she thus spoke, she turned upon her companion a countenance whose faded cheek attested the reality of her sufferings, even while it glowed with the temporary animation which accompanied her language. The horseman was not insensible to the appeal ; he raised his hand to his brow with the sudden motion of one who feels a pang shoot along his brain, passed it hastily over his face, and then pulled the shadowing hat still deeper on his forehead. The movement, and the feelings which it excited, did not escape Edith, nor did she remark them without emotion.

" And yet," she said, " should the person of whom I speak seem to you too deeply affected by the hard opinion of—of—an early friend, say to him that sincere repentance is next to innocence ; that, though fallen from a height not easily recovered, and the author of much mischief, because gilded by his example, he may still atone in some measure for the evil he has done."

" And in what manner ?" asked the cavalier, in the same suppressed and almost choked voice.

" By lending his efforts to restore the blessings of peace to his distracted countrymen, and to induce the deluded rebels to lay down their arms. By saving their blood, he may atone for that which has been already spilled ; and he that shall be most active in accomplishing this great end will best deserve the thanks of this age and an honored remembrance in the next."

" And in such a peace," said her companion, with a firm voice, " Miss Bellenden would not wish, I think, that the interests of the people were sacrificed unreservedly to those of the crown ?"

" I am but a girl," was the young lady's reply ; " and I scarce can speak on the subject without presumption. But, since I have gone so far, I will fairly add, I would wish to see a peace which should give rest to all parties, and secure the subjects from military rapine, which I detest as much as I do the means now adopted to resist it."

" Miss Bellenden," answered Henry Morton, raising his face and speaking in his natural tone, " the person who has lost such a highly valued place in your esteem has yet too much spirit to plead his cause as a criminal ; and, conscious that he can no longer claim a friend's interest in your bosom, he would be silent under your hard censure, were it not that he can refer to the honored testimony of Lord Evandale, that his earnest wishes and most active exertions are, even now, directed to the accomplishment of such a peace as the most loyal cannot censure."

He bowed with dignity to Miss Bellenden, who, though her language intimated that she well knew to whom she had been speaking, probably had not expected that he would justify himself with so much animation. She returned his salute, confused and in silence. Morton then rode forward to the head of the party.

"Henry Morton !" exclaimed Major Bellenden, surprised at the sudden apparition.

"The same," answered Morton ; "who is sorry that he labors under the harsh construction of Major Bellenden and his family. He commits to my Lord Evandale," he continued, turning towards the young nobleman and bowing to him, "the charge of undeceiving his friends, both regarding the particulars of his conduct and the purity of his motives. Farewell, Major Bellenden. All happiness attend you and yours ! May we meet again in happier and better times !"

"Believe me," said Lord Evandale, "your confidence, Mr. Morton, is not misplaced ; I will endeavor to repay the great services I have received from you by doing my best to place your character on its proper footing with Major Bellenden and all whose esteem you value."

"I expected no less from your generosity, my lord," said Morton.

He then called his followers, and rode off along the heath in the direction of Hamilton, their feathers waving and their steel caps glancing in the beams of the rising sun. Cuddie Headrigg alone remained an instant behind his companions to take an affectionate farewell of Jenny Dennison, who had contrived, during this short morning's ride, to re-establish her influence over his susceptible bosom. A straggling tree or two obscured, rather than concealed, their *téte-à-téte*, as they halted their horses to bid adieu.

"Fare ye weel, Jenny," said Cuddie, with a loud exertion of his lungs, intended perhaps to be a sigh, but rather resembling the intonation of a groan. "Ye'll think o' puir Cuddie sometimes, an honest lad that lo'es ye, Jenny—ye'll think o' him now and then ?"

"Whiles—at brose-time," answered the malicious damsel,

unable either to suppress the repartee or the arch smile which attended it.

Cuddie took his revenge as rustic lovers are wont, and as Jenny probably expected,—caught his mistress round the neck, kissed her cheeks and lips heartily, and then turned his horse and trotted after his master.

"Deil's in the fallow," said Jenny, wiping her lips and adjusting her head-dress, "he has twice the spunk o' Tam Halliday, after a'. Coming, my leddy, coming. Lord have a care o' us, I trust the auld leddy didna see us!"

"Jenny," said Lady Margaret, as the damsel came up, "was not that young man who commanded the party the same that was captain of the popinjay, and who was afterwards prisoner at Tillietudlem on the morning Claverhouse came there?"

Jenny, happy that the query had no reference to her own little matters, looked at her young mistress to discover, if possible, whether it was her cue to speak truth or not. Not being able to catch any hint to guide her, she followed her instinct as a lady's-maid, and lied.

"I dinna believe it was him, my leddy," said Jenny, as confidently as if she had been saying her catechism; "he was a little black man, that."

"You must have been blind, Jenny," said the Major: "Henry Morton is tall and fair, and that youth is the very man."

"I had ither thing ado than be looking at him," said Jenny, tossing her head; "he may be as fair as a farthing candle for me."

"Is it not," said Lady Margaret, "a blessed escape which we have made out of the hands of so desperate and bloodthirsty a fanatic?"

"You are deceived, madam," said Lord Evandale; "Mr. Morton merits such a title from no one, but least from us. That I am now alive, and that you are now on your safe retreat to your friends, instead of being prisoners to a real fanatical homicide, is solely and entirely owing to the prompt, active, and energetic humanity of this young gentleman."

He then went into a particular narrative of the events with which the reader is acquainted, dwelling upon the merits of Morton, and expatiating on the risk at which he had rendered them these important services, as if he had been a brother instead of a rival.

"I were worse than ungrateful," he said, "were I silent on the merits of the man who has twice saved my life."

"I would willingly think well of Henry Morton, my lord," replied Major Bellenden ; "and I own he has behaved handsomely to your lordship and to us ; but I cannot have the same allowances which it pleases your lordship to entertain for his present courses."

"You are to consider," replied Lord Evandale, "that he has been partly forced upon them by necessity ; and I must add, that his principles, though differing in some degree from my own, are such as ought to command respect. Claverhouse, whose knowledge of men is not to be disputed, spoke justly of him as to his extraordinary qualities, but with prejudice and harshly concerning his principles and motives."

"You have not been long in learning all his extraordinary qualities, my lord," answered Major Bellenden. "I, who have known him from boyhood, could, before this affair, have said much of his good principles and good-nature ; but as to his high talents——"

"They were probably hidden, Major," replied the generous Lord Evandale, "even from himself until circumstances called them forth ; and, if I have detected them, it was only because our intercourse and conversation turned on momentous and important subjects. He is now laboring to bring this rebellion to an end, and the terms he has proposed are so moderate that they shall not want my hearty recommendation."

"And have you hopes," said Lady Margaret, "to accomplish a scheme so comprehensive ?"

"I should have, madam, were every Whig as moderate as Morton, and every loyalist as disinterested as Major Bellenden. But such is the fanaticism and violent irritation of both parties, that I fear nothing will end this civil war save the edge of the sword."

It may be readily supposed that Edith listened with the deepest interest to this conversation. While she regretted that she had expressed herself harshly and hastily to her lover, she felt a conscious and proud satisfaction that his character was, even in the judgment of his noble-minded rival, such as her own affection had once spoke it.

"Civil feuds and domestic prejudices," she said, "may render it necessary for me to tear his remembrance from my heart ; but it is no small relief to know assuredly that it is worthy of the place it has so long retained there."

While Edith was thus retracting her unjust resentment, her lover arrived at the camp of the insurgents near Hamilton, which he found in considerable confusion. Certain advices had arrived that the royal army, having been recruited from England by a large detachment of the King's Guards, were about to take the field. Fame magnified their numbers and their high state of equipment and discipline, and spread abroad other circumstances which dismayed the courage of the insurgents. What favor they might have expected from Monmouth was likely to be intercepted by the influence of those associated with him in command. His lieutenant-general was the celebrated General Thomas Dalzell, who, having practised the art of war in the then barbarous country of Russia, was as much feared for his cruelty and indifference to human life and human sufferings as respected for his steady loyalty and undaunted valor. This man was second in command to Monmouth, and the horse were commanded by Claverhouse, burning with desire to revenge the death of his nephew and his defeat at Drumclog. To these accounts was added the most formidable and terrific description of the train of artillery and the cavalry force with which the royal army took the field.*

Large bodies composed of the Highland clans, having in language, religion, and manners no connection with the insurgents, had been summoned to join the royal army under their various chieftains; and these Amorites, or Philistines, as the insurgents termed them, came like eagles to the slaughter. In fact, every person who could ride or run at the king's command was summoned to arms, apparently with the purpose of forfeiting and fining such men of property whom their principles might deter from joining the royal standard, though prudence prevented them from joining that of the insurgent Presbyterians. In short, every rumor tended to increase the apprehension among the insurgents that the king's vengeance had only been delayed in order that it might fall more certain and more heavy.

Morton endeavored to fortify the minds of the common people by pointing out the probable exaggeration of these reports, and by reminding them of the strength of their own situation, with an unfordable river in front only passable by a long and narrow bridge. He called to their remembrance their victory over Claverhouse when their numbers were few, and then much worse disciplined and appointed for battle than now; showed them that the ground on which they lay afforded, by its undulation and the thickets which intersected it, considerable protection against artillery, and even against cavalry,

---

* See Royal Army at Bothwell Bridge. Note 27.

if stoutly defended ; and that their safety, in fact, depended on their own spirit and resolution.

But while Morton thus endeavored to keep up the courage of the army at large, he availed himself of those discouraging rumors to endeavor to impress on the minds of the leaders the necessity of proposing to the government moderate terms of accommodation, while they were still formidable as commanding an unbroken and numerous army. He pointed out to them that, in the present humor of their followers, it could hardly be expected that they would engage, with advantage, the well-appointed and regular force of the Duke of Monmouth; and that if they chanced, as was most likely, to be defeated and dispersed, the insurrection in which they had engaged, so far from being useful to the country, would be rendered the apology for oppressing it more severely.

Pressed by these arguments, and feeling it equally dangerous to remain together or to dismiss their forces, most of the leaders readily agreed that, if such terms could be obtained as had been transmitted to the Duke of Monmouth by the hands of Lord Evandale, the purpose for which they had taken up arms would be, in a great measure, accomplished. They then entered into similar resolutions, and agreed to guarantee the petition and remonstrance which had been drawn up by Morton. On the contrary, there were still several leaders, and those men whose influence with the people exceeded that of persons of more apparent consequence, who regarded every proposal of treaty which did not proceed on the basis of the Solemn League and Covenant of 1640 as utterly null and void, impious, and unchristian. These men diffused their feelings among the multitude, who had little foresight and nothing to lose, and persuaded many that the timid counsellors who recommended peace upon terms short of the dethronement of the royal family, and the declared independence of the church with respect to the state, were cowardly laborers, who were about to withdraw their hands from the plough, and despicable trimmers, who sought only a specious pretext for deserting their brethren in arms. These contradictory opinions were fiercely argued in each tent of the insurgent army, or rather in the huts or cabins which served in the place of tents. Violence in language often led to open quarrels and blows, and the divisions into which the army of sufferers was rent served as too plain a presage of their future fate.

CHAPTER XXX

THE prudence of Morton found sufficient occupation in stemming the furious current of these contending parties, when, two days after his return to Hamilton, he was visited by his friend and colleague, the Reverend Mr. Poundtext, flying, as he presently found, from the face of John Balfour of Burley, whom he left not a little incensed at the share he had taken in the liberation of Lord Evandale. When the worthy divine had somewhat recruited his spirits, after the hurry and fatigue of his journey, he proceeded to give Morton an account of what had passed in the vicinity of Tillietudlem after the memorable morning of his departure.

The night march of Morton had been accomplished with such dexterity, and the men were so faithful to their trust, that Burley received no intelligence of what had happened until the morning was far advanced. His first inquiry was, whether Macbriar and Kettledrummle had arrived, agreeably to the summons which he had despatched at midnight. Macbriar had come, and Kettledrummle, though a heavy traveller, might, he was informed, be instantly expected. Burley then despatched a messenger to Morton's quarters to summon him to an immediate council. The messenger returned with news that he had left the place. Poundtext was next summoned ; but he thinking, as he said himself, that it was ill dealing with fractious folk, had withdrawn to his own quiet manse, preferring a dark ride, though he had been on horseback the whole preceding day, to a renewal in the morning of a controversy with Burley, whose ferocity overawed him when unsupported by the firmness of Morton. Burley's next inquiries were directed after Lord Evandale ; and great was his rage when he learned that he had been conveyed away overnight by a party of the Marksmen of Milnwood, under the immediate command of Henry Morton himself.

" The villain !" exclaimed Burley, addressing himself to

Macbriar, "the base, mean-spirited traitor, to curry favor for himself with the government, hath set at liberty the prisoner taken by my own right hand, through means of whom, I have little doubt, the possession of the place of strength which hath wrought us such trouble might now have been in our hands!"

"But is it not in our hands?" said Macbriar, looking up towards the keep of the castle; "and are not these the colors of the Covenant that float over its walls?"

"A stratagem, a mere trick," said Burley, "an insult over our disappointment, intended to aggravate and embitter our spirits."

He was interrupted by the arrival of one of Morton's followers, sent to report to him the evacuation of the place, and its occupation by the insurgent forces. Burley was rather driven to fury than reconciled by the news of this success.

"I have watched," he said, "I have fought, I have plotted, I have striven for the reduction of this place, I have forborne to seek to head enterprises of higher command and of higher honor, I have narrowed their outgoings, and cut off the springs, and broken the staff of bread within their walls; and when the men were about to yield themselves to my hand, that their sons might be bondsmen and their daughters a laughing-stock to our whole camp, cometh this youth without a beard on his chin, and takes it on him to thrust his sickle into the harvest, and to rend the prey from the spoiler! Surely the laborer is worthy of his hire, and the city, with its captives, should be given to him that wins it?"

"Nay," said Macbriar, who was surprised at the degree of agitation which Balfour displayed, "chafe not thyself because of the ungodly. Heaven will use its own instruments; and who knows but this youth——"

"Hush! hush!" said Burley; "do not discredit thine own better judgment. It was thou that first badest me beware of this painted sepulchre, this lacquered piece of copper, that passed current with me for gold. It fares ill, even with the elect, when they neglect the guidance of such pious pastors as thou. But our carnal affections will mislead us: this ungrateful boy's father was mine ancient friend. They must be as earnest in their struggles as thou, Ephraim Macbriar, that would shake themselves clear of the clogs and chains of humanity."

This compliment touched the preacher in the most sensible part; and Burley deemed, therefore, he should find little difficulty in moulding his opinions to the support of his own views, more especially as they agreed exactly in their high-strained opinions of church government.

"Let us instantly," he said, "go up to the Tower ; there is that among the records in yonder fortress which, well used as I can use it, shall be worth to us a valiant leader and an hundred horsemen."

"But will such be the fitting aids of the children of the Covenant ?" said the preacher. "We have already among us too many who hunger after lands, and silver and gold, rather than after the Word ; it is not by such that our deliverance shall be wrought out."

"Thou errest," said Burley ; "we must work by means, and these worldly men shall be our instruments. At all events, the Moabitish woman shall be despoiled of her inheritance, and neither the Malignant Evandale nor the Erastian Morton shall possess yonder castle and lands, though they may seek in marriage the daughter thereof."

So saying, he led the way to Tillietudlem, where he seized upon the plate and other valuables for the use of the army, ransacked the charter-room and other receptacles for family papers, and treated with contempt the remonstrances of those who reminded him that the terms granted to the garrison had guaranteed respect to private property.

Burley and Macbriar, having established themselves in their new acquisition, were joined by Kettledrummle in the course of the day, and also by the Laird of Langcale, whom that active divine had contrived to seduce, as Poundtext termed it, from the pure light in which he had been brought up. Thus united, they sent to the said Poundtext an invitation, or rather a summons, to attend a council at Tillietudlem. He remembered, however, that the door had an iron grate and the keep a dungeon, and resolved not to trust himself with his incensed colleagues. He therefore retreated, or rather fled, to Hamilton, with the tidings that Burley, Macbriar, and Kettledrummle were coming to Hamilton as soon as they could collect a body of Cameronians sufficient to overawe the rest of the army.

"And ye see," concluded Poundtext, with a deep sigh, "that they will then possess a majority in the council ; for Langcale, though he has always passed for one of the honest and rational party, cannot be suitably or preceesely termed either fish, or flesh, or gude red-herring ; whoever has the stronger party has Langcale."

Thus concluded the heavy narrative of honest Poundtext, who sighed deeply, as he considered the danger in which he was placed betwixt unreasonable adversaries among themselves, and the common enemy from without. Morton exhorted him to patience, temper, and composure ; informed him of the good hope he had of negotiating for peace and indemnity through means of Lord Evandale, and made out to him a very fair prospect that he should again return to his own parchment-bound Calvin, his evening pipe of tobacco, and his noggin of inspiring ale, providing always he would afford his effectual support and concurrence to the measures which he, Morton, had taken for a general pacification.* Thus backed and comforted, Poundtext resolved magnanimously to await the coming of the Cameronians to the general rendezvous.

Burley and his confederates had drawn together a considerable body of these sectaries, amounting to a hundred horse and about fifteen hundred foot, clouded and severe in aspect, morose and jealous in communication, haughty of heart, and confident, as men who believed that the pale of salvation was open for them exclusively, while all other Christians, however slight were the shades of difference of doctrine from their own, were in fact little better than outcasts or reprobates. These men entered the Presbyterian camp rather as dubious and suspicious allies, or possibly antagonists, than as men who were heartily embarked in the same cause, and exposed to the same dangers, with their more moderate brethren in arms. Burley made no private visits to his colleagues, and held no communication with them on the subject of the public affairs, otherwise than by sending a dry invitation to them to attend a meeting of the general council for that evening.

On the arrival of Morton and Poundtext at the place of assembly they found their brethren already seated. Slight greeting passed between them, and it was easy to see that no amicable conference was intended by those who convoked the council. The first question was put by Macbriar, the sharp eagerness of whose zeal urged him to the van on all occasions. He desired to know by whose authority the Malignant called Lord Evandale had been freed from the doom of death justly denounced against him.

" By my authority and Mr. Morton's," replied Poundtext, who, besides being anxious to give his companion a good opinion of his courage, confided heartily in his support, and, moreover, had much less fear of encountering one of his own profession, and who confined himself to the weapons of theological controversy, in which Poundtext feared no man, than of entering into debate with the stern homicide Balfour.

* See Moderate Presbyterians. Note 28.

"And who, brother," said Kettledrummle—"who gave you authority to interpose in such a high matter ?"

"The tenor of our commission," answered Poundtext, "gives us authority to bind and to loose. If Lord Evandale was justly doomed to die by the voice of one of our number, he was of a surety lawfully redeemed from death by the warrant of two of us."

" Go to, go to," said Burley ; " we know your motives : it was to send that silkworm, that gilded trinket, that embroidered trifle of a lord to bear terms of peace to the tyrant."

"It was so," replied Morton, who saw his companion begin to flinch before the fierce eye of Balfour—" it was so ; and what then ? Are we to plunge the nation in endless war in order to pursue schemes which are equally wild, wicked, and unattainable ?"

" Hear him !" said Balfour ; " he blasphemeth."

" It is false," said Morton ; " they blaspheme who pretend to expect miracles, and neglect the use of the human means with which Providence has blessed them. I repeat it—Our avowed object is the re-establishment of peace on fair and honorable terms of security to our religion and our liberty. We disclaim any desire to tyrannize over those of others."

The debate would now have run higher than ever, but they were interrupted by intelligence that the Duke of Monmouth had commenced his march towards the west, and was already advanced half-way from Edinburgh. This news silenced their divisions for the moment, and it was agreed that the next day should be held as a fast of general humiliation for the sins of the land ; that the Reverend Mr. Poundtext should preach to the army in the morning, and Kettledrummle in the afternoon ; that neither should touch upon any topics of schism or of division, but animate the soldiers to resist to the blood, like brethren in a good cause. This healing overture having been agreed to, the Moderate party ventured upon another proposal, confiding that it would have the support of Langcale, who looked extremely blank at the news which they had just received, and might be supposed reconverted to Moderate measures. It was to be presumed, they said, that since the king had not intrusted the command of his forces upon the present occasion to any of their active oppressors, but, on the contrary, had employed a nobleman distinguished by gentleness of temper and a disposition favorable to their cause, there must be some better intention entertained towards them than they had yet experienced. They contended that it was not only prudent but necessary to ascertain, from a communication with the Duke of Monmouth, whether he was not charged with some secret instructions in their favor. This could only be learned by despatching an envoy to his army.

"And who will undertake the task ?" said Burley, evading a proposal too reasonable to be openly resisted—"who will go up to their camp, knowing that John Grahame of Claverhouse hath sworn to hang up whomsoever we shall despatch towards them, in revenge of the death of the young man his nephew ?"

"Let that be no obstacle," said Morton; "I will with pleasure encounter any risk attached to the bearer of your errand."

"Let him go," said Balfour, apart to Macbriar; "our councils will be well rid of his presence."

The motion, therefore, received no contradiction even from those who were expected to have been most active in opposing it; and it was agreed that Henry Morton should go to the camp of the Duke of Monmouth, in order to discover upon what terms the insurgents would be admitted to treat with him. As soon as his errand was made known several of the more Moderate party joined in requesting him to make terms upon the footing of the petition intrusted to Lord Evandale's hands; for the approach of the king's army spread a general trepidation, by no means allayed by the high tone assumed by the Cameronians, which had so little to support it excepting their own headlong zeal. With these instructions, and with Cuddie as his attendant, Morton set forth towards the royal camp, at all the risks which attend those who assume the office of mediator during the heat of civil discord.

Morton had not proceeded six or seven miles before he perceived that he was on the point of falling in with the van of the royal forces; and, as he ascended a height, saw all the roads in the neighborhood occupied by armed men marching in great order towards Bothwell Muir, an open common, on which they proposed to encamp for that evening, at the distance of scarcely two miles from the Clyde, on the further side of which river the army of the insurgents was encamped. He gave himself up to the first advanced guard of cavalry which he met, as bearer of a flag of truce, and communicated his desire to obtain access to the Duke of Monmouth. The non-commissioned officer who commanded the party made his report to his superior, and he again to another in still higher command, and both immediately rode to the spot where Morton was detained.

"You are but losing your time, my friend, and risking your life," said one of them, addressing Morton ; "the Duke of Monmouth will receive no terms from traitors with arms in their hands, and your cruelties have been such as to authorize retaliation of every kind. Better trot your nag back and save his mettle to-day, that he may save your life to-morrow."

"I cannot think," said Morton, "that, even if the Duke of Monmouth should consider us as criminals, he would condemn so large a body of his fellow-subjects without even hearing what they have to plead for themselves. On my part I fear nothing. I am conscious of having consented to, or authorized, no cruelty, and the fear of suffering innocently for the crimes of others shall not deter me from executing my commission."

The two officers looked at each other.

"I have an idea," said the younger, "that this is the young man of whom Lord Evandale spoke."

"Is my Lord Evandale in the army?" said Morton.

"He is not," replied the officer ; "we left him at Edinburgh, too much indisposed to take the field. Your name, sir, I presume, is Henry Morton?"

"It is, sir," answered Morton.

"We will not oppose your seeing the Duke, sir," said the officer, with more civility of manner ; "but you may assure yourself it will be to no purpose ; for, were his Grace disposed to favor your people, others are joined in commission with him who will hardly consent to his doing so."

"I shall be sorry to find it thus," said Morton ; "but my duty requires that I should persevere in my desire to have an interview with him."

"Lumley," said the superior officer, "let the Duke know of Mr. Morton's arrival, and remind his Grace that this is the person of whom Lord Evandale spoke so highly."

The officer returned with a message that the General could not see Mr. Morton that evening, but would receive him by times in the ensuing morning. He was detained in a neighboring cottage all night, but treated with civility, and everything provided for his accommodation.

Early on the next morning the officer he had first seen came to conduct him to his audience. The army was drawn out, and in the act of forming column for march, or attack. The Duke was in the centre, nearly a mile from the place where Morton had passed the night. In riding towards the General, he had an opportunity of estimating the force which had been assembled for the suppression of the hasty and ill-concerted insurrection. There were three or four regiments of English, the flower of Charles's army ; there were the Scottish Life Guards, burning with desire to revenge their late defeat ; other Scottish regiments of regulars were also assembled ; and a large body of cavalry, consisting partly of gentlemen volunteers, partly of the tenants of the crown who did military duty for their fiefs. Morton also observed several strong parties of Highlanders drawn from the points nearest to the Lowland frontiers, a people, as already mentioned, particularly obnoxious to the western Whigs, and who hated and despised them in the same proportion. These were assembled under their chiefs, and made part of this formidable array. A complete train of field artillery accompanied these troops ; and the whole had an air so imposing that it seemed nothing short of an actual miracle could prevent the ill-equipped, ill-modelled, and tumultuary army of the insurgents from being utterly destroyed. The officer who accompanied Morton endeavored to gather from his looks the feelings with which this splendid and awful parade of military force had impressed him. But, true to the cause he had espoused, he labored successfully to prevent the anxiety which he felt from appearing in his countenance, and looked around him on the warlike display as on a sight which he expected, and to which he was indifferent.

"You see the entertainment prepared for you," said the officer.

"If I had no appetite for it," replied Morton, "I should not have been accompanying you at this moment. But I shall be better pleased with a more peaceful regale, for the sake of all parties."

As they spoke thus, they approached the commander-in-chief, who, surrounded by several officers, was seated upon a knoll commanding an extensive prospect of the distant country, and from which could be easily discovered the windings of the majestic Clyde, and the distant camp of the insurgents on the opposite bank. The officers of the royal army appeared to be surveying the ground, with the purpose of directing an immediate attack. When Captain Lumley, the officer who accompanied Morton, had whispered in Monmouth's ear his name and errand, the Duke made a signal for all around him to retire, excepting only two general officers of distinction. While they spoke together in whispers for a few minutes before Morton was permitted to advance, he had time to study the appearance of the persons with whom he was to treat.

It was impossible for any one to look upon the Duke of

Monmouth without being captivated by his personal graces
and accomplishments, of which the great High Priest of all
the Nine afterwards recorded—

> Whate'er he did was done with so much ease,
> In him alone 'twas natural to please ;
> His motions all accompanied with grace,
> And Paradise was open'd in his face.*

Yet to a strict observer the manly beauty of Monmouth's face
was occasionally rendered less striking by an air of vacillation
and uncertainty, which seemed to imply hesitation and
doubt at moments when decisive resolution was most necessary.

Beside him stood Claverhouse, whom we have already
fully described, and another general officer whose appearance was singularly striking. His dress was of the antique
fashion of Charles the First's time, and composed of chamois
leather, curiously slashed, and covered with antique lace and
garniture. His boots and spurs might be referred to the
same distant period. He wore a breastplate, over which descended a gray beard of venerable length, which he cherished
as a mark of mourning for Charles the First, having never
shaved since that monarch was brought to the scaffold. His
head was uncovered, and almost perfectly bald. His high
and wrinkled forehead, piercing gray eyes, and marked features evinced age unbroken by infirmity, and stern resolution unsoftened by humanity. Such is the outline, however
feebly expressed, of the celebrated General Thomas Dalzell,†
a man more feared and hated by the Whigs than even Claverhouse himself, and who executed the same violences against
them out of a detestation of their persons, or perhaps an innate severity of temper, which Grahame only resorted to on
political accounts, as the best means of intimidating the followers of Presbytery, and of destroying that sect entirely.

The presence of these two generals, one of whom he knew
by person and the other by description, seemed to Morton
decisive of the fate of his embassy. But, notwithstanding
his youth and inexperience, and the unfavorable reception
which his proposals seemed likely to meet with, he advanced
boldly towards them upon receiving a signal to that purpose,
determined that the cause of his country, and of those with
whom he had taken up arms, should suffer nothing from
being intrusted to him. Monmouth received him with the

---

* Dryden's *Absalom and Achitophel* (*Laing*).
† See Note 29.

graceful courtesy which attended even his slightest actions; Dalzell regarded him with a stern, gloomy, and impatient frown; and Claverhouse, with a sarcastic smile and inclination of his head, seemed to claim him as an old acquaintance.

"You come, sir, from these unfortunate people now assembled in arms," said the Duke of Monmouth, "and your name, I believe, is Morton; will you favor us with the purport of your errand?"

"It is contained, my lord," answered Morton, "in a paper, termed a Remonstrance and Supplication, which my Lord Evandale has placed, I presume, in your Grace's hands?"

"He has done so, sir," answered the Duke; "and I understand from Lord Evandale that Mr. Morton has behaved in these unhappy matters with much temperance and generosity, for which I have to request his acceptance of my thanks."

Here Morton observed Dalzell shake his head indignantly and whisper something into Claverhouse's ear, who smiled in return, and elevated his eyebrows, but in a degree so slight as scarce to be perceptible. The Duke, taking the petition from his pocket, proceeded, obviously struggling between the native gentleness of his own disposition, and perhaps his conviction that the petitioners demanded no more than their rights, and the desire, on the other hand, of enforcing the king's authority, and complying with the sterner opinions of the colleagues in office, who had been assigned for the purpose of controlling as well as advising him.

"There are, Mr. Morton, in this paper, proposals as to the abstract propriety of which I must now waive delivering any opinion. Some of them appear to me reasonable and just; and, although I have no express instructions from the King upon the subject, yet I assure you, Mr. Morton, and I pledge my honor, that I will interpose in your behalf, and use my utmost influence to procure you satisfaction from his Majesty. But you must distinctly understand that I can only treat with supplicants, not with rebels; and, as a preliminary to every act of favor on my side, I must insist upon your followers laying down their arms and dispersing themselves."

"To do so, my Lord Duke," replied Morton, undauntedly, "were to acknowledge ourselves the rebels that our enemies term us. Our swords are drawn for recovery of a birthright wrested from us; your Grace's moderation and good sense has admitted the general justice of our demand—a demand which would never have been listened to had it not been accompanied with the sound of the trumpet. We cannot, therefore, and dare not, lay down our arms, even on your Grace's assurance of indemnity, unless it were accompanied with some reasonable prospect of the redress of the wrongs which we complain of."

"Mr. Morton," replied the Duke, "you are young, but you must have seen enough of the world to perceive that requests, by no means dangerous or unreasonable in themselves, may become so by the way in which they are pressed and supported."

"We may reply, my lord," answered Morton, "that this disagreeable mode has not been resorted to until all others have failed."

"Mr. Morton," said the Duke, "I must break this conference short.   We are in readiness to commence the attack ; yet I will suspend it for an hour, until you can communicate my answer to the insurgents.   If they please to disperse their followers, lay down their arms, and send a peaceful deputation to me, I will consider myself bound in honor to do all I can to procure redress of their grievances ; if not, let them stand on their guard and expect the consequences.   I think, gentlemen," he added, turning to his two colleagues, "this is the utmost length to which I can stretch my instructions in favor of these misguided persons ? "

" By my faith," answered Dalzell, suddenly, " and it is a length to which my poor judgment durst not have stretched them, considering I had both the King and my conscience to answer to !   But, doubtless, your Grace knows more of the King's private mind than we, who have only the letter of our instructions to look to."

Monmouth blushed deeply.   " You hear," he said, addressing Morton, " General Dalzell blames me for the length which I am disposed to go in your favor."

" General Dalzell's sentiments, my lord," replied Morton, " are such as we expected from him; your Grace's such as we were prepared to hope you might please to entertain.   Indeed, I cannot help adding that, in the case of the absolute submission upon which you are pleased to insist, it might still remain something less than doubtful how far, with such counsellors around the King, even your Grace's intercession might procure us effectual relief.   But I will communicate to our leaders your Grace's answer to our supplication ; and, since we cannot obtain peace, we must bid war welcome as well as we may."

" Good morning, sir," said the Duke ; "I suspend the movements of attack for one hour, and for one hour only.   If you have an answer to return within that space of time, I will receive it here, and earnestly entreat it may be such as to save the effusion of blood."

At this moment another smile of deep meaning passed between Dalzell and Claverhouse.

The Duke observed it, and repeated his words with great dignity. "Yes, gentlemen, I said I trusted the answer might be such as would save the effusion of blood. I hope the sentiment neither needs your scorn nor incurs your displeasure."

Dalzell returned the Duke's frown with a stern glance, but made no answer. Claverhouse, his lip just curled with an ironical smile, bowed, and said, "It was not for him to judge the propriety of his Grace's sentiments."

The Duke made a signal to Morton to withdraw. He obeyed, and, accompanied by his former escort, rode slowly through the army to return to the camp of the nonconformists. As he passed the fine corps of Life Guards, he found Claverhouse was already at their head. That officer no sooner saw Morton than he advanced and addressed him with perfect politeness of manner.

"I think this is not the first time I have seen Mr. Morton of Milnwood ?"

"It is not Colonel Grahame's fault," said Morton, smiling sternly, "that he or any one else should be now incommoded by my presence."

"Allow me at least to say," replied Claverhouse, "that Mr. Morton's present situation authorizes the opinion I have entertained of him, and that my proceedings at our last meeting only squared to my duty."

"To reconcile your actions to your duty, and your duty to your conscience, is your business, Colonel Grahame, not mine," said Morton, justly offended at being thus, in a manner, required to approve of the sentence under which he had so nearly suffered.

"Nay, but stay an instant," said Claverhouse; "Evandale insists that I have some wrongs to acquit myself of in your instance. I trust I shall always make some difference between a high-minded gentleman who, though misguided, acts upon generous principles and the crazy fanatical clowns yonder, with the bloodthirsty assassins who head them. Therefore, if they do not disperse upon your return, let me pray you, instantly come over to our army and surrender yourself, for, be assured, they cannot stand our assault for half an hour. If you will be ruled and do this, be sure to inquire for me. Monmouth, strange as it may seem, cannot protect you; Dalzell will not; I both can and will, and I have promised to Evandale to do so if you will give me an opportunity."

"I should owe Lord Evandale my thanks," answered Morton, coldly, "did not his scheme imply an opinion that I might be prevailed on to desert those with whom I am engaged. For you, Colonel Grahame, if you will honor me with a different species of satisfaction, it is probable that, in an hour's time, you will find me at the west end of Bothwell Bridge with my sword in my hand."

"I shall be happy to meet you there," said Claverhouse, "but still more so should you think better on my first proposal."

They then saluted and parted.

"That is a pretty lad, Lumley," said Claverhouse, addressing himself to the other officer; "but he is a lost man, his blood be upon his head."

So saying, he addressed himself to the task of preparation for instant battle.

CHAPTER XXXI

But, hark ! the tent has changed its voice,
  There's peace and rest nae langer.
                                        BURNS.

The Lowdien mallisha they
  Came with their coats of blew ;
Five hundred men from London came,
  Claid in a reddish hue.
                              Bothwell Lines.

WHEN Morton had left the well-ordered outposts of the regular army, and arrived at those which were maintained by his own party, he could not but be peculiarly sensible of the difference of discipline, and entertain a proportional degree of fear for the consequences. The same discords which agitated the counsels of the insurgents raged even among their meanest followers ; and their pickets and patrols were more interested and occupied in disputing the true occasion and causes of wrath, and defining the limits of Erastian heresy, than in looking out for and observing the motions of their enemies, though within hearing of the royal drums and trumpets.

There was a guard, however, of the insurgent army, posted at the long and narrow bridge of Bothwell, over which the enemy must necessarily advance to the attack ; but, like the others, they were divided and disheartened ; and entertaining the idea that they were posted on a desperate service, they even meditated withdrawing themselves to the main body. This would have been utter ruin ; for on the defense or loss of this pass the fortune of the day was most likely to depend. All beyond the bridge was a plain open field, excepting a few thickets of no great depth, and, consequently, was ground on which the undisciplined forces of the insurgents, deficient as they were in cavalry and totally unprovided with artillery, were altogether unlikely to withstand the shock of regular troops.

Morton, therefore, viewed the pass carefully, and formed the hope that, by occupying two or three houses on the left bank of the river, with the copse and thickets of alders and hazels that lined its side, and by blockading the passage itself, and shutting the gates of a portal which, according to the old fashion, was built on the central arch of the Bridge of Bothwell, it might be easily defended against a very superior force. He issued directions accordingly, and commanded the parapets of the bridge, on the further side of the portal, to be thrown down, that they might afford no protection to the enemy when they should attempt the passage. Morton then conjured the party at this important post to be watchful and upon their guard, and promised them a speedy and strong reinforcement. He caused them to advance videttes beyond the river to watch the progress of the enemy, which outposts he directed should be withdrawn to the left bank as soon as they approached; finally, he charged them to send regular information to the main body of all that they should observe. Men under arms, and in a situation of danger, are usually sufficiently alert in appreciating the merit of their officers. Morton's intelligence and activity gained the confidence of these men, and with better hope and heart than before, they began to fortify their position in the manner he recommended, and saw him depart with three loud cheers.

Morton now galloped hastily towards the main body of the insurgents, but was surprised and shocked at the scene of confusion and clamor which it exhibited at the moment when good order and concord were of such essential consequence. Instead of being drawn up in line of battle and listening to the commands of their officers, they were crowding together in a confused mass, that rolled and agitated itself like the waves of the sea, while a thousand tongues spoke, or rather vociferated, and not a single ear was found to listen. Scandalized at a scene so extraordinary, Morton endeavored to make his way through the press to learn, and if possible to remove, the cause of this so untimely disorder. While he is thus engaged we shall make the reader acquainted with that which he was some time in discovering.

The insurgents had proceeded to hold their day of humiliation, which, agreeably to the practice of the Puritans during the earlier Civil War, they considered as the most effectual mode of solving all difficulties and waiving all discussions. It was usual to name an ordinary week-day for this purpose; but on this occasion the Sabbath itself was adopted, owing to the pressure of the time and the vicinity of the enemy. A temporary pulpit or tent was erected in the middle of the encampment; which, according to the fixed arrangement, was first to be occupied by the Reverend Peter Poundtext, to whom the post of honor was assigned as the eldest clergyman present. But as the worthy divine, with slow and stately steps, was advancing towards the rostrum which had been prepared for him, he was prevented by the unexpected apparition of Habakkuk Mucklewrath, the insane preacher, whose appearance had so much startled Morton at the first council of the insurgents after their victory at Loudon Hill. It is not known whether he was acting under the influence and instigation of the Cameronians, or whether he was merely compelled by his own agitated imagination and the temptation of a vacant pulpit before him, to seize the opportunity of exhorting so respectable a congregation. It is only certain that he took occasion by the forelock, sprang into the pulpit, cast his eyes wildly round him, and, undismayed by the murmurs of many of the audience, opened the Bible, read forth as his text from the thirteenth chapter of Deuteronomy, " Certain men, the children of Belial, are gone out from among you, and have withdrawn the inhabitants of their city, saying, Let us go and serve other gods, which you have not known ; " and then rushed at once into the midst of his subject.

The harangue of Mucklewrath was as wild and extravagant as his intrusion was unauthorized and untimely ; but it was provokingly coherent, in so far as it turned entirely upon the very subjects of discord of which it had been agreed to adjourn the consideration until some more suitable opportunity. Not a single topic did he omit which had offence in it ; and, after charging the Moderate party with heresy, with crouching to tyranny, with seeking to be at peace with God's enemies, he applied to Morton by name the charge that he had been one of those men of Belial who, in the words of his text, had gone out from among them, to withdraw the inhabitants of his city, and to go astray after false gods. To him, and all who followed him or approved of his conduct, Mucklewrath denounced fury and vengeance, and exhorted those who would hold themselves pure and undefiled to come up from the midst of them.

" Fear not," he said, " because of the neighing of horses or the glittering of breastplates. Seek not aid of the Egyptians, because of the enemy, though they may be numerous as locusts and fierce as dragons. Their trust is not as our trust, nor their rock as our rock ; how else shall a thousand fly before one, and two put ten thousand to the flight ? I dreamed it in the visions of the night, and the voice said, ' Habakkuk, take thy fan and purge the wheat from the chaff, that they be not both consumed with the fire of indignation and the lightning of fury.'   Wherefore, I say, take this Henry Morton—this wretched Achan, who hath brought the accursed thing among ye, and made himself brethren in the camp of the enemy—take him and stone him with stones, and thereafter burn him with fire, that the wrath may depart from the children of the Covenant.   He hath not taken a Babylonish garment, but he hath sold the garment of righteousness to the woman of Babylon ; he hath not taken two hundred shekels of fine silver, but he hath bartered the truth, which is more precious than shekels of silver or wedges of gold."

At this furious charge, brought so unexpectedly against one of their most active commanders, the audience broke out into open tumult, some demanding that there should instantly be a new election of officers, into which office none should hereafter be admitted who had, in their phrase, touched of that which was accursed, or temporized more or less with the heresies and corruptions of the times.   While such was the demand of the Cameronians, they vociferated loudly that those who were not with them were against them ; that it was no time to relinquish the substantial part of the covenanted testimony of the church if they expected a blessing on their arms and their cause ; and that, in their eyes, a lukewarm Presbyterian was little better than a Prelatist, an Anti-Covenanter, and a Nullifidian.

The parties accused repelled the charge of criminal compliance and defection from the truth with scorn and indignation, and charged their accusers with breach of faith, as well as with wrong-headed and extravagant zeal in introducing such divisions into an army the joint strength of which could not, by the most sanguine, be judged more than sufficient to face their enemies.   Poundtext and one or two others made some faint efforts to stem the increasing fury of the factious, exclaiming to those of the other party, in the words of the Patriarch—" Let there be no strife, I pray thee, between me and thee, and between thy herdsmen and my herdsmen, for we be brethren."   No pacific overture could possibly obtain audience.   It was in vain that even Burley himself, when he saw the dissension proceed to such ruinous lengths, exerted his stern and deep voice, commanding silence and obedience to discipline.   The spirit of insubordination had gone forth, and it seemed as if the exhortation of Habakkuk Mucklewrath had communicated a part of his frenzy to all who heard him.   The wiser, or more timid, part of the assembly were already withdrawing themselves from the field, and giving up their cause as lost.   Others were moderating a harmonious call, as they somewhat improperly termed it, to new officers, and dismissing those formerly chosen, and that with a tumult and clamor worthy of the deficiency of good sense and good order implied in the whole transaction. It was at this moment, when Morton arrived in the field and joined the army, in total confusion, and on the point of dissolving itself. His arrival occasioned loud exclamations of applause on the one side and of imprecation on the other.

"What means this ruinous disorder at such a moment ?" he exclaimed to Burley, who, exhausted with his vain exertions to restore order, was now leaning on his sword and regarding the confusion with an eye of resolute despair.

"It means," he replied, "that God has delivered us into the hands of our enemies."

"Not so," answered Morton, with a voice and gesture which compelled many to listen ; "it is not God who deserts us, it is we who desert Him, and dishonor ourselves by disgracing and betraying the cause of freedom and religion. Hear me, " he exclaimed, springing to the pulpit which Mucklewrath had been compelled to evacuate by actual exhaustion— "I bring from the enemy an offer to treat, if you incline to lay down your arms. I can assure you the means of making an honorable defence, if you are of more manly tempers. The time flies fast on.   Let us resolve either for peace or war ; and let it not be said of us, in future days, that six thousand Scottish men in arms had neither courage to stand their ground and fight it out, nor prudence to treat for peace, nor even the coward's wisdom to retreat in good time and with safety. What signifies quarrelling on minute points of church discipline, when the whole edifice is threatened with total destruction ? O, remember, my brethren, that the last and worst evil which God brought upon the people whom He had once chosen—the last and worst punishment of their blindness and hardness of heart—was the bloody dissensions which rent asunder their city, even when the enemy were thundering at its gates !"

Some of the audience testified their feeling of this exhortation by loud exclamations of applause ; others by hooting and exclaiming—"To your tents, O Israel !"

Morton, who beheld the columns of the enemy already beginning to appear on the right bank, and directing their march upon the bridge, raised his voice to its utmost pitch, and, pointing at the same time with his hand, exclaimed, "Silence your senseless clamors, yonder is the enemy ! On maintaining the bridge against him depend our lives, as well as our hope to reclaim our laws and liberties. There shall at least one Scottish man die in their defence. Let any one who loves his country follow me !"

The multitude had turned their heads in the direction to which he pointed. The sight of the glittering files of the English Foot Guards, supported by several squadrons of horse, of the cannon which the artillerymen were busily engaged in planting against the bridge, of the plaided clans who seemed to search for a ford, and of the long succession of troops which were destined to support the attack, silenced at once their clamorous uproar, and struck them with as much consternation as if it were an unexpected apparition, and not the very thing which they ought to have been looking out for. They gazed on each other and on their leaders with looks resembling those that indicate the weakness of a patient when exhausted by a fit of frenzy. Yet when Morton, springing from the rostrum, directed his steps towards the bridge, he was followed by about a hundred of the young men who were particularly attached to his command.

Burley turned to Macbriar. "Ephraim," he said, "it is Providence points us the way, through the worldly wisdom of this latitudinarian youth. He that loves the light, let him follow Burley !"

"Tarry," replied Macbriar; " it is not by Henry Morton, or such as he, that our goings-out and our comings-in are to be meted ; therefore tarry with us. I fear treachery to the host from this Nullifidian Achan. Thou shalt not go with him. Thou art our chariots and our horsemen."

" Hinder me not," replied Burley ; " he hath well said that all is lost if the enemy win the bridge ; therefore let me not. Shall the children of this generation be called wiser or braver than the children of the sanctuary ? Array yourselves under your leaders ; let us not lack supplies of men and ammunition ; and accursed be he who turneth back from the work on this great day !"

Having thus spoken, he hastily marched towards the bridge, and was followed by about two hundred of the most gallant and zealous of his party. There was a deep and disheartened pause when Morton and Burley departed. The commanders availed themselves of it to display their lines in some sort of order, and exhorted those who were most exposed to throw themselves upon their faces to avoid the cannonade which they might presently expect. The insurgents ceased to resist or to remonstrate ; but the awe which had silenced their discords had dismayed their courage. They suffered themselves to be formed into ranks with the docility of a flock of sheep, but without possessing, for the time, more resolution or energy ; for they experienced a sinking of the heart, imposed by the sudden and imminent approach of the danger which they had neglected to provide against while it was yet distant.   They were, however, drawn out with some regularity ; and as they still possessed the appearance of an army, their leaders had only to hope that some favorable circumstance would restore their spirits and courage.

Kettledrummle, Poundtext, Macbriar, and other preachers busied themselves in their ranks, and prevailed on them to raise a psalm.   But the superstitious among them observed, as an ill omen, that their song of praise and triumph sunk into "a quaver of consternation," and resembled rather a penitentiary stave sung on the scaffold of a condemned criminal than the bold strain which had resounded along the wild heath of Loudon Hill in anticipation of that day's victory.   The melancholy melody soon received a rough accompaniment ; the royal soldiers shouted, the Highlanders yelled, the cannon began to fire on one side, and the musketry on both, and the Bridge of Bothwell, with the banks adjacent, were involved in wreaths of smoke.

CHAPTER XXXII

As e'er ye saw the rain doun fa',
  Or yet the arrow from the bow,
Sae our Scots lads fell even down,
  And they lay slain on every knowe.
                              Old Ballad.

ERE Morton or Burley had reached the post to be defended, the enemy had commenced an attack upon it with great spirit. The two regiments of Foot Guards, formed into a close column, rushed forward to the river ; one corps, deploying along the right bank, commenced a galling fire on the defenders of the pass, while the other pressed on to occupy the bridge. The insurgents sustained the attack with great constancy and courage ; and while part of their number returned the fire across the river, the rest maintained a discharge of musketry upon the further end of the bridge itself, and every avenue by which the soldiers endeavored to approach it. The latter suffered severely, but still gained ground, and the head of their column was already upon the bridge, when the arrival of Morton changed the scene ; and his Marksmen, commencing upon the pass a fire as well aimed as it was sustained and regular, compelled the assailants to retire with much loss. They were a second time brought up to the charge, and a second time repulsed with still greater loss, as Burley had now brought his party into action. The fire was continued with the utmost vehemence on both sides, and the issue of the action seemed very dubious.

Monmouth, mounted on a superb white charger, might be discovered on the top of the right bank of the river, urging, entreating, and animating the exertions of his soldiers. By his orders, the cannon, which had hitherto been employed in annoying the distant main body of the Presbyterians, were now turned upon the defenders of the bridge. But these tremendous engines, being wrought much more slowly than in modern times, did not produce the effect of annoying or terrifying the enemy to the extent proposed. The insurgents, sheltered by copsewood along the bank of the river, or stationed in the houses already mentioned, fought under cover, while the Royalists, owing to the precautions of Morton, were entirely exposed. The defence was so protracted and obstinate that the royal generals began to fear it might be ultimately successful. While Monmouth threw himself from his horse, and, rallying the Foot Guards, brought them on to another close and desperate attack, he was warmly seconded by Dalzell, who, putting himself at the head of a body of Lennox Highlanders, rushed forward with their tremendous war-cry of Loch Sloy.* The ammunition of the defenders of the bridge began to fail at this important crisis ; messages, commanding and imploring succors and supplies, were in vain despatched, one after the other, to the main body of the Presbyterian army, which remained inactively drawn up on the open fields in the rear. Fear, consternation, and misrule had gone abroad among them, and while the post on which their safety depended required to be instantly and powerfully reinforced, there remained none either to command or to obey.

As the fire of the defenders of the bridge began to slacken, that of the assailants increased, and in its turn became more fatal. Animated by the example and exhortations of their generals, they obtained a footing upon the bridge itself, and began to remove the obstacles by which it was blockaded. The portal-gate was broken open, the beams, trunks of trees, and other materials of the barricade pulled down and thrown into the river. This was not accomplished without opposition. Morton and Burley fought in the very front of their followers, and encouraged them with their pikes, halberds, and partizans to encounter the bayonets of the Guards and the broadswords of the Highlanders. But those behind the leaders began to shrink from the unequal combat, and fly singly, or in parties of two or three, towards the main body, until the remainder were, by the mere weight of the hostile column as much as by their weapons, fairly forced from the bridge. The passage being now open, the enemy began to pour over. But the bridge was long and narrow, which rendered the manœuvre slow as well as dangerous ; and those who first passed had still to force the houses, from the windows of which the Covenanters continued to fire.

Burley and Morton were near each other at this critical moment.

" There is yet time," said the former, " to bring down horse to attack them, ere they can get into order ; and, with the aid of God, we may thus regain the bridge ; hasten thou to bring them down, while I make the defence good with this old and wearied body."

* See Note 30.

Morton saw the importance of the advice, and, throwing himself on the horse which Cuddie held in readiness for him behind the thicket, galloped towards a body of cavalry which chanced to be composed entirely of Cameronians. Ere he could speak his errand or utter his orders, he was saluted by the execrations of the whole body.

"He flies!" they exclaimed—"the cowardly traitor flies like a hart from the hunters, and hath left valiant Burley in the midst of the slaughter!"

"I do not fly," said Morton. "I come to lead you to the attack. Advance boldly, and we shall yet do well."

"Follow him not! Follow him not!"—such were the tumultuous exclamations which resounded from the ranks; "he hath sold you to the sword of the enemy!"

And while Morton argued, entreated, and commanded in vain, the moment was lost in which the advance might have been useful; and the outlet from the bridge, with all its defences, being in complete possession of the enemy, Burley and his remaining followers were driven back upon the main body, to whom the spectacle of their hurried and harassed retreat was far from restoring the confidence which they so much wanted.

In the meanwhile, the forces of the king crossed the bridge at their leisure, and, securing the pass, formed in line of battle; while Claverhouse, who, like a hawk perched on a rock, and eying the time to pounce on its prey, had watched the event of the action from the opposite bank, now passed the bridge at the head of his cavalry, at full trot, and, leading them in squadrons through the intervals and round the flanks of the royal infantry, formed them in line on the moor, and led them to the charge, advancing in front with one large body, while other two divisions threatened the flanks of the Covenanters. Their devoted army was now in that situation when the slightest demonstration towards an attack was certain to inspire panic. Their broken spirits and disheartened courage were unable to endure the charge of the cavalry, attended with all its terrible accompaniments of sight and sound —the rush of the horses at full speed, the shaking of the earth under their feet, the glancing of the swords, the waving of the plumes, and the fierce shouts of the cavaliers. The front ranks hardly attempted one ill-directed and disorderly fire, and their rear were broken and flying in confusion ere the charge had been completed; and in less than five minutes the horsemen were mixed with them, cutting and hewing without mercy. The voice of Claverhouse was heard, even above the din of conflict, exclaiming to his soldiers—"Kill—kill! no quarter! think on Richard Grahame!" The dragoons, many of whom had shared the disgrace of Loudon Hill, required no exhortations to vengeance as easy as it was complete. Their swords drank deep of slaughter among the unresisting fugitives. Screams for quarter were only answered by the shouts with which the pursuers accompanied their blows, and the whole field presented one general scene of confused slaughter, flight, and pursuit.

About twelve hundred of the insurgents who remained in a body a little apart from the rest, and out of the line of the charge of cavalry, threw down their arms and surrendered at discretion, upon the approach of the Duke of Monmouth at the head of the infantry. That mild-tempered nobleman instantly allowed them the quarter which they prayed for; and, galloping about through the field, exerted himself as much to stop the slaughter as he had done to obtain the victory. While busied in this humane task he met with General Dalzell, who was encouraging the fierce Highlanders and royal volunteers to show their zeal for king and country by quenching the flame of the rebellion with the blood of the rebels.

"Sheathe your sword, I command you, General!" exclaimed the Duke, "and sound the retreat. Enough of blood has been shed; give quarter to the king's misguided subjects."

"I obey your Grace," said the old man, wiping his bloody sword and returning it to the scabbard; "but I warn you, at the same time, that enough has *not* been done to intimidate these desperate rebels. Has not your Grace heard that Basil Olifant has collected several gentlemen and men of substance in the west, and is in the act of marching to join them?"

"Basil Olifant!" said the Duke. "Who or what is he?"

"The next male heir to the last Earl of Torwood. He is disaffected to government from his claim to the estate being set aside in favor of Lady Margaret Bellenden; and I suppose the hope of getting the inheritance has set him in motion."

"Be his motives what they will," replied Monmouth, "he must soon disperse his followers, for this army is too much broken to rally again. Therefore, once more, I command that the pursuit be stopped."

"It is your Grace's province to command, and to be responsible for your commands," answered Dalzell, as he gave reluctant orders for checking the pursuit.

But the fiery and vindictive Grahame was already far out of hearing of the signal of retreat, and continued with his cavalry an unwearied and bloody pursuit, breaking, dispersing, and cutting to pieces all the insurgents whom they could come up with.

Burley and Morton were both hurried off the field by the confused tide of fugitives. They made some attempt to defend the streets of the town of Hamilton ; but, while laboring to induce the fliers to face about and stand to their weapons, Burley received a bullet which broke his sword-arm.

"May the hand be withered that shot the shot!" he exclaimed, as the sword which he was waving over his head fell powerless to his side. "I can fight no longer."*

Then, turning his horse's head, he retreated out of the confusion. Morton also now saw that the continuing his unavailing efforts to rally the fliers could only end in his own death or captivity, and, followed by the faithful Cuddie, he extricated himself from the press, and, being well mounted, leaped his horse over one or two enclosures and got into the open country.

From the first hill which they gained in their flight they looked back, and beheld the whole country covered with their fugitive companions, and with the pursuing dragoons, whose wild shouts and halloo, as they did execution on the groups whom they overtook, mingled with the groans and screams of their victims, rose shrilly up the hill.

"It is impossible they can ever make head again," said Morton.

"The head's taen aff them, as clean as I wad bite it aff a sybo!" rejoined Cuddie. "Eh, Lord! see how the broadswords are flashing! war's a fearsome thing. They'll be cunning that catches me at this wark again. But, for God's sake, sir, let us mak for some strength!"

Morton saw the necessity of following the advice of his trusty squire. They resumed a rapid pace, and continued it without intermission, directing their course towards the wild and mountainous country, where they thought it likely some part of the fugitives might draw together, for the sake either of making defence or of obtaining terms.

* This incident, and Burley's exclamation, are taken from the records.

Rout and slaughter of the Puritans after the battle of Bothwell Bridge.

CHAPTER XXXIII

They require
Of Heaven the hearts of lions, breath of tigers,
Yea and the fierceness too.

FLETCHER.

EVENING had fallen; and for the last two hours they had seen none of their ill-fated companions, when Morton and his faithful attendant gained the moorland, and approached a large and solitary farmhouse, situated in the entrance of a wild glen, far remote from any other habitation.

"Our horses," said Morton, "will carry us no farther without rest or food, and we must try to obtain them here, if possible."

So speaking, he led the way to the house. The place had every appearance of being inhabited. There was smoke issuing from the chimney in a considerable volume, and the marks of recent hoofs were visible around the door. They could even hear the murmuring of human voices within the house. But all the lower windows were closely secured; and when they knocked at the door no answer was returned. After vainly calling and entreating admittance, they withdrew to the stable or shed in order to accommodate their horses, ere they used further means of gaining admission. In this place they found ten or twelve horses, whose state of fatigue, as well as the military yet disordered appearance of their saddles and accoutrements, plainly indicated that their owners were fugitive insurgents in their own circumstances.

"This meeting bodes luck," said Cuddie; "and they hae walth o' beef, that's ae thing certain, for here's a raw hide that has been about the hurdies o' a stot not half an hour syne: it's warm yet."

Encouraged by these appearances, they returned again to the house, and, announcing themselves as men in the same predicament with the inmates, clamored loudly for admittance.

"Whoever ye be," answered a stern voice from the window, after a long and obdurate silence, "disturb not those who mourn for the desolation and captivity of the land, and search out the causes of wrath and of defection, that the stumbling-blocks may be removed over which we have stumbled."

" They are wild western Whigs," said Cuddie, in a whisper to his master, " I ken by their language. Fiend hae me, if I like to venture on them ! "

Morton, however, again called to the party within, and insisted on admittance; but, finding his entreaties still disregarded, he opened one of the lower windows, and pushing asunder the shutters, which were but slightly secured, stepped into the large kitchen from which the voice had issued. Cuddie followed him, muttering betwixt his teeth, as he put his head within the window, " That he hoped there was nae scalding brose on the fire ; " and master and servant both found them-. selves in the company of ten or twelve armed men, seated around the fire, on which refreshments were preparing, and busied apparently in their devotions,

In the gloomy countenances, illuminated by the firelight, Morton had no difficulty in recognizing several of those zealots who had most distinguished themselves by their intemperate opposition to all moderate measures, together with their noted pastor, the fanatical Ephraim Macbriar, and the maniac, Habakkuk Mucklewrath. The Cameronians neither stirred tongue nor hand to welcome their brethren in misfortune, but continued to listen to the low murmured exercise of Macbriar, as he prayed that the Almighty would lift up His hand from His people, and not make an end in the day of His anger. That they were conscious of the presence of the intruders only appeared from the sullen and indignant glances which they shot at them, from time to time, as their eyes encountered.

Morton, finding into what unfriendly society he had unwittingly intruded, began to think of retreating ; but, on turning his head, observed with some alarm that two strong men had silently placed themselves beside the window through which they had entered. One of these ominous sentinels whispered to Cuddie, " Son of that precious woman, Mause Headrigg, do not cast thy lot farther with this child of treachery and perdition. Pass on thy way, and tarry not, for the avenger of blood is behind thee."

With this he pointed to the window, out of which Cuddie jumped without hesitation ; for the intimation he had received plainly implied the personal danger he would otherwise incur.

" Winnocks are no lucky wi' me," was his first reflection

when he was in the open air ; his next was upon the probable fate of his master. " They'll kill him, the murdering loons, and think they're doing a gude turn ! but I'se tak the back road for Hamilton, and see if I canna get some o' our ain folk to bring help in time of needcessity."

So saying, Cuddie hastened to the stable, and taking the best horse he could find instead of his own tired animal, he galloped off in the direction he proposed.

The noise of his horse's tread alarmed for an instant the devotion of the fanatics. As it died in the distance, Macbriar brought his exercise to a conclusion, and his audience raised themselves from the stooping posture and lowering, downward look with which they had listened to it, and all fixed their eyes sternly on Henry Morton.

" You bend strange countenances on me, gentlemen," said he, addressing them. " I am totally ignorant in what manner I can have deserved them."

" Out upon thee ! out upon thee !" exclaimed Muckle-wrath, starting up : " the Word that thou hast spurned shall become a rock to crush and to bruise thee ; the spear which thou wouldst have broken shall pierce thy side ; we have prayed, and wrestled, and petitioned for an offering to atone the sins of the congregation, and lo ! the very head of the offence is delivered into our hand. He hath burst in like a thief through the window ; he is a ram caught in the thicket, whose blood shall be a drink-offering to redeem vengeance from the church, and the place shall from henceforth be called Jehovah-Jireh, for the sacrifice is provided. Up, then, and bind the victim with cords to the horns of the altar !"

There was a movement among the party ; and deeply did Morton regret at that moment the incautious haste with which he had ventured into their company. He was armed only with his sword, for he had left his pistols at the bow of his saddle ; and, as the Whigs were all provided with fire-arms, there was little or no chance of escaping from them by resistance.

The interposition, however, of Macbriar protected him for the moment. " Tarry yet a while, brethren ; let us not use the sword rashly, lest the load of innocent blood lie heavy on us. Come," he said, addressing himself to Morton, " we will reckon with thee ere we avenge the cause thou hast betrayed. Hast thou not," he continued, " made thy face as hard as flint against the truth in all the assemblies of the host ?"

" He has—he has," murmured the deep voices of the as-sistants.

"He hath ever urged peace with the Malignants," said one.

"And pleaded for the dark and dismal guilt of the Indulgence," said another.

"And would have surrendered the host into the hands of Monmouth," echoed a third; "and was the first to desert the honest and manly Burley, while he yet resisted at the pass. I saw him on the moor, with his horse bloody with spurring, long ere the firing had ceased at the bridge."

"Gentlemen," said Morton, "if you mean to bear me down by clamor, and take my life without hearing me, it is perhaps a thing in your power; but you will sin before God and man by the commission of such a murder."

"I say, hear the youth," said Macbriar; "for Heaven knows our bowels have yearned for him, that he might be brought to see the truth, and exert his gifts in its defence. But he is blinded by his carnal knowledge, and has spurned the light when it blazed before him."

Silence being obtained, Morton proceeded to assert the good faith which he had displayed in the treaty with Monmouth, and the active part he had borne in the subsequent action.

"I may not, gentlemen," he said, "be fully able to go the lengths you desire, in assigning to those of my own religion the means of tyrannizing over others; but none shall go farther in asserting our own lawful freedom. And I must needs aver that, had others been of my mind in counsel, or disposed to stand by my side in battle, we should this evening, instead of being a defeated and discordant remnant, have sheathed our weapons in an useful and honorable peace, or brandished them triumphantly after a decisive victory."

"He hath spoken the word," said one of the assembly; "he hath avowed his carnal self-seeking and Erastianism: let him die the death!"

"Peace yet again," said Macbriar, "for I will try him further. Was it not by thy means that the Malignant Evandale twice escaped from death and captivity? Was it not through thee that Miles Bellenden and his garrison of cutthroats were saved from the edge of the sword?"

"I am proud to say that you have spoken the truth in both instances," replied Morton.

"Lo! you see," said Macbriar, "again hath his mouth spoken it. And didst thou not do this for the sake of a Midianitish woman, one of the spawn of Prelacy, a toy with which the arch-enemy's trap is baited? Didst thou not do all this for the sake of Edith Bellenden?"

"You are incapable," answered Morton, boldly, "of appreciating my feelings towards that young lady; but all that I have done I would have done had she never existed."

" Thou art a hardy rebel to the truth," said another dark-browed man ; "and didst thou not so act that, by conveying away the aged woman, Margaret Bellenden, and her granddaughter, thou mightest thwart the wise and godly project of John Balfour of Burley for bringing forth to battle Basil Olifant, who had agreed to take the field if he were insured possession of these women's worldly endowments ? "

"I never heard of such a scheme," said Morton, "and therefore I could not thwart it. But does your religion permit you to take such uncreditable and immoral modes of recruiting ? "

" Peace," said Macbriar, somewhat disconcerted ; "it is not for thee to instruct tender professors, or to construe Covenant obligations. For the rest, you have acknowledged enough of sin and sorrowful defection to draw down defeat on a host, were it as numerous as the sands on the sea-shore. And it is our judgment that we are not free to let you pass from us safe and in life, since Providence hath given you into our hands at the moment that we prayed with godly Joshua, saying, ' What shall we say when Israel turneth their backs before their enemies ? ' Then camest thou, delivered to us as it were by lot, that thou mightest sustain the punishment of one that hath wrought folly in Israel. Therefore, mark my words. This is the Sabbath, and our hand shall not be on thee to spill thy blood upon this day ; but when the twelfth hour shall strike, it is a token that thy time on earth hath run ! Wherefore improve thy span, for it flitteth fast away. Seize on the prisoner, brethren, and take his weapon."

The command was so unexpectedly given, and so suddenly executed by those of the party who had gradually closed behind and around Morton, that he was overpowered, disarmed, and a horse-girth passed round his arms before he could offer any effectual resistance. When this was accomplished, a dead and stern silence took place. The fanatics ranged themselves around a large oaken table, placing Morton among them bound and helpless, in such a manner as to be opposite to the clock which was to strike his knell. Food was placed before them, of which they offered their intended victim a share ; but, it will readily be believed, he had little appetite. When this was removed, the party resumed their devotions. Macbriar, whose fierce zeal did not perhaps exclude some feelings of doubt and compunction, began to expostulate in prayer, as if to wring from the Deity a signal that the bloody sacrifice they proposed was an acceptable service. The eyes and ears of his hearers were anxiously strained, as if to gain some sight or sound which might be converted or wrested into a type of approbation, and ever and anon dark looks were turned on the dial-plate of the timepiece, to watch its progress towards the moment of execution.

Morton's eye frequently took the same course, with the sad reflection that there appeared no possibility of his life being expanded beyond the narrow segment which the index had yet to travel on the circle until it arrived at the fatal hour. Faith in his religion, with a constant unyielding principle of honor, and the sense of conscious innocence, enabled him to pass through this dreadful interval with less agitation than he himself could have expected had the situation been prophesied to him. Yet there was a want of that eager and animating sense of right which supported him in similar circumstances, when in the power of Claverhouse. Then he was conscious that amid the spectators were many who were lamenting his condition, and some who applauded his conduct. But now, among these pale-eyed and ferocious zealots, whose hardened brows were soon to be bent, not merely with indifference, but with triumph, upon his execution—without a friend to speak a kindly word, or give a look either of sympathy or encouragement—awaiting till the sword destined to slay him crept out of the scabbard gradually, and as it were by straw-breadths, and condemned to drink the bitterness of death drop by drop —it is no wonder that his feelings were less composed than they had been on any former occasion of danger. His destined executioners, as he gazed around them, seemed to alter their forms and features, like spectres in a feverish dream; their figures became larger, and their faces more disturbed; and, as an excited imagination predominated over the realities which his eyes received, he could have thought himself surrounded rather by a band of demons than of human beings; the walls seemed to drop with blood, and the light tick of the clock thrilled on his ear with such loud, painful distinctness as if each sound were the prick of a bodkin inflicted on the naked nerve of the organ.

It was with pain that he felt his mind wavering while on the brink between this and the future world. He made a strong effort to compose himself to devotional exercises, and, unequal, during that fearful strife of nature, to arrange his own thoughts into suitable expressions, he had, instinctively, recourse to the petition for deliverance and for composure of spirit which is to be found in the Book of Common Prayer of the Church of England. Macbriar, whose family were of that persuasion, instantly recognized the words, which the unfortunate prisoner pronounced half aloud.

"There lacked but this," he said, his pale cheek kindling with resentment, "to root out my carnal reluctance to see his blood spilled He is a Prelatist, who has sought the camp under the disguise of an Erastian, and all, and more than all, that has been said of him must needs be verity. His blood be on his head, the deceiver ! let him go down to Tophet with the ill-mumbled mass which he calls a prayer-book in his right hand."

"I take up my song against him !" exclaimed the maniac. "As the sun went back on the dial ten degrees for intimating the recovery of holy Hezekiah, so shall it now go forward, that the wicked may be taken away from among the people, and the Covenant established in its purity."

He sprang to a chair with an attitude of frenzy, in order to anticipate the fatal moment by putting the index forward ; and several of the party began to make ready their slaughter-weapons for immediate execution, when Mucklewrath's hand was arrested by one of his companions.

"Hist !" he said ; "I hear a distant noise."

"It is the rushing of the brook over the pebbles," said one.

"It is the sough of the wind among the bracken," said another.

"It is the galloping of horse," said Morton to himself, his sense of hearing rendered acute by the dreadful situation in which he stood. "God grant they may come as my deliverers !"

The noise approached rapidly, and became more and more distinct.

"It is horse," cried Macbriar. "Look out and descry who they are."

"The enemy are upon us !" cried one who had opened the window in obedience to his order.

A thick trampling and loud voices were heard immediately round the house. Some rose to resist, and some to escape ; the doors and windows were forced at once, and the red coats of the troopers appeared in the apartment.

"Have at the bloody rebels ! Remember Cornet Grahame !" was shouted on every side.

The lights were struck down, but the dubious glare of the fire enabled them to continue the fray. Several pistol-shots

were fired ; the Whig who stood next to Morton received a
shot as he was rising, stumbled against the prisoner, whom he
bore down with his weight, and lay stretched above him a
dying man.   This accident probably saved Morton from the
damage he might otherwise have received in so close a struggle, where firearms were discharged and sword-blows given for
upwards of five minutes.

"Is the prisoner safe ?" exclaimed the well-known voice
of Claverhouse ; "look about for him, and despatch the Whig
dog who is groaning there."

Both orders were executed.   The groans of the wounded
man were silenced by a thrust with a rapier, and Morton, disencumbered of his weight, was speedily raised and in the arms
of the faithful Cuddie, who blubbered for joy when he found
that the blood with which his master was covered had not
flowed from his own veins.   A whisper in Morton's ear, while
his trusty follower relieved him from his bonds, explained
the secret of the very timely appearance of the soldiers.*

"I fell into Claverhouse's party when I was seeking for
some o' our ain folk to help ye out o' the hands of the Whigs,
sae being atween the deil and the deep sea, I e'en thought it
best to bring him on wi' me, for he'll be wearied wi' felling
folk the night, and the morn's a new day, and Lord Evandale
awes ye a day in har'st ; and Monmouth gies quarter, the dragoons tell me, for the asking.   Sae haud up your heart, an'
I'se warrant we'll do a' weel eneugh yet."

* See Morton's Capture and Release.   Note 31.

CHAPTER XXXIV

WHEN the desperate affray had ceased, Claverhouse commanded his soldiers to remove the dead bodies, to refresh themselves and their horses, and prepare for passing the night at the farmhouse, and for marching early in the ensuing morning. He then turned his attention to Morton, and there was politeness, and even kindness, in the manner in which he addressed him.

"You would have saved yourself risk from both sides, Mr. Morton, if you had honored my counsel yesterday morning with some attention; but I respect your motives. You are a prisoner-of-war at the disposal of the king and council, but you shall be treated with no incivility; and I will be satisfied with your parole that you will not attempt an escape."

When Morton had passed his word to that effect, Claverhouse bowed civilly, and, turning away from him, called for his sergeant-major.

"How many prisoners, Halliday, and how many killed?"

"Three killed in the house, sir, two cut down in the court, and one in the garden—six in all; four prisoners."

"Armed or unarmed?" said Claverhouse.

"Three of them armed to the teeth," answered Halliday; "one without arms, he seems to be a preacher."

"Ay, the trumpeter to the long-ear'd rout, I suppose," replied Claverhouse, glancing slightly round upon his victims; "I will talk with him to-morrow. Take the other three down to the yard, draw out two files, and fire upon them; and, d'ye hear, make a memorandum in the orderly book of three rebels taken in arms and shot, with the date and name of the place— Drumshinnel, I think, they call it. Look after the preacher till to-morrow; as he was not armed, he must undergo a short examination; or better, perhaps, take him before the privy council; I think they should relieve me of a share of this disgusting drudgery. Let Mr. Morton be civilly used, and see that the men look well after their horses; and let my groom wash Wildblood's shoulder with some vinegar, the saddle has touched him a little."

All these various orders—for life and death, the securing of his prisoners, and the washing his charger's shoulder—were given in the same unmoved and equable voice, of which no accent or tone intimated that the speaker considered one direction as of more importance than another.

The Cameronians, so lately about to be the willing agents of a bloody execution, were now themselves to undergo it. They seemed prepared alike for either extremity, nor did any of them show the least sign of fear, when ordered to leave the room for the purpose of meeting instant death. Their severe enthusiasm sustained them in that dreadful moment, and they departed with a firm look and in silence, excepting that one of them, as he left the apartment, looked Claverhouse full in the face, and pronounced, with a stern and steady voice—"Mischief shall haunt the violent man!" to which Grahame only answered by a smile of contempt.

They had no sooner left the room than Claverhouse applied himself to some food, which one or two of his party had hastily provided, and invited Morton to follow his example, observing, it had been a busy day for them both. Morton declined eating; for the sudden change of circumstances— the transition from the verge of the grave to a prospect of life—had occasioned a dizzy revulsion in his whole system. But the same confused sensation was accompanied by a burning thirst, and he expressed his wish to drink.

"I will pledge you, with all my heart," said Claverhouse; "for here is a black-jack full of ale, and good it must be, if there be good in the country, for the Whigs never miss to find it out. My service to you, Mr. Morton," he said, filling one horn of ale for himself and handing another to his prisoner.

Morton raised it to his head, and was just about to drink when the discharge of carabines beneath the window, followed by a deep and hollow groan, repeated twice or thrice, and more faint at each interval, announced the fate of the three men who had just left them. Morton shuddered and set down the untasted cup.

"You are but young in these matters, Mr. Morton," said Claverhouse, after he had very composedly finished his draught; "and I do not think the worse of you as a young soldier for appearing to feel them acutely. But habit, duty, and necessity reconcile men to everything."

" I trust," said Morton, " they will never reconcile me to such scenes as these."

" You would hardly believe," said Claverhouse, in reply, " that, in the beginning of my military career, I had as much aversion to seeing blood spilled as ever man felt ; it seemed to me to be wrung from my own heart ; and yet, if you trust one of those Whig fellows, he will tell you I drink a warm cup of it every morning before I breakfast.* But in truth, Mr. Morton, why should we care so much for death, light upon us or around us whenever it may ? Men die daily : not a bell tolls the hour but it is the death-note of some one or other ; and why hesitate to shorten the span of others, or take over-anxious care to prolong our own ? It is all a lottery : when the hour of midnight came, you were to die ; it has struck, you are alive and safe, and the lot has fallen on those fellows who were to murder you. It is not the expiring pang that is worth thinking of in an event that must happen one day, and may befall us on any given moment ; it is the memory which the soldier leaves behind him, like the long train of light that follows the sunken sun, that is all which is worth caring for, which distinguishes the death of the brave or the ignoble. When I think of death, Mr. Morton, as a thing worth thinking of, it is in the hope of pressing one day some well-fought and hard-won field of battle, and dying with the shout of victory in my ear ; *that* would be worth dying for, and more, it would be worth having lived for !"

At the moment when Grahame delivered these sentiments, his eye glancing with the martial enthusiasm which formed such a prominent feature in his character, a gory figure, which seemed to rise out of the floor of the apartment, stood upright before him, and presented the wild person and hideous feat-ures of the maniac so often mentioned. His face, where it was not covered with blood-streaks, was ghastly pale, for the hand of death was on him. He bent upon Claverhouse eyes in which the gray light of insanity still twinkled, though just about to flit forever, and exclaimed, with his usual wildness of ejaculation, " Wilt thou trust in thy bow and in thy spear, in thy steed and in thy banner ? And shall not God visit thee for innocent blood ? Wilt thou glory in thy wisdom, and in thy courage, and in thy might ? And shall not the Lord judge thee ? Behold the princes, for whom thou hast

---

* The Author is uncertain whether this was ever said of Claverhouse. But it was currently reported of Sir Robert Grierson of Lagg, another of the persecutors, that a cup of wine placed in his hand turned to clotted blood.

sold thy soul to the destroyer, shall be removed from their
place, and banished to other lands, and their names shall be
a desolation, and an astonishment, and a hissing, and a curse.
And thou, who hast partaken of the wine-cup of fury, and
hast been drunken and mad because thereof, the wish of thy
heart shall be granted to thy loss, and the hope of thine own
pride shall destroy thee. I summon thee, John Grahame, to
appear before the tribunal of God, to answer for this innocent
blood, and the seas besides which thou hast shed."

He drew his right hand across his bleeding face and held
it up to heaven as he uttered these words, which he spoke
very loud, and then added more faintly, "How long, O Lord,
holy and true, dost thou not judge and avenge the blood of
thy saints !"

As he uttered the last word he fell backwards without an
attempt to save himself, and was a dead man ere his head
touched the floor.

Morton was much shocked at this extraordinary scene, and
the prophecy of the dying man, which tallied so strangely
with the wish which Claverhouse had just expressed ; and he
often thought of it afterwards when that wish seemed to be
accomplished. Two of the dragoons who were in the apartment, hardened as they were, and accustomed to such scenes,
showed great consternation at the sudden apparition, the event,
and the words which preceded it. Claverhouse alone was unmoved. At the first instant of Mucklewrath's appearance he
had put his hand to his pistol, but on seeing the situation of
the wounded wretch, he immediately withdrew it, and listened
with great composure to his dying exclamation.

When he dropped, Claverhouse asked in an unconcerned
tone of voice—"How came the fellow here ? Speak, you
staring fool !" he added, addressing the nearest dragoon,
"unless you would have me think you such a poltroon as to
fear a dying man."

The dragoon crossed himself, and replied with a faltering
voice—"That the dead fellow had escaped their notice when
they removed the other bodies, as he chanced to have fallen
where a cloak or two had been flung aside and covered him."

"Take him away now, then, you gaping idiot, and see
that he does not bite you, to put an old proverb to shame.
This is a new incident, Mr. Morton, that dead men should
rise and push us from our stools. I must see that my blackguards grind their swords sharper ; they used not to do their
work so slovenly. But we have had a busy day ; they are
tired, and their blades blunted with their bloody work ; and

I suppose you, Mr. Morton, as well as I, are well disposed for a few hours' repose."

So saying, he yawned, and taking a candle which a soldier had placed ready, saluted Morton courteously, and walked to the apartment which had been prepared for him.

Morton was also accommodated for the evening with a separate room. Being left alone, his first occupation was the returning thanks to Heaven for redeeming him from danger, even through the instrumentality of those who seemed his most dangerous enemies; he also prayed sincerely for the Divine assistance in guiding his course through times which held out so many dangers and so many errors. And having thus poured out his spirit in prayer before the Great Being who gave it, he betook himself to the repose which he so much required.

CHAPTER XXXV

The charge is prepared, the lawyers are met,
The judges all ranged—a terrible show !

Beggar's Opera.

So deep was the slumber which succeeded the agitation and
embarrassment of the preceding day, that Morton hardly knew
where he was when it was broken by the tramp of horses, the
hoarse voice of men, and the wild sound of the trumpets blowing the reveille.   The sergeant-major immediately afterwards
came to summon him, which he did in a very respectful manner, saying the General (for Claverhouse now held that rank)
hoped for the pleasure of his company upon the road.   In
some situations an intimation is a command, and Morton
considered that the present occasion was one of these.   He
waited upon Claverhouse as speedily as he could, found his
own horse saddled for his use, and Cuddie in attendance.
Both were deprived of their firearms, though they seemed,
otherwise, rather to make part of the troop than of the prisoners ; and Morton was permitted to retain his sword, the
wearing which was, in those days, the distinguishing mark
of a gentleman.   Claverhouse seemed also to take pleasure in
riding beside him, in conversing with him, and in confound-
ing his ideas when he attempted to appreciate his real character.   The gentleness and urbanity of that officer's general
manners, the high and chivalrous sentiments of military devotion which he occasionally expressed, his deep and accurate
insight into the human bosom, demanded at once the approbation and the wonder of those who conversed with him ;
while, on the other hand, his cold indifference to military
violence and cruelty seemed altogether inconsistent with the
social, and even admirable, qualities which he displayed.
Morton could not help in his heart contrasting him with Balfour of Burley ; and so deeply did the idea impress him, that
he dropped a hint of it as they rode together at some distance
from the troop.

" You are right," said Claverhouse, with a smile—" you

are very right, we are both fanatics; but there is some distinction between the fanaticism of honor and that of dark and sullen superstition."

"Yet you both shed blood without mercy or remorse," said Morton, who could not suppress his feelings.

"Surely," said Claverhouse, with the same composure; "but of what kind? There is a difference, I trust, between the blood of learned and reverend prelates and scholars, of gallant soldiers and noble gentlemen, and the red puddle that stagnates in the veins of psalm-singing mechanics, crack-brained demagogues, and sullen boors; some distinction, in short, between spilling a flask of generous wine and dashing down a can full of base muddy ale?"

"Your distinction is too nice for my comprehension," replied Morton. "God gives every spark of life, that of the peasant as well as of the prince; and those who destroy His work recklessly or causelessly must answer in either case. What right, for example, have I to General Grahame's protection now more than when I first met him?"

"And narrowly escaped the consequences, you would say?" answered Claverhouse. "Why, I will answer you frankly. Then I thought I had to do with the son of an old Roundheaded rebel, and the nephew of a sordid Presbyterian laird; now I know your points better, and there is that about you which I respect in an enemy as much as I like in a friend. I have learned a good deal concerning you since our first meeting, and I trust that you have found that my construction of the information has not been unfavorable to you."

"But yet," said Morton——

"But yet," interrupted Grahame, taking up the word, "you would say you were the same when I first met you that you are now? True; but then, how could I know that? though, by the by, even my reluctance to suspend your execution may show you how high your abilities stood in my estimation."

"Do you expect, General," said Morton, "that I ought to be particularly grateful for such a mark of your esteem?"

"Poh! poh! you are critical," returned Claverhouse. "I tell you I thought you a different sort of person. Did you ever read Froissart?"

"No," was Morton's answer.

"I have half a mind," said Claverhouse, "to contrive you should have six months' imprisonment in order to procure you that pleasure. His chapters inspire me with more enthusiasm than even poetry itself. And the noble canon, with what true chivalrous feeling he confines his beautiful expressions of sorrow to the death of the gallant and high-bred knight, of whom it was a pity to see the fall, such was his loyalty to his king, pure faith to his religion, hardihood towards his enemy, and fidelity to his lady-love! Ah, *benedicite!* how he will mourn over the fall of such a pearl of knighthood, be it on the side he happens to favor or on the other! But, truly, for sweeping from the face of the earth some few hundreds of villain churls, who are born but to plough it, the high-born and inquisitive historian has marvellous little sympathy; as little, or less, perhaps, than John Grahame of Claverhouse."

"There is one ploughman in your possession, General, for whom," said Morton, "in despite of the contempt in which you hold a profession which some philosophers have considered as useful as that of a soldier, I would humbly request your favor."

"You mean," said Claverhouse, looking at a memorandum-book, "one Hatherick—Hedderick—or—or—Headrigg. Ay, Cuthbert, or Cuddie Headrigg—here I have him. O, never fear him, if he will be but tractable. The ladies of Tillietudlem made interest with me on his account some time ago. He is to marry their waiting-maid, I think. He will be allowed to slip off easy, unless his obstinacy spoils his good fortune."

"He has no ambition to be a martyr, I believe," said Morton.

"'Tis the better for him," said Claverhouse. "But, besides, although the fellow had more to answer for. I should stand his friend for the sake of the blundering gallantry which threw him into the midst of our ranks last night, when seeking assistance for you. I never desert any man who trusts me with such implicit confidence. But, to deal sincerely with you, he has been long in our eye. Here, Halliday; bring me up the black book."

The sergeant, having committed to his commander this ominous record of the disaffected, which was arranged in alphabetical order, Claverhouse, turning over the leaves as he rode on, began to read names as they occurred.

"Gumblegumption, a minister, aged 50, indulged, close, sly, and so forth—pooh! pooh! He—He—I have him here—Heathercat; outlawed—a preacher—a zealous Cameronian—keeps a conventicle among the Campsie Hills—tush! O, here is Headrigg—Cuthbert; his mother a bitter Puritan—himself a simple fellow, like to be forward in action, but of no genius for plots, more for the hand than the head, and might be drawn to the right side, but for his attachment to——" Here Claverhouse looked at Morton, and then shut the book and changed his tone. "Faithful and true are words never thrown away upon me, Mr. Morton. You may depend on the young man's safety."

" Does it not revolt a mind like yours," said Morton, " to follow a system which is to be supported by such minute inquiries after obscure individuals ?"

" You do not suppose *we* take the trouble ?" said the General, haughtily. "The curates, for their own sakes, willingly collect all these materials for their own regulation in each parish ; they know best the black sheep of the flock. I have had your picture for three years."

"Indeed !" replied Morton. "Will you favor me by imparting it ?"

"Willingly," said Claverhonse ; "it can signify little, for you cannot avenge yourself on the curate, as you will probably leave Scotland for some time."

This was spoken in an indifferent tone. Morton felt an involuntary shudder at hearing words which implied a banishment from his native land ; but ere he answered, Claverhouse proceeded to read, "Henry Morton, son of Silas Morton, colonel of horse for the Scottish Parliament, nephew and apparent heir of Morton of Milnwood ; imperfectly educated, but with spirit beyond his years ; excellent at all exercises ; indifferent to forms of religion, but seems to incline to the Presbyterian ; has high-flown and dangerous notions about liberty of thought and speech, and hovers between a latitudinarian and an enthusiast. Much admired and followed by the youth of his own age ; modest, quiet, and unassuming in manner, but in his heart peculiarly bold and intractable. He is—— Here follow three red crosses, Mr. Morton, which signify triply dangerous. You see how important a person you are. But what does this fellow want ?"

A horseman rode up as he spoke, and gave a letter. Claverhouse glanced it over, laughed scornfully, bade him tell his master to send his prisoners to Edinburgh, for there was no answer ; and, as the man turned back, said contemptuously to Morton—"Here is an ally of yours deserted from you, or rather, I should say, an ally of your good friend Burley. Hear how he sets forth : '*Dear Sir*'—I wonder when we were such intimates—'may it please your Excellency to accept my humble congratulations on the victory'—hum—hum— 'blessed his Majesty's army. I pray you to understand I have my people under arms to take and intercept all fugitives, and have already several prisoners,' and so forth.   Subscribed Basil Olifant.   You know the fellow by name, I suppose ?"

" A relative of Lady Margaret Bellenden," replied Morton, " is he not ?"

" Ay," replied Grahame, " and heir-male of her father's family, though a distant one, and moreover a suitor to the fair Edith, though discarded as an unworthy one ; but, above all, a devoted admirer of the estate of Tillietudlem and all thereunto belonging."

" He takes an ill mode of recommending himself," said Morton, suppressing his feelings, " to the family at Tillietudlem by corresponding with our unhappy party."

" O, this precious Basil will turn cat in pan with any man !" replied Claverhouse.   " He was displeased with the government because they would not overturn in his favor a settlement of the late Earl of Torwood, by which his lordship gave his own estate to his own daughter ; he was displeased with Lady Margaret because she avowed no desire for his alliance, and with the pretty Edith because she did not like his tall ungainly person.   So he held a close correspondence with Burley, and raised his followers with the purpose of helping him, providing always he needed no help—that is, if you had beat us yesterday. And now the rascal pretends he was all the while proposing the king's service, and, for aught I know, the council will receive his pretext for current coin, for he knows how to make friends among them ; and a dozen scores of poor vagabond fanatics will be shot or hanged, while this cunning scoundrel lies hid under the double cloak of loyalty, well-lined with the fox-fur of hypocrisy."

With conversation on this and other matters they beguiled the way, Claverhouse all the while speaking with great frankness to Morton, and treating him rather as a friend and companion than as a prisoner ; so that, however uncertain of his fate, the hours he passed in the company of this remarkable man were so much lightened by the varied play of his imagination and the depth of his knowledge of human nature, that, since the period of his becoming a prisoner of war, which relieved him at once from the cares of his doubtful and dangerous station among the insurgents, and from the consequences of their suspicious resentment, his hours flowed on less anxiously than at any time since his having commenced actor in public life.   He was now, with respect to his fortune, like a rider who has flung his reins on the horse's neck, and, while he abandoned himself to circumstances, was at least relieved from the task of attempting to direct them.   In this mood he journeyed on, the number of his companions being continually augmented by detached parties of horse who came in from every quarter of the country, bringing with them, for the most part, the unfortunate persons who had fallen into their power.

At length they approached Edinburgh.

"Our council," said Claverhouse, "being resolved, I suppose, to testify by their present exultation the extent of their former terror, have decreed a kind of triumphal entry to us victors and our captives; but, as I do not quite approve the taste of it, I am willing to avoid my own part in the show, and at the same time to save you from yours."

So saying, he gave up the command of the forces to Allan (now a lieutenant-colonel), and turning his horse into a by-lane, rode into the city privately, accompanied by Morton and two or three servants. When Claverhouse arrived at the quarters which he usually occupied in the Canongate, he assigned to his prisoner a small apartment, with an intimation that his parole confined him to it for the present.

After about a quarter of an hour spent in solitary musing on the strange vicissitudes of his late life, the attention of Morton was summoned to the window by a great noise in the street beneath. Trumpets, drums, and kettle-drums contended in noise with the shouts of a numerous rabble, and apprised him that the royal cavalry were passing in the triumphal attitude which Claverhouse had mentioned. The magistrates of the city, attended by their guard of halberds, had met the victors with their welcome at the gate of the city, and now preceded them as a part of the procession. The next object was two heads borne upon pikes; and before each bloody head were carried the hands of the dismembered sufferers, which were, by the brutal mockery of those who bore them, often approached towards each other as if in the attitude of exhortation or prayer. These bloody trophies belonged to two preachers who had fallen at Bothwell Bridge. After them came a cart led by the executioner's assistant, in which were placed Macbriar and other two prisoners, who seemed of the same profession. They were bareheaded and strongly bound, yet looked around them with an air rather of triumph than dismay, and appeared in no respect moved either by the fate of their companions, of which the bloody evidences were carried before them, or by dread of their own approaching execution, which these preliminaries so plainly indicated.

Behind these prisoners, thus held up to public infamy and derision, came a body of horse, brandishing their broadswords,

and filling the wide street with acclamations, which were answered by the tumultuous outcries and shouts of the rabble,
who, in every considerable town, are too happy in being permitted to huzza for anything whatever which calls them together.   In the rear of these troopers came the main body of
the prisoners, at the head of whom were some of their leaders,
who were treated with every circumstance of inventive mockery and insult.   Several were placed on horseback with their
faces to the animal's tail ; others were chained to long bars of
iron, which they were obliged to support in their hands, like
the galley-slaves in Spain when travelling to the port where
they are to be put on shipboard.   The heads of others who
had fallen were borne in triumph before the survivors, some
on pikes and halberds, some in sacks, bearing the names of
the slaughtered persons labelled on the outside.   Such were
the objects who headed the ghastly procession, who seemed as
effectually doomed to death as if they wore the *sanbenitos* of
the condemned heretics in an *auto-da-fe.**

Behind them came on the nameless crowd to the number
of several hundreds, some retaining under their misfortunes
a sense of confidence in the cause for which they suffered captivity, and were about to give a still more bloody testimony ;
others seemed pale, dispirited, dejected, questioning in their
own minds their prudence in espousing a cause which Providence seemed to have disowned, and looking about for some
avenue through which they might escape from the consequences of their rashness.   Others there were who seemed incapable of forming an opinion on the subject, or of entertaining either hope, confidence, or fear, but who, foaming with
thirst and fatigue, stumbled along like over-driven oxen, lost
to everything but their present sense of wretchedness, and
without having any distinct idea whether they were led to the
shambles or to the pasture.   These unfortunate men were
guarded on each hand by troopers, and behind them came the
main body of the cavalry, whose military music resounded
back from the high houses on each side of the street, and mingled with their own songs of jubilee and triumph, and the
wild shouts of the rabble.

Morton felt himself heart-sick while he gazed on the dismal
spectacle, and recognized in the bloody heads, and still more
miserable and agonized features of the living sufferers, faces
which had been familiar to him during the brief insurrection.
He sunk down in a chair in a bewildered and stupefied state,
from which he was awakened by the voice of Cuddie.

* See Prisoners' Procession. Note 32.

" Lord forgie us, sir ! " said the poor fellow, his teeth chattering like a pair of nut-crackers, his hair erect like boar's bristles, and his face as pale as that of a corpse—"Lord forgie us, sir ! we maun instantly gang before the council ! O Lord, what made them send for a puir body like me, sae mony braw lords and gentles ! And there's my mither come on the lang tramp frae Glasgow to see to gar me testify, as she ca's it, that is to say, confess and be hanged ; but deil tak me if they mak sic a guse o' Cuddie, if I can do better. But here's Claverhouse himsell—the Lord preserve and forgie us, I say anes mair ! "

" You must immediately attend the council, Mr. Morton," said Claverhouse, who entered while Cuddie spoke, " and your servant must go with you. You need be under no apprehension for the consequences to yourself personally. But I warn you that you will see something that will give you much pain, and from which I would willingly have saved you, if I had possessed the power. My carriage waits us ; shall we go ? "

It will be readily supposed that Morton did not venture to dispute this invitation, however unpleasant. He rose and accompanied Claverhouse.

" I must apprise you," said the latter, as he led the way downstairs, " that you will get off cheap ; and so will your servant, provided he can keep his tongue quiet."

Cuddie caught these last words to his exceeding joy.

" Deil a fear o' me," said he, " an my mither disna pit her finger in the pie."

At that moment his shoulder was seized by old Mause, who had contrived to thrust herself forward into the lobby of the apartment.

" O, hinny, hinny ! " said she to Cuddie, hanging upon his neck, " glad and proud, and sorry and humbled am I, a' in ane and the same instant, to see my bairn ganging to testify for the truth gloriously with his mouth in council, as he did with his weapon in the field ! "

" Whist, whist, mither ! " cried Cuddie, impatiently. " Odd, ye daft wife, is this a time to speak o' thae things ? I tell ye I'll testify naething either ae gate or another. I hae spoken to Mr. Poundtext, and I'll tak the declaration, or whate'er they ca' it, and we're a' to win free off if we do that. He's gotten life for himsell and a' his folk, and that's a minister for my siller ; I like nane o' your sermons that end in a psalm at the Grassmarket."

" O, Cuddie, man, laith wad I be they suld hurt ye," said old Mause, divided grievously between the safety of her son's soul and that of his body ; " but mind, my bonny bairn, ye hae battled for the faith, and dinna let the dread o' losing creature comforts withdraw ye frae the gude fight."

" Hout tout, mither," replied Cuddie, " I hae fought e'en ower muckle already, and, to speak plain, I'm wearied o' the trade. I hae swaggered wi' a' thae arms, and muskets, and pistols, buff-coats, and bandoliers, lang eneugh, and I like the pleugh-paidle a hantle better. I ken naething suld gar a man fight—that's to say, when he's no angry—bye and out-taken the dread o' being hanged or killed if he turns back."

" But, my dear Cuddie," continued the persevering Mause, " your bridal garment ! Oh, hinny, dinna sully the marriage garment !" .

" Awa', awa', mither," replied Cuddie ; " dinna ye see the folks waiting for me ? Never fear me ; I ken how to turn this far better than ye do ; for ye're bleezing awa' about marriage, and the job is how we are to win bye hanging."

So saying, he extricated himself out of his mother's embraces, and requested the soldiers who took him in charge to conduct him to the place of examination without delay. He had been already preceded by Claverhouse and Morton.

CHAPTER XXXVI

My native land, good night!
LORD BYRON.

THE privy council of Scotland, in whom the practice since
the union of the crowns vested great judicial powers, as well
as the general superintendence of the executive department,
was met in the ancient dark Gothic room adjoining to the
House of Parliament in Edinburgh, when General Grahame
entered and took his place among the members at the council
table.

"You have brought us a leash of game to-day, General,"
said a nobleman of high place among them. "Here is a
craven to confess, a cock of the game to stand at bay, and
what shall I call the third, General?"

"Without further metaphor, I will entreat your Grace to
call him a person in whom I am specially interested," replied
Claverhouse.

"And a Whig into the bargain?" said the nobleman, loll-
ing out a tongue which was at all times too big for his mouth,
and accommodating his coarse features to a sneer, to which
they seemed to be familiar.

"Yes, please your Grace, a Whig, as your Grace was in
1641," replied Claverhouse, with his usual appearance of imperturbable civility.

"He has you there, I think, my Lord Duke," said one of
the privy councillors.

"Ay, ay," returned the Duke, laughing, "there's no
speaking to him since Drumclog; but come, bring in the
prisoners; and do you, Mr. Clerk, read the record."

The clerk read forth a bond, in which General Grahame
of Claverhouse and Lord Evandale entered themselves securities that Henry Morton, younger of Milnwood, should go
abroad and remain in foreign parts until his Majesty's pleasure
was further known, in respect of the said Henry Morton's accession to the late rebellion, and that under penalty of life and
limb to the said Henry Morton, and of ten thousand merks
to each of his securities.

"Do you accept of the king's mercy upon these terms, Mr. Morton ?" said the Duke of Lauderdale, who presided in the council.

"I have no other choice, my lord," replied Morton.

"Then subscribe your name in the record."

Morton did so without reply, conscious that, in the circumstances of his case, it was impossible for him to have escaped more easily. Macbriar, who was at the same instant brought to the foot of the council table, bound upon a chair, for his weakness prevented him from standing, beheld Morton in the act of what he accounted apostasy.

"He hath summed his defection by owning the carnal power of the tyrant !" he exclaimed, with a deep groan. "A fallen star ! a fallen star !"

"Hold your peace, sir," said the Duke, "and keep your ain breath to cool your ain porridge ; ye'll find them scalding hot, I promise you. Call in the other fellow, who has some common sense. One sheep will leap the ditch when another goes first."

Cuddie was introduced unbound, but under the guard of two halberdiers, and placed beside Macbriar at the foot of the table. The poor fellow cast a piteous look around him, in which were mingled awe for the great men in whose presence he stood, and compassion for his fellow-sufferers, with no small fear of the personal consequences which impended over himself. He made his clownish obeisances with a double portion of reverence, and then awaited the opening of the awful scene.

"Were you at the battle of Bothwell Brig ?" was the first question which was thundered in his ears.

Cuddie meditated a denial, but had sense enough, upon reflection, to discover that the truth would be too strong for him ; so he replied, with true Caledonian indirectness of response, " I'll no say but it may be possible that I might hae been there."

"Answer directly, you knave—yes or no ? You know you were there."

"It's no for me to contradict your Lordship's Grace's honor," said Cuddie.

"Once more, sir, were you there ?—yes or no ?" said the Duke, impatiently.

"Dear stir," again replied Cuddie, "how can ane mind preceesely where they hae been a' the days o' their life ?"

"Speak out, you scoundrel," said General Dalzell,* " or

* See Dalzell's Brutality. Note 33.

I'll dash your teeth out with my dudgeon-haft!   Do you think we can stand here all day to be turning and dodging with you, like greyhounds after a hare?"

"Aweel, then," said Cuddie, "since naething else will please ye, write down that I cannot deny but I was there."

"Well, sir," said the Duke, "and do you think that the rising upon that occasion was rebellion or not?"

"I'm no just free to gie my opinion, stir," said the cautious captive, "on what might cost my neck; but I doubt it will be very little better."

"Better than what?"

"Just than rebellion, as your honor ca's it," replied Cuddie.

"Well, sir, that's speaking to the purpose," replied his Grace.   "And are you content to accept of the king's pardon for your guilt as a rebel, and to keep the church, and pray for the king?"

"Blithely, stir," answered the unscrupulous Cuddie; "and drink his health into the bargain when the ale's gude."

"Egad," said the Duke, "this is a hearty cock.   What brought you into such a scrape, mine honest friend?"

"Just ill example, stir," replied the prisoner, "and a daft auld jaud of a mither, wi' reverence to your Grace's honor."

"Why, God-a-mercy, my friend," replied the Duke, "take care of bad advice another time; I think you are not likely to commit treason on your own score.   Make out his free pardon, and bring forward the rogue in the chair."

Macbriar was then moved forward to the post of examination.

"Were you at the battle of Bothwell Bridge?" was, in like manner, demanded of him.

"I was," answered the prisoner, in a bold and resolute tone.

"Were you armed?"

"I was not: I went in my calling as a preacher of God's Word, to encourage them that drew the sword in His cause."

"In other words, to aid and abet the rebels?" said the Duke.

"Thou hast spoken it," replied the prisoner.

"Well, then," continued the interrogator, "let us know if you saw John Balfour of Burley among the party?   I presume you know him?"

"I bless God that I do know him," replied Macbriar; "he is a zealous and a sincere Christian."

"And when and where did you last see this pious personage?" was the query which immediately followed.

"I am here to answer for myself," said Macbriar, in the same dauntless manner, "and not to endanger others."

"We shall know," said Dalzell, "how to make you find your tongue."

"If you can make him fancy himself in a conventicle," answered Lauderdale, "he will find it without you. Come, laddie, speak while the play is good ; you're too young to bear the burden will be laid on you else."

"I defy you," retorted Macbriar. "This has not been the first of my imprisonments or of my sufferings ; and, young as I may be, I have lived long enough to know how to die when I am called upon."

"Ay, but there are some things which must go before an easy death, if you continue obstinate," said Lauderdale, and rung a small silver bell which was placed before him on the table.

A dark crimson curtain, which covered a sort of niche or Gothic recess in the wall, rose at the signal, and displayed the public executioner, a tall, grim, and hideous man, having an oaken table before him, on which lay thumb-screws, and an iron case, called the Scottish boot, used in those tyrannical days to torture accused persons. Morton, who was unprepared for this ghastly apparition, started when the curtain arose ; but Macbriar's nerves were more firm. He gazed upon the horrible apparatus with much composure ; and if a touch of nature called the blood from his cheek for a second, resolution sent it back to his brow with greater energy.

"Do you know who that man is ?" said Lauderdale, in a low, stern voice, almost sinking into a whisper.

"He is, I suppose," replied Macbriar, "the infamous executioner of your bloodthirsty commands upon the persons of God's people. He and you are equally beneath my regard ; and, I bless God, I no more fear what he can inflict than what you can command. Flesh and blood may shrink under the sufferings you can doom me to, and poor frail nature may shed tears, or send forth cries ; but I trust my soul is anchored firmly on the rock of ages."

"Do your duty," said the Duke to the executioner.

The fellow advanced, and asked, with a harsh and discordant voice, upon which of the prisoner's limbs he should first employ his engine.

"Let him choose for himself," said the Duke ; "I should like to oblige him in anything that is reasonable."

"Since you leave it to me," said the prisoner, stretching

forth his right leg, "take the best ; I willingly bestow it in the cause for which I suffer." *

The executioner, with the help of his assistants, enclosed the leg and knee within the tight iron boot or case, and then placing a wedge of the same metal between the knee and the edge of the machine, took a mallet in his hand, and stood waiting for further orders. A well-dressed man, by profession a surgeon, placed himself by the other side of the prisoner's chair, bared the prisoner's arm, and applied his thumb to the pulse in order to regulate the torture according to the strength of the patient. When these preparations were made, the president of the council repeated with the same stern voice the question, " When and where did you last see John Balfour of Burley ?"

The prisoner, instead of replying to him, turned his eyes to Heaven as if imploring Divine strength, and muttered a few words, of which the last were distinctly audible, " Thou hast said Thy people shall be willing in the day of Thy power !"

The Duke of Lauderdale glanced his eye around the council as if to collect their suffrages, and, judging from their mute signs, gave on his own part a nod to the executioner, whose mallet instantly descended on the wedge, and, forcing it between the knee and the iron boot, occasioned the most exquisite pain, as was evident from the flush which instantly took place on the brow and on the cheeks of the sufferer. The fellow then again raised his weapon and stood prepared to give a second blow.

" Will you yet say," repeated the Duke of Lauderdale, " where and when you last parted from Balfour of Burley ?"

" You have my answer," said the sufferer, resolutely, and the second blow fell. The third and fourth succeeded ; but at the fifth, when a larger wedge had been introduced, the prisoner set up a scream of agony.

Morton, whose blood boiled within him at witnessing such cruelty, could bear no longer, and, although unarmed and himself in great danger, was springing forward, when Claverhouse, who observed his emotion, withheld him by force, laying one hand on his arm and the other on his mouth, while he whispered, " For God's sake, think where you are !"

This movement, fortunately for him, was observed by no other of the councillors, whose attention was engaged with the dreadful scene before them.

" He is gone," said the surgeon—" he has fainted, my lords, and human nature can endure no more."

* This was the reply actually made by James Mitchell when subjected to the torture of the boot for an attempt to assassinate Archbishop Sharp.

"Release him," said the Duke; and added, turning to Dalzell, "He will make an old proverb good, for he'll scarce ride to-day, though he has had his boots on. I suppose we must finish with him?"

"Ay, despatch his sentence and have done with him; we have plenty of drudgery behind."

Strong waters and essences were busily employed to recall the senses of the unfortunate captive; and when his first faint gasps intimated a return of sensation, the Duke pronounced sentence of death upon him, as a traitor taken in the act of open rebellion, and adjudged him to be carried from the bar to the common place of execution, and there hanged by the neck; his head and hands to be stricken off after death, and disposed of according to the pleasure of the council,* and all and sundry his movable goods and gear escheat and inbrought to his Majesty's use.

"Doomster," he continued, "repeat the sentence to the prisoner."

The office of doomster was in those days, and till a much later period, held by the executioner *in commendam* with his ordinary functions.† The duty consisted in reciting to the unhappy criminal the sentence of the law as pronounced by the judge, which acquired an additional and horrid emphasis from the recollection that the hateful personage by whom it was uttered was to be the agent of the cruelties he denounced. Macbriar had scarce understood the purport of the words as first pronounced by the Lord President of the Council; but he was sufficiently recovered to listen and to reply to the sentence when uttered by the harsh and odious voice of the ruffian who was to execute it, and at the last awful words, "And this I pronounce for doom," he answered boldly, "My lords, I thank you for the only favor I looked for, or would accept at your hands, namely, that you have sent the crushed and maimed carcass, which has this day sustained your cruelty, to this hasty end. It were indeed little to me whether I perish on the gallows or in the prison-house; but if death, following close on what I have this day suffered, had found me in my cell of darkness and bondage, many might have lost the sight how a Christian man can suffer in the good cause. For the rest, I forgive you, my lords, for what you have appointed and I have sustained. And why should I not? Ye send me to a happy exchange, to the company of angels and the spirits of the just for that of frail dust and ashes. Ye send me from

---

* See Heads of the Executed. Note 34.
† See a note on the subject of this office in the *Heart of Midlothian.*

darkness into day, from mortality to immortality, and, in a word, from earth to heaven! If the thanks, therefore, and pardon of a dying man can do you good, take them at my hand, and may your last moments be as happy as mine!"

As he spoke thus, with a countenance radiant with joy and triumph, he was withdrawn by those who had brought him into the apartment, and executed within half an hour, dying with the same enthusiastic firmness which his whole life had evinced.

The council broke up, and Morton found himself again in the carriage with General Grahame.

"Marvellous firmness and gallantry!" said Morton, as he reflected upon Macbriar's conduct; "what a pity it is that with such self-devotion and heroism should have been mingled the fiercer features of his sect!"

"You mean," said Claverhouse, "his resolution to condemn you to death? To that he would have reconciled himself by a single text; for example, 'And Phinehas arose and executed judgment,' or something to the same purpose. But wot ye where you are now bound, Mr. Morton?"

"We are on the road to Leith, I observe," answered Morton. "Can I not be permitted to see my friends ere I leave my native land?"

"Your uncle," replied Grahame, "has been spoken to, and declines visiting you. The good gentleman is terrified, and not without some reason, that the crime of your treason may extend itself over his lands and tenements; he sends you, however, his blessing, and a small sum of money. Lord Evandale continues extremely indisposed. Major Bellenden is at Tillietudlem putting matters in order. The scoundrels have made great havoc there with Lady Margaret's muniments of antiquity, and have desecrated and destroyed what the good lady called the Throne of his most Sacred Majesty. Is there any one else whom you would wish to see?"

Morton sighed deeply as he answered, "No; it would avail nothing. But my preparations—small as they are, some must be necessary."

"They are all ready for you," said the General. "Lord Evandale has anticipated all you wish. Here is a packet from him with letters of recommendation for the court of the Stadtholder Prince of Orange, to which I have added one or two. I made my first campaigns under him, and first saw fire at the battle of Seneff.* There are also bills of exchange for

* August, 1674. Claverhouse greatly distinguished himself in this action, and was made captain.

your immediate wants, and more will be sent when you require it."

Morton heard all this and received the parcel with an astounded and confused look, so sudden was the execution of the sentence of banishment.

"And my servant?" he said.

"He shall be taken care of, and replaced, if it be practicable, in the service of Lady Margaret Bellenden; I think he will hardly neglect the parade of the feudal retainers, or go a-Whigging a second time. But here we are upon the quay, and the boat waits you."

It was even as Claverhouse said. A boat waited for Captain Morton, with the trunks and baggage belonging to his rank. Claverhouse shook him by the hand, and wished him good fortune, and a happy return to Scotland in quieter times.

"I shall never forget," he said, "the gallantry of your behavior to my friend Evandale, in circumstances when many men would have sought to rid him out of their way."

Another friendly pressure, and they parted. As Morton descended the pier to get into the boat, a hand placed in his a letter folded up in very small space. He looked round. The person who gave it seemed much muffled up; he pressed his finger upon his lip, and then disappeared among the crowd. The incident awakened Morton's curiosity; and when he found himself on board of a vessel bound for Rotterdam, and saw all his companions of the voyage busy making their own arrangements, he took an opportunity to open the billet thus mysteriously thrust upon him. It ran thus: "Thy courage on the fatal day when Israel fled before his enemies hath in some measure atoned for thy unhappy owning of the Erastian interest. These are not days for Ephraim to strive with Israel. I know thy heart is with the daughter of the stranger. But turn from that folly; for in exile, and in flight, and even in death itself, shall my hand be heavy against that bloody and Malignant house, and Providence hath given me the means of meting unto them with their own measure of ruin and confiscation. The resistance of their stronghold was the main cause of our being scattered at Bothwell Bridge, and I have bound it upon my soul to visit it upon them. Wherefore, think of her no more, but join with our brethren in banishment, whose hearts are still towards this miserable land to save and to relieve her. There is an honest remnant in Holland whose eyes are looking out for deliverance. Join thyself unto them like the true son of the stout and worthy Silas

Morton, and thou wilt have good acceptance among them for his sake and for thine own working. Shouldst thou be found worthy again to labor in the vineyard, thou wilt at all times hear of my incomings and outgoings, by inquiring after Quintin Mackell of Irongray, at the house of that singular Christian woman, Bessie Maclure, near to the place called the Howff, where Niel Blane entertaineth guests. So much from him who hopes to hear again from thee in brotherhood, resisting unto blood, and striving against sin. Meanwhile, possess thyself in patience. Keep thy sword girded, and thy lamp burning, as one that wakes in the night; for He who shall judge the Mount of Esau, and shall make false professors as straw and Malignants as stubble, will come in the fourth watch with garments dyed in blood, and the house of Jacob shall be for spoil, and the house of Joseph for fire. I am he that hath written it, whose hand hath been on the mighty in the waste field."

This extraordinary letter was subscribed J. B. of B.; but the signature of these initials was not necessary for pointing out to Morton that it could come from no other than Burley. It gave him new occasion to admire the indomitable spirit of this man, who, with art equal to his courage and obstinacy, was even now endeavoring to re-establish the web of conspiracy which had been so lately torn to pieces. But he felt no sort of desire in the present moment to sustain a correspondence which must be perilous, or to renew an association which, in so many ways, had been nearly fatal to him. The threats which Burley held out against the family of Bellenden, he considered as a mere expression of his spleen on account of their defence of Tillietudlem; and nothing seemed less likely than that, at the very moment of their party being victorious, their fugitive and distressed adversary could exercise the least influence over their fortunes.

Morton, however, hesitated for an instant whether he should not send the Major or Lord Evandale intimation of Burley's threats. Upon consideration, he thought he could not do so without betraying his confidential correspondence; for to warn them of his menaces would have served little purpose, unless he had given them a clue to prevent them, by apprehending his person; while, by doing so, he deemed he should commit an ungenerous breach of trust to remedy an evil which seemed almost imaginary. Upon mature consideration, therefore, he tore the letter, having first made a memorandum of the name and place where the writer was to be heard of, and threw the fragments into the sea.

While Morton was thus employed the vessel was unmoored, and the white sails swelled out before a favorable north-west wind. The ship leaned her side to the gale, and went roaring through the waves, leaving a long and rippling furrow to track her course. The city and port from which he had sailed became undistinguishable in the distance ; the hills by which they were surrounded melted finally into the blue sky, and Morton was separated for several years from the land of his nativity.

CHAPTER XXXVII

Whom does time gallop withal?
As You Like It.

IT is fortunate for tale-tellers that they are not tied down like
theatrical writers to the unities of time and place, but may
conduct their personages to Athens and Thebes at their pleasure, and bring them back at their convenience. Time, to
use Rosalind's simile, has hitherto paced with the hero of our
tale; for, betwixt Morton's first appearance as a competitor
for the popinjay and his final departure for Holland hardly
two months elapsed. Years, however, glided away ere we find
it possible to resume the thread of our narrative, and Time
must be held to have galloped over the interval. Craving,
therefore, the privilege of my cast, I entreat the reader's attention to the continuation of the narrative, as it starts from
a new era, being the year immediately subsequent to the British
Revolution.

Scotland had just begun to repose from the convulsion occasioned by a change of dynasty, and, through the prudent
tolerance of King William, had narrowly escaped the horrors
of a protracted civil war. Agriculture began to revive; and
men, whose minds had been disturbed by the violent political
concussions and the general change of government in church
and state, had begun to recover their ordinary temper, and to
give the usual attention to their own private affairs in lieu of
discussing those of the public. The Highlanders alone resisted
the newly established order of things, and were in arms in a
considerable body under the Viscount of Dundee, whom our
readers have hitherto known by the name of Grahame of
Claverhouse. But the usual state of the Highlands was so
unruly that their being more or less disturbed was not supposed greatly to affect the general tranquillity of the country, so long as their disorders were confined within their own
frontiers. In the Lowlands, the Jacobites, now the undermost
party, had ceased to expect any immediate advantage by open
resistance, and were, in their turn, driven to hold private

meetings and form associations for mutual defence, which the government termed treason, while *they* cried out persecution.

The triumphant Whigs, while they re-established Presbytery as the national religion, and assigned to the General Assemblies of the Kirk their natural influence, were very far from going the lengths which the Cameronians and more extravagant portion of the Nonconformists under Charles and James loudly demanded. They would listen to no proposal for re-establishing the Solemn League and Covenant ; and those who had expected to find in King William a zealous covenanted monarch were grievously disappointed when he intimated, with the phlegm peculiar to his country, his intention to tolerate all forms of religion which were consistent with the safety of the state. The principles of indulgence thus espoused and gloried in by the government gave great offence to the more violent party, who condemned them as diametrically contrary to Scripture ; for which narrow-spirited doctrine they cited various texts, all, as it may well be supposed, detached from their context, and most of them derived from the charges given to the Jews in the Old Testament dispensation to extirpate idolaters out of the promised land. They also murmured highly against the influence assumed by secular persons in exercising the rights of patronage, which they termed a rape upon the chastity of the church. They censured and condemned as Erastian many of the measures by which government after the Revolution showed an inclination to interfere with the management of the church, and they positively refused to take the oath of allegiance to King William and Queen Mary until they should, on their part, have sworn to the Solemn League and Covenant—the Magna Charta, as they termed it—of the Presbyterian Church.

This party, therefore, remained grumbling and dissatisfied, and made repeated declarations against defections and causes of wrath, which, had they been prosecuted as in the two former reigns, would have led to the same consequence of open rebellion. But as the murmurers were allowed to hold their meetings uninterrupted, and to testify as much as they pleased against Socinianism, Erastianism, and all the compliances and defections of the time, their zeal, unfanned by persecution, died gradually away, their numbers became diminished, and they sunk into the scattered remnant of serious, scrupulous, and harmless enthusiasts of whom Old Mortality, whose legends have afforded the groundwork of my tale, may be taken as no bad representative. But in the years which immediately succeeded the Revolution, the Camero-

nians continued a sect strong in numbers and vehement in their
political opinions, whom government wished to discourage,
while they prudently temporized with them.   These men
formed one violent party in the state ; and the Episcopalian
and Jacobite interest, notwithstanding their ancient and national animosity, yet repeatedly endeavored to intrigue among
them, and avail themselves of their discontents to obtain their
assistance in recalling the Stewart family.   The Revolution-
ary government, in the meanwhile, was supported by the
great bulk of the Lowland interest, who were chiefly disposed
to a moderate Presbytery, and formed in a great measure the
party who, in the former oppressive reigns, were stigmatized
by the Cameronians for having exercised that form of worship
under the declaration of Indulgence issued by Charles II.
Such was the state of parties in Scotland immediately subsequent to the Revolution.

It was on a delightful summer evening that a stranger,
well mounted, and having the appearance of a military man
of rank, rode down a winding descent which terminated in
view of the romantic ruins of Bothwell Castle and the river
Clyde, which winds so beautifully between rocks and woods
to sweep around the towers formerly built by Aymer de Valence.
Bothwell Bridge was at a little distance, and also in sight.
The opposite field, once the scene of slaughter and conflict,
now lay as placid and quiet as the surface of a summer lake.
The trees and bushes, which grew around in romantic variety of
shade, were hardly seen to stir under the influence of the evening breeze.   The very murmur of the river seemed to soften
itself into unison with the stillness of the scene around.
The path through which the traveller descended was occasionally shaded by detached trees of great size, and elsewhere
by the hedges and boughs of flourishing orchards, now laden
with summer fruits.   The nearest object of consequence was
a farmhouse, or, it might be, the abode of a small proprietor,
situated on the side of a sunny bank, which was covered by
apple and pear trees.   At the foot of the path which led up
to this modest mansion was a small cottage, pretty much in
the situation of a porter's lodge, though obviously not designed
for such a purpose.   The hut seemed comfortable, and more
neatly arranged than is usual in Scotland.   It had its little
garden, where some fruit-trees and bushes were mingled with
kitchen herbs ; a cow and six sheep fed in a paddock hard by ;
the cock strutted and crowed, and summoned his family around
him, before the door ; a heap of brushwood and turf, neatly

made up, indicated that the winter fuel was provided ; and the thin blue smoke which ascended from the straw-bound chimney, and winded slowly out from among the green trees, showed that the evening meal was in the act of being made ready. To complete the little scene of rural peace and comfort, a girl of about five years old was fetching water in a pitcher from a beautiful fountain of the purest transparency, which bubbled up at the root of a decayed old oak-tree, about twenty yards from the end of the cottage.

The stranger reined up his horse and called to the little nymph, desiring to know the way to Fairy Knowe. The child set down her water-pitcher, hardly understanding what was said to her, put her fair flaxen hair apart on her brows, and opened her round blue eyes with the wondering, "What's your wull ?" which is usually a peasant's first answer, if it can be called one, to all questions whatever.

"I wish to know the way to Fairy Knowe."

"Mammie, mammie," exclaimed the little rustic, running towards the door of the hut, "come out and speak to the gentleman."

Her mother appeared—a handsome young countrywoman, to whose features, originally sly and *espiègle* in expression, matrimony had given that decent matronly air which peculiarly marks the peasant's wife of Scotland. She had an infant in one arm, and with the other she smoothed down her apron, to which hung a chubby child of two years old. The elder girl, whom the traveller had first seen, fell back behind her mother as soon as she appeared, and kept that station, occasionally peeping out to look at the stranger.

"What was your pleasure, sir ?" said the woman, with an air of respectful breeding, not quite common in her rank of life, but without anything resembling forwardness.

The stranger looked at her with great earnestness for a moment, and then replied, "I am seeking a place called Fairy Knowe, and a man called Cuthbert Headrigg. You can probably direct me to him ?"

"It's my gudeman, sir," said the young woman, with a smile of welcome ; "will you alight, sir, and come into our puir dwelling? Cuddie, Cuddie [a white-headed rogue of four years appeared at the door of the hut]. Rin awa', my bonny man, and tell your father a gentleman wants him. Or, stay—Jenny, ye'll hae mair sense, rin ye awa' and tell him ; he's down at the Four-acres Park. Winna ye light down and bide a blink, sir ? Or would ye take a mouthfu' o' bread and cheese, or a drink o' ale, till our gudeman comes ? It's gude ale, though I shouldna say sae that brews it ; but ploughman lads work hard, and maun hae something to keep their hearts abune by ordinar, sae I aye pit a gude gowpen o' maut to the browst."

As the stranger declined her courteous offers, Cuddie, the reader's old acquaintance, made his appearance in person.   His countenance still presented the same mixture of apparent dulness with occasional sparkles which indicated the craft so often found in the clouted shoe.   He looked on the rider as on one whom he never had before seen ; and, like his daughter and wife, opened the conversation with the regular query, "What's your wull wi' me, sir ?"

"I have a curiosity to ask some questions about this country," said the traveller, "and I was directed to you as an intelligent man who can answer them."

"Nae doubt, sir," said Cuddie, after a moment's hesitation.   "But I would first like to ken what sort of questions they are.   I hae had sae many questions speered at me in my day, and in sic queer ways, that if ye kenn'd a' ye wadna wonder at my jalousing a'thing about them.   My mother gar'd me learn the Single Carritch, whilk was a great vex ; then I behoved to learn about my godfathers and godmothers to please the auld leddy ; and whiles I jumbled them thegither and pleased nane o' them ; and when I cam to man's yestate, cam another kind o' questioning in fashion, that I liked waur than 'effectual calling ;' and the 'did promise and vow' of the tane were yokit to the end o' the tother.   Sae ye see, sir, I aye like to hear questions asked before I answer them."

"You have nothing to apprehend from mine, my good friend ; they only relate to the state of the country."

"Country !" replied Cuddie.   "Ou, the country's weel eneugh, and it werena that dour deevil, Claver'se—they ca' him Dundee now—that's stirring about yet in the Highlands, they say, wi' a' the Donalds, and Duncans, and Dugalds that ever wore bottomless breeks driving about wi' him, to set things asteer again, now we hae gotten them a' reasonably weel settled.   But Mackay will pit him down, there's little doubt o' that ; he'll gie him his fairing, I'll be caution for it."

"What makes you so positive of that, my friend ?" asked the horseman.

"I heard it wi' my ain lugs," answered Cuddie, "foretauld to him by a man that had been three hours stane dead, and came back to this earth again just to tell him his mind.   It was at a place they ca' Drumshinnel."

"Indeed ?" said the stranger ; "I can hardly believe you, my friend."

"Ye might ask my mither, then, if she were in life," said Cuddie ; "it was her explained it a' to me, for I thought the man had only been wounded. At ony rate, he spake of the casting out of the Stewarts by their very names, and the vengeance that was brewing for Claver'se and his dragoons. They ca'd the man Habakkuk Mucklewrath ; his brain was a wee ajee, but he was a braw preacher for a' that."

"You seem," said the stranger, "to live in a rich and peaceful country."

"It's no to compleen o', sir, an we get the crap weel in," quoth Cuddie ; "but if ye had seen the bluid rinnin' as fast on the tap o' that brig yonder as ever the water ran below it, ye wadna hae thought it sae bonny a spectacle."

"You mean the battle some years since ? I was waiting upon Monmouth that morning, my good friend, and did see some part of the action," said the stranger.

"Then ye saw a bonny stour," said Cuddie, "that sall serve me for fighting a' the days o' my life. I judged ye wad be a trooper by your red scarlet lace-coat and your looped hat."

"And which side were you upon, my friend ?" continued the inquisitive stranger.

"Aha, lad," retorted Cuddie, with a knowing look, or what he designed for such, "there's nae use in telling that, unless I kenn'd wha was asking me."

"I commend your prudence, but it is unnecessary ; I know you acted on that occasion as servant to Henry Morton."

"Ay !" said Cuddie, in surprise, "how cam ye by that secret ? No that I need care a bodle about it, for the sun's on our side o' the hedge now. I wish my master were living to get a blink o't."

"And what became of him ?" said the rider.

"He was lost in the vessel gaun to that weary Holland— clean lost, and a'body perished, and my poor master amang them. Neither man nor mouse was ever heard o' mair." Then Cuddie uttered a groan.

"You had some regard for him, then ?" continued the stranger.

"How could I help it ? His face was made of a fiddle, as they say, for a'body that looked on him liked him. And a braw soldier he was. O, an ye had but seen him down at the brig there, fleeing about like a fleeing dragon to gar folk fight that had unco little will till't ! There was he and that sour

Whigamore they ca'd Burley—if twa men could hae won a field, we wadna hae gotten our skins paid that day."

"You mention Burley. Do you know if he yet lives?"

"I kenna muckle about him. Folk say he was abroad and our sufferers wad hold no communion wi' him, because o' his having murdered the Archbishop. Sae he cam hame ten times dourer than ever, and broke aff wi' mony o' the Presbyterians; and, at this last coming of the Prince of Orange, he could get nae countenance nor command for fear of his deevilish temper, and he hasna been heard of since; only some folk say that pride and anger hae driven him clean wud."

"And—and," said the traveller, after considerable hesitation, "do you know anything of Lord Evandale?"

"Div I ken onything o' Lord Evandale? Div I no? Is not my young leddy up-bye yonder at the house, that's as gude as married to him?"

"And are they not married, then?" said the rider, hastily.

"No, only what they ca' betrothed; me and my wife were witnesses, it's no mony months by-past. It was a lang courtship; few folk kenn'd the reason bye Jenny and mysell. But will ye no light down? I downa bide to see ye sitting up there, and the clouds are casting up thick in the west ower Glasgowward, and maist skeely folk think that bodes rain."

In fact, a deep black cloud had already surmounted the setting sun; a few large drops of rain fell, and the murmurs of distant thunder were heard.

"The deil's in this man," said Cuddie to himself; "I wish he would either light aff or ride on, that he may quarter himsell in Hamilton or the shower begin."

But the rider sat motionless on his horse for two or three moments after his last question, like one exhausted by some uncommon effort. At length, recovering himself as if with a sudden and painful effort, he asked Cuddie "if Lady Margaret Bellenden still lived."

"She does," replied Cuddie, "but in a very sma' way. They hae been a sad changed family since thae rough times began; they hae suffered eneugh first and last; and to lose the auld Tower and a' the bonny barony and the holms that I hae pleughed sae often, and the mains, and my kale-yard, that I suld hae gotten back again, and a' for naething, as a body may say, but just the want o' some bits of sheepskin that were lost in the confusion of the taking of Tillietudlem."

"I have heard something of this," said the stranger, deepening his voice and averting his head. "I have some interest in the family, and would willingly help them if 1 could. Can you give me a bed in your house to-night, my friend ?"

"It's but a corner of a place, sir," said Cuddie, "but we'se try, rather than ye suld ride on in the rain and thunner ; for, to be free wi' ye, sir, I think ye seem no that ower weel."

"I am liable to a dizziness," said the stranger, "but it will soon wear off."

"I ken we can gie ye a decent supper, sir," said Cuddie ; "and we'll see about a bed as weel as we can. We wad be laith a stranger suld lack what we have, though we are jimply provided for in beds rather; for Jenny has sae mony bairns—God bless them and her—that troth I maun speak to Lord Evandale to gie us a bit eik or outshot o' some sort to the onstead."

"I shall be easily accommodated," said the stranger, as he entered the house.

"And ye may rely on your naig being weel sorted," said Cuddie ; "I ken weel what belangs to suppering a horse, and this is a very gude ane."

Cuddie took the horse to the little cow-house, and called to his wife to attend in the meanwhile to the stranger's accommodation. The officer entered and threw himself on a settle at some distance from the fire, carefully turning his back to the little lattice window. Jenny, or Mrs. Headrigg, if the reader pleases, requested him to lay aside the cloak, belt, and flapped hat which he wore upon his journey, but he excused himself under pretence of feeling cold ; and to divert the time till Cuddie's return he entered into some chat with the children, carefully avoiding, during the interval, the inquisitive glances of his landlady.

CHAPTER XXXVIII

What tragic tears bedim the eye !
What deaths we suffer ere we die !
Our broken friendships we deplore,
And loves of youth that are no more.
LOGAN.

CUDDIE soon returned, assuring the stranger, with a cheerful voice, "that the horse was properly suppered up, and that the gudewife should make a bed up for him at the house, mair purpose-like and comfortable than the like o' them could gie him."

"Are the family at the house ?" said the stranger, with an interrupted and broken voice.

"No, stir ; they're awa' wi' a' the servants—they keep only twa nowadays—and my gudewife there has the keys and the charge, though she's no a fee'd servant. She has been born and bred in the family, and has a' trust and management. If they were there we behovedna to take sic freedom without their order ; but when they are awa' they will be weel pleased we serve a stranger gentleman. Miss Bellenden wad help a' the haill warld, an her power were as gude as her will ; and her grandmother, Leddy Margaret, has an unco respect for the gentry, and she's no ill to the poor bodies neither. And now, wife, what for are ye no getting forrit wi' the sowens ?"

"Never mind, lad," rejoined Jenny, "ye sall hae them in gude time ; I ken weel that ye like your brose het."

Cuddie fidgeted, and laughed with a peculiar expression of intelligence at this repartee, which was followed by a dialogue of little consequence betwixt his wife and him, in which the stranger took no share. At length he suddenly interrupted them by the question—"Can you tell me when Lord Evandale's marriage takes place ?"

"Very soon, we expect," answered Jenny, before it was possible for her husband to reply ; "it wad hae been ower afore now, but for the death o' auld Major Bellenden."

"The excellent old man !" said the stranger ; "I heard at Edinburgh he was no more. Was he long ill ?"

"He couldna be said to haud up his head after his

331

brother's wife and his niece were turned out o' their ain house ; and he had himsell sair borrowing siller to stand the law ; but it was in the latter end o' King James's days, and Basil Olifant, who claimed the estate, turned a Papist to please the managers, and then naething was to be refused him ; sae the law gaed again the leddies at last, after they had fought a weary sort o' years about it ; and, as I said before, the Major ne'er held up his head again.　And then cam the pitting awa' o' the Stewart line ; and, though he had but little reason to like them, he couldna brook that, and it clean broke the heart o' him, and creditors cam to Charnwood and cleaned out a' that was there : he was never rich, the gude auld man, for he dow'd na see onybody want."

"He was indeed," said the stranger, with a faltering voice, "an admirable man ; that is, I have heard that he was so. So the ladies were left without fortune as well as without a protector ?"

"They will neither want the tane nor the tother while Lord Evandale lives," said Jenny ; "he has been a true friend in their griefs.　E'en to the house they live in is his lordship's ; and never man, as my auld gudemother used to say, since the days of the patriarch Jacob, served sae lang and sae sair for a wife as gude Lord Evandale has dune."

"And why," said the stranger, with a voice that quivered with emotion—"why was he not sooner rewarded by the object of his attachment ?"

"There was the lawsuit to be ended," said Jenny, readily, "forbye many other family arrangements."

"Na, but," said Cuddie, "there was another reason forbye ; for the young leddy——"

"Whisht, haud your tongue and sup your sowens," said his wife.　"I see the gentleman's far frae weel, and downa eat our coarse supper ; I wad kill him a chicken in an instant."

"There is no occasion," said the stranger ; "I shall want only a glass of water, and to be left alone."

"You'll gie yoursell the trouble then to follow me," said Jenny, lighting a small lantern, "and I'll show you the way."

Cuddie also proffered his assistance ; but his wife reminded him, "That the bairns would be left to fight thegither and coup ane anither into the fire," so that he remained to take charge of the menage.

His wife led the way up a little winding path, which, after threading some thickets of sweetbriar and honeysuckle, conducted to the back-door of a small garden.　Jenny undid the latch, and they passed through an old-fashioned flower-

garden, with its clipped yew hedges and formal parterres, to
a glass-sashed door, which she opened with a master-key, and
lighting a candle, which she placed upon a small work-table,
asked pardon for leaving him there for a few minutes until
she prepared his apartment.   She did not exceed five minutes
in these preparations ; but when she returned was startled to
find that the stranger had sunk forward with his head upon
the table, in what she at first apprehended to be a swoon.   As
she advanced to him, however, she could discover by his short-
drawn sobs that it was a paroxysm of mental agony.   She
prudently drew back until he raised his head, and then showing herself, without seeming to have observed his agitation,
informed him that his bed was prepared.   The stranger
gazed at her a moment as if to collect the sense of her words.
She repeated them, and only bending his head as an indication that he understood her, he entered the apartment, the
door of which she pointed out to him.   It was a small bedchamber, used, as she informed him, by Lord Evandale when
a guest at Fairy Knowe, connecting on one side with a little
china-cabinet which opened to the garden, and on the other
with a saloon, from which it was only separated by a thin
wainscot partition.   Having wished the stranger better
health and good rest, Jenny descended as speedily as she could
to her own mansion.

"O, Cuddie !" she exclaimed to her helpmate as she entered, " I doubt we're ruined folk ! "

" How can that be ?   What's the matter wi' ye ?" returned
the imperturbed Cuddie, who was one of those persons who
do not easily take alarm at anything.

" Wha d'ye think yon gentleman is ?   O, that ever ye
suld hae asked him to light here !" exclaimed Jenny.

" Why, wha the muckle deil d'ye say he is ?   There's nae
law against harboring and intercommunicating now," said
Cuddie ; " sae, Whig or Tory, what need we care wha he be ?"

" Ay, but it's ane will ding Lord Evandale's marriage ajee
yet, if it's no the better looked to," said Jenny ; "it's Miss
Edith's first jo, your ain auld maister, Cuddie."

" The deil, woman !" exclaimed Cuddie, starting up,
" trow ye that I am blind ?   I wad hae kenn'd Mr. Harry
Morton amang a hunder."

" Ay, but, Cuddie lad," replied Jenny, "though ye are no
blind, ye are no sae notice-taking as I am."

" Weel, what for needs ye cast that up to me just now ? or
what did ye see about the man that was like our Maister
Harry ?"

"I will tell ye," said Jenny. "I jaloused his keeping his face frae us, and speaking wi' a made-like voice, sae I e'en tried him wi' some tales o' lang syne, and when I spake o' the brose, ye ken, he didna just laugh—he's ower grave for that nowadays—but he gae a gledge wi' his ee that I kenn'd he took up what I said. And a' his distress is about Miss Edith's marriage, and I ne'er saw a man mair taen down wi' true love in my days—I might say man or woman, only I mind how ill Miss Edith was when she first gat word that him and you—ye muckle graceless loon—were coming against Tillietudlem wi' the rebels. But what's the matter wi' the man now?"

"What's the matter wi' me, indeed!" said Cuddie, who was again hastily putting on some of the garments he had stripped himself of. "Am I no gaun up this instant to see my maister?"

"Atweel, Cuddie, ye are gaun nae sic gate," said Jenny, coolly and resolutely.

"The deil's in the wife!" said Cuddie; "d'ye think I am to be Joan Tamson's man, and maistered by women a' the days o' my life?"

"And whase man wad ye be? And wha wad ye hae to maister ye but me, Cuddie lad?" answered Jenny. "I'll gar ye comprehend in the making of a hay-band. Naebody kens that this young gentleman is living but oursells, and frae that he keeps himsell up sae close, I am judging that he's purposing if he fand Miss Edith either married or just gaun to be married, he wad just slide awa' easy, and gie them nae mair trouble. But if Miss Edith kenn'd that he was living, and if she were standing before the very minister wi' Lord Evandale when it was tauld to her, I'se warrant she wad say 'No' when she suld say 'Yes.'"

"Weel," replied Cuddie, "and what's my business wi' that? If Miss Edith likes her auld jo better than her new ane, what for suld she no be free to change her mind like other folk? Ye ken, Jenny, Halliday aye threeps he had a promise frae yoursell."

"Halliday's a liar, and ye're naething but a gomeril to hearken till him, Cuddie. And then for this leddy's choice, lack-a-day! ye may be sure a' the gowd Mr. Morton has is on the outside o' his coat, and how can he keep Leddy Margaret and the young leddy?"

"Isna there Milnwood?" said Cuddie. "Nae doubt, the auld laird left his housekeeper the life-rent, as he heard naught o' his nephew; but it's but speaking the auld wife fair, and they may a' live brawly thegither, Leddy Margaret and a'."

"Hout tout, lad," replied Jenny, "ye ken them little to think leddies o' their rank wad set up house wi' auld Ailie Wilson, when they're maist ower proud to take favors frae Lord Evandale himsell. Na, na, they maun follow the camp, if she tak Morton."

"That wad sort ill wi' the auld leddy, to be sure," said Cuddie; "she wad hardly win ower a lang day in the baggage-wain."

"Then sic a flyting as there wad be between them, a' about Whig and Tory," continued Jenny.

"To be sure," said Cuddie, "the auld leddy's unco kittle in thae points."

"And then, Cuddie," continued his helpmate, who had reserved her strongest argument to the last, "if this marriage wi' Lord Evandale is broken off, what comes o' our ain bit free house, and the kale-yard, and the cow's grass? I trow that baith us and thae bonny bairns will be turned on the wide warld!"

Here Jenny began to whimper. Cuddie writhed himself this way and that way, the very picture of indecision. At length he broke out, "Weel, woman, canna ye tell us what we suld do, without a' this din about it?"

"Just do naething at a'," said Jenny. "Never seem to ken onything about this gentleman, and for your life say a word that he suld hae been here, or up at the house! An I had kenn'd, I wad hae gien him my ain bed and sleepit in the byre or he had gane up-bye: but it canna be helpit now. The neist thing's to get him cannily awa' the morn, and I judge he'll be in nae hurry to come back again."

"My puir maister!" said Cuddie; "and maun I no speak to him, then?"

"For your life, no," said Jenny; "ye're no obliged to ken him; and I wadna hae tauld ye, only I feared ye wad ken him in the morning."

"Aweel," said Cuddie, sighing heavily, "I'se awa' to pleugh the outfield, then; for, if I am no to speak to him, I wad rather be out o' the gate."

"Very right, my dear hinny," replied Jenny; "naebody has better sense than you when ye crack a bit wi' me ower your affairs, but ye suld ne'er do onything aff-hand out o' your ain head."

"Ane wad think it's true," quoth Cuddie; "for I hae aye had some carline or quean or another to gar me gang their gate instead o' my ain. There was first my mither," he continued, as he undressed and tumbled himself into bed; "then there was Leddy Margaret didna let me ca' my soul my ain; then my mither and her quarrelled, and pu'ed me twa ways at anes, as if ilk ane had an end o' me, like Punch and the Deevil rugging about the Baker at the fair; and now I hae gotten a wife," he murmured in continuation, as he stowed the blankets around his person, "and she's like to tak the guiding o' me a' thegither."

"And amna I the best guide ye ever had in a' your life?" said Jenny, as she closed the conversation by assuming her place beside her husband and extinguishing the candle.

Leaving this couple to their repose, we have next to inform the reader that, early on the next morning, two ladies on horseback, attended by their servants, arrived at the house of Fairy Knowe, whom, to Jenny's utter confusion, she instantly recognized as Miss Bellenden and Lady Emily Hamilton, a sister of Lord Evandale.

"Had I no better gang to the house to put things to rights?" said Jenny, confounded with this unexpected apparition.

"We want nothing but the pass-key," said Miss Bellenden. "Gudyill will open the windows of the little parlor."

"The little parlor's locked, and the lock's spoiled," answered Jenny, who recollected the local sympathy between that apartment and the bedchamber of her guest.

"In the red parlor, then," said Miss Bellenden, and rode up to the front of the house, but by an approach different from that through which Morton had been conducted.

"All will be out," thought Jenny, "unless I can get him smuggled out of the house the back way."

So saying, she sped up the bank in great tribulation and uncertainty.

"I had better hae said at ance there was a stranger there," was her next natural reflection. "But then they wad hae been for asking him to breakfast. O, safe us! what will I do? And there's Gudyill walking in the garden, too!" she exclaimed internally, on approaching the wicket, "and I daurna gang in the back way till he's aff the coast. O, sirs! what will become of us?"

In this state of perplexity she approached the *ci-devant* butler, with the purpose of decoying him out of the garden. But John Gudyill's temper was not improved by his decline in rank and increase in years. Like many peevish people, too, he seemed to have an intuitive perception as to what was most likely to teaze those whom he conversed with; and on the present occasion all Jenny's efforts to remove him from the garden served only to root him in it as fast as if he had

been one of the shrubs.   Unluckily, also, he had commenced
florist during his residence at Fairy Knowe, and, leaving all
other things to the charge of Lady Emily's servant, his first
care was dedicated to the flowers, which he had taken under
his special protection, and which he propped, dug, and watered,
prosing all the while upon their respective merits to poor Jenny,
who stood by him trembling, and almost crying, with anxiety,
fear, and impatience.

Fate seemed determined to win a match against Jenny this
unfortunate morning.   As soon as the ladies entered the house
they observed that the door of the little parlor, the very apartment out of which she was desirous of excluding them on account of its contiguity to the room in which Morton slept,
was not only unlocked, but absolutely ajar.   Miss Bellenden
was too much engaged with her own immediate subjects of
reflection to take much notice of the circumstance, but, desiring the servant to open the window-shutters, walked into the
room along with her friend.

"He is not yet come," she said.   "What can your brother
possibly mean?   Why express so anxious a wish that we
should meet him here?   And why not come to Castle Din-
nan, as he proposed?   I own, my dear Emily, that, even engaged as we are to each other, and with the sanction of your
presence, I do not feel that I have done quite right in indulging him."

"Evandale was never capricious," answered his sister; "I
am sure he will satisfy us with his reasons, and if he does not
I will help you to scold him."

"What I chiefly fear," said Edith, "is his having engaged
in some of the plots of this fluctuating and unhappy time.   I
know his heart is with that dreadful Claverhouse and his army,
and I believe he would have joined them ere now but for my
uncle's death, which gave him so much additional trouble on
our account.   How singular that one so rational and so deeply
sensible of the errors of the exiled family should be ready to
risk all for their restoration!"

"What can I say?" answered Lady Emily; "it is a point
of honor with Evandale.   Our family have always been loyal;
he served long in the Guards; the Viscount of Dundee was
his commander and his friend for years; he is looked on with
an evil eye by many of his own relations, who set down his
inactivity to the score of want of spirit.   You must be aware,
my dear Edith, how often family connections and early
predilections influence our actions more than abstract arguments.   But I trust Evandale will continue quiet, though, to

tell you truth, I believe you are the only one who can keep him so."

"And how is it in my power?" said Miss Bellenden.

"You can furnish him with the Scriptural apology for not going forth with the host: 'He has married a wife, and therefore cannot come.'"

"I have promised," said Edith, in a faint voice; "but I trust I shall not be urged on the score of time."

"Nay," said Lady Emily, "I will leave Evandale—and here he comes—to plead his own cause."

"Stay, stay, for God's sake!" said Edith, endeavoring to detain her.

"Not I—not I," said the young lady, making her escape; "the third person makes a silly figure on such occasions. When you want me for breakfast I will be found in the willow-walk by the river."

As she tripped out of the room, Lord Evandale entered. "Good-morrow, brother, and good-bye till breakfast-time," said the lively young lady; "I trust you will give Miss Bellenden some good reasons for disturbing her rest so early in the morning."

And so saying, she left them together, without waiting a reply.

"And now, my lord," said Edith, "may I desire to know the meaning of your singular request to meet you here at so early an hour?"

She was about to add, that she hardly felt herself excusable in having complied with it; but, upon looking at the person whom she addressed, she was struck dumb by the singular and agitated expression of his countenance, and interrupted herself to exclaim—"For God's sake, what is the matter?"

"His Majesty's faithful subjects have gained a great and most decisive victory near Blair of Athole; but, alas! my gallant friend, Lord Dundee——"

"Has fallen?" said Edith, anticipating the rest of his tidings.

"True—most true; he has fallen in the arms of victory, and not a man remains of talents and influence sufficient to fill up his loss in King James's service. This, Edith, is no time for temporizing with our duty. I have given directions to raise my followers, and I must take leave of you this evening."

"Do not think of it, my lord," answered Edith; "your life is essential to your friends; do not throw it away in an adventure so rash. What can your single arm, and the few tenants or servants who might follow you, do against the force of almost all Scotland, the Highland clans only excepted ?"

"Listen to me, Edith," said Lord Evandale. "I am not so rash as you may suppose me, nor are my present motives of such light importance as to affect only those personally dependent on myself. The Life Guards, with whom I served so long, although new-modelled and new-officered by the Prince of Orange, retain a predilection for the cause of their rightful master ; and [and here he whispered as if he feared even the walls of the apartment had ears] when my foot is known to be in the stirrup two regiments of cavalry have sworn to renounce the usurper's service and fight under my orders. They delayed only till Dundee should descend into the Lowlands ; but, since he is no more, which of his successors dare take that decisive step, unless encouraged by the troops declaring themselves ? Meantime, the zeal of the soldiers will die away. I must bring them to a decision while their hearts are glowing with the victory their old leader has obtained, and burning to avenge his untimely death."

" And will you, on the faith of such men as you know these soldiers to be," said Edith, " take a part of such dreadful moment ?"

" I will," said Lord Evandale—"I must ; my honor and loyalty are both pledged for it."

"And all for the sake," continued Miss Bellenden, " of a prince whose measures, while he was on the throne, no one could condemn more than Lord Evandale ?"

" Most true," replied Lord Evandale ; " and as I resented, even during the plenitude of his power, his innovations on church and state, like a freeborn subject, I am determined I will assert his real rights when he is in adversity, like a loyal one. Let courtiers and sycophants flatter power and desert misfortune ; I will neither do the one nor the other."

" And if you are determined to act what my feeble judgment must still term rashly, why give yourself the pain of this untimely meeting ?"

"Were it not enough to answer," said Lord Evandale, " that, ere rushing on battle, I wished to bid adieu to my betrothed bride ? Surely it is judging coldly of my feelings, and showing too plainly the indifference of your own, to question my motive for a request so natural."

" But why in this place, my lord ?" said Edith ; " and why with such peculiar circumstances of mystery ?"

" Because," he replied, putting a letter into her hand, " I

have yet another request, which I dare hardly proffer, even when prefaced by these credentials."

In haste and terror Edith glanced over the letter, which was from her grandmother.

"My dearest childe," such was its tenor in style and spelling, "I never more deeply regretted the reumatizm, which disqualified me from riding on horseback, than at this present writing, when I would most have wished to be where this paper will soon be, that is at Fairy Knowe, with my poor dear Willie's only child. But it is the will of God I should not be with her, which I conclude to be the case, as much for the pain I now suffer as because it hath now not given way either to cammomile poultices or to decoxion of wild mustard, wherewith I have often relieved others. Therefore, I must tell you, by writing instead of word of mouth, that, as my young Lord Evandale is called to the present campaign both by his honor and his duty, he hath earnestly solicited me that the bonds of holy matrimony be knitted before his departure to the wars between you and him, in implement of the indenture formerly entered into for that effeck, whereuntill, as I see no raisonable objexion, so I trust that you, who have been always a good and obedient childe, will not devize any which has less than raison. It is trew that the contrax of our house have heretofore been celebrated in a manner more befitting our Rank, and not in private, and with few witnesses, as a thing done in a corner. But it has been Heaven's own freewill, as well as those of the kingdom where we live, to take away from us our estate, and from the King his throne. Yet I trust He will yet restore the rightful heir to the throne, and turn his heart to the true Protestant Episcopal faith, which I have the better right to expect to see even with my old eyes, as I have beheld the royal family when they were struggling as sorely with masterful usurpers and rebels as they are now : that is to say, when his most sacred Majesty, Charles the Second of happy memory, honored our poor house of Tillietudlem by taking his disjune therein," etc., etc., etc.

We will not abuse the reader's patience by quoting more of Lady Margaret's prolix epistle. Suffice it to say, that it closed by laying her commands on her grandchild to consent to the solemnization of her marriage without loss of time.

"I never thought till this instant," said Edith, dropping the letter from her hand, "that Lord Evandale would have acted ungenerously."

"Ungenerously, Edith!" replied her lover. "And how

can you apply such a term to my desire to call you mine ere I
part from you perhaps forever ? ”

“Lord Evandale ought to have remembered,” said Edith,
“that when his perseverance, and, I must add, a due sense of
his merit and of the obligations we owed him, wrung from me
a slow consent that I would one day comply with his wishes,
I made it my condition that I should not be pressed to a hasty
accomplishment of my promise ; and now he avails himself of
his interest with my only remaining relative to hurry me with
precipitate and even indelicate importunity. There is more
selfishness then generosity, my lord, in such eager and urgent
solicitation.”

Lord Evandale, evidently much hurt, took two or three
turns through the apartment ere he replied to this accusation ;
at length he spoke—“I should have escaped this painful charge,
durst I at once have mentioned to Miss Bellenden my principal reason for urging this request. It is one which she will
probably despise on her own account, but which ought to
weigh with her for the sake of Lady Margaret. My death in
battle must give my whole estate to my heirs of entail ; my
forfeiture as a traitor, by the usurping government, may vest
it in the Prince of Orange or some Dutch favorite. In either
case, my venerable friend and betrothed bride must remain
unprotected and in poverty. Vested with the rights and provisions of Lady Evandale, Edith will find, in the power of
supporting her aged parent, some consolation for having condescended to share the titles and fortunes of one who does
not pretend to be worthy of her.”

Edith was struck dumb by an argument which she had not
expected, and was compelled to acknowledge that Lord Evandale’s suit was urged with delicacy as well as with consideration.

“And yet,” she said, “such is the waywardness with
which my heart reverts to former times, that I cannot [she
burst into tears] suppress a degree of ominous reluctance at
fulfilling my engagement upon such a brief summons.”

“We have already fully considered this painful subject,”
said Lord Evandale ; “and I hoped, my dear Edith, your
own inquiries, as well as mine, had fully convinced you that
these regrets were fruitless.”

“Fruitless indeed !” said Edith, with a deep sigh, which,
as if by an unexpected echo, was repeated from the adjoining
apartment. Miss Bellenden started at the sound, and scarcely
composed herself upon Lord Evandale’s assurances that she
had heard but the echo of her own respiration.

"It sounded strangely distinct," she said, "and almost ominous ; but my feelings are so harassed that the slightest trifle agitates them."

Lord Evandale eagerly attempted to soothe her alarm, and reconcile her to a measure which, however hasty, appeared to him the only means by which he could secure her independence. He urged his claim in virtue of the contract, her grandmother's wish and command, the propriety of insuring her comfort and independence, and touched lightly on his own long attachment, which he had evinced by so many and such varied services. These Edith felt the more the less they were insisted upon ; and at length, as she had nothing to oppose to his ardor excepting a causeless reluctance, which she herself was ashamed to oppose against so much generosity, she was compelled to rest upon the impossibility of having the ceremony performed upon such hasty notice at such a time and place. But for all this Lord Evandale was prepared, and he explained with joyful alacrity that the former chaplain of his regiment was in attendance at the lodge with a faithful domestic, once a non-commissioned officer in the same corps ; that his sister was also possessed of the secret ; and that Headrigg and his wife might be added to the list of witnesses, if agreeable to Miss Bellenden. As to the place, he had chosen it on very purpose. The marriage was to remain a secret, since Lord Evandale was to depart in disguise very soon after it was solemnized, a circumstance which, had their union been public, must have drawn upon him the attention of the government, as being altogether unaccountable, unless from his being engaged in some dangerous design. Having hastily urged these motives and explained his arrangements, he ran, without waiting for an answer, to summon his sister to attend his bride, while he went in search of the other persons whose presence was necessary.

When Lady Emily arrived, she found her friend in an agony of tears, of which she was at some loss to comprehend the reason, being one of those damsels who think there is nothing either wonderful or terrible in matrimony, and joining with most who knew him in thinking that it could not be rendered peculiarly alarming by Lord Evandale being the bridegroom. Influenced by these feelings, she exhausted in succession all the usual arguments for courage, and all the expressions of sympathy and condolence ordinarily employed on such occasions. But when Lady Emily beheld her future sister-in-law deaf to all those ordinary topics of consolation ; when she beheld tears follow fast and without intermission down cheeks as pale as marble ; when she felt that the hand which she pressed in order to enforce her arguments turned cold within her grasp, and lay, like that of a corpse, insensible and unresponsive to her caresses, her feelings of sympathy gave way to those of hurt pride and pettish displeasure.

"I must own," she said, "that I am something at a loss to understand all this, Miss Bellenden. Months have passed since you agreed to marry my brother, and you have postponed the fulfilment of your engagement from one period to another, as if you had to avoid some dishonorable or highly disagreeable connection. I think I can answer for Lord Evandale that he will seek no woman's hand against her inclination ; and, though his sister, I may boldly say that he does not need to urge any lady further than her inclinations carry her. You will forgive me, Miss Bellenden, but your present distress augurs ill for my brother's future happiness, and I must needs say that he does not merit all these expressions of dislike and dolor, and that they seem an odd return for an attachment which he has manifested so long and in so many ways."

"You are right, Lady Emily," said Edith, drying her eyes and endeavoring to resume her natural manner, though still betrayed by her faltering voice and the paleness of her cheeks —"you are quite right ; Lord Evandale merits such usage from no one, least of all from her whom he has honored with his regard. But if I have given way, for the last time, to a sudden and irresistible burst of feeling, it is my consolation, Lady Emily, that your brother knows the cause, that I have hid nothing from him, and that he at least is not apprehensive of finding in Edith Bellenden a wife undeserving of his affection. But still you are right, and I merit your censure for indulging for a moment fruitless regret and painful remembrances. It shall be so no longer ; my lot is cast with Evandale, and with him I am resolved to bear it. Nothing shall in future occur to excite his complaints or the resentment of his relations ; no idle recollections of other days shall intervene to prevent the zealous and affectionate discharge of my duty ; no vain illusions recall the memory of other days——"

As she spoke these words, she slowly raised her eyes, which had before been hidden by her hand, to the latticed window of her apartment, which was partly open, uttered a dismal shriek, and fainted. Lady Emily turned her eyes in the same direction, but saw only the shadow of a man, which seemed to disappear from the window, and terrified more by the state of Edith than by the apparition she had herself witnessed, she uttered shriek upon shriek for assistance. Her brother soon arrived with the chaplain and Jenny Dennison ; but strong and vigorous remedies were necessary ere they could recall Miss Bellenden to sense and motion. Even then her language was wild and incoherent.

"Press me no further," she said to Lord Evandale ; "it cannot be : Heaven and earth, the living and the dead, have leagued themselves against this ill-omened union. Take all I can give, my sisterly regard, my devoted friendship. I will love you as a sister and serve you as a bondswoman, but never speak to me more of marriage."

The astonishment of Lord Evandale may easily be conceived.

"Emily," he said to his sister, "this is your doing ; I was accursed when I thought of bringing you here ; some of your confounded folly has driven her mad !"

"On my word, brother," answered Lady Emily, "you're sufficient to drive all the women in Scotland mad. Because your mistress seems much disposed to jilt you, you quarrel with your sister, who has been arguing in your cause, and had brought her to a quiet hearing, when all of a sudden a man looked in at a window, whom her crazed sensibility mistook either for you or some one else, and has treated us gratis with an excellent tragic scene."

"What man ? What window ?" said Lord Evandale, in impatient displeasure. "Miss Bellenden is incapable of trifling with me ; and yet what else could have——"

"Hush ! hush !" said Jenny, whose interest lay particularly in shifting further inquiry ; "for Heaven's sake, my lord, speak low, for my lady begins to recover."

Edith was no sooner somewhat restored to herself than she begged, in a feeble voice, to be left alone with Lord Evandale. All retreated, Jenny with her usual air of officious simplicity, Lady Emily and the chaplain with that of awakened curiosity. No sooner had they left the apartment than Edith beckoned Lord Evandale to sit beside her on the couch ; her next motion was to take his hand, in spite of his surprised resistance, to her lips ; her last was to sink from her seat and to clasp his knees.

"Forgive me, my lord !" she exclaimed—"forgive me ! I must deal most untruly by you, and break a solemn engagement. You have my friendship, my highest regard, my most sincere gratitude. You have more : you have my word and my faith. But, O, forgive me, for the fault is not mine—you have not my love, and I cannot marry you without a sin !"

"You dream, my dearest Edith !" said Evandale, perplexed in the utmost degree ; "you let your imagination beguile you ; this is but some delusion of an over-sensitive mind. The person whom you preferred to me has been long in a better world, where your unavailing regret cannot follow him, or, if it could, would only diminish his happiness."

"You are mistaken, Lord Evandale," said Edith, solemnly, "I am not a sleep-walker or a madwoman. No ; I could not have believed from any one what I have seen. But, having seen him, I must believe mine own eyes."

"Seen *him?*—seen whom ?" asked Lord Evandale, in great anxiety.

"Henry Morton," replied Edith, uttering these two words as if they were her last, and very nearly fainting when she had done so.

"Miss Bellenden," said Lord Evandale, "you treat me like a fool or a child. If you repent your engagement to me," he continued, indignantly, "I am not a man to enforce it against your inclination ; but deal with me as a man, and forbear this trifling."

He was about to go on, when he perceived, from her quivering eye and pallid cheek, that nothing was less intended than imposture, and that by whatever means her imagination had been so impressed, it was really disturbed by unaffected awe and terror. He changed his tone, and exerted all his eloquence in endeavoring to soothe and extract from her the secret cause of such terror.

"I saw him !" she repeated—"I saw Henry Morton stand at that window, and look into the apartment at the moment I was on the point of abjuring him forever. His face was darker, thinner, and paler than it was wont to be ; his dress was a horseman's cloak, and hat looped down over his face ; his expression was like that he wore on that dreadful morning when he was examined by Claverhouse at Tillietudlem. Ask your sister—ask Lady Emily, if she did not see him as well as I. I know what has called him up ; he came to upbraid me, that, while my heart was with him in the deep and dead sea, I was about to give my hand to another. My lord, it is ended between you and me ; be the consequences what they will, *she* cannot marry whose union disturbs the repose of the dead."*

"Good heaven !" said Evandale, as he paced the room, half mad himself with surprise and vexation, "her fine understanding must be totally overthrown, and that by the effort which she has made to comply with my ill-timed, though well-

* See Supposed Apparition of Morton. Note 35.

meant, request. Without rest and attention her health is ruined forever."

At this moment the door opened, and Halliday, who had been Lord Evandale's principal personal attendant since they both left the Guards on the Revolution, stumbled into the room with a countenance as pale and ghastly as terror could paint it.

"What is the matter next, Halliday?" cried his master, starting up. "Any discovery of the——"

He had just recollection sufficient to stop short in the midst of the dangerous sentence.

"No, sir," said Halliday, "it is not that, nor anything like that; but I have seen a ghost!"

"A ghost! you eternal idiot!" said Lord Evandale, forced altogether out of his patience. "Has all mankind sworn to go mad in order to drive me so? What ghost, you simpleton?"

"The ghost of Henry Morton, the Whig captain at Bothwell Bridge," replied Halliday. "He passed by me like a fireflaught when I was in the garden!"

"This is midsummer madness," said Lord Evandale, "or there is some strange villany afloat. Jenny, attend your lady to her chamber, while I endeavor to find a clue to all this."

But Lord Evandale's inquiries were in vain. Jenny, who might have given, had she chosen, a very satisfactory explanation, had an interest to leave the matter in darkness; and interest was a matter which now weighed principally with Jenny, since the possession of an active and affectionate husband in her own proper right had altogether allayed her spirit of coquetry. She had made the best use of the first moments of confusion hastily to remove all traces of any one having slept in the apartment adjoining to the parlor, and even to erase the mark of footsteps beneath the window, through which she conjectured Morton's face had been seen, while attempting, ere he left the garden, to gain one look at her whom he had so long loved, and was now on the point of losing forever. That he had passed Halliday in the garden was equally clear; and she learned from her elder boy, whom she had employed to have the stranger's horse saddled and ready for his departure, that he had rushed into the stable, thrown the child a broad gold piece, and, mounting his horse, had ridden with fearful rapidity down towards the Clyde. The secret was, therefore, in their own family, and Jenny was resolved it should remain so.

"For, to be sure," she said, "although her lady and Halliday kenn'd Mr. Morton by broad daylight, that was nae reason I suld own to kenning him in the gloaming and by candle-light, and him keeping his face frae Cuddie and me a' the time."

So she stood resolutely upon the negative when examined by Lord Evandale. As for Halliday, he could only say that, as he entered the garden-door, the supposed apparition met him walking swiftly, and with a visage on which anger and grief appeared to be contending.

"He knew him well," he said, "having been repeatedly guard upon him, and obliged to write down his marks of stature and visage in case of escape. And there were few faces like Mr. Morton's." But what should make him haunt the country where he was neither hanged nor shot, he, the said Halliday, did not pretend to conceive.

Lady Emily confessed she had seen the face of a man at the window, but her evidence went no further. John Gudyill deponed *nil novit in causa*. He had left his gardening to get his morning dram just at the time when the apparition had taken place. Lady Emily's servant was waiting orders in the kitchen, and there was not another being within a quarter of a mile of the house.

Lord Evandale returned perplexed and dissatisfied in the highest degree at beholding a plan which he thought necessary not less for the protection of Edith in contingent circumstances than for the assurance of his own happiness, and which he had brought so very near perfection, thus broken off without any apparent or rational cause. His knowledge of Edith's character set her beyond the suspicion of covering any capricious change of determination by a pretended vision. But he would have set the apparition down to the influence of an overstrained imagination, agitated by the circumstances in which she had so suddenly been placed, had it not been for the coinciding testimony of Halliday, who had no reason for thinking of Morton more than any other person, and knew nothing of Miss Bellenden's vision when he promulgated his own. On the other hand, it seemed in the highest degree improbable that Morton, so long and so vainly sought after, and who was, with such good reason, supposed to be lost when the "Vryheid" of Rotterdam went down with crew and passengers, should be alive and lurking in this country, where there was no longer any reason why he should not openly show himself, since the present government favored his party in politics. When Lord Evandale reluctantly brought himself to communicate these doubts to the chaplain,

in order to obtain his opinion, he could only obtain a long lecture
on demonology, in which, after quoting Delrio, and Burthoog, and De L'Ancre, on the subject of apparitions, together
with sundry civilians and common lawyers on the nature of
testimony, the learned gentleman expressed his definite and
determined opinion to be, either that there had been an
actual apparition of the deceased Henry Morton's spirit, the
possibility of which he was, as a divine and a philosopher,
neither fully prepared to admit nor to deny; or else, that the
said Henry Morton, being still *in rerum natura*, had appeared
in his proper person that morning; or, finally, that some
strong *deceptio visus*, or striking similitude of person, had
deceived the eyes of Miss Bellenden and of Thomas Halliday.
Which of these was the most probable hypothesis, the Doctor
declined to pronounce, but expressed himself ready to die in
the opinion that one or other of them had occasioned that
morning's disturbance.

Lord Evandale soon had additional cause for distressful
anxiety. Miss Bellenden was declared to be dangerously ill.

"I will not leave this place," he exclaimed, "till she is
pronounced to be in safety. I neither can nor ought to do
so; for, whatever may have been the immediate occasion of
her illness, I gave the first cause for it by my unhappy solicitation."

He established himself, therefore, as a guest in the family,
which the presence of his sister as well as of Lady Margaret
Bellenden—who, in despite of her rheumatism, caused herself
to be transported thither when she heard of her granddaughter's illness—rendered a step equally natural and delicate.
And thus he anxiously awaited until, without injury to her
health, Edith could sustain a final explanation ere his departure on his expedition.

"She shall never," said the generous young man, "look
on her engagement with me as the means of fettering her to
a union the idea of which seems almost to unhinge her understanding."

CHAPTER XXXIX

Ode on a Distant Prospect of Eton College.

IT is not by corporal wants and infirmities only that men of the most distinguished talents are levelled, during their lifetime, with the common mass of mankind. There are periods of mental agitation when the firmest of mortals must be ranked with the weakest of his brethren ; and when, in paying the general tax of humanity, his distresses are even aggravated by feeling that he transgresses, in the indulgence of his grief, the rules of religion and philosophy by which he endeavors in general to regulate his passions and his actions. It was during such a paroxysm that the unfortunate Morton left Fairy Knowe. To know that his long-loved and still-beloved Edith, whose image had filled his mind for so many years, was on the point of marriage to his early rival, who had laid claim to her heart by so many services as hardly left her a title to refuse his addresses, bitter as the intelligence was, yet came not as an unexpected blow.

During his residence abroad he had once written to Edith. It was to bid her farewell forever, and to conjure her to forget him. He had requested her not to answer his letter, yet he half hoped for many a day that she might transgress his injunction. The letter never reached her to whom it was addressed, and Morton, ignorant of its miscarriage, could only conclude himself laid aside and forgotten, according to his own self-denying request. All that he had heard of their mutual relations since his return to Scotland prepared him to expect that he could only look upon Miss Bellenden as the betrothed bride of Lord Evandale ; and, even if freed from the burden of obligation to the latter, it would still have been inconsistent with Morton's generosity of disposition to disturb their arrangements, by attempting the assertion of a claim, proscribed by absence, never sanctioned by the consent of friends, and barred by a thousand circumstances of difficulty. Why, then, did he seek the cottage which their broken fortunes had now rendered the retreat of Lady Margaret Bellenden and her granddaughter ? He yielded, we are under the necessity of acknowledging, to the impulse of an inconsistent wish, which many might have felt in his situation.

Accident apprised him, while travelling towards his native district, that the ladies, near whose mansion he must necessarily pass, were absent ; and learning that Cuddie and his wife acted as their principal domestics, he could not resist pausing at their cottage to learn, if possible, the real progress which Lord Evandale had made in the affections of Miss Bellenden—alas ! no longer his Edith. This rash experiment ended as we have related, and he parted from the house of Fairy Knowe conscious that he was still beloved by Edith, yet compelled by faith and honor to relinquish her forever. With what feelings he must have listened to the dialogue between Lord Evandale and Edith, the greater part of which he involuntarily overheard, the reader must conceive, for we dare not attempt to describe them. An hundred times he was tempted to burst upon their interview, or to exclaim aloud —"Edith, I yet live !" and as often the recollection of her plighted troth, and of the debt of gratitude which he owed Lord Evandale, to whose influence with Claverhouse he justly ascribed his escape from torture and from death, withheld him from a rashness which might indeed have involved all in further distress, but gave little prospect of forwarding his own happiness. He repressed forcibly these selfish emotions, though with an agony which thrilled his every nerve.

"No, Edith !" was his internal oath, "never will I add a thorn to thy pillow. That which Heaven has ordained, let it be ; and let me not add, by my selfish sorrows, one atom's weight to the burden thou hast to bear. I was dead to thee when thy resolution was adopted ; and never—never shalt thou know that Henry Morton still lives !"

. As he formed this resolution, diffident of his own power to keep it, and seeking that firmness in flight which was every moment shaken by his continuing within hearing of Edith's voice, he hastily rushed from his apartment by the little closet and the sashed door which led to the garden.

But firmly as he thought his resolution was fixed, he could not leave the spot where the last tones of a voice so beloved still vibrated on his ear, without endeavoring to avail himself of the opportunity which the parlor window afforded, to steal one last glance at the lovely speaker. It was in this attempt, made while Edith seemed to have her eyes unalterably bent upon the ground, that Morton's presence was detected by her raising them suddenly. So soon as her wild scream made this known to the unfortunate object of a passion so constant, and which seemed so ill-fated, he hurried from the place, as if pursued by the furies. He passed Halliday in the garden without recognizing, or even being sensible that he had seen him, threw himself on his horse, and, by a sort of instinct rather than recollection, took the first by-road in preference to the public route to Hamilton.

In all probability this prevented Lord Evandale from learning that he was actually in existence; for the news that the Highlanders had obtained a decisive victory at Killie-crankie had occasioned an accurate lookout to be kept, by order of the government, on all the passes, for fear of some commotion among the Lowland Jacobites. They did not omit to post sentinels on Bothwell Bridge, and as these men had not seen any traveller pass westward in that direction, and as, besides, their comrades stationed in the village of Bothwell were equally positive that none had gone eastward, the apparition, in the existence of which Edith and Halliday were equally positive, became yet more mysterious in the judgment of Lord Evandale, who was finally inclined to settle in the belief that the heated and disturbed imagination of Edith had summoned up the phantom she stated herself to have seen, and that Halliday had in some unaccountable manner been infected by the same superstition.

Meanwhile, the by-path which Morton pursued, with all the speed which his vigorous horse could exert, brought him in a very few seconds to the brink of the Clyde, at a spot marked with the feet of horses, who were conducted to it as a watering-place. The steed, urged as he was to the gallop, did not pause a single instant, but, throwing himself into the river, was soon beyond his depth. The plunge which the animal made as his feet quitted the ground, with the feeling that the cold water rose above his sword-belt, were the first incidents which recalled Morton, whose movements had been hitherto mechanical, to the necessity of taking measures for preserving himself and the noble animal which he bestrode. A perfect master of all manly exercises, the management of a horse in water was as familiar to him as when upon a meadow. He directed the animal's course somewhat down the stream towards a low plain or holm, which seemed to promise an easy egress from the river. In the first and second attempt to get on shore, the horse was frustrated by the nature of the ground, and nearly fell backwards on his rider. The instinct of self-preservation seldom fails, even in the most desperate circumstances, to recall the human mind to some degree of equipoise, unless when altogether distracted by terror, and Morton was obliged to the danger in which he was placed for complete recovery of his self-possession. A third attempt, at a spot more carefully and judiciously selected, succeeded better than the former, and placed the horse and his rider in safety upon the further and left-hand bank of the Clyde.

"But whither," said Morton, in the bitterness of his heart, "am I now to direct my course ? or rather, what does it signify to which point of the compass a wretch so forlorn betakes himself ? I would to God, could the wish be without a sin, that these dark waters had flowed over me, and drowned my recollection of that which was and that which is !"

The sense of impatience which the disturbed state of his feelings had occasioned scarcely had vented itself in these violent expressions ere he was struck with shame at having given way to such a paroxysm. He remembered how signally the life which he now held so lightly, in the bitterness of his disappointment, had been preserved through the almost incessant perils which had beset him since he entered upon his public career.

"I am a fool !" he said, " and worse than a fool, to set light by that existence which Heaven has so often preserved in the most marvellous manner. Something there yet remains for me in this world, were it only to bear my sorrows like a man, and to aid those who need my assistance. What have I seen—what have I heard, but the very conclusion of that which I knew was to happen ? They [he durst not utter their names even in soliloquy]—they are embarrassed and in difficulties. She is stripped of her inheritance, and he seems rushing on some dangerous career, with which, but for the low voice in which he spoke, I might have become acquainted. Are there no means to aid or to warn them ?"

As he pondered upon this topic, forcibly withdrawing his mind from his own disappointment and compelling his attention to the affairs of Edith and her betrothed husband, the letter of Burley, long forgotten, suddenly rushed on his memory like a ray of light darting through a mist.

"Their ruin must have been his work," was his internal conclusion. "If it can be repaired, it must be through his means, or by information obtained from him. I will search him out. Stern, crafty, and enthusiastic as he is, my plain and downright rectitude of purpose has more than once prevailed with him. I will seek him out, at least; and who knows what influence the information I may acquire from him may have on the fortunes of those whom I shall never see more, and who will probably never learn that I am now suppressing my own grief to add, if possible, to their happiness!"

Animated by these hopes, though the foundation was but slight, he sought the nearest way to the high-road; and as all the tracks through the valley were known to him since he hunted through them in youth, he had no other difficulty than that of surmounting one or two enclosures ere he found himself on the road to the small burgh where the feast of the popinjay had been celebrated. He journeyed in a state of mind sad indeed and dejected, yet relieved from its earlier and more intolerable state of anguish; for virtuous resolution and manly disinterestedness seldom fail to restore tranquillity even where they cannot create happiness. He turned his thoughts with strong effort upon the means of discovering Burley, and the chance there was of extracting from him any knowledge which he might possess favorable to her in whose cause he interested himself, and at length formed the resolution of guiding himself by the circumstances in which he might discover the object of his quest, trusting that, from Cuddie's account of a schism betwixt Burley and his brethren of the Presbyterian persuasion, he might find him less rancorously disposed against Miss Bellenden, and inclined to exert the power which he asserted himself to possess over her fortunes more favorably than heretofore.

Noontide had passed away when our traveller found himself in the neighborhood of his deceased uncle's habitation of Milnwood. It rose among glades and groves that were checkered with a thousand early recollections of joy and sorrow, and made upon Morton that mournful impression, soft and affecting, yet withal soothing, which the sensitive mind usually receives from a return to the haunts of childhood and early youth, after having experienced the vicissitudes and tempests of public life. A strong desire came upon him to visit the house itself.

"Old Alison," he thought, "will not know me, more than the honest couple whom I saw yesterday. I may indulge my curiosity and proceed on my journey, without her having any knowledge of my existence. I think they said my uncle had bequeathed to her my family mansion; well, be it so. I have enough to sorrow for, to enable me to dispense with lamenting such a disappointment as that; and yet methinks he has chosen an odd successor in my grumbling old dame to a line of respectable, if not distinguished, ancestry.　Let it be as it may, I will visit the old mansion at least once more."

The house of Milnwood, even in its best days, had nothing cheerful about it, but its gloom appeared to be double under the auspices of the old housekeeper.　Everything, indeed, was in repair; there were no slates deficient upon the steep gray roof, and no panes broken in the narrow windows.　But the grass in the courtyard looked as if the foot of man had not been there for years; the doors were carefully locked, and that which admitted to the hall seemed to have been shut for a length of time, since the spiders had fairly drawn their webs over the doorway and the staples.　Living sight or sound there was none, until, after much knocking, Morton heard the little window, through which it was usual to reconnoitre visitors, open with much caution.　The face of Alison, puckered with some score of wrinkles, in addition to those with which it was furrowed when Morton left Scotland, now presented itself, enveloped in a "toy," from under the protection of which some of her gray tresses had escaped in a manner more picturesque than beautiful, while her shrill tremulous voice demanded the cause of the knocking.

"I wish to speak an instant with one Alison Wilson who resides here," said Henry.

"She's no at hame the day," answered Mrs. Wilson *in propria persona*, the state of whose head-dress, perhaps, inspired her with this direct mode of denying herself; "and ye are but a mislear'd person to speer for her in sic a manner.　Ye might hae had an M under your belt for *Mistress* Wilson of Milnwood."

"I beg pardon," said Morton, internally smiling at finding in old Ailie the same jealousy of disrespect which she used to exhibit upon former occasions—"I beg pardon; I am but a stranger in this country, and have been so long abroad that I have almost forgotten my own language."

"Did ye come frae foreign parts?" said Ailie; "then maybe ye may hae heard of a young gentleman of this country that they ca' Henry Morton?"

"I have heard," said Morton, "of such a name in Germany."

"Then bide a wee bit where ye are, friend—or stay, gang round by the back o' the house, and ye'll find a laigh door; it's on the latch; for it's never barred till sunset.　Ye'll open't—and tak care ye dinna fa' ower the tub, for the entry's dark—and then ye'll turn to the right, and then ye'll haud straught forward, and then ye'll turn to the right again, and ye'll tak heed o' the cellar stairs, and then ye'll be at the door o' the little kitchen—it's a' the kitchen that's at Milnwood now—and I'll come down t'ye, and whate'er ye wad say to Mistress Wilson ye may very safely tell it to me."

A stranger might have had some difficulty, notwithstanding the minuteness of the directions supplied by Ailie, to pilot himself in safety through the dark labyrinth of passages that led from the back door to the little kitchen, but Henry was too well acquainted with the navigation of these straits to experience danger, either from the Scylla which lurked on one side in shape of a bucking-tub, or the Charybdis which yawned on the other in the profundity of a winding cellar stair. His only impediment arose from the snarling and vehement barking of a small cocking spaniel, once his own property, but which, unlike to the faithful Argus, saw his master return from his wanderings without any symptom of recognition.

"The little dogs and all!" said Morton to himself, on being disowned by his former favorite. "I am so changed that no breathing creature that I have known and loved will now acknowledge me!"

At this moment he had reached the kitchen, and soon after the tread of Alison's high heels, and the pat of the crutch-handled cane, which served at once to prop and to guide her footsteps, were heard upon the stairs, an annunciation which continued for some time ere she fairly reached the kitchen.

Morton had, therefore, time to survey the slender preparations for housekeeping which were now sufficient in the house of his ancestors. The fire, though coals are plenty in that neighborhood, was husbanded with the closest attention to economy of fuel, and the small pipkin, in which was preparing the dinner of the old woman and her maid-of-all-work, a girl of twelve years old, intimated, by its thin and watery vapor, that Ailie had not mended her cheer with her improved fortune.

When she entered, the head which nodded with self-importance, the features in which an irritable peevishness, acquired by habit and indulgence, strove with a temper naturally affectionate and good-natured, the coif, the apron, the blue checked gown, were all those of old Ailie ; but laced pinners, hastily put on to meet the stranger, with some other trifling articles of decoration, marked the difference between Mrs. Wilson, life-rentrix of Milnwood, and the housekeeper of the late proprietor.

"What were ye pleased to want wi' Mrs. Wilson, sir? I am Mrs. Wilson," was her first address; for the five minutes' time which she had gained for the business of the toilet entitled her, she conceived, to assume the full merit of her illustrious name, and shine forth on her guest in unchastened splendor.

Morton's sensations, confounded between the past and present, fairly confused him so much that he would have had difficulty in answering her, even if he had known well what to say. But as he had not determined what character he was to adopt while concealing that which was properly his own, he had an additional reason for remaining silent.

Mrs. Wilson, in perplexity, and with some apprehension, repeated her question. "What were ye pleased to want wi' me, sir? Ye said ye kenn'd Mr. Harry Morton?"

"Pardon me, madam," answered Henry; "it was of one Silas Morton I spoke."

The old woman's countenance fell.

"It was his father, then, ye kent o', the brother o' the late Milnwood? Ye canna mind him abroad, I wad think; he was come hame afore ye were born. I thought ye had brought me news of poor Maister Harry."

"It was from my father I learned to know Colonel Morton," said Henry. "Of the son I know little or nothing; rumor says he died abroad on his passage to Holland."

"That's ower like to be true," said the old woman, with a sigh, "and mony a tear it's cost my auld een. His uncle, poor gentleman, just sough'd awa' wi' it in his mouth. He had been gieing me preceeze directions anent the bread, and the wine, and the brandy, at his burial, and how often it was to be handed round the company—for, dead or alive, he was a prudent, frugal, painstaking man—and then he said, said he, 'Ailie'—he aye ca'd me Ailie, we were auld acquaintance— 'Ailie, take ye care and haud the gear weel thegither; for the name of Morton of Milnwood's gane out like the last sough of an auld sang.' And sae he fell out o' ae dwam into another, and ne'er spak a word mair unless it were something we cou'dna mak out, about a dipped candle being gude eneugh to see to dee wi'. He cou'd ne'er bide to see a moulded ane, and there was ane, by ill luck, on the table."

While Mrs. Wilson was thus detailing the last moments of the old miser, Morton was pressingly engaged in diverting the assiduous curiosity of the dog, which, recovered from his first surprise, and combining former recollections, had, after much snuffing and examination, begun a course of capering and jumping upon the stranger which threatened every instant to betray him. At length, in the urgency of his impatience, Morton could not forbear exclaiming, in a tone of hasty impatience, "Down, Elphin! Down, sir!"

"Ye ken our dog's name," said the old lady, struck with great and sudden surprise—"ye ken our dog's name, and it's no a common ane. And the creature kens you too," she continued, in a more agitated and shriller tone. "God guide us! it's my ain bairn!" So saying, the poor old woman threw herself around Morton's neck, clung to him, kissed him as if he had been actually her child, and wept for joy.

There was no parrying the discovery, if he could have had the heart to attempt any further disguise. He returned the embrace with the most grateful warmth, and answered—"I do indeed live, dear Ailie, to thank you for all your kindness, past and present, and to rejoice that there is at least one friend to welcome me to my native country."

"Friends!" exclaimed Ailie, "ye'll hae mony friends—ye'll hae mony friends; for ye will hae gear, hinny—ye will hae gear. Heaven mak ye a gude guide o't! But, eh, sirs!" she continued, pushing him back from her with her trembling hand and shrivelled arm, and gazing in his face as if to read, at more convenient distance, the ravages which sorrow rather than time had made on his face—"eh, sirs! ye're sair altered, hinny: your face is turned pale, and your een are sunken, and your bonny red-and-white cheeks are turned a' dark and sunburnt. O, weary on the wars! mony's the comely face they destroy. And when cam ye here, hinny? And where hae ye been? And what hae ye been doing? And what for did ye na write to us? And how cam ye to pass yoursell for dead? And what for did ye come creepin' to your ain house as if ye had been an unco body, to gie poor auld Ailie sic a start?" she concluded, smiling through her tears.

It was some time ere Morton could overcome his own emotion so as to give the kind old woman the information which we shall communicate to our readers in the next chapter.

CHAPTER XL

Aumerle that was,
But that is gone for being Richard's friend ;
And, madam, you must call him Rutland now.
Richard II.

THE scene of explanation was hastily removed from the little
kitchen to Mrs. Wilson's own matted room, the very same
which she had occupied as housekeeper, and which she continued to retain. "It was," she said, "better secured against
sifting winds than the hall, which she had found dangerous
to her rheumatisms, and it was more fitting for her use than
the late Milnwood's apartment, honest man, which gave her
sad thoughts ;" and as for the great oak parlor, it was never
opened but to be aired, washed, and dusted, according to the
invariable practice of the family, unless upon their most solemn festivals. In the matted room, therefore, they were settled, surrounded by pickle-pots and conserves of all kinds,
which the *ci-devant* housekeeper continued to compound out
of mere habit, although neither she herself nor any one else
ever partook of the comfits which she so regularly prepared.

Morton, adapting his narrative to the comprehension of
his auditor, informed her briefly of the wreck of the vessel
and the loss of all hands, excepting two or three common seamen, who had early secured the skiff, and were just putting
off from the vessel when he leaped from the deck into their
boat, and unexpectedly, as well as contrary to their inclination, made himself partner of their voyage and of their safety.
Landed at Flushing, he was fortunate enough to meet with
an old officer who had been in service with his father. By his
advice, he shunned going immediately to The Hague, but forwarded his letters to the court of the Stadtholder.

"Our Prince," said the veteran, "must as yet keep terms
with his father-in-law and with your King Charles; and to
approach him in the character of a Scottish malcontent would
render it imprudent for him to distinguish you by his favor.
Wait, therefore, his orders, without forcing yourself on his
notice ; observe the strictest prudence and retirement ; assume
for the present a different name ; shun the company of the

British exiles; and, depend upon it, you will not repent your prudence."

The old friend of Silas Morton argued justly. After a considerable time had elapsed, the Prince of Orange, in a progress through the United States, came to the town where Morton, impatient at his situation and the incognito which he was obliged to observe, still continued, nevertheless, to be a resident. He had an hour of private interview assigned, in which the Prince expressed himself highly pleased with his intelligence, his prudence, and the liberal view which he seemed to take of the factions of his native country, their motives and their purposes.

"I would gladly," said William, "attach you to my own person, but that cannot be without giving offence in England. But I will do as much for you, as well out of respect for the sentiments you have expressed as for the recommendations you have brought me. Here is a commission in a Swiss regiment at present in garrison in a distant province, where you will meet few or none of your countrymen. Continue to be Captain Melville, and let the name of Morton sleep till better days."

"Thus began my fortune," continued Morton; "and my services have, on various occasions, been distinguished by his Royal Highness, until the moment that brought him to Britain as our political deliverer. His commands must excuse my silence to my few friends in Scotland; and I wonder not at the report of my death, considering the wreck of the vessel, and that I found no occasion to use the letters of exchange with which I was furnished by the liberality of some of them, a circumstance which must have confirmed the belief that I had perished."

"But, dear hinny," asked Mrs. Wilson, "did ye find nae Scotch body at the Prince of Oranger's court that kenn'd ye? I wad hae thought Morton o' Milnwood was kenn'd a' through the country."

"I was purposely engaged in distant service," said Morton, "until a period when few, without as deep and kind a motive of interest as yours, Ailie, would have known the stripling Morton in Major-General Melville."

"Malville was your mother's name," said Mrs. Wilson; "but Morton sounds far bonnier in my auld lugs. And when ye tak up the lairdship ye maun tak the auld name and designation again."

"I am like to be in no haste to do either the one or the other, Ailie, for I have some reasons for the present to conceal my being alive from every one but you ; and as for the lairdship of Milnwood, it is in as good hands."

"As gude hands, hinny !" re-echoed Ailie ; "I'm hopefu' ye are no meaning mine ? The rents and the lands are but a sair fash to me. And I'm ower failed to tak a helpmate, though Wylie Mactrickit, the writer, was very pressing, and spak very civilly ; but I'm ower auld a cat to draw that strae before me. He canna whilly-wha me as he's dune mony a ane. And then I thought aye ye wad come back, and I wad get my pickle meal and my soup milk, and keep a' things right about ye as I used to do in your puir uncle's time, and it wad be just pleasure eneugh for me to see ye thrive and guide the gear canny. Ye'll hae learned that in Holland, I'se warrant, for they're thrifty folk there, as I hear tell. But ye'll be for keeping rather a mair house than puir auld Milnwood that's gane ; and, indeed, I would approve o' your eating butcher-meat maybe as aften as three times a week, it keeps the wind out o' the stamack."

"We will talk of all this another time," said Morton, surprised at the generosity upon a large scale which mingled in Ailie's thoughts and actions with habitual and sordid parsimony, and at the odd contrast between her love of saving and indifference to self-acquisition. "You must know," he continued, "that I am in this country only for a few days on some special business of importance to the government, and therefore, Ailie, not a word of having seen me. At some other time I will acquaint you fully with my motives and intentions."

"E'en be it sae, my jo," replied Ailie, "I can keep a secret like my neighbors ; and weel auld Milnwood kenn'd it, honest man, for he tauld me where he keepit his gear, and that's what maist folk like to hae as private as possibly may be. But come awa' wi' me, hinny, till I show ye the oak parlor how grandly it's keepit, just as if ye had been expected hame every day ; I loot naebody sort it but my ain hands. It was a kind o' divertisement to me, though whiles the tear wan into my ee, and I said to mysell, what needs I fash wi' grates, and carpets, and cushions, and the muckle brass candle-sticks, ony mair ? for they'll ne'er come hame that aught it rightfully."

With these words she hauled him away to this *sanctum sanctorum*, the scrubbing and cleaning whereof was her daily employment, as its high state of good order constituted the very pride of her heart. Morton, as he followed her into the room, underwent a rebuke for not "dighting his shune,"

which showed that Ailie had not relinquished her habits of
authority.   On entering the oak parlor, he could not but recollect the feelings of solemn awe with which, when a boy,
he had been affected at his occasional and rare admission to
an apartment which he then supposed had not its equal save
in the halls of princes.   It may be readily supposed that the
worked-worsted chairs, with their short ebony legs and long
upright backs, had lost much of their influence over his mind ;
that the large brass andirons seemed diminished in splendor ;
that the green worsted tapestry appeared no masterpiece of
the Arras loom ; and that the room looked, on the whole,
dark, gloomy, and disconsolate.   Yet there were two objects,
"the counterfeit presentment of two brothers," which, dissimilar as those described by Hamlet, affected his mind with
a variety of sensations.   One full-length portrait represented
his father, in complete armor, with a countenance indicating
his masculine and determined character ; and the other set
forth his uncle, in velvet and brocade, looking as if he were
ashamed of his own finery, though entirely indebted for it to
the liberality of the painter.

"It was an idle fancy," Ailie said, "to dress the honest auld
man in thae expensive fal-lalls that he ne'er wore in his life,
instead o' his douce raploch gray, and his band wi' the narrow edging."

In private Morton could not help being much of her opinion ; for anything approaching to the dress of a gentleman
sat as ill on the ungainly person of his relative as an open or
generous expression would have done on his mean and money-
making features.   He now extricated himself from Ailie to
visit some of his haunts in the neighboring wood, while her
own hands made an addition to the dinner she was preparing ;
an incident no otherwise remarkable than as it cost the life of
a fowl, which for any event of less importance than the arrival
of Henry Morton might have cackled on to a good old age ere
Ailie could have been guilty of the extravagance of killing
and dressing it.   The meal was seasoned by talk of old times,
and by the plans which Ailie laid out for futurity, in which
she assigned her young master all the prudential habits of her
old one, and planned out the dexterity with which she was to
exercise her duty as governante.   Morton let the old woman
enjoy her day-dreams and castle-building during moments of
such pleasure, and deferred till some fitter occasion the communication of his purpose again to return and spend his life
upon the Continent.

His next care was to lay aside his military dress, which he

considered likely to render more difficult his researches after
Burley.   He exchanged it for a gray doublet and cloak, formerly his usual attire at Milnwood, and which Mrs. Wilson
produced from a chest of walnut-tree, wherein she had laid
them aside, without forgetting carefully to brush and air them
from time to time.   Morton retained his sword and firearms,
without which few persons travelled in those unsettled times.

When he appeared in his new attire, Mrs. Wilson was first
thankful "that they fitted him sae decently, since, though
he was nae fatter, yet he looked mair manly than when he was
taen frae Milnwood."   Next she enlarged on the advantage of
saving old clothes to be what she called "beet-masters to the
new," and was far advanced in the history of a velvet cloak
belonging to the late Milnwood, which had first been converted
to a velvet doublet, and then into a pair of breeches, and appeared each time as good as new, when Morton interrupted her
account of its transmigration to bid her good-bye.

He gave, indeed, a sufficient shock to her feelings by expressing the necessity he was under of proceeding on his journey that evening.

"And where are ye gaun ?   And what wad ye do that for ?
And whar wad ye sleep but in your ain house, after ye hae been
sae mony years frae hame ?"

"I feel all the unkindness of it, Ailie, but it must be so ;
and that was the reason that I attempted to conceal myself
from you, as I suspected you would not let me part from you
so easily."

"But whar are ye gaun, then ?" said Ailie, once more.
"Saw e'er mortal een the like o' you, just to come ae moment
and flee awa' like an arrow out of a bow the neist ?"

"I must go down," replied Morton, "to Niel Blane, the
Piper's Howff.   He can give me a bed, I suppose ?"

"A bed !   I'se warrant can he," replied Ailie, "and gar
ye pay weel for't into the bargain.   Laddie, I dare say ye hae
lost your wits in thae foreign parts, to gang and gie siller for
a supper and a bed, and might hae baith for naething, and
thanks t'ye for accepting them."

"I assure you, Ailie," said Morton, desirous to silence her
remonstrances, "that this is a business of great importance,
in which I may be a great gainer, and cannot possibly be a
loser."

"I dinna see how that can be, if ye begin by gieing maybe
the feck o' twal shillings Scots for your supper ; but young
folks are aye venturesome, and think to get siller that way.

My puir auld master took a surer gate, and never parted wi'
it when he had anes gotten't."

Persevering in his desperate resolution, Morton took leave
of Ailie and mounted his horse to proceed to the little town,
after exacting a solemn promise that she would conceal his return until she again saw or heard from him.

"I am not very extravagant," was his natural reflection,
as he trotted slowly towards the town ; "but were Ailie and
I to set up house together, as she proposes, I think my profusion would break the good old creature's heart before a week
were out."

CHAPTER XLI

Where's the jolly host
You told me of ?   'T has been my custom eve
To parley with mine host.

Lover's Progress.

MORTON reached the borough-town without meeting with any remarkable adventure, and alighted at the little inn.   It had occurred to him more than once, while upon his journey, that his resumption of the dress which he had worn while a youth, although favorable to his views in other respects, might render it more difficult for him to remain incognito. But a few years of campaigns and wandering had so changed his appearance that he had great confidence that in the grown man, whose brows exhibited the traces of resolution and considerate thought, none would recognize the raw and bashful stripling who won the game of the popinjay.   The only chance was, that here and there some Whig whom he had led to battle might remember the Captain of the Milnwood Marksmen ; but the risk, if there was any, could not be guarded against.

The Howff seemed full and frequented as if possessed of all its old celebrity.   The person and demeanor of Niel Blane, more fat and less civil than of yore, intimated that he had increased as well in purse as in corpulence ; for in Scotland a landlord's complaisance for his guests decreases in exact proportion to his rise in the world   His daughter had acquired the air of a dexterous barmaid, undisturbed by the circumstances of love and war, so apt to perplex her in the exercise of her vocation.   Both showed Morton the degree of attention which could have been expected by a stranger travelling without attendants, at a time when they were particularly the badges of distinction.   He took upon himself exactly the character his appearance presented—went to the stable and saw his horse accommodated, then returned to the house, and, seating himself in the public room (for to request one to himself would, in those days, have been thought an overweening degree of conceit), he found himself in the very apartment in which he had some years before celebrated his victory at the game of the popinjay, a jocular preferment which led to so many serious consequences.

He felt himself, as may well be supposed, a much changed man since that festivity ; and yet, to look around him, the groups assembled in the Howff seemed not dissimilar to those which the same scene had formerly presented. Two or three burghers husbanded their "dribbles o' brandy ; " two or three dragoons lounged over their muddy ale, and cursed the in-active times that allowed them no better cheer. Their cornet did not, indeed, play at backgammon with the curate in his cassock, but he drank a little modicum of *aqua mirabilis* with the gray-cloaked Presbyterian minister. The scene was an-other, and yet the same, differing only in persons, but corre-sponding in general character.

"Let the tide of the world wax or wane as it will," Morton thought, as he looked around him, "enough will be found to fill the places which chance renders vacant ; and, in the usual occupations and amusements of life, human beings will suc-ceed each other, as leaves upon the same tree, with the same individual difference and the same general resemblance."

After pausing a few minutes, Morton, whose experience had taught him the readiest mode of securing attention, ordered a pint of claret, and, as the smiling landlord appeared with the pewter measure foaming fresh from the tap (for bottling wine was not then in fashion), he asked him to sit down and take a share of the good cheer. This invitation was peculiarly acceptable to Niel Blane, who, if he did not positively expect it from every guest not provided with better company, yet received it from many, and was not a whit abashed or surprised at the summons. He sat down along with his guest, in a secluded nook near the chimney ; and while he received encouragement to drink by far the greater share of the liquor before them, he entered at length, as a part of his expected functions, upon the news of the country—the births, deaths, and marriages, the change of property, the downfall of old families, and the rise of new. But politics, now the fertile source of eloquence, mine host did not care to mingle in his theme ; and it was only in answer to a question of Morton that he replied with an air of indifference, "Um ! ay we aye hae sodgers amang us, mair or less. There's a wheen German horse down at Glasgow yonder ; they ca' their com-mander Wittybody, or some sic name, though he's as grave and grewsome an auld Dutchman as e'er I saw."

"Wittenbold, perhaps ?" said Morton ; "an old man, with gray hair and short black moustaches ; speaks seldom ?"

"And smokes forever," replied Niel Blane. "I see your honor kens the man. He may be a very gude man too, for aught I see, that is, considering he is a sodger and a Dutchman; but if he were ten generals, and as mony Wittybodies, he has nae skill in the pipes; he gar'd me stop in the middle of 'Torphichen's Rant,' the best piece o' music that ever bag gae wind to."

"But these fellows," said Morton, glancing his eye towards the soldiers that were in the apartment, "are not of his corps?"

"Na, na, these are Scotch dragoons," said mine host; "our ain auld caterpillars; these were Claver'se's lads a while syne, and wad be again, maybe, if he had the lang ten in his hand."

"Is there not a report of his death?" inquired Morton.

"Troth is there," said the landlord; "your honor is right: there is sic a fleeing rumor; but, in my puir opinion, it's lang or the deil die. I wad hae the folks here look to themsells. If he makes an outbreak, he'll be doun frae the Hielands or I could drink this glass; and whare are they then? A' thae hell-rakers o' dragoons wad be at his whistle in a moment. Nae doubt they're Willie's men e'en now, as they were James's a while syne; and reason good—they fight for their pay; what else hae they to fight for? They hae neither lands nor houses, I trow. There's ae gude thing o' the change—or the Revolution, as they ca' it—folks may speak out afore thae birkies now, and nae fear o' being hauled awa' to the guard-house, or having the thumikins screwed on your finger-ends, just as I wad drive the screw through a cork."

There was a little pause, when Morton, feeling confident in the progress he had made in mine host's familiarity, asked, though with the hesitation proper to one who puts a question on the answer to which rests something of importance— "Whether Blane knew a woman in that neighborhood called Elizabeth Maclure?"

"Whether I ken Bessie Maclure?" answered the landlord, with a landlord's laugh. "How can I *but* ken my ain wife's—haly be her rest!—my ain wife's first gudeman's sister, Bessie Maclure? An honest wife she is, but sair she's been trysted wi' misfortunes—the loss o' twa decent lads o' sons, in the time o' the persecution, as they ca' it nowadays; and doucely and decently she has borne her burden, blaming nane and condemning nane. If there's an honest woman in the world, it's Bessie Maclure. And to lose her twa sons, as I was saying, and to hae dragoons clinked down on her for a month by-past, for, be Whig or Tory uppermost, they

aye quarter thae loons on victuallers—to lose, as I was saying——"

"This woman keeps an inn, then ?" interrupted Morton.

"A public, in a puir way," replied Blane, looking round
at his own superior accommodations—"a sour browst o' sma'
ale that she sells to folk that are ower drouthy wi' travel to be
nice ; but naething to ca' a stirring trade or a thriving change-
house."

"Can you get me a guide there ?" said Morton.

"Your honor will rest here a' the night ? ye'll hardly get
accommodation at Bessie's," said Niel, whose regard for his
deceased wife's relative by no means extended to sending
company from his own house to hers.

"There is a friend," answered Morton, "whom I am to
meet with there, and I only called here to take a stirrup-cup
and inquire the way."

"Your honor had better," answered the landlord, with the
perseverance of his calling, "send some ane to warn your
friend to come on here."

"I tell you, landlord," answered Morton, impatiently,
"that will not serve my purpose ; I must go straight to this
woman Maclure's house, and I desire you to find me a guide."

"Aweel, sir, ye'll choose for yoursell, to be sure," said Niel
Blane, somewhat disconcerted ; "but deil a guide ye'll need,
if ye gae doun the water for twa mile or sae, as gin ye were
bound for Milnwood House, and then tak the first broken dis-
jasked-looking road that makes for the hills—ye'll ken't by a
broken ash-tree that stands at the side o' a burn just where
the roads meet—and then travel out the path ; ye canna miss
Widow Maclure's public, for deil another house or hauld is on
the road for ten lang Scots miles, and that's worth twenty
English. I am sorry your honor would think o' gaun out o'
my house the night. But my wife's gude-sister is a decent
woman, and it's no lost that a friend gets."

Morton accordingly paid his reckoning and departed. The
sunset of the summer day placed him at the ash-tree, where
the path led up towards the moors.

"Here," he said to himself, "my misfortunes commenced ; for just here, when Burley and I were about to separate on the first night we ever met, he was alarmed by the
intelligence that the passes were secured by soldiers lying in
wait for him. Beneath that very ash sat the old woman
who apprised him of his danger. How strange that my whole
fortunes should have become inseparably interwoven with
that man's, without anything more on my part than the dis-

charge of an ordinary duty of humanity ! Would to Heaven it were possible I could find my humble quiet and tranquillity of mind upon the spot where I lost them !"

Thus arranging his reflections betwixt speech and thought, he turned his horse's head up the path.

Evening lowered around him as he advanced up the narrow dell which had once been a wood, but was now a ravine divested of trees, unless where a few, from their inaccessible situation on the edge of precipitous banks, or clinging among rocks and huge stones, defied the invasion of men and of cattle, like the scattered tribes of a conquered country, driven to take refuge in the barren strength of its mountains. These too, wasted and decayed, seemed rather to exist than to flourish, and only served to indicate what the landscape had once been. But the stream brawled down among them in all its freshness and vivacity, giving the life and animation which a mountain rivulet alone can confer on the barest and most savage scenes, and which the inhabitants of such a country miss when gazing even upon the tranquil winding of a majestic stream through plains of fertility, and beside palaces of splendor. The track of the road followed the course of the brook, which was now visible, and now only to be distinguished by its brawling heard among the stones, or in the clefts of the rock, that occasionally interrupted its course.

" Murmurer that thou art," said Morton, in the enthusiasm of his reverie, " why chafe with the rocks that stop thy course for a moment ? There is a sea to receive thee in its bosom ; and there is an eternity for man when his fretful and hasty course through the vale of time shall be ceased and over. What thy petty fuming is to the deep and vast billows of a shoreless ocean, are our cares, hopes, fears, joys, and sorrows to the objects which must occupy us through the awful and boundless succession of ages."

Thus moralizing, our traveller passed on till the dell opened, and the banks, receding from the brook, left a little green vale, exhibiting a croft or small field, on which some corn was growing, and a cottage, whose walls were not above five feet high, and whose thatched roof, green with moisture, age, house-leek, and grass, had in some places suffered damage from the encroachment of two cows, whose appetite this appearance of verdure had diverted from their more legitimate pasture. An ill-spelled and worse-written inscription intimated to the traveller that he might here find refreshment for man and horse ; no unacceptable intimation, rude as the hut appeared to be, considering the wild path he had trod in approaching it, and the high and waste mountains which rose in desolate dignity behind this humble asylum.

"It must indeed have been," thought Morton, "in some such spot as this that Burley was likely to find a congenial confidant."

As he approached, he observed the good dame of the house herself seated by the door; she had hitherto been concealed from him by a huge alder-bush.

"Good evening, mother," said the traveller. "Your name is Mistress Maclure?"

"Elizabeth Maclure, sir, a poor widow," was the reply.

"Can you lodge a stranger for a night?"

"I can, sir, if he will be pleased with the widow's cake and the widow's cruise."

"I have been a soldier, good dame," answered Morton, "and nothing can come amiss to me in the way of entertainment."

"A sodger, sir?" said the old woman, with a sigh. "God send ye a better trade!"

"It is believed to be an honorable profession, my good dame. I hope you do not think the worse of me for having belonged to it?"

"I judge no one, sir," replied the woman, "and your voice sounds like that of a civil gentleman; but I hae witnessed sae muckle ill wi' sodgering in this puir land that I am e'en content that I can see nae mair o't wi' these sightless organs."

As she spoke thus, Morton observed that she was blind.

"Shall I not be troublesome to you, my good dame?" said he, compassionately; "your infirmity seems ill calculated for your profession."

"Na, sir," answered the old woman; "I can gang about the house readily eneugh; and I hae a bit lassie to help me, and the dragoon lads will look after your horse when they come hame frae their patrol, for a sma' matter; they are civiller now than lang syne."

Upon these assurances, Morton alighted.

"Peggy, my bonny bird," continued the hostess, addressing a little girl of twelve years old, who had by this time appeared, "tak the gentleman's horse to the stable, and slack his girths, and tak aff the bridle, and shake down a lock o' hay before him, till the dragoons come back. Come this way, sir," she continued; "ye'll find my house clean, though it's a puir ane."

Morton followed her into the cottage accordingly.

CHAPTER XLII

Then out and spake the auld mother,
    And fast her tears did fa—
" Ye wadna be warn'd, my son Johnie,
    Frae the hunting to bide awa ! "
                              Old Ballad.

WHEN he entered the cottage, Morton perceived that the old
hostess had spoken truth. The inside of the hut belied its
outward appearance, and was neat, and even comfortable, especially the inner apartment, in which the hostess informed
her guest that he was to sup and sleep. Refreshments were
placed before him, such as the little inn afforded ; and, though
he had small occasion for them, he accepted the offer, as the
means of maintaining some discourse with the landlady. Notwithstanding her blindness, she was assiduous in her attendance, and seemed, by a sort of instinct, to find her way to
what she wanted.

" Have you no one but this pretty little girl to assist you in
waiting on your guests ? " was the natural question.

" None, sir," replied his old hostess ; " I dwell alone, like
the widow of Zarephath. Few guests come to this puir place ;
and I haena custom eneugh to hire servants. I had anes twa
fine sons that lookit after a'thing. But God gives and takes
away, His name be praised ! " she continued, turning her
clouded eyes towards Heaven. " I was anes better off, that is,
warldly speaking, even since I lost them ; but that was before
this last change."

" Indeed ! " said Morton, " and yet you are a Presbyterian,
my good mother ? "

" I am, sir, praised be the light that showed me the right
way," replied the landlady.

" Then I should have thought," continued the guest, " the
Revolution would have brought you nothing but good."

" If," said the old woman, " it has brought the land gude,
and freedom of worship to tender consciences, it's little matter
what it has brought to a puir blind worm like me."

" Still," replied Morton, " I cannot see how it could possibly injure you."

"It's a lang story, sir," answered his hostess, with a sigh. "But ae night, sax weeks or thereby afore Bothwell Brig, a young gentleman stopped at this puir cottage, stiff and bloody with wounds, pale and dune out wi' riding, and his horse sae weary he couldna drag ae foot after the other, and his foes were close ahint him, and he was ane o' our enemies. What could I do, sir? You that's a sodger will think me but a silly auld wife; but I fed him and relieved him, and keepit him hidden till the pursuit was ower."

"And who," said Morton, "dares disapprove of your having done so?"

"I kenna," answered the blind woman; "I gat ill-will about it amang some o' our ain folk. They said I should hae been to him what Jael was to Sisera. But weel I wot I had nae divine command to shed blood, and to save it was baith like a woman and a Christian. And then they said I wanted natural affection, to relieve ane that belanged to the band that murdered my twa sons."

"That murdered your two sons?"

"Ay, sir; though maybe ye'll gie their deaths another name. The tane fell wi' sword in hand, fighting for a broken National Covenant; the tother—O, they took him and shot him dead on the green before his mother's face! My auld een dazzled when the shots were looten off, and, to my thought, they waxed weaker and weaker ever since that weary day; and sorrow, and heartbreak, and tears that would not be dried might help on the disorder. But, alas! betraying Lord Evandale's young blood to his enemies' sword wad ne'er hae brought my Ninian and Johnie alive again."

"Lord Evandale!" said Morton, in surprise. "Was it Lord Evandale whose life you saved?"

"In troth, even his," she replied. "And kind he was to me after, and gae me a cow and calf, malt, meal, and siller, and nane durst steer me when he was in power. But we live on an outside bit of Tillietudlem land, and the estate was sair plea'd between Leddy Margaret Bellenden and the present Laird, Basil Olifant, and Lord Evandale backed the auld leddy for love o' her daughter Miss Edith, as the country said, ane o' the best and bonniest lasses in Scotland. But they behuved to gie way, and Basil gat the Castle and land, and on the back o' that came the Revolution, and wha to turn coat faster than the Laird? for he said he had been a true Whig a' the time, and turned Papist only for fashion's sake. And then he got favor, and Lord Evandale's head was under water; for he was ower proud and manfu' to bend

to every blast o' wind, though mony a ane may ken as weel
as me that, be his ain principles as they might, he was nae
ill friend to our folk when he could protect us, and far kinder
than Basil Olifant, that aye keepit the cobble head doun the
stream.   But he was set by and ill looked on, and his word ne'er
asked ; and then Basil, wha's a revengefu' man, set himsell
to vex him in a' shapes, and especially by oppressing and de-
spoiling the auld blind widow, Bessie Maclure, that saved
Lord Evandale's life, and that he was sae kind to.   But he's
mistaen, if that's his end ; for it will be lang or Lord Evandale hears a word frae me about the selling my kye for rent
or e'er it was due, or the putting the dragoons on me when
the country's quiet, or onything else that will vex him ; I can
bear my ain burden patiently, and warld's loss is the least
part o't."

Astonished and interested at this picture of patient,
grateful, and high-minded resignation, Morton could not
help bestowing an execration upon the poor-spirited rascal
who had taken such a dastardly course of vengeance.

"Dinna curse him, sir," said the old woman ; "I have
heard a good man say that a curse was like a stone flung up to
the heavens, and maist like to return on the head that sent it.
But if ye ken Lord Evandale, bid him look to himsell, for I
hear strange words pass atween the sodgers that are lying here,
and his name is often mentioned ; and the tane o' them has
been twice up at Tillietudlem.   He's a kind of favorite wi'
the Laird, though he was in former times ane o' the maist
cruel oppressors ever rade through a country—out-taken
Sergeant Bothwell—they ca' him Inglis." *

"I have the deepest interest in Lord Evandale's safety,"
said Morton, "and you may depend on my finding some
mode to apprise him of these suspicious circumstances.   And
in return, my good friend, will you indulge me with another
question ? Do you know anything of Quintin Mackell of
Irongray ?"

"Do I know *whom ?* " echoed the blind woman, in a tone
of great surprise and alarm.

"Quintin Mackell of Irongray," repeated Morton ; "is
there anything so alarming in the sound of that name ?"

"Na, na," answered the woman, with hesitation, "but to
hear him asked after by a stranger and a sodger—Gude protect us, what mischief is to come next !"

"None by my means, I assure you," said Morton ; "the
subject of my inquiry has nothing to fear from me, if, as I

* See Note 36.

suppose, this Quintin Mackell is the same with John Bal——"

"Do not mention his name," said the widow, pressing his lips with her fingers. "I see you have his secret and his password, and I'll be free wi' you. But, for God's sake, speak lound and low. In the name of Heaven, I trust ye seek him not to his hurt! Ye said ye were a sodger?"

"I said truly; but one he has nothing to fear from. I commanded a party at Bothwell Bridge."

"Indeed!" said the woman. "And verily there is something in your voice I can trust. Ye speak prompt and readily, and like an honest man."

"I trust I am so," said Morton.

"But nae displeasure to you, sir, in thae waefu' times," continued Mrs. Maclure, "the hand of brother is against brother, and he fears as mickle almaist frae this government as e'er he did frae the auld persecutors."

"Indeed?" said Morton, in a tone of inquiry; "I was not aware of that. But I am only just now returned from abroad."

"I'll tell ye," said the blind woman, first assuming an attitude of listening that showed how effectually her powers of collecting intelligence had been transferred from the eye to the ear; for, instead of casting a glance of circumspection around, she stooped her face, and turned her head slowly around, in such a manner as to insure that there was not the slightest sound stirring in the neighborhood, and then continued—"I'll tell ye. Ye ken how he has labored to raise up again the Covenant, burned, broken, and buried in the hard hearts and selfish devices of this stubborn people. Now, when he went to Holland, far from the countenance and thanks of the great, and the comfortable fellowship of the godly, both whilk he was in right to expect, the Prince of Orange wad show him no favor, and the ministers no godly communion. This was hard to bide for ane that had suffered and done mickle—ower mickle, it may be—but why suld I be a judge? He came back to me and to the auld place o' refuge that had often received him in his distresses, mair especially before the great day of victory at Drumclog, for I sall ne'er forget how he was bending hither of a' nights in the year on that e'ening after the play, when young Milnwood wan the popinjay; but I warned him off for that time."

"What!" exclaimed Morton, "it was you that sat in your red cloak by the high-road and told him there was a lion in the path?"

"In the name of Heaven! wha are ye?" said the old woman, breaking off her narrative in astonishment. "But be wha ye may," she continued, resuming it with tranquillity, "ye can ken naething waur o' me than that I hae been willing to save the life o' friend and foe."

"I know no ill of you, Mrs. Maclure, and I mean no ill by you; I only wished to show you that I know so much of this person's affairs, that I might be safely intrusted with the rest. Proceed, if you please, in your narrative."

"There is a strange command in your voice," said the blind woman, "though its tones are sweet. I have little mair to say. The Stewarts hae been dethroned, and William and Mary reign in their stead, but nae mair word of the Covenant than if it were a dead letter. They hae taen the Indulged clergy, and an Erastian General Assembly of the ance pure and triumphant Kirk of Scotland even into their very arms and bosoms. Our faithfu' champions o' the testimony agree e'en waur wi' this than wi' the open tyranny and apostasy of the persecuting times, for souls are hardened and deadened, and the mouths of fasting multitudes are crammed wi' fizzenless bran instead of the sweet word in season; and mony an hungry, starving creature, when he sits down on a Sunday forenoon to get something that might warm him to the great work, has a dry clatter o' morality driven about his lugs, and——"

"In short," said Morton desirous to stop a discussion which the good old woman, as enthusiastically attached to her religious profession as to the duties of humanity, might probably have indulged longer—"in short, you are not disposed to acquiesce in this new government, and Burley is of the same opinion?"

"Many of our brethren, sir, are of belief we fought for the Covenant, and fasted, and prayed, and suffered for that grand national league, and now we are like neither to see nor hear tell of that which we suffered, and fought, and fasted, and prayed for. And anes it was thought something might be made by bringing back the auld family on a new bargain and a new bottom, as, after a', when King James went awa', I understand the great quarrel of the English against him was in behalf of seven unhallowed prelates; and sae, though ae part of our people were free to join wi' the present model, and levied an armed regiment under the Yerl of Angus, yet our honest friend, and others that stude up for purity of doctrine and freedom of conscience, were determined to hear the breath o' the Jacobites before they took part again them, fearing to fa' to the ground like a wall built with unslaked mortar, or from sitting between twa stools."

"They chose an odd quarter," said Morton, "from which to expect freedom of conscience and purity of doctrine."

"O, dear sir!" said the landlady, "the natural dayspring rises in the east, but the spiritual dayspring may rise in the north, for what we blinded mortals ken."

"And Burley went to the north to seek it?" replied the guest.

"Truly ay, sir; and he saw Claver'se himsell, that they ca' Dundee now."

"What!" exclaimed Morton, in amazement; "I would have sworn that meeting would have been the last of one of their lives."

"Na, na, sir; in troubled times, as I understand," said Mrs. Maclure, "there's sudden changes—Montgomery, and Ferguson, and mony ane mair that were King James's greatest faes, are on his side now; Claver'se spake our friend fair, and sent him to consult with Lord Evandale. But then there was a break-off, for Lord Evandale wadna look at, hear, or speak wi' him; and now he's anes wud and aye waur, and roars for revenge again Lord Evandale, and will hear naught of onything but burn and slay; and O thae starts o' passion! they unsettle his mind, and gie the Enemy sair advantages."

"The enemy?" said Morton. "What enemy?"

"What enemy? Are ye acquainted familiarly wi' John Balfour o' Burley, and dinna ken that he has had sair and frequent combats to sustain against the Evil One? Did ye ever see him alone but the Bible was in his hand and the drawn sword on his knee? Did ye never sleep in the same room wi' him, and hear him strive in his dreams with the delusions of Satan? O, ye ken little o' him, if ye have seen him only in fair daylight, for nae man can put the face upon his doleful visits and strifes that he can do. I hae seen him, after sic a strife of agony, tremble, that an infant might hae held him, while the hair on his brow was drapping as fast as ever my puir thatched roof did in a heavy rain."

As she spoke, Morton began to recollect the appearance of Burley during his sleep in the hay-loft at Milnwood, the report of Cuddie that his senses had become impaired, and some whispers current among the Cameronians, who boasted frequently of Burley's soul-exercises, and his strifes with the foul fiend; which several circumstances led him to conclude that this man himself was a victim to those delusions, though his mind, naturally acute and forcible, not only disguised his superstition from those in whose opinion it might have discredited his judgment, but by exerting such a force as is said to be proper to those afflicted with epilepsy, could postpone the fits which it occasioned until he was either freed from superintendence or surrounded by such as held him more highly on account of these visitations. It was natural to suppose, and could easily be inferred from the narrative of Mrs. Maclure, that disappointed ambition, wrecked hopes, and the downfall of the party which he had served with such desperate fidelity, were likely to aggravate enthusiasm into temporary insanity. It was, indeed, no uncommon circumstance in those singular times, that men like Sir Harry Vane, Harrison, Overton, and others, themselves slaves to the wildest and most enthusiastic dreams, could, when mingling with the world, conduct themselves not only with good sense in difficulties and courage in dangers, but with the most acute sagacity and determined valor. The subsequent part of Mrs. Maclure's information confirmed Morton in these impressions.

"In the gray of the morning," she said, "my little Peggy sall show ye the gate to him before the sodgers are up. But ye maun let his hour of danger, as he ca's it, be ower, afore ye venture on him in his place of refuge. Peggy will tell ye when to venture in. She kens his ways weel, for whiles she carries him some little helps that he canna do without to sustain life."

"And in what retreat, then," said Morton, "has this unfortunate person found refuge ?"

"An awsome place," answered the blind woman, "as ever living creature took refuge in. They ca' it the Black Linn of Linklater. It's a doleful place ; but he loves it abune a' others, because he has sae often been in safe hiding there ; and it's my belief he prefers it to a tapestried chamber and a down bed. But ye'll see't. I hae seen it mysell mony a day syne. I was a daft hempie lassie then, and little thought what was to come o't. Wad ye choose onything, sir, ere ye betake yoursell to your rest, for ye maun stir wi' the first dawn o' the gray light ?"

"Nothing more, my good mother," said Morton ; and they parted for the evening.

Morton recommended himself to Heaven, threw himself on the bed, heard, between sleeping and waking, the trampling of the dragoon horses at the riders' return from their patrol, and then slept soundly after such painful agitation.

CHAPTER XLIII

The darksome cave they enter, where they found
The accursed man, low sitting on the ground,
Musing full sadly in his sullen mind.

SPENSER.

As the morning began to appear on the mountains, a gentle knock was heard at the door of the humble apartment in which Morton slept, and a girlish treble voice asked him from without, "If he wad please gang to the Linn or the folk raise?"

He arose upon the invitation, and, dressing himself hastily, went forth and joined his little guide. The mountain maid tripped lightly before him, through the gray haze, over hill and moor. It was a wild and varied walk, unmarked by any regular or distinguishable track, and keeping, upon the whole, the direction of the ascent of the brook, though without tracing its windings. The landscape, as they advanced, became waster and more wild, until nothing but heath and rock encumbered the side of the valley.

"Is the place still distant?" said Morton.

"Nearly a mile off," answered the girl. "We'll be there belyve."

"And do you often go this wild journey, my little maid?"

"When grannie sends me wi' milk and meal to the Linn," answered the child.

"And are you not afraid to travel so wild a road alone?"

"Hout na, sir," replied the guide; "nae living creature wad touch sic a bit thing as I am, and grannie says we need never fear onything else when we are doing a gude turn."

"Strong in innocence as in triple mail!" said Morton to himself, and followed her steps in silence.

They soon came to a decayed thicket, where brambles and thorns supplied the room of the oak and birches of which it had once consisted. Here the guide turned short off the open heath, and by a sheep track conducted Morton to the brook. A hoarse and sullen roar had in part prepared him for the scene which presented itself, yet it was not to be viewed without surprise and even terror.   When he emerged from the devious path which conducted him through the thicket, he found himself placed on a ledge of flat rock, projecting over one side of a chasm not less than a hundred feet deep, where the dark mountain-stream made a decided and rapid shoot over the precipice, and was swallowed up by a deep, black, yawning gulf.   The eye in vain strove to see the bottom of the fall ; it could catch but one sheet of foaming uproar and sheer descent, until the view was obstructed by the projecting crags which enclosed the bottom of the waterfall, and hid from sight the dark pool which received its tortured waters; far beneath, at the distance of perhaps a quarter of a mile, the eye caught the winding of the stream as it emerged into a more open course.   But for that distance they were lost to sight as much as if a cavern had been arched over them ; and indeed the steep and projecting ledges of rock through which they wound their way in darkness were very nearly closing and over-roofing their course.

While Morton gazed at this scene of tumult, which seemed, by the surrounding thickets and the clefts into which the waters descended, to seek to hide itself from every eye, his little attendant, as she stood beside him on the platform of rock which commanded the best view of the fall, pulled him by the sleeve, and said, in a tone which he could not hear without stooping his ear near the speaker, " Hear till him ! Eh ! hear till him !"

Morton listened more attentively, and out of the very abyss into which the brook fell, and amidst the tumultuary sounds of the cataract, thought he could distinguish shouts, screams, and even articulate words, as if the tortured demon of the stream had been mingling his complaints with the roar of his broken waters.

" This is the way," said the little girl; " follow me, gin ye please, sir, but tak tent to your feet;" and, with the daring agility which custom had rendered easy, she vanished from the platform on which she stood, and, by notches and slight projections in the rock, scrambled down its face into the chasm which it overhung.   Steady, bold, and active, Morton hesitated not to follow her ; but the necessary attention to secure his hold and footing in a descent where both foot and hand were needful for security, prevented him from looking around him, till, having descended nigh twenty feet, and being sixty or seventy above the pool which received the fall, his guide made a pause, and he again found himself by her side in a situation that appeared equally romantic and pre-

The Cataract of Linklater.

carious. They were nearly opposite to the waterfall, and in point of level situated at about one-quarter's depth from the point of the cliff over which it thundered, and three-fourths of the height above the dark, deep, and restless pool which received its fall. Both these tremendous points, the first shoot, namely, of the yet unbroken stream, and the deep and sombre abyss into which it was emptied, were full before him, as well as the whole continuous stream of billowy froth, which, dashing from the one, was eddying and boiling in the other. They were so near this grand phenomenon that they were covered with its spray, and well-nigh deafened by the incessant roar. But crossing in the very front of the fall, and at scarce three yards' distance from the cataract, an old oak-tree, flung across the chasm in a manner that seemed accidental, formed a bridge of fearfully narrow dimensions and uncertain footing. The upper end of the tree rested on the platform on which they stood, the lower or uprooted extremity extended behind a projection on the opposite side, and was secured, Morton's eye could not discover where. From behind the same projection glimmered a strong red light, which, glancing in the waves of the falling water, and tingeing them partially with crimson, had a strange preternatural and sinister effect when contrasted with the beams of the rising sun, which glanced on the first broken waves of the fall, though even its meridian splendor could not gain the third of its full depth. When he had looked around him for a moment, the girl again pulled his sleeve, and pointing to the oak and the projecting point beyond it (for hearing speech was now out of the question), indicated that there lay his further passage.

Morton gazed at her with surprise ; for, although he well knew that the persecuted Presbyterians had in the preceding reigns sought refuge among dells and thickets, caves and cataracts, in spots the most extraordinary and secluded, although he had heard of the champions of the Covenant who had long abidden beside Dob's Linn on the wild heights of Polmoodie, and others who had been concealed in the yet more terrific cavern called Crichope Linn, in the parish of Closeburn,* yet his imagination had never exactly figured out the horrors of such a residence, and he was surprised how the strange and romantic scene which he now saw had remained concealed from him, while a curious investigator of such natural phenomena. But he readily conceived that, lying in a remote and wild district, and being destined as a place of concealment to the persecuted preachers and professors of nonconformity, the secret of

* See The Retreats of the Covenanters. Note 37.

its existence was carefully preserved by the few shepherds to whom it might be known.

As, breaking from these meditations, he began to consider how he should traverse the doubtful and terrific bridge, which, skirted by the cascade, and rendered wet and slippery by its constant drizzle, traversed the chasm above sixty feet from the bottom of the fall, his guide, as if to give him courage, tripped over and back without the least hesitation. Envying for a moment the little bare feet which caught a safer hold of the rugged side of the oak than he could pretend to with his heavy boots, Morton nevertheless resolved to attempt the passage, and, fixing his eye firm on a stationary object on the other side, without allowing his head to become giddy, or his attention to be distracted by the flash, the foam, and the roar of the waters around him, he strode steadily and safely along the uncertain bridge, and reached the mouth of a small cavern on the further side of the torrent. Here he paused ; for a light, proceeding from a fire of red-hot charcoal, permitted him to see the interior of the cave, and enabled him to contemplate the appearance of its inhabitant, by whom he himself could not be so readily distinguished, being concealed by the shadow of the rock. What he observed would by no means have encouraged a less determined man to proceed with the task which he had undertaken.

Burley, only altered from what he had been formerly by the addition of a grisly beard, stood in the midst of the cave, with his clasped Bible in one hand and his drawn sword in the other. His figure, dimly ruddied by the light of the red charcoal, seemed that of a fiend in the lurid atmosphere of Pandemonium, and his gestures and words, as far as they could be heard, seemed equally violent and irregular. All alone, and in a place of almost unapproachable seclusion, his demeanor was that of a man who strives for life and death with a mortal enemy. "Ha ! ha ! there—there !" he exclaimed, accompanying each word with a thrust, urged with his whole force against the impassible and empty air. "Did I not tell thee so ? I have resisted, and thou fleest from me ! Coward as thou art, come in all thy terrors—come with mine own evil deeds, which render thee most terrible of all ; there is enough betwixt the boards of this book to rescue me ! What mutterest thou of gray hairs ? It was well done to slay him : the more ripe the corn the readier for the sickle. Art gone ?—art gone ? I have ever known thee but a coward—ha ! ha ! ha !"

With these wild exclamations he sunk the point of his

sword, and remained standing still in the same posture, like a maniac whose fit is over.

"The dangerous time is by now," said the little girl, who had followed ; "it seldom lasts beyond the time that the sun's ower the hill. Ye may gang in and speak wi' him now. I'll wait for you at the other side of the Linn ; he canna bide to see twa folk at anes."

Slowly and cautiously, and keeping constantly upon his guard, Morton presented himself to the view of his old associate in command.

"What! comest thou again when thine hour is over?" was his first exclamation ; and flourishing his sword aloft, his countenance assumed an expression in which ghastly terror seemed mingled with the rage of a demoniac.

"I am come, Mr. Balfour," said Morton, in a steady and composed tone, "to renew an acquaintance which has been broken off since the fight of Bothwell Bridge."

As soon as Burley became aware that Morton was before him in person—an idea which he caught with marvellous celerity—he at once exerted that mastership over his heated and enthusiastic imagination the power of enforcing which was a most striking part of his extraordinary character. He sunk his sword-point at once, and as he stole it composedly into the scabbard, he muttered something of the damp and cold which sent an old soldier to his fencing exercise to prevent his blood from chilling. This done, he proceeded in the cold determined manner which was peculiar to his ordinary discourse.

"Thou hast tarried long, Henry Morton, and hast not come to the vintage before the twelfth hour has struck. Art thou yet willing to take the right hand of fellowship, and be one with those who look not to thrones or dynasties, but to the rule of Scripture, for their directions ?"

"I am surprised," said Morton, evading the direct answer to his question, "that you should have known me after so many years."

"The features of those who ought to act with me are engraved on my heart," answered Burley ; "and few but Silas Morton's son durst have followed me into this my castle of retreat. Seest thou that drawbridge of Nature's own construction ?" he added, pointing to the prostrate oak-tree ; "one spurn of my foot, and it is overwhelmed in the abyss below, bidding foemen on the farther sidest and at defiance, and leaving enemies on this at the mercy of one who never yet met his equal in single fight."

"Of such defences," said Morton, " I should have thought you would now have had little need."

" Little need ? " said Burley, impatiently. " What little need, when incarnate fiends are combined against me on earth, and Satan himself—— But it matters not," added he, checking himself. " Enough that I like my place of refuge —my cave of Adullam—and would not change its rude ribs of limestone rock for the fair chambers of the castle of the Earls of Torwood, with their broad bounds and barony. Thou, unless the foolish fever-fit be over, mayst think differently."

" It was of those very possessions I came to speak," said Morton ; " and I doubt not to find Mr. Balfour the same rational and reflecting person which I knew him to be in times when zeal disunited brethren."

" Ay ? " said Burley ; " indeed ? Is such truly your hope ? wilt thou express it more plainly ? "

" In a word, then," said Morton, " you have exercised, by means at which I can guess, a secret but most prejudicial influence over the fortunes of Lady Margaret Bellenden and her granddaughter, and in favor of that base, oppressive apostate, Basil Olifant, whom the law, deceived by thy operations, has placed in possession of their lawful property."

" Sayest thou ? " said Balfour.

" I do say so," replied Morton ; " and face to face you will not deny what you have vouched by your handwriting."

" And suppose I deny it not ? " said Balfour, " and suppose that thy eloquence were found equal to persuade me to retrace the steps I have taken on matured resolve, what will be thy meed ? Dost thou still hope to possess the fair-haired girl, with her wide and rich inheritance ? "

" I have no such hope," answered Morton, calmly.

" And for whom, then, hast thou ventured to do this great thing, to seek to rend the prey from the valiant, to bring forth food from the den of the lion, and to extract sweetness from the maw of the devourer ? For whose sake hast thou undertaken to read this riddle, more hard than Samson's ? "

" For Lord Evandale's and that of his bride," replied Morton, firmly. " Think better of mankind, Mr. Balfour, and believe there are some who are willing to sacrifice their happiness to that of others." .

" Then, as my soul liveth," replied Balfour, " thou art, to wear beard, and back a horse, and draw a sword, the tamest and most gall-less puppet that ever sustained injury unavenged. What ! thou wouldst help that accursed Evandale to the arms of the woman that thou lovest ? thou wouldst endow them with wealth and with heritages, and thou think'st that there lives another man, offended even more deeply than thou, yet equally cold-livered and mean-spirited, crawling upon the face of the earth, and hast dared to suppose that one other to be John Balfour ?"

" For my own feelings," said Morton, composedly, " I am answerable to none but Heaven. To you, Mr. Balfour, I should suppose it of little consequence whether Basil Olifant or Lord Evandale possess these estates."

" Thou art deceived," said Burley ; " both are indeed in outer darkness, and strangers to the light, as he whose eyes have never been opened to the day. But this Basil Olifant is a Nabal, a Demas, a base churl, whose wealth and power are at the disposal of him who can threaten to deprive him of them. He became a professor because he was deprived of these lands of Tillietudlem ; he turned a Papist to obtain possession of them ; he called himself an Erastian, that he might not again lose them ; and he will become what I list while I have in my power the document that may deprive him of them. These lands are a bit between his jaws and a hook in his nostrils, and the rein and the line are in my hands to guide them as I think meet ; and his they shall therefore be, unless I had assurance of bestowing them on a sure and sincere friend. But Lord Evandale is a Malignant, of heart like flint and brow like adamant ; the goods of the world fall on him like leaves on the frost-bound earth, and unmoved he will see them whirled off by the first wind. The heathen virtues of such as he are more dangerous to us than the sordid cupidity of those who, governed by their interest, must follow where it leads, and who, therefore, themselves the slaves of avarice, may be compelled to work in the vineyard, were it but to earn the wages of sin."

" This might have been all well some years since," replied Morton ; " and I could understand your argument, although I could never acquiesce in its justice. But at this crisis it seems useless to you to persevere in keeping up an influence which can no longer be directed to an useful purpose. The land has peace, liberty, and freedom of conscience, and what would you more ? "

" More ! " exclaimed Burley, again unsheathing his sword, with a vivacity which nearly made Morton start. " Look at the notches upon that weapon ; they are three in number, are they not ? "

" It seems so," answered Morton ; " but what of that ? "

" The fragment of steel that parted from this first gap

rested on the skull of the perjured traitor who first introduced
Episcopacy into Scotland ; this second notch was made in the
rib-bone of an impious villain, the boldest and best soldier that
upheld the prelatic cause at Drumclog ; this third was broken on the steel headpiece of the captain who defended the
Chapel of Holyrood when the people rose at the Revolution.
I cleft him to the teeth through steel and bone.   It has done
great deeds this little weapon, and each of these blows was a
deliverance to the church.   This sword," he said, again sheath-
ing it, " has yet more to do—to weed out this base and pesti-
lential heresy of Erastianism, to vindicate the true liberty of
the kirk in her purity, to restore the Covenant in its glory ;
then let it moulder and rust beside the bones of its master." *

" You have neither men nor means, Mr. Balfour, to disturb the government as now settled," argued Morton ; " the
people are in general satisfied, excepting only the gentlemen
of the Jacobite interest ; and surely you would not join with
those who would only use you for their own purposes ? "

" It is they," answered Burley, " that should serve ours.
I went to the camp of the Malignant Claver'se, as the future
King of Israel sought the land of the Philistines ; I arranged
with him a rising, and, but for the villain Evandale, the Erastians ere now had been driven from the west.   I could slay
him," he added, with a vindictive scowl, " were he grasping
the horns of the altar ! "   He then proceeded in a calmer
tone : " If thou, son of mine ancient comrade, wert suitor for
thyself to this Edith Bellenden, and wert willing to put thy
hand to the great work with zeal equal to thy courage, think
not I would prefer the friendship of Basil Olifant to thine ;
thou shouldst then have the means that this document [he
produced a parchment] affords to place her in possession of
the lands of her fathers.   This have I longed to say to thee
ever since I saw thee fight the good fight so strongly at the
fatal Bridge.   The maiden loved thee and thou her."

Morton replied firmly, " I will not dissemble with you,
Mr. Balfour, even to gain a good end.   I came in hopes to
persuade you to do a deed of justice to others, not to gain
any selfish end of my own.   I have failed.   I grieve for your
sake more than for the loss which others will sustain by your
injustice."

" You refuse my proffer, then ? " said Burley, with kindling eyes.

" I do," said Morton.   " Would you be really, as you are
desirous to be thought, a man of honor and conscience, you

---

* See Predictions of the Covenanters.   Note 38.

would, regardless of all other considerations, restore that parchment to Lord Evandale, to be used for the advantage of the lawful heir."

"Sooner shall it perish!" said Balfour; and, casting the deed into the heap of red charcoal beside him, pressed it down with the heel of his boot.

While it smoked, shrivelled, and crackled in the flames, Morton sprang forward to snatch it, and Burley catching hold of him, a struggle ensued. Both were strong men, but although Morton was much the more active and younger of the two, yet Balfour was the most powerful, and effectually prevented him from rescuing the deed until it was fairly reduced to a cinder. They then quitted hold of each other. and the enthusiast, rendered fiercer by the contest, glared on Morton with an eye expressive of frantic revenge.

"Thou hast my secret," he exclaimed; "thou must be mine or die!"

"I contemn your threats," said Morton; "I pity you, and leave you."

But, as he turned to retire, Burley stepped before him, pushed the oak-trunk from its resting-place, and, as it fell thundering and crashing into the abyss beneath, drew his sword, and cried out, with a voice that rivalled the roar of the cataract and the thunder of the falling oak—"Now thou art at bay! fight, yield, or die!" and standing in the mouth of the cavern, he flourished his naked sword.

"I will not fight with the man that preserved my father's life," said Morton; "I have not yet learned to say the words, 'I yield;' and my life I will rescue as I best can."

So speaking, and ere Balfour was aware of his purpose, he sprang past him, and, exerting that youthful agility of which he possessed an uncommon share, leaped clear across the fearful chasm which divided the mouth of the cave from the projecting rock on the opposite side, and stood there safe and free from his incensed enemy. He immediately ascended the ravine, and, as he turned, saw Burley stand for an instant aghast with astonishment, and then, with the frenzy of disappointed rage, rush into the interior of his cavern.

It was not difficult for him to perceive that this unhappy man's mind had been so long agitated by desperate schemes and sudden disappointments that it had lost its equipoise, and that there was now in his conduct a shade of lunacy, not the less striking from the vigor and craft with which he pursued his wild designs. Morton soon joined his guide, who had been terrified by the fall of the oak. This he represented as acci-

dental; and she assured him in return that the inhabitant of
the cave would experience no inconvenience from it, being
always provided with materials to construct another bridge.

The adventures of the morning were not yet ended. As
they approached the hut, the little girl made an exclamation
of surprise at seeing her grandmother groping her way towards
them, at a greater distance from her home than she could have
been supposed capable of travelling.

"O, sir, sir!" said the old woman, when she heard them
approach, "gin e'er ye loved Lord Evandale, help now, or
never! God be praised that left my hearing when He took
my poor eyesight! Come this way—this way. And O! tread
lightly. Peggy, hinny, gang saddle the gentleman's horse,
and lead him cannily ahint the thorny shaw, and bide him
there."

She conducted him to a small window, through which,
himself unobserved, he could see two dragoons seated at their
morning draught of ale, and conversing earnestly together.

"The more I think of it," said the one, "the less I like it,
Inglis. Evandale was a good officer, and the soldier's friend;
and though we were punished for the mutiny at Tillietudlem,
yet, by ——, Frank, you must own we deserved it."

"D——n seize me, if I forgive him for it, though!" replied the other; "and I think I can sit in his skirts now."

"Why, man, you should forget and forgive. Better take
the start with him along with the rest, and join the ranting
Highlanders. We have all eat King James's bread."

"Thou art an ass; the start, as you call it, will never happen; the day's put off. Halliday's seen a ghost, or Miss Bellenden's fallen sick of the pip, or some blasted nonsense or
another; the thing will never keep two days longer, and the
first bird that sings out will get the reward."

"That's true, too," answered his comrade; "and will this
fellow—this Basil Olifant—pay handsomely?"

"Like a prince, man," said Inglis. "Evandale is the
man on earth whom he hates worst, and he fears him, besides,
about some law business, and were he once rubbed out of the
way, all, he thinks, will be his own."

"But shall we have warrants and force enough?" said the
other fellow. "Few people here will stir against my lord, and
we may find him with some of our own fellows at his back."

"Thou'rt a cowardly fool, Dick," returned Inglis; "he is
living quietly down at Fairy Knowe to avoid suspicion. Olifant
is a magistrate, and will have some of his own people that he
can trust along with him. There are us two, and the Laird

says he can get a desperate fighting Whig fellow, called Quintin Mackell, that has an old grudge at Evandale."

"Well, well, you are my officer, you know," said the private, with true military conscience, "and if anything is wrong——"

"I'll take the blame," said Inglis. "Come, another pot of ale, and let us to Tillietudlem. Here, blind Bess! why, where the devil has the old hag crept to?"

"Delay them as long as you can," whispered Morton, as he thrust his purse into the hostess's hand; "all depends on gaining time."

Then, walking swiftly to the place where the girl held his horse ready—"To Fairy Knowe? no; alone I could not protect them. I must instantly to Glasgow. Wittenbold, the commandant there, will readily give me the support of a troop and procure me the countenance of the civil power. I must drop a caution as I pass. Come, Moorkopf," he said, addressing his horse as he mounted him, "this day must try your breath and speed."

CHAPTER XLIV

Yet could he not his closing eyes withdraw,
Though less and less of Emily he saw ;
So, speechless for a little space he lay,
Then grasp'd the hand he held, and sigh'd his soul away.
                              Palamon and Arcite.

THE indisposition of Edith confined her to bed during the
eventful day on which she had received such an unexpected
shock from the sudden apparition of Morton.   Next morning, however, she was reported to be so much better that
Lord Evandale resumed his purpose of leaving Fairy Knowe.
At a late hour in the forenoon, Lady Emily entered the apartment of Edith with a peculiar gravity of manner.   Having
received and paid the compliments of the day, she observed it
would be a sad one for her, though it would relieve Miss Bellenden of an encumbrance—" My brother leaves us to-day,
Miss Bellenden."

" Leaves us ! " exclaimed Edith, in surprise ; " for his own
house, I trust ? "

" I have reason to think he meditates a more distant journey," answered Lady Emily ; " he has little to detain him in
this country."

" Good Heaven ! " exclaimed Edith, " why was I born to
become the wreck of all that is manly and noble ?   What can
be done to stop him from running headlong on ruin ?   I will
come down instantly.   Say that I implore he will not depart
until I speak with him."

" It will be in vain, Miss Bellenden ; but I will execute
your commission ; " and she left the room as formally as she
had entered it, and informed her brother, Miss Bellenden was
so much recovered as to propose coming downstairs ere he
went away.

" I suppose," she added, pettishly, " the prospect of being
speedily released from our company has wrought a cure on her
shattered nerves."

" Sister," said Lord Evandale, " you are unjust, if not
envious."

" Unjust I may be, Evandale, but I should not have

dreamt," glancing her eye at a mirror, "of being thought envious without better cause. But let us go to the old lady; she is making a feast in the other room, which might have dined all your troop when you had one."

Lord Evandale accompanied her in silence to the parlor, for he knew it was in vain to contend with her prepossessions and offended pride. They found the table covered with refreshments, arranged under the careful inspection of Lady Margaret.

"Ye could hardly weel be said to breakfast this morning, my Lord Evandale, and ye maun e'en partake of a small collation before ye ride, such as this poor house, whose inmates are so much indebted to you, can provide in their present circumstances. For my ain part, I like to see young folk take some refection before they ride out upon their sports or their affairs, and I said as much to his most sacred Majesty when he breakfasted at Tillietudlem in the year of grace 1651; and his most sacred Majesty was pleased to reply, drinking to my health at the same time in a flagon of Rhenish wine, 'Lady Margaret, ye speak like a Highland oracle.' These were his Majesty's very words; so that your lordship may judge whether I have not good authority to press young folk to partake of their vivers."

It may be well supposed that much of the good lady's speech failed Lord Evandale's ears, which were then employed in listening for the light step of Edith. His absence of mind on this occasion, however natural, cost him very dear. While Lady Margaret was playing the kind hostess, a part she delighted and excelled in, she was interrupted by John Gudyill, who, in the natural phrase for announcing an inferior to the mistress of a family, said, "There was ane wanting to speak to her leddyship."

"Ane! what ane? Has he nae name? Ye speak as if I kept a shop, and was to come at everybody's whistle."

"Yes, he has a name," answered John, "but your leddyship likes ill to hear't."

"What is it, you fool?"

"It's Calf Gibbie, my leddy," said John, in a tone rather above the pitch of decorous respect, on which he occasionally trespassed, confiding in his merit as an ancient servant of the family, and a faithful follower of their humble fortunes—"it's Calf Gibbie, an your leddyship will hae't, that keeps Edie Henshaw's kye down yonder at the brig end; that's him that was Guse Gibbie at Tillietudlem, and gaed to the wappinshaw, and that——"

"Hold your peace, John," said the old lady, rising in dignity ; "you are very insolent to think I wad speak wi' a person like that. Let him tell his business to you or Mrs. Headrigg."

"He'll no hear o' that, my leddy ; he says, them that sent him bade him gie the thing to your leddyship's ain hand direct, or to Lord Evandale's, he wots na whilk. But, to say the truth, he's far frae fresh, and he's but an idiot an he were."

"Then turn him out," said Lady Margaret, "and tell him to come back to-morrow when he is sober. I suppose he comes to crave some benevolence, as an ancient follower o' the house."

"Like eneugh, my leddy, for he's a' in rags, poor creature."

Gudyill made another attempt to get at Gibbie's commission, which was indeed of the last importance, being a few lines from Morton to Lord Evandale, acquainting him with the danger in which he stood from the practices of Olifant, and exhorting him either to instant flight, or else to come to Glasgow and surrender himself, where he could assure him of protection. This billet, hastily written, he intrusted to Gibbie, whom he saw feeding his herd beside the bridge, and backed with a couple of dollars his desire that it might instantly be delivered into the hand to which it was addressed.

But it was decreed that Goose Gibbie's intermediation, whether as an emissary or as a man-at-arms, should be unfortunate to the family of Tillietudlem. He unluckily tarried so long at the ale-house, to prove if his employer's coin was good, that, when he appeared at Fairy Knowe, the little sense which nature had given him was effectually drowned in ale and brandy, and instead of asking for Lord Evandale, he demanded to speak with Lady Margaret, whose name was more familiar to his ear. Being refused admittance to her presence, he staggered away with the letter undelivered, perversely faithful to Morton's instructions in the only point in which it would have been well had he departed from them.

A few minutes after he was gone, Edith entered the apartment. Lord Evandale and she met with mutual embarrassment, which Lady Margaret, who only knew in general that their union had been postponed by her granddaughter's indisposition, set down to the bashfulness of a bride and bridegroom, and, to place them at ease, began to talk to Lady Emily on indifferent topics. At this moment, Edith, with a countenance as pale as death, muttered, rather than whispered, to

Lord Evandale a request to speak with him. He offered his arm, and supported her into the small anteroom, which, as we have noticed before, opened from the parlor. He placed her in a chair, and, taking one himself, awaited the opening of the conversation.

"I am distressed, my lord," were the first words she was able to articulate, and those with difficulty; "I scarce know what I would say, nor how to speak it."

"If I have any share in occasioning your uneasiness," said Lord Evandale, mildly, "you will soon, Edith, be released from it."

"You are determined, then, my lord," she replied, " to run this desperate course with desperate men, in spite of your own better reason, in spite of your friends' entreaties, in spite of the almost inevitable ruin which yawns before you?"

"Forgive me, Miss Bellenden; even your solicitude on my account must not detain me when my honor calls. My horses stand ready saddled, my servants are prepared, the signal for rising will be given so soon as I reach Kilsyth. If it is my fate that calls me, I will not shun meeting it. It will be something," he said, taking her hand, "to die deserving your compassion, since I cannot gain your love."

"O, my lord, remain!" said Edith, in a tone which went to his heart; "time may explain the strange circumstance which has shocked me so much; my agitated nerves may recover their tranquillity. O, do not rush on death and ruin! Remain to be our prop and stay, and hope everything from time."

"It is too late, Edith," answered Lord Evandale; "and I were most ungenerous could I practice on the warmth and kindliness of your feelings towards me. I know you cannot love me; nervous distress, so strong as to conjure up the appearance of the dead or absent, indicates a predilection too powerful to give way to friendship and gratitude alone. But were it otherwise, the die is now cast."

As he spoke thus, Cuddie burst into the room, terror and haste in his countenance. "O, my lord, hide yoursell! they hae beset the outlets o' the house," was his first exclamation.

"They? Who?" said Lord Evandale.

"A party of horse, headed by Basil Olifant," answered Cuddie.

"O, hide yourself, my lord!" echoed Edith, in an agony of terror.

"I will not, by Heaven!" answered Lord Evandale. "What right has the villain to assail me, or stop my passage?

I will make my way, were he backed by a regiment; tell
Halliday and Hunter to get out the horses. And now, farewell, Edith!" He clasped her in his arms and kissed her
tenderly; then, bursting from his sister, who, with Lady
Margaret, endeavored to detain him, rushed out and mounted
his horse.

All was in confusion: the women shrieked and hurried in
consternation to the front windows of the house, from which
they could see a small party of horsemen, of whom two only
seemed soldiers. They were on the open ground before Cuddie's cottage, at the bottom of the descent from the house,
and showed caution in approaching it, as if uncertain of the
strength within.

"He may escape—he may escape!" said Edith, "O, would
he but take the by-road!"

But Lord Evandale, determined to face a danger which his
high spirit undervalued, commanded his servants to follow
him, and rode composedly down the avenue. Old Gudyill ran
to arm himself, and Cuddie snatched down a gun which was
kept for the protection of the house, and, although on foot,
followed Lord Evandale. It was in vain his wife, who had
hurried up on the alarm, hung by his skirts, threatening him
with death by the sword or halter for meddling with other
folks' matters.

"Haud your peace, ye b——," said Cuddie, "and that's
braid Scotch, or I wotna what is; is it ither folks' matters to
see Lord Evandale murdered before my face?" and down the
avenue he marched. But considering on the way that he
composed the whole infantry, as John Gudyill had not appeared, he took his vantage-ground behind the hedge, ham-
mered his flint, cocked his piece, and, taking a long aim at
Laird Basil, as he was called, stood prompt for action.

As soon as Lord Evandale appeared, Olifant's party spread
themselves a little, as if preparing to enclose him. Their
leader stood fast, supported by three men, two of whom were
dragoons, the third in dress and appearance a countryman,
all well armed. But the strong figure, stern features, and
resolved manner of the third attendant, made him seem the
most formidable of the party; and whoever had before seen
him could have no difficulty in recognizing Balfour of Burley.

"Follow me," said Lord Evandale to his servants, "and if
we are forcibly opposed, do as I do." He advanced at a hand
gallop towards Olifant, and was in the act of demanding why
he had thus beset the road, when Olifant called out, "Shoot
the traitor!" and the whole four fired their carabines upon the

unfortunate nobleman. He reeled in the saddle, advanced his hand to the holster, and drew a pistol, but, unable to discharge it, fell from his horse mortally wounded. His servants had presented their carabines. Hunter fired at random ; but Halliday, who was an intrepid fellow, took aim at Inglis, and shot him dead on the spot. At the same instant a shot from behind the hedge still more effectually avenged Lord Evandale, for the ball took place in the very midst of Basil Olifant's forehead, and stretched him lifeless on the ground. His followers, astonished at the execution done in so short a time, seemed rather disposed to stand inactive, when Burley, whose blood was up with the contest, exclaimed, "Down with the Midianites !" and attacked. Halliday sword in hand. At this instant the clatter of horses' hoofs was heard, and a party of horse, rapidly advancing on the road from Glasgow, appeared on the fatal field. They were foreign dragoons, led by the Dutch commandant Wittenbold, accompanied by Morton and a civil magistrate.

A hasty call to surrender, in the name of God and King William, was obeyed by all except Burley, who turned his horse, and attempted to escape. Several soldiers pursued him by command of their officer, but, being well mounted, only the two headmost seemed likely to gain on him. He turned deliberately twice, and discharging first one of his pistols and then the other, rid himself of the one pursuer by mortally wounding him, and of the other by shooting his horse, and then continued his flight to Bothwell Bridge, where, for his misfortune, he found the gates shut and guarded. Turning from thence, he made for a place where the river seemed passable, and plunged into the stream, the bullets from the pistols and carabines of his pursuers whizzing around him. Two balls took effect when he was past the middle of the stream, and he felt himself dangerously wounded. He reined his horse round in the midst of the river, and returned towards the bank he had left, waving his hand, as if with the purpose of intimating that he surrendered. The troopers ceased firing at him accordingly, and awaited his return, two of them riding a little way into the river to seize and disarm him. But it presently appeared that his purpose was revenge, not safety. As he approached the two soldiers, he collected his remaining strength and discharged a blow on the head of one, which tumbled him from his horse. The other dragoon, a strong muscular man, had in the meanwhile laid hands on him. Burley, in requital, grasped his throat, as a dying tiger seizes his prey, and both, losing the saddle in the struggle, came headlong into the river, and were swept down the stream.　Their course might be traced by the blood which bubbled up to the surface.　They were twice seen to rise, the Dutchman striving to swim, and Burley * clinging to him in a manner that showed his desire that both should perish.　Their corpses were taken out about a quarter of a mile down the river.　As Balfour's grasp could not have been unclinched without cutting off his hands, both were thrown into a hasty grave, still marked by a rude stone and a ruder epitaph. †

While the soul of this stern enthusiast flitted to its account, that of the brave and generous Lord Evandale was also released. Morton had flung himself from his horse upon perceiving his situation, to render his dying friend all the aid in his power. He knew him, for he pressed his hand, and, being unable to speak, intimated by signs his wish to be conveyed to the house. This was done with all the care possible, and he was soon surrounded by his lamenting friends.　But the clamorous grief of Lady Emily was far exceeded in intensity by the silent agony of Edith.　Unconscious even of the presence of Morton, she hung over the dying man; nor was she aware that Fate, who was removing one faithful lover, had restored another as if from the grave, until Lord Evandale, taking their hands in his, pressed them both affectionately, united them together, raised his face as if to pray for a blessing on them, and sunk back and expired in the next moment.

* See John Balfour called Burley.　Note 39.
† See Balfour's Grave.　Note 40.

CONCLUSION

I HAD determined to waive the task of a concluding chapter, leaving to the reader's imagination the arrangements which must necessarily take place after Lord Evandale's death. But as I was aware that precedents are wanting for a practice which might be found convenient both to readers and compilers, I confess myself to have been in a considerable dilemma, when fortunately I was honored with an invitation to drink tea with Miss Martha Buskbody, a young lady who has carried on the profession of mantua-making at Gandercleugh and in the neighborhood, with great success, for about forty years. Knowing her taste for narratives of this description, I requested her to look over the loose sheets the morning before I waited on her, and enlighten me by the experience which she must have acquired in reading through the whole stock of three circulating libraries in Gandercleugh and the two next market-towns. When, with a palpitating heart, I appeared before her in the evening, I found her much disposed to be complimentary.

"I have not been more affected," said she, wiping the glasses of her spectacles, "by any novel, excepting the *Tale of Jemmy and Jenny Jessamy*, which is indeed pathos itself; but your plan of omitting a formal conclusion will never do. You may be as harrowing to our nerves as you will in the course of your story, but, unless you had the genius of the author of *Julia de Roubigné*, never let the end be altogether overclouded. Let us see a glimpse of sunshine in the last chapter; it is quite essential."

"Nothing would be more easy for me, madam, than to comply with your injunctions; for, in truth, the parties in whom you have had the goodness to be interested did live long and happily, and begot sons and daughters."

"It is unnecessary, sir," she said, with a slight nod of reprimand, "to be particular concerning their matrimonial comforts. But what is your objection to let us have, in a general way, a glimpse of their future felicity?"

"Really, madam," said I, "you must be aware that every

volume of a narrative turns less and less interesting as the author draws to a conclusion ; just like your tea, which, though excellent hyson, is necessarily weaker and more insipid in the last cup. Now, as I think the one is by no means improved by the luscious lump of half-dissolved sugar usually found at the bottom of it, so I am of opinion that a history, growing already vapid, is but dully crutched up by a detail of circumstances which every reader must have anticipated, even though the author exhaust on them every flowery epithet in the language."

"This will not do, Mr. Pattieson," continued the lady ; " you have, as I may say, basted up your first story very hastily and clumsily at the conclusion ; and, in my trade, I would have cuffed the youngest apprentice who had put such a horrid and bungled spot of work out of her hand. And if you do not redeem this gross error by telling us all about the marriage of Morton and Edith, and what became of the other personages of the story, from Lady Margaret down to Goose Gibbie, I apprise you that you will not be held to have accomplished your task handsomely."

"Well, madam," I replied, " my materials are so ample that I think I can satisfy your curiosity, unless it descend to very minute circumstances indeed."

"First, then," said she, " for that is most essential—Did Lady Margaret get back her fortune and her castle ?"

"She did, madam, and in the easiest way imaginable, as heir, namely, to her worthy cousin, Basil Olifant, who died without a will ; and thus, by his death, not only restored, but even augmented, the fortune of her whom, during his life, he had pursued with the most inveterate malice. John Gudyill, reinstated in his dignity, was more important than ever ; and Cuddie, with rapturous delight, entered upon the cultivation of the mains of Tillietudlem, and the occupation of his original cottage. But, with the shrewd caution of his character, he was never heard to boast of having fired the lucky shot which repossessed his lady and himself in their original habitations. "After a'," he said to Jenny, who was his only confidant, " auld Basil Olifant was my leddy's cousin, and a grand gentleman ; and though he was acting again the law, as I understand, for he ne'er showed ony warrant, or required Lord Evandale to surrender, and though I mind killing him nae mair than I wad do a muir-cock, yet it's just as weel to keep a calm sough about it." He not only did so, but ingeniously enough countenanced a report that old Gudyill had done the deed, which was worth many a gill of brandy to him from the old butler, who, far different in disposition from Cuddie, was much more inclined to exaggerate than suppress his exploits of manhood. The blind widow was provided for in the most comfortable manner, as well as the little guide to the Linn ; and——"

"But what is all this to the marriage—the marriage of the principal personages ?" interrupted Miss Buskbody, impatiently tapping her snuff-box.

"The marriage of Morton and Miss Bellenden was delayed for several months, as both went into deep mourning on account of Lord Evandale's death. They were then wedded."

"I hope, not without Lady Margaret's consent, sir ?" said my fair critic. "I love books which teach a proper deference in young persons to their parents. In a novel the young people may fall in love without their countenance, because it is essential to the necessary intricacy of the story, but they must always have the benefit of their consent at last. Even old Delville received Cecilia, though the daughter of a man of low birth."

"And even so, madam," replied I, "Lady Margaret was prevailed on to countenance Morton, although the old Covenanter, his father, stuck sorely with her for some time. Edith was her only hope, and she wished to see her happy ; Morton, or Melville Morton, as he was more generally called, stood so high in the reputation of the world, and was in every other respect such an eligible match, that she put her prejudice aside, and consoled herself with the recollection that 'marriage went by destiny, as was observed to her,' she said, 'by his most sacred Majesty, Charles the Second of happy memory, when she showed him the portrait of her grandfather Fergus, third Earl of Torwood, the handsomest man of his time, and that of Countess Jane, his second lady, who had a humpback and only one eye. This was his Majesty's observation,' she said, 'on one remarkable morning when he deigned to take his disjune——'"

"Nay," said Miss Buskbody, again interrupting me, "if she brought such authority to countenance her acquiescing in a misalliance, there was no more to be said. And what became of old Mrs. What's-her-name, the housekeeper ?"

"Mrs. Wilson, madam ?" answered I. "She was perhaps the happiest of the party ; for once a year, and not oftener, Mr. and Mrs. Melville Morton dined in the great wainscotted chamber in solemn state, the hangings being all displayed, the carpet laid down, and the huge brass candlestick set on the table, stuck round with leaves of laurel. The preparing the room for this yearly festival employed her mind for six months before it came about, and the putting matters to rights occupied old Alison the other six, so that a single day of rejoicing found her business for all the year round."

"And Niel Blane?" said Miss Buskbody.

"Lived to a good old age, drank ale and brandy with guests of all persuasions, played Whig or Jacobite tunes as best pleased his customers, and died worth as much money as married Jenny to a cock laird. I hope, ma'am, you have no other inquiries to make, for really——"

"Goose Gibbie, sir?" said my persevering friend—"Goose Gibbie, whose ministry was fraught with such consequences to the personages of the narrative?"

"Consider, my dear Miss Buskbody—I beg pardon for the familiarity—but pray consider, even the memory of the renowned Scheherazade, that Empress of Tale-tellers, could not preserve every circumstance. I am not quite positive as to the fate of Goose Gibbie, but am inclined to think him the same with one Gilbert Dudden, *alias* Calf Gibbie, who was whipped through Hamilton for stealing poultry."

Miss Buskbody now placed her left foot on the fender, crossed her right leg over her knee, lay back on the chair, and looked towards the ceiling. When I observed her assume this contemplative mood, I concluded she was studying some further cross-examination, and therefore took my hat and wished her a hasty good-night, ere the Demon of Criticism had supplied her with any more queries. In like manner, gentle Reader, returning you my thanks for the patience which has conducted you thus far, I take the liberty to withdraw myself from you for the present.

PERORATION

IT was mine earnest wish, most courteous Reader, that the
Tales of my Landlord should have reached thine hands in
one entire succession of tomes, or volumes. But as I sent
some few more manuscript quires, containing the continuation of these most pleasing narratives, I was apprised, somewhat unceremoniously, by my publisher, that he did not approve of novels, as he injuriously called these real histories,
extending beyond four volumes, and, if I did not agree to
the first four being published separately, he threatened to
decline the article. (O, ignorance ! as if the vernacular
article of our mother English were capable of declension !)
Whereupon, somewhat moved by his remonstrances, and
more by heavy charges for print and paper which he stated
to have been already incurred, I have resolved that these
four volumes shall be the heralds or avant-couriers of the
Tales which are yet in my possession, nothing doubting
that they will be eagerly devoured, and the remainder anxiously demanded, by the unanimous voice of a discerning
public. I rest, esteemed Reader, thine as thou shalt construe me,

JEDEDIAH CLEISHBOTHAM.

GANDERCLEUGH, *Nov.* 15, 1816.

NOTES TO OLD MORTALITY

NOTE 1.—PETER PATTIESON'S GRAVE, p. 2

Note by Mr. Jedediah Cleishbotham.—That I kept my plight in this melancholy matter with my deceased and lamented friend, appeareth from a handsome headstone, erected at my proper charges in this spot, bearing the name and calling of Peter Pattieson, with the date of his nativity and sepulture, together also with a testimony of his merits, attested by myself, as his superior and patron.—J. C.

NOTE 2.—A MARCH-DIKE BOUNDARY, p. 4.

I deem it fitting that the reader should be apprised that this limitary boundary between the conterminous heritable property of his honour the Laird of Gandercleugh and his honour the Laird of Gusedub was to have been in fashion an agger, or rather murus, of uncemented granite, called by the vulgar a 'dry-stane dyke,' surmounted or cope, cospite, viridi, i. e. with a sod-turf. Truly their honours fell into discord concerning two roods of marshy ground, near the cove culled the Bedral's Beild; and the controversy, having some years bygone been removed from before the judges of the land (with whom it abode long), even unto the Great City of London and the Assembly of the Nobles therein, is, as I may say, adhuc in pendente.—J. C.

NOTE 3.—THE PROPHET'S CHAMBER, p. 8.

He might have added, and for the rich also; since, I laud my stars, the great of the earth have also taken harbourage in my poor domicile. And during the service of my handmaiden, Dorothy, who was buxom and comely of aspect, his Honour the Laird of Smackawa, in his peregrinations to and from the metropolis, was wont to prefer my Prophet's Chamber even to the sanded chamber of dais in the Wallace Inn, and to bestow a mutchkin, as he would jocosely say, to obtain the freedom of the house, but, in reality, to assure himself of my company during the evening.—J. C.

NOTE 4.—FESTIVAL OF THE POPINJAY, p. 13.

The Festival of the Popinjay is still, I believe, practised at Maybole, in Ayrshire. The following passage in the history of the Somerville family suggested the scenes in the text. The author of that curious manuscript* thus celebrates his father's demeanor at such an assembly:—

'Haveing now passed his infancie, in the tenth year of his age, he was by his grandfather putt to the grammar scholl, ther bein then att the toune of Delserf a very able master that taught the grammar, and fitted boyes for the colledge. Dureing his educating in this place, they had then a custome every year to solemnize the first Sunday of

---

*Published by Sir Walter Scott in 1814. Edin. 2 vols.

May with danceing about a May-pole, fyreing of pieces, and all manner of ravelling then in use. Ther being at that tyme few or noe
merchants in this pettie village, to furnish necessaries for the schoil-
ars sports, this youth resolves to furnish himself elsewhere, that so
he may appear with the bravest. In order to this, by break of day
he ryses and goes to Hamiltoune, and there bestowes all the money
that for a long tyme before he had gotten from his friends, or had
otherwayes purchased, upon ribbones of diverse coloures, a new hatt
and gloves. But in nothing he bestowed his money more liberall'e
than upon gunpowder, a great quantitie whereof he buyes for his
oune use, and to supply the wantes of his comrades; thus furnished
with these commodities, but ane empty purse, he returnes to Delserf
be seven a clock (haveing travelled that Sabbath morning above
eight myles), puttes on his [best] cloathes and new hatt, flying with
ribbones of all culloures; in this equipag, with this little phizie (fuzee)
upon his shoulder, he marches to the church-yaird, where the May-
pole was sett up, and the solemnitie of that day was to be kept.
Ther first at the foot-ball he equalled anyone that played; but for han-
dleing of his piece, in chargeing and dischargeing, he was so ready,
and shott soe near the marke, that he faire surpassed all his fellow
schollars, and became a teacher of that art to them before the thret-
tenth year of his oune age. And really, I have often admired his
dexterity in this, both at the exercizeing of his souldiers, and when
for recreatione I have gone to the gunning with him when I was but
a stripeling myself; for albeit that pessetyme was the exercize I delighted most in, yet could I never attaine to any perfectione compar-
able to him. This dayes sport being over, he had the applause of all
the spectatores, the kyndenesse of his fellow-condisciples, and the
favour of the wholl inhabitants of that litle village [vol. ii. p. 144].

NOTE 5.—SERGEANT BOTHWELL, p. 28.

The history of the restless and ambitious Francis Stewart, Earl of
Bothwell, makes a considerable figure in the reign of James VI. of
Scotland and First of England. After being repeatedly pardoned for
acts of treason, he was at length obliged to retire abroad, where he
died in great misery. Great part of his forfeited estate was bestowed
on Walter Scott, first Lord of Buccleuch, and on the first Earl of
Roxburghe.

Francis Stewart, son of the forfeited earl, obtained from the favour
of Charles I. a decreet-arbitral, appointing the two noblemen, gran-
tees of his father's estate, to restore the same, or make some compen-
sation for retaining it. The barony of Crichton, with its beautiful
castle, was surrendered by the curaors of Francis, Earl of Buccleuch, but he retained the far more extensive property Liddesdale.
James Stewart also, as appears from writings in the Author's possession, made an advantageous composition with the Earl of Roxburghe. 'But,' says the satirical Scotstarvet, 'male parta pejus
dilabunter; for he never brooked them (enjoyed them) nor was anything the richer, since they accresced to his creditors, and now are
in the possession of one Dr. Seaton. His eldest son Francis became
a trooper in the late war; as for the other brother, John, who was
Abbot of Coldingham, he also disponed all that estate, and now has
nothing, but lives on the charity of his friends.'*

Francis Stewart, who had been a trooper during the great Civil
War, seems to have received no preferment after the Restoration
suited to his high birth, though, in fact, third cousin to Charles II.
Captain Creichton, the friend of Dean Swift, who published his
Memoirs, found him a private gentleman in the King's Life Guards.
At the same time this was no degrading condition; for Fountainhall
records a duel fought between a Life Guardsman and an officer in the
militia, because the latter had taken upon him to assume superior
rank as an officer to a gentleman private in the Life Guards. The Life
Guardsman was killed in the rencontre, and his antagonist was executed for murder.

The character of Bothwell, except in relation to the name, is
entirely ideal.

---

*The Staggering State of the Scots Statesman for One Hundred Years, by Sir John
Scot of Scotstarvet. Edinburgh, 1754, p. 154.

NOTE 6.—ASSASSINATION OF ARCHBISHOP SHARP, p. 32

The general account of this act of assassination is to be found in all histories of the period. A more particular narrative may be found in the words of one of the actors, James Russell, in the Appendix to Kirkton's History of the Church of Scotland, published by Charles Kirkpatrick Sharpe, Esquire, 4to, Edinburgh, 1817.

NOTE 7.—SHERIFF-DEPUTE CARMICHAEL, p. 33.

One Carmichael, sheriff-depute in Fife, who had been active in enforcing the penal measures against nonconformists. He was on the moors hunting, but receiving accidental information that a party was out in quest of him, he returned home, and escaped the fate designed for him, which befell his patron the Archbishop.

NOTE 8.—MURDERERS OF ARCHBISHOP SHARP, p. 33

The leader of this party was David Hackston, of Rathillet, a gentleman of ancient birth and good estate. He had been profligate in his younger days, but having been led from curiosity to attend the conveticles of the non-conforming clergy, he adopted their principles in the fullest extent. It appears that Hackston had some personal quarrel with Archbishop Sharp which induced him to decline the command of the party when the slaughter was determined upon, fearing his acceptance might be ascribed to motives of personal enmity. He felt himself free in conscience, however, to be present; and when the archbishop, dragged from his carriage, crawled towards him on his knees for protection, he replied coldly, "Sir, I will never lay a finger on you." It is remarkable that Hackston, as well as a shepherd who was also present, but passive, on the occasion, were the only two of the party of assassins who suffered death by the hands of the executioner.

On Hackston refusing the command it was by universal suffrage conferred on John Balfour of Kinloch, called Burley, who was Hackston's brother-in-law. He is described as "a little man, squint-eyed, and of a very fierce aspect." "He was," adds the same author, "by some reckoned none of the most religious; yet he was always zealous and honest-hearted, courageous in every enterprise, and a brave soldier, seldom any escaping that came into his hands. He was the principal actor in killing that arch-traitor to the Lord and His Christ, James Sharp."*

NOTE 9.—OLD FAMILY SERVANTS, p. 41

A masculine retainer of this kind, having offended his master extremely was commanded to leave his service instantly. "In troth, and that will I not," answered the domestic; "if your honour disna ken when ye hae a gude servant, I ken when I hae a gude master, and go away I will not." On another occasion of the same nature the master said, "John, you and I shall never sleep under the same roof again"; to which John replied, with much naivete, "Where the deil can your honour be ganging?"

NOTE 10.—MILITARY MUSIC AT NIGHT, p. 42

Regimental music is never played at night. But who can assure us that such was not the custom in Charles the Second's time? Till I am well informed on this point, the kettledrums shall clash on, as adding something to the picturesque effect of the night march.

NOTE 11.—WINNOWING MACHINE, p. 57

Probably something similar to the barn-fanners now used for winnowing corn, which were not, however, used in their present shape

---

*See Scots Worthies, 8vo, Leith, 1816, p. 522.

until about 1730. They were objected to by the more rigid sectaries on their first introduction upon such reasoning as that of honest Mause in the text.

NOTE 12.—LOCKING THE DOOR DURING DINNER, p. 66

The custom of keeping the door of a house or chateau locked during the time of dinner probably arose from the family being anciently assembled in the hall at that meal and liable to surprise. But it was in many instances continued as a point of high etiquette, of which the following is an example:

A considerable landed proprietor in Dumfriesshire, being a bachelor, without near relations, and determined to make his will, resolved previously to visit his two nearest kinsmen and decide which should be his heir according to the degree of kindness with which he should be received. Like a good clansman, he first visited his own chief, a baronet in rank, descendant and representative of one of the oldest families in Scotland. Unhappily, the dinner bell had rung, and the door of the castle had been locked before his arrival. The visitor in vain announced his name and requested admittance; but his chief adhered to the ancient etiquette and would on no account suffer the doors to be unbarred. Irritated at this cold reception, the old Laird rode on to Sanquhar Castle, then the residence of the Duke of Queensberry, who no sooner heard his name than, knowing well he had a will to make, the drawbridge dropped and the gates flew open; the table was covered anew; His Grace's bachelor and intestate kinsman was received with the utmost attention and respect; and it is scarcely necessary to add that, upon his death some years after, the visitor's considerable landed property went to augment the domains of the Ducal House of Queensberry. This happened about the end of the seventeenth century.

NOTE 13.—LANDWARD TOWN, p. 67

The Scots retain the use of the word "town" in its comprehensive Saxon meaning as a place of habitation. A mansion or a farm-house, though solitary, is called "the town." A "landward town" is a dwelling situated in the country.

NOTE 14.—THROWING THE PURSE OVER THE GATE, p. 81

A Highland laird, whose peculiarities still live in the recollection of his countrymen, used to regulate his residence at Edinburgh in the following manner: Every day he visited the Water Gate, as it is called, of the Canongate, over which is extended a wooden arch. Specie being then the general currency, he threw his purse over the gate, and as long as it was heavy enough to be thrown over he continued his round of pleasure in the metropolis; when it was too light, he thought it time to retire to the Highlands. Query—How often would he have repeated this experiment at Temple Bar?

NOTE 15—WOODEN MARE, P. 82.

The punishment of riding the wooden mare was, in the days of Charles and long after, one of the various and cruel modes of enforcing military discipline. In front of the old guard-house in the High Street of Edinburgh a large horse of this kind was placed, on which now and then in the more ancient times a veteran might be seen mounted, with a firelock tied to each foot, atoning for some small offense.

There is a singular work, entitled Memoirs of Prince William Henry, Duke of Gloucester (son of Queen Anne), from his birth to his ninth year, in which Jenkin Lewis, an honest Welshman in attendance on the royal infant's person, is pleased to record that his Royal Highness laughed, cried, crow'd, and said 'Gig' and 'Dy' very like a babe of plebeian descent. He had also a premature taste for the discipline as well as the show of war, and had a corps of twenty-two boys arrayed with paper caps and wooden swords. For the maintenance of discipline in this juvenile corps a wooden horse was established in the presence-chamber, and was sometimes employed in the punishment of offenses not strictly military. Hughes, the Duke's tailor, having made him a suit of clothes which were too tight, was appointed, in an order of the day issued by the young prince, to be placed on this penal steed. The man of remnants, by dint of supplication and mediation, escaped from the penance, which was likely to equal the inconveniences of his brother artist's equestrian trip to Brentford. But an attendant named Weatherby, who had presumed to bring the young prince a toy after he had discarded the use of them, was actually mounted on the wooden horse without a saddle, with his face to the tail, while he was plied by four servants of the household with syringes and squirts till he had a thorough wetting. "He was a waggish fellow," says Lewis, "and would not lose anything for the joke's sake when he was putting his tricks upon others, so he was obliged to submit cheerfully to what was inflicted upon him, being at our mercy to pay him off well, which we did accordingly." Amid much such nonsense, Lewis's book shows that this poor child, the heir of the British monarchy, who died when he was eleven years old, was, in truth, of promising parts, and of a good disposition. The volume, which rarely occurs, is an octavo, published in 1789, the editor being Dr. Philip Hayes, of Oxford.

NOTE 16.—CONCEALING THE FACE, P. 91.

Concealment of an individual while in public or promiscuous society was then very common. In England, where no plaids were worn, the ladies used vizard masks for the same purpose, and the gallants drew the skirts of their cloaks over the right shoulder, so as cover part of the face. This is repeatedly alluded to in Pepys's Diary.

NOTE 17.—ROMANCES OF THE SEVENTEENTH CENTURY, P. 106.

As few in the present age are acquainted with the ponderous folios to which the age of Louis XIV. gave rise, we need only say that they combine the dulness of the metaphysical courtship with all the improbabilities of the ancient romance of chivalry. Their character will be most easily learned from Boileau's Dramatic Satire or Mrs. Lennox's Female Quixote.

NOTE 18.—SIR JAMES TURNER, P. 106.

Sir James Turner was a soldier of fortune, bred in the civil wars. He was intrusted with a commission to levy the fines imposed by the privy council for nonconformity in the district of Dumfries and Galloway. In this capacity he vexed the country so much by his exactions that the people rose and made him prisoner, and then proceeded in arms toward Midlothian, where they were defeated at Pentland Hills in 1666. Besides his treatise on the military art, Sir James Turner wrote several other works, the most curious of which is his Memoirs of His Own Life and Times, which has just been printed under the charge of the Bannatyne Club. (See Legend of Montrose, pp. 143-145.)

NOTE 19.—TILLIETUDLEM CASTLE, P. 106.

The Castle of Tillietudlem is imaginary; but the ruins of Craignethan Castle, situated on the Nethan, about three miles from its junction with the Clyde, have something of the character of the description in the text.

NOTE 20.—JOHN GRAHAME OF CLAVERHOUSE, P. 108.

This remarkable person united the seemingly inconsistent qualities of courage and cruelty, a disinterested and devoted loyalty to his prince with a disregard of the rights of his fellow-subjects. He was the unscrupulous agent of the Scottish privy council in executing the merciless severities of the government in Scotland during the reigns of Charles II. and James II.; but he redeemed his character by the zeal with which he asserted the cause of the latter monarch after the Revolution, the military skill with which he supported it at the battle of Killiecrankie, and by his own death in the arms of victory.

It is said by tradition that he was very desirous to see, and be introduced to, a certain Lady Elphinstoun, who had reached the advanced age of one hundred years and upward. The noble matron, being a stanch Whig, was rather unwilling to receive Claver'se (as he was called from his title), but at length consented. After the usual compliments, the officer observed to the lady that, having lived so much beyond the usual term of humanity, she must in her time have seen many strange changes. "Hout na, sir," said Lady Elphinstoun, "the world is just to end with me as it began. When I was entering life there was ane Knox deaving us a' wi' his clavers, and now I am ganging out there is ane Claver'se deaving us a' wi' his knocks." Clavers signifying, in common parlance, idle chat, the double pun does credit to the ingenuity of a lady of a hundred years old.

NOTE 21.—CORNET GRAHAME, P. 153.

There was actually a young cornet of the Life Guards named Grahame, and probably some relation of Claverhouse, slain in the skirmish of Drumclog. In the old ballad on the "Battle of Bothwell Bridge," Claverhouse is said to have continued the slaughter of the fugitives in revenge of this gentleman's death.

> "Haud up your hand," then Monmouth said;
> "Gie quarters to these men for me";
> But bloody Claver'se swore an oath,
> His kinsman's death avenged should be.

The body of this young man was found shockingly mangled after the battle, his eyes pulled out and his features so much defaced that it was impossible to recognize him. The Tory writers say that this was done by the Whigs; because, finding the name Grahame wrought in the young gentleman's neckcloth, they took the corpse for that of Claver'se himself. The Whig authorities give a different account, from tradition, of the cause of Cornet Grahame's body being thus mangled. He had, they say, refused his own dog any food on the morning of the battle, affirming with an oath that he should have no breakfast but upon the flesh of the Whigs. The ravenous animal, it is said, flew at his master as soon as he fell and lacerated his face and throat.

These two stories are presented to the reader, leaving it to him to judge whether it is most likely that a party of persecuted and insurgent fanatics should mangle a body supposed to be that of their chief enemy, in the same manner as several persons present at Drumclog had shortly before treated the person of Archbishop Sharp, or that a domestic dog should, for want of a single breakfast, become so ferocious as to feed on his own master, selecting his body from scores that were lying around equally accessible to his ravenous appetite.

NOTE 22.—PROOF AGAINST SHOT GIVEN BY SATAN, p. 158

The belief of the Covenanters that their principal enemies, and Claverhouse in particular, had obtained from the Devil a charm which rendered them proof against leaden bullets, led them to pervert even the circumstances of his death. Howie, of Lochgoin, after giving some account of the battle of Killiecrankie, adds:

'The battle was very bloody, and by Mackay's third fire Claverhouse fell, of whom historians give little account; but it has been said for certain that his own waiting-servant, taking a resolution to rid the world of this truculent bloody monster, and knowing he had proof of lead, shot him with a silver button he had before taken off his own coat for that purpose. However, he fell, and with him

Popery and King James's interest in Scotland.'—God's Judgment on
Persecutors, p. 38.

Original Note.—'Perhaps some may think this anent proof of shot
a paradox, and be ready to object here, as formerly, concerning
Bishop Sharp and Dalziel—"How can the Devil have or give a power
to save life?" etc. Without entering upon the thing in its reality, I
shall only observe—1st, That it is neither in his power or of his
nature to be a savious of men's lives; he is called Apollyon the destroyer. 2d, That even in this case he is said only to give inchant-
ment against one kind of mettle, and this does not save life: for the
lead would not take Sharp and Claverhouse's lives, yet steel and
silver could do it; and for Dalziel, though he died not on the field,
he did not escape the arrows of the Almighty.'—Ibidem.

NOTE 23.—CLAVERHOUSE'S CHARGER, p. 160

It appears, from the letter of Claverhouse afterwards quoted,
that the horse on which he rode to Drumclog was not black, but
sorrel. The Author has been misled as to the colour by the many
extraordinary traditions current in Scotland concerning Claverhouse's famous black charger, which was generally believed to have
been a gift to its rider from the Author of Evil, who is said to have
performed the Caesarian operation upon its dam. This horse was so
fleet, and its rider so expert, that they are said to have outstripped
and 'coted,' or turned, a hare upon the Bran Law, near the head of
Moffat Water, where the descent is so precipitous that no merely
earthly horse could keep its feet, or merely mortal rider could keep
the saddle.

There is a curious passage in the testimony of John Dick, one of
the suffering Presbyterians, in which the author, by describing each
of the persecutors by their predominant qualities or passions, shows
how little their best-loved attributes would avail them in the great
day of judgment. When he introduces Claverhouse, it is to reproach
him with his passion for horses in general, and for that steed in particular which was killed at Drumclog in the manner described in the
text:

'And for that blood thirsty wretch, Claver-house, how thinks he
to shelter himself that day? Is it possible the pitiful thing can be so
mad as to think to secure himself by the fleetness of his horse (a
creature he has so much respect for, that he regarded more the loss
of his horse at Drumclog than all the men that fell there, and sure
on either party there fell prettier men than himself)? No, sure,
though he could fall upon a chymist that could extract the spirits
out of all the horse in the world and infuse them into his one,
though he were on that horse back never so well mounted, he need
not dream of escaping.'—A Testimony to the Doctrine, Worship, Discipline, and Government of the Church of Scotland, etc., as it was
left in Write by that truly Pious and emmently Faithfull, and now
Glorified Martyr, Mr. John Dick. To which is added, his Last Speech
and Behaviour on the Scaffold, on the fifth day of March 1684, which
Day he Sealed this Testimony. 58 pp. 4to. No year or place of publication.

The reader may perhaps receive some farther information on the
subject of Cornet Grahame's death and the flight of Claverhouse
from the following Latin lines, a part of a poem entitled Bellum
Bothuellianum, by Andrew Guild, which exists in manuscript in the
Advocates' Library:—

> Mons est occiduus surgit qui celsus in oris,
>   (Nomine Loudunum) fossis puteisque profundis
> Quo scatet hic tellus, et aprico gramine tectus.
>   Huc collecta fuit, numeroso milite cincta,
> Turba ferox, matres, pueri, innuptaeque puellae,
> Quam parat egregia Graemus dispersere turma.
> Venit et primo campo discedere cogit;
> Post hos et alios, coeno provolvit inerti;
> At numerosa cohors, campum dispersa per omnem
> Circumfusa ruit; turmasque, indagine captas,
> Aggreditur; virtus non hic, nec profuit ensis;
> Corripuere fugam, viridi sed gramine tectis
> Precipitata perit fossis pars ultima, quorum
> Cornipedes haesere luto, sessore rejecto:

Tum rabiosa cohors, misereri nescia, stratos
  Invadit laceratque viros: hic signifer, eheu!
Trajectus globulo, Graemus, quo fortior alter,
Inter Scotigenas fuerat, nec justior ullus:
Hunc manibus rapuere feris, faciemque virilem
Foedarunt, lingua, auriculis, manibusque resectis,
Aspera diffuso spargentes saxa cerebro.
Vix dux ipse fuga salvus, namque exta trahebat
Vulnere tardatus sonipes generosus hiante:
Insequitur clamore cohors fanatica, namque
Crudelis semper timidus, si vicerit unquam.
                                    MS. Bellum Bothuellianum.

NOTE 24.—SKIRMISH AT DRUMCLOG, p. 168

This affair, the only one in which Claverhouse was defeated or the insurgent Cameronians successful, was fought pretty much in the manner mentioned in the text. The Royalists lost about thirty or forty men. The commander of the Presbyterian, or rather Covenanting, party was Mr. Robert Hamilton, of the honourable house of Preston, brother of Sir William Hamilton, to whose title and estate he afterwards succeeded; but, according to his biographer, Howie of Lochgoin, he never took possession of either, as he could not do so without acknowledging the right of King William (an uncovenanted monarch) to the crown. Hamilton had been bred by Bishop Burnet, while the latter lived at Glasgow, his brother, Sir Thomas, having married a sister of that historian. 'He was then,' says the Bishop, 'a lively, hopeful young man; but getting into that company, and into their notions, he became a crack-brained enthusiast.'

Several well-meaning persons have been much scandalised at the manner in which the victors are said to have conducted themselves towards the prisoners at Drumclog. But the principle of these poor fanatics (I mean the high-flying, or Cameronian party) was to obtain not merely toleration for their church, but the same supremacy which Presbytery had acquired in Scotland after the treaty of Ripon betwixt Charles I. and his Scottish subjects in 1640. The fact is, that they conceived themselves a chosen people sent forth to extirpate the heathen, like the Jews of old, and under a similar charge to show no quarter.

The historian of the Insurrection of Bothwell makes the following explicit avowal of the principles on which their General acted:—

'Mr. Hamilton discovered a great deal of bravery and valour, both in the conflict with and pursuit of the enemy; but when he and some others were pursuing the enemy, others flew too greedily upon the spoil, small as it was, instead of pursuing the victory; and some, without Mr. Hamilton's knowledge, and directly contrary to his express command, gave five of these bloody enemies quarters, and then let them go; this greatly grieved Mr. Hamilton when he saw some of Babel's brats spared, after that the Lord had delivered them into their hands, that they might dash them against the stones—Psalm cxxxvii. 9. In his own account of this he reckons the sparing of these enemies, and letting them go, to be among their first stepping aside, for which he feared that the Lord would not honour them to do much more for Him; and says that he was neither for taking favours from, nor giving favours to, the Lord's enemies.'—See A True and Impartial Account [Relation] of the Persecuted Presbyterians in Scotland, their being [rising] in arms, and Defeat at Bothwell Brigg in 1679, by William Wilson, late Schoolmaster in the Parish of Douglas. The reader who would authenticate the quotation, must not consult any other edition than that of 1697 [or that of 1809]; for somehow or other the publisher of the last edition [1825] has omitted this remarkable part of the narrative.

Sir Robert Hamilton himself felt neither remorse nor shame for having put to death one of the prisoners after the battle with his own hand, which appears to have been a charge against him by some whose fanaticism was less exalted than his own—

'As for that accusation they bring against me of killing that poor man (as they call him) at Drumclog, I may easily guess that my accusers can be other but some of the house of Saul or Shimei, or some such risen again to espouse that poor gentleman's (Saul) his quarrel

against honest Samuel, for his offering to kill that poor man Agag,
after the king's giving him quarters. But I, being to command that
day, gave out the word that no quarter should be g.ven; and returning
from pursuing Claverhouse, one or two of these fellows were standing
in the midst of a company of our friends, and some were debating for
quarters, others against it. None could blame me to decide the controversy, and I bless the Lord for it to this day. There were five more
that without my knowledge got quarters, who were brought to me
after we were a mile from the place as having got quarters, which I
reckoned among the first steppings aside; and seeing that spirit
amongst us at that time, I then told it to some that were with me (to
my best remembrance, it was honest old John Nisbet), that I feared
the Lord would not honour us to do much for Him. I shall only say
this, I desire to bless His holy name, that ever since He helped me to
set my face to His work, I never had, nor would take, a favour from
enemies, either on right or left hand, and desired to give as iew'
[p. 201].

The preceding passage is extracted from a long vindication of his
own 'conduct, sent by Sir Robert Hamilton, 7th December 1685, addressed to the anti-Popish, anti-Prelatic, anti-Erastian, anti-Sectarian
true Presbyterian remnant of the Church of Scotland'; and the substance is to be found in the work or collection called Faithful Contendings Displayed, collected and transcribed by John Howie.

As the skirmish of Drumclog has been of late the subject of some
inquiry, the reader may be curious to see Claverhouse's own account
of the affair, in a letter to the Earl of Linlithgow, written immediately
after the action. This gazette, as it may be called, occurs in the volume called Dundee's Letters, printed by Mr. Smythe of Methven, as a
contribution to the Bannatyne Club. The original is in the library of
the Duke of Buckingham. Claverhouse, it may be observed, spells like
a chambermaid.

'FOR THE EARL OF LINLITHGOW

[COMMANDER-IN-CHIEF OF KING CHARLES II.'S FORCES IN SCOTLAND]

'Glaskow, Jun. the 1, 1679.

'MY LORD,—Upon Saturday's night, when my Lord Rosse came in
to this place, I marched out, and because of the insolency that had
been done tue nights before at Rugien, I went thither and inquyred for
the names. So soon as I got them, I sent out partys to sease on them,
and found not only three of those rogues, but also ane intercomend
minister called King. We had them at Streven about six in the morning yesterday, and resolving to convey them to this, I thought that
we might mak a little tour to see if we could fall upon a conventicle;
which we did, litle to our advantage; for when we came in sight of
them, we found them drawen up in batell, upon a most adventagious
ground, to which there was no coming but throgh moses and lakes.
They wer not preaching, and had gat away all there women and
shildring. They consisted of four bataillons of foot, and all well
armed with fusils and pitch forks, and three squadrons of horse. We
sent both partys to skirmish, they of foot and we of dragoons; they
run for it, and sent down a bataillon of foot against them; we sent
threescor of dragoons, who mad them run again shamfully; but in end
they percaiving that we had the better of them in skirmish, they resolved a generall engadgment, and imediatly advanced with there foot,
the horse folouing; they came throght the lotche, and the greatest
body of all made up against my troupe; we keeped our fyr till they
wer within ten pace of us: they received our fyr, and advanced to
shok; the first they gave us broght doun the Coronet Mr. Crafford
and Captain Bleith, besides that with a pitch fork they mad such an
opening in my sorre horses belly, that his guts hung out half an elle,
and yet he caryed me af an myl; which so discoroged our men, that
they sustined not the shok, but fell into disorder. There horse took
the occasion of this, and purseud us so hotly that we got no tym to
rayly. I saved the standarts, but lost on the place about aight or ten
men, besides wounded; but the dragoons lost many mor. They ar not
com easily af on the other side, for I sawe severall of them fall befor
we cam to the shok. I mad the best retraite the confusion of our

people would suffer, and I am now laying with my Lord Ross. The
toun of Streven drou up as we was making our retrait, and thoght of
a pass to cut us of, but we took couradge and fell to them, made them
run, leaving a dousain on the place. What these rogues will dou yet
I know not, but the contry was fioking to them from all hands. This
may be counted the begining of the rebellion, in my opinion.

'I am, my lord,

'Your lordships most humble servant,

'J. GRAHAME.

'My lord, I am so wearied, and so sleapy, that I have wryton this
very confusedly.'

NOTE 25.—DISSENSIONS AMONG THE COVENANTERS, p. 238

These feuds, which tore to pieces the little army of insurgents,
turned mainly on the point whether the king's interest or royal
authority was to be owned or not, and whether the party in arms
were to be contented with a free exercise of their own religion, or insist upon the re-establishment of Presbytery in its supreme authority,
and with full power to predominate over all other forms of worship.
The few country gentlemen who joined the insurrection, with the most
sensible part of the clergy, thought it best to limit their demands to
what it might be possible to attain. But the party who urged these
moderate views were termed by the more zealous bigots the Erastian
party, men, namely, who were willing to place the church under the
influence of the civil government, and therefore they accounted them
'a snare upon Mizpah, and a net spread upon Tabor.' See the 'Life of
Sir Robert Hamilton' in the Scots Worthies, and his account of the
Battle of Bothwell Bridge, Passim.

NOTE 26.—THE CAMERONIANS' GIBBET, p. 245

The Cameronians had suffered persecution, but it was without
learning mercy. We are informed by Captain Crichton that they had
set up in their camp a huge gibbet, or gallows, having many hooks
upon it, with a coil of new ropes lying beside it, for the execution of
such Royalists as they might make prisoners. Guild, in his Bellum
Bothuellianum, describes this machine particularly.

NOTE 27.—ROYAL ARMY AT BOTHWELL BRIDGE, p. 264

A Cameronian muse was awakened from slumber on this doleful
occasion, and gave the following account of the muster of the royal
forces, in poetry nearly as melancholy as the subject:—

They marched east throw Lithgow-town
For to enlarge their forces;
And sent for all the north country
To come, both foot and horses.

Montrose did come and Athole both,
And with them many more;
And all the Highland Amorites
That had been there before.

The Lowdien mallisha they
Came with their coats of blew;
Five hundred men from London came,
Claid in a reddish hue.

When they were assembled one and all,
A full bragade were they;
Like to a pack of hellish hounds,
Roreing after their prey.

When they were all provided well,
In armour and amonition,
Then thither wester did they come,
Most cruel of intention.

The Royalists celebrated their victory in strains of equal merit.
Specimens of both may be found in the curious collection of Fugitive
Scottish Poetry, principally of the Seventeenth Century, printed for
the Messrs. Laing, Edinburgh [1825-53].

NOTE 28.—MODERATE PRESBYTERIANS, p. 269

The Author does not by any means desire that Poundtext should
be regarded as a just representative of the moderate Presbyterians,
among whom were many ministers whose courage was equal to their
good sense and sound views of religion. Were he to write the tale
anew, he would probably endeavour to give the character a higher
turn. It is certain, however, that the Cameronians imputed to their
opponents in opinion concerning the Indulgence, or others of their
strained and fanatical notions, a disposition not only to seek their
own safety, but to enjoy themselves. Hamilton speaks of three clergymen of this description as follows:—

'They pretended great zeal against the Indulgence; but, alas! that
was all, their practice otherwise being but very gross, which I shall
but hint at in short. When great Cameron and those with him were
taking many a cold blast and storm in the fields and among the cot-
houses in Scotland, these three had, for the most part, their residence
in Glasgow, where they found good quarters and a full table (which
I doubt not but some bestowed upon them from real affection to the
Lord's cause); and when these three were together, their greatest
work was who should make the finest and sharpest roundels, and
break the quickest jests upon one another, and to tell what valiant
acts they were to do, and who could laugh loudest and most heartily
among them; and when at any time they came out to the country,
whatever other thing they had, they were careful each of them to
have a great flask of brandy with them, which was very heavy to
some, particularly to Mr. Cameron, Mr. Cargill, and Henry Hall; I
shall name no more.'—Faithful Contendings, p. 198.

NOTE 29.—GENERAL DALZELL, USUALLY CALLED TOM DALZELL, p. 274

In Creichton's Memoirs, edited by Swift, where a particular account of this remarkable person's dress and habits is given, he is said
never to have worn boots. The following account of his rencounter
with John Paton of Meadowhead showed that in action at least he
wore pretty stout ones, unless the reader be inclined to believe in the
truth of his having a charm which made him proof against lead.

'Dalziel,' says Paton's biographer, 'advanced the whole left wing
of his army on Colonel Wallace's right. Here Captain Paton behaved
with great courage and gallantry. Dalzell, knowing him in the former
wars, advanced upon him himself, thinking to take him prisoner.
Upon his approach each presented their pistols. Upon their first discharge, Captain Paton, perceiving the pistol ball to hoop down upon
Dalziel's boots, and knowing what was the cause (he having proof),
put his hand to his pocket for some small pieces of silver he had
there for the purpose, and put one of them into his other pistol. But
Dalziel, having his eye on him in the meanwhile, retired behind his
own man, who by that means was slain' [Scots Worthies, p. 415, con-
densed somewhat].

NOTE 30.—LOCH SLOY, p. 287

This was the slogan or war-cry of the MacFarlanes, taken from a
lake near the head of Loch Lomond, in the centre of their ancient
possession of the western banks, of that beautiful inland sea.

NOTE 31.—MORTON'S CAPTURE AND RELEASE, p. 298

The principal incident of the foregoing chapter was suggested by
an occurrence of a similar kind, told me by a gentleman, now deceased, who held an important situation in the Excise, to which he
had been raised by active and resolute exertions in an inferior de-

partment. When employed as a supervisor on the coast of Galloway. at a time when the immunities of the Isle of Man rendered smuggling almost universal in that district, this gentleman had the fortune to offend highly several of the leaders in the contraband trade, by his zeal in serving the revenue.

This rendered his situation a dangerous one, and, on more than one occasion, placed his life in jeopardy. At one time in particular, as he was riding after sunset on a summer evening, he came suddenly upon a gang of the most desperate smugglers in that part of the country. They surrounded him without violence, but in such a manner as to show that it would be resorted to if he offered resistance, and gave him to understand he must spend the evening with them, since they had met so happily. The officer did not attempt opposition, but only asked leave to send a country lad to tell his wife and family that he should be detained later than he expected. As he had to charge the boy with this message in the presence of the smugglers, he could found no hope of deliverance from it, save what might arise from the sharpness of the lad's observation and the natural anxiety and affection of his wife. But if his errand should be delivered and received literally, as he was conscious the smugglers expected, it was likely that it might, by suspending alarm about his absence from home, postpone all search after him till it might be useless. Making a merit of necessity, therefore, he instructed and despatched his messenger, and went with the contraband traders, with seeming willingness, to one of their ordinary haunts. He sat down at table with them, and they began to drink and indulge themselves in gross jokes, while, like Mirabel in the Inconstant, their prisoner had the heavy task of receiving their insolence as wit, answering their insults with good humour, and withholding from them the opportunity which they sought of engaging him in a quarrel, that they might have a pretense for misusing him. He succeeded for some time, but soon became satisfied it was their purpose to murder him outright, or else to beat him in such a manner as scarce to leave him with life. A regard for the sanctity of the Sabbath evening, which still oddly subsisted among these ferocious men, amidst their habitual violation of divine and social law, prevented their commencing their intended cruelty until the Sabbath should be terminated. They were sitting around their anxious prisoner, muttering to each other words of terrible import, and watching the index of a clock, which was shortly to strike the hour at which, in their apprehension, murder would become lawful, when their intended victim heard a distant rustling like the wind among withered leaves. It came nearer, and resembled the sound of a brook in flood chafing within its banks; it came nearer yet, and was plainly distinguished as the galloping of a party of horse. The absence of her husband. and the account given by the boy of the suspicious appearance of those with whom he had remained, had induced Mrs. —— to apply to the neighbouring town for a party of dragoons, who thus providentially arrived in time to save him from extreme violence, if not from actual destruction.

NOTE 32.—PRISONERS' PROCESSION, p. 310

David Hackston of Rathillet, who was wounded and made prisoner in the skirmish of Air's Moss, in which the celebrated Cameron fell, was, on entering Edinburgh, 'by order of the Council, received by the magistrates at the Water Gate, and set on a horse's bare back with his face to the tail, and the other three laid on a goad of iron, and carried up the street, Mr. Cameron's hand being on a halberd before them.'

NOTE 33.—DALZELL'S BRUTALITY, p. 314

The General is said to have struck one of the captive Whigs when under examination, with the hilt of his sabre, so that the blood gushed out. The provocation for this unmanly violence was, that the prisoner had called the fierce veteran 'a Muscovy beast, who used to roast men.' Dalzell had been long in the Russian service, which in those days was 'no school of humanity.'

NOTE 34.—HEADS OF THE EXECUTED, p. 318

The pleasure of the Council respecting the relics of their victims was often as savage as the rest of their conduct. The heads of the preachers were frequently exposed on pikes between their two hands, the palms displayed as in the attitude of prayer. When the celebrated Richard Cameron's head was exposed in this manner, a spectator bore testimony to it as that of one who lived praying and preaching, and died praying and fighting.

NOTE 35.—SUPPOSED APPARITION OF MORTON, p. 345

This incident is taken from a story in the History of Apparitions written by Daniel Defoe, under the assumed name of Morton. To abridge the narrative, we are under the necessity of omitting many of these particular circumstances which gave the fictions of this most ingenious author such a lively air of truth.

A gentleman married a lady of family and fortune, and had one son by her, after which the lady died. The widower afterwards united himself in a second marriage; and his wife proved such a very stepmother to the heir of the first marriage that, discontented with his situation, he left his father's house and set out on distant travels. His father heard from him occasionally, and the young man for some time drew regularly for certain allowances which were settled upon him. At length, owing to the instigation of his mother-in-law, one of his draughts was refused, and the bill returned dishonoured.

After receiving this affront, the youth drew no bills and wrote no more letters, nor did his father know in what part of the world he was. The stepmother seized the opportunity to represent the young man as deceased, and to urge her husband to settle his estate anew upon her children, of whom she had several. The father for a length of time positively refused to disinherit his son, convinced as he was, in his own mind, that he was still alive.

At length, worn out by his wife's importunities, he agreed to execute the new deeds if his son did not return within a year.

During the interval there were many violent disputes between the husband and wife upon the subject of the family settlements. In the midst of one of these altercations, the lady was startled by seeing a hand at a casement of the window; but as the iron hasps, according to the ancient fashion, fastened in the inside, the hand seemed to essay the fastenings, and being unable to undo them, was immediately withdrawn. The lady, forgetting the quarrel with her husband, exclaimed that there was some one in the garden. The husband rushed out but could find no trace of any intruder, while the walls of the garden seemed to render it impossible for any such to have made his escape. He therefore taxed his wife with having fancied that which she supposed she saw. She maintained the accuracy of her sight; on which her husband observed, that it must have been the devil, who was apt to haunt those who had evil consciences. This tart remark brought back the matrimonial dialogue to its original current. 'It was no devil,' said the lady, 'but the ghost of your son come to tell you he is dead, and that you may give your estate to your bastards, since you will not settle it on the lawful heirs.' 'It was my son,' said he, 'come to tell me that he is alive, and ask you how you can be such a devil as to urge me to disinherit him'; with that he started up and exclaimed, 'Alexander, Alexander! if you are alive, show yourself, and do not let me be insulted every day with being told you are dead.'

At these words, the casement which the hand had been seen at opened of itself, and his son Alexander looked in with a full face and, staring directly on the mother with an angry countenance, cried, 'Here!' and then vanished in a moment.

The lady, though much frightened at the apparition, had wit enough to make it serve her own purpose; for, as the spectre appeared at her husband's summons, she made affidavit that he had a familiar spirit who appeared when he called it. To escape from this discreditable charge the poor husband agreed to make the new settlement of the estate in the terms demanded by the unreasonable lady.

A meeting of friends was held for that purpose, the new deed was executed, and the wife was about to cancel the former settlement by tearing the seal, when on a sudden they heard a rushing noise in the parlour in which they sat, as if something had come in at the door of the room which opened from the hall, and then had gone through the room towards the garden-door, which was shut; they were all surprised at it, for the sound was very distinct, but they saw nothing.

This rather interrupted the business of the meeting, but the persevering lady brought them back to it. "I am not frightened," said she, "not I. Come," said she to her husband, haughtily, "I'll cancel the old writing if forty devils were in the room;" with that she took up one of the deeds and was about to tear off the seal. But the double-ganger, or eidolon, of Alexander was as pertinacious in guarding the rights of his principal as his stepmother in invading them.

The same moment she raised the paper to destroy it, the casement flew open, though it was fast in the inside just as it was before, and the shadow of a body was seen as standing in the garden without, the face looking into the room, and staring directly at the woman with a stern and angry countenance. "Hold," said the spectre, as if speaking to the lady, and immediately closed the window and vanished. After this second interruption, the new settlement was cancelled by the consent of all concerned, and Alexander, in about four or five months after, arrived from the East Indies, to which he had gone four years before from London in a Portuguese ship. He could give no explanation of what had happened, excepting that he dreamed his father had written him an angry letter, threatening to disinherit him.—The History and Reality of Apparitions, chap. viii.

NOTE 36.—CAPTAIN INGLIS. p. 372

The deeds of a man, or rather a monster, of this name, are recorded upon the tombstone of one of those martyrs which it was Old Mortality's delight to repair. I do not remember the name of the murdered person, but the circumstances of the crime were so terrible to my childish imagination that I am confident the following copy of the epitaph will be found nearly correct, although I have not seen the original for forty years at least:—

> This martyr was by Peter Inglis shot,
> By birth a tiger rather than a Scot;
> Who, that his hellish offspring might be seen,
> Cut off his head, then kick'd it o'er the green;
> Thus was the head which was to wear the croun,
> A foot-ball made by a profane dragoon.

In Dundee's Letters, Captain Inglish, or Inglis, is repeatedly mentioned as commanding a troop of horse. The murdered person here referred to was James White, of the parish of Fenwick, Ayrshire. The epitaph appeared in the Cloud of Witnesses, a well-known work published in 1714; but the brutal conduct of Inglis is thus stated in a pamphlet or Memorial printed in 1690:—"Item—The said Peter or Patrick Inglis killed one James White, struck off his head with an ax, brought it to Newmills, and played at the foot-ball with it; he killed him at the Little Black Wood, the foresaid year 1685."

As proof of the Author's singular memory, it may be stated that the epitaph as quoted above is almost verbatim with the original, except in the third line, which runs thus, "who, that his monstruous extract might be seen" (Laing).

NOTE 37.—THE RETREATS OF THE COVENANTERS, p. 379

The severity of persecution often drove the sufferers to hide themselves in dens and caves of the earth, where they had not only to struggle with the real dangers of damp, darkness, and famine, but were called upon in their disordered imaginations to oppose the infernal powers by whom such caverns were believed to be haunted. A very romantic scene of rocks, thickets, and cascades, called

Crichope Linn, on the estate of Mr. Menteath of Closeburn, is said to have been the retreat of some of these enthusiasts, who judged it safer to face the apparitions by which the place was thought to be haunted than to expose themselves to the rage of their mortal enemies.

Another remarkable encounter betwixt the Foul Fiend and the champions of the Covenant is preserved in certain rude rhymes, not yet forgotten in Ettrick Forest. Two men, it is said, by name Halbert Dobson and David Dun, constructed for themselves a place of refuge in a hidden ravine of a very savage character, by the side of a considerable waterfall, near the head of Moffat Water. Here, concealed from human foes, they were assailed by Satan himself, who came upon them grinning and making mouths, as if trying to frighten them, and disturb their devotions. The wanderers, more incensed than astonished at this supernatural visitation, assailed their ghostly visitor, buffeted him soundly with their Bibles, and compelled him at length to change himself into the resemblance of a pack of dried hides, in which shape he rolled down the cascade. The shape which he assumed was probably designed to excite the cupidity of the assailants, who, as souters of Selkirk, might have been disposed to attempt something to save a package of good leather. Thus,

> Hab Dab and David Din,
> Dang the Deil ower Dabson's Linn.

The popular verses recording this feat, to which Burns seems to have been indebted for some hints in his "Address to the Deil," may be found in the Minstrelsy of the Scottish Border, vol. ii.

It cannot be matter of wonder to any one at all acquainted with human nature, that superstition should have aggravated, by its terrors, the apprehensions to which men of enthusiastic character were disposed by the gloomy haunts to which they had fled for refuge.

NOTE 38.—PREDICTIONS OF THE COVENANTERS, p. 384

The sword of Captain John Paton of Meadowhead, a Cameronian, famous for his personal prowess, bore testimony to his exertions in the cause of the Covenant, and was typical of the oppressions of the times. "Their sword or short shabble (sciabbola, Italian) yet remains," says Mr. Howie of Lochgoin. "It was then by his progenitors (meaning descendants, a rather unusual use of the word) counted to have twenty-eight gaps in its edge; which made them afterwards observe, that there were just as many years of the persecution as there were steps or broken pieces in its edge."—Scots Worthies, edit. 1796, p. 416.

The persecuted party, as their circumstances led to their placing a due and sincere reliance on heaven, when earth was scarce permitted to bear them, fell naturally into enthusiastic credulity, and, as they imagined, direct contention with the powers of darkness, so they conceived some amongst them to be possessed of a power of prediction, which, though they did not exactly call it inspired prophecy, seems to have approached, in their opinion, very nearly to it. The subject of these predictions was generally of a melancholy nature; for it is during such times of blood and confusion that

> Pale-eyed prophets whisper fearful change.

The celebrated Alexander Peden was haunted by the terrors of a French invasion, and was often heard to exclaim, 'Oh, the Monzies, the French Monzies (for Mounsiers, doubtless), how they run! How long will they run? Oh Lord, cut their houghs and stay their running!' He afterwards declared, that French blood would run thicker in the waters of Ayr and Clyde than ever did that of the Highlandmen. Upon another occasion, he said he had been made to see the French marching with their armies through the length and breadth of the land in the blood of all ranks, up to the bridle-reins, and that for a burned, broken, and buried Covenant.

Gabriel Semple also prophesied. In passing by the house of Kenmure, to which workmen were making some additions, he said, 'Lads, you are very busy enlarging and repairing that house, but it will be burned like a crow's nest in a misty May morning'; which accordingly came to pass, the house being burned by the English forces in a cloudy May morning.

Other instances might be added, but these are enough to show the character of the people and times.

NOTE 39.—JOHN BALFOUR, CALLED BURLEY, p. 394

The return of John Balfour of Kinloch, called Burley, to Scotland, as well as his violent death in the manner described, is entirely fictitious. He was wounded at Bothwell Bridge, when he uttered the execration transferred to the text, not much in unison with his religious pretensions. He aferwards escaped to Holland, where he found refuge, with other fugitives of that disturbed period. His biographer seems simple enough to believe that he rose high in the Prince of Orange's favour, and observes, 'That having still a desire to be avenged upon those who persecuted the Lord's cause and people in Scotland, it is said he obtained liberty from the Prince for that purpose, but died at sea before their arrival in Scotland; whereby that design was never accomplished, and so the land was never purged by the blood of them who had shed innocent blood, according to the law of the Lord—Gen. ix. 6, Whoso sheddeth man's blood, by man shall his blood be shed.'—Scots Worthies, p. 552.

It was reserved for this historian to discover that the moderation of King William, and his prudent anxiety to prevent that perpetuating of factious quarrels which is called in modern times reaction, were only adopted in consequence of the death of John Balfour, called Burley.

The late Mr. Wemyss, of Wemyss Hall, in Fifeshire, succeeded to Balfour's property in late times, and had several accounts, papers, articles of dress, etc., which belonged to the old homicide.

His name seems still to exist in Holland or Flanders; for in the Brussels papers of 28th July 1828, Lieutenant-Colonel Balfour de Burleigh is named Commandant of the troops of the King of the Netherlands in the West Indies.

NOTE 40.—BALFOUR'S GRAVE, p. 394

Gentle reader, I did request of mine honest friend Peter Proudfoot, travelling merchant, known to many of this land for his faithful and just dealings, as well in muslins and cambrics as in small wares, to procure me on his next peregrination to that vicinage a copy of the epitaphion alluded to. And, according to his report, which I see no ground to discredit, it runneth thus:

> Here lyes ane saint to prelates surly,
> Being John Balfour, sometime of Burley,
> Who stirred up to vengeance take,
> For Solemn League and Cov'nant's sake,
> Upon the Magus Moor in Fife
> Did tak James Sharpe the apostate's life;
> By Dutchman's hands was hacked and shot,
> Then drowned in Clyde near this saam spot.

GLOSSARY

OF

WORDS, PHRASES, AND ALLUSIONS

ABULYIEMENTS, habiliments, equipments

ABUNE, ABOON, above; MALT ABUNE THE MEAL, the ale begins to take effect

ACQUENT, acquainted

ADHUC IN PENDENTE, still pending

AE, one

AGAIN, against, until, before

AGGER, a rampart, mound

AIN, own

AIR, early

AITMEAL, oatmeal

AJEE, awry

AMAIST, almost

ANABAPTISTS OF MUNSTER. Bockhold, Knipperdolling, and others, disciples of one John Matthiesen, were guilty of the wildest excesses at Munster in Westphalia in 1534-35

ANCE, ANES, once

AQUA MIRABILIS, the wonderful water, a cordial compounded of spirit of wine, nutmegs, cardamons, ginger, mace, etc.

ARK, a meal-chest

ARLES, earnest-money

ARM-GAUNT, with gaunt or lean limbs (Shakespeare, Antony and Cleopatra, Act i. Sc. 5)

ARTAMINES, or ARTAMENE, a character in Mdlle. Scudery's Grand Cyrus, supposed to represent Conde

ASTEER, in confusion

AUCHLET, two stones weight, or peck measure

AUGHT, to own

AUTO-DA-FE, the execution of heretics by the Inquisition

AVA, at all

BAB, a bunch, knot

BACK-SWORD, a sword with only one cutting edge; a single-stick

BAFF, bang

BAKER, DEVIL, AND PUNCH. See Punch

BARKING AND FLEEING, going to wreck and ruin

BASS. See Tower of the Bass

BATTS, the colic

BAWBEE, a halfpenny

BEAR, a kind of barley

BEDRAL, a beadle, gravedigger

BEET-MASTER, a substitute

BEHADDEN, beholden, obliged

BEILD, shelter

BELYVE, directly

BEN, BROUGHT FARTHER, better treated, made intimate; WIN FARTHER BEN, get farther in

BENEDICITE! bless ye!

BENNISON, blessing

BESTIAL, cattle

BICKER, wooden bowl, cup

BIDE, to wait, stay; suffer

BIEN, or BEIN, well provided

BIGGIT WA'S, built, i. e. stone, walls

BILBO, a sword with an elastic, finely-tempered blade

BIRKIES, lively 'blades'

BIRL, to drink, tipple

BITTOCK, a good bit more

BLACK-A-VISED, dark-complexioned.

BLACK-FISHERS, salmon-poachers

BLACK-JACK, a large jug of waxed leather, for ale

BLATE, ashamed, bashful

BLEEZE, blaze, flame; to make an outcry

BLETHERING, chattering, idly but volubly talking

BLINK, a glance; a moment, short while

BLYTHE, glad

BODDLE, or BODLE, a small copper coin, worth 1-3d. halfpenny

BOLE, an aperture

BON CAMARADO, a chum, boon companion

BOOTS, a contrivance for torturing the feet

BORE, an aperture, crevice

BOROUGH-TOWN, a royal borough

BOW, a boll

BOWIE, a wooden pail, tub

BRAW, fine, brave; BRAWS, fine things

BRECHAM, the collar of a working-horse

BREERING, sprouting

BRENTFORD, EQUESTRIAN TRIP TO, that of John Gilpin, linen-draper of London; but he rode to Ware and Edmonton, not to Brentford

BRICKLE, ticklish, troublesome

BROGUE, a Highland shoe

BROO, a favorable opinion, liking

BROSE, oatmeal over which boiling water has been poured.

BROWST, a brewing

BUCKING-TUB, a tub for steeping, in the old process of bleaching clothes

BUDGET, a socket for a carabine

BURTHOOG, or BURTHOGGE, RICHARD, an English doctor of medicine who wrote An Essay Upon Reason and the Nature of Spirits (1694)

BUSK, to deck, attire

BYE, past, besides

BY ORDINAR, above the common, more than usual

BYRE, a cow-house

417

CA', to call, drive

CAESAREAN OPERA-TION, a surgical operation to secure delivery (as in the case of Caesar.)

CALLANT, a lad

CALPRENEDE, LA, author of Cleopatre (10 vols., 1647) and other extravagant, long-winded romances, much read in their day

CANNA HEAR DAY NOR DOOR, deaf as a post

CANNY, prudent, knowing, cautious; CANNILY, nicely, civilly, quietly

CARCAGES, carcases, dead bodies

CARLE, a fellow

CARLINE, old woman, witch

CAST, an old spelling of caste, an exclusive party or social class

CAST O' A CART, chance use of a cart, a lift

CATERAN, a robber

CATERPILLARS, rapacious persons

CATES, viands, victuals

CAT IN PAN, TO TURN THE, to act the turncoat

CAULD, cold

CAUP, or CAP, a wooden bowl for containing food

CAUSEWAYED, burnt so as to be stiff and hard like a causeway or causey

CECILIA. See Delville

CESS, land tax

CHAINZIE, or CHAINYIE, a diminutive for chain

CHAMBER OF DAIS, the best bedroom

CHANCY, lucky, fortunate

CHANGE-HOUSE, a small inn or ale-house

CHANTER, that pipe of a bagpipe in which are the finger-holes

CHAPPIN, a quart measure

CHASSEUR, a sportsman

CHEEK O' THE INGLE. See Ingle

CHIELD, a fellow

CHIMLEY-NEUK, the chimney-corner

CLACHAN, village, hamlet

CLAES, clothes.

CLASHES, gossip, nonsense, scandal

CLAVERING, gossiping; CLAVERS, gossip, nonsense

CLELAND, a poet and soldier, distinguished himself at Drumclog, and was killed in 1689 in the defence of Dunkeld, at the head of the Cameronian Regiment

CLEUGH, a ravine

CLOUR, to thump

CLOUTED SHOE, a shoe the sole of which is studded with big nails, also a mended or cobbled shoe

CLOW - GILLIEFLOWER, the clove gillyflower

COCKERNONY, a topknot on the head, bound by a fillet

DOCKING (SPANIEL), snarling, fighting

COCK LAIRD, a small landholder who cultivates his estate himself, yeoman

COGUE, a wooden pail

COLT FOALED OF AN ACORN, the wooden mare, timber horse. See Note 15, p. 417

COMMINATION, threatening of Divine punishments, a special form of service in the Church of England

CORRA LINN, one of the Falls of the Clyde, near Lanark

COT-HOUSE, a cottage

COUP, to barter, buy and sell; tumble; also a bowl

CRACK, talk, friendly chat

CREEL, a basket for the back; IN A CREEL, crazy

CROWDY, oatmeal and water stirred together

CUITTLE, to wheedle

CURCH, a woman's kerchief or head-covering

CURMURRING, murmuring in the stomach, slight gripes

CURNEY, large-grained

CUTTER'S LAW, the law of the sharper, robber

CUTTIE, a pert, impudent girl, a wanton

CUTTY - SPOON, short spoon

DAFFING, larking, flirting

DAFT, crazy

DAIDLING, trifling, inactive, useless

DAIS, CHAMBER OF. See Chamber

DANG, knocked, thrust

DARGUE, a day's work

DAUR, dare

DAY NOR DOOR, CANNA HEAR, deaf as a post

DEAVE, to deafen

DECEPTIO VISUS, optical illusion

DEER-HAIR, the heath club-rush

DELL GIN, devil may care if

DE L'ANCRE, PIERRE, a stern enemy of witchcraft and author of Tableau de l'Inconstance des Mauvais Anges et Demons (1613)

DELRIO, MARTIN ANTONY, Dutch theologian of the 16th century, wrote Disquisitionum Magicanum Libri Sex (1599), a celebrated work on sorcery and kindred topics

DELVILLE AND CECILIA, in Miss Burney's Cecilia (1782)

DEMAS. See 2 Tim. iv. 10

DENTY, dainty

DEVIL, PUNCH AND BAKER. See Punch

DIE, BONNY, a petty toy, gewgaw

DIGHTING, winnowing, sifting; cleaning, wiping

DING, to knock off; DING AJEE, upset, mar

DINGWALL. A man of this name was of the party who murdered Archbishop Sharp, and was himself killed at Drumclog

DINNA, do not

DIOTREPHES. See Third Epistle of John, ver. 9

DIRDUM, an ado, mess

DISJASKED, decayed or miserable-looking

DISJUNE, dejeune, breakfast

DIV, do

DIVERTISEMENT, amusement, pastime

DOOMS, confoundedly

DOOMSTER. See Note to Heart of Midlothian

DOUBLE-GANGER, a spectral double of a person

DOUCE, quiet, sensible

DOUDLE THE BAG O' WIND, to daudle, hug, and caress, the bagpipes

DOUR, stubborn, obstinate

DOW, DOO, dove

DOWNA BIDE, cannot bear, don't like; DOW'D NA, did not like

DRAMMOCK, raw meal and water mixed

DREE, to suffer

DREELING, drilling

DROUTHY, dry, thirsty

DRUCKEN, drunken

DUDGEON-HAFT, the haft or hilt of a dagger ornamented with graven lines.

DUDS, clothes

DUNBAR, RACE OF, Cromwell's defeat of Leslie at Dunbar in 1650

DUNG OWER, overcome, beaten

DWAM, a swoon

EARLSHALL, BRUCE OF, Claverhouse's lieutenant

EE, eye; EEN, eyes

E'ENOW, just now

EFFECTUAL CALLING. See The Shorter Catechism, Qu. 31

BIDENT, attentive, diligent

EIDOLON, a spectral image

EIK, an addition

ELIHU. See Job xxxii.

ENEUCH, ENEUGH, ENOW, enough

ESPIEGLE, roguish

FAILED, failing, feeble

FAIRING, GIE HIM A, settle him, give him something to remember one by

FARD, to colour, embellish

FASH, trouble; to trouble, bother

FAULD-DIKE, the wall of a sheep-fold

FAUT, fault

FAUT O'FUDE, want of food

FECK, the greatest part

FECKLESS, harmless, feeble

FEE AND BOUNTITH, wages and perquisites

FEMALE QUIXOTE. See Mrs. Lennox

FEND, to provide

FERGUSON, ROBERT, styled the Plotter, from having been concerned in the Rye-House and other plots against James II., was a leading partisan of the Duke of Monmouth, and afterwards plotted against William III.

FIRE-FLAUGHT, a flash of lightning

FISSENLESS, FIZZENLESS, FOISONLESS, without energy, spiritless, lacking pith

FITBA', football

FLEECH, to wheedle, cajole

FLYTE, to scold

FOISONLESS. See Fissenless

FORBYE, besides

FORE-A-HAND, leading, going first

FORGATHER, to come together, put their heads together

FORRIT, forward

FOUL FA' YE, ill befall ye

FOUNTAINHALL, LORD. i. c., Sir John Lauder, Bart., a law lord, author of Chronological Notes of Scottish Affairs, etc.

FRAIM, strange

FRIAR'S CHICKEN, chicken broth, with eggs mixed in it

FURS, furrows

FUSEE, a flint-lock musket

GAED, went; GANE, gone; GANG, go

GALLIO, proconsul of Achaia, or Southern Greece. See Acts xviii. 12-27

GALLOWAY, a breed of horses in the south-west of Scotland

GAR, to make, oblige

GATE, GAIT, way, mode, direction

GAUN, going

GAUNTREES a stand for casks

GAY, pretty, considerably

GEAR, property, goods

GILPY a frolicsome lassie

GIN, if

GIRNEL, a granary, meal-chest

GLEDGE, a sly side glance

GLEG, quick, sharp

GLENKENS. See Kens

GLIFF, an instant; also fright

GLOWRING, staring, gazing hard at

GOMERIL, a fool, simpleton, lout

GOVERNANTE, house-keeper

GOWK a fool

GOWPEN, a handful

GRAMASHES, leggings

GRANE, to groan

GRASSMARKET, the place of public execution in Edinburgh

GUDEMAN, husband

GUDEWIFE, wife

GUIDE (good or ill), to treat, behave to

HAFTED, settled

HAILL, HALE, whole

HANTLE, a good deal

HARLE, to trail, drag

HARNS, brains

HARRISON, THOMAS, the Parliamentarian and regicide

HAR'ST, OWE A DAY IN, to owe a great deal in time of need

HASH, a lout, blockhead

HAUD, to hold

HAUD, IMMEMOR, not unmindful

HAUGH, a level plain

HAULD, a habitation

HAUSE, the throat

HAVINGS, behaviour, demeanour

HELLICAT, violent, wild

HEMPIE giddy, romping

HERITORS, owners of land or other heritable property in Scotland

HEUGH a steep hill

HICKERY-PICKERY, hiera-picra, a warm purgative, made of aloes, cinnamon and honey

HIGHLANDMEN IN 1677. A "Highland host," 6,000 to 8,000 were quartered in Ayrshire and adjacent counties to pun-

ish those who upheld conventicles

HILL-FOLK, the Covenanters (as they worshipped among the hills)

HINNY, honey, a term of endearment

HIT, a special kind of move in backgammon

HOAST, a cough

HODDEN-GREY, the natural colour of wool

HOLME, low ground by a stream

HORNING, a legal injunction to a debtor to pay a debt, under penalty of being proclaimed a rebel to the king

HOSTING, mustering of armed men

HOUSE OF MUIR, a place where markets were held, on the Pentland Hills, near Glencorse

HOWFF, a place of resort

HUMLIE, or HUMBLE, COW, a cow without horns

HUP NOR WIND, go to right nor left, used to a horse

HURCHEON, a hedgehog

HURDIES, the buttocks

ILK, ILKA, each, every; ILKA-DAYS, week days

ILL-FAUR'D, ill-favoured, ugly

IN COMMENDAM, in trust, along with

INCONSTANT. See Mirabel

INGLE, fire; INGLE-NOOK, fireside corner; CHEEK OF THE INGLE, the fireside

IN RERUM NATURA, in existence

ITHER, other

JALOUSE, to suspect, be suspicious of

JAUD, jade

JEMMY AND JENNY JESSAMY by Eliza Haywood (1753)

JENNYFLECTION, genuflexion, kneeling down

JIMPLY, scantily

JO, JOE, a sweetheart

JOAN TAMSON'S MAN, a hen-pecked husband

JULIA DE RUBIGNE, by Henry Mackenzie. The Man of Feeling (1795)

JUSTICE OVERDO, in Ben Jonson's Bartholomew Fair

JUSTIFIED, executed

KAIL, KALE, cabbage greens, broth; KAIL-BROSE, pottage of meal made with the scum of broth; KALE (soup) THROUGH THE REEK (smoke), to take over the coals, storm and rail at; KAIL-WORM, a term of contempt; KALE-YARD, a vegetable garden

KAISAR, Caesar, that is, any emperor

KEBBIE, a hook-headed staff

KEEK, to peep

KEELYVINE, a lead pencil

KENS OF GALLOWAY, a rugged district, known as Glenkens, in Kirkcudbrightshire, where many of the Cameronians found refuge

KENT, a staff

KINDLY TENANTS, those whose ancestors have long held the same land

KITTLE, ticklish, difficult, touchy

KNAPPING, mouthing, talking in an affected manner

KYE, kine, cows

LAIGH, low

LAITH, loth

LANE, THEIR, alone by themselves; MY LANE, by myself

LANG TEN, the ten of trumps in Scotch whist

LANRICK, Lanark

LASSOCK, a little girl

LAVE, the remainder, rest

LAVROCKS, SANDY, sand-larks

LAWING, the reckoning

LEASING-MAKING, falsehood against the sovereign to the people, or vice versa, high treason

LESLEY, or LESLIE, ALEXANDER, afterwards Earl of Leven; was field-marshal in the army of Gustavus Adolphus

LET, to hinder

LICK, a blow

LIPPEN, to trust

LIPPIE, the fourth part of a peck

LITHGOW-TOWN, Linlithgow

LOCALITIES, the shares of an increase of the parochial stipend that fall on the several landowners

LOCK, a handful

LOOF, palm of the hand

LOON, a fellow

LOOP DOUN (A HAT), let down the cocked points

LOOT, allowed, let; LOOTEN, discharged

LOUND, quiet

LOUNDER, to thump

LOUP, to leap

LOW, a flame

LOWDIEN MALLISHA, Lothian militia

LUG, the ear; BLAW IN ONE'S LUG, cajole, flatter; PU' OUT BY LUG AND HORN, drag out as a shepherd drags out a horned sheep

LUKEWARM LAODICEAN. See Revelation iii. 16

LUM, a chimney

LUPPEN, leapt

MAGOR-MISSABIB. See Jeremiah xx. 3

MAIN, a hand or throw at dice

MAINS, the home-farm

MAIR BY TOKEN, especially

MAIR HOUSE, a better table and establishment

MAIST, almost

MAJORING, strutting, prancing with a military air

MALCAIAH, SON OF HAMELMELECH. See Jeremiah xxxviii. 6. The 'king's son,' or Hammelech, was apparently the title of an officer of the royal household.

MALE PARTA PEJUS DILABUNTUR, ill-gotten, worse spent

MALLISHA, militia

MALT ABUNE THE MEAL. See Abune

MARAVEDI, an old Spanish copper coin, worth less than ¼th penny

MARGRAVE, originally an officer of the German empire, the count (graf, grave) of a frontier province (mark, march); afterwards a title of nobility

MART, a fatted cow, ox

MASHLUM, mixed grain

MASK, to brew

MASSY, full of conceit

MASTER SILENCE. See Shakespeare's Henry IV. Part II. Act. v. Sc. 3

MAUNDER, to mutter and grumble, talk for talking's sake

MAUT, malt

MAWKIN, a hare

MEAL-ARK, meal-tub or bin

MEARNS, the ancient name of Kincardineshire

MELVIN, JAMES, should be James Melville, one of the assisins of Cardinal Beaton in 1546

MENSEFU', becoming, suitable

MERK, 1s. 1⅓d.

MEROZ, CURSE OF. See Judges v. 23

MILE, SCOTS, nearly 9 furlongs

MINNIE, mother

MIRABEL IN THE INCONSTANT, a play by G. Farquhar, 1702, but taken in great part from Fletcher's Wild-goose Chase

MIRLIGOES, dizziness

MISLEAR'D, unmannerly

MONRO, MAJOR-GENERAL ROBERT, frequently alluded to in Legend of Montrose

MONSIEUR SCUDERI, Grand Cyrus was originally published under the name of Georges de Scudery, Madeleine's brother, though he only contributed the outline of the story

MONTGOMERY, SIR JAMES, of Skelmorlie, one of the commissioners sent to offer the crown to the Prince of Orange; being disappointed of the office he coveted, he plotted against William in the interests of James II.

MONZIES, probably monsieurs. The words were apparently spoken during apprehensions of invasion from France. See Note 38, p. 439

MOSS-FLOW, a boggy place; MOSS-HAG, a bog-pit

MOUSQUETAIRES, FRENCH, companies of gentlemen who formed the king's guard and enjoyed many privileges

MRS LENNOX'S FEMALE QUIXOT an imitation of Don Quixote, ridiculing the long-winded French romances of the time

MUIR, TAK THE, to flee to the moors

MURGEONS, contortions, violent gestures

MURUS, a wall

MUTCHKIN, pint measure

NABAL. See 1 Sam. xxv.

NASH-GAB, trashy, insolent talk

NEIST, next

NEUK, a nook, corner

NEVOY, a nephew

NIECE, according to old custom, frequently means granddaughter

NIL NOVIT IN CAUSA, he knew nothing about it

NOBLE, an old English coin, worth at first 6s. 8d., later 10s.

NULLIFIDIAN, an unbeliever

ONSTEAD, a farm-steading

ORLANDO, the hero of Ariosto's romantic epic

OUTFIELD AND IN-FIELD. Land constantly manured and cultivated was called 'infield'; land cropped, without manure, until exhausted, 'outfield'

OUTSHOT, a projecting addition to a building

OUT-TAKEN, excepting

OVERTON, RICHARD, Leveller and pamphleteer (1642-49), was imprisoned in Newgate for attacking the House of Lords

OWSEN, oxen

PADUASOY, a lady's habit made of Padua silk

PARENT, a kinswoman

PARRITCH, porridge

PATON OF MEADOWHEAD, an Ayrshire Covenanter, distinguished himself in the German wars and at the battle of Worcester; he was executed after Bothwell Brig

PEARLINGS, a kind of lace, made of thread or silk

PEAT-HAG, a hollow in a moor left from digging peats

PEEL-HOUSE, a small fortified house, or tower

PEINE FORTE ET DURE, stern necessity

PENNY-FEE, wages

PENTLAND HILLS, BATTLE OF, or RULLION GREEN, where in 1666 General Dalziel defeated the Galloway Cameronians

PERDU, hidden

PICKLE, a small quantity, little bit

PINNERS AND PEARLINGS, caps and laces

PIT, to put

PIT AND GALLOWS, PRIVILEGE OF, the right to inflict capital punishment—to drown women in a pit and to hang men on a gallows

PLACK, 1-3d penny

PLENISHING, furnishing

PLEUGH-PAIDLE, a stick for clearing earth from the plough

POCKMANTLE, portmanteau

POCK-PUDDING, a Scotchman's contemptuous epithet for an Englishman

PORT ROYAL, the port of Kingston in Jamaica

POSE, a secret hoard, treasure

POUSS, to push

PU', to pull

PULE, a pool

PUNCH, THE DEVIL, AND THE BAKER, an allusion to the popular puppet-plays of the day

PUND SCOTS, 1s. 8d.

QUAIGH, shallow drinking cup

QUEAN, a young woman

RACE OF DUNBAR. See Dunbar

RANDY, RANDIE, a scold, beggar, disorderly, vagrant

RAPLOCH, coarse, undyed homespun

RAX, to stretch, reach

REDDER, an adviser, settler of disputes, peacemaker

REEK, smoke

REIVING, thieving

RENT-MAIL, a pleonasm for rent

RESET, to harbour, entertain

RIG, a ridge of land; field

RIPE, to search, examine

ROUND, to whisper

ROUT, to bellow

ROW, to roll, wrap

RUE, TO TAKE THE, to rue, repent a proposal, intention

RUGGING, pulling, scuffing

RUGLEN, Rutherglen, on the Clyde, 2 miles from Glasgow

RUTHVEN, SIR PATRICK, sometime governor of Ulm, on the Danube, afterwards Earl of Forth and Branford

SAE, so

ST. JOHNSTONE'S TIPPET, a halter

SAIR, sore, very

SAN BENITOS, robes worn by the victims of the Inquisition, and cut like those worn by the monks of St. Benedict (San Benito)

SANCTUM SANCTORUM, holy of holies, a very jealously kept apartment

SARK, a shirt

SAUT, salt

SCAFF AND RAFF, tagrag and bobtail

SCALED, cleaned the inside of a cannon by firing a small charge from it

SCAUR, a steep bank

SCOTS MILE, nearly 9 furlongs

SCOTS SHILLINGS, equivalent to English pennies

SCREED, a long harangue

SCUDERI, or SCUDERY, MDLLE. DE, an amiable but long-winded and extravagant writer of romances, Grand Cyrus (10 vols., 1649-53), etc., which enjoyed great popularity in their day

SETS, becomes, suits

SHAMENA, are not ashamed

SHAMOY, chamois

SHAW, a wood, flat ground at the bottom of a hill

SHEELING-HILL, a mound where grain was shelled or winnowed by hand in the open air

SHEFFIELD, JOHN, Duke of Buckinghamshire, commanded a force sent in 1680 to the relief of Tangiers, then an English possession and besieged by the Moors

SHILLINGS, SCOTS, equal to English pennies

SIEUR D'URFE, author of Astree and other romances

SILENCE, MASTER. See Master Silence

SINGLE CARRITCH, Single or Shorter Catechism of the Church of Scotland

SINGLE SODGER, a private soldier

SIN' SYNE, since

SKAITH, harm

SKEEL, skill

SKEELY, knowing, skilful

SKELLIE, to squint

SKELPING, beating, thrashing; trotting, cantering

SKINKER, one who serves out liquor

SKIRL, to scream

SKIRL-IN-THE-PAN, a fry

SOMEGATE, somehow

SORN, to demand bed and board, sponge on

SORT, to arrange, make tidy and clean

SOUGH, a whistling sound, sigh; to sigh; CALM SOUGH, an easy mind, a quiet tongue

SOUP, a spoonful

SOUTERS, shoemakers

SOWENS, a sort of flummery made of oatmeal

SPANG, to spring, leap

SPEEL, to scramble, slide

SPEER, to inquire, ask

SPENCE, a pantry, larder

STAP, to push, cram

STARKLY, strongly, stoutly

STAW, to surfeit

STEEK, STEEKIT, shut

STEER, to disturb, interfere with

STILTS (OF A PLOUGH), handles

STING AND LING, entirely

STIR, sir

'STONE WALLS DO NOT,' FOUR etc., from Lovelace's To Althea

STOT, a bullock

STOUP, a liquid measure

STOUR, conflict, strife

STOUR-LOOKING, gruff-looking, austere, surly-looking

STRAFFING UP, hanging

STRAUGHT, or STRAUCHT, straight

STRAVEN, or STRAT-HAVEN, a town some 16 miles south of Glasgow

STUDE, hesitated; STAND, hesitate, shrink from

SULDNA, should not

SUNE AS SYNE, the sooner the better

SUNK, a cushion of straw

SWEAL (OF A CANDLE), to melt and run down

SYBO, a young onion

SYKE, a streamlet dry in summer

SYNE, since, ago

TASS, a glass, cup

TAWPIE, an awkward girl

TENT, care; TAK TENT, take care, heed

TEUGH, tough

THACK AND RAPE, tight in, well cared for, attended to, like a farmer's well-thatched stacks

THEEKING, thatch, roof

THOWLESS, sluggish, inactive

THRANG, thronged, busy

THRAPPLE, throat

THRAW, to thwart

THREEP, aver stoutly, assert

THUMBIKINS, a contrivance for torturing the hands

TIRAILLEUR, sharpshooter

TIRL, to strip, strip off

TITTIE, sister

TOUZLE, to disorder

TOW a rope

TOWER OF THE BASS, the Bass Rock, at the entrance to the Firth of Forth. In its dungeons many Covenanters were imprisoned during the reigns of Charles II. and James II.

TOWN, a country house, with its farm, cottages, and other dependencies. See Note 13, p. 416

TOY, a woman's linen or woollen headdress hanging over the shoulders

TRAGEDY, ONLY SCOTTISH, John Home's Douglas, in Act i. Sc. 1

TRICK-TRACK, a kind of backgammon

TRYSTED, tried, afflicted

TWA, two

TWAL, twelve

UMQUHILE, deceased, late

UNCE, ounce

UNCO, uncommon, strange, queer-looking

UNITED STATES, the United Provinces of the Netherlands

UP-BYE, up, up yonder

UPTAKE, UPTAK, AT THE, at catching up the meaning

VANE, SIR HARRY, the republican, chief commissioner for treating with the Scots in 1643

VIVERS, victuals

WAD, would

WAE, sorry

WALLIE, a valet

WAME, belly, stomach

WAN, got, reached

WARE, to spend

WASSAIL, ale

WATER, DOWN THE, down the valley; WATER-SIDE, the entire district, valley

WATER-BROO, broth, water in which meat has been boiled

WAUGHT, a draught

WAUR, worse

WERSH, tasteless, insipid

WESTPORT, the western gate of Edinburgh, on which the heads of criminals and traitors were exposed

WHAT'S YOUR WULL? what's your will? what do you want?

WHEEN, a few

WHIG AWA, to jog on, move at an easy, steady pace

WHILES, sometimes, occasionally

WHILLY-WHA, wheedling, cajolery

WHIRRY, to hurry, whir

WIN, to get, reach, begin

WINDELSTRAE, bent-grass

WINNOCK, a window

WOODIE, a halter

WUD, mad; CLEAN WUD, stark mad

WUNNA WANT, will not go with

WYTE, blame

YAIRD, YARD, a cottage garden

YILL, YELL, ale

YOKING, the time a horse is in yoke

YOKIT, yoked, fastened

YULE EVE, Christmas Eve

INDEX

TALES OF MY LANDLORD

Second Series

Hear, Land o' Cakes and brither Scots,
Frae Maidenkirk to Johnny Groat's,
If there's a hole in a' your coats,
       I rede ye tent it ;
A chiel's amang you takin' notes,
       An' faith he'll prent it !
BURNS

Ahora bien, dixo il Cura, traedme, senor huésped, aquesos libros, que los quiero ver. Que me place, respondió el, y entrando en su aposento, sacó dél una maletilla vieja cerrada con una cadenilla, y abriéndola halló en ella tres libros grandes y unos papeles de muy buena letra escritos de mano.—DON QUIXOTE, Parte I., Capitulo xxxii.

It is mighty well, said the priest ; pray, landlord, bring me those books, for I have a mind to see them.   With all my heart, answered the host ; and going to his chamber, he brought out a little old cloke-bag, with a padlock and chain to it, and opening it, he took out three large volumes, and some manuscript papers written in a fine character.—JARVIS'S *Translation.*

INTRODUCTION

TO

THE HEART OF MIDLOTHIAN

THE Author has stated in the preface to the *Chronicles of the Canongate*, 1827, that he received from an anonymous correspondent an account of the incident upon which the following story is founded. He is now at liberty to say that the information was conveyed to him by a late amiable and ingenious lady, whose wit and power of remarking and judging of character still survive in the memory of her friends. Her maiden name was Miss Helen Lawson, of Girthhead, and she was wife of Thomas Goldie, Esq., of Craigmuie, Commissary of Dumfries.

Her communication was in these words :

"I had taken for summer lodgings a cottage near the old Abbey of Lincluden. It had formerly been inhabited by a lady who had pleasure in embellishing cottages, which she found perhaps homely and even poor enough ; mine therefore possessed many marks of taste and elegance unusual in this species of habitation in Scotland, where a cottage is literally what its name declares.

"From my cottage door I had a partial view of the old Abbey before mentioned ; some of the highest arches were seen over, and some through, the trees were scattered along a lane which led down to the ruin, and the strange fantastic shapes of almost all those old ashes accorded wonderfully well with the building they at once shaded and ornamented.

"The Abbey itself from my door was almost on a level with the cottage ; but on coming to the end of the lane, it was discovered to be situated on a high perpendicular bank, at the foot of which run the clear waters of the Cluden, where they hasten to join the sweeping Nith,

Whose distance roaring swells and fa's.

As my kitchen and parlor were not very far distant, I one
day went in to purchase some chickens from a person I heard
offering them for sale. It was a little, rather stout-looking
woman, who seemed to be between seventy and eighty years
of age ; she was almost covered with a tartan plaid, and her
cap had over it a black silk hood tied under the chin, a
piece of dress still much in use among elderly women of that
rank of life in Scotland ; her eyes were dark, and remarkably lively and intelligent. I entered into conversation with
her, and began by asking how she maintained herself, etc.

"She said that in winter she footed stockings, that is,
knit feet to country people's stockings, which bears about
the same relation to stocking-knitting that cobbling does to
shoemaking, and is of course both less profitable and less
dignified ; she likewise taught a few children to read, and
in summer she whiles reared a few chickens.

I said I could venture to guess from her face she had
never been married. She laughed heartily at this, and said,
"I maun hae the queerist face that ever was seen, that ye
could guess that. Now, do tell me, madam, how ye cam to
think sae ?" I told her it was from her cheerful disengaged
countenance. She said, "Mem, have ye na far mair reason
to be happy than me, wi' a gude husband and a fine family
o' bairns, and plenty o' everything ? For me, I'm the
puirest o' a' puir bodies, and can hardly contrive to keep
mysell alive in a' thae wee bits o' ways I hae tell't ye."
After some more conversation, during which I was more
and more pleased with the old woman's sensible conversation and the *naïveté* of her remarks, she rose to go away,
when I asked her name. Her countenance suddenly
clouded, and she said gravely, rather coloring, "My name
is Helen Walker ; but your husband kens weel about
me."

"In the evening I related how much I had been pleased, and
inquired what was extraordinary in the history of the poor woman. Mr. —— said, there were perhaps few more remarkable
people than Helen Walker. She had been left an orphan, with
the charge of a sister considerably younger than herself, and
who was educated and maintained by her exertions. Attached to her by so many ties, therefore, it will not be easy to
conceive her feelings when she found that this only sister
must be tried by the laws of her country for child-murder, and
upon being called as principal witness against her. The

counsel for the prisoner told Helen, that if she could declare that her sister had made any preparations, however slight, or had given her any intimation on the subject, such a statement would save her sister's life, as she was the principal witness against her. Helen said, 'It is impossible for me to swear to a falsehood; and, whatever may be the consequence, I will give my oath according to my conscience.'

"The trial came on, and the sister was found guilty and condemned; but, in Scotland, six weeks must elapse between the sentence and the execution, and Helen Walker availed herself of it. The very day of her sister's condemnation, she got a petition drawn up, stating the peculiar circumstances of the case, and that very night set out on foot to London.

"Without introduction or recommendation, with her simple, perhaps ill-expressed, petition, drawn up by some inferior clerk of the court, she presented herself, in her tartan plaid and country attire, to the late Duke of Argyle, who immediately procured the pardon she petitioned for, and Helen returned with it on foot, just in time to save her sister.

"I was so strongly interested by this narrative, that I determined immediately to prosecute my acquaintance with Helen Walker; but as I was to leave the country next day, I was obliged to defer it till my return in spring, when the first walk I took was to Helen Walker's cottage.

"She had died a short time before. My regret was extreme, and I endeavored to obtain some account of Helen from an old woman who inhabited the other end of her cottage. I inquired if Helen ever spoke of her past history, her journey to London, etc. 'Na,' the old woman said, 'Helen was a wily body, and whene'er ony o' the neebors asked anything about it, she aye turned the conversation.'

"In short, every answer I received only tended to increase my regret, and raise my opinion of Helen Walker, who could unite so much prudence with so much heroic virtue."

This narrative was enclosed in the following letter to the Author, without date or signature:

"SIR—The occurrence just related happened to me twenty-six years ago. Helen Walker lies buried in the churchyard of Irongray, about six miles from Dumfries. I once proposed that a small monument should have been erected to commemorate so remarkable a character, but I now prefer leaving it to you to perpetuate her memory in a more durable manner."

The reader is now able to judge how far the Author has improved upon, or fallen short of, the pleasing and interesting sketch of high principle and steady affection displayed by Helen Walker, the prototype of the fictitious Jeanie Deans. Mrs. Goldie was unfortunately dead before the Author had given his name to these volumes, so he lost all opportunity of thanking that lady for her highly valuable communication. But her daughter, Miss Goldie, obliged him with the following additional information :

" Mrs. Goldie endeavored to collect further particulars of Helen Walker, particularly concerning her journey to London, but found this nearly impossible ; as the natural dignity of her character, and a high sense of family respectability, made her so indissolubly connect her sister's disgrace with her own exertions, that none of her neighbors durst ever question her upon the subject. One old woman, a distant relation of Helen's, and who is still living, says she worked an harvest with her, but that she never ventured to ask her about her sister's trial, or her journey to London. 'Helen,' she added, 'was a lofty body, and used a high style o' language.' The same old woman says that every year Helen received a cheese from her sister, who lived at Whitehaven, and that she always sent a liberal portion of it to herself or to her father's family. This fact, though trivial in itself, strongly marks the affection subsisting between the two sisters, and the complete conviction on the mind of the criminal that her sister had acted solely from high principle, not from any want of feeling, which another small but characteristic trait will further illustrate. A gentleman, a relation of Mrs. Goldie's, who happened to be travelling in the North of England, on coming to a small inn, was shown into the parlor by a female servant, who, after cautiously shutting the door, said, 'Sir, I'm Nelly Walker's sister.' Thus practically showing that she considered her sister as better known by her high conduct than even herself by a different kind of celebrity.

" Mrs. Goldie was extremely anxious to have a tombstone and an inscription upon it erected in Irongray churchyard ; and if Sir Walter Scott will condescend to write the last, a little subscription could be easily raised in the immediate neighborhood, and Mrs. Goldie's wish be thus fulfilled."

It is scarcely necessary to add, that the request of Miss Goldie will be most willingly complied with, and without the necessity of any tax on the public.* Nor is there much oc-

---

* See Tombstone to Helen Walker. Note 1.

casion to repeat how much the Author conceives himself obliged to his unknown correspondent, who thus supplied him with a theme affording such a pleasing view of the moral dignity of virtue, though unaided by birth, beauty, or talent. If the picture has suffered in the execution, it is from the failure of the Author's powers to present in detail the same simple and striking portrait exhibited in Mrs. Goldie's letter.

ABBOTSFORD, *April* 1, 1830.

ALTHOUGH it would be impossible to add much to Mrs. Goldie's picturesque and most interesting account of Helen Walker, the prototype of the imaginary Jeanie Deans, the Editor may be pardoned for introducing two or three anecdotes respecting that excellent person, which he has collected from a volume entitled *Sketches from Nature*, by John M'Diarmid, a gentleman who conducts an able provincial paper in the town of Dumfries.

Helen was the daughter of a small farmer in a place called Dalquhairn, in the parish of Irongray ; where, after the death of her father, she continued, with the unassuming piety of a Scottish peasant, to support her mother by her own unremitted labor and privations ; a case so common that even yet, I am proud to say, few of my countrywomen would shrink from the duty.

Helen Walker was held among her equals " pensy," that is, proud or conceited ; but the facts brought to prove this accusation seem only to evince a strength of character superior to those around her. Thus it was remarked, that when it thundered, she went with her work and her Bible to the front of the cottage, alleging that the Almighty could smite in the city as well as in the field.

Mr. M'Diarmid mentions more particularly the misfortune of her sister, which he supposes to have taken place previous to 1736. Helen Walker, declining every proposal of saving her relation's life at the expense of truth, borrowed a sum of money sufficient for her journey, walked the whole distance to London barefoot, and made her way to John Duke of Argyle. She was heard to say that, by the Almighty's strength, she had been enabled to meet the Duke at the most critical moment, which, if lost, would have caused the inevitable forfeiture of her sister's life.

Isabella, or Tibby Walker, saved from the fate which impended over her, was married by the person who had wronged her (named Waugh), and lived happily for great part of a century, uniformly acknowledging the extraordinary affection to which she owed her preservation.

Helen Walker died about the end of the year 1791, and her remains are interred in the churchyard of her native parish of Irongray, in a romantic cemetery on the banks of the Cairn. That a character so distinguished for her undaunted love of virtue lived and died in poverty, if not want, serves only to show us how insignificant, in the sight of Heaven, are our principal objects of ambition upon earth.

TO THE BEST OF PATRONS,

A PLEASED AND INDULGENT READER,

JEDEDIAH CLEISHBOTHAM

WISHES HEALTH, AND INCREASE, AND CONTENTMENT

Courteous Reader,

If ingratitude comprehendeth every vice, surely so foul a
stain worst of all beseemeth him whose life has been devoted to instructing youth in virtue and in humane letters.
Therefore have I chosen, in this prolegomenon, to unload
my burden of thanks at thy feet, for the favor with which
thou hast kindly entertained the *Tales of my Landlord.*
Certes, if thou hast chuckled over their facetious and fes-
tivous descriptions, or hast thy mind filled with pleasure at
the strange and pleasant turns of fortune which they record,
verily, I have also simpered when I beheld a second story
with attics, that has arisen on the basis of my small domicile at Gandercleugh, the walls having been aforehand pronounced by Deacon Barrow to be capable of enduring such
an elevation. Nor has it been without delectation that I
have endued a new coat (snuff-brown, and with metal buttons), having all nether garments corresponding thereto.
We do therefore lie, in respect of each other, under a re-
ciprocation of benefits, whereof those received by me being
the most solid, in respect that a new house and a new coat
are better than a new tale and an old song, it is meet that
my gratitude should be expressed with the louder voice and
more preponderating vehemence. And how should it be so
expressed? Certainly not in words only, but in act and
deed. It is with this sole purpose, and disclaiming all intention of purchasing that pendicle or poffle of land called
the Carlinescroft, lying adjacent to my garden, and measuring seven acres, three roods, and four perches, that I have committed to the eyes of those who thought well of the former
tomes, these four additional volumes * of the *Tales of my*

* [*The Heart of Midlothian* was originally published in four
volumes.]

xv

Landlord.   Not the less, if Peter Prayfort be minded to sell the said poffle, it is at his own choice to say so ; and, peradventure, he may meet with a purchaser ; unless, gentle Reader, the pleasing pourtraictures of Peter Pattieson, now given unto thee in particular, and unto the public in general, shall have lost their favor in thine eyes, whereof I am no way distrustful.   And so much confidence do I repose in thy continued favor, that, should thy lawful occasions call thee to the town of Gandercleugh, a place frequented by most at one time or other in their lives, I will enrich thine eyes with a sight of those precious manuscripts whence thou hast derived so much delectation, thy nose with a snuff from my mull, and thy palate with a dram from my bottle of strong waters, called by the learned of Gandercleugh the Dominie's Dribble o' Drink.

It is there, O highly esteemed and beloved Reader, thou wilt be able to bear testimony, through the medium of thine own senses, against the children of vanity, who have sought to identify thy friend and servant with I know not what inditer of vain fables ; who hath cumbered the world with his devices, but shrunken from the responsibility thereof. Truly, this hath been well termed a generation hard of faith; since what can a man do to assert his property in a printed tome, saving to put his name in the title-page thereof, with his description, or designation, as the lawyers term it, and place of abode ?   Of a surety I would have such sceptics consider how they themselves would brook to have their works ascribed to others, their names and professions imputed as forgeries, and their very existence brought into question ; even although, peradventure, it may be it is of little consequence to any but themselves, not only whether they are living or dead, but even whether they ever lived or no.   Yet have my maligners carried their uncharitable censures still farther. These cavillers have not only doubted mine identity, although thus plainly proved, but they have impeached my veracity and the authenticity of my historical narratives !   Verily, I can only say in answer, that I have been cautelous in quoting mine authorities.   It is true, indeed, that if I had hearkened with only one ear, I might have rehearsed my tale with more acceptation from those who love to hear but half the truth. It is, it may hap, not altogether to the discredit of our kindly nation of Scotland, that we are apt to take an interest, warm, yea partial, in the deeds and sentiments of our forefathers. He whom his adversaries describe as a perjured Prelatist, is desirous that his predecessors should be held moderate in their power, and just in their execution of its privileges, when, truly, the unimpassioned peruser of the annals of those times shall deem them sanguinary, violent, and tyrannical.

Again, the representatives of the suffering nonconformists desire that their ancestors, the Cameronians, shall be represented not simply as honest enthusiasts, oppressed for conscience' sake, but persons of fine breeding, and valiant heroes. Truly, the historian cannot gratify these predilections. He must needs describe the Cavaliers as proud and high-spirited, cruel, remorseless, and vindictive ; the suffering party as honorably tenacious of their opinions under persecution, their own tempers being, however, sullen, fierce, and rude, their opinions absurd and extravagant, and their whole course of conduct that of persons whom hellebore would better have suited than prosecutions unto death for high treason. Natheless, while such and so preposterous were the opinions on either side, there were, it cannot be doubted, men of virtue and worth on both, to entitle either party to claim merit from its martyrs. It has been demanded of me, Jedediah Cleishbotham, by what right I am entitled to constitute myself an impartial judge of their discrepancies of opinions, seeing (as it is stated) that I must necessarily have descended from one or other of the contending parties, and be, of course, wedded for better or for worse, according to the reasonable practice of Scotland, to its dogmata, or opinions, and bound, as it were, by the tie matrimonial, or, to speak without metaphor, *ex jure sanguinis,* to maintain them in preference to all others.

But, nothing denying the rationality of the rule, which calls on all now living to rule their political and religious opinions by those of their great-grandfathers, and inevitable as seems the one or the other horn of the dilemma betwixt which my adversaries conceive they have pinned me to the wall, I yet spy some means of refuge, and claim a privilege to write and speak of both parties with impartiality. For, O ye powers of logic ! when the Prelatists and Presbyterians of old times went together by the ears in this unlucky country, my ancestor—venerated be his memory !—was one of the people called Quakers,* and suffered severe handling from either side, even to the extenuation of his purse and the incarceration of his person.

Craving thy pardon, gentle Reader, for these few words concerning me and mine, I rest, as above expressed, thy sure and obligated friend, J. C.

GANDERCLEUGH, *this* 1st *of April,* 1818.

* See Sir Walter Scott's Relations with the Quakers. Note 2.

THE HEART OF MIDLOTHIAN

CHAPTER I

BEING INTRODUCTORY

So down thy hill, romantic Ashbourn, glides
The Derby dilly, carrying six insides.

FRERE.

THE times have changed in nothing more—we follow as we were wont the manuscript of Peter Pattieson—than in the rapid conveyance of intelligence and communication betwixt one part of Scotland and another. It is not above twenty or thirty years, according to the evidence of many credible witnesses now alive, since a little miserable horse-cart, performing with difficulty a journey of thirty miles *per diem*, carried our mails from the capital of Scotland to its extremity. Nor was Scotland much more deficient in these accommodations than our richer sister had been about eighty years before. Fielding, in his *Tom Jones,* and Farquhar, in a little farce called the *Stage-Coach,* have ridiculed the slowness of these vehicles of public accommodation. According to the latter authority, the highest bribe could only induce the coachman to promise to anticipate by half an hour the usual time of his arrival at the Bull and Mouth.

But in both countries these ancient, slow, and sure modes of conveyance are now alike unknown: mail-coach races against mail-coach, and high-flier against high-flier, through the most remote districts of Britain. And in our village alone, three post-coaches, and four coaches with men armed, and in scarlet cassocks, thunder through the streets each day, and rival in brilliancy and noise the invention of the celebrated tyrant:

Demens, qui nimbos et non imitabile fulmen,
Ære et cornipedum pulsu, simularat, equorum.

Now and then, to complete the resemblance, and to correct the presumption of the venturous charioteers, it does happen that the career of these dashing rivals of Salmoneus meets with as undesirable and violent a termination as that of their prototype. It is on such occasions that the "insides" and "outsides," to use the appropriate vehicular phrases, have reason to rue the exchange of the slow and safe motion of the ancient fly-coaches, which, compared with the chariots of Mr. Palmer, so ill deserve the name. The ancient vehicle used to settle quietly down, like a ship scuttled and left to sink by the gradual influx of the waters, while the modern is smashed to pieces with the velocity of the same vessel hurled against breakers, or rather with the fury of a bomb bursting at the conclusion of its career through the air. The late ingenious Mr. Pennant, whose humor it was to set his face in stern opposition to these speedy conveyances, had collected, I have heard, a formidable list of such casualties, which, joined to the imposition of innkeepers, whose charges the passengers had no time to dispute, the sauciness of the coachman, and the uncontrolled and despotic authority of the tyrant called the guard, held forth a picture of horror, to which murder, theft, fraud, and peculation lent all their dark coloring. But that which gratifies the impatience of the human disposition will be practised in the teeth of danger, and in defiance of admonition ; and, in despite of the Cambrian antiquary, mail-coaches not only roll their thunders round the base of Penmen-Maur and Cader-Edris, but

> Frighted Skiddaw hears afar
> The rattling of the unscythed car.

And perhaps the echoes of Ben Nevis may soon be awakened by the bugle, not of a warlike chieftain, but of the guard of a mail-coach.

It was a fine summer day, and our little school had obtained a half-holiday, by the intercession of a good-humored visitor.* I expected by the coach a new number of an interesting periodical publication, and walked forward on the highway to meet it, with the impatience which Cowper has described as actuating the resident in the country when longing for intelligence from the mart of news :

> The grand debate,
> The popular harangue, the tart reply,
> The logic, and the wisdom, and the wit,
> And the loud laugh,—I long to know them all ;
> I burn to set the imprison'd wranglers free,
> And give them voice and utterance again.

* His honor Gilbert Goslinn of Gandercleugh ; for I love to be precise in matters of importance.—J. C.

It was with such feelings that I eyed the approach of the new coach, lately established on our road, and known by the name of the Somerset, which, to say truth, possesses some interest for me, even when it conveys no such important information. The distant tremulous sound of its wheels was heard just as I gained the summit of the gentle ascent, called the Goslin brae, from which you command an extensive view down the valley of the river Gander. The public road, which comes up the side of that stream, and crosses it at a bridge about a quarter of a mile from the place where I was standing, runs partly through enclosures and plantations, and partly through open pasture land. It is a childish amusement perhaps—but my life has been spent with children, and why should not my pleasures be like theirs ?—childish as it is, then, I must own I have had great pleasure in watching the approach of the carriage, where the openings of the road permit it to be seen. The gay glancing of the equipage, its diminished and toy-like appearance at a distance, contrasted with the rapidity of its motion, its appearance and disappearance at intervals, and the progressively increasing sounds that announce its nearer approach, have all to the idle and listless spectator, who has nothing more important to attend to, something of awakening interest. The ridicule may attach to me, which is flung upon many an honest citizen, who watches from the window of his villa the passage of the stage-coach ; but it is a very natural source of amusement notwithstanding, and many of those who join in the laugh are perhaps not unused to resort to it in secret.

On the present occasion, however, fate had decreed that I should not enjoy the consummation of the amusement by seeing the coach rattle past me as I sat on the turf, and hearing the hoarse grating voice of the guard as he skimmed forth for my grasp the expected packet, without the carriage checking its course for an instant. I had seen the vehicle thunder down the hill that leads to the bridge with more than its usual impetuosity, glittering all the while by flashes from a cloudy tabernacle of the dust which it had raised, and leaving a train behind it on the road resembling a wreath of summer mist. But it did not appear on the top of the nearer bank within the usual space of three minutes, which frequent observation had enabled me to ascertain was the medium time for crossing the bridge and mounting the ascent. When double that space had elapsed, I became alarmed, and walked hastily forward. As I came in sight of the bridge, the cause of delay was too manifest, for the Somerset had made a summerset in good earnest, and overturned so completely, that it was literally resting upon the ground, with the roof undermost, and the four wheels in the air. The " exertions of the guard and coach-man," both of whom were gratefully commemorated in the newspapers, having succeeded in disentangling the horses by cutting the harness, were now proceeding to extricate the " in-sides " by a sort of summary and Cæsarean process of delivery, forcing the hinges from one of the doors which they could not open otherwise. In this manner were two disconsolate damsels set at liberty from the womb of the leathern conveniency. As they immediately began to settle their clothes, which were a little deranged, as may be presumed, I concluded they had re-ceived no injury, and did not venture to obtrude my services at their toilet, for which, I understand, I have since been reflected upon by the fair sufferers. The " outsides," who must have been discharged from their elevated situation by a shock resembling the springing of a mine, escaped, neverthe-less, with the usual allowance of scratches and bruises, except-ing three, who, having been pitched into the river Gander, were dimly seen contending with the tide, like the relics of Æneas's shipwreck—

Rari apparent nantes in gurgite vasto.

I applied my poor exertions where they seemed to be most needed, and with the assistance of one or two of the company who had escaped unhurt, easily succeeded in fishing out two of the unfortunate passengers, who were stout active young fellows ; and but for the preposterous length of their great-coats, and the equally fashionable latitude and longitude of their Wellington trousers, would have required little assist-ance from any one. The third was sickly and elderly, and might have perished but for the efforts used to preserve him.

When the two greatcoated gentlemen had extricated them-selves from the river, and shaken their ears like huge water-dogs, a violent altercation ensued betwixt them and the coach-man and guard, concerning the cause of their overthrow. In the course of the squabble, I observed that both my new ac-quaintances belonged to the law, and that their professional sharpness was likely to prove an overmatch for the surly and official tone of the guardians of the vehicle. The dispute ended in the guard assuring the passengers that they should have seats in a heavy coach which would pass that spot in less than half a hour, providing it were not full. Chance seemed to favor this arrangement, for when the expected vehicle ar-rived, there were only two places occupied in a carriage which professed to carry six. The two ladies who had been disin terred out of the fallen vehicle were readily admitted, but positive objections were stated by those previously in possession to the admittance of the two lawyers, whose wetted garments being much of the nature of well-soaked sponges, there was every reason to believe they would refund a considerable part of the water they had collected, to the inconvenience of their fellow-passengers. On the other hand, the lawyers rejected a seat on the roof, alleging that they had only taken that station for pleasure for one stage, but were entitled in all respects to free egress and regress from the interior, to which their contract positively referred. After some altercation, in which something was said upon the edict *Nautæ, caupones, stabularii*, the coach went off, leaving the learned gentlemen to abide by their action of damages.

They immediately applied to me to guide them to the next village and the best inn ; and from the account I gave them of the Wallace Head, declared they were much better pleased to stop there than to go forward upon the terms of that impudent scoundrel the guard of the Somerset. All that they now wanted was a lad to carry their travelling bags, who was easily procured from an adjoining cottage ; and they prepared to walk forward, when they found there was another passenger in the same deserted situation with themselves. This was the elderly and sickly-looking person who had been precipitated into the river along with the two young lawyers. He, it seems, had been too modest to push his own plea against the coachman when he saw that of his betters rejected, and now remained behind with a look of timid anxiety, plainly intimating that he was deficient in those means of recommendation which are necessary passports to the hospitality of an inn.

I ventured to call the attention of the two dashing young blades, for such they seemed, to the desolate condition of their fellow-traveller. They took the hint with ready good-nature.

"O, true, Mr. Dunover," said one of the youngsters, "you must not remain on the *pavé* here ; you must go and have some dinner with us ; Halkit and I must have a post-chaise to go on, at all events, and we will set you down wherever suits you best."

The poor man, for such his dress, as well as his diffidence, bespoke him, made the sort of acknowledging bow by which says a Scotchman, "It's too much honor for the like of me ;" and followed humbly behind his gay patrons, all three besprinkling the dusty road as they walked along with the moisture of their drenched garments, and exhibiting the singular and somewhat ridiculous appearance of three persons suffering from the opposite extreme of humidity, while the summer sun was at its height, and everything else around them had the expression of heat and drought. The ridicule did not escape the young gentlemen themselves, and they had made what might be received as one or two tolerable jests on the subject before they had advanced far on their peregrination.

"We cannot complain, like Cowley," said one of them, "that Gideon's fleece remains dry, while all around is moist; this is the reverse of the miracle."

"We ought to be received with gratitude in this good town; we bring a supply of what they seem to need most," said Halkit.

"And distribute it with unparalleled generosity," replied his companion; "performing the part of three water-carts for the benefit of their dusty roads."

"We come before them, too," said Halkit, "in full professional force—counsel and agent——"

"And client," said the young advocate, looking behind him. And then added, lowering his voice, "that looks as if he had kept such dangerous company too long."

It was, indeed, too true, that the humble follower of the gay young men had the threadbare appearance of a worn-out litigant, and I could not but smile at the conceit, though anxious to conceal my mirth from the object of it.

When we arrived at the Wallace Inn, the elder of the Edinburgh gentlemen, and whom I understood to be a barrister, insisted that I should remain and take part of their dinner; and their inquiries and demands speedily put my Landlord and his whole family in motion to produce the best cheer which the larder and cellar afforded, and proceed to cook it to the best advantage, a science in which our entertainers seemed to be admirably skilled. In other respects they were lively young men, in the heyday of youth and good spirits, playing the part which is common to the higher classes of the law at Edinburgh, and which nearly resembles that of the young Templars in the days of Steele and Addison. An air of giddy gayety mingled with the good sense, taste, and information which their conversation exhibited; and it seemed to be their object to unite the character of men of fashion and lovers of the polite arts. A fine gentleman, bred up in the thorough idleness and inanity of pursuit which I understand is absolutely necessary to the character in perfection, might in all probability have traced a tinge of professional pedantry which marked the barrister in spite of his efforts, and something of

active bustle in his companion, and would certainly have detected more than a fashionable mixture of information and
animated interest in the language of both.   But to me, who
had no pretensions to be so critical, my companions seemed to
form a very happy mixture of good-breeding and liberal information, with a disposition to lively rattle, pun, and jest,
amusing to a grave man, because it is what he himself can
least easily command.

The thin pale-faced man, whom their good-nature had
brought into their society, looked out of place, as well as out
of spirits, sat on the edge of his seat, and kept the chair at
two feet distance from the table, thus incommoding himself
considerably in conveying the victuals to his mouth, as if by
way of penance for partaking of them in the company of his
superiors.   A short time after dinner, declining all entreaty
to partake of the wine, which circulated freely round, he informed himself of the hour when the chaise had been ordered
to attend ; and saying he would be in readiness, modestly
withdrew from the apartment.

"Jack," said the barrister to his companion, "I remember
that poor fellow's face ; you spoke more truly than you were
aware of ; he really is one of my clients, poor man."

"Poor man !" echoed Halkit.   "I suppose you mean he
is your one and only client ?"

"That's not my fault, Jack," replied the other, whose
name I discovered was Hardie.   "You are to give me all your
business, you know ; and if you have none, the learned gentleman here knows nothing can come of nothing."

"You seem to have brought something to nothing, though,
in the case of that honest man.   He looks as if he were
just about to honor with his residence the HEART OF MID-
LOTHIAN."

"You are mistaken : he is just delivered from it.   Our
friend here looks for an explanation.   Pray, Mr. Pattieson,
have you been in Edinburgh ?"

I answered in the affirmative.

"Then you must have passed, occasionally at least, though
probably not so faithfully as I am doomed to do, through a
narrow intricate passage, leading out of the north-west corner
of the Parliament Square, and passing by a high and antique
building, with turrets and iron grates,

> "Making good the saying odd,
> Near the church and far from God——"

Mr. Halkit broke in upon his learned counsel to contrib-

ute his moiety to the riddle—"Having at the door the sign
of the Red Man——"

"And being on the whole," resumed the counsellor, interrupting his friend in his turn, "a sort of place where misfortune is happily confounded with guilt, where all who are in
wish to get out——"

"And where none who have the good luck to be out wish
to get in," added his companion.

"I conceive you, gentlemen," replied I: "you mean the
prison."

"The prison," added the young lawyer. "You have hit
it—the very reverend tolbooth itself; and let me tell you,
you are obliged to us for describing it with so much modesty
and brevity; for with whatever amplifications we might have
chosen to decorate the subject, you lay entirely at our mercy,
since the Fathers Conscript of our city have decreed that the
venerable edifice itself shall not remain in existence to confirm
or to confute us."

"Then the tolbooth of Edinburgh is called the Heart of
Midlothian?" said I.

"So termed and reputed, I assure you."

"I think," said I, with the bashful diffidence with which
a man lets slip a pun in presence of his superiors, "the met-
ropolitan county may, in that case, be said to have a sad
heart."

"Right as my glove, Mr. Pattieson," added Mr. Hardie;
"and a close heart, and a hard heart. Keep it up, Jack."

"And a wicked heart, and a poor heart," answered Halkit, doing his best.

"And yet it may be called in some sort a strong heart,
and a high heart," rejoined the advocate. "You see I can
put you both out of heart."

"I have played all my hearts," said the younger gentleman.

"Then we'll have another lead," answered his companion.
"And as to the old and condemned tolbooth, what pity the
same honor cannot be done to it as has been done to many of
its inmates. Why should not the tolbooth have its "Last
Speech, Confession, and Dying Words?" The old stones
would be just as conscious of the honor as many a poor devil
who has dangled like a tassel at the west end of it, while the
hawkers were shouting a confession the culprit had never
heard of."

"I am afraid," said I, "if I might presume to give my
opinion, it would be a tale of unvaried sorrow and guilt."

"Not entirely, my friend," said Hardie ; "a prison is a world within itself, and has its own business, griefs, and joys, peculiar to its circle. Its inmates are sometimes short-lived, but so are soldiers on service ; they are poor relatively to the world without, but there are degrees of wealth and poverty among them, and so some are relatively rich also. They cannot stir abroad, but neither can the garrison of a besieged fort, nor the crew of a ship at sea ; and they are not under a dispensation quite so desperate as either, for they may have as much food as they have money to buy, and are not obliged to work whether they have food or not."

"But what variety of incident," said I, not without a secret view to my present task, "could possibly be derived from such a work as you are pleased to talk of ?"

"Infinite," replied the young advocate. "Whatever of guilt, crime, imposture, folly, unheard-of misfortunes, and unlooked-for change of fortune, can be found to checker life, my Last Speech of the Tolbooth should illustrate with examples sufficient to gorge even the public's all-devouring appetite for the wonderful and horrible. The inventor of fictitious narratives has to rack his brains for means to diversify his tale, and after all can hardly hit upon characters or incidents which have not been used again and again, until they are familiar to the eye of the reader, so that the development, *enlèvement*, the desperate wound of which the hero never dies, the burning fever from which the heroine is sure to recover, become a mere matter of course. I join with my honest friend Crabbe, and have an unlucky propensity to hope when hope is lost, and to rely upon the cork-jacket, which carries the heroes of romance safe through all the billows of affliction." He then declaimed the following passage, rather with too much than too little emphasis :

> Much have I fear'd, but am no more afraid,
> When some chaste beauty, by some wretch betray'd,
> Is drawn away with such distracted speed,
> That she anticipates a dreadful deed.
> Not so do I. Let solid walls impound
> The captive fair, and dig a moat around ;
> Let there be brazen locks and bars of steel,
> And keepers cruel, such as never feel ;
> With not a single note the purse supply,
> And when she begs, let men and maids deny ;
> Be windows those from which she dares not fall
> And help so distant, 'tis in vain to call ;
> Still means of freedom will some Power devise,
> And from the baffled ruffian snatch his prize.

"The end of uncertainty," he concluded, "is the death of interest; and hence it happens that no one now reads novels."

"Hear him, ye gods!" returned his companion. "I assure you, Mr. Pattieson, you will hardly visit this learned gentleman but you are likely to find the new novel most in repute lying on his table—snugly intrenched, however, beneath Stair's *Institutes,* or an open volume of Morison's *Decisions.*"

"Do I deny it?" said the hopeful jurisconsult, "or wherefore should I, since it is well known these Delilahs seduced my wisers and my betters? May they not be found lurking amidst the multiplied memorials of our most distinguished counsel, and even peeping from under the cushion of a judge's arm-chair? Our seniors at the bar, within the bar, and even on the bench, read novels; and, if not belied, some of them have written novels into the bargain. I only say, that I read from habit and from indolence, not from real interest; that, like Ancient Pistol devouring his leek, I read and swear till I get to the end of the narrative. But not so in the real records of human vagaries, not so in the *State Trials,* or in the *Books of Adjournal,* where every now and then you read new pages of the human heart, and turns of fortune far beyond what the boldest novelist ever attempted to produce from the coinage of his brain."

"And for such narratives," I asked, "you suppose the history of the prison of Edinburgh might afford appropriate materials?"

"In a degree unusually ample, my dear sir," said Hardie. "Fill your glass, however, in the meanwhile. Was it not for many years the place in which the Scottish Parliament met? Was it not James's place of refuge, when the mob, inflamed by a seditious preacher, broke forth on him with the cries of 'The sword of the Lord and of Gideon; bring forth the wicked Haman?' Since that time how many hearts have throbbed within these walls, as the tolling of the neighboring bell announced to them how fast the sands of their life were ebbing; how many must have sunk at the sound; how many were supported by stubborn pride and dogged resolution; how many by the consolations of religion? Have there not been some, who, looking back on the motives of their crimes, were scarce able to understand how they should have had such temptation as to seduce them from virtue? and have there not, perhaps, been others, who, sensible of their innocence, were divided between indignation at the undeserved doom which they were to undergo, consciousness that they had not deserved it, and racking anxiety to discover some way in which they might yet vindicate themselves? Do you suppose any of these deep, powerful, and agitating feelings can be recorded and perused without exciting a corresponding depth of deep, powerful, and agitating interest? O! do but wait till I publish the *causes célèbres* of Caledonia, and you will find no want of a novel or a tragedy for some time to come. The true thing will triumph over the brightest inventions of the most ardent imagination. *Magna est veritas, et prœvalebit.*"

"I have understood," said I, encouraged by the affability of my rattling entertainer, "that less of this interest must attach to Scottish jurisprudence than to that of any other country. The general morality of our people, their sober and prudent habits——"

"Secure them," said the barrister, "against any great increase of professional thieves and depredators, but not against wild and wayward starts of fancy and passion, producing crimes of an extraordinary description, which are precisely those to the detail of which we listen with thrilling interest. England has been much longer a highly civilized country ; her subjects have been very strictly amenable to laws administered without fear or favor ; a complete division of labor has taken place among her subjects ; and the very thieves and robbers form a distinct class in society, subdivided among themselves according to the subject of their depredations, and the mode in which they carry them on, acting upon regular habits and principles, which can be calculated and anticipated at Bow Street, Hatton Garden, or the Old Bailey. Our sister kingdom is like a cultivated field : the farmer expects that, in spite of all his care, a certain number of weeds will rise with the corn, and can tell you beforehand their names and appearance. But Scotland is like one of her own Highland glens, and the moralist who reads the records of her criminal jurisprudence will find as many curious anomalous facts in the history of mind as the botanist will detect rare specimens among her dingles and cliffs."

"And that's all the good you have obtained from three perusals of the *Commentaries on Scottish Criminal Jurisprudence?*" said his companion. "I suppose the learned author very little thinks that the facts which his erudition and acuteness have accumulated for the illustration of legal doctrines might be so arranged as to form a sort of appendix to the half-bound and slipshod volumes of the circulating library."

"I'll bet you a pint of claret," said the elder lawyer,

"that he will not feel sore at the comparison. But as we say at the bar, 'I beg I may not be interrupted;' I have much more to say upon my Scottish collection of *causes célèbres*. You will please recollect the scope and motive given for the contrivance and execution of many extraordinary and daring crimes, by the long civil dissensions of Scotland ; by the hereditary jurisdictions, which, until 1748, rested the investigation of crimes in judges, ignorant, partial, or interested ; by the habits of the gentry, shut up in their distant and solitary mansion-houses, nursing their revengeful passions just to keep their blood from stagnating ; not to mention that amiable national qualification, called the *perfervidum ingenium Scotorum*, which our lawyers join in alleging as a reason for the severity of some of our enactments. When I come to treat of matters so mysterious, deep, and dangerous as these circumstances have given rise to, the blood of each reader shall be curdled, and his epidermis crisped into goose-skin. But, hist ! here comes the landlord, with tidings, I suppose, that the chaise is ready."

It was no such thing : the tidings bore, that no chaise could be had that evening, for Sir Peter Plyem had carried forward my Landlord's two pair of horses that morning to the ancient royal borough of Bubbleburgh, to look after his interest there. But as Bubbleburgh is only one of a set of five boroughs which club their shares for a member of Parliament, Sir Peter's adversary had judiciously watched his departure, in order to commence a canvass in the no less royal borough of Bitem, which, as all the world knows, lies at the very termination of Sir Peter's avenue, and has been held in leading-strings by him and his ancestors for time immemorial. Now, Sir Peter was thus placed in the situation of an ambitious monarch who, after having commenced a daring inroad into his enemies' territories, is suddenly recalled by an invasion of his own hereditary dominions. He was obliged in consequence to return from the half-won borough of Bubbleburgh to look after the half-lost borough of Bitem, and the two pairs of horses which had carried him that morning to Bubbleburgh were now forcibly detained to transport him, his agent, his valet, his jester, and his hard-drinker across the country to Bitem. The cause of this detention, which to me was of as little consequence as it may be to the reader, was important enough to my companions to reconcile them to the delay. Like eagles, they smelled the battle afar off, ordered a magnum of claret and beds at the Wallace, and entered at full career into the Bubbleburgh and Bitem politics, with all the probable

" petitions and complaints " to which they were likely to give rise.

In the midst of an anxious, animated, and, to me, most unintelligible discussion, concerning provosts, bailies, deacons, sets of boroughs, leets, town clerks, burgesses resident and non-resident, all of a sudden the lawyer recollected himself. " Poor Dunover, we must not forget him; " and the landlord was despatched in quest of the *pauvre honteux*, with an earnestly civil invitation to him for the rest of the evening. I could not help asking the young gentlemen if they knew the history of this poor man ; and the counsellor applied himself to his pocket to recover the memorial or brief from which he had stated his cause.

" He has been a candidate for our *remedium miserabile*," said Mr. Hardie, " commonly called a *cessio bonorum*. As there are divines who have doubted the eternity of future punishments, so the Scotch lawyers seem to have thought that the crime of poverty might be atoned for by something short of perpetual imprisonment. After a month's confinement, you must know, a prisoner for debt is entitled, on a sufficient statement to our Supreme Court, setting forth the amount of his funds, and the nature of his misfortunes, and surrendering all his effects to his creditors, to claim to be discharged from prison."

" I had heard," I replied, " of such a humane regulation."

" Yes," said Halkit, " and the beauty of it is, as the foreign fellow said, you may get the *cessio* when the *bonorums* are all spent. But what, are you puzzling in your pockets to seek your only memorial among old play-bills, letters requesting a meeting of the faculty, rules of the Speculative Society,* syllabus of lectures—all the miscellaneous contents of a young advocate's pocket, which contains everything but briefs and bank-notes ? Can you not state a case of *cessio* without your memorial ? Why, it is done every Saturday. The events follow each other as regularly as clockwork, and one form of condescendence might suit every one of them."

" This is very unlike the variety of distress which this gentleman stated to fall under the consideration of your judges," said I.

" True," replied Halkit ; " but Hardie spoke of criminal jurisprudence, and this business is purely civil. I could plead a *cessio* myself without the inspiring honors of a gown and three-tailed periwig. Listen. My client was bred a journeyman weaver—made some little money—took a farm—(for con-

* A well-known debating club in Edinburgh (*Laing*).

ducting a farm, like driving a gig, comes by nature)—late severe times—induced to sign bills for a friend, for which he received no value—landlord sequestrates—creditors accept a composition—pursuer sets up a public-house—fails a second time—is incarcerated for a debt of ten pounds, seven shillings and sixpence—his debts amount to blank—his losses to blank—his funds to blank—leaving a balance of blank in his favor. There is no opposition; your lordships will please grant commission to take his oath."

Hardie now renounced his ineffectual search, in which there was perhaps a little affectation, and told us the tale of poor Dunover's distresses, with a tone in which a degree of feeling, which he seemed ashamed of as unprofessional, mingled with his attempts at wit, and did him more honor. It was one of those tales which seem to argue a sort of ill-luck or fatality attached to the hero. A well-informed, industrious, and blameless, but poor and bashful, man had in vain essayed all the usual means by which others acquire independence, yet had never succeeded beyond the attainment of bare subsistence. During a brief gleam of hope, rather than of actual prosperity, he had added a wife and family to his cares, but the dawn was speedily overcast. Everything retrograded with him towards the verge of the miry Slough of Despond, which yawns for insolvent debtors; and after catching at each twig, and experiencing the protracted agony of feeling them one by one elude his grasp, he actually sunk into the miry pit whence he had been extricated by the professional exertions of Hardie.

" And, I suppose, now you have dragged this poor devil ashore, you will leave him half naked on the beach to provide for himself?" said Halkit. " Hark ye," and he whispered something in his ear, of which the penetrating and insinuating words, "Interest with my lord," alone reached mine.

"It is *pessimi exempli*," said Hardie, laughing, "to provide for a ruined client; but I was thinking of what you mention, provided it can be managed. But hush! here he comes."

The recent relation of the poor man's misfortunes had given him, I was pleased to observe, a claim to the attention and respect of the young men, who treated him with great civility, and gradually engaged him in a conversation which, much to my satisfaction, again turned upon the *causes célèbres* of Scotland. Emboldened by the kindness with which he was treated, Mr. Dunover began to contribute his share to the amusement of the evening. Jails, like other places, have their ancient traditions, known only to the inhabitants, and handed down from one set of the melancholy lodgers to the next who occupy their cells. Some of these, which Dunover mentioned, were interesting, and served to illustrate the narratives of remarkable trials which Hardie had at his finger-ends, and which his companion was also well skilled in. This sort of conversation passed away the evening till the early hour when Mr. Dunover chose to retire to rest, and I also retreated to take down memorandums of what I had learned, in order to add another narrative to those which it had been my chief amusement to collect, and to write out in detail. The two young men ordered a broiled bone, Madeira negus, and a pack of cards, and commenced a game at picquet.

Next morning the travellers left Gandercleugh. I afterwards learned from the papers that both have been since engaged in the great political cause of Bubbleburgh and Bitem, a summary case, and entitled to particular despatch ; but which, it is thought, nevertheless, may outlast the duration of the parliament to which the contest refers. Mr. Halkit, as the newspapers informed me, acts as agent or solicitor ; and Mr. Hardie opened for Sir Peter Plyem with singular ability, and to such good purpose, that I understand he has since had fewer play-bills and more briefs in his pocket. And both the young gentlemen deserve their good fortune ; for I learned from Dunover, who called on me some weeks afterwards, and communicated the intelligence with tears in his eyes, that their interest had availed to obtain him a small office for the decent maintenance of his family ; and that, after a train of constant and uninterrupted misfortune, he could trace a dawn of prosperity to his having the good fortune to be flung from the top of a mail-coach into the river Gander, in company with an advocate and a writer to the signet. The reader will not perhaps deem himself equally obliged to the accident, since it brings upon him the following narrative, founded upon the conversation of the evening.

CHAPTER II

Whoe'er's been at Paris must needs know the Grêve,
The fatal retreat of the unfortunate brave,
Where honor and justice most oddly contribute,
To ease heroes' pains by an halter and gibbet.

There death breaks the shackles which force had put on,
And the hangman completes what the judge but began ;
There the squire of the pad, and knight of the post,
Find their pains no more baulk'd, and their hopes no more cross'd.
PRIOR.

In former times, England had her Tyburn, to which the devoted victims of justice were conducted in solemn procession up what is now called Oxford Road. In Edinburgh, a large open street, or rather oblong square, surrounded by high houses, called the Grassmarket, was used for the same melancholy purpose. It was not ill chosen for such a scene, being of considerable extent, and therefore fit to accommodate a great number of spectators, such as are usually assembled by this melancholy spectacle. On the other hand, few of the houses which surround it were, even in early times, inhabited by persons of fashion ; so that those likely to be offended or over deeply affected by such unpleasant exhibitions were not in the way of having their quiet disturbed by them. The houses in the Grassmarket are, generally speaking, of a mean description ; yet the place is not without some features of grandeur, being overhung by the southern side of the huge rock on which the castle stands, and by the moss-grown battlements and turreted walls of that ancient fortress.

It was the custom, until within these thirty years or thereabouts, to use this esplanade for the scene of public executions. The fatal day was announced to the public by the appearance of a huge black gallows-tree towards the eastern end of the Grassmarket. This ill-omened apparition was of great height, with a scaffold surrounding it, and a double ladder placed against it, for the ascent of the unhappy criminal and the executioner. As this apparatus was always arranged before dawn, it seemed as if the gallows had grown out of the earth in the course of one night, like the production of some foul demon ; and I well remember the fright with which the schoolboys, when I was one of their number, used to regard these ominous signs of deadly preparation. On the night after the execution the gallows again disappeared, and was conveyed in silence and darkness to the place where it was usually deposited, which was one of the vaults under the Parliament House, or courts of justice. This mode of execution is now exchanged for one similar to that in front of Newgate, with what beneficial effect is uncertain. The mental sufferings of the convict are indeed shortened. He no longer stalks between the attendant clergymen, dressed in his graveclothes, through a considerable part of the city, looking like a moving and walking corpse, while yet an inhabitant of this world ; but as the ultimate purpose of punishment has in view the prevention of crimes, it may at least be doubted whether, in abridging the melancholy ceremony, we have not in part diminished that appalling effect upon the spectators which is the useful end of all such inflictions, and in consideration of which alone, unless in very particular cases, capital sentences can be altogether justified.

On the 7th day of September, 1736, these ominous preparations for execution were descried in the place we have described, and at an early hour the space around began to be occupied by several groups, who gazed on the scaffold and gibbet with a stern and vindictive show of satisfaction very seldom testified by the populace, whose good-nature in most cases forgets the crime of the condemned person, and dwells only on his misery. But the act of which the expected culprit had been convicted was of a description calculated nearly and closely to awaken and irritate the resentful feelings of the multitude. The tale is well known ; yet it is necessary to recapitulate its leading circumstances, for the better understanding what is to follow ; and the narrative may prove long, but I trust not uninteresting, even to those who have heard its general issue. At any rate, some detail is necessary, in order to render intelligible the subsequent events of our narrative.

Contraband trade, though it strikes at the root of legitimate government, by encroaching on its revenues ; though it injures the fair trader, and debauches the minds of those engaged in it, is not usually looked upon, either by the vulgar or by their betters, in a very heinous point of view. On the contrary, in those counties where it prevails, the cleverest, boldest, and most intelligent of the peasantry are uniformly

engaged in illicit transactions, and very often with the sanction of the farmers and inferior gentry. Smuggling was almost universal in Scotland in the reigns of George I. and II.;
for the people, unaccustomed to imposts, and regarding them
as an unjust aggression upon their ancient liberties, made no
scruple to elude them whenever it was possible to do so.

The county of Fife, bounded by two firths on the south
and north, and by the sea on the east, and having a number
of small seaports, was long famed for maintaining successfully
a contraband trade ; and as there were many seafaring men
residing there, who had been pirates and buccaneers in their
youth, there were not wanting a sufficient number of daring
men to carry it on. Among these, a fellow called Andrew
Wilson, originally a baker in the village of Pathhead, was
particularly obnoxious to the revenue officers. He was possessed of great personal strength, courage, and cunning, was
perfectly acquainted with the coast, and capable of conducting
the most desperate enterprises. On several occasions he succeeded in baffling the pursuit and researches of the king's
officers ; but he became so much the object of their suspicions
and watchful attention that at length he was totally ruined
by repeated seizures. The man became desperate. He considered himself as robbed and plundered, and took it into his
head that he had a right to make reprisals, as he could find
opportunity. Where the heart is prepared for evil, opportunity is seldom long wanting. This Wilson learned that the
collector of the customs at Kirkcaldy had come to Pittenweem, in the course of his official round of duty, with a considerable sum of public money in his custody. As the amount
was greatly within the value of the goods which had been
seized from him, Wilson felt no scruple of conscience in
resolving to reimburse himself for his losses at the expense
of the collector and the revenue. He associated with himself
one Robertson and two other idle young men, whom, having
been concerned in the same illicit trade, he persuaded to view
the transaction in the same justifiable light in which he himself
considered it. They watched the motions of the collector ;
they broke forcibly into the house where he lodged, Wilson,
with two of his associates, entering the collector's apartment,
while Robertson, the fourth, kept watch at the door with a
drawn cutlass in his hand. The officer of the customs, conceiving his life in danger, escaped out of his bedroom window,
and fled in his shirt, so that the plunderers, with much ease,
possessed themselves of about two hundred pounds of public
money. This robbery was committed in a very audacious

manner, for several persons were passing in the street at the time. But Robertson, representing the noise they heard as a dispute or fray betwixt the collector and the people of the house, the worthy citizens of Pittenweem felt themselves no way called on to interfere in behalf of the obnoxious revenue officer ; so, satisfying themselves with this very superficial account of the matter, like the Levite in the parable, they passed on the opposite side of the way. An alarm was at length given, military were called in, the depredators were pursued, the booty recovered, and Wilson and Robertson tried and condemned to death, chiefly on the evidence of an accomplice.

Many thought that, in consideration of the men's erroneous opinion of the nature of the action they had committed, justice might have been satisfied with a less forfeiture than that of two lives. On the other hand, from the audacity of the fact, a severe example was judged necessary ; and such was the opinion of the government. When it became apparent that the sentence of death was to be executed, files, and other implements necessary for their escape, were transmitted secretly to the culprits by a friend from without. By these means they sawed a bar out of one of the prison windows, and might have made their escape, but for the obstinacy of Wilson, who, as he was daringly resolute, was doggedly pertinacious of his opinion. His comrade, Robertson, a young and slender man, proposed to make the experiment of passing the foremost through the gap they had made, and enlarging it from the outside, if necessary, to allow Wilson free passage. Wilson, however, insisted on making the first experiment, and being a robust and lusty man, he not only found it impossible to get through betwixt the bars, but, by his struggles, he jammed himself so fast that he was unable to draw his body back again. In these circumstances discovery became unavoidable ; and sufficient precautions were taken by the jailer to prevent any repetition of the same attempt. Robertson uttered not a word of reflection on his companion for the consequences of his obstinacy ; but it appeared from the sequel that Wilson's mind was deeply impressed with the recollection that, but for him, his comrade, over whose mind he exercised considerable influence, would not have engaged in the criminal enterprise which had terminated thus fatally ; and that now he had become his destroyer a second time, since, but for his obstinacy, Robertson might have effected his escape. Minds like Wilson's, even when exercised in evil practices, sometimes retain the power of thinking and resolving with enthusiastic generosity.

His whole thoughts were now bent on the possibility of saving Robertson's life, without the least respect to his own. The resolution which he adopted, and the manner in which he carried it into effect, were striking and unusual.

Adjacent to the tolbooth or city jail of Edinburgh is one of three churches into which the cathedral of St. Giles is now divided, called, from its vicinity, the Tolbooth Church. It was the custom that criminals under sentence of death were brought to this church, with a sufficient guard, to hear and join in public worship on the Sabbath before execution. It was supposed that the hearts of these unfortunate persons, however hardened before against feelings of devotion, could not but be accessible to them upon uniting their thoughts and voices, for the last time, along with their fellow-mortals, in addressing their Creator. And to the rest of the congregation it was thought it could not but be impressive and affecting to find their devotions mingling with those who, sent by the doom of an earthly tribunal to appear where the whole earth is judged, might be considered as beings trembling on the verge of eternity. The practice, however edifying, has been discontinued, in consequence of the incident we are about to detail.

The clergyman whose duty it was to officiate in the Tolbooth Church had concluded an affecting discourse, part of which was particularly directed to the unfortunate men, Wilson and Robertson, who were in the pew set apart for the persons in their unhappy situation, each secured betwixt two soldiers of the City Guard. The clergyman had reminded them that the next congregation they must join would be that of the just or of the unjust; that the psalms they now heard must be exchanged, in the space of two brief days, for eternal hallelujahs or eternal lamentations; and that this fearful alternative must depend upon the state to which they might be able to bring their minds before the moment of awful preparation; that they should not despair on account of the suddenness of the summons, but rather to feel this comfort in their misery, that, though all who now lifted the voice, or bent the knee, in conjunction with them lay under the same sentence of certain death, *they* only had the advantage of knowing the precise moment at which it should be executed upon them. "Therefore," urged the good man, his voice trembling with emotion, "redeem the time, my unhappy brethren, which is yet left; and remember that, with the grace of Him to whom space and time are but as nothing, salvation may yet be assured, even in the pittance of delay which the laws of your country afford you."

Robertson was observed to weep at these words; but Wilson seemed as one whose brain had not entirely received their meaning, or whose thoughts were deeply impressed with some different subject; an expression so natural to a person in his situation that it excited neither suspicion nor surprise.

The benediction was pronounced as usual, and the congregation was dismissed, many lingering to indulge their curiosity with a more fixed look at the two criminals, who now, as well as their guards, rose up, as if to depart when the crowd should permit them. A murmur of compassion was heard to pervade the spectators, the more general, perhaps, on account of the alleviating circumstances of the case; when all at once, Wilson, who, as we have already noticed, was a very strong man, seized two of the soldiers, one with each hand, and calling at the same time to his companion, " Run, Geordie, run!" threw himself on a third, and fastened his teeth on the collar of his coat. Robertson stood for a second as if thunderstruck, and unable to avail himself of the opportunity of escape; but the cry of "Run, run!" being echoed from many around, whose feelings surprised them into a very natural interest in his behalf, he shook off the grasp of the remaining soldier, threw himself over the pew, mixed with the dispersing congregation, none of whom felt inclined to stop a poor wretch taking this last chance for his life, gained the door of the church, and was lost to all pursuit.

The generous intrepidity which Wilson had displayed on this occasion augmented the feeling of compassion which attended his fate. The public, where their own prejudices are not concerned being easily engaged on the side of disinterestedness and humanity, admired Wilson's behavior, and rejoiced in Robertson's escape. This general feeling was so great that it excited a vague report that Wilson would be rescued at the place of execution, either by the mob or by some of his old associates, or by some second extraordinary and unexpected exertion of strength and courage on his own part. The magistrates thought it their duty to provide against the possibility of disturbance. They ordered out, for protection of the execution of the sentence, the greater part of their own City Guard, under the command of Captain Porteous, a man whose name became too memorable from the melancholy circumstances of the day and subsequent events. It may be necessary to say a word about this person and the corps which he commanded. But the subject is of importance sufficient to deserve another chapter.

CHAPTER III

And thou, great god of aqua-vitæ !
Wha sways the empire of this city,
(When fou we're sometimes capernoity),
Be thou prepared,
To save us frae that black banditti,
The City Guard !
FERGUSON'S *Daft Days.*

CAPTAIN JOHN PORTEOUS, a name memorable in the traditions
of Edinburgh, as well as in the records of criminal jurisprudence, was the son of a citizen of Edinburgh, who endeavored
to breed him up to his own mechanical trade of a tailor. The
youth, however, had a wild and irreclaimable propensity to dissipation, which finally sent him to serve in the corps long maintained in the service of the States of Holland, and called the
Scotch Dutch. Here he learned military discipline ; and returning afterwards, in the course of an idle and wandering life,
to his native city, his services were required by the magistrates
of Edinburgh, in the disturbed year 1715, for disciplining their
City Guard, in which he shortly afterwards received a captain's
commission. It was only by his military skill, and an alert and
resolute character as an officer of police, that he merited this
promotion, for he is said to have been a man of profligate
habits, an unnatural son, and a brutal husband. He was,
however, useful in his station, and his harsh and fierce habits
rendered him formidable to rioters or disturbers of the public
peace.

The corps in which he held his command is, or perhaps we
should rather say *was*, a body of about one hundred and twenty
soldiers, divided into three companies, and regularly armed,
clothed, and embodied. They were chiefly veterans who enlisted in this corps, having the benefit of working at their
trades when they were off duty. These men had the charge
of preserving public order, repressing riots and street robber-
ies, acting, in short, as an armed police, and attending on all
public occasions where confusion or popular disturbance
might be expected.* Poor Ferguson, whose irregularities

* See Edinburgh City Guard. Note 3.

somtimes led him into unpleasant *rencontres* with these military conservators of public order, and who mentions them so often that he may be termed their poet laureate, thus admonishes his readers, warned doubtless by his own experience:

> Gude folk, as ye come frae the fair,
>   Bide yont frae this black squad;
> There's nae sic savages elsewhere
>   Allow'd to wear cockad.

In fact, the soldiers of the City Guard, being, as we have said, in general discharged veterans, who had strength enough remaining for this municipal duty, and being, moreover, for the greater part, Highlanders, were neither by birth, education, nor former habits trained to endure with much patience the insults of the rabble, or the provoking petulance of truant schoolboys, and idle debauchees of all descriptions, with whom their occupation brought them into contact. On the contrary, the tempers of the poor old fellows were soured by the indignities with which the mob distinguished them on many occasions, and frequently might have required the soothing strains of the poet we have just quoted—

> O soldiers! for your ain dear sakes,
> For Scotland's love, the Land o' Cakes,
> Gie not her bairns sic deadly paiks,
>   Nor be sae rude,
> Wi' firelock or Lochaber axe,
>   As spill their bluid!

On all occasions when a holiday licensed some riot and irregularity, a skirmish with these veterans was a favorite recreation with the rabble of Edinburgh. These pages may perhaps see the light when many have in fresh recollection such onsets as we allude to. But the venerable corps with whom the contention was held may now be considered as totally extinct. Of late the gradual diminution of these civic soldiers reminds one of the abatement of King Lear's hundred knights. The edicts of each succeeding set of magistrates have, like those of Goneril and Regan, diminished this venerable band with the similar question, "What need we five and twenty?—ten?—or five?" And it is now nearly come to, "What need one?" A spectre may indeed here and there still be seen, of an old gray-headed and gray-bearded Highlander, with war-worn features, but bent double by age; dressed in an old-fashioned cocked hat, bound with white tape instead of silver lace, and in coat, waistcoat, and breeches of a muddy-colored red, bearing in

his withered hand an ancient weapon, called a Lochaber axe,
a long pole, namely, with an axe at the extremity and a hook
at the back of the hatchet.*   Such a phantom of former days
still creeps, I have been informed, round the statue of Charles
the Second, in the Parliament Square, as if the image of a
Stuart were the last refuge for any memorial of our ancient
manners ; and one or two others are supposed to glide around
the door of the guard-house assigned to them in the Luckenbooths when their ancient refuge in the High Street was laid
low.†   But the fate of manuscripts bequeathed to friends and
executors is so uncertain, that the narrative containing these
frail memorials of the old Town Guard of Edinburgh, who,
with their grim and valiant corporal, John Dhu, the fiercest-
looking fellow I ever saw, were, in my boyhood, the alternate
terror and derision of the petulant brood of the High School,
may, perhaps, only come to light when all memory of the in-
stitution has faded away, and then serve as an illustration of
Kay's caricatures, who has preserved the features of some of
their heroes.   In the preceding generation, when there was a
perpetual alarm for the plots and activity of the Jacobites,
some pains were taken by the magistrates of Edinburgh to
keep this corps, though composed always of such materials as
we have noticed, in a more effective state than was afterwards
judged necessary, when their most dangerous service was to
skirmish with the rabble on the king's birthday.   They were,
therefore, more the objects of hatred, and less that of scorn,
than they were afterwards accounted.

To Captain John Porteous the honor of his command and
of his corps seems to have been a matter of high interest and
importance.   He was exceedingly incensed against Wilson for
the affront which he construed him to have put upon his soldiers, in the effort he made for the liberation of his companion, and expressed himself most ardently on the subject.   He
was no less indignant at the report that there was an intention to rescue Wilson himself from the gallows, and uttered
many threats and imprecations upon that subject, which were
afterwards remembered to his disadvantage.   In fact, if a good
deal of determination and promptitude rendered Porteous, in
one respect, fit to command guards designed to suppress popular commotion, he seems, on the other, to have been disqualified for a charge so delicate by a hot and surly temper, always
too ready to come to blows and violence, a character void of

* This hook was to enable the bearer of the Lochaber axe to scale a gateway, by
grappling the top of the door and swinging himself up by the staff of his weapon.
† See Last March of the City Guard.   Note 4.

principle, and a disposition to regard the rabble, who seldom failed to regale him and his soldiers with some marks of their displeasure, as declared enemies, upon whom it was natural and justifiable that he should seek opportunities of vengeance. Being, however, the most active and trustworthy among the captains of the City Guard, he was the person to whom the magistrates confided the command of the soldiers appointed to keep the peace at the time of Wilson's execution. He was ordered to guard the gallows and scaffold, with about eighty men, all the disposable force that could be spared for that duty.

But the magistrates took further precautions, which affected Porteous's pride very deeply. They requested the assistance of part of a regular infantry regiment, not to attend upon the execution, but to remain drawn up on the principal street of the city, during the time that it went forward, in order to intimidate the multitude, in case they should be disposed to be unruly, with a display of force which could not be resisted without desperation. It may sound ridiculous in our ears, considering the fallen state of this ancient civic corps, that its officer should have felt punctiliously jealous of its honor. Yet so it was. Captain Porteous resented as an indignity the introducing the Welsh Fusileers within the city, and drawing them up in the street where no drums but his own were allowed to be sounded without the special command or permission of the magistrates. As he could not show his ill-humor to his patrons the magistrates, it increased his indignation and his desire to be revenged on the unfortunate criminal Wilson, and all who favored him. These internal emotions of jealousy and rage wrought a change on the man's mien and bearing, visible to all who saw him on the fatal morning when Wilson was appointed to suffer. Porteous's ordinary appearance was rather favorable. He was about the middle size, stout, and well made, having a military air, and yet rather a gentle and mild countenance. His complexion was brown, his face somewhat fretted with the scars of the smallpox, his eyes rather languid than keen or fierce. On the present occasion, however, it seemed to those who saw him as if he were agitated by some evil demon. His step was irregular, his voice hollow and broken, his countenance pale, his eyes staring and wild, his speech imperfect and confused, and his whole appearance so disordered that many remarked he seemed to be "fey," a Scottish expression, meaning the state of those who are driven on to their impending fate by the strong impulse of some irresistible necessity.

One part of his conduct was truly diabolical, if, indeed, it has not been exaggerated by the general prejudice entertained against his memory. When Wilson, the unhappy criminal, was delivered to him by the keeper of the prison, in order that he might be conducted to the place of execution, Porteous, not satisfied with the usual precautions to prevent escape, ordered him to be manacled. This might be justifiable from the character and bodily strength of the malefactor, as well as from the apprehensions so generally entertained of an expected rescue. But the handcuffs which were produced being found too small for the wrists of a man so big-boned as Wilson, Porteous proceeded with his own hands, and by great exertion of strength, to force them till they clasped together, to the exquisite torture of the unhappy criminal. Wilson remonstrated against such barbarous usage, declaring that the pain distracted his thoughts from the subjects of meditation proper to his unhappy condition.

"It signifies little," replied Captain Porteous ; "your pain will be soon at an end."

"Your cruelty is great," answered the sufferer. "You know not how soon you yourself may have occasion to ask the mercy which you are now refusing to a fellow-creature. May God forgive you !"

These words, long afterwards quoted and remembered, were all that passed between Porteous and his prisoner ; but as they took air and became known to the people, they greatly increased the popular compassion for Wilson, and excited a proportionate degree of indignation against Porteous, against whom, as strict, and even violent, in the discharge of his unpopular office, the common people had some real, and many imaginary, causes of complaint.

When the painful procession was completed, and Wilson, with the escort, had arrived at the scaffold in the Grassmarket, there appeared no signs of that attempt to rescue him which had occasioned such precautions. The multitude, in general, looked on with deeper interest than at ordinary executions ; and there might be seen on the countenances of many a stern and indignant expression, like that with which the ancient Cameronians might be supposed to witness the execution of their brethren, who glorified the Covenant on the same occasion, and at the same spot. But there was no attempt at violence. Wilson himself seemed disposed to hasten over the space that divided time from eternity. The devotions proper and usual on such occasions were no sooner finished than he submitted to his fate, and the sentence of the law was fulfilled.

He had been suspended on the gibbet so long as to be totally deprived of life, when at once, as if occasioned by some newly received impulse, there arose a tumult among the multitude. Many stones were thrown at Porteous and his guards; some mischief was done ; and the mob continued to press forward with whoops, shrieks, howls, and exclamations. A young fellow, with a sailor's cap slouched over his face, sprung on the scaffold and cut the rope by which the criminal was suspended. Others approached to carry off the body, either to secure for it a decent grave, or to try, perhaps, some means of resuscitation. Captain Porteous was wrought, by this appearance of insurrection against his authority, into a rage so headlong as made him forget that, the sentence having been fully executed, it was his duty not to engage in hostilities with the misguided multitude, but to draw off his men as fast as possible. He sprung from the scaffold, snatched a musket from one of his soldiers, commanded the party to give fire, and, as several eye-witnesses concurred in swearing, set them the example by discharging his piece and shooting a man dead on the spot. Several soldiers obeyed his command or followed his example ; six or seven persons were slain, and a great many were hurt and wounded.

After this act of violence, the Captain proceeded to withdraw his men towards their guard-house in the High Street. The mob were not so much intimidated as incensed by what had been done. They pursued the soldiers with execrations, accompanied by volleys of stones. As they pressed on them, the rearmost soldiers turned and again fired with fatal aim and execution. It is not accurately known whether Porteous commanded this second act of violence ; but of course the odium of the whole transactions of the fatal day attached to him, and to him alone. He arrived at the guard-house, dismissed his soldiers, and went to make his report to the magistrates concerning the unfortunate events of the day.

Apparently by this time Captain Porteous had begun to doubt the propriety of his own conduct, and the reception he met with from the magistrates was such as to make him still more anxious to gloss it over. He denied that he had given orders to fire ; he denied he had fired with his own hand ; he even produced the fusee which he carried as an officer for examination : it was found still loaded. Of three cartridges which he was seen to put in his pouch that morning, two were still there ; a white handkerchief was thrust into the muzzle

of the piece, and returned unsoiled or blackened. To the
defence founded on these circumstances it was answered, that
Porteous had not used his own piece, but had been seen to
take one from a soldier. Among the many who had been
killed and wounded by the unhappy fire, there were several
of better rank ; for even the humanity of such soldiers as fired
over the heads of the mere rabble around the scaffold proved
in some instances fatal to persons who were stationed in windows, or observed the melancholy scene from a distance.
The voice of public indignation was loud and general ; and,
ere men's tempers had time to cool, the trial of Captain Porteous took place before the High Court of Justiciary. After
a long and patient hearing, the jury had the difficult duty of
balancing the positive evidence of many persons, and those
of respectability, who deposed positively to the prisoner's
commanding his soldiers to fire, and himself firing his piece,
of which some swore that they saw the smoke and flash, and
beheld a man drop at whom it was pointed, with the negative
testimony of others, who, though well stationed for seeing
what had passed, neither heard Porteous give orders to fire,
nor saw him fire himself ; but, on the contrary, averred that
the first shot was fired by a soldier who stood close by him.
A great part of his defence was also founded on the turbulence of the mob, which witnesses, according to their feelings,
their predilections, and their opportunities of observation,
represented differently ; some describing as a formidable riot
what others represented as a trifling disturbance, such as
always used to take place on the like occasions, when the executioner of the law and the men commissioned to protect
him in his task were generally exposed to some indignities.
The verdict of the jury sufficiently shows how the evidence
preponderated in their minds. It declared that John Porteous fired a gun among the people assembled at the execution ;
that he gave orders to his soldiers to fire, by which many persons were killed and wounded ; but, at the same time, that
the prisoner and his guard had been wounded and beaten by
stones thrown at them by the multitude. Upon this verdict,
the Lords of Justiciary passed sentence of death against Captain John Porteous, adjudging him, in the common form, to
be hanged on a gibbet at the common place of execution, on
Wednesday, 8th September, 1736, and all his movable property to be forfeited to the king's use, according to the Scottish law in cases of wilful murder.

CHAPTER IV

The hour's come, but not the man. *
                                  Kelpie.

On the day when the unhappy Porteous was expected to suffer the sentence of the law, the place of execution, extensive as it is, was crowded almost to suffocation. There was not a window in all the lofty tenements around it, or in the steep and crooked street, called the Bow, by which the fatal procession was to descend from the High Street, that was not absolutely filled with spectators. The uncommon height and antique appearance of these houses, some of which were formerly the property of the Knights Templars and the Knights of St. John, and still exhibit on their fronts and gables the iron cross of these orders, gave additional effect to a scene in itself so striking. The area of the Grassmarket resembled a huge dark lake or sea of human heads, in the centre of which arose the fatal tree, tall, black, and ominous, from which dangled the deadly halter. Every object takes interest from its uses and associations, and the erect beam and empty noose, things so simple in themselves, became, on such an occasion, objects of terror and of solemn interest.

Amid so numerous an assembly there was scarcely a word spoken, save in whispers. The thirst of vengeance was in some degree allayed by its supposed certainty ; and even the populace, with deeper feeling than they are wont to entertain, suppressed all clamorous exultation, and prepared to enjoy the scene of retaliation in triumph, silent and decent, though stern and relentless. It seemed as if the depth of their hatred to the unfortunate criminal scorned to display itself in anything resembling the more noisy current of their ordinary feelings. Had a stranger consulted only the evidence of his ears, he might have supposed that so vast a multitude were assembled for some purpose which affected them with the deepest sorrow, and stilled those noises which, on all ordinary occasions, arise from such a concourse ; but if he gazed upon

---

* See The Kelpie's Voice. Note 5.

their faces he would have been instantly undeceived. The compressed lip, the bent brow, the stern and flashing eye of almost every one on whom he looked, conveyed the expression of men come to glut their sight with triumphant revenge. It is probable that the appearance of the criminal might have somewhat changed the temper of the populace in his favor, and that they might in the moment of death have forgiven the man against whom their resentment had been so fiercely heated. It had, however, been destined that the mutability of their sentiments was not to be exposed to this trial.

The usual hour for producing the criminal had been past for many minutes, yet the spectators observed no symptom of his appearance. "Would they venture to defraud public justice?" was the question which men began anxiously to ask at each other. The first answer in every case was bold and positive—"They dare not." But when the point was further canvassed, other opinions were entertained, and various causes of doubt were suggested. Porteous had been a favorite officer of the magistracy of the city, which, being a numerous and fluctuating body, requires for its support a degree of energy in its functionaries which the individuals who compose it cannot at all times alike be supposed to possess in their own persons. It was remembered that in the information for Porteous (the paper, namely, in which his case was stated to the judges of the criminal court), he had been described by his counsel as the person on whom the magistrates chiefly relied in all emergencies of uncommon difficulty. It was argued, too, that his conduct, on the unhappy occasion of Wilson's execution, was capable of being attributed to an imprudent excess of zeal in the execution of his duty, a motive for which those under whose authority he acted might be supposed to have great sympathy. And as these considerations might move the magistrates to make a favorable representation of Porteous's case, there were not wanting others in the higher departments of government which would make such suggestions favorably listened to.

The mob of Edinburgh, when thoroughly excited, had been at all times one of the fiercest which could be found in Europe; and of late years they had risen repeatedly against the government, and sometimes not without temporary success. They were conscious, therefore, that they were no favorites with the rulers of the period, and that, if Captain Porteous's violence was not altogether regarded as good service, it might certainly be thought that to visit it with a capital punishment would render it both delicate and dangerous for future officers, in the same circumstances, to act with effect in repressing tumults. There is also a natural feeling, on the part of all members of government, for the general maintenance of authority; and it seemed not unlikely that what to the relatives of the sufferers appeared a wanton and unprovoked massacre, should be otherwise viewed in the cabinet of St. James's. It might be there supposed that, upon the whole matter, Captain Porteous was in the exercise of a trust delegated to him by the lawful civil authority; that he had been assaulted by the populace, and several of his men hurt; and that, in finally repelling force by force, his conduct could be fairly imputed to no other motive than self-defence in the discharge of his duty.

These considerations, of themselves very powerful, induced the spectators to apprehend the possibility of a reprieve; and to the various causes which might interest the rulers in his favor the lower part of the rabble added one which was peculiarly well adapted to their comprehension. It was averred, in order to increase the odium against Porteous, that, while he repressed with the utmost severity the slightest excesses of the poor, he not only overlooked the license of the young nobles and gentry, but was very willing to lend them the countenance of his official authority in execution of such loose pranks as it was chiefly his duty to have restrained. This suspicion, which was perhaps much exaggerated, made a deep impression on the minds of the populace; and when several of the higher rank joined in a petition recommending Porteous to the mercy of the crown, it was generally supposed he owed their favor not to any conviction of the hardship of his case, but to the fear of losing a convenient accomplice in their debaucheries. It is scarcely necessary to say how much this suspicion augmented the people's detestation of this obnoxious criminal, as well as their fear of his escaping the sentence pronounced against him.

While these arguments were stated and replied to, and canvassed and supported, the hitherto silent expectation of the people became changed into that deep and agitating murmur which is sent forth by the ocean before the tempest begins to howl. The crowded populace, as if their motions had corresponded with the unsettled state of their minds, fluctuated to and fro without any visible cause of impulse, like the agitation of the waters called by sailors the ground-swell. The news, which the magistrates had almost hesitated to communicate to them, were at length announced, and spread among the spectators with a rapidity like lightning. A reprieve from the Secretary of State's office, under the hand of his Grace the Duke of Newcastle, had arrived, intimating the pleasure of Queen Caroline (regent of the kingdom during the absence of George II. on the Continent), that the execution of the sentence of death pronounced against John Porteous, late Captain-Lieutenant of the City Guard of Edinburgh, present prisoner in the tolbooth of that city, be respited for six weeks from the time appointed for his execution.

The assembled spectators of almost all degrees, whose minds had been wound up to the pitch which we have described, uttered a groan, or rather a roar of indignation and disappointed revenge, similar to that of a tiger from whom his meal has been rent by his keeper when he was just about to devour it. This fierce exclamation seemed to forebode some immediate explosion of popular resentment, and, in fact, such had been expected by the magistrates, and the necessary measures had been taken to repress it. But the shout was not repeated, nor did any sudden tumult ensue, such as it appeared to announce. The populace seemed to be ashamed of having expressed their disappointment in a vain clamor, and the sound changed, not into the silence which had preceded the arrival of these stunning news, but into stifled mutterings, which each group maintained among themselves, and which were blended into one deep and hoarse murmur which floated above the assembly.

Yet still, though all expectation of the execution was over the mob remained assembled, stationary, as it were, through very resentment, gazing on the preparations for death, which had now been made in vain, and stimulating their feelings by recalling the various claims which Wilson might have had on royal mercy, from the mistaken motives on which he acted, as well as from the generosity he had displayed towards his accomplice. "This man," they said, "the brave, the resolute, the generous, was executed to death without mercy for stealing a purse of gold, which in some sense he might consider as a fair reprisal; while the profligate satellite, who took advantage of a trifling tumult, inseparable from such occasions, to shed the blood of twenty of his fellow-citizens, is deemed a fitting object for the exercise of the royal prerogative of mercy. Is this to be borne? Would our fathers have borne it? Are not we, like them, Scotsmen and burghers of Edinburgh?"

The officers of justice began now to remove the scaffold and other preparations which had been made for the execution, in hopes, by doing so, to accelerate the dispersion of the multitude. The measure had the desired effect ; for no sooner had the fatal tree been unfixed from the large stone pedestal or socket in which it was secured, and sunk slowly down upon the wain intended to remove it to the place where it was usually deposited, than the populace, after giving vent to their feelings in a second shout of rage and mortification, began slowly to disperse to their usual abodes and occupations.

The windows were in like manner gradually deserted, and groups of the more decent class of citizens formed themselves, as if waiting to return homewards when the streets should be cleared of the rabble. Contrary to what is frequently the case, this description of persons agreed in general with the sentiments of their inferiors, and considered the cause as common to all ranks. Indeed, as we have already noticed, it was by no means among the lowest class of the spectators, or those most likely to be engaged in the riot at Wilson's execution, that the fatal fire of Porteous's soldiers had taken effect. Several persons were killed who were looking out at windows at the scene, who could not of course belong to the rioters, and were persons of decent rank and conditions. The burghers, therefore, resenting the loss which had fallen on their own body, and proud and tenacious of their rights, as the citizens of Edinburgh have at all times been, were greatly exasperated at the unexpected respite of Captain Porteous.

It was noticed at the time, and afterwards more particularly remembered, that, while the mob were in the act of dispersing, several individuals were seen busily passing from one place and one group of people to another, remaining long with none, but whispering for a little time with those who appeared to be declaiming most violently against the conduct of government. These active agents had the appearance of men from the country, and were generally supposed to be old friends and confederates of Wilson, whose minds were of course highly excited against Porteous.

If, however, it was the intention of these men to stir the multitude to any sudden act of mutiny, it seemed for the time to be fruitless. The rabble, as well as the more decent part of the assembly, dispersed, and went home peaceably ; and it was only by observing the moody discontent on their brows, or catching the tenor of the conversation they held with each other, that a stranger could estimate the state of their minds. We will give the reader this advantage, by associating ourselves with one of the numerous groups who were painfully ascending the steep declivity of the West Bow, to return to their dwellings in the Lawnmarket.

"An unco thing this, Mrs. Howden," said old Peter Plumdamas to his neighbor the rouping-wife, or saleswoman, as he offered her his arm to assist her in the toilsome ascent, "to see the grit folk at Lunnon set their face against law and gospel, and let loose sic a reprobate as Porteous upon a peaceable town!"

"And to think o' the weary walk they hae gien us," answered Mrs. Howden, with a groan; "and sic a comfortable window as I had gotten, too, just within a pennystane cast of the scaffold—I could hae heard every word the minister said—and to pay twal pennies for my stand, and a' for naething!"

"I am judging," said Mr. Plumdamas, "that this reprieve wadna stand gude in the auld Scots law, when the kingdom *was* a kingdom."

"I dinna ken muckle about the law," answered Mrs. Howden; "but I ken, when we had a king, and a chancellor, and parliament men o' our ain, we could aye peeble them wi' stanes when they werena gude bairns. But naebody's nails can reach the length o' Lunnon."

"Weary on Lunnon, and a' that e'er came out o't!" said Miss Grizel Damahoy, an ancient seamstress; "they hae taen awa' our parliament, and they hae oppressed our trade. Our gentles will hardly allow that a Scots needle can sew ruffles on a sark, or lace on an owerlay."

"Ye may say that, Miss Damahoy, and I ken o' them that hae gotten raisins frae Lunnon by forpits at ance," responded Plumdamas; "and then sic an host of idle English gaugers and excisemen as hae come down to vex and torment us, that an honest man canna fetch sae muckle as a bit anker o' brandy frae Leith to the Lawnmarket, but he's like to be rubbit o' the very gudes he's bought and paid for. Weel, I winna justify Andrew Wilson for pitting hands on what wasna his; but if he took nae mair than his ain, there's an awfu' difference between that and the fact this man stands for."

"If ye speak about the law," said Mrs. Howden, "here comes Mr. Saddletree, that can settle it as weel as ony on the bench."

The party she mentioned, a grave elderly person, with a superb periwig, dressed in a decent suit of sad-colored clothes, came up as she spoke, and courteously gave his arm to Miss Grizel Damahoy.

It may be necessary to mention that Mr. Bartoline Saddletree kept an excellent and highly esteemed shop for harness, saddles, etc., etc., at the sign of the Golden Nag, at the head of Bess Wynd.* His genius, however (as he himself and most of his neighbors conceived), lay towards the weightier matters of the law, and he failed not to give frequent attendance upon the pleadings and arguments of the lawyers and judges in the neighboring square, where, to say the truth, he was oftener to be found than would have consisted with his own emolument; but that his wife, an active painstaking person, could, in his absence, make an admirable shift to please the customers and scold the journeymen. This good lady was in the habit of letting her husband take his way, and go on improving his stock of legal knowledge without interruption; but, as if in requital, she insisted upon having her own will in the domestic and commercial departments which he abandoned to her. Now, as Bartoline Saddletree had a considerable gift of words, which he mistook for eloquence, and conferred more liberally upon the society in which he lived than was at all times gracious and acceptable, there went forth a saying, with which wags used sometimes to interrupt his rhetoric, that, as he had a golden nag at his door, so he had a gray mare in his shop. This reproach induced Mr. Saddletree, on all occasions, to assume rather a haughty and stately tone towards his good woman, a circumstance by which she seemed very little affected, unless he attempted to exercise any real authority, when she never failed to fly into open rebellion. But such extremes Bartoline seldom provoked; for, like the gentle King Jamie, he was fonder of talking of authority than really exercising it. This turn of mind was on the whole lucky for him; since his substance was increased without any trouble on his part, or any interruption of his favorite studies.

This word in explanation has been thrown in to the reader while Saddletree was laying down, with great precision, the law upon Porteous's case, by which he arrived at this conclusion, that, if Porteous had fired five minutes sooner, before Wilson was cut down, he would have been *versans in licito*, engaged, that is, in a lawful act, and only liable to be punished *propter excessum*, or for lack of discretion, which might have mitigated the punishment to *pœna ordinaria.*

"Discretion!" echoed Mrs. Howden, on whom, it may well be supposed, the fineness of this distinction was entirely thrown away, "whan had Jock Porteous either grace, discretion, or gude manners? I mind when his father——"

*See Bess Wynd. Note 6.

"But, Mrs. Howden——" said Saddletree.

"And I," said Miss Damahoy, "mind when his mother——"

"Miss Damahoy——" entreated the interrupted orator.

"And I," said Plumdamas, "mind when his wife——"

"Mr. Plumdamas—Mrs. Howden—Miss Damahoy," again implored the orator, "mind the distinction," as Counsellor Crossmyloof says—'I,' says he, 'take a distinction.' Now, the body of the criminal being cut down, and the execution ended, Porteous was no longer official; the act which he came to protect and guard being done and ended, he was no better than *cuivis ex populo.*"

"*Quivis—quivis*, Mr. Saddletree, craving your pardon," said, with a prolonged emphasis on the first syllable, Mr. Butler, the deputy schoolmaster of a parish near Edinburgh, who at that moment came up behind them as the false Latin was uttered.

"What signifies interrupting me, Mr. Butler ?—but I am glad to see ye notwithstanding. I speak after Counsellor Crossmyloof, and he said *cuivis.*"

"If Counsellor Crossmyloof used the dative for the nominative, I would have crossed *his* loof with a tight leathern strap, Mr. Saddletree; there is not a boy on the booby form but should have been scourged for such a solecism in grammar."

"I speak Latin like a lawyer, Mr. Butler, and not like a schoolmaster," retorted Saddletree.

"Scarce like a schoolboy, I think," rejoined Butler.

"It matters little," said Bartoline; "all I mean to say is, that Porteous has become liable to the *pœna extra ordinem* or capital punishment, which is to say, in plain Scotch, the gallows, simply because he did not fire when he was in office, but waited till the body was cut down, the execution whilk he had in charge to guard implemented, and he himself exonered of the public trust imposed on him."

"But, Mr. Saddletree," said Plumdamas, "do ye really think John Porteous's case wad hae been better if he had begun firing before ony stanes were flung at a' ?"

"Indeed do I, neighbor Plumdamas," replied Bartoline, confidently, "he being then in point of trust and in point of power, the execution being but inchoate, or, at least, not implemented, or finally ended ; but after Wilson was cut down it was a' ower—he was clean exauctorate, and had nae mair ado but to get awa' wi' his Guard up this West Bow as fast as if there had been a caption after him.   And this is law, for I heard it laid down by Lord Vincovincentem."

"Vincovincentem !   Is he a lord of state or a lord of seat ? " inquired Mrs. Howden.

"A lord of seat—a lord of session.   I fash mysell little wi' lords o' state ; they vex me wi' a wheen idle questions about their saddles, and curpels, and holsters, and horse-furniture, and what they'll cost, and whan they'll be ready.   A wheen galloping geese ! my wife may serve the like o' them."

"And so might she, in her day, hae served the best lord in the land, for as little as ye think o' her, Mr. Saddletree," said Mrs. Howden, somewhat indignant at the contemptuous way in which her gossip was mentioned ; " when she and I were twa gilpies, we little thought to hae sitten doun wi' the like o' my auld Davie Howden, or you either, Mr. Saddletree."

While Saddletree, who was not bright at a reply, was cudgelling his brains for an answer to this home-thrust, Miss Damahoy broke in on him.

" And as for the lords of state," said Miss Damahoy, "ye suld mind the riding o' the parliament, Mr. Saddletree, in the gude auld time before the Union : a year's rent o' mony a gude estate gaed for horse-graith and harnessing, forbye broidered robes and foot-mantles, that wad hae stude by their lane wi' gold brocade, and that were muckle in my ain line."

" Ay, and then the lusty banqueting, with sweetmeats and comfits wet and dry, and dried fruits of divers sorts," said Plumdamas.   " But Scotland was Scotland in these days."

" I'll tell ye what it is, neighbors," said Mrs. Howden, " I'll ne'er believe Scotland is Scotland ony mair, if our kindly Scots sit doun with the affront they hae gien us this day.   It's not only the bluid that *is* shed, but the bluid that might hae been shed, that's required at our hands.   There was my daughter's wean, little Eppie Daidle—my oe, ye ken, Miss Grizel—had played the truant frae the school, as bairns will do, ye ken, Mr. Butler——"

" And for which," interjected Mr. Butler, "they should be soundly scourged by their well-wishers."

" And had just cruppen to the gallows' foot to see the hanging, as was natural for a wean ; and what for mightna she hae been shot as weel as the rest o' them, and where wad we a' hae been then ?   I wonder how Queen Carline—if her name be Carline—wad hae liked to hae had ane o' her ain bairns in sic a venture ? "

" Report says," answered Butler, " that such a circumstance would not have distressed her Majesty beyond endurance "

"Aweel," said Mrs. Howden, "the sum o' the matter is, that, were I a man, I wad hae amends o' Jock Porteous, be the upshot what like o't, if a' the carles and carlines in England had sworn to the nay-say."

"I would claw down the tolbooth door wi' my nails," said Miss Grizel, "but I wad be at him."

"Ye may be very right, ladies," said Butler, "but I would not advise you to speak so loud."

"Speak!" exclaimed both the ladies together, "there will be naething else spoken about frae the Weigh House to the Water Gate till this is either ended or mended."

The females now departed to their respective places of abode. Plumdamas joined the other two gentlemen in drinking their "meridian," a bumper-dram of brandy, as they passed the well-known low-browed shop in the Lawnmarket where they were wont to take that refreshment. Mr. Plumdamas then departed towards his shop, and Mr. Butler, who happened to have some particular occasion for the rein of an old bridle— the truants of that busy day could have anticipated its application—walked down the Lawnmarket with Mr. Saddletree, each talking as he could get a word thrust in, the one on the laws of Scotland, the other on those of syntax, and neither listening to a word which his companion uttered.

CHAPTER V

"THERE has been Jock Driver, the carrier, here, speering about his new graith," said Mrs. Saddletree to her husband, as he crossed his threshold, not with the purpose, by any means, of consulting him upon his own affairs, but merely to intimate, by a gentle recapitulation, how much duty she had gone through in his absence.

"Weel," replied Bartoline, and deigned not a word more.

"And the Laird of Girdingburst has had his running footman here, and ca'd himsell—he's a civil pleasant young gentleman—to see when the broidered saddle-cloth for his sorrel horse will be ready, for he wants it again the Kelso races."

"Weel, aweel," replied Bartoline, as laconically as before.

"And his lordship, the Earl of Blazonbury, Lord Flash and Flame, is like to be clean daft that the harness for the six Flanders mears, wi' the crests, coronets, housings, and mountings conform, are no sent hame according to promise gien."

"Weel, weel, weel—weel, weel, gudewife," said Saddletree, "if he gangs daft, we'll hae him cognosced—it's a' very weel."

"It's weel that ye think sae, Mr. Saddletree," answered his helpmate, rather nettled at the indifference with which her report was received; "there's mony ane wad hae thought themselves affronted if sae mony customers had ca'd and naebody to answer them but womenfolk; for a' the lads were aff, as soon as your back was turned, to see Porteous hanged, that might be counted upon; and sae, you no being at hame——"

"Houts, Mrs. Saddletree," said Bartoline, with an air of consequence, "dinna deave me wi' your nonsense; I was under the necessity of being elsewhere: *non omnia*, as Mr. Crossmyloof said, when he was called by two macers at once—*non omnia possumus—pessimus—possimis*—I ken our law Latin offends Mr. Butler's ears, but it means 'Naebody,' an it were the Lord President himsell, 'can do twa turns at ance.'"

"Very right, Mr. Saddletree," answered his careful helpmate, with a sarcastic smile; "and nae doubt it's a decent thing to leave your wife to look after young gentlemen's saddles and bridles, when ye gang to see a man that never did ye nae ill raxing a halter."

"Woman," said Saddletree, assuming an elevated tone, to which the "meridian" had somewhat contributed, "desist— I say forbear, from intromitting with affairs thou canst not understand. D'ye think I was born to sit here broggin an elshin through bend-leather, when sic men as Duncan Forbes and that other Arniston chield there, without muckle greater parts, if the close-head speak true, than mysell, maun be presidents and king's advocates, nae doubt, and wha but they ? Whereas, were favor equally distribute, as in the days of the wight Wallace——"

"I ken naething we wad hae gotten by the wight Wallace," said Mrs. Saddletree, "unless, as I hae heard the auld folk tell, they fought in thae days wi' bend-leather guns, and then it's a chance but what, if he had bought them, he might have forgot to pay for them.   And as for the greatness of your parts, Bartley, the folk in the close-head maun ken mair about them than I do, if they make sic a report of them."

"I tell ye, woman," said Saddletree, in high dudgeon, "that ye ken naething about these matters. In Sir William Wallace's days there was nae man pinned down to sic a slavish wark as a saddler's, for they got ony leather graith that they had use for ready-made out of Holland."

"Well," said Butler, who was, like many of his profession, something of a humorist and dry joker, "if that be the case, Mr. Saddletree, I think we have changed for the better ; since we make our own harness, and only import our lawyers from Holland."

"It's ower true, Mr. Butler," answered Bartoline, with a sigh ; "if I had had the luck—or rather, if my father had had the sense to send me to Leyden and Utrecht to learn the *Substitutes* and *Pandex*——"

"You mean the *Institutes*—Justinian's *Institutes*, Mr. Saddletree ?" said Butler.

"Institutes and substitutes are synonymous words, Mr. Butler, and used indifferently as such in deeds of tailzie, as you may see in Balfour's *Practiques*, or Dallas of St. Martin's *Styles*.   I understand these things pretty weel, I thank God ; but I own I should have studied in Holland."

"To comfort you, you might not have been farther forward than you are now, Mr. Saddletree," replied Mr. Butler; "for our Scottish advocates are an aristocratic race. Their brass is of the right Corinthian quality, and *Non cuivis contigit adire Corinthum.* Aha, Mr. Saddletree!"

"And aha, Mr. Butler," rejoined Bartoline, upon whom, as may be well supposed, the jest was lost, and all but the sound of the words, "ye said a gliff syne it was *quivis,* and now I heard ye say *cuivis* with my ain ears, as plain as ever I heard a word at the fore-bar."

"Give me your patience, Mr. Saddletree, and I'll explain the discrepancy in three words," said Butler, as pedantic in his own department, though with infinitely more judgment and learning, as Bartoline was in his self-assumed profession of the law. "Give me your patience for a moment. You'll grant that the nominative case is that by which a person or thing is nominated or designed, and which may be called the primary case, all others being formed from it by alterations of the termination in the learned languages, and by prepositions in our modern Babylonian jargons? You'll grant me that, I suppose, Mr. Saddletree?"

"I dinna ken whether I will or no—*ad avisandum,* ye ken—naebody should be in a hurry to make admissions, either in point of law or in point of fact," said Saddletree, looking, or endeavoring to look, as if he understood what was said.

"And the dative case——" continued Butler.

"I ken what a tutor dative is," said Saddletree, "readily enough."

"The dative case," resumed the grammarian, "is that in which anything is given or assigned as properly belonging to a person or thing. You cannot deny that, I am sure."

"I am sure I'll no grant it though," said Saddletree.

"Then, what the *deevil* d'ye take the nominative and the dative cases to be?" said Butler, hastily, and surprised at once out of his decency of expression and accuracy of pronunciation.

"I'll tell you that at leisure, Mr. Butler," said Saddletree, with a very knowing look. "I'll take a day to see and answer every article of your condescendence, and then I'll hold you to confess or deny, as accords."

"Come, come, Mr. Saddletree," said his wife, "we'll hae nae confessions and condescendences here, let them deal in thae sort o' wares that are paid for them; they suit the like o' us as ill as a demi-pique saddle would set a draught ox."

"Aha!" said Mr. Butler, "*Optat ephippia bos piger,*

nothing new under the sun. But it was a fair hit of Mrs. Saddletree, however."

"And it wad far better become ye, Mr. Saddletree," continued his helpmate, "since ye say ye hae skeel o' the law, to try if ye can do onything for Effie Deans, puir thing, that's lying up in the tolbooth yonder, cauld, and hungry, and comfortless. A servant lass of ours, Mr. Butler, and as innocent a lass, to my thinking, and as usefu' in the shop. When Mr. Saddletree gangs out—and ye're aware he's seldom at hame when there's ony o' the plea-houses open—puir Effie used to help me to tumble the bundles o' barkened leather up and down, and range out the gudes, and suit a'body's humors. And troth, she could aye please the customers wi' her answers, for she was aye civil, and a bonnier lass wasna in Auld Reekie. And when folk were hasty and unreasonable, she could serve them better than me, that am no sae young as I hae been, Mr. Butler, and a wee bit short in the temper into the bargain; for when there's ower mony folks crying on me at anes, and nane but ae tongue to answer them, folk maun speak hastily, or they'll ne'er get through their wark. Sae I miss Effie daily."

"*De die in diem*," added Saddletree.

"I think," said Butler, after a good deal of hesitation, "I have seen the girl in the shop, a modest-looking, fair-haired girl?"

"Ay, ay, that's just puir Effie," said her mistress. "How she was abandoned to hersell, or whether she was sackless o' the sinfu' deed, God in Heaven knows; but if she's been guilty, she's been sair tempted, and I wad amaist take my Bible aith she hasna been hersell at the time."

Butler had by this time become much agitated; he fidgeted up and down the shop, and showed the greatest agitation that a person of such strict decorum could be supposed to give way to. "Was not this girl," he said, "the daughter of David Deans, that had the parks at St. Leonard's taken? and has she not a sister?"

"In troth has she—puir Jeanie Deans, ten years aulder than hersell; she was here greeting a wee while syne about her tittie. And what could I say to her, but that she behoved to come and speak to Mr. Saddletree when he was at hame? It wasna that I thought Mr. Saddletree could do her or ony other body muckle gude or ill, but it wad aye serve to keep the puir thing's heart up for a wee while; and let sorrow come when sorrow maun."

"Ye're mistaen, though, gudewife," said Saddletree, scornfully, "for I could hae gien her great satisfaction; I could hae proved to her that her sister was indicted upon the statute 1690, chap. 1 [21]—for the mair ready prevention of child-murder, for concealing her pregnancy, and giving no account of the child which she had borne."

"I hope," said Butler—"I trust in a gracious God, that she can clear herself."

"And sae do I, Mr. Butler," replied Mrs. Saddletree. "I am sure I wad hae answered for her as my ain daughter; but, wae's my heart, I had been tender a' the simmer, and scarce ower the door o' my room for twal weeks. And as for Mr. Saddletree, he might be in a lying-in hospital, and ne'er find out what the women cam there for. Sae I could see little or naething o' her, or I wad hae had the truth o' her situation out o' her, I'se warrant ye. But we a' think her sister maun be able to speak something to clear her."

"The haill Parliament House," said Saddletree, "was speaking o' naething else, till this job o' Porteous's put it out o' head. It's a beautiful point of presumptive murder, and there's been nane like it in the Justiciar Court since the case of Luckie Smith, the howdie, that suffered in the year 1679."

"But what's the matter wi' you, Mr. Butler?" said the good woman; "ye are looking as white as a sheet; will ye take a dram?"

"By no means," said Butler, compelling himself to speak. "I walked in from Dumfries yesterday, and this is a warm day."

"Sit down," said Mrs. Saddletree, laying hands on him kindly, "and rest ye; ye'll kill yoursell, man, at that rate. And are we to wish you joy o' getting the scule, Mr. Butler?"

"Yes—no—I do not know," answered the young man, vaguely. But Mrs. Saddletree kept him to the point, partly out of real interest, partly from curiosity.

"Ye dinna ken whether ye are to get the free scule o' Dumfries or no, after hinging on and teaching it a' the simmer?"

"No, Mrs. Saddletree, I am not to have it," replied Butler, more collectedly. "The Laird of Black-at-the-Bane had a natural son bred to the kirk, that the presbytery could not be prevailed upon to license; and so——"

"Ay, ye need say nae mair about it; if there was a laird that had a puir kinsman or a bastard that it wad suit, there's eneugh said. And ye're e'en come back to Liberton to wait for dead men's shoon? and, for as frail as Mr. Whackbairn is, he may live as lang as you, that are his assistant and successor."

"Very like," replied Butler, with a sigh; "I do not know if I should wish it otherwise."

"Nae doubt it's a very vexing thing," continued the good lady, "to be in that dependent station; and you that hae right and title to sae muckle better, I wonder how ye bear these crosses."

"*Quos diligit castigat*," answered Butler; "even the pagan Seneca could see an advantage in affliction. The heathens had their philosophy and the Jews their revelation, Mrs. Saddletree, and they endured their distresses in their day. Christians have a better dispensation than either, but doubtless——"

He stopped and sighed.

"I ken what ye mean," said Mrs. Saddletree, looking toward her husband; "there's whiles we lose patience in spite of baith book and Bible. But ye are no gaun awa', and looking sae poorly; ye'll stay and take some kail wi' us?"

Mr. Saddletree laid aside Balfour's *Practiques* (his favorite study, and much good may it do him), to join in his wife's hospitable importunity. But the teacher declined all entreaty, and took his leave upon the spot.

"There's something in a' this," said Mrs. Saddletree, looking after him as he walked up the street. "I wonder what makes Mr. Butler sae distressed about Effie's misfortune; there was nae acquaintance atween them that ever I saw or heard of; but they were neighbors when David Deans was on the Laird o' Dumbiedikes' land. Mr. Butler wad ken her father, or some o' her folk. Get up, Mr. Saddletree; ye have set yoursell down on the very brecham that wants stitching; and here's little Willie, the prentice. Ye little rinthereout deil that ye are, what takes you raking through the gutters to see folk hangit? How wad ye like when it comes to be your ain chance, as I winna insure ye, if ye dinna mend your manners? And what are ye maundering and greeting for, as if a word were breaking your banes? Gang in bye, and be a better bairn another time, and tell Peggy to gie ye a bicker o' broth, for ye'll be as gleg as a gled, I'se warrant ye. It's a fatherless bairn, Mr. Saddletree, and motherless, whilk in some cases may be waur, and ane would take care o' him if they could; it's a Christian duty."

"Very true, gudewife," said Saddletree, in reply, "we are *in loco parentis* to him during his years of pupillarity, and I hae had thoughts of applying to the court for a commission as factor *loco tutoris*, seeing there is nae tutor nominate, and the tutor-at-law declines to act ; but only I fear the expense of the procedure wad not be *in rem versam,* for I am not aware if Willie has ony effects whereof to assume the administration."

He concluded this sentence with a self-important cough, as one who has laid down the law in an indisputable manner.

"Effects ! " said Mrs. Saddletree ; "what effects has the puir wean ?   He was in rags when his mother died ; and the blue polonie that Effie made for him out of an auld mantle of my ain was the first decent dress the bairn ever had on. Puir Effie ! can ye tell me now really, wi' a' your law, will her life be in danger, Mr. Saddletree, when they arena able to prove that ever there was a bairn ava ? "

"Whoy," said Mr. Saddletree, delighted at having for once in his life seen his wife's attention arrested by a topic of legal discussion—"whoy, there are two sorts of *murdrum,* or *murdragium,* or what you *populariter et vulgariter* call murther.   I mean there are many sorts ; for there's your *murthrum per vigilias et insidias* and your *murthrum* under trust."

"I am sure," replied his moiety, "that murther by trust is the way that the gentry murther us merchants, and whiles make us shut the booth up ; but that has naething to do wi' Effie's misfortune."

"The case of Effie—or Euphemia—Deans," resumed Saddletree, "is one of those cases of murder presumptive, that is, a murder of the law's inferring or construction, being derived from certain *indicia* or grounds of suspicion."

"So that," said the good woman, "unless puir Effie has communicated her situation, she'll be hanged by the neck, if the bairn was still-born, or if it be alive at this moment ? "

"Assuredly," said Saddletree, "it being a statute made by our sovereign Lord and Lady to prevent the horrid delict of bringing forth children in secret.   The crime is rather a favorite of the law, this species of murther being one of its ain creation." *

"Then, if the law makes murders," said Mrs. Saddletree, "the law should be hanged for them ; or if they wad hang a lawyer instead, the country wad find nae faut."

A summons to their frugal dinner interrupted the further progress of the conversation, which was otherwise like to take a turn much less favorable to the science of jurisprudence and its professors than Mr. Bartoline Saddletree, the fond admirer of both, had at its opening anticipated.

* See Law relating to Child-Murder.   Note 7.

CHAPTER VI

BUTLER, on his departure from the sign of the Golden Nag, went in quest of a friend of his connected with the law, of whom he wished to make particular inquiries concerning the circumstances in which the unfortunate young woman mentioned in the last chapter was placed, having, as the reader has probably already conjectured, reasons much deeper than those dictated by mere humanity for interesting himself in her fate. He found the person he sought absent from home, and was equally unfortunate in one or two other calls which he made upon acquaintances whom he hoped to interest in her story. But everybody was, for the moment, stark mad on the subject of Porteous, and engaged busily in attacking or defending the measures of government in reprieving him; and the ardor of dispute had excited such universal thirst that half the young lawyers and writers, together with their very clerks, the class whom Butler was looking after, had adjourned the debate to some favorite tavern. It was computed by an experienced arithmetician that there was as much twopenny ale consumed on the discussion as would have floated a first-rate man-of-war.

Butler wandered about until it was dusk, resolving to take that opportunity of visiting the unfortunate young woman, when his doing so might be least observed; for he had his own reasons for avoiding the remarks of Mrs. Saddletree, whose shop-door opened at no great distance from that of the jail, though on the opposite or south side of the street, and a little higher up. He passed, therefore, through the narrow and partly covered passage leading from the north-west end of the Parliament Square.

He stood now before the Gothic entrance of the ancient prison, which, as is well known to all men, rears its ancient front in the very middle of the High Street, forming, as it were, the termination to a huge pile of buildings called the Luckenbooths, which, for some inconceivable reason, our ancestors had jammed into the midst of the principal street of the town, leaving for passage a narrow street on the north, and on the south, into which the prison opens, a narrow crooked lane, winding betwixt the high and sombre walls of the tolbooth and the adjacent houses on the one side, and the buttresses and projections of the old Cathedral upon the other. To give some gayety to this sombre passage, well known by the name of the Krames, a number of little booths or shops, after the fashion of cobblers' stalls, are plastered, as it were, against the Gothic projections and abutments, so that it seemed as if the traders had occupied with nests, bearing the same proportion to the building, every buttress and coign of vantage, as the martlet did in Macbeth's castle. Of later years these booths have degenerated into mere toy-shops, where the little loiterers chiefly interested in such wares are tempted to linger, enchanted by the rich display of hobby-horses, babies, and Dutch toys, arranged in artful and gay confusion ; yet half-scared by the cross looks of the withered pantaloon, or spectacled old lady, by whom these tempting stores are watched and superintended. But in the times we write of the hosiers, the glovers, the hatters, the mercers, the milliners, and all who dealt in the miscellaneous wares now termed haberdashers' goods, were to be found in this narrow alley.

To return from our digression. Butler found the outer turnkey, a tall, thin old man, with long silver hair, in the act of locking the outward door of the jail. He addressed himself to this person, and asked admittance to Effie Deans, confined upon accusation of child-murder. The turnkey looked at him earnestly, and, civilly touching his hat out of respect to Butler's black coat and clerical appearance, replied, " It was impossible any one could be admitted at present."

" You shut up earlier than usual, probably on account of Captain Porteous's affair ? " said Butler.

The turnkey, with the true mystery of a person in office, gave two grave nods, and withdrawing from the wards a ponderous key of about two feet in length, he proceeded to shut a strong plate of steel which folded down above the keyhole, and was secured by a steel spring and catch. Butler stood still instinctively while the door was made fast, and then looking at his watch, walked briskly up the street, muttering to himself almost unconsciously—

> Porta adversa, ingens, solidoque adamante columnæ ;
> Vis ut nulla virum, non ipsi exscindere ferro
> Cœlicolæ valeant. Stat ferrea turris ad auras, etc.*

* See Translation. Note 8.

Having wasted half an hour more in a second fruitless attempt to find his legal friend and adviser, he thought it time to leave the city and return to his place of residence in a small village about two miles and a half to the southward of Edinburgh. The metropolis was at this time surrounded by a high wall, with battlements and flanking projections at some intervals, and the access was through gates, called in the Scottish language "ports," which were regularly shut at night. A small fee to the keepers would indeed procure egress and ingress at any time, through a wicket left for that purpose in the large gate, but it was of some importance to a man so poor as Butler to avoid even this slight pecuniary mulct; and fearing the hour of shutting the gates might be near, he made for that to which he found himself nearest, although by doing so he somewhat lengthened his walk homewards. Bristo Port was that by which his direct road lay, but the West Port, which leads out of the Grassmarket, was the nearest of the city gates to the place where he found himself, and to that, therefore, he directed his course.

He reached the port in ample time to pass the circuit of the walls, and enter a suburb called Portsburgh, chiefly inhabited by the lower order of citizens and mechanics. Here he was unexpectedly interrupted. He had not gone far from the gate before he heard the sound of a drum, and, to his great surprise, met a number of persons, sufficient to occupy the whole front of the street, and form a considerable mass behind, moving with great speed towards the gate he had just come from, and having in front of them a drum beating to arms. While he considered how he should escape a party assembled, as it might be presumed, for no lawful purpose, they came full on him and stopped him.

"Are you a clergyman?" one questioned him.

Butler replied that "he was in orders, but was not a placed minister."

"It's Mr. Butler from Liberton," said a voice from behind; "he'll discharge the duty as weel as ony man."

"You must turn back with us, sir," said the first speaker, in a tone civil but peremptory.

"For what purpose, gentlemen?" said Mr. Butler. "I live at some distance from town; the roads are unsafe by night; you will do me a serious injury by stopping me."

"You shall be sent safely home, no man shall touch a hair of your head; but you must and shall come along with us."

"But to what purpose or end, gentlemen?" said Butler. "I hope you will be so civil as to explain that to me?"

"You shall know that in good time. Come along, for come you must, by force or fair means; and I warn you to look neither to the right hand nor the left, and to take no notice of any man's face, but consider all that is passing before you as a dream."

"I would it were a dream I could awaken from," said Butler to himself; but having no means to oppose the violence with which he was threatened, he was compelled to turn round and march in front of the rioters, two men partly supporting and partly holding him. During this parley the insurgents had made themselves masters of the West Port, rushing upon the waiters (so the people were called who had the charge of the gates), and possessing themselves of the keys. They bolted and barred the folding doors, and commanded the person whose duty it usually was to secure the wicket, of which they did not understand the fastenings. The man, terrified at an incident so totally unexpected, was unable to perform his usual office, and gave the matter up, after several attempts. The rioters, who seemed to have come prepared for every emergency, called for torches, by the light of which they nailed up the wicket with long nails, which, it appeared probable, they had provided on purpose.

While this was going on, Butler could not, even if he had been willing, avoid making remarks on the individuals who seemed to lead this singular mob. The torch-light, while it fell on their forms and left him in the shade, gave him an opportunity to do so without their observing him. Several of those who appeared most active were dressed in sailors' jackets, trowsers, and sea-caps; others in large loose-bodied greatcoats, and slouched hats; and there were several who, judging from their dress, should have been called women, whose rough deep voices, uncommon size, and masculine deportment and mode of walking, forbade them being so interpreted. They moved as if by some well-concerted plan of arrangement. They had signals by which they knew, and nicknames by which they distinguished, each other. Butler remarked that the name of Wildfire was used among them, to which one stout amazon seemed to reply.

The rioters left a small party to observe the West Port, and directed the waiters, as they valued their lives, to remain within their lodge, and make no attempt for that night to repossess themselves of the gate. They then moved with rapidity along the low street called the Cowgate, the mob of the city everywhere rising at the sound of their drum and joining them. When the multitude arrived at the Cowgate Port,

they secured it with as little opposition as the former, made
it fast, and left a small party to observe it. It was afterwards remarked as a striking instance of prudence and precaution, singularly combined with audacity, that the parties
left to guard those gates did not remain stationary on their
posts, but flitted to and fro, keeping so near the gates as to
see that no efforts were made to open them, yet not remaining so long as to have their persons closely observed. The
mob, at first only about one hundred strong, now amounted
to thousands, and were increasing every moment. They
divided themselves so as to ascend with more speed the various
narrow lanes which lead up from the Cowgate to the High
Street ; and still beating to arms as they went, and calling on
all true Scotsmen to join them, they now filled the principal
street of the city.

The Netherbow Port might be called the Temple Bar of
Edinburgh, as, intersecting the High Street at its termination, it divided Edinburgh, properly so called, from the suburb
named the Canongate, as Temple Bar separates London from
Westminster. It was of the utmost importance to the rioters
to possess themselves of this pass, because there was quartered
in the Canongate at that time a regiment of infantry, commanded by Colonel Moyle, which might have occupied the
city by advancing through this gate, and would possess the
power of totally defeating their purpose. The leaders therefore hastened to the Netherbow Port, which they secured in
the same manner, and with as little trouble, as the other gates,
leaving a party to watch it, strong in proportion to the importance of the post.

The next object of these hardy insurgents was at once to
disarm the City Guard and to procure arms for themselves ;
for scarce any weapons but staves and bludgeons had been yet
seen among them. The guard-house was a long, low, ugly
building (removed in 1787), which to a fanciful imagination
might have suggested the idea of a long black snail crawling
up the middle of the High Street, and deforming its beautiful
esplanade. This formidable insurrection had been so unexpected that there were no more than the ordinary sergeant's
guard of the city corps upon duty ; even these were without
any supply of powder and ball ; and sensible enough what had
raised the storm, and which way it was rolling, could hardly
be supposed very desirous to expose themselves by a valiant
defence to the animosity of so numerous and desperate a mob,
to whom they were on the present occasion much more than
usually obnoxious.

There was a sentinel upon guard, who, that one town guard soldier might do his duty on that eventful evening, presented his piece, and desired the foremost of the rioters to stand off. The young amazon, whom Butler had observed particularly active, sprung upon the soldier, seized his musket, and after a struggle succeeded in wrenching it from him, and throwing him down on the causeway. One or two soldiers, who endeavored to turn out to the support of their sentinel, were in the same manner seized and disarmed, and the mob without difficulty possessed themselves of the guard-house, disarming and turning out-of-doors the rest of the men on duty. It was remarked that, notwithstanding the city soldiers had been the instruments of the slaughter which this riot was designed to revenge, no ill-usage or even insult was offered to them. It seemed as if the vengeance of the people disdained to stoop at any head meaner than that which they considered as the source and origin of their injuries.

On possessing themselves of the guard, the first act of the multitude was to destroy the drums, by which they supposed an alarm might be conveyed to the garrison in the Castle; for the same reason they now silenced their own, which was beaten by a young fellow, son to the drummer of Portsburgh, whom they had forced upon that service. Their next business was to distribute among the boldest of the rioters the guns, bayonets, partizans, halberds, and battle or Lochaber axes. Until this period the principal rioters had preserved silence on the ultimate object of their rising, as being that which all knew, but none expressed. Now, however, having accomplished all the preliminary parts of their design, they raised a tremendous shout of "Porteous! Porteous! To the tolbooth! To the tolbooth!"

They proceeded with the same prudence when the object seemed to be nearly in their grasp as they had done hitherto when success was more dubious. A strong party of the rioters, drawn up in front of the Luckenbooths, and facing down the street, prevented all access from the eastward, and the west end of the defile formed by the Luckenbooths was secured in the same manner; so that the tolbooth was completely surrounded, and those who undertook the task of breaking it open effectually secured against the risk of interruption.

The magistrates, in the meanwhile, had taken the alarm, and assembled in a tavern, with the purpose of raising some strength to subdue the rioters. The deacons, or presidents of the trades, were applied to, but declared there was little chance of their authority being respected by the craftsmen, where it was the object to save a man so obnoxious. Mr. Lindsay, member of parliament for the city, volunteered the perilous task of carrying a verbal message from the Lord Provost to Colonel Moyle, the commander of the regiment lying in the Canongate, requesting him to force the Netherbow Port, and enter the city to put down the tumult. But Mr. Lindsay declined to charge himself with any written order, which, if found on his person by an enraged mob, might have cost him his life ; and the issue of the application was, that Colonel Moyle, having no written requisition from the civil authorities, and having the fate of Porteous before his eyes as an example of the severe construction put by a jury on the proceedings of military men acting on their own responsibility, declined to encounter the risk to which the Provost's verbal communication invited him.

More than one messenger was despatched by different ways to the Castle, to require the commanding officer to march down his troops, to fire a few cannon-shot, or even to throw a shell among the mob, for the purpose of clearing the streets. But so strict and watchful were the various patrols whom the rioters had established in different parts of the street, that none of the emissaries of the magistrates could reach the gate of the Castle. They were, however, turned back without either injury or insult, and with nothing more of menace than was necessary to deter them from again attempting to accomplish their errand.

The same vigilance was used to prevent everybody of the higher, and those which, in this case, might be deemed the more suspicious, orders of society from appearing in the street, and observing the movements, or distinguishing the persons, of the rioters. Every person in the garb of a gentleman was stopped by small parties of two or three of the mob, who partly exhorted, partly required of them, that they should return to the place from whence they came. Many a quadrille table was spoiled that memorable evening ; for the sedan chairs of ladies, even of the highest rank, were interrupted in their passage from one point to another, in despite of the laced footmen and blazing flambeaux. This was uniformly done with a deference and attention to the feelings of the terrified females which could hardly have been expected from the videttes of a mob so desperate. Those who stopped the chair usually made the excuse that there was much disturbance on the streets, and that it was absolutely necessary for the lady's safety that the chair should turn back. They offered themselves to escort the vehicles which they had thus interrupted in their progress, from the apprehension, probably, that some of those who had casually united themselves to the riot might disgrace their systematic and determined plan of vengeance, by those acts of general insult and license which are common on similar occasions.

Persons are yet living who remember to have heard from the mouths of ladies thus interrupted on their journey in the manner we have described, that they were escorted to their lodgings by the young men who stopped them, and even handed out of their chairs, with a polite attention far beyond what was consistent with their dress, which was apparently that of journeymen mechanics.*   It seemed as if the conspirators, like those who assassinated the Cardinal Beatoun in former days, had entertained the opinion that the work about which they went was a judgment of Heaven, which, though unsanctioned by the usual authorities, ought to be proceeded in with order and gravity.

While their outposts continued thus vigilant, and suffered themselves neither from fear nor curiosity to neglect that part of the duty assigned to them, and while the main guards to the east and west secured them against interruption, a select body of the rioters thundered at the door of the jail, and demanded instant admission. No one answered, for the outer keeper had prudently made his escape with the keys at the commencement of the riot, and was nowhere to be found. The door was instantly assailed with sledge-hammers, iron crows, and the coulters of ploughs, ready provided for the purpose, with which they prized, heaved, and battered for some time with little effect; for, being of double oak planks, clinched, both end-long and athwart, with broad-headed nails, the door was so hung and secured as to yield to no means of forcing, without the expenditure of much time. The rioters, however, appeared determined to gain admittance. Gang after gang relieved each other at the exercise, for, of course, only a few could work at a time ; but gang after gang retired, exhausted with their violent exertions, without making much progress in forcing the prison door. Butler had been led up near to this the principal scene of action ; so near, indeed, that he was almost deafened by the unceasing clang of the heavy fore-hammers against the iron-bound portals of the prison. He began to entertain hopes, as the task seemed protracted, that the populace might give it over in despair, or that some rescue might arrive to disperse them. There was a moment at which the latter seemed probable.

* See Note 9.

The magistrates, having assembled their officers and some of the citizens who were willing to hazard themselves for the public tranquillity, now sallied forth from the tavern where they held their sitting, and approached the point of danger. Their officers went before them with links and torches, with a herald to read the Riot Act, if necessary. They easily drove before them the outposts and videttes of the rioters; but when they approached the line of guard which the mob, or rather, we should say, the conspirators, had drawn across the street in the front of the Luckenbooths, they were received with an unintermitted volley of stones, and, on their nearer approach, the pikes, bayonets, and Lochaber axes of which the populace had possessed themselves were presented against them. One of their ordinary officers, a strong resolute fellow, went forward, seized a rioter, and took from him a musket; but, being unsupported, he was instantly thrown on his back in the street, and disarmed in his turn. The officer was too happy to be permitted to rise and run away without receiving any further injury; which afforded another remarkable instance of the mode in which these men had united a sort of moderation towards all others with the most inflexible invetcracy against the object of their resentment. The magistrates, after vain attempts to make themselves heard and obeyed, possessing no means of enforcing their authority, were constrained to abandon the field to the rioters, and retreat in all speed from the showers of missiles that whistled around their ears.

The passive resistance of the tolbooth gate promised to do more to baffle the purpose of the mob than the active interference of the magistrates. The heavy sledge-hammers continued to din against it without intermission, and with a noise which, echoed from the lofty buildings around the spot, seemed enough to have alarmed the garrison in the Castle. It was circulated among the rioters that the troops would march down to disperse them, unless they could execute their purpose without loss of time; or that, even without quitting the fortress, the garrison might obtain the same end by throwing a bomb or two upon the street.

Urged by such motives for apprehension, they eagerly relieved each other at the labor of assailing the tolbooth door; yet such was its strength that it still defied their efforts. At length a voice was heard to pronounce the words, "Try it with fire." The rioters, with a unanimous shout, called for combustibles, and as all their wishes seemed to be instantly supplied, they were soon in possession of two or three empty tar-barrels.

A huge red glaring bonfire speedily arose close to the door of the prison, sending up a tall column of smoke and flame against its antique turrets and strongly grated windows, and illuminating the ferocious and wild gestures of the rioters who surrounded the place, as well as the pale and anxious groups of those who, from windows in the vicinage, watched the progress of this alarming scene. The mob fed the fire with whatever they could find fit for the purpose. The flames roared and crackled among the heaps of nourishment piled on the fire, and a terrible shout soon announced that the door had kindled, and was in the act of being destroyed. The fire was suffered to decay, but long ere it was quite extinguished the most forward of the rioters rushed, in their impatience, one after another, over its yet smoldering remains. Thick showers of sparkles rose high in the air as man after man bounded over the glowing embers and disturbed them in their passage. It was now obvious to Butler and all others who were present that the rioters would be instantly in possession of their victim, and have it in their power to work their pleasure upon him, whatever that might be.*

* See The Old Tolbooth. Note 10.

CHAPTER VII

The evil you teach us, we will execute ; and it shall go hard
but we will better the instruction.

Merchant of Venice.

THE unhappy object of this remarkable disturbance had been
that day delivered from the apprehension of a public execution, and his joy was the greater, as he had some reason to
question whether government would have run the risk of unpopularity by interfering in his favor, after he had been legally
convicted, by the verdict of a jury, of a crime so very obnoxious. Relieved from this doubtful state of mind, his heart
was merry within him, and he thought, in the emphatic words
of Scripture on a similar occasion, that surely the bitterness
of death was past. Some of his friends, however, who had
watched the manner and behavior of the crowd when they
were made acquainted with the reprieve, were of a different
opinion. They augured, from the unusual sternness and silence
with which they bore their disappointment, that the populace
nourished some scheme of sudden and desperate vengeance ;
and they advised Porteous to lose no time in petitioning the
proper authorities that he might be conveyed to the Castle
under a sufficient guard, to remain there in security until his
ultimate fate should be determined. Habituated, however,
by his office to overawe the rabble of the city, Porteous could
not suspect them of an attempt so audacious as to storm a
strong and defensible prison ; and, despising the advice by
which he might have been saved, he spent the afternoon of
the eventful day in giving an entertainment to some friends
who visited him in jail, several of whom, by the indulgence
of the captain of the tolbooth, with whom he had an old intimacy, arising from their official connection, were even permitted to remain to supper with him, though contrary to the
rules of the jail.

It was, therefore, in the hour of unalloyed mirth, when
this unfortunate wretch was "full of bread," hot with wine,

56

and high in mistimed and ill-grounded confidence, and, alas ! with all his sins full blown, when the first distant shouts of the rioters mingled with the song of merriment and intemperance. The hurried call of the jailer to the guests, requiring them instantly to depart, and his yet more hasty intimation that a dreadful and determined mob had possessed themselves of the city gates and guard-house, were the first explanation of these fearful clamors.

Porteous might, however, have eluded the fury from which the force of authority could not protect him, had he thought of slipping on some disguise and leaving the prison along with his guests. It is probable that the jailer might have connived at his escape, or even that, in the hurry of this alarming contingency, he might not have observed it. But Porteous and his friends alike wanted presence of mind to suggest or execute such a plan of escape. The latter hastily fled from a place where their own safety seemed compromised, and the former, in a state resembling stupefaction, awaited in his apartment the termination of the enterprise of the rioters. The cessation of the clang of the instruments with which they had at first attempted to force the door gave him momentary relief. The flattering hopes that the military had marched into the city, either from the Castle or from the suburbs, and that the rioters were intimidated and dispersing, were soon destroyed by the broad and glaring light of the flames, which, illuminating through the grated window every corner of his apartment, plainly showed that the mob, determined on their fatal purpose, had adopted a means of forcing entrance equally desperate and certain.

The sudden glare of light suggested to the stupefied and astonished object of popular hatred the possibility of concealment or escape. To rush to the chimney, to ascend it at the risk of suffocation, were the only means which seem to have occurred to him ; but his progress was speedily stopped by one of those iron gratings which are, for the sake of security, usually placed across the vents of buildings designed for imprisonment. The bars, however, which impeded his further progress served to support him in the situation which he had gained, and he seized them with the tenacious grasp of one who esteemed himself clinging to his last hope of existence. The lurid light which had filled the apartment lowered and died away ; the sound of shouts was heard within the walls, and on the narrow and winding stair, which, cased within one of the turrets, gave access to the upper apartments of the prison. The huzza of the rioters was answered by a shout wild and des-

perate as their own, the cry, namely, of the imprisoned felons, who, expecting to be liberated in the general confusion,
welcomed the mob as their deliverers.   By some of these the
apartment of Porteous was pointed out to his enemies.   The
obstacle of the lock and bolts was soon overcome, and from
his hiding-place the unfortunate man heard his enemies search
every corner of the apartment, with oaths and maledictions,
which would but shock the reader if we recorded them, but
which served to prove, could it have admitted of doubt, the
settled purpose of soul with which they sought his destruction.

A place of concealment so obvious to suspicion and scrutiny as that which Porteous had chosen could not long screen
him from detection.   He was dragged from his lurking-place,
with a violence which seemed to argue an intention to put him
to death on the spot.   More than one weapon was directed
towards him, when one of the rioters, the same whose female
disguise had been particularly noticed by Butler, interfered in
an authoritative tone.   "Are ye mad ?" he said, " or would
ye execute an act of justice as if it were a crime and a cruelty ?   This sacrifice will lose half its savor if we do not offer
it at the very horns of the altar.   We will have him die
where a murderer should die, on the common gibbet.   We
will have him die where he spilled the blood of so many in-
nocents !"

A loud shout of applause followed the proposal, and the
cry, "To the gallows with the murderer !   To the Grassmarket with him !" echoed on all hands.

"Let no man hurt him," continued the speaker ; "let him
make his peace with God, if he can ; we will not kill both his
soul and body."

"What time did he give better folk for preparing their account ?" answered several voices." Let us mete to him with
the same measure he measured to them."

But the opinion of the spokesman better suited the temper
of those he addressed, a temper rather stubborn than impetu-
ous, sedate though ferocious, and desirous of coloring their
cruel and revengeful action with a show of justice and moderation.

For an instant this man quitted the prisoner, whom he
consigned to a selected guard, with instructions to permit him
to give his money and property to whomsoever he pleased.   A
person confined in the jail for debt received this last deposit from
the trembling hand of the victim, who was at the same time
permitted to make some other brief arrangements to meet his

approaching fate.   The felons, and all others who wished to leave the jail, were now at full liberty to do so ; not that their liberation made any part of the settled purpose of the rioters, but it followed as almost a necessary consequence of forcing the jail doors.   With wild cries of jubilee they joined the mob, or disappeared among the narrow lanes to seek out the hidden receptacles of vice and infamy where they were accustomed to lurk and conceal themselves from justice.

Two persons, a man about fifty years old and a girl about eighteen, were all who continued within the fatal walls, excepting two or three debtors, who probably saw no advantage in attempting their escape.   The persons we have mentioned remained in the strong-room of the prison, now deserted by all others.   One of their late companions in misfortune called out to the man to make his escape, in the tone of an acquaintance. "Rin for it, Ratcliffe ; the road's clear."

"It may be sae, Willie," answered Ratcliffe, composedly, "but I have taen a fancy to leave aff trade, and set up for an honest man."

"Stay there and be hanged, then, for a donnard auld deevil !" said the other, and ran down the prison stair.

The person in female attire whom we have distinguished as one of the most active rioters was about the same time at the ear of the young woman.   "Flee, Effie, flee !" was all he had time to whisper.   She turned towards him an eye of mingled fear, affection, and upbraiding, all contending with a sort of stupefied surprise.   He again repeated, "Flee, Effie, flee, for the sake of all that's good and dear to you !"   Again she gazed on him, but was unable to answer.   A loud noise was now heard, and the name of Madge Wildfire was repeatedly called from the bottom of the staircase.

"I am coming—I am coming," said the person who answered to that appellative ; and then reiterating hastily, "For God's sake—for your own sake—for my sake, flee, or they'll take your life !" he left the strong-room.

The girl gazed after him for a moment, and then faintly muttering, "Better tyne life, since tint is gude fame," she sunk her head upon her hand, and remained seemingly unconscious as a statue of the noise and tumult which passed around her.

That tumult was now transferred from the inside to the outside of the tolbooth.   The mob had brought their destined victim forth, and were about to conduct him to the common place of execution, which they had fixed as the scene of his death.   The leader whom they distinguished by the name of

Madge Wildfire had been summoned to assist at the procession by the impatient shouts of his confederates.

"I will insure you five hundred pounds," said the unhappy man, grasping Wildfire's hand—"five hundred pounds for to save my life."

The other answered in the same undertone, and returning his grasp with one equally convulsive, "Five hundred-weight of coined gold should not save you. Remember Wilson!"

A deep pause of a minute ensued, when Wildfire added, in a more composed tone, "Make your peace with Heaven. Where is the clergyman?"

Butler, who, in great terror and anxiety, had been detained within a few yards of the tolbooth door, to wait the event of the search after Porteous, was now brought forward and commanded to walk by the prisoner's side, and to prepare him for immediate death. His answer was a supplication that the rioters would consider what they did. "You are neither judges nor jury," said he. "You cannot have, by the laws of God or man, power to take away the life of a human creature, however deserving he may be of death. If it is murder even in a lawful magistrate to execute an offender otherwise than in the place, time, and manner which the judges' sentence prescribes, what must it be in you, who have no warrant for interference but your own wills? In the name of Him who is all mercy, show mercy to this unhappy man, and do not dip your hands in his blood, nor rush into the very crime which you are desirous of avenging!"

"Cut your sermon short, you are not in your pulpit," answered one of the rioters.

"If we hear more of your clavers," said another, "we are like to hang you up beside him."

"Peace! hush!" said Wildfire. "Do the good man no harm; he discharges his conscience, and I like him the better."

He then addressed Butler. "Now, sir, we have patiently heard you, and we just wish you to understand, in the way of answer, that you may as well argue to the ashler-work and iron stanchels of the tolbooth as think to change our purpose. Blood must have blood. We have sworn to each other by the deepest oaths ever were pledged, that Porteus shall die the death he deserves so richly; therefore, speak no more to us, but prepare him for death as well as the briefness of his change will permit."

They had suffered the unfortunate Porteous to put on his

night-gown and slippers, as he had thrown off his coat and shoes in order to facilitate his attempted escape up the chimney. In this garb he was now mounted on the hands of two of the rioters, clasped together, so as to form what is called in Scotland " The King's Cushion." Butler was placed close to his side, and repeatedly urged to perform a duty always the most painful which can be imposed on a clergyman deserving of the name, and now rendered more so by the peculiar and horrid circumstances of the criminal's case. Porteous at first uttered some supplications for mercy, but when he found that there was no chance that these would be attended to, his military education, and the natural stubbornness of his disposition, combined to support his spirits.

" Are you prepared for this dreadful end ? " said Butler, in a faltering voice. " O turn to Him in whose eyes time and space have no existence, and to whom a few minutes are as a lifetime, and a lifetime as a minute."

"I believe I know what you would say," answered Porteous, sullenly. " I was bred a soldier ; if they will murder me without time, let my sins as well as my blood lie at their door."

" Who was it," said the stern voice of Wildfire, " that said to Wilson at this very spot, when he could not pray, owing to the galling agony of his fetters, that his pains would soon be over ? I say to you, take your own tale home ; and if you cannot profit by the good man's lessons, blame not them that are still more merciful to you than you were to others."

The procession now moved forward with a slow and determined pace. It was enlightened by many blazing links and torches ; for the actors of this work were so far from affecting any secrecy on the occasion that they seemed even to court observation. Their principal leaders kept close to the person of the prisoner, whose pallid yet stubborn features were seen distinctly by the torch-light, as his person was raised considerably above the concourse which thronged around him. Those who bore swords, muskets, and battle-axes marched on each side, as if forming a regular guard to the procession. The windows, as they went along, were filled with the inhabitants, whose slumbers had been broken by this unusual disturbance. Some of the spectators muttered accents of encouragement ; but in general they were so much appalled by a sight so strange and audacious, that they looked on with a sort of stupefied astonishment. No one offered, by act or word, the slightest interruption.

The rioters, on their part, continued to act with the same

air of deliberate confidence and security which had marked
all their proceedings. When the object of their resentment
dropped one of his slippers, they stopped, sought for it, and
replaced it upon his foot with great deliberation.* As they
descended the Bow towards the fatal spot where they designed
to complete their purpose, it was suggested that there should
be a rope kept in readiness. For this purpose the booth of a
man who dealt in cordage was forced open, a coil of rope
fit for their purpose was selected to serve as a halter, and the
dealer next morning found that a guinea had been left on his
counter in exchange ; so anxious were the perpetrators of this
daring action to show that they meditated not the slightest
wrong for infraction of law, excepting so far as Porteous was
himself concerned.

Leading, or carrying along with them, in this determined
and regular manner, the object of their vengeance, they at
length reached the place of common execution, the scene of
his crime, and destined spot of his sufferings. Several of the
rioters (if they should not rather be described as conspirators)
endeavored to remove the stone which filled up the socket in
which the end of the fatal tree was sunk when it was erected
for its fatal purpose ; others sought for the means of con-
structing a temporary gibbet, the place in which the gallows
itself was deposited being reported too secure to be forced,
without much loss of time.

Butler endeavored to avail himself of the delay afforded by
these circumstances to turn the people from their desperate
design. "For God's sake," he exclaimed, "remember it is
the image of your Creator which you are about to deface in
the person of this unfortunate man ! Wretched as he is, and
wicked as he may be, he has a share in every promise of Scripture, and you cannot destroy him in impenitence without
blotting his name from the Book of Life. Do not destroy
soul and body ; give time for preparation."

" What time had they," returned a stern voice, " whom
he murdered on this very spot ? The laws both of God and
man call for his death."

" But what, my friends," insisted Butler, with a generous
disregard to his own safety—" what hath constituted you his
judges ?"

" We are not his judges," replied the same person ; "he
has been already judged and condemned by lawful authority.
We are those whom Heaven, and our righteous anger, have

* This little incident, characteristic of the extreme composure of this extraordinary mob, was witnessed by a lady who, disturbed, like others, from her slumbers, had gone to the window. It was told to the Author by the lady's daughter.

stirred up to execute judgment, when a corrupt government would have protected a murderer."

"I am none," said the unfortunate Porteous; "that which you charge upon me fell out in self-defence, in the lawful exercise of my duty."

"Away with him—away with him!" was the general cry. "Why do you trifle away time in making a gallows? that dyester's pole is good enough for the homicide."

The unhappy man was forced to his fate with remorseless rapidity. Butler, separated from him by the press, escaped the last horrors of his struggles. Unnoticed by those who had hitherto detained him as a prisoner, he fled from the fatal spot, without much caring in what direction his course lay. A loud shout proclaimed the stern delight with which the agents of this deed regarded its completion. Butler then, at the opening into the low street called the Cowgate, cast back a terrified glance, and by the red and dusky light of the torches he could discern a figure wavering and struggling as it hung suspended above the heads of the multitude, and could even observe men striking at it with their Lochaber axes and partizans. The sight was of a nature to double his horror and to add wings to his flight.

The street down which the fugitive ran opens to one of the eastern ports or gates of the city. Butler did not stop till he reached it, but found it still shut. He waited nearly an hour, walking up and down in inexpressible perturbation of mind. At length he ventured to call out and rouse the attention of the terrified keepers of the gate, who now found themselves at liberty to resume their office without interruption. Butler requested them to open the gate. They hesitated. He told them his name and occupation.

"He is a preacher," said one; "I have heard him preach in Haddo's Hole."

"A fine preaching has he been at the night," said another; "but maybe least said is sunest mended."

Opening then the wicket of the main gate, the keepers suffered Butler to depart, who hastened to carry his horror and fear beyond the walls of Edinburgh. His first purpose was instantly to take the road homeward; but other fears and cares, connected with the news he had learned in that remarkable day, induced him to linger in the neighborhood of Edinburgh until daybreak. More than one group of persons passed him as he was whiling away the hours of darkness that yet remained, whom, from the stifled tones of their discourse, the unwonted hour when they travelled, and the hasty pace at which they walked, he conjectured to have been engaged in the late fatal transaction.

Certain it was, that the sudden and total dispersion of the rioters, when their vindictive purpose was accomplished, seemed not the least remarkable feature of this singular affair. In general, whatever may be the impelling motive by which a mob is at first raised, the attainment of their object has usually been only found to lead the way to further excesses. But not so in the present case. They seemed completely satiated with the vengeance they had prosecuted with such stanch and sagacious activity. When they were fully satisfied that life had abandoned their victim, they dispersed in every direction, throwing down the weapons which they had only assumed to enable them to carry through their purpose. At daybreak there remained not the least token of the events of the night, excepting the corpse of Porteous, which still hung suspended in the place where he had suffered, and the arms of various kinds which the rioters had taken from the City Guard-house, which were found scattered about the streets as they had thrown them from their hands, when the purpose for which they had seized them was accomplished.*

The ordinary magistrates of the city resumed their power, not without trembling at the late experience of the fragility of its tenure. To march troops into the city, and commence a severe inquiry into the transactions of the preceding night, were the first marks of returning energy which they displayed. But these events had been conducted on so secure and well-calculated a plan of safety and secrecy, that there was little or nothing learned to throw light upon the authors or principal actors in a scheme so audacious. An express was despatched to London with the tidings, where they excited great indignation and surprise in the council of regency, and particularly in the bosom of Queen Caroline, who considered her own authority as exposed to contempt by the success of this singular conspiracy. Nothing was spoke of for some time save the measure of vengeance which should be taken, not only on the actors of this tragedy, so soon as they should be discovered, but upon the magistrates who had suffered it to take place, and upon the city which had been the scene where it was exhibited. On this occasion, it is still recorded in popular tradition that her Majesty, in the height of her displeasure, told the celebrated John, Duke of Argyle, that, sooner than submit to such an insult, she would make Scotland a hunting-field. "In that case, Madam," answered that high-spirited noble-

<hr>

* See The Murder of Captain Porteous.　Note 11.

man, with a profound bow, "I will take leave of your Majesty, and go down to my own country to get my hounds ready."

The import of the reply had more than met the ear; and as most of the Scottish nobility and gentry seemed actuated by the same national spirit, the royal displeasure was necessarily checked in mid-volley, and milder courses were recommended and adopted, to some of which we may hereafter have occasion to advert.

CHAPTER VIII

Arthur's Seat shall be my bed,
  The sheets shall ne'er be press'd by me ;
St. Anton's well shall be my drink,
  Sin' my true-love's forsaken me.

Old Song.

IF I were to choose a spot from which the rising or setting sun could be seen to the greatest possible advantage, it would be that wild path winding around the foot of the high belt of semicircular rocks called Salisbury Crags, and marking the verge of the steep descent which slopes down into the glen on the south-eastern side of the city of Edinburgh. The prospect, in its general outline, commands a close-built, high-piled city, stretching itself out beneath in a form which, to a romantic imagination, may be supposed to represent that of a dragon ; now a noble arm of the sea, with its rocks, isles, distant shores, and boundary of mountains ; and now a fair and fertile champaign country, varied with hill, dale, and rock, and skirted by the picturesque ridge of the Pentland Mountains. But as the path gently circles around the base of the cliffs, the prospect, composed as it is of these enchanting and sublime objects, changes at every step, and presents them blended with, or divided from, each other in every possible variety which can gratify the eye and the imagination. When a piece of scenery so beautiful, yet so varied, so exciting by its intricacy, and yet so sublime, is lighted up by the tints of morning or of evening, and displays all that variety of shadowy depth, exchanged with partial brilliancy, which gives character even to the tamest of landscapes, the effect approaches near to enchantment. This path used to be my favorite evening and morning resort, when engaged with a favorite author or new subject of study. It is, I am informed, now become totally impassable, a circumstance which, if true, reflects little credit on the taste of the Good Town or its leaders.*

---

* A beautiful and solid pathway has, within a few years, been formed around these romantic rocks ; and the Author has the pleasure to think that the passage in the text gave rise to the undertaking.

It was from this fascinating path—the scene to me of so much delicious musing, when life was young and promised to be happy, that I have been unable to pass it over without an episodical description—it was, I say, from this romantic path that Butler saw the morning arise the day after the murder of Porteous. It was possible for him with ease to have found a much shorter road to the house to which he was directing his course, and, in fact, that which he chose was extremely circuitous. But to compose his own spirits, as well as to while away the time, until a proper hour for visiting the family without surprise or disturbance, he was induced to extend his circuit by the foot of the rocks, and to linger upon his way until the morning should be considerably advanced. While, now standing with his arms across and waiting the slow progress of the sun above the horizon, now sitting upon one of the numerous fragments which storms had detached from the rocks above him, he is meditating alternately upon the horrible catastrophe which he had witnessed, and upon the melancholy, and to him most interesting, news which he had learned at Saddletree's, we will give the reader to understand who Butler was, and how his fate was connected with that of Effie Deans, the unfortunate handmaiden of the careful Mrs. Saddletree.

Reuben Butler was of English extraction, though born in Scotland. His grandfather was a trooper in Monk's army, and one of the party of dismounted dragoons which formed the forlorn hope at the storming of Dundee in 1651. Stephen Butler (called, from his talents in reading and expounding, Scripture Stephen and Bible Butler) was a stanch Independent, and received in its fullest comprehension the promise that the saints should inherit the earth. As hard knocks were what had chiefly fallen to his share hitherto in the division of this common property, he lost not the opportunity, which the storm and plunder of a commercial place afforded him, to appropriate as large a share of the better things of this world as he could possibly compass. It would seem that he had succeeded indifferently well, for his exterior circumstances appeared, in consequence of this event, to have been much mended.

The troop to which he belonged was quartered at the village of Dalkeith, as forming the body-guard of Monk, who, in the capacity of general for the Commonwealth, resided in the neighboring castle. When, on the eve of the Restoration, the general commenced his march from Scotland, a measure pregnant with such important consequences, he new-modelled his troops, and more especially those immediately about his person, in order that they might consist chiefly of individuals devoted to himself. On this occasion Scripture Stephen was weighed in the balance and found wanting. It was supposed he felt no call to any expedition which might endanger the reign of the military sainthood, and that he did not consider himself as free in conscience to join with any party which might be likely ultimately to acknowledge the interest of Charles Stuart, the son of "the last man," as Charles I. was familiarly and irreverently termed by them in their common discourse, as well as in their more elaborate predications and harangues. As the time did not admit of cashiering such dissidents, Stephen Butler was only advised in a friendly way to give up his horse and accoutrements to one of Middleton's old troopers, who possessed an accommodating conscience of a military stamp, and which squared itself chiefly upon those of the colonel and paymaster. As this hint came recommended by a certain sum of arrears presently payable, Stephen had carnal wisdom enough to embrace the proposal, and with great indifference saw his old corps depart for Coldstream, on their route for the south, to establish the tottering government of England on a new basis.

The "zone" of the ex-trooper, to use Horace's phrase, was weighty enough to purchase a cottage and two or three fields (still known by the name of Beersheba), within about a Scottish mile of Dalkeith ; and there did Stephen establish himself with a youthful helpmate, chosen out of the said village, whose disposition to a comfortable settlement on this side of the grave reconciled her to the gruff manners, serious temper, and weather-beaten features of the martial enthusiast. Stephen did not long survive the falling on "evil days and evil tongues" of which Milton, in the same predicament, so mournfully complains. At his death his consort remained an early widow, with a male child of three years old, which, in the sobriety wherewith it demeaned itself, in the old-fashioned and even grim cast of its features, and in its sententious mode of expressing itself, would sufficiently have vindicated the honor of the widow of Beersheba, had any one thought proper to challenge the babe's descent from Bible Butler.

Butler's principles had not descended to his family, or extended themselves among his neighbors. The air of Scotland was alien to the growth of Independency, however favorable to fanaticism under other colors. But, nevertheless, they were not forgotten ; and a certain neighboring laird, who piqued himself upon the loyalty of his principles "in the worst of times" (though I never heard they exposed him to more peril than that of a broken head, or a night's lodging in the main guard, when wine and Cavalierism predominated in his upper story), had found it a convenient thing to rake up all matter of accusation against the deceased Stephen. In this enumeration his religious principles made no small figure, as, indeed, they must have seemed of the most exaggerated enormity to one whose own were so small and so faintly traced as to be well-nigh imperceptible. In these circumstances, poor widow Butler was supplied with her full proportion of fines for nonconformity, and all the other oppressions of the time, until Beersheba was fairly wrenched out of her hands and became the property of the laird who had so wantonly, as it had hitherto appeared, persecuted this poor forlorn woman. When his purpose was fairly achieved, he showed some remorse or moderation, or whatever the reader may please to term it, in permitting her to occupy her husband's cottage, and cultivate, on no very heavy terms, a croft of land adjacent. Her son, Benjamin, in the meanwhile, grew up to man's estate, and, moved by that impulse which makes men seek marriage even when its end can only be the perpetuation of misery, he wedded and brought a wife, and eventually a son, Reuben, to share the poverty of Beersheba.

The Laird of Dumbiedikes * had hitherto been moderate in his exactions, perhaps because he was ashamed to tax too highly the miserable means of support which remained to the widow Butler. But when a stout active young fellow appeared as the laborer of the croft in question, Dumbiedikes began to think so broad a pair of shoulders might bear an additional burden. He regulated, indeed, his management of his dependants (who fortunately were but few in number) much upon the principle of the carters whom he observed loading their carts at a neighboring coal-hill, and who never failed to clap an additional brace of hundredweights on their burden, so soon as by any means they had compassed a new horse of somewhat superior strength to that which had broken down the day before. However reasonable this practice appeared to the Laird of Dumbiedikes, he ought to have observed that it may be overdone, and that it infers, as a matter of course, the destruction and loss of both horse, cart, and loading. Even so it befell when the additional "prestations" came to be demanded of Benjamin Butler. A man of few words and few ideas, but attached to Beersheba with a feeling like that which a vegetable entertains to the spot in which it chances

* See Dumbiedikes. Note 12.

to be planted, he neither remonstrated with the Laird nor endeavored to escape from him, but, toiling night and day to accomplish the terms of his taskmaster, fell into a burning fever and died. His wife did not long survive him ; and, as if it had been the fate of this family to be left orphans, our Reuben Butler was, about the year 1704–5, left in the same circumstances in which his father had been placed, and under the same guardianship, being that of his grandmother, the widow of Monk's old trooper.

The same prospect of misery hung over the head of another tenant of this hard-hearted lord of the soil. This was a tough true-blue Presbyterian, called Deans, who, though most obnoxious to the Laird on account of principles in church and state, contrived to maintain his ground upon the estate by regular payment of mail-duties, kain, arriage, carriage, dry multure, lock, gowpen, and knaveship, and all the various exactions now commuted for money, and summed up in the emphatic word RENT. But the years 1700 and 1701, long remembered in Scotland for dearth and general distress, subdued the stout heart of the agricultural Whig. Citations by the ground-officer, decreets of the Baron Court, sequestrations, poindings of outsight and insight plenishing, flew about his ears as fast as ever the Tory bullets whistled around those of the Covenanters at Pentland, Bothwell Brig, or Aird's Moss. Struggle as he might, and he struggled gallantly, "Douce Davie Deans " was routed horse and foot, and lay at the mercy of his grasping landlord just at the time that Benjamin Butler died. The fate of each family was anticipated ; but they who prophesied their expulsion to beggary and ruin were disappointed by an accidental circumstance.

On the very term-day when their ejection should have taken place, when all their neighbors were prepared to pity and not one to assist them, the minister of the parish, as well as a doctor from Edinburgh, received a hasty summons to attend the Laird of Dumbiedikes. Both were surprised, for his contempt for both faculties had been pretty commonly his theme over an extra bottle, that is to say, at least once every day. The leech for the soul and he for the body alighted in the court of the little old manor-house at almost the same time ; and when they had gazed a moment at each other with some surprise, they in the same breath expressed their conviction that Dumbiedikes must needs be very ill indeed, since he summoned them both to his presence at once. Ere the servant could usher them to his apartment the party was augmented by a man of law, Nichil Novit, writing himself procurator before the sheriff court, for in those days there were no solicitors. This latter personage was first summoned to the apartment of the Laird, where, after some short space, the soul-curer and the body-curer were invited to join him.

Dumbiedikes had been by this time transported into the best bedroom, used only upon occasions of death and marriage, and called, from the former of these occupations, the Dead Room. There were in this apartment, besides the sick person himself and Mr. Novit, the son and heir of the patient, a tall gawky silly-looking boy of fourteen or fifteen, and a housekeeper, a good buxom figure of a woman, betwixt forty and fifty, who had kept the keys and managed matters at Dumbiedikes since the lady's death. It was to these attendants that Dumbiedikes addressed himself pretty nearly in the following words; temporal and spiritual matters, the care of his health and his affairs, being strangely jumbled in a head which was never one of the clearest:

"These are sair times wi' me, gentlemen and neighbors! amaist as ill as at the aughty-nine, when I was rabbled by the collegeaners.* They mistook me muckle: they ca'd me a Papist, but there was never a Papist bit about me, minister. Jock, ye'll take warning. It's a debt we maun a' pay, and there stands Nichil Novit that will tell ye I was never gude at paying debts in my life. Mr. Novit, ye'll no forget to draw the annual rent that's due on the yerl's band ; if I pay debt to other folk, I think they suld pay it to me—that equals aquals. Jock, when ye hae naething else to do, ye may be aye sticking in a tree ; it will be growing, Jock, when ye're sleeping.† My father tauld me sae forty years sin', but I ne'er fand time to mind him. Jock, ne'er drink brandy in the morning, it files the stamach sair ; gin ye take a morning's draught, let it be *aqua mirabilis ;* Jenny there makes it weel. Doctor, my breath is growing as scant as a broken-winded piper's, when he has played for four-and-twenty hours at a penny-wedding. Jenny, pit the cod aneath my head ; but it's a' needless ! Mass John, could ye think o' rattling ower some bit short prayer ; it wad do me gude maybe, and keep some queer thoughts out o' my head. Say something, man."

"I cannot use a prayer like a ratt-rhyme," answered the honest clergyman; "and if you would have your soul redeemed like a prey from the fowler, Laird, you must needs show me your state of mind."

"And shouldna ye ken that without my telling you ?"

* See College Students. Note 13.
† See Recommendation to Arboriculture. Note 14.

answered the patient. "What have I been paying stipend and teind, parsonage and vicarage for, ever sin' the aughty-nine, an I canna get a spell of a prayer for't, the only time I ever asked for ane in my life? Gang awa' wi' your Whiggery, if that's a' ye can do ; auld Curate Kiltstoup wad hae read half the Prayer Book to me by this time. Awa' wi' ye! Doctor, let's see if ye can do onything better for me."

The Doctor, who had obtained some information in the meanwhile from the housekeeper on the state of his complaints, assured him the medical art could not prolong his life many hours.

"Then damn Mass John and you baith !" cried the furious and intractable patient. "Did ye come here for naething but to tell me that ye canna help me at the pinch? Out wi' them, Jenny—out o' the house! and, Jock, my curse, and the curse of Cromwell, go wi' ye, if ye gie them either fee or bountith, or sae muckle as a black pair o' cheverons !"

The clergyman and doctor made a speedy retreat out of the apartment, while Dumbiedikes fell into one of those transports of violent and profane language which had procured him the surname of Damn-me-dikes. "Bring me the brandy bottle, Jenny, ye b——," he cried, with a voice in which passion contended with pain. "I can die as I have lived, without fashing ony o' them. But there's ae thing," he said, sinking his voice—"there's ae fearful thing hings about my heart, and an anker of brandy winna wash it away. The Deanses at Woodend! I sequestered them in the dear years, and now they are to flit, they'll starve ; and that Beersheba, and that auld trooper's wife and her oe, they'll starve—they'll starve ! Look out, Jock ; what kind o' night is't ?"

"On-ding o' snaw, father," answered Jock, after having opened the window and looked out with great composure.

"They'll perish in the drifts !" said the expiring sinner—"they'll perish wi' cauld ! but I'll be het eneugh, gin a' tales be true."

This last observation was made under breath, and in a tone which made the very attorney shudder. He tried his hand at ghostly advice, probably for the first time in his life, and recommended, as an opiate for the agonized conscience of the Laird, reparation of the injuries he had done to these distressed families, which, he observed by the way, the civil law called *restitutio in integrum.* But Mammon was struggling with Remorse for retaining his place in a bosom he had so long possessed ; and he partly succeeded, as an old tyrant proves often too strong for his insurgent rebels.

" I canna do't," he answered, with a voice of despair. " It would kill me to do't; how can ye bid me pay back siller, when ye ken how I want it ? or dispone Beersheba, when it lies sae weel into my ain plaid-nuik ? Nature made Dumbiedikes and Beersheba to be ae man's land. She did, by ——. Nichil, it wad kill me to part them."

" But ye maun die whether or no, Laird," said Mr. Novit ; " and maybe ye wad die easier ; it's but trying. I'll scroll the disposition in nae time."

"Dinna speak o't, sir," replied Dumbiedikes, "or I'll fling the stoup at your head. But, Jock, lad, ye see how the warld warstles wi' me on my death-bed ; be kind to the puir creatures, the Deanses and the Butlers—be kind to them, Jock. Dinna let the warld get a grip o' ye, Jock ; but keep the gear thegither ! and whate'er ye do, dispone Beersheba at no rate. Let the creatures stay at a moderate mailing, and hae bite and soup ; it will maybe be the better wi' your father whare he's gaun, lad."

After these contradictory instructions, the Laird felt his mind so much at ease that he drank three bumpers of brandy continuously, and " soughed awa'," as Jenny expressed it, in an attempt to sing " Deil stick the minister."

His death made a revolution in favor of the distressed families. John Dumbie, now of Dumbiedikes, in his own right, seemed to be close and selfish enough ; but wanted the grasping spirit and active mind of his father ; and his guardian happened to agree with him in opinion that his father's dying recommendation should be attended to. The tenants, therefore, were not actually turned out-of-doors among the snow wreaths, and were allowed wherewith to procure buttermilk and pease bannocks, which they ate under the full force of the original malediction. The cottage of Deans, called Woodend, was not very distant from that of Beersheba. Formerly there had been little intercourse between the families. Deans was a sturdy Scotchman, with all sorts of prejudices against the Southern, and the spawn of the Southern. Moreover, Deans was, as we have said, a stanch Presbyterian, of the most rigid and unbending adherence to what he conceived to be the only possible straight line, as he was wont to express himself, between right-hand heats and extremes and left-hand defections ; and, therefore, he held in high dread and horror all Independents, and whomsoever he supposed allied to them.

But, notwithstanding these national prejudices and religious professions, Deans and the widow Butler were placed in such a situation as naturally and at length created some intimacy between the families.   They had shared a common danger and a mutual deliverance.   They needed each other's assistance, like a company who, crossing a mountain stream, are compelled to cling close together, lest the current should be too powerful for any who are not thus supported.

On nearer acquaintance, too, Deans abated some of his prejudices.   He found old Mrs. Butler, though not thoroughly grounded in the extent and bearing of the real testimony against the defections of the times, had no opinions in favor of the Independent party ; neither was she an Englishwoman. Therefore, it was to be hoped that, though she was the widow of an enthusiastic corporal of Cromwell's dragoons, her grandson might be neither schismatic nor anti-national, two qualities concerning which Goodman Deans had as wholesome a terror as against Papists and Malignants.   Above all, for Douce Davie Deans had his weak side, he perceived that widow Butler looked up to him with reverence, listened to his advice, and compounded for an occasional fling at the doctrines of her deceased husband, to which, as we have seen, she was by no means warmly attached, in consideration of the valuable counsels which the Presbyterian afforded her for the management of her little farm.   These usually concluded with, "they may do otherwise in England, neighbor Butler, for aught I ken ;" or, "it may be different in foreign parts ;" or, "they wha think differently on the great foundation of our covenanted reformation, overturning and misguggling the government and discipline of the kirk, and breaking down the carved work of our Zion, might be for sawing the craft wi' aits ; but I say pease, pease."   And as his advice was shrewd and sensible, though conceitedly given, it was received with gratitude, and followed with respect.

The intercourse which took place betwixt the families at Beersheba and Woodend became strict and intimate, at a very early period, betwixt Reuben Butler, with whom the reader is already in some degree acquainted, and Jeanie Deans, the only child of Douce Davie Deans by his first wife, "that singular Christian woman," as he was wont to express himself, "whose name was savory to all that knew her for a desirable professor, Christian Menzies in Hochmagirdle."   The manner of which intimacy, and the consequences thereof, we now proceed to relate.

CHAPTER IX

Reuben and Rachel, though as fond as doves,
Were yet discreet and cautious in their loves,
Nor would attend to Cupid's wild commands,
Till cool reflection bade them join their hands.
When both were poor, they thought it argued ill
Of hasty love to make them poorer still.
CRABBE'S *Parish Register.*

WHILE widow Butler and widower Deans struggled with poverty, and the hard and sterile soil of those "parts and portions" of the lands of Dumbiedikes which it was their lot to occupy, it became gradually apparent that Deans was to gain the strife, and his ally in the conflict was to lose it. The former was a man, and not much past the prime of life; Mrs. Butler a woman, and declined into the vale of years. This, indeed, ought in time to have been balanced by the circumstance that Reuben was growing up to assist his grandmother's labors, and that Jeanie Deans, as a girl, could be only supposed to add to her father's burdens. But Douce Davie Deans knew better things, and so schooled and trained the young minion, as he called her, that from the time she could walk, upwards, she was daily employed in some task or other suitable to her age and capacity; a circumstance which, added to her father's daily instructions and lectures, tended to give her mind, even when a child, a grave, serious, firm, and reflecting cast. An uncommonly strong and healthy temperament, free from all nervous affection and every other irregularity, which, attacking the body in its more noble functions, so often influences the mind, tended greatly to establish this fortitude, simplicity, and decision of character.

On the other hand, Reuben was weak in constitution, and, though not timid in temper, might be safely pronounced anxious, doubtful, and apprehensive. He partook of the temperament of his mother, who had died of a consumption in early age. He was a pale, thin, feeble, sickly boy, and somewhat lame, from an accident in early youth. He was, besides, the child of a doting grandmother, whose too solicitous attention to him soon taught him a sort of diffidence in himself, with a disposition to overrate his own importance, which is one of the very worst consequences that children deduce from over-indulgence.

Still, however, the two children clung to each other's society, not more from habit than from taste. They herded together the handful of sheep, with the two or three cows, which their parents turned out rather to seek food than actually to feed upon the unenclosed common of Dumbiedikes. It was there that the two urchins might be seen seated beneath a blooming bush of whin, their little faces laid close together under the shadow of the same plaid drawn over both their heads, while the landscape around was embrowned by an overshadowing cloud, big with the shower which had driven the children to shelter. On other occasions they went together to school, the boy receiving that encouragement and example from his companion, in crossing the little brooks which intersected their path, and encountering cattle, dogs, and other perils upon their journey, which the male sex in such cases usually consider it as their prerogative to extend to the weaker. But when, seated on the benches of the school-house, they began to con their lessons together, Reuben, who was as much superior to Jeanie Deans in acuteness of intellect as inferior to her in firmness of constitution, and in that insensibility to fatigue and danger which depends on the conformation of the nerves, was able fully to requite the kindness and countenance with which, in other circumstances, she used to regard him. He was decidedly the best scholar at the little parish school; and so gentle was his temper and disposition, that he was rather admired than envied by the little mob who occupied the noisy mansion, although he was the declared favorite of the master. Several girls, in particular (for in Scotland they are taught with the boys), longed to be kind to and comfort the sickly lad, who was so much cleverer than his companions. The character of Reuben Butler was so calculated as to offer scope both for their sympathy and their admiration, the feelings, perhaps, through which the female sex, the more deserving part of them at least, is more easily attached.

But Reuben, naturally reserved and distant, improved none of these advantages; and only became more attached to Jeanie Deans, as the enthusiastic approbation of his master assured him of fair prospects in future life, and awakened his ambition. In the meantime, every advance that Reuben made in learning (and, considering his opportunities, they were uncommonly great) rendered him less capable of attending to the domestic duties of his grandmother's farm. While studying the *pons asinorum* in Euclid, he suffered every "cuddie" upon the common to trespass upon a large field of pease belonging to the Laird, and nothing but the active exertions of Jeanie Deans, with her little dog Dustiefoot, could have saved great loss and consequent punishment. Similar miscarriages marked his progress in his classical studies. He read Virgil's *Georgics* till he did not know bear from barley ; and had nearly destroyed the crofts of Beersheba while attempting to cultivate them according to the practice of Columella and Cato the Censor.

These blunders occasioned grief to his grand-dame, and disconcerted the good opinion which her neighbor, Davie Deans, had for some time entertained of Reuben.

"I see naething ye can make of that silly callant, neighbor Butler," said he to the old lady, "unless ye train him to the wark o' the ministry. And ne'er was there mair need of poorfu' preachers than e'en now in these cauld Gallio days, when men's hearts are hardened like the nether millstone, till they come to regard none of these things. It's evident this puir callant of yours will never be able to do an usefu' day's wark, unless it be as an ambassador from our Master ; and I will make it my business to procure a license when he is fit for the same, trusting he will be a shaft cleanly polished, and meet to be used in the body of the kirk, and that he shall not turn again, like the sow, to wallow in the mire of heretical extremes and defections, but shall have the wings of a dove, though he hath lain among the pots."

The poor widow gulped down the affront to her husband's principles implied in this caution, and hastened to take Butler from the High School, and encourage him in the pursuit of mathematics and divinity, the only physics and ethics that chanced to be in fashion at the time.

Jeanie Deans was now compelled to part from the companion of her labor, her study, and her pastime, and it was with more than childish feeling that both children regarded the separation. But they were young, and hope was high, and they separated like those who hope to meet again at a more auspicious hour.

While Reuben Butler was acquiring at the University of St. Andrews the knowledge necessary for a clergyman, and macerating his body with the privations which were necessary in seeking food for his mind, his grand-dame became daily less able to struggle with her little farm, and was at length obliged to throw it up to the new Laird of Dumbiedikes.

That great personage was no absolute Jew, and did not cheat her in making the bargain more than was tolerable. He even gave her permission to tenant the house in which she had lived with her husband, as long as it should be "tenantable;" only he protested against paying for a farthing of repairs, any benevolence which he possessed being of the passive, but by no means of the active mood.

In the meanwhile, from superior shrewdness, skill, and other circumstances, some of them purely accidental, Davie Deans gained a footing in the world, the possession of some wealth, the reputation of more, and a growing disposition to preserve and increase his store, for which, when he thought upon it seriously, he was inclined to blame himself. From his knowledge in agriculture, as it was then practised, he became a sort of favorite with the Laird, who had no pleasure either in active sports or in society, and was wont to end his daily saunter by calling at the cottage of Woodend.

Being himself a man of slow ideas and confused utterance, Dumbiedikes used to sit or stand for half an hour with an old laced hat of his father's upon his head, and an empty tobacco-pipe in his mouth, with his eyes following Jeanie Deans, or "the lassie," as he called her, through the course of her daily domestic labor; while her father, after exhausting the subject of bestial, of ploughs, and of harrows, often took an opportunity of going full-sail into controversial subjects, to which discussions the dignitary listened with much seeming patience, but without making any reply, or, indeed, as most people thought, without understanding a single word of what the orator was saying. Deans, indeed, denied this stoutly, as an insult at once to his own talents for expounding hidden truths, of which he was a little vain, and to the Laird's capacity of understanding them. He said, "Dumbiedikes was nane of these flashy gentles, wi' lace on their skirts and swords at their tails, that were rather for riding on horseback to hell than ganging barefooted to Heaven. He wasna like his father—nae profane company-keeper, nae swearer, nae drinker, nae frequenter of play-house, or music-house, or dancing-house, nae Sabbath-breaker, nae imposer of aiths, or bonds, or denier of liberty to the flock. He clave to the warld, and the warld's gear, a wee ower muckle, but then there was some breathing of a gale upon his spirit," etc., etc. All this honest Davie said and believed.

It is not to be supposed that, by a father and a man of sense and observation, the constant direction of the Laird's eyes towards Jeanie was altogether unnoticed. This circumstance, however, made a much greater impression upon another member of his family, a second helpmate, to wit, whom he had chosen to take to his bosom ten years after the death of his first. Some people were of opinion that Douce Davie had been rather surprised into this step, for in general he was no friend to marriages or giving in marriage, and seemed rather to regard that state of society as a necessary evil—a thing lawful, and to be tolerated in the imperfect state of our nature, but which clipped the wings with which we ought to soar upwards, and tethered the soul to its mansion of clay, and the creature comforts of wife and bairns. His own practice, however, had in this material point varied from his principles, since, as we have seen, he twice knitted for himself this dangerous and ensnaring entanglement.

Rebecca, his spouse, had by no means the same horror of matrimony, and as she made marriages in imagination for every neighbor round, she failed not to indicate a match betwixt Dumbiedikes and her stepdaughter Jeanie. The goodman used regularly to frown and pshaw whenever this topic was touched upon, but usually ended by taking his bonnet and walking out of the house to conceal a certain gleam of satisfaction which, at such a suggestion, involuntarily diffused itself over his austere features.

The more youthful part of my readers may naturally ask whether Jeanie Deans was deserving of this mute attention of the Laird of Dumbiedikes ; and the historian, with due regard to veracity, is compelled to answer that her personal attractions were of no uncommon description. She was short, and rather too stoutly made for her size, had gray eyes, light-colored hair, a round good-humored face, much tanned with the sun, and her only peculiar charm was an air of inexpressible serenity, which a good conscience, kind feelings, contented temper, and the regular discharge of all her duties, spread over her features. There was nothing, it may be supposed, very appalling in the form or manners of this rustic heroine ; yet, whether from sheepish bashfulness, or from want of decision and imperfect knowledge of his own mind on the subject, the Laird of Dumbiedikes, with his old laced hat and empty tobacco-pipe, came and enjoyed the beatific vision of Jeanie Deans day after day, week after week, year after year, without proposing to accomplish any of the prophecies of the stepmother.

This good lady began to grow doubly impatient on the subject when, after having been some years married, she herself presented Douce Davie with another daughter, who was named Euphemia, by corruption, Effie. It was then that Rebecca began to turn impatient with the slow pace at which the Laird's wooing proceeded, judiciously arguing that, as Lady Dumbiedikes would have but little occasion for tocher, the principal part of her gudeman's substance would naturally descend to the child by the second marriage. Other step-dames have tried less laudable means for clearing the way to the succession of their own children; but Rebecca, to do her justice, only sought little Effie's advantage through the promotion, or which must have generally been accounted such, of her elder sister. She therefore tried every female art within the compass of her simple skill to bring the Laird to a point; but had the mortification to perceive that her efforts, like those of an unskilful angler, only scared the trout she meant to catch. Upon one occasion, in particular, when she joked with the Laird on the propriety of giving a mistress to the house of Dumbiedikes, he was so effectually startled that neither laced hat, tobacco-pipe, nor the intelligent proprietor of these movables, visited Woodend for a fortnight. Rebecca was therefore compelled to leave the Laird to proceed at his own snail's pace, convinced by experience of the grave-digger's aphorism, that your dull ass will not mend his pace for beating.

Reuben in the meantime pursued his studies at the university, supplying his wants by teaching the younger lads the knowledge he himself acquired, and thus at once gaining the means of maintaining himself at the seat of learning and fixing in his mind the elements of what he had already obtained. In this manner, as is usual among the poorer students of divinity at Scottish universities, he contrived not only to maintain himself according to his simple wants, but even to send considerable assistance to his sole remaining parent, a sacred duty of which the Scotch are seldom negligent. His progress in knowledge of a general kind, as well as in the studies proper to his profession, was very considerable, but was little remarked, owing to the retired modesty of his disposition, which in no respect qualified him to set off his learning to the best advantage. And, thus had Butler been a man given to make complaints, he had his tale to tell, like others, of unjust preferences, bad luck, and hard usage. On these subjects, however, he was habitually silent, perhaps from modesty, perhaps from a touch of pride, or perhaps from a conjunction of both.

He obtained his license as a preacher of the Gospel, with some compliments from the presbytery by whom it was be-

The Laird of Dumbiedykes in Dean's cottage, Woodend.

stowed ; but this did not lead to any preferment, and he found it necessary to make the cottage at Beersheba his residence for some months, with no other income than was afforded by the precarious occupation of teaching in one or other of the neighboring families. After having greeted his aged grandmother, his first visit was to Woodend, where he was received by Jeanie with warm cordiality, arising from recollections which had never been dismissed from her mind, by Rebecca with good-humored hospitality, and by old Deans in a mode peculiar to himself.

Highly as Douce Davie honored the clergy, it was not upon each individual of the cloth that he bestowed his approbation ; and, a little jealous, perhaps, at seeing his youthful acquaintance erected into the dignity of a teacher and preacher, he instantly attacked him upon various points of controversy, in order to discover whether he might not have fallen into some of the snares, defections, and desertions of the time. Butler was not only a man of stanch Presbyterian principles, but was also willing to avoid giving pain to his old friend by disputing upon points of little importance ; and therefore he might have hoped to have come like refined gold out of the furnace of Davie's interrogatories. But the result on the mind of that strict investigator was not altogether so favorable as might have been hoped and anticipated. Old Judith Butler, who had hobbled that evening as far as Woodend, in order to enjoy the congratulations of her neighbors upon Reuben's return, and upon his high attainments, of which she was herself not a little proud, was somewhat mortified to find that her old friend Deans did not enter into the subject with the warmth she expected. At first, indeed, he seemed rather silent than dissatisfied ; and it was not till Judith had essayed the subject more than once that it led to the following dialogue :

" Aweel, neibor Deans, I thought ye wad hae been glad to see Reuben amang us again, poor fallow."

" I *am* glad, Mrs. Butler," was the neighbor's concise answer.

" Since he has lost his grandfather and his father—praised be Him that giveth and taketh !—I ken nae friend he has in the world that's been sae like a father to him as the sell o' ye, neibor Deans."

" God is the only Father of the fatherless," said Deans, touching his bonnet and looking upwards. " Give honor where it is due, gudewife, and not to an unworthy instrument."

" Aweel, that's your way o' turning it, and nae doubt ye

ken best.   But I hae kenn'd ye, Davie, send a forpit o' meal to Beersheba when there wasna a bow left in the meal-ark at Woodend ; ay, and I hae kenn'd ye——"

"Gudewife," said Davie, interrupting her, " these are but idle tales to tell me, fit for naething but to puff up our inward man wi' our ain vain acts.   I stude beside blessed Alexander Peden, when I heard him call the death and testimony of our happy martyrs but draps of bluid and scarts of ink in respect of fitting discharge of our duty ; and what suld I think of onything the like of me can do ?"

"Weel, neibor Deans, ye ken best ; but I maun say that I am sure you are glad to see my bairn again.   The halt's gane now, unless he has to walk ower mony miles at a stretch ; and he has a wee bit color in his cheek, that glads my auld een to see it ; and he has as decent a black coat as the minister ; and——"

"I am very heartily glad he is weel and thriving," said Mr. Deans, with a gravity that seemed intended to cut short the subject ; but a woman who is bent upon a point is not easily pushed aside from it.

"And," continued Mrs. Butler, " he can wag his head in a pulpit now, neibor Deans, think but of that—my ain oe—and a'body maun sit still and listen to him, as if he were the Paip of Rome."

"The what ? the who, woman ?" said Deans, with a sternness far beyond his usual gravity, as soon as these offensive words had struck upon the tympanum of his ear.

"Eh, guide us !" said the poor woman ; " I had forgot what an ill will ye had aye at the Paip, and sae had my puir gudeman, Stephen Butler.   Mony an afternoon he wad sit and take up his testimony again the Paip, and again baptising of bairns, and the like."

"Woman," reiterated Deans, " either speak about what ye ken something o', or be silent.   I say that Independency is a foul heresy, and Anabaptism a damnable and deceiving error, whilk suld be rooted out of the land wi' the fire o' the spiritual and the sword o' the civil magistrate."

"Weel, weel, neibor, I'll no say that ye mayna be right," answered the submissive Judith.   "I am sure ye are right about the sawing and the mawing, the shearing and the leading, and what for suld ye no be right about kirk-wark, too ?   But concerning my oe, Reuben Butler——"

"Reuben Butler, gudewife," said David, with solemnity, "is a lad I wish heartily weel to, even as if he were mine ain son ; but I doubt there will be outs and ins in the track of his walk. I muckle fear his gifts will get the heels of his grace. He has ower muckle human wit and learning, and thinks as muckle about the form of the bicker as he does about the healsomeness of the food ; he maun broider the marriage-garment with lace and passments, or it's no gude eneugh for him. And it's like he's something proud o' his human gifts and learning, whilk enables him to dress up his doctrine in that fine airy dress. But," added he, at seeing the old woman's uneasiness at his discourse, "affliction may gie him a jagg, and let the wind out o' him, as out o' a cow that's eaten wet clover, and the lad may do weel, and be a burning and a shining light ; and I trust it will be yours to see, and his to feel it, and that soon."

Widow Butler was obliged to retire, unable to make anything more of her neighbor, whose discourse, though she did not comprehend it, filled her with undefined apprehensions on her grandson's account, and greatly depressed the joy with which she had welcomed him on his return. And it must not be concealed, in justice to Mr. Deans's discernment, that Butler, in their conference, had made a greater display of his learning than the occasion called for, or than was likely to be acceptable to the old man, who, accustomed to consider himself as a person pre-eminently entitled to dictate upon theological subjects of controversy, felt rather humbled and mortified when learned authorities were placed in array against him. In fact, Butler had not escaped the tinge of pedantry which naturally flowed from his education, and was apt, on many occasions, to make parade of his knowledge, when there was no need of such vanity.

Jeanie Deans, however, found no fault with this display of learning, but on the contrary, admired it ; perhaps on the same score that her sex are said to admire men of courage, on account of their own deficiency in that qualification. The circumstances of their families threw the young people constantly together ; their old intimacy was renewed, though upon a footing better adapted to their age ; and it became at length understood betwixt them that their union should be deferred no longer than until Butler should obtain some steady means of support, however humble. This, however, was not a matter speedily to be accomplished. Plan after plan was formed, and plan after plan failed. The good-humored cheek of Jeanie lost the first flush of juvenile freshness ; Reuben's brow assumed the gravity of manhood ; yet the means of obtaining a settlement seemed remote as ever. Fortunately for the lovers, their passion was of no ardent or enthusiastic cast ;

and a sense of duty on both sides induced them to bear with patient fortitude the protracted interval which divided them from each other.

In the meanwhile, time did not roll on without effecting his usual changes. The widow of Stephen Butler, so long the prop of the family of Beersheba, was gathered to her fathers ; and Rebecca, the careful spouse of our friend Davie Deans, was also summoned from her plans of matrimonial and domestic economy. The morning after her death, Reuben Butler went to offer his mite of consolation to his old friend and benefactor. He witnessed, on this occasion, a remarkable struggle betwixt the force of natural affection and the religious stoicism which the sufferer thought it was incumbent upon him to maintain under each earthly dispensation, whether of weal or woe.

On his arrival at the cottage, Jeanie, with her eyes overflowing with tears, pointed to the little orchard, " in which," she whispered with broken accents, " my poor father has been since his misfortune." Somewhat alarmed at this account, Butler entered the orchard, and advanced slowly towards his old friend, who, seated in a small rude arbor, appeared to be sunk in the extremity of his affliction. He lifted his eyes somewhat sternly as Butler approached, as if offended at the interruption ; but as the young man hesitated whether he ought to retreat or advance, he arose and came forward to meet him with a self-possessed and even dignified air.

" Young man," said the sufferer, " lay it not to heart though the righteous perish and the merciful are removed, seeing, it may well be said, that they are taken away from the evils to come. Woe to me, were I to shed a tear for the wife of my bosom, when I might weep rivers of water for this afflicted church, cursed as it is with carnal seekers and with the dead of heart."

" I am happy," said Butler, " that you can forget your private affliction in your regard for public duty."

" Forget, Reuben ? " said poor Deans, putting his handkerchief to his eyes. " She's not to be forgotten on this side of time ; but He that gives the wound can send the ointment. I declare there have been times during this night when my meditation has been so wrapped that I knew not of my heavy loss. It has been with me as with the worthy John Semple, called Carspharn John,* upon a like trial : I have been this night on the banks of Ulai, plucking an apple here and there."

Notwithstanding the assumed fortitude of Deans, which

* See Note 15.

he conceived to be the discharge of a great Christian duty, he had too good a heart not to suffer deeply under this heavy loss. Woodend became altogether distasteful to him ; and as he had obtained both substance and experience by his management of that little farm, he resolved to employ them as a dairy-farmer, or cow-feeder, as they are called in Scotland. The situation he chose for his new settlement was at a place called St. Leonard's Crags, lying betwixt Edinburgh and the mountain called Arthur's Seat, and adjoining to the extensive sheep pasture still named the King's Park, from its having been formerly dedicated to the preservation of the royal game. Here he rented a small lonely house, about half a mile distant from the nearest point of the city, but the site of which, with all the adjacent ground, is now occupied by the buildings which form the south-eastern suburb. An extensive pasture-ground adjoining, which Deans rented from the keeper of the Royal Park, enabled him to feed his milk-cows ; and the unceasing industry and activity of Jeanie, his eldest daughter, was exerted in making the most of their produce.

She had now less frequent opportunities of seeing Reuben, who had been obliged, after various disappointments, to accept the subordinate situation of assistant in a parochial school of some eminence, at three or four miles' distance from the city. Here he distinguished himself, and became acquainted with several respectable burgesses, who, on account of health or other reasons, chose that their children should commence their education in this little village. His prospects were thus gradually brightening, and upon each visit which he paid at St. Leonard's he had an opportunity of gliding a hint to this purpose into Jeanie's ear. These visits were necessarily very rare, on account of the demands which the duties of the school made upon Butler's time. Nor did he dare to make them even altogether so frequent as these avocations would permit. Deans received him with civility indeed, and even with kindness ; but Reuben, as is usual in such cases, imagined that he read his purpose in his eyes, and was afraid too premature an explanation on the subject would draw down his positive disapproval. Upon the whole, therefore, he judged it prudent to call at St. Leonard's just so frequently as old acquaintance and neighborhood seemed to authorize, and no oftener. There was another person who was more regular in his visits.

When Davie Deans intimated to the Laird of Dumbiedikes his purpose of "quitting wi' the land and house at Woodend,"

the Laird stared and said nothing. He made his usual visits at
the usual hour without remark, until the day before the term,
when, observing the bustle of moving furniture already commenced, the great east-country "awmrie" dragged out of its
nook, and standing with its shoulder to the company, like an
awkward booby about to leave the room, the Laird again stared
mightily, and was heard to ejaculate, "Hegh, sirs!" Even
after the day of departure was past and gone, the Laird of Dumbiedikes, at his usual hour, which was that at which David
Deans was wont to "loose the pleugh," presented himself before
the closed door of the cottage at Woodend, and seemed as much
astonished at finding it shut against his approach as if it was
not exactly what he had to expect. On this occasion he was
heard to ejaculate, "Gude guide us!" which, by those who knew
him, was considered as a very unusual mark of emotion. From
that moment forward, Dumbiedikes became an altered man,
and the regularity of his movements, hitherto so exemplary,
was as totally disconcerted as those of a boy's watch when he
has broken the main-spring. Like the index of the said watch,
did Dumbiedikes spin round the whole bounds of his little
property, which may be likened unto the dial of the timepiece, with unwonted velocity. There was not a cottage into
which he did not enter, nor scarce a maiden on whom he did
not stare. But so it was, that although there were better farm-
houses on the land than Woodend, and certainly much prettier
girls than Jeanie Deans, yet it did somehow befall that the
blank in the Laird's time was not so pleasantly filled up as it
had been. There was no seat accommodated him so well as the
"bunker" at Woodend, and no face he loved so much to gaze
on as Jeanie Deans's. So, after spinning round and round his
little orbit, and then remaining stationary for a week, it seems
to have occurred to him that he was not pinned down to cir-
culate on a pivot, like the hands of the watch, but possessed
the power of shifting his central point and extending his circle
if he thought proper. To realize which privilege of change
of place, he bought a pony from a Highland drover, and with
its assistance and company stepped, or rather stumbled, as far
as St. Leonard's Crags.

Jeanie Deans, though so much accustomed to the Laird's
staring that she was sometimes scarce conscious of his presence,
had nevertheless some occasional fears lest he should call in
the organ of speech to back those expressions of admiration
which he bestowed on her through his eyes. Should this
happen, farewell, she thought, to all chance of a union with
Butler. For her father, however stout-hearted and inde-

pendent in civil and religious principles, was not without that respect for the laird of the land so deeply imprinted on the Scottish tenantry of the period. Moreover, if he did not positively dislike Butler, yet his fund of carnal learning was often the object of sarcasms on David's part, which were perhaps founded in jealousy, and which certainly indicated no partiality for the party against whom they were launched. And, lastly, the match with Dumbiedikes would have presented irresistible charms to one who used to complain that he felt himself apt to take "ower grit an armfu' o' the warld." So that, upon the whole, the Laird's diurnal visits were disagreeable to Jeanie from apprehension of future consequences, and it served much to console her, upon removing from the spot where she was bred and born, that she had seen the last of Dumbiedikes, his laced hat, and tobacco-pipe. The poor girl no more expected he could muster courage to follow her to St. Leonard's Crags than that any of her apple-trees or cabbages, which she had left rooted in the "yard" at Woodend, would spontaneously, and unaided, have undertaken the same journey. It was, therefore, with much more surprise than pleasure that, on the sixth day after their removal to St. Leonard's, she beheld Dumbiedikes arrive, laced hat, tobacco-pipe, and all, and, with the self-same greeting of "How's a' wi' ye, Jeanie? Whare's the gudeman?" assume as nearly as he could the same position in the cottage at St. Leonard's which he had so long and so regularly occupied at Woodend. He was no sooner, however, seated than, with an unusual exertion of his powers of conversation, he added, "Jeanie—I say, Jeanie, woman;" here he extended his hand towards her shoulder with all the fingers spread out as if to clutch it, but in so bashful and awkward a manner that, when she whisked herself beyond its reach, the paw remained suspended in the air with the palm open, like the claw of an heraldic griffin. "Jeanie," continued the swain, in this moment of inspiration —"I say, Jeanie, it's a braw day out-bye, and the roads are no that ill for boot-hose."

"The deil's in the daidling body," muttered Jeanie between her teeth; "wha wad hae thought o' his daikering out this length?" And she afterwards confessed that she threw a little of this ungracious sentiment into her accent and manner; for her father being abroad, and the "body," as she irreverently termed the landed proprietor, "looking unco gleg and canty, she didna ken what he might be coming out wi' next."

Her frowns, however, acted as a complete sedative, and

the Laird relapsed from that day into his former taciturn habits, visiting the cow-feeder's cottage three or four times every week, when the weather permitted, with apparently no other purpose than to stare at Jeanie Deans, while Douce Davie poured forth his eloquence upon the controversies and testimonies of the day.

CHAPTER X

Her air, her manners, all who saw admired,
Courteous, though coy, and gentle, though retired;
The joy of youth and health her eyes display'd,
And ease of heart her every look convey'd.

CRABBE.

THE visits of the Laird thus again sunk into matters of ordinary course, from which nothing was to be expected or apprehended. If a lover could have gained a fair one as a snake is said to fascinate a bird, by pertinaciously gazing on her with great stupid greenish eyes, which began now to be occasionally aided by spectacles, unquestionably Dumbiedikes would have been the person to perform the feat. But the art of fascination seems among the *artes perditæ*, and I cannot learn that this most pertinacious of starers produced any effect by his attentions beyond an occasional yawn.

In the meanwhile, the object of his gaze was gradually attaining the verge of youth, and approaching to what is called in females the middle age, which is impolitely held to begin a few years earlier with their more fragile sex than with men. Many people would have been of opinion that the Laird would have done better to have transferred his glances to an object possessed of far superior charms to Jeanie's, even when Jeanie's were in their bloom, who began now to be distinguished by all who visited the cottage at St. Leonard's Crags.

Effie Deans, under the tender and affectionate care of her sister, had now shot up into a beautiful and blooming girl. Her Grecian-shaped head was profusely rich in waving ringlets of brown hair, which, confined by a blue snood of silk, and shading a laughing Hebe countenance, seemed the picture of health, pleasure, and contentment. Her brown russet short-gown set off a shape which time, perhaps, might be expected to render too robust, the frequent objection to Scottish beauty, but which, in her present early age, was slender and taper, with that graceful and easy sweep of outline which at once indicates health and beautiful proportion of parts.

These growing charms, in all their juvenile profusion, had

no power to shake the steadfast mind, or divert the fixed gaze, of the constant Laird of Dumbiedikes. But there was scarce another eye that could behold this living picture of health and beauty without pausing on it with pleasure. The traveller stopped his weary horse on the eve of entering the city which was the end of his journey, to gaze at the sylph-like form that tripped by him, with her milk-pail poised on her head, bearing herself so erect, and stepping so light and free under her burden, that it seemed rather an ornament than an encumbrance. The lads of the neighboring suburb, who held their evening rendezvous for putting the stone, casting the hammer, playing at long bowls, and other athletic exercises, watched the motions of Effie Deans, and contended with each other which should have the good fortune to attract her attention. Even the rigid Presbyterians of her father's persuasion, who held each indulgence of the eye and sense to be a snare at least, if not a crime, were surprised into a moment's delight while gazing on a creature so exquisite—instantly checked by a sigh, reproaching at once their own weakness, and mourning that a creature so fair should share in the common and hereditary guilt and imperfection of our nature. She was currently entitled the Lily of St. Leonard's, a name which she deserved as much by her guileless purity of thought, speech, and action as by her uncommon loveliness of face and person.

Yet there were points in Effie's character which gave rise not only to strange doubt and anxiety on the part of Douce David Deans, whose ideas were rigid, as may easily be supposed, upon the subject of youthful amusements, but even of serious apprehension to her more indulgent sister. The children of the Scotch of the inferior classes are usually spoiled by the early indulgence of their parents; how, wherefore, and to what degree, the lively and instructive narrative of the amiable and accomplished authoress * of *Glenburnie* has saved me and all future scribblers the trouble of recording. Effie had had a double share of this inconsiderate and misjudged kindness. Even the strictness of her father's principles could not condemn the sports of infancy and childhood; and to the good old man his younger daughter, the child of his old age, seemed a child for some years after she attained the years of womanhood, was still called the " bit lassie " and "little Effie," and was permitted to run up and down uncontrolled, unless upon the Sabbath or at the times of family worship. Her sister, with all the love and care of a mother, could not be supposed to possess the same authoritative in-

* Mrs. Elizabeth Hamilton.

fluence; and that which she had hitherto exercised became gradually limited and diminished as Effie's advancing years entitled her, in her own conceit at least, to the right of independence and free agency.   With all the innocence and goodness of disposition, therefore, which we have described, the Lily of St. Leonard's possessed a little fund of self-conceit and obstinacy, and some warmth and irritability of temper, partly natural perhaps, but certainly much increased by the unrestrained freedom of her childhood.   Her character will be best illustrated by a cottage evening scene.

The careful father was absent in his well-stocked byre, foddering those useful and patient animals on whose produce his living depended, and the summer evening was beginning to close in, when Jeanie Deans began to be very anxious for the appearance of her sister, and to fear that she would not reach home before her father returned from the labor of the evening, when it was his custom to have " family exercise," and when she knew that Effie's absence would give him the most serious displeasure.   These apprehensions hung heavier upon her mind because, for several preceding evenings, Effie had disappeared about the same time, and her stay, at first so brief as scarce to be noticed, had been gradually protracted to half an hour, and an hour, and on the present occasion had considerably exceeded even this last limit.   And now Jeanie stood at the door, with her hand before her eyes to avoid the rays of the level sun, and looked alternately along the various tracks which led towards their dwelling, to see if she could descry the nymph-like form of her sister.   There was a wall and a stile which separated the royal domain, or King's Park, as it is called, from the public road; to this pass she frequently directed her attention, when she saw two persons appear there somewhat suddenly, as if they had walked close by the side of the wall to screen themselves from observation. One of them, a man, drew back hastily; the other, a female, crossed the stile and advanced towards her.   It was Effie. She met her sister with that affected liveliness of manner which, in her rank, and sometimes in those above it, females occasionally assume to hide surprise or confusion; and she carolled as she came—

> " The elfin knight sate on the brae,
>   The broom grows bonny, the broom grows fair ;
>   And by there came lilting a lady so gay,
>   And we daurna gang down to the broom nae mair."

" Whisht, Effie," said her sister; " our father's coming

out o' the byre."   The damsel stinted in her song.   " Whare
hae ye been sae late at e'en ? "

" It's no late, lass," answered Effie.

" It's chappit eight on every clock o' the town, and the
sun's gaun down ahint the Corstorphine Hills.   Whare can
ye hae been sae late ? "

" Nae gate," answered Effie.

" And wha was that parted wi' you at the stile ? "

" Naebody," replied Effie once more.

" Nae gate !   Naebody !   I wish it may be a right gate,
and a right body, that keeps folk out sae late at e'en,
Effie."

" What needs ye be aye speering, then, at folk ? " retorted
Effie.   " I'm sure, if ye'll ask nae questions, I'll tell ye nae
lees.   I never ask what brings the Laird of Dumbiedikes
glowering here like a wull-cat—only his een's greener, and
no sae gleg—day after day, till we are a' like to gaunt our
chafts aff."

" Because ye ken very weel he comes to see our father,"
said Jeanie, in answer to this pert remark.

" And Dominie Butler—does he come to see our father,
that's sae taen wi' his Latin words ? " said Effie, delighted to
find that, by carrying the war into the enemy's country, she
could divert the threatened attack upon herself, and with the
petulance of youth she pursued her triumph over her prudent
elder sister.   She looked at her with a sly air, in which there
was something like irony, as she chanted, in a low but marked
tone, a scrap of an old Scotch song—

> " Through the kirkyard
> I met wi' the Laird ;
> The silly puir body he said me nae harm.
> But just ere 'twas dark,
> I met wi the clerk— "

Here the songstress stopped, looked full at her sister, and,
observing the tear gather in her eyes, she suddenly flung her
arms round her neck and kissed them away.   Jeanie, though
hurt and displeased, was unable to resist the caresses of this
untaught child of nature, whose good and evil seemed to flow
rather from impulse than from reflection.   But as she returned
the sisterly kiss, in token of perfect reconciliation, she could
not suppress the gentle reproof—" Effie, if ye will learn fule
sangs, ye might make a kinder use of them."

" And so I might, Jeanie," continued the girl, clinging to
her sister's neck ; " and I wish I had never learned ane o' them,

and I wish we had never come here, and I wish my tongue had been blistered or I had vexed ye."

"Never mind that, Effie," replied the affectionate sister. "I canna be muckle vexed wi' onything ye say to me ; but O dinna vex our-father ! "

"I will not—I will not," replied Effie ; "and if there were as mony dances the morn's night as there are merry dancers in the north firmament on a frosty e'en, I winna budge an inch to gang near ane o' them."

"Dance ! " echoed Jeanie Deans in astonishment. "O, Effie, what could take ye to a dance ? "

It is very possible that, in the communicative mood into which the Lily of St. Leonard's was now surprised, she might have given her sister her unreserved confidence, and saved me the pain of telling a melancholy tale ; but at the moment the word "dance" was uttered, it reached the ear of old David Deans, who had turned the corner of the house, and came upon his daughters ere they were aware of his presence. The word "prelate," or even the word "pope," could hardly have produced so appalling an effect upon David's ear; for, of all exercises, that of dancing, which he termed a voluntary and regular fit of distraction, he deemed most destructive of serious thoughts, and the readiest inlet to all sort of licentiousness ; and he accounted the encouraging, and even permitting, assemblies or meetings, whether among those of high or low degree, for this fantastic and absurd purpose, or for that of dramatic representations, as one of the most flagrant proofs of defection and causes of wrath. The pronouncing of the word "dance" by his own daughters, and at his own door, now drove him beyond the verge of patience. "Dance ! " he exclaimed. "Dance—dance, said ye ? I daur ye, limmers that ye are, to name sic a word at my door-cheek ! It's a dissolute profane pastime, practised by the Israelites only at their base and brutal worship of the Golden Calf at Bethel, and by the unhappy lass wha danced aff the head of John the Baptist, upon whilk chapter I will exercise this night for your farther instruction, since ye need it sae muckle, nothing doubting that she has cause to rue the day, lang or this time, that e'er she suld hae shook a limb on sic an errand. Better for her to hae been born a cripple, and carried frae door to door, like auld Bessie Bowie, begging bawbees, than to be a king's daughter, fiddling and flinging the gate she did. I hae often wondered that ony ane that ever bent a knee for the right purpose should ever daur to crook a hough to fyke and fling at piper's wind and fiddler's squealing. And I bless God, with that singular worthy, Peter [Patrick] Walker,* the packman, at Bristo Port, that ordered my lot in my dancing days so that fear of my head and throat, dread of bloody rope and swift bullet, and trenchant swords and pain of boots and thumkins, cauld and hunger, wetness and weariness, stopped the lightness of my head and the wantonness of my feet. And now, if I hear ye, quean lassies, sae muckle as name dancing, or think there's sic a thing in this warld as flinging to fiddler's sounds and piper's springs, as sure as my father's spirit is with the just, ye shall be no more either charge or concern of mine! Gang in, then —gang in, then, hinnies," he added, in a softer tone, for the tears of both daughters, but especially those of Effie, began to flow very fast—"gang in, dears, and we'll seek grace to preserve us frae all manner of profane folly, whilk causeth to sin, and promoteth the kingdom of darkness, warring with the kingdom of light."

The objurgation of David Deans, however well meant, was unhappily timed. It created a division of feelings in Effie's bosom, and deterred her from her intended confidence in her sister. "She wad haud me nae better than the dirt below her feet," said Effie to herself, "were I to confess I hae danced wi' him four times on the green down-bye, and ance at Maggie Macqueen's ; and she'll maybe hing it ower my head that she'll tell my father, and then she wad be mistress and mair. But I'll no gang back there again. I'm resolved I'll no gang back. I'll lay in a leaf of my Bible,† and that's very near as if I had made an aith, that I winna gang back." And she kept her vow for a week, during which she was unusually cross and fretful, blemishes which had never before been observed in her temper, except during a moment of contradiction.

There was something in all this so mysterious as considerably to alarm the prudent and affectionate Jeanie, the more so as she judged it unkind to her sister to mention to their father grounds of anxiety which might arise from her own imagination. Besides, her respect for the good old man did not prevent her from being aware that he was both hot-tempered and positive, and she sometimes suspected that he carried his dislike to youthful amusements beyond the verge that religion and reason demanded. Jeanie had sense enough to see that a sudden and severe curb upon her sister's hitherto unrestrained freedom might be rather productive of harm than good, and that Effie, in the headstrong wilfulness of youth,

---

* See Patrick Walker. Note 16.

† This custom, of making a mark by folding a leaf in the party's Bible when a solemn resolution is formed, is still held to be, in some sense, an appeal to Heaven for his or her sincerity.

was likely to make what might be overstrained in her father's precepts an excuse to herself for neglecting them altogether. In the higher classes a damsel, however giddy, is still under the dominion of etiquette, and subject to the surveillance of mammas and chaperons ; but the country girl, who snatches her moment of gayety during the intervals of labor, is under no such guardianship or restraint, and her amusement becomes so much the more hazardous. Jeanie saw all this with much distress of mind, when a circumstance occurred which appeared calculated to relieve her anxiety.

Mrs. Saddletree, with whom our readers have already been made acquainted, chanced to be a distant relation of Douce David Deans, and as she was a woman orderly in her life and conversation, and, moreover, of good substance, a sort of acquaintance was formally kept up between the families. Now this careful dame, about a year and a half before our story commences, chanced to need, in the line of her profession, a better sort of servant, or rather shop-woman. "Mr. Saddletree," she said, "was never in the shop when he could get his nose within the Parliament House, and it was an awkward thing for a woman-body to be standing among bundles o' barkened leather her lane, selling saddles and bridles ; and she had cast her eyes upon her far-awa' cousin, Effie Deans, as just the very sort of lassie she would want to keep her in countenance on such occasions."

In this proposal there was much that pleased old David : there was bed, board, and bountith ; it was a decent situation ; the lassie would be under Mrs. Saddletree's eye, who had an upright walk, and lived close by the Tolbooth Kirk, in which might still be heard the comforting doctrines of one of those few ministers of the Kirk of Scotland who had not bent the knee unto Baal, according to David's expression, or become accessory to the course of national defections—union, toleration, patronages, and a bundle of prelatical Erastian oaths which had been imposed on the church since the Revolution, and particularly in the reign of "the late woman," as he called Queen Anne, the last of that unhappy race of Stuarts. In the good man's security concerning the soundness of the theological doctrine which his daughter was to hear, he was nothing disturbed on account of the snares of a different kind to which a creature so beautiful, young, and wilful might be exposed in the centre of a populous and corrupted city. The fact is, that he thought with so much horror on all approaches to irregularities of the nature most to be dreaded in such cases, that he would as soon have suspected and guarded against Effie's being induced to become guilty of the crime of murder. He only regretted that she should live under the same roof with such a worldly-wise man as Bartoline Saddletree, whom David never suspected of being an ass as he was, but considered as one really endowed with all the legal knowledge to which he made pretension, and only liked him the worse for possessing it. The lawyers, especially those among them who sat as ruling elders in the General Assembly of the Kirk, had been forward in promoting the measures of patronage, of the abjuration oath, and others, which in the opinion of David Deans were a breaking down of the carved work of the sanctuary, and an intrusion upon the liberties of the kirk. Upon the dangers of listening to the doctrines of a legalized formalist, such as Saddletree, David gave his daughter many lectures; so much so, that he had time to touch but slightly on the dangers of chambering, company-keeping, and promiscuous dancing, to which, at her time of life, most people would have thought Effie more exposed than to the risk of theoretical error in her religious faith.

Jeanie parted from her sister with a mixed feeling of regret, and apprehension, and hope. She could not be so confident concerning Effie's prudence as her father, for she had observed her more narrowly, had more sympathy with her feelings, and could better estimate the temptations to which she was exposed. On the other hand, Mrs. Saddletree was an observing, shrewd, notable woman, entitled to exercise over Effie the full authority of a mistress, and likely to do so strictly, yet with kindness. Her removal to Saddletree's, it was most probable, would also serve to break off some idle acquaintances which Jeanie suspected her sister to have formed in the neighboring suburb. Upon the whole, then, she viewed her departure from St. Leonard's with pleasure, and it was not until the very moment of their parting for the first time in their lives, that she felt the full force of sisterly sorrow. While they repeatedly kissed each other's cheeks and wrung each other's hands, Jeanie took that moment of affectionate sympathy to press upon her sister the necessity of the utmost caution in her conduct while residing in Edinburgh. Effie listened, without once raising her large dark eyelashes, from which the drops fell so fast as almost to resemble a fountain. At the conclusion she sobbed again, kissed her sister, promised to recollect all the good counsel she had given her, and they parted.

During the first few weeks, Effie was all th‑ her kinswoman expected, and even more. But with time there came a relaxation of that early zeal which she manifested in Mrs. Saddletree's service. To borrow once again from the poet who so correctly and beautifully describes living manners—

> Something there was,—what, none presumed to say,—
> Clouds lightly passing on a summer's day ;
> Whispers and hints, which went from ear to ear,
> And mix'd reports no judge on earth could clear.

During this interval, Mrs. Saddletree was sometimes displeased by Effie's lingering when she was sent upon errands about the shop business, and sometimes by a little degree of impatience which she manifested at being rebuked on such occasions. But she good-naturedly allowed that the first was very natural to a girl to whom everything in Edinburgh was new, and the other was only the petulance of a spoiled child when subjected to the yoke of domestic discipline for the first time. Attention and submission could not be learned at once ; Holy-Rood was not built in a day ; use would make perfect.

It seemed as if the considerate old lady had presaged truly. Ere many months had passed, Effie became almost wedded to her duties, though she no longer discharged them with the laughing cheek and light step which at first had attracted every customer. Her mistress sometimes observed her in tears ; but they were signs of secret sorrow, which she concealed as often as she saw them attract notice. Time wore on, her cheek grew pale, and her step heavy. The cause of these changes could not have escaped the matronly eye of Mrs. Saddletree, but she was chiefly confined by indisposition to her bedroom for a considerable time during the latter part of Effie's service. This interval was marked by symptoms of anguish almost amounting to despair. The utmost efforts of the poor girl to command her fits of hysterical agony were often totally unavailing, and the mistakes which she made in the shop the while were so numerous and so provoking, that Bartoline Saddletree, who, during his wife's illness, was obliged to take closer charge of the business than consisted with his study of the weightier matters of the law, lost all patience with the girl, who, in his law Latin, and without much respect to gender, he declared ought to be cognosced by inquest of a jury, as *fatuus, furiosus,* and *naturaliter idiota.* Neighbors, also, and fellow-servants, remarked, with malicious curiosity or degrading pity, the disfigured shape, loose dress, and pale cheeks of the once beautiful and still interesting girl. But to no one would she grant her confidence, answering all taunts with bitter sarcasm, and all serious expostulation with sullen denial, or with floods of tears.

At length, when Mrs. Saddletree's recovery was likely to permit her wonted attention to the regulation of her household, Effie Deans, as if unwilling to face an investigation made by the authority of her mistress, asked permission of Bartoline to go home for a week or two, assigning indisposition, and the wish of trying the benefit of repose and the change of air, as the motives of her request. Sharp-eyed as a lynx, or conceiving himself to be so, in the nice sharp quillets of legal discussion, Bartoline was as dull at drawing inferences from the occurrences of common life as any Dutch professor of mathematics. He suffered Effie to depart without much suspicion, and without any inquiry.

It was afterwards found that a period of a week intervened betwixt her leaving her master's house and arriving at St. Leonard's. She made her appearance before her sister in a state rather resembling the specter than the living substance of the gay and beautiful girl who had left her father's cottage for the first time scarce seventeen months before. The lingering illness of her mistress had, for the last few months given her a plea for confining herself entirely to the dusky precincts of the shop in the Lawnmarket, and Jeanie was so much occupied, during the same period, with the concerns of her father's household, that she had rarely found leisure for a walk into the city, and a brief and hurried visit to her sister. The young women, therefore, had scarcely seen each other for several months, nor had a single scandalous surmize reached the ears of the secluded inhabitants of the cottage at St. Leonard's. Jeanie, therefore, terrified to death at her sister's appearance, at first overwhelmed her with inquiries, to which the unfortunate young woman returned for a time incoherent and rambling answers, and finally fell into a hysterical fit. Rendered too certain of her sister's misfortune, Jeanie had now the dreadful alternative of communicating her ruin to her father or of endeavoring to conceal it from him. To all questions concerning the name or rank of her seducer, and the fate of the being to whom her fall had given birth, Effie remained mute as the grave, to which she seemed hastening; and indeed the least allusion to either seemed to drive her to distraction. Her sister, in distress and in despair, was about to repair to Mrs. Saddletree to consult her experience, and at the same time to obtain what lights she could upon this most unhappy affair, when she was saved that trouble by a new stroke of fate, which seemed to carry misfortune to the uttermost.

David Deans had been alarmed at the state of health in which his daughter had returned to her paternal residence ; but Jeanie had contrived to divert him from particular and specific inquiry. It was, therefore, like a clap of thunder to the poor old man when, just as the hour of noon had brought the visit of the Laird of Dumbiedikes as usual, other and sterner, as well as most unexpected, guests arrived at the cottage of St. Leonard's. These were the officers of justice, with a warrant of justiciary to search for and apprehend Euphemia or Effie Deans, accused of the crime of child-murder. The stunning weight of a blow so totally unexpected bore down the old man, who had in his early youth resisted the brow of military and civil tyranny, though backed with swords and guns, tortures and gibbets. He fell extended and senseless upon his own hearth ; and the men, happy to escape from the scene of his awakening, raised, with rude humanity, the object of their warrant from her bed, and placed her in a coach, which they had brought with them. The hasty remedies which Jeanie had applied to bring back her father's senses were scarce begun to operate when the noise of the wheels in motion recalled her attention to her miserable sister. To run shrieking after the carriage was the first vain effort of her distraction, but she was stopped by one or two female neighbors, assembled by the extraordinary appearance of a coach in that sequestered place, who almost forced her back to her father's house. The deep and sympathetic affliction of these poor people, by whom the little family at St. Leonard's were held in high regard, filled the house with lamentation. Even Dumbiedikes was moved from his wonted apathy, and, groping for his purse as he spoke, ejaculated, " Jeanie, woman !— Jeanie, woman ! dinna greet. It's sad wark ; but siller will help it," and he drew out his purse as he spoke.

The old man had now raised himself from the ground, and, looking about him as if he missed something, seemed gradually to recover the sense of his wretchedness. " Where," he said, with a voice that made the roof ring—" where is the vile harlot that has disgraced the blood of an honest man ? Where is she that has no place among us, but has come foul with her sins, like the Evil One, among the children of God ? Where is she, Jeanie ? Bring her before me, that I may kill her with a word and a look ! "

All hastened around him with their appropriate sources of consolation—the Laird with his purse, Jeanie with burned feathers and strong waters, and the women with their exhortations. "O neighbor—O Mr. Deans, it's a sair trial, doubtless; but think of the Rock of Ages, neighbor, think of the promise!"

"And I do think of it, neighbors, and I bless God that I can think of it, even in the wrack and ruin of a' that's nearest and dearest to me. But to be the father of a castaway, a profligate, a bloody Zipporah, a mere murderess! O, how will the wicked exult in the high places of their wickedness! —the prelatists, and the latitudinarians, and the hand-waled murderers, whose hands are hard as horn wi' hauding the slaughter-weapons; they will push out the lip, and say that we are even such as themselves. Sair, sair I am grieved, neighbors, for the poor castaway, for the child of mine old age; but sairer for the stumbling-block and scandal it will be to all tender and honest souls!"

"Davie, winna siller do't?" insinuated the Laird, still proffering his green purse, which was full of guineas.

"I tell ye, Dumbiedikes," said Deans, "that if telling down my haill substance could hae saved her frae this black snare, I wad hae walked out wi' naething but my bonnet and my staff to beg an awmous for God's sake, and ca'd mysell an happy man. But if a dollar, or a plack, or the nineteenth part of a boddle wad save her open guilt and open shame frae open punishment, that purchase wad David Deans never make. Na, na; an eye for an eye, a tooth for a tooth, life for life, blood for blood: it's the law of man, and it's the law of God. Leave me, sirs—leave me; I maun warstle wi' this trial in privacy and on my knees."

Jeanie, now in some degree restored to the power of thought, joined in the same request. The next day found the father and daughter still in the depth of affliction, but the father sternly supporting his load of ill through a proud sense of religious duty, and the daughter anxiously suppressing her own feelings to avoid again awakening his. Thus was it with the afflicted family until the morning after Porteous's death, a period at which we are now arrived.

CHAPTER XI

Is all the counsel that we two have shared,
The sisters' vows, the hours that we have spent
When we have chid the hasty-footed time
For parting us—Oh! and is all forgot?
       Midsummer Night's Dream.

WE have been a long while in conducting Butler to the door
of the cottage at St. Leonard's; yet the space which we have
occupied in the preceding narrative does not exceed in length
that which he actually spent on Salisbury Crags on the morning which succeeded the execution done upon Porteous by the
rioters. For this delay he had his own motives. He wished
to collect his thoughts, strangely agitated as they were, first
by the melancholy news of Effie Deans's situation, and afterwards by the frightful scene which he had witnessed. In the
situation also in which he stood with respect to Jeanie and her
father, some ceremony, at least some choice of fitting time
and season, was necessary to wait upon them. Eight in the
morning was then the ordinary hour for breakfast, and he resolved that it should arrive before he made his appearance in
their cottage.

Never did hours pass so heavily. Butler shifted his place
and enlarged his circle to while away the time, and heard the
huge bell of St. Giles's toll each successive hour in swelling
tones, which were instantly attested by those of the other
steeples in succession. He had heard seven struck in this
manner, when he began to think he might venture to approach
nearer to St. Leonard's, from which he was still a mile distant. Accordingly he descended from his lofty station as low
as the bottom of the valley which divides Salisbury Crags
from those small rocks which take their name from St.
Leonard. It is, as many of my readers may know, a deep,
wild, grassy valley, scattered with huge rocks and fragments
which have descended from the cliffs and steep ascent to the
east.

This sequestered dell, as well as other places of the open
pasturage of the King's Park, was, about this time, often the

resort of the gallants of the time who had affairs of honor to discuss with the sword. Duels were then very common in Scotland, for the gentry were at once idle, haughty, fierce, divided by faction, and addicted to intemperance, so that there lacked neither provocation nor inclination to resent it when given ; and the sword, which was part of every gentleman's dress, was the only weapon used for the decision of such differences. When, therefore, Butler observed a young man skulking, apparently to avoid observation, among the scattered rocks at some distance from the footpath, he was naturally led to suppose that he had sought this lonely spot upon that evil errand. He was so strongly impressed with this that, notwithstanding his own distress of mind, he could not, according to his sense of duty as a clergyman, pass this person without speaking to him. "There are times," thought he to himself, "when the slightest interference may avert a great calamity— when a word spoken in season may do more for prevention than the eloquence of Tully could do for remedying evil. And for my own griefs, be they as they may, I shall feel them the lighter if they divert me not from the prosecution of my duty."

Thus thinking and feeling, he quitted the ordinary path and advanced nearer the object he had noticed. The man at first directed his course towards the hill, in order, as it appeared, to avoid him ; but when he saw that Butler seemed disposed to follow him, he adjusted his hat fiercely, turned round and came forward, as if to meet and defy scrutiny.

Butler had an opportunity of accurately studying his features as they advanced slowly to meet each other. The stranger seemed about twenty-five years old. His dress was of a kind which could hardly be said to indicate his rank with certainty, for it was such as young gentlemen sometimes wore while on active exercise in the morning, and which, therefore, was imitated by those of the inferior ranks, as young clerks and tradesmen, because its cheapness rendered it attainable, while it approached more nearly to the apparel of youths of fashion than any other which the manners of the times permitted them to wear. If his air and manner could be trusted, however, this person seemed rather to be dressed under than above his rank ; for his carriage was bold and somewhat supercilious, his step easy and free, his manner daring and unconstrained. His stature was of the middle size, or rather above it, his limbs well-proportioned, yet not so strong as to infer the reproach of clumsiness. His features were uncommonly handsome, and all about him would have been interesting and prepossessing, but for that indescribable expression which habitual dissipation gives to the countenance, joined with a certain audacity in look and manner, of that kind which is often assumed as a mask for confusion and apprehension.

Butler and the stranger met, surveyed each other; when, as the latter, slightly touching his hat, was about to pass by him, Butler, while he returned the salutation, observed, "A fine morning, sir. You are on the hill early."

"I have business here," said the young man, in a tone meant to repress further inquiry.

"I do not doubt it, sir," said Butler. "I trust you will forgive my hoping that it is of a lawful kind?"

"Sir," said the other with marked surprise, "I never forgive impertinence, nor can I conceive what title you have to hope anything about what no way concerns you."

"I am a soldier, sir," said Butler, "and have a charge to arrest evil-doers in the name of my Master."

"A soldier!" said the young man, stepping back and fiercely laying his hand on his sword—"a soldier, and arrest me? Did you reckon what your life was worth before you took the commission upon you?"

"You mistake me, sir," said Butler, gravely; "neither my warfare nor my warrant are of this world. I am a preacher of the Gospel, and have power, in my Master's name, to command the peace upon earth and good-will towards men which was proclaimed with the Gospel."

"A minister!" said the stranger, carelessly, and with an expression approaching to scorn. "I know the gentlemen of your cloth in Scotland claim a strange right of intermeddling with men's private affairs. But I have been abroad, and know better than to be priest-ridden."

"Sir, if it be true that any of my cloth, or, it might be more decently said, of my calling, interfere with men's private affairs, for the gratification either of idle curiosity or for worse motives, you cannot have learned a better lesson abroad than to contemn such practices. But, in my Master's work, I am called to be busy in season and out of season; and, conscious as I am of a pure motive, it were better for me to incur your contempt for speaking than the correction of my own conscience for being silent."

"In the name of the devil!" said the young man, impatiently, "say what you have to say, then; though whom you take me for, or what earthly concern you can have with me, a stranger to you, or with my actions and motives, of which you can know nothing, I cannot conjecture for an instant."

"You are about," said Butler, "to violate one of your country's wisest laws, you are about—which is much more dreadful—to violate a law which God Himself has implanted within our nature, and written, as it were, in the table of our hearts, to which every thrill of our nerves is responsive."

"And what is the law you speak of?" said the stranger, in a hollow and somewhat disturbed accent.

"Thou shalt do no MURDER," said Butler, with a deep and solemn voice.

The young man visibly started, and looked considerably appalled. Butler perceived he had made a favorable impression, and resolved to follow it up. "Think," he said, "young man," laying his hand kindly upon the stranger's shoulder, "what an awful alternative you voluntarily choose for yourself, to kill or be killed. Think what it is to rush uncalled into the presence of an offended Deity, your heart fermenting with evil passions, your hand hot from the steel you had been urging, with your best skill and malice, against the breast of a fellow-creature. Or, suppose yourself the scarce less wretched survivor, with the guilt of Cain, the first murderer, in your heart, with his stamp upon your brow—that stamp, which struck all who gazed on him with unutterable horror, and by which the murderer is made manifest to all who look upon him. Think——"

The stranger gradually withdrew himself from under the hand of his monitor; and, pulling his hat over his brows, thus interrupted him. "Your meaning, sir, I dare say, is excellent, but you are throwing your advice away. I am not in this place with violent intentions against any one. I may be bad enough—you priests say all men are so—but I am here for the purpose of saving life, not of taking it away. If you wish to spend your time rather in doing a good action than in talking about you know not what, I will give you an opportunity. Do you see yonder crag to the right, over which appears the chimney of a lone house? Go thither, inquire for one Jeanie Deans, the daughter of the goodman; let her know that he she wots of remained here from daybreak till this hour, expecting to see her, and that he can abide no longer. Tell her she *must* meet me at the Hunter's Bog to-night, as the moon rises behind St. Anthony's Hill, or that she will make a desperate man of me."

"Who or what are you," replied Butler, exceedingly and most unpleasantly surprised, "who charge me with such an errand?"

"I am the devil!" answered the young man, hastily.

Butler stepped instinctively back and commended himself internally to Heaven; for, though a wise and strong-minded man, he was neither wiser nor more strong-minded than those of his age and education, with whom to disbelieve witchcraft or spectres was held an undeniable proof of atheism.

The stranger went on without observing his emotion. "Yes! call me Apollyon, Abaddon, whatever name you shall choose, as a clergyman acquainted with the upper and lower circles of spiritual denomination, to call me by, you shall not find an appellation more odious to him that bears it than is mine own."

This sentence was spoken with the bitterness of self-upbraiding, and a contortion of visage absolutely demoniacal. Butler, though a man brave by principle, if not by constitution, was overawed; for intensity of mental distress has in it a sort of sublimity which repels and overawes all men, but especially those of kind and sympathetic dispositions. The stranger turned abruptly from Butler as he spoke, but instantly returned, and, coming up to him closely and boldly, said, in a fierce, determined tone, "I have told you who and what I am; who and what are you? What is your name?"

"Butler," answered the person to whom this abrupt question was addressed, surprised into answering it by the sudden and fierce manner of the querist—"Reuben Butler, a preacher of the Gospel."

At this answer, the stranger again plucked more deep over his brows the hat which he had thrown back in his former agitation. "Butler!" he repeated; "the assistant of the schoolmaster at Liberton?"

"The same," answered Butler, composedly.

The stranger covered his face with his hand, as if on sudden reflection, and then turned away; but stopped when he had walked a few paces, and seeing Butler follow him with his eyes, called out in a stern yet suppressed tone, just as if he had exactly calculated that his accents should not be heard a yard beyond the spot on which Butler stood. "Go your way and do mine errand. Do not look after me. I will neither descend through the bowels of these rocks, nor vanish in a flash of fire; and yet the eye that seeks to trace my motions shall have reason to curse it was ever shrouded by eyelid or eyelash. Begone, and look not behind you. Tell Jeanie Deans that when the moon rises I shall expect to meet her at Nicol Muschat's Cairn, beneath St. Anthony's Chapel."

As he uttered these words, he turned and took the road

against the hill, with a haste that seemed as peremptory as his tone of authority.

Dreading he knew not what of additional misery to a lot which seemed little capable of receiving augmentation, and desperate at the idea that any living man should dare to send so extraordinary a request, couched in terms so imperious, to the half-betrothed object of his early and only affection, Butler strode hastily towards the cottage, in order to ascertain how far this daring and rude gallant was actually entitled to press on Jeanie Deans a request which no prudent, and scarce any modest, young woman was likely to comply with.

Butler was by nature neither jealous nor superstitious; yet the feelings which lead to those moods of the mind were rooted in his heart, as a portion derived from the common stock of humanity. It was maddening to think that a profligate gallant, such as the manner and tone of the stranger evinced him to be, should have it in his power to command forth his future bride and plighted true-love, at a place so improper and an hour so unseasonable. Yet the tone in which the stranger spoke had nothing of the soft, half-breathed voice proper to the seducer who solicits an assignation; it was bold, fierce, and imperative, and had less of love in it than of menace and intimidation.

The suggestions of superstition seemed more plausible, had Butler's mind been very accessible to them. Was this indeed the Roaring Lion, who goeth about seeking whom he may devour? This was a question which pressed itself on Butler's mind with an earnestness that cannot be conceived by those who live in the present day. The fiery eye, the abrupt demeanor, the occasionally harsh, yet studiously subdued, tone of voice; the features, handsome, but now clouded with pride, now disturbed by suspicion, now inflamed with passion; those dark hazel eyes which he sometimes shaded with his cap, as if he were averse to have them seen while they were occupied with keenly observing the motions and bearing of others—those eyes that were now turbid with melancholy, now gleaming with scorn, and now sparkling with fury—was it the passions of a mere mortal they expressed, or the emotions of a fiend, who seeks, and seeks in vain, to conceal his fiendish designs under the borrowed mask of manly beauty? The whole partook of the mien, language, and port of the ruined archangel; and, imperfectly as we have been able to describe it, the effect of the interview upon Butler's nerves, shaken as they were at the time by the horrors of the preceding night, was greater than his understanding warranted, or his pride cared to submit to.

The very place where he had met this singular person was desecrated, as it were, and unhallowed, owing to many violent deaths, both in duels and by suicide, which had in former times taken place there ; and the place which he had named as a rendezvous at so late an hour was held in general to be accursed, from a frightful and cruel murder which had been there committed, by the wretch from whom the place took its name, upon the person of his own wife.* It was in such places, according to the belief of that period, when the laws against witchcraft were still in fresh observance, and had even lately been acted upon, that evil spirits had power to make themselves visible to human eyes, and to practise upon the feelings and senses of mankind. Suspicions, founded on such circumstances, rushed on Butler's mind, unprepared as it was, by any previous course of reasoning, to deny that which all of his time, country, and profession believed ; but common sense rejected these vain ideas as inconsistent, if not with possibility, at least with the general rules by which the universe is governed—a deviation from which, as Butler well argued with himself, ought not to be admitted as probable upon any but the plainest and most incontrovertible evidence. An earthly lover, however, or a young man who, from whatever cause, had the right of exercising such summary and unceremonious authority over the object of his long-settled, and apparently sincerely returned, affection, was an object scarce less appalling to his mind than those which superstition suggested.

His limbs exhausted with fatigue, his mind harassed with anxiety, and with painful doubts and recollections, Butler dragged himself up the ascent from the valley to St. Leonard's Crags and presented himself at the door of Deans's habitation, with feelings much akin to the miserable reflections and fears of its inhabitants.

* See Muschat's Cairn. Note 17.

CHAPTER XII

Old Ballad.

"COME in," answered the low and sweet-toned voice he loved
best to hear, as Butler tapped at the door of the cottage. He
lifted the latch, and found himself under the roof of affliction.
Jeanie was unable to trust herself with more than one glance
towards her lover, whom she now met under circumstances so
agonizing to her feelings, and at the same time so humbling
to her honest pride. It is well known that much both of
what is good and bad in the Scottish national character arises
out of the intimacy of their family connections. " To be
come of honest folk," that is, of people who have borne a fair
and unstained reputation, is an advantage as highly prized
among the lower Scotch as the emphatic counterpart, " to be
of a good family," is valued among their gentry. The worth
and respectability of one member of a peasant's family is always accounted by themselves and others not only a matter of
honest pride, but a guarantee for the good conduct of the
whole. On the contrary, such a melancholy stain as was now
flung on one of the children of Deans extended its disgrace to
all connected with him, and Jeanie felt herself lowered at
once in her own eyes and in those of her lover. It was in
vain that she repressed this feeling, as far subordinate and too
selfish to be mingled with her sorrow for her sister's calamity.
Nature prevailed; and while she shed tears for her sister's
distress and danger, there mingled with them bitter drops of
grief for her own degradation.

As Butler entered, the old man was seated by the fire with
his well-worn pocket Bible in his hands, the companion of the
wanderings and dangers of his youth, and bequeathed to him
on the scaffold by one of those who, in the year 1686, sealed
their enthusiastic principles with their blood. The sun sent
its rays through a small window at the old man's back, and,
" shining motty through the reek," to use the expression of a

bard of that time and country, illumined the gray hairs of the old man and the sacred page which he studied. His features, far from handsome, and rather harsh and severe, had yet, from their expression of habitual gravity and contempt for earthly things, an expression of stoical dignity amid their sternness. He boasted, in no small degree, the attributes which Southey ascribes to the ancient Scandinavians, whom he terms " firm to inflict and stubborn to endure." The whole formed a picture, of which the lights might have been given by Rembrandt, but the outline would have required the force and vigor of Michael Angelo.

Deans lifted his eye as Butler entered, and instantly withdrew it, as from an object which gave him at once surprise and sudden pain. He had assumed such high ground with this carnal-witted scholar, as he had in his pride termed Butler, that to meet him of all men under feelings of humiliation aggravated his misfortune, and was a consummation like that of the dying chief in the old ballad—" Earl Percy sees my fall !"

Deans raised the Bible with his left hand, so as partly to screen his face, and putting back his right as far as he could, held it towards Butler in that position, at the same time turning his body from him, as if to prevent his seeing the working of his countenance. Butler clasped the extended hand which had supported his orphan infancy, wept over it, and in vain endeavored to say more than the words—" God comfort you—God comfort you !"

" He will—He doth, my friend," said Deans, assuming firmness as he discovered the agitation of his guest ; " He doth now, and He will yet more, in His own gude time. I have been ower proud of my sufferings in a gude cause, Reuben, and now I am to be tried with those whilk will turn my pride and glory into a reproach and a hissing. How muckle better I hae thought mysell than them that lay saft, fed sweet, and drank deep, when I was in the moss-hags and moors, wi' precious Donald [Richard] Cameron, and worthy Mr. Blackadder, called Guessagain ; and how proud I was o' being made a spectacle to men and angels, having stood on their pillory at the Canongate afore I was fifteen years old, for the cause of a National Covenant ! To think, Reuben, that I, wha hae been sae honored and exalted in my youth, nay, when I was but a hafflins callant, and that hae borne testimony again the defections o' the times, yearly, monthly, daily, hourly, minutely, striving and testifying with uplifted hand and voice, crying aloud, and sparing not, against all great

national snares, as the nation-wasting and church-sinking
abomination of union, toleration, and patronage, imposed by
the last woman of that unhappy race of Stuarts, also against
the infringements and invasions of the just powers of elder-
ship, whereanent I uttered my paper, called a 'Cry of an
Howl in the Desert,' printed at the Bow-head, and sold by
all flying stationers in town and country—and *now*——"

Here he paused. It may well be supposed that Butler,
though not absolutely coinciding in all the good old man's
ideas about church government, had too much consideration
and humanity to interrupt him, while he reckoned up with
conscious pride his sufferings, and the constancy of his testimony. On the contrary, when he paused under the influence
of the bitter recollections of the moment, Butler instantly
threw in his mite of encouragement.

"You have been well known, my old and revered friend,
a true and tried follower of the Cross ; one who, as St. Jerome
hath it, '*per infamiam et bonam famam grassari ad immor-
talitatem*,' which may be freely rendered, 'who rusheth on
to immortal life, through bad report and good report.' You
have been one of those to whom the tender and fearful souls
cry during the midnight solitude—'Watchman, what of the
night ?—Watchman, what of the night ?' And, assuredly,
this heavy dispensation, as it comes not without Divine permission, so it comes not without its special commission and
use."

"I do receive it as such," said poor Deans, returning the
grasp of Butler's hand ; "and, if I have not been taught to
read the Scripture in any other tongue but my native Scottish (even in his distress Butler's Latin quotation had not escaped his notice), I have, nevertheless, so learned them, that
I trust to bear even this crook in my lot with submission.
But O, Reuben Butler, the kirk, of whilk, though unworthy,
I have yet been thought a polished shaft, and meet to be a
pillar, holding, from my youth upward, the place of ruling
elder—what will the lightsome and profane think of the guide
that cannot keep his own family from stumbling ? How will
they take up their song and their reproach, when they see
that the children of professors are liable to as foul backsliding
as the offspring of Belial ! But I will bear my cross with the
comfort that whatever showed like goodness in me or mine
was but like the light that shines frae creeping insects, on
the brae-side, in a dark night ; it kythes bright to the ee, because all is dark around it ; but when the morn comes on
the mountains, it is but a puir crawling kail-worm after a'.

And sae it shows wi' ony rag of human righteousness, or formal law-work, that we may pit round us to cover our shame."

As he pronounced these words, the door again opened, and Mr. Bartoline Saddletree entered, his three-pointed hat set far back on his head, with a silk handkerchief beneath it, to keep it in that cool position, his gold-headed cane in his hand, and his whole deportment that of a wealthy burgher, who might one day look to have a share in the magistracy, if not actually to hold the curule chair itself.

Rochefoucault, who has torn the veil from so many foul gangrenes of the human heart, says, we find something not altogether unpleasant to us in the misfortunes of our best friends. Mr. Saddletree would have been very angry had any one told him that he felt pleasure in the disaster of poor Effie Deans and the disgrace of her family ; and yet there is great question whether the gratification of playing the person of importance, inquiring, investigating, and laying down the law on the whole affair, did not offer, to say the least, full consolation for the pain which pure sympathy gave him on account of his wife's kinswoman. He had now got a piece of real judicial business by the end, instead of being obliged, as was his common case, to intrude his opinion where it was neither wished nor wanted ; and felt as happy in the exchange as a boy when he gets his first new watch, which actually goes when wound up, and has real hands and a true dial-plate. But besides this subject for legal disquisition, Bartoline's brains were also overloaded with the affair of Porteous, his violent death, and all its probable consequences to the city and community. It was what the French call *l'embarras des richesses,* the confusion arising from too much mental wealth. He walked in with a consciousness of double importance, full fraught with the superiority of one who possesses more information than the company into which he enters, and who feels a right to discharge his learning on them without mercy. " Good morning, Mr. Deans. Good-morrow to you, Mr. Butler ; I was not aware that you were acquainted with Mr. Deans."

Butler made some slight answer ; his reasons may be readily imagined for not making his connection with the family, which, in his eyes, had something of tender mystery, a frequent subject of conversation with indifferent persons, such as Saddletree.

The worthy burgher, in the plenitude of self-importance, now sat down upon a chair, wiped his brow, collected his breath, and made the first experiment of the resolved pith of his lungs, in a deep and dignified sigh, resembling a groan in

sound and intonation—"Awfu' times these, neighbor Deans
—awfu' times!"

"Sinfu', shamefu', Heaven-daring times," answered Deans,
in a lower and more subdued tone.

"For my part," continued Saddletree, swelling with importance, "what between the distress of my friends and my
poor auld country, ony wit that ever I had may be said to
have abandoned me, sae that I sometimes think myself as ignorant as if I were *inter rusticos*. Here when I arise in the
morning, wi' my mind just arranged touching what's to be
done in puir Effie's misfortune, and hae gotten the haill
statute at my finger-ends, the mob maun get up and string
Jock Porteous to a dyester's beam, and ding a'thing out of my
head again."

Deeply as he was distressed with his own domestic calamity, Deans could not help expressing some interest in the
news. Saddletree immediately entered on details of the insurrection and its consequences, while Butler took the occasion to seek some private conversation with Jeanie Deans.
She gave him the opportunity he sought, by leaving the
room, as if in prosecution of some part of her morning labor.
Butler followed her in a few minutes, leaving Deans so
closely engaged by his busy visitor that there was little chance
of his observing their absence.

The scene of their interview was an outer apartment,
where Jeanie was used to busy herself in arranging the productions of her dairy. When Butler found an opportunity
of stealing after her into this place, he found her silent, dejected, and ready to burst into tears. Instead of the active
industry with which she had been accustomed, even while in
the act of speaking, to employ her hands in some useful
branch of household business, she was seated listless in a corner, sinking apparently under the weight of her own thoughts.
Yet the instant he entered, she dried her eyes, and, with the
simplicity and openness of her character, immediately entered
on conversation.

"I am glad you have come in, Mr. Butler," said she,
"for—for—for I wished to tell ye, that all maun be ended
between you and me; it's best for baith our sakes."

"Ended!" said Butler, in surprise; "and for what should
it be ended? I grant this is a heavy dispensation, but it lies
neither at your door nor mine : it's an evil of God's sending,
and it must be borne; but it cannot break plighted troth,
Jeanie, while they that plighted their word wish to keep it."

"But, Reuben," said the young woman, looking at him

affectionately, " I ken weel that ye think mair of me than yourself ; and, Reuben, I can only in requital think mair of your weal than of my ain. Ye are a man of spotless name, bred to God's ministry, and a' men say that ye will some day rise high in the kirk, though poverty keep ye down e'en now. Poverty is a bad back-friend, Reuben, and that ye ken ower weel ; but ill-fame is a waur ane, and that is a truth ye sall never learn through my means."

" What do you mean ? " said Butler, eagerly and impatiently ; " or how do you connect your sister's guilt, if guilt there be, which, I trust in God, may yet be disproved, with our engagement ? How can that affect you or me ? "

" How can you ask me that, Mr. Butler ? Will this stain, d'ye think, ever be forgotten, as lang as our heads are abune the grund ? Will it not stick to us, and to our bairns, and to their very bairns' bairns ? To hae been the child of an honest man might hae been saying something for me and mine ; but to be the sister of a—— O my God ! " With this exclamation her resolution failed, and she burst into a passionate fit of tears.

The lover used every effort to induce her to compose herself, and at length succeeded ; but she only resumed her composure to express herself with the same positiveness as before. " No, Reuben, I'll bring disgrace hame to nae man's hearth ; my ain distresses I can bear, and I maun bear, but there is nae occasion for buckling them on other folks' shouthers. I will bear my load alone ; the back is made for the burden."

A lover is by charter wayward and suspicious ; and Jeanie's readiness to renounce their engagement, under pretence of zeal for his peace of mind and respectability of character, seemed to poor Butler to form a portentous combination with the commission of the stranger he had met with that morning. His voice faltered as he asked, " Whether nothing but a sense of her sister's present distress occasioned her to talk in that manner ? "

" And what else can do sae ? " she replied, with simplicity. " Is it not ten long years since we spoke together in this way ? "

" Ten years ? " said Butler. " It's a long time, sufficient perhaps for a woman to weary——"

" To weary of her auld gown," said Jeanie, " and to wish for a new ane, if she likes to be brave, but not long enough to weary of a friend. The eye may wish change, but the heart never."

" Never ! " said Reuben ; " that's a bold promise."

"But not more bauld than true," said Jeanie, with the same quiet simplicity which attended her manner in joy and grief, in ordinary affairs, and in those which most interested her feelings.

Butler paused, and looking at her fixedly, "I am charged," he said," with a message to you, Jeanie."

"Indeed! From whom? Or what can ony ane have to say to me?"

"It is from a stranger," said Butler, affecting to speak with an indifference which his voice belied, "a young man whom I met this morning in the Park."

"Mercy!" said Jeanie, eagerly; "and what did he say?"

"That he did not see you at the hour he expected, but required you should meet him alone at Muschat's Cairn this night, so soon as the moon rises."

"Tell him," said Jeanie, hastily, "I shall certainly come."

"May I ask," said Butler, his suspicions increasing at the ready alacrity of the answer, "who this man is to whom you are so willing to give the meeting at a place and hour so uncommon?"

"Folk maun do muckle they have little will to do in this world," replied Jeanie.

"Granted," said her lover; "but what compels you to this? Who is this person? What I saw of him was not very favorable. Who or what is he?"

"I do not know!" replied Jeanie, composedly.

"You do not know?" said Butler, stepping impatiently through the apartment. "You purpose to meet a young man whom you do not know, at such a time and in a place so lonely; you say you are compelled to do this, and yet you say you do not know the person who exercises such an influence over you! Jeanie, what am I to think of this?"

"Think only, Reuben, that I speak truth, as if I were to answer at the last day. I do not ken this man, I do not even ken that I ever saw him; and yet I must give him the meeting he asks; there's life and death upon it."

"Will you not tell your father, or take him with you?" said Butler.

"I cannot," said Jeanie; "I have no permission."

"Will you let *me* go with you? I will wait in the Park till nightfall, and join you when you set out."

"It is impossible," said Jeanie; "there maunna be mortal creature within hearing of our conference."

"Have you considered well the nature of what you are going to do?—the time, the place, an unknown and suspicious

character ? Why, if he had asked to see you in this house,
your father sitting in the next room, and within call, at such
an hour, you should have refused to see him."

"My weird maun be fulfilled, Mr. Butler. My life and
my safety are in God's hands, but I'll not spare to risk either
of them on the errand I am gaun to do."

"Then, Jeanie," said Butler, much displeased, "we must
indeed break short off, and bid farewell. When there can be
no confidence betwixt a man and his plighted wife on such a
momentous topic, it is a sign that she has no longer the
regard for him that makes their engagement safe and suitable."

Jeanie looked at him and sighed. "I thought," she said,
"that I had brought myself to bear this parting ; but—but—
I did not ken that we were to part in unkindness. But I am
a woman and you are a man, it may be different wi' you ; if
your mind is made easier by thinking sae hardly of me, I
would not ask you to think otherwise."

"You are," said Butler, "what you have always been—
wiser, better, and less selfish in your native feelings than I
can be with all the helps philosophy can give to a Christian.
But why—why will you persevere in an undertaking so desperate ? Why will you not let me be your assistant, your protector, or at least your adviser ?"

"Just because I cannot, and I dare not," answered Jeanie.
"But hark, what's that ? Surely my father is no weel ?"

In fact, the voices in the next room became obstreperously
loud of a sudden, the cause of which vociferation it is necessary to explain before we go further.

When Jeanie and Butler retired, Mr. Saddletree entered
upon the business which chiefly interested the family. In
the commencement of their conversation he found old Deans,
who, in his usual state of mind, was no granter of propositions,
so much subdued by a deep sense of his daughter's danger and
disgrace that he heard without replying to, or perhaps without understanding, one or two learned disquisitions on the
nature of the crime imputed to her charge, and on the steps
which ought to be taken in consequence. His only answer at
each pause was, "I am no misdoubting that you wuss us weel,
your wife's our far-awa' cousin."

Encouraged by these symptoms of acquiescence, Saddletree, who, as an amateur of the law, had a supreme deference
for all constituted authorities, again recurred to his other topic
of interest, the murder, namely, of Porteous, and pronounced
a severe censure on the parties concerned.

"These are kittle times—kittle times, Mr. Deans, when the people take the power of life and death out of the hands of the rightful magistrate into their ain rough grip. I am of opinion, and so, I believe, will Mr. Crossmyloof and the privy council, that this rising in effeir of war, to take away the life of a reprieved man, will prove little better than perduellion."

"If I hadna that on my mind whilk is ill to bear, Mr. Saddletree," said Deans, "I wad make bold to dispute that point wi' you."

"How could ye dispute what's plain law, man?" said Saddletree, somewhat contemptuously; "there's no a callant that e'er carried a pock wi' a process in't but will tell you that perduellion is the warst and maist virulent kind of treason, being an open convocating of the king's lieges against his authority, mair especially in arms, and by touk of drum, to baith whilk accessories my een and lugs bore witness, and muckle warse than lese-majesty, or the concealment of a treasonable purpose. It winna bear a dispute, neighbor."

"But it will, though," retorted Douce Davie Deans; "I tell ye it will bear a dispute. I never like your cauld, legal, formal doctrines, neighbor Saddletree. I haud unco little by the Parliament House, since the awfu' downfall of the hopes of honest folk that followed the Revolution."

"But what wad ye hae had, Mr. Deans?" said Saddletree, impatiently; "didna ye get baith liberty and conscience made fast, and settled by tailzie on you and your heirs forever?"

"Mr. Saddletree," retorted Deans, "I ken ye are one of those that are wise after the manner of this world, and that ye haud your part, and cast in your portion, wi' the lang-heads and lang-gowns, and keep with the smart witty-pated lawyers of this our land. Weary on the dark and dolefu' cast that they hae gien this unhappy kingdom, when their black hands of defection were clasped in the red hands of our sworn murtherers ; when those who had numbered the towers of our Zion, and marked the bulwarks of our Reformation, saw their hope turn into a snare and their rejoicing into weeping."

"I canna understand this, neighbor," answered Saddletree. "I am an honest Presbyterian of the Kirk of Scotland, and stand by her and the General Assembly, and the due administration of justice by the fifteen Lords o' Session and the five Lords o' Justiciary."

"Out upon ye, Mr. Saddletree !" exclaimed David, who, in an opportunity of giving his testimony on the offences and backslidings of the land, forgot for a moment his own domestic calamity—"out upon your General Assembly, and the back of my hand to your Court o' Session ! What is the tane but a waefu' bunch o' cauldrife professors and ministers, that sat bien and warm when the persecuted remnant were warstling wi' hunger, and cauld, and fear of death, and danger of fire and sword, upon wet brae-sides, peat-hags, and flow-mosses, and that now creep out of their holes, like bluebottle flees in a blink of sunshine, to take the pu'pits and places of better folk—of them that witnessed, and testified, and fought, and endured pit, prison-house, and transportation beyond seas ? A bonny bike there's o' them ! And for your Court o' Session——"

"Ye may say what ye will o' the General Assembly," said Saddletree, interrupting him, "and let them clear them that kens them ; but as for the Lords o' Session, forbye that they are my next-door neighbors, I would have ye ken, for your ain regulation, that to raise scandal anent them, whilk is termed, to 'murmur again' them, is a crime *sui generis—sui generis*, Mr. Deans ; ken ye what that amounts to ?"

"I ken little o' the language of Antichrist," said Deans ; "and I care less than little what carnal courts may call the speeches of honest men. And as to murmur again them, it's what a' the folk that loses their pleas, and nine-tenths o' them that win them, will be gay sure to be guilty in. Sae I wad hae ye ken that I haud a' your gleg-tongued advocates, that sell their knowledge for pieces of silver, and your worldly-wise judges, that will gie three days of hearing in presence to a debate about the peeling of an ingan, and no ae half-hour to the Gospel testimony, as legalists and formalists, countenancing, by sentences, and quirks, and cunning terms of law, the late begun courses of national defections—union, toleration, patronages, and Yerastian prelatic oaths. As for the soul and body-killing Court o' Justiciary——"

The habit of considering his life as dedicated to bear testimony in behalf of what he deemed the suffering and deserted cause of true religion had swept honest David along with it thus far ; but with the mention of the criminal court, the recollection of the disastrous condition of his daughter rushed at once on his mind ; he stopped short in the midst of his triumphant declamation, pressed his hands against his forehead, and remained silent.

Saddletree was somewhat moved, but apparently not so much so as to induce him to relinquish the privilege of prosing in his turn, afforded him by David's sudden silence. "Nae doubt, neighbor," he said, "it's a sair thing to hae to do wi'

courts of law, unless it be to improve ane's knowledge and
practique, by waiting on as a hearer ; and touching this unhappy affair of Effie—ye'll hae seen the dittay, doubtless ?"
He dragged out of his pocket a bundle of papers, and began
to turn them over.   "This is no it : this is the information
of Mungo Marsport, of that ilk, against Captain Lackland,
for coming on his lands of Marsport with hawks, hounds,
lying-dogs, nets, guns, cross-bows, hagbuts of found, or other
engines more or less for destruction of game, sic as red-deer,
fallow-deer, caper-cailzies, gray-fowl, moor-fowl, paitricks,
herons, and sic-like ; he the said defender not being ane qualified person, in terms of the statute 1621 ; that is, not having
ane plough-gate of land.   Now, the defences proponed say
that *non constat* at this present what is a plough-gate of land,
whilk uncertainty is sufficient to elide the conclusions of the
libel.   But then the answers to the defences—they are signed
by Mr. Crossmyloof, but Mr. Younglad drew them — they
propone that it signifies naething, *in hoc statu,* what or how
muckle a plough-gate of land may be, in respect the defender
has nae lands whatsoe'er, less or mair.   'Sae grant a plough-
gate [here Saddletree read from the paper in his hand] to be
less than the nineteenth part of a guse's grass'—I trow Mr.
Crossmyloof put in that, I ken his style—'of a guse's grass,
what the better will the defender be, seeing he hasna a divot-
cast of land in Scotland ?   *Advocatus* for Lackland duplies
that, *nihil interest de possessione,* the pursuer must put his
case under the statute'—now this is worth your notice, neighbor—'and must show, *formaliter et specialiter,* as well as *gen-
eraliter,* what is the qualification that defender Lackland does
not possess : let him tell me what a plough-gate of land is,
and I'll tell him if I have one or no.   Surely the pursuer is
bound to understand his own libel and his own statute that
he founds upon.   Titius pursues Mævius for recovery of ane
black horse lent to Mævius ; surely he shall have judgment.
But if Titius pursue Mævius for ane *scarlet* or *crimson* horse,
doubtless he shall be bound to show that there is sic ane animal *in rerum natura.*   No man can be bound to plead to
nonsense, that is to say, to a charge which cannot be explained
or understood'—he's wrang there, the better the pleadings
the fewer understand them—'and so the reference unto this
undefined and unintelligible measure of land is, as if a penalty
was inflicted by statute for any man who suld hunt or hawk,
or use lying-dogs, and wearing a sky-blue pair of breeches,
without having——'   But I am wearying you, Mr. Deans ;
we'll pass to your ain business, though this case of Marsport

against Lackland has made an unco din in the Outer House. Weel, here's the dittay against puir Effie: 'Whereas it is humbly meant and shown to us,' etc.—they are words of mere style—'that whereas, by the laws of this and every other well-regulated realm, the murder of any one, more especially of an infant child, is a crime of ane high nature, and severely punishable: And whereas, without prejudice to the foresaid generality, it was, by ane act made in the second session of the First Parliament of our most High and Dread Soveraigns William and Mary, especially enacted, that ane woman who shall have concealed her condition, and shall not be able to show that she hath called for help at the birth, in case that the child shall be found dead or amissing, shall be deemed and held guilty of the murder thereof ; and the said facts of concealment and pregnancy being found proven or confessed, shall sustain the pains of law accordingly ; yet, nevertheless, you, Effie or Euphemia Deans——' "

"Read no farther !" said Deans, raising his head up; " I would rather ye thrust a sword into my heart than read a word farther !"

"Weel, neighbor," said Saddletree, "I thought it wad hae comforted ye to ken the best and the warst o't. But the question is, what's to be dune ?"

"Nothing," answered Deans, firmly, "but to abide the dispensation that the Lord sees meet to send us. O, if it had been His will to take the gray head to rest before this awful visitation on my house and name ! But His will be done. I can say that yet, though I can say little mair."

"But, neighbor," said Saddletree, " ye'll retain advocates for the puir lassie ? it's a thing maun needs be thought of."

"If there was ae man of them," answered Deans, "that held fast his integrity—but I ken them weel, they are a' carnal, crafty, and warld-hunting self-seekers, Yerastians and Arminians, every ane o' them."

"Hout tout, neighbor, ye maunna take the warld at its word," said Saddletree ; "the very deil is no sae ill as he's ca'd ; and I ken mair than ae advocate that may be said to hae some integrity as weel as their neighbors ; that is, after a sort o' fashion o' their ain."

" It is indeed but a fashion of integrity that ye will find amang them," replied David Deans, "and a fashion of wisdom, and fashion of carnal learning—gazing glancing-glasses they are, fit only to fling the glaiks in folks' een, wi' their pawky policy, and earthly ingine, their flights and refinements, and periods of eloquence, frae heathen emperors and popish canons. They canna, in that daft trash ye were reading to me, sae muckle as ca' men that are sae ill-starred as to be amang their hands by ony name o' the dispensation o' grace, but maun new baptise them by the names of the accursed Titus, wha was made the instrument of burning the holy Temple, and other sic-like heathens."

" It's Tishius," interrupted Saddletree, " and no Titus. Mr. Crossmyloof cares as little about Titus or the Latin learning as ye do. But it's a case of necessity : she maun hae counsel. Now, I could speak to Mr. Crossmyloof ; he's weel kenn'd for a round-spun Presbyterian, and a ruling elder to boot."

" He's a rank Yerastian," replied Deans; " one of the public and polititious warldly-wise men that stude up to prevent ane general owning of the cause in the day of power."

" What say ye to the auld Laird of Cuffabout ?" said Saddletree ; " he whiles thumps the dust out of a case gay and weel."

" He ! the fause loon !" answered Deans. " He was in his bandaliers to hae joined the ungracious Highlanders in 1715, an they had ever had the luck to cross the Firth."

" Weel, Arniston ? there's a clever chield for ye !" said Bartoline, triumphantly.

" Ay, to bring popish medals in till their very library from that schismatic woman in the north, the Duchess of Gordon."*

" Weel, weel, but somebody ye maun hae. What think ye o' Kittlepunt ?"

" He's an Arminian."

" Woodsetter ?"

" He's, I doubt, a Cocceian."

" Auld Whilliewhaw ?"

" He's onything ye like."

" Young Næmmo ?"

" He's naething at a'."

" Ye're ill to please, neighbor," said Saddletree. " I hae run ower the pick o' them for you, ye maun e'en choose for yoursell ; but bethink ye that in the multitude of counsellors there's safety. What say ye to try young Mackenyie ? he has a' his uncle's practiques at the tongue's end."

" What, sir, wad ye speak to me," exclaimed the sturdy Presbyterian, in excessive wrath, " about a man that has the blood of the saints at his fingers' ends ? Didna his eme die

---

* James Dundas, younger of Arniston, was tried in the year 1711 upon a charge of leasing-making, in having presented. from the Duchess of Gordon, a medal of the Pretender, for the purpose, it was said, of affronting Queen Anne (*Laing*).

and gang to his place wi' the name of the Bluidy Mackenyie?
and winna he be kenn'd by that name sae lang as there's a
Scots tongue to speak the word? If the life of the dear
bairn that's under a suffering dispensation, and Jeanie's, and
my ain, and a' mankind's, depended on my asking sic a slave
o' Satan to speak a word for me or them, they should a' gae
down the water thegither for Davie Deans!"

It was the exalted tone in which he spoke this last sentence that broke up the conversation between Butler and
Jeanie, and brought them both " ben the house," to use the
language of the country. Here they found the poor old man
half frantic between grief and zealous ire against Saddletree's
proposed measures, his cheek inflamed, his hand clenched,
and his voice raised, while the tear in his eye, and the occasional quiver of his accents, showed that his utmost efforts
were inadequate to shaking off the consciousness of his misery.
Butler, apprehensive of the consequences of his agitation to
an aged and feeble frame, ventured to utter to him a recommendation to patience.

"I *am* patient," returned the old man, sternly, " more
patient than any one who is alive to the woful backslidings
of a miserable time can be patient; and in so much, that I
need neither sectarians, nor sons nor grandsons of sectarians,
to instruct my gray hairs how to bear my cross."

" But, sir," continued Butler, taking no offence at the slur
cast on his grandfather's faith, "we must use human means.
When you call in a physician, you would not, I suppose,
question him on the nature of his religious principles?"

" Wad I *no?*" answered David. " But I wad, though;
and if he didna satisfy me that he had a right sense of the
right-hand and left-hand defections of the day, not a goutte
of his physic should gang through my father's son."

It is a dangerous thing to trust to an illustration. Butler
had done so and miscarried; but, like a gallant soldier when
his musket misses fire, he stood his ground and charged with
the bayonet. " This is too rigid an interpretation of your
duty, sir. The sun shines, and the rain descends, on the just
and unjust, and they are placed together in life in circumstances
which frequently render intercourse between them indispensa-
ble, perhaps that the evil may have an opportunity of being
converted by the good, and perhaps, also, that the righteous
might, among other trials, be subjected to that of occasional
converse with the profane."

" Ye're a silly callant, Reuben," answered Deans, "with
your bits of argument. Can a man touch pitch and not be de-

filed ?   Or what think ye of the brave and worthy champions
of the Covenant, that wadna sae muckle as hear a minister
speak, be his gifts and graces as they would, that hadna witnessed against the enormities of the day ?   Nae lawyer shall
ever speak for me and mine that hasna concurred in the testimony of the scattered yet lovely remnant which abode in the
clifts of the rocks."

So saying, and as if fatigued both with the arguments and
presence of his guests, the old man arose, and seeming to bid
them adieu with a motion of his head and hand, went to shut
himself up in his sleeping-apartment.

"It's thrawing his daughter's life awa'," said Saddletree
to Butler, "to hear him speak in that daft gate.   Where will
he ever get a Cameronian advocate ?   Or wha ever heard of a
lawyer's suffering either for ae religion or another ?   The
lassie's life is clean flung awa'."

During the latter part of this debate, Dumbiedikes had
arrived at the door, dismounted, hung the pony's bridle on the
usual hook, and sunk down on his ordinary settle.   His eyes,
with more than their usual animation, followed first one speaker, then another, till he caught the melancholy sense of the
whole from Saddletree's last words.   He rose from his seat,
stumped slowly across the room, and, coming close up to Saddletree's ear, said, in a tremulous, anxious voice, "Will—will
siller do naething for them, Mr. Saddletree ?"

"Umph !" said Saddletree, looking grave, "siller will certainly do it in the Parliament House, if onything *can* do it ;
but whare's the siller to come frae ?   Mr. Deans, ye see, will do
naething ; and though Mrs. Saddletree's their far-awa' friend
and right good weel-wisher, and is weel disposed to assist, yet
she wadna like to stand to be bound *singuli in solidum* to such
an expensive wark.   An ilka friend wad bear a share o' the
burden, something might be dune, ilka ane to be liable for
their ain input.   I wadna like to see the case fa' through without being pled ; it wadna be creditable, for a' that daft Whig
body says."

"I'll—I will—yes (assuming fortitude), I will be answerable," said Dumbiedikes, "for a score of punds sterling."
And he was silent, staring in astonishment at finding himself
capable of such unwonted resolution and excessive generosity.

"God Almighty bless ye, Laird !" said Jeanie, in a transport of gratitude.

"Ye may ca' the twenty punds thretty," said Dumbiedikes,
looking bashfully away from her, and towards Saddletree.

"That will do bravely," said Saddletree, rubbing his hands ;

"and ye sall hae a' my skill and knowledge to gar the siller gang far. I'll tape it out weel ; I ken how to gar the birkies tak short fees, and be glad o' them too : it's only garring them trow ye hae twa or three cases of importance coming on, and they'll work cheap to get custom. Let me alane for whilly-whaing an advocate. It's nae sin to get as muckle frae them for our siller as we can ; after a', it's but the wind o' their mouth, it costs them naething ; whereas, in my wretched occupation of a saddler, horse-milliner, and harness-maker, we are out unconscionable sums just for barkened hides and leather."

"Can I be of no use ? " said Butler. "My means, alas ! are only worth the black coat I wear ; but I am young, I owe much to the family. Can I do nothing ?"

"Ye can help to collect evidence, sir," said Saddletree ; "if we could but find ony ane to say she had gien the least hint o' her condition, she wad be brought aff wi' a wat finger. Mr. Crossmyloof tell'd me sae. 'The crown,' says he, 'canna be craved to prove a positive'—was't a positive or a negative they couldna be ca'd to prove ? it was the tane or the tither o' them, I am sure, and it maksna muckle matter whilk. 'Wherefore,' says he, 'the libel maun be redargued by the panel proving her defences. And it canna be done otherwise.'"

"But the fact, sir," argued Butler—"the fact that this poor girl has borne a child ; surely the crown lawyers must prove that ?" said Butler.

Saddletree paused a moment, while the visage of Dumbiedikes, which traversed, as if it had been placed on a pivot, from the one spokesman to the other, assumed a more blithe expression.

"Ye—ye—ye—es," said Saddletree, after some grave hesitation ; "unquestionably that is a thing to be proved, as the court will more fully declare by an interlocutor of relevancy in common form ; but I fancy that job's done already, for she has confessed her guilt."

"Confessed the murder ?" exclaimed Jeanie, with a scream that made them all start.

"No, I didna say that," replied Bartoline. "But she confessed bearing the babe."

"And what became of it, then ?" said Jeanie ; "for not a word could I get from her but bitter sighs and tears."

"She says it was taken away from her by the woman in whose house it was born, and who assisted her at the time."

"And who was that woman ?" said Butler. "Surely by

her means the truth might be discovered.   Who was she ?   I
will fly to her directly."

"I wish," said Dumbiedikes, "I were as young and as
supple as you, and had the gift of the gab as weel."

"Who is she ?" again reiterated Butler, impatiently.
"Who could that woman be ?"

"Ay, wha kens that but hersell," said Saddletree ; "she
deponed further, and declined to answer that interrogatory."

"Then to herself will I instantly go," said Butler ; "farewell, Jeanie."   Then coming close up to her—"Take no *rash
steps* till you hear from me.   Farewell !" and he immediately
left the cottage.

"I wad gang too," said the landed proprietor in an anxious, jealous, and repining tone, "but my powny winna for
the life o' me gang ony other road than just frae Dumbiedikes
to this house-end, and sae straight back again."

"Ye'll do better for them," said Saddletree, as they left
the house together, "by sending me the thretty punds."

"Thretty punds ?" hesitated Dumbiedikes, who was now
out of the reach of those eyes which had inflamed his generosity.   "I only said *twenty* punds."

"Ay ; but," said Saddletree, "that was under protesta-
tion to add and eik ; and so ye craved leave to amend your
libel, and made it thretty."

"Did I ?   I dinna mind that I did," answered Dumbiedikes.   "But whatever I said I'll stand to."   Then bestrid-
ing his steed with some difficulty, he added, "Dinna ye think
poor Jeanie's een wi' the tears in them glanced like lamor
beads, Mr. Saddletree ?"

"I kenna muckle about women's een, Laird," replied the
insensible Bartoline ; "and I care just as little.   I wuss I
were as weel free o' their tongues ; though few wives," he
added, recollecting the necessity of keeping up his character
for domestic rule, "are under better command than mine,
Laird.   I allow neither perduellion nor lese-majesty against
my sovereign authority."

The Laird saw nothing so important in this observation as
to call for a rejoinder, and when they had exchanged a mute
salutation, they parted in peace upon their different errands.

CHAPTER XIII

I'll warrant that fellow from drowning, were the ship no stronger
than a nut-shell.

The Tempest.

BUTLER felt neither fatigue nor want of refreshment, although,
from the mode in which he had spent the night, he might
well have been overcome with either. But in the earnestness
with which he hastened to the assistance of the sister of
Jeanie Deans he forgot both.

In his first progress he walked with so rapid a pace as
almost approached to running, when he was surprised to hear
behind him a call upon his name, contending with an asth-
matic cough, and half drowned amid the resounding trot of
a Highland pony. He looked behind, and saw the Laird of
Dumbiedikes making after him with what speed he might, for
it happened, fortunately for the Laird's purpose of conversing
with Butler, that his own road homeward was for about two
hundred yards the same with that which led by the nearest
way to the city. Butler stopped when he heard himself thus
summoned, internally wishing no good to the panting equestrian who thus retarded his journey.

"Uh! uh! uh!" ejaculated Dumbiedikes, as he checked
the hobbling pace of the pony by our friend Butler. "Uh!
uh! it's a hard-set willyard beast this o' mine." He had in
fact just overtaken the object of his chase at the very point
beyond which it would have been absolutely impossible for
him to have continued the pursuit, since there Butler's road
parted from that leading to Dumbiedikes, and no means of
influence or compulsion which the rider could possibly have
used towards his Bucephalus could have induced the Celtic
obstinacy of Rory Bean (such was the pony's name) to have
diverged a yard from the path that conducted him to his own
paddock.

Even when he had recovered from the shortness of breath
occasioned by a trot much more rapid than Rory or he were
accustomed to, the high purpose of Dumbiedikes seemed to
stick as it were in his throat, and impede his utterance, so
that Butler stood for nearly three minutes ere he could utter

a syllable; and when he did find voice, it was only to say, after one or two efforts, "Uh! uh! uhm! I say, Mr.—Mr. Butler, it's a braw day for the har'st."

"Fine day, indeed," said Butler. "I wish you good morning, sir."

"Stay—stay a bit," rejoined Dumbiedikes; "that was no what I had gotten to say."

"Then, pray be quick and let me have your commands," rejoined Butler. "I crave your pardon, but I am in haste, and *Tempus nemini*—you know the proverb."

Dumbiedikes did not know the proverb, nor did he even take the trouble to endeavor to look as if he did, as others in his place might have done. He was concentrating all his intellects for one grand proposition, and could not afford any detachment to defend outposts. "I say, Mr. Butler," said he, "ken ye if Mr. Saddletree's a great lawyer?"

"I have no person's word for it but his own," answered Butler, dryly; "but undoubtedly he best understands his own qualities."

"Umph!" replied the taciturn Dumbiedikes, in a tone which seemed to say, "Mr. Butler, I take your meaning." "In that case," he pursued, "I'll employ my ain man o' business, Nichil Novit—auld Nichil's son, and amaist as gleg as his father—to agent Effie's plea."

And having thus displayed more sagacity than Butler expected from him, he courteously touched his gold-laced cocked hat, and by a punch on the ribs conveyed to Rory Bean it was his rider's pleasure that he should forthwith proceed homewards; a hint which the quadruped obeyed with that degree of alacrity with which men and animals interpret and obey suggestions that entirely correspond with their own inclinations.

Butler resumed his pace, not without a momentary revival of that jealousy which the honest Laird's attention to the family of Deans had at different times excited in his bosom. But he was too generous long to nurse any feeling which was allied to selfishness. "He is," said Butler to himself, "rich in what I want; why should I feel vexed that he has the heart to dedicate some of his pelf to render them services which I can only form the empty wish of executing? In God's name, let us each do what we can. May she be but happy! saved from the misery and disgrace that seems impending! Let me but find the means of preventing the fearful experiment of this evening, and farewell to other thoughts, though my heart-strings break in parting with them!"

He redoubled his pace, and soon stood before the door **of** the tolbooth, or rather before the entrance where the door had formerly been placed. His interview with the mysterious stranger, the message to Jeanie, his agitating conversation with her on the subject of breaking off their mutual engagements, and the interesting scene with old Deans, had so entirely occupied his mind as to drown even recollection of the tragical event which he had witnessed the preceding evening. His attention was not recalled to it by the groups who stood scattered on the street in conversation, which they hushed when strangers approached, or by the bustling search of the agents of the city police, supported by small parties of the military, or by the appearance of the guard-house, before which were treble sentinels, or, finally, by the subdued and intimidated looks of the lower orders of society, who, conscious that they were liable to suspicion, if they were not guilty, of accession to a riot likely to be strictly inquired into, glided about with a humble and dismayed aspect, like men whose spirits being exhausted in the revel and the dangers of a desperate debauch overnight, are nerve-shaken, timorous, and unenterprising on the succeeding day.

None of these symptoms of alarm and trepidation struck Butler, whose mind was occupied with a different, and to him still more interesting, subject, until he stood before the entrance to the prison, and saw it defended by a double file of grenadiers, instead of bolts and bars. Their "Stand, stand !" the blackened appearance of the doorless gateway, and the winding staircase and apartments of the tolbooth, now open to the public eye, recalled the whole proceedings of the eventful night. Upon his requesting to speak with Effie Deans, the same tall, thin, silver-haired turnkey whom he had seen on the preceding evening made his appearance.

"I think," he replied to Butler's request of admission, with true Scottish indirectness, "ye will be the same lad that was for in to see her yestreen ?"

Butler admitted he was the same person.

"And I am thinking," pursued the turnkey, "that ye speered at me when we locked up, and if we locked up earlier on account of Porteous ?"

"Very likely I might make some such observation," said Butler ; "but the question now is, can I see Effie Deans ?"

"I dinna ken ; gang in bye, and up the turnpike stair, and turn till the ward on the left hand."

The old man followed close behind him, with his keys in his hand, not forgetting even that huge one which had once

opened and shut the outward gate of his dominions, though
at present it was but an idle and useless burden. No sooner
had Butler entered the room to which he was directed, than
the experienced hand of the warder selected the proper key,
and locked it on the outside. At first Butler conceived this
manœuvre was only an effect of the man's habitual and official
caution and jealousy. But when he heard the hoarse command, "Turn out the guard!" and immediately afterwards
heard the clash of a sentinel's arms, as he was posted at the
door of his apartment, he again called out to the turnkey,
"My good friend, I have business of some consequence with
Effie Deans, and I beg to see her as soon as possible." No answer was returned. "If it be against your rules to admit me,"
repeated Butler in a still louder tone, "to see the prisoner, I
beg you will tell me so, and let me go about my business.
Fugit irrevocabile tempus!" muttered he to himself.

"If ye had business to do, ye suld hae dune it before ye
cam here," replied the man of keys from the outside ; "ye'll
find it's easier wunnin in than wunnin out here. There's
sma' likelihood o' another Porteous Mob coming to rabble us
again : the law will haud her ain now, neighbor, and that
ye'll find to your cost."

"What do you mean by that, sir?" retorted Butler.
"You must mistake me for some other person. My name is
Reuben Butler, preacher of the Gospel."

"I ken that weel eneugh," said the turnkey.

"Well, then, if you know me, I have a right to know from
you, in return, what warrant you have for detaining me ; that,
I know, is the right of every British subject."

"Warrant!" said the jailer. "The warrant's awa' to
Liberton wi' twa sheriff officers seeking ye. If ye had stayed
at hame, as honest men should do, ye wad hae seen the warrant ; but if ye come to be incarcerated of your ain accord,
wha can help it, my jo?"

"So I cannot see Effie Deans, then," said Butler ; "and
you are determined not to let me out?"

"Troth will I no, neighbor," answered the old man, doggedly ; "as for Effie Deans, ye'll hae eneugh ado to mind your
ain business, and let her mind hers ; and for letting you out,
that maun be as the magistrate will determine. And fare ye
weel for a bit, for I maun see Deacon Sawyers put on ane or
twa o' the doors that your quiet folk broke down yesternight,
Mr. Butler."

There was something in this exquisitely provoking, but
there was also something darkly alarming. To be imprisoned,

even on a false accusation, has something in it disagreeable and menacing even to men of more constitutional courage than Butler had to boast; for although he had much of that resolution which arises from a sense of duty and an honorable desire to discharge it, yet, as his imagination was lively and his frame of body delicate, he was far from possessing that cool insensibility to danger which is the happy portion of men of stronger health, more firm nerves, and less acute sensibility. An indistinct idea of peril, which he could neither understand nor ward off, seemed to float before his eyes. He tried to think over the events of the preceding night, in hopes of discovering some means of explaining or vindicating his conduct for appearing among the mob, since it immediately occurred to him that his detention must be founded on that circumstance. And it was with anxiety that he found he could not recollect to have been under the observation of any disinterested witness in the attempts that he made from time to time to expostulate with the rioters, and to prevail on them to release him. The distress of Deans's family, the dangerous rendezvous which Jeanie had formed, and which he could not now hope to interrupt, had also their share in his unpleasant reflections. Yet impatient as he was to receive an *éclaircissement* upon the cause of his confinement, and if possible to obtain his liberty, he was affected with a trepidation which seemed no good omen, when, after remaining an hour in this solitary apartment, he received a summons to attend the sitting magistrate. He was conducted from prison strongly guarded by a party of soldiers, with a parade of precaution that, however ill-timed and unnecessary, is generally displayed *after* an event, which such precaution, if used in time, might have prevented.

He was introduced into the Council Chamber, as the place is called where the magistrates hold their sittings, and which was then at a little distance from the prison. One or two of the senators of the city were present, and seemed about to engage in the examination of an individual who was brought forward to the foot of the long green-covered table round which the council usually assembled.

"Is that the preacher?" said one of the magistrates, as the city officer in attendance introduced Butler. The man answered in the affirmative. "Let him sit down there an instant; we will finish this man's business very briefly."

"Shall we remove Mr. Butler?" queried the assistant.

"It is not necessary. Let him remain where he is."

Butler accordingly sat down on a bench at the bottom of the apartment, attended by one of his keepers.

It was a large room, partially and imperfectly lighted ; but by chance, or the skill of the architect, who might happen to remember the advantage which might occasionally be derived from such an arrangement, one window was so placed as to throw a strong light at the foot of the table at which prisoners were usually posted for examination, while the upper end, where the examinants sat, was thrown into shadow.   Butler's eyes were instantly fixed on the person whose examination was at present proceeding, in the idea that he might recognize some one of the conspirators of the former night.   But though the features of this man were sufficiently marked and striking, he could not recollect that he had ever seen them before.

The complexion of this person was dark, and his age somewhat advanced.   He wore his own hair, combed smooth down, and cut very short.   It was jet black, slightly curled by nature, and already mottled with gray.   The man's face expressed rather knavery than vice, and a disposition to sharpness, cunning, and roguery, more than the traces of stormy and indulged passions.   His sharp, quick black eyes, acute features, ready sardonic smile, promptitude, and effrontery, gave him altogether what is called among the vulgar a *knowing* look, which generally implies a tendency to knavery.   At a fair or market, you could not for a moment have doubted that he was a horse-jockey, intimate with all the tricks of his trade ; yet had you met him on a moor, you would not have apprehended any violence from him.   His dress was also that of a horse-dealer—a close-buttoned jockey-coat, or wrap-rascal, as it was then termed, with huge metal buttons, coarse blue upper stockings, called boot-hose, because supplying the place of boots, and a slouched hat.   He only wanted a loaded whip under his arm and a spur upon one heel to complete the dress of the character he seemed to represent.

"Your name is James Ratcliffe ?" said the magistrate.

"Ay, always wi' your honor's leave."

"That is to say, you could find me another name if I did not like that one ?"

"Twenty to pick and choose upon, always with your honor's leave," resumed the respondent.

"But James Ratcliffe is your present name ?   What is your trade ?"

"I canna just say, distinctly, that I have what ye wad ca' preceesely a trade."

"But," repeated the magistrate, "what are your means of living—your occupation ?"

"Hout tout, your honor, wi' your leave, kens that as weel as I do," replied the examined.

"No matter, I want to hear you describe it," said the examinant.

"Me describe ? and to your honor ? Far be it from Jemmie Ratcliffe," responded the prisoner.

"Come, sir, no trifling ; I insist on an answer."

"Weel, sir," replied the declarant, "I maun make a clean breast, for ye see, wi' your leave, I am looking for favor. Describe my occupation, quo' ye ? Troth it will be ill to do that, in a feasible way, in a place like this ; but what is't again that the aught command says ?"

"Thou shalt not steal," answered the magistrate.

"Are you sure o' that ?" replied the accused. "Troth, then, my occupation and that command are sair at odds, for I read it, thou *shalt* steal ; and that makes an unco difference, though there's but a wee bit word left out."

"To cut the matter short, Ratcliffe, you have been a most notorious thief," said the examinant.

"I believe Highlands and Lowlands ken that, sir, forbye England and Holland," replied Ratcliffe, with the greatest composure and effrontery.

"And what d'ye think the end of your calling will be ?" said the magistrate.

"I could have gien a braw guess yesterday ; but I dinna ken sae weel the day," answered the prisoner.

"And what would you have said would have been your end had you been asked the question yesterday ?"

"Just the gallows," replied Ratcliffe, with the same composure.

"You are a daring rascal, sir," said the magistrate ; "and how dare you hope times are mended with you to-day ?"

"Dear, your honor," answered Ratcliffe, "there's muckle difference between lying in prison under sentence of death and staying there of ane's ain proper accord, when it would have cost a man naething to get up and rin awa'. What was to hinder me from stepping out quietly, when the rabble walked awa' wi' Jock Porteous yestreen ? And does your honor really think I stayed on purpose to be hanged ?"

"I do not know what you may have proposed to yourself ; but I know," said the magistrate, "what the law proposes for you, and that is to hang you next Wednesday eight days."

"Na, na, your honor," said Ratcliffe, firmly ; "craving

your honor's pardon, I'll ne'er believe that till I see it.   I have
kenn'd the law this mony a year, and mony a thrawart job
I hae had wi' her first and last; but the auld jaud is no sae
ill as that comes to ; I aye fand her bark waur than her bite."

"And if you do not expect the gallows, to which you are
condemned—for the fourth time to my knowledge—may I beg
the favor to know," said the magistrate, "what it is that you
do expect, in consideration of your not having taken your flight
with the rest of the jail-birds, which I will admit was a line of
conduct little to have been expected ?"

"I would never have thought for a moment of staying in
that auld gousty toom house," answered Ratcliffe, "but that
use and wont had just gien me a fancy to the place, and I'm
just expecting a bit post in't."

"A post !" exclaimed the magistrate ; "a whipping-post,
I suppose, you mean ?"

"Na, na, sir, I had nae thoughts o' a whuppin-post.   After
having been four times doomed to hang by the neck till I was
dead, I think I am far beyond being whuppit."

"Then, in Heaven's name, what *did* you expect ?"

"Just the post of under-turnkey, for I understand there's
a vacancy," said the prisoner.   "I wadna think of asking the
lockman's * place ower his head ; it wadna suit me sae weel as
ither folk, for I never could put a beast out o' the way, much
less deal wi' a man."

"That's something in your favor," said the magistrate,
making exactly the inference to which Ratcliffe was desirous
to lead him, though he mantled his art with an affectation of
oddity.   "But," continued the magistrate, "how do you think
you can be trusted with a charge in the prison, when you have
broken at your own hand half the jails in Scotland ?"

"Wi' your honor's leave," said Ratcliffe, "if I kenn'd sae
weel how to wun out mysell, it's like I wad be a' the better a
hand to keep other folk in.   I think they wad ken their business weel that held me in when I wanted to be out, or wan
out when I wanted to haud them in."

The remark seemed to strike the magistrate, but he made
no further immediate observation, only desired Ratcliffe to be
removed.

When this daring and yet sly freebooter was out of hearing,
the magistrate asked the city clerk, "what he thought of the
fellow's assurance ?"

"It's no for me to say, sir," replied the clerk ; "but if
James Ratcliffe be inclined to turn to good, there is not a man

* See Note 18.

e'er came within the ports of the burgh could be of sae muckle use to the Good Town in the thief and lock-up line of business. I'll speak to Mr. Sharpitlaw about him."

Upon Ratcliffe's retreat, Butler was placed at the table for examination. The magistrate conducted his inquiry civilly, but yet in a manner which gave him to understand that he labored under strong suspicion. With a frankness which at once became his calling and character, Butler avowed his involuntary presence at the murder of Porteous, and, at the request of the magistrate, entered into a minute detail of the circumstances which attended that unhappy affair. All the particulars, such as we have narrated, were taken minutely down by the clerk from Butler's dictation.

When the narrative was concluded, the cross-examination commenced, which it is a painful task even for the most candid witness to undergo, since a story, especially if connected with agitating and alarming incidents, can scarce be so clearly and distinctly told but that some ambiguity and doubt may be thrown upon it by a string of successive and minute interrogatories.

The magistrate commenced by observing that Butler had said his object was to return to the village of Liberton, but that he was interrupted by the mob at the West Port. "Is the West Port your usual way of leaving town when you go to Liberton ?" said the magistrate, with a sneer.

" No, certainly," answered Butler, with the haste of a man anxious to vindicate the accuracy of his evidence ; " but I chanced to be nearer that port than any other, and the hour of shutting the gates was on the point of striking."

" That was unlucky," said the magistrate, dryly. " Pray, being, as you say, under coercion and fear of the lawless multitude, and compelled to accompany them through scenes disagreeable to all men of humanity, and more especially irreconcilable to the profession of a minister, did you not attempt to struggle, resist, or escape from their violence ?"

Butler replied, " that their numbers prevented him from attempting resistance, and their vigilance from effecting his escape."

" That was unlucky," again repeated the magistrate, in the same dry inacquiescent tone of voice and manner. He proceeded with decency and politeness, but with a stiffness which argued his continued suspicion, to ask many questions concerning the behavior of the mob, the manners and dress of the ringleaders ; and when he conceived that the caution of Butler, if he was deceiving him, must be lulled asleep, the magistrate suddenly and artfully returned to former parts of his declaration, and required a new recapitulation of the circumstances, to the minutest and most trivial point, which attended each part of the melancholy scene. No confusion or contradiction, however, occurred, that could countenance the suspicion which he seemed to have adopted against Butler. At length the train of his interrogatories reached Madge Wildfire, at whose name the magistrate and town clerk exchanged significant glances. If the fate of the Good Town had depended on her careful magistrate's knowing the features and dress of this personage, his inquiries could not have been more particular. But Butler could say almost nothing of this person's features, which were disguised apparently with red paint and soot, like an Indian going to battle, besides the projecting shade of a curch or coif, which muffled the hair of the supposed female. He declared that he thought he could not know this Madge Wildfire, if placed before him in a different dress, but that he believed he might recognize her voice.

The magistrate requested him again to state by what **gate** he left the city.

" By the Cowgate Port," replied Butler.

" Was that the nearest road to Liberton ? "

" No," answered Butler, with embarrassment; " but it was the nearest way to extricate myself from the mob."

The clerk and magistrate again exchanged glances.

" Is the Cowgate Port a nearer way to Liberton from the Grassmarket than Bristo Port ? "

" No," replied Butler ; " but I had to visit a friend."

" Indeed ? " said the interrogator. " You were in a hurry to tell the sight you had witnessed, I suppose ? "

" Indeed I was not," replied Butler ; " nor did I speak on the subject the whole time I was at St. Leonard's Crags."

" Which road did you take to St. Leonard's Crags ? "

" By the foot of Salisbury Crags," was the reply.

" Indeed ? you seem partial to circuitous routes," again said the magistrate. " Whom did you see after you left the city ? "

One by one he obtained a description of every one of the groups who had passed Butler, as already noticed, their number, demeanor, and appearance, and at length came to the circumstance of the mysterious stranger in the King's Park. On this subject Butler would fain have remained silent. But the magistrate had no sooner got a slight hint concerning the incident than he seemed bent to possess himself of the most minute particulars.

"Look ye, Mr. Butler," said he, "you are a young man, and bear an excellent character; so much I will myself testify in your favor. But we are aware there has been, at times, a sort of bastard and fiery zeal in some of your order, and those men irreproachable in other points, which has led them into doing and countenancing great irregularities, by which the peace of the country is liable to be shaken. I will deal plainly with you. I am not at all satisfied with this story of your setting out again and again to seek your dwelling by two several roads, which were both circuitous. And, to be frank, no one whom we have examined on this unhappy affair could trace in your appearance anything like your acting under compulsion. Moreover, the waiters at the Cowgate Port observed something like the trepidation of guilt in your conduct, and declare that you were the first to command them to open the gate, in a tone of authority, as if still presiding over the guards and outposts of the rabble who had besieged them the whole night."

"God forgive them!" said Butler. "I only asked free passage for myself; they must have much misunderstood, if they did not wilfully misrepresent, me."

"Well, Mr. Butler," resumed the magistrate, "I am inclined to judge the best and hope the best, as I am sure I wish the best; but you must be frank with me, if you wish to secure my good opinion, and lessen the risk of inconvenience to yourself. You have allowed you saw another individual in your passage through the King's Park to St. Leonard's Crags; I must know every word which passed betwixt you."

Thus closely pressed, Butler, who had no reason for concealing what passed at that meeting, unless because Jeanie Deans was concerned in it, thought it best to tell the whole truth from beginning to end.

"Do you suppose," said the magistrate, pausing, "that the young woman will accept an invitation so mysterious?"

"I fear she will," replied Butler.

"Why do you use the word 'fear' it?" said the magistrate.

"Because I am apprehensive for her safety in meeting, at such a time and place, one who had something of the manner of a desperado, and whose message was of a character so inexplicable."

"Her safety shall be cared for," said the magistrate.

"Mr. Butler, I am concerned I cannot immediately discharge you from confinement, but I hope you will not be long detained. Remove Mr. Butler, and let him be provided with decent accommodation in all respects."

He was conducted back to the prison accordingly; but, in the food offered to him, as well as in the apartment in which he was lodged, the recommendation of the magistrate was strictly attended to.

CHAPTER XIV

Dark and eerie was the night,
And lonely was the way,
As Janet, wi' her green mantell,
To Miles' Cross she did gae.
Old Ballad.

LEAVING Butler to all the uncomfortable thoughts attached to his new situation, among which the most predominant was his feeling that he was, by his confinement, deprived of all possibility of assisting the family at St. Leonard's in their greatest need, we return to Jeanie Deans, who had seen him depart, without an opportunity of further explanation, in all that agony of mind with which the female heart bids adieu tc the complicated sensations so well described by Coleridge—

Hopes, and fears that kindle hope,
An undistinguishable throng ;
And gentle wishes long subdued—
Subdued and cherish'd long.

It is not the firmest heart (and Jeanie, under her russet rokelay, had one that would not have disgraced Cato's daughter) that can most easily bid adieu to these soft and mingled emotions. She wept for a few minutes bitterly, and without attempting to refrain from this indulgence of passion. But a moment's recollection induced her to check herself for a grief selfish and proper to her own affections, while her father and sister were plunged into such deep and irretrievable affliction. She drew from her pocket the letter which had been that morning flung into her apartment through an open window, and the contents of which were as singular as the expression was violent and energetic. "If she would save a human being from the most damning guilt, and all its desperate consequences ; if she desired the life and honor of her sister to be saved from the bloody fangs of an unjust law ; if she desired not to forfeit peace of mind here, and happiness hereafter," such was the frantic style of the conjuration, "she was entreated to give a sure, secret, and solitary meeting to the writer. She alone could rescue him," so ran the

letter, "and he only could rescue her."   He was in such circumstances, the billet further informed her, that an attempt
to bring any witness of their conference, or even to mention to
her father, or any other person whatsoever, the letter which
requested it, would inevitably prevent its taking place, and
insure the destruction of her sister.   The letter concluded
with incoherent but violent protestations that in obeying this
summons she had nothing to fear personally.

The message delivered to her by Butler from the stranger
in the Park tallied exactly with the contents of the letter,
but assigned a later hour and a different place of meeting.
Apparently the writer of the letter had been compelled to
let Butler so far into his confidence, for the sake of announcing this change to Jeanie.   She was more than once on the
point of producing the billet, in vindication of herself from
her lover's half-hinted suspicions.   But there is something in
stooping to justification which the pride of innocence does not
at all times willingly submit to ; besides that the threats contained in the letter, in case of her betraying the secret, hung
heavy on her heart.   It is probable, however, that, had they
remained longer together, she might have taken the resolution to submit the whole matter to Butler, and be guided by
him as to the line of conduct which she should adopt.   And
when, by the sudden interruption of their conference, she
lost the opportunity of doing so, she felt as if she had been
unjust to a friend whose advice might have been highly useful, and whose attachment deserved her full and unreserved
confidence.

To have recourse to her father upon this occasion, she
considered as highly imprudent.   There was no possibility of
conjecturing in what light the matter might strike old David,
whose manner of acting and thinking in extraordinary circumstances depended upon feelings and principles peculiar to
himself, the operation of which could not be calculated upon
even by those best acquainted with him.   To have requested
some female friend to have accompanied her to the place of
rendezvous would perhaps have been the most eligible expedient ; but the threats of the writer, that betraying his secret
would prevent their meeting, on which her sister's safety was
said to depend, from taking place at all, would have deterred
her from making such a confidence, even had she known a
person in whom she thought it could with safety have been
reposed.   But she knew none such.   Their acquaintance with
the cottagers in the vicinity had been very slight, and limited
to trifling acts of good neighborhood.   Jeanie knew little of

them, and what she knew did not greatly incline her to trust any of them. They were of the order of loquacious good-humored gossips usually found in their situation of life ; and their conversation had at all times few charms for a young woman to whom nature and the circumstances of a solitary life had given a depth of thought and force of character superior to the frivolous part of her sex whether in high or low degree.

Left alone and separated from all earthly counsel, she had recourse to a Friend and Adviser whose ear is open to the cry of the poorest and most afflicted of His people. She knelt and prayed with fervent sincerity that God would please to direct her what course to follow in her arduous and distressing situation. It was the belief of the time and sect to which she belonged that special answers to prayer, differing little in their character from divine inspiration, were, as they expressed it, "borne in upon their minds" in answer to their earnest petitions in a crisis of difficulty. Without entering into an abstruse point of divinity, one thing is plain ; namely, that the person who lays open his doubts and distresses in prayer, with feeling and sincerity, must necessarily, in the act of doing so, purify his mind from the dross of worldly passions and interests, and bring it into that state when the resolutions adopted are likely to be selected rather from a sense of duty than from any inferior motive. Jeanie arose from her devotions with her heart fortified to endure affliction and encouraged to face difficulties.

"I will meet this unhappy man," she said to herself—"unhappy he must be, since I doubt he has been the cause of poor Effie's misfortune ; but I will meet him, be it for good or ill. My mind shall never cast up to me that, for fear of what might be said or done to myself, I left that undone that might even yet be the rescue of her."

With a mind greatly composed since the adoption of this resolution, she went to attend her father. The old man, firm in the principles of his youth, did not, in outward appearance at least, permit a thought of his family distress to interfere with the stoical reserve of his countenance and manners. He even chid his daughter for having neglected, in the distress of the morning, some trifling domestic duties which fell under her department.

"Why, what meaneth this, Jeanie ?" said the old man. "The brown four-year-auld's milk is not seiled yet, nor the bowies put up on the bink. If ye neglect your warldly duties in the day of affliction, what confidence have I that ye mind the greater matters that concern salvation ? God knows, our bowies, and our pipkins, and our draps o' milk, and our bits o' bread are nearer and dearer to us than the bread of life."

Jeanie, not unpleased to hear her father's thoughts thus expand themselves beyond the sphere of his immediate distress, obeyed him, and proceeded to put her household matters in order ; while old David moved from place to place about his ordinary employments, scarce showing, unless by a nervous impatience at remaining long stationary, an occasional convulsive sigh, or twinkle of the eyelid, that he was laboring under the yoke of such bitter affliction.

The hour of noon came on, and the father and child sat down to their homely repast. In his petition for a blessing on the meal, the poor old man added to his supplication a prayer that the bread eaten in sadness of heart, and the bitter waters of Merah, might be made as nourishing as those which had been poured forth from a full cup and a plentiful basket and store ; and having concluded his benediction, and resumed the bonnet which he had laid "reverently aside," he proceeded to exhort his daughter to eat, not by example, indeed, but at least by precept.

" The man after God's own heart," he said, " washed and anointed himself, and did eat bread, in order to express his submission under a dispensation of suffering, and it did not become a Christian man or woman so to cling to creature-comforts of wife or bairns [here the words became too great, as it were, for his utterance] as to forget the first duty—submission to the Divine will."

To add force to his precept, he took a morsel on his plate, but nature proved too strong even for the powerful feelings with which he endeavored to bridle it. Ashamed of his weakness, he started up and ran out of the house, with haste very unlike the deliberation of his usual movements. In less than five minutes he returned, having successfully struggled to recover his ordinary composure of mind and countenance, and affected to color over his late retreat by muttering that he thought he heard the " young staig loose in the byre."

He did not again trust himself with the subject of his former conversation, and his daughter was glad to see that he seemed to avoid further discourse on that agitating topic. The hours glided on, as on they must and do pass, whether winged with joy or laden with affliction. The sun set beyond the dusky eminence .of the Castle and the screen of western hills, and the close of evening summoned David Deans and his daughter to the family duty of the evening. It came bitterly upon Jeanie's recollection how often, when the hour of worship approached, she used to watch the lengthening shadows, and look out from the door of the house, to see if she could spy her sister's return homeward. Alas! this idle and thoughtless waste of time, to what evils had it not finally led? And was she altogether guiltless, who, noticing Effie's turn to idle and light society, had not called in her father's authority to restrain her? "But I acted for the best," she again reflected, "and who could have expected such a growth of evil from one grain of human leaven in a disposition so kind, and candid, and generous?"

As they sat down to the "exercise," as it is called, a chair happened accidentally to stand in the place which Effie usually occupied. David Deans saw his daughter's eyes swim in tears as they were directed towards this object, and pushed it aside with a gesture of some impatience, as if desirous to destroy every memorial of earthly interest when about to address the Deity. The portion of Scripture was read, the psalm was sung, the prayer was made; and it was remarkable that, in discharging these duties, the old man avoided all passages and expressions, of which Scripture affords so many, that might be considered as applicable to his own domestic misfortune. In doing so it was perhaps his intention to spare the feelings of his daughter, as well as to maintain, in outward show at least, that stoical appearance of patient endurance of all the evil which earth could bring, which was, in his opinion, essential to the character of one who rated all earthly things at their own just estimate of nothingness. When he had finished the duty of the evening, he came up to his daughter, wished her good-night, and, having done so, continued to hold her by the hands for half a minute; then drawing her towards him, kissed her forehead, and ejaculated, "The God of Israel bless you, even with the blessings of the promise, my dear bairn!"

It was not either in the nature or habits of David Deans to seem a fond father; nor was he often observed to experience, or at least to evince, that fulness of the heart which seeks to expand itself in tender expressions or caresses even to those who were dearest to him. On the contrary, he used to censure this as a degree of weakness in several of his neighbors, and particularly in poor widow Butler. It followed, however, from the rarity of such emotions in this self-denied and reserved man, that his children attached to occasional marks of his affection and approbation a degree of high interest and solemnity, well considering them as evidences of

feelings which were only expressed when they became too intense for suppression or concealment.

With deep emotion, therefore, did he bestow, and his
daughter receive, this benediction and paternal caress. "And
you, my dear father," exclaimed Jeanie, when the door had
closed upon the venerable old man, "may you have purchased
and promised blessings multiplied upon you—upon *you*, who
walk in this world as though ye were not of the world, and
hold all that it can give or take away but as the *midges* that
the sun-blink brings out and the evening wind sweeps away !"

She now made preparation for her night-walk. Her
father slept in another part of the dwelling, and, regular in
all his habits, seldom or never left his apartment when he had
betaken himself to it for the evening. It was therefore easy
for her to leave the house unobserved, so soon as the time
approached at which she was to keep her appointment. But
the step she was about to take had difficulties and terrors in
her own eyes, though she had no reason to apprehend her
father's interference. Her life had been spent in the quiet,
uniform, and regular seclusion of their peaceful and monotonous household. The very hour which some damsels
of the present day, as well of her own as of higher degree,
would consider as the natural period of commencing an evening of pleasure, brought, in her opinion, awe and solemnity
in it ; and the resolution she had taken had a strange, daring
and adventurous character, to which she could hardly reconcile herself when the moment approached for putting it into
execution. Her hands trembled as she snooded her fair
hair beneath the ribbon, then the only ornament or cover
which young unmarried women wore on their head, and as
she adjusted the scarlet tartan screen or muffler made of
plaid, which the Scottish women wore, much in the fashion
of the black silk veils still a part of female dress in the Netherlands. A sense of impropriety as well as of danger pressed
upon her, as she lifted the latch of her paternal mansion to
leave it on so wild an expedition, and at so late an hour, unprotected, and without the knowledge of her natural guardian.

When she found herself abroad and in the open fields, additional subjects of apprehension crowded upon her. The
dim cliffs and scattered rocks, interspersed with greensward,
through which she had to pass to the place of appointment,
as they glimmered before her in a clear autumn night, recalled
to her memory many a deed of violence, which, according to
tradition, had been done and suffered among them. In earlier
days they had been the haunt of robbers and assassins, the

memory of whose crimes is preserved in the various edicts which the council of the city, and even the parliament of Scotland, had passed for dispersing their bands, and insuring safety to the lieges, so near the precincts of the city. The names of these criminals, and of their atrocities, were still remembered in traditions of the scattered cottages and the neighboring suburb. In latter times, as we have already noticed, the sequestered and broken character of the ground rendered it a fit theatre for duels and *rencontres* among the fiery youth of the period. Two or three of these incidents, all sanguinary, and one of them fatal in its termination, had happened since Deans came to live at St. Leonard's. His daughter's recollections, therefore, were of blood and horror as she pursued the small scarce-tracked solitary path, every step of which conveyed her to a greater distance from help, and deeper into the ominous seclusion of these unhallowed precincts.

As the moon began to peer forth on the scene with a doubtful, flitting, and solemn light, Jeanie's apprehensions took another turn, too peculiar to her rank and country to remain unnoticed. But to trace its origin will require another chapter.

CHAPTER XV

The spirit I have seen
May be the devil.   And the devil has power
To assume a pleasing shape.

Hamlet.

WITCHCRAFT and demonology, as we haye had already occasion
to remark, were at this period believed in by almost all ranks,
but more especially among the stricter classes of Presbyterians,
whose government, when their party were at the head of the
state, had been much sullied by their eagerness to inquire into
and persecute these imaginary crimes.   Now, in this point of
view, also, St. Leonard's Crags and the adjacent chase were a
dreaded and ill-reputed district.   Not only had witches held
their meetings there, but even of very late years the enthusiast, or impostor, mentioned in the *Pandæmonium* of Richard
Bovet, Gentleman,* had, among the recesses of these romantic
cliffs, found his way into the hidden retreats where the fairies
revel in the bowels of the earth.

With all these legends Jeanie Deans was too well acquainted
to escape that strong impression which they usually make on
the imagination.   Indeed, relations of this ghostly kind had
been familiar to her from her infancy, for they were the only
relief which her father's conversation afforded from controversial argument, or the gloomy history of the strivings and
testimonies, escapes, captures, tortures, and executions of
those martyrs of the Covenant with whom it was his chiefest
boast to say he had been acquainted.   In the recesses of
mountains, in caverns, and in morasses, to which these persecuted enthusiasts were so ruthlessly pursued, they conceived
they had often to contend with the visible assaults of the
Enemy of mankind, as in the cities and in the cultivated fields
they were exposed to those of the tyrannical government and
their soldiery.   Such were the terrors which made one of their
gifted seers exclaim, when his companion returned to him,
after having left him alone in a haunted cavern in Sorn in
Galloway, "It is hard living in this world—incarnate devils
above the earth, and devils under the earth !   Satan has been

* See The Fairy Boy of Leith.   Note 19.

144

here since ye went away, but I have dismissed him by resistance ; we will be no more troubled with him this night." David Deans believed this, and many other such ghostly encounters and victories, on the faith of the ansars, or auxiliaries of the banished prophets. This event was beyond David's remembrance. But he used to tell with great awe, yet not without a feeling of proud superiority to his auditors, how he himself had been present at a field-meeting at Crochmade, when the duty of the day was interrupted by the apparition of a tall black man, who, in the act of crossing a ford to join the congregation, lost ground, and was carried down apparently by the force of the stream. All were instantly at work to assist him, but with so little success that ten or twelve stout men, who had hold of the rope which they had cast in to his aid, were rather in danger to be dragged into the stream, and lose their own lives, than likely to save that of the supposed perishing man. "But famous John Semple of Carspharn," David Deans used to say with exultation, "saw the whaup in the rape. 'Quit the rope,' he cried to us—for I that was but a callant had a haud o' the rape mysell—'it is the Great Enemy ! he will burn, but not drown ; his design is to disturb the good wark, by raising wonder and confusion in your minds, to put off from your spirits all that ye hae heard and felt.' Sae we let go the rape," said David, "and he went adown the water screeching and bullering like a Bull of Bashan, as he's ca'd in Scripture."*

Trained in these and similar legends, it was no wonder that Jeanie began to feel an ill-defined apprehension, not merely of the phantoms which might beset her way, but of the quality, nature, and purpose of the being who had thus appointed her a meeting at a place and hour of horror, and at a time when her mind must be necessarily full of those tempting and ensnaring thoughts of grief and despair which were supposed to lay sufferers particularly open to the temptations of the Evil One. If such an idea had crossed even Butler's well-informed mind, it was calculated to make a much stronger impression upon hers. Yet firmly believing the possibility of an encounter so terrible to flesh and blood, Jeanie, with a degree of resolution of which we cannot sufficiently estimate the merit, because the incredulity of the age has rendered us strangers to the nature and extent of her feelings, persevered in her determination not to omit an opportunity of doing something towards saving her sister, although, in the attempt to avail herself of it, she might be

* See Intercourse of the Covenanters with the Invisible World. Note 20.

exposed to dangers so dreadful to her imagination. So, like Christiana in the *Pilgrim's Progress,* when traversing with a timid yet resolved step the terrors of the Valley of the Shadow of Death, she glided on by rock and stone, "now in glimmer and now in gloom," as her path lay through moonlight or shadow, and endeavored to overpower the suggestions of fear, sometimes by fixing her mind upon the distressed condition of her sister, and the duty she lay under to afford her aid, should that be in her power, and more frequently by recurring in mental prayer to the protection of that Being to whom night is as noonday.

Thus drowning at one time her fears by fixing her mind on a subject of overpowering interest, and arguing them down at others by referring herself to the protection of the Deity, she at length approached the place assigned for this mysterious conference.

It was situated in the depth of the valley behind Salisbury Crags, which has for a background the north-western shoulder of the mountain called Arthur's Seat, on whose descent still remain the ruins of what was once a chapel, or hermitage, dedicated to St. Anthony the Eremite. A better site for such a building could hardly have been selected ; for the chapel, situated among the rude and pathless cliffs, lies in a desert, even in the immediate vicinity of a rich, populous, and tumultuous capital ; and the hum of the city might mingle with the orisons of the recluses, conveying as little of worldly interest as if it had been the roar of the distant ocean. Beneath the steep ascent on which these ruins are still visible, was, and perhaps is still, pointed out the place where the wretch Nicol Muschat, who has been already mentioned in these pages, had closed a long scene of cruelty towards his unfortunate wife by murdering her, with circumstances of uncommon barbarity. The execration in which the man's crime was held extended itself to the place where it was perpetrated, which was marked by a small cairn, or heap of stones, composed of those which each chance passenger had thrown there in testimony of abhorrence, and on the principle, it would seem, of the ancient British malediction, "May you have a cairn for your burial-place !"

As our heroine approached this ominous and unhallowed spot, she paused and looked to the moon, now rising broad on the north-west, and shedding a more distinct light than it had afforded during her walk thither. Eying the planet for a moment, she then slowly and fearfully turned her head towards the cairn, from which it was at first averted. She was at first disappointed. Nothing was visible beside the little pile of stones, which shone gray in the moonlight. A multitude of confused suggestions rushed on her mind. Had her correspondent deceived her, and broken his appointment ? was he too tardy at the appointment he had made ? or had some strange turn of fate prevented him from appearing as he proposed ? or, if he were an unearthly being, as her secret apprehensions suggested, was it his object merely to delude her with false hopes, and put her to unnecessary toil and terror, according to the nature, as she had heard, of those wandering demons ? or did he purpose to blast her with the sudden horrors of his presence when she had come close to the place of rendezvous ? These anxious reflections did not prevent her approaching to the cairn with a pace that, though slow, was determined

When she was within two yards of the heap of stones, a figure rose suddenly up from behind it, and Jeanie scarce forbore to scream aloud at what seemed the realization of the most frightful of her anticipations. She constrained herself to silence, however, and, making a dead pause, suffered the figure to open the conversation, which he did by asking, in a voice which agitation rendered tremulous and hollow, " Are you the sister of that ill-fated young woman ? "

" I am ; I am the sister of Effie Deans ! " exclaimed Jeanie. " And as ever you hope God will hear you at your need, tell me, if you can tell, what can be done to save her ! "

" I do *not* hope God will hear me at my need," was the singular answer. " I do not deserve—I do not expect He will." This desperate language he uttered in a tone calmer than that with which he had at first spoken, probably because the shock of first addressing her was what he felt most difficult to overcome.

Jeanie remained mute with horror to hear language expressed so utterly foreign to all which she had ever been acquainted with, that it sounded in her ears rather like that of a fiend than of a human being.

The stranger pursued his address to her without seeming to notice her surprise. " You see before you a wretch predestined to evil here and hereafter."

" For the sake of Heaven, that hears and sees us," said Jeanie, " dinna speak in this desperate fashion. The Gospel is sent to the chief of sinners—to the most miserable among the miserable."

" Then should I have my own share therein," said the stranger, " if you call it sinful to have been the destruction of the mother that bore me, of the friend that loved me, of the woman that trusted me, of the innocent child that was born

to me.   If to have done all this is to be a sinner, and to survive it is to be miserable, then am I most guilty and most miserable indeed."

"Then you are the wicked cause of my sister's ruin ?" said
Jeanie, with a natural touch of indignation expressed in her
tone of voice.

"Curse me for it if you will," said the stranger; "I have
well deserved it at your hand."

"It is fitter for me," said Jeanie, "to pray to God to forgive you."

"Do as you will, how you will, or what you will," he replied, with vehemence ; "only promise to obey my directions,
and save your sister's life."

"I must first know," said Jeanie, "the means you would
have me use in her behalf."

"No! you must first swear—solemnly swear—that you
will employ them, when I make them known to you."

"Surely it is needless to swear that I will do all that is lawful to a Christian to save the life of my sister ?"

"I will have no reservation !" thundered the stranger.
"Lawful or unlawful, Christian or heathen, you shall swear
to do my hest and act by my counsel, or—you little know
whose wrath you provoke !"

"I will think on what you have said," said Jeanie, who began to get much alarmed at the frantic vehemence of his manner, and disputed in her own mind whether she spoke to a
maniac or an apostate spirit incarnate—"I will think on what
you say, and let you ken to-morrow."

"To-morrow !" exclaimed the man, with a laugh of scorn.
"And where will I be to-morrow ? or where will you be to-
night, unless you swear to walk by my counsel ? There was
one accursed deed done at this spot before now ; and there
shall be another to match it unless you yield up to my guidance body and soul."

As he spoke, he offered a pistol at the unfortunate young
woman.   She neither fled nor fainted, but sunk on her knees
and asked him to spare her life.

"Is that all you have to say ?" said the unmoved ruffian.

"Do not dip your hands in the blood of a defenceless creature that has trusted to you," said Jeanie, still on her knees.

"Is that all you can say for your life?   Have you no promise to give ?   Will you destroy your sister, and compel me to
shed more blood ?"

"I can promise nothing," said Jeanie, "which is unlawful for a Christian."

He cocked the weapon and held it towards **her.**

"May God forgive you!" she said, pressing her hands forcibly against her eyes.

"D———n!" muttered the man; and, turning aside from her, he uncocked the pistol and replaced it in his pocket. "I am a villain," he said, "steeped in guilt and wretchedness, but not wicked enough to do you any harm! I only wished to terrify you into my measures. She hears me not—she is gone! Great God! what a wretch am I become!"

As he spoke, she recovered herself from an agony which partook of the bitterness of death; and in a minute or two, through the strong exertion of her natural sense and courage, collected herself sufficiently to understand he intended her no personal injury.

"No!" he repeated; "I would not add to the murder of your sister, and of her child, that of any one belonging to her! Mad, frantic, as I am, and unrestrained by either fear or mercy, given up to the possession of an evil being, and forsaken by all that is good, I would not hurt you, were the world offered me for a bribe! But, for the sake of all that is dear to you, swear you will follow my counsel. Take this weapon, shoot me through the head, and with your own hand revenge your sister's wrong, only follow the course—the only course, by which her life can be saved."

"Alas! is she innocent or guilty?"

"She is guiltless—guiltless of everything but of having trusted a villain! Yet, had it not been for those that were worse than I am—yes, worse than I am, though I am bad indeed—this misery had not befallen."

"And my sister's child—does it live?" said Jeanie.

"No; it was murdered—the new-born infant was barbarously murdered," he uttered in a low yet stern and sustained voice; "but," he added, hastily, "not by her knowledge or consent."

"Then why cannot the guilty be brought to justice, and the innocent freed?"

"Torment me not with questions which can serve no purpose," he sternly replied. "The deed was done by those who are far enough from pursuit, and safe enough from discovery! No one can save Effie but yourself."

"Woe's me! how is it in my power?" asked Jeanie, in despondency.

"Hearken to me! You have sense—you can apprehend my meaning—I will trust you. Your sister is innocent of the crime charged against her———"

" Thank God for that ! " said Jeanie.

" Be still and hearken ! The person who assisted her in her illness murdered the child ; but it was without the mother's knowledge or consent. She is therefore guiltless—as guiltless as the unhappy innocent that but gasped a few minutes in this unhappy world ; the better was its hap to be so soon at rest. She is innocent as that infant, and yet she must die ; it is impossible to clear her of the law ! "

" Cannot the wretches be discovered and given up to punishment ? " said Jeanie.

" Do you think you will persuade those who are hardened in guilt to die to save another ? Is that the reed you would lean to ? "

" But you said there was a remedy," again gasped out the terrified young woman.

" There is," answered the stranger, " and it is in your own hands. The blow which the law aims cannot be broken by directly encountering it, but it may be turned aside. You saw your sister during the period preceding the birth of her child ; what is so natural as that she should have mentioned her condition to you ? The doing so would, as their cant goes, take the case from under the statute, for it removes the quality of concealment. I know their jargon, and have had sad cause to know it ; and the quality of concealment is essential to this statutory offence. Nothing is so natural as that Effie should have mentioned her condition to you ; think—reflect— I am positive that she did."

" Woe's me ! " said Jeanie, " she never spoke to me on the subject, but grat sorely when I spoke to her about her altered looks and the change on her spirits."

" You asked her questions on the subject ? " he said, eagerly. " You *must* remember her answer was a confession that she had been ruined by a villain—yes, lay a strong emphasis on that—a cruel false villain call it—any other name is unnecessary ; and that she bore under her bosom the consequences of his guilt and her folly ; and that he had assured her he would provide safely for her approaching illness. Well he kept his word ! " These last words he spoke as it were to himself, and with a violent gesture of self-accusation, and then calmly proceeded, " You will remember all this ? That is all that is necessary to be said."

" But I cannot remember," answered Jeanie, with simplicity, " that which Effie never told me."

" Are you so dull—so very dull of apprehension ? " he exclaimed, suddenly grasping her arm, and holding it firm in his hand. "I tell you [speaking between his teeth, and under his breath, but with great energy], you *must* remember that she told you all this, whether she ever said a syllable of it or no. You must repeat this tale, in which there is no falsehood, except in so far as it was not told to you, before these Justices —Justiciary—whatever they call their bloodthirsty court, and save your sister from being murdered, and them from becoming murderers. Do not hesitate ; I pledge life and salvation, that in saying what I have said, you will only speak the simple truth."

"But," replied Jeanie, whose judgment was too accurate not to see the sophistry of this argument, "I shall be mansworn in the very thing in which my testimony is wanted, for it is the concealment for which poor Effie is blamed, and you would make me tell a falsehood anent it."

"I see," he said, "my first suspicions of you were right, and that you will let your sister, innocent, fair, and guiltless, except in trusting a villain, die the death of a murderess, rather than bestow the breath of your mouth and the sound of your voice to save her."

"I wad ware the best blood in my body to keep her skaithless," said Jeanie, weeping in bitter agony ; "but I canna change right into wrang, or make that true which is false."

"Foolish, hard-hearted girl," said the stranger, "are you afraid of what they may do to you ? I tell you, even the retainers of the law, who course life as greyhounds do hares, will rejoice at the escape of a creature so young—so beautiful ; that they will not suspect your tale ; that, if they did suspect it, they would consider you as deserving, not only of forgiveness, but of praise for your natural affection."

"It is not man I fear," said Jeanie, looking upward ; "the God, whose name I must call on to witness the truth of what I say, He will know the falsehood."

"And He will know the motive," said the stranger, eagerly; "He will know that you are doing this, not for lucre of gain, but to save the life of the innocent and prevent the commission of a worse crime than that which the law seeks to avenge."

"He has given us a law," said Jeanie, "for the lamp of our path ; if we stray from it we err against knowledge. I may not do evil, even that good may come out of it. But you—you that ken all this to be true, which I must take on your word—you that, if I understood what you said e'en now, promised her shelter and protection in her travail, why do not *you* step forward and bear leal and soothfast evidence in her behalf, as ye may with a clear conscience ?"

"To whom do you talk of a clear conscience, woman?" said he, with a sudden fierceness which renewed her terrors— "to *me?* I have not known one for many a year. Bear witness in her behalf?—a proper witness, that even to speak these few words to a woman of so little consequence as yourself, must choose such an hour and such a place as this. When you see owls and bats fly abroad, like larks, in the sunshine, you may expect to see such as I am in the assemblies of men. Hush! listen to that."

A voice was heard to sing one of those wild and monotonous strains so common in Scotland, and to which the natives of that country chant their old ballads. The sound ceased, then came nearer and was renewed; the stranger listened attentively, still holding Jeanie by the arm (as she stood by him in motionless terror), as if to prevent her interrupting the strain by speaking or stirring. When the sounds were renewed, the words were distinctly audible:

> " When the glede's in the blue cloud,
>   The lavrock lies still;
>   When the hound's in the green-wood,
>   The hind keeps the hill."

The person who sung kept a strained and powerful voice at its highest pitch, so that it could be heard at a very considerable distance. As the song ceased, they might hear a stifled sound, as of steps and whispers of persons approaching them. The song was again raised, but the tune was changed:

> "O sleep ye sound, Sir James, she said,
>   When ye suld rise and ride?
>   There's twenty men, wi' bow and blade,
>   Are seeking where ye hide."

"I dare stay no longer," said the stranger. "Return home, or remain till they come up, you have nothing to fear; but do not tell you saw me: your sister's fate is in your hands." So saying, he turned from her, and with a swift yet cautiously noiseless step plunged into the darkness on the side most remote from the sounds which they heard approaching, and was soon lost to her sight. Jeanie remained by the cairn terrified beyond expression, and uncertain whether she ought to fly homeward with all the speed she could exert, or wait the approach of those who were advancing towards her. This uncertainty detained her so long that she now distinctly saw two or three figures already so near to her that a precipitate flight would have been equally fruitless and impolitic.

CHAPTER XVI

> She speaks things in doubt,
> That carry but half sense : her speech is nothing,
> Yet the unshaped use of it doth move
> The hearers to collection ; they aim at it,
> And botch the words up to fit their own thoughts.
> *Hamlet.*

LIKE the digressive poet Ariosto, I find myself under the necessity of connecting the branches of my story, by taking up the adventures of another of the characters, and bringing them down to the point at which we have left those of Jeanie Deans. It is not, perhaps, the most artificial way of telling a story, but it has the advantage of sparing the necessity of resuming what a knitter (if stocking-looms have left such a person in the land) might call our "dropped stitches ;" a labor in which the author generally toils much, without getting credit for his pains.

"I could risk a sma' wad," said the clerk to the magistrate, "that this rascal Ratcliffe, if he were insured of his neck's safety, could do more than ony ten of our police-people and constables to help us to get out of this scrape of Porteous's. He is weel acquent wi' a' the smugglers, thieves, and banditti about Edinburgh ; and, indeed, he may be called the father of a' the misdoers in Scotland, for he has passed amang them for these twenty years by the name of Daddie Rat."

"A bonny sort of a scoundrel," replied the magistrate, "to expect a place under the city !"

"Begging your honor's pardon," said the city's procurator-fiscal, upon whom the duties of superintendent of police devolved, "Mr. Fairscrieve is perfectly in the right. It is just sic as Ratcliffe that the town needs in my department ; an' if sae be that he's disposed to turn his knowledge to the city service, ye'll no find a better man. Ye'll get nae saints to be searchers for uncustomed goods, or for thieves and sic-like ; and your decent sort of men, religious professors and broken tradesmen, that are put into the like o' sic trust, can do nae gude ava. They are feared for this, and they are scrupulous about that, and they arena free to tell a lie, though it may be

for the benefit of the city; and they dinna like to be out at
irregular hours, and in a dark cauld night, and they like a
clout ower the croun far waur; and sae between the fear o'
God, and the fear o' man, and the fear o' getting a sair throat,
or sair banes, there's a dozen o' our city-folk, baith waiters,
and officers, and constables, that can find out naething but a
wee bit sculduddery for the benefit of the kirk-treasurer.
Jock Porteous, that's stiff and stark, puir fallow, was worth
a dozen o' them; for he never had ony fears, or scruples, or
doubts, or conscience, about onything your honors bade him."

"He was a gude servant o' the town," said the bailie,
"though he was an ower free-living man. But if you really
think this rascal Ratcliffe could do us ony service in discovering these malefactors, I would insure him life, reward, and
promotion.   It's an awsome thing this mischance for the
city, Mr. Fairscrieve.   It will be very ill taen wi' abune stairs.
Queen Caroline, God bless her! is a woman—at least I judge
sae, and it's nae treason to speak my mind sae far—and ye
maybe ken as weel as I do, for ye hae a housekeeper, though
ye arena a married man, that women are wilfu', and downa
bide a slight.   And it will sound ill in her ears that sic a
confused mistake suld come to pass, and naebody sae muckle
as to be put into the tolbooth about it."

"If ye thought that, sir," said the procurator-fiscal, "we
could easily clap into the prison a few blackguards upon suspicion.   It will have a gude active look, and I hae aye plenty
on my list, that wadna be a hair the waur of a week or twa's
imprisonment; and if ye thought it no strictly just, ye could
be just the easier wi' them the neist time they did onything
to deserve it; they arena the sort to be lang o' gieing ye an
opportunity to clear scores wi' them on that account."

"I doubt that will hardly do in this case, Mr. Sharpitlaw," returned the town clerk; "they'll run their letters,*
and be adrift again, before ye ken where ye are."

"I will speak to the Lord Provost," said the magistrate,
"about Ratcliffe's business.   Mr. Sharpitlaw, you will go
with me and receive instructions.   Something may be made
too out of this story of Butler's and his unknown gentleman.
I know no business any man has to swagger about in the
King's Park, and call himself the devil, to the terror of honest folks, who dinna care to hear mair about the devil than is
said from the pulpit on the Sabbath.   I cannot think the
preacher himsell wad be heading the mob, though the time

* A Scottish form of procedure, answering, in some respects, to the English
Habeas Corpus.

has been they hae been as forward in a bruilzie as their neighbors."

"But these times are lang bye," said Mr. Sharpitlaw. "In my father's time there was mair search for silenced ministers about the Bow-head and the Covenant Close, and all the tents of Kedar, as they ca'd the dwellings o' the godly in those days, than there's now for thieves and vagabonds in the Laigh Calton and the back o' the Canongate. But that time's weel bye, an it bide. And if the bailie will get me directions and authority from the provost, I'll speak wi' Daddie Rat mysell; for I'm thinking I'll make mair out o' him than ye'll do."

Mr. Sharpitlaw, being necessarily a man of high trust, was accordingly empowered, in the course of the day, to make such arrangements as might seem in the emergency most advantageous for the Good Town. He went to the jail accordingly, and saw Ratcliffe in private.

The relative positions of a police-officer and a professed thief bear a different complexion according to circumstances. The most obvious simile of a hawk pouncing upon his prey is often least applicable. Sometimes the guardian of justice has the air of a cat watching a mouse, and, while he suspends his purpose of springing upon the pilferer, takes care so to calculate his motions that he shall not get beyond his power. Sometimes, more passive still, he uses the art of fascination ascribed to the rattlesnake, and contents himself with glaring on the victim through all his devious flutterings ; certain that his terror, confusion, and disorder of ideas will bring him into his jaws at last. The interview between Ratcliffe and Sharpitlaw had an aspect different from all these. They sat for five minutes silent, on opposite sides of a small table, and looked fixedly at each other, with a sharp, knowing, and alert cast of countenance, not unmingled with an inclination to laugh, and resembled more than anything else two dogs who, preparing for a game at romps, are seen to couch down and remain in that posture for a little time, watching each other's movements, and waiting which shall begin the game.

"So, Mr. Ratcliffe," said the officer, conceiving it suited his dignity to speak first, "you give up business, I find ?"

"Yes, sir," replied Ratcliffe ; "I shall be on that lay nae mair ; and I think that will save your folk some trouble, Mr. Sharpitlaw ?"

"Which Jock Dalgleish * [then finisher of the law in the Scottish metropolis] wad save them as easily," returned the procurator-fiscal.

* See Note 21.

"Ay; if I waited in the tolbooth here to have him fit my cravat; but that's an idle way o' speaking, Mr. Sharpitlaw."

"Why, I suppose you know you are under sentence of death, Mr. Ratcliffe?" replied Mr. Sharpitlaw.

"Ay, so are a', as that worthy minister said in the Tolbooth Kirk the day Robertson wan off; but naebody kens when it will be executed. Gude faith, he had better reason to say sae than he dreamed of, before the play was played out that morning!"

"This Robertson," said Sharpitlaw, in a lower and something like a confidential tone, "d'ye ken, Rat—that is, can ye gie us ony inkling where he is to be heard tell o'?"

"Troth, Mr. Sharpitlaw, I'll be frank wi' ye: Robertson is rather a cut abune me. A wild deevil he was, and mony a daft prank he played; but, except the collector's job that Wilson led him into, and some tuilzies about run goods wi' the gaugers and the waiters, he never did onything that came near our line o' business."

"Umph! that's singular, considering the company he kept."

"Fact, upon my honor and credit," said Ratcliffe, gravely. "He keepit out o' our little bits of affairs, and that's mair than Wilson did; I hae dune business wi' Wilson afore now. But the lad will come on in time, there's nae fear o' him; naebody will live the life he has led but what he'll come to sooner or later."

"Who or what is he, Ratcliffe? you know, I suppose?" said Sharpitlaw.

"He's better born, I judge, than he cares to let on; he's been a soldier, and he has been a play-actor, and I watna what he has been or hasna been, for as young as he is, sae that it had daffing and nonsense about it."

"Pretty pranks he has played in his time, I suppose?"

"Ye may say that," said Ratcliffe, with a sardonic smile; "and [touching his nose] a deevil amang the lasses."

"Like enough," said Sharpitlaw. "Weel, Ratcliffe, I'll no stand niffering wi' ye: ye ken the way that favor's gotten in my office; ye maun be usefu'."

"Certainly, sir, to the best of my power: naething for naething—I ken the rule of the office," said the ex-depredator.

"Now the principal thing in hand e'en now," said the official person, "is this job of Porteous's. An ye can gie us a lift—why, the inner turnkey's office to begin wi', and the captainship in time; ye understand my meaning?"

"Ay, troth do I, sir; a wink's as gude as a nod to a blind

horse.   But Jock Porteous's job—Lord help ye !—I was under sentence the haill time.   God ! but I couldna help laughing when I heard Jock skirling for mercy in the lads' hands ! 'Mony a het skin ye hae gien me, neighbor,' thought I, 'tak ye what's gaun : time about's fair play ; ye'll ken now what hanging's gude for.' "

"Come, come, this is all nonsense, Rat," said the procurator.   "Ye canna creep out at that hole, lad ; you must speak to the point, you understand me, if you want favor ; gif-gaf makes gude friends, ye ken."

"But how can I speak to the point, as your honor ca's it," said Ratcliffe, demurely, and with an air of great simplicity, "when ye ken I was under sentence, and in the strong-room a' the while the job was going on ? "

"And how can we turn ye loose on the public again, Daddie Rat, unless ye do or say something to deserve it ? "

"Well, then, d—n it !" answered the criminal, "since it maun be sae, I saw Geordie Robertson among the boys that brake the jail ; I suppose that will do me some gude ? "

"That's speaking to the purpose, indeed," said the office-bearer ; "and now, Rat, where think ye we'll find him ? "

"Deil haet o' me kens," said Ratcliffe ; "he'll no likely gang back to ony o' his auld howffs ; he'll be off the country by this time.   He has gude friends some gate or other, for a' the life he's led ; he's been weel educate."

"He'll grace the gallows the better," said Mr. Sharpitlaw ; "a desperate dog, to murder an officer of the city for doing his duty ! wha kens wha's turn it might be next ?   But you saw him plainly ? "

"As plainly as I see you."

"How was he dressed ? " said Sharpitlaw.

"I couldna weel see ; something of a woman's bit mutch on his head ; but ye never saw sic a ca'-throw.   Ane couldna hae een to a'thing."

"But did he speak to no one ? " said Sharpitlaw.

"They were a' speaking and gabbling through other," said Ratcliffe, who was obviously unwilling to carry his evidence further than he could possibly help.

"This will not do, Ratcliffe," said the procurator ; "you must speak *out—out—out*," tapping the table emphatically, as he repeated that impressive monosyllable.

"It's very hard, sir," said the prisoner ; "and but for the under turnkey's place——"

"And the reversion of the captaincy—the captaincy of the tolbooth, man—that is, in case of gude behavior."

"Ay, ay," said Ratcliffe, "gude behavior! there's the deevil. And then it's waiting for dead folks' shoon into the bargain."

"But Robertson's head will weigh something," said Sharpitlaw—"something gay and heavy, Rat; the town maun show cause—that's right and reason—and then ye'll hae freedom to enjoy your gear honestly."

"I dinna ken," said Ratcliffe; "it's a queer way of beginning the trade of honesty—but deil ma care. Weel, then, I heard and saw him speak to the wench Effie Deans, that's up there for child-murder."

"The deil ye did? Rat, this is finding a mare's nest wi' a witness. And the man that spoke to Butler in the Park, and that was to meet wi' Jeanie Deans at Muschat's Cairn—whew! lay that and that thegither! As sure as I live he's been the father of the lassie's wean."

"There hae been waur guesses than that, I'm thinking," observed Ratcliffe, turning his quid of tobacco in his cheek and squirting out the juice. "I heard something a while syne about his drawing up wi' a bonny quean about the Pleasaunts, and that it was a' Wilson could do to keep him frae marrying her."

Here a city officer entered, and told Sharpitlaw that they had the woman in custody whom he had directed them to bring before him.

"It's little matter now," said he, "the thing is taking another turn; however, George, ye may bring her in."

The officer retired, and introduced, upon his return, a tall, strapping wench of eighteen or twenty, dressed fantastically, in a sort of blue riding-jacket, with tarnished lace, her hair clubbed like that of a man, a Highland bonnet, and a bunch of broken feathers, a riding-skirt (or petticoat) of scarlet camlet, embroidered with tarnished flowers. Her features were coarse and masculine, yet at a little distance, by dint of very bright wild-looking black eyes, an aquiline nose, and a commanding profile, appeared rather handsome. She flourished the switch she held in her hand, dropped a courtesy as low as a lady at a birthnight introduction, recovered herself seemingly according to Touchstone's directions to Audrey, and opened the conversation without waiting till any questions were asked.

"God gie your honor gude-e'en, and mony o' them, bonny Mr. Sharpitlaw! Gude e'en to ye, Daddie Ratton; they tauld me ye were hanged, man; or did ye get out o' John Dalgleish's hands like half-hangit Maggie Dickson?"

"Whisht, ye daft jaud," said Ratcliffe, "and hear what's said to ye."

"Wi' a' my heart, Ratton. Great preferment for poor Madge to be brought up the street wi' a grand man, wi' a coat a' passemented wi' worset-lace, to speak wi' provosts, and bailies, and town clerks, and prokitors, at this time o' day ; and the haill town looking at me too. This is honor on earth for anes !"

"Ay, Madge," said Mr. Sharpitlaw, in a coaxing tone ; "and ye're dressed out in your braws, I see ; these are not your every-day's claiths ye have on ?"

"Deil be in my fingers, then !" said Madge. "Eh, sirs ! [observing Butler come into the apartment], there's a minister in the tolbooth ; wha will ca' it a graceless place now ? I'se warrant he's in for the gude auld cause ; but it's be nae cause o' mine," and off she went into a song :

> "Hey for cavaliers, ho for cavaliers,
> Dub a dub, dub a dub ;
> Have at old Beelzebub,—
> Oliver's squeaking for fear."

"Did you ever see that madwoman before ?" said Sharpitlaw to Butler.

"Not to my knowledge, sir," replied Butler.

"I thought as much," said the procurator-fiscal, looking towards Ratcliffe, who answered his glance with a nod of acquiescence and intelligence.

"But that is Madge Wildfire, as she calls herself," said the man of law to Butler.

"Ay, that I am," said Madge, "and that I have been ever since I was something better—heigh ho ! [and something like melancholy dwelt on her features for a minute]. But I canna mind when that was ; it was lang syne, at ony rate, and I'll ne'er fash my thumb about it :

> "I glance like the wildfire through country and town ;
> I'm seen on the causeway—I'm seen on the down ;
> The lightning that flashes so bright and so free,
> Is scarcely so blithe or so bonny as me."

"Haud your tongue, ye skirling limmer !" said the officer who had acted as master of the ceremonies to this extraordinary performer, and who was rather scandalized at the freedom of her demeanor before a person of Mr. Sharpitlaw's importance —"haud your tongue, or I'se gie ye something to skirl for !"

"Let her alone, George," said Sharpitlaw, "dinna put

her out o' tune; I hae some questions to ask her. But first, Mr. Butler, take another look of her."

"Do sae, minister—do sae," cried Madge; "I am as weel worth looking at as ony book in your aught. And I can say the Single Carritch, and the Double Carritch, and justification, and effectual calling, and the Assembly of Divines at Westminster—that is," she added in a low tone, "I could say them anes; but it's lang syne, and ane forgets, ye ken." And poor Madge heaved another deep sigh.

"Weel, sir," said Mr. Sharpitlaw to Butler, "what think ye now?"

"As I did before," said Butler; "that I never saw the poor demented creature in my life before."

"Then she is not the person whom you said the rioters last night described as Madge Wildfire?"

"Certainly not," said Butler. "They may be near the same height, for they are both tall; but I see little other resemblance."

"Their dress, then, is not alike?" said Sharpitlaw.

"Not in the least," said Butler.

"Madge, my bonny woman," said Sharpitlaw, in the same coaxing manner, "what did ye do wi' your ilka-day's claise yesterday?"

"I dinna mind," said Madge.

"Where was ye yesterday at e'en, Madge?"

"I dinna mind onything about yesterday," answered Madge; "ae day is eneugh for onybody to wun ower wi' at a time, and ower muckle sometimes."

"But maybe, Madge, ye wad mind something about it if I was to gie ye this half-crown?" said Sharpitlaw, taking out the piece of money.

"That might gar me laugh, but it couldna gar me mind."

"But, Madge," continued Sharpitlaw, "were I to send you to the warkhouse in Leith Wynd, and gar Jock Dalgleish lay the tawse on your back——"

"That wad gar me greet," said Madge, sobbing, "but it couldna gar me mind, ye ken."

"She is ower far past reasonable folks' motives, sir," said Ratcliffe, "to mind siller, or John Dalgleish, or the cat and nine tails either; but I think I could gar her tell us something."

"Try her, then, Ratcliffe," said Sharpitlaw, "for I am tired of her crazy prate, and be d—d to her."

"Madge," said Ratcliffe, "hae ye ony joes now?"

"An onybody ask ye, say ye dinna ken. Set him to be speaking of my joes, auld Daddie Ratton!"

"I dare say ye hae deil ane?"

"See if I haena, then," said Madge, with the toss of the head of affronted beauty; "there's Rob the Ranter, and Will Fleming, and then there's Geordie Robertson, lad—that's Gentleman Geordie; what think ye o' that?"

Ratcliffe laughed, and, winking to the procurator-fiscal, pursued the inquiry in his own way. "But, Madge, the lads only like ye when ye hae on your braws; they wadna touch you wi' a pair o' tangs when you are in your auld ilka-day rags."

"Ye're a leeing auld sorrow, then," replied the fair one; "for Gentle Geordie Robertson put my ilka-day's claise on his ain bonny sell yestreen, and gaed a' through the town wi' them; and gawsie and grand he lookit, like ony queen in the land."

"I dinna believe a word o't," said Ratcliffe, with another wink to the procurator. "Thae duds were a' o' the color o' moonshine in the water, I'm thinking, Madge. The gown wad be a sky-blue scarlet, I'se warrant ye?"

"It was nae sic thing," said Madge, whose unretentive memory let out, in the eagerness of contradiction, all that she would have most wished to keep concealed, had her judgment been equal to her inclination. "It was neither scarlet nor sky-blue, but my ain auld brown threshie-coat of a short-gown, and my mother's auld mutch, and my red rokelay; and he gaed me a croun and a kiss for the use o' them, blessing on his bonny face—though it's been a dear ane to me."

"And where did he change his clothes again, hinny?" said Sharpitlaw, in his most conciliatory manner.

"The procurator's spoiled a'," observed Ratcliffe, dryly.

And it was even so; for the question, put in so direct a shape, immediately awakened Madge to the propriety of being reserved upon those very topics on which Ratcliffe had indirectly seduced her to become communicative.

"What was't ye were speering at us, sir?" she resumed, with an appearance of stolidity, so speedily assumed as showed there was a good deal of knavery mixed with her folly.

"I asked you," said the procurator, "at what hour, and to what place, Robertson brought back your clothes."

"Robertson! Lord haud a care o' us! what Robertson?"

"Why, the fellow we were speaking of, Gentle Geordie, as you call him."

"Geordie Gentle!" answered Madge, with well-feigned

amazement. "I dinna ken naebody they ca' Geordie Gentle."

"Come, my jo," said Sharpitlaw, "this will not do ; you must tell us what you did with these clothes of yours."

Madge Wildfire made no answer, unless the question may seem connected with the snatch of a song with which she indulged the embarrassed investigator :

"What did ye wi' the bridal ring—bridal ring—bridal ring?
What did ye wi' your wedding ring, ye little cutty quean, O?
I gied it till a sodger, a sodger, a sodger,
I gied it till a sodger, an auld true love o' mine, O."

Of all the madwomen who have sung and said, since the days of Hamlet the Dane, if Ophelia be the most affecting, Madge Wildfire was the most provoking.

The procurator-fiscal was in despair. "I'll take some measures with this d—d Bess of Bedlam," said he, "that shall make her find her tongue."

"Wi' your favor, sir," said Ratcliffe, "better let her mind settle a little. Ye have aye made out something."

"True," said the official person ; "a brown short-gown, mutch, red rokelay—that agrees with your Madge Wildfire, Mr. Butler?" Butler agreed that it did so. "Yes, there was a sufficient motive for taking this crazy creature's dress and name, while he was about such a job."

"And I am free to say *now*——" said Ratcliffe.

"When you see it has come out without you," interrupted Sharpitlaw.

"Just sae, sir," reiterated Ratcliffe. "I am free to say now, since it's come out otherwise, that these were the clothes I saw Robertson wearing last night in the jail, when he was at the head of the rioters."

"That's direct evidence," said Sharpitlaw ; "stick to that, Rat. I will report favorably of you to the provost, for I have business for you to-night. It wears late ; I must home and get a snack, and I'll be back in the evening. Keep Madge with you, Ratcliffe, and try to get her into a good tune again." So saying, he left the prison.

CHAPTER XVII

And some they whistled, and some they sang,
  And some did loudly say,
Whenever Lord Barnard's horn it blew,
  "Away, Musgrave, away!"
          Ballad of Little Musgrave.

WHEN the man of office returned to the Heart of Midlothian, he resumed his conference with Ratcliffe, of whose experience and assistance he now held himself secure. "You must speak with this wench, Rat—this Effie Deans—you must sift her a wee bit; for as sure as a tether she will ken Robertson's haunts; till her, Rat—till her, without delay."

"Craving your pardon, Mr. Sharpitlaw," said the turnkey-elect, "that's what I am not free to do."

"Free to do, man! what the deil ails ye now? I thought we had settled a' that."

"I dinna ken, sir," said Ratcliffe; "I hae spoken to this Effie. She's strange to this place and to its ways, and to a' our ways, Mr. Sharpitlaw; and she greets, the silly tawpie, and she's breaking her heart already about this wild chield; and were she the means o' taking him, she wad break it outright."

"She wunna hae time, lad," said Sharpitlaw: "the woodie will hae its ain o' her before that; a woman's heart takes a lang time o' breaking."

"That's according to the stuff they are made o', sir," replied Ratcliffe. "But to make a lang tale short, I canna undertake the job. It gangs against my conscience."

"*Your* conscience, Rat!" said Sharpitlaw, with a sneer, which the reader will probably think very natural upon the occasion.

"Ou ay, sir," answered Ratcliffe, calmly, "just *my* conscience; a body has a conscience, though it may be ill wunnin at it. I think mine's as weel out o' the gate as maist folks' are; and yet it's just like the noop of my elbow: it whiles gets a bit dirl on a corner."

"Weel, Rat," replied Sharpitlaw, "since ye are nice, I'll speak to the hussy mysell."

Sharpitlaw accordingly caused himself to be introduced into the little dark apartment tenanted by the unfortunate Effie Deans. The poor girl was seated on her little flock-bed, plunged in a deep reverie. Some food stood on the table, of a quality better than is usually supplied to prisoners, but it was untouched. The person under whose care she was more particularly placed said, "that sometimes she tasted naething from the tae end of the four-and-twenty hours to the t'other, except a drink of water."

Sharpitlaw took a chair, and, commanding the turnkey to retire, he opened the conversation, endeavoring to throw into his tone and countenance as much commiseration as they were capable of expressing, for the one was sharp and harsh, the other sly, acute, and selfish.

"How's a' wi' ye, Effie? How d'ye find yoursell, hinny?"

A deep sigh was the only answer.

"Are the folk civil to ye, Effie? it's my duty to inquire."

"Very civil, sir," said Effie, compelling herself to answer, yet hardly knowing what she said.

"And your victuals," continued Sharpitlaw, in the same condoling tone—"do you get what you like? or is there ony-thing you would particularly fancy, as your health seems but silly?"

"It's a' very weel, sir, I thank ye," said the poor prisoner, in a tone how different from the sportive vivacity of those of the Lily of St. Leonard's!—"it's a' very gude, ower gude for me."

"He must have been a great villain, Effie, who brought you to this pass," said Sharpitlaw.

The remark was dictated partly by a natural feeling, of which even he could not divest himself, though accustomed to practise on the passions of others, and keep a most heedful guard over his own, and partly by his wish to introduce the sort of conversation which might best serve his immediate purpose. Indeed, upon the present occasion these mixed motives of feeling and cunning harmonized together won-derfully; "for," said Sharpitlaw to himself, "the greater rogue Robertson is, the more will be the merit of bringing him to justice." "He must have been a great villain, in-deed," he again reiterated; "and I wish I had the skelping o' him."

"I may blame mysell mair than him," said Effie. "I

was bred up to ken better ; but he, poor fellow——" She stopped.

"Was a thorough blackguard a' his life, I dare say," said Sharpitlaw. "A stranger he was in this country, and a companion of that lawless vagabond, Wilson, I think, Effie ?"

"It wad hae been dearly telling him that he had ne'er seen Wilson's face."

"That's very true that you are saying, Effie," said Sharpitlaw. "Where was't that Robertson and you used to howff thegither ? Somegate about the Laigh Calton, I am thinking."

The simple and dispirited girl had thus far followed Mr. Sharpitlaw's lead because he had artfully adjusted his observations to the thoughts he was pretty certain must be passing through her own mind, so that her answers became a kind of thinking aloud, a mood into which those who are either constitutionally absent in mind, or are rendered so by the temporary pressure of misfortune, may be easily led by a skilful train of suggestions. But the last observation of the procurator-fiscal was too much of the nature of a direct interrogatory, and it broke the charm accordingly.

"What was it that I was saying ?" said Effie, starting up from her reclining posture, seating herself upright, and hastily shading her dishevelled hair back from her wasted, but still beautiful, countenance. She fixed her eyes boldly and keenly upon Sharpitlaw—"You are too much of a gentleman, sir— too much of an honest man, to take any notice of what a poor creature like me says, that can hardly ca' my senses my ain— God help me !"

"Advantage ! I would be of some advantage to you if I could," said Sharpitlaw, in a soothing tone ; "and I ken naething sae likely to serve ye, Effie, as gripping this rascal, Robertson."

"O dinna misca' him, sir, that never misca'd you ! Robertson ! I am sure I had naething to say against ony man o' the name, and naething will I say."

"But if you do not heed your own misfortune, Effie, you should mind what distress he has brought on your family," said the man of law.

"O, Heaven help me !" exclaimed poor Effie. "My poor father—my dear Jeanie ! O, that's sairest to bide of a' ! O, sir, if you hae ony kindness—if ye hae ony touch of compassion—for a' the folk I see here are as hard as the wa'-stanes—if ye wad but bid them let my sister Jeanie in the next time she ca's ! for when I hear them put her awa' frae the door, and canna climb up to that high window to see sae muckle as her gown-tail, it's like to pit me out o' my judgment." And she looked on him with a face of entreaty so earnest, yet so humble, that she fairly shook the steadfast purpose of his mind.

"You shall see your sister," he began, "if you'll tell me"—then interrupting himself, he added, in a more hurried tone—"no, d—n it, you shall see your sister whether you tell me anything or no." So saying, he rose up and left the apartment.

When he had rejoined Ratcliffe, he observed, "You are right, Ratton; there's no making much of that lassie. But ae thing I have cleared—that is, that Robertson has been the father of the bairn, and so I will wager a boddle it will be he that's to meet wi' Jeanie Deans this night at Muschat's Cairn, and there we'll nail him, Rat, or my name is not Gideon Sharpitlaw."

"But," said Ratcliffe, perhaps because he was in no hurry to see anything which was like to be connected with the discovery and apprehension of Robertson, "an that were the case, Mr. Butler wad hae kenn'd the man in the King's Park to be the same person wi' him in Madge Wildfire's claise that headed the mob."

"That makes nae difference, man," replied Sharpitlaw. "The dress, the light, the confusion, and maybe a touch o' a blackit cork, or a slake o' paint—hout, Ratton, I have seen ye dress your ainsell that the deevil ye belang to durstna hae made oath t'ye."

"And that's true, too," said Ratcliffe.

"And besides, ye donnard carle," continued Sharpitlaw, triumphantly, "the minister *did* say, that he thought he knew something of the features of the birkie that spoke to him in the Park, though he could not charge his memory where or when he had seen them."

"It's evident, then, your honor will be right," said Ratcliffe.

"Then, Rat, you and I will go with the party oursells this night, and see him in grips, or we are done wi' him."

"I seena muckle use I can be o' to your honor," said Ratcliffe, reluctantly.

"Use!" answered Sharpitlaw. "You can guide the party; you ken the ground. Besides, I do not intend to quit sight o' you, my good friend, till I have him in hand."

"Weel, sir," said Ratcliffe, but in no joyful tone of acquiescence, "ye maun hae it your ain way; but mind he's a desperate man."

"We shall have that with us," answered Sharpitlaw, "that will settle him, if it is necessary."

"But, sir," answered Ratcliffe, "I am sure I couldna undertake to guide you to Muschat's Cairn in the night-time; I ken the place, as mony does, in fair daylight, but how to find it by moonshine, amang sae mony crags and stanes, as like to each other as the collier to the deil, is mair than I can tell. I might as soon seek moonshine in water."

"What's the meaning o' this, Ratcliffe?" said Sharpitlaw, while he fixed his eye on the recusant, with a fatal and ominous expression. "Have you forgotten that you are still under sentence of death?"

"No, sir," said Ratcliffe, "that's a thing no easily put out o' memory; and if my presence be judged necessary, nae doubt I maun gang wi' your honor. But I was gaun to tell your honor of ane that has mair skeel o' the gate than me, and that's e'en Madge Wildfire."

"The devil she has! Do you think me as mad as she is, to trust to her guidance on such an occasion?"

"Your honor is the best judge," answered Ratcliffe; "but I ken I can keep her in tune, and gar her haud the straight path; she aften sleeps out, or rambles about amang thae hills the haill simmer night, the daft limmer."

"Well, Ratcliffe," replied the procurator-fiscal, "if you think she can guide us the right way, but take heed to what you are about, your life depends on your behavior."

"It's a sair judgment on a man," said Ratcliffe, "when he has ance gane sae far wrang as I hae done that deil a bit he can be honest, try't whilk way he will."

Such was the reflection of Ratcliffe, when he was left for a few minutes to himself, while the retainer of justice went to procure a proper warrant, and give the necessary directions.

The rising moon saw the whole party free from the walls of the city, and entering upon the open ground. Arthur's Seat, like a couchant lion of immense size, Salisbury Crags, like a huge belt or girdle of granite, were dimly visible. Holding their path along the southern side of the Canongate, they gained the Abbey of Holyrood House, and from thence found their way by step and stile into the King's Park. They were at first four in number—an officer of justice and Sharpitlaw, who were well armed with pistols and cutlasses; Ratcliffe, who was not trusted with weapons, lest he might, peradventure, have used them on the wrong side; and the female. But at the last stile, when they entered the chase, they were joined by other two officers, whom Sharpitlaw, desirous to secure sufficient force for his purpose, and at the same time to avoid observation, had directed to wait for him at this place. Ratcliffe saw this accession of strength with some disquietude, for he had hitherto thought it likely that Robertson, who was a bold, stout, and active young fellow, might have made his escape from Sharpitlaw and the single officer, by force or agility, without his being implicated in the matter. But the present strength of the followers of justice was overpowering, and the only mode of saving Robertson, which the old sinner was well disposed to do, providing always he could accomplish his purpose without compromising his own safety, must be by contriving that he should have some signal of their approach. It was probably with this view that Ratcliffe had requested the addition of Madge to the party, having considerable confidence in her propensity to exert her lungs. Indeed, she had already given them so many specimens of her clamorous loquacity, that Sharpitlaw half determined to send her back with one of the officers, rather than carry forward in his company a person so extremely ill qualified to be a guide in a secret expedition. It seemed, too, as if the open air, the approach to the hills, and the ascent of the moon, supposed to be so portentous over those whose brain is infirm, made her spirits rise in a degree tenfold more loquacious than she had hitherto exhibited. To silence her by fair means seemed impossible; authoritative commands and coaxing entreaties she set alike at defiance; and threats only made her sulky, and altogether intractable.

"Is there no one of you," said Sharpitlaw, impatiently, "that knows the way to this accursed place—this Nicol Muschat's Cairn—excepting this mad clavering idiot?"

"Deil ane o' them kens it, except mysell," exclaimed Madge; "how suld they, the poor fule cowards? But I hae sat on the grave frae bat-fleeing time till cock-crow, and had mony a fine crack wi' Nicol Muschat, and Ailie Muschat, that are lying sleeping below."

". The devil take your crazy brain," said Sharpitlaw; "will you not allow the men to answer a question?"

The officers, obtaining a moment's audience while Ratcliffe diverted Madge's attention, declared, that though they had a general knowledge of the spot, they could not undertake to guide the party to it by the uncertain light of the moon, with such accuracy as to insure success to their expedition.

"What shall we do, Ratcliffe?" said Sharpitlaw. "If he sees us before we see him—and that's what he is certain to do, if we go strolling about, without keeping the straight road—we may bid gude day to the job; and I wad rather lose one hundred pounds, baith for the credit of the police, and because the Provost says somebody maun be hanged for this job o' Porteous, come o't what likes."

"I think," said Ratcliffe, "we maun just try Madge; and I'll see if I can get her keepit in ony better order. And at ony rate, if he suld hear her skirling her auld ends o' sangs, he's no to ken for that that there's onybody wi' her."

"That's true," said Sharpitlaw; "and if he thinks her alone he's as like to come towards her as to rin frae her. So set forward, we hae lost ower muckle time already; see to get her to keep the right road."

"And what sort o' house does Nicol Muschat and his wife keep now?" said Ratcliffe to the mad woman, by way of humoring her vein of folly; "they were but thrawn folk lang syne, an a' tales be true."

"Ou, ay, ay, ay; but a's forgotten now," replied Madge, in the confidential tone of a gossip giving the history of her next-door neighbor. "Ye see, I spoke to them mysell, and tauld them byganes suld be byganes. Her throat's sair misguggled and mashackered, though; she wears her corpse-sheet drawn weel up to hide it, but that canna hinder the bluid seiping through, ye ken. I wussed her to wash it in St. Anthony's Well, and that will cleanse if onything can. But they say bluid never bleaches out o' linen claith. Deacon Sanders's new cleansing draps winna do't; I tried them mysell on a bit rag we hae at hame, that was mailed wi' the bluid of a bit skirling wean that was hurt some gate, but out it winna come. Weel, ye'll say that's queer; but I will bring it out to St. Anthony's blessed Well some braw night just like this, and I'll cry up Ailie Muschat, and she and I will hae a grand bouking-washing, and bleach our claise in the beams of the bonny Lady Moon, that's far pleasanter to me than the sun; the sun's ower het, and ken ye, cummers, my brains are het eneugh already. But the moon, and the dew, and the night-wind, they are just like a caller kail-blade laid on my brow; and whiles I think the moon just shines on purpose to pleasure me, when naebody sees her but mysell."

This raving discourse she continued with prodigious volubility, walking on at a great pace, and dragging Ratcliffe along with her while he endeavored, in appearance at least, if not in reality, to induce her to moderate her voice.

All at once she stopped short upon the top of a little hillock, gazed upward fixedly, and said not one word for the space of five minutes. "What the devil is the matter with her now?" said Sharpitlaw to Ratcliffe. "Can you not get her forward?"

"Ye maun just take a grain o' patience wi' her, sir," said Ratcliffe. "She'll no gae a foot faster than she likes hersell."

"D—n her," said Sharpitlaw, "I'll take care she has her time in Bedlam or Bridewell, or both, for she's both mad and mischievous."

In the meanwhile, Madge, who had looked very pensive when she first stopped, suddenly burst into a vehement fit of laughter, then paused and sighed bitterly, then was seized with a second fit of laughter, then, fixing her eyes on the moon, lifted up her voice and sung—

> "Good even, good fair moon, good even to thee;
> I prithee, dear moon, now show to me
> The form and the features, the speech and degree,
> Of the man that true lover of mine shall be.

But I need not ask that of the bonny Lady Moon; I ken that weel eneugh mysell—*true*-love though he wasna. But naebody shall say that I ever tauld a word about the matter. But whiles I wish the bairn had lived. Weel, God guide us, there's a heaven aboon us a' [here she sighed bitterly], and a bonny moon, and sterns in it forbye," and here she laughed once more.

"Are we to stand here all night?" said Sharpitlaw, very impatiently. "Drag her forward."

"Ay, sir," said Ratcliffe, "if we kenn'd whilk way to drag her that would settle it at ance. Come, Madge, hinny," addressing her, "we'll no be in time to see Nicol and his wife unless ye show us the road."

"In troth and that I will, Ratton," said she, seizing him by the arm, and resuming her route with huge strides, considering it was a female who took them. "And I'll tell ye, Ratton, blithe will Nicol Muschat be to see ye, for he says he kens weel there isna sic a villain out o' hell as ye are, and he wad be ravished to hae a crack wi' you—like to like, ye ken—it's a proverb never fails; and ye are baith a pair o' the deevil's peats, I trow—hard to ken whilk deserves the hettest corner o' his ingle-side."

Ratcliffe was conscience-struck, and could not forbear

making an involuntary protest against this classification. "I never shed blood," he replied.

"But ye hae sauld it, Ratton—ye hae sauld blood mony a time. Folk kill wi' the tongue as weel as wi' the hand—wi' the word as weel as wi' the gulley !—

> "It is the bonny butcher lad,
>   That wears the sleeves of blue,
> He sells the flesh on Saturday,
>   On Friday that he slew."

"And what is that I am doing now ?" thought Ratcliffe. "But I'll hae nae wyte of Robertson's young bluid, if I can help it." Then speaking apart to Madge, he asked her, "Whether she did not remember ony o' her auld sangs ?"

"Mony a dainty ane," said Madge; "and blithely can I sing them, for lightsome sangs make merry gate." And she sung—

> "When the glede's in the blue cloud,
>   The lavrock lies still ;
> When the hound's in the green-wood,
>   The hind keeps the hill."

"Silence her cursed noise, if you should throttle her," said Sharpitlaw ; "I see somebody yonder. Keep close, my boys, and creep round the shoulder of the height. George Poinder, stay you with Ratcliffe and that mad yelling bitch ; and you other two, come with me round under the shadow of the brae."

And he crept forward with the stealthy pace of an Indian savage, who leads his band to surprise an unsuspecting party of some hostile tribe. Ratcliffe saw them glide off, avoiding the moonlight, and keeping as much in the shade as possible. "Robertson's done up," said he to himself ; "thae young lads are aye sae thoughtless. What deevil could he hae to say to Jeanie Deans, or to ony woman on earth, that he suld gang awa' and get his neck raxed for her ? And this mad quean, after cracking like a pen-gun and skirling like a pea-hen for the haill night, behoves just to hae hadden her tongue when her clavers might have done some gude ! But it's aye the way wi' women ; if they ever haud their tongues ava, ye may swear it's for mischief. I wish I could set her on again without this blood-sucker kenning what I am doing. But he's as gleg as MacKeachan's elshin, that ran through sax plies of bend-leather and half an inch into the king's heel."

He then began to hum, but in a very low and suppressed tone, the first stanza of a favorite ballad of Wildfire's, the

words of which bore some distant analogy with the situation
of Robertson, trusting that the power of association would not
fail to bring the rest to her mind :

> " There's a bloodhound ranging Tinwald wood,
>   There's harness glancing sheen ;
>   There's a maiden sits on Tinwald brae,
>   And she sings loud between."

Madge had no sooner received the catchword than she
vindicated Ratcliffe's sagacity by setting off at score with the
song :

> " O sleep ye sound, Sir James, she said,
>   When ye suld rise and ride ?
>   There's twenty men, wi' bow and blade,
>   Are seeking where ye hide."

Though Ratcliffe was at a considerable distance from the
spot called Muschat's Cairn, yet his eyes, practised like those
of a cat to penetrate darkness, could mark that Robertson
had caught the alarm. George Poinder, less keen of sight
or less attentive, was not aware of his flight any more than
Sharpitlaw and his assistants, whose view, though they were
considerably nearer to the cairn, was intercepted by the broken
nature of the ground under which they were screening themselves. At length, however, after the interval of five or six
minutes, they also perceived that Robertson had fled, and
rushed hastily towards the place, while Sharpitlaw called out
aloud, in the harshest tones of a voice which resembled a
saw-mill at work, " Chase, lads—chase—haud the brae; I
see him on the edge of the hill ! " Then hallooing back to
the rear-guard of his detachment, he issued his further orders :
" Ratcliffe, come here and detain the woman ; George, run
and keep the stile at the Duke's Walk ; Ratcliffe, come here
directly, but first knock out that mad bitch's brains ! "
 " Ye had better rin for it, Madge," said Ratcliffe, " for
it's ill dealing wi' an angry man."
 Madge Wildfire was not so absolutely void of common sense
as not to understand this innuendo ; and while Ratcliffe, in
seemingly anxious haste of obedience, hastened to the spot
where Sharpitlaw waited to deliver up Jeanie Deans to his
custody, she fled with all the despatch she could exert in an
opposite direction. Thus the whole party were separated,
and in rapid motion of flight or pursuit, excepting Ratcliffe
and Jeanie, whom, although making no attempt to escape,
he held fast by the cloak, and who remained standing by
Muschat's Cairn.

CHAPTER XVIII

You have paid the heavens your function, and the prisoner the
very debt of your calling.
Measure for Measure.

JEANIE DEANS—for here our story unites itself with that part
of the narrative which broke off at the end of the fifteenth
chapter—while she waited, in terror and amazement, the hasty
advance of three or four men towards her, was yet more startled
at their suddenly breaking asunder, and giving chase in different directions to the late object of her terror, who became
at that moment, though she could not well assign a reasonable
cause, rather the cause of her interest. One of the party—it
was Sharpitlaw—came straight up to her, and saying, "Your
name is Jeanie Deans, and you are my prisoner," immediately
added, "but if you will tell me which way he ran I will let
you go."

"I dinna ken, sir," was all the poor girl could utter ; and,
indeed, it is the phrase which rises most readily to the lips of
any person in her rank, as the readiest reply to any embarrassing question.

"But," said Sharpitlaw, "ye *ken* wha it was ye were speaking wi', my leddy, on the hillside, and midnight sae near ; ye
surely ken *that*, my bonny woman ?"

"I dinna ken, sir," again iterated Jeanie, who really did
not comprehend in her terror the nature of the questions which
were so hastily put to her in this moment of surprise.

"We will try to mend your memory by and by, hinny,"
said Sharpitlaw, and shouted, as we have already told the
reader, to Ratcliffe to come up and take charge of her, while
he himself directed the chase after Robertson, which he still
hoped might be successful. As Ratcliffe approached, Sharpitlaw pushed the young woman towards him with some rudeness,
and betaking himself to the more important object of his
quest, began to scale crags and scramble up steep banks, with
an agility of which his profession and his general gravity of
demeanor would previously have argued him incapable. In a
few minutes there was no one within sight, and only a distant
halloo from one of the pursuers to the other, faintly heard on
the side of the hill, argued that there was any one within

hearing. Jeanie Deans was left in the clear moonlight, standing under the guard of a person of whom she knew nothing, and, what was worse, concerning whom, as the reader is well aware, she could have learned nothing that would not have increased her terror.

When all in the distance was silent, Ratcliffe for the first time addressed her, and it was in that cold sarcastic indifferent tone familiar to habitual depravity, whose crimes are instigated by custom rather than by passion. "This is a braw night for ye, dearie," he said, attempting to pass his arm across her shoulder, "to be on the green hill wi' your jo." Jeanie extricated herself from his grasp, but did not make any reply. "I think lads and lasses," continued the ruffian, "dinna meet at Muschat's Cairn at midnight to crack nuts," and he again attempted to take hold of her.

"If ye are an officer of justice, sir," said Jeanie, again eluding his attempt to seize her, "ye deserve to have your coat stripped from your back."

"Very true, hinny," said he, succeeding forcibly in his attempt to get hold of her, "but suppose I should strip your cloak off first?"

"Ye are more a man, I am sure, than to hurt me, sir," said Jeanie; "for God's sake have pity on a half-distracted creature!"

"Come, come," said Ratcliffe, "you're a good-looking wench, and should not be cross-grained. I was going to be an honest man, but the devil has this very day flung first a lawyer and then a woman in my gate. I'll tell you what, Jeanie, they are out on the hillside; if you'll be guided by me, I'll carry you to a wee bit corner in the Pleasaunts that I ken o' in an auld wife's, that a' the prokitors o' Scotland wot naething o', and we'll send Robertson word to meet us in Yorkshire, for there is a set o' braw lads about the midland counties, that I hae dune business wi' before now, and sae we'll leave Mr. Sharpitlaw to whistle on his thumb."

It was fortunate for Jeanie, in an emergency like the present, that she possessed presence of mind and courage, so soon as the first hurry of surprise had enabled her to rally her recollection. She saw the risk she was in from a ruffian, who not only was such by profession, but had that evening been stupefying, by means of strong liquors, the internal aversion which he felt at the business on which Sharpitlaw had resolved to employ him.

"Dinna speak sae loud," said she, in a low voice, "he's up yonder."

"Who? Robertson?" said Ratcliffe, eagerly.

"Ay," replied Jeanie—"up yonder;" and she pointed to the ruins of the hermitage and chapel.

"By G—d, then," said Ratcliffe, "I'll make my ain of him, either one way or other; wait for me here."

But no sooner had he set off, as fast as he could run, towards the chapel, than Jeanie started in an opposite direction, over high and low, on the nearest path homeward. Her juvenile exercise as a herdswoman had put "life and mettle" in her heels, and never had she followed Dustiefoot, when the cows were in the corn, with half so much speed as she now cleared the distance betwixt Muschat's Cairn and her father's cottage at St. Leonard's. To lift the latch, to enter, to shut, bolt, and double bolt the door, to draw against it a heavy article of furniture, which she could not have moved in a moment of less energy, so as to make yet further provision against violence, was almost the work of a moment, yet done with such silence as equalled the celerity.

Her next anxiety was upon her father's account, and she drew silently to the door of his apartment, in order to satisfy herself whether he had been disturbed by her return. He was awake—probably had slept but little; but the constant presence of his own sorrows, the distance of his apartment from the outer door of the house, and the precautions which Jeanie had taken to conceal her departure and return, had prevented him from being sensible of either. He was engaged in his devotions, and Jeanie could distinctly hear him use these words : "And for the other child Thou hast given me to be a comfort and stay to my old age, may her days be long in the land, according to the promise Thou hast given to those who shall honor father and mother; may all her purchased and promised blessings be multiplied upon her; keep her in the watches of the night, and in the uprising of the morning, that all in this land may know that Thou hast not utterly hid Thy face from those that seek Thee in truth and in sincerity." He was silent, but probably continued his petition in the strong fervency of mental devotion.

His daughter retired to her apartment, comforted, that while she was exposed to danger, her head had been covered by the prayers of the just as by a helmet, and under the strong confidence that, while she walked worthy of the protection of Heaven, she would experience its countenance. It was in that moment that a vague idea first darted across her mind, that something might yet be achieved for her sister's safety, conscious as she now was of her innocence of the unnatural murder with which she stood charged. It came, as she described it, on her mind like a sun-blink on a stormy sea; and although it instantly vanished, yet she felt a degree of composure which she had not experienced for many days, and could not help being strongly persuaded that, by some means or other, she would be called upon and directed to work out her sister's deliverance. She went to bed, not forgetting her usual devotions, the more fervently made on account of her late deliverance, and she slept soundly in spite of her agitation.

We must return to Ratcliffe, who had started, like a greyhound from the slips when the sportsman cries halloo, so soon as Jeanie had pointed to the ruins. Whether he meant to aid Robertson's escape or to assist his pursuers may be very doubtful; perhaps he did not himself know, but had resolved to be guided by circumstances. He had no opportunity, however, of doing either; for he had no sooner surmounted the steep ascent, and entered under the broken arches of the ruins, than a pistol was presented at his head, and a harsh voice commanded him, in the king's name, to surrender himself prisoner.

"Mr. Sharpitlaw!" said Ratcliffe, surprised, "is this your honor?"

"Is it only you, and be d—d to you?" answered the fiscal, still more disappointed; "what made you leave the woman?"

"She told me she saw Robertson go into the ruins, so I made what haste I could to cleek the callant."

"It's all over now," said Sharpitlaw, "we shall see no more of him to-night; but he shall hide himself in a bean-hool, if he remains on Scottish ground without my finding him. Call back the people, Ratcliffe."

Ratcliffe hallooed to the dispersed officers, who willingly obeyed the signal; for probably there was no individual among them who would have been much desirous of a *rencontre* hand to hand, and at a distance from his comrades, with such an active and desperate fellow as Robertson.

"And where are the two women?" said Sharpitlaw.

"Both made their heels serve them, I suspect," replied Ratcliffe, and he hummed the end of the old song—

> "Then hey play up the rin-awa' bride,
> For she has taen the gee."

"One woman," said Sharpitlaw, for, like all rogues, he was a great calumniator of the fair sex *—"one woman is enough

* See Note 22.

to dark the fairest ploy that ever was planned ; and how could I be such an ass as to expect to carry through a job that had two in it ? But we know how to come by them both, if they are wanted, that's one good thing."

Accordingly, like a defeated general, sad and sulky, he led back his discomfited forces to the metropolis, and dismissed them for the night.

The next morning early, he was under the necessity of making his report to the sitting magistrate of the day. The gentleman who occupied the chair of office on this occasion, for the bailies (*Anglicé*, aldermen) take it by rotation, chanced to be the same by whom Butler was committed, a person very generally respected among his fellow-citizens. Something he was of a humorist, and rather deficient in general education ; but acute, patient, and upright, possessed of a fortune acquired by honest industry, which made him perfectly independent ; and, in short, very happily qualified to support the respectability of the office which he held.

Mr. Middleburgh had just taken his seat, and was debating in an animated manner, with one of his colleagues, the doubtful chances of a game at golf which they had played the day before, when a letter was delivered to him, addressed "For Bailie Middleburgh—These : to be forwarded with speed." It contained these words :

"Sir, ·

"I know you to be a sensible and a considerate magistrate, and one who, as such, will be content to worship God though the devil bid you. I therefore expect that, notwithstanding the signature of this letter acknowledges my share in an action which, in a proper time and place, I would not fear either to avow or to justify, you will not on that account reject what evidence I place before you. The clergyman, Butler, is innocent of all but involuntary presence at an action which he wanted spirit to approve of, and from which he endeavored, with his best set phrases, to dissuade us. But it was not for him that it is my hint to speak. There is a woman in your jail, fallen under the edge of a law so cruel that it has hung by the wall, like unscoured armor, for twenty years, and is now brought down and whetted to spill the blood of the most beautiful and most innocent creature whom the walls of a prison ever girdled in. Her sister knows of her innocence, as she communicated to her that she was betrayed by a villain. O that high Heaven

    " Would put in every honest hand a whip,
     To scourge me such a villain through the world !

"I write distractedly. But this girl—this Jeanie Deans, is a peevish Puritan, superstitious and scrupulous after the manner of her sect; and I pray your honor, for so my phrase must go, to press upon her that her sister's life depends upon her testimony. But though she should remain silent, do not dare to think that the young woman is guilty, far less to permit her execution. Remember, the death of Wilson was fearfully avenged; and those yet live who can compel you to drink the dregs of your poisoned chalice. I say, remember Porteous—and say that you had good counsel from

"ONE OF HIS SLAYERS."

The magistrate read over this extraordinary letter twice or thrice. At first he was tempted to throw it aside as the production of a madman, so little did "the scraps from playbooks," as he termed the poetical quotation, resemble the correspondence of a rational being. On a re-perusal, however, he thought that, amid its incoherence, he could discover something like a tone of awakened passion, though expressed in a manner quaint and unusual.

"It is a cruelly severe statute," said the magistrate to his assistant, "and I wish the girl could be taken from under the letter of it. A child may have been born, and it may have been conveyed away while the mother was insensible, or it may have perished for want of that relief which the poor creature herself—helpless, terrified, distracted, despairing, and exhausted—may have been unable to afford to it. And yet it is certain, if the woman is found guilty under the statute, execution will follow. The crime has been too common, and examples are necessary."

"But if this other wench," said the city clerk, "can speak to her sister communicating her situation, it will take the case from under the statute."

"Very true," replied the bailie; "and I will walk out one of these days to St. Leonard's and examine the girl myself. I know something of their father Deans—an old true-blue Cameronian, who would see house and family go to wreck ere he would disgrace his testimony by a sinful complying with the defections of the times; and such he will probably uphold the taking an oath before a civil magistrate. If they are to go on and flourish with their bull-headed obstinacy, the legislature must pass an act to take their affirmations, as in the case of Quakers. But surely neither a father nor a sister will scruple in a case of this kind. As I said before, I will go speak with them myself, when the hurry of this Porteous investigation is somewhat over;

their pride and spirit of contradiction will be far less alarmed than if they were called into a court of justice at once."

"And I suppose Butler is to remain incarcerated?" said the city clerk.

"For the present, certainly," said the magistrate. "But I hope soon to set him at liberty upon bail."

"Do you rest upon the testimony of that light-headed letter?" asked the clerk.

"Not very much," answered the bailie; "and yet there is something striking about it too; it seems the letter of a man beside himself, either from great agitation or some great sense of guilt."

"Yes," said the town clerk, "it is very like the letter of a mad strolling play-actor, who deserves to be hanged with all the rest of his gang, as your honor justly observes."

"I was not quite so bloodthirsty," continued the magistrate. "But to the point. Butler's private character is excellent; and I am given to understand, by some inquiries I have been making this morning, that he did actually arrive in town only the day before yesterday, so that it was impossible he could have been concerned in any previous machinations of these unhappy rioters, and it is not likely that he should have joined them on a suddenty."

"There's no saying anent that; zeal catches fire at a slight spark as fast as a brunstane match," observed the secretary. "I hae kenn'd a minister wad be fair gude-day and fair gude-e'en wi' ilka man in the parochine, and hing just as quiet as a rocket on a stick, till ye mentioned the word abjuration oath, or patronage, or sic-like, and then, whiz, he was off, and up in the air an hundred miles beyond common manners, common sense, and common comprehension."

"I do not understand," answered the burgher magistrate, "that the young man Butler's zeal is of so inflammable a character. But I will make further investigation. What other business is there before us?"

And they proceeded to minute investigations concerning the affair of Porteous's death, and other affairs through which this history has no occasion to trace them.

In the course of their business they were interrupted by an old woman of the lower rank, extremely haggard in look and wretched in her apparel, who thrust herself into the council room.

"What do you want, gudewife? Who are you?" said Bailie Middleburgh.

"What do I want!" replied she, in a sulky tone   "I

want my bairn, or I want naething frae nane o' ye, for as grand's ye are." And she went on muttering to herself, with the wayward spitefulness of age—"They maun hae lordships and honors nae doubt; set them up, the gutter-bloods! and deil a gentleman amang them." Then again addressing the sitting magistrate—"Will *your honor* gie me back my puir crazy bairn? *His* honor! I hae kenn'd the day when less wad ser'd him, the oe of a Campvere skipper."

"Good woman," said the magistrate to this shrewish supplicant, "tell us what it is you want, and do not interrupt the court."

"That's as muckle as till say, 'Bark, Bawtie, and be dune wi't!' I tell ye," raising her termagant voice, "I want my bairn! is na that braid Scots?"

"Who *are* you? who is your bairn?" demanded the magistrate.

"Wha am I? Wha suld I be, but Meg Murdockson, and wha suld my bairn be but Magdalen Murdockson? Your guard soldiers, and your constables, and your officers ken us weel eneugh when they rive the bits o' duds aff our backs, and take what penny o' siller we hae, and harle us to the correction-house in Leith Wynd, and pettle us up wi' bread and water, and sic-like sunkets."

"Who is she?" said the magistrate, looking round to some of his people.

"Other than a gude ane, sir," said one of the city officers, shrugging his shoulders and smiling.

"Will ye say sae?" said the termagant, her eye gleaming with impotent fury; "an I had ye amang the Frigate Whins, wadna I set my ten talents in your wuzzent face for that very word?" and she suited the word to the action, by spreading out a set of claws resembling those of St. George's dragon on a country sign-post.

"What does she want here?" said the impatient magistrate. "Can she not tell her business, or go away?"

"It's my bairn—it's Magdalen Murdockson I'm wantin'," answered the beldam, screaming at the highest pitch of her cracked and mistuned voice; "havena I been tellin' ye sae this half-hour? And if ye are deaf, what needs ye sit cockit up there, and keep folk scraughin' t'ye this gate?"

"She wants her daughter, sir," said the same officer whose interference had given the hag such offence before—"her daughter, who was taken up last night—Madge Wildfire, as they ca' her."

"Madge HELLFIRE, as they ca' her!" echoed the beldam;

"and what business has a blackguard like you to ca' an honest woman's bairn out o' her ain name ?"

"An *honest* woman's bairn, Maggie ?" answered the peace-officer, smiling and shaking his head with an ironical emphasis on the adjective, and a calmness calculated to provoke to madness the furious old shrew.

"If I am no honest now, I was honest ance," she replied ; "and that's mair than ye can say, ye born and bred thief, that never kenn'd ither folks' gear frae your ain since the day ye was cleckit. Honest, say ye ? Ye pykit your mother's pouch o' twal pennies Scotch when ye were five years auld, just as she was taking leave o' your father at the fit o' the gallows."

"She has you there, George," said the assistants, and there was a general laugh ; for the wit was fitted for the meridian of the place where it was uttered. This general applause somewhat gratified the passions of the old hag ; the "grim feature" smiled, and even laughed, but it was a laugh of bitter scorn. She condescended, however, as if appeased by the success of her sally, to explain her business more distinctly, when the magistrate, commanding silence, again desired her either to speak out her errand or to leave the place.

"Her bairn," she said, "*was* her bairn, and she came to fetch her out of ill haft and waur guiding. If she wasna sae wise as ither folk, few ither folk had suffered as muckle as she had done ; forbye that she could fend the waur for hersell within the four wa's of a jail. She could prove by fifty witnesses, and fifty to that, that her daughter had never seen Jock Porteous, alive or dead, since he had gien her a loundering wi' his cane, the neger that he was ! for driving a dead cat at the provost's wig on the Elector of Hanover's birthday."

Notwithstanding the wretched appearance and violent demeanor of this woman, the magistrate felt the justice of her argument, that her child might be as dear to her as to a more fortunate and more amiable mother. He proceeded to investigate the circumstances which had led to Madge Murdockson's (or Wildfire's) arrest, and as it was clearly shown that she had not been engaged in the riot, he contented himself with directing that an eye should be kept upon her by the police, but that for the present she should be allowed to return home with her mother. During the interval of fetching Madge from the jail, the magistrate endeavored to discover whether her mother had been privy to the change of dress betwixt that young woman and Robertson. But on this point he could obtain no light. She persisted in declaring that she had never seen Robertson since his remarkable escape during service-time; and that, if her daughter had changed clothes with him, it must have been during her absence at a hamlet about two miles out of town, called Duddingstone, where she could prove that she passed that eventful night. And, in fact, one of the town officers, who had been searching for stolen linen at the cottage of a washerwoman in that village, gave his evidence, that he had seen Maggie Murdockson there, whose presence had considerably increased his suspicion of the house in which she was a visitor, in respect that he considered her as a person of no good reputation.

"I tauld ye sae," said the hag; "see now what it is to hae a character, gude or bad! Now, maybe after a', I could tell ye something about Porteous that you council-chamber bodies never could find out, for as muckle stir as ye mak."

All eyes were turned towards her, all ears were alert. "Speak out!" said the magistrate.

"It will be for your ain gude," insinuated the town clerk.

"Dinna keep the bailie waiting," urged the assistants.

She remained doggedly silent for two or three minutes, casting around a malignant and sulky glance, that seemed to enjoy the anxious suspense with which they waited her answer. And then she broke forth at once—"A' that I ken about him is, that he was neither soldier nor gentleman, but just a thief and a blackguard, like maist o' yoursells, dears. What will ye gie me for that news, now? He wad hae served the Gude Town lang or provost or bailie wad hae fund that out, my jo!"

While these matters were in discussion, Madge Wildfire entered, and her first exclamation was, "Eh! see if there isna our auld ne'er-do-weel deevil's buckie o' a mither. Hegh, sirs! but we are a hopefu' family, to be twa o' us in the guard at ance. But there were better days wi' us ance; were there na, mither?"

Old Maggie's eyes had glistened with something like an expression of pleasure when she saw her daughter set at liberty. But either her natural affection, like that of the tigress, could not be displayed without a strain of ferocity, or there was something in the ideas which Madge's speech awakened that again stirred her cross and savage temper. "What signifies what we were, ye street-raking limmer!" she exclaimed, pushing her daughter before her to the door, with no gentle degree of violence. "I'se tell thee what thou is now: thou's a crazed hellicat Bess o' Bedlam, that sall taste naething but bread and

Madge Wildfire before Bailie Middleburgh.

water for a fortnight, to serve ye for the plague ye hae gien me ; and ower gude for ye, ye idle tawpie ! ''

Madge, however, escaped from her mother at the door, ran back to the foot of the table, dropped a very low and fantastic courtesy to the judge, and said, with a giggling laugh—'' Our minnie's sair mis-set, after her ordinar, sir. She'll hae had some quarrel wi' her auld gudeman—that's Satan, ye ken, sirs.'' This explanatory note she gave in a low confidential tone, and the spectators of that credulous generation did not hear it without an involuntary shudder. '' The gudeman and her disna aye gree weel, and then I maun pay the piper ; but my back's broad eneugh to bear't a', an if she hae nae havings, that's nae reason why wiser folk shouldna hae some.'' Here another deep courtesy, when the ungracious voice of her mother was heard.

'' Madge, ye limmer ! If I come to fetch ye ! ''

'' Hear till her,'' said Madge. '' But I'll wun out a gliff the night for a' that, to dance in the moonlight, when her and the gudeman will be whirrying through the blue lift on a broom-shank, to see Jean Jap, that they hae putten intill the Kirkcaldy tolbooth ; ay, they will hae a merry sail ower Inchkeith, and ower a' the bits o' bonny waves that are poppling and plashing against the rocks in the gowden glimmer o' the moon, ye ken. I'm coming, mither—I'm coming,'' she concluded, on hearing a scuffle at the door betwixt the beldam and the officers, who were endeavoring to prevent her re-entrance. Madge then waved her hand wildly towards the ceiling, and sung, at the topmost pitch of her voice—

> Up in the air,
> On my bonny gray mare,
> And I see, and I see, and I see her yet ;''

and with a hop, skip, and jump, sprung out of the room, as the witches of *Macbeth* used, in less refined days, to seem to fly upwards from the stage.

Some weeks intervened before Mr. Middleburgh, agreeably to his benevolent resolution, found an opportunity of taking a walk towards St. Leonard's, in order to discover whether it might be possible to obtain the evidence hinted at in the anonymous letter respecting Effie Deans.

In fact, the anxious perquisitions made to discover the murderers of Porteous occupied the attention of all concerned with the administration of justice.

In the course of these inquiries, two circumstances happened material to our story. Butler, after a close investigation of his conduct, was declared innocent of accession to the death of Porteous ; but, as having been present during the whole transaction, was obliged to find bail not to quit his usual residence at Liberton, that he might appear as a witness when called upon. The other incident regarded the disappearance of Madge Wildfire and her mother from Edinburgh. When they were sought, with the purpose of subjecting them to some further interrogatories, it was discovered by Mr. Sharpitlaw that they had eluded the observation of the police, and left the city so soon as dismissed from the council-chamber. No efforts could trace the place of their retreat.

In the meanwhile, the excessive indignation of the council of regency, at the slight put upon their authority by the murder of Porteous, had dictated measures, in which their own extreme desire of detecting the actors in that conspiracy were consulted, in preference to the temper of the people and the character of their churchmen. An act of parliament was hastily passed, offering two hundred pounds reward to those who should inform against any person concerned in the deed, and the penalty of death, by a very unusual and severe enactment, was denounced against those who should harbor the guilty. But what was chiefly accounted exceptionable, was a clause, appointing the act to be read in churches by the officiating clergyman, on the first Sunday of every month, for a certain period, immediately before the sermon. The ministers who should refuse to comply with this injunction were declared, for the first offense, incapable of sitting or voting in any church judicature, and for the second, incapable of holding any ecclesiastical preferment in Scotland.

This last order united in a common cause those who might privately rejoice in Porteous's death, though they dared not vindicate the manner of it, with the more scrupulous Presbyterians, who held that even the pronouncing the name of the "Lords Spiritual" in a Scottish pulpit was *quodammodo*, an acknowledgment of Prelacy, and that the injunction of the legislature was an interference of the civil government with the *jus divinum* of Presbytery, since to the General Assembly alone, as representing the invisible head of the kirk, belonged to the sole and exclusive right of regulating whatever pertained to public worship. Very many also, of different political or religious sentiments, and therefore not much moved by these considerations, thought they saw, in so violent an act of parliament, a more vindictive spirit than became the legislature of a great country, and something like an attempt to trample

upon the rights and independence of Scotland.   The various
steps adopted for punishing the city of Edinburgh, by taking
away her charter and liberties, for what a violent and over-
mastering mob had done within her walls, were resented by
many, who thought a pretext was too hastily taken for degrading the ancient metropolis of Scotland.   In short, there was
much heart-burning, discontent, and disaffection occasioned
by these ill-considered measures.*

Amidst these heats and dissensions, the trial of Effie
Deans, after she had been many weeks imprisoned, was at
length about to be brought forward, and Mr. Middleburgh
found leisure to inquire into the evidence concerning her.
For this purpose, he chose a fine day for his walk towards her
father's house.

The excursion into the country was somewhat distant, in
the opinion of a burgess of those days, although many of the
present inhabit suburban villas considerably beyond the
spot to which we allude.   Three-quarters of an hour's walk,
however, even at a pace of magisterial gravity, conducted our
benevolent office-bearer to the Crags of St. Leonard's, and the
humble mansion of David Deans.

The old man was seated on the deas, or turf-seat, at the
end of his cottage, busied in mending his cart-harness with
his own hands; for in those days any sort of labor which required a little more skill than usual fell to the share of the
goodman himself, and that even when he was well-to-pass in
the world.   With stern and austere gravity he persevered in
his task, after having just raised his head to notice the advance
of the stranger.   It would have been impossible to have discovered, from his countenance and manner, the internal feelings of agony with which he contended.   Mr. Middleburgh
waited an instant, expecting Deans would in some measure
acknowledge his presence, and lead into conversation; but, as
he seemed determined to remain silent, he was himself obliged
to speak first.

"My name is Middleburgh—Mr. James Middleburgh, one
of the present magistrates of the city of Edinburgh."

"It may be sae," answered Deans, laconically, and without interrupting his labor.

"You must understand," he continued, "that the duty
of a magistrate is sometimes an unpleasant one."

"It may be sae," replied David; "I hae naething to say
in the contrair;" and he was again doggedly silent.

"You must be aware," pursued the magistrate, "that

* See The Magistrates and the Porteous Mob.   Note 23.

persons in my situation are often obliged to make painful and disagreeable inquiries of individuals, merely because it is their bounden duty."

"It may be sae," again replied Deans; "I hae naething to say anent it, either the tae way or the t'other. But I do ken there was ance in a day a just and God-fearing magistracy in yon town o' Edinburgh, that did not bear the sword in vain, but were a terror to evil-doers, and a praise to such as kept the path. In the glorious days of auld worthy faithfu' Provost Dick,* when there was a true and faithfu' General Assembly of the Kirk, walking hand in hand with the real noble Scottish-hearted barons, and with the magistrates of this and other towns, gentles, burgesses, and commons of all ranks, seeing with one eye, hearing with one ear, and upholding the ark with their united strength. And then folk might see men deliver up their silver to the state's use, as if it had been as muckle sclate stanes. My father saw them toom the sacks of dollars out o' Provost Dick's window intill the carts that carried them to the army at Dunse Law; and if ye winna believe his testimony, there is the window itsell still standing in the Luckenbooths—I think it's a claith-merchant's booth the day†—at the airn stanchells, five doors abune Gossford's Close. But now we haena sic spirit amang us; we think mair about the warst wally-draigle in our ain byre than about the blessing which the angel of the covenant gave to the Patriarch, even at Peniel and Mahanaim, or the binding obligation of our national vows; and we wad rather gie a pund Scots to buy an unguent to clear our auld rannel-trees and our beds o' the English bugs, as they ca' them, than we wad gie a plack to rid the land of the swarm of Arminian caterpillars, Socinian pismires, and deistical Miss Katies, that have ascended out of the bottomless pit to plague this perverse, insidious, and lukewarm generation."

It happened to Davie Deans on this occasion, as it has done to many other habitual orators, when once he became embarked on his favorite subject, the stream of his own enthusiasm carried him forward in spite of his mental distress, while his well-exercised memory supplied him amply with all the types and tropes of rhetoric peculiar to his sect and cause.

Mr. Middleburgh contented himself with answering—"All this may be very true, my friend; but, as you said just now,

* See Sir William Dick of Braid. Note 24.

† I think so too; but if the reader be curious, he may consult **Mr. Chambers's** *Traditions of Edinburgh.*

I have nothing to say to it at present, either one way or other. You have two daughters, I think, Mr. Deans ?"

The old man winced, as one whose smarting sore is suddenly galled ; but instantly composed himself, resumed the work which, in the heat of his declamation, he had laid down, and answered with sullen resolution, "Ae daughter, sir—only *ane.*"

"I understand you," said Mr. Middleburgh ; "you have only one daughter here at home with you ; but this unfortunate girl who is a prisoner—she is, I think, your youngest daughter ?"

The Presbyterian sternly raised his eyes. "After the world, and according to the flesh, she *is* my daughter ; but when she became a child of Belial, and a company-keeper, and a trader in guilt and iniquity, she ceased to be a bairn of mine."

"Alas, Mr. Deans," said Middleburgh, sitting down by him and endeavoring to take his hand, which the old man proudly withdrew, "we are ourselves all sinners ; and the errors of our offspring, as they ought not to surprise us, being the portion which they derive of a common portion of corruption inherited through us, so they do not entitle us to cast them off because they have lost themselves."

"Sir," said Deans, impatiently, "I ken a' that as weel as —I mean to say," he resumed, checking the irritation he felt at being schooled—a discipline of the mind which those most ready to bestow it on others do themselves most reluctantly submit to receive—"I mean to say, that what ye observe may be just and reasonable ; but I hae nae freedom to enter into my ain private affairs wi' strangers. And now, in this great national emergency, when there's the Porteous Act has come doun frae London, that is a deeper blow to this poor sinfu' kingdom and suffering kirk than ony that has been heard of since the foul and fatal Test—at a time like this——"

"But, goodman," interrupted Mr. Middleburgh, "you must think of your own household first, or else you are worse even than the infidels."

"I tell ye, Bailie Middleburgh," retorted David Deans, "if ye be a bailie, as there is little honor in being ane in these evil days—I tell ye, I heard the gracious Saunders Peden—I wotna whan it was ; but it was in killing time, when the plowers were drawing alang their furrows on the back of the Kirk of Scotland—I heard him tell his hearers, gude and waled Christians they were too, that some o' them wad greet mair for a bit drowned calf or stirk than for a' the defections and oppressions of the day ; and that they were some o' them thinking o' ae thing, some o' anither, and there was Lady Hundleslope thinking o' greeting Jock at the fireside !　And the lady confessed in my hearing that a drow of anxiety had come ower her for her son that she had left at hame of a decay.*　And what wad he hae said of me, if I had ceased to think of the gude cause for a castaway—a—— It kills me to think of what she is !"

"But the life of your child, goodman—think of that; if her life could be saved," said Middleburgh.

"Her life !" exclaimed David.　"I wadna gie ane o' my gray hairs for her life, if her gude name be gane.　And yet," said he, relenting and retracting as he spoke, "I wad make the niffer, Mr. Middleburgh—I wad gie a' these gray hairs that she has brought to shame and sorrow—I wad gie the auld head they grow on, for her life, and that she might hae time to amend and return, for what hae the wicked beyond the breath of their nostrils ?　But I'll never see her mair.　No ! that—that I am determined in—I'll never see her mair !"　His lips continued to move for a minute after his voice ceased to be heard, as if he were repeating the same vow internally.

"Well, sir," said Mr. Middleburgh, "I speak to you as a man of sense ; if you would save your daughter's life you must use human means."

"I understand what you mean ; but Mr. Novit, who is the procurator and doer of an honorable person, the Laird of Dumbiedikes, is to do what carnal wisdom can do for her in the circumstances.　Mysell am not clear to trinquet and traffic wi' courts o' justice, as they are now constituted ; I have a tenderness and scruple in my mind anent them."

"That is to say," said Middleburgh, "that you are a Cameronian, and do not acknowledge the authority of our courts of judicature, or present government ?"

"Sir, under your favor," replied David, who was too proud of his own polemical knowledge to call himself the follower of any one, "ye take me up before I fall down.　I canna see why I suld be termed a Cameronian, especially now that ye hae given the name of that famous and savory sufferer, not only until a regimental band of soldiers, whereof I am told many can now curse, swear, and use profane language as fast as ever Richard Cameron could preach or pray, but also because ye have, in as far as it is in your power, rendered that martyr's name vain and contemptible, by pipes, drums, and fifes, playing the vain carnal spring, called the Cameronian Rant, which too many professors of religion dance to—a practice maist unbecoming a professor to dance to any tune

* See *Life of Peden,* v. 111.

whatsoever, more especially promiscuously, that is, with the female sex.* A brutish fashion it is, whilk is the beginning of defection with many, as I may hae as muckle cause as maist folk to testify."

"Well, but, Mr. Deans," replied Mr. Middleburgh, "I only meant to say that you were a Cameronian, or Mac-Millanite, one of the society people, in short, who think it inconsistent to take oaths under a government where the Covenant is not ratified."

"Sir," replied the controversialist, who forgot even his present distress in such discussions as these, "you cannot fickle me sae easily as you do opine. I am *not* a MacMillanite, or a Russelite, or a Hamiltonian, or a Harleyite, or a Howdenite ; † I will be led by the nose by none ; I take my name as a Christian from no vessel of clay. I have my own principles and practice to answer for, and am an humble pleader for the gude auld cause in a legal way."

"That is to say, Mr. Deans," said Middleburgh, "that you are *Deanite,* and have opinions peculiar to yourself."

"It may please you to say sae," replied David Deans ; but I have maintained my testimony before as great folk, and in sharper times ; and though I will neither exalt myself nor pull down others, I wish every man and woman in this land had kept the true testimony, and the middle and straight path, as it were, on the ridge of a hill, where wind and water shears, avoiding right-hand snares and extremes and left-hand way-slidings, as weel as Johnny Dodds of Farthing's Acre and ae man mair that shall be nameless."

"I suppose," replied the magistrate, "that is as much as to say, that Johnny Dodds of Farthing's Acre and David Deans of St. Leonards constitute the only members of the true, real, unsophisticated Kirk of Scotland ?"

"God forbid that I suld make sic a vainglorious speech, when there are sae mony professing Christians !" answered David ; "but this I maun say, that all men act according to their gifts and their grace, sae that it is nae marvel that——"

"This is all very fine," interrupted Mr. Middleburgh ; "but I have no time to spend in hearing it. The matter in hand is this—I have directed a citation to be lodged in your daughter's hands. If she appears on the day of trial and gives evidence, there is reason to hope that she may save her sister's life ; if, from any constrained scruples about the legality of her performing the office of an affectionate sister and a good subject, by appearing in a court held under the

* See note to Patrick Walker.
† All various species of the great genus Cameronian.

authority of the law and government, you become the means
of deterring her from the discharge of this duty, I must
say, though the truth may sound harsh in your ears, that
you, who gave life to this unhappy girl, will became the
means of her losing it by a premature and violent death."

So saying Mr. Middleburgh turned to leave him.

" Bide a wee—bide a wee, Mr. Middleburgh," said Deans in
great perplexity and distress of mind ; but the bailie, who was
probably sensible that protracted discussion might diminish
the effect of his best and most forcible argument, took a hasty
leave, and declined entering farther into the controversy.

Deans sunk down upon his seat, stunned with a variety of
conflicting emotions. It had been a great source of controversy among those holding his opinions in religious matters,
how far the government which suceeeded the Revolution
could be, without sin, acknowledged by true Presbyterians,
seeing that it did not recognize the great national testimony
of the Solemn League and Covenant. And latterly, those
agreeing in this general doctrine, and assuming the sounding title of the anti-Popish, anti-Prelatic, anti-Erastian,
anti-Sectarian, true Presbyterian remnant, were divided into
many petty sects among themselves, even as to the extent of
submission to the existing laws aud rulers which constituted
such an acknowledgment as amounted to sin.

At a very stormy and tumultous meeting, held in 1682, to
discuss these important and delicate points, the testimonies of
the faithful few were found utterly inconsistent with each
other.* The place where this conference took place was remarkably well adapted for such an assembly. It was a wild
and very sequestered dell in Tweeddale, surrounded by high
hills, and far removed from human habitation. A small
river, or rather a mountain torrent, called the Talla, breaks
down the glen with great fury, dashing successively over a
number of small cascades, which has procured the spot the
name of Talla Linns. Here the leaders among the scattered
adherents to the Covenant, men who, in their banishment
from human society, and in the recollection of the severities
to which they had been exposed, had become at once sullen
in their tempers and fantastic in their religious opinions,
met with arms in their hands and by the side of the torrent
discussed, with a turbulence which the noise of the stream
could not drown, points of controversy as empty and un-
substantial as its foam.

It was the fixed judgment of most of the meeting, that all
payment of cess or tribute to the existing government was

<hr>

*See Meeting at Talla Linns. Note 25.

utterly unlawful, and a sacrificing to idols. About other impositions and degrees of submission there were various opinions ; and perhaps it is the best illustration of the spirit of those military fathers of the church to say, that while all allowed it was impious to pay the cess employed for maintaining the standing army and militia, there was a fierce controversy on the lawfulness of paying the duties levied at ports and bridges, for maintaining roads and other necessary purposes that there were some who, repugnant to these imposts for turnpikes and pontages, were nevertheless free in conscience to make payment of the usual freight at public ferries, and that a person of exceeding and punctilious zeal, James Russel, one of the slayers of the Archbishop of St. Andrews, had given his testimony with great warmth even against this last faint shade of subjection to constituted authority. This ardent and enlightened person and his followers had also great scruples about the lawfulness of bestowing the ordinary names upon the days of the week and the months of the year, which savored in their nostrils so strongly of paganism, that at length they arrived at the conclusion that they who owned such names as Monday, Tuesday, January, February, and so forth, "served themselves heirs to the same, if not greater, punishment than had been denounced against the idolators of old."

David Deans had been present on this memorable occasion, although too young to be a speaker among the polemical combatants. His, brain, however, had been thoroughly heated by the noise, clamor, and metaphysical ingenuity of the discussion, and it was a controversy to which his mind had often returned ; and though he carefully disguised his vacillation from others, and perhaps from himself, he had never been able to come to any precise line of decision on the subject. Iu fact, his natural sense had acted as a counterpoise to his controversial zeal. He was by no means pleased with the quiet and indifferent manner in which King William's government slurred over the errors of the times, when, far from restoring the Presbyterian Kirk to its former supremacy, they passed an act of oblivion even to those who had been its persecutors, and bestowed on many of them titles, favors, and employments. When, in the first General Assembly which succeeded the Revolution, an overture was made for the revival of the League and Covenant, it was with horror that Douce David heard the proposal eluded by the men of carnal wit and policy, as he called them, as being inapplicable to the present times, and not falling under the modern model of the church. The reign of Queen Anne had increased his conviction that the Revolution government was not one of the true Presbyterian complexion. But then, more sensible than the bigots of his sect, he did not confound the moderation and tolerance of these two reigns with the active tyranny and oppression exercised in those of Charles II. and James II. The Presbyterian form of religion, though deprived of the weight formerly attached to its sentences and excommunications, and compelled to tolerate the co-existence of the Episcopacy, and of sects of various descriptions, was still the National Church ; and though the glory of the second temple was far inferior to that which had flourished from 1639 till the battle of Dunbar, still it was a structure that, wanting the strength and the terrors, retained at least the form and symmetry, of the original model. Then came the insurrection of 1715, and David Deans's horror for the revival of the popish and pre-latical faction reconciled him greatly to the government of King George, although he grieved that that monarch might be suspected of a leaning unto Erastianism. In short, moved by so many different considerations, he had shifted his ground at different times concerning the degree of freedom which he felt in adopting any act of immediate acknowledgment or submission to the present government, which, however mild and paternal, was still uncovenanted ; and now he felt himself called upon by the most powerful motive conceivable to authorize his daughter's giving testimony in a court of justice, which all who have since been called Cameronians accounted a step of lamentable and direct defection. The voice of nature, however, exclaimed loud in his bosom against the dictates of fanaticism ; and his imagination, fertile in the solution of polemical difficulties, devised an expedient for extricating himself from the fearful dilemma, in which he saw, on the one side, a falling off from principle, and on the other, a scene from which a father's thoughts could not but turn in shuddering horror.

"I have been constant and unchanged in my testimony," said David Deans ; "but then who has said it of me, that I have judged my neighbor over closely, because he hath had more freedom in his walk than I have found in mine ? I never was a separatist, nor for quarreling with tender souls about mint, cummin, or other the lesser tithes. My daughter Jean may have a light in this subject that is hid frae my auld een ; it is laid on her conscience, and not on mine. If she hath freedom to gang before the judiciary, and hold up her hand for this poor castaway, surely I will not say she steppeth over her bounds ; and if not——" He paused in his mental argument, while a pang of unutterable anguish convulsed his features, yet, shaking it off, he firmly resumed the strain of his reasoning—"And IF NOT, God forbid that she should go into defection at bidding of mine ! I wunna fret the tender conscience of one bairn—no, not to save the life of the other."

A Roman would have devoted his daughter to death from different feelings and motives, but not upon a more heroic principle of duty.

CHAPTER XIX

IT was with a firm step that Deans sought his daughter's apartment, determined to leave her to the light of her own conscience in the dubious point of casuistry in which he supposed her to be placed.

The little room had been the sleeping-apartment of both sisters, and there still stood there a small occasional bed which had been made for Effie's accommodation, when, complaining of illness, she had declined to share, as in happier times, her sister's pillow. The eyes of Deans rested involuntarily, on entering the room, upon this little couch, with its dark green coarse curtains, and the ideas connected with it rose so thick upon his soul as almost to incapacitate him from opening his errand to his daughter. Her occupation broke the ice. He found her gazing on a slip of paper, which contained a citation to her to appear as a witness upon her sister's trial in behalf of the accused. For the worthy magistrate, determined to omit no chance of doing Effie justice, and to leave her sister no apology for not giving the evidence which she was supposed to possess, had caused the ordinary citation, or *subpœna*, of the Scottish criminal court, to be served upon her by an officer during his conference with David.

This precaution was so far favorable to Deans, that it saved him the pain of entering upon a formal explanation with his daughter; he only said, with a hollow and tremulous voice, "I perceive ye are aware of the matter."

"O father, we are cruelly sted between God's laws and man's laws. What shall we do? What can we do?"

Jeanie, it must be observed, had no hesitation whatever about the mere act of appearing in a court of justice. She might have heard the point discussed by her father more than once; but we have already noticed, that she was accustomed to listen with reverence to much which she was incapable of understanding, and that subtle arguments of casuistry found her a patient but unedified hearer. Upon receiving the citation, therefore, her thoughts did not turn upon the chimerical scruples which alarmed her father's mind, but to the language which had been held to her by the stranger at Muschat's Cairn. In a word, she never doubted but she was to be dragged forward into the court of justice, in order to place her in the cruel position of either sacrificing her sister by telling the truth, or committing perjury in order to save her life. And so strongly did her thoughts run in this channel that she applied her father's words, "Ye are aware of the matter," to his acquaintance with the advice that had been so fearfully enforced upon her. She looked up with anxious surprise, not unmingled with a cast of horror, which his next words, as she interpreted and applied them, were not qualified to remove.

"Daughter," said David, "it has ever been my mind, that in things of ane doubtful and controversial nature ilk Christian's conscience suld be his ain guide. Wherefore descend into yourself, try your ain mind with sufficiency of soul exercise, and as you sall finally find yourself clear to do in this matter, even so be it."

"But, father," said Jeanie, whose mind revolted at the construction which she naturally put upon his language, "can this—THIS be a doubtful or controversial matter? Mind, father, the ninth command—'Thou shalt not bear false witness against thy neighbor.'"

David Deans paused ; for, still applying her speech to his preconceived difficulties, it seemed to him as if *she*, a woman and a sister, was scarce entitled to be scrupulous upon this occasion, where *he*, a man, exercised in the testimonies of that testifying period, had given indirect countenance to her following what must have been the natural dictates of her own feelings. But he kept firm his purpose, until his eyes involuntarily rested upon the little settle-bed, and recalled the form of the child of his old age, as she sat upon it, pale, emaciated, and broken-hearted. His mind, as the picture arose before him, involuntarily conceived, and his tongue involuntarily uttered—but in a tone how different from his usual dogmatical precision !—arguments for the course of conduct likely to insure his child's safety.

"Daughter," he said, "I did not say that your path was free from stumbling ; and, questionless, this act may be in the opinion of some a transgression, since he who beareth witness unlawfully, and against his conscience, doth in some sort bear false witness against his neighbor. Yet in matters of compliance, the guilt lieth not in the compliance sae muckle as in the mind and conscience of him that doth comply; and, therefore, although my testimony hath not been spared upon public defections, I haena felt freedom to separate mysell from the communion of many who have been clear to hear those ministers who have taken the fatal indulgence, because they might get good of them, though I could not."

When David had proceeded thus far, his conscience reproved him, that he might be indirectly undermining the purity of his daughter's faith, and smoothing the way for her falling off from strictness of principle. He, therefore, suddenly stopped, and changed his tone : " Jeanie, I perceive that our vile affections—so I call them in respect of doing the will of our Father—cling too heavily to me in this hour of trying sorrow, to permit me to keep sight of my ain duty, or to airt you to yours. I will speak nae mair anent this overtrying matter. Jeanie, if ye can, wi' God and gude conscience, speak in favor of this puir unhappy—— [Here his voice faltered.] She is your sister in the flesh : worthless and castaway as she is, she is the daughter of a saint in heaven, that was a mother to you, Jeanie, in place of your ain ; but if ye arena free in conscience to speak for her in the court of judicature, follow your conscience, Jeanie, and let God's will be done." After this adjuration he left the apartment, and his daughter remained in a state of great distress and perplexity.

It would have been no small addition to the sorrows of David Deans, even in this extremity of suffering, had he known that his daughter was applying the casuistical arguments which he had been using, not in the sense of a permission to follow her own opinion on a dubious and disputed point of controversy, but rather as an encouragement to transgress one of those divine commandments which Christians of all sects and denominations unite in holding most sacred.

" Can this be ? " said Jeanie, as the door closed on her father—" can these be his words that I have heard, or has the Enemy taken his voice and features to give weight unto the counsel which causeth to perish ? A sister's life, and a father pointing out how to save it ! O God deliver me ! this is a fearfu' temptation."

Roaming from thought to thought, she at one time imagined her father understood the ninth commandment literally, as prohibiting false witness *against* our neighbor, without extending the denunciation against falsehood uttered *in favor* of the criminal. But her clear and unsophisticated power of discriminating between good and evil instantly rejected an interpretation so limited and so unworthy of the Author of the law. She remained in a state of the most agitating terror and uncertainty—afraid to communicate her thoughts freely to her father, lest she should draw forth an opinion with which she could not comply; wrung with distress on her sister's account, rendered the more acute by reflecting that the means of saving her were in her power, but were such as her conscience prohibited her from using; tossed, in short, like a vessel in an open roadstead during a storm, and, like that vessel, resting on one only sure cable and anchor—faith in Providence, and a resolution to discharge her duty.

Butler's affection and strong sense of religion would have been her principal support in these distressing circumstances, but he was still under restraint, which did not permit him to come to St. Leonard's Crags; and her distresses were of a nature which, with her indifferent habits of scholarship, she found it impossible to express in writing. She was therefore compelled to trust for guidance to her own unassisted sense of what was right or wrong.

It was not the least of Jeanie's distresses that, although she hoped and believed her sister to be innocent, she had not the means of receiving that assurance from her own mouth.

The double-dealing of Ratcliffe in the matter of Robertson had not prevented his being rewarded, as double-dealers frequently have been, with favor and preferment. Sharpitlaw, who found in him something of a kindred genius, had been intercessor in his behalf with the magistrates, and the circumstance of his having voluntarily remained in the prison, when the doors were forced by the mob, would have made it a hard measure to take the life which he had such easy means of saving. He received a full pardon; and soon afterwards, James Ratcliffe, the greatest thief and housebreaker in Scotland, was, upon the faith, perhaps, of an ancient proverb, selected as a person to be intrusted with the custody of other delinquents.

When Ratcliffe was thus placed in a confidential situation, he was repeatedly applied to by the sapient Saddletree and others who took some interest in the Deans family, to procure an interview between the sisters; but the magistrates, who were extremely anxious for the apprehension of Robertson, had given strict orders to the contrary, hoping that, by keeping them separate, they might, from the one or the other, ex-

tract some information respecting that fugitive. On this subject Jeanie had nothing to tell them. She informed Mr.
Middleburgh that she knew nothing of Robertson, except
having met him that night by appointment to give her some
advice respecting her sister's concern, the purport of which,
she said, was betwixt God and her conscience. Of his motions,
purposes, or plans, past, present, or future, she knew nothing,
and so had nothing to communicate.

Effie was equally silent, though from a different cause. It
was in vain that they offered a commutation and alleviation
of her punishment, and even a free pardon, if she would confess what she knew of her lover. She answered only with
tears ; unless, when at times driven into pettish sulkiness by
the persecution of the interrogators, she made them abrupt
and disrespectful answers.

At length, after her trial had been delayed for many weeks,
in hopes she might be induced to speak out on a subject
infinitely more interesting to the magistracy than her own
guilt or innocence, their patience was worn out, and even Mr.
Middleburgh finding no ear lent to further intercession in her
behalf, the day was fixed for the trial to proceed.

It was now, and not sooner, that Sharpitlaw, recollecting
his promise to Effie Deans, or rather being dinned into compliance by the unceasing remonstrances of Mrs. Saddletree,
who was his next-door neighbor, and who declared "it was
heathen cruelty to keep the twa broken-hearted creatures separate," issued the important mandate permitting them to see
each other.

On the evening which preceded the eventful day of trial,
Jeanie was permitted to see her sister—an awful interview,
and occurring at a most distressing crisis. This, however,
formed a part of the bitter cup which she was doomed to
drink, to atone for crimes and follies to which she had no accession ; and at twelve o'clock noon, being the time appointed
for admission to the jail, she went to meet, for the first time
for several months, her guilty, erring, and most miserable
sister, in that abode of guilt, error, and utter misery.

CHAPTER XX

Sweet sister, let me live !
What sin you do to save a brother's life,
Nature dispenses with the deed so far,
That it becomes a virtue.
Measure for Measure.

JEANIE DEANS was admitted into the jail by Ratcliffe. This
fellow, as void of shame as of honesty, as he opened the now
trebly secured door, asked her, with a leer which made her
shudder, " whether she remembered him ? "

A half-pronounced and timid " No " was her answer.

" What ! not remember moonlight, and Muschat's Cairn,
and Rob and Rat ? " said he, with the same sneer. " Your
memory needs redding up, my jo."

If Jeanie's distresses had admitted of aggravation, it must
have been to find her sister under the charge of such a profligate as this man. He was not, indeed, without something
of good to balance so much that was evil in his character and
habits. In his misdemeanors he had never been bloodthirsty
or cruel ; and in his present occupation he had shown himself,
in a certain degree, accessible to touches of humanity. But
these good qualities were unknown to Jeanie, who, remembering the scene at Muschat's Cairn, could scarce find voice to
acquaint him that she had an order from Bailie Middleburgh,
permitting her to see her sister.

" I ken that fu' weel, my bonny doo ; mair by token I have
a special charge to stay in the ward with you a' the time ye
are thegither."

" Must that be sae ? " asked Jeanie, with an imploring
voice.

" Hout, ay, hinny," replied the turnkey ; " and what the
waur will you and your tittie be of Jim Ratcliffe hearing what
ye hae to say to ilk other ? Deil a word ye'll say that will
gar him ken your kittle sex better than he kens them already ;
and another thing is, that, if ye dinna speak o' breaking the
tolbooth, deil a word will I tell ower, either to do ye good
or ill."

Thus saying, Ratcliffe marshalled her the way to the apartment where Effie was confined.

Shame, fear, and grief had contended for mastery in the poor prisoner's bosom during the whole morning, while she had looked forward to this meeting; but when the door opened, all gave way to a confused and strange feeling that had a tinge of joy in it, as, throwing herself on her sister's neck, she ejaculated, " My dear Jeanie ! my dear Jeanie ! it's lang since I hae seen ye." Jeanie returned the embrace with an earnestness that partook almost of rapture, but it was only a flitting emotion like a sunbeam unexpectedly penetrating betwixt the clouds of a tempest, and obscured almost as soon as visible. The sisters walked together to the side of the pallet bed, and sat down side by side, took hold of each other's hands, and looked each other in the face, but without speaking a word. In this posture they remained for a minute, while the gleam of joy gradually faded from their features, and gave way to the most intense expression, first of melancholy, and then of agony, till, throwing themselves again into each other's arms, they, to use the language of Scripture, lifted up their voices and wept bitterly.

Even the hard-hearted turnkey, who had spent his life in scenes calculated to stifle both conscience and feeling, could not witness this scene without a touch of human sympathy. It was shown in a trifling action, but which had more delicacy in it than seemed to belong to Ratcliffe's character and station. The unglazed window of the miserable chamber was open, and the beams of a bright sun fell right upon the bed where the sufferers were seated. With a gentleness that had something of reverence in it, Ratcliffe partly closed the shutter, and seemed thus to throw a veil over a scene so sorrowful.

" Ye are ill, Effie," were the first words Jeanie could utter —" ye are very ill."

" O, what wad I gie to be ten times waur, Jeanie !" was the reply—" what wad I gie to be cauld dead afore the ten o'clock bell the morn ! And our father—but I am his bairn nae langer now ! O, I hae nae friend left in the warld ! O that I were lying dead at my mother's side in Newbattle kirkyard !"

" Hout, lassie," said Ratcliffe, willing to show the interest which he absolutely felt, " dinna be sae dooms down-hearted as a' that ; there's mony a tod hunted that's no killed. Advocate Langtale has brought folk through waur snappers than a' this, and there's no a cleverer agent than Nichil Novit e'er drew a bill of suspension. Hanged or unhanged, they are weel aff has sic an agent and counsel ; ane's sure o' fair play. Ye are a bonny lass, too, an ye wad busk up your cocker-nonie a bit ; and a bonny lass will find favor wi' judge and jury, when they would strap up a grewsome carle like me for the fifteenth part of a flea's hide and tallow, d—n them."

To this homely strain of consolation the mourners returned no answer ; indeed, they were so much lost in their own sorrows as to have become insensible of Ratcliffe's presence. "O, Effie," said her elder sister, "how could you conceal your situation from me ? O, woman, had I deserved this at your hand ? Had ye spoke but ae word—sorry we might hae been, and shamed we might hae been, but this awfu' dispensation had never come ower us."

"And what gude wad that hae dune ?" answered the prisoner. "Na, na, Jeanie, a' was ower when ance I forgot what I promised when I faulded down the leaf of my Bible. See," she said, producing the sacred volume, "the book opens aye at the place o' itsell. O see, Jeanie, what a fearfu' scripture !"

Jeanie took her sister's Bible, and found that the fatal mark was made at this impressive text in the Book of Job : "He hath stripped me of my glory, and taken the crown from my head. He hath destroyed me on every side, and I am gone. And mine hope hath he removed like a tree."

"Isna that ower true a doctrine ?" said the prisoner : "isna my crown, my honor removed ? And what am I but a poor wasted, wan-thriven tree, dug up by the roots and flung out to waste in the highway, that man and beast may tread it under foot ? I thought o' the bonny bit thorn that our father rooted out o' the yard last May, when it had a' the flush o' blossoms on it ; and then it lay in the court till the beasts had trod them a' to pieces wi' their feet. I little thought, when I was wae for the bit silly green bush and its flowers, that I was to gang the same gate mysell."

"O, if ye had spoken a word," again sobbed Jeanie—"if I were free to swear that ye had said but ae word of how it stude wi' ye, they couldna hae touched your life this day."

"Could they na ?" said Effie, with something like awakened interest, for life is dear even to those who feel it as a burden. "Wha tauld ye that, Jeanie ?"

"It was ane that kenn'd what he was saying weel eneugh," replied Jeanie, who had a natural reluctance at mentioning even the name of her sister's seducer.

"Wha was it ? I conjure ye to tell me," said Effie, seating herself upright. "Wha could tak interest in sic a cast-bye as I am now? Was it—was it *him?*"

"Hout," said Ratcliffe, "what signifies keeping the poor lassie in a swither? I'se uphaud it's been Robertson that learned ye that doctrine when ye saw him at Muschat's Cairn."

"Was it him?" said Effie, catching eagerly at his words—"was it him, Jeanie, indeed? O, I see it was him, poor lad; and I was thinking his heart was as hard as the nether mill-stane; and him in sic danger on his ain part—poor George!"

Somewhat indignant at this burst of tender feeling towards the author of her misery, Jeanie could not help exclaiming—"O, Effie, how can ye speak that gate of sic a man as that?"

"We maun forgie our enemies, ye ken," said poor Effie, with a timid look and a subdued voice; for her conscience told her what a different character the feelings with which she still regarded her seducer bore, compared with the Christian charity under which she attempted to veil it.

"And ye hae suffered a' this for him, and ye can think of loving him still?" said her sister, in a voice betwixt pity and blame.

"Love him!" answered Effie. "If I hadna loved as woman seldom loves, I hadna been within these wa's this day; and trow ye that love sic as mine is lightly forgotten? Na, na, ye may hew down the tree, but ye canna change its bend. And O, Jeanie, if ye wad do good to me at this moment, tell me every word that he said, and whether he was sorry for poor Effie or no!"

"What needs I tell ye onything about it," said Jeanie. "Ye may be sure he had ower muckle to do to save himsell, to speak lang or muckle about onybody beside."

"That's no true, Jeanie, though a saunt had said it," replied Effie, with a sparkle of her former lively and irritable temper. "But ye dinna ken, though I do, how far he pat his life in venture to save mine." And looking at Ratcliffe, she checked herself and was silent.

"I fancy," said Ratcliffe, with one of his familiar sneers, "the lassie thinks that naebody has een but hersell. Didna I see when Gentle Geordie was seeking to get other folk out of the tolbooth forbye Jock Porteous? But ye are of my mind, hinny: better sit and rue than flit and rue. Ye needna look in my face sae amazed. I ken mair things than that, maybe."

"O my God! my God!" said Effie, springing up and throwing herself down on her knees before him. "D'ye ken where they hae putten my bairn? O my bairn! my bairn! the poor sackless innocent new-born wee ane—bone of my bone, and flesh of my flesh ! O man, if ye wad e'er deserve a portion in heaven, or a broken-hearted creature's blessing upon earth, tell me where they hae put my bairn—the sign of my shame, and the partner of my suffering ! tell me wha has taen't away, or what they hae dune wi't !"

"Hout tout," said the turnkey, endeavoring to extricate himself from the firm grasp with which she held him, "that's taking me at my word wi' a witness. Bairn, quo' she? How the deil suld I ken onything of your bairn, huzzy? Ye maun ask that of auld Meg Murdockson, if ye dinna ken ower muckle about it yoursell."

As his answer destroyed the wild and vague hope which had suddenly gleamed upon her, the unhappy prisoner let go her hold of his coat, and fell with her face on the pavement of the apartment in a strong convulsion fit.

Jeanie Deans possessed, with her excellently clear understanding, the concomitant advantage of pomptitude of spirit, even in the extremity of distress.

She did not suffer herself to be overcome by her own feelings of exquisite sorrow, but instantly applied herself to her sister's relief, with the readiest remedies which circumstances afforded ; and which, to do Ratcliffe justice, he showed himself anxious to suggest, and alert in procuring. He had even the delicacy to withdraw to the furthest corner of the room, so as to render his official attendance upon them as little intrusive as possible, when Effie was composed enough again to resume her conference with her sister.

The prisoner once more, in the most earnest and broken tones, conjured Jeanie to tell her the particulars of the conference with Robertson, and Jeanie felt it was impossible to refuse her this gratification.

"Do ye mind," she said, "Effie, when ye were in the fever before we left Woodend, and how angry your mother, that's now in a better place, was wi' me for gieing ye milk and water to drink, because ye grat for it ? Ye were a bairn then, and ye are a woman now, and should ken better than ask what canna but hurt you. But come weal or woe, I canna refuse ye onything that ye ask me wi' the tear in your ee."

Again Effie threw herself into her arms, and kissed her cheek and forehead, murmuring, "O if ye kenn'd how lang it is since I heard his name mentioned ! if ye but kenn'd how muckle good it does me but to ken onything o' him that's like goodness or kindness, ye wadna wonder that I wish to hear o' him !"

Jeanie sighed, and commenced her narrative of all that had passed betwixt Robertson and her, making it as brief as possible. Effie listened in breathless anxiety, holding her sister's hand in hers, and keeping her eye fixed upon her face, as if devouring every word she uttered. The interjections of " Poor fellow ! "—" Poor George ! " which escaped in whispers, and betwixt sighs, were the only sounds with which she interrupted the story. When it was finished she made a long pause.

" And this was his advice ? " were the first words she uttered.

" Just sic as I hae tell'd ye," replied her sister.

" And he wanted you to say something to yon folks that wad save my young life ? "

" He wanted," answered Jeanie, " that I suld be mansworn."

" And you tauld him," said Effie, " that ye wadna hear o' coming between me and the death that I am to die, and me no aughteen year auld yet ? "

" I told him," replied Jeanie, who now trembled at the turn which her sister's reflections seemed about to take, " that I daured na swear to an untruth."

" And what d'ye ca' an untruth ? " said Effie, again showing a touch of her former spirit. " Ye are muckle to blame, lass, if ye think a mother would, or could, murder her ain bairn. Murder ! I wad hae laid down my life just to see a blink o' its ee ! "

" I do believe," said Jeanie, " that ye are as innocent of sic a purpose as the new-born babe itsell."

" I am glad ye do me that justice," said Effie, haughtily ; " it's whiles the faut of very good folk like you, Jeanie, that they think a' the rest of the warld are as bad as the warst temptations can make them."

" I dinna deserve this frae ye, Effie," said her sister, sobbing, and feeling at once the injustice of the reproach and compassion for the state of mind which dictated it.

" Maybe no, sister," said Effie. " But ye are angry because I love Robertson. How can I help loving him, that loves me better that body and soul baith ? Here he put his life in a niffer, to break the prison to let me out ; and sure am I, had it stood wi' him as it stands wi' you——" Here she paused and was silent.

" O, if it stude wi' me to save ye wi' risk of *my* life ! " said Jeanie.

" Ay, lass," said her sister, " that's lightly said, but no sae lightly credited, frae ane that winna ware a word for me ; and if it be a wrang word, ye'll hae time eneugh to repent o't."

"But that word is a grievous sin, and it's a deeper offence when it's a sin wilfully and presumptuously committed."

"Weel, weel, Jeanie," said Effie, "I mind a' about the sins o' presumption in the questions ; we'll speak nae mair about this matter, and ye may save your breath to say your carritch ; and for me, I'll soon hae nae breath to waste on onybody."

"I must needs say," interposed Ratcliffe, "that it's d—d hard, when three words of your mouth would give the girl the chance to nick Moll Blood, that you make such scrupling about rapping to them. D—n me, if they would take me, if I would not rap to all Whatd'yecallum's—Hyssop's Fables —for her life ; I am us'd to't, b—t me, for less matters. Why, I have smacked calfskin fifty times in England for a keg of brandy."

"Never speak mair o't," said the prisoner. "It's just as weel as it is ; and gude day, sister, ye keep Mr. Ratcliffe waiting on. Ye'll come back and see me, I reckon, before——" Here she stopped, and became deadly pale.

"And are we to part in this way," said Jeanie, "and you in sic deadly peril ? O, Effie, look but up and say what ye wad hae me do, and I could find in my heart amaist to say that I wad do't."

"No, Jeanie," replied her sister, after an effort, "I am better minded now. At my best, I was never half sae gude as ye were, and what for suld you begin to mak yoursell waur to save me, now that I am no worth saving ? God knows, that in my sober mind I wadna wuss ony living creature to do a wrang thing to save my life. I might have fled frae this tolbooth on that awfu' night wi' ane wad hae carried me through the warld, and friended me, and fended for me. But I said to them, let life gang when gude fame is gane before it. But this lang imprisonment has broken my spirit, and I am whiles sair left to mysell, and then I wad gie the Indian mines of gold and diamonds just for life and breath ; for I think, Jeanie, I have such roving fits as I used to hae in the fever ; but instead of the fiery een, and wolves, and Widow Butler's bullsegg, that I used to see speiling up on my bed, I am thinking now about a high black gibbet, and me standing up, and such seas of faces all looking up at poor Effie Deans, and asking if it be her that George Robertson used to call the Lily of St. Leonard's. And then they stretch out their faces, and make mouths, and girn at me, and whichever way I look, I see a face laughing like Meg Murdockson, when she tauld me I had seen the last of my wean. God preserve us, Jeanie, that carline has a fearsome face !" She clapped her hands before her eyes as she uttered this exclamation, as if to secure herself against seeing the fearful object she had alluded to.

Jeanie Deans remained with her sister for two hours, during which she endeavored, if possible, to extract something from her that might be serviceable in her exculpation. But she had nothing to say beyond what she had declared on her first examination, with the purport of which the reader will be made acquainted in proper time and place. "They wadna believe her," she said, "and she had naething mair to tell them."

At length Ratcliffe, though reluctantly, informed the sisters that there was a necessity that they should part. "Mr. Novit," he said, "was to see the prisoner, and maybe Mr. Langtale too. Langtale likes to look at a bonny lass, whether in prison or out o' prison."

Reluctantly, therefore, and slowly, after many a tear and many an embrace, Jeanie retired from the apartment, and heard its jarring bolts turned upon the dear being from whom she was separated. Somewhat familiarized now even with her rude conductor, she offered him a small present in money, with a request he would do what he could for her sister's accommodation. To her surprise, Ratcliffe declined the fee. "I wasna bloody when I was on the pad," he said, "and I winna be greedy—that is, beyond what's right and reasonable —now that I am in the lock. Keep the siller ; and for civility, your sister sall hae sic as I can bestow. But I hope you'll think better on it, and rap an oath for her ; deil a hair ill there is in it, if ye are rapping again the crown. I kenn'd a worthy minister, as gude a man, bating the deed they deposed him for, as ever ye heard claver in a pu'pit, that rapped to a hogshead of pigtail tobacco, just for as muckle as filled his spleuchan. But maybe ye are keeping your ain counsel ; weel, weel, there's nae harm in that. As for your sister, I'se see that she gets her meat clean and warm, and I'll try to gar her lie down and take a sleep after dinner, for deil a ee she'll close the night. I hae gude experience of these matters. The first night is aye the warst o't. I hae never heard o' ane that sleepit the night afore trial, but of mony a ane that sleepit as sound as a tap the night before their necks were straughted. And it's nae wonder: the warst may be tholed when it's kenn'd. Better a finger aff as aye wagging."

CHAPTER XXI

AFTER spending the greater part of the morning in his devotions, for his benevolent neighbors had kindly insisted upon discharging his task of ordinary labor, David Deans entered the apartment when the breakfast meal was prepared. His eyes were involuntarily cast down, for he was afraid to look at Jeanie, uncertain as he was whether she might feel herself at liberty, with a good conscience, to attend the Court of Justiciary that day, to give the evidence which he understood that she possessed in order to her sister's exculpation. At length, after a minute of apprehensive hesitation, he looked at her dress to discover whether it seemed to be in her contemplation to go abroad that morning. Her apparel was neat and plain, but such as conveyed no exact intimation of her intentions to go abroad. She had exchanged her usual garb for morning labor for one something inferior to that with which, as her best, she was wont to dress herself for church, or any more rare occasion of going into society. Her sense taught her, that it was respectful to be decent in her apparel on such an occasion, while her feelings induced her to lay aside the use of the very few and simple personal ornaments which, on other occasions, she permitted herself to wear. So that there occurred nothing in her external appearance which could mark out to her father, with anything like certainty, her intentions on this occasion.

The preparations for their humble meal were that morning made in vain. The father and daughter sat, each assuming the appearance of eating when the other's eyes were turned to them, and desisting from the effort with disgust when the affectionate imposture seemed no longer necessary.

At length these moments of constraint were removed. The sound of St. Giles's heavy toll announced the hour previous to the commencement of the trial; Jeanie arose, and, with a degree of composure for which she herself could not account, assumed her plaid, and made her other preparations for a distant walking. It was a strange contrast between the firmness of her demeanor and the vacillation and cruel uncertainty of purpose indicated in all her father's motions ; and one unacquainted with both could scarcely have supposed that the former was, in her ordinary habits of life, a docile, quiet, gentle, and even timid country maiden, while her father, with a mind naturally proud and strong, and supported by religious opinions of a stern, stoical, and unyielding character, had in his time undergone and withstood the most severe hardships and the most imminent peril, without depression of spirit or subjugation of his constancy. The secret of this difference was, that Jeanie's mind had already anticipated the line of conduct which she must adopt, with all its natural and necessary consequences ; while her father, ignorant of every other circumstance, tormented himself with imagining what the one sister might say or swear, or what effect her testimony might have upon the awful event of the trial.

He watched his daughter with a faltering and indecisive look, until she looked back upon him with a look of unutterable anguish, as she was about to leave the apartment.

"My dear lassie," said he, "I will——" His action, hastily and confusedly searching for his worsted mittens and staff, showed his purpose of accompanying her, though his tongue failed distinctly to announce it.

"Father," said Jeanie, replying rather to his action than his words, "ye had better not."

"In the strength of my God," answered Deans, assuming firmness, "I will go forth."

And, taking his daughter's arm under his, he began to walk from the door with a step so hasty that she was almost unable to keep up with him. A trifling circumstance, but which marked the perturbed state of his mind, checked his course. "Your bonnet, father ?" said Jeanie, who observed · he had come out with his gray hairs uncovered. He turned back with a slight blush on his cheek, being ashamed to have been detected in an omission which indicated so much mental confusion, assumed his large blue Scottish bonnet, and with a step slower, but more composed, as if the circumstance had obliged him to summon up his resolution and collect his scattered ideas, again placed his daughter's arm under his, and resumed the way to Edinburgh.

The courts of justice were then, and are still, held in what is called the Parliament Close, or, according to modern phrase, the Parliament Square, and occupied the buildings intended for the accommodation of the Scottish Estates. This edifice, though in an imperfect and corrupted style of architecture, had then a grave, decent, and, as it were, a judicial aspect, which was at least entitled to respect from its antiquity ; for which venerable front, I observed, on my last occasional visit to the metropolis, that modern taste had substituted, at great apparent expense, a pile so utterly inconsistent with every monument of antiquity around, and in itself so clumsy at the same time and fantastic, that it may be likened to the decorations of Tom Errand, the porter, in the *Trip to the Jubilee,* when he appears bedizened with the tawdry finery of Beau Clincher. *Sed transeat cum cæteris erroribus.*

The small quadrangle, or close, if we may presume still to give it that appropriate though antiquated title, which at Litchfield, Salisbury, and elsewhere is properly applied to designate the enclosure adjacent to a cathedral, already evinced tokens of the fatal scene which was that day to be acted. The soldiers of the City Guard were on their posts, now enduring, and now rudely repelling with the butts of their muskets, the motley crew who thrust each other forward, to catch a glance at the unfortunate object of trial, as she should pass from the adjacent prison to the court in which her fate was to be determined. All must have occasionally observed, with disgust, the apathy with which the vulgar gaze on scenes of this nature, and how seldom, unless when their sympathies are called forth by some striking and extraordinary circumstance, the crowd evince any interest deeper than that of callous, unthinking bustle and brutal curiosity. They laugh, jest, quarrel, and push each other to and fro, with the same unfeeling indifference as if they were assembled for some holiday sport, or to see an idle procession. Occasionally, however, this demeanor, so natural to the degraded populace of a large town, is exchanged for a temporary touch of human affections ; and so it chanced on the present occasion.

When Deans and his daughter presented themselves in the close, and endeavored to make their way forward to the door of the court-house, they became involved in the mob, and subject, of course, to their insolence. As Deans repelled with some force the rude pushes which he received on all sides, his figure and antiquated dress caught the attention of the rabble, who often show an intuitive sharpness in ascribing the proper character from external appearance.

" Ye're welcome, Whigs,
Frae Bothwell Briggs,"

sung one fellow, for the mob of Edinburgh were at that time
Jacobitically disposed, probably because that was the line of
sentiment most diametrically opposite to existing authority.

> " Mess David Williamson,
>   Chosen of twenty,
>   Ran up the pu'pit stair,
>   And sang Killiecrankie,"

chanted a siren, whose profession might be guessed by her appearance. A tattered cadie or errand porter, whom David
Deans had jostled in his attempt to extricate himself from the
vicinity of these scorners, exclaimed in a strong north-country tone, " Ta deil ding out her Cameronian een ! What gies
her titles to dunch gentlemans about ?"

" Make room for the ruling elder," said yet another; "he
comes to see a precious sister glorify God in the Grassmarket !"

" Whisht ! shame's in ye, sirs," said the voice of a man very
loudly, which, as quickly sinking, said in a low, but distinct
tone, " It's her father and sister."

All fell back to make way for the sufferers; and all, even
the very rudest and most profligate, were struck with shame
and silence. In the space thus abandoned to them by the
mob, Deans stood, holding his daughter by the hand, and said
to her, with a countenance strongly and sternly expressive of
his internal emotion, " Ye hear with your ears, and ye see
with your eyes, where and to whom the backslidings and defections of professors are ascribed by the scoffers. Not to
themselves alone, but to the kirk of which they are members,
and to its blessed and invisible Head. Then, weel may we take
wi' patience our share and portion of this outspreading reproach."

The man who had spoken, no other than our old friend
Dumbiedikes, whose mouth, like that of the prophet's ass,
had been opened by the emergency of the case, now joined
them, and, with his usual taciturnity, escorted them into the
court-house. No opposition was offered to their entrance,
either by the guards or doorkeepers; and it is even said that
one of the latter refused a shilling of civility-money, tendered
him by the Laird of Dumbiedikes, who was of opinion that
" siller wad mak a' easy." But this last incident wants confirmation.

Admitted within the precincts of the court-house, they
found the usual number of busy office-bearers and idle loiterers, who attend on these scenes by choice or from duty. Burghers gaped and stared ; young lawyers sauntered, sneered, and

laughed, as in the pit of the theatre; while others apart sat on a bench retired and reasoned highly, *inter apices juris*, on the doctrines of constructive crime and the true import of the statute. The bench was prepared for the arrival of the judges. The jurors were in attendance. The crown counsel, employed in looking over their briefs and notes of evidence, looked grave and whispered with each other. They occupied one side of a large table placed beneath the bench; on the other sat the advocates, whom the humanity of the Scottish law, in this particular more liberal than that of the sister country, not only permits, but enjoins, to appear and assist with their advice and skill all persons under trial. Mr. Nichil Novit was seen actively instructing the counsel for the panel —so the prisoner is called in Scottish law-phraseology— busy, bustling, and important. When they entered the court-room, Deans asked the Laird, in a tremulous whisper, "Where will *she* sit?"

Dumbiedikes whispered Novit, who pointed to a vacant space at the bar, fronting the judges, and was about to conduct Deans towards it.

"No!" he said; "I cannot sit by her; I cannot own her —not as yet, at least. I will keep out of her sight, and turn mine own eyes elsewhere; better for us baith."

Saddletree, whose repeated interference with the counsel had procured him one or two rebuffs, and a special request that he would concern himself with his own matters, now saw with pleasure an opportunity of playing the person of importance. He bustled up to the poor old man, and proceeded to exhibit his consequence, by securing, through his interest with the barkeepers and macers, a seat for Deans in a situation where he was hidden from the general eye by the projecting corner of the bench.

"It's gude to have a friend at court," he said, continuing his heartless harangues to the passive auditor, who neither heard nor replied to them; "few folk but mysell could hae sorted ye out a seat like this. The Lords will be here incontinent, and proceed *instanter* to trial. They wunna fence the court as they do at the circuit. The High Court of Justiciary is aye fenced. But, Lord's sake, what's this o't? Jeanie, ye are a cited witness. Macer, this lass is a witness; she maun be enclosed; she maun on nae account be at large. Mr. Novit, suldna Jeanie Deans be enclosed?"

Novit answered in the affirmative, and offered to conduct Jeanie to the apartment where, according to the scrupulous practice of the Scottish court, the witnesses remain in readi-

ness to be called into court to give evidence ; and separated,
at the same time, from all who might influence their testimony, or give them information concerning that which was
passing upon the trial.

"Is this necessary ?" said Jeanie, still reluctant to quit
her father's hand.

"A matter of absolute needcessity," said Saddletree;
" wha ever heard of witnesses no being inclosed ?"

"It is really a matter of necessity," said the younger
counsellor retained for her sister ; and Jeanie reluctantly followed the macer of the court to the place appointed.

"This, Mr. Deans," said Saddletree, "is ca'd sequestering
a witness ; but it's clean different, whilk maybe ye wadna fund
out o' yoursell, frae sequestering ane's estate or effects, as in
cases of bankruptcy. I hae aften been sequestered as a witness, for the sheriff is in the use whiles to cry me in to witness
the declarations at precognitions, and so is Mr. Sharpitlaw ;
but I was ne'er like to be sequestered o' land and gudes but
ance, and that was lang syne, afore I was married. But
whisht, whisht ! here's the Court coming."

As he spoke, the five Lords of Justiciary, in their long
robes of scarlet, faced with white, and preceded by their mace-
bearer, entered with the usual formalities, and took their places
upon the bench of judgment.

The audience rose to receive them ; and the bustle occasioned by their entrance was hardly composed, when a great
noise and confusion of persons struggling, and forcibly endeavoring to enter at the doors of the court-room and of the
galleries, announced that the prisoner was about to be placed
at the bar. This tumult takes place when the doors, at first
only opened to those either having right to be present or to
the better and more qualified ranks, are at length laid open to
all whose curiosity induces them to be present on the occasion.
With inflamed countenances and dishevelled dresses, struggling with and sometimes tumbling over each other, in rushed
the rude multitude, while a few soldiers, forming, as it were,
the centre of the tide, could scarce, with all their efforts, clear
a passage for the prisoner to the place which she was to occupy. By the authority of the Court and the exertions of
its officers, the tumult among the spectators was at length appeased, and the unhappy girl brought forward, and placed
betwixt two sentinels with drawn bayonets, as a prisoner at
the bar, where she was to abide her deliverance for good or
evil, according to the issue of her trial.

CHAPTER XXII

We have strict statutes, and most biting laws—
The needful bits and curbs for headstrong steeds—
Which, for these fourteen years, we have let sleep,
Like to an o'ergrown lion in a cave
That goes not out to prey.

Measure for Measure.

"Euphemia Deans," said the presiding Judge, in an accent in which pity was blended with dignity, "stand up and listen to the criminal indictment now to be preferred against you."

The unhappy girl, who had been stupefied by the confusion through which the guards had forced a passage, cast a bewildered look on the multitude of faces around her which seemed to tapestry, as it were, the walls, in one broad slope from the ceiling to the floor, with human countenances, and instinctively obeyed a command which rung in her ears like the trumpet of the judgment-day.

"Put back your hair, Effie," said one of the macers. For her beautiful and abundant tresses of long fair hair, which, according to the costume of the country, unmarried women were not allowed to cover with any sort of cap, and which, alas! Effie dared no longer confine with the snood or ribbon which implied purity of maiden-fame, now hung unbound and dishevelled over her face, and almost concealed her features. On receiving this hint from the attendant, the unfortunate young woman, with a hasty, trembling, and apparently mechanical compliance, shaded back from her face her luxuriant locks, and showed to the whole court, excepting one individual, a countenance which, though pale and emaciated, was so lovely amid its agony that it called forth a universal murmur of compassion and sympathy. Apparently the expressive sound of human feeling recalled the poor girl from the stupor of fear which predominated at first over every other sensation, and awakened her to the no less painful sense of shame and exposure attached to her present situation. Her eye, which had at first glanced wildly around, was turned on the ground ; her cheek, at first so deadly pale, began gradually to be overspread with a faint blush, which increased so fast that, when in agony of shame she strove to conceal her face, her temples, her brow, her neck, and all that her slender fingers and small palms could not cover, became of the deepest crimson.

All marked and were moved by these changes, excepting one. It was old Deans, who, motionless in his seat, and concealed, as we have said, by the corner of the bench, from seeing or being seen, did nevertheless keep his eyes firmly fixed on the ground, as if determined that, by no possibility whatever, would he be an ocular witness of the shame of his house.

"Ichabod !" he said to himself—"Ichabod ! my glory is departed !"

While these reflections were passing through his mind, the indictment, which set forth in technical form the crime of which the panel stood accused, was read as usual, and the prisoner was asked if she was Guilty or Not Guilty.

"Not guilty of my poor bairn's death," said Effie Deans, in an accent corresponding in plaintive softness of tone to the beauty of her features, and which was not heard by the audience without emotion.

The presiding Judge next directed the counsel to plead to the relevancy ; that is, to state on either part the arguments in point of law, and evidence in point of fact, against and in favor of the criminal, after which it is the form of the Court to pronounce a preliminary judgment, sending the cause to the cognizance of the jury or assize.

The counsel for the crown briefly stated the frequency of the crime of infanticide, which had given rise to the special statute under which the panel stood indicted. He mentioned the various instances, many of them marked with circumstances of atrocity, which had at length induced the King's Advocate, though with great reluctance, to make the experiment, whether, by strictly enforcing the Act of Parliament which had been made to prevent such enormities, their occurrence might be prevented. "He expected," he said, "to be able to establish by witnesses, as well as by the declaration of the panel herself, that she was in the state described by the statute. According to his information, the panel had communicated her pregnancy to no one, nor did she allege in her own declaration that she had done so. This secrecy was the first requisite in support of the indictment. The same declaration admitted that she had borne a male child, in cir-

cumstances which gave but too much reason to believe it had
died by the hands, or at least with the knowledge or consent,
of the unhappy mother. It was not, however, necessary for
him to bring positive proof that the panel was accessory to
the murder, nay, nor even to prove that the child was murdered at all. It was sufficient to support the indictment,
that it could not be found. According to the stern but necessary severity of this statute, she who should conceal her pregnancy, who should omit to call that assistance which is most
necessary on such occasions, was held already to have medi-
ted the death of her offspring, as an event most likely to be
the consequence of her culpable and cruel concealment. And
if, under such circumstances, she could not alternatively show
by proof that the infant had died a natural death, or produce
it still in life, she must, under the construction of the law,
be held to have murdered it, and suffer death accordingly."

The counsel for the prisoner, Mr. Fairbrother, a man of
considerable fame in his profession, did not pretend directly
to combat the arguments of the King's Advocate. He began
by lamenting that his senior at the bar, Mr. Langtale, had
been suddenly called to the county of which he was sheriff,
and that he had been applied to, on short warning, to give
the panel his assistance in this interesting case. He had had
little time, he said, to make up for his inferiority to his
learned brother by long and minute research ; and he was
afraid he might give a specimen of his incapacity by being
compelled to admit the accuracy of the indictment under the
statute. "It was enough for their Lordships," he observed,
"to know, that such was the law, and he admitted the Advocate had a right to call for the usual interlocutor of relevancy." But he stated, "that when he came to establish
his case by proof, he trusted to make out circumstances
which would satisfactorily elide the charge in the libel.
His client's story was a short but most melancholy one. She
was bred up in the strictest tenets of religion and virtue, the
daughter of a worthy and conscientious person, who, in evil
times, had established a character for courage and religion,
by becoming a sufferer for conscience' sake."

David Deans gave a convulsive start at hearing himself
thus mentioned, and then resumed the situation in which,
with his face stooped against his hands, and both resting
against the corner of the elevated bench on which the Judges
sat, he had hitherto listened to the procedure in the trial.
The Whig lawyers seemed to be interested ; the Tories put
up their lip.

" Whatever may be our difference of opinion," resumed the lawyer, whose business it was to carry his whole audience with him if possible, " concerning the peculiar tenets of these people [here Deans groaned deeply], it is impossible to deny them the praise of sound, and even rigid, morals, or the merit of training up their children in the fear of God ; and yet it was the daughter of such a person whom a jury would shortly be called upon, in the absence of evidence, and upon mere presumptions, to convict of a crime more properly belonging to a heathen or a savage than to a Christian and civilized country. It was true," he admitted, " that the excellent nurture and early instruction which the poor girl had received had not been sufficient to preserve her from guilt and error. She had fallen a sacrifice to an inconsiderate affection for a young man of prepossessing manners, as he had been informed, but of a very dangerous and desperate character. She was seduced under promise of marriage—a promise which the fellow might have, perhaps, done her justice by keeping, had he not at that time been called upon by the law to atone for a crime, violent and desperate in itself, but which became the preface to another eventful history, every step of which was marked by blood and guilt, and the final termination of which had not even yet arrived. He believed that no one would hear him without surprise, when he stated that the father of this infant now amissing, and said by the learned Advocate to have been murdered, was no other than the notorious George Robertson, the accomplice of Wilson, the hero of the memorable escape from the Tolbooth Church, and, as no one knew better than his learned friend the Advocate, the principal actor in the Porteous conspiracy."

" I am sorry to interrupt a counsel in such a case as the present," said the presiding Judge ; " but I must remind the learned gentleman that he is travelling out of the case before us."

The counsel bowed, and resumed. " He only judged it necessary," he said, " to mention the name and situation of Robertson, because the circumstance in which that character was placed went a great way in accounting for the silence on which his Majesty's counsel had laid so much weight, as affording proof that his client proposed to allow no fair play for its life to the helpless being whom she was about to bring into the world. She had not announced to her friends that she had been seduced from the path of honor, and why had she not done so ? Because she expected daily to be restored to character, by her seducer doing her that justice which she knew to be in his power, and believed to be in his inclination.   Was it natural, was it reasonable, was it fair, to expect that she should, in the interim, become *felo de se* of her own character, and proclaim her frailty to the world, when she had every reason to expect that, by concealing it for a season, it might be veiled forever ?   Was it not, on the contrary, pardonable that, in such an emergency, a young woman, in such a situation, should be found far from disposed to make a confidante of every prying gossip who, with sharp eyes and eager ears, pressed upon her for an explanation of suspicious circum-stances, which females in the lower—he might say which females of all ranks are so alert in noticing, that they sometimes discover them where they do not exist ?   Was it strange, or was it criminal, that she should have repelled their inquisitive impertinence with petulant denials ?   The sense and feeling of all who heard him would answer directly in the negative.   But although his client had thus remained silent towards those to whom she was not called upon to communicate her situation—to whom," said the learned gentleman, " I will add, it would have been unadvised and improper in her to have done so ; yet I trust I shall remove this case most triumphantly from under the statute, and obtain the unfortunate young woman an honorable dismission from your Lordships' bar, by showing that she did, in due time and place, and to a person most fit for such confidence, mention the calamitous circumstances in which she found herself.   This occurred after Robertson's conviction, and when he was lying in prison in expectation of the fate which his comrade Wilson afterwards suffered, and from which he himself so strangely escaped.   It was then, when all hopes of having her honor repaired by wedlock vanished from her eyes—when a union with one in Robertson's situation, if still practicable, might perhaps have been regarded rather as an addition to her disgrace—it was *then*, that I trust to be able to prove that the prisoner communicated and consulted with her sister, a young woman several years older than herself, the daughter of her father, if I mistake not, by a former marriage, upon the perils and distress of her unhappy situation."

" If, indeed, you are able to instruct *that* point, Mr. Fairbrother——" said the presiding Judge.

" If I am indeed able to instruct that point, my lord," resumed Mr. Fairbrother, " I trust not only to serve my client, but to relieve your Lordships from that which I know you feel the most painful duty of your high office ; and to give all who now hear me the exquisite pleasure of beholding a creature so young, so ingenuous, and so beautiful as she that is now at the bar of your Lordships' Court, dismissed from thence in safety and in honor."

This address seemed to affect many of the audience, and was followed by a slight murmur of applause. Deans, as he heard his daughter's beauty and innocent appearance appealed to, was involuntarily about to turn his eyes towards her; but, recollecting himself, he bent them again on the ground with stubborn resolution.

"Will not my learned brother on the other side of the bar," continued the advocate, after a short pause, "share in this general joy, since I know, while he discharges his duty in bringing an accused person here, no one rejoices more in their being freely and honorably sent hence? My learned brother shakes his head doubtfully, and lays his hand on the panel's declaration. I understand him perfectly: he would insinuate that the facts now stated to your Lordships are inconsistent with the confession of Euphemia Deans herself. I need not remind your Lordships, that her present defence is no whit to be narrowed within the bounds of her former confession; and that it is not by any account which she may formerly have given of herself, but by what is now to be proved for or against her, that she must ultimately stand or fall. I am not under the necessity of accounting for her choosing to drop out of her declaration the circumstances of her confession to her sister. She might not be aware of its importance; she might be afraid of implicating her sister; she might even have forgotten the circumstance entirely, in the terror and distress of mind incidental to the arrest of so young a creature on a charge so heinous. Any of these reasons are sufficient to account for her having suppressed the truth in this instance, at whatever risk to herself; and I incline most to her erroneous fear of criminating her sister, because I observe she has had a similar tenderness towards her lover, however undeserved on his part, and has never once mentioned Robertson's name from beginning to end of her declaration.

"But, my lords," continued Fairbrother, "I am aware the King's Advocate will expect me to show that the proof I offer is consistent with other circumstances of the case which I do not and cannot deny. He will demand of me how Effie Deans's confession to her sister, previous to her delivery, is reconcilable with the mystery of the birth—with the disappearance, perhaps the murder—for I will not deny a possibility which I cannot disprove—of the infant. My lords, the explanation of this is to be found in the placability, perchance I may say in the facility and pliability, of the female sex. The *dulcis Amaryllidis iræ*, as your Lordships well know, are easily appeased ; nor is it possible to conceive a woman so atrociously offended by the man whom she has loved, but what she will retain a fund of forgiveness upon which his penitence, whether real or affected, may draw largely, with a certainty that his bills will be answered. We can prove, by a letter produced in evidence, that this villain Robertson, from the bottom of the dungeon whence he already probably meditated the escape which he afterwards accomplished by the assistance of his comrade, contrived to exercise authority over the mind, and to direct the motions, of this unhappy girl. It was in compliance with his injunctions, expressed in that letter, that the panel was prevailed upon to alter the line of conduct which her own better thoughts had suggested ; and, instead of resorting, when her time of travail approached, to the protection of her own family, was induced to confide herself to the charge of some vile agent of this nefarious seducer, and by her conducted to one of those solitary and secret purlieus of villany, which, to the shame of our police, still are suffered to exist in the suburbs of this city, where, with the assistance, and under the charge, of a person of her own sex, she bore a male child, under circumstances which added treble bitterness to the woe denounced against our original mother. What purpose Robertson had in all this, it is hard to tell or even to guess. He may have meant to marry the girl, for her father is a man of substance. But for the termination of the story, and the conduct of the woman whom he had placed about the person of Euphemia Deans, it is still more difficult to account. The unfortunate young woman was visited by the fever incidental to her situation. In this fever she appears to have been deceived by the person that waited on her, and, on recovering her senses, she found that she was childless in that abode of misery. Her infant had been carried off, perhaps for the worst purposes, by the wretch that waited on her. It may have been murdered for what I can tell."

He was here interrupted by a piercing shriek, uttered by the unfortunate prisoner. She was with difficulty brought to compose herself. Her counsel availed himself of the tragical interruption to close his pleading with effect.

" My lords," said he, " in that piteous cry you heard the eloquence of maternal affection, far surpassing the force of my poor words : Rachel weeping for her children ! Nature herself bears testimony in favor of the tenderness and acuteness

of the prisoner's parental feelings.   I will not dishonor her
plea by adding a word more."

   " Heard ye ever the like o' that, Laird ?" said Saddletree
to Dumbiedikes, when the counsel had ended his speech.
" There's a chield can spin a muckle pirn out of a wee tait of
tow !   Deil haet he kens mair about it than what's in the
declaration, and a surmise that Jeanie Deans suld hae been
able to say something about her sister's situation, whilk surmise, Mr. Crossmyloof says, rests on sma' authority.   And
he's cleckit this great muckle bird out o' this wee egg !   He
could wile the very flounders out o' the Firth.   What garr'd
my father no send me to Utrecht ?   But whisht ! the Court
is gaun to pronounce the interlocutor of relevancy."

   And accordingly the Judges, after a few words, recorded
their judgment, which bore, that the indictment, if proved,
was relevant to infer the pains of law ; and that the defence,
that the panel had communicated her situation to her sister,
was a relevant defence ; and, finally, appointed the said indictment and defence to be submitted to the judgment of an
assize.

CHAPTER XXIII

Most righteous judge ! a sentence.   Come, prepare.
Merchant of Venice.

It is by no means my intention to describe minutely the
forms of a Scottish criminal trial, nor am I sure that I could
draw up an account so intelligible and accurate as to abide
the criticism of the gentlemen of the long robe.   It is enough
to say that the jury was impanelled, and the case proceeded.
The prisoner was again required to plead to the charge, and
she again replied, "Not Guilty," in the same heart-thrilling
tone as before.

The crown counsel then called two or three female witnesses,
by whose testimony it was established that Effie's situation had
been remarked by them, that they had taxed her with the
fact, and that her answers had amounted to an angry and
petulant denial of what they charged her with.   But, as very
frequently happens, the declaration of the panel or accused
party herself was the evidence which bore hardest upon her
case.

In the event of these Tales ever finding their way across
the Border, it may be proper to apprise the southern reader
that it is the practice in Scotland, on apprehending a suspected person, to subject him to a judicial examination before a magistrate.   He is not compelled to answer any of the
questions asked of him, but may remain silent if he sees it his
interest to do so.   But whatever answers he chooses to give
are formally written down, and being subscribed by himself
and the magistrate, are produced against the accused in case
of his being brought to trial.   It is true, that these declarations are not produced as being in themselves evidence properly so called, but only as *adminicles* of testimony, tending to
corroborate what is considered as legal and proper evidence.
Notwithstanding this nice distinction, however, introduced
by lawyers to reconcile this procedure to their own general
rule, that a man cannot be required to bear witness against
himself, it nevertheless usually happens that these declarations become the means of condemning the accused, as it

were, out of their own mouths. The prisoner, upon these previous examinations, has indeed the privilege of remaining silent if he pleases ; but every man necessarily feels that a refusal to answer natural and pertinent interrogatories, put by judicial authority, is in itself a strong proof of guilt, and will certainly lead to his being committed to prison ; and few can renounce the hope of obtaining liberty by giving some specious account of themselves, and showing apparent frankness in explaining their motives and accounting for their conduct. It therefore seldom happens that the prisoner refuses to give a judicial declaration, in which, nevertheless, either by letting out too much of the truth, or by endeavoring to substitute a fictitious story, he almost always exposes himself to suspicion and to contradictions, which weigh heavily in the minds of the jury.

The declaration of Effie Deans was uttered on other principles, and the following is a sketch of its contents, given in the judicial form in which they may still be found in the *Books of Adjournal.*

The declarant admitted a criminal intrigue with an individual whose name she desired to conceal. "Being interrogated, what her reason was for secrecy on this point ? She declared, that she had no right to blame that person's conduct more than she did her own, and that she was willing to confess her own faults, but not to say anything which might criminate the absent. Interrogated, if she confessed her situation to any one, or made any preparation for her confinement ? Declares, she did not. And being interrogated, why she forbore to take steps which her situation so peremptorily required ? Declares, she was ashamed to tell her friends, and she trusted the person she has mentioned would provide for her and the infant. Interrogated, if he did so ? Declares, that he did not do so personally ; but that it was not his fault, for that the declarant is convinced he would have laid down his life sooner than the bairn or she had come to harm. Interrogated, what prevented him from keeping his promise ? Declares, that it was impossible for him to do so, he being under trouble at the time, and declines further answer to this question. Interrogated, where she was from the period she left her master, Mr. Saddletree's family, until her appearance at her father's, at St. Leonard's, the day before she was apprehended ? Declares, she does not remember. And, on the interrogatory being repeated, declares, she does not mind muckle about it, for she was very ill. On the question being again repeated, she declares, she will tell the truth, if it should be the undoing of her, so long as she is not asked to tell on other folk ; and admits, that she passed that interval of time in the lodging of a woman, an acquaintance of that person who had wished her to that place to be delivered, and that she was there delivered accordingly of a male child. Interrogated, what was the name of that person ? Declares and refuses to answer this question. Interrogated, where she lives ? Declares, she has no certainty, for that she was taken to the lodging aforesaid under cloud of night. Interrogated, if the lodging was in the city or suburbs ? Declares and refuses to answer that question. Interrogated, whether, when she left the house of Mr. Saddletree, she went up or down the street ? Declares and refuses to answer the question. Interrogated, whether she had ever seen the woman before she was wished to her, as she termed it, by the person whose name she refuses to answer ? Declares and replies, not to her knowledge. Interrogated, whether this woman was introduced to her by the said person verbally, or by word of mouth ? Declares, she has no freedom to answer this question. Interrogated, if the child was alive when it was born ? Declares, that—God help her and it !—it certainly was alive. Interrogated, if it died a natural death after birth ? Declares, not to her knowledge. Interrogated, where it now is ? Declares, she would give her right hand to ken, but that she never hopes to see mair than the banes of it. And being interrogated, why she supposes it is now dead ? the declarant wept bitterly, and made no answer. Interrogated, if the woman in whose lodging she was seemed to be a fit person to be with her in that situation ? Declares, she might be fit .enough for skill, but that she was a hard-hearted bad woman. Interrogated, if there was any other person in the lodging excepting themselves two ? Declares, that she thinks there was another woman ; but her head was so carried with pain of body and trouble of mind that she minded her very little. Interrogated, when the child was taken away from her ? Declared, that she fell in a fever, and was light-headed, and when she came to her own mind the woman told her the bairn was dead ; and that the declarant answered, if it was dead it had had foul play. That, thereupon, the woman was very sair on her, and gave her much ill language ; and that the deponent was frightened, and crawled out of the house when her back was turned, and went home to St. Leonard's Crags, as well as a woman in her condition dought. Interrogated, why she did not tell her story to her sister and father, and get force to search the house for her child, dead or alive ? Declares, it was her purpose to do so, but she had not time.　Interrogated, why she now conceals the name of the woman, and the place of her abode ?　The declarant remained silent for a time, and then said, that to do so could not repair the skaith that was done, but might be the occasion of more.　Interrogated, whether she had herself, at any time, had any purpose of putting away the child by violence ?　Declares, never ; so might God be merciful to her ; and then again declares, never, when she was in her perfect senses ; but what bad thoughts the Enemy might put into her brain when she was out of herself, she cannot answer.　And again solemnly interrogated, declares, that she would have been drawn with wild horses rather than have touched the bairn with an unmotherly hand.　Interrogated, declares, that among the ill language the woman gave her, she did say sure enough that the declarant had hurt the bairn when she was in the brain fever ; but that the declarant does not believe that she said this from any other cause than to frighten her, and make her be silent.　Interrogated, what else the woman said to her ?　Declares, that when the declarant cried loud for her bairn, and was like to raise the neighbors, the woman threatened her, that they that could stop the wean's skirling would stop hers, if she did not keep a' the lounder.　And that this threat, with the manner of the woman, made the declarant conclude that the bairn's life was gone, and her own in danger, for that the woman was a desperate bad woman, as the declarant judged, from the language she used.　Interrogated, declares, that the fever and delirium were brought on her by hearing bad news, suddenly told to her, but refuses to say what the said news related to.　Interrogated, why she does not now communicate these particulars, which might, perhaps, enable the magistrate to ascertain whether the child is living or dead, and requested to observe, that her refusing to do so exposes her own life, and leaves the child in bad hands, as also, that her present refusal to answer on such points is inconsistent with her alleged intention to make a clean breast to her sister ?　Declares, that she kens the bairn is now dead, or, if living, there is one that will lock after it ; that for her own living or dying, she is in God's hands, who knows her innocence of harming her bairn with her will or knowledge ; and that she has altered her resolution of speaking out, which she entertained when she left the woman's lodging, on account of a matter which she has since learned. And declares, in general, that she is wearied, and will answer no more questions at this time."

Upon a subsequent examination, Euphemia Deans adhered

to the declaration she had formerly made, with this addition, that a paper found in her trunk being shown to her, she admitted that it contained the credentials in consequence of which she resigned herself to the conduct of the woman at whose lodgings she was delivered of the child. Its tenor ran thus:

"DEAREST EFFIE,

"I have gotten the means to send to you by a woman who is well qualified to assist you in your approaching streight; she is not what I could wish her, but I cannot do better for you in my present condition. I am obliged to trust to her in this present calamity, for myself and you too. I hope for the best, though I am now in a sore pinch; yet thought is free. I think Handie Dandie and I may queer the stifler for all that is come and gone. You will be angry for me writing this to my little Cameronian Lily; but if I can but live to be a comfort to you, and a father to your baby, you will have plenty of time to scold. Once more, let none know your counsel. My life depends on this hag, d—n her; she is both deep and dangerous, but she has more wiles and wit than ever were in a beldam's head, and has cause to be true to me. Farewell, my Lily. Do not droop on my account; in a week I will be yours, or no more my own."

Then followed a postscript. "If they must truss me, I will repent of nothing so much, even at the last hard pinch, as of the injury I have done my Lily."

Effie refused to say from whom she had received this letter, but enough of the story was now known to ascertain that it came from Robertson; and from the date it appeared to have been written about the time when Andrew Wilson, called for a nickname Handie Dandie, and he were meditating their first abortive attempt to escape, which miscarried in the manner mentioned in the beginning of this history.

The evidence of the crown being concluded, the counsel for the prisoner began to lead a proof in her defence. The first witnesses were examined upon the girl's character. All gave her an excellent one, but none with more feeling than worthy Mrs. Saddletree, who, with the tears on her cheeks, declared, that she could not have had a higher opinion of Effie Deans, nor a more sincere regard for her, if she had been her own daughter. All present gave the honest woman credit for her goodness of heart, excepting her husband, who whispered to Dumbiedikes, "That Nichil Novit of yours is but a raw hand at leading evidence, I'm thinking. What signified his bringing a woman here to snotter and snivel, and bather their Lordships ? He should hae ceeted me, sir, and I should hae gien them sic a screed o' testimony, they shouldna hae touched a hair o' her head."

"Hadna ye better get up and try't yet ?" said the Laird. "I'll mak a sign to Novit."

"Na, na," said Saddletree, "thank ye for naething, neighbor : that would be ultroneous evidence, and I ken what belangs to that; but Nichil Novit suld hae had me ceeted *debito tempore.*" And wiping his mouth with his silk handkerchief with great importance, he resumed the port and manner of an edified and intelligent auditor.

Mr. Fairbrother now premised, in a few words, "that he meant to bring forward his most important witness, upon whose evidence the cause must in a great measure depend. What his client was, they had learned from the preceding witnesses ; and so far as general character, given in the most forcible terms, and even with tears, could interest every one in her fate, she had already gained that advantage. It was necessary, he admitted, that he should produce more positive testimony of her innocence than what arose out of general character, and this he undertook to do by the mouth of the person to whom she had communicated her situation—by the mouth of her natural counsellor and guardian—her sister. Macer, call into court Jean or Jeanie Deans, daughter of David Deans, cow-feeder, at St. Leonard's Crags."

When he uttered these words, the poor prisoner instantly started up and stretched herself half-way over the bar, towards the side at which her sister was to enter. And when, slowly following the officer, the witness advanced to the foot of the table, Effie, with the whole expression of her countenance altered from that of confused shame and dismay to an eager, imploring, and almost ecstatic earnestness of entreaty, with outstretched hands, hair streaming back, eyes raised eagerly to her sister's face, and glistening through tears, exclaimed, in a tone which went through the heart of all who heard her— "O Jeanie—Jeanie, save me—save me !"

With a different feeling, yet equally appropriated to his proud and self-dependent character, old Deans drew himself back still further under the cover of the bench ; so that when Jeanie, as she entered the court, cast a timid glance towards the place at which she had left him seated, his venerable figure was no longer visible. He sat down on the other side of Dumbiedikes, wrung his hand hard, and whispered, "Ah,

Laird, this is warst of a'—if I can but win ower this part! I feel my head unco dizzy; but my Master is strong in His servant's weakness." After a moment's mental prayer, he again started up, as if impatient of continuing in any one posture, and gradually edged himself forward towards the place he had just quitted.

Jeanie in the meantime had advanced to the bottom of the table, when, unable to resist the impulse of affection, she suddenly extended her hand to her sister. Effie was just within the distance that she could seize it with both hers, press it to her mouth, cover it with kisses, and bathe it in tears, with the fond devotion that a Catholic would pay to a guardian saint descended for his safety; while Jeanie, hiding her own face with her other hand, wept bitterly. The sight would have moved a heart of stone, much more of flesh and blood. Many of the spectators shed tears, and it was some time before the presiding Judge himself could so far subdue his emotion as to request the witness to compose herself, and the prisoner to forbear those marks of eager affection, which, however natural, could not be permitted at that time and in that presence.

The solemn oath—"the truth to tell, and no truth to conceal, as far as she knew or should be asked," was then administered by the Judge "in the name of God, and as the witness should answer to God at the great day of judgment;" an awful adjuration, which seldom fails to make impression even on the most hardened characters, and to strike with fear even the most upright. Jeanie, educated in deep and devout reverence for the name and attributes of the Deity, was, by the solemnity of a direct appeal to His person and justice, awed, but at the same time elevated above all considerations save those which she could, with a clear conscience, call HIM to witness. She repeated the form in a low and reverent, but distinct, tone of voice after the Judge, to whom, and not to any inferior officer of the court, the task is assigned in Scotland of directing the witness in that solemn appeal which is the sanction of his testimony.

When the Judge had finished the established form, he added, in a feeling, but yet a monitory, tone, an advice which the circumstances appeared to him to call for.

"Young woman," these were his words, "you come before this Court in circumstances which it would be worse than cruel not to pity and to sympathize with. Yet it is my duty to tell you, that the truth, whatever its consequences may be —the truth is what you owe to your country, and to that God whose word is truth, and whose name you have now invoked. Use your own time in answering the questions that gentleman [pointing to the counsel] shall put to you. But remember, that for what you may be tempted to say beyond what is the actual truth, you must answer both here and hereafter."

The usual questions were then put to her : Whether any one had instructed her what evidence she had to deliver? Whether any one had given or promised her any good deed, hire, or reward for her testimony? Whether she had any malice or ill-will at his Majesty's Advocate, being the party against whom she was cited as a witness? To which questions she successively answered by a quiet negative. But their tenor gave great scandal and offence to her father, who was not aware that they are put to every witness as a matter of form.

"Na, na," he exclaimed, loud enough to be heard, "my bairn is no like the widow of Tekoah : nae man has putten words into her mouth."

"One of the Judges, better acquainted, perhaps, with the *Books of Adjournal* than with the Book of Samuel, was disposed to make some instant inquiry after this widow of Tekoah, who, as he construed the matter, had been tampering with the evidence. But the presiding Judge, better versed in Scripture history, whispered to his learned brother the necessary explanation ; and the pause occasioned by this mistake had the good effect of giving Jeanie Deans time to collect her spirits for the painful task she had to perform.

Fairbrother, whose practice and intelligence were considerable, saw the necessity of letting the witness compose herself. In his heart he suspected that she came to bear false witness in her sister's cause.

"But that is her own affair," thought Fairbrother ; "and it is my business to see that she has plenty of time to regain composure, and to deliver her evidence, be it true or be it false, *valeat quantum.*"

Accordingly, he commenced his interrogatories with uninteresting questions, which admitted of instant reply.

"You are, I think, the sister of the prisoner ?"

"Yes, sir."

"Not the full sister, however ?"

"No, sir ; we are by different mothers."

"True ; and you are, I think, several years older than your sister ?"

"Yes, sir," etc.

After the advocate had conceived that, by these preliminary and unimportant questions, he had familiarized the witness with the situation in which she stood, he asked, " whether she had not remarked her sister's state of health to be altered, during the latter part of the term when she had lived with Mrs. Saddletree ? "

Jeanie answered in the affirmative.

" And she told you the cause of it, my dear, I suppose ? " said Fairbrother, in an easy, and, as one may say, an inductive sort of tone.

" I am sorry to interrupt my brother," said the Crown Counsel, rising, " but I am in your Lordships' judgment, whether this be not a leading question ? "

" If this point is to be debated," said the presiding Judge, " the witness must be removed."

For the Scottish lawyers regard with a sacred and scrupulous horror every question so shaped by the counsel examining as to convey to a witness the least intimation of the nature of the answer which is desired from him.   These scruples, though founded on an excellent principle, are sometimes carried to an absurd pitch of nicety, especially as it is generally easy for a lawyer who has his wits about him to elude the objection. Fairbrother did so in the present case.

" It is not necessary to waste the time of the Court, my lord ; since the King's Counsel thinks it worth while to object to the form of my question, I will shape it otherwise. Pray, young woman, did you ask your sister any question when you observed her looking unwell ? Take courage—speak out."

" I asked her," replied Jeanie, " what ailed her."

" Very well—take your own time—and what was the answer she made ? " continued Mr. Fairbrother.   ·

Jeanie was silent, and looked deadly pale.   It was not that she at any one instant entertained an idea of the possibility of prevarication : it was the natural hesitation to extinguish the last spark of hope that remained for her sister.

" Take courage, young woman," said Fairbrother.   " I asked what your sister said ailed her when you inquired ? "

" Nothing," answered Jeanie, with a faint voice, which was yet heard distinctly in the most distant corner of the court-room—such an awful and profound silence had been preserved during the anxious interval which had interposed betwixt the lawyer's question and the answer of the witness.

Fairbrother's countenance fell ; but with that ready presence of mind which is as useful in civil as in military emergencies, he immediately rallied.   " Nothing ? True ; you mean nothing at *first;* but when you asked her again, did she not tell you what ailed her ?"

The question was put in a tone meant to make her comprehend the importance of her answer, had she not been already aware of it. The ice was broken, however, and with less pause than at first, she now replied—"Alack! alack! she never breathed word to me about it."

A deep groan passed through the Court. It was echoed by one deeper and more agonized from the unfortunate father. The hope, to which unconsciously, and in spite of himself, he had still secretly clung, had now dissolved, and the venerable old man fell forward senseless on the floor of the court-house, with his head at the foot of his terrified daughter. The unfortunate prisoner, with impotent passion, strove with the guards betwixt whom she was placed. "Let me gang to my father! I *will* gang to him—I *will* gang to him ; he is dead—he is killed ; I hae killed him !" she repeated, in frenzied tones of grief, which those who heard them did not speedily forget.

Even in this moment of agony and general confusion, Jeanie did not lose that superiority which a deep and firm mind assures to its possessor under the most trying circumstances.

"He is my father—he is our father," she mildly repeated to those who endeavored to separate them, as she stooped, shaded aside his gray hairs, and began assiduously to chafe his temples.

The Judge, after repeatedly wiping his eyes, gave directions that they should be conducted into a neighboring apartment, and carefully attended. The prisoner, as her father was borne from the court, and her sister slowly followed, pursued them with her eyes so earnestly fixed, as if they would have started from their sockets. But when they were no longer visible, she seemed to find, in her despairing and deserted state, a courage which she had not yet exhibited.

"The bitterness of it is now past," she said, and then boldly addressed the Court. "My lords, if it is your pleasure to gang on wi' this matter, the weariest day will hae its end at last."

The Judge, who, much to his honor, had shared deeply in the general sympathy, was surprised at being recalled to his duty by the prisoner. He collected himself, and requested to know if the panel's counsel had more evidence to produce. Fairbrother replied, with an air of dejection, that his proof was concluded.

The King's Counsel addressed the jury for the crown. He said in few words, that no one could be more concerned than he was for the distressing scene which they had just witnessed.

But it was the necessary consequence of great crimes to bring distress and ruin upon all connected with the perpetrators. He briefly reviewed the proof, in which he showed that all the circumstances of the case concurred with those required by the act under which the unfortunate prisoner was tried : that the counsel for the panel had totally failed in proving that Euphemia Deans had communicated her situation to her sister ; that, respecting her previous good character, he was sorry to observe, that it was females who possessed the world's good report, and to whom it was justly valuable, who were most strongly tempted, by shame and fear of the world's censure, to the crime of infanticide ; that the child was murdered, he professed to entertain no douht. The vacillating and inconsistent declaration of the prisoner herself, marked as it was by numerous refusals to speak the truth on subjects when, according to her own story, it would have been natural, as well as advantageous, to have been candid—even this imperfect declaration left no doubt in his mind as to the fate of the unhappy infant. Neither could he doubt that the panel was a partner in this guilt. Who else had an interest in a deed so inhuman ? Surely neither Robertson, nor Robertson's agent, in whose house she was delivered, had the least temptation to commit such a crime, unless upon her account, with her connivance, and for the sake of saving her reputation. But it was not required of him by the law that he should bring precise proof of the murder, or of the prisoner's accession to it. It was the very purpose of the statute to substitute a certain chain of presumptive evidence in place of a probation, which, in such cases, it was peculiarly difficult to obtain. The jury might peruse the statute itself, and they had also the libel and interlocutor of relevancy to direct them in point of law. He put it to the conscience of the jury, that under both he was entitled to a verdict of Guilty.

The charge of Fairbrother was much cramped by his having failed in the proof which he expected to lead. But he fought his losing cause with courage and constancy. He ventured to arraign the severity of the statute under which the young woman was tried. "In all other cases," he said, "the first thing required of the criminal prosecutor was, to prove unequivocally that the crime libelled had actually been committed, which lawyers called proving the *corpus delicti*. But this statute, made doubtless with the best intentions, and under the impulse of a just horror for the unnatural crime of infanticide, run the risk of itself occasioning the worst of murders, the death of an innocent person, to atone for a sup-

posed crime which may never have been committed by any one.
He was so far from acknowledging the alleged probability of
the child's violent death, that he could not even allow that
there was evidence of its having ever lived."

The King's Counsel pointed to the woman's declaration ;
to which the counsel replied—"A production concocted in
a moment of terror and agony, and which approached to insanity," he said, "his learned brother well knew was no
sound evidence against the party who emitted it. It was
true, that a judicial confession, in presence of the justices
themselves, was the strongest of all proof, in so much that it
is said in law, that '*in confitentem nullæ sunt partes judicis.*'
But this was true of judicial confession only, by which law
meant that which is made in presence of the justices and the
sworn inquest. Of extrajudicial confession, all authorities
held with the illustrious Farinaceus and Matheus, '*confessio
extrajudicialis in se nulla est; et quod nullum est, non po-
test adminiculari.*' It was totally inept, and void of all
strength and effect from the beginning ; incapable, therefore,
of being bolstered up or supported, or, according to the law-
phrase, adminiculated, by other presumptive circumstances.
In the present case, therefore, letting the extrajudicial confession go, as it ought to go, for nothing," he contended,
" the prosecutor had not made out the second quality of the
statute, that a live child had been born ; and *that*, at least,
ought to be established before presumptions were received
that it had been murdered. If any of the assize," he said,
"should be of opinion that this was dealing rather narrowly
with the statute, they ought to consider that it was in its
nature highly penal, and therefore entitled to no favorable
construction."

He concluded a learned speech with an eloquent perora-
tion on the scene they had just witnessed, during which Saddletree fell fast asleep.

It was now the presiding Judge's turn to address the jury.
He did so briefly and distinctly.

"It was for the jury," he said, "to consider whether the
prosecutor had made out his plea. For himself, he sincerely
grieved to say that a shadow of doubt remained not upon his
mind concerning the verdict which the inquest had to bring
in. He would not follow the prisoner's counsel through the
impeachment which he had brought against the statute of
King William and Queen Mary. He and the jury were sworn
to judge according to the laws as they stood, not to criticise,
or to evade, or even to justify them. In no civil case would
a counsel have been permitted to plead his client's case in the

teeth of the law; but in the hard situation in which counsel were often placed in the Criminal Court, as well as out of favor to all presumptions of innocence, he had not inclined to interrupt the learned gentleman, or narrow his plea. The present law, as it now stood, had been instituted by the wisdom of their fathers, to check the alarming progress of a dreadful crime; when it was found too severe for its purpose, it would doubtless be altered by the wisdom of the legislature; at present it was the law of the land, the rule of the court, and, according to the oath which they had taken, it must be that of the jury. This unhappy girl's situation could not be doubted: that she had borne a child, and that the child had disappeared, were certain facts. The learned counsel had failed to show that she had communicated her situation. All the requisites of the case required by the statute were therefore before the jury. The learned gentleman had, indeed, desired them to throw out of consideration the panel's own confession, which was the plea usually urged, in penury of all others, by counsel in his situation, who usually felt that the declarations of their clients bore hard on them. · But that the Scottish law designed that a certain weight should be laid on these declarations, which, he admitted, were *quodammodo* extrajudicial, was evident from the universal practice by which they were always produced and read, as part of the prosecutor's probation. In the present case, no person who had heard the witnesses describe the appearance of the young woman before she left Saddletree's house, and contrasted it with that of her state and condition at her return to her father's, could have any doubt that the fact of delivery had taken place, as set forth in her own declaration, which was, therefore, not a solitary piece of testimony, but adminiculated and supported by the strongest circumstantial proof.

"He did not," he said, "state the impression upon his own mind with the purpose of biassing theirs. He had felt no less than they had done from the scene of domestic misery which had been exhibited before them; and if they, having God and a good conscience, the sanctity of their oath, and the regard due to the law of the country, before their eyes, could come to a conclusion favorable to this unhappy prisoner, he should rejoice as much as any one in Court; for never had he found his duty more distressing than in discharging it that day, and glad he would be to be relieved from the still more painful task which would otherwise remain for him."

The jury, having heard the Judge's address, bowed and retired, preceded by a macer of Court, to the apartment destined for their deliberation.

CHAPTER XXIV

Law, take thy victim. May she find the mercy
In yon mild heaven, which this hard world denies her!

IT was an hour ere the jurors returned, and as they traversed
the crowd with slow steps, as men about to discharge themselves of a heavy and painful responsibility, the audience was
hushed into profound, earnest, and awful silence.

"Have you agreed on your chancellor, gentlemen?" was
the first question of the Judge.

The foreman, called in Scotland the chancellor of the jury,
usually the man of best rank and estimation among the as-
sizers, stepped forward, and, with a low reverence, delivered
to the Court a sealed paper, containing the verdict, which,
until of late years that verbal returns are in some instances
permitted, was always couched in writing. The jury remained
standing while the Judge broke the seals, and, having perused
the paper, handed it, with an air of mournful gravity, down
to the Clerk of Court, who proceeded to engross in the record
the yet unknown verdict, of which, however, all omened the
tragical contents. A form still remained, trifling and unimportant in itself, but to which imagination adds a sort of solemnity, from the awful occasion upon which it is used. A
lighted candle was placed on the table, the original paper
containing the verdict was enclosed in a sheet of paper, and,
sealed with the Judge's own signet, was transmitted to the
Crown Office, to be preserved among other records of the same
kind. As all this is transacted in profound silence, the producing and extinguishing the candle seems a type of the human
spark which is shortly afterwards doomed to be quenched, and
excites in the spectators something of the same effect which
in England is obtained by the Judge assuming the fatal cap
of judgment. When these preliminary forms had been gone
through, the Judge required Euphemia Deans to attend to the
verdict to be read.

After the usual words of style, the verdict set forth, that
the jury, having made choice of John Kirk, Esq., to be
their chancellor, and Thomas Moore, merchant, to be their

clerk, did, by a plurality of voices, find the said Euphemia Deans GUILTY of the crime libelled; but, in consideration of her extreme youth, and the cruel circumstances of her case, did earnestly entreat that the Judge would recommend her to the mercy of the Crown.

"Gentlemen," said the Judge, "you have done your duty, and a painful one it must have been to men of humanity like you. I will, undoubtedly, transmit your recommendation to the throne. But it is my duty to tell all who now hear me, but especially to inform that unhappy young woman, in order that her mind may be settled accordingly, that I have not the least hope of a pardon being granted in the present case. You know the crime has been increasing in this land, and I know further, that this has been ascribed to the lenity in which the laws have been exercised, and that there is therefore no hope whatever of obtaining a remission for this offence." The jury bowed again, and, released from their painful office, dispersed themselves among the mass of bystanders.

The Court then asked Mr. Fairbrother whether he had anything to say, why judgment should not follow on the verdict? The counsel had spent some time in perusing and re-perusing the verdict, counting the letters in each juror's name, and weighing every phrase, nay, every syllable, in the nicest scales of legal criticism. But the clerk of the jury had understood his business too well. No flaw was to be found, and Fairbrother mournfully intimated that he had nothing to say in arrest of judgment.

The presiding Judge then addressed the unhappy prisoner: "Euphemia Deans, attend to the sentence of the Court now to be pronounced against you."

She rose from her seat, and, with a composure far greater than could have been augured from her demeanor during some parts of the trial, abode the conclusion of the awful scene. So nearly does the mental portion of our feelings resemble those which are corporal, that the first severe blows which we receive bring with them a stunning apathy, which renders us indifferent to those that follow them. Thus said Mandrin,* when he was undergoing the punishment of the wheel; and so have all felt upon whom successive inflictions have descended with continuous and reiterated violence.

"Young woman," said the Judge, "it is my painful duty to tell you, that your life is forfeited under a law which, if it may seem in some degree severe, is yet wisely so, to render those of

* He was known as captain-general of French smugglers. See a Tract on his exploits, printed 1753 (*Laing*).

your unhappy situation aware what risk they run, by concealing, out of pride or false shame, their lapse from virtue, and making no preparation to save the lives of the unfortunate infants whom they are to bring into the world. When you concealed your situation from your mistress, your sister, and other worthy and compassionate persons of your own sex, in whose favor your former conduct had given you a fair place, you seem to me to have had in your contemplation, at least, the death of the helpless creature for whose life you neglected to provide. How the child was disposed of—whether it was dealt upon by another, or by yourself; whether the extraordinary story you have told is partly false, or altogether so, is between God and your own conscience. I will not aggravate your distress by pressing on that topic, but I do most solemnly adjure you to employ the remaining space of your time in making your peace with God, for which purpose such reverend clergyman as you yourself may name shall have access to you. Notwithstanding the humane recommendation of the jury, I cannot afford to you, in the present circumstances of the country, the slightest hope that your life will be prolonged beyond the period assigned for the execution of your sentence. Forsaking, therefore, the thoughts of this world, let your mind be prepared by repentance for those of more awful moments—for death, judgment, and eternity. Doomster,* read the sentence."

When the doomster showed himself, a tall haggard figure, arrayed in a fantastic garment of black and gray, passemented with silver lace, all fell back with a sort of instinctive horror, and made wide way for him to approach the foot of the table. As this office was held by the common executioner, men shouldered each other backward to avoid even the touch of his garment, and some were seen to brush their own clothes, which had accidentally become subject to such contamination. A sound went through the court, produced by each person drawing in their breath hard, as men do when they expect or witness what is frightful, and at the same time affecting. The caitiff villain yet seemed, amid his hardened brutality, to have some sense of his being the object of public detestation, which made him impatient of being in public, as birds of evil omen are anxious to escape from daylight and from pure air.

Repeating after the Clerk of Court, he gabbled over the words of the sentence, which condemned Euphemia Deans to be conducted back to the tolbooth of Edinburgh, and detained there until Wednesday the —— day of ——; and upon that

* See Note 26

day, betwixt the hours of two and four o'clock afternoon, to be conveyed to the common place of execution, and there hanged by the neck upon a gibbet. "And this," said the doomster, aggravating his harsh voice, "I pronounce for *doom.*"

He vanished when he had spoken the last emphatic word, like a foul fiend after the purpose of his visitation has been accomplished; but the impression of horror excited by his presence and his errand remained upon the crowd of spectators.

The unfortunate criminal—for so she must now be termed —with more susceptibility and more irritable feelings than her father and sister, was found, in this emergence, to possess a considerable share of their courage. She had remained standing motionless at the bar while the sentence was pronounced, and was observed to shut her eyes when the doomster appeared. But she was the first to break silence when that evil form had left his place.

"God forgive ye, my lords," she said, "and dinna be angry wi' me for wishing it—we a' need forgiveness. As for myself, I canna blame ye, for ye act up to your lights; and if I havena killed my poor infant, ye may witness a' that hae seen it this day, that I hae been the means of killing my gray-headed father. I deserve the warst frae man, and frae God too. But God is mair mercifu' to us than we are to each other."

With these words the trial concluded. The crowd rushed, bearing forward and shouldering each other, out of the court in the same tumultuary mode in which they had entered; and, in the excitation of animal motion and animal spirits, soon forgot whatever they had felt as impressive in the scene which they had witnessed. The professional spectators, whom habit and theory had rendered as callous to the distress of the scene as medical men are to those of a surgical operation, walked homeward in groups, discussing the general principle of the statute under which the young woman was condemned, the nature of the evidence, and the arguments of the counsel, without considering even that of the Judge as exempt from their criticism.

The female spectators, more compassionate, were loud in exclamation against that part of the Judge's speech which seemed to cut off the hope of pardon.

"Set him up, indeed," said Mrs. Howden, "to tell us that the poor lassie behoved to die, when Mr. John Kirk, as civil a gentleman as is within the ports of the town, took the pains to prigg for her himsell."

"Ay, but, neighbor," said Miss Damahoy, drawing up her

thin maidenly form to its full height of prim dignity, "I really think this unnatural business of having bastard bairns should be putten a stop to. There isna a hussy now on this side of thirty that you can bring within your doors, but there will be chields—writer-lads, prentice-lads, and what not—coming traiking after them for their destruction, and discrediting ane's honest house into the bargain. I hae nae patience wi' them."

"Hout, neighbor," said Mrs. Howden, "we suld live and let live ; we hae been young oursells, and we are no aye to judge the warst when lads and lasses forgather."

"Young oursells ! and judge the warst !" said Miss Damahoy. "I am no sae auld as that comes to, Mrs. Howden ; and as for what ye ca' the warst, I ken neither good nor bad about the matter, I thank my stars !"

"Ye are thankfu' for sma' mercies, then," said Mrs. Howden, with a toss of her head ; "and as for *you* and *young*—I trow ye were doing for yoursell at the last riding of the Scots Parliament, and that was in the gracious year seven, sae ye can be nae sic chicken at ony rate."

Plumdamas, who acted as squire of the body to the two contending dames, instantly saw the hazard of entering into such delicate points of chronology, and being a lover of peace and good neighborhood, lost no time in bringing back the conversation to its original subject. "The Judge didna tell us a' he could hae tell'd us, if he had liked, about the application for pardon, neighbors," said he ; "there is aye a wimple in a lawyer's clue ; but it's a wee bit of a secret."

"And what is't ?—what is't, neighbor Plumdamas ?" said Mrs. Howden and Miss Damahoy at once, the acid fermentation of their dispute being at once neutralized by the powerful alkali implied in the word "secret."

"Here's Mr. Saddletree can tell ye that better than me, for it was him that tauld me," said Plumdamas, as Saddletree came up, with his wife hanging on his arm and looking very disconsolate.

When the question was put to Saddletree, he looked very scornful. "They speak about stopping the frequency of child-murder," said he, in a contemptuous tone ; "do ye think our auld enemies of England, as Glendook aye ca's them in his printed Statute-book, care a boddle whether we didna kill ane anither, skin and birn, horse and foot, man, woman, and bairns, all and sindry, *omnes et singulos*, as Mr. Crossmyloof says ? Na, na, it's no *that* hinders them frae pardoning the bit lassie. But here is the pinch of the plea. The king and queen are sae ill pleased wi' that mistak about Porteous, that deil a kindly Scot will they pardon again, either by reprieve or remission, if the haill town o' Edinburgh should be a' hanged on ae tow."

"Deil that they were back at their German kale-yard, then, as my neighbor MacCroskie ca's it," said Mrs. Howden, "an that's the way they're gaun to guide us!"

"They say for certain," said Miss Damahoy, "that King George flang his periwig in the fire when he heard o' the Porteous mob."

"He has done that, they say," replied Saddletree, "for less thing."

"Aweel," said Miss Damahoy, "he might keep mair wit in his anger; but it's a' the better for his wigmaker, I'se warrant."

"The queen tore her biggonets for perfect anger, ye'll hae heard o' that too?" said Plumdamas. "And the king, they say, kickit Sir Robert Walpole for no keeping down the mob of Edinburgh; but I dinna believe he wad behave sae ungenteel."

"It's dooms truth, though," said Saddletree; "and he was for kickin' the Duke of Argyle* too."

"Kickin' the Duke of Argyle!" exclaimed the hearers at once, in all the various combined keys of utter astonishment.

"Ay, but MacCallummore's blood wadna sit down wi' that; there was risk of Andro Ferrara coming in thirdsman."

"The Duke is a real Scotsman—a true friend to the country," answered Saddletree's hearers.

"Ay, troth is he, to king and country baith, as ye sall hear," continued the orator, "if ye will come in bye to our house, for it's safest speaking of sic things *inter parietes*."

When they entered his shop he thrust his prentice boy out of it, and, unlocking his desk, took out, with an air of grave and complacent importance, a dirty and crumpled piece of printed paper. He observed, "This is new corn; it's no everybody could show ye the like o' this. It's the Duke's speech about the Porteous mob, just promulgated by the hawkers. Ye shall hear what Ian Roy Cean † says for himsell. My correspondent bought it in the palace-yard, that's like just under the king's nose. I think he claws up their mittens! It came in a letter about a foolish bill of exchange that the man wanted me to renew for him. I wish ye wad see about it, Mrs. Saddletree."

* See John Duke of Argyle and Greenwich. Note 27.
† Red John the Warrior, a name personal and proper in the Highlands to John Duke of Argyle and Greenwich, as MacCummin was that of his race or dynasty.

Honest Mrs. Saddletree had hitherto been so sincerely distressed about the situation of her unfortunate *protégée*, that she had suffered her husband to proceed in his own way, witnout attending to what he was saying. The words "bill" and "renew" had, however, an awakening sound in them; and she snatched the letter which her husband held towards her, and wiping her eyes, and putting on her spectacles, endeavored, as fast as the dew which collected on her glasses would permit, to get at the meaning of the needful part of the epistle; while her husband, with pompous elevation, read an extract from the speech.

"I am no minister, I never was a minister, and I never will be one——"

"I didna ken his Grace was ever designed for the ministry," interrupted Mrs. Howden.

"He disna mean a minister of the Gospel, Mrs. Howden, but a minister of state," said Saddletree, with condescending goodness, and then proceeded: "The time was when I might have been a piece of a minister, but I was too sensible of my own incapacity to engage in any state affair. And I thank God that I had always too great a value for those few abilities which nature has given me, to employ them in doing any drudgery, or any job of what kind soever. I have, ever since I set out in the world—and I believe few have set out more early—served my prince with my tongue; I have served him with any little interest I had; and I have served him with my sword, and in my profession of arms. I have held employments which I have lost, and were I to be to-morrow deprived of those which still remain to me, and which I have endeavored honestly to deserve, I would still serve him to the last acre of my inheritance, and to the last drop of my blood——"

Mrs. Saddletree here broke in upon the orator. "Mr. Saddletree, what *is* the meaning of a' this? Here are ye clavering about the Duke of Argyle, and this man Martingale gaun to break on our hands, and lose us gude sixty pounds. I wonder what duke will pay that, quotha. I wish the Duke of Argyle would pay his ain accounts. He is in a thousand punds Scots on thae very books when he was last at Roystoun. I'm no saying but he's a just nobleman, and that it's gude siller; but it wad drive ane daft to be confused wi' deukes and drakes, and thae distressed folk upstairs, that's Jeanie Deans and her father. And then, putting the very callant that was sewing the curpel out o' the shop, to play wi' blackguards in the close. Sit still, neighbors, it's no that I mean to disturb *you ;* but what between courts o' law and courts o' state, and upper and under parliaments, and parliament houses, here and in London, the gudeman's gane clean gyte, I think."

The gossips understood civility, and the rule of doing as they would be done by, too well to tarry upon the slight invitation implied in the conclusion of this speech, and therefore made their farewells and departure as fast as possible, Saddletree whispering to Plumdamas that he would "meet him at MacCroskie's (the low-browed shop in the Luckenbooths [Lawnmarket], already mentioned) in the hour of cause, and put MacCallummore's speech in his pocket, for a' the gudewife's din."

When Mrs. Saddletree saw the house freed of her importunate visitors, and the little boy reclaimed from the pastimes of the wynd to the exercise of the awl, she went to visit her unhappy relative, David Deans, and his elder daughter, who had found in her house the nearest place of friendly refuge.

CHAPTER XXV

WHEN Mrs. Saddletree entered the apartment in which her
guests had shrouded their misery, she found the window darkened.   The feebleness which followed his long swoon had
rendered it necessary to lay the old man in bed.   The curtains
were drawn around him, and Jeanie sat motionless by the side
of the bed.   Mrs. Saddletree was a woman of kindness, nay,
of feeling, but not of delicacy.   She opened the half-shut window, drew aside the curtain, and taking her kinsman by the
hand, exhorted him to sit up and bear his sorrow like a good
man, and a Christian man, as he was.   But when she quitted
his hand it fell powerless by his side, nor did he attempt the
least reply.

"Is all over ? " asked Jeanie, with lips and cheeks as pale
as ashes.   "And is there nae hope for her ? "

"Nane, or next to nane," said Mrs. Saddletree ; "I heard
the Judge-carle say it with my ain ears.   It was a burning
shame to see sae mony o' them set up yonder in their red gowns
and black gowns, and a' to take the life o' a bit senseless lassie.
I had never muckle broo o' my gudeman's gossips, and now I
like them waur than ever.   The only wise-like thing I heard
onybody say was decent Mr. John Kirk, of Kirk Knowe, and
he wussed them just to get the king's mercy, and nae mair
about it.   But he spake to unreasonable folk ; he might just
hae keepit his breath to hae blawn on his porridge."

"But *can* the king gie her mercy ? " said Jeanie, earnestly.   "Some folk tell me he canna gie mercy in cases of
mur——in cases like hers."

"*Can* he gie mercy, hinny ?   I weel I wot he *can*, when
he likes.   There was young Singlesword, that stickit the
Laird of Ballencleuch ; and Captain Hackum, the Englishman, that killed Lady Colgrain's gudeman ; and the Master
of St. Clair, that shot the twa Shaws ;* and mony mair in

* See Murder of the Two Shaws.   Note 28.

my time—to be sure they were gentle bluid, and had their kin
to speak for them—and there was Jock Porteous, the other
day.   I'se warrant there's mercy, an folk could win at it."

"Porteous!" said Jeanie; "very true.   I forget a' that I
suld maist mind.   Fare ye weel, Mrs. Saddletree; and may
ye never want a friend in the hour o' distress!"

"Will ye no stay wi' your father, Jeanie, bairn?   Ye had
better," said Mrs. Saddletree.

"I will be wanted ower yonder," indicating the tolbooth
with her hand, "and I maun leave him now, or I will never
be able to leave him.   I fearna for his life; I ken how strong-
hearted he is—I ken it," she said, laying her hand on her
bosom, "by my ain heart at this minute."

"Weel, hinny, if ye think it's for the best, better he stay
here and rest him than gang back to St. Leonard's."

"Muckle better—muckle better; God bless you—God
bless you!   At no rate let him gang till ye hear frae me,"
said Jeanie.

"But ye'll be back belyve?" said Mrs. Saddletree, detaining her; "they wunna let ye stay yonder, hinny."

"But I maun gang to St. Leonard's; there's muckle to be
dune and little time to do it in.   And I have friends to speak
to.   God bless you! take care of my father."

She had reached the door of the apartment when, suddenly
turning, she came back and knelt down by the bedside.   "O
father, gie me your blessing; I dare not go till ye bless me.
Say but 'God bless ye and prosper ye, Jeanie;' try but to
say that!"

Instinctively, rather than by an exertion of intellect, the
old man murmured a prayer that "purchased and promised
blessings might be multiplied upon her."

"He has blessed mine errand," said his daughter, rising
from her knees, "and it is borne in upon my mind that I
shall prosper."

So saying, she left the room.

Mrs. Saddletree looked after her, and shook her head.   "I
wish she binna roving, poor thing.   There's something queer
about a' thae Deanses.   I dinna like folk to be sae muckle
better than other folk; seldom comes gude o't.   But if she's
gaun to look after the kye at St. Leonard's, that's another
story; to be sure they maun be sorted.   Grizzie, come up here
and take tent to the honest auld man, and see he wants naething.   Ye silly tawpie [addressing the maid-servant as she
entered], what garr'd ye busk up your cockernony that gate?
I think there's been eneugh the day to gie an awfu' warning

about your cock-ups and your fal-lal duds; see what they a'
come to," etc., etc., etc.

Leaving the good lady to her lecture upon worldly vanities,
we must transport our reader to the cell in which the unfortunate Effie Deans was now immured, being restricted of several
liberties which she had enjoyed before the sentence was pronounced.

When she had remained about an hour in the state of stupefied horror so natural in her situation, she was disturbed by
the opening of the jarring bolts of her place of confinement,
and Ratcliffe showed himself. "It's your sister," he said,
"wants to speak t'ye, Effie."

"I canna see naebody," said Effie, with the hasty irritability which misery had rendered more acute—"I canna see
naebody, and least of a' her. Bid her take care of the auld
man: I am naething to ony o' them now, nor them to me."

"She says she maun see ye, though," said Ratcliffe; and
Jeanie, rushing into the apartment, threw her arms round
her sister's neck, who writhed to extricate herself from her
embrace.

"What signifies coming to greet ower me," said poor Effie,
"when you have killed me? killed me, when a word of your
mouth would have saved me; killed me, when I am an innocent creature—innocent of that guilt, at least—and me that
wad hae wared body and soul to save your finger from being
hurt!"

"You shall not die," said Jeanie, with enthusiastic firmness; "say what ye like o' me, think what ye like o' me, only
promise—for I doubt your proud heart—that ye wunna harm
yourself, and you shall not die this shameful death."

"A *shameful* death I will not die, Jeanie, lass. I have
that in my heart, though it has been ower kind a ane, that
wunna bide shame. Gae hame to our father, and think nae
mair on me: I have eat my last earthly meal."

"O, this was what I feared!" said Jeanie.

"Hout, tout, hinny," said Ratcliffe; "it's but little ye
ken o' thae things. Ane aye thinks at the first dinnle o' the
sentence, they hae heart eneugh to die rather than bide out
the sax weeks; but they aye bide the sax weeks out for a'
that. I ken the gate o't weel; I hae fronted the doomster
three times, and here I stand, Jim Ratcliffe, for a' that. Had
I tied my napkin strait the first time, as I had a great mind
till't—and it was a' about a bit gray cowt, wasna worth ten
punds sterling—where would I have been now?"

"And how *did* you escape?" said Jeanie, the fates of

this man, at first so odious to her, having acquired a sudden interest in her eyes from their correspondence with those of her sister.

"*How* did I escape?" said Ratcliffe, with a knowing wink. "I tell ye I 'scapit in a way that naebody will escape from this tolbooth while I keep the keys."

"My sister shall come out in the face of the sun," said Jeanie; "I will go to London and beg her pardon from the king and queen. If they pardoned Porteous, they may pardon her; if a sister asks a sister's life on her bended knees, they *will* pardon her—they *shall* pardon her—and they will win a thousand hearts by it."

Effie listened in bewildered astonishment, and so earnest was her sister's enthusiastic assurance, that she almost involuntarily caught a gleam of hope; but it instantly faded away.

"Ah, Jeanie! the king and queen live in London, a thousand miles from this—far ayont the saut sea; I'll be gane before ye win there!"

"You are mistaen," said Jeanie; "it is no sae far, and they.go to it by land: I learned something about thae things from Reuben Butler."

"Ah, Jeanie! ye never learned onything but what was gude frae the folk ye keepit company wi'; but I—but I——" She wrung her hands and wept bitterly.

"Dinna think on that now," said Jeanie; "there will be time for that if the present space be redeemed. Fare ye weel! Unless I die by the road, I will see the king's face that gies grace. O, sir [to Ratcliffe], be kind to her. She ne'er kenn'd what it was to need stranger's kindness till now. Fareweel—fareweel, Effie! Dinna speak to me; I maunna greet now, my head's ower dizzy already!"

She tore herself from her sister's arms, and left the cell. Ratcliffe followed her, and beckoned her into a small room. She obeyed his signal, but not without trembling.

"What's the fule thing shaking for?" said he; "I mean nothing but civility to you. D—n me, I respect you, and I can't help it. You have so much spunk, that—d—n me, but I think there's some chance of your carrying the day. But you must not go to the king till you have made some friend; try the Duke—try MacCallummore; he's Scotland's friend. I ken that the great folks dinna muckle like him; but they fear him, and that will serve your purpose as weel. D'ye ken naebody wad gie ye a letter to him?"

"Duke of Argyle!" said Jeanie, recollecting herself suddenly. " What was he to that Argyle that suffered in my father's time—in the persecution ? "

" His son or grandson, I'm thinking," said Ratcliffe ; " but what o' that ? "

" Thank God ! " said Jeanie, devoutly clasping her hands.

" You Whigs are aye thanking God for something," said the ruffian. " But hark ye, hinny, I'll tell ye a secret. Ye may meet wi' rough customers on the Border, or in the Midland, afore ye get to Lunnon. Now, deil ane o' them will touch an acquaintance o' Daddie Ratton's ; for though I am retired frae public practice, yet they ken I can do a gude or an ill turn yet ; and deil a gude fellow that has been but a twelvemonth on the lay, be he ruffler or padder, but he knows my gybe as well as the jark of e'er a queer cuffin in England —and there's rogue's Latin for you."

It was, indeed, totally unintelligible to Jeanie Deans, who was only impatient to escape from him. He hastily scrawled a line or two on a dirty piece of paper, and said to her, as she drew back when he offered it, " Hey ! what the deil ! it wunna bite you, my lass ; if it does nae gude, it can do nae ill. But I wish you to show it if you have ony fasherie wi' ony o' St. Nicholas's clerks."

" Alas ! " said she, " I do not understand what you mean ? "

" I mean, if ye fall among thieves, my precious ; that is a Scripture phrase, if ye will hae ane. The bauldest of them will ken a scart o' my guse feather. And now awa' wi' ye, and stick to Argyle ; if onybody can do the job, it maun be him."

After casting an anxious look at the grated windows and blackened walls of the old tolbooth, and another scarce less anxious at the hospitable lodging of Mrs. Saddletree, Jeanie turned her back on that quarter, and soon after on the city itself. She reached St. Leonard's Crags without meeting any one whom she knew, which, in the state of her mind, she considered as a great blessing. " I must do naething," she thought, as she went along, " that can soften or weaken my heart : it's ower weak already for what I hae to do. I will think and act as firmly as I can, and speak as little."

There was an ancient servant, or rather cottar, of her father's, who had lived under him for many years, and whose fidelity was worthy of full confidence. She sent for this woman, and explaining to her that the circumstances of her family required that she should undertake a journey which would detain her for some weeks from home, she gave her full instructions concerning the management of the domestic affairs in her absence. With a precision which, upon reflection, she herself could not help wondering at, she described and detailed the most minute steps which were to be taken, and especially such as were necessary for her father's comfort. "It was probable," she said, "that he would return to St. Leonard's to-morrow—certain that he would return very soon ; all must be in order for him. He had eneugh to distress him, without being fashed about warldly matters."

In the meanwhile she toiled busily, along with May Hettly, to leave nothing unarranged.

It was deep in the night when all these matters were settled; and when they had partaken of some food, the first which Jeanie had tasted on that eventful day, May Hettly, whose usual residence was a cottage at a little distance from Deans's house, asked her young mistress whether she would not permit her to remain in the house all night. "Ye hae had an awfu' day," she said, "and sorrow and fear are but bad companions in the watches of the night, as I hae heard the gudeman say himsell."

"They are ill companions indeed," said Jeanie ; "but I maun learn to abide their presence, and better begin in the house than in the field."

She dismissed her aged assistant accordingly—for so slight was the gradation in their rank of life that we can hardly term May a servant—and proceeded to make a few preparations for her journey.

The simplicity of her education and country made these preparations very brief and easy. Her tartan screen served all the purposes of a riding-habit and of an umbrella ; a small bundle contained such changes of linen as were absolutely necessary. Barefooted, as Sancho says, she had come into the world, and barefooted she proposed to perform her pilgrimage ; and her clean shoes and change of snow-white thread stockings were to be reserved for special occasions of ceremony. She was not aware that the English habits of *comfort* attach an idea of abject misery to the idea of a barefooted traveller ; and if the objection of cleanliness had been made to the practice, she would have been apt to vindicate herself upon the very frequent ablutions to which, with Mahometan scrupulosity, a Scottish damsel of some condition usually subjects herself. Thus far, therefore, all was well.

From an oaken press or cabinet, in which her father kept a few old books, and two or three bundles of papers, besides his ordinary accounts and receipts, she sought out and extracted from a parcel of notes of sermons, calculations of interest, records of dying speeches of the martyrs, and the like, one or two documents which she thought might be of some use to her upon her mission. But the most important difficulty remained behind, and it had not occurred to her until that very evening. It was the want of money, without which it was impossible she could undertake so distant a journey as she now meditated.

David Deans, as we have said, was easy, and even opulent, in his circumstances. But his wealth, like that of the patriarchs of old, consisted in his kine and herds, and in two or three sums lent out at interest to neighbors or relatives, who, far from being in circumstances to pay anything to account of the principal sums, thought they did all that was incumbent on them when, with considerable difficulty, they discharged "the annual rent." To these debtors it would be in vain, therefore, to apply, even with her father's concurrence ; nor could she hope to obtain such concurrence, or assistance in any mode, without such a series of explanations and debates as she felt might deprive her totally of the power of taking the step, which, however daring and hazardous, she knew was absolutely necessary for trying the last chance in favor of her sister. Without departing from filial reverence, Jeanie had an inward conviction that the feelings of her father, however just, and upright, and honorable, were too little in unison with the spirit of the time to admit of his being a good judge of the measures to be adopted in this crisis. Herself more flexible in manner, though no less upright in principle, she felt that to ask his consent to her pilgrimage would be to encounter the risk of drawing down his positive prohibition, and under that she believed her journey could not be blessed in its progress and event. Accordingly, she had determined upon the means by which she might communicate to him her undertaking and its purpose shortly after her actual departure. But it was impossible to apply to him for money without altering this arrangement, and discussing fully the propriety of her journey ; pecuniary assistance from that quarter, therefore, was laid out of the question.

It now occurred to Jeanie that she should have consulted with Mrs. Saddletree on this subject. But, besides the time that must now necessarily be lost in recurring to her assistance, Jeanie internally revolted from it. Her heart acknowledged the goodness of Mrs. Saddletree's general character, and the kind interest she took in their family misfortunes ; but still she felt that Mrs. Saddletree was a woman of an ordinary and worldly way of thinking, incapable, from habit and temperament, of taking a keen or enthusiastic view of such a resolution as she had formed ; and to debate the point with her, and to rely upon her conviction of its propriety for the means of carrying it into execution, would have been gall and worm-wood.

Butler, whose assistance she might have been assured of, was greatly poorer than herself. In these circumstances, she formed a singular resolution for the purpose of surmounting this difficulty, the execution of which will form the subject of the next chapter.

CHAPTER XXVI

'Tis the voice of the sluggard, I've heard him complain,
" You have waked me too soon, I must slumber again ; "
As the door on its hinges, so he on his bed,
Turns his side and his shoulders, and his heavy head.
DR. WATTS.

THE mansion-house of Dumbiedikes, to which we are now to introduce our readers, lay three or four miles—no matter for the exact topography—to the southward of St. Leonard's. It had once borne the appearance of some little celebrity ; for the Auld Laird, whose humors and pranks were often mentioned in the alehouses for about a mile round it, wore a sword, kept a good horse, and a brace of greyhounds ; brawled, swore, and betted at cock-fights and horse-matches ; followed Somerville of Drum's hawks and the Lord Ross's hounds ; and called himself point devise a gentleman. But the line had been veiled of its splendor in the present proprietor, who cared for no rustic amusements, and was as saving, timid, and retired as his father had been at once grasping and selfishly extravagant, daring, wild, and intrusive.

Dumbiedikes was what is called in Scotland a "single" house ; that is, having only one room occupying its whole depth from back to front, each of which single apartments was illuminated by six or eight cross lights, whose diminutive panes and heavy frames permitted scarce so much light to enter as shines through one well-constructed modern window. This inartificial edifice, exactly such as a child would build with cards, had a steep roof flagged with coarse gray stones instead of slates ; a half-circular turret, battlemented, or, to use the appropriate phrase, bartizan'd on the top, served as a case for a narrow turnpike-stair, by which an ascent was gained from story to story ; and at the bottom of the said turret was a door studded with large-headed nails. There was no lobby at the bottom of the tower, and scarce a landing-place opposite to the doors which gave access to the apartments. One or two low and dilapidated out-houses, connected by a courtyard wall equally ruinous, surrounded the mansion. The court had been paved, but the flags being partly displaced and partly renewed, a gallant crop of docks and thistles sprung up between them, and the small garden, which opened by a postern through the wall, seemed not to be in a much more orderly condition. Over the low-arched gateway which led into the yard, there was a carved stone, exhibiting some attempt at armorial bearings; and above the inner entrance hung, and had hung for many years, the mouldering hatchment, which announced that umquhile Laurence Dumbie of Dumbiedikes had been gathered to his fathers in Newbattle kirkyard. The approach to this palace of pleasure was by a road formed by the rude fragments of stone gathered from the fields, and it was surrounded by ploughed but unenclosed land. Upon a baulk, that is, an un-ploughed ridge of land interposed among the corn, the Laird's trusty palfrey was tethered by the head, and picking a meal of grass. The whole argued neglect and discomfort, the con-sequence, however, of idleness and indifference, not of poverty.

In this inner court, not without a sense of bashfulness and timidity, stood Jeanie Deans, at an early hour in a fine spring morning. She was no heroine of romance, and therefore looked with some curiosity and interest on the mansion-house and domains, of which, it might at that moment occur to her, a little encouragement, such as women of all ranks know by instinct how to apply, might have made her mistress. More-over, she was no person of taste beyond her time, rank, and country, and certainly thought the house of Dumbiedikes, though inferior to Holyrood House or the palace at Dalkeith, was still a stately structure in its way, and the land a "very bonny bit, if it were better seen to and done to." But Jeanie Deans was a plain, true-hearted, honest girl, who, while she acknowledged all the splendor of her old admirer's habitation, and the value of his property, never for a moment harbored a thought of doing the Laird, Butler, or herself the injustice which many ladies of higher rank would not have hesitated to do to all three on much less temptation.

Her present errand being with the Laird, she looked round the offices to see if she could find any domestic to announce that she wished to see him. As all was silence, she ventured to open one door: it was the old Laird's dog-kennel, now de-serted, unless when occupied, as one or two tubs seemed to testify, as a washing-house. She tried another: it was the roofless shed where the hawks had been once kept, as appeared from a perch or two not yet completely rotten, and a lure and jesses which were mouldering on the wall. A third door led to the coal-house, which was well stocked. To keep a very good fire was one of the few points of domestic management in which Dumbiedikes was positively active; in all other matters of domestic economy he was completely passive, and at the mercy of his housekeeper, the same buxom dame whom his father had long since bequeathed to his charge, and who, if fame did her no injustice, had feathered her nest pretty well at his expense.

Jeanie went on opening doors, like the second Calender wanting an eye, in the castle of the hundred obliging damsels, until, like the said prince-errant, she came to a stable. The Highland Pegasus, Rory Bean, to which belonged the single entire stall, was her old acquaintance, whom she had seen grazing on the baulk, as she failed not to recognize by the well-known ancient riding furniture and demi-pique saddle, which half hung on the walls, half trailed on the litter. Beyond the "treviss," which formed one side of the stall, stood a cow, who turned her head and lowed when Jeanie came into the stable, an appeal which her habitual occupations enabled her perfectly to understand, and with which she could not refuse complying, by shaking down some fodder to the animal, which had been neglected like most things else in this castle of the sluggard.

While she was accommodating "the milky mother" with the food which she should have received two hours sooner, a slipshod wench peeped into the stable, and perceiving that a stranger was employed in discharging the task which she, at length, and reluctantly, had quitted her slumbers to perform, ejaculated, "Eh, sirs! the brownie! the brownie!" and fled, yelling as if she had seen the devil.

To explain her terror, it may be necessary to notice that the old house of Dumbiedikes had, according to report, been long haunted by a brownie, one of those familiar spirits who were believed in ancient times to supply the deficiencies of the ordinary laborer—

Whirl the long mop and ply the airy flail.

Certes, the convenience of such a supernatural assistant could have been nowhere more sensibly felt than in a family where the domestics were so little disposed to personal activity; yet this serving maiden was so far from rejoicing in seeing a supposed aerial substitute discharging a task which she should have long since performed herself, that she proceeded to raise the family by her screams of horror, uttered as thick as if the brownie had been flaying her. Jeanie, who had immediately resigned her temporary occupation and followed the yelling damsel into the courtyard, in order to undeceive and appease her, was there met by Mrs. Janet Balchristie, the favorite sultana of the last Laird, as scandal went—the housekeeper of the present.　The good-looking buxom woman, betwixt forty and fifty (for such we described her at the death of the last Laird), was now a fat, red-faced, old dame of seventy, or thereabouts, fond of her place, and jealous of her authority.　Conscious that her administration did not rest on so sure a basis as in the time of the old proprietor, this considerate lady had introduced into the family the screamer aforesaid, who added good features and bright eyes to the powers of her lungs.　She made no conquest of the Laird, however, who seemed to live as if there was not another woman in the world but Jeanie Deans, and to bear no very ardent or overbearing affection even to her.　Mrs. Janet Balchristie, notwithstanding, had her own uneasy thoughts upon the almost daily visits to St. Leonard's Crags, and often, when the Laird looked at her wistfully and paused, according to his custom, before utterance, she expected him to say, "Jenny, I am gaun to change my condition;" but she was relieved by "Jenny, I am gaun to change my shoon."

Still, however, Mrs. Balchristie regarded Jeanie Deans with no small portion of malevolence, the customary feeling of such persons towards any one who they think has the means of doing them an injury.　But she had also a general aversion to any female, tolerably young and decently well-looking, who showed a wish to approach the house of Dumbiedikes and the proprietor thereof.　And as she had raised her mass of mortality out of bed two hours earlier than usual, to come to the rescue of her clamorous niece, she was in such extreme bad humor against all and sundry, that Saddletree would have pronounced that she harbored *inimicitiam contra omnes mortales.*

"Wha the deil are ye ?" said the fat dame to poor Jeanie, whom she did not immediately recognize, "scouping about a decent house at sic an hour in the morning ?"

"It was ane wanting to speak to the Laird," said Jeanie, who felt something of the intuitive terror which she had formerly entertained for this termagant, when she was occasionally at Dumbiedikes on business of her father's.

"Ane ! And what sort of ane are ye ? hae ye nae name ? D'ye think his honor has naething else to do than to speak wi' ilka idle tramp that comes about the town, and him in his bed yet, honest man ?"

"Dear, Mrs. Balchristie," replied Jeanie, in a submissive tone, "d'ye no mind me ?—d'ye no mind Jeanie Deans ?"

"Jeanie Deans!!" said the termagant, in accents affecting the utmost astonishment; then, taking two strides nearer to her, she peered into her face with a stare of curiosity, equally scornful and malignant. "I say Jeanie Deans, indeed—Jeanie Deevil, they had better hae ca'd ye! A bonny spot o' wark your tittie and you hae made out, murdering ae puir wean, and your light limmer of a sister's to be hanged for't, as weel she deserves! And the like o' you to come to ony honest man's house, and want to be into a decent bachelor gentleman's room at this time in the morning, and him in his bed? Gae wa'—gae wa'!"

Jeanie was struck mute with shame at the unfeeling brutality of this accusation, and could not even find words to justify herself from the vile construction put upon her visit, when Mrs. Balchristie, seeing her advantage, continued in the same tone, "Come, come, bundle up your pipes and tramp awa' wi' ye! ye may be seeking a father to another wean for onything I ken. If it warna that your father, auld David Deans, had been a tenant on our land, I would cry up the menfolk and hae ye dookit in the burn for your impudence."

Jeanie had already turned her back and was walking towards the door of the courtyard, so that Mrs. Balchristie, to make her last threat impressively audible to her, had raised her stentorian voice to its utmost pitch. But, like many a general, she lost the engagement by pressing her advantage too far.

The Laird had been disturbed in his morning slumbers by the tones of Mrs. Balchristie's objurgation, sounds in themselves by no means uncommon, but very remarkable in respect to the early hour at which they were now heard. He turned himself on the other side, however, in hopes the squall would blow by, when, in the course of Mrs. Balchristie's second explosion of wrath, the name of Deans distinctly struck the tympanum of his ear. As he was, in some degree, aware of the small portion of benevolence with which his housekeeper regarded the family at St. Leonard's, he instantly conceived that some message from thence was the cause of this untimely ire, and getting out of his bed, he slipped as speedily as possible into an old brocaded nightgown and some other necessary integuments, clapped cn his head his father's gold-laced hat (for though he was seldom seen without it, yet it is proper to contradict the popular report that he slept in it, as Don Quixote did in his helmet), and opening the window of his bedroom, beheld, to his great astonishment, the well-known figure of Jeanie Deans herself retreating from his gate; while his housekeeper, with arms akimbo, fists clinched and ex-

tended, body erect, and head shaking with rage, sent after her
a volley of Billingsgate oaths.   His choler rose in proportion
to the surprise, and, perhaps, to the disturbance of his repose.
"Hark ye," he exclaimed from the window, "ye auld limb
of Satan! wha the deil gies you commission to guide an honest man's daughter that gate?"

Mrs. Balchristie was completely caught in the manner.
She was aware, from the unusual warmth with which the Laird
expressed himself, that he was quite serious in this matter,
and she knew that, with all his indolence of nature, there were
points on which he might be provoked, and that, being provoked, he had in him something dangerous, which her wisdom
taught her to fear accordingly.   She began, therefore, to re-
tract her false step as fast as she could.   "She was but speaking for the house's credit, and she couldna think of disturbing his honor in the morning sae early, when the young woman
might as weel wait or call again; and, to be sure, she might
make a mistake between the twa sisters, for ane o' them wasna
sae creditable an acquaintance."

"Haud your peace, ye auld jade," said Dumbiedikes; "the
warst quean e'er stude in their shoon may ca' you cousin, an
a' be true that I have heard.   Jeanie, my woman, gang into
the parlor—but stay, that winna be redd up yet; wait there a
minute till I come doun to let ye in.   Dinna mind what Jenny
says to ye."

"Na, na," said Jenny, with a laugh of affected heartiness,
"never mind me, lass.   A' the warld kens my bark's waur
than my bite; if ye had had an appointment wi' the Laird, ye
might hae tauld me, I am nae urcivil person.   Gang your
ways in bye, hinny."   And she opened the door of the house
with a master-key.

"But I had no appointment wi' the Laird," said Jeanie,
drawing back; "I want just to speak twa words to him, and
I wad rather do it standing here, Mrs. Balchristie."

"In the open courtyard?   Na, na, that wad never do, lass;
we maunna guide ye that gate neither.   And how's that douce
honest man, your father?"

Jeanie was saved the pain of answering this hypocritical
question by the appearance of the Laird himself.

"Gang in and get breakfast ready," said he to his housekeeper; "and, d'ye hear, breakfast wi' us yoursell; ye ken
how to manage thae porringers of tea-water; and, hear ye, see
abune a' that there's a gude fire.   Weel, Jeanie, my woman,
gang in bye—gang in bye, and rest ye."

"Na, Laird," Jeanie replied, endeavoring as much as she

could to express herself with composure, notwithstanding she still trembled, "I canna gang in : I have a lang day's darg afore me ; I maun be twenty mile o' gate the night yet, if feet will carry me."

"Guide and deliver us ! twenty mile—twenty mile on your feet !" ejaculated Dumbiedikes, whose walks were of a very circumscribed diameter. "Ye maun never think o' that ; come in bye."

"I canna do that, Laird," replied Jeanie. "The twa words I hae to say to ye I can say here ; forbye that Mrs. Balchristie——"

"The deil flee awa' wi' Mrs. Balchristie," said Dumbiedikes, "and he'll hae a heavy lading o' her ! I tell ye, Jeanie Deans, I am a man of few words, but I am laird at hame as weel as in the field : deil a brute or body about my house but I can manage when I like, except Rory Bean, my powny ; but I can seldom be at the plague, an it binna when my bluid's up."

"I was wanting to say to ye, Laird," said Jeanie, who felt the necessity of entering upon her business, "that I was gaun a lang journey, outbye of my father's knowledge."

"Outbye his knowledge, Jeanie ! Is that right ? Ye maun think o't again ; it's no right," said Dumbiedikes, with a countenance of great concern.

"If I were anes at Lunnon," said Jeanie, in exculpation, "I am amaist sure I could get means to speak to the queen about my sister's life."

"Lunnon, and the queen, and her sister's life !" said Dumbiedikes, whistling for very amazement ; "the lassie's demented."

"I am no out o' my mind," said she, "and, sink or swim, I am determined to gang to Lunnon, if I suld beg my way frae door to door ; and so I maun, unless ye wad lend me a small sum to pay my expenses. Little thing will do it ; and ye ken my father's a man of substance, and wad see nae man, far less you, Laird, come to loss by me."

Dumbiedikes, on comprehending the nature of this application, could scarce trust his ears ; he made no answer whatever, but stood with his eyes riveted on the ground.

"I see ye are no for assisting me, Laird," said Jeanie ; "sae fare ye weel ; and gang and see my poor father as aften as ye can, he will be lonely eneugh now."

"Where is the silly bairn gaun ?" said Dumbiedikes ; and, laying hold of her hand, he led her into the house. "It's no that I didna think o't before," he said, "but it stack in my throat."

Thus speaking to himself, he led her into an old-fashioned parlor, shut the door behind them, and fastened it with a bolt. While Jeanie, surprised at this manœuvre, remained as near the door as possible, the Laird quitted her hand, and pressed upon a spring lock fixed in an oak panel in the wainscot, which instantly slipped aside. An iron strong-box was discovered in a recess of the wall; he opened this also, and, pulling out two or three drawers, showed that they were filled with leathern bags, full of gold and silver coin.

"This is my bank, Jeanie, lass," he said, looking first at her and then at the treasure, with an air of great complacency; "nane o' your goldsmith's bills for me; they bring folk to ruin."

Then suddenly changing his tone, he resolutely said— "Jeanie, I will make ye Leddy Dumbiedikes afore the sun sets, and ye may ride to Lunnon in your ain coach, if ye like."

"Na, Laird," said Jeanie, "that can never be : my father's grief, my sister's situation, the discredit to you——"

"That's *my* business," said Dumbiedikes. "Ye wad say naething about that if ye werena a fule; and yet I like ye the better for't : ae wise body's eneugh in the married state. But if your heart's ower fu', take what siller will serve ye, and let it be when ye come back again, as gude syne as sune."

"But, Laird," said Jeanie, who felt the necessity of being explicit with so extraordinary a lover, "I like another man better than you, and I canna marry ye."

"Another man better than me, Jeanie!" said Dumbiedikes; "how is that possible? It's no possible, woman; ye hae kenn'd me sae lang."

"Ay, but, Laird," said Jeanie, with persevering simplicity, "I hae kenn'd him langer."

"Langer! It's no possible!" exclaimed the poor Laird. "It canna be; ye were born on the land. O Jeanie, woman, ye haena lookit—ye haena seen the half o' the gear." He drew out another drawer. "A' gowd, Jeanie, and there's bands for siller lent. And the rental book, Jeanie—clear three hunder sterling; deil a wadset, heritable band, or burden. Ye haena lookit at them, woman. And then my mother's wardrobe, and my grandmother's forbye—silk gowns wad stand on their ends, pearlin-lace as fine as spiders' webs, and rings and earrings to the boot of a' that; they are a' in the chamber of deas. Oh, Jeanie, gang up the stair and look at them!"

But Jeanie held fast her integrity, though beset with

temptations which perhaps the Laird of Dumbiedikes did not greatly err in supposing were those most affecting to her sex.

"It canna be, Laird: I have said it, and I canna break my word till him, if ye wad gie me the haill barony of Dalkeith, and Lugton into the bargain."

"Your word to *him,*" said the Laird, somewhat pettishly; "but wha is he, Jeanie?—wha is he? I haena heard his name yet. Come now, Jeanie, ye are but queering us. I am no trowing that there is sic a ane in the warld; ye are but making fashion. What is he? wha is he?"

"Just Reuben Butler, that's schulemaster at Liberton," said Jeanie.

"Reuben Butler! Reuben Butler!" echoed the Laird of Dumbiedikes, pacing the apartment in high disdain. "Reuben Butler, the dominie at Liberton, and a dominie depute too! Reuben, the son of my cottar! Very weel, Jeanie, lass, wilfu' woman will hae her way. Reuben Butler! he hasna in his pouch the value o' the auld black coat he wears —but it disna signify." And, as he spoke, he shut successively, and with vehemence, the drawers of his treasury. "A fair offer, Jeanie, is nae cause of feud. Ae man may bring a horse to the water, but twenty wunna gar him drink. And as for wasting my substance on other folks' joes——"

There was something in the last hint that nettled Jeanie's honest pride. "I was begging nane frae your honor," she said; "least of a' on sic a score as ye pit it on. Gude morning to ye, sir; ye hae been kind to my father, and it isna in my heart to think otherwise than kindly of you."

So saying, she left the room, without listening to a faint "But, Jeanie—Jeanie—stay, woman!" and traversing the courtyard with a quick step, she set out on her forward journey, her bosom glowing with that natural indignation and shame which an honest mind feels at having subjected itself to ask a favor which had been unexpectedly refused. When out of the Laird's ground, and once more upon the public road, her pace slackened, her anger cooled, and anxious anticipations of the consequence of this unexpected disappointment began to influence her with other feelings. Must she then actually beg her way to London? for such seemed the alternative; or must she turn back and solicit her father for money; and by doing so lose time, which was precious, besides the risk of encountering his positive prohibition respecting her journey? Yet she saw no medium between these alternatives; and, while she walked slowly on, was still meditating whether it were not better to return.

While she was thus in an uncertainty, she heard the clatter of a horse's hoofs, and a well-known voice calling her name. She looked round, and saw advancing towards her on a pony, whose bare back and halter assorted ill with the nightgown, slippers, and laced cocked hat of the rider, a cavalier of no less importance than Dumbiedikes himself. In the energy of his pursuit, he had overcome even the Highland obstinacy of Rory Bean, and compelled that self-willed palfrey to canter the way his rider chose ; which Rory, however, performed with all the symptoms of reluctance, turning his head, and accompanying every bound he made in advance with a sidelong motion, which indicated his extreme wish to turn round—a manœuvre which nothing but the constant exercise of the Laird's heels and cudgel could possibly have counteracted.

When the Laird came up with Jeanie, the first words he uttered were—"Jeanie, they say ane shouldna aye take a woman at her first word ?"

"Aye, but ye maun take me at mine, Laird," said Jeanie, looking on the ground, and walking on without a pause. "I hae but ae word to bestow on onybody, and that's aye a true ane."

"Then," said Dumbiedikes, "at least ye suldna aye take a man at *his* first word. Ye maunna gang this wilfu' gate sillerless, come o't what like." He put a purse into her hand. "I wad gie you Rory too, but he's as wilfu' as yoursell, and he's ower weel used to a gate that maybe he and I hae gaen ower aften, and he'll gang nae road else."

"But, Laird," said Jeanie, "though I ken my father will satisfy every penny of this siller, whatever there's o't, yet I wadna like to borrow it frae ane that maybe thinks of something mair than the paying o't back again."

"There's just twenty-five guineas o't," said Dumbiedikes, with a gentle sigh, "and whether your father pays or disna pay, I make ye free till't without another word. Gang where ye like, do what ye like, and marry a' the Butlers in the country gin ye like. And sae, gude morning to you, Jeanie."

"And God bless you, Laird, wi' mony a gude morning," said Jeanie, her heart more softened by the unwonted generosity of this uncouth character than perhaps Butler might have approved, had he known her feelings at that moment ; "and comfort, and the Lord's peace, and the peace of the world, be with you, if we suld never meet again !"

Dumbiedikes turned and waved his hand ; and his pony, much more willing to return than he had been to set out, hurried him homewards so fast that, wanting the aid of a regular bridle, as well as of saddle and stirrups, he was too much puzzled to keep his seat to permit of his looking behind, even to give the parting glance of a forlorn swain. I am ashamed to say that the sight of a lover, run away with in nightgown and slippers and a laced hat, by a barebacked Highland pony, had something in it of a sedative, even to a grateful and deserved burst of affectionate esteem. The figure of Dumbiedikes was too ludicrous not to confirm Jeanie in the original sentiments she entertained towards him.

"He's a gude creature," said she, "and a kind; it's a pity he has sae willyard a powny." And she immediately turned her thoughts to the important journey which she had commenced, reflecting with pleasure that, according to her habits of life and of undergoing fatigue, she was now amply, or even superfluously, provided with the means of encountering the expenses of the road up and down from London, and all other expenses whatever.

CHAPTER XXVII

IN pursuing her solitary journey, our heroine, soon after passing the house of Dumbiedikes, gained a little eminence, from which, on looking to the eastward down a prattling brook, whose meanders were shaded with straggling willows and alder-trees, she could see the cottages of Woodend and Beersheba, the haunts and habitation of her early life, and could distinguish the common on which she had so often herded sheep, and the recesses of the rivulet where she had pulled rushes with Butler, to plait crowns and sceptres for her sister Effie, then a beautiful but spoiled child of about three years old. The recollections which the scene brought with them were so bitter that, had she indulged them, she would have sat down and relieved her heart with tears.

"But I kenn'd," said Jeanie, when she gave an account of her pilgrimage, "that greeting would do but little good, and that it was mair beseeming to thank the Lord, that had showed me kindness and countenance by means of a man that mony ca'd a Nabal and churl, but wha was free of his gudes to me as ever the fountain was free of the stream. And I minded the Scripture about the sin of Israel at Meribah, when the people murmured, although Moses had brought water from the dry rock that the congregation might drink and live. Sae, I wad not trust mysell with another look at puir Woodend, for the very blue reek that came out of the lum-head pat me in mind of the change of market days with us."

In this resigned and Christian temper she pursued her journey, until she was beyond this place of melancholy recollections, and not distant from the village where Butler dwelt, which, with its old-fashioned church and steeple, rises among a tuft of trees, occupying the ridge of an eminence to the south

of Edinburgh.   At a quarter of a mile's distance is a clumsy
square tower, the residence of the Laird of Liberton, who, in
former times, with the habits of the predatory chivalry of
Germany, is said frequently to have annoyed the city of Edinburgh by intercepting the supplies and merchandise which
came to the town from the southward.

This village, its tower, and its church, did not lie precisely
in Jeanie's road towards England; but they were not much
aside from it, and the village was the abode of Butler. She
had resolved to see him in the beginning of her journey, because she conceived him the most proper person to write to
her father concerning her resolution and her hopes. There
was probably another reason latent in her affectionate bosom.
She wished once more to see the object of so early and so sincere an attachment, before commencing a pilgrimage, the perils of which she did not disguise from herself, although she
did not allow them so to press upon her mind as to diminish the strength and energy of her resolution. A visit to a
lover from a young person in a higher rank of life than Jeanie's would have had something forward and improper in its
character. But the simplicity of her rural habits was unacquainted with these punctilious ideas of decorum, and no
notion, therefore, of impropriety crossed her imagination as,
setting out upon a long journey, she went to bid adieu to an
early friend.

There was still another motive that pressed upon her mind
with additional force as she approached the village. She had
looked anxiously for Butler in the court-house, and had expected that certainly, in some part of that eventful day, he
would have appeared to bring such countenance and support
as he could give to his old friend and the protector of his
youth, even if her own claims were laid aside. She knew, indeed, that he was under a certain degree of restraint; but
she still had hoped that he would have found means to eman-
cipate himself from it, at least for one day. In short, the
wild and wayward thoughts which Wordsworth has described
as rising in an absent lover's imagination suggested, as the
only explanation of his absence, that Butler must be very
ill. And so much had this wrought on her imagination, that
when she approached the cottage in which her lover occupied
a small apartment, and which had been pointed out to her by
a maiden with a milk-pail on her head, she trembled at anticipating the answer she might receive on inquiring for him.

Her fears in this case had, indeed, only hit upon the truth.
Butler, whose constitution was naturally feeble, did not soon

recover the fatigue of body and distress of mind which he had suffered in consequence of the tragical events with which our narrative commenced. The painful idea that his character was breathed on by suspicion was an aggravation to his distress.

But the most cruel addition was the absolute prohibition laid by the magistrates on his holding any communication with Deans or his family. It had unfortunately appeared likely to them that some intercourse might be again attempted with that family by Robertson, through the medium of Butler, and this they were anxious to intercept, or prevent, if possible. The measure was not meant as a harsh or injurious severity on the part of the magistrates; but, in Butler's circumstances, it pressed cruelly hard. He felt he must be suffering under the bad opinion of the person who was dearest to him, from an imputation of unkind desertion, the most alien to his nature.

This painful thought, pressing on a frame already injured, brought on a succession of slow and lingering feverish attacks, which greatly impaired his health, and at length rendered him incapable even of the sedentary duties of the school, on which his bread depended. Fortunately, old Mr. Whackbairn, who was the principal teacher of the little parochial establishment, was sincerely attached to Butler. Besides that he was sensible of his merits and value as an assistant, which had greatly raised the credit of his little school, the ancient pedagogue, who had himself been tolerably educated, retained some taste for classical lore, and would gladly relax, after the drudgery of the school was past, by conning over a few pages of Horace or Juvenal with his usher. A similarity of taste begot kindness, and he accordingly saw Butler's increasing debility with great compassion, roused up his own energies to teaching the school in the morning hours, insisted upon his assistant's reposing himself at that period, and, besides, supplied him with such comforts as the patient's situation required, and his own means were inadequate to compass.

Such was Butler's situation, scarce able to drag himself to the place where his daily drudgery must gain his daily bread, and racked with a thousand fearful anticipations concerning the fate of those who were dearest to him in the world, when the trial and condemnation of Effie Deans put the copestone upon his mental misery.

He had a particular account of these events from a fellow-student who resided in the same village, and who, having been present on the melancholy occasion, was able to place it in all its agony of horrors before his excruciated imagination. That sleep should have visited his eyes, after such a curfew-note, was impossible. A thousand dreadful visions haunted his imagination all night, and in the morning he was awaked from a feverish slumber by the only circumstance which could have added to his distress—the visit of an intrusive ass.

This unwelcome visitant was no other than Bartoline Saddletree. The worthy and sapient burgher had kept his appointment at MacCroskie's, with Plumdamas and some other neighbors, to discuss the Duke of Argyle's speech, the justice of Effie Deans's condemnation, and the improbability of her obtaining a reprieve. This sage conclave disputed high and drank deep, and on the next morning Bartoline felt, as he expressed it, as if his head was like a "confused progress of writs."

To bring his reflective powers to their usual serenity, Saddletree resolved to take a morning's ride upon a certain hackney which he, Plumdamas, and another honest shopkeeper combined to maintain by joint subscription, for occasional jaunts for the purpose of business or exercise. As Saddletree had two children boarded with Whackbairn, and was, as we have seen, rather fond of Butler's society, he turned his palfrey's head towards Liberton, and came, as we have already said, to give the unfortunate usher that additional vexation of which Imogen complains so feelingly when she says,

> I'm sprighted with a fool—
> Sprighted and anger'd worse.

If anything could have added gall to bitterness, it was the choice which Saddletree made of a subject for his prosing harangues, being the trial of Effie Deans, and the probability of her being executed. Every word fell on Butler's ear like the knell of a death-bell or the note of a screech-owl.

Jeanie paused at the door of her lover's humble abode upon hearing the loud and pompous tones of Saddletree sounding from the inner apartment—"Credit me, it will be sae, Mr. Butler. Brandy cannot save her. She maun gang down the Bow wi' the lad in the pioted coat* at her heels. I am sorry for the lassie, but the law, sir, maun hae its course—

> Vivat rex,
> Currat lex,

as the poet has it, in whilk of Horace's *Odes* I know not."

Here Butler groaned, in utter impatience of the brutality and ignorance which Bartoline had contrived to amalgamate into one sentence. But Saddletree, like other prosers, was

---

* The executioner, in a livery of black or dark gray and silver, likened by low wit to a magpie.

blessed with a happy obtuseness of perception concerning the unfavorable impression which he generally made on his auditors. He proceeded to deal forth his scraps of legal knowledge without mercy, and concluded by asking Butler with great self-complacency, "Was it na a pity my father didna send me to Utrecht? Havena I missed the chance to turn out as *clarissimus* an *ictus* as auld Grunwiggin himsell? What for dinna ye speak, Mr. Butler? Wad I no hae been a *clarissimus ictus?* Eh, man?"

"I really do not understand you, Mr. Saddletree," said Butler, thus pushed hard for an answer. His faint and exhausted tone of voice was instantly drowned in the sonorous bray of Bartoline.

"No understand me, man? *Ictus* is Latin for a lawyer, is it not?"

"Not that ever I heard of," answered Butler, in the same dejected tone.

"The deil ye didna! See, man, I got the word but this morning out of a memorial of Mr. Crossmyloof's; see, there it is, *ictus clarissimus et perti—peritissimus;* it's a' Latin, for it's printed in the Italian types."

"O, you mean *juris-consultus? Ictus* is an abbreviation for *juris-consultus.*"

"Dinna tell me, man," persevered Saddletree; "there's nae abbreviates except in adjudications; and this is a' about a servitude of water-drap, that is to say, *tillicidian**—maybe ye'll say that's no Latin neither—in Mary King's Close in the High Street."

"Very likely," said poor Butler, overwhelmed by the noisy perseverance of his visitor. "I am not able to dispute with you."

"Few folk are—few folk are, Mr. Butler, though I say it that shouldna say it," returned Bartoline, with great delight. "Now, it will be twa hours yet or ye're wanted in the schule, and as ye are no weel, I'll sit wi' you to divert ye, and explain t'ye the nature of a *tillicidian*. Ye maun ken, the petitioner, Mrs. Crombie, a very decent woman, is a friend of mine, and I hae stude her friend in this case, and brought her wi' credit into the court, and I doubtna that in due time she will win out o't wi' credit, win she or lose she. Ye see, being an inferior tenement or laigh house, we grant ourselves to be burdened wi' the *tillicide*, that is, that we are obligated to receive the natural water-drap of the superior tenement, sae far as the same fa's frae the heavens, or the roof of our neighbor's

---

* He meant, probably. *stillicidium.*

house, and from thence by the gutters or eaves upon our laigh
tenement.   But the other night comes a Highland quean of
a lass, and she flashes, God kens what, out at the eastmost
window of Mrs. MacPhail's house, that's the superior tenement.   I believe the auld women wad hae greed, for Luckie
MacPhail sent down the lass to tell my friend Mrs. Crombie
that she had made the gardyloo out of the wrang window,
from respect for twa Highlandmen that were speaking Gaelic in the close below the right ane.   But luckily for Mrs.
Crombie, I just chanced to come in in time to break aff the
communing, for it's a pity the point sulda be tried.   We had
Mrs. MacPhail into the Ten-Mark Court.   The Hieland limmer of a lass wanted to swear herself free ; but 'Haud ye
there,' says I——"

The detailed account of this important suit might have
lasted until poor Butler's hour of rest was completely exhausted, had not Saddletree been interrupted by the noise of
voices at the door.   The woman of the house where Butler
lodged, on returning with her pitcher from the well, whence
she had been fetching water for the family, found our heroine Jeanie Deans standing at the door, impatient of the prolix
harangue of Saddletree, yet unwilling to enter until he should
have taken his leave.

The good woman abridged the period of hesitation by inquiring, "Was ye wanting the gudeman or me, lass ?"

"I wanted to speak with Mr. Butler, if he's at leisure,"
replied Jeanie.

"Gang in bye, then, my woman," answered the goodwife ;
and opening the door of a room, she announced the additional visitor with—"Mr. Butler, here's a lass wants to speak
t'ye."

The surprise of Butler was extreme when Jeanie, who
seldom stirred half a mile from home, entered his apartment
upon this annunciation.

"Good God !" he said, starting from his chair, while
alarm restored to his cheek the color of which sickness had
deprived it ; "some new misfortune must have happened !"

"None, Mr. Reuben, but what you must hae heard of ;
but O, ye are looking ill yoursell !" for "the hectic of a
moment" had not concealed from her affectionate eye the
ravages which lingering disease and anxiety of mind had
made in her lover's person.

"No ; I am well—quite well," said Butler, with eagerness ; "if I can do anything to assist you, Jeanie—or your
father."

"Ay, to be sure," said Saddletree; "the family may be considered as limited to them twa now, just as if Effie had never been in the tailzie, puir thing. But, Jeanie, lass, what brings you out to Liberton sae air in the morning, and your father lying ill in the Luckenbooths?"

"I had a message frae my father to Mr. Butler," said Jeanie, with embarrassment; but instantly feeling ashamed of the fiction to which she had resorted, for her love of and veneration for truth was almost Quaker-like, she corrected herself—"That is to say, I wanted to speak with Mr. Butler about some business of my father's and puir Effie's."

"Is it law business?" said Bartoline; "because, if it be, ye had better take my opinion on the subject than his."

"It is not just law business," said Jeanie, who saw considerable inconvenience might arise from letting Mr. Saddletree into the secret purpose of her journey; "but I want Mr. Butler to write a letter for me."

"Very right," said Mr. Saddletree; "and if ye'll tell me what it is about, I'll dictate to Mr. Butler as Mr. Crossmyloof does to his clerk. Get your pen and ink *in initialibus*, Mr. Butler."

Jeanie looked at Butler, and wrung her hands with vexation and impatience.

"I believe, Mr. Saddletree," said Butler, who saw the necessity of getting rid of him at all events, "that Mr. Whackbairn will be somewhat affronted if you do not hear your boys called up to their lessons."

"Indeed, Mr. Butler, and that's as true; and I promised to ask a half play-day to the schule, so that the bairns might gang and see the hanging, which canna but have a pleasing effect on their young minds, seeing there is no knowing what they may come to themselves. Odd so, I didna mind ye were here, Jeanie Deans; but ye maun use yoursell to hear the matter spoken o'. Keep Jeanie here till I come back, Mr. Butler; I wunna bide ten minutes."

And with this unwelcome assurance of an immediate return, he relieved them of the embarrassment of his presence.

"Reuben," said Jeanie, who saw the necessity of using the interval of his absence in discussing what had brought her there, "I am bound on a lang journey. I am gaun to Lunnon to ask Effie's life of the king and of the queen."

"Jeanie! you are surely not yourself," answered Butler, in the utmost surprise; "*you* go to London—*you* address the king and queen!"

"And what for no, Reuben?" said Jeanie, with all the

composed simplicity of her character ; "it's but speaking to
a mortal man and woman when a' is done.　And their hearts
maun be made o' flesh and blood like other folks', and Effie's
story wad melt them were they stane.　Forbye, I hae heard
that they are no sic bad folk as what the Jacobites ca' them."

"Yes, Jeanie," said Butler ; "but their magnificence,
their retinue, the difficulty of getting audience ?"

"I have thought of a' that, Reuben, and it shall not break
my spirit.　Nae doubt their claiths will be very grand, wi'
their crowns on their heads, and their sceptres in their hands,
like the great King Ahasuerus when he sat upon his royal
throne foranent the gate of his house, as we are told in Scripture.　But I have that within me that will keep my heart
from failing, and I am amaist sure that I will be strengthened
to speak the errand I came for."

"Alas ! alas !" said Butler, "the kings nowadays do not
sit in the gate to administer justice, as in patriarchal times.
I know as little of courts as you do, Jeanie, by experience ;
but by reading and report I know that the King of Britain
does everything by means of his ministers."

"And if they be upright, God-fearing ministers," said
Jeanie, "it's sae muckle the better chance for Effie and me."

"But you do not even understand the most ordinary words
relating to a court," said Butler ; "by the ministry is meant
not clergymen, but the king's official servants."

"Nae doubt," returned Jeanie, "he maun hae a great number mair, I daur to say, than the Duchess has at Dalkeith ;
and great folks' servants are aye mair saucy than themselves.
But I'll be decently put on, and I'll offer them a trifle o' siller, as if I came to see the palace.　Or, if they scruple that,
I'll tell them I'm come on a business of life and death, and
then they will surely bring me to speech of the king and
queen ?"

Butler shook his head.　"O, Jeanie, this is entirely a wild
dream.　You can never see them but through some great lord's
intercession, and I think it is scarce possible even then."

"Weel, but maybe I can get that too," said Jeanie, "with
a little helping from you."

"From me, Jeanie ! this is the wildest imagination of all."

"Ay, but it is not, Reuben.　Havena I heard you say that
your grandfather, that my father never likes to hear about,
did some gude lang syne to the forbear of this MacCallummore, when he was Lord of Lorn ?"

"He did so," said Butler, eagerly, "and I can prove it.
I will write to the Duke of Argyle—report speaks him a good

kindly man, as he is known for a brave soldier and true patriot—I will conjure him to stand between your sister and this cruel fate.   There is but a poor chance of success, but we will try all means."

"We *must* try all means," replied Jeanie; "but writing winna do it : a letter canna look, and pray, and beg, and beseech, as the human voice can do to the human heart.   A letter's like the music that the ladies have for their spinets : naething but black scores, compared to the same tune played or sung.   It's word of mouth maun do it, or naething, Reuben."

"You are right," said Reuben, recollecting his firmness, "and I will hope that Heaven has suggested to your kind heart and firm courage the only possible means of saving the life of this unfortunate girl.   But, Jeanie, you must not take this most perilous journey alone ; I have an interest in you, and I will not agree that my Jeanie throws herself away.   You must, even in the present circumstances, give me a husband's right to protect you, and I will go with you myself on this journey, and assist you to do your duty by your family."

"Alas, Reuben !" said Jeanie, in her turn, "this must not be ; a pardon will not gie my sister her fair fame again, or mak me a bride fitting for an honest man and an usefu' minister.   Wha wad mind what he said in the pu'pit, that had to wife the sister of a woman that was condemned for sic wickedness ?"

"But, Jeanie," pleaded her lover, "I do not believe, and I cannot believe, that Effie has done this deed."

"Heaven bless you for saying sae, Reuben !" answered Jeanie ; "but she maun bear the blame o't, after all."

"But that blame, were it even justly laid on her, does not fall on you."

"Ah, Reuben, Reuben," replied the young woman, "ye ken it is a blot that spreads to kith and kin.   Ichabod, as my poor father says, the glory is departed from our house ; for the poorest man's house has a glory, where there are true hands, a divine heart, and an honest fame.   And the last has gane frae us a'."

"But, Jeanie, consider your word and plighted faith to me ; and would ye undertake such a journey without a man to protect you ? and who should that protector be but your husband ?"

"You are kind and good, Reuben, and wad tak me wi' a' my shame, I doubtna.   But ye canna but own that this is no time to marry or be given in marriage.   Na, if that suld ever

be, it maun be in another and a better season. And, dear
Reuben, ye speak of protecting me on my journey. Alas !
who will protect and take care of you ? Your very limbs
tremble with standing for ten minutes on the floor ; how
could you undertake a journey as far as Lunnon ?"

"But I am strong—I am well," continued Butler, sinking in his seat totally exhausted ; "at least I shall be quite
well to-morrow."

"Ye see, and ye ken, ye maun just let me depart," said
Jeanie, after a pause ; and then taking his extended hand,
and gazing kindly in his face, she added, "It's e'en a grief
the mair to me to see you in this way. But ye maun keep
up your heart for Jeanie's sake, for if she isna your wife, she
will never be the wife of living man. And now gie me the
paper for MacCallummore and bid God speed me on my way."

There was something of romance in Jeanie's venturous resolution ; yet, on consideration, as it seemed impossible to alter it
by persuasion, or to give her assistance but by advice, Butler,
after some further debate, put into her hands the paper she
desired, which, with the muster-roll in which it was folded up,
were the sole memorials of the stout and enthusiastic Bible
Butler, his grandfather.   While Butler sought this document,
Jeanie had time to take up his pocket Bible. "I have marked
a scripture," she said, as she again laid it down, "with your
keelyvine pen, that will be useful to us baith. And ye maun
tak the trouble, Reuben, to write a' this to my father, for, God
help me, I have neither head nor hand for lang letters at ony
time, forbye now ; and I trust him entirely to you, and I trust
you will soon be permitted to see him. And, Reuben, when ye
do win to the speech o' him, mind a' the auld man's bits o' ways,
for Jeanie's sake ; and dinna speak o' Latin or English terms
to him, for he's o' the auld warld, and downa bide to be fashed
wi' them, though I dare say he may be wrang. And dinna ye
say muckle to him, but set him on speaking himsell, for he'll
bring himsell mair comfort that way. And O, Reuben, the
poor lassie in yon dungeon !—but I needna bid your kind heart
—gie her what comfort ye can as soon as they will let ye see
her ; tell her—— But I maunna speak mair about her, for I
maunna take leave o' ye wi' the tear in my ee, for that wadna
be canny. God bless ye, Reuben !"

To avoid so ill an omen she left the room hastily, while her
features yet retained the mournful and affectionate smile which
she had compelled them to wear in order to support Butler's
spirits.

It seemed as if the power of sight, of speech, and of reflection had left him as she disappeared from the room, which she had entered and retired from so like an apparition. Saddletree, who entered immediately afterwards, overwhelmed him with questions, which he answered without understanding them, and with legal disquisitions, which conveyed to him no iota of meaning. At length the learned burgess recollected that there was a baron court to be held at Loanhead that day, and though it was hardly worth while, "he might as weel go to see if there was onything doing, as he was acquainted with the baron-bailie, who was a decent man, and would be glad of a word of legal advice."

So soon as he departed, Butler flew to the Bible, the last book which Jeanie had touched. To his extreme surprise, a paper, containing two or three pieces of gold, dropped from the book. With a black-lead pencil she had marked the sixteenth and twenty-fifth verses of the thirty-seventh Psalm—"A little that a righteous man hath is better than the riches of the wicked." "I have been young and am now old, yet have I not seen the righteous forsaken, nor his seed begging their bread."

Deeply impressed with the affectionate delicacy which shrouded its own generosity under the cover of a providential supply to his wants, he pressed the gold to his lips with more ardor than ever the metal was greeted with by a miser. To emulate her devout firmness and confidence seemed now the pitch of his ambition, and his first task was to write an account to David Deans of his daughter's resolution and journey southward. He studied every sentiment, and even every phrase, which he thought could reconcile the old man to her extraordinary resolution. The effect which this epistle produced will be hereafter adverted to. Butler committed it to the charge of an honest clown, who had frequent dealings with Deans in the sale of his dairy produce, and who readily undertook a journey to Edinburgh to put the letter into his own hands.*

* By dint of assiduous research, I am enabled to certiorate the reader that the name of this person was Saunders Broadfoot, and that he dealt in the wholesome commodity called kirn-milk (*Anglicé*, buttermilk).—J. C.

CHAPTER XXVIII

My native land, good night!
LORD BYRON.

IN the present day, a journey from Edinburgh to London is a
matter at once safe, brief, and simple, however inexperienced
or unprotected the traveller. Numerous coaches of different
rates of charge, and as many packets, are perpetually passing
and repassing betwixt the capital of Britain and her northern
sister, so that the most timid or indolent may execute such a
journey upon a few hours' notice. But it was different in 1737.
So slight and infrequent was then the intercourse betwixt
London and Edinburgh that men still alive remember, that
upon one occasion the mail from the former city arrived at
the General Post-Office in Scotland with only one letter in it.*
The usual mode of travelling was by means of post-horses, the
traveller occupying one and his guide another, in which manner, by relays of horses from stage to stage, the journey might
be accomplished in a wonderfully short time by those who
could endure fatigue. To have the bones shaken to pieces by
a constant change of those hacks was a luxury for the rich;
the poor were under the necessity of using the mode of conveyance with which nature had provided them.

With a strong heart, and a frame patient of fatigue, Jeanie
Deans, travelling at the rate of twenty miles a day, and sometimes further, traversed the southern part of Scotland and advanced as far as Durham.

Hitherto she had been either among her own country-folk,
or those to whom her bare feet and tartan screen were objects
too familiar to attract much attention. But as she advanced,
she perceived that both circumstances exposed her to sarcasm
and taunts which she might otherwise have escaped; and although in her heart she thought it unkind and inhospitable
to sneer at a passing stranger on account of the fashion of her
attire, yet she had the good sense to alter those parts of her
dress which attracted ill-natured observation. Her checked

* The fact is certain. The single epistle was addressed to the principal director
of the British Linen Company.

screen was deposited carefully in her bundle, and she conformed to the national extravagance of wearing shoes and stockings for the whole day. She confessed afterwards that, "besides the wastrife, it was lang or she could walk sae comfortably with the shoes as without them ; but there was often a bit saft heather by the roadside, and that helped her weel on." The want of the screen, which was drawn over the head like a veil, she supplied by a *bon-grace*, as she called it—a large straw bonnet, like those worn by the English maidens when laboring in the fields. "But I thought unco shame o' mysell," she said, "the first time I put on a married woman's *bon-grace*, and me a single maiden."

With these changes she had little, as she said, to make "her kenspeckle when she didna speak," but her accent and language drew down on her so many jests and gibes, couched in a worse *patois* by far than her own, that she soon found it was her interest to talk as little and as seldom as possible. She answered, therefore, civil salutations of chance passengers with a civil courtesy, and chose, with anxious circumspection, such places of repose as looked at once most decent and sequestered. She found the common people of England, although inferior in courtesy to strangers, such as was then practised in her own more unfrequented country, yet, upon the whole, by no means deficient in the real duties of hospitality. She readily obtained food, and shelter, and protection at a very moderate rate, which sometimes the generosity of mine host altogether declined, with a blunt apology—"Thee hast a lang way afore thee, lass ; and I'se ne'er take penny out o' a single woman's purse ; it's the best friend thou can have on the road."

It often happened, too, that mine hostess was struck with "the tidy, nice Scotch body," and procured her an escort, or a cast in a wagon, for some part of the way, or gave her useful advice and recommendation respecting her resting-places.

At York our pilgrim stopped for the best part of a day—partly to recruit her strength, partly because she had the good luck to obtain a lodging in an inn kept by a countrywoman, partly to indite two letters to her father and Reuben Butler, an operation of some little difficulty, her habits being by no means those of literary composition. That to her father was in the following words :

"DEAREST FATHER,

"I make my present pilgrimage more heavy and burdensome through the sad occasion to reflect that it is without your knowledge, which, God knows, was far contrary to my heart; for Scripture says that 'the vow of the daughter should not be binding without the consent of the father,' wherein it may be I have been guilty to tak this wearie journey without your consent.   Nevertheless, it was borne in upon my mind that I should be an instrument to help my poor sister in this extremity of needcessity, otherwise I wad not, for wealth or for world's gear, or for the haill lands of Da'keith and Lugton, have done the like o' this, without your free will and knowledge.   O, dear father, as ye wad desire a blessing on my journey, and upon your household, speak a word or write a line of comfort to yon poor prisoner.   If she has sinned, she has sorrowed and suffered, and ye ken better than me that we maun forgie others, as we pray to be forgien.   Dear father, forgive my saying this muckle, for it doth not become a young head to instruct gray hairs; but I am sae far frae ye, that my heart yearns to ye a', and fain wad I hear that ye had forgien her trespass, and sae I nae doubt say mair than may become me. The folk here are civil, and, like the barbarians unto the holy apostle, hae shown me much kindness; and there are a sort of chosen people in the land, for they hae some kirks without organs that are like ours, and are called meeting-houses, where the minister preaches without a gown.   But most of the country are prelatists, whilk is awfu' to think; and I saw twa men that were ministers following hunds, as bauld as Roslin or Driden, the young Laird of Loup-the-Dike, or ony wild gallant in Lothian.   A sorrowfu' sight to behold!   O, dear father, may a blessing be with your down-lying and up-rising, and remember in your prayers your affectionate daughter to command,

" JEAN DEANS."

A postscript bore—" I learned from a decent woman, a grazier's widow, that they hae a cure for the muir-ill in Cumberland, whilk is ane pint, as they ca't, of yill—whilk is a dribble in comparison of our gawsie Scots pint, and hardly a mutchkin—boil'd wi' sope and hartshorn draps, and toomed doun the creature's throat wi' ane whorn.   Ye might try it on the bauson-faced year-auld quey; an it does nae gude, it can do nae ill.   She was a kind woman, and seemed skeely about horned beasts.   When I reach Lunnon, I intend to gang to our cousin Mistress Glass, the tobacconist, at the sign o' the Thistle, wha is so ceevil as to send you down your spleuchan-fu' anes a year; and as she must be weel kenn'd in Lunnon, I doubt not easily to find out where she lives."

Being seduced into betraying our heroine's confidence thus far, we will stretch our communication a step beyond, and impart to the reader her letter to her lover.

"MR. REUBEN BUTLER,

"Hoping this will find you better, this comes to say, that I have reached this great town safe, and am not wearied with walking, but the better for it. And I have seen many things which I trust to tell you one day, also the muckle kirk of this place ; and all around the city are mills, whilk havena muckle wheels nor mill-dams, but gang by the wind—strange to behold. Ane miller asked me to gang in and see it work, but I wad not, for I am not come to the south to make acquaintance with strangers. I keep the straight road, and just beck if onybody speaks to me ceevilly, and answers naebody with the tong but women of mine ain sect. I wish, Mr. Butler, I kenn'd onything that wad mak ye weel, for they hae mair medicines in this town of York than wad cure a' Scotland, and surely some of them wad be gude for your complaints. If ye had a kindly motherly body to nurse ye, and no to let ye waste yoursell wi' reading—whilk ye read mair than eneugh with the bairns in the schule—and to gie ye warm milk in the morning, I wad be mair easy for ye. Dear Mr. Butler, keep a good heart, for we are in the hands of Ane that kens better what is gude for us than we ken what is for ourwells. I hae nae doubt to do that for which I am come : I canna doubt it—I winna think to doubt it ; because, if I haena full assurance, how shall I bear myself with earnest entreaties in the great folks' presence ? But to ken that ane's purpose is right, and to make their heart strong, is the way to get through the warst day's darg. The bairns' rime says, the warst blast of the borrowing days* couldna kill the three silly poor hog-lambs. And if it be God's pleasure, we that are sindered in sorrow may meet again in joy, even on this hither side of Jordan. I dinna bid ye mind what I said at our partin' anent my poor father and that misfortunate lassie, for I ken you will do sae for the sake of Christian charity, whilk is mair than the entreaties of her that is your servant to command,

"JEANIE DEANS."

This letter also had a postscript. "Dear Reuben, If ye think that it wad hae been right for me to have said mair and kinder things to ye, just think that I hae written sae, since I

* See Note 29.

am sure that I wish a' that is kind and right to ye and by ye. Ye will think I am turned waster, for I wear clean hose and shoon every day; but it's the fashion here for decent bodies, and ilka land has its ain lauch.   Ower and aboon a', if laughing days were e'er to come back again till us, ye wad laugh weel to see my round face at the far end of a strae *bon-grace*, that looks as muckle and round as the middell aisle in Liberton kirk.   But it sheds the sun weel aff, and keeps un-ceevil folk frae staring as if ane were a worriecow.   I sall tell ye by writ how I come on wi' the Duke of Argyle, when I won up to Lunnon.   Direct a line, to say how ye are, to me, to the charge of Mrs. Margaret Glass, tobacconist, at the sign of the Thistle, Lunnon, whilk, if it assures me of your health, will make my mind sae muckle easier.   Excuse bad spelling and writing, as I have ane ill pen."

The orthography of these epistles may seem to the south-ron to require a better apology than the letter expresses, though a bad pen was the excuse of a certain Galwegian laird for bad spelling ; but, on behalf of the heroine, I would have them to know that, thanks to the care of Butler, Jeanie Deans wrote and spelled fifty times better than half the women of rank in Scotland at that period, whose strange orthography and singular diction form the strongest contrast to the good sense which their correspondence usually intimates.

For the rest, in the tenor of these epistles, Jeanie expressed, perhaps, more hopes, a firmer courage, and better spirits than she actually felt.   But this was with the amiable idea of reliev-ing her father and lover from apprehensions on her account, which she was sensible must greatly add to their other troubles. "If they think me weel, and like to do weel," said the poor pilgrim to herself, "my father will be kinder to Effie, and But-ler will be kinder to himself.   For I ken weel that they will think mair o' me than I do o' mysell."

Accordingly, she sealed her letters carefully, and put them into the post-office with her own hand, after many inquiries con-cerning the time in which they were likely to reach Edinburgh. When this duty was performed, she readily accepted her land-lady's pressing invitation to dine with her, and remain till the next morning.   The hostess, as we have said, was her country-woman, and the eagerness with which Scottish people meet, communicate, and, to the extent of their power, assist each other, although it is often objected to us as a prejudice and narrowness of sentiment, seems, on the contrary, to arise from a most justifiable and honorable feeling of patriotism, combined with a conviction, which, if undeserved, would long since have been confuted by experience, that the habits and principles of the nation are a sort of guarantee for the character of the individual. At any rate, if the extensive influence of this national partiality be considered as an additional tie, binding man to man, and calling forth the good offices of such as can render them to the countryman who happens to need them, we think it must be found to exceed, as an active and efficient motive to generosity, that more impartial and wider principle of general benevolence, which we have sometimes seen pleaded as an excuse for assisting no individual whatever.

Mrs. Bickerton, lady of the ascendant of the Seven Stars, in the Castle Gate, York, was deeply infected with the unfortunate prejudices of her country. Indeed, she displayed so much kindness to Jeanie Deans (because she herself, being a Merse woman, "marched" with Midlothian, in which Jeanie was born), showed such motherly regard to her, and such anxiety for her further progress, that Jeanie thought herself safe, though by temper sufficiently cautious, in communicating her whole story to her.

Mrs. Bickerton raised her hands and eyes at the recital, and exhibited much wonder and pity. But she also gave some effectual good advice.

She required to know the strength of Jeanie's purse, reduced by her deposit at Liberton and the necessary expense of her journey to about fifteen pounds. "This," she said, "would do very well, providing she could carry it a' safe to London."

"Safe !" answered Jeanie. "I'se warrant my carrying it safe, bating the needful expenses."

"Ay, but highwaymen, lassie," said Mrs. Bickerton ; "for ye are come into a more civilized, that is to say, a more ro-guish, country than the north, and how ye are to get forward I do not profess to know. If ye could wait here eight days, our wagons would go up, and I would recommend you to Joe Broadwheel, who would see you safe to the Swan and Two Necks. And dinna sneeze at Joe, if he should be for drawing up wi' you," continued Mrs. Bickerton, her acquired English mingling with her national or original dialect ; "he's a handy boy, and a wanter, and no lad better thought o' on the road ; and the English make good husbands enough, witness my poor man, Moses Bickerton, as is i' the kirkyard."

Jeanie hastened to say that she could not possibly wait for the setting forth of Joe Broadwheel ; being internally by no means gratified with the idea of becoming the object of his attention during the journey.

"Aweel, lass," answered the good landlady, "then thou must pickle in thine ain poke-nook, and buckle thy girdle thine ain gate. But take my advice, and hide thy gold in thy stays, and keep a piece or two and some silver, in case thou be'st spoke withal; for there's as wud lads haunt within a day's walk from hence as on the Braes of Doune in Perthshire. And, lass, thou maunna gang staring through Lunnon, asking wha kens Mrs. Glass at the sign o' the Thistle; marry, they would laugh thee to scorn. But gang thou to this honest man," and she put a direction into Jeanie's hand, "he kens maist part of the 'sponsible Scottish folk in the city, and he will find out your friend for thee."

Jeanie took the little introductory letter with sincere thanks; but, something alarmed on the subject of the highway robbers, her mind recurred to what Ratcliffe had mentioned to her, and briefly relating the circumstances which placed a document so extraordinary in her hands, she put the paper he had given her into the hand of Mrs. Bickerton.

The Lady of the Seven Stars did not, indeed, ring a bell, because such was not the fashion of the time, but she whistled on a silver-call, which was hung by her side, and a tight serv- ing-maiden entered the room.

"Tell Dick Ostler to come here," said Mrs. Bickerton.

Dick Ostler accordingly made his appearance—a queer, knowing, shambling animal, with a hatchet-face, a squint, a game arm, and a limp.

"Dick Ostler," said Mrs. Bickerton, in a tone of author- ity that showed she was, at least by adoption, Yorkshire too, "thou knowest most people and most things o' the road."

"Eye, eye, God help me, mistress," said Dick, shrugging his shoulders betwixt a repentant and a knowing expression— "eye! I ha' know'd a thing or twa i' ma day, mistress." He looked sharp and laughed, looked grave and sighed, as one who was prepared to take the matter either way.

"Kenst thou this wee bit paper amang the rest, man?" said Mrs. Bickerton, handing him the protection which Rat- cliffe had given Jeanie Deans.

When Dick had looked at the paper, he winked with one eye, extended his grotesque mouth from ear to ear, like a navigable canal, scratched his head powerfully, and then said, "Ken! Ay, maybe we ken summat, an it werena for harm to him, mistress."

"None in the world," said Mrs. Bickerton; "only a dram of Hollands to thyself, man, an thou will't speak."

"Why, then," said Dick, giving the head-band of his

breeches a knowing hoist with one hand, and kicking out one foot behind him to accommodate the adjustment of that important habiliment, "I dares to say the pass will be kenn'd weel eneugh on the road, an that be all."

"But what sort of a lad was he ?" said Mrs. Bickerton, winking to Jeanie, as proud of her knowing hostler.

"Why, what ken I ? Jim the Rat ! why he was cock o' the North within this twelmonth, he and Scotch Wilson—Handie Dandie, as they called him. But he's been out o' this country a while, as I rackon ; but ony gentleman as keeps the road o' this side Stamford will respect Jim's pass."

Without asking further questions, the landlady filled Dick Ostler a bumper of Hollands. He ducked with his head and shoulders, scraped with his more advanced hoof, bolted the alcohol, to use the learned phrase, and withdrew to his own domains.

" I would advise thee, Jeanie," said Mrs. Bickerton, " an thou meetest with ugly customers o' the road, to show them this bit paper, for it will serve thee, assure thyself."

A neat little supper concluded the evening. The exported Scotswoman, Mrs. Bickerton by name, eat heartily of one or two seasoned dishes, drank some sound old ale, and a glass of stiff negus, while she gave Jeanie a history of her gout, admiring how it was possible that she, whose fathers and mothers for many generations had been farmers in Lammermuir, could have come by a disorder so totally unknown to them. Jeanie did not choose to offend her friendly landlady by speaking her mind on the probable origin of this complaint ; but she thought on the flesh-pots of Egypt, and, in spite of all entreaties to better fare, made her evening meal upon vegetables, with a glass of fair water.

Mrs. Bickerton assured her that the acceptance of any reckoning was entirely out of the question, furnished her with credentials to her correspondent in London, and to several inns upon the road where she had some influence or interest, reminded her of the precautions she should adopt for concealing her money, and, as she was to depart early in the morning, took leave of her very affectionately, taking her word that she would visit her on her return to Scotland, and tell her how she had managed, and that *summum bonum* for a gossip, "all how and about it." This Jeanie faithfully promised.

CHAPTER XXIX

And Need and Misery, Vice and Danger, **bind,**
In sad alliance, each degraded mind.

As our traveller set out early on the ensuing morning to prosecute her journey, and was in the act of leaving the inn-yard, Dick Ostler, who either had risen early or neglected to go to bed, either circumstance being equally incident to his calling, hallooed out after her—"The top of the morning to you, Moggie ! Have a care o' Gunnerby Hill, young one. Robin Hood's dead and gwone, but there be takers yet in the vale of Beever." Jeanie looked at him as if to request a further explanation, but, with a leer, a shuffle, and a shrug, inimitable (unless by Emery), Dick turned again to the raw-boned steed which he was currying, and sung as he employed the comb and brush—

> "Robin Hood was a yeoman good,
>   And his bow was of trusty yew ;
>   And if Robin said stand on the king's lea-land,
>   Pray, why should not we say so too?"

Jeanie pursued her journey without further inquiry, for there was nothing in Dick's manner that inclined her to prolong their conference. A painful day's journey brought her to Ferrybridge, the best inn, then and since, upon the great northern road ; and an introduction from Mrs. Bickerton, added to her own simple and quiet manners, so propitiated the landlady of the Swan in her favor that the good dame procured her the convenient accommodation of a pillion and post-horse then returning to Tuxford ; so that she accomplished, upon the second day after leaving York, the longest journey she had yet made. She was a good deal fatigued by a mode of travelling to which she was less accustomed than to walking, and it was considerably later than usual on the ensuing morning that she felt herself able to resume her pilgrimage. At noon the hundred armed Trent, and the blackened ruins of Newark Castle, demolished in the great Civil War, lay before her. It may easily be supposed that Jeanie had no curiosity to make antiquarian researches, but, entering the town, went

280

straight to the inn to which she had been directed at Ferry-bridge. While she procured some refreshment, she observed the girl who brought it to her looked at her several times with fixed and peculiar interest, and at last, to her infinite surprise, inquired if her name was not Deans, and if she was not a Scotchwoman, going to London upon justice business. Jeanie, with all her simplicity of character, had some of the caution of her country, and, according to Scottish universal custom, she answered the question by another, requesting the girl would tell her why she asked these questions.

The Maritornes of the Saracen's Head, Newark, replied, "Two women had passed that morning, who had made inquiries after one Jeanie Deans, travelling to London on such an errand, and could scarce be persuaded that she had not passed on."

Much surprised, and somewhat alarmed, for what is inexplicable is usually alarming, Jeanie questioned the wench about the particular appearance of these two women, but could only learn that the one was aged and the other young; that the latter was the taller, and that the former spoke most and seemed to maintain an authority over her companion, and that both spoke with the Scottish accent.

This conveyed no information whatever, and with an indescribable presentiment of evil designed towards her, Jeanie adopted the resolution of taking post-horses for the next stage. In this, however, she could not be gratified; some accidental circumstances had occasioned what is called a run upon the road, and the landlord could not accommodate her with a guide and horses. After waiting some time in hopes that a pair of horses that had gone southward would return in time for her use, she at length, feeling ashamed of her own pusillanimity, resolved to prosecute her journey in her usual manner.

"It was all plain road," she was assured, "except a high mountain, called Gunnerby Hill, about three miles from Grantham, which was her stage for the night."

"I'm glad to hear there's a hill," said Jeanie, "for baith my sight and my very feet are weary o' sic tracts o' level ground; it looks a' the way between this and York as if a' the land had been trenched and levelled, whilk is very wearisome to my Scotch een. When I lost sight of a muckle blue hill they ca' Ingleboro', I thought I hadna a friend left in this strange land."

"As for the matter of that, young woman," said mine host, "and you be so fond o' hill, I carena an thou couldst carry Gunnerby away with thee in thy lap, for it's a murder to post-horses. But here's to thy journey, and mayst thou win well through it, for thou is a bold and a canny lass."

So saying, he took a powerful pull at a solemn tankard of home-brewed ale.

"I hope there is nae bad company on the road, sir ?" said Jeanie.

" Why, when it's clean without them I'll thatch Groby pool wi' pancakes. But there arena sae mony now ; and since they hae lost Jim the Rat, they hold together no better than the men of Marsham when they lost their common. Take a drop ere thou goest," he concluded, offering her the tankard ; " thou wilt get naething at night save Grantham gruel, nine grots and a gallon of water."

Jeanie courteously declined the tankard, and inquired what was her "lawing."

"Thy lawing ! Heaven help thee, wench ! what ca'st thou that ? "

" It is—I was wanting to ken what was to pay," replied Jeanie.

" Pay ! Lord help thee ! why, nought, woman ; we hae drawn no liquor but a gill o' beer, and the Saracen's Head can spare a mouthful o' meat to a stranger like o' thee, that cannot speak Christian language. So here's to thee once more. 'The same again, quoth Mark of Bellgrave,' " and he took another profound pull at the tankard.

The travellers who have visited Newark more lately will not fail to remember the remarkably civil and gentlemanly manners of the person who now keeps the principal inn there, and may find some amusement in contrasting them with those of his more rough predecessor. But we believe it will be found that the polish has worn off none of the real worth of the metal.

Taking leave of her Lincolnshire Gaius, Jeanie resumed her solitary walk, and was somewhat alarmed when evening and twilight overtook her in the open ground which extends to the foot of Gunnerby Hill, and is intersected with patches of copse and with swampy spots. The extensive commons on the north road, most of which are now enclosed, and in general a relaxed state of police, exposed the traveller to a highway robbery in a degree which is now unknown, excepting in the immediate vicinity of the metropolis. Aware of this circumstance, Jeanie mended her pace when she heard the trampling of a horse behind, and instinctively drew to one side of the road, as if to allow as much room for the rider to pass as might be possible. When the animal came up, she found that it was bearing two women, the one placed on a side-saddle, the other on a pillion behind her, as may still occasionally be seen in England.

"A braw gude night to ye, Jeanie Deans," said the foremost female, as the horse passed our heroine. "What think ye o' yon bonny hill yonder, lifting its brow to the moon? Trow ye yon's the gate to Heaven, that ye are sae fain of? Maybe we may win there the night yet, God sain us, though our minnie here's rather dreich in the upgang."

The speaker kept changing her seat in the saddle, and half stopping the horse, as she brought her body round, while the woman that sat behind her on the pillion seemed to urge her on, in words which Jeanie heard but imperfectly.

"Haud your tongue, ye moon-raised b—— ! what is your business with——, or with Heaven or Hell either?"

"Troth, mither, no muckle wi' Heaven, I doubt, considering wha I carry ahint me; and as for Hell, it will fight its ain battle at its ain time, I'se be bound. Come, naggie, trot awa', man, an as thou wert a broomstick, for a witch rides thee—

With my curch on my foot, and my shoe on my hand,
I glance like the wildfire through brugh and through land."

The tramp of the horse, and the increasing distance, drowned the rest of her song, but Jeanie heard for some time the inarticulate sounds ring along the waste.

Our pilgrim remained stupefied with undefined apprehensions. The being named by her name in so wild a manner, and in a strange country, without further explanation or communing, by a person who thus strangely flitted forward and disappeared before her, came near to the supernatural sounds in *Comus:*

The airy tongues, which syllable men's names
On sands, and shores, and desert wildernesses.

And although widely different in features, deportment, and rank from the Lady of that enchanting masque, the continuation of the passage may be happily applied to Jeanie Deans upon this singular alarm:

These thoughts may startle well, but not astound
The virtuous mind, that ever walks attended
By a strong siding champion—Conscience.

In fact, it was, with the recollection of the affectionate

and dutiful errand on which she was engaged, her right, if such a word could be applicable, to expect protection in a task so meritorious. She had not advanced much further, with a mind calmed by these reflections, when she was disturbed by a new and more instant subject of terror. Two men who had been lurking among some copse started up as she advanced, and met her on the road in a menacing manner. "Stand and deliver," said one of them, a short stout fellow, in a smock-frock, such as are worn by wagoners.

"The woman," said the other, a tall thin figure, "does not understand the words of action. Your money, my precious, or your life!"

"I have but very little money, gentlemen," said poor Jeanie, tendering that portion which she had separated from her principal stock, and kept apart for such an emergency; "but if you are resolved to have it, to be sure you must have it."

"This won't do, my girl. D——n me if it shall pass!" said the shorter ruffian; "do ye think gentlemen are to hazard their lives on the road to be cheated in this way? We'll have every farthing you have got, or we will strip you to the skin, curse me."

His companion, who seemed to have something like compassion for the horror which Jeanie's countenance now expressed, said, "No, no, Tom, this is one of the precious sisters, and we'll take her word, for once, without putting her to the stripping proof. Hark ye, my lass, if you'll look up to heaven and say this is the last penny you have about ye, why, hang it, we'll let you pass."

"I am not free," answered Jeanie, "to say what I have about me, gentlemen, for there's life and death depends on my journey; but if you leave me as much as finds me in bread and water, I'll be satisfied, and thank you, and pray for you."

"D——n your prayers!" said the shorter fellow; "that's a coin that won't pass with us;" and at the same time made a motion to seize her.

"Stay, gentlemen," Ratcliffe's pass suddenly occurring to her; "perhaps you know this paper."

"What the devil is she after now, Frank?" said the more savage ruffian. "Do you look at it, for d——n me if I could read it, if it were for the benefit of my clergy."

"This is a jark from Jim Ratcliffe," said the taller, having looked at the bit of paper. "The wench must pass by our cutter's law."

"I say no," answered his companion. "Rat has left the lay, and turned bloodhound, they say."

"We may need a good turn from him all the same," said the taller ruffian again.

"But what are we to do then?" said the shorter man. "We promised, you know, to strip the wench and send her begging back to her own beggarly country, and now you are for letting her go on."

"I did not say that," said the other fellow, and whispered to his companion, who replied, "Be alive about it, then, and don't keep chattering till some travellers come up to nab us."

"You must follow us off the road, young woman," said the taller.

"For the love of God!" exclaimed Jeanie, "as you were born of woman, dinna ask me to leave the road! rather take all I have in the world."

"What the devil is the wench afraid of?" said the other fellow. "I tell you you shall come to no harm; but if you will not leave the road and come with us, d—n me, but I'll beat your brains out where you stand."

"Thou art a rough bear, Tom," said his companion. "An ye touch her, I'll give ye a shake by the collar shall make the Leicester beans rattle in thy guts. Never mind him, girl; I will not allow him to lay a finger on you, if you walk quietly on with us; but if you keep jabbering there, d—n me, but I'll leave him to settle it with you."

This threat conveyed all that is terrible to the imagination of poor Jeanie, who saw in him that "was of milder mood" her only protection from the most brutal treatment. She, therefore, not only followed him, but even held him by the sleeve, lest he should escape from her; and the fellow, hardened as he was, seemed something touched by these marks of confidence, and repeatedly assured her that he would suffer her to receive no harm.

They conducted their prisoner in a direction leading more and more from the public road, but she observed that they kept a sort of track or by-path, which relieved her from part of her apprehensions, which would have been greatly increased had they not seemed to follow a determined and ascertained route. After about half an hour's walking, all three in profound silence, they approached an old barn, which stood on the edge of some cultivated ground, but remote from everything like an habitation. It was itself, however, tenanted, for there was light in the windows.

One of the footpads scratched at the door, which was

opened by a female, and they entered with their unhappy
prisoner.   An old woman, who was preparing food by the assistance of a stifling fire of lighted charcoal, asked them, in
the name of the devil, what they brought the wench there for,
and why they did not strip her and turn her abroad on the
common.

"Come, come, Mother Blood," said the tall man, "we'll
do what's right to oblige you, and we'll do no more; we are
bad enough, but not such as you would make us—devils incarnate."

"She has got a jark from Jim Ratcliffe," said the short
fellow, "and Frank here won't hear of our putting her through
the mill."

"No, that will I not, by G—d!" answered Frank; "but
if old Mother Blood could keep her here for a little while, or
send her back to Scotland, without hurting her, why, I see no
harm in that, not I."

"I'll tell you what, Frank Levitt," said the old woman,
"if you call me Mother Blood again, I'll paint this gulley
[and she held a knife up as if about to make good her threat]
in the best blood in your body, my bonny boy."

"The price of ointment must be up in the north," said
Frank, "that puts Mother Blood so much out of humor."

Without a moment's hesitation the fury darted her knife
at him with the vengeful dexterity of a wild Indian.   As he
was on his guard, he avoided the missile by a sudden motion
of his head, but it whistled past his ear and stuck deep in the
clay wall of a partition behind.

"Come, come, mother," said the robber, seizing her by
both wrists, "I shall teach you who's master;" and so saying,
he forced the hag backwards by main force, who strove vehe-
mently until she sunk on a bunch of straw, and then letting
go her hands, he held up his finger towards her in the menacing posture by which a maniac is intimidated by his keeper.
It appeared to produce the desired effect; for she did not attempt to rise from the seat on which he had placed her, or to
resume any measures of actual violence, but wrung her
withered hands with impotent rage, and brayed and howled
like a demoniac.

"I will keep my promise with you, you old devil," said
Frank; "the wench shall not go forward on the London road,
but I will not have you touch a hair of her head, if it were
but for your insolence."

This intimation seemed to compose in some degree the
vehement passion of the old hag; and while her exclamations

and howls sunk into a low, maundering, growling tone of voice, another personage was added to this singular party.

"Eh, Frank Levitt," said this new-comer, who entered with a hop, step, and jump, which at once conveyed her from the door into the centre of the party, "were ye killing our mother ? or were ye cutting the grunter's weasand t'at Tam brought in this morning ? or have ye been reading your prayers backward, to bring up my auld acquaintance the deil amang ye ?"

The tone of the speaker was so particular that Jeanie immediately recognized the woman who had rode foremost of the pair which passed her just before she met the robbers ; a circumstance which greatly increased her terror, as it served to show that the mischief designed against her was premeditated, though by whom, or for what cause, she was totally at a loss to conjecture. From the style of her conversation, the reader also may probably acknowledge in this female an old acquaintance in the earlier part of our narrative.

"Out, ye mad devil !" said Tom, whom she had disturbed in the middle of a draught of some liquor with which he had found means of accommodating himself ; "betwixt your Bess of Bedlam pranks and your dam's frenzies a man might live quieter in the devil's den than here." And he again resumed the broken jug out of which he had been drinking.

"And what's this o't ?" said the madwoman, dancing up to Jeanie Deans, who, although in great terror, yet watched the scene with a resolution to let nothing pass unnoticed which might be serviceable in assisting her to escape, or informing her as to the true nature of her situation, and the danger attending it. "What's this o't ?" again exclaimed Madge Wildfire. "Douce Davie Deans, the auld doited Whig body's daughter in a gypsy's barn, and the night setting in ; this is a sight for sair een ! Eh, sirs, the falling off o' the godly ! And the t'other sister's in the tolbooth at Edinburgh ! I am very sorry for her, for my share ; it's my mother wusses ill to her, and no me, though maybe I hae as muckle cause."

"Hark ye, Madge," said the taller ruffian, "you have not such a touch of the devil's blood as the hag your mother, who may be his dam for what I know ; take this young woman to your kennel, and do not let the devil enter, though he should ask in God's name."

"Ou ay, that I will, Frank," said Madge, taking hold of Jeanie by the arm, and pulling her along ; "for it's no for decent Christian young leddies, like her and me, to be keeping the like o' you and Tyburn Tam company at this time o' night.   Sae gude e'en t'ye, sirs, and mony o' them ; and may ye a' sleep till the hangman wauken ye, and then it will be weel for the country."

She then, as her wild fancy seemed suddenly to prompt her, walked demurely towards her mother, who, seated by the charcoal fire, with the reflection of the red light on her withered and distorted features, marked by every evil passion, seemed the very picture of Hecate at her infernal rites ; and suddenly dropping on her knees, said, with the manner of a six-years-old child, "Mammie, hear me say my prayers before I go to bed, and say God bless my bonny face, as ye used to do lang syne."

"The deil flay the hide o' it to sole his brogues wi' !" said the old lady, aiming a buffet at the supplicant in answer to her duteous request.

The blow missed Madge, who, being probably acquainted by experience with the mode in which her mother was wont to confer her maternal benedictions, slipped out of arm's-length with great dexterity and quickness.   The hag then started up, and, seizing a pair of old fire-tongs, would have amended her motion by beating out the brains either of her daughter or Jeanie, she did not seem greatly to care which, when her hand was once more arrested by the man whom they called Frank Levitt, who, seizing her by the shoulder, flung her from him with great violence, exclaiming, "What, Mother Damnable, again, and in my sovereign presence ? Hark ye, Madge of Bedlam, get to your hole with your playfellow, or we shall have the devil to pay here, and nothing to pay him with."

Madge took Levitt's advice, retreating as fast as she could, and dragging Jeanie along with her, into a sort of recess, partitioned off from the rest of the barn, and filled with straw, from which it appeared that it was intended for the purpose of slumber.   The moonlight shone through an open hole upon a pillion, a pack-saddle, and one or two wallets, the travelling furniture of Madge and her amiable mother. "Now, saw ye e'er in your life," said Madge, "sae dainty a chamber of deas ? See as the moon shines down sae caller on the fresh strae ! There's no a pleasanter cell in Bedlam, for as braw a place as it is on the outside. Were ye ever in Bedlam ?"

"No," answered Jeanie, faintly, appalled by the question and the way in which it was put, yet willing to soothe her insane companion ; being in circumstances so unhappily precarious that even the society of this gibbering madwoman seemed a species of protection.

"Never in Bedlam!" said Madge, as if with some surprise. "But ye'll hae been in the cells at Edinburgh?"

"Never," repeated Jeanie.

"Weel, I think thae daft carles the magistrates send naebody to Bedlam but me; they maun hae an unco respect for me, for whenever I am brought to them they aye hae me back to Bedlam. But troth, Jeanie [she said this in a very confidential tone], to tell ye my private mind about it, I think ye are at nae great loss; for the keeper's a cross patch, and he maun hae it a' his ain gate, to be sure, or he makes the place waur than hell: I often tell him he's the daftest in a' the house. But what are they making sic a skirling for? Deil ane o' them's get in here; it wadna be mensefu'! I will sit wi' my back again the door; it winna be that easy stirring me."

"Madge!"—"Madge!"—"Madge Wildfire!"—"Madge devil! what have ye done with the horse?" was repeatedly asked by the men without.

"He's e'en at his supper, puir thing," answered Madge; "deil an ye were at yours too, an it were scauding brimstane, and then we wad hae less o' your din."

"His supper!" answered the more sulky ruffian. "What d'ye mean by that? Tell me where he is, or I will knock your Bedlam brains out!"

"He's in Gaffer Gabblewood's wheat-close, an ye maun ken."

"His wheat-close, you crazed jilt!" answered the other, with an accent of great indignation.

"O, dear Tyburn Tam, man, what ill will the blades of the young wheat do to the puir naig?"

"That is not the question," said the other robber; "but what the country will say to us to-morrow when they see him in such quarters. Go, Tom, and bring him in; and avoid the soft ground, my lad; leave no hoof-track behind you."

"I think you give me always the fag of it, whatever is to be done," grumbled his companion.

"'Leap, Laurence, you're long enough,'" said the other; and the fellow left the barn accordingly, without further remonstrance.

In the meanwhile, Madge had arranged herself for repose on the straw; but still in a half-sitting posture, with her back resting against the door of the hovel, which, as it opened inwards, was in this manner kept shut by the weight of her person.

"There's mair shifts bye stealing, Jeanie," said Madge Wildfire; "though whiles I can hardly get our mother to think sae. Wha wad hae thought but mysell of making a bolt of my ain backbane ? But it's no sae strong as thae that I hae seen in the tolbooth at Edinburgh. The hammermen of Edinburgh are to my mind afore the world for making stanchions, ring-bolts, fetter-bolts, bars, and locks. And they arena that bad at girdles for carcakes neither, though the Cu'ross hammermen have the gree for that. My mother had ance a bonny Cu'ross girdle, and I thought to have baked car-cakes on it for my puir wean that's dead and gane nae fair way ; but we maun a' dee, ye ken, Jeanie. You Cameronian bodies ken that brawly ; and ye're for making a hell upon earth that ye may be less unwillin' to part wi' it. But as touching Bedlam, that ye were speaking about, I'se ne'er recommend it muckle the tae gate or the tother, be it right, be it wrang. But ye ken what the sang says ?" And, pursuing the unconnected and floating wanderings of her mind, she sung aloud—

> "In the bonny cells of Bedlam,
> Ere I was ane-and-twenty,
> I had hempen bracelets strong,
> And merry whips, ding-dong,
> And prayer and fasting plenty.

Weel, Jeanie, I am something herse the night, and I canna sing muckle mair ; and troth, I think I am gaun to sleep."

She drooped her head on her breast, a posture from which Jeanie, who would have given the world for an opportunity of quiet to consider the means and the probability of her escape, was very careful not to disturb her. After nodding, however, for a minute or two, with her eyes half closed, the unquiet and restless spirit of her malady again assailed Madge. She raised her head and spoke, but with a lowered tone, which was again gradually overcome by drowsiness, to which the fatigue of a day's journey on horseback had probably given unwonted occasion—"I dinna ken what makes me sae sleepy ; I amaist never sleep till my bonny Lady Moon gangs till her bed, mair by token when she's at the full, ye ken, rowing aboon us yonder in her grand silver coach. I have danced to her my lane sometimes for very joy, and whiles dead folk came and danced wi' me, the like o' Jock Porteous, or onybody I had kenn'd when I was living ; for ye maun ken I was ance dead mysell." Here the poor maniac sung in a low and wild tone—

> "My banes are buried in yon kirkyard
> Sae far ayont the sea,
> And it is but my blithesome ghaist
> That's speaking now to thee.

But, after a', Jeanie, my woman, naebody kens weel wha's living and wha's dead—or wha's gane to Fairyland, there's another question.   Whiles I think my puir bairn's dead ; ye ken very weel it's buried, but that signifies naething.   I have had it on my knee a hundred times, and a hundred till that, since it was buried ; and how could that be were it dead, ye ken ?   It's merely impossible."   And here, some conviction half overcoming the reveries of her imagination, she burst into a fit of crying and ejaculation, "Wae's me ! wae's me ! wae's me !" till at length she moaned and sobbed herself into a deep sleep, which was soon intimated by her breathing hard, leaving Jeanie to her own melancholy reflections and observations.

CHAPTER XXX

Bind her quickly ; or, by this steel,
I'll tell, although I truss for company.
                                    FLETCHER.

THE imperfect light which shone into the window enabled
Jeanie to see that there was scarcely any chance of making
her escape in that direction ; for the aperture was high in the
wall, and so narrow that, could she have climbed up to it, she
might well doubt w' ether it would have permitted her to
pass her body through it. An unsuccessful attempt to escape
would be sure to draw down worse treatment than she now
received, and she therefore resolved to watch her opportunity
carefully ere making such a perilous effort. For this purpose she applied herself to the ruinous clay partition which
divided the hovel in which she now was from the rest of the
waste barn. It was decayed, and full of cracks and chinks,
one of which she enlarged with her fingers, cautiously and
without noise, until she could obtain a plain view of the old
hag and the taller ruffian, whom they called Levitt, seated
together beside the decayed fire of charcoal, and apparently
engaged in close conference. She was at first terrified by the
sight, for the features of the old woman had a hideous cast
of hardened and inveterate malice and ill-humor, and those
of the man, though naturally less unfavorable, were such as
corresponded well with licentious habits and a lawless profession.

"But I remembered," said Jeanie, "my worthy father's
tales of a winter evening, how he was confined with the
blessed martyr, Mr. James Renwick, who lifted up the fallen
standard of the true reformed Kirk of Scotland, after the
worthy and renowned Daniel [Richard] Cameron, our last
blessed bannerman, had fallen among the swords of the
wicked at Aird's Moss, and how the very hearts of the wicked
malefactors and murderers whom they were confined withal
were melted like wax at the sound of their doctrine, and I
bethought mysell, that the same help that was wi' them in
their strait, wad be wi' me in mine, an I could but watch the

Lord's time and opportunity for delivering my feet from their snare ; and I minded the Scripture of the blessed Psalmist, whilk he insisteth on, as weel in the forty-second as in the forty-third psalm, 'Why art thou cast down, O my soul, and why art thou disquieted within me ? Hope in God, for I shall yet praise him, who is the health of my countenance, and my God.'"

Strengthened in a mind naturally calm, sedate, and firm, by the influence of religious confidence, this poor captive was enabled to attend to, and comprehend, a great part of an interesting conversation which passed betwixt those into whose hands she had fallen, notwithstanding that their meaning was partly disguised by the occasional use of cant terms, of which Jeanie knew not the import, by the low tone in which they spoke, and by their mode of supplying their broken phrases by shrugs and signs, as is usual among those of their disorderly profession.

The man opened the conversation by saying, "Now, dame, you see I am true to my friend. I have not forgot that you planked a chury which helped me through the bars of the Castle of York, and I came to do your work without asking questions, for one good turn deserves another. But now that Madge, who is as loud as Tom of Lincoln, is somewhat still, and this same Tyburn Neddie is shaking his heels after the old nag, why, you must tell me what all this is about, and what's to be done ; for d—n me if I touch the girl, or let her be touched, and she with Jim Rat's pass too."

"Thou art an honest lad, Frank," answered the old woman, "but e'en too kind for thy trade ; thy tender heart will get thee into trouble. I will see ye gang up Holborn Hill backward, and a' on the word of some silly loon that could never hae rapped to ye had ye drawn your knife across his weasand."

"You may be balked there, old one," answered the robber ; "I have known many a pretty lad cut short in his first summer upon the road, because he was something hasty with his flats and sharps. Besides, a man would fain live out his two years with a good conscience. So, tell me what all this is about, and what's to be done for you that one can do decently ?"

"Why, you must know, Frank—but first taste a snap of right Hollands." She drew a flask from her pocket, and filled the fellow a large bumper, which he pronounced to be the right thing. "You must know, then, Frank—wunna ye mend your hand ?" again offering the flask.

"No, no; when a woman wants mischief from you, she always begins by filling you drunk. D—n all Dutch courage. What I do I will do soberly. I'll last the longer for that too."

"Well, then, you must know," resumed the old woman, without any further attempts at propitiation, "that this girl is going to London."

Here Jeanie could only distinguish the word "sister."

The robber answered in a louder tone, "Fair enough that; and what the devil is your business with it?"

"Business enough, I think. If the b—— queers the noose, that silly cull will marry her."

"And who cares if he does?" said the man.

"Who cares, ye donnard Neddie? *I* care; and I will strangle her with my own hands rather than she should come to Madge's preferment."

"Madge's preferment! Does your old blind eyes see no further than that? If he is as you say, d'ye think he'll ever marry a moon-calf like Madge? Ecod, that's a good one. Marry Madge Wildfire! ha! ha! ha!"

"Hark ye, ye crack-rope padder, born beggar, and bred thief!" replied the hag; "suppose he never marries the wench, is that a reason he should marry another, and that other to hold my daughter's place, and she crazed, and I a beggar, and all along of him? But I know that of him will hang him—I know that of him will hang him, if he had a thousand lives—I know that of him will hang—hang—hang him!"

She grinned as she repeated and dwelt upon the fatal monosyllable with the emphasis of a vindictive fiend.

"Then why don't you hang—hang—hang him?" said Frank, repeating her words contemptuously. "There would be more sense in that, than in wreaking yourself here upon two wenches that have done you and your daughter no ill."

"No ill!" answered the old woman; "and he to marry this jail-bird, if ever she gets her foot loose!"

"But as there is no chance of his marrying a bird of your brood, I cannot, for my soul, see what you have to do with all this," again replied the robber, shrugging his shoulders. "Where there is aught to be got, I'll go as far as my neighbors, but I hate mischief for mischief's sake."

"And would you go nae length for revenge?" said the hag—"for revenge, the sweetest morsel to the mouth that ever was cooked in hell!"

"The devil may keep it for his own eating, then," said

the robber; "for hang me if I like the sauce he dresses it with."

"Revenge!" continued the old woman; "why, it is the best reward the devil gives us for our time here and hereafter. I have wrought hard for it, I have suffered for it, and I have sinned for it, and I will have it—or there is neither justice in Heaven nor in Hell!"

Levitt had by this time lighted a pipe, and was listening with great composure to the frantic and vindictive ravings of the old hag. He was too much hardened by his course of life to be shocked with them; too indifferent, and probably too stupid, to catch any part of their animation or energy. "But, mother," he said, after a pause, "still I say, that if revenge is your wish, you should take it on the young fellow himself."

"I wish I could," she said, drawing in her breath, with the eagerness of a thirsty person while mimicking the action of drinking—"I wish I could! but no, I cannot—I cannot."

"And why not? You would think little of peaching and hanging him for this Scotch affair. Rat me, one might have milled the Bank of England, and less noise about it."

"I have nursed him at this withered breast," answered the old woman, folding her hands on her bosom, as if pressing an infant to it, "and though he has proved an adder to me, though he has been the destruction of me and mine, though he has made me company for the devil, if there be a devil, and food for hell, if there be such a place, yet I cannot take his life. No, I cannot," she continued, with an appearance of rage against herself; "I have thought of it, I have tried it, but, Francis Levitt, I canna gang through wi't! Na, na, he was the first bairn I ever nurst; ill I had been—but man can never ken what woman feels for the bairn she has held first to her bosom!"

"To be sure," said Levitt, "we have no experience. But, mother, they say you ha'n't been so kind to other *bairns*, as you call them, that have come in your way. Nay, d—n me, never lay your hand on the whittle, for I am captain and leader here, and I will have no rebellion."

The hag, whose first motion had been, upon hearing the question, to grasp the haft of a large knife, now unclosed her hand, stole it away from the weapon, and suffered it to fall by her side, while she proceeded with a sort of smile—"Bairns! ye are joking, lad, wha wad touch bairns? Madge, puir thing, had a misfortune wi' ane; and the tother——" Here her voice sunk so much that Jeanie, though anxiously upon the watch, could not catch a word she said, until she raised her tone at the conclusion of the sentence—"So Madge, in her daffin', threw it into the Nor' Loch, I trow."

Madge, whose slumbers, like those of most who labor under mental malady, had been short, and were easily broken, now made herself heard from her place of repose.

"Indeed, mother, that's a great lee, for I did nae sic thing."

"Hush, thou hellicat devil," said her mother. "By Heaven! the other wench will be waking too!"

"That may be dangerous," said Frank; and he rose and followed Meg Murdockson across the floor.

"Rise," said the hag to her daughter, "or I sall drive the knife between the planks into the Bedlam back of thee!"

Apparently she at the same time seconded her threat, by pricking her with the point of a knife, for Madge, with a faint scream, changed her place, and the door opened.

The old woman held a candle in one hand and a knife in the other. Levitt appeared behind her; whether with a view of preventing or assisting her in any violence she might meditate could not be well guessed. Jeanie's presence of mind stood her friend in this dreadful crisis. She had resolution enough to maintain the attitude and manner of one who sleeps profoundly, and to regulate even her breathing, notwithstanding the agitation of instant terror, so as to correspond with her attitude.

The old woman passed the light across her eyes; and, although Jeanie's fears were so powerfully awakened by this movement, that she often declared afterwards that she thought she saw the figures of her destined murderers through her closed eyelids, she had still the resolution to maintain the feint on which her safety perhaps depended.

Levitt looked at her with fixed attention; he then turned the old woman out of the place, and followed her himself. Having regained the outer apartment, and seated themselves, Jeanie heard the highwayman say, to her no small relief, "She's as fast as if she were in Bedfordshire. Now, old Meg, d—n me if I can understand a glim of this story of yours, or what good it will do you to hang the one wench and torment the other; but, rat me, I will be true to my friend, and serve ye the way ye like it. I see it will be a bad job; but I do think I could get her down to Surfleet on the Wash, and so on board Tom Moonshine's neat lugger, and keep her out of the way three or four weeks, if that will please ye. But d—n me if any one shall harm her, unless they have a mind to choke on a brace of blue plums. It's a cruel bad job, and I wish you and it, Meg, were both at the devil."

" Never mind, hinny Levitt," said the old woman ; "you are a ruffler, and will have a' your ain gate. She shanna gang to Heaven an hour sooner for me ; I carena whether she live or die : it's her sister—ay, her sister !"

" Well, we'll say no more about it, I hear Tom coming in. We'll couch a hogshead, and so better had you."

They retired to repose, accordingly, and all was silent in this asylum of iniquity.

Jeanie lay for a long time awake. At break of day she heard the two ruffians leave the barn, after whispering with the old woman for some time. The sense that she was now guarded only by persons of her own sex gave her some confidence, and irresistible lassitude at length threw her into slumber.

When the captive awakened, the sun was high in heaven, and the morning considerably advanced. Madge Wildfire was still in the hovel which had served them for the night, and immediately bid her good morning, with her usual air of insane glee. "And d'ye ken, lass," said Madge, "there's queer things chanced since ye hae been in the land of Nod. The constables hae been here, woman, and they met wi' my minnie at the door, and they whirl'd her awa' to the Justice's about the man's wheat. Dear! thae English churls think as muckle about a blade of wheat or grass as a Scots laird does about his maukins and his muir-poots. Now, lass, if ye like, we'll play them a fine jink : we will awa' out and take a walk ; they will make unco wark when they miss us, but we can easily be back by dinner time, or before dark night at ony rate, and it will be some frolic and fresh air. But maybe ye wad like to take some breakfast, and then lie down again ? I ken by mysell there's whiles I can sit wi' my head on my hand the haill day, and havena a word to cast at a dog, and other whiles that I canna sit still a moment. That's when the folk think me warst ; but I am aye canny eneugh—ye needna be feared to walk wi' me."

Had Madge Wildfire been the most raging lunatic, instead of possessing a doubtful, uncertain, and twilight sort of rationality, varying, probably, from the influence of the most trivial causes, Jeanie would hardly have objected to leave a place of captivity where she had so much to apprehend. She eagerly assured Madge that she had no occasion for further sleep, no desire whatever for eating ; and hoping internally that she was not guilty of sin in doing so, she flattered her keeper's crazy humor for walking in the woods.

"It's no a'thegither for that neither," said poor Madge ; "but I am judging ye will wun the better out o' thae folks' hands ; no that they are a'thegither bad folk neither, but they have queer ways wi' them, and I whiles dinna think it has been ever very weel wi' my mother and me since we kept sic-like company."

With the haste, the joy, the fear, and the hope of a liberated captive, Jeanie snatched up her little bundle, followed Madge into the free air, and eagerly looked round her for a human habitation ; but none was to be seen. The ground was partly cultivated, and partly left in its natural state, according as the fancy of the slovenly agriculturists had decided. In its natural state it was waste, in some places covered with dwarf trees and bushes, in others swamp, and elsewhere firm and dry downs or pasture-grounds.

Jeanie's active mind next led her to conjecture which way the high-road lay, whence she had been forced. If she regained that public road, she imagined she must soon meet some person, or arrive at some house, where she might tell her story, and request protection. But after a glance around her, she saw with regret that she had no means whatever of directing her course with any degree of certainty, and that she was still in dependence upon her crazy companion. "Shall we not walk upon the high-road ?" said she to Madge, in such a tone as a nurse uses to coax a child. "It's brawer walking on the road than amang thae wild bushes and whins."

Madge, who was walking very fast, stopped at this question, and looked at Jeanie with a sudden and scrutinizing glance, that seemed to indicate complete acquaintance with her purpose. "Aha, lass !" she exclaimed, "are ye gaun to guide us that gate ? Ye'll be for making your heels save your head, I am judging."

Jeanie hesitated for a moment, on hearing her companion thus express herself, whether she had not better take the hint, and try to outstrip and get rid of her. But she knew not in which direction to fly ; she was by no means sure that she would prove the swiftest, and perfectly conscious that, in the event of her being pursued and overtaken, she would be inferior to the madwoman in strength. She therefore gave up thoughts for the present of attempting to escape in that manner, and, saying a few words to allay Madge's suspicions, she followed in anxious apprehension the wayward path by which her guide thought proper to lead her. Madge, infirm of purpose, and easily reconciled to the present scene, whatever it was, began soon to talk with her usual diffuseness of ideas.

"It's a dainty thing to be in the woods on a fine morning

like this. I like it far better than the town, for there isna a wheen duddy bairns to be crying after ane, as if ane were a warld's wonder, just because ane maybe is a thought bonnier and better put-on than their neighbors ; though, Jeanie, ye suld never be proud o' braw claiths, or beauty neither ; wae's me ! they're but a snare. I anes thought better o' them, and what came o't ? "

"Are ye sure ye ken the way ye are taking us ? " said Jeanie, who began to imagine that she was getting deeper into the woods, and more remote from the high-road.

"Do I ken the road ? Wasna I mony a day living here, and what for shouldna I ken the road ? I might hae forgotten, too, for it was afore my accident ; but there are some things ane can never forget, let them try it as muckle as they like."

By this time they had gained the deepest part of a patch of woodland. The trees were a little separated from each other, and at the foot of one of them, a beautiful poplar, was a variegated hillock of wild flowers and moss, such as the poet of Grasmere has described in his verses on "The Thorn." So soon as she arrived at this spot, Madge Wildfire, joining her hands above her head, with a loud scream that resembled laughter, flung herself all at once upon the spot, and remained lying there motionless.

Jeanie's first idea was to take the opportunity of flight ; but her desire to escape yielded for a moment to apprehension for the poor insane being, who, she thought, might perish for want of relief. With an effort which, in her circumstances, might be termed heroic, she stooped down, spoke in a soothing tone, and endeavored to raise up the forlorn creature. She effected this with difficulty, and, as she placed her against the tree in a sitting posture, she observed with surprise that her complexion, usually florid, was now deadly pale, and that her face was bathed in tears. Notwithstanding her own extreme danger, Jeanie was affected by the situation of her companion ; and the rather that, through the whole train of her wavering and inconsistent state of mind and line of conduct, she discerned a general color of kindness towards herself, for which she felt grateful.

"Let me alane !—let me alane !" said the poor young woman, as her paroxysm of sorrow began to abate. "Let me alane ; it does me good to weep. I canna shed tears but maybe anes or twice a year, and I aye come to wet this turf with them, that the flowers may grow fair, and the grass may be green."

"But what is the matter with you ?" said Jeanie. "**Why** do you weep so bitterly ?"

"There's matter enow," replied the lunatic ; "mair than ae puir mind can bear. I trow. Stay a bit, and I'll tell you a' about it ; for I like ye, Jeanie Deans ; a'body spoke weel about ye when we lived in the Pleasaunts. And I mind aye the drink o' milk ye gae me yon day, when I had been on Arthur's Seat for four-and-twenty hours, looking for the ship that somebody was sailing in."

These words recalled to Jeanie's recollection that, in fact, she had been one morning much frightened by meeting a crazy young woman near her father's house at an early hour, and that, as she appeared to be harmless, her apprehension had been changed into pity, and she had relieved the unhappy wanderer with some food, which she devoured with the haste of a famished person. The incident, trifling in itself, was at present of great importance, if it should be found to have made a favorable and permanent impression on the mind of the object of her charity.

"Yes," said Madge, "I'll tell ye all about it, for ye are a decent man's daughter—Douce Davie Deans, ye ken ; and maybe ye'll can teach me to find out the narrow way and the strait path ; for I have been burning bricks in Egypt, and walking through the weary wilderness of Sinai, for lang and mony a day. But whenever I think about mine errors, I am like to cover my lips for shame." Here she looked up and smiled. "It's a strange thing now—I hae spoke mair gude words to you in ten minutes, than I wad speak to my mother in as mony years. It's no that I dinna think on them, and whiles they are just at my tongue's end ; but then comes the devil and brushes my lips with his black wing, and lays his broad black loof on my mouth—for a black loof it is, Jeanie —and sweeps away a' my gude thoughts, and dits up my gude words, and pits a wheen fule sangs and idle vanities in their place."

"Try, Madge," said Jeanie—"try to settle your mind and make your breast clean, and you'll find your heart easier. Just resist the devil, and he will flee from you ; and mind that, as my worthy father tells me, there is nae devil sae deceitfu' as our ain wandering thoughts."

"And that's true too, lass," said Madge, starting up ; "and I'll gang a gate where the devil daurna follow me ; and it's a gate that you will like dearly to gang ; but I'll keep a fast haud o' your arm, for fear Apollyon should stride across the path, as he did in the *Pilgrim's Progress*."

Accordingly, she got up, and, taking Jeanie by the arm, began to walk forward at a great pace ; and soon, to her companion's no small joy, came into a marked path, with the meanders of which she seemed perfectly acquainted. Jeanie endeavored to bring her back to the confessional, but the fancy was gone by. In fact, the mind of this deranged being resembled nothing so much as a quantity of dry leaves, which may for a few minutes remain still, but are instantly discomposed and put in motion by the first casual breath of air. She had now got John Bunyan's parable into her head, to the exclusion of everything else, and on she went with great volubility.

"Did ye never read the *Pilgrim's Progress?* And you shall be the woman Christiana, and I will be the maiden Mercy ; for ye ken Mercy was of the fairer countenance, and the more alluring than her companion ; and if I had my little messan dog here, it would be Great-Heart, their guide, ye ken, for he was e'en as bauld that he wad bark at onything twenty times his size ; and that was e'en the death of him, for he bit Corporal MacAlpine's heels ae morning when they were hauling me to the guard-house, and Corporal MacAlpine killed the bit faithfu' thing wi' his Lochaber axe—deil pike the Highland banes o' him !"

"O fie, Madge," said Jeanie, "ye should not speak such words."

"It's very true," said Madge, shaking her head ; "but then I maunna think on my puir bit doggie, Snap, when I saw it lying dying in the gutter. But it's just as weel, for it suffered baith cauld and hunger when it was living, and in the grave there is rest for a' things—rest for the doggie, and my puir bairn, and me."

"Your bairn ?" said Jeanie, conceiving that by speaking on such a topic, supposing it to be a real one, she could not fail to bring her companion to a more composed temper.

She was mistaken, however, for Madge colored, and replied with some anger, "*My* bairn ? ay, to be sure, *my* bairn. What for shouldna I hae a bairn, and lose a bairn too, as weel as your bonny tittie, the Lily of St. Leonard's ?"

The answer struck Jeanie with some alarm, and she was anxious to soothe the irritation she had unwittingly given occasion to. "I am very sorry for your misfortune——"

"Sorry ! what wad ye be sorry for ?" answered Madge. "The bairn was a blessing—that is, Jeanie, it wad hae been a blessing if it hadna been for my mother ; but my mother's a queer woman. Ye see. there was an auld carle wi' a bit land,

and a gude clat o' siller besides, just the very picture of old Mr. Feeblemind or Mr. Ready-to-halt, that Great-Heart delivered from Slaygood the giant, when he was rifling him and about to pick his bones, for Slaygood was of the nature of the flesh-eaters ; and Great-Heart killed Giant Despair too ; but I am doubting Giant Despair's come alive again, for a' the story-book ; I find him busy at my heart whiles."

"Weel, and so the auld carle——" said Jeanie, for she was painfully interested in getting to the truth of Madge's history, which she could not but suspect was in some extraordinary way linked and entwined with the fate of her sister. She was also desirous, if possible, to engage her companion in some narrative which might be carried on in a lower tone of voice, for she was in great apprehension lest the elevated notes of Madge's conversation should direct her mother or the robbers in search of them.

"And so the auld carle," said Madge, repeating her words--"I wish you had seen him stoiting about, aff ae leg on to the other, wi' a kind o' dot-and-go-one sort o' motion, as if ilk ane o' his twa legs had belonged to sindry folk. But Gentle George could take him aff brawly. Eh, as I used to laugh to see George gang hip-hop like him ! I dinna ken, I think I laughed heartier then than what I do now, though maybe no just sae muckle."

"And who was Gentle George ? " said Jeanie, endeavoring to bring her back to her story.

"O, he was Geordie Robertson, ye ken, when he was in Edinburgh ; but that's no his right name neither. His name is—— But what is your business wi' his name ? " said she, as if upon sudden recollection. "What have ye to do asking for folks' names ? Have ye a mind I should scour my knife between your ribs, as my mother says ?"

As this was spoken with a menacing tone and gesture, Jeanie hastened to protest her total innocence of purpose in the accidental question which she had asked, and Madge Wildfire went on, somewhat pacified.

"Never ask folks' names, Jeanie : it's no civil. I hae seen half a dozen o' folk in my mother's at anes, and ne'er ane o' them ca'd the ither by his name ; and Daddie Ratton says it is the most uncivil thing may be, because the bailie bodies are aye asking fashious questions, when ye saw sic a man or sic a man ; and if ye dinna ken their names, ye ken there can be nae mair speer'd about it."

"In what strange school," thought Jeanie to herself, "has this poor creature been bred up, where such remote precautions are taken against the pursuits of justice ? What would my father or Reuben Butler think, if I were to tell them there are sic folk in the world ? And to abuse the simplicity of this demented creature ! O, that I were but safe at hame amang mine ain leal and true people ! and I'll bless God, while I have breath, that placed me among those who live in His fear, and under the shadow of His wing."

She was interrupted by the insane laugh of Madge Wildfire, as she saw a magpie hop across the path.

"See there ! that was the gate my old jo used to cross the country, but no just sae lightly : he hadna wings to help his auld legs, I trow ; but I behoved to have married him for a' that, Jeanie, or my mother wad hae been the dead o' me. But then came in the story of my poor bairn, and my mother thought he wad be deaved wi' its skirling, and she pat it away in below the bit bourock of turf yonder, just to be out o' the gate ; and I think she buried my best wits with it, for I have never been just mysell since. And only think, Jeanie, after my mother had been at a' this pains, the auld doited body Johnny Drottle turned up his nose, and wadna hae aught to say to me ! But it's little I care for him, for I have led a merry life ever since, and ne'er a braw gentleman looks at me but ye wad think he was gaun to drop off his horse for mere love of me. I have kenn'd some o' them put their hand in their pocket and gie me as muckle as sixpence at a time, just for my weel-faur'd face."

This speech gave Jeanie a dark insight into Madge's history. She had been courted by a wealthy suitor, whose addresses her mother had favored, notwithstanding the objection of old age and deformity. She had been seduced by some profligate, and, to conceal her shame and promote the advantageous match she had planned, her mother had not hesitated to destroy the offspring of their intrigue. That the consequence should be the total derangement of a mind which was constitutionally unsettled by giddiness and vanity was extremely natural ; and such was, in fact, the history of Madge Wildfire's insanity.

CHAPTER XXXI

PURSUING the path which Madge had chosen, Jeanie Deans observed, to her no small delight, that marks of more cultivation appeared, and the thatched roofs of houses, with their blue smoke arising in little columns, were seen embosomed in a tuft of trees at some distance. The track led in that direction, and Jeanie therefore resolved, while Madge continued to pursue it, that she would ask her no questions; having had the penetration to observe that by doing so she ran the risk of irritating her guide, or awakening suspicions, to the impressions of which persons in Madge's unsettled state of mind are particularly liable.

Madge therefore, uninterrupted, went on with the wild disjointed chat which her rambling imagination suggested; a mood in which she was much more communicative respecting her own history and that of others than when there was any attempt made, by direct queries or cross-examinations, to extract information on these subjects.

"It's a queer thing," she said, "but whiles I can speak about the bit bairn and the rest of it, just as if it had been another body's and no my ain; and whiles I am like to break my heart about it. Had you ever a bairn, Jeanie?"

Jeanie replied in the negative.

"Ay, but your sister had, though; and I ken what came o't too."

"In the name of Heavenly mercy," said Jeanie, forgetting the line of conduct which she had hitherto adopted, "tell me but what became of that unfortunate babe, and——"

Madge stopped, looked at her gravely and fixedly, and then broke into a great fit of laughing. "Aha, lass, catch me if you can. I think it's easy to gar you trow onything. How suld I ken onything o' your sister's wean? Lasses suld hae naething to do wi' weans till they are married; and then a' the gossips and cummers come in and feast as if it were the blithest day in the warld. They say maidens' bairns are weel

304

guided. I wot that wasna true of your tittie's and mine ;
but these are sad tales to tell, I maun just sing a bit to
keep up my heart. It's a sang that Gentle George made on
me lang syne, when I went with him to Lockington wake, to
see him act upon a stage, in fine clothes, with the player folk.
He might have dune waur than married me that night as he
promised : ' Better wed over the mixen as over the moor,' as
they say in Yorkshire—he may gang farther and fare waur ;
but that's a' ane to the sang—

> " I'm Madge of the country, I'm Madge of the town,
> And I'm Madge of the lad I am blithest to own.
> The Lady of Beever in diamonds may shine,
> But has not a heart half so lightsome as mine.

> " I am Queen of the Wake, and I'm Lady of May,
> And I lead the blithe ring round the May-pole to-day.
> The wildfire that flashes so fair and so free
> Was never so bright or so bonny as me.

I like that the best o' a' my sangs," continued the maniac,
"because *he* made it. I am often singing it, and that's maybe
the reason folk ca' me Madge Wildfire. I aye answer to the
name, though it's no my ain, for what's the use of making a
fash ? "

" But ye shouldna sing upon the Sabbath at least," said
Jeanie, who, amid all her distress and anxiety, could not help
being scandalized at the deportment of her companion, especially as they now approached near to the little village.

" Ay ! is this Sunday ? " said Madge. " My mother leads
sic a life, wi' turning night into day, that ane loses a' count
o' the days o' the week, and disna ken Sunday frae Saturday.
Besides, it's a' your Whiggery : in England folks sing when
they like. And then, ye ken, you are Christiana and I am
Mercy ; and ye ken, as they went on their way, they sang."
And she immediately raised one of John Bunyan's ditties :

> " He that is down need fear no fall,
> He that is low no pride ;
> He that is humble ever shall
> Have God to be his guide.

> " Fulness to such a burthen is
> That go on pilgrimage ;
> Here little, and hereafter bliss,
> Is best from age to age.

And do ye ken, Jeanie, I think there's much truth in that
book, the *Pilgrim's Progress*. The boy that sings that song

was feeding his father's sheep in the Valley of Humiliation, and Mr. Great-Heart says that he lived a merrier life, and had more of the herb called heart's-ease in his bosom, than they that wear silk and velvet like me, and are as bonny as I am."

Jeanie Deans had never read the fanciful and delightful parable to which Madge alluded. Bunyan was, indeed, a rigid Calvinist, but then he was also a member of a Baptist congregation, so that his works had no place on David Deans's shelf of divinity. Madge, however, at some time of her life had been well acquainted, as it appeared, with the most popular of his performances, which, indeed, rarely fails to make a deep impression upon children and people of the lower rank.

"I am sure," she continued, "I may weel say I am come out of the City of Destruction, for my mother is Mrs. Bat's-eyes, that dwells at Deadman's Corner; and Frank Levitt and Tyburn Tam, they may be likened to Mistrust and Guilt, that came galloping up, and struck the poor pilgrim to the ground with a great club, and stole a bag of silver, which was most of his spending money, and so have they done to many, and will do to more. But now we will gang to the Interpreter's house, for I ken a man that will play the Interpreter right weel; for he has eyes lifted up to heaven, the best of books in his hand, the law of truth written on his lips, and he stands as if he pleaded wi' men. O if I had minded what he had said to me, I had never been the castaway creature that I am! But it is all over now. But we'll knock at the gate, and then the keeper will admit Christiana, but Mercy will be left out; and then I'll stand at the door trembling and crying, and then Christiana—that's you, Jeanie—will intercede for me; and then Mercy—that's me, ye ken—will faint; and then the Interpreter—yes, the Interpreter, that's Mr. Staunton himself—will come out and take me—that's poor, lost, demented me—by the hand, and give me a pomegranate, and a piece of honeycomb, and a small bottle of spirits, to stay my fainting; and then the good times will come back again, and we'll be the happiest folk you ever saw."

In the midst of the confused assemblage of ideas indicated in this speech, Jeanie thought she saw a serious purpose on the part of Madge to endeavor to obtain the pardon and countenance of some one whom she had offended; an attempt the most likely of all others to bring them once more into contact with law and legal protection. She therefore resolved to be guided by her while she was in so hopeful a disposition, and act for her own safety according to circumstances.

They were now close by the village, one of those beautiful
scenes which are so often found in Merry England, where the
cottages, instead of being built in two direct lines on each
side of a dusty high-road, stand in detached groups, interspersed not only with large oaks and elms, but with fruit trees,
so many of which were at this time in flourish that the grove
seemed enamelled with their crimson and white blossoms. In
the centre of the hamlet stood the parish church and its little
Gothic tower, from which at present was heard the Sunday
chime of bells.

"We will wait here until the folk are a' in the church—
they ca' the kirk a church in England, Jeanie, be sure you
mind that—for if I was gaun forward amang them, a' the
gaitts o' boys and lasses wad be crying at Madge Wildfire's
tail, the little hellrakers! and the beadle would be as hard
upon us as if it was our fault. I like their skirling as ill as
he does, I can tell him; I'm sure I often wish there was a het
peat doun their throats when they set them up that gate."

Conscious of the disorderly appearance of her own dress
after the adventure of the preceding night, and of the grotesque habit and demeanor of her guide, and sensible how important it was to secure an attentive and patient audience to
her strange story from some one who might have the means to
protect her, Jeanie readily acquiesced in Madge's proposal to rest
under the trees, by which they were still somewhat screened,
until the commencement of service should give them an opportunity of entering the hamlet without attracting a crowd
around them. She made the less opposition, that Madge had
intimated that this was not the village where her mother was
in custody, and that the two squires of the pad were absent in
a different direction.

She sat herself down, therefore, at the foot of an oak, and
by the assistance of a placid fountain which had been dammed
up for the use of the villagers, and which served her as a natural mirror, she began—no uncommon thing with a Scottish
maiden of her rank—to arrange her toilet in the open air, and
bring her dress, soiled and disordered as it was, into such order
as the place and circumstances admitted.

She soon perceived reason, however, to regret that she had
set about this task, however decent and necessary, in the present time and society. Madge Wildfire, who, among other indications of insanity, had a most overweening opinion of those
charms to which, in fact, she had owed her misery, and whose
mind, like a raft upon a lake, was agitated and driven about
at random by each fresh impulse, no sooner beheld Jeanie be-

gin to arrange her hair, place her bonnet in order, rub the dust from her shoes and clothes, adjust her neck-handkerchief and mittens, and so forth, than with imitative zeal she began to bedizen and trick herself out with shreds and remnants of beggarly finery, which she took out of a little bundle, and which, when disposed around her person, made her appearance ten times more fantastic and apish than it had been before.

Jeanie groaned in spirit, but dared not interfere in a matter so delicate. Across the man's cap or riding-hat which she wore, Madge placed a broken and soiled white feather, intersected with one which had been shed from the train of a peacock. To her dress, which was a kind of riding-habit, she stitched, pinned, and otherwise secured a large furbelow of artificial flowers, all crushed, wrinkled, and dirty, which had first bedecked a lady of quality, then descended to her abigail, and dazzled the inmates of the servants' hall. A tawdry scarf of yellow silk, trimmed with tinsel and spangles, which had seen as hard service and boasted as honorable a transmission, was next flung over one shoulder, and fell across her person in the manner of a shoulder-belt, or baldrick. Madge then stripped off the coarse ordinary shoes which she wore, and replaced them by a pair of dirty satin ones, spangled and embroidered to match the scarf, and furnished with very high heels. She had cut a willow switch in her morning's walk, almost as long as a boy's fishing-rod. This she set herself seriously to peel, and when it was transformed into such a wand as the Treasurer or High Steward bears on public occasions, she told Jeanie that she thought they now looked decent, as young women should do upon the Sunday morning, and that, as the bells had done ringing, she was willing to conduct her to the Interpreter's house.

Jeanie sighed heavily to think it should be her lot on the Lord's day, and during kirk-time too, to parade the street of an inhabited village with so very grotesque a comrade; but necessity had no law, since, without a positive quarrel with the madwoman, which, in the circumstances, would have been very unadvisable, she could see no means of shaking herself free of her society.

As for poor Madge, she was completely elated with personal vanity, and the most perfect satisfaction concerning her own dazzling dress and superior appearance. They entered the hamlet without being observed, except by one old woman, who, being nearly "high-gravel blind," was only conscious that something very fine and glittering was passing by, and dropped as deep a reverence to Madge as she would have done to a countess. This filled up the measure of Madge's self-approbation. She minced, she ambled, she smiled, she simpered, and waved Jeanie Deans forward with the condescension of a noble chaperon, who has undertaken the charge of a country miss on her first journey to the capital.

Jeanie followed in patience, and with her eyes fixed on the ground, that she might save herself the mortification of seeing her companion's absurdities; but she started when, ascending two or three steps, she found herself in the churchyard, and saw that Madge was making straight for the door of the church. As Jeanie had no mind to enter the congregation in such company, she walked aside from the pathway, and said in a decided tone, " Madge, I will wait here till the church comes out; you may go in by yourself if you have a mind."

As she spoke these words, she was about to seat herself upon one of the gravestones.

Madge was a little before Jeanie when she turned aside; but suddenly changing her course, she followed her with long strides, and, with every feature inflamed with passion, overtook and seized her by the arm. " Do ye think, ye ungratefu' wretch, that I am gaun to let you sit doun upon my father's grave ? The deil settle ye doun ! if ye dinna rise and come into the Interpreter's house, that's the house of God, wi' me, but I'll rive every dud aff your back !"

She adapted the action to the phrase; for with one clutch she stripped Jeanie of her straw bonnet and a handful of her hair to boot, and threw it up into an old yew-tree, where it stuck fast. Jeanie's first impulse was to scream, but conceiving she might receive deadly harm before she could obtain the assistance of any one, notwithstanding the vicinity of the church, she thought it wiser to follow the madwoman into the congregation, where she might find some means of escape from her, or at least be secured against her violence. But when she meekly intimated her consent to follow Madge, her guide's uncertain brain had caught another train of ideas. She held Jeanie fast with one hand, and with the other pointed to the inscription on the gravestone, and commanded her to read it. Jeanie obeyed, and read these words:

"THIS MONUMENT WAS ERECTED TO THE MEMORY OF DONALD MURDOCKSON OF THE KING'S XXVI., OR CAMERONIAN REGIMENT, A SINCERE CHRISTIAN, A BRAVE SOLDIER, AND A FAITHFUL SERVANT, BY HIS GRATEFUL AND SORROWING MASTER, ROBERT STAUNTON."

"It's very weel read, Jeanie ; it's just the very words," said Madge, whose ire had now faded into deep melancholy, and with a step which, to Jeanie's great joy, was uncommonly quiet and mournful, she led her companion towards the door of the church.

It was one of those old-fashioned Gothic parish churches which are frequent in England, the most cleanly, decent, and reverential places of worship that. are, perhaps, anywhere to be found in the Christian world.   Yet, notwithstanding the decent solemnity of its exterior, Jeanie was too faithful to the directory of the Presbyterian Kirk to have entered a prelatic place of worship, and would, upon any other occasion, have thought that she beheld in the porch the venerable figure of her father waving her back from the entrance, and pronouncing in a solemn tone, "Cease, my child, to hear the instruction which causeth to err from the words of knowledge." But in her present agitating and alarming situation, she looked for safety to this forbidden place of assembly, as the hunted animal will sometimes seek shelter from imminent danger in the human habitation, or in other places of refuge most alien to its nature and habits.   Not even the sound of the organ, and of one or two flutes which accompanied the psalmody, prevented her from following her guide into the chancel of the church.

No sooner had Madge put her foot upon the pavement, and become sensible that she was the object of attention to the spectators, than she resumed all the fantastic extravagance of deportment which some transient touch of melancholy had banished for an instant.   She swam rather than walked up the centre aisle, dragging Jeanie after her, whom she held fast by the hand.   She would, indeed, have fain slipped aside into the pew nearest to the door, and left Madge to ascend in her own manner and alone to the high places of the synagogue ; but this was impossible, without a degree of violent resistance which seemed to her inconsistent with the time and place, and she was accordingly led in captivity up the whole length of the church by her grotesque conductress, who, with half-shut eyes, a prim smile upon her lips, and a mincing motion with her hands, which corresponded with the delicate and affected pace at which she was pleased to move, seemed to take the general stare of the congregation which such an exhibition necessarily excited as a high compliment, and which she returned by nods and half courtesies to individuals among the audience whom she seemed to distinguish as acquaintances.   Her absurdity was enhanced in the eyes of the spectators by the strange contrast which she formed to her companion, who, with dishevelled hair, downcast eyes, and a face glowing with shame, was dragged, as it were, in triumph after her.

Madge's airs were at length fortunately cut short by her encountering in her progress the looks of the clergyman, who fixed upon her a glance at once steady, compassionate, and admonitory. She hastily opened an empty pew which happened to be near her, and entered, dragging in Jeanie after her. Kicking Jeanie on the shins by way of hint that she should follow her example, she sunk her head upon her hand for the space of a minute. Jeanie, to whom this posture of mental devotion was entirely new, did not attempt to do the like, but looked round her with a bewildered stare, which her neighbors, judging from the company in which they saw her, very naturally ascribed to insanity. Every person in their immediate vicinity drew back from this extraordinary couple as far as the limits of their pew permitted ; but one old man could not get beyond Madge's reach ere she had snatched the prayer-book from his hand and ascertained the lesson of the day. She then turned up the ritual, and, with the most over-strained enthusiasm of gesture and manner, showed Jeanie the passages as they were read in the service, making, at the same time, her own responses so loud as to be heard above those of every other person.

Notwithstanding the shame and vexation which Jeanie felt in being thus exposed in a place of worship, she could not and durst not omit rallying her spirits so as to look around her and consider to whom she ought to appeal for protection so soon as the service should be concluded. Her first ideas naturally fixed upon the clergyman, and she was confirmed in the resolution by observing that he was an aged gentleman, of a dignified appearance and deportment, who read the service with an undisturbed and decent gravity, which brought back to becoming attention those younger members of the congregation who had been disturbed by the extravagant behavior of Madge Wildfire. To the clergyman, therefore, Jeanie resolved to make her appeal when the service was over.

It is true, she felt disposed to be shocked at his surplice, of which she had heard so much, but which she had never seen upon the person of a preacher of the Word. Then she was confused by the change of posture adopted in different parts of the ritual, the more so as Madge Wildfire, to whom they seemed familiar, took the opportunity to exercise authority over her, pulling her up and pushing her down with a bustling assiduity which Jeanie felt must make them both the objects of painful attention.   But, notwithstanding these prejudices, it was her prudent resolution, in this dilemma, to imitate as nearly as she could what was done around her. "The prophet," she thought, "permitted Naaman the Syrian to bow even in the house of Rimmon.   Surely if I, in this streight, worship the God of my fathers in mine own language, although the manner thereof be strange to me, the Lord will pardon me in this thing."

In this resolution she became so much confirmed that, withdrawing herself from Madge as far as the pew permitted, she endeavored to evince, by serious and undeviating attention to what was passing, that her mind was composed to devotion. Her tormentor would not long have permitted her to remain quiet, but fatigue overpowered her, and she fell fast asleep in the other corner of the pew.

Jeanie, though her mind in her own despite sometimes reverted to her situation, compelled herself to give attention to a sensible, energetic, and well-composed discourse upon the practical doctrines of Christianity, which she could not help approving, although it was every word written down and read by the preacher, and although it was delivered in a tone and gesture very different from those of Boanerges Stormheaven, who was her father's favorite preacher.   The serious and placid attention with which Jeanie listened did not escape the clergyman.   Madge Wildfire's entrance had rendered him apprehensive of some disturbance, to provide against which, as far as possible, he often turned his eyes to the part of the church where Jeanie and she were placed, and became soon aware that, although the loss of her head-gear and the awkwardness of her situation had given an uncommon and anxious air to the features of the former, yet she was in a state of mind very different from that of her companion. When he dismissed the congregation, he observed her look around with a wild and terrified look, as if uncertain what course she ought to adopt, and noticed that she approached one or two of the most decent of the congregation, as if to address them, and then shrunk back timidly, on observing that they seemed to shun and to avoid her.   The clergyman was satisfied there must be something extraordinary in all this, and as a benevolent man, as well as a good Christian pastor, he resolved to inquire into the matter more minutely.

CHAPTER XXXII

There govern'd in that year
A stern, stout churl—an angry overseer.
CRABBE.

WHILE Mr. Staunton, for such was this worthy clergyman's
name, was laying aside his gown in the vestry, Jeanie was in
the act of coming to an open rupture with Madge.

"We must return to Mummer's barn directly," said Madge;
"we'll be ower late, and my mother will be angry."

"I am not going back with you, Madge," said Jeanie, taking out a guinea and offering it to her; "I am much obliged to
you, but I maun gang my ain road."

"And me coming a' this way out o' my gate to pleasure
you, ye ungratefu' cutty," answered Madge; "and me to be
brained by my mother when I gang hame, and a' for your sake!
But I will gar ye as good——"

"For God's sake," said Jeanie to a man who stood beside
them, "keep her off; she is mad!"

"Ey, ey," answered the boor; "I hae some guess of that,
and I trow thou be'st a bird of the same feather. Howsomever, Madge, I red thee keep hand off her, or I'se lend thee a
whisterpoop."

Several of the lower class of the parishioners now gathered
round the strangers, and the cry arose among the boys that
"there was a-going to be a fite between mad Madge Murdockson and another Bess of Bedlam." But while the fry assembled
with the humane hope of seeing as much of the fun as possible, the laced cocked hat of the beadle was discerned among
the multitude, and all made way for that person of awful authority. His first address was to Madge.

"What's brought thee back again, thou silly donnot, to
plague this parish? Hast thou brought ony more bastards wi'
thee to lay to honest men's doors? or does thou think to burden us with this goose, that's as gare-brained as thysell, as if
rates were no up enow? Away wi' thee to thy thief of a
mother; she's fast in the stocks at Barkston town-end. Away
wi' ye out o' the parish, or I'se be at ye with the rattan."

Madge stood sulky for a minute ; but she had been too often taught submission to the beadle's authority by ungentle means to feel courage enough to dispute it.

" And my mother—my puir auld mother, is in the stocks at Barkston ! This is a' your wyte, Miss Jeanie Deans ; but I'll be upsides wi' you, as sure as my name's Madge Wildfire—I mean Murdockson. God help me, I forget my very name in this confused waste ! "

So saying, she turned upon her heel and went off, followed by all the mischievous imps of the village, some crying, "Madge, canst thou tell thy name yet ? " some pulling the skirts of her dress, and all, to the best of their strength and ingenuity, exercising some new device or other to exasperate her into frenzy.

Jeanie saw her departure with infinite delight, though she wished that, in some way or other, she could have requited the service Madge had conferred upon her.

In the meantime, she applied to the beadle to know whether " there was any house in the village where she could be civilly entertained for her money, and whether she could be permitted to speak to the clergyman ? "

" Ay, ay, we'se ha' reverend care on thee ; and I think," answered the man of constituted authority, "that, unless thou answer the Rector all the better, we'se spare thy money, and gie thee lodging at the parish charge, young woman."

" Where am I to go, then ? " said Jeanie, in some alarm.

" Why, I am to take thee to his Reverence, in the first place, to gie an account o' thysell, and to see thou comena to be a burden upon the parish."

" I do not wish to burden any one," replied Jeanie ; " I have enough for my own wants, and only wish to get on my journey safely."

" Why, that's another matter," replied the beadle, " an if it be true ; and I think thou dost not look so pollrumptious as thy playfellow yonder. Thou wouldst be a mettle lass enow, an thou wert snog and snod a bit better. Come thou away, then ; the Rector is a good man."

" Is that the minister," said Jeanie, " who preached——"

" The minister ! Lord help thee ! What kind o' Presbyterian art thou ? Why, 'tis the Rector—the Rector's sell, woman, and there isna the like o' him in the county, nor the four next to it. Come away—away with thee ; we munna bide here."

" I am sure I am very willing to go to see the minister," said Jeanie ; " for, though he read his discourse, and wore that surplice, as they call it here, I cannot but think he must be a very worthy God-fearing man, to preach the root of the matter in the way he did."

The disappointed rabble, finding that there was like to be no further sport, had by this time dispersed, and Jeanie, with her usual patience, followed her consequential and surly, but not brutal, conductor towards the rectory.

This clerical mansion was large and commodious, for the living was an excellent one, and the advowson belonged to a very wealthy family in the neighborhood, who had usually bred up a son or nephew to the church, for the sake of inducting him, as opportunity offered, into this very comfortable provision. In this manner the rectory of Willingham had always been considered as a direct and immediate appanage of Willingham Hall; and as the rich baronets to whom the latter belonged had usually a son, or brother, or nephew, settled in the living, the utmost care had been taken to render their habitation not merely respectable and commodious, but even dignified and imposing.

It was situated about four hundred yards from the village, and on a rising ground which sloped gently upward, covered with small enclosures, or closes, laid out irregularly, so that the old oaks and elms, which were planted in hedge-rows, fell into perspective, and were blended together in beautiful irregularity. When they approached nearer to the house, a handsome gateway admitted them into a lawn, of narrow dimensions, indeed, but which was interspersed with large sweet-chestnut trees and beeches, and kept in handsome order. The front of the house was irregular. Part of it seemed very old, and had, in fact, been the resident of the incumbent in Romish times. Successive occupants had made considerable additions and improvements, each in the taste of his own age, and without much regard to symmetry. But these incongruities of architecture were so graduated and happily mingled, that the eye, far from being displeased with the combinations of various styles, saw nothing but what was interesting in the varied and intricate pile which they exhibited. Fruit trees displayed on the southern wall, outer staircases, various places of entrance, a combination of roofs and chimneys of different ages, united to render the front, not indeed beautiful or grand, but intricate, perplexed, or, to use Mr. Price's appropriate phrase, picturesque. The most considerable addition was that of the present Rector, who, " being a bookish man, " as the beadle was at the pains to inform Jeanie, to augment, perhaps, her reverence for the person before whom she was to appear, had built a handsome library and parlor, and no less than two additional bedrooms.

"Mony men would hae scrupled such expense," continued the parochial officer, "seeing as the living mun go as it pleases Sir Edmund to will it; but his Reverence has a canny bit land of his own, and need not look on two sides of a penny."

Jeanie could not help comparing the irregular yet extensive and commodious pile of building before her to the "manses" in her own country, where a set of penurious heritors, professing all the while the devotion of their lives and fortunes to the Presbyterian establishment, strain their inventions to discover what may be nipped, and clipped, and pared from a building which forms but a poor accommodation even for the present incumbent, and, despite the superior advantage of stone masonry, must, in the course of forty or fifty years, again burden their descendants with an expense which, once liberally and handsomely employed, ought to have freed their estates from a recurrence of it for more than a century at least.

Behind the Rector's house the ground sloped down to a small river, which, without possessing the romantic vivacity and rapidity of a northern stream, was, nevertheless, by its occasional appearance through the ranges of willows and poplars that crowned its banks, a very pleasing accompaniment to the landscape. "It was the best trouting stream," said the beadle, whom the patience of Jeanie, and especially the assurance that she was not about to become a burden to the parish, had rendered rather communicative—"the best trouting stream in all Lincolnshire; for when you got lower there was nought to be done wi' fly-fishing."

Turning aside from the principal entrance, he conducted Jeanie towards a sort of portal connected with the older part of the building, which was chiefly occupied by servants, and knocking at the door, it was opened by a servant in grave purple livery, such as befitted a wealthy and dignified clergyman.

"How dost do, Tummas?" said the beadle; "and how's young Measter Staunton?"

"Why, but poorly—but poorly, Measter Stubbs. Are you wanting to see his Reverence?"

"Ay, ay, Tummas; please to say I ha' brought up the young woman as came to service to-day with mad Madge Murdockson; she seems to be a decentish koind o' body; but I ha' asked her never a question. Only I can tell his Reverence that she is a Scotchwoman, I judge, and as flat as the fens of Holland."

Tummas honored Jeanie Deans with such a stare as the pampered domestics of the rich, whether spiritual or temporal, usually esteem it part of their privilege to bestow upon the poor, and then desired Mr. Stubbs and his charge to step in till he informed his master of their presence.

The room into which he showed them was a sort of steward's parlor, hung with a county map or two, and three or four prints of eminent persons connected with the county, as Sir William Monson, James York the blacksmith of Lincoln,* and the famous Peregrine, Lord Willoughby, in complete armor, looking as when he said, in the words of the legend below the engraving—

> " Stand to it, noble pikemen,
>   And face ye well about :
> And shoot ye sharp, bold bowmen,
>   And we will keep them out.
> Ye musquet and calliver-men,
>   Do you prove true to me,
> I'll be the foremost man in fight,
>   Said brave Lord Willoughbee."

When they had entered this apartment, Tummas as a matter of course offered, and as a matter of course Mr. Stubbs accepted, a "summat" to eat and drink, being the respectable relics of a gammon of bacon, and a *whole whiskin*, or blackpot, of sufficient double ale. To these eatables Mr. Beadle seriously inclined himself, and (for we must do him justice) not without an invitation to Jeanie, in which Tummas joined, that his prisoner or charge would follow his good example. But although she might have stood in need of refreshment, considering she had tasted no food that day, the anxiety of the moment, her own sparing and abstemious habits, and a bashful aversion to eat in company of the two strangers, induced her to decline their courtesy. So she sat in a chair apart, while Mr. Stubbs and Mr. Tummas, who had chosen to join his friend in consideration that dinner was to be put back till the afternoon service was over, made a hearty luncheon, which lasted for half an hour, and might not then have concluded, had not his Reverence rung his bell, so that Tummas was obliged to attend his master. Then, and no sooner, to save himself the labor of a second journey to the other end of the house, he announced to his master the arrival of Mr. Stubbs, with the other madwoman, as he chose to designate Jeanie, as an event which had just taken place. He returned with an

* Author of the *Union of Honor*, a treatise on English Heraldry, London, 1641 (*Laing*).

order that Mr. Stubbs and the young woman should be instantly ushered up to the library.

The beadle bolted in haste his last mouthful of fat bacon, washed down the greasy morsel with the last rinsings of the pot of ale, and immediately marshalled Jeanie through one or two intricate passages, which led from the ancient to the more modern buildings, into a handsome little hall, or ante-room, adjoining to the library, and out of which a glass door opened to the lawn.

"Stay here," said Stubbs, "till I tell his Reverence you are come."

So saying, he opened a door and entered the library.

Without wishing to hear their conversation, Jeanie, as she was circumstanced, could not avoid it; for as Stubbs stood by the door, and his Reverence was at the upper end of a large room, their conversation was necessarily audible in the ante-room.

"So you have brought the young woman here at last, Mr. Stubbs. I expected you some time since. You know I do not wish such persons to remain in custody a moment without some inquiry into their situation."

"Very true, your Reverence," replied the beadle; "but the young woman had eat nought to-day, and soa Measter Tummas did set down a drap of drink and a morsel, to be sure."

"Thomas was very right, Mr. Stubbs; and what has become of the other most unfortunate being?"

"Why," replied Mr. Stubbs, "I did think the sight on her would but vex your Reverence, and soa I did let her go her ways back to her mother, who is in trouble in the next parish."

"In trouble! that signifies in prison, I suppose?" said Mr. Staunton.

"Ay, truly; something like it, an it like your Reverence."

"Wretched, unhappy, incorrigible woman!" said the clergyman. "And what sort of person is this companion of hers?"

"Why, decent enow, an it like your Reverence," said Stubbs; "for aught I sees of her, there's no harm of her, and she says she has cash enow to carry her out of the county."

"Cash! that is always what you think of, Stubbs. But has she sense?—has she her wits?—has she the capacity of taking care of herself?"

"Why, your Reverence," replied Stubbs, "I cannot just

say: I will be sworn she was not born at Witt-ham ;* for
Gaffer Gibbs looked at her all the time of service, and he says
she could not turn up a single lesson like a Christian, even
though she had Madge Murdockson to help her ; but then,
as to fending for hersell, why, she's a bit of a Scotchwoman,
your Reverence, and they say the worst donnot of them can
look out for their own turn ; and she is decently put on enow,
and not bechounched like t'other."

"Send her in here, then, and do you remain below, Mr.
Stubbs."

This colloquy had engaged Jeanie's attention so deeply that
it was not until it was over that she observed that the sashed
door, which, we have said, led from the ante-room into the
garden, was opened, and that there entered, or rather was
borne in by two assistants, a young man of a very pale and
sickly appearance, whom they lifted to the nearest couch, and
placed there, as if to recover from the fatigue of an unusual
exertion.   Just as they were making this arrangement, Stubbs
came out of the library and summoned Jeanie to enter it.   She
obeyed him, not without tremor; for, besides the novelty of
the situation to a girl of her secluded habits, she felt also as if
the successful prosecution of her journey was to depend upon
the impression she should be able to make on Mr. Staunton.

It is true, it was difficult to suppose on what pretext a person
travelling on her own business, and at her own charge, could
be interrupted upon her route.   But the violent detention she
had already undergone was sufficient to show that there existed
persons at no great distance who had the interest, the inclination, and the audacity forcibly to stop her journey, and she
felt the necessity of having some countenance and protection,
at least till she should get beyond their reach.   While these
things passed through her mind, much faster than our pen and
ink can record, or even the reader's eye collect the meaning
of its traces, Jeanie found herself in a handsome library, and
in presence of the Rector of Willingham.   The well-furnished
presses and shelves which surrounded the large and handsome
apartment contained more books than Jeanie imagined existed
in the world, being accustomed to consider as an extensive collection two fir shelves, each about three feet long, which contained
her father's treasured volumes, the whole pith and marrow, as
he used sometimes to boast, of modern divinity.   An orrery,
globes, a telescope, and some other scientific implements conveyed to Jeanie an impression of admiration and wonder, not

* A proverbial and punning expression in that county, to intimate that a person
is not very clever.

unmixed with fear; for, in her ignorant apprehension, they seemed rather adapted for magical purposes than any other; and a few stuffed animals (as the Rector was fond of natural history) added to the impressive character of the apartment.

Mr. Staunton spoke to her with great mildness. He observed that, although her appearance at church had been uncommon, and in strange, and, he must add, discreditable society, and calculated, upon the whole, to disturb the congregation during divine worship, he wished, nevertheless, to hear her own account of herself before taking any steps which his duty might seem to demand. He was a justice of peace, he informed her, as well as a clergyman.

"His honor [for she would not say his reverence] was very civil and kind," was all that poor Jeanie could at first bring out.

"Who are you, young woman?" said the clergyman, more peremptorily, "and what do you do in this country, and in such company? We allow no strollers or vagrants here."

"I am not a vagrant or a stroller, sir," said Jeanie, a little roused by the supposition. "I am a decent Scotch lass, travelling through the land on my own business and my own expenses; and I was so unhappy as to fall in with bad company, and was stopped a' night on my journey. And this puir creature, who is something light-headed, let me out in the morning."

"Bad company!" said the clergyman. "I am afraid, young woman, you have not been sufficiently anxious to avoid them."

"Indeed, sir," returned Jeanie, "I have been brought up to shun evil communication. But these wicked people were thieves, and stopped me by violence and mastery."

"Thieves!" said Mr. Staunton; "then you charge them with robbery, I suppose?"

"No, sir; they did not take so much as a boddle from me," answered Jeanie; "nor did they use me ill, otherwise than by confining me."

The clergyman inquired into the particulars of her adventure, which she told him from point to point.

"This is an extraordinary, and not a very probable, tale, young woman," resumed Mr. Staunton. "Here has been, according to your account, a great violence committed without any adequate motive. Are you aware of the law of this country—that if you lodge this charge you will be bound over to prosecute this gang?"

Jeanie did not understand him, and he explained that the

English law, in addition to the inconvenience sustained by persons who have been robbed or injured, has the goodness to intrust to them the care and the expense of appearing as prosecutors.

Jeanie said, "that her business at London was express ; all she wanted was, that any gentleman would, out of Christian charity, protect her to some town where she could hire horses and a guide ; and, finally," she thought, "it would be her father's mind that she was not free to give testimony in an English court of justice, as the land was not under a direct Gospel dispensation."

Mr. Staunton stared a little, and asked if her father was a Quaker.

"God forbid, sir," said Jeanie. "He is nae schismatic nor sectary, nor ever treated for sic black commodities as theirs, and that's weel kenn'd o' him."

"And what is his name, pray ?" said Mr. Staunton.

"David Deans, sir, the cow-feeder at St. Leonard's Craigs, near Edinburgh."

A deep groan from the ante-room prevented the Rector from replying, and, exclaiming, "Good God ! that unhappy boy !" he left Jeanie alone, and hastened into the outer apartment.

Some noise and bustle was heard, but no one entered the library for the best part of an hour.

CHAPTER XXXIII

Fantastic passions' maddening brawl !
And shame and terror over all !
Deeds to be hid which were not hid,
Which, all confused, I could not know
Whether I suffer'd or I did,
For all seem'd guilt, remorse, or woe ;
My own, or others, still the same
Life-stifling fear, soul-stifling shame.
COLERIDGE.

DURING the interval while she was thus left alone, Jeanie anxiously revolved in her mind what course was best for her to pursue. She was impatient to continue her journey, yet she feared she could not safely adventure to do so while the old hag and her assistants were in the neighborhood, without risking a repetition of their violence. She thought she could collect from the conversation which she had partly overheard, and also from the wild confessions of Madge Wildfire, that her mother had a deep and revengeful motive for obstructing her journey if possible. And from whom could she hope for assistance if not from Mr. Staunton ? His whole appearance and demeanor seemed to encourage her hopes. His features were handsome, though marked with a deep cast of melancholy ; his tone and language were gentle and encouraging ; and, as he had served in the army for several years during his youth, his air retained that easy frankness which is peculiar to the profession of arms. He was, besides, a minister of the Gospel ; and although a worshipper, according to Jeanie's notions, in the court of the Gentiles, and so benighted as to wear a surplice ; although he read the Common Prayer, and wrote down every word of his sermon before delivering it ; and although he was, moreover, in strength of lungs, as well as pith and marrow of doctrine, vastly inferior to Boanerges Stormheaven, Jeanie still thought he must be a very different person from Curate Kiltstoup and other prelatical divines of her father's earlier days, who used to get drunk in their canonical dress, and hound out the dragoons against the wandering Cameronians. The house seemed to be in some disturbance, but as she could not suppose she was

322 "

altogether forgotten, she thought it better to remain quiet in the apartment where she had been left till some one should take notice of her.

The first who entered was, to her no small delight, one of her own sex, a motherly-looking aged person of a housekeeper. To her Jeanie explained her situation in a few words, and begged her assistance.

The dignity of a housekeeper did not encourage too much familiarity with a person who was at the rectory on justice business, and whose character might seem in her eyes somewhat precarious ; but she was civil, although distant.

"Her young master," she said, " had had a bad accident by a fall from his horse, which made him liable to fainting fits ; he had been taken very ill just now, and it was impossible his Reverence could see Jeanie for some time ; but that she need not fear his doing all that was just and proper in her behalf the instant he could get her business attended to." She concluded by offering to show Jeanie a room, where she might remain till his Reverence was at leisure.

Our heroine took the opportunity to request the means of adjusting and changing her dress.

The housekeeper, in whose estimation order and cleanliness ranked high among personal virtues, gladly complied with a request so reasonable ; and the change of dress which Jeanie's bundle furnished made so important an improvement in her appearance, that the old lady hardly knew the soiled and disordered traveller, whose attire showed the violence she had sustained, in the neat, clean, quiet-looking little Scotchwoman who now stood before her. Encouraged by such a favorable alteration in her appearance, Mrs. Dalton ventured to invite Jeanie to partake of her dinner, and was equally pleased with the decent propriety of her conduct during that meal.

"Thou canst read this book, canst thou, young woman ?" said the old lady, when their meal was concluded, laying her hand upon a large Bible.

"I hope sae, madam," said Jeanie, surprised at the question ; "my father wad hae wanted mony a thing ere I had wanted *that* schuling."

"The better sign of him, young woman. There are men here, well-to-pass in the world, would not want their share of a Leicester plover, and that's a bag-pudding, if fasting for three hours would make all their poor children read the Bible from end to end. Take thou the book, then, for my eyes are something dazed, and read where thou listest : it's the only book thou canst not happen wrong in."

Jeanie was at first tempted to turn up the parable of the good Samaritan, but her conscience checked her, as if it were a use of Scripture not for her own edification, but to work upon the mind of others for the relief of her worldly afflictions ; and under this scrupulous sense of duty she selected, in preference, a chapter of the prophet Isaiah, and read it, notwithstanding her northern accent and tone, with a devout propriety which greatly edified Mrs. Dalton.

"Ah," she said, "an all Scotchwomen were sic as thou ! But it was our luck to get born devils of thy country, I think, every one worse than t'other. If thou knowest of any tidy lass like thysell, that wanted a place, and could bring a good character, and would not go laiking about to wakes and fairs, and wore shoes and stockings all the day round—why, I'll not say but we might find room for her at the rectory. Hast no cousin or sister, lass, that such an offer would suit ? "

This was touching upon a sore point, but Jeanie was spared the pain of replying by the entrance of the same man-servant she had seen before.

"Measter wishes to see the young woman from Scotland," was Tummas's address.

"Go to his Reverence, my dear, as fast as you can, and tell him all your story ; his Reverence is a kind man," said Mrs. Dalton. "I will fold down the leaf, and make you a cup of tea, with some nice muffin, against you come down, and that's what you seldom see in Scotland, girl."

"Measter's waiting for the young woman," said Tummas, impatiently.

"Well, Mr. Jack Sauce, and what is your business to put in your oar ? And how often must I tell you to call Mr. Staunton his Reverence, seeing as he is a dignified clergyman, and not be meastering, meastering him, as if he were a little petty squire ? "

As Jeanie was now at the door, and ready to accompany Tummas, the footman said nothing till he got into the passage, when he muttered, "There are moe masters than one in this house, and I think we shall have a mistress too, an Dame Dalton carries it thus."

Tummas led the way through a more intricate range of passages than Jeanie had yet threaded, and ushered her into an apartment which was darkened by the closing of most of the window-shutters, and in which was a bed with the curtains partly drawn.

"Here is the young woman, sir," said Tummas.

"Very well," said a voice from the bed, but not that of

his Reverence ; "be ready to answer the bell, and leave the room."

"There is some mistake," said Jeanie, confounded at finding herself in the apartment of an invalid ; "the servant told me that the minister——"

"Don't trouble yourself," said the invalid, "there is no mistake. I know more of your affairs than my father, and I can manage them better. Leave the room, Tom." The servant obeyed. "We must not," said the invalid, "lose time, when we have little to lose. Open the shutter of that window."

She did so, and as he drew aside the curtain of his bed the light fell on his pale countenance, as, turbaned with bandages and dressed in a nightgown, he lay, seemingly exhausted, upon the bed.

"Look at me," he said, "Jeanie Deans ; can you not recollect me ?"

"No, sir," said she, full of surprise. "I was never in this country before."

"But I may have been in yours. Think—recollect. I should faint did I name the name you are most dearly bound to loathe and to detest. Think—remember !"

A terrible recollection flashed on Jeanie, which every tone of the speaker confirmed, and which his next words rendered certainty.

"Be composed—remember Muschat's Cairn and the moonlight night !"

Jeanie sunk down on a chair, with clasped hands, and gasped in agony.

"Yes, here I lie," he said, "like a crushed snake, writhing with impatience at my incapacity of motion ; here I lie, when I ought to have been in Edinburgh, trying every means to save a life that is dearer to me than my own. How is your sister ? how fares it with her ?—condemned to death, I know it, by this time ! O, the horse that carried me safely on a thousand errands of folly and wickedness—that he should have broke down with me on the only good mission I have undertaken for years ! But I must rein in my passion; my frame cannot endure it, and I have much to say. Give me some of the cordial which stands on that table. Why do you tremble ? But you have too good cause. Let it stand; I need it not."

Jeanie, however reluctant, approached him with the cup into which she had poured the draught, and could not forbear saying, "There is a cordial for the mind, sir, if the wicked will turn from their transgressions and seek to the Physician of souls."

"Silence !" he said, sternly; "and yet I thank you.   But
tell me, and lose no time in doing so, what you are doing in
this country ?   Remember, though I have been your sister's
worst enemy, yet I will serve her with the best of my blood,
and I will serve you for her sake; and no one can serve you to
such purpose, for no one can know the circumstances so well;
so speak without fear."

"I am not afraid, sir," said Jeanie, collecting her spirits.
"I trust in God; and if it pleases Him to redeem my sister's
captivity, it is all I seek, whosoever be the instrument.   But,
sir, to be plain with you, I dare not use your counsel, unless
I were enabled to see that it accords with the law which I
must rely upon."

"The devil take the Puritan !" cried George Staunton, for
so we must now call him.   "I beg your pardon; but I am
naturally impatient, and you drive me mad !   What harm
can it possibly do you to tell me in what situation your sister
stands, and your own expectations of being able to assist her?
It is time enough to refuse my advice when I offer any which
you may think improper.   I speak calmly to you, though 'tis
against my nature; but don't urge me to impatience : it will
only render me incapable of serving Effie."

There was in the looks and words of this unhappy young
man a sort of restrained eagerness and impetuosity, which
seemed to prey upon itself, as the impatience of a fiery steed
fatigues itself with churning upon the bit.   After a moment's
consideration, it occurred to Jeanie that she was not entitled
to withhold from him, whether on her sister's account or her
own, the account of the fatal consequences of the crime
which he had committed, nor to reject such advice, being in
itself lawful and innocent, as he might be able to suggest in
the way of remedy.   Accordingly, in as few words as she
could express it, she told the history of her sister's trial and
condemnation, and of her own journey as far as Newark.
He appeared to listen in the utmost agony of mind, yet repressed every violent symptom of emotion, whether by gesture
or sound, which might have interrupted the speaker, and,
stretched on his couch like the Mexican monarch on his bed
of live coals, only the contortions of his cheek, and the
quivering of his limbs, gave indication of his sufferings.   To
much of what she said he listened with stifled groans, as if
he were only hearing those miseries confirmed whose fatal
reality he had known before; but when she pursued her tale
through the circumstances which had interrupted her journey,
extreme surprise and earnest attention appeared to succeed

to the symptoms of remorse which he had before exhibited. He questioned Jeanie closely concerning the appearance of the two men, and the conversation which she had overheard between the taller of them and the woman.

When Jeanie mentioned the old woman having alluded to her foster-son—"It is too true," he said; "and the source from which I derived food, when an infant, must have communicated to me the wretched—the fated—propensity to vices that were strangers in my own family. But go on."

Jeanie passed slightly over her journey in company with Madge, having no inclination to repeat what might be the effect of mere raving on the part of her companion, and therefore her tale was now closed.

Young Staunton lay for a moment in profound meditation, and at length spoke with more composure than he had yet displayed during their interview. "You are a sensible, as well as a good, young woman, Jeanie Deans, and I will tell you more of my story than I have told to any one. Story did I call it? it is a tissue of folly, guilt, and misery. But take notice, I do it because I desire your confidence in return—that is, that you will act in this dismal matter by my advice and direction. Therefore do I speak."

"I will do what is fitting for a sister, and a daughter, and a Christian woman to do," said Jeanie; "but do not tell me any of your secrets. It is not good that I should come into your counsel, or listen to the doctrine which causeth to err."

"Simple fool!" said the young man. "Look at me. My head is not horned, my foot is not cloven, my hands are not garnished with talons; and, since I am not the very devil himself, what interest can any one else have in destroying the hopes with which you comfort or fool yourself? Listen to me, patiently, and you will find that, when you have heard my counsel, you may go to the seventh heaven with it in your pocket, if you have a mind, and not feel yourself an ounce heavier in the ascent."

At the risk of being somewhat heavy, as explanations usually prove, we must here endeavor to combine into a distinct narrative information which the invalid communicated in a manner at once too circumstantial, and too much broken by passion, to admit of our giving his precise words. Part of it, indeed, he read from a manuscript, which he had perhaps drawn up for the information of his relations after his decease.

"To make my tale short—this wretched hag, this Margaret Murdockson, was the wife of a favorite servant of my father;

she had been my nurse; her husband was dead; she resided in a cottage near this place; she had a daughter who grew up and was then a beautiful but very giddy girl; her mother endeavored to promote her marriage with an old and wealthy churl in the neighborhood.   The girl saw me frequently; she was familiar with me, as our connection seemed to permit, and I— in a word, I wronged her cruelly.   It was not so bad as your sister's business, but it was sufficiently villanous; her folly should have been her protection.   Soon after this I was sent abroad.   To do my father justice, if I have turned out a fiend, it is not his fault: he used the best means.   When I returned, I found the wretched mother and daughter had fallen into disgrace, and were chased from this country.   My deep share in their shame and misery was discovered; my father used very harsh language; we quarrelled.   I left his house, and led a life of strange adventure, resolving never again to see my father or my father's home.

"And now comes the story!   Jeanie, I put my life into your hands, and not only my own life, which, God knows, is not worth saving, but the happiness of a respectable old man, and the honor of a family of consideration.   My love of low society, as such propensities as I was cursed with are usually termed, was, I think, of an uncommon kind, and indicated a nature which, if not depraved by early debauchery, would have been fit for better things.   I did not so much delight in the wild revel, the low humor, the unconfined liberty of those with whom I associated, as in the spirit of adventure, presence of mind in peril, and sharpness of intellect which they displayed in prosecuting their maraudings upon the revenue, or similar adventures.—Have you looked round this rectory? Is it not a sweet and pleasant retreat?"

Jeanie, alarmed at his sudden change of subject, replied in the affirmative.

"Well! I wish it had been ten thousand fathoms under ground, with its church lands, and tithes, and all that belongs to it!   Had it not been for this cursed rectory, I should have been permitted to follow the bent of my own inclinations and the profession of arms, and half the courage and address that I have displayed among smugglers and deer-stealers would have secured me an honorable rank among my contemporaries.   Why did I not go abroad when I left this house?   Why did I leave it at all?—why?   But it came to that point with me that it is madness to look back, and misery to look forward."

He paused, and then proceeded with more composure.

" The chances of a wandering life brought me unhappily to Scotland, to embroil myself in worse and more criminal actions than I had yet been concerned in. It was now I became acquainted with Wilson, a remarkable man in his station of life— quiet, composed, and resolute, firm in mind, and uncommonly strong in person, gifted with a sort of rough eloquence which raised him above his companions. Hitherto I had been

> As dissolute as desperate, yet through both
> Were seen some sparkles of a better hope.

But it was this man's misfortune, as well as mine, that, notwithstanding the difference of our rank and education, he acquired an extraordinary and fascinating influence over me, which I can only account for by the calm determination of his character being superior to the less sustained impetuosity of mine. Where he led, I felt myself bound to follow ; and strange was the courage and address which he displayed in his pursuits. While I was engaged in desperate adventures, under so strange and dangerous a preceptor, I became acquainted with your unfortunate sister at some sports of the young people in the suburbs, which she frequented by stealth ; and her ruin proved an interlude to the tragic scenes in which I was now deeply engaged. Yet this let me say : the villany was not premeditated, and I was firmly resolved to do her all the justice which marriage could do, so soon as I should be able to extricate myself from my unhappy course of life, and embrace some one more suited to my birth. I had wild visions —visions of conducting her as if to some poor retreat, and introducing her at once to rank and fortune she never dreamed of. A friend, at my request, attempted a negotiation with my father, which was protracted for some time, and renewed at different intervals. At length, and just when I expected my father's pardon, he learned by some means or other my infamy, painted in even exaggerated colors, which was, God knows, unnecessary. He wrote me a letter—how it found me out I know not—enclosing me a sum of money, and disowning me forever. I became desperate—I became frantic—I readily joined Wilson in a perilous smuggling adventure in which we miscarried, and was willingly blinded by his logic to consider the robbery of the officer of the customs in Fife as a fair and honorable reprisal. Hitherto I had observed a certain line in my criminality, and stood free of assaults upon personal property, but now I felt a wild pleasure in disgracing myself as much as possible.

" The plunder was no object to me. I abandoned that to

my comrades, and only asked the post of danger. I remember well, that when I stood with my drawn sword guarding the door while they committed the felony, I had not a thought of my own safety. I was only meditating on my sense of supposed wrong from my family, my impotent thirst of vengeance, and how it would sound in the haughty ears of the family of Willingham, that one of their descendants, and the heir-apparent of their honors, should perish by the hands of the hangman for robbing a Scottish gauger of a sum not equal to one-fifth part of the money I had in my pocket-book. We were taken; I expected no less. We were condemned; that also I looked for. But death, as he approached nearer, looked grimly; and the recollection of your sister's destitute condition determined me on an effort to save my life. I forgot to tell you that in Edinburgh I again met the woman Murdockson and her daughter. She had followed the camp when young, and had now, under pretence of a trifling traffic, resumed predatory habits, with which she had already been too familiar. Our first meeting was stormy; but I was liberal of what money I had, and she forgot, or seemed to forget, the injury her daughter had received. The unfortunate girl herself seemed hardly even to know her seducer, far less to retain any sense of the injury she had received. Her mind is totally alienated, which, according to her mother's account, is sometimes the consequence of an unfavorable confinement. But it was *my doing.* Here was another stone knitted round my neck to sink me into the pit of perdition. Every look, every word of this poor creature, her false spirits, her imperfect recollections, her allusions to things which she had forgotten, but which were recorded in my conscience, were stabs of a poniard. Stabs did I say? they were tearing with hot pincers, and scalding the raw wound with burning sulphur; they were to be endured, however, and they *were* endured. I return to my prison thoughts.

" It was not the least miserable of them that your sister's time approached. I knew her dread of you and of her father. She often said she would die a thousand deaths ere you should know her shame; yet her confinement must be provided for. I knew this woman Murdockson was an infernal hag, but I thought she loved me, and that money would make her true. She had procured a file for Wilson and a spring-saw for me; and she undertook readily to take charge of Effie during her illness, in which she had skill enough to give the necessary assistance. I gave her the money which my father had sent me. It was settled that she should receive Effie into her house in the meantime, and wait for further directions from me, when I should effect my escape. I communicated this purpose, and recommended the old hag to poor Effie by a letter, in which I recollect that I endeavored to support the character of Macheath under condemnation—a fine, gay, bold-faced ruffian, who is game to the last. Such, and so wretchedly poor, was my ambition ! Yet I had resolved to forsake the courses I had been engaged in, should I be so fortunate as to escape the gibbet. My design was to marry your sister and go over to the West Indies. I had still a considerable sum of money left, and I trusted to be able, in one way or other, to provide for myself and my wife.

"We made the attempt to escape, and by the obstinacy of Wilson, who insisted upon going first, it totally miscarried. The undaunted and self-denied manner in which he sacrificed himself to redeem his error, and accomplish my escape from the Tolbooth Church, you must have heard of : all Scotland rang with it. It was a gallant and extraordinary deed. All men spoke of it ; all men, even those who most condemned the habits and crimes of this self-devoted man, praised the heroism of his friendship. I have many vices, but cowardice or want of gratitude are none of the number. I resolved to requite his generosity, and even your sister's safety became a secondary consideration with me for the time. To effect Wilson's liberation was my principal object, and I doubted not to find the means.

"Yet I did not forget Effie neither. The bloodhounds of the law were so close after me, that I dared not trust myself near any of my old haunts ; but old Murdockson met me by appointment, and informed me that your sister had happily been delivered of a boy. I charged the hag to keep her patient's mind easy, and let her want for nothing that money could purchase, and I retreated to Fife, where, among my old associates of Wilson's gang, I hid myself in those places of concealment where the men engaged in that desperate trade are used to find security for themselves and their uncustomed goods. Men who are disobedient both to human and divine laws are not always insensible to the claims of courage and generosity. We were assured that the mob of Edinburgh, strongly moved with the hardships of Wilson's situation and the gallantry of his conduct, would back any bold attempt that might be made to rescue him even from the foot of the gibbet. Desperate as the attempt seemed, upon my declaring myself ready to lead the onset on the guard, I found no want of followers who engaged to stand by me, and returned to

Lothian, soon joined by some steady associates, prepared to act whenever the occasion might require.

"I have no doubt I should have rescued him from the very noose that dangled over his head," he continued, with animation, which seemed a flash of the interest which he had taken in such exploits ; "but among other precautions, the magistrates had taken one—suggested, as we afterwards learned, by the unhappy wretch Porteous—which effectually disconcerted my measures. They anticipated by half an hour the ordinary period for execution ; and, as it had been resolved among us that, for fear of observation from the officers of justice, we should not show ourselves upon the street until the time of action approached, it followed that all was over before our attempt at a rescue commenced. It did commence, however, and I gained the scaffold and cut the rope with my own hand. It was too late ! The bold, stout-hearted, generous criminal was no more, and vengeance was all that remained to us—a vengeance, as I then thought, doubly due from my hand, to whom Wilson had given life and liberty when he could as easily have secured his own."

"O, sir," said Jeanie, "did the Scripture never come into your mind, ' Vengeance is mine, and I will repay it ?'"

"Scripture ! Why, I had not opened a Bible for five years," answered Staunton.

"Wae's me, sirs," said Jeanie, "and a minister's son too !"

"It is natural for you to say so ; yet do not interrupt me, but let me finish my most accursed history. The beast, Porteous, who kept firing on the people long after it had ceased to be necessary, became the object of their hatred for having overdone his duty, and of mine for having done it too well. We—that is, I and the other determined friends of Wilson— resolved to be avenged ; but caution was necessary. I thought I had been marked by one of the officers, and therefore continued to lurk about the vicinity of Edinburgh, but without daring to venture within the walls. At length I visited, at the hazard of my life, the place where I hoped to find my future wife and my son ; they were both gone. Dame Murdockson informed me that, so soon as Effie heard of the miscarriage of the attempt to rescue Wilson, and the hot pursuit after me, she fell into a brain fever ; and that, being one day obliged to go out on some necessary business and leave her alone, she had taken that opportunity to escape, and she had not seen her since. I loaded her with reproaches, to which she listened with the most provoking and callous composure ; for it is one of her attributes that, violent and fierce as she is upon most occasions, there are some in which she shows the most imperturbable calmness. I threatened her with justice ; she said I had more reason to fear justice than she had. I felt she was right, and was silenced. I threatened her with vengeance ; she replied in nearly the same words, that, to judge by injuries received, I had more reason to fear her vengeance than she to dread mine. She was again right, and I was left without an answer. I flung myself from her in indignation, and employed a comrade to make inquiry in the neighborhood of St. Leonard's concerning your sister ; but ere I received his answer, the opening quest of a well-scented terrier of the law drove me from the vicinity of Edinburgh to a more distant and secluded place of concealment. A secret and trusty emissary at length brought me the account of Porteous's condemnation, and of your sister's imprisonment on a criminal charge ; thus astounding one of mine ears, while he gratified the other.

"I again ventured to the Pleasance—again charged Murdockson with treachery to the unfortunate Effie and her child, though I could conceive no reason, save that of appropriating the whole of the money I had lodged with her. Your narrative throws light on this, and shows another motive, not less powerful because less evident—the desire of wreaking vengeance on the seducer of her daughter, the destroyer at once of her reason and reputation. Great God ! how I wish that, instead of the revenge she made choice of, she had delivered me up to the cord !"

"But what account did the wretched woman give of Effie and the bairn ? " said Jeanie, who, during this long and agitating narrative, had firmness and discernment enough to keep her eye on such points as might throw light on her sister's misfortunes.

"She would give none," said Staunton ; "she said the mother made a moonlight flitting from her house, with the infant in her arms ; that she had never seen either of them since ; that the lass might have thrown the child into the North Loch or the Quarry Holes, for what she knew, and it was like enough she had done so."

"And how came you to believe that she did not speak the fatal truth ? " said Jeanie, trembling.

"Because, on this second occasion, I saw her daughter, and I understood from her that, in fact, the child had been removed or destroyed during the illness of the mother. But all knowledge to be got from her is so uncertain and indirect, that I could not collect any further circumstances. Only the diabolical character of old Murdockson makes me augur the worst."

"The last account agrees with that given by my poor sister," said Jeanie ; "but gang on wi' your ain tale, sir."

"Of this I am certain," said Staunton, "that Effie, in her senses, and with her knowledge, never injured living creature. But what could I do in her exculpation ? Nothing ; and therefore my whole thoughts were turned towards her safety. I was under the cursed necessity of suppressing my feelings towards Murdockson : my life was in the hag's hand—that I cared not for ; but on my life hung that of your sister. I spoke the wretch fair ; I appeared to confide in her ; and to me, so far as I was personally concerned, she gave proofs of extraordinary fidelity. I was at first uncertain what measures I ought to adopt for your sister's liberation, when the general rage excited among the citizens of Edinburgh on account of the reprieve of Porteous suggested to me the daring idea of forcing the jail, and at once carrying off your sister from the clutches of the law, and bringing to condign punishment a miscreant who had tormented the unfortunate Wilson even in the hour of death, as if he had been a wild Indian taken captive by a hostile tribe. I flung myself among the multitude in the moment of fermentation ; so did others among Wilson's mates, who had, like me, been disappointed in the hope of glutting their eyes with Porteous's execution. All was organized, and I was chosen for the captain. I felt not— I do not now feel—compunction for what was to be done, and has since been executed."

"O, God forgive ye, sir, and bring ye to a better sense of your ways !" exclaimed Jeanie, in horror at the avowal of such violent sentiments.

"Amen," replied Staunton, "if my sentiments are wrong. But I repeat that, although willing to aid the deed, I could have wished them to have chosen another leader ; because I foresaw that the great and general duty of the night would interfere with the assistance which I proposed to render Effie. I gave a commission, however, to a trusty friend to protect her to a place of safety, so soon as the fatal procession had left the jail. But for no persuasions which I could use in the hurry of the moment, or which my comrade employed at more length, after the mob had taken a different direction, could the unfortunate girl be prevailed upon to leave the prison. His arguments were all wasted upon the infatuated victim, and he was obliged to leave her in order to attend to his own safety. Such was his account ; but perhaps he persevered less steadily in his attempt to persuade her than I would have done."

"Effie was right to remain," said Jeanie ; "and I love her the better for it."

"Why will you say so ?" said Staunton.

"You cannot understand my reasons, sir, if I should render them," answered Jeanie, composedly ; "they that thirst for the blood of their enemies have no taste for the well-spring of life."

"My hopes," said Staunton, "were thus a second time disappointed. My next efforts were to bring her through her trial by means of yourself. How I urged it, and where, you cannot have forgotten. I do not blame you for your refusal ; it was founded, I am convinced, on principle, and not on indifference to your sister's fate. For me, judge of me as a man frantic ; I knew not what hand to turn to, and all my efforts were unavailing. In this condition, and close beset on all sides, I thought of what might be done by means of my family and their influence. I fled from Scotland ; I reached this place ; my miserably wasted and unhappy appearance procured me from my father that pardon which a parent finds it so hard to refuse, even to the most undeserving son. And here I have awaited in anguish of mind, which the condemned criminal might envy, the event of your sister's trial."

"Without taking any steps for her relief ?" said Jeanie.

"To the last I hoped her case might terminate more favorably ; and it is only two days since that the fatal tidings reached me. My resolution was instantly taken. I mounted my best horse with the purpose of making the utmost haste to London, and there compounding with Sir Robert Walpole for your sister's safety, by surrendering to him, in the person of the heir of the family of Willingham, the notorious George Robertson, the accomplice of Wilson, the breaker of the Tolbooth prison, and the well-known leader of the Porteous mob."

"But would that save my sister ?" said Jeanie, in astonishment.

"It would, as I should drive my bargain," said Staunton. "Queens love revenge as well as their subjects. Little as you seem to esteem it, it is a poison which pleases all palates, from the prince to the peasant. Prime ministers love no less the power of pleasing sovereigns by gratifying their passions. The life of an obscure village girl ! Why, I might ask the best of the crown jewels for laying the head of such an insolent conspiracy at the foot of her Majesty, with a certainty of being gratified. All my other plans have failed, but this could not. Heaven is just, however, and would not honor me with making this voluntary atonement for the injury I have done your sister. I had not rode ten miles, when my horse, the best and most sure-footed animal in this country, fell with me on a level piece of road, as if he had been struck by a cannon-shot. I was greatly hurt, and was brought back here in the miserable condition in which you now see me."

As young Staunton had come to the conclusion, the servant opened the door, and, with a voice which seemed intended rather for a signal than merely the announcing of a visit, said, "His Reverence, sir, is coming upstairs to wait upon you."

"For God's sake, hide yourself, Jeanie," exclaimed Staunton, "in that dressing-closet !"

"No, sir," said Jeanie ; "as I am here for nae ill, I canna take the shame of hiding mysell frae the master o' the house."

"But, good Heavens !" exclaimed George Staunton, "do but consider——"

Ere he could complete the sentence, his father entered the apartment.

CHAPTER XXXIV

And now, will pardon, comfort, kindness, draw
The youth from vice? will honor, duty, law?
CRABBE.

JEANIE arose from her seat and made her quiet reverence when
the elder Mr. Staunton entered the apartment. His astonishment was extreme at finding his son in such company.

"I perceive, madam," he said, "I have made a mistake respecting you, and ought to have left the task of interrogating
you, and of righting your wrongs, to this young man, with
whom, doubtless, you have been formerly acquainted."

"It's unwitting on my part that I am here," said Jeanie;
"the servant told me his master wished to speak with me."

"There goes the purple coat over my ears," murmured
Tummas. "D—n her, why must she needs speak the truth,
when she could have as well said anything else she had a
mind?"

"George," said Mr. Staunton, "if you are still, as you
have ever been, lost to all self-respect, you might at least have
spared your father, and your father's house, such a disgraceful
scene as this."

"Upon my life—upon my soul, sir!" said George, throwing
his feet over the side of the bed, and starting from his recumbent posture.

"Your life, sir!" interrupted his father, with melancholy
sternness—"what sort of life has it been? Your soul! alas!
what regard have you ever paid to it? Take care to reform
both ere offering either as pledges of your sincerity."

"On my honor, sir, you do me wrong," answered George
Staunton; "I have been all that you can call me that's bad,
but in the present instance you do me injustice. By my
honor, you do!"

"Your honor!" said his father, and turned from him, with
a look of the most upbraiding contempt, to Jeanie. "From
you, young woman, I neither ask nor expect any explanation;
but, as a father alike and as a clergyman, I request your departure from this house. If your romantic story has been
other than a pretext to find admission into it—which, from
the society in which you first appeared, I may be permitted to

doubt—you will find a justice of peace within two miles, with whom, more properly than with me, you may lodge your complaint."

" This shall not be," said George Staunton, starting up to his feet. " Sir, you are naturally kind and humane ; you shall not become cruel and inhospitable on my account. Turn out that eavesdropping rascal," pointing to Thomas, "and get what hartshorn drops, or what better receipt you have against fainting, and I will explain to you in two words the connection betwixt this young woman and me. She shall not lose her fair character through me. I have done too much mischief to her family already, and I know too well what belongs to the loss of fame."

" Leave the room, sir," said the Rector to the servant ; and when the man had obeyed, he carefully shut the door behind him. Then addressing his son, he said, sternly, " Now, sir, what new proof of your infamy have you to impart to me ?"

Young Staunton was about to speak, but it was one of those moments when persons who, like Jeanie Deans, possess the advantage of a steady courage and unruffled temper, can assume the superiority over more ardent but less determined spirits.

" Sir," she said to the elder Staunton, " ye have an undoubted right to ask your ain son to render a reason of his conduct. But respecting me, I am but a wayfaring traveller, no ways obligated or indebted to you, unless it be for the meal of meat, which, in my ain country, is willingly gien by rich or poor, according to their ability, to those who need it ; and for which, forbye that, I am willing to make payment, if I didna think it would be an affront to offer siller in a house like this, only I dinna ken the fashions of the country."

" This is all very well, young woman," said the Rector, a good deal surprised, and unable to conjecture whether to impute Jeanie's language to simplicity or impertinence—" this may be all very well, but let me bring it to a point. Why do you stop this young man's mouth, and prevent his communicating to his father and his best friend an explanation, since he says he has one, of circumstances which seem in themselves not a little suspicious ?"

" He may tell of his ain affairs what he likes," answered Jeanie ; " but my family and friends have nae right to hae ony stories told anent them without their express desire ; and, as they canna be here to speak for themselves, I entreat ye wadna ask Mr. George Rob—I mean Staunton, or whatever his name is—ony questions anent me or my folk ; for I maun be free to tell you, that he will neither have the bearing of a Christian or a gentleman if he answers you against my express desire."

"This is the most extraordinary thing I ever met with," said the Rector, as, after fixing his eyes keenly on the placid yet modest countenance of Jeanie, he turned them suddenly upon his son. "What have you to say, sir?"

"That I feel I have been too hasty in my promise, sir," answered George Staunton. "I have no title to make any communications respecting the affairs of this young person's family without her assent."

The elder Mr. Staunton turned his eyes from one to the other with marks of surprise.

"This is more and worse, I fear," he said, addressing his son, "than one of your frequent and disgraceful connections. I insist upon knowing the mystery."

"I have already said, sir," replied his son, rather sullenly, "that I have no title to mention the affairs of this young woman's family without her consent."

"And I hae nae mysteries to explain, sir," said Jeanie, "but only to pray you, as a preacher of the Gospel and a gentleman, to permit me to go safe to the next public-house on the Lunnon road."

"I shall take care of your safety," said young Staunton; "you need ask that favor from no one."

"Do you say so before my face?" said the justly incensed father. "Perhaps, sir, you intend to fill up the cup of disobedience and profligacy by forming a low and disgraceful marriage? But let me bid you beware."

"If you were feared for sic a thing happening wi' me, sir," said Jeanie, "I can only say, that not for all the land that lies between the twa ends of the rainbow wad I be the woman that should wed your son."

"There is something very singular in all this," said the elder Staunton; "follow me into the next room, young woman."

"Hear me speak first," said the young man. "I have but one word to say. I confide entirely in your prudence; tell my father as much or as little of these matters as you will, he shall know neither more nor less from me."

His father darted to him a glance of indignation, which softened into sorrow as he saw him sink down on the couch, exhausted with the scene he had undergone. He left the apartment, and Jeanie followed him, George Staunton raising himself as she passed the doorway, and pronouncing the word

"Remember!" in a tone as monitory as it was uttered by Charles I. upon the scaffold. The elder Staunton led the way into a small parlor, and shut the door.

"Young woman," said he, "there is something in your face and appearance that marks both sense and simplicity, and, if I am not deceived, innocence also. Should it be otherwise, I can only say, you are the most accomplished hypocrite I have ever seen. I ask to know no secret that you have unwillingness to divulge, least of all those which concern my son. His conduct has given me too much unhappiness to permit me to hope comfort or satisfaction from him. If you are such as I suppose you, believe me, that whatever unhappy circumstances may have connected you with George Staunton, the sooner you break them through the better."

"I think I understand your meaning, sir," replied Jeanie; "and as ye are sae frank as to speak o' the young gentleman in sic a way, I must needs say that it is but the second time of my speaking wi' him in our lives, and what I hae heard frae him on these twa occasions has been such that I never wish to hear the like again."

"Then it is your real intention to leave this part of the country, and proceed to London?" said the Rector.

"Certainly, sir; for I may say, in one sense, that the avenger of blood is behind me; and if I were but assured against mischief by the way——"

"I have made inquiry," said the clergyman, "after the suspicious characters you described. They have left their place of rendezvous; but as they may be lurking in the neighborhood, and as you say you have special reason to apprehend violence from them, I will put you under the charge of a steady person, who will protect you as far as Stamford, and see you into a light coach, which goes from thence to London."

"A coach is not for the like of me, sir," said Jeanie, to whom the idea of a stage-coach was unknown, as, indeed, they were then only used in the neighborhood of London.

Mr. Staunton briefly explained that she would find that mode of conveyance more commodious, cheaper, and more safe than travelling on horseback. She expressed her gratitude with so much singleness of heart, that he was induced to ask her whether she wanted the pecuniary means of prosecuting her journey. She thanked him, but said she had enough for her purpose; and, indeed, she had husbanded her stock with great care. This reply served also to remove some doubts which naturally enough still floated in Mr. Staunton's mind, respecting her character and real purpose, and satisfied him, at least, that money did not enter into her scheme of deception, if an impostor she should prove. He next requested to know what part of the city she wished to go to.

" To a very decent merchant, a cousin o' my ain, a Mrs. Glass, sir, that sells snuff and tobacco, at the sign o' the Thistle, somegate in the town."

Jeanie communicated this intelligence with a feeling that a connection so respectable ought to give her consequence in the eyes of Mr. Staunton ; and she was a good deal surprised when he answered—"And is this woman your only acquaintance in London, my poor girl ? and have you really no better knowledge where she is to be found ? "

" I was gaun to see the Duke of Argyie, forbye Mrs. Glass," said Jeanie ; "and if your honor thinks it would be best to go there first, and get some of his Grace's folk to show me my cousin's shop——"

" Are you acquainted with any of the Duke of Argyle's people ? " said the Rector.

"No, sir."

"Her brain must be something touched after all, or it would be impossible for her to rely on such introductions. Well," said he aloud, "I must not inquire into the cause of your journey, and so I cannot be fit to give you advice how to manage it. But the landlady of the house where the coach stops is a very decent person ; and as I use her house sometimes, I will give you a recommendation to her."

Jeanie thanked him for his kindness with her best courtesy, and said, "That with his honor's line, and ane from worthy Mrs. Bickerton, that keeps the Seven Stars at York, she did not doubt to be well taken out in Lunnon."

" And now," said he, "I presume you will be desirous to set out immediately."

" If I had been in an inn, sir, or any suitable resting-place," answered Jeanie, "I wad not have presumed to use the Lord's day for travelling ; but as I am on a journey of mercy, I trust my doing so will not be imputed."

" You may, if you choose, remain with Mrs. Dalton for the evening ; but I desire you will have no further correspondence with my son, who is not a proper counsellor for a person of your age, whatever your difficulties may be."

" Your honor speaks ower truly in that," said Jeanie ; "it was not with my will that I spoke wi' him just now, and—not to wish the gentleman onything but gude—I never wish to see him between the een again."

" If you please," added the Rector, "as you seem to be a

seriously disposed young woman, you may attend family worship in the hall this evening."

"I thank your honor," said Jeanie; "but I am doubtful if my attendance would be to edification."

"How!" said the Rector; "so young, and already unfortunate enough to have doubts upon the duties of religion!"

"God forbid, sir," replied Jeanie; "it is not for that; but I have been bred in the faith of the suffering remnant of the Presbyterian doctrine in Scotland, and I am doubtful if I can lawfully attend upon your fashion of worship, seeing it has been testified against by many precious souls of our kirk, and specially by my worthy father."

"Well, my good girl," said the Rector, with a good-humored smile, "far be it from me to put any force upon your conscience; and yet you ought to recollect that the same divine grace dispenses its streams to other kingdoms as well as to Scotland. As it is as essential to our spiritual as water to our earthly wants, its springs, various in character, yet alike efficacious in virtue, are to be found in abundance throughout the Christian world."

"Ah, but," said Jeanie, "though the waters may be alike, yet, with your worship's leave, the blessing upon them may not be equal. It would have been in vain for Naaman the Syrian leper to have bathed in Pharphar and Abana, rivers of Damascus, when it was only the waters of Jordan that were sanctified for the cure."

"Well," said the Rector, "we will not enter upon the great debate betwixt our national churches at present. We must endeavor to satisfy you that at least, among our errors, we preserve Christian charity, and a desire to assist our brethren."

He then ordered Mrs. Dalton into his presence, and consigned Jeanie to her particular charge, with directions to be kind to her, and with assurances that, early in the morning, a trusty guide and a good horse should be ready to conduct her to Stamford. He then took a serious and dignified, yet kind leave of her, wishing her full success in the objects of her journey, which he said he doubted not were laudable, from the soundness of thinking which she had displayed in conversation.

Jeanie was again conducted by the housekeeper to her own apartment. But the evening was not destined to pass over without further torment from young Staunton. A paper was slipped into her hand by the faithful Tummas, which intimated his young master's desire, or rather demand, to see her instantly, and assured her he had provided against interruption.

"Tell your young master," said Jeanie, openly, and regardless of all the winks and signs by which Tummas strove to make her comprehend that Mrs. Dalton was not to be admitted into the secret of the correspondence, "that I promised faithfully to his worthy father that I would not see him again."

"Tummas," said Mrs. Dalton, "I think you might be much more creditably employed, considering the coat you wear and the house you live in, than to be carrying messages between your young master and girls that chance to be in this house."

"Why, Mrs. Dalton, as to that, I was hired to carry messages, and not to ask any questions about them ; and it's not for the like of me to refuse the young gentleman's bidding, if he were a little wildish or so. If there was harm meant, there's no harm done, you see."

"However," said Mrs. Dalton, "I gie you fair warning, Tummas Ditton, that an I catch thee at this work again, his Reverence shall make a clear house of you."

Tummas retired, abashed and in dismay. The rest of the evening passed away without anything worthy of notice.

Jeanie enjoyed the comforts of a good bed and a sound sleep with grateful satisfaction, after the perils and hardships of the preceding day ; and such was her fatigue, that she slept soundly until six o'clock, when she was awakened by Mrs. Dalton, who acquainted her that her guide and horse were ready and in attendance. She hastily rose, and, after her morning devotions, was soon ready to resume her travels. The motherly care of the housekeeper had provided an early breakfast, and, after she had partaken of this refreshment, she found herself safe seated on a pillion behind a stout Lincolnshire peasant, who was, besides, armed with pistols, to protect her against any violence which might be offered.

They trudged on in silence for a mile or two along a country road, which conducted them, by hedge and gateway, into the principal highway, a little beyond Grantham. At length her master of the horse asked her whether her name was not Jean, or Jane, Deans. She answered in the affirmative, with some surprise. "Then here's a bit of a note as concerns you," said the man, handing it over his left shoulder. "It's from young master, as I judge, and every man about Willingham is fain to pleasure him either for love or fear ; for he'll come to be landlord at last, let them say what they like."

Jeanie broke the seal of the note, which was addressed to her, and read as follows:

"You refuse to see me. I suppose you are shocked at my character; but, in painting myself such as I am, you should give me credit for my sincerity. I am, at least, no hypocrite. You refuse, however, to see me, and your conduct may be natural; but is it wise? I have expressed my anxiety to repair your sister's misfortunes at the expense of my honor—my family's honor—my own life; and you think me too debased to be admitted even to sacrifice what I have remaining of honor, fame, and life in her cause. Well, if the offerer be despised, the victim is still equally at hand; and perhaps there may be justice in the decree of Heaven that I shall not have the melancholy credit of appearing to make this sacrifice out of my own free good-will. You, as you have declined my concurrence, must take the whole upon yourself. Go, then, to the Duke of Argyle, and, when other arguments fail you, tell him you have it in your power to bring to condign punishment the most active conspirator in the Porteous mob. He will hear you on this topic, should he be deaf to every other. Make your own terms, for they will be at your own making. You know where I am to be found; and you may be assured I will not give you the dark side of the hill, as at Muschat's Cairn: I have no thoughts of stirring from the house I was born in; like the hare, I shall be worried in the seat I started from. I repeat it—make your own terms. I need not remind you to ask your sister's life, for that you will do of course; but make terms of advantage for yourself: ask wealth and reward—office and income for Butler—ask anything, you will get anything, and all for delivering to the hands of the executioner a man most deserving of his office—one who, though young in years, is old in wickedness, and whose most earnest desire is, after the storms of an unquiet life, to sleep and be at rest."

This extraordinary letter was subscribed with the initials "G. S."

Jeanie read it over once or twice with great attention, which the slow pace of the horse, as he stalked through a deep lane, enabled her to do with facility.

When she had perused this billet, her first employment was to tear it into as small pieces as possible, and disperse these pieces in the air by a few at a time, so that a document containing so perilous a secret might not fall into any other person's hand.

The question how far, in point of extremity, she was entitled to save her sister's life by sacrificing that of a person who, though guilty towards the state, had done her no injury, formed the next earnest and most painful subject of consideration. In one sense, indeed, it seemed as if denouncing the guilt of Staunton, the cause of her sister's errors and misfortunes, would have been an act of just, and even providential, retribution. But Jeanie, in the strict and severe tone of morality in which she was educated, had to consider not only the general aspect of a proposed action, but its justness and fitness in relation to the actor, before she could be, according to her own phrase, free to enter upon it. What right had she to make a barter between the lives of Staunton and of Effie, and to sacrifice the one for the safety of the other? His guilt—that guilt for which he was amenable to the laws— was a crime against the public indeed, but it was not against her.

Neither did it seem to her that his share in the death of Porteous, though her mind revolted at the idea of using violence to any one, was in the relation of a common murder, against the perpetrator of which every one is called to aid the public magistrate. That violent action was blended with many circumstances which, in the eyes of those of Jeanie's rank in life, if they did not altogether deprive it of the character of guilt, softened, at least, its most atrocious features. The anxiety of the government to obtain conviction of some of the offenders had but served to increase the public feeling which connected the action, though violent and irregular, with the idea of ancient national independence. The rigorous procedure adopted or proposed against the city of Edinburgh, the ancient metropolis of Scotland, the extremely unpopular and injudicious measure of compelling the Scottish clergy, contrary to their principles and sense of duty, to promulgate from the pulpit the reward offered for the discovery of the perpetrators of this slaughter, had produced on the public mind the opposite consequences from what were intended; and Jeanie felt conscious that, whoever should lodge information concerning that event, and for whatsoever purpose it might be done, it would be considered as an act of treason against the independence of Scotland. With the fanaticism of the Scotch Presbyterians there was always mingled a glow of national feeling, and Jeanie trembled at the idea of her name being handed down to posterity with that of the " fause Monteath," and one or two others, who, having deserted and betrayed the cause of their country, are damned to perpetual remembrance and execration among its peasantry. Yet, to part with Effie's life once more, when a word spoken might save it, pressed severely on the mind of her affectionate sister.

"The Lord support and direct me!" said Jeanie, "for it seems to be His will to try me with difficulties far beyond my ain strength."

While this thought passed through Jeanie's mind, her guard, tired of silence, began to show some inclination to be communicative. He seemed a sensible, steady peasant, but not having more delicacy or prudence than is common to those in his situation, he, of course, chose the Willingham family as the subject of his conversation. From this man Jeanie learned some particulars of which she had hitherto been ignorant, and which we will briefly recapitulate for the information of the reader.

The father of George Staunton had been bred a soldier, and, during service in the West Indies, had married the heiress of a wealthy planter. By this lady he had an only child, George Staunton, the unhappy young man who has been so often mentioned in this narrative. He passed the first part of his early youth under the charge of a doting mother, and in the society of negro slaves, whose study it was to gratify his every caprice. His father was a man of worth and sense ; but, as he alone retained tolerable health among the officers of the regiment he belonged to, he was much engaged with his duty. Besides, Mrs. Staunton was beautiful and wilful, and enjoyed but delicate health ; so that it was difficult for a man of affection, humanity, and a quiet disposition to struggle with her on the point of her over-indulgence to an only child. Indeed, what Mr. Staunton did do towards counteracting the baneful effects of his wife's system, only tended to render it more pernicious ; for every restraint imposed on the boy in his father's presence was compensated by treble license during his absence. So that George Staunton acquired, even in childhood, the habit of regarding his father as a rigid censor, from whose severity he was desirous of emancipating himself as soon and absolutely as possible.

When he was about ten years old, and when his mind had received all the seeds of those evil weeds which afterwards grew apace, his mother died, and his father, half heart-broken, returned to England. To sum up her imprudence and unjustifiable indulgence, she had contrived to place a considerable part of her fortune at her son's exclusive control or disposal ; in consequence of which management, George Staunton had not been long in England till he learned his independence, and how to abuse it. His father had endeavored to rectify the defects of his education by placing him in a well-regulated seminary. But although he showed some capacity for learning, his riotous conduct soon became intolerable to his teachers. He found means (too easily afforded to all youths who have certain expectations) of procuring such a command of money as enabled him to anticipate in boyhood the frolics and follies of a more mature age, and, with these accomplishments, he was returned on his father's hands as a profligate boy, whose example might ruin a hundred.

The elder Mr. Staunton, whose mind, since his wife's death, had been tinged with a melancholy which certainly his son's conduct did not tend to dispel, had taken orders, and was inducted by his brother, Sir William Staunton, into the family living of Willingham. The revenue was a matter of consequence to him, for he derived little advantage from the estate of his late wife ; and his own fortune was that of a younger brother.

He took his son to reside with him at the rectory ; but he soon found that his disorders rendered him an intolerable inmate. And as the young men of his own rank would not endure the purse-proud insolence of the Creole, he fell into that taste for low society which is worse than " pressing to death, whipping, or hanging." His father sent him abroad, but he only returned wilder and more desperate than before. It is true, this unhappy youth was not without his good qualities. He had lively wit, good temper, reckless generosity, and manners which, while he was under restraint, might pass well in society. But all these availed him nothing. He was so well acquainted with the turf, the gaming-table, the cock-pit, and every worse rendezvous of folly and dissipation, that his mother's fortune was spent before he was twenty-one, and he was soon in debt and in distress. His early history may be concluded in the words of our British Juvenal, when describing a similar character :

> Headstrong, determined in his own career,
> He thought reproof unjust, and truth severe.
> The soul's disease was to its crisis come,
> He first abused and then abjured his home ;
> And when he chose a vagabond to be,
> He made his shame his glory, " I'll be free ! "*

" And yet 'tis pity on Measter George, too," continued the honest boor, " for he has an open hand, and winna let a poor body want an he has it."

* Crabbe's *Borough*, Letter xii. (*Laing*).

The virtue of profuse generosity, by which, indeed, they themselves are most directly advantaged, is readily admitted by the vulgar as a cloak for many sins.

At Stamford our heroine was deposited in safety by her communicative guide. She obtained a place in the coach, which, although termed a light one, and accommodated with no fewer than six horses, only reached London on the afternoon of the second day. The recommendation of the elder Mr. Staunton procured Jeanie a civil reception at the inn where the carriage stopped, and, by the aid of Mrs. Bickerton's correspondent, she found out her friend and relative Mrs. Glass, by whom she was kindly received and hospitably entertained.

CHAPTER XXXV

My name is Argyle, you may well think it strange,
To live at the court and never to change.
Ballad.

FEW names deserve more honorable mention in the history of
Scotland, during this period, than that of John Duke of Argyle and Greenwich. His talents as a statesman and a soldier
were generally admitted; he was not without ambition, but
"without the illness that attends it"—without that irregularity of thought and aim which often excites great men, in
his peculiar situation (for it was a very peculiar one), to grasp
the means of raising themselves to power at the risk of throwing a kingdom into confusion. Pope has distinguished him as

Argyle, the state's whole thunder born to wield,
And shake alike the senate and the field.

He was alike free from the ordinary vices of statesmen, falsehood, namely, and dissimulation; and from those of warriors,
inordinate and violent thirst after self-aggrandizement.

Scotland, his native country, stood at this time in a very
precarious and doubtful situation. She was indeed united to
England, but the cement had not had time to acquire consist-
ence. The irritation of ancient wrongs still subsisted, and betwixt the fretful jealousy of the Scottish and the supercilious
disdain of the English, quarrels repeatedly occurred, in the
course of which the national league, so important to the safety
of both, was in the utmost danger of being dissolved. Scotland had, besides, the disadvantage of being divided into in-
testine factions, which hated each other bitterly, and waited
but a signal to break forth into action.

In such circumstances, another man, with the talents and
rank of Argyle, but without a mind so happily regulated,
would have sought to rise from the earth in the whirlwind,
and direct its fury. He chose a course more safe and more
honorable.

Soaring above the petty distinctions of faction, his voice
was raised, whether in office or opposition, for those measures
which were at once just and lenient. His high military talents

enabled him, during the memorable year 1715, to render such
services to the house of Hanover as, perhaps, were too great
to be either acknowledged or repaid. He had employed, too,
his utmost influence in softening the consequences of that insurrection to the unfortunate gentlemen whom a mistaken
sense of loyalty had engaged in the affair, and was rewarded
by the esteem and affection of his country in an uncommon
degree. This popularity with a discontented and warlike
people was supposed to be a subject of jealousy at court, where
the power to become dangerous is sometimes of itself obnoxious, though the inclination is not united with it. Besides,
the Duke of Argyle's independent and somewhat haughty
mode of expressing himself in Parliament, and acting in public, were ill calculated to attract royal favor. He was, therefore, always respected, and often employed ; but he was not a
favorite of George the Second, his consort, or his ministers.
At several different periods in his life, the Duke might be
considered as in absolute disgrace at court, although he could
hardly be said to be a declared member of opposition. This
rendered him the dearer to Scotland, because it was usually
in her cause that he incurred the displeasure of his sovereign;
and upon this very occasion of the Porteous mob, the animated
and eloquent opposition which he had offered to the severe
measures which were about to be adopted towards the city of
Edinburgh was the more gratefully received in that metropolis as it was understood that the Duke's interposition had
given personal offence to Queen Caroline.

His conduct upon this occasion, as, indeed, that of all the
Scottish members of the legislature, with one or two unworthy
exceptions, had been in the highest degree spirited. The
popular tradition concerning his reply to Queen Caroline has
been given already, and some fragments of his speech against
the Porteous bill are still remembered. He retorted upon
the Chancellor, Lord Hardwicke, the insinuation that he had
stated himself in this case rather as a party than as a judge.
"I appeal," said Argyle, "to the House—to the nation, if
I can be justly branded with the infamy of being a jobber or
a partisan. Have I been a briber of votes—a buyer of boroughs—the agent of corruption for any purpose, or on behalf of any party ? Consider my life, examine my actions
in the field and in the cabinet, and see where there lies a blot
that can attach to my honor. I have shown myself the friend
of my country, the loyal subject of my king. I am ready to
do so again, without an instant's regard to the frowns or
smiles of a court. I have experienced both, and am pre-

pared with indifference for either. I have given my reasons
for opposing this bill, and have made it appear that it is repugnant to the international treaty of union, to the liberty
of Scotland, and, reflectively, to that of England, to common
justice, to common sense, and to the public interest. Shall
the metropolis of Scotland, the capital of an independent
nation, the residence of a long line of monarchs, by whom
that noble city was graced and dignified—shall such a city,
for the fault of an obscure and unknown body of rioters, be
deprived of its honors and its privileges, its gates and its
guards ? and shall a native Scotsman tamely behold the havoc?
I glory, my lords, in opposing such unjust rigor, and reckon
it my dearest pride and honor to stand up in defence of my
native country, while thus laid open to undeserved shame and
unjust spoliation.''

Other statesmen and orators, both Scottish and English,
used the same arguments ; the bill was gradually stripped of
its most oppressive and obnoxious clauses, and at length ended
in a fine upon the city of Edinburgh in favor of Porteous's
widow ; so that, as somebody observed at the time, the whole
of these fierce debates ended in making the fortune of an old
cook-maid, such having been the good woman's original capacity.

The court, however, did not forget the baffle they had received in this affair, and the Duke of Argyle, who had contributed so much to it, was thereafter considered as a person in
disgrace. It is necessary to place these circumstances under
the reader's observation, both because they are connected with
the preceding and subsequent part of our narrative.

The Duke was alone in his study, when one of his gentlemen acquainted him that a country-girl from Scotland was
desirous of speaking with his Grace.

"A country-girl, and from Scotland !" said the Duke ;
"what can have brought the silly fool to London ? Some
lover pressed and sent to sea, or some stock sunk in the South
Sea funds, or some such hopeful concern, I suppose, and then
nobody to manage the matter but MacCallummore. Well,
this same popularity has its inconveniences. However, show
our countrywoman up, Archibald ; it is ill manners to keep
her in attendance.''

A young woman of rather low stature, and whose countenance might be termed very modest and pleasing in expression, though sun-burnt, somewhat freckled, and not possessing regular features, was ushered into the splendid library.

She wore the tartan plaid of her country, adjusted so as partly to cover her head, and partly to fall back over her shoulders. A quantity of fair hair, disposed with great simplicity and neatness, appeared in front of her round and good-humored face, to which the solemnity of her errand, and her sense of the Duke's rank and importance, gave an appearance of deep awe, but not of slavish fear or fluttered bashfulness. The rest of Jeanie's dress was in the style of Scottish maidens of her own class, but arranged with that scrupulous attention to neatness and cleanliness which we often find united with that purity of mind of which it is a natural emblem.

She stopped near the entrance of the room, made her deepest reverence, and crossed her hands upon her bosom, without uttering a syllable. The Duke of Argyle advanced towards her ; and if she admired his graceful deportment and rich dress, decorated with the orders which had been deservedly bestowed on him, his courteous manner, and quick and intelligent cast of countenance, he, on his part, was not less, or less deservedly, struck with the quiet simplicity and modesty expressed in the dress, manners, and countenance of his humble countrywoman.

"Did you wish to speak with me, my bonny lass ?" said the Duke, using the encouraging epithet which at once acknowledged the connection betwixt them as country-folk ; " or did you wish to see the Duchess ? "

"My business is with your honor, my Lord—I mean your Lordship's Grace."

"And what is it, my good girl ?" said the Duke, in the same mild and encouraging tone of voice. Jeanie looked at the attendant. "Leave us, Archibald," said the Duke, "and wait in the ante-room." The domestic retired. "And now sit down, my good lass," said the Duke ; "take your breath—take your time, and tell me what you have got to say. I guess by your dress you are just come up from poor old Scotland. Did you come through the streets in your tartan plaid ?"

"No, sir," said Jeanie ; "a friend brought me in ane o' their street coaches—a very decent woman," she added, her courage increasing as she became familiar with the sound of her own voice in such a presence ; "your Lordship's Grace kens her : it's Mrs. Glass, at the sign o' the Thistle."

"O, my worthy snuff merchant ! I have always a chat with Mrs. Glass when I purchase my Scotch high-dried. Well, but your business, my bonny woman : time and tide, you know, wait for no one."

"Your honor—I beg your Lordship's pardon, I mean your

Grace "—for it must be noticed that this matter of addressing the Duke by his appropriate title had been anxiously inculcated upon Jeanie by her friend Mrs. Glass, in whose eyes it was a matter of such importance that her last words, as Jeanie left the coach were, "Mind to say your Grace;" and Jeanie, who had scarce ever in her life spoke to a person of higher quality than the Laird of Dumbiedikes, found great difficulty in arranging her language according to the rules of ceremony.

The Duke, who saw her embarrassment, said, with his usual affability, "Never mind my Grace, lassie; just speak out a plain tale, and show you have a Scotch tongue in your head."

"Sir, I am muckle obliged. Sir, I am the sister of that poor unfortunate criminal, Effie Deans, who is ordered for execution at Edinburgh."

"Ah!" said the Duke, "I have heard of that unhappy story, I think—a case of child-murder, under a special Act of Parliament. Duncan Forbes mentioned it at dinner the other day."

"And I was come up frae the North, sir, to see what could be done for her in the way of getting a reprieve or pardon, sir, or the like of that."

"Alas! my poor girl," said the Duke, "you have made a long and a sad journey to very little purpose. Your sister is ordered for execution."

"But I am given to understand that there is law for reprieving her, if it is in the king's pleasure," said Jeanie.

"Certainly there is," said the Duke; "but that is purely in the king's breast. The crime has been but too common; the Scotch crown lawyers think it is right there should be an example. Then the late disorders in Edinburgh have excited a prejudice in government against the nation at large, which they think can only be managed by measures of intimidation and severity. What argument have you, my poor girl, except the warmth of your sisterly affection to offer against all this? What is your interest? What friends have you at court?"

"None, excepting God and your Grace," said Jeanie, still keeping her ground resolutely, however.

"Alas!" said the Duke, "I could almost say with old Ormond, that there could not be any whose influence was smaller with kings and ministers. It is a cruel part of our situation, young woman—I mean of the situation of men in my circumstances—that the public ascribe to them influence which they do not possess; and that individuals are led to expect from them assistance which we have no means of rendering. But candor and plain dealing is in the power of every one, and I must not let you imagine you have resources in **my** influence which do not exist, to make your distress the heavier. I have no means of averting your sister's fate.   She must die."

"We must a' die, sir," said Jeanie; "it is our common doom for our father's transgression; but we shouldna hasten ilk other out o' the world, that's what your honor kens better than me."

"My good young woman," said the Duke, mildly, "we are all apt to blame the law under which we immediately suffer; but you seem to have been well educated in your line of life, and you must know that it is alike the law of God and man that the murderer shall surely die."

"But, sir, Effie—that is, my poor sister, sir—canna be proved to be a murderer; and if she be not, and the law take her life notwithstanding, wha is it that is the murderer then?"

"I am no lawyer," said the Duke; "and I own I think the statute a very severe one."

"You are a law-maker, sir, with your leave; and therefore ye have power over the law," answered Jeanie.

"Not in my individual capacity," said the Duke; "though, as one of a large body, I have a voice in the legislation.   But that cannot serve you; nor have I at present—I care not who knows it—so much personal influence with the sovereign as would entitle me to ask from him the most insignificant favor. What could tempt you, young woman, to address yourself to me?"

"It was yoursell, sir."

"Myself?" he replied.   "I am sure you have never seen me before."

"No, sir; but a' the world kens that the Duke of Argyle is his country's friend; and that ye fight for the right, and speak for the right, and that there's nane like you in our present Israel, and so they that think themselves wranged draw to refuge under your shadow; and if ye wunna stir to save the blood of an innocent countrywoman of your ain, what should we expect frae Southrons and strangers?   And maybe I had another reason for troubling your honor."

"And what is that?" asked the Duke.

"I hae understood from my father that your honor's house, and especially your gudesire and his father, laid down their lives on the scaffold in the persecuting time.   And my father was honored to gie his testimony baith in the cage and in the pillory, as is specially mentioned in the books of Peter [Patrick] Walker, the packman, that your honor, I dare say, kens, for he uses maist partly the westland of Scotland.

And, sir, there's ane that takes concern in me that wished me to gang to your Grace's presence, for his gudesire had done your gracious gudesire some good turn, as ye will see frae these papers."

With these words, she delivered to the Duke the little parcel which she had received from Butler. He opened it, and in the envelope read with some surprise, "Muster-roll of the men serving in the troop of that godly gentleman, Captain Salathiel Bangtext—Obadiah Muggleton, Sin-Despise Double-knock, Stand-fast-in-faith Gipps, Turn-to-the-right Thwack-away. What the deuce is this? A list of Praise-God Barebones' Parliament, I think, or of old Noll's evangelical army; that last fellow should understand his wheelings, to judge by his name. But what does all this mean, my girl?"

"It was the other paper, sir," said Jeanie, somewhat abashed at the mistake.

"O, this is my unfortunate grandfather's hand sure enough: 'To all who may have friendship for the house of Argyle, these are to certify that Benjamin [Stephen] Butler, of Monk's regiment of dragoons, having been, under God, the means of saving my life from four English troopers who were about to slay me, I, having no other present means of recompense in my power, do give him this acknowledgment, hoping that it may be useful to him or his during these troublesome times; and do conjure my friends, tenants, kinsmen, and whoever will do aught for me, either in the Highlands or Lowlands, to protect and assist the said Benjamin [Stephen] Butler, and his friends or family, on their lawful occasions, giving them such countenance, maintenance, and supply as may correspond with the benefit he hath bestowed on me. Witness my hand—   LORNE.'

"This is a strong injunction. This Benjamin [Stephen] Butler was your grandfather, I suppose? You seem too young to have been his daughter."

"He was nae akin to me, sir; he was grandfather to ane —to a neighbor's son—to a sincere weel-wisher of mine, sir," dropping her little courtesy as she spoke.

"O, I understand," said the Duke—"a true-love affair. He was the grandsire of one you are engaged to?"

"One I *was* engaged to, sir," said Jeanie, sighing; "but this unhappy business of my poor sister——"

"What!" said the Duke, hastily; "he has not deserted you on that account, has he?"

"No, sir; he wad be the last to leave a friend in difficulties," said Jeanie ; " but I maun think for him as weel as for mysell. He is a clergyman, sir, and it would not beseem him to marry the like of me, wi' this disgrace on my kindred."

" You are a singular young woman," said the Duke. " You seem to me to think of every one before yourself. And have you really come up from Edinburgh on foot to attempt this hopeless solicitation for your sister's life ?"

" It was not a'thegither on foot, sir," answered Jeanie ; " for I sometimes got a cast in a wagon, and I had a horse from Ferrybridge, and then the coach——"

" Well, never mind all that," interrupted the Duke. " What reason have you for thinking your sister innocent ?"

" Because she has not been proved guilty, as will appear from looking at these papers."

She put into his hand a note of the evidence and copies of her sister's declaration. These papers Butler had procured after her departure, and Saddletree had them forwarded to London, to Mrs. Glass's care ; so that Jeanie found the documents, so necessary for supporting her suit, lying in readiness at her arrival.

"Sit down in that chair, my good girl," said the Duke, "until I glance over the papers."

She obeyed, and watched with the utmost anxiety each change in his countenance as he cast his eye through the papers briefly, yet with attention, and making memoranda as he went along. After reading them hastily over, he looked up, and seemed about to speak, yet changed his purpose, as if afraid of committing himself by giving too hasty an opinion, and read over again several passages which he had marked as being most important. All this he did in shorter time than can be supposed by men of ordinary talents ; for his mind was of that acute and penetrating character which discovers, with the glance of intuition, what facts bear on the particular point that chances to be subjected to consideration. At length he rose, after a few minutes' deep reflection. " Young woman," said he, " your sister's case must certainly be termed a hard one."

" God bless you, sir, for that very word !" said Jeanie.

" It seems contrary to the genius of British law," continued the Duke, " to take that for granted which is not proved, or to punish with death for a crime which, for aught the prosecutor has been able to show, may not have been committed at all."

" God bless you, sir !" again said Jeanie, who had risen from her seat, and, with clasped hands, eyes glittering through tears, and features which trembled with anxiety, drank in every word which the Duke uttered.

"But, alas! my poor girl," he continued, "what good will my opinion do you, unless I could impress it upon those in whose hands your sister's life is placed by the law? Besides, I am no lawyer; and I must speak with some of our Scottish gentlemen of the gown about the matter."

"O, but, sir, what seems reasonable to your honor will certainly be the same to them," answered Jeanie.

"I do not know that," replied the Duke; "ilka man buckles his belt his ain gate—you know our old Scotch proverb? But you shall not have placed this reliance on me altogether in vain. Leave these papers with me, and you shall hear from me to-morrow or next day. Take care to be at home at Mrs. Glass's, and ready to come to me at a moment's warning. It will be unnecessary for you to give Mrs. Glass the trouble to attend you; and, by the by, you will please to be dressed just as you are at present."

"I wad hae putten on a cap, sir," said Jeanie, "but your honor kens it isna the fashion of my country for single women; and I judged that being sae mony hundred miles frae hame, your Grace's heart wad warm to the tartan," looking at the corner of her plaid.

"You judged quite right," said the Duke. "I know the full value of the snood; and MacCallummore's heart will be as cold as death can make it when it does *not* warm to the tartan. Now, go away, and don't be out of the way when I send."

Jeanie replied, "There is little fear of that, sir, for I have little heart to go to see sights amang this wilderness of black houses. But if I might say to your gracious honor, that if ye ever condescend to speak to ony ane that is of greater degree than yoursell, though maybe it is nae civil in me to say sae, just if you would think there can be nae sic odds between you and them as between poor Jeanie Deans from St. Leonard's and the Duke of Argyle; and so dinna be chappit back or cast down wi' the first rough answer."

"I am not apt," said the Duke, laughing, "to mind rough answers much. Do not you hope too much from what I have promised. I will do my best; but God has the hearts of kings in His own hand."

Jeanie courtesied reverently and withdrew, attended by the Duke's gentleman, to her hackney-coach, with a respect which her appearance did not demand, but which was perhaps paid to the length of the interview with which his master had honored her.

CHAPTER XXXVI

FROM her kind and officious, but somewhat gossiping friend,
Mrs. Glass, Jeanie underwent a very close catechism on their
road to the Strand, where the Thistle of the good lady flourished in full glory, and, with its legend of *Nemo me impune*,
distinguished a shop then well known to all Scottish folk of
high and low degree.

"And were you sure aye to say 'Your Grace' to him ?"
said the good old lady ; "for ane should make a distinction
between MacCallummore and the bits o' southern bodies that
they ca' lords here : there are as mony o' them, Jeanie, as
would'gar ane think they maun cost but little fash in the making.   Some of them I wadna trust wi' six penniesworth of
black rappee ; some of them I wadna gie mysell the trouble to
put up a hapnyworth in brown paper for.   But I hope you
showed your breeding to the Duke of Argyle, for what sort of
folk would he think your friends in London, if you had been
lording him, and him a duke ?"

"He didna seem muckle to mind," said Jeanie ; "he
kenn'd that I was landward bred."

"Weel, weel," answered the good lady.   "His Grace kens
me weel ; so I.am the less anxious about it.   I never fill his
snuff-box but he says, 'How d'ye do, good Mrs. Glass ?   How
are all our friends in the North ?' or it may be—'Have ye
heard from the North lately ?'   And you may be sure I make
my best courtesy, and answer, 'My Lord Duke, I hope your
Grace's noble Duchess and your Grace's young ladies are well ;
and I hope the snuff continues to give your Grace satisfaction.'
And then ye will see the people in the shop begin to look about
them ; and if there's a Scotchman, as there may be three or
half a dozen, aff go the hats, and mony a look after him, and
'There goes the Prince of Scotland, God bless him !'   But
ye have not told me yet the very words he said t'ye."

Jeanie had no intention to be quite so communicative She had, as the reader may have observed, some of the caution and shrewdness, as well as of the simplicity, of her country. She answered generally, that the Duke had received her very compassionately, and had promised to interest himself in her sister's affair, and to let her hear from him in the course of the next day, or the day after. She did not choose to make any mention of his having desired her to be in readiness to attend him, far less of his hint that she should not bring her landlady. So that honest Mrs. Glass was obliged to remain satisfied with the general intelligence above mentioned, after having done all she could to extract more.

It may easily be conceived that, on the next day, Jeanie declined all invitations and inducements, whether of exercise or curiosity,[to walk abroad, and continued to inhale the close and somewhat professional atmosphere of Mrs. Glass's small parlor. The latter flavor it owed to a certain cupboard, containing, among other articles, a few canisters of real Havana, which, whether from respect to the manufacturer or out of a reverent fear of the exciseman, Mrs. Glass did not care to trust in the open shop below, and which communicated to the room a scent that, however fragrant to the nostrils of the connoisseur, was not very agreeable to those of Jeanie.

" Dear sirs," she said to herself, " I wonder how my cousin's silk manty, and her gowd watch, or onything in the world, can be worth sitting sneezing all her life in this little stifling room, and might walk on green braes if she liked."

Mrs. Glass was equally surprised at her cousin's reluctance to stir abroad and her indifference to the fine sights of London. " It would always help to pass away the time," she said, " to have something to look at, though ane *was* in distress."

But Jeanie was unpersuadable.

The day after her interview with the Duke was spent in that " hope delayed, which maketh the heart sick." Minutes glided after minutes ; hours fled after hours ; it became too late to have any reasonable expectation of hearing from the Duke that day ; yet the hope which she disowned, she could not altogether relinquish, and her heart throbbed, and her ears tingled, with every casual sound in the shop below. It was in vain. The day wore away in the anxiety of protracted and fruitless expectation.

The next morning commenced in the same manner. But before noon a well-dressed gentleman entered Mrs. Glass's shop, and requested to see a young woman from Scotland.

"That will be my cousin, Jeanie Deans, Mr. Archibald," said Mrs. Glass, with a courtesy of recognizance. "Have you any message for her from his Grace the Duke of Argyle, Mr. Archibald? I will carry it to her in a moment."

"I believe I must give her the trouble of stepping down, Mrs. Glass."

"Jeanie—Jeanie Deans!" said Mrs. Glass, screaming at the bottom of the little staircase, which ascended from the corner of the shop to the higher regions. "Jeanie—Jeanie Deans, I say! come downstairs instantly; here is the Duke of Argyle's groom of the chambers desires to see you directly." This was announced in a voice so loud as to make all who chanced to be within hearing aware of the important communication.

It may easily be supposed that Jeanie did not tarry long in adjusting herself to attend the summons, yet her feet almost failed her as she came downstairs.

"I must ask the favor of your company a little way," said Archibald, with civility.

"I am quite ready, sir," said Jeanie.

"Is my cousin going out, Mr. Archibald? then I will hae to go wi' her, no doubt. James Rasper—look to the shop, James. Mr. Archibald," pushing a jar towards him, "you take his Grace's mixture, I think? Please to fill your box, for old acquaintance sake, while I get on my things."

Mr. Archibald transposed a modest parcel of snuff from the jar to his own mull, but said he was obliged to decline the pleasure of Mrs. Glass's company, as his message was particularly to the young person.

"Particularly to the young person!" said Mrs. Glass; "is not that uncommon, Mr. Archibald? But his Grace is the best judge; and you are a steady person, Mr. Archibald. It is not every one that comes from a great man's house I would trust my cousin with. But, Jeanie, you must not go through the streets with Mr. Archibald with your tartan what-d'ye-call-it there upon your shoulders, as if you had come up with a drove of Highland cattle. Wait till I bring down my silk cloak. Why, we'll have the mob after you!"

"I have a hackney-coach in waiting, madam," said Mr. Archibald, interrupting the officious old lady, from whom Jeanie might otherwise have found it difficult to escape, "and I believe I must not allow her time for any change of dress."

So saying, he hurried Jeanie into the coach, while she internally praised and wondered at the easy manner in which he shifted off Mrs. Glass's officious offers and inquiries, without mentioning his master's orders, or going into any explanation whatever.

On entering the coach, Mr. Archibald seated himself in the front seat, opposite to our heroine, and they drove on in silence. After they had proceeded nearly half an hour, without a word on either side, it occurred to Jeanie that the distance and time did not correspond with that which had been occupied by her journey on the former occasion to and from the residence of the Duke of Argyle. At length she could not help asking her taciturn companion, "Whilk way they were going?"

"My Lord Duke will inform you himself, madam," answered Archibald, with the same solemn courtesy which marked his whole demeanor. Almost as he spoke the hackney-coach drew up, and the coachman dismounted and opened the door. Archibald got out and assisted Jeanie to get down. She found herself in a large turnpike road, without the bounds of London, upon the other side of which road was drawn up a plain chariot and four horses, the panels without arms, and the servants without liveries.

"You have been punctual, I see, Jeanie," said the Duke of Argyle, as Archibald opened the carriage door. "You must be my companion for the rest of the way. Archibald will remain here with the hackney-coach till your return."

Ere Jeanie could make answer, she found herself, to her no small astonishment, seated by the side of a duke, in a carriage which rolled forward at a rapid yet smooth rate, very different in both particulars from the lumbering, jolting vehicle which she had just left; and which, lumbering and jolting as it was, conveyed to one who had seldom been in a coach before a certain feeling of dignity and importance.

"Young woman," said the Duke, "after thinking as attentively on your sister's case as is in my power, I continue to be impressed with the belief that great injustice may be done by the execution of her sentence. So are one or two liberal and intelligent lawyers of both countries whom I have spoken with. Nay, pray hear me out before you thank me. I have already told you my personal conviction is of little consequence, unless I could impress the same upon others. Now I have done for you what I would certainly not have done to serve any purpose of my own: I have asked an audience of a lady whose interest with the king is deservedly very high. It has been allowed me, and I am desirous that you should see her and speak for yourself. You have no occasion to be abashed; tell your story simply as you did to me."

"I am much obliged to your Grace," said Jeanie, remembering Mrs. Glass's charge; "and I am sure, since I have had the courage to speak to your Grace in poor Effie's cause, I have less reason to be shamefaced in speaking to a leddy.   But, sir, I would like to ken what to ca' her, whether 'Your Grace,' or 'Your Honor,' or 'Your leddyship,' as we say to lairds and leddies in Scotland, and I will take care to mind it; for I ken leddies are full mair particular than gentlemen about their titles of honor."

"You have no occasion to call her anything but 'Madam.' Just say what you think is likely to make the best impression. Look at me from time to time: if I put my hand to my cravat so [showing her the motion], you will stop; but I shall only do this when you say anything that is not likely to please."

"But, sir, your Grace," said Jeanie, "if it wasna ower muckle trouble, wad it no be better to tell me what I should say, and I could get it by heart?"

"No, Jeanie, that would not have the same effect: that would be like reading a sermon, you know, which we good Presbyterians think has less unction than when spoken without book," replied the Duke.   "Just speak as plainly and boldly to this lady as you did to me the day before yesterday; and if you can gain her consent, I'll wad ye a plack, as we say in the North, that you get the pardon from the king."

As he spoke he took a pamphlet from his pocket and began to read.   Jeanie had good sense and tact, which constitute betwixt them that which is called natural good-breeding.   She interpreted the Duke's manœuvre as a hint that she was to ask no more questions, and she remained silent accordingly.

The carriage rolled rapidly onward through fertile meadows ornamented with splendid old oaks, and catching occasionally a glance of the majestic mirror of a broad and placid river. After passing through a pleasant village, the equipage stopped on a commanding eminence, where the beauty of English landscape was displayed in its utmost luxuriance.   Here the Duke alighted, and desired Jeanie to follow him.   They paused for a moment on the brow of a hill, to gaze on the unrivalled landscape which it presented.   A huge sea of verdure, with crossing and intersecting promontories of massive and tufted groves, was tenanted by numberless flocks and herds, which seemed to wander unrestrained and unbounded through the rich pastures.   The Thames, here turreted with villas and there garlanded with forests, moved on slowly and placidly like the mighty monarch of the scene, to whom all its other beauties were but accessories, and bore on his bosom a hundred

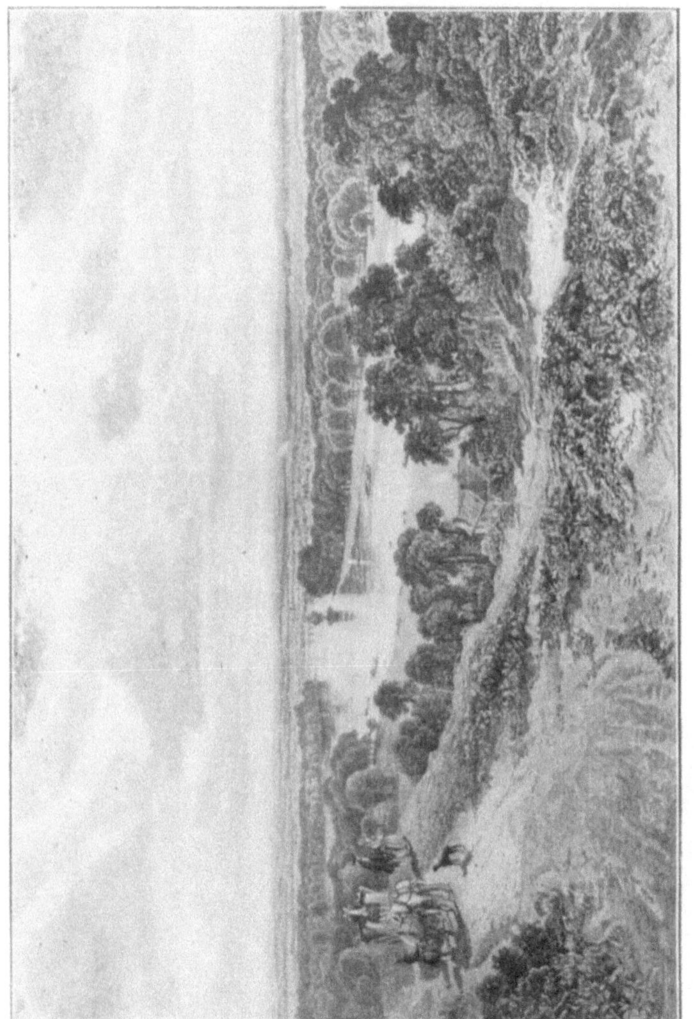

View from Richmond Hill.

barks and skiffs, whose white sails and gayly fluttering pennons gave life to the whole.

The Duke of Argyle was, of course, familiar with this scene ; but to a man of taste it must be always new. Yet, as he paused and looked on this inimitable landscape with the feeling of delight which it must give to the bosom of every admirer of nature, his thoughts naturally reverted to his own more grand, and scarce less beautiful, domains of Inverary. " This is a fine scene," he said to his companion, curious, perhaps, to draw out her sentiments ; " we have nothing like it in Scotland."

" It's braw rich feeding for the cows, and they have a fine breed o' cattle here," replied Jeanie ; " but I like just as weel to look at the craigs of Arthur's Seat, and the sea coming in ayont them, as at a' thae muckle trees."

The Duke smiled at a reply equally professional and national, and made a signal for the carriage to remain where it was. Then adopting an unfrequented footpath, he conducted Jeanie through several complicated mazes to a postern-door in a high brick wall. It was shut ; but as the Duke tapped slightly at it, a person in waiting within, after reconnoitring through a small iron grate contrived for the purpose, unlocked the door and admitted them. They entered, and it was immediately closed and fastened behind them. This was all done quickly, the door so instantly closing, and the person who opened it so suddenly disappearing, that Jeanie could not even catch a glimpse of his exterior.

They found themselves at the extremity of a deep and narrow alley, carpeted with the most verdant and close-shaven turf, which felt like velvet under their feet, and screened from the sun by the branches of the lofty elms which united over the path, and caused it to resemble, in the solemn obscurity of the light which they admitted, as well as from the range of columnar stems, and intricate union of their arched branches, one of the narrow side aisles in an ancient Gothic cathedral.

CHAPTER XXXVII

I beseech you ;
These tears beseech you, and these chaste hands woo you,
That never yet were heaved but to things holy—
Things like yourself.   You are a God above us ;
Be as a God, then, full of sav ing mercy !
The Bloody Brother.

ENCOURAGED as she was by the courteous manners of her noble countryman, it was not without a feeling of something like terror that Jeanie felt herself in a place apparently so lonely, with a man of such high rank.   That she should have been permitted to wait on the Duke in his own house, and have been there received to a private interview, was in itself an uncommon and distinguished event in the annals of a life so simple as hers ; but to find herself his travelling companion in a journey, and then suddenly to be left alone with him in so secluded a situation, had something in it of awful mystery. A romantic heroine might have suspected and dreaded the power of her own charms ; but Jeanie was too wise to let such a silly thought intrude on her mind.   Still, however, she had a most eager desire to know where she now was, and to whom she was to be presented.

.She remarked that the Duke's dress, though still such as indicated rank and fashion (for it was not the custom of men of quality at that time to dress themselves like their own coach-men or grooms) was nevertheless plainer than that in which she had seen him upon a former occasion, and was divested, in particular, of all those badges of external decoration which intimated superior consequence.   Iu short, he was attired as plainly as any gentleman of fashion could appear in the streets of London in a morning ; and this circumstance helped to shake an opinion which Jeanie began to entertain, that per-haps he intended she should plead her cause in the presence of royalty itself.   "But, surely," said she to herself, "he wad hae putten on his braw star and garter, an he had thought o' coming before the face of Majesty ; and after a', this is mair like a gentleman's policy than a royal palace."

There was some sense in Jeanie's reasoning ;   yet she was

864

not sufficiently mistress either of the circumstances of etiquette, or the particular relations which existed betwixt the
government and the Duke of Argyle, to form an accurate
judgment. The Duke, as we have said, was at this time in
open opposition to the administration of Sir Robert Walpole,
and was understood to be out of favor with the royal family,
to whom he had rendered such important services. But it was
a maxim of Queen Caroline to bear herself towards her political friends with such caution as if there was a possibility of
their one day being her enemies, and towards political opponents with the same degree of circumspection, as if they might
again become friendly to her measures. Since Margaret of
Anjou, no queen-consort had exercised such weight in the
political affairs of England, and the personal address which
she displayed on many occasions had no small share in reclaiming from their political heresy many of those determined
Tories who, after the reign of the Stuarts had been extinguished in the person of Queen Anne, were disposed rather
to transfer their allegiance to her brother, the Chevalier de
St. George, than to acquiesce in the settlement of the crown
on the Hanover family. Her husband, whose most shining
quality was courage in the field of battle, and who endured
the office of King of England without ever being able to acquire English habits, or any familiarity with English dispositions, found the utmost assistance from the address of his
partner ; and while he jealously affected to do everything according to his own will and pleasure, was in secret prudent
enough to take and follow the advice of his more adroit consort. He intrusted to her the delicate office of determining
the various degrees of favor necessary to attach the wavering,
or to confirm such as were already friendly, or to regain those
whose good will had been lost.

With all the winning address of an elegant, and, according
to the times, an accomplished woman, Queen Caroline possessed the masculine soul of the other sex. She was proud
by nature, and even her policy could not always temper her
expressions of displeasure, although few were more ready at
repairing any false step of this kind, when her prudence came
up to the aid of her passions. She loved the real possession
of power rather than the show of it, and whatever she did herself that was either wise or popular she always desired that
the king should have the full credit as well as the advantage
of the measure, conscious that, by adding to his respectability, she was most likely to maintain her own. And so
desirous was she to comply with all his tastes, that, when

threatened with the gout, she had repeatedly had recourse to checking the fit by the use of the cold bath, thereby endangering her life, that she might be able to attend the king in his walks.

It was a very consistent part of Queen Caroline's character to keep up many private correspondences with those to whom in public she seemed unfavorable, or who, for various reasons, stood ill with the court. By this means she kept in her hands the thread of many a political intrigue, and, without pledging herself to anything, could often prevent discontent from becoming hatred and opposition from exaggerating itself into rebellion. If by any accident her correspondence with such persons chanced to be observed or discovered, which she took all possible pains to prevent, it was represented as a mere intercourse of society, having no reference to politics ; an answer with which even the prime minister, Sir Robert Walpole, was compelled to remain satisfied, when he discovered that the Queen had given a private audience to Pulteney, afterwards Earl of Bath, his most formidable and most inveterate enemy.

In thus maintaining occasional intercourse with several persons who seemed most alienated from the crown, it may readily be supposed that Queen Caroline had taken care not to break entirely with the Duke of Argyle. His high birth, his great talents, the estimation in which he was held in his own country, the great services which he had rendered the house of Brunswick in 1715, placed him high in that rank of persons who were not to be rashly neglected. He had, almost by his single and unassisted talents, stopped the irruption of the banded force of all the Highland chiefs ; there was little doubt that, with the slightest encouragement, he could put them all in motion and renew the civil war ; and it was well known that the most flattering overtures had been transmitted to the Duke from the court of St. Germains. The character and temper of Scotland were still little known, and it was considered as a volcano which might, indeed, slumber for a series of years, but was still liable, at a moment the least expected, to break out into a wasteful eruption. It was therefore of the highest importance to retain some hold over so important a personage as the Duke of Argyle, and Caroline preserved the power of doing so by means of a lady with whom, as wife of George II., she might have been supposed to be on less intimate terms.

It was not the least instance of the Queen's address that she had contrived that one of her principal attendants, Lady

Suffolk, should unite in her own person the two apparently inconsistent characters of her husband's mistress and her own very obsequious and complaisant confidante. By this dexterous management the Queen secured her power against the danger which might most have threatened it—the thwarting influence of an ambitious rival; and if she submitted to the mortification of being obliged to connive at her husband's infidelity, she was at least guarded against what she might think its most dangerous effects, and was besides at liberty now and then to bestow a few civil insults upon " her good Howard," whom, however, in general, she treated with great decorum.* Lady Suffolk lay under strong obligations to the Duke of Argyle, for reasons which may be collected from Horace Walpole's *Reminiscences* of that reign, and through her means the Duke had some occasional correspondence with Queen Caroline, much interrupted, however, since the part he had taken in the debate concerning the Porteous mob, an affair which the Queen, though somewhat unreasonably, was disposed to resent rather as an intended and premeditated insolence to her own person and authority than as a sudden ebullition of popular vengeance. Still, however, the communication remained open betwixt them, though it had been of late disused on both sides. These remarks will be found necessary to understand the scene which is about to be presented to the reader.

From the narrow alley which they had traversed, the Duke turned into one of the same character, but broader and still longer. Here, for the first time since they had entered these gardens, Jeanie saw persons approaching them.

They were two ladies, one of whom walked a little behind the other, yet not so much as to prevent her from hearing and replying to whatever observation was addressed to her by the lady who walked foremost, and that without her having the trouble to turn her person. As they advanced very slowly, Jeanie had time to study their features and appearance. The Duke also slackened his pace, as if to give her time to collect herself, and repeatedly desired her not to be afraid. The lady who seemed the principal person had remarkably good features, though somewhat injured by the small-pox, that venomous scourge which each village Esculapius (thanks to Jenner) can now tame as easily as their tutelary deity subdued the python. The lady's eyes were brilliant, her teeth good, and her countenance formed to express at will either majesty or courtesy. Her form, though rather *embonpoint,* was nevertheless grace-

* See Horace Walpole's *Reminiscences.*

ful; and the elasticity and firmness of her step gave no room to suspect, what was actually the case, that she suffered occasionally from a disorder the most unfavorable to pedestrian exercise. Her dress was rather rich than gay, and her manner commanding and noble.

Her companion was of lower stature, with light brown hair and expressive blue eyes. Her features, without being absolutely regular, were perhaps more pleasing than if they had been critically handsome. A melancholy, or at least a pensive, expression, for which her lot gave too much cause, predominated when she was silent, but gave way to a pleasing and good-humored smile when she spoke to any one.

When they were within twelve or fifteen yards of these ladies, the Duke made a sign that Jeanie should stand still, and stepping forward himself, with the grace which was natural to him, made a profound obeisance, which was formally, yet in a dignified manner, returned by the personage whom he approached.

"I hope," she said, with an affable and condescending smile, "that I see so great a stranger at court as the Duke of Argyle has been of late in as good health as his friends there and elsewhere could wish him to enjoy."

The Duke replied, "That he had been perfectly well;" and added, "that the necessity of attending to the public business before the House, as well as the time occupied by a late journey to Scotland, had rendered him less assiduous in paying his duty at the levee and drawing-room than he could have desired."

"When your Grace *can* find time for a duty so frivolous," replied the Queen, "you are aware of your title to be well received. I hope my readiness to comply with the wish which you expressed yesterday to Lady Suffolk is a sufficient proof that one of the royal family, at least, has not forgotten ancient and important services, in resenting something which resembles recent neglect." This was said apparently with great good-humor, and in a tone which expressed a desire of conciliation.

The Duke replied, "That he would account himself the most unfortunate of men, if he could be supposed capable of neglecting his duty, in modes and circumstances when it was expected and would have been agreeable. He was deeply gratified by the honor which her Majesty was now doing to him personally; and he trusted she would soon perceive that it was in a matter essential to his Majesty's interest that he had the boldness to give her this trouble."

"You cannot oblige me more, my Lord Duke," replied the Queen, " than by giving me the advantage of your lights and experience on any point of the King's service. Your Grace is aware that I can only be the medium through which the matter is subjected to his Majesty's superior wisdom ; but if it is a suit which respects your Grace personally, it shall lose no support by being preferred through me."

"It is no suit of mine, madam," replied the Duke ; "nor have I any to prefer for myself personally, although I feel in full force my obligation to your Majesty. It is a business which concerns his Majesty, as a lover of justice and of mercy, and which, I am convinced, may be highly useful in conciliating the unfortunate irritation which at present subsists among his Majesty's good subjects in Scotland."

There were two parts of this speech disagreeable to Caroline. In the first place, it removed the flattering notion she had adopted, that Argyle designed to use her personal intercession in making his peace with the administration, and recovering the employments of which he had been deprived ; and next, she was displeased that he should talk of the discontents in Scotland as irritations to be conciliated, rather than suppressed.

Under the influence of these feelings, she answered hastily, "That his Majesty has good subjects in England, my Lord Duke, he is bound to thank God and the laws ; that he has subjects in Scotland, I think he may thank God and his sword."

The Duke, though a courtier, colored slightly, and the Queen, instantly sensible of her error, added, without displaying the least change of countenance, and as if the words had been an original branch of the sentence—" And the swords of those real Scotchmen who are friends to the house of Brunswick, particularly that of his Grace of Argyle."

" My sword, madam," replied the Duke, " like that of my fathers, has been always at the command of my lawful king and of my native country : I trust it is impossible to separate their real rights and interests. But the present is a matter of more private concern, and respects the person of an obscure individual."

" What is the affair, my Lord ? " said the Queen. " Let us find out what we are talking about, lest we should misconstrue and misunderstand each other."

" The matter, madam," answered the Duke of Argyle, " regards the fate of an unfortunate young woman in Scotland, now lying under sentence of death, for a crime of which

I think it highly probable that she is innocent. And my humble petition to your Majesty is, to obtain your powerful intercession with the King for a pardon."

It was now the Queen's turn to color, and she did so over cheek and brow, neck and bosom. She paused a moment, as if unwilling to trust her voice with the first expression of her displeasure ; and on assuming an air of dignity and an austere regard of control, she at length replied, " My Lord Duke, I will not ask your motives for addressing to me a request which circumstances have rendered such an extraordinary one. Your road to the King's closet, as a peer and a privy-councillor, entitled to request an audience, was open, without giving me the pain of this discussion. *I*, at least, have had enough of Scotch pardons."

The Duke was prepared for this burst of indignation, and he was not shaken by it. He did not attempt a reply while the Queen was in the first heat of displeasure, but remained in the same firm yet respectful posture which he had assumed during the interview. The Queen, trained from her situation to self-command, instantly perceived the advantage she might give against herself by yielding to passion ; and added, in the same condescending and affable tone in which she had opened the interview, " You must allow me some of the privileges of the sex, my Lord ; and do not judge uncharitably of me, though I am a little moved at the recollection of the gross insult and outrage done in your capital city to the royal authority, at the very time when it was vested in my unworthy person. Your Grace cannot be surprised that I should both have felt it at the time and recollected it now."

" It is certainly a matter not speedily to be forgotten," answered the Duke. " My own poor thoughts of it have been long before your Majesty, and I must have expressed myself very ill if I did not convey my detestation of the murder which was committed under such extraordinary circumstances. I might, indeed, be so unfortunate as to differ with his Majesty's advisers on the degree in which it was either just or politic to punish the innocent instead of the guilty. But I trust your Majesty will permit me to be silent on a topic in which my sentiments have not the good fortune to coincide with those of more able men."

" We will not prosecute a topic on which we may probably differ," said the Queen. " One word, however, I may say in private—you know our good Lady Suffolk is a little deaf— the Duke of Argyle, when disposed to renew his acquaintance with his master and mistress, will hardly find many topics on which we should disagree."

"Let me hope," said the Duke, bowing profoundly to so flattering an intimation, "that I shall not be so unfortunate as to have found one on the present occasion."

"I must first impose on your Grace the duty of confession," said the Queen, "before I grant you absolution. What is your particular interest in this young woman? She does not seem [and she scanned Jeanie, as she said this, with the eye of a connoisseur] much qualified to alarm my friend the Duchess's jealousy."

"I think your Majesty," replied the Duke, smiling in his turn, "will allow my taste may be a pledge for me on that score."

"Then, though she has not much the air *d'une grande dame*, I suppose she is some thirtieth cousin in the terrible chapter of Scottish genealogy?"

"No, madam," said the Duke; "but I wish some of my nearer relations had half her worth, honesty, and affection."

"Her name must be Campbell, at least?" said Queen Caroline.

"No, madam; her name is not quite so distinguished, if I may be permitted to say so," answered the Duke.

"Ah! but she comes from Inverary or Argyleshire?" said the Sovereign.

"She has never been further north in her life than Edinburgh, madam."

"Then my conjectures are all ended," said the Queen, "and your Grace must yourself take the trouble to explain the affair of your *protégée*."

With that precision and easy brevity which is only acquired by habitually conversing in the higher ranks of society, and which is the diametrical opposite of that protracted style of disquisition

<blockquote>Which squires call potter, and which men call prose,</blockquote>

the Duke explained the singular law under which Effie Deans had received sentence of death, and detailed the affectionate exertions which Jeanie had made in behalf of a sister for whose sake she was willing to sacrifice all but truth and conscience.

Queen Caroline listened with attention; she was rather fond, it must be remembered, of an argument, and soon found matter in what the Duke told her for raising difficulties to his request.

"It appears to me, my Lord," she replied, "that this is a severe law. But still it is adopted upon good grounds, I am bound to suppose, as the law of the country, and the girl has been convicted under it. The very presumptions which the law construes into a positive proof of guilt exist in her case; and all that your Grace has said concerning the possibility of her innocence may be a very good argument for annulling the Act of Parliament, but cannot, while it stands good, be admitted in favor of any individual convicted upon the statute."

The Duke saw and avoided the snare; for he was conscious that, by replying to the argument, he must have been inevitably led to a discussion, in the course of which the Queen was likely to be hardened in her own opinion, until she became obliged, out of mere respect to consistency, to let the criminal suffer. "If your Majesty," he said, "would condescend to hear my poor countrywoman herself, perhaps she may find an advocate in your own heart more able than I am to combat the doubts suggested by your understanding."

The Queen seemed to acquiesce, and the Duke made a signal for Jeanie to advance from the spot where she had hitherto remained watching countenances which were too long accustomed to suppress all apparent signs of emotion to convey to her any interesting intelligence. Her Majesty could not help smiling at the awe-struck manner in which the quiet, demure figure of the little Scotchwoman advanced towards her, and yet more at the first sound of her broad northern accent. But Jeanie had a voice low and sweetly toned, an admirable thing in woman, and eke besought "her Leddyship to have pity on a poor misguided young creature," in tones so affecting that, like the notes of some of her native songs, provincial vulgarity was lost in pathos.

"Stand up, young woman," said the Queen, but in a kind tone, "and tell me what sort of a barbarous people your country-folk are, where child-murder is become so common as to require the restraint of laws like yours?"

"If your Leddyship pleases," answered Jeanie, "there are mony places beside Scotland where mothers are unkind to their ain flesh and blood."

It must be observed, that the disputes between George the Second and Frederick, Prince of Wales, were then at the highest, and that the good-natured part of the public laid the blame on the Queen. She colored highly, and darted a glance of a most penetrating character first at Jeanie and then at the Duke. Both sustained it unmoved—Jeanie from total unconsciousness of the offence she had given, and the Duke from his habitual composure.   But in his heart he thought, "My unlucky *protégée* has, with this luckless answer, shot dead, by a kind of chance-medley, her only hope of success."

Lady Suffolk good-humoredly and skilfully interposed in this awkward crisis.   "You should tell this lady," she said to Jeanie, "the particular causes which render this crime common in your country."

"Some thinks it's the kirk-session ; that is, it's the—it's the cutty-stool, if your Leddyship pleases," said Jeanie, looking down and courtesying.

"The what ?" said Lady Suffolk, to whom the phrase was new, and who besides was rather deaf.

"That's the stool of repentance, madam, if it please your Leddyship," answered Jeanie, "for light life and conversation, and for breaking the seventh command."   Here she raised her eyes to the Duke, saw his hand at his chin, and, totally unconscious of what she had said out of joint, gave double effect to the innuendo by stopping short and looking embarrassed.

As for Lady Suffolk, she retired like a covering party which, having interposed betwixt their retreating friends and the enemy, have suddenly drawn on themselves a fire unexpectedly severe.

"The deuce take the lass," thought the Duke of Argyle to himself ; "there goes another shot, and she has hit with both barrels right and left !"

Indeed, the Duke had himself his share of the confusion, for, having acted as master of ceremonies to this innocent offender, he felt much in the circumstances of a country squire who, having introduced his spaniel into a well-appointed drawing-room, is doomed to witness the disorder and damage which arises to china and to dress-gowns in consequence of its untimely frolics.   Jeanie's last chance-hit, however, obliterated the ill impression which had arisen from the first ; for her Majesty had not so lost the feelings of a wife in those of a Queen but that she could enjoy a jest at the expense of "her good Suffolk."   She turned towards the Duke of Argyle with a smile, which marked that she enjoyed the triumph, and observed, "The Scotch are a rigidly moral people."   Then again applying herself to Jeanie, she asked how she travelled up from Scotland.

"Upon my foot mostly, madam," was the reply.

"What, all that immense way upon foot ?   How far can you walk in a day ?"

"Five-and-twenty miles and a bittock."

"And a what?" said the Queen, looking towards the Duke of Argyle.

"And about five miles more," replied the Duke.

"I thought I was a good walker," said the Queen, "but this shames me sadly."

"May your Leddyship never hae sae weary a heart that ye canna be sensible of the weariness of the limbs!" said Jeanie.

"That came better off," thought the Duke; "it's the first thing she has said to the purpose."

"And I didna just a'thegither walk the haill way neither, for I had whiles the cast of a cart; and I had the cast of a horse from Ferrybridge, and divers other easements," said Jeanie, cutting short her story, for she observed the Duke made the sign he had fixed upon.

"With all these accommodations," answered the Queen, "you must have had a very fatiguing journey, and, I fear, to little purpose; since, if the King were to pardon your sister, in all probability it would do her little good, for I suppose your people of Edinburgh would hang her out of spite."

"She will sink herself now outright," thought the Duke.

But he was wrong. The shoals on which Jeanie had touched in this delicate conversation lay underground, and were unknown to her; this rock was above water, and she avoided it.

"She was confident," she said, "that baith town and country wad rejoice to see his Majesty taking compassion on a poor unfriended creature."

"His Majesty has not found it so in a late instance," said the Queen; "but I suppose my Lord Duke would advise him to be guided by the votes of the rabble themselves who should be hanged and who spared?"

"No, madam," said the Duke; "but I would advise his Majesty to be guided by his own feelings, and those of his royal consort; and then, I am sure, punishment will only attach itself to guilt, and even then with cautious reluctance."

"Well, my Lord," said her Maj:sty, "all these fine speeches do not convince me of the propriety of so soon showing any mark of favor to your—I suppose I must not say rebellious?—but, at least, your very disaffected and intractable metropolis. Why, the whole nation is in a league to screen the savage and abominable murderers of that unhappy man; otherwise, how is it possible but that, of so many perpetrators, and engaged in so public an action for such a length of time, one at least must have been recognized? Even this wench, for aught I can tell, may be a depository of the secret. Hark you, young woman, had you any friends engaged in the Porteous mob?"

"No, madam," answered Jeanie, happy that the question was so framed that she could, with a good conscience, answer it in the negative.

"But I suppose," continued the Queen, "if you were possessed of such a secret you would hold it matter of conscience to keep it to yourself?"

"I would pray to be directed and guided what was the line of duty, madam," answered Jeanie.

"Yes, and take that which suited your own inclinations," replied her Majesty.

"If it like you, madam," said Jeanie, "I would hae gaen to the end of the earth to save the life of John Porteous, or any other unhappy man in his condition; but I might lawfully doubt how far I am called upon to be the avenger of his blood, though it may become the civil magistrate to do so. He is dead and gane to his place, and they that have slain him must answer for their ain act. But my sister—my puir sister Effie, still lives, though her days and hours are numbered! She still lives, and a word of the King's mouth might restore her to a broken-hearted auld man, that never, in his daily and nightly exercise, forgot to pray that his Majesty might be blessed with a long and a prosperous reign, and that his throne, and the throne of his posterity, might be established in righteousness. O, madam, if ever ye kenn'd what it was to sorrow for and with a sinning and a suffering creature, whose mind is sae tossed that she can be neither ca'd fit to live or die, have some compassion on our misery! Save an honest house from dishonor, and an unhappy girl, not eighteen years of age, from an early and dreadful death! Alas! it is not when we sleep soft and wake merrily ourselves, that we think on other people's sufferings. Our hearts are waxed light within us then, and we are for righting our ain wrangs and fighting our ain battles. But when the hour of trouble comes to the mind or to the body—and seldom may it visit your Leddyship—and when the hour of death comes, that comes to high and low—lang and late may it be yours— O, my Leddy, then it isna what we hae dune for oursells, but what we hae dune for others, that we think on maist pleasantly. And the thoughts that ye hae intervened to spare the puir thing's life will be sweeter in that hour, come when it may, than if a word of your mouth could hang the haill Porteous mob at the tail of ae tow."

Tear followed tear down Jeanie's cheeks, as, her features

glowing and quivering with emotion, she pleaded her sister's cause with a pathos which was at once simple and solemn.

"This is eloquence," said her Majesty to the Duke of Argyle. "Young woman," she continued, addressing herself to Jeanie, "*I* cannot grant a pardon to your sister, but you shall not want my warm intercession with his Majesty. Take this housewife case," she continued, putting a small embroidered needle-case into Jeanie's hands; "do not open it now, but at your leisure you will find something in it which will remind you that you have had an interview with Queen Caroline."

Jeanie, having her suspicions thus confirmed, dropped on her knees, and would have expanded herself in gratitude; but the Duke, who was upon thorns lest she should say more or less than just enough, touched his chin once more.

"Our business is, I think, ended for the present, my Lord Duke," said the Queen, "and, I trust, to your satisfaction. Hereafter, I hope to see your Grace more frequently, both at Richmond and St. James's. Come, Lady Suffolk, we must wish his Grace good morning."

They exchanged their parting reverences, and the Duke, so soon as the ladies had turned their backs, assisted Jeanie to rise from the ground, and conducted her back through the avenue, which she trod with the feeling of one who walks in her sleep.

CHAPTER XXXVIII

So soon as I can win the offended King,
I will be known your advocate.

Cymbeline.

THE Duke of Argyle led the way in silence to the small postern by which they had been admitted into Richmond Park, so long the favorite residence of Queen Caroline. It was opened by the same half-seen janitor, and they found themselves beyond the precincts of the royal demesne. Still not a word was spoken on either side. The Duke probably wished to allow his rustic *protégée* time to recruit her faculties, dazzled and sunk with colloquy sublime; and betwixt what she had guessed, had heard, and had seen, Jeanie Deans's mind was too much agitated to permit her to ask any questions.

They found the carriage of the Duke in the place where they had left it; and when they resumed their places, soon began to advance rapidly on their return to town.

"I think, Jeanie," said the Duke, breaking silence, "you have every reason to congratulate yourself on the issue of your interview with her Majesty."

"And that leddy *was* the Queen hersell?" said Jeanie; "I misdoubted it when I saw that your honor didna put on your hat. And yet I can hardly believe it, even when I heard her speak it hersell."

"It was certainly Queen Caroline," replied the Duke. "Have you no curiosity to see what is in the little pocket-book?"

"Do you think the pardon will be in it, sir?" said Jeanie, with the eager animation of hope.

"Why, no," replied the Duke; "that is unlikely. They seldom carry these things about them, unless they were likely to be wanted; and, besides, her Majesty told you it was the King, not she, who was to grant it."

"That is true too," said Jeanie; "but I am so confused in my mind. But does your honor think there is a certainty of Effie's pardon, then?" continued she, still holding in her hand the unopened pocket-book.

"Why, kings are kittle cattle to shoe behind, as we say in the North," replied the Duke; "but his wife knows his trim, and I have not the least doubt that the matter is quite certain."

"O, God be praised! God be praised!" ejaculated Jeanie; "and may the gude leddy never want the heart's ease she has gien me at this moment. And God bless you too, my Lord! without your help I wad ne'er hae won near her."

The Duke let her dwell upon this subject for a considerable time, curious, perhaps, to see how long the feelings of gratitude would continue to supersede those of curiosity. But so feeble was the latter feeling in Jeanie's mind, that his Grace, with whom, perhaps, it was for the time a little stronger, was obliged once more to bring forward the subject of the Queen's present. It was opened accordingly. In the inside of the case was the usual assortment of silk and needles, with scissors, tweezers, etc.; and in the pocket was a bank-bill for fifty pounds.

The Duke had no sooner informed Jeanie of the value of this last document, for she was unaccustomed to see notes for such sums, than she expressed her regret at the mistake which had taken place. "For the hussy itsell," she said, "was a very valuable thing for a keepsake, with the Queen's name written in the inside with her ain hand, doubtless—Caroline—as plain as could be, and a crown drawn aboon it." She therefore tendered the bill to the Duke, requesting him to find some mode of returning it to the royal owner.

"No, no, Jeanie," said the Duke, "there is no mistake in the case. Her Majesty knows you have been put to great expense, and she wishes to make it up to you."

"I am sure she is even ower gude," said Jeanie, "and it glads me muckle that I can pay back Dumbiedikes his siller, without distressing my father, honest man."

"Dumbiedikes! What, a freeholder of Midlothian, is he not?" said his Grace, whose occasional residence in that country made him acquainted with most of the heritors, as landed persons are termed in Scotland. "He has a house not far from Dalkeith, wears a black wig and a laced hat?"

"Yes, sir," answered Jeanie, who had her reasons for being brief in her answers upon this topic.

"Ah! my old friend Dumbie!" said the Duke; "I have thrice seen him fou, and only once heard the sound of his voice. Is he a cousin of yours, Jeanie?"

"No, sir—my Lord."

"Then he must be a well-wisher, I suspect?"

" Ye—yes, my Lord, sir,"answered Jeanie, blushing, and with hesitation.

" Aha ! then, if the Laird starts, I suppose my friend But‑ ler must be in some danger ? "

" O no, sir," answered Jeanie much more readily, but at the same time blushing much more deeply.

" Well, Jeanie," said the Duke, "you are a girl may be safely trusted with your own matters, and I shall inquire no further about them.   But as to this same pardon, I must see to get it passed through the proper forms ; and I have a friend in office who will, for auld lang syne, do me so much favor. And then, Jeanie, as I shall have occasion to send an express down to Scotland who will travel with it safer and more swiftly than you can do, I will take care to have it put into the proper channel ; meanwhile, you may write to your friends, by post, of your good success."

" And does your honor think,"said Jeanie, " that will do as weel as if I were to take my tap in my lap and slip my ways hame again on my ain errand ? "

" Much better, certainly," said the Duke.   " You know the roads are not very safe for a single woman to travel."

Jeanie internally acquiesced in this observation.

"And I have a plan for you besides.   One of the Duch‑ ess's attendants, and one of mine—your acquaintance Archi‑ bald—are going down to Inverary in a light calash, with four horses I have bought, and there is room enough in the car‑ riage for you to go with them as far as Glasgow, where Archi‑ bald will find means of sending you safely to Edinburgh. And in the way, I beg you will teach the woman as much as you can of the mystery of cheese-making, for she is to have a charge in the dairy, and I dare swear you are as tidy about your milk-pail as about your dress."

" Does your honor like cheese ?" said Jeanie, with a gleam of conscious delight as she asked the question.

" Like it !" said the Duke, whose good-nature anticipated what was to follow—" cakes and cheese are a dinner for an emperor, let alone a Highlandman."

" Because," said Jeanie, with modest confidence, and great and evident self-gratulation, " we have been thought so particular in making cheese, that some folk think it as gude as the real Dunlop ; and if your Honor's Grace wad but ac‑ cept a stane or twa, blithe, and fain, and proud it wad make us !   But maybe ye may like the ewe-milk, that is, the Buck‑ holmside * cheese better ; or maybe the gait-milk, as ye come

* See Buckholmside Cheese.   Note 30.

frae the Highlands—and I canna pretend just to the same skeel o' them; but my cousin Jean, that lives at Locker-machus in Lammermuir, I could speak to her, and——"

"Quite unnecessary," said the Duke; "the Dunlop is the very cheese of which I am so fond, and I will take it as the greatest favor you can do me to send one to Caroline Park. But remember, be on honor with it, Jeanie, and make it all yourself, for I am a real good judge."

"I am not feared," said Jeanie, confidently, "that I may please your honor; for I am sure you look as if you could hardly find fault wi' onybody that did their best; and weel is it my part, I trow, to do mine."

This discourse introduced a topic upon which the two travellers, though so different in rank and education, found each a good deal to say. The Duke, besides his other patriotic qualities, was a distinguished agriculturist, and proud of his knowledge in that department. He entertained Jeanie with his observations on the different breeds of cattle in Scotland, and their capacity for the dairy, and received so much information from her practical experience in return, that he promised her a couple of Devonshire cows in reward for the lesson. In short, his mind was so transported back to his rural employments and amusements, that he sighed when his carriage stopped opposite to the old hackney-coach, which Archibald had kept in attendance at the place where they had left it. While the coachman again bridled his lean cattle, which had been indulged with a bite of musty hay, the Duke cautioned Jeanie not to be too communicative to her landlady concerning what had passed. "There is," he said, "no use of speaking of matters till they are actually settled; and you may refer the good lady to Archibald, if she presses you hard with questions. She is his old acquaintance, and he knows how to manage with her."

He then took a cordial farewell of Jeanie, and told her to be ready in the ensuing week to return to Scotland, saw her safely established in her hackney-coach, and rolled off in his own carriage, humming a stanza of the ballad which he is said to have composed:

> "At the sight of Dunbarton once again,
> I'll cock up my bonnet and march amain,
> With my claymore hanging down to my heel,
> To whang at the bannocks of barley meal."

Perhaps one ought to be actually a Scotchman to conceive how ardently, under all distinctions of rank and situation, they feel their mutual connection with each other as natives of the same country.   There are, I believe, more associations common to the inhabitants of a rude and wild than of a well-cultivated and fertile country : their ancestors have more seldom changed their place of residence ; their mutual recollection of remarkable objects is more accurate ; the high and the low are more interested in each other's welfare ; the feelings of kindred and relationship are more widely extended ; and, in a word, the bonds of patriotic affection, always honorable even when a little too exclusively strained, have more influence on men's feelings and actions.

The rumbling hackney-coach, which tumbled over the (then) execrable London pavement at a rate very different from that which had conveyed the ducal carriage to Richmond, at length deposited Jeanie Deans and her attendant at the national sign of the Thistle.   Mrs. Glass, who had been in long and anxious expectation, now rushed, full of eager curiosity and open-mouthed interrogation, upon our heroine, who was positively unable to sustain the overwhelming cataract of her questions, which burst forth with the sublimity of a grand gardyloo—"Had she seen the Duke, God bless him ! —the Duchess—the young ladies ?   Had she seen the King, God bless him !—the Queen—the Prince of Wales—the Princess—or any of the rest of the royal family ?   Had she got her sister's pardon ?   Was it out and out, or was it only a commutation of punishment ?   How far had she gone—where had she driven to—whom had she seen—what had been said—what had kept her so long ?"

Such were the various questions huddled upon each other by a curiosity so eager that it could hardly wait for its own gratification.   Jeanie would have been more than sufficiently embarrassed by this overbearing tide of interrogations, had not Archibald, who had probably received from his master a hint to that purpose, advanced to her rescue.   "Mrs. Glass," said Archibald, "his Grace desired me particularly to say, that he would take it as a great favor if you would ask the young woman no questions, as he wishes to explain to you more distinctly than she can do how her affairs stand, and consult you on some matters which she cannot altogether so well explain.   The Duke will call at the Thistle to-morrow or next day for that purpose."

"His Grace is very condescending," said Mrs. Glass, her zeal for inquiry slaked for the present by the dexterous administration of this sugar-plum ; "his Grace is sensible that I am in a manner accountable for the conduct of my young kinswoman, and no doubt his Grace is the best judge how far he should intrust her or me with the management of her affairs."

" His Grace is quite sensible of that," answered Archibald, with national gravity, " and will certainly trust what he has to say to the most discreet of the two ; and therefore, Mrs. Glass, his Grace relies you will speak nothing to Mrs. Jean Deans, either of her own affairs or her sister's, until he sees you himself. He desired me to assure you, in the meanwhile, that all was going on as well as your kindness could wish, Mrs. Glass."

" His Grace is very kind—very considerate ; certainly, Mr. Archibald, his Grace's commands shall be obeyed, and—— But you have had a far drive, Mr. Archibald, as I guess by the time of your absence, and I guess [with an engaging smile] you winna be the waur o' a glass of the right Rosa Solis."

" I thank you, Mrs. Glass," said the great man's great man, " but I am under the necessity of returning to my Lord directly." And making his adieus civilly to both cousins, he left the shop of the lady of the Thistle.

"I am glad your affairs have prospered so well, Jeanie, my love," said Mrs. Glass ; " though, indeed, there was little fear of them so soon as the Duke of Argyle was so condescending as to take them into hand. I will ask you no questions about them, because his Grace, who is most considerate and prudent in such matters, intends to tell me all that you ken yourself, dear, and doubtless a great deal more ; so that anything that may lie heavily on your mind may be imparted to me in the meantime, as you see it is his Grace's pleasure that I should be made acquainted with the whole matter forthwith, and whether you or he tells it will make no difference in the world, ye ken. If I ken what he is going to say beforehand, I will be much more ready to give my advice, and whether you or he tell me about it cannot much signify after all, my dear. So you may just say whatever you like, only mind I ask you no questions about it."

Jeanie was a little embarrassed. She thought that the communication she had to make was perhaps the only means she might have in her power to gratify her friendly and hospitable kinswoman. But her prudence instantly suggested that her secret interview with Queen Caroline, which seemed to pass under a certain sort of mystery, was not a proper subject for the gossip of a woman like Mrs. Glass, of whose heart she had a much better opinion than of her prudence. She therefore answered in general, "That the Duke had had the extraordinary kindness to make very particular inquiries into her sister's bad affair, and that he thought he had found the means of putting it a' straight again, but that he proposed to tell all that he thought about the matter to Mrs. Glass herself."

This did not quite satisfy the penetrating mistress of the Thistle. Searching as her own small rappee, she, in spite of her promise, urged Jeanie with still further questions. "Had she been a' that time at Argyle House? Was the Duke with her the whole time? and had she seen the Duchess? and had she seen the young ladies, and specially Lady Caroline Campbell?" To these questions Jeanie gave the general reply, "That she knew so little of the town that she could not tell exactly where she had been; that she had not seen the Duchess to her knowledge; that she had seen two ladies, one of whom, she understood, bore the name of Caroline; and more," she said, "she could not tell about the matter."

"It would be the Duke's eldest daughter, Lady Caroline Campbell, there is no doubt of that," said Mrs. Glass; "but, doubtless, I shall know more particularly through his Grace. And so, as the cloth is laid in the little parlor above stairs, and it is past three o'clock—for I have been waiting this hour for you, and I have had a snack myself—and, as they used to say in Scotland in my time—I do not ken if the word be used now—there is ill talking between a full body and a fasting——"

CHAPTER XXXIX

Heaven first sent letters to some wretch's aid—
Some banish'd lover, or some captive maid.

POPE.

BY dint of unwonted labor with the pen, Jeanie Deans contrived to indite, and give to the charge of the postman on the ensuing day, no less than three letters, an exertion altogether strange to her habits; insomuch so that, if milk had been plenty, she would rather have made thrice as many Dunlop cheeses. The first of them was very brief. It was addressed to George Staunton, Esq., at the Rectory, Willingham, by Grantham; the address being part of the information which she had extracted from the communicative peasant who rode before her to Stamford. It was in these words:

"SIR,

"To prevent farder mischieves, whereof there hath been enough, comes these: Sir, I have my sister's pardon from the Queen's Majesty, whereof I do not doubt you will be glad, having had to say naut of matters whereof you know the purport. So, sir, I pray for your better welfare in bodie and soul, and that it will please the fisycian to visit you in His good time. Alwaies, sir, I pray you will never come again to see my sister, whereof there has been too much. And so, wishing you no evil, but even your best good, that you may be turned from your iniquity—for why suld ye die?—I rest your humble servant to command, YE KEN WHA."

The next letter was to her father. It was too long altogether for insertion, so we only give a few extracts. It commenced—

"DEAREST AND TRULY HONORED FATHER,

"This comes with my duty to inform you, that it has pleased God to redeem that captivitie of my poor sister, in respect the Queen's blessed Majesty, for whom we are ever bound to pray, hath redeemed her soul from the slayer, granting the ransom of her, whilk is ane pardon or reprieve. And I spoke with the Queen face to face, and yet live ; for she is not muckle differing from other grand leddies, saving that she has a stately presence, and een like a blue huntin'-hawk's, whilk gaed throu' and throu' me like a Hieland durk. And all this good was, alway under the Great Giver, to whom all are but instruments, wrought forth for us by the Duk of Argile, wha is ane native true-hearted Scotsman, and not pridefu', like other folk we ken of ; and likewise skeely enow in bestial, whereof he has promised to gie me twa Devonshire kye, of which he is enamoured, although I do still haud by the real hawkit Airshire breed ; and I have promised him a cheese ; and I wad wuss ye, if Gowans, the brockit cow, has a quey, that she suld suck her fill of milk, as I am given to understand he has none of that breed, and is not scornfu', but will take a thing frae a puir body, that it may lighten their heart of the loading of debt that they awe him. Also his Honor the Duke will accept ane of our Dunlop cheeses, and it sall be my faut if a better was ever yearned in Lowden. [Here follow some observations respecting the breed of cattle and the produce of the dairy, which it is our intention to forward to the Board of Agriculture.] Nevertheless, these are but matters of the after-harvest, in respect of the great good which Providence hath gifted us with, and, in especial, poor Effie's life. And O, my dear father, since it hath pleased God to be merciful to her, let her not want your free pardon, whilk will make her meet to be ane vessel of grace, and also a comfort to your ain graie hairs. Dear father, will ye let the Laird ken that we have had friends strangely raised up to us, and that the talent whilk he lent me will be thankfully repaid ? I hae some of it to the fore ; and the rest of it is not knotted up in ane purse or napkin, but in ane wee bit paper, as is the fashion heir, whilk I am assured is gude for the siller. And, dear father, through Mr. Butler's means I hae gude friendship with the Duke, for there had been kindness between their forbears in the auld troublesome time by-past. And Mrs. Glass has been kind like my very mother. She has a braw house here, and lives bien and warm, wi' twa servant lasses, and a man and a callant in the shop. And she is to send you doun a pound of her hie-dried, and some other tobaka, and we maun think of some propine for her, since her kindness hath been great. And the Duk is to send the pardun doun by an express messenger, in respect that I canna travel sae fast ; and I am to come doun wi' twa of his Honor's servants —that is, John Archibald, a decent elderly gentleman, that says he has seen you lang syne, when ye were buying beasts in the west frae the Laird of Aughtermuggitie—but maybe ye winna mind him—ony way, he's a civil man—and Mrs. Dolly Dutton, that is to be dairymaid at Inverara; and they bring me on as far as Glasgo', whilk will make it nae pinch to win hame, whilk I desire of all things.　May the Giver of all good things keep ye in your outgauns and incomings, whereof devoutly prayeth your loving dauter,

"JEAN DEANS."

The third letter was to Butler, and its tenor as follows :

"MASTER BUTLER,

"SIR—It will be pleasure to you to ken that all I came for is, thanks be to God, weel dune and to the gude end, and that your forbear's letter was right welcome to the Duke of Argile, and that he wrote your name down with a keelyvine pen in a leathern book, whereby it seems like he will do for you either wi' a scule or a kirk ; he has enow of baith, as I am assured. And I have seen the Queen, which gave me a hussy-case out of her own hand.　She had not her crown and skeptre, but they are laid by for her, like the bairns' best claise, to be worn when she needs them.　And they are keepit in a tour, whilk is not like the tour of Liberton, nor yet Craigmillar, but mair like to the castell of Edinburgh, if the buildings were taen and set down in the midst of the Nor' Loch.　Also the Queen was very bounteous, giving me a paper worth fiftie pounds, as I am assured, to pay my expenses here and back agen.　Sae, Master Butler, as we were aye neebours' bairns, forbye ony-thing else that may hae been spoken between us, I trust you winna skrimp yoursell for what is needfu' for your health, since it signifies not muckle whilk o' us has the siller, if the other wants it.　And mind this is no meant to haud ye to ony-thing whilk ye wad rather forget, if ye suld get a charge of a kirk or a scule, as above said.　Only I hope it will be a scule, and not a kirk, because of these difficulties anent aiths and patronages, whilk might gang ill doun wi' my honest father. Only if ye could compass a harmonious call frae the parish of Skreegh-me-dead, as ye anes had hope of, I trow it wad please him weel ; since I hae heard him say that the root of the mat-ter was mair deeply hafted in that wild muirland parish than in the Canongate of Edinburgh.　I wish I had whaten books ye wanted, Mr. Butler, for they hae haill houses of them here, and they are obliged to set sum out in the street, whilk are sald cheap, doubtless to get them out of the weather.　It is a muckle place, and I hae seen sae muckle of it that my poor head turns round. And ye ken lang syne I am nae great pen-woman, and it is near eleven o'clock o' the night. I am cumming down in good company, and safe ; and I had troubles in gaun up, whilk makes me blyther of travelling wi' kenn'd folk. My cousin, Mrs. Glass, has a braw house here, but a'thing is sae poisoned wi' snuff that I am like to be scomfished whiles. But what signifies these things, in comparison of the great deliverance whilk has been vouchsafed to my father's house, in whilk you, as our auld and dear well-wisher, will, I doubt not, rejoice and be exceedingly glad ? And I am, dear Mr. Butler, your sincere well-wisher in temporal and eternal things, J. D."

After these labors of an unwonted kind, Jeanie retired to her bed, yet scarce could sleep a few minutes together, so often was she awakened by the heart-stirring consciousness of her sister's safety, and so powerfully urged to deposit her burden of joy where she had before laid her doubts and sorrows, in the warm and sincere exercises of devotion.

All the next, and all the succeeding day, Mrs. Glass fidgeted about her shop in the agony of expectation, like a pea—to use a vulgar simile which her profession renders appropriate—upon one of her own tobacco-pipes. With the third morning came the expected coach, with four servants clustered behind on the foot-board, in dark brown and yellow liveries ; the Duke in person, with laced coat, gold-headed cane, star and garter—all, as the story-book says, very grand.

He inquired for his little countrywoman of Mrs. Glass, but without requesting to see her, probably because he was unwilling to give an appearance of personal intercourse betwixt them which scandal might have misinterpreted. "The Queen," he said to Mrs. Glass, "had taken the case of her kinswoman into her gracious consideration, and being specially moved by the affectionate and resolute character of the elder sister, had condescended to use her powerful intercession with his Majesty, in consequence of which a pardon had been despatched to Scotland to Effie Deans, on condition of her banishing herself forth of Scotland for fourteen years. The King's Advocate had insisted," he said, "upon this qualification of the pardon, having pointed out to his Majesty's ministers that, within the course of only seven years, twenty-one instances of child-murder had occurred in Scotland."

"Weary on him !" said Mrs. Glass, "what for needed he to have telled that of his ain country, and to the English folk

abune a'?   I used aye to think the Advocate * a douce decent
man, but it is an ill bird—begging your Grace's pardon for
speaking of such a coorse by-word.   And then what is the
poor lassie to do in a foreign land?   Why, wae's me, it's just
sending her to play the same pranks ower again, out of sight
or guidance of her friends."

"Pooh! pooh!" said the Duke, "that need not be anticipated.   Why, she may come up to London, or she may go
over to America, and marry well for all that is come and
gone."

"In troth, and so she may, as your Grace is pleased to intimate," replied Mrs. Glass; "and now I think upon it, there is
my old correspondent in Virginia, Ephraim Buckskin, that has
supplied the Thistle this forty years with tobacco, and it is not
a little that serves our turn, and he has been writing to me
this ten years to send him out a wife.   The carle is not above
sixty, and hale and hearty, and well-to-pass in the world, and
a line from my hand would settle the matter, and Effie Deans's
misfortune—forbye that there is no special occasion to speak
about it—would be thought little of there."

"Is she a pretty girl?" said the Duke; "her sister does
not get beyond a good comely sonsy lass."

"Oh, far prettier is Effie than Jeanie," said Mrs. Glass,
"though it is long since I saw her mysell; but I hear of the
Deanses by all my Lowden friends when they come; your
Grace kens we Scots are clannish bodies."

"So much the better for us," said the Duke, "and the
worse for those who meddle with us, as your good old-fashioned
Scots sign says, Mrs. Glass.   And now I hope you will approve
of the measures I have taken for restoring your kinswoman to
her friends."   These he detailed at length, and Mrs. Glass
gave her unqualified approbation, with a smile and a courtesy at
every sentence.   "And now, Mrs. Glass, you must tell Jeanie
I hope she will not forget my cheese when she gets dowr to
Scotland.   Archibald has my orders to arrange all her expenses."

"Begging your Grace's humble pardon," said Mrs. Glass,
"it's a pity to trouble yourself about them; the Deanses are
wealthy people in their way, and the lass has money in her
pocket."

"That's all very true," said the Duke; "but you know,
where MacCallummore travels he pays all: it is our Highland privilege to take from all what *we* want, and to give to
all what *they* want."

<hr>

* The celebrated Duncan Forbes, soon afterwards Lord President of the College
of Justice, was at this time Lord Advocate.

"Your Grace's better at giving than taking," said Mrs. Glass.

"To show you the contrary," said the Duke, "I will fill my box out of this canister without paying you a bawbee;" and again desiring to be remembered to Jeanie, with his good wishes for her safe journey, he departed, leaving Mrs. Glass uplifted in heart and in countenance, the proudest and happiest of tobacco and snuff dealers.

Reflectively, his Grace's good-humor and affability had a favorable effect upon Jeanie's situation. Her kinswoman, though civil and kind to her, had acquired too much of London breeding to be perfectly satisfied with her cousin's rustic and national dress, and was, besides, something scandalized at the cause of her journey to London. Mrs. Glass might, therefore, have been less sedulous in her attentions towards Jeanie, but for the interest which the foremost of the Scottish nobles (for such, in all men's estimation, was the Duke of Argyle) seemed to take in her fate. Now, however, as a kinswoman whose virtues and domestic affections had attracted the notice and approbation of royalty itself, Jeanie stood to her relative in a light very different and much more favorable, and was not only treated with kindness, but with actual observance and respect.

It depended upon herself alone to have made as many visits, and seen as many sights, as lay within Mrs. Glass's power to compass. But, excepting that she dined abroad with one or two "far-away kinsfolk," and that she paid the same respect, on Mrs. Glass's strong urgency, to Mrs. Deputy Dabby, wife of the Worshipful Mr. Deputy Dabby, of Farringdon Without, she did not avail herself of the opportunity. As Mrs. Dabby was the second lady of great rank whom Jeanie had seen in London, she used sometimes afterwards to draw a parallel betwixt her and the Queen, in which she observed, that "Mrs. Dabby was dressed twice as grand, and was twice as big, and spoke twice as loud, and twice as muckle, as the Queen did, but she hadna the same goss-hawk glance that makes the skin creep and the knee bend; and though she had very kindly gifted her with a loaf of sugar and twa punds of tea, yet she hadna a'thegither the sweet look that the Queen had when she put the needle-book into her hand."

Jeanie might have enjoyed the sights and novelties of this great city more, had it not been for the qualification added to her sister's pardon, which greatly grieved her affectionate disposition. On this subject, however, her mind was somewhat relieved by a letter which she received in return of post, in answer to that which she had written to her father. With his affectionate blessing, it brought his full approbation of the step which she had taken, as one inspired by the immediate dictates of Heaven, and which she had been thrust upon in order that she might become the means of safety to a perishing household.

"If ever a deliverance was dear and precious, this," said the letter, "is a dear and precious deliverance; and if life saved can be made more sweet and savory, it is when it cometh by the hands of those whom we hold in the ties of affection. And do not let your heart be disquieted within you, that this victim, who is rescued from the horns of the altar, whereuntil she was fast bound by the chains of human law, is now to be driven beyond the bounds of our land. Scotland is a blessed land to those who love the ordinances of Christianity, and it is a fair land to look upon, and dear to them who have dwelt in it a' their days; and weel said that judicious Christian, worthy John Livingstone, a sailor in Borrowstounness, as the famous Patrick Walker reporteth his words, that howbeit he thought Scotland was a Gehennah of wickedness when he was at home, yet, when he was abroad, he accounted it ane paradise; for the evils of Scotland he found everywhere, and the good of Scotland he found nowhere. But we are to hold in remembrance that Scotland, though it be our native land, and the land of our fathers, is not like Goshen in Egypt, on whilk the sun of the heavens and of the Gospel shineth allenarly, and leaveth the rest of the world in utter darkness. Therefore, and also because this increase of profit at St. Leonard's Crags may be a cauld waff of wind blawing from the frozen land of earthly self, where never plant of grace took root or grew, and because my concerns make me take something ower muckle a grip of the gear of the warld in mine arms, I receive this dispensation anent Effie as a call to depart out of Haran, as righteous Abraham of old, and leave my father's kindred and my mother's house, and the ashes and mould of them who have gone to sleep before me, and which wait to be mingled with these auld crazed bones of mine own. And my heart is lightened to do this, when I call to mind the decay of active and earnest religion in this land, and survey the height and the depth, the length and the breadth, of national defections, and how the love of many is waxing lukewarm and cold; and I am strengthened in this resolution to change my domicile likewise, as I hear that store-farms are to be set at an easy mail in Northumberland, where there are many precious souls that are of our true though suffering persuasion. And sic part of the kye or stock as I judge it fit to keep may be driven thither without incommodity—say about Wooler, or that gate, keeping aye a shouther to the hills—and the rest may be sauld to gude profit and advantage, if we had grace weel to use and guide these gifts of the warld. The Laird has been a true friend on our unhappy occasions, and I have paid him back the siller for Effie's misfortune, whereof Mr. Nichil Novit returned him no balance, as the Laird and I did expect he wad hae done. But law licks up a', as the common folk say. I have had the siller to borrow out of sax purses. Mr. Saddletree advised to give the Laird of Lounsbeck a charge on his band for a thousand merks. But I hae nae broo' of charges, since that awfu' morning that a tout of a horn at the Cross of Edinburgh blew half the faithfu' ministers of Scotland out of their pulpits. However, I sall raise an adjudication, whilk Mr. Saddletree says comes instead of the auld apprisings, and will not lose weel-won gear with the like of him if it may be helped. As for the Queen, and the credit that she hath done to a poor man's daughter, and the mercy and the grace ye found with her, I can only pray for her weel-being here and hereafter, for the establishment of her house now and forever upon the throne of these kingdoms. I doubt not but what you told her Majesty that I was the same David Deans of whom there was a sport at the Revolution, when I noited thegither the heads of twa false prophets, these ungracious Graces the prelates, as they stood on the Hie Street, after being expelled from the Convention Parliament.* The Duke of Argyle is a noble and true-hearted nobleman, who pleads the cause of the poor, and those who have none to help them; verily his reward shall not be lacking unto him. I have been writing of many things, but not of that whilk lies nearest mine heart. I have seen the misguided thing; she will be at freedom the morn, on enacted caution that she shall leave Scotland in four weeks. Her mind is in an evil frame—casting her eye backward on Egypt, I doubt, as if the bitter waters of the wilderness were harder to endure than the brick furnaces, by the side of which there were savory flesh-pots. I need not bid you make haste down, for you are, excepting always my Great Master, my only comfort in these straits. I charge you to withdraw your feet from the delusion of that Vanity Fair in whilk ye are a sojourner, and not to go to their worship, whilk is an ill-mumbled mass, as it was weel termed by James the Sext, though he afterwards, with his unhappy son, strove to bring it ower back and belly into his native kingdom, wherethrough their race

* See Expulsion of the Bishops from the Scottish Convention. Note 31.

have been cut off as foam upon the water, and shall be as wanderers among the nations; see the prophecies of Hosea, ninth and seventeenth, and the same, tenth and seventh. But us and our house, let us say with the same prophet: 'Let us return to the Lord; for he hath torn and he will heal us, he hath smitten and he will bind us up.'"

He proceeded to say, that he approved of her proposed mode of returning by Glasgow, and entered into sundry minute particulars not necessary to be quoted. A single line in the letter, but not the least frequently read by the party to whom it was addressed, intimated that "Reuben Butler had been as a son to him in his sorrows." As David Deans scarce ever mentioned Butler before without some gibe, more or less direct, either at his carnal gifts and learning or at his grandfather's heresy, Jeanie drew a good omen from no such qualifying clause being added to this sentence respecting him.

A lover's hope resembles the bean in the nursery tale: let it once take root, and it will grow so rapidly that in the course of a few hours the giant Imagination builds a castle on the top, and by and by comes Disappointment with the "curtal axe," and hews down both the plant and the superstructure. Jeanie's fancy, though not the most powerful of her faculties, was lively enough to transport her to a wild farm in Northumberland, well stocked with milk-cows, yeald beasts, and sheep; a meeting-house hard by, frequented by serious Presbyterians, who had united in an harmonious call to Reuben Butler to be their spiritual guide; Effie restored, not to gayety, but to cheerfulness at least; their father, with his gray hairs smoothed down, and spectacles on his nose; herself, with the maiden snood exchanged for a matron's curch—all arranged in a pew in the said meeting-house, listening to words of devotion, rendered sweeter and more powerful by the affectionate ties which combined them with the preacher. She cherished such visions from day to day, until her residence in London began to become insupportable and tedious to her; and it was with no ordinary satisfaction that she received a summons from Argyle House, requiring her in two days to be prepared to join their northward party.

CHAPTER XL

> **One** was a female, who had grievous ill
> Wrought in revenge, and she enjoy'd it still;
> Sullen she was, and threatening ; in her eye
> Glared the stern triumph that she dared to die.
> CRABBE.

THE summons of preparation arrived after Jeanie Deans had resided in the metropolis about three weeks.

On the morning appointed she took a grateful farewell of Mrs. Glass, as that good woman's attention to her particularly required, placed herself and her movable goods, which purchases and presents had greatly increased, in a hackney-coach, and joined her travelling companions in the housekeeper's apartment at Argyle House. While the carriage was getting ready, she was informed that the Duke wished to speak with her; and being ushered into a splendid saloon, she was surprised to find that he wished to present her to his lady and daughters.

"I bring you my little countrywoman, Duchess," these were the words of the introduction. "With an army of young fellows as gallant and steady as she is, and a good cause, I would not fear two to one."

"Ah, papa!" said a lively young lady, about twelve years old, "remember you were full one to two at Sheriffmuir, and yet [singing the well-known ballad]—

> "Some say that we wan, and some say that they wan,
> And some say that nane wan at a', man ;
> But of ae thing I'm sure, that on Sheriffmuir
> A battle there was that I saw, man. "

"What, little Mary turned Tory on my hands ? This will be fine news for our countrywoman to carry down to Scotland !"

"We may all turn Tories for the thanks we have got for remaining Whigs," said the second young lady.

"Well, hold your peace, you discontented monkeys, and go dress your babies ; and as for the Bob of Dumblane,

> "If it wasna weel bobbit, weel bobbit, weel bobbit,
> If it wasna weel bobbit, we'll bobb it again."

"Papa's wit is running low," said Lady Mary ; "the poor gentleman is repeating himself ; he sang that on the field of battle, when he was told the Highlanders had cut his left wing to pieces with their claymores."

A pull by the hair was the repartee to this sally.

"Ah ! brave Highlanders and bright claymores," said the Duke, "well do I wish them, 'for a' the ill they've done me yet,' as the song goes. But come, madcaps, say a civil word to your countrywoman. I wish ye had half her canny hamely sense ; I think you may be as leal and true-hearted."

The Duchess advanced, and, in few words, in which there was as much kindness as civility, assured Jeanie of the respect which she had for a character so affectionate, and yet so firm, and added, "When you get home, you will perhaps hear from me."

"And from me." "And from me." "And from me, Jeanie," added the young ladies one after the other, "for you are a credit to the land we love so well."

Jeanie, overpowered with these unexpected compliments, and not aware that the Duke's investigation had made him acquainted with her behavior on her sister's trial, could only answer by blushing, and courtesying round and round, and uttering at intervals, "Mony thanks ! mony thanks !"

"Jeanie," said the Duke, "you must have *doch an' dor-roch*, or you will be unable to travel."

There was a salver with cake and wine on the table. He took up a glass, drank "to all true hearts that lo'ed Scotland," and offered a glass to his guest.

Jeanie, however, declined it, saying, "that she had never tasted wine in her life."

"How comes that, Jeanie ?" said the Duke ; "wine maketh glad the heart, you know."

"Ay, sir, but my father is like Jonadab the son of Rechab, who charged his children that they should drink no wine."

"I thought your father would have had more sense," said the Duke, "unless, indeed, he prefers brandy. But, however, Jeanie, if you will not drink, you must eat, to save the character of my house."

He thrust upon her a large piece of cake, nor would he permit her to break off a fragment and lay the rest on the salver. "Put it in your pouch, Jeanie," said he ; "you will be glad of it before you see St. Giles's steeple. I wish to Heaven I were to see it as soon as you ! and so my best service to all my friends at and about Auld Reekie, and a blithe journey to you."

And, mixing the frankness of a soldier with his natural affability, he shook hands with his *protégée*, and committed her to the charge of Archibald, satisfied that he had provided sufficiently for her being attended to by his domestics, from the unusual attention with which he had himself treated her.

Accordingly, in the course of her journey, she found both her companions disposed to pay her every possible civility, so that her return, in point of comfort and safety, formed a strong contrast to her journey to London.

Her heart also was disburdened of the weight of grief, shame, apprehension, and fear which had loaded her before her interview with the Queen at Richmond. But the human mind is so strangely capricious that, when freed from the pressure of real misery, it becomes open and sensitive to the apprehension of ideal calamities. She was now much disturbed in mind that she had heard nothing from Reuben Butler, to whom the operation of writing was so much more familiar than it was to herself.

"It would have cost him sae little fash," she said to herself; "for I hae seen his pen gang as fast ower the paper as ever it did ower the water when it was in the gray goose's wing. Wae's me! maybe he may be badly; but then my father wad likely hae said something about it. Or maybe he may hae taen the rue, and kensna how to let me wot of his change of mind. He needna be at muckle fash about it," she went on, drawing herself up, though the tear of honest pride and injured affection gathered in her eye, as she entertained the suspicion; "Jeanie Deans is no the lass to pu' him by the sleeve, or put him in mind of what he wishes to forget. I sall wish him weel and happy a' the same; and if he has the luck to get a kirk in our country, I sall gang and hear him just the very same, to show that I bear nae malice." And as she imagined the scene, the tear stole over her eye.

In these melancholy reveries Jeanie had full time to indulge herself; for her travelling companions, servants in a distinguished and fashionable family, had, of course, many topics of conversation in which it was absolutely impossible she could have either pleasure or portion. She had, therefore, abundant leisure for reflection, and even for self-tormenting, during the several days which, indulging the young horses the Duke was sending down to the North with sufficient ease and short stages, they occupied in reaching the neighborhood of Carlisle.

In approaching the vicinity of that ancient city, they discerned a considerable crowd upon an eminence at a little distance from the high-road, and learned from some passengers who were gathering towards that busy scene from the southward, that the cause of the concourse was the laudable public desire " to see a domned Scotch witch and thief get half of her due upo' Haribee Broo' yonder : for she was only to be hanged ; she should hae been boorned aloive, an' cheap on't."

" Dear Mr. Archibald," said the dame of the dairy elect, " I never seed a woman hanged in a' my life, and only four men, as made a goodly spectacle."

Mr. Archibald, however, was a Scotchman, and promised himself no exuberant pleasure in seeing his countrywoman undergo " the terrible behests of law."   Moreover, he was a man of sense and delicacy in his way, and the late circumstances of Jeanie's family, with the cause of her expedition to London, were not unknown to him ; so that he answered dryly, it was impossible to stop, as he must be early at Carlisle on some business of the Duke's, and he accordingly bid the postilions get on.

The road at that time passed at about a quarter of a mile's distance from the eminence called Haribee or Harabee Brow, which, though it is very moderate in size and height, is nevertheless seen from a great distance around, owing to the flatness of the country through which the Eden flows.   Here many an outlaw and border-rider of both kingdoms had wavered in the wind during the wars, and scarce less hostile truces, between the two countries.   Upon Harabee, in latter days, other executions had taken place with as little ceremony as compassion ; for these frontier provinces remained long unsettled, and, even at the time of which we write, were ruder than those in the centre of England.

The postilions drove on, wheeling, as the Penrith road led them, round the verge of the rising ground.   Yet still the eyes of Mrs. Dolly Dutton, which, with the head and substantial person to which they belonged, were all turned towards the scene of action, could discern plainly the outline of the gallows-tree, relieved against the clear sky, the dark shade formed by the persons of the executioner and the criminal upon the light rounds of the tall aerial ladder, until one of the objects, launched into the air, gave unequivocal signs of mortal agony, though appearing in the distance not larger than a spider dependent at the extremity of his invisible thread, while the remaining form descended from its elevated situation, and regained with all speed an undistinguished place among the crowd.   This termination of the tragic scene drew forth, of course, a squall from Mrs. Dutton, and Jeanie, with instinctive curiosity, turned her head in the same direction.

The sight of a female culprit in the act of undergoing the fatal punishment from which her beloved sister had been so recently rescued was too much, not perhaps for her nerves, but for her mind and feelings. She turned her head to the other side of the carriage, with a sensation of sickness, of loathing, and of fainting. Her female companion overwhelmed her with questions, with proffers of assistance, with requests that the carriage might be stopped, that a doctor might be fetched, that drops might be gotten, that burnt feathers and asafœtida, fair water, and hartshorn might be procured, all at once, and without one instant's delay. Archibald, more calm and considerate, only desired the carriage to push forward; and it was not till they had got beyond sight of the fatal spectacle that, seeing the deadly paleness of Jeanie's countenance, he stopped the carriage, and jumping out himself, went in search of the most obvious and most easily procured of Mrs. Dutton's pharmacopœia—a draught, namely, of fair water.

While Archibald was absent on this good-natured piece of service, damning the ditches which produced nothing but mud, and thinking upon the thousand bubbling springlets of his own mountains, the attendants on the execution began to pass the stationary vehicle in their way back to Carlisle.

From their half-heard and half-understood words, Jeanie, whose attention was involuntarily riveted by them, as that of children is by ghost stories, though they know the pain with which they will afterwards remember them—Jeanie, I say, could discern that the present victim of the law had died "game," as it is termed by those unfortunates; that is, sullen, reckless, and impenitent, neither fearing God nor regarding man.

"A sture woife, and a dour," said one Cumbrian peasant, as he clattered by in his wooden brogues, with a noise like the trampling of a dray-horse.

"She has gone to ho master, with ho's name in her mouth," said another. "Shame the country should be harried wi' Scotch witches and Scotch bitches this gate; but I say hang and drown."

"Ay, ay, Gaffer Tramp, take awa' yealdon, take awa' low; hang the witch, and there will be less scathe amang us; mine owsen hae been reckan this towmont."

"And mine bairns hae been crining too, mon," replied his neighbor.

"Silence wi' your fule tongues, ye churls," said an old woman who hobbled past them as they stood talking near the carriage ; "this was nae witch, but a bluidy-fingered thief and murderess."

"Ay ? was it e'en sae, Dame Hinchup ?" said one in a civil tone, and stepping out of his place to let the old woman pass along the footpath.   "Nay, you know best, sure ; but at ony rate we hae but tint a Scot of her, and that's a thing better lost than found."

The old woman passed on without making any answer.

"Ay, ay, neighbor," said Gaffer Tramp, "seest thou how one witch will speak for t'other—Scots or English, the same to them."

His companion shook his head, and replied in the same subdued tone, "Ay, ay, when a Sark-foot wife gets on her broomstick, the dames of Allonby are ready to mount, just as sure as the by-word gangs o' the hills—

> "If Skiddaw hath a cap,
>   Criffel wots full weel of that."

"But," continued Gaffer Tramp, "thinkest thou the daughter o' yon hangit body isna as rank a witch as ho ?"

"I kenna cloarly," returned tho fellow, "but the folk are speaking o' swimming her i' the Eden."   And they passed on their several roads, after wishing each other good morning.

Just as the clowns left the place, and as Mr. Archibald returned with some fair water, a crowd of boys and girls, and some of the lower rabble of more mature age, came up from the place of execution, grouping themselves with many a yell of delight around a tall female fantastically dressed, who was dancing, leaping, and bounding in the midst of them.   A horrible recollection pressed on Jeanie as she looked on this unfortunate creature ; and the reminiscence was mutual, for, by a sudden exertion of great strength and agility, Madge Wildfire broke out of the noisy circle of tormentors who surrounded her, and clinging fast to the door of the calash, uttered, in a sound betwixt laughter and screaming, "Eh, d'ye ken, Jeanie Deans, they hae hangit our mother ?"   Then suddenly changing her tone to that of the most piteous entreaty, she added, "O gar them let me gang to cut her down ! —let me but cut her down !   She is my mother, if she was waur than the deil, and she'll be nae mair kenspeckle than half-hangit Maggie Dickson,* that cried saut mony a day after she had been hangit; her voice was roupit and hoarse, and her neck was a wee agee, or ye wad hae kenn'd nae odds on her frae ony other saut-wife."

Mr. Archibald, embarrassed by the madwoman's clinging to the carriage, and detaining around them her noisy and mischievous attendants, was all this while looking out for a constable or beadle, to whom he might commit the unfortunate creature. But seeing no such person of authority, he endeavored to loosen her hold from the carriage, that they might escape from her by driving on. This, however, could hardly be achieved without some degree of violence; Madge held fast, and renewed her frantic entreaties to be permitted to cut down her mother. "It was but a tenpenny tow lost," she said, "and what was that to a woman's life?" There came up, however, a parcel of savage-looking fellows, butchers and graziers chiefly, among whose cattle there had been of late a very general and fatal distemper, which their wisdom imputed to witchcraft. They laid violent hands on Madge, and tore her from the carriage, exclaiming, "What, doest stop folk o' king's highway? Hast no done mischief enow already, wi' thy murders and thy witcherings?"

"Oh, Jeanie Deans—Jeanie Deans!" exclaimed the poor maniac, "save my mother, and I will take ye to the Interpreter's house again; and I will teach ye a' my bonny sangs; and I will tell ye what came o' the——" The rest of her entreaties were drowned in the shouts of the rabble.

"Save her, for God's sake!—save her from those people!" exclaimed Jeanie to Archibald.

"She is mad, but quite innocent—she is mad, gentlemen," said Archibald; "do not use her ill, take her before the mayor."

"Ay, ay, we'se hae care enow on her," answered one of the fellows; "gang thou thy gate, man, and mind thine own matters."

"He's a Scot by his tongue," said another; "and an he will come out o' his whirligig there, I'se gie him his tartan plaid fu' o' broken banes."

It was clear nothing could be done to rescue Madge; and Archibald, who was a man of humanity, could only bid the postilions hurry on to Carlisle, that he might obtain some assistance to the unfortunate woman. As they drove off, they heard the hoarse roar with which the mob preface acts of riot or cruelty, yet even above that deep and dire note they could

* See Note 32.

discern the screams of the unfortunate victim. They were
soon out of hearing of the cries, but had no sooner entered
the streets of Carlisle than Archibald, at Jeanie's earnest
and urgent entreaty, went to a magistrate, to state the cruelty which was likely to be exercised on this unhappy creature.

In about an hour and a half he returned, and reported to
Jeanie that the magistrate had very readily gone in person,
with some assistants, to the rescue of the unfortunate woman,
and that he had himself accompanied him ; that when they
came to the muddy pool in which the mob were ducking her,
according to their favorite mode of punishment, the magistrate succeeded in rescuing her from their hands, but in a
state of insensibility, owing to the cruel treatment which she
had received. He added, that he had seen her carried to the
workhouse, and understood that she had been brought to herself, and was expected to do well.

This last averment was a slight alteration in point of fact,
for Madge Wildfire was not expected to survive the treatment
she had received ; but Jeanie seemed so much agitated that
Mr. Archibald did not think it prudent to tell her the worst
at once. Indeed, she appeared so fluttered and disordered by
this alarming accident that, although it had been their intention to proceed to Longtown that evening, her companions
judged it most advisable to pass the night at Carlisle.

This was particularly agreeable to Jeanie, who resolved, if
possible, to procure an interview with Madge Wildfire. Connecting some of her wild flights with the narrative of George
Staunton, she was unwilling to omit the opportunity of extracting from her, if possible, some information concerning
the fate of that unfortunate infant which had cost her sister
so dear. Her acquaintance with the disordered state of poor
Madge's mind did not permit her to cherish much hope that
she could acquire from her any useful intelligence ; but then,
since Madge's mother had suffered her deserts, and was silent
forever, it was her only chance of obtaining any kind of information, and she was loath to lose the opportunity.

She colored her wish to Mr. Archibald by saying that she
had seen Madge formerly, and wished to know, as a matter of
humanity, how she was attended to under her present misfortunes. That complaisant person immediately went to the
workhouse, or hospital, in which he had seen the sufferer
lodged, and brought back for reply, that the medical attendants positively forbade her seeing any one. When the application for admittance was repeated next day, Mr. Archibald

was informed that she had been very quiet and composed, insomuch that the clergyman who acted as chaplain to the establishment, thought it expedient to read prayers beside her bed, but that her wandering fit of mind had returned soon after his departure; however, her countrywoman might see her if she chose it. She was not expected to live above an hour or two.

Jeanie had no sooner received this information than she hastened to the hospital, her companions attending her. They found the dying person in a large ward, where there were ten beds, of which the patient's was the only one occupied.

Madge was singing when they entered—singing her own wild snatches of songs and obsolete airs, with a voice no longer overstrained by false spirits, but softened, saddened, and subdued by bodily exhaustion. She was still insane, but was no longer able to express her wandering ideas in the wild notes of her former state of exalted imagination. There was death in the plaintive tones of her voice, which yet, in this moderated and melancholy mood, had something of the lulling sound with which a mother sings her infant asleep. As Jeanie entered, she heard first the air, and then a part of the chorus and words, of what had been, perhaps, the song of a jolly harvest-home:

> " Our work is over—over now,
> The goodman wipes his weary brow,
> The last long wain wends slow away,
> And we are free to sport and play.
>
> " The night comes on when sets the sun,
> And labor ends when day is done.
> When Autumn's gone and Winter's come,
> We hold our jovial harvest-home."

Jeanie advanced to the bedside when the strain was finished, and addressed Madge by her name. But it produced no symptoms of recollection. On the contrary, the patient, like one provoked by interruption, changed her posture, and called out, with an impatient tone, " Nurse—nurse, turn my face to the wa', that I may never answer to that name ony mair, and never see mair of a wicked world."

The attendant on the hospital arranged her in her bed as she desired, with her face to the wall and her back to the light. So soon as she was quiet in this new position, she began again to sing in the same low and modulated strains, as if she was recovering the state of abstraction which the interruption of her visitants had disturbed. The strain, however, was different, and rather resembled the music of the Methodist hymns, though the measure of the song was similar to that of the former :

> "When the fight of grace is fought,
>   When the marriage vest is wrought,
>   When Faith hath chased cold Doubt away,
>   And Hope but sickens at delay,
>   When Charity, imprisoned here,
>   Longs for a more expanded sphere,
>   Doff thy robes of sin and clay,
>   Christian, rise, and come away."

The strain was solemn and affecting, sustained as it was by the pathetic warble of a voice which had naturally been a fine one, and which weakness, if it diminished its power, had improved in softness.   Archibald, though a follower of the court, and a *pococurante* by profession, was confused, if not affected ; the dairymaid blubbered ; and Jeanie felt the tears rise spontaneously to her eyes.   Even the nurse, accustomed to all modes in which the spirit can pass, seemed considerably moved.

The patient was evidently growing weaker, as was intimated by an apparent difficulty of breathing which seized her from time to time, and by the utterance of low, listless moans, intimating that nature was succumbing in the last conflict.   But the spirit of melody, which must originally have so strongly possessed this unfortunate young woman, seemed, at every interval of ease, to triumph over her pain and weakness. And it was remarkable that there could always be traced in her songs something appropriate, though perhaps only obliquely or collaterally so, to her present situation.   Her next seemed to be the fragment of some old ballad :

> "Cauld is my bed, Lord Archibald,
>   And sad my sleep of sorrow ;
> But thine sall be as sad and cauld,
>   My fause true-love, to-morrow.
>
> "And weep ye not, my maidens free,
>   Though death your mistress borrow ;
> For he for whom I die to-day
>   Sall die for me to-morrow."

Again she changed the tune to one wilder, less monotonous, and less regular.   But of the words only a fragment or two could be collected by those who listened to this singular scene :

> "Proud Maisie is in the wood,
>   Walking so early.
> Sweet Robin sits on the bush,
>   Singing so rarely.

> " ' Tell me, thou bonny bird,
>   When shall I marry me?
>   ' When six braw gentlemen
>   Kirkward shall carry ye.'
>
> .   .   .
>
> " ' Who makes the bridal bed,
>   Birdie, say truly ? '
>   ' The gray-headed sexton,
>   That delves the grave duly.'
>
> .   .   .
>
> " The glowworm o'er grave and stone
>   Shall light thee steady ;
>   The owl from the steeple sing,
>   ' Welcome, proud lady.' "

Her voice died away with the last notes, and she fell into a slumber, from which the experienced attendant assured them that she never would awake at all, or only in the death-agony.

The nurse's prophecy proved true. The poor maniac parted with existence without again uttering a sound of any kind. But our travellers did not witness this catastrophe. They left the hospital as soon as Jeanie had satisfied herself that no elucidation of her sister's misfortunes was to be hoped from the dying person.*

* See Madge Wildfire. Note 38.

CHAPTER XLI

> Wilt thou go on with me?
> The moon is bright, the sea is calm,
> And I know well the ocean paths . . .
> Thou wilt go on with me !
>
> *Thalaba.*

THE fatigue and agitation of these various scenes had agitated Jeanie so much, notwithstanding her robust strength of constitution, that Archibald judged it necessary that she should have a day's repose at the village of Longtown. It was in vain that Jeanie herself protested against any delay. The Duke of Argyle's man of confidence was of course consequential ; and as he had been bred to the medical profession in his youth—at least he used this expression to describe his having, thirty years before, pounded for six months in the mortar of old Mungo Mangleman, the surgeon at Greenock—he was obstinate whenever a matter of health was in question.

In this case he discovered febrile symptoms, and having once made a happy application of that learned phrase to Jeanie's case, all further resistance became in vain ; and she was glad to acquiesce, and even to go to bed and drink water-gruel, in order that she might possess her soul in quiet, and without interruption.

Mr. Archibald was equally attentive in another particular. He observed that the execution of the old woman, and the miserable fate of her daughter, seemed to have had a more powerful effect upon Jeanie's mind than the usual feelings of humanity might naturally have been expected to occasion. Yet she was obviously a strong-minded, sensible young woman, and in no respect subject to nervous affections, and therefore Archibald, being ignorant of any special connection between his master's *protégée* and these unfortunate persons, excepting that she had seen Madge formerly in Scotland, naturally imputed the strong impression these events had made upon her to her associating them with the unhappy circumstances in which her sister had so lately stood. He became anxious, therefore, to prevent anything occurring which might recall these associations to Jeanie's mind.

Archibald had speedily an opportunity of exercising this precaution. A peddler brought to Longtown that evening, among other wares, a large broadside sheet, giving an account of the "Last Speech and Execution of Margaret Murdockson, and of the Barbarous Murder of her Daughter, Magdalene or Madge Murdockson, called Madge Wildfire ; and of her Pious Conversation with his Reverence Archdeacon Fleming ;" which authentic publication had apparently taken place on the day they left Carlisle, and being an article of a nature peculiarly acceptable to such country-folk as were within hearing of the transaction, the itinerant bibliopolist had forthwith added them to his stock in trade. He found a merchant sooner than he expected ; for Archibald, much applauding his own prudence, purchased the whole lot for two shillings and ninepence ; and the peddler, delighted with the profit of such a wholesale transaction, instantly returned to Carlisle to supply himself with more.

The considerate Mr. Archibald was about to commit his whole purchase to the flames, but it was rescued by the yet more considerate dairy-damsel, who said, very prudently, it was a pity to waste so much paper, which might crepe hair, pin up bonnets, and serve many other useful purposes ; and who promised to put the parcel into her own trunk, and keep it carefully out of the sight of Mrs. Jeanie Deans : " Though, by the by, she had no great notion of folk being so very nice. Mrs. Deans might have had enough to think about the gallows all this time to endure a sight of it, without all this to do about it."

Archibald reminded the dame of the dairy of the Duke's very particular charge that they should be attentive and civil to Jeanie ; as also that they were to part company soon, and consequently would not be doomed to observing any one's health or temper during the rest of the journey ; with which answer Mrs. Dolly Dutton was obliged to hold herself satisfied.

On the morning they resumed their journey, and prosecuted it successfully, travelling through Dumfriesshire and part of Lanarkshire, until they arrived at the small town of Rutherglen, within about four miles of Glasgow. Here an express brought letters to Archibald from the principal agent of the Duke of Argyle in Edinburgh.

He said nothing of their contents that evening ; but when they were seated in the carriage the next day, the faithful squire informed Jeanie that he had received directions from the Duke's factor, to whom his Grace had recommended him to carry her, if she had no objection, for a stage or two beyond Glasgow.   Some temporary causes of discontent had occasioned tumults in that city and the neighborhood, which would render it unadvisable for Mrs. Jeanie Deans to travel alone and unprotected betwixt that city and Edinburgh; whereas, by going forward a little further, they would meet one of his Grace's sub-factors, who was coming down from the Highlands to Edinburgh with his wife, and under whose charge she might journey with comfort and in safety.

Jeanie remonstrated against this arrangement.   "She had been lang," she said, "frae hame: her father and her sister behoved to be very anxious to see her; there were other friends she had that werena weel in health.   She was willing to pay for man and horse at Glasgow, and surely naebody wad meddle wi' sae harmless and feckless a creature as she was. She was muckle obliged by the offer; but never hunted deer langed for its resting-place as I do to find myself at St. Leonard's."

The groom of the chambers exchanged a look with his female companion, which seemed 'so full of meaning that Jeanie screamed aloud—" O, Mr. Archibald—Mrs. Dutton, if ye ken of onything that has happened at St. Leonard's, for God's sake—for pity's sake, tell me, and dinna keep me in suspense!"

"I really know nothing, Mrs. Deans," said the groom of the chambers.

"And I—I—I am sure I knows as little," said the dame of the dairy, while some communication seemed to tremble on her lips, which, at a glance of Archibald's eye, she appeared to swallow down, and compressed her lips thereafter into a state of extreme and vigilant firmness, as if she had been afraid of its bolting out before she was aware.

Jeanie saw that there was to be something concealed from her, and it was only the repeated assurances of Archibald that her father—her sister—all her friends were, as far as he knew, well and happy, that at all pacified her alarm.   From such respectable people as those with whom she travelled she could apprehend no harm, and yet her distress was so obvious that Archibald, as a last resource, pulled out and put into her hand a slip of paper, on which these words were written:

"JEANIE DEANS—You will do me a favor by going with Archibald and my female domestic a day's journey beyond Glasgow, and asking them no questions, which will greatly oblige your friend,

"ARGYLE & GREENWICH."

Although this laconic epistle, from a nobleman to whom she was bound by such inestimable obligations, silenced all Jeanie's objections to the proposed route, it rather added to than diminished the eagerness of her curiosity. The proceeding to Glasgow seemed now no longer to be an object with her fellow-travellers. On the contrary, they kept the left-hand side of the river Clyde, and travelled through a thousand beautiful and changing views down the side of that noble stream, till, ceasing to hold its inland character, it began to assume that of a navigable river.

"You are not for gaun intill Glasgow, then?" said Jeanie, as she observed that the drivers made no motion for inclining their horses' heads towards the ancient bridge, which was then the only mode of access to St. Mungo's capital.

"No," replied Archibald; "there is some popular commotion, and as our Duke is in opposition to the court, perhaps we might be too well received; or they might take it in their heads to remember that the Captain of Carrick came down upon them with his Highlandmen in the time of Shawfield's mob * in 1725, and then we would be too ill received. And, at any rate, it is best for us, and for me in particular, who may be supposed to possess his Grace's mind upon many particulars, to leave the good people of the Gorbals to act according to their own imaginations, without either provoking or encouraging them by my presence."

To reasoning of such tone and consequence Jeanie had nothing to reply, although it seemed to her to contain fully as much self-importance as truth.

The carriage meantime rolled on; the river expanded itself, and gradually assumed the dignity of an estuary, or arm of the sea. The influence of the advancing and retiring tides became more and more evident, and in the beautiful words of him of the laurel wreath, the river waxed

> A broader and a broader stream.
>
> .   .   .   .   .   .
>
> The cormorant stands upon its shoals,
> His black and dripping wings
> Half open'd to the wind.†

"Which way lies Inverary?" said Jeanie, gazing on the dusky ocean of Highland hills, which now, piled above each other, and intersected by many a lake, stretched away on the opposite side of the river to the northward. "Is yon high castle the Duke's hoose?"

* See Note 34.
† From Southey's *Thalaba*, Bk. XI., stanza 36 (*Laing*).

"That, Mrs. Deans?   Lud help thee," replied Archibald; "that's the old Castle of Dunbarton, the strongest place in Europe, be the other what it may.   Sir William Wallace was governor of it in the old wars with the English, and his Grace is governor just now.   It is always intrusted to the best man in Scotland."

"And does the Duke live on that high rock, then?" demanded Jeanie.

"No, no, he has his deputy-governor, who commands in his absence; he lives in the white house you see at the bottom of the rock.   His Grace does not reside there himself."

"I think not, indeed," said the dairywoman, upon whose mind the road, since they had left Dumfries, had made no very favorable impression; "for if he did, he might go whistle for a dairywoman, an he were the only duke in England.   I did not leave my place and my friends to come down to see cows starve to death upon hills as they be at that pig-stye of Elfinfoot, as you call it, Mr. Archibald, or to be perched up on the top of a rock, like a squirrel in his cage, hung out of a three pair of stairs window."

Inwardly chuckling that these symptoms of recalcitration had not taken place until the fair malcontent was, as he mentally termed it, under his thumb, Archibald coolly replied, "That the hills were none of his making, nor did he know how to mend them; but as to lodging, they would soon be in a house of the Duke's in a very pleasant island called Roseneath, where they went to wait for shipping to take them to Inverary, and would meet the company with whom Jeanie was to return to Edinburgh."

"An island!" said Jeanie, who, in the course of her various and adventurous travels, had never quitted *terra firma,* "then I am doubting we maun gang in ane of these boats; they look unco sma', and the waves are something rough, and——"

"Mr. Archibald," said Mrs. Dutton, "I will not consent to it; I was never engaged to leave the country, and I desire you will bid the boys drive round the other way to the Duke's house."

"There is a safe pinnace belonging to his Grace, ma'am, close by," replied Archibald, "and you need be under no apprehensions whatsoever."

"But I *am* under apprehensions," said the damsel; "and I insist upon going round by land, Mr. Archibald, were it ten miles about."

"I am sorry I cannot oblige you, madam, as Roseneath happens to be an island."

"If it were ten islands," said the incensed dame, "that's no reason why I should be drowned in going over the seas to it."

"No reason why you should be drowned, certainly, ma'am," answered the unmoved groom of the chambers, "but an admirable good one why you cannot proceed to it by land." And, fixed his master's mandates to perform, he pointed with his hand, and the drivers, turning off the high-road, proceeded towards a small hamlet of fishing huts, where a shallop, somewhat more gayly decorated than any which they had yet seen, having a flag which displayed a boar's head, crested with a ducal coronet, waited with two or three seamen and as many Highlanders.

The carriage stopped, and the men began to unyoke their horses, while Mr. Archibald gravely superintended the removal of the baggage from the carriage to the little vessel. "Has the 'Caroline' been long arrived?" said Archibald to one of the seamen.

"She has been here in five days from Liverpool, and she's lying down at Greenock," answered the fellow.

"Let the horses and carriage go down to Greenock, then," said Archibald, "and be embarked there for Inverary when I send notice: they may stand in my cousin's, Duncan Archibald the stabler's. Ladies," he added, "I hope you will get yourselves ready, we must not lose the tide."

"Mrs. Deans," said the Cowslip of Inverary, "you may do as you please, but I will sit here all night, rather than go into that there painted egg-shell. Fellow—fellow! [this was addressed to a Highlander who was lifting a travelling trunk], that trunk is *mine,* and that there bandbox, and that pillion mail, and those seven bundles, and the paper bag ; and if you venture to touch one of them, it shall be at your peril."

The Celt kept his eye fixed on the speaker, then turned his head towards Archibald, and receiving no countervailing signal, he shouldered the portmanteau, and without further notice of the distressed damsel, or paying any attention to remonstrances, which probably he did not understand, and would certainly have equally disregarded whether he understood them or not, moved off with Mrs. Dutton's wearables, and deposited the trunk containing them safely in the boat.

The baggage being stowed in safety, Mr. Archibald handed Jeanie out of the carriage, and, not without some tremor on her part, she was transported through the surf and placed in

the boat. He then offered the same civility to his fellow-servant, but she was resolute in her refusal to quit the carriage, in which she now remained in solitary state, threatening all concerned or unconcerned with actions for wages and board-wages, damages and expenses, and numbering on her fingers the gowns and other habiliments from which she seemed in the act of being separated forever. Mr. Archibald did not give himself the trouble of making many remonstrances, which, indeed, seemed only to aggravate the damsel's indignation, but spoke two or three words to the Highlanders in Gaelic ; and the wily mountaineers, approaching the carriage cautiously, and without giving the slightest intimation of their intention, at once seized the recusant so effectually fast that she could neither resist nor struggle, and hoisting her on their shoulders in nearly an horizontal posture, rushed down with her to the beach, and through the surf, and, with no other inconvenience than ruffling her garments a little, deposited her in the boat ; but in a state of surprise, mortification, and terror at her sudden transportation which rendered her absolutely mute for two or three minutes. The men jumped in themselves ; one tall fellow remained till he had pushed off the boat, and then tumbled in upon his companions. They took their oars and began to pull from the shore, then spread their sail and drove merrily across the firth.

"You Scotch villain !" said the infuriated damsel to Archibald, "how dare you use a person like me in this way ?"

"Madam," said Archibald, with infinite composure, "it's high time you should know you are in the Duke's country, and that there is not one of these fellows but would throw you out of the boat as readily as into it, if such were his Grace's pleasure."

"Then the Lord have mercy on me !" said Mrs. Dutton. "If I had had any on myself I would never have engaged with you."

"It's something of the latest to think of that now, Mrs. Dutton," said Archibald ; "but I assure you, you will find the Highlands have their pleasures. You will have a dozen of cow-milkers under your own authority at Inverary, and you may throw any of them into the lake if you have a mind, for the Duke's head people are almost as great as himself."

"This is a strange business, to be sure, Mr. Archibald," said the lady ; "but I suppose I must make the best on't. Are you sure the boat will not sink ? it leans terribly to one side, in my poor mind."

"Fear nothing," said Mr. Archibald, taking a most important pinch of snuff ; "this same ferry on Clyde knows us very well, or we know it, which is all the same ; no fear of any of our people meeting with any accident. We should have crossed from the opposite shore, but for the disturbances at Glasgow, which made it improper for his Grace's people to pass through the city."

"Are you not afeard, Mrs. Deans," said the dairy vestal, addressing Jeanie, who sat, not in the most comfortable state of mind, by the side of Archibald, who himself managed the helm—"are you not afeard of these wild men with their naked knees, and of this nutshell of a thing, that seems bobbing up and down like a skimming-dish in a milk-pail ?"

"No—no, madam," answered Jeanie, with some hesitation, "I am not feared ; for I hae seen Hielandmen before, though I never was sae near them ; and for the danger of the deep waters, I trust there is a Providence by sea as well as by land."

"Well," said Mrs. Dutton, "it is a beautiful thing to have learned to write and read, for one can always say such fine words whatever should befall them."

Archibald, rejoicing in the impression which his vigorous measures had made upon the intractable dairymaid, now applied himself, as a sensible and good-natured man, to secure by fair means the ascendency which he had obtained by some wholesome violence ; and he succeeded so well in representing to her the idle nature of her fears, and the impossibility of leaving her upon the beach enthroned in an empty carriage, that the good understanding of the party was completely revived ere they landed at Roseneath.

CHAPTER XLII

Did Fortune guide,
Or rather Destiny, our bark, to which
We could appoint no port, to this best place?
FLETCHER.

THE islands in the Firth of Clyde, which the daily passage of
so many smoke-pennoned steamboats now renders so easily
accessible, were in our fathers' times secluded spots, frequented
by no travellers, and few visitants of any kind. They are of
exquisite yet varied beauty. Arran, a mountainous region, or
Alpine island, abounds with the grandest and most romantic
scenery. Bute is of a softer and more woodland character.
The Cumrays, as if to exhibit a contrast to both, are green,
level, and bare, forming the links of a sort of natural bar,
which is drawn along the mouth of the firth, leaving large
intervals, however, of ocean. Roseneath, a smaller isle, lies
much higher up the firth, and towards its western shore, near
the opening of the lake called the Gare Loch, and not far
from Loch Long and Loch Seant, or the Holy Loch, which
wind from the mountains of the Western Highlands to join
the estuary of the Clyde.

In these isles the severe frost winds which tyrannize over
the vegetable creation during a Scottish spring are comparatively little felt ; nor, excepting the gigantic strength of Arran,
are they much exposed to the Atlantic storms, lying land-
locked and protected to the westward by the shores of Ayrshire [Argyllshire]. Accordingly, the weeping-willow, the
weeping-birch, and other trees of early and pendulous shoots,
flourish in these favored recesses in a degree unknown in our
eastern districts ; and the air is also said to possess that mildness which is favorable to consumptive cases.

The picturesque beauty of the island of Roseneath, in
particular, had such recommendations that the Earls and
Dukes of Argyle from an early period made it their occasional
residence, and had their temporary accommodation in a fishing or hunting lodge, which succeeding improvements have

since transformed into a palace. It was in its original simplicity when the little bark which we left traversing the firth at the end of last chapter approached the shores of the isle.

When they touched the landing-place, which was partly shrouded by some old low but wide-spreading oak trees, intermixed with hazel-bushes, two or three figures were seen as if awaiting their arrival. To these Jeanie paid little attention, so that it was with a shock of surprise almost electrical that, upon being carried by the rowers out of the boat to the shore, she was received in the arms of her father!

It was too wonderful to be believed—too much like a happy dream to have the stable feeling of reality. She extricated herself from his close and affectionate embrace, and held him at arm's length to satisfy her mind that it was no illusion. But the form was indisputable—Douce David Deans himself, in his best light blue Sunday's coat, with broad metal buttons, and waistcoat and breeches of the same ; his strong gramashes or leggins of thick gray cloth ; the very copper buckles ; the broad Lowland blue bonnet, thrown back as he lifted his eyes to Heaven in speechless gratitude ; the gray locks that straggled from beneath it down his weather-beaten "haffets ; " the bald and furrowed forehead ; the clear blue eye, that, undimmed by years, gleamed bright and pale from under its shaggy gray pent-house ; the features, usually so stern and stoical, now melted into the unwonted expression of rapturous joy, affection, and gratitude—were all those of David Deans ; and so happily did they assort together, that, should I ever again see my friends Wilkie or Allan, I will try to borrow or steal from them a sketch of this very scene.

"Jeanie—my ain Jeanie—my best—my maist dutiful bairn ! The Lord of Israel be thy father, for I am hardly worthy of thee ! Thou hast redeemed our captivity, brought back the honor of our house. Bless thee, my bairn, with mercies promised and purchased ! But He *has* blessed thee, in the good of which He has made thee the instrument."

These words broke from him not without tears, though David was of no melting mood. Archibald had, with delicate attention, withdrawn the spectators from the interview, so that the wood and setting sun alone were witnesses of the expansion of their feelings.

"And Effie ?—and Effie, dear father ? " was an eager interjectional question which Jeanie repeatedly threw in among her expressions of joyful thankfulness.

"Ye will hear—ye will hear," said David, hastily, and ever and anon renewed his grateful acknowledgments to

Heaven for sending Jeanie safe down from the land of prelatic deadness and schismatic heresy; and had delivered her from the dangers of the way, and the lions that were in the path.

"And Effie?" repeated her affectionate sister again and again. "And—and [fain would she have said Butler, but she modified the direct inquiry]—and Mr. and Mrs. Saddletree—and Dumbiedikes—and a' friends?"

"A' weel—a' weel, praise to His name!"

"And—and Mr. Butler? He wasna weel when I gaed awa'."

"He is quite mended—quite weel," replied her father.

"Thank God! but O, dear father, Effie?—Effie?"

"You will never see her mair, my bairn," answered Deans in a solemn tone. "You are the ae and only leaf left now on the auld tree; heal be your portion!"

"She is dead! She is slain! It has come ower late!" exclaimed Jeanie, wringing her hands.

"No, Jeanie," returned Deans, in the same grave, melancholy tone. "She lives in the flesh, and is at freedom from earthly restraint, if she were as much alive in faith and as free from the bonds of Satan."

"The Lord protect us!" said Jeanie. "Can the unhappy bairn hae left you for that villain?"

"It is ower truly spoken," said Deans. "She has left her auld father, that has wept and prayed for her. She has left her sister, that travailed and toiled for her like a mother. She has left the bones of her mother, and the land of her people, and she is ower the march wi' that son of Belial. She has made a moonlight flitting of it." He paused, for a feeling betwixt sorrow and strong resentment choked his utterance.

"And wi' that man—that fearfu' man?" said Jeanie. "And she has left us to gang aff wi' him? O Effie, Effie, wha could hae thought it, after sic a deliverance as you had been gifted wi'!"

"She went out from us, my bairn, because she was not of us," replied David. "She is a withered branch will never bear fruit of grace—a scapegoat gone forth into the wilderness of the world, to carry wi' her, as I trust, the sins of our little congregation. The peace of the warld gang wi' her, and a better peace when she has the grace to turn to it! If she is of His elected, His ain hour will come. What would her mother have said, that famous and memorable matron, Rebecca M'Naught, whose memory is like a flower of sweet savor in Newbattle and a pot of frankincense in Lugton? But be it sae; let her part—let her gang her gate—let her bite on her ain bridle. The Lord kens His time. She was the bairn of prayers, and may not prove an utter castaway. But never, Jeanie—never more let her name be spoken between you and me. She hath passed from us like the brook which vanisheth when the summer waxeth warm, as patient Job saith; let her pass, and be forgotten."

There was a melancholy pause which followed these expressions. Jeanie would fain have asked more circumstances relating to her sister's departure, but the tone of her father's prohibition was positive. She was about to mention her interview with Staunton at his father's rectory; but, on hastily running over the particulars in her memory, she thought that, on the whole, they were more likely to aggravate than diminish his distress of mind. She turned, therefore, the discourse from this painful subject, resolving to suspend further inquiry until she should see Butler, from whom she expected to learn the particulars of her sister's elopement.

But when was she to see Butler? was a question she could not forbear asking herself, especially while her father, as if eager to escape from the subject of his youngest daughter, pointed to the opposite shore of Dunbartonshire, and asking Jeanie "if it werena a pleasant abode?" declared to her his intention of removing his earthly tabernacle to that country, "in respect he was solicited by his Grace the Duke of Argyle, as one well skilled in country labor and a' that appertained to flocks and herds, to superintend a store farm whilk his Grace had taen into his ain hand for the improvement of stock."

Jeanie's heart sunk within her at this declaration. "She allowed it was a goodly and pleasant land, and sloped bonnily to the western sun; and she doubtedna that the pasture might be very gude, for the grass looked green, for as drouthy as the weather had been. But it was far frae hame, and she thought she wad be often thinking on the bonny spots of turf, sae fu' of gowans and yellow kingcups, amang the Crags at St. Leonard's."

"Dinna speak on't, Jeanie," said her father; "I wish never to hear it named mair—that is, after the rouping is ower, and the bills paid. But I brought a' the beasts ower-bye that I thought ye wad like best. There is Gowans, and there's your ain brockit cow, and the wee hawkit ane, that ye ca'd—I needna tell ye how ye ca'd it; but I couldna bid them sell the petted creature, though the sight o't may sometimes gie us a sair heart: it's no the poor dumb creature's fault. And ane or twa beasts mair I hae reserved, and I caused them to be driven before the other beasts, that men might say, as when the son of Jesse returned from battle, ‘ This is David's spoil.' "

Upon more particular inquiry, Jeanie found new occasion to admire the active beneficence of her friend the Duke of Argyle. While establishing a sort of experimental farm on the skirts of his immense Highland estates, he had been somewhat at a loss to find a proper person in whom to vest the charge of it.   The conversation his Grace had upon country matters with Jeanie Deans during their return from Richmond had impressed him with a belief that the father, whose experience and success she so frequently quoted, must be exactly the sort of person whom he wanted.   When the condition annexed to Effie's pardon rendered it highly probable that David Deans would choose to change his place of residence, this idea again occurred to the Duke more strongly, and as he was an enthusiast equally in agriculture and in benevolence, he imagined he was serving the purposes of both when he wrote to the gentleman in Edinburgh intrusted with his affairs to inquire into the character of David Deans, cow-feeder, and so forth, at St. Leonard's Crags ; and if he found him such as he had been represented, to engage him without delay, and on the most liberal terms, to superintend his fancy-farm in Dunbartonshire.

The proposal was made to old David by the gentleman so commissioned on the second day after his daughter's pardon had reached Edinburgh.   His resolution to leave St. Leonard's had been already formed ; the honor of an express invitation from the Duke of Argyle to superintend a department where so much skill and diligence was required was in itself extremely flattering ; and the more so, because honest David, who was not without an excellent opinion of his own talents, persuaded himself that, by accepting this charge, he would in some sort repay the great favor he had received at the hands of the Argyle family.   The appointments, including the right of sufficient grazing for a small stock of his own, were amply liberal ; and David's keen eye saw that the situation was convenient for trafficking to advantage in Highland cattle.   There was risk of " hership " from the neighboring mountains, indeed, but the awful name of the Duke of Argyle would be a great security, and a trifle of blackmail would, David was aware, assure his safety.

Still, however, there were two points on which he haggled. The first was the character of the clergyman with whose worship he was to join ; and on this delicate point he received, as we will presently show the reader, perfect satisfaction.

The next obstacle was the condition of his youngest daughter, obliged as she was to leave Scotland for so many years.

The gentleman of the law smiled, and said, "There was no occasion to interpret that clause very strictly ; that if the young woman left Scotland for a few months, or even weeks, and came to her father's new residence by sea from the western side of England, nobody would know of her arrival, or at least nobody who had either the right or inclination to give her disturbance. The extensive heritable jurisdictions of his Grace excluded the interference of other magistrates with those living on his estates, and they who were in immediate dependence on him would receive orders to give the young woman no disturbance. Living on the verge of the Highlands, she might, indeed, be said to be out of Scotland, that is, beyond the bounds of ordinary law and civilization."

Old Deans was not quite satisfied with this reasoning ; but the elopement of Effie, which took place on the third night after her liberation, rendered his residence at St. Leonard's so detestable to him that he closed at once with the proposal which had been made him, and entered with pleasure into the idea of surprising Jeanie, as had been proposed by the Duke, to render the change of residence more striking to her. The Duke had apprised Archibald of these circumstances, with orders to act according to the instructions he should receive from Edinburgh, and by which accordingly he was directed to bring Jeanie to Roseneath.

The father and daughter communicated these matters to each other, now stopping, now walking slowly towards the Lodge, which showed itself among the trees, at about half a mile's distance from the little bay in which they had landed.

As they approached the house, David Deans informed his daughter, with somewhat like a grim smile, which was the utmost advance he ever made towards a mirthful expression of visage, that "there was baith a worshipful gentleman and ane reverend gentleman residing therein. The worshipful gentleman was his honor the Laird of Knocktarlitie, who was bailie of the lordship under the Duke of Argyle, ane Hieland gentleman, tarred wi' the same stick." David doubted, "as mony of them, namely, a hasty and choloric temper, and a neglect of the higher things that belong to salvation, and also a gripping unto the things of this world, without muckle distinction of property ; but, however, ane gude hospitable gentleman, with whom it would be a part of wisdom to live on a gude understanding ; for Hielandmen were hasty—ower hasty. As for the reverend person of whom he had spoken, he was candidate by favor of the Duke of Argyle (for David would not for the universe have called him presentee) for the kirk of the parish in which their farm was situated, and he was likely to be highly acceptable unto the Christian souls of the parish, who were hungering for spiritual manna, having been fed but upon sour Hieland sowens by Mr. Duncan MacDonought, the last minister, who began the morning duly, Sunday and Saturday, with a mutchkin of usquebaugh. But I need say the less about the present lad," said David, again grimly grimacing, "as I think ye may hae seen him afore; and here he is come to meet us."

She had indeed seen him before, for it was no other than Reuben Butler himself.

CHAPTER XLIII

No more shalt thou behold thy sister's face ;
Thou hast already had her last embrace.
Elegy on Mrs. Anne Killigrew.

THIS second surprise had been accomplished for Jeanie Deans
by the rod of the same benevolent enchanter whose power
had transplanted her father from the Crags of St. Leonard's
to the banks of the Gare Loch.   The Duke of Argyle was
not a person to forget the hereditary debt of gratitude which
had been bequeathed to him by his grandfather in favor of
the grandson of old Bible Butler.   He had internally resolved to provide for Reuben Butler in this kirk of Knocktarlitie, of which the incumbent had just departed this life.
Accordingly, his agent received the necessary instructions
for that purpose, under the qualifying condition always that
the learning and character of Mr. Butler should be found
proper for the charge.   Upon inquiry, these were found as
highly satisfactory as had been reported in the case of David
Deans himself.

By this preferment, the Duke of Argyle more essentially
benefitted his friend and *protégée*, Jeanie, than he himself
was aware of, since he contributed to remove objections in
her father's mind to the match, which he had no idea had
been in existence.

We have already noticed that Deans had something of a
prejudice against Butler, which was, perhaps, in some degree
owing to his possessing a sort of consciousness that the poor
usher looked with eyes of affection upon his eldest daughter.
This, in David's eyes, was a sin of presumption, even although it should not be followed by any overt act or actual
proposal.   But the lively interest which Butler had displayed in his distresses since Jeanie set forth on her London
expedition, and which, therefore, he ascribed to personal
respect for himself individually, had greatly softened the
feelings of irritability with which David had sometimes regarded him.   And, while he was in this good disposition
towards Butler, another incident took place which had great
influence on the old man's mind.

So soon as the shock of Effie's second elopement was over, it was Deans's early care to collect and refund to the Laird of Dumbiedikes the money which he had lent for Effie's trial and for Jeanie's traveling expenses. The Laird, the pony, the cocked hat, and the tobacco-pipe had not been seen at St. Leonard's Crags for many a day; so that, in order to pay this debt, David was under the necessity of repairing in person to the mansion of Dumbiedikes.

He found it in a state of unexpected bustle. There were workmen pulling down some of the old hangings and replacing them with others, altering, repairing, scrubbing, painting, and whitewashing. There was no knowing the old house, which had been so long the mansion of sloth and silence. The Laird himself seemed in some confusion, and his reception, though kind, lacked something of the reverential cordiality with which he used to greet David Deans. There was a change also, David did not very well know of what nature, about the exterior of this landed proprietor—an improvement in the shape of his garments, a spruceness in the air with which they were put on, that were both novelties. Even the old hat looked smarter; the cock had been newly pointed, the lace had been refreshed, and instead of slouching backward or forward on the Laird's head as it happened to be thrown on, it was adjusted with a knowing inclination over one eye.

David Deans opened his business and told down the cash. Dumbiedikes steadily inclined his ear to the one, and counted the other with great accuracy, interrupting David, while he was talking of the redemption of the captivity of Judah, to ask him whether he did not think one or two of the guineas looked rather light. When he was satisfied on this point, had pocketed his money, and had signed a receipt, he addressed David with some little hesitation—"Jeanie wad be writing ye something, gudeman?"

"About the siller?" replied Davie. "Nae doubt she did."

"And did she say nae mair about me?" asked the Laird.

"Nae mair but kind and Christian wishes; what suld she hae said?" replied David, fully expecting that the Laird's long courtship, if his dangling after Jeanie deserves so active a name, was now coming to a point. And so indeed it was, but not to that point which he wished or expected.

"Aweel, she kens her ain mind best, gudeman. I hae made a clean house o' Jenny Balchristie and her niece. They were a bad pack—stealed meat and mault, and loot

the carters magg the coals. I'm to be married the morn,
and kirkit on Sunday."

Whatever David felt, he was too proud and too steady-
minded to show any unpleasant surprise in his countenance
and manner.

"I wuss ye happy, sir, through Him that gies happiness;
marriage is an honorable state."

"And I am wedding into an honorable house, David—the
Laird of Lickpelf's youngest daughter; she sits next us in
the kirk, and that's the way I came to think on't."

There was no more to be said, but again to wish the Laird
joy, to taste a cup of his liquor, and to walk back again to
St. Leonard's, musing on the mutability of human affairs
and human resolutions. The expectation that one day or
other Jeanie would be Lady Dumbiedikes had, in spite of
himself, kept a more absolute possession of David's mind
than he himself was aware of. At least it had hitherto
seemed an union at all times within his daughter's reach,
whenever she might choose to give her silent lover any degree of encouragement, and now it was vanished forever.
David returned, therefore, in no very gracious humor for
so good a man. He was angry with Jeanie for not having
encouraged the Laird; he was angry with the Laird for requiring encouragement; and he was angry with himself for
being angry at all on the occasion.

On his return he found the gentleman who managed the
Duke of Argyle's affairs was desirous of seeing him, with a
view to completing the arrangement between them. Thus,
after a brief repose, he was obliged to set off anew for Edinburgh, so that old May Hattly declared, "That a' this was
to end with the master just walking himself aff his feet."

When the business respecting the farm had been talked
over and arranged, the professional gentleman acquainted
David Deans, in answer to his inquiries concerning the state
of public worship, that it was the pleasure of the Duke to
put an excellent young clergyman called Reuben Butler into
the parish, which was to be his future residence.

"Reuben Butler!" exclaimed David—"Reuben Butler,
the usher at Liberton?"

"The very same," said the Duke's commissioner. "His
Grace has heard an excellent character of him, and has some
hereditary obligations to him besides; few ministers will be
so comfortable as I am directed to make Mr. Butler."

"Obligations! The Duke! Obligations to Reuben
Butler! Reuben Butler a placed minister of the Kirk of

Scotland!" exclaimed David, in interminable astonishment, for somehow he had been led by the bad success which Butler had hitherto met with in all his undertakings to consider him as one of those stepsons of Fortune whom she treats with unceasing rigor, and ends with disinheriting altogether.

There is, perhaps, no time at which we are disposed to think so highly of a friend as when we find him standing higher than we expected in the esteem of others. When assured of the reality of Butler's change of prospects, David expressed his great satisfaction at his success in life, which he observed, was entirely owing to himself (David). "I advised his puir grandmother, who was but a silly woman, to breed him up to the ministry; and I prophesied that, with a blessing on his endeavors, he would become a polished shaft in the temple. He may be something ower proud o' his carnal learning, but a gude lad, and has the root of the matter; as ministers gang now, where ye'll find ane better, ye'll find ten waur than Reuben Butler."

He took leave of the man of business and walked homeward, forgetting his weariness in the various speculations to which this wonderful piece of intelligence gave rise. Honest David had now, like other great men, to go to work to reconcile his speculative principles with existing circumstances; and, like other great men, when they set seriously about that task, he was tolerably successful.

"Ought Reuben Butler in conscience to accept of this preferment in the Kirk of Scotland, subject (as David at present thought that establishment was) to the Erastian encroachments of the civil power?" This was the leading question, and he considered it carefully. "The Kirk of Scotland was shorn of its beams, and deprived of its full artillery and banners of authority; but still it contained zealous and fructifying pastors, attentive congregations, and with all her spots and blemishes, the like of this kirk was nowhere else to be seen upon earth."

David's doubts had been too many and too critical to permit him ever unequivocally to unite himself with any of the dissenters, who, upon various accounts absolutely seceded from the national church. He had often joined in communion with such of the established clergy as approached nearest to the old Presbyterian model and principles of 1640. And although there were many things to be amended in that system, yet he remembered that he, David Deans, had himself ever been a humble pleader for the good old cause in a legal way, but without rushing into right-hand excesses, divisions, and separations.   But, as an enemy to separation, he might join the right-hand of fellowship with a minister of the Kirk of Scotland in its present model.   *Ergo*, Reuben Butler might take possession of the parish of Knocktarlitie without forfeiting his friendship or favor—Q. E. D. But, secondly came the trying point of lay patronage, which David Deans had ever maintained to be a coming in by the window and over the wall, a cheating and starving the souls of a whole parish, for the purpose of clothing the back and filling the belly of the incumbent.

This presentation, therefore, from the Duke of Argyle, whatever was the worth and high character of that nobleman, was a limb of the brazen image, a portion of the evil thing, and with no kind of consistency could David bend his mind to favor such a transaction.   But if the parishioners themselves joined in a general call to Reuben Butler to be their pastor, it did not seem quite so evident that the existence of this unhappy presentation was a reason for his refusing them the comforts of his doctrine.   If the presbytery admitted him to the kirk in virtue rather of that act of patronage than of the general call of the congregation, that might be their error, and David allowed it was a heavy one. But if Reuben Butler accepted of the cure as tendered to him by those whom he was called to teach, and who had expressed themselves desirous to learn, David, after considering and reconsidering the matter, came, through the great virtue of "if," to be of opinion that he might safely so act in that matter.

There remained a third stumbling-block—the oaths to government exacted from the established clergymen, in which they acknowledge an Erastian king and parliament, and homologate the incorporating Union between England and Scotland, through which the latter kingdom had become part and portion of the former, wherein Prelacy, the sister of Popery, had made fast her throne and elevated the horns of her miter.   These were symptoms of defection which had often made David cry out, "My bowels—my bowels!   I am pained at the very heart!"   And he remembered that a godly Bow-head matron had been carried out of the Tolbooth Church in a swoon, beyond the reach of brandy and burnt feathers, merely on hearing these fearful words, 'It is enacted by the Lords *spiritual* and temporal," pronounced from a Scottish pulpit, in the proem to the Porteous proclamation.   These oaths were, therefore, a deep compliance

and dire abomination—a sin and a snare, and a danger and
a defection. But this shibboleth was not always exacted.
Ministers had respect to their own tender consciences and
those of their brethren ; and it was not till a later period
that the reins of discipline were taken up tight by the General
Assemblies and presbyteries. The peacemaking particle
came again to David's assistance. *If* an incumbent was not
called upon to make such compliances, and *if* he got a right
entry into the church without intrusion, and by orderly
appointment, why, upon the whole, David Deans came to
be of opinion that the said incumbent might lawfully enjoy
the spirituality and temporality of the cure of souls at
Knocktarlitie, with stipend, manse, glebe, and all thereunto
appertaining.

The best and most upright-minded men are so strongly
influenced by existing circumstances, that it would be somewhat cruel to inquire too nearly what weight paternal affection gave to these ingenious trains of reasoning. Let David
Deans's situation be considered. He was just deprived of
one daughter, and his eldest, to whom he owed so much,
was cut off, by the sudden resolution of Dumbiedikes, from
the high hope which David had entertained that she might
one day be mistress of that fair lordship. Just while this
disappointment was bearing heavy on his spirits, Butler
comes before his imagination—no longer the half-starved
threadbare usher, but fat and sleek and fair, the beneficed
minister of Knocktarlitie, beloved by his congregation, exemplary in his life, powerful in his doctrine, doing the duty
of the kirk as never Highland minister did it before, turning sinners as a collie dog turns sheep, a favorite of the
Duke of Argyle, and drawing a stipend of eight hundred
punds Scots and four chalders of victual. Here was a match
making up, in David's mind, in a tenfold degree, the disappointment in the case of Dumbiedikes, in so far as the goodman of St. Leonard's held a powerful minister in much
greater admiration than a mere landed proprietor. It did
not occur to him, as an additional reason in favor of the
match, that Jeanie might herself have some choice in the
matter ; for the idea of consulting her feelings never once
entered into the honest man's head, any more than the
possibility that her inclination might perhaps differ from
his own.

The result of his meditations was, that he was called upon
to take the management of the whole affair into his own
hand, and give, if it should be found possible without sinful

compliance, or backsliding, or defection of any kind, a worthy pastor to the kirk of Knocktarlitie. Accordingly, by the intervention of the honest dealer in buttermilk who dwelt in Liberton, David summoned to his presence Reuben Butler. Even from this worthy messenger he was unable to conceal certain swelling emotions of dignity, insomuch that, when the carter had communicated his message to the usher, he added, that "Certainly the gudeman of St. Leonard's had some grand news to tell him, for he was as uplifted as a midden-cock upon pattens."

Butler, it may readily be conceived, immediately obeyed the summons. His was a plain character, in which worth and good sense and simplicity were the principal ingredients; but love on this occasion, gave him a certain degree of address. He had received an intimation of the favor designed him by the Duke of Argyle, with what feelings those only can conceive who have experienced a sudden prospect of being raised to independence and respect, from penury and toil. He resolved, however, that the old man should retain all the consequences of being, in his own opinion, the first to communicate the important intelligence. At the same time, he also determined that in the expected conference he would permit David Deans to expatiate at length upon the proposal in all its bearings, without irritating him either by interruption or contradiction. This last plan was the most prudent he could have adopted; because, although there were many doubts which David Deans could himself clear up to his own satisfaction, yet he might have been by no means disposed to accept the solution of any other person; and to engage him in an argument would have been certain to confirm him at once and forever in the opinion which Butler chanced to impugn.

He received his friend with an appearance of important gravity, which real misfortune had long compelled him to lay aside, and which belonged to those days of awful authority in which he predominated over Widow Butler, and dictated the mode of cultivating the crofts at Beersheba. He made known to Reuben with great prolixity the prospect of his changing his present residence for the charge of the Duke of Argyle's stock farm in Dunbartonshire, and enumerated the various advantages of the situation with obvious self-congratulation; but assured the patient hearer that nothing had so much moved him to acceptance as the sense "That, by his skill in bestial, he could render the most important services to his Grace the Duke of Argyle, to whom, in the late unhappy circumstances (here a tear dimmed the sparkle of pride in the old man's eye), he had been sae muckle obliged. To put a rude 'Hielandman into sic a charge," he continued, "what could be expected but that he suld be sic a chiefest herdsman as wicked Doeg the Edomite ; whereas, while this gray head is to the fore, not a clute o' them but sall be as weel cared for if they were the fatted kine of Pharaoh.   And now, Reuben, lad, seeing we maun remove our tent to a strange country, ye'll be casting a dolefu' look after us, and thinking with whom ye are to hold council anent your government in thae slippery and backsliding times ; and nae doubt remembering that the auld man, David Deans, was made the instrument to bring you out of the mire of schism and heresy, wherein your father's house delighted to wallow ; aften also, nae doubt, when ye are pressed wi' ensnaring trials and temptations and heart-plagues, you, that are like a recruit that is marching for the first time to the took of drum, will miss the auld, bauld, and experienced veteran soldier that has felt the brunt of mony a foul day, and heard the bullets whistle as aften as he has hairs left on his auld pow."

It is very possible that Butler might internally be of opinion that the reflection on his ancestor's peculiar tenets might have been spared, or that he might be presumptuous enough even to think that, at his years and with his own lights, he must be able to hold his course without the pilotage of honest David.   But he only replied by expressing his regret that anything should separate him from an ancient, tried, and affectionate friend.

"But how can it be helped, man ?" said David, twisting his features into a sort of smile—"how can we help it ?   I trow ye canna tell me that.   Ye maun leave that to ither folk—to the Duke of Argyle and me, Reuben.   It's a gude thing to hae friends in this warld ; how muckle better to hae an interest beyond it !"   And David, whose piety, though not always quite rational, was as sincere as it was habitual and fervent, looked reverentially upward and paused.

Mr. Butler intimated the pleasure with which he would receive his friend's advice on a subject so important, and David resumed.

"What think ye now, Reuben, of a kirk—a regular kirk under the present establishment ?   Were sic offered to ye, wad ye be free to accept it, and under whilk provisions ?   I am speaking but by way of query."

Butler replied, "That if such a prospect were held out to him, he would probably first consult whether he was likely to be useful to the parish he should be called to ; and if there appeared a fair prospect of his proving so, his friend must be aware that, in every other point of view, it would be highly advantageous for him."

"Right, Reuben—very right, lad," answered the monitor, "your ain conscience is the first thing to be satisfied ; for how sall he teach others that has himsell sae ill learned the Scriptures as to grip for the lucre of foul earthly preferment, sic as gear and manse, money and victual, that which is not his in a spiritual sense ; or wha makes his kirk a stalking-horse, from behind which he may tak aim at his stipend ? But I look for better things of you ; and specially ye maun be minded not to act altogether on your ain judgment, for therethrough comes sair mistakes, backslidings, and defections on the left and on the right. If there were sic a day of trial put to you, Reuben, you, who are a young lad, although it may be ye are gifted wi' the carnal tongues, and those whilk were spoken at Rome, whilk is now the seat of the scarlet abomination, and by the Greeks, to whom the Gospel was as foolishness, yet natheless ye may be entreated by your weel-wisher to take the counsel of those prudent and resolved and weather-withstanding professors wha hae kenn'd what it was to lurk on banks and in mosses, in bogs and in caverns, and to risk the peril of the head rather than renunce the honesty of the heart."

Butler replied, "That certainly, possessing such a friend as he hoped and trusted he had in the goodman himself, who had seen so many changes in the preceding century, he should be much to blame if he did not avail himself of his experience and friendly counsel."

"Eneugh said—enough said, Reuben," said David Deans, with internal exultation ; "and say that ye were in the predicament whereof I hae spoken, of a surety I would deem it my duty to gang to the root o' the matter, and lay bare to you the ulcers and imposthumes, and the sores and the leprosies, of this our time, crying aloud and sparing not."

David Deans was now in his element. He commenced his examination of the doctrines and belief of the Christian Church with the very Culdees, from whom he passed to John Knox ; from John Knox to the recusants in James the Sixth's time—Bruce, Black, Blair, Livingstone ; from them to the brief, and at length triumphant, period of the Presbyterian Church's splendor, until it was overrun by the English Independents. Then followed the dismal times of Prelacy, the indulgences, seven in number, with all their shades and bearings, until he arrived at the reign of King James the Second, in which he himself had been, in his own mind, neither an obscure actor nor an obscure sufferer. Then was Butler doomed to hear the most detailed and annotated edition of what he had so often heard before— David Dean's confinement, namely, in the iron cage in the Canongate tolbooth, and the cause thereof.

We should be very unjust to our friend David Deans if we should "pretermit," to use his own expression, a narrative which he held essential to his fame. A drunken trooper of the Royal Guards, Francis Gordon by name, had chased five or six of the skulking Whigs, among whom was our friend David ; and after he had compelled them to stand, and was in the act of brawling with them, one of their number fired a pocket-pistol and shot him dead. David used to sneer and shake his head when any one asked him whether *he* had been the instrument of removing this wicked persecutor from the face of the earth. In fact, the merit of the deed lay between him and his friend, Patrick Walker, the pedler, whose works he was so fond of quoting. Neither of them cared directly to claim the merit of silencing Mr. Francis Gordon of the Life Guards, there being some wild cousins of his about Edinburgh, who might have been even yet addicted to revenge, but yet neither of them chose to disown or yield to the other the merit of this active defense of their religious rights. David said, that if he had fired a pistol then, it was what he never did after or before. And as for Mr. Patrick Walker, he has left it upon record that his great surprise was that so small a pistol could kill so big a man. These are the words of that venerable biographer, whose trade had not taught him by experience that an inch was as good as an ell : " He (Francis Gordon) got a shot in his head out of a pocket-pistol, rather fit for diverting a boy than killing such a furious, mad, brisk man, which notwithstanding killed him dead !"*

Upon the extensive foundation which the history of the kirk afforded, during its short-lived triumph and long tribulation, David, with length of breath and of narrative which would have astounded any one but a lover of his daughter, proceeded to lay down his own rules for guiding the conscience of his friend as an aspirant to serve in the ministry. Upon this subject the good man went through such a variety of nice and casuistical problems, supposed so many extreme

* See Death of Francis Gordon.   Note 35.

cases, made the distinctions so critical and nice betwixt the right hand and the left hand, betwixt compliance and de· fection, holding back and stepping aside, slipping and stumbling, snares and errors, that at length, after having limited the path of truth to a mathematical line, he was brought to the broad admission that each man's conscience, after he had gained a certain view of the difficult navigation which he was to encounter, would be the best guide for his pilotage. He stated the examples and arguments for and against the acceptance of a kirk on the present revolution model with much more impartiality to Butler than he had been able to place them before his own view. And he concluded, that his young friend ought to think upon these things, and be guided by the voice of his own conscience, whether he could take such an awful trust as the charge of souls without doing injury to his own internal conviction of what is right or wrong.

When David had finished his very long harangue, which was only interrupted by monosyllables, or little more, on the part of Butler, the orator himself was greatly astonished to find that the conclusion at which he very naturally wished to arrive seemed much less decisively attained than when he had argued the case in his own mind.

In this particular David's current of thinking and speaking only illustrated the very important and general proposition concerning the excellence of the publicity of debate. For, under the influence of any partial feeling, it is certain that most men can more easily reconcile themselves to any favorite measure when agitating it in their own mind than when obliged to expose its merits to a third party, when the necessity of seeming impartial procures from the opposite arguments a much more fair statement than that which he affords it in tacit meditation. Having finished what he had to say, David thought himself obliged to be more explicit in point of fact, and to explain that this was no hypothetical case, but one on which, by his own influence and that of the Duke of Argyle, Reuben Butler would soon be called to decide.

It was even with something like apprehension that David Deans heard Butler announce, in return to this communication, that he would take that night to consider on what he had said with such kind intentions, and return him an answer the next morning. The feelings of the father mastered David on this occasion. He pressed Butler to spend the evening with him. He produced, most unusual at his meals, one, nay, two bottles of aged strong ale. He

spoke of his daughter—of her merits, her housewifery, her
thrift, her affection.   He led Butler so decidedly up to a
declaration of his feelings towards Jeanie, that, before nightfall, it was distinctly understood she was to be the bride of
Reuben Butler ; and if they thought it indelicate to abridge
the period of deliberation which Reuben had stipulated, it
seemed to be sufficiently understood betwixt them that
there was a strong probability of his becoming minister of
Knocktarlitie, providing the congregation were as willing
to accept of him as the Duke to grant him the presentation.
The matter of the oaths, they agreed, it was time enough
to dispute about whenever the shibboleth should be tendered.

Many arrangements were adopted that evening, which
were afterwards ripened by correspondence with the Duke
of Argyle's man of business, who entrusted Deans and
Butler with the benevolent wish of his principal that they
should all meet with Jeanie, on her return from England,
at the Duke's hunting-lodge in Roseneath.

This retrospect, so far as the placid loves of Jeanie Deans
and Ruben Butler are concerned, forms a full explanation
of the preceding narrative up to their meeting on the island
as already mentioned.

CHAPTER XLIV

"I come," he said, "my love, my life,
And—nature's dearest name—my wife.
Thy father's house and friends resign,
My home, my friends, my sire, are thine."
LOGAN.

THE meeting of Jeanie and Butler, under circumstances promising to crown an affection so long delayed, was rather affecting from its simple sincerity than from its uncommom vehemence of feeling. David Deans, whose practise was sometimes a little different from his theory, appalled them at first by giving them the opinion of sundry of the suffer-ing preachers and champions of his younger days, that marriage though honorable by the laws of Scripture, was yet a state over-rashly coveted by professors, and specially by young ministers, whose desire, he said, was at whiles too inordinate for kirks, stipends, and wives, which had fre-quently occasioned over-ready compliance with the general defections of the times. He endeavored to make them aware also, that hasty wedlock had been the bane of many a savory professor ; that the unbelieving wife had too often reversed the text, and perverted the believing husband ; that when the famous Donald Cargill, being then hiding in Lee Wood, in Lanarkshire, it being "killing time," did, upon importunity, marry Robert Marshal of Starry Shaw, he had thus expressed himself : "What hath induced Robert to marry this woman ? Her ill will overcome his good ; he will not keep the way long : his thriving days are done." To the sad accomplishment of which prophecy David said he was himself a living witness, for Robert Marshal, having fallen into foul compliances with the enemy, went home, and heard the curates, declined into other steps of defection, and became lightly esteemed. Indeed, he observed that the great upholders of the standard, Cargill, Peden, Cameron, and Renwick, had less delight in tying the bonds of matrimony than in any other piece of their ministerial work ; and although they would neither dissuade the parties nor refuse their office, they considered the being called to it as an evidence of indifference on the part of those between whom it was solemnized to the many grievous things of the day. Notwithstanding, however, that marriage was a snare unto many, David was of opinion, as, indeed, he had showed in his practise, "that it was in itself honorable, especially if times were such that honest men could be secure against being shot, hanged, or banished, and had ane competent livelihood to maintain themselves and those that might come after them. And, therefore," as he concluded something abruptly, addressing Jeanie and Butler, who, with faces as high-colored as crimson, had been listening to his lengthened argument for and against the holy state of matrimony, "I will leave ye to your ain cracks."

As their private conversation, however interesting to themselves, might probably be very little so to the reader, so far as it respected their present feelings and future prospects, we shall pass it over, and only mention the information which Jeanie received from Butler concerning her sister's elopement, which contained many particulars that she had been unable to extract from her father.

Jeanie learned, therefore, that for three days, after her pardon had arrived, Effie had been the inmate of her father's house at St. Leonard's; that the interviews betwixt David and his erring child which had taken place before she was liberated from prison had been touching in the extreme; but Butler could not suppress his opinion that, when he was freed from the apprehension of losing her in a manner so horrible, her father had tightened the bands of discipline, so as, in some degree, to gall the feelings and aggravate the irritability of a spirit naturally impatient and petulant, and now doubly so from the sense of merited disgrace.

On the third night, Effie disappeared from St. Leonard's leaving no information whatever of the route she had taken. Butler, however, set out in pursuit of her, and with much trouble traced her towards a little landing-place, formed by a small brook which enters the sea betwixt Musselburgh and Edinburgh. This place, which has been since made into a small harbor, surrounded by many villas and lodging-houses, is now termed Portobello. At this time it was surrounded by a waste common, covered with firs, and unfrequented, save by fishing boats, and now and then a smuggling lugger. A vessel of this description had been hovering in the firth at the time of Effie's elopement, and, as Butler ascertained, a boat had come ashore in the evening on which the fugitive had disappeared, and had carried on board a female. As the vessel made sail immediately, and landed no part of their cargo, there seemed little doubt that they were accomplices of the notorious Robertson, and that the vessel had only come into the Firth to carry off his paramour.

This was made clear by a letter which Butler himself soon afterwards received by post, signed "E. D.," but without bearing any date of place or time. It was miserably ill written and spelt; sea sickness having apparently aided the derangement of Effie's very irregular orthography and mode of expression. In this epistle, however, as in all that that unfortunate girl said or did, there was something to praise as well as to blame. She said in her letter. "That she could not endure that her father and her sister should go into banishment, or be partakers of her shame; that if her burden was a heavy one, it was of her own binding, and she had the more right to bear it alone; that in future they could not be a comfort to her, or she to them, since every look and word of her father put her in mind of her transgression, and was like to drive her mad; that she had nearly lost her judgment during the three days she was at St. Leonard's: her father meant weel by her, and all men, but he did not know the dreadful pain he gave her in casting up her sins. If Jeanie had been at hame, it might hae dune better; Jeanie was ane, like the angels in heaven, that rather weep for sinners than reckon their transgressions. But she should never see Jeanie ony mair, and that was the thought that gave her the sairest heart of a' that had come and gane yet. On her bended knees would she pray for Jeanie, night and day, baith for what she had done and what she had scorned to do in her behalf; for what a thought would it have been to her at that moment o' time, if that upright creature had made a fault to save her! She desired her father would give Jeanie a' the gear—her ain (*i. e.* Effie's) mother's and a'. She had made a deed giving up her right, and it was in Mr. Novit's hand. Warld's gear was henceforward the least of her care, nor was it likely to be muckle her mister." She hoped this would make it easy for her sister to settle;" and immediately after this expression, she wished Butler himself all good things, in return for his kindness to her. "For herself," she said, "she kenn'd her lot would be a waesome ane, but it was of her own framing, sae she desired the less pity. But, for her friends' satisfaction, she wished them to know that she was gaun nae ill gate; that they who had done her maist wrong were now willing to do her what justice was in their power; and she would, in some warldly respects, be far better off than she deserved. But she desired her family to remain satisfied with this assurance, and give themselves no trouble in making further inquiries after her."

To David Deans and to Butler this letter gave very little comfort; for what was to be expected from this unfortunate girl's uniting her fate to that of a character so notorious as Robertson, who they readily guessed was alluded to in the last sentence, excepting that she should become the partner and victim of his future crimes? Jeanie, who knew George Staunton's character and real rank, saw her sister's situation under a ray of better hope. She augured well of the haste he had shown to reclaim his interest in Effie, and she trusted he had made her his wife. If so, it seemed improbable that, with his expected fortune and high connections, he should again resume the life of criminal adventure which he had led, especially since, as matters stood, his life depended upon his keeping his own secret, which could only be done by an entire change of his habits, and particularly by avoiding all those who had known the heir of Willingham under the character of the audacious, criminal, and condemned Robertson.

She thought it most likely that the couple would go abroad for a few years, and not return to England until the affair of Porteous was totally forgotten. Jeanie, therefore, saw more hopes for her sister than Butler or her father had been able to perceive; but she was not at liberty to impart the comfort which she felt in believing that she would be secure from the pressure of poverty, and in little risk of being seduced into the paths of guilt. She could not have explained this without making public what it was essentially necessary for Effie's chance of comfort to conceal, the identity, namely, of George Staunton and George Robertson. After all, it was dreadful to think that Effie had united herself to a man condemned for felony, and liable to trial for murder, whatever might be his rank in life, and the degree of his repentance. Besides, it was melancholy to reflect that, she herself being in possession of the whole dreadful secret, it was most probable he would, out of regard to his own feelings and fear for his safety, never again permit her to see poor Effie. After perusing and re-perusing her sister's valedictory letter, she gave ease to her feelings in a flood of tears, which Butler in vain endeavored to check by every soothing attention in his power. She was obliged, however, at length to look up and wipe her eyes, for her father, thinking he had allowed the lovers time enough for conference, was now advancing towards them from the Lodge, accompanied by the Captain of Knockdunder, or, as his friends called him for brevity's sake, Duncan Knock, a title which some youthful exploits had rendered peculiarly appropriate.

This Duncan of Knockdunder was a person of first-rate importance in the island * of Roseneath and the continental parishes of Knocktarlitie, Kilmun, and so forth ; nay, his influence extended as far as Cowall, where, however, it was obscured by that of another factor. The Tower of Knockdunder still occupies, with its remains, a cliff overhanging the Holy Loch. Duncan swore it had been a royal castle ; if so, it was one of the smallest, the space within only forming a square of sixteen feet, and bearing therefore a ridiculous proportion to the thickness of the walls, which was ten feet at least. Such as it was, however, it had long given the title of Captain, equivalent to that of Chatelain, to the ancestors of Duncan, who were retainers of the house of Argyle, and held a hereditary jurisdiction under them, of little extent indeed, but which had great consequence in their own eyes, and was usually administered with a vigor somewhat beyond the law.

The present representative of that ancient family was a stout short man about fifty, whose pleasure it was to unite in his own person the dress of the Highlands and Lowlands, wearing on his head a black tie-wig, surmounted by a fierce cocked hat, deeply guarded with gold lace, while the rest of his dress consisted of the plaid and philabeg. Duncan superintended a district which was partly Highland, partly Lowland, and therefore might be supposed to combine their national habits, in order to show his impartiality to Trojan or Tyrian. The incongruity, however, had a whimsical and ludicrous effect, as it made his head and body look as if belonging to different individuals ; or, as some one said who had seen the executions of the insurgent prisoners in 1715, it seemed as if some Jacobite enchanter, having recalled the sufferers to life, had clapped, in his haste, an Englishman's head on a Highlander's body. To finish the portrait, the bearing of the gracious Duncan was brief, bluff, and consequential, and the upward turn of his short copper-colored nose indicated that he was somewhat addicted to wrath and usquebaugh.

* This is, more correctly speaking, a peninsula (*Laing*).

When this dignitary had advanced up to Butler and to Jeanie, "I take the freedom, Mr. Deans," he said, in a very consequential manner, " to salute your daughter, whilk I presume this young lass to be. I kiss every pretty girl that comes to Roseneath, in virtue of my office." Having made this gallant speech, he took out his quid, saluted Jeanie with a hearty smack, and bade her welcome to Argyle's country. Then addressing Butler, he said, "Ye maun gang ower and meet the carle ministers yonder the morn, for they will want to do your job; and synd it down with usquebaugh doubtless : they seldom make dry wark in this kintra."

"And the Laird——" said David Deans, addressing Butler in further explanation.

"The Captain, man," interrupted Duncan ; "folk winna ken wha ye are speaking aboot, unless ye gie shentlemens their proper title."

"The Captain, then," said David, "assures me that the call is unanimous on the part of the parishioners—a real harmonious call, Reuben."

"I pelieve," said Duncan, "it was as harmonious as could pe expected, when the tae half o' the bodies were clavering Sassenach and the t'other skirling Gaelic, like sea-maws and clack-geese before a storm. Ane wad hae needed the gift of tongues to ken preceesely what they said ; but I pelieve the best end of it was, 'Long live MacCallummore and Knockdunder!' And as to its being an unanimous call, I wad be glad to ken fat business the carles have to call ony thing or ony body but what the Duke and mysell likes!"

"Nevertheless," said Mr. Butler, "if any of the parishioners have any scruples, which sometimes happens in the mind of sincere professors, I should be happy of an opportunity of trying to remove——"

"Never fash your peard about it, man," interrupted Duncan Knock. "Leave it a' to me. Scruple! deil ane o' them has been bred up to scruple ony thing that they're bidden to do. And if sic a thing suld happen as ye speak o', ye sall see the sincere professor, as ye ca' him, towed at the stern of my boat for a few furlongs. I'll try if the water of the Haly Loch winna wash off scruples as weel as fleas. Cot tam——!"

The rest of Duncan's threats was lost in a growling gurgling sort of sound which he made in his throat, and which menaced recusants with no gentle means of conversion. David Deans would certainly have given battle in defence of the right of the Christian congregation to be consulted in the choice of their own pastor, which, in his estimation, was one of the choicest and most inalienable of their privileges ; but he had again engaged in close conversation with Jeanie, and, with more interest than he was in use to take in affairs foreign alike to his occupation and to his religious tenets, was inquiring into the particulars of her London journey. This was, perhaps, fortunate for the new-formed friendship betwixt him and the Captain of Knockdunder, which rested, in David's estimation, upon the proofs he had given of his skill in managing stock ; but, in reality, upon the special charge transmitted to Duncan from the Duke and his agent to behave with the utmost attention to Deans and his family.

"And now, sirs," said Duncan, in a commanding tone, "I am to pray ye a' to come in to your supper, for yonder is Mr. Archibald half famished, and a Saxon woman, that looks as if her een were fleeing out o' her head wi' fear and wonder, as if she had never seen a shentleman in a philabeg pefore."

"And Reuben Butler," said David, "will doubtless desire instantly to retire, that he may prepare his mind for the exercise of to-morrow, that his work may suit the day, and be an offering of a sweet savor in the nostrils of the reverend presbytery."

"Hout tout, man, it's but little ye ken about them," interrupted the Captain. "Teil a ane o' them wad gie the savor of the hot venison pasty which I smell (turning his squad nose up in the air) a' the way frae the Lodge, for a' that Mr. Putler, or you either, can say to them."

David groaned ; but judging he had to do with a Gallio, as he said, did not think it worth his while to give battle. They followed the Captain to the house, and arranged themselves with great ceremony round a well-loaded supper-table. The only other circumstance of the evening worthy to be recorded is, that Butler pronounced the blessing ; that Knockdunder found it too long, and David Deans censured it as too short ; from which the charitable reader may conclude it was exactly the proper length.

CHAPTER XLV.

Now turn the Psalms of David ower
  And lilt wi' holy clangor;
Of double verse come gie us four
  And skirl up the Bangor.

BURNS.

THE next was the important day when, according to the forms of ritual of the Scottish Kirk, Reuben Butler was to be ordained minister of Knocktarlitie by the presbytery of——. And so eager were the whole party, that all, excepting Mrs. Dutton, the destined Cowslip of Inverary, were stirring at an early hour.

Their host, whose appetite was as quick and keen as his temper, was not long in summoning them to a substantial breakfast, where there were at least a dozen of different preparations of milk, plenty of cold meat, scores boiled and roasted eggs, a huge cag of butter, half a firkin herrings boiled and broiled, fresh and salt, and tea and coffee for them that liked it, which, as their landlord assured them, with a nod and a wink, pointing at the same time to a little cutter which seemed dodging under the lee of the island, cost them little beside the fetching ashore.

"Is the contraband trade permitted here so openly?" said Butler. "I should think it very unfavorable to the people's morals."

"The Duke, Mr. Putler, has gien nae orders concerning the putting of it down," said the magistrate, and seemed to think that he had said all that was necessary to justify his connivance.

Butler was a man of prudence, and aware that real good can only be obtained by remonstrance when remonstrance is well-timed; so for the present he said nothing more on the subject.

When breakfast was half over, in flounced Mrs. Dolly, as fine as a blue sacque and cherry-colored ribbons could make her.

"Good morrow to you, madam," said the master of ceremonies; "I trust your early rising will not scaith ye."

The dame apologized to Captain Knockunder, as she was

438

pleased to term their entertainer; "but, as we say in Cheshire," she added, "I was like the mayor of Altringham, who lies in bed while his breeches are mending, for the girl did not bring up the right bundle to my room till she had brought up all the others by mistake one after t'other. Well, I suppose we are all for church to-day, as I understand. Pray may I be so bold as to ask if it is the fashion for you North-Country gentlemen to go to church in your petticoats, Captain Knockunder!"

"Captain of Knockdunder, madam, if you please, for I knock under to no man ; and in respect of my garb, I shall go to church as I am, at your service, madam ; for if I were to lie in bed, like your Major What-d'ye-callum, till my breeches were mended, I might be there all my life, seeing I never had a pair of them on my person but twice in my life, which I am pound to remember, it peing when the Duke brought his Duchess here, when her Grace pehoved to be pleasured ; so I e'en porrowed the minister's trews for the twa days his Grace was pleased to stay ; but I will put myself under sic confinement again for no man on earth, or woman either, but her Grace being always excepted, as in duty pound."

The mistress of the milking-pail stared, but, making no answer to this round declaration, immediately proceeded to show that the alarm of the preceding evening had in no degree injured her appetite.

When the meal was finished, the Captain proposed to them to take boat, in order that Mistress Jeanie might see her new place of residence, and that he himself might inquire whether the necessary preparations had been made there and at the manse for receiving the future inmates of these mansions.

The morning was delightful, and the huge mountain-shadows slept upon the mirrored wave of the firth, almost as little disturbed as if it had been an inland lake. Even Mrs. Dutton's fears no longer annoyed her. She had been informed by Archibald that there was to be some sort of junketting after the sermon, and that was what she loved dearly ; and as for the water, it was so still that it would look quite like a pleasuring on the Thames.

The whole party being embarked, therefore, in a large boat, which the Captain called his coach and six, and attended by a smaller one termed his gig, the gallant Duncan steered straight upon the little tower of the old-fashioned church of Knocktarlitie, and the exertions of six stout

rowers sped them rapidly on their voyage. As they neared
the land, the hills appeared to recede from them, and a little
valley, formed by the descent of a small river from the
mountains, evolved itself as it were upon their approach.
The style of the country on each side was simply pastoral,
and resembled, in appearance and character, the description
of a forgotten Scottish poet, which runs nearly thus :—

> The water gently down a level slid,
> With little din, but couthy what it made ;
> On ilka side the trees grew thick and lang,
> And wi' the wild birds' notes were a' in sang ;
> On either side, a full bow-shot and mair,
> The green was even, gowany, and fair ;
> With easy slope on every hand the braes
> To the hills' feet with scattered bushes raise ;
> With goats and sheep aboon, and kye below,
> The bonny banks all in a swarm did go. *

They landed in this Highland Arcadia, at the mouth of
the small stream which watered the delightful and peaceable
valley. Inhabitants of several descriptions came to pay their
respects to the Captain of Knockdunder, a homage which
he was very peremptory in exacting, and to see the new set-
tlers. Some of these were men after David Deans's own heart,
elders of the kirk-session, zealous professors, from the Lennox, Lanarkshire, and Ayrshire, to whom the preceding
Duke of Argyle had given " rooms " in this corner of his
estate, because they had suffered for joining his father, the
unfortunate Earl, during his ill-fated attempt in 1686.
These were cakes of the right leaven for David regaling himself with ; and, had it not been for this circumstance, he
has been heard to say, " that the Captain of Knockdunder
would have sworn him out of the country in twenty-four
hours, sae awsome it was to ony thinking soul to hear his
imprecations, upon the slightest temptation that crossed his
humor."
Besides these, there were a wilder set of parishioners,
mountaineers from the upper glen and adjacent hill, who
spoke Gaelic, went about armed, and wore the Highland
dress. But the strict commands of the Duke had established such good order in this part of his territories, that
the Gael and Saxons lived upon the best possible terms of
good neighborhood.
They first visited the manse, as the parsonage is termed
in Scotland. It was old, but in good repair, and stood

* Ross's *Fortunate Shepherdess*. **Edit. 1778, p. 23.**

snugly embosomed in a grove of sycamore, with a well-stocked garden in front, bounded by the small river, which was partly visible from the windows, partly concealed by the bushes, trees, and bounding hedge. Within, the house looked less comfortable than it might have been, for it had been neglected by the late incumbent; but workmen had been laboring under the directions of the Captain of Knockdunder, and at the expense of the Duke of Argyle, to put it into some order. The old "plenishing" had been removed, and neat but plain household furniture had been sent down by the Duke in a brig of his own, called the "Caroline," and was now ready to be placed in order in the apartments.

The gracious Duncan, finding matters were at a stand among the workmen, summoned before him the delinquents, and impressed all who heard him with a sense of his authority by the penalties with which he threatened them for their delay. Mulcting them in half their charge, he assured them, would be the least of it; for, if they were to neglect his pleasure and the Duke's, "he would be tamn'd if he paid them the t'other half either, and they might seek law for it where they could get it." The workpeople humbled themselves before the offended dignitary, and spake him soft and fair; and at length, upon Mr. Butler recalling to his mind that it was the ordination-day, and that the workmen were probably thinking of going to church, Knockdunder agreed to forgive them, out of respect to their new minister.

"But an I catch them neglecting my duty again, Mr. Putler, the teil pe in me if the kirk shall be an excuse; for what has the like o' them rapparees to do at the kirk ony day put Sundays, or then either, if the Duke and I has the necessitous uses for them?"

It may be guessed with what feelings of quiet satisfaction and delight Butler looked forward to spending his days, honored and useful as he trusted to be, in this sequestered valley, and how often an intelligent .glance was exchanged betwixt him and Jeanie, whose good-humored face looked positively handsome, from the expression of modesty, and at the same time of satisfaction, which she wore when visiting the apartments of which she was soon to call herself mistress. She was left at liberty to give more open indulgence to her feelings of delight and admiration when, leaving the manse, the company proceeded to examine the destined habitation of David Deans.

Jeanie found with pleasure that it was not above a musket-shot from the manse; for it had been a bar to her happiness to think she might be obliged to reside at a distance from her father, and she was aware that there were strong objections to his actually living in the same house with Butler. But this brief distance was the very thing which she could have wished.

The farm-house was on the plan of an improved cottage, and contrived with great regard to convenience ; an excellent little garden, an orchard, and a set of offices complete, according to the best ideas of the time, combined to render it a most desirable habitation for the practical farmer, and far superior to the hovel at Woodend and the small house at St Leonard's Crags. The situation was considerably higher than that of the manse, and fronted to the west. The windows commanded an enchanting view of the little vale over which the mansion seemed to preside, the windings of the stream, and the firth, with its associated lakes and romantic islands. The hills of Dunbartonshire, once possessed by the fierce clan of MacFarlanes, formed a crescent behind the valley, and far to the right were seen the dusky and more gigantic mountains of Argyleshire, with a seaward view of the shattered and thunder-splitten peaks of Arran.

But to Jeanie, whose taste for the picturesque, if she had any by nature, had never been awakened or cultivated, the sight of the faithful old May Hettly, as she opened the door to receive them in her clean toy, Sunday's russet-gown, and blue apron, nicely smoothed down before her, was worth the whole varied landscape. The raptures of the faithful old creature at seeing Jeanie were equal to her own, as she hastened to assure her " that baith the gudeman and the beasts had been as weel seen after as she possibly could contrive." Separating her from the rest of the company, May then hurried her young mistress to the offices, that she might receive the compliments she expected for her care of the cows. Jeanie rejoiced, in the simplicity of her heart, to see her charge once more ; and the mute favorites of our heroine, Gowans and the others, acknowledged her presence by lowing, turning round their broad and decent brows when they heard her well-known ' Pruh, my leddy—pruh, my woman," and by various indications, known only to those who have studied the habits of the milky mothers showing sensible pleasure as she approached to caress them in their turn.

"The very brute beasts are glad to see ye again," said May; "but nae wonder, Jeanie, for ye were aye kind to beast and body. And I maun learn to ca' ye *mistress* now, Jeanie, since ye hae been up to Lunnon, and seen the Duke, and the King, and a' the braw folk. But wha kens," added the old dame slyly, "what I'll hae to ca' ye forbye mistress, for I am thinking it wunna lang be Deans."

"Ca' me your ain Jeanie, May, and then ye can never gang wrang."

In the cow-house which they examined there was one animal which Jeanie looked at till the tears gushed from her eyes. May, who had watched her with a sympathizing expression, immediately observed, in an undertone, "The gudeman aye sorts that beast himsell, and is kinder to it than ony beast in the byre ; and I noticed he was that way e'en when he was angriest, and had maist cause to be angry. Eh, sirs ! a parent's heart's a queer thing ! Mony a warsle he has had for that puir lassie. I am thinking he petitions mair for her than for yoursell, hinny ; for what can he plead for you but just to wish you the blessing ye deserve ? And when I sleepit ayont the hallan, when we came first here, he was often earnest a' night, and I could hear him come ower and ower again wi', 'Effie—puir blinded misguided thing !' it was aye 'Effie ! Effie !' If that puir wandering lamb comena into the sheepfauld in the Shepherd's ain time, it will be an unco wonder, for I wot she has been a child of prayers. O, if the puir prodigal wad return, sae blithely as the goodman wad kill the fatted calf !—though Brockie's calf will no be fit for killing this three weeks yet."

And then, with the discursive talent of persons of her description, she got once more afloat in her account of domestic affairs, and left this delicate and affecting topic.

Having looked at everything in the offices and the dairy, and expressed her satisfaction with the manner in which matters had been managed in her absence, Jeanie rejoined the rest of the party, who were surveying the interior of the house, all excepting David Deans and Butler, who had gone down to the church to meet the kirk-session and the clergymen of the presbytery, and arrange matters for the duty of the day.

In the interior of the cottage all was clean, neat, and suitable to the exterior. It had been originally built and furnished by the Duke as a retreat for a favorite domestic of the higher class, who did not long enjoy it, and had been dead only a few months, so that everything was in excellent taste and good order. But in Jeanie's bedroom was a neat trunk, which had greatly excited Mrs. Dutton's curiosity, for she was sure that the direction, "For Mrs. Jean Deans, at Auchingower, parish of Knocktarlitie," was the writing of Mrs. Semple, the Duchess's own woman. May Hettly produced the key in a sealed parcel, which bore the same address, and attached to the key was a label, intimating that the trunk and its contents were " a token of remembrance to Jeanie Deans from her friends the Duchess of Argyle and the young ladies." The trunk, hastily opened, as the reader will not doubt, was found to be full of wearing apparel of the best quality, suited to Jeanie's rank in life ; and to most of the articles the names of the particular donors were attached, as if to make Jeanie sensible not only of the general but of the individual interest she had excited in the noble family. To name the various articles by their appropriate names would be to attempt things unattempted yet in prose or rhyme ; besides, that the old-fashioned terms of manteaus, sacques, kissing-strings, and so forth would convey but little information even to the milliners of the present day. (I shall deposit, however, an accurate inventory of the contents of the trunk with my kind friend, Miss Martha Buskbody, who has promised, should the public curiosity seem interested in the subject, to supply me with a professional glossary and commentary.) Suffice it to say, that the gift was such as became the donors, and was suited to the situation of the receiver ; that everything was handsome and appropriate, and nothing forgotten which belonged to the wardrobe of a young person in Jeanie's situation in life, the destined bride of a respectable clergyman.

Article after article was displayed, commented upon, and admired, to the wonder of May, who declared, " she didna think the Queen had mair or better claise," and somewhat to the envy of the northern Cowslip. This unamiable, but not very unnatural, disposition of mind broke forth in sundry unfounded criticisms to the disparagement of the articles, as they were severally exhibited. But it assumed a more direct character when, at the bottom of all, was found a dress of white silk, very plainly made, but still of white silk, and French silk to boot, with a paper pinned to it, bearing, that it was a present from the Duke of Argyle to his traveling companion, to be worn on the day when she should change her name.

Mrs. Dutton could forbear no longer, but whispered into Mr. Archibald's ear, that it was a clever thing to be a Scotchwoman : "She supposed all *her* sisters, and she had half a dozen, might have been hanged, without any one sending her a present of a pocket handkerchief."

"Or without your making any exertion to save them, Mrs. Dolly," answered Archibald, drily. "But I am surprised we do not hear the bell yet," said he, looking at his watch.

"Fat ta deil, Mr. Archibald," answered the Captain of Knockdunder, "wad ye hae them ring the bell before I am ready to gang to kirk ? I wad gar the bedral eat the bell-rope if he took ony sic freedom. But if ye want to hear the bell, I will just show mysell on the knowe-head, and it will begin jowing forthwith."

Accordingly, so soon as they sallied out, and the gold-laced hat of the Captain was seen rising like Hesper above the dewy verge of the rising ground, the clash—for it was rather a clash than a clang—of the bell was heard from the old moss-grown tower, and the clapper continued to thump its cracked sides all the while they advanced towards the kirk, Duncan exhorting them to take their own time, "for teil ony sport wad be till he came."*

Accordingly, the bell only changed to the final and impatient chime when they crossed the stile ; and "rang in," that is, concluded its mistuned summons, when they had entered the Duke's seat in the little kirk, where the whole party arranged themselves, with Duncan at their head, excepting David Deans, who already occupied a seat among the elders.

The business of the day, with a particular detail of which it is unnecessary to trouble the reader, was gone through according to the established form, and the sermon pronounced upon the occasion had the good fortune to please even the critical David Deans, though it was only an hour and a quarter long, which David termed a short allowance of spiritual provender.

The preacher, who was a divine that held many of David's opinions, privately apologized for his brevity by saying, "That he observed the Captain was gaunting grievously, and that if he had detained him longer, there was no knowing how long he might be in paying the next term's victual stipend."

David groaned to find that such carnal motives could have influence upon the mind of a powerful preacher. He had, indeed, been scandalized by another circumstance during the service.

* See Tolling to Service in Scotland. Note 36.

So soon as the congregation were seated after prayers, and the clergyman had read his text, the gracious Duncan, after rummaging the leathern purse which hung in front of his petticoat, produced a short tobacco-pipe made of iron, and observed, almost aloud, "I hae forgotten my spleuchan. Lachlan, gang down to the clachan and bring me up a penny-worth of twist." Six arms, the nearest within reach, presented, with an obedient start, as many tobacco-pouches to the man of office. He made choice of one with a nod of acknowledgment, filled his pipe, lighted it with the assistance of his pistol-flint, and smoked with infinite composure during the whole time of the sermon. When the discourse was finished, he knocked the ashes out of his pipe, replaced it in its sporran, returned the tobacco pouch or spleuchan to its owner, and joined in the prayer with decency and attention.

At the end of the service, when Butler had been admitted minister of the kirk of Knocktarlitie, with all its spiritual immunities and privileges, David, who had frowned, groaned, and murmured at Knockdunder's irreverent demeanor, communicated his plain thoughts of the matter to Isaac Meiklehose, one of the elders, with whom a reverential aspect and huge grizzle wig had especially disposed him to seek fraternization. "It didna become a wild Indian," David said, "much less a Christian and a gentleman, to sit in the kirk puffing tobacco-reek, as if he were in a change-house."

Meiklehose shook his head, and allowed it was "far frae beseeming. But what will ye say? The Captain's a queer hand, and to speak to him about that or ony thing else that crosses the maggot, wad be to set the kiln a-low. He keeps a high hand ower the country, and we couldna deal wi' the Hielandmen without his protection, sin' a' the keys o' the kintray hings at his belt; and he's no an ill body in the main, and maistry, ye ken, maws the meadows doun."

"That may be very true, neighbor," said David; "but Reuben Butler isna the man I take him to be if he disna learn the Captain to fuff his pipe some other gate than in God's house or the quarter be ower."

"Fair and softly gangs far," said Meiklehose; "and if a fule may gie a wise man a counsel, I wad hae him think twice or he mells wi' Knockdunder. He suld hae a lang-shankit spune that wad sup kail wi' the deil. But they are a' away to their dinner to the change-house, and if we dinna mend our pace, we'll come short at meal-time."

David accompanied his friend without answer; but began

to feel from experience that the glen of Knocktarlitie, like the rest of the world, was haunted by its own special subjects of regret and discontent. His mind was so much occupied by considering the best means of converting Duncan of Knock to a sense of reverent decency during public worship, that he altogether forgot to inquire whether Butler was called upon to subscribe the oaths to government.

Some have insinuated that his neglect on this head was, in some degree, intentional; but I think this explanation inconsistent with the simplicity of my friend David's character. Neither have I ever been able, by the most minute inquiries, to know whether the formula at which he so much scrupled had been exacted from Butler, aye or no. The books of the kirk-session might have thrown some light on this matter; but unfortunately they were destroyed in the year 1746, by one Donacha Dhu na Dunaigh, at the instance, it was said, or at least by the connivance, of the gracious Duncan of Knock, who had a desire to obliterate the recorded foibles of a certain Kate Finlayson.

CHAPTER XLVI

Now butt and ben the change-house fills
Wi' yill-caup commentators ;
Here's crying out for bakes and gills,
And there the pint-stoup clatters.
While thick and thrang, and loud and lang,
Wi' logic and wi' Scripture,
They raise a din that in the end
Is like to breed a rupture
     O' wrath that day.
      BURNS.

A PLENTIFUL entertainment, at the Duke of Argyle's cost, regaled the reverend gentlemen who had assisted at the ordination of Reuben Butler, and almost all the respectable part of the parish. The feast was, indeed, such as the country itself furnished ; for plenty of all the requisites for "a rough and round" dinner were always at Duncan of Knock's command. There was the beef and mutton on the braes, the fresh and saltwater fish in the lochs, the brooks, and firth ; game of every kind, from the deer to the leveret, were to be had for the killing in the Duke's forests, moors, heaths, and mosses ; and for liquor, home-brewed ale flowed as freely as water ; brandy and usquebaugh both were had in those happy times without duty ; even white wine and claret were got for nothing, since the Duke's extensive rights of admiralty gave him a title to all the wine in cask which is drifted ashore on the western coast and isles of Scotland, when shipping have suffered by severe weather. In short, as Duncan boasted, the entertainment did not cost MacCallummore a plack out of his sporran, and was nevertheless not only liberal, but overflowing.

The Duke's health was solemnized in a *bona fide* bumper, and David Deans himself added perhaps the first huzza that his lungs had ever uttered to swell the shout with which the pledge was received. Nay, so exalted in heart was he upon this memorable occasion, and so much disposed to be indulgent, that he expressed no dissatisfaction when three bagpipers struck up, "The Campbells are coming." The health of the reverend minister of Knocktarlitie was received with similar honors ; and there was a roar of laughter when one of his brethren slyly subjoined the addition of, "A good wife to our brother to keep the manse in order."   On this occasion David Deans was delivered of his first-born joke; and apparently the parturition was accompanied with many throes, for sorely did he twist about his physiognomy, and much did he stumble in his speech, before he could express his idea, "That the lad being now wedded to his spiritual bride, it was hard to threaten him with a temporal spouse in the same day."   He then laughed a hoarse and brief laugh, and was suddenly grave and silent, as if abashed at his own vivacious effort.

After another toast or two, Jeanie, Mrs. Dolly, and such of the female natives as had honored the feast with their presence, retired to David's new dwelling at Auchingower, and left the gentlemen to their potations.

The feast proceeded with great glee.   The conversation, where Duncan had it under his direction, was not indeed always strictly canonical, but David Deans escaped any risk of being scandalized by engaging with one of his neighbors in a racapitulation of the sufferings of Ayrshire and Lanarkshire, during what was called the invasion of the Highland Host; the prudent Mr. Meiklehose cautioning them from time to time to lower their voices, for "that Duncan Knock's father had been at that onslaught, and brought back muckle gude plenishing, and that Duncan was no unlikely to hae been there himself, for what he kenn'd."

Meanwhile, as the mirth grew fast and furious, the graver members of the party began to escape as well as they could. David Deans accomplished his retreat, and Butler anxiously watched an opportunity to follow him.   Knockdunder, however, desirous, he said, of knowing what stuff was in the new minister, had no intention to part with him so easily, but kept him pinned to his side, watching him sedulously, and with obliging violence filling his glass to the brim as often as he could seize an opportunity of doing so.   At length, as the evening was wearing late, a venerable brother chanced to ask Mr. Archibald when they might hope to see the Duke, *tam carum caput*, as he would venture to term him, at the Lodge of Roseneath.   Duncan of Knock, whose ideas were somewhat conglomerated, and who, it may be believed, was no great scholar, catching up some imperfect sound of the words, conceived the speaker was drawing a parallel between the Duke and Sir Donald Gorme of Sleat; and being of opinion that such comparison was odious, snorted thrice, and prepared himself to be in a passion.

29

To the explanation of the venerable divine the Captain answered, "I heard the word "Gorme" myself, sir, with my ain ears. D'ye think I do not know Gaelic from Latin ?"

"Apparently not, sir," so the clergyman, offended in his turn, and taking a pinch of snuff, answered with great coolness.

The copper nose of the gracious Duncan now became heated like the bull of Phalaris, and while Mr. Archibald mediated betwixt the offended parties, and the attention of the company was engaged by their dispute, Butler took an opportunity to effect his retreat.

He found the females at Auchingower very anxious for the breaking up of the convivial party ; for it was a part of the arrangement that, although David Deans was to remain at Auchingower, and Butler was that night to take possession of the manse, yet Jeanie, for whom complete accommodations were not yet provided in her father's house, was to return for a day or two to the Lodge at Roseneath, and the boats had been held in readiness accordingly. They waited, therefore, for Knockdunder's return, but twilight came and they still waited in vain.   At length Mr. Archibald, who, as a man of decorum, had taken care not to exceed in his conviviality, made his appearance, and advised the females strongly to return to the island under his escort ; observing that, from the humor in which he had left the Captain, it was a great chance whether he budged out of the public-house that night, and it was absolutely certain that he would not be very fit company for ladies. The gig was at their disposal, he said, and there was still pleasant twilight for a party on the water.

Jeanie, who had considerable confidence in Archibald's prudence, immediately acquiesced in this proposal ; but Mrs. Dolly positively objected to the small boat. If the big boat could be gotten, she agreed to set out, otherwise she would sleep on the floor, rather than stir a step. Reasoning with Dolly was out of the question, and Archibald did not think the difficulty so pressing as to require compulsion. He observed, "It was not using the Captain very politely to deprive him of his coach and six ; but as it was in the ladies' service," he gallantly said, "he would use so much freedom ; besides, the gig would serve the Captain's purpose better, as it could come off at any hour of the tide ; the large boat should, therefore, be at Mrs. Dolly's service."

They walked to the beach accordingly, accompanied by Butler. It was some time before the boatmen could be assembled, and ere they were well embarked, and ready to depart, the pale moon was come over the hill, and flinging a trembling reflection on the broad and glittering waves. But so soft and pleasant was the night, that Butler, in bidding farewell to Jeanie, had no apprehension for her safety; and, what is yet more extraordinary, Mrs. Dolly felt no alarm for her own. The air was soft, and came over the cooling wave with something of summer fragrance. The beautiful scene of headlands, and capes, and bays around them, with the broad blue chain of mountains, was dimly visible in the moonlight; while every dash of the oars made the waters glance and sparkle with the brilliant phenomenon called the sea fire.

This last circumstance filled Jeanie with wonder, and served to amuse the mind of her companion, until they approached the little bay, which seemed to stretch its dark and wooded arms into the sea as if to welcome them.

The usual landing-place was at a quarter of a mile's distance from the Lodge, and although the tide did not admit of the large boat coming quite close to the jetty of loose stones which served as a pier, Jeanie, who was both bold and active, easily sprung ashore; but Mrs. Dolly positively refusing to commit herself to the same risk, the complaisant Mr. Archibald ordered the boat round to a more regular landing-place, at a considerable distance along the shore. He then prepared to land himself, that he might, in the meanwhile, accompany Jeanie to the Lodge. But as there was no mistaking the woodland lane which led from thence to the shore, and as the moonlight showed her one of the white chimneys rising out of the wood which embosomed the building, Jeanie declined this favor with thanks, and requested him to proceed with Mrs. Dolly, who, being "in a country where the ways were strange to her, had mair need of countenance."

This, indeed, was a fortunate circumstance, and might even be said to save poor Cowslip's life, if it was true, as she herself used solemnly to aver, that she must positively have expired for fear if she had been left alone in the boat with six wild Highlanders in kilts.

The night was so exquisitely beautiful that Jeanie, instead of immediately directing her course towards the Lodge, stood looking after the boat as it again put off from the side, and rowed out into the little bay, the dark figures of her companions growing less and less distinct as they diminished in the distance, and the jorram, or melancholy boat-song,

of the rowers coming on the ear with softened and sweeter
sound, until the boat rounded the headland and was lost to
her observation.

Still Jeanie remained in the same posture, looking our
upon the sea. It would, she was aware, be some time ere
her companions could reach the Lodge, as the distance by
the more convenient landing-place was considerably greater
than from the point where she stood, and she was not sorry
to have an opportunity to spend the interval by herself.

The wonderful change which a few weeks had wrought
in her situation, from shame and grief, and almost despair,
to honor, joy, and a fair prospect of future happiness, passed
before her eyes with a sensation which brought the tears
into them. Yet they flowed at the same time from another
source. As human happiness is never perfect, and as well-
constructed minds are never more sensible of the distresses
of those whom they love than when their own situation
forms a contrast with them, Jeanie's affectionate regrets
turned to the fate of the poor sister—the child of so many
hopes, the fondled nursling of so many years—now an exile,
and, what was worse, dependent on the will of a man of
whose habits she had every reason to entertain the worst
opinion, and who, even in his strongest paroxysms of remorse,
had appeared too much a stranger to the feelings of real
penitence.

While her thoughts were occupied with these melancholy
reflections, a shadowy figure seemed to detach itself from the
copsewood on her right hand. Jeanie started, and the
stories of apparitions and wraiths, seen by solitary travelers
in wild situations, as such times and in such an hour, suddenly came full upon her imagination. The figure glided
on, and as it came betwixt her and the moon, she was aware
that it had the appearance of a woman. A soft voice twice
repeated, "Jeanie—Jeanie!" Was it indeed—could it be
the voice of her sister? Was she still among the living, or
had the grave given up its tenant? Ere she could state
these questions to her own mind, Effie, alive and in the
body, had clasped her in her arms, and was straining her
to her bosom and devouring her with kisses. "I have wandered here," she said, "like a ghaist, to see you, and nae
wonder you take me for ane. I thought but to see you
gang by, or to hear the sound of your voice; but to speak
to yoursell again, Jeanie, was mair than I deserved, and
mair than I durst pray for."

"O, Effie! how came ye here alone, and at this hour, and

on the wild sea-beach? Are you sure it's your ain living sell?"

There was something of Effie's former humor in her practically answering the question by a gentle pinch, more beseeming the fingers of a fairy than of a ghost.

And again the sisters embraced, and laughed, and wept by turns.

"But ye maun gang up wi' me to the Lodge, Effie," said Jeanie, "and tell me a' your story. I hae gude folk there that will make ye welcome for my sake."

"Na, na, Jeanie," replied her sister, sorrowfully: "ye hae forgotten what I am—a banished outlawed creature, scarce escaped the gallows by your being the bauldest and the best sister that ever lived. I'll gae near nane o' your grand friends, if ever there was nae danger to me."

"There is nae danger—there shall be nae danger," said Jeanie, eagerly. "O, Effie, dinna be wilfu': be guided for anes ; we will be sae happy a' thegither !"

"I have a' the happiness I deserve on this side of the grave, now that I hae seen you," answered Effie ; "and whether there were danger to mysell or no, naebody should ever say that I come with my cheat-the-gallows face to shame my sisters amang her grand friends."

"I hae nae grand friends," said Jeanie ; "nae friends but what are friends of yours—Reuben Butler and my father. O, unhappy lassie, dinna be dour, and turn your back on your happiness again ! We wunna see another acquaintance. Come hame to us, your ain dearest friends ; "it's better sheltering under an auld hedge than under a new-planted wood."

"It's in vain speaking, Jeanie : I maun drink as I hae brewed. I am married, and I maun follow my husband for better for worse."

"Married, Effie !" exclaimed Jeanie. "Misfortunate creature ! and to that awfu'——"

"Hush, hush !" said Effie, clapping one hand on her mouth, and pointing to the thicket with the other ; "he is yonder." She said this in a tone which showed that her husband had found means to inspire her with awe as well as affection.

At this moment a man issued from the wood. It was young Staunton. Even by the imperfect light of the moon, Jeanie could observe that he was handsomely dressed, and had the air of a person of rank.

"Effie," he said, "our time is well-nigh spent ; the skiff

will be aground in the creek, and I dare not stay longer. I
hope your sister will allow me to salute her ?” But Jeanie
shrunk back from him with a feeling of internal abhorrence.
“Well,” he said, “it does not much signify ; if you keep up
the feeling of ill-will, at least you do not act upon it, and I
thank you for your respect to my secret, when a word—
which in your place I would have spoken at once—would
have cost me my life. People say you should keep from the
wife of your bosom the secret that concerns your neck : my
wife and her sister both know mine, and I shall not sleep a
wink the less sound.”

“But are you really married to my sister, sir ?” asked
Jeanie, in great doubt and anxiety ; for the haughty, careless tone in which he spoke seemed to justify her worst
apprehensions.

“I really am legally married, and by own name,” replied
Staunton, more gravely.

“And your father—and your friends——? ”

“And my father and my friends must just reconcile themselves to that which is done and cannot be undone,” replied
Staunton. “However, it is my intention, in order to break
off dangerous connections, and to let my friends come to
their temper, to conceal my marriage for the present, and
stay abroad for some years. So you will not hear of us for
some time, if ever you hear of us again at all. It would be
dangerous, you must be aware, to keep up the correspondence ; for all would guess that the husband of Effie was the
—what shall I call myself ?—the slayer of Porteous.”

“Hard-hearted, light man ! ” thought Jeanie ; “to what
a charactor she has entrusted her happiness ! She has sown
the wind, and maun reap the whirlwind.”

“Dinna think ill o’ him,” said Effie, breaking away from
her husband, and leading Jeanie a step or two out of hearing
—dinna think *very* ill o’ him ; he’s gude to me, Jeanie—as
gude as I deserve. And he is determined to gie up his bad
courses. Sae, after a’, dinna greet for Effie ; she is better
off than she has wrought for. But you—O you !—how can
you be happy enough ! Never till ye get to Heaven, where
a’body is as gude as yoursell. Jeanie, if I live and thrive ye
shall hear of me ; if not, just forget that sic a creature ever
lived to vex ye. Fare ye weel—fare—fare ye weel ! ”

“She tore herself from her sister’s arms ; rejoined her
husband ; they plunged into the copsewood, and she saw
them no more.

The whole scene had the effect of a vision, and she could

almost have believed it such, but that very soon after they quitted her she heard the sounds of oars, and a skiff was seen on the firth, pulling swiftly towards the small smuggling sloop which lay in the offing. It was on board of such a vessel that Effie had embarked at Portobello, and Jeanie had no doubt that the same conveyance was destined, as Staunton had hinted, to transport them to a foreign country.

Although it was impossible to determine whether this interview, while it was passing, gave more pain or pleasure to Jeanie Deans, yet the ultimate impression which remained on her mind was decidedly favorable. Effie was married—made, according to the common phrase, an honest woman; that was one main point. It seemed also as if her husband were about to abandon the path of gross vice, in which he had run so long and so desperately; that was another; for his final and effectual conversion, he did not want understanding, and God knew His own hour.

Such were the thoughts with which Jeanie endeavored to console her anxiety respcting her sister's future fortune. On her arrival at the lodge, she found Archibald in some anxiety at her stay, and about to walk out in quest of her. A headache served as an a apology for retiring to rest, in order to conceal her visible agitation of mind from her companions.

By this secession also, she escaped another scene of a different sort. For, as if there were danger in all gigs, whether by sea or land, that of Knockdunder had been run down by another boat, an accident owing chiefly to the drunkenness of the Captain, his crew, and passengers. Knockdunder, and two or three guests whom he was bringing along with him to finish the conviviality of the evening at the Lodge, got a sound ducking; but, being rescued by the crew of the boat which endangered them, there was no ultimate loss, excepting that of the Captain's laced hat, which, greatly to the satisfaction of the Highland part of the district, as well as to the improvement of the conformity of his own personal appearance, he replaced by a smart Highland bonnet next day. Many were the vehement threats of vengeance which, on the succeeding morning, the gracious Duncan threw out against the boat which had upset him; but as neither she nor the small smuggling vessel to which she belonged was any longer to be seen in the firth, he was compelled to sit down with the affront. This was the more hard, he said, as he was assured the mischief was done on purpose, these scoundrels having lurked about after they had landed every drop of brandy and every bag of tea they had on board ; and he understood the coxswain had been on shore making par-ticular inquiries concerning the time when his boat was to cross over, and to return, and so forth.

"Put the neist time they meet me on the firth," said Duncan, with great majesty, "I will teach the moonlight rapscallions and vagabonds to keep their ain side of the road, and be tamn'd to them!"

CHAPTER XLVII

WITHIN a reasonable time after Butler was safely and comfortably settled in his living, and Jeanie had taken up her abode at Auchingower with her father—the precise extent of which interval we request each reader to settle according to his own sense of what is decent and proper upon the occasion—and after due proclamation of banns and all other formalities, the long wooing of this worthy pair was ended by their union in the holy bands of matrimony. On this occasion, David Deans stoutly withstood the iniquities of pipes, fiddles, and promiscuous dancing, to the great wrath of the Captain of Knockdunder, who said, if he "had guessed it was to be sic a tamn'd Quakers' meeting, he wad hae seen them peyont the cairn before he wad hae darkened their doors."

And so much rancor remained on the spirits of the gracious Duncan upon this occasion, that various "picqueerings," as David called them, took place upon the same and similar topics ; and it was only in consequence of an accidental visit of the Duke to his Lodge at Roseneath that they were put a stop to. But upon that occasion his Grace showed such particular respect to Mr. and Mrs. Butler, and such favor even to aid David, that Knockdunder held it prudent to change his course towards the latter. He in future used to express himself among friends concerning the minister and his wife, as " very worthy decent folk, just a little over strict in their notions ; put it was pest for thae plack cattle to err on the safe side." And respecting David, he allowed that "he was an excellent judge of nowte and sheep, and a sensible eneugh carle, an it werena for his tamn'd Cameronian nonsense, whilk it is not worth while of a shentleman to knock out of an auld silly head, either by force of reason or otherwise." So that, by avoiding topics of dispute, the personages of our tale lived in great good habits with the gracious Duncan, only that he still grieved David's soul, and set a perilous example to the congregation, by sometimes bringing his pipe to the church during a cold winter day, and almost always sleeping during sermon in the summer-time.

Mrs. Butler, whom we must no longer, if we can help it, term by the familiar name of Jeanie, brought into the married state the same firm mind and affectionate disposition, the same natural and homely good sense, and spirit of useful exertion—in a word, all the domestic good qualities of which she had given proof during her maiden life. She did not indeed rival Butler in learning ; but then no woman more devoutly venerated the extent of her husband's erudition. She did not pretend to understand his expositions of divinity; but no minister of the presbytery had his humble dinner so well arranged, his clothes and linen in equal good order, his fireside so neatly swept, his parlor so clean, and his books so well dusted.

If he talked to Jeanie of what she did not understand—and (for the man was mortal, and had been a schoolmaster) he sometimes did harangue more scholarly and wisely than was necessary—she listened in placid silence ; and whenever the point referred to common life, and was such as came under the grasp of a strong natural understanding, her views were more forcible, and her observations more acute, than his own. In acquired politeness of manners, when it happened that she mingled a little in society, Mrs. Butler was, of course, judged deficient. But then she had that obvious wish to oblige, and that real and natural good-breeding depending on good sense and good-humor, which, joined to a considerable degree of archness and liveliness of manner, rendered her behavior acceptable to all with whom she was called upon to associate. Notwithstanding her strict attention to all domestic affairs, she always appeared the clean well-dressed mistress of the house, never the sordid household drudge. When complimented on this occasion by Duncan Knock, who swore, "that he thought the fairies must help her, since her house was always clean, and nobody ever saw anybody sweeping it," she modestly replied, "That much might be dune by timing ane's turns."

Duncan replied, "He heartily wished she could teach that art to the huzzies at the Lodge, for he could never discover that the house was washed at a', except now and then by breaking his shins over the pail, Cot tamn the jauds !"

Of lesser matters there is no occasion to speak much. It may easily be believed that the Duke's cheese was carefully made, and so graciously accepted that the offering became annual. Remembrances and acknowledgments of past favors were sent to Mrs. Bickerton and Mrs. Glass, and an amicable intercourse maintained from time to time with these two respectable and benevolent persons.

It is especially necessary to mention that, in the course of five years, Mrs. Butler, had three children, two boys and a girl, all stout healthy babes of grace, fair-haired, blue-eyed, and strong-limbed. The boys were named David and Reuben, an order of nomenclature which was much to the satisfaction of the old hero of the Covenant, and the girl, by her mother's special desire, was christened Euphemia, rather contrary to the wish of both her father and husband, who nevertheless loved Mrs. Butler too well, and were too much indebted to her for their hours of happiness, to withstand any request which she made with earnestness, and as a gratification to herself. But from some feeling, I know not of what kind, the child was never distinguished by the name of Effie, but by the abbreviation of Femie, which in Scotland is equally commonly applied to persons called Euphemia.

In this state of quiet and unostentatious enjoyment there were, besides the ordinary rubs and ruffles which disturbed even the most uniform life, two things which particularly chequered Mrs. Butler's happiness. "Without these," she said to our informer, "her life would have been but too happy ; and perhaps," she added, "she had need of some crosses in this world to remind her that there was a better to come behind it."

The first of these related to certain polemical skirmishes betwixt her father and her husband, which notwithstanding the mutual respect and affection they entertained for each other, and their great love for her ; notwithstanding also their general agreement in strictness, and even severity, of Presbyterian principle, often threatened unpleasant weather between them. David Deans, as our readers must be aware, was sufficiently opinionative and intractable, and having prevailed on himself to become a member of a kirk-session under the established church, he felt doubly obliged to evince that, in so doing, he had not compromised any whit of his former professions, either in practise or principle. Now Mr. Butler, doing all credit to his father-in-law's motives, was frequently of opinion that it was better to drop out of memory points of division and separation, and to act in the manner most likely to attract and unite all parties who were serious in religion. Moreover, he was not pleased, as a man and a scholar, to be always dictated to by his unlettered father-in-law ; and as a clergyman he did not think it fit to seem forever under the thumb of an elder of his own kirk-session.　A proud but honest thought carried his opposition now and then a little farther than it would otherwise have gone.　" My brethren," he said, " will suppose I am flattering and conciliating the old man for the sake of his succession, if I defer and give way to him on every occasion ; and, besides, there are many on which I neither can nor will conscientiously yield to his notions.　I cannot be persecuting old women for witches, or ferreting out matter of scandal among the young ones, which might otherwise remained concealed."

From this difference of opinion it happened that, in many cases of nicety, such as in owning certain defections, and failing to testify against certain backslidings of the time ; in not always severely tracing forth little matters of scandal and *fama clamosa*, which David called a loosening of the reins of discipline ; and in failing to demand clear testimonies in other points of controversy which had, as it were, drifted to leeward with the change of times, Butler incurred the censure of his father-in-law ; and sometimes the disputes betwixt them became eager and almost unfriendly.　In all such cases Mrs. Butler was a mediating spirit, who endeavored, by the alkaline smoothness of her own disposition, to neutralize the acidity of theological controversy.　To the complaints of both she lent an unprejudiced and attentive ear, and sought always rather to excuse than absolutely to defend the other party.

She reminded her father that Butler had not " his experience of the auld and wrastling times, when folk were gifted wi' a far look into eternity, to make up for the oppressions whilk they suffered here below in time.　She freely allowed that many devout ministers and professors in times past had enjoyed downright revelation, like the blessed Peden, and Lundie, and Cameron, and Renwick, and John Caird the tinkler, wha entered into the secrets ; and Elizabeth Melvil, Lady Culross who prayed in her bed, surrounded by a great many Christians in a large room, in whilk it was placed on purpose, and that for three hours' time, with wonderful assistance ; and Lady Robertland, whilk got six sure outgates of grace ; and mony other in times past ; and of a specialty, Mr. John Scrimgeour, minister of Kinghorn, who, having a beloved child sick to death of the crewels, was free to expostulate with his Maker with such impatience of displeasure, and complaining so bitterly, that at length it was said unto him that he was heard for this time, but that he was requested to use no such boldness in time coming; so that, when he returned, he found the child sitting up in the bed hale and fair, with all its wounds closed, and supping its parritch, whilk babe he had left at the time of death. But though these things might be true in these needful times, she contended that those ministers who had not seen such vouchsafed and especial mercies were to seek their rule in the record of ancient times; and therefore Reuben was carefu' both to search the Scriptures and the books written by wise and good men of old; and sometimes in this way it wad happen that twa precious saints might pu' sundry wise, like twa cows riving at the same hay-band."

To this David used to reply, with a sigh, "Ah, hinny, thou kenn'st little o't; but that same John Scrimgeour, that blew open the gates of Heaven as an it had been wi' a sax-pund cannon-ball, used devoutly to wish that most part of books were burned, except the Bible. Reuben's a gude lad and a kind—I have aye allowed that; but as to his not allowing inquiry anent the scandal of Margery Kittlesides and Rory MacRand, under pretense that they have southered sin wi' marriage, it's clear agane the Christian discipline o' the kirk. And then there's Ailie MacClure of Deepheugh, that practises her abominations, spaeing folks fortunes wi' egg-shells, and mutton-banes, and dreams and divinations, whilk is a scandal to ony Christian land to suffer sic a wretch to live; and I'll uphaud that in a' judicatures, civil or ecclesiastical."

"I daresay ye are very right, father," was the general style of Jeanie's answer; "but ye maun come down to the manse to your dinner the day. The bits o' bairns, puir things, are wearying to see their luckie-dad; and Reuben never sleeps weel, nor I neither, when you and he hae had ony bit outcast."

"Nae outcast, Jeanie; God forbid I suld cast out wi' thee, or aught that is dear to thee!" And he put on his Sunday's coat and came to the manse accordingly.

With her husband, Mrs. Butler had a more direct conciliatory process. Reuben had the utmost respect for the old man's motives, and affection for his person, as well as gratitude for his early friendship; so that, upon any such occasion of accidental irritation, it was only necessary to remind him with delicacy of his father-in-law's age, of his scanty education, strong prejudices, and family distresses. The least of these considerations always inclined Butler to measures of conciliation, in so far as he could accede to them without compromising principle ; and thus our simple and unpretending heroine had the merit of those peace-makers to whom it is pronounced as a benediction that they shall inherit the earth.

The second crook in Mrs. Butler's lot, to use the language of her father, was the distressing circumstance that she had never heard of her sister's safety, or of the circumstances in which she found herself, though betwixt four and five years had elapsed since they had parted on the beach of the island of Roseneath. Frequent intercourse was not to be expected—not to be desired, perhaps, in their relative situa-tions ; but Effie had promised that, if she lived and pros-pered, her sister should hear from her. She must then be no more, or sunk into some abyss of misery, since she had never redeemed her pledge. Her silence seemed strange and portentous, and wrung from Jeanie, who could never forget the early years of their intimacy, the most painful anticipa-tion concerning her fate. At length, however, the veil was drawn aside.

One day, as the Captain of Knockdunder had called in at the manse, on his return from some business in the High-land part of the parish, and had been accommodated, accord-ing to his special request, with a mixture of milk, brandy, honey, and water, which he said Mrs. Butler compounded "petter than ever a woman in Scotland"—for in all inno-cent matters she studied the taste of every one around her—he said to Butler, "Py the py, minister, I have a letter here either for your canny pody of a wife or you, which I got when I was last at Glasco ; the postage comes to fourpence, which you may either pay me forthwith, or give me tooble or quits in a hit at packcammon."

The playing at backgammon and draughts had been a frequent amusement of Mr. Whackbairn, Butler's principal, when at Liberton school. The minister, therefore, still piqued himself on his skill at both games, and occasionally practised them, as strictly canonical, although David Deans, whose notions of every kind were more rigorous, used to shake his head and groan grievously when he espied the tables lying in the parlor, or the children playing with the dice-boxes or backgammon men. Indeed, Mrs. Butler was sometimes chidden for removing these implements of pas-time into some closet or corner out of sight. "Let them be where they are, Jeanie," would Butler say upon such occasions; "I am not conscious of following this or any other trifling relaxation to the interruption of my more serious studies and still more serious duties. I will not, therefore, have it supposed that I am indulging by stealth, and against my conscience, in an amusement which, using it so little as I do, I may well practise openly, and without any check of mind. *Nil conscire sibi*, Jeanie, that is my motto; which signifies, my love, the honest and open confidence which a man ought to entertain when he is acting openly, and without any sense of doing wrong."

Such being Butler's humor, he accepted the Captain's defiance to a twopenny hit at backgammon, and handed the letter to his wife, observing, "the post-mark was York, but if it came from her friend Mrs. Bickerton, she had considerably improved her handwriting, which was uncommon at her years."

Leaving the gentlemen to their game, Mrs. Butler went to order something for supper, for Captain Duncan had proposed kindly to stay the night with them, and then carelessly broke open her letter. It was not from Mrs. Bickerton, and, after glancing over the first few lines, she soon found it necessary to retire into her own bedroom, to read the document at leisure.

CHAPTER XLVIII.

THE letter, which Mrs. Butler, when retired into her own apartment, perused with anxious wonder, was certainly from Effie, although it had no other signature than the letter E.; and although the orthography, style, and penmanship were very far superior not only to anything which Effie could produce, who, though a lively girl, had been a remarkably careless scholar, but even to her more considerate sister's own powers of composition and expression. The manuscript was a fair Italian hand, though something stiff and constrained ; the spelling and the diction that of a person who had been accustomed to read good composition, and mix in good society.

The tenor of the letter was as follows :—

" MY DEAREST SISTER,

" At many risks I venture to write to you, to inform you that I am still alive, and, as to worldly situation, that I rank higher than I could expect or merit. If wealth and distinction, and an honorable rank could make a woman happy, I have them all ; but you, Jeanie, whom the world might think placed far beneath me in all these respects, are far happier than I am.   I have had means of hearing of your welfare, my dearest Jeanie, from time to time ; I think I should have broken my heart otherwise. I have learned with great pleasure of your increasing family. We have not been worthy of such a blessing ; two infants have been successively removed, and we are now childless—God's will be done ! But if we had a child it would perhaps divert him from the gloomy thoughts which make him terrible to himself and others.   Yet do not let me frighten you, Jeanie, he continues to be kind, and I am far better off than I deserve. You will wonder at my better scholarship ; but when I was abroad I had the best teachers, and I worked hard because my progress pleased him. He is kind, Jeanie, only he has much to distress him, especially when he looks backward. When I look backward myself I have always a ray of comfort; it is in the generous conduct of a sister who forsook me not when I was forsaken by every one. You have had your reward. You live happy in the esteem and love of all who know you, and I drag on the life of a miserable impostor, indebted for the marks of regard I receive to a tissue of deceit and lies, which the slightest accident may unravel. He has produced me to his friends, since the estate opened to him, as the daughter of a Scotchman of rank, banished on account of the Viscount of Dundee's wars —that is our Fr's old friend Clavers, you know—and he says I was educated in a Scotch convent; indeed, I lived in such a place long enough to enable me to support the character. But when a countryman approaches me, and begins to talk, as they all do, of the various families engaged in Dundee's affair, and to make inquiries into my connections, and when I see *his* eye bent on mine with such an expression of agony, my terror brings me to the very risk of detection. Good-nature and politeness have hitherto saved me, as they prevented people from pressing on me with distressing questions. But how long—O how long will this be the case! And if I bring this disgrace on him, he will hate me; he will kill me, for as much as he loves me; he is as jealous of his family honor now as ever he was careless about it. I have been in England four months, and have often thought of writing to you; and yet such are the dangers that might arise from an intercepted letter that I have hitherto forborne. But now I am obliged to run the risk. Last week I saw your great friend, the D. of A. He came to my box, and sate by me; and something in the play put him in mind of you. Gracious Heaven! he told over your whole London journey to all who were in the box, but particularly to the wretched creature who was the occasion of it all. If he had known—if he could have conceived, beside whom he was sitting, and to whom the story was told! I suffered with courage, like an Indian at the stake, while they are rending his fibers and boring his eyes, and while he smiles applause at each well-imagined contrivance of his torturers. It was too much for me at last, Jeanie: I fainted; and my agony was imputed partly to the heat of the place, and partly to my extreme sensibility; and, hypocrite all over, I encouraged both opinions—anything but discovery! Luckily *he* was not there. But the incident has led to more alarms. I am obliged to meet your great

30

man often ; and he seldom sees me without talking of E. D.
and J. D., and R. B. and D. D., as persons in whom my
amiable sensibility is interested.   My amiable sensibility ! ! !
And then the cruel tone of light indifference with which
persons in the fashionable world speak together on the
most affecting subjects ! To hear my guilt, my folly, my
agony, the foibles and weaknesses of my friends, even your
heroic exertions, Jeanie, spoken of in the drolling style
which is the present tone in fashionable life ! Scarce all .
that I formerly endured is equal to this state of irritation :
then it was blows and stabs ; now it is pricking to death
with needles and pins.   He—I mean the D.—goes down
next month to spend the shooting-season in Scotland.   He
says he makes a point of always dining one day at the
manse ; be on your guard, and do not betray yourself, should
he mention me.   Yourself—alas ! *you* have nothing to betray—nothing to fear ; you, the pure, the virtuous, the
heroine of unstained faith, unblemished purity, what can
you have to fear from the world or its proudest minions ?
It is E. whose life is once more in your hands ; it is E.
whom you are to save from being plucked of her borrowed
plumes, discovered, branded, and trodden down—first by
him, perhaps, who has raised her to this dizzy pinnacle.
The inclosure will reach you twice a-year.   Do not refuse
it ; it is out of my own allowance, and may be twice as
much when you want it.   With you it may do good ; with
me it never can.

"Write to me soon, Jeanie, or I shall remain in the
agonizing apprehension that this has fallen into wrong hands.
Address simply to "L. S.," under cover to the Reverend
George Whiterose, in the Minster Close, York.   He thinks
I correspond with some of my noble Jacobite relations who
are in Scotland.   How High Church and Jacobitical zeal
would burn in his cheeks if he knew he was the agent, not
of Euphemia Setoun, of the honorable house of Winton,
but of E. D., daughter of a Cameronian cow-feeder !
Jeanie, I can laugh yet sometimes—but God protect you
from such mirth.   My father—I mean your father—
would say it was like the idle crackling of thorns ; but
the thorns keep their poignancy, they remain unconsumed.
Farewell, my dearest Jeanie.   Do not show this even to
Mr. Butler, much less to any one else.   I have every respect for him ; but his principles are over strict, and my
case will not endure severe handling.—I rest your affectionate sister, E."

In this long letter there was much to surprise as well as distress Mrs. Butler. That Effie—her sister Effie should be mingling freely in society, and apparently on not unequal terms with the Duke of Argyle, sounded like something so extraordinary that she even doubted if she read truly. Nor was it less marvelous that, in the space of four years, her education should have made such progress. Jeanie's humility readily allowed that Effie had always, when she chose it, been smarter at her book than she herself was , but then she was very idle, and, upon the whole, had made much less proficiency. Love, or fear, or necessity, however, had proved an able schoolmistress, and completely supplied all her deficiencies.

What Jeanie least liked in the tone of the letter was a smothered degree of egotism. "We should have heard little about her," said Jeanie to herself, "but that she was feared the Duke might come to learn wha she was, and a' about her puir friends here ; but Effe, puir thing, aye looks her ain way, and folk that do that think mair o' themselves than of their neighbors. I am no clear about keeping her siller," she added, taking up a £50 note which had fallen out of the paper to the floor. " We hae eneugh, and it looks unco like theft-boot, or hush-money, as they ca' it : she might hae been sure that I wad say naething wad harm her, for a' the gowd in Lunnon. And I maun tell the minister about it. I dinna see that she suld be sae feared for her ain bonny bargain o' a gudeman, and that I shouldna reverence Mr. Butler just as much ; and sae I'll e'en tell him when that tippling body, the Captain, has ta'en boat in the morning. But I wonder at my ain state of mind," she added, turning back, after she had made a step or two to the door to join the gentlemen ; "surely I am no sic a fule as to be angry that Effie's a braw lady, while I am only a minister's wife ? and yet I am as petted as a bairn, when I should bless God, that has redeemed her from shame, and poverty, and guilt, as ower likely she might hae been plunged into."

Sitting down upon a stool at the foot of the bed, she folded her arms upon her bosom, saying within herself, " From this place will I not rise till I am in a better frame of mind ; " and so placed, by dint of tearing the veil from the motives of her little temporary spleen against her sister, she compelled herself to be ashamed of them, and to view as blessings the advantages of her sister's lot, while its embarrassments were the necessary consequences of errors long since committed. And thus she fairly vanquished the feeling of pique which she naturally enough entertained at seeing Effie, so long the object of her care and her pity, soar suddenly so high above her in life as to reckon amongst the chief objects of her apprehension the risk of their relationship being discovered.

When this unwonted burst of *amour propre* was thoroughly subdued, she walked down to the little parlor where the gentlemen were finishing their game, and heard from the Captain a confirmation of the news intimated in her letter, that the Duke of Argyle was shortly expected at Roseneath.

"He'll find plenty of moor-fowls and plack-cock on the moors of Auchingower, and he'll pe nae doubt for taking a late dinner and a ped at the manse, as he has done pefore now."

"He has a gude right, Captain," said Jeanie.

"Teil ane petter to ony ped in the kintra," answered the Captain. "And ye had petter tell your father, puir body, to get his beasts a' in order, and put his tamn'd Cameronian nonsense out o' his head for twa or three days, if he can pe so opliging; for fan I speak to him apout prute pestial, he answers me out o' the Pible, whilk is not using a shentleman weel, unless it be a person of your cloth, Mr. Putler."

No one understood better than Jeanie the merit of the soft answer which turneth away wrath; and she only smiled, and hoped that his Grace would find everything that was under her father's care to his entire satisfaction.

But the Captain, who had lost the whole postage of the letter at backgammon, was in the pouting mood not unusual to losers, and which, says the proverb, must be allowed to them.

"And, Master Putler, though you know I never meddle with the things of your kirk-sessions, yet I must be allowed to say that I will not pe pleased to allow Ailie MacClure of Deepheugh to be poonished as a witch, in respect she only spaes fortunes, and does not lame, or plind, or pedevil any persons, or coup cadgers' carts, or ony sort of mischief; put only tells people good fortunes, as anent our poats killing so many seals and doug-fishes, whilk is very pleasant to hear."

"The woman," said Butler, "is, I believe, no witch, but a cheat; and it is only on that head that she is summoned to the kirk-session, to cause her to desist in future from practising her impostures upon ignorant persons."

" I do not know," replied the gracious Duncan, "what her practices or her postures are, but I pelieve that if the poys take hould on her to duck her in the clachan purn, it will be a very sorry practise ; and I pelieve, moreover, that if I come in thirdsman among you at the kirk-sessions, you will be all in a tamn'd pad posture indeed."

Without noticing this threat, Mr. Butler replied, " That he had not attended to the risk of ill-usage which the poor woman might undergo at the hands of the rabble, and that he would give her the necessary admonition in private, instead of bringing her before the assembled session."

"This," Duncan said, " was speaking like a reasonable shentleman ;" and so the evening passed peaceably off.

Next morning, after the Captain had swallowed his morning draught of Athole brose, and departed in his coach and six, Mrs. Butler anew deliberated upon communicating to her husband her sister's letter. But she was deterred by the recollection that, in doing so, she would unveil to him the whole of a dreadful secret, of which, perhaps, his public character might render him an unfit depository. Butler already had reason to believe that Effie had eloped with that same Robertson who had been a leader in the Porteous mob, and who lay under sentence of death for the robbery at Kirkcaldy. But he did not know his identity with George Staunton, a man of birth and fortune, who had now apparently reassumed his natural rank in society. Jeanie had respected Staunton's own confession as sacred, and upon reflection she considered the letter of her sister as equally so, and resolved to mention the contents to no one.

On reperusing the letter, she could not help observing the staggering and unsatisfactory condition of those who have risen to distinction by undue paths, and the outworks and bulwarks of fiction and falsehood by which they are under the necessity of surrounding and defending their precarious advantages. But she was not called upon, she thought to unveil her sister's original history : it would restore no right to any one, for she was usurping none ; it would only destroy her happiness, and degrade her in the public estimation. Had she been wise, Jeanie thought she would have chosen seclusion and privacy, in place of public life and gaiety ; but the power of choice might not be hers. The money, she thought, could not be returned without her seeming haughty and unkind. She resolved, therefore, upon reconsidering this point, to employ it as occasion should serve, either in educating her children better than her own means could compass, or for their future portion. Her sister had enough, was strongly bound to assist Jeanie by any means in her power, and the arrangement was so natural and proper, that it ought not to be declined out of fastidious or romantic delicacy. Jeanie accordingly wrote to her sister, acknowledging her letter, and requesting to hear from her as often as she could. In entering into her own little details of news, chiefly respecting domestic affairs, she experienced a singular vacillation of ideas ; for sometimes she apologized for mentioning things unworthy the notice of a lady of rank, and then recollected that everything which concerned her should be interesting to Effie. Her letter, under the cover of Mr. Whiterose, she committed to the post-office at Glasgow, by the intervention of a parishioner who had business at that city.

The next week brought the Duke to Roseneath, and shortly afterwards he intimated his intention of sporting in their neighborhood, and taking his bed at the manse ; an honor which he had once or twice done to its inmates on former occasions.

Effie proved to be perfectly right in her anticipations. The Duke had hardly set himself down at Mrs. Butler's right hand, and taken upon himself the task of carving the excellent "barndoor chucky," which had been selected as the high dish upon this honorable occasion, before he began to speak of Lady Staunton of Willingham, in Lincolnshire, and the great noise which her wit and beauty made in London. For much of this Jeanie was, in some measure, prepared ; but Effie's wit ! that would never have entered into her imagination, being ignorant how exactly raillery in the higher rank resembles flippancy among their inferiors.

"She has been the ruling belle—the blazing star—the universal toast of the winter," said the Duke ; "and is really the most beautiful creature that was seen at court upon the birthday."

The birthday ! and at court ! Jeanie was annihilated, remembering well her own presentation, all its extraordinary circumstances, and particularly the cause of it.

"I mention this lady particularly to you, Mrs. Butler," said the Duke, "because she has something in the sound of her voice and cast of her countenance that reminded me of you : not when you look so pale though ; you have over-fatigued yourself ; you must pledge me in a glass of wine."

She did so, and Butler observed, "It was dangerous flattery in his Grace to tell a poor minister's wife that she was like a court-beauty."

"Oho ! Mr. Butler," said the Duke, "I find you are growing jealous ; but it's rather too late in the day, for you know how long I have admired your wife. But seriously, there is betwixt them one of those inexplicable likenesses which we see in countenances that do not otherwise resemble each other."

"The perilous part of the compliment has flown off," thought Mr. Butler.

His wife, feeling the awkwardness of silence, forced herself to say, "That perhaps the lady might be her countrywoman, and the language might make some resemblance."

"You are quite right," replied the Duke. "She is a Scotchwoman, and speaks with a Scotch accent, and now and then a provincial word drops out so prettily that it is quite Doric, Mr. Butler."

"I should have thought," said the clergyman, "that would have sounded vulgar in the great city."

"Not at all," replied the Duke ; "you must suppose it is not the broad coarse Scotch that is spoken in the Cowgate of Edinburgh, or in the Gorbals. This lady has been very little in Scotland, in fact. She was educated in a convent abroad, and speaks that pure court-Scotch which was common in my younger days ; but it is so generally disused now, that it sounds like a different dialect, entirely distinct from our modern *patois*."

Notwithstanding her anxieties, Jeanie could not help admiring within herself, how the most correct judges of life and manners can be imposed on by their own preconceptions, while the Duke proceeded thus : "She is of the unfortunate house of Winton, I believe ; but, being bred abroad, she had missed the opportunity of learning her own pedigree, and was obliged to me for informing her that she must certainly come of the Setouns of Windygoul. I wish you could have seen how prettily she blushed at her own ignorance. Amidst her noble and elegant manners, there is now and then a little touch of bashfulness and conventual rusticity, if I may call it so, that makes her quite enchanting. You see at once the rose that had bloomed untouched amid the chaste precincts of the cloister, Mr. Butler."

True to the hint, Mr. Butler failed not to start with his

"Ut flos in septis secretus nascitur hortis," etc. ;

while his wife could hardly persuade herself that all this was spoken of Effie Deans, and by so competent a judge as the Duke of Argyle ; and had she been acquainted with Catullus, would have thought the fortunes of her sister had reversed the whole passage.

She was, however, determined to obtain some indemnification for the anxious feelings of the moment, by gaining all the intelligence she could ; and therefore ventured to make some inquiry about the husband of the lady his Grace admired so much.

" He is very rich," replied the Duke ; " of an ancient family, and has good manners ; but he is far from being such a general favorite as his wife.   Some people say he can be very pleasant.   I never saw him so ; but should rather judge him reserved, and gloomy, and capricious.   He was very wild in his youth, they say, and has bad health ; yet he is a good-looking man enough—a great friend of your Lord High Commissioner of the Kirk, Mr. Butler."

" Then he is the friend of a very worthy and honorable nobleman," said Butler.

" Does he admire his lady as much as other people do ? " said Jeanie, in a low voice.

" Who—Sir George ?   They say he is very fond of her," said the Duke ; " but I observe she trembles a little when he fixes his eye on her, and that is no good sign.   But it is strange how I am haunted by this resemblance of yours to Lady Staunton, in look and tone of voice.   One would almost swear you were sisters."

Jeanie's distress became uncontrollable, and beyond concealment.   The Duke of Argyle was much disturbed, good-naturedly ascribing it to his having unwittingly recalled to her remembrance her family misfortunes.   He was too well-bred to attempt to apologize ; but hastened to change the subject, and arrange certain points of dispute which had occurred betwixt Duncan of Knock and the minister, acknowledging that his worthy substitute was sometimes a little too obstinate, as well as too energetic, in his executive measures.

Mr. Butler admitted his general merits ; but said, " He would presume to apply to the worthy gentleman the words of the poet to Marrucinus Asinius,

Manu . . .
Non belle uteris in joco atcue vino.'

The discourse being thus turned on parish business, nothing farther occurred that can interest the reader.

CHAPTER XLIX

AFTER this period, but under the most strict precautions against discovery, the sisters corresponded occasionally, exchanging letters about twice every year. Those of Lady Staunton spoke of her husband's health and spirits as being deplorably uncertain ; her own seemed also to be sinking, and one of the topics on which she most frequently dwelt was their want of family. Sir George Staunton, always violent, had taken some aversion at the next heir, whom he suspected of having irritated his friends against him during his absence ; and he declared, he would bequeath Willingham and all its lands to an hospital, ere that fetch-and-carry tell-tale should inherit an acre of it.

"Had he but a child," said the unfortunate wife, "or had that luckless infant survived, it would be some motive for living and for exertion. But Heaven has denied us a blessing which we have not deserved."

Such complaints, in varied form, but turning frequently on the same topic, filled the letters which passed from the spacious but melancholy halls of Willingham to the quiet and happy parsonage at Knocktarlitie. Years meanwhile rolled on amid these fruitless repinings. John Duke of Argyle and Greenwich died in the year 1743, universally lamented, but by none more than by the Butlers, to whom his benevolence had been so distinguished. He was succeeded by his brother Duke Archibald, with whom they had not the same intimacy ; but who continued the protection which his brother had extended towards them. This, indeed, became more necessary than ever ; for, after the breaking out and suppression of the rebellion in 1745, the peace of the country adjacent to the Highlands was considerably disturbed. Marauders, or men that had been driven to that desperate mode of life, quartered themselves in the fastnesses nearest to the Lowlands, which were their scene of plunder ; and there is scarce a glen in the romantic and now peaceable Highlands of Perth, Stirling, and Dunbartonshire where one or more did not take up their residence.

The prime pest of the parish of Knocktarlitie was a certain Donacha Dhu na Dunaigh, or Black Duncan the Mischievous, whom we have already casually mentioned. This fellow had been originally a tinkler or " caird," many of whom stroll about these districts ; but when all police was disorganized by the civil war, he threw up his profession, and from half thief became whole robber ; and being generally at the head of three or four active young fellows, and he himself artful, bold, and well acquainted with the passes, he plied his new profession with emolument to himself and infinite plague to the country.

All were convinced that Duncan of Knock could have put down his namesake Donacha any morning he had a mind ; for there were in the parish a set of stout young men who had joined Argyle's banner in the war under his old friend, and behaved very well upon several occasions. And as for their leader, as no one doubted his courage, it was generally supposed that Donacha had found out the mode of conciliating his favor, a thing not very uncommon in that age and country. This was the more readily believed, as David Deans's cattle, being the property of the Duke, were left untouched, when the minister's cows were carried off by the thieves. Another attempt was made to renew the same act of rapine, and the cattle were in the act of being driven off, when Butler, laying his profession aside in a case of such necessity, put himself at the head of some of his neighbors, and rescued the creagh ; an exploit at which Deans attended in person, notwithstanding his extreme old age, mounted on a Highland pony, and girded with an old broadsword, likening himself (for he failed not to arrogate the whole merit of the expedition) to David the son of Jesse, when he recovered the spoil of Ziklag from the Amalekites. This spirited behavior had so far a good effect, that Donacha Dhu da Dunaigh kept his distance for some time to come ; and, though his distant exploits were frequently spoken of, he did not exercise any depredations in that part of the country. He continued to flourish, and to be heard of occasionally, until the year 1751, when, if the fear of the second David had kept him in check, fate released him from that restraint, for the venerable patriarch of St. Leonard's was that year gathered to his fathers.

David Deans died full of years and of honor. He is be-**lieved,** for the exact time of his birth is not known, to have lived upwards of ninety years ; for he used to speak of events as falling under his own knowledge which happened about the time of the battle of Bothwell Bridge. It was said that he even bore arms there, for once, when a drunken Jacobite laird wished for a Bothwell Brig Whig, that " he might stow the lugs out of his head," David informed him with a peculiar austerity of countenance that, if he liked to try such a prank, there was one at his elbow ; and it required the interference of Butler to preserve the peace.

He expired in the arms of his beloved daughter, thankful for all the blessings which Providence had vouchsafed to him while in this valley of strife and toil, and thankful also for the trials he had been visited with ; having found them, he said, needful to mortify that spiritual pride and confidence in his own gifts which was the side on which the wily Enemy did most sorely beset him. He prayed in the most affecting manner for Jeanie, her husband, and her family, and that her affectionate duty to " the puir auld man " might purchase her length of days here and happiness hereafter ; then in a pathetic petition, too well understood by those who knew his family circumstances, he besought the Shepherd of souls, while gathering His flock, not to forget the little one that had strayed from the fold, and even then might be in the hands of the ravening wolf. He prayed for the national Jerusalem, that peace might be in her land and prosperity in her palaces ; for the welfare of the honorable house of Argyle, and for the conversion of Duncan of Knockdunder. After this he was silent, being exhausted, nor did he again utter anything distinctly. He was heard, indeed, to mutter something about national defections, right-hand extremes, and left-hand fallings off ; but as May Hettly observed, his head was " carried " at the time ; and it is probable that these expressions occurred to him merely out of general habit, and that he died in the full spirit of charity with all men. About an hour afterwards he slept in the Lord.

Notwithstanding her father's advanced age, his death was a severe shock to Mrs. Butler. Much of her time had been dedicated to attending to his health and his wishes, and she felt as if part of her business in the world was ended when the good old man was no more. His wealth, which came nearly to £1500, in disposable capital, served to raise the fortunes of the family at the manse. How to dispose of this sum for the best advantage of his family was matter of anxious consideration to Butler.

" If we put it on heritable bond, we shall maybe lose the

interest ; for there's that bond over Lounsbeck's land, your father could neither get principal nor interest for it. If we bring it into the funds, we shall maybe lose the principal and all, as many did in the South Sea scheme. The little estate of Craigsture is in the market ; it lies within two miles of the manse, and Knock says his Grace has no thought to buy it. But they ask £2500, and they may, for it is worth the money ; and were I to borrow the balance, the creditor might call it up suddenly, or in case of my death my family might be distressed."

"And so, if we had mair siller, we might buy that bonny pasture-ground, where the grass comes so early ? " asked Jeanie.

"Certainly, my dear ; and Knockdunder, who is a good judge, is strongly advising me to it. To be sure it is his nephew that is selling it."

"Aweel, Reuben," said Jeanie, "ye maun just look up a text in Scripture, as ye did when ye wanted siller before. Just look up a text in the Bible."

"Ah, Jeanie," said Butler, laughing and pressing her hand at the same time, "the best people in these times can only work miracles once."

"We will see," said Jeanie, composedly ; and going to the closet in which she kept her honey, her sugar, her pots of jelly, her vials of the more ordinary medicines, and which served her, in short, as a sort of store-room, she jangled vials and gallipots, till, from out the darkest nook, well flanked by a triple row of bottles and jars, which she was under the necessity of displacing, she brought a cracked brown can, with a piece of leather tied over the top. Its contents seemed to be written papers, thrust in disorder into this uncommon *secretaire.* But from among these Jeanie brought an old clasped Bible, which had been David Deans's companion in his earlier wanderings, and which he had given to his daughter when the failure of his eyes had compelled him to use one of a larger print. This she gave to Butler, who had been looking at her motions with some surprise, and desired him to see what that book could do for him. He opened the clasps, and to his astonishment a parcel of £50 bank-notes dropped out from betwixt the leaves, where they had been separately lodged, and fluttered upon the floor. "I didna think to hae tauld you o' my wealth, Reuben," said his wife, smiling at his surprise, "till on my deathbed, or maybe on some family pinch ; but it wad be better laid out on yon bonny grass-holms, than lying useless here in this auld pigg."

"How on earth came ye by that siller, Jeanie ? Why, here is more than a thousand pounds," said Butler, lifting up and counting the notes.

"If it were ten thousand, it's a' honestly come by," said Jeanie ; "and troth I kenna how muckle there is o't, but it's a' there that ever I got. And as for how I came by it, Reuben—it's weel come by and honestly, as I said before. And it's mair folks' secret than mine, or ye wad hae kenn'd about it lang syne ; and as for ony thing else, I am not free to answer mair questions about it, and ye maun just ask me nane."

"Answer me but one," said Butler. "Is it all freely and indisputably your own property, to dispose of it as you think fit ? Is it possible no one has a claim in so large a sum except you ?"

"It *was* mine, free to dispose of it as I like," answered Jeanie ; "and I have disposed of it already, for now it is yours, Reuben. You are Bible Butler now, as weel as your forbear, that my puir father had sic an ill-will at. Only, if ye like, I wad wish Femie to get a gude share o't when we are gane."

"Certainly, it shall be as you choose. But who on earth ever pitched on such a hiding-place for temporal treasures ?"

"That is just ane o' my auld-fashioned gates, as you ca' them, Reuben. I thought, if Donacha Dhu was to make an outbreak upon us, the Bible was the last thing in the house he wad meddle wi'. But an ony mair siller should drap in, as it is not unlikely, I shall e'en pay it ower to you, and ye may lay it out your ain way."

"And I positively must not ask you how you have come by all this money ?" said the clergyman.

"Indeed, Reuben, you must not ; for if you were 'asking me very sair I wad maybe tell you, and then I am sure I would do wrong."

"But tell me," said Butler, "is it anything that distresses your own mind ?"

"There is baith weal and woe come aye wi' warld's gear, Reuben ; but ye maun ask me naething mair. This siller binds me to naething, and can never be speered back again."

"Surely," said Mr. Butler, when he had again counted over the money, as if to assure himself that the notes were real, "there was never man in the world had a wife like mine : a blessing seems to follow her."

"Never," said Jeanie, "since the enchanted Princess in the bairns' fairy tale, that kamed gold nobles out o' the tae side of her haffit locks and Dutch dollars out o' the tother. But gang away now, minister, and put by the siller, and dinna keep the notes wampishing in your hand that gate, or I shall wish them in the brown pigg again, for fear we get a back-cast about them : we're ower near the hills in these times to be thought to hae siller in the house. And, besides, ye maun gree wi' Knockdunder, that has the selling o' the lands ; and dinna you be simple and let him ken o' this windfa', but keep him to the very lowest penny, as if ye had to borrow siller to make the price up."

In the last admonition Jeanie showed distinctly that, although she did not understand how to secure the money which came into her hands otherwise than by saving and hoarding it, yet she had some part of her father David's shrewdness, even upon worldly subjects. And Reuben Butler was a prudent man, and went and did even as his wife had advised him.

The news quickly went abroad into the parish that the minister had bought Craigsture ; and some wished him joy, and some "were sorry it had gane out of the auld name." However, his clerical brethren, understanding that he was under the necessity of going to Edinburgh about the ensuing Whitsunday, to get together David Deans's cash to make up the purchase-money of his new acquisition, took the opportunity to name him their delegate to the General Assembly, or Convocation of the Scottish Church, which takes place usually in the latter end of the month of May.

CHAPTER L

But who is this what thing of sea or land—
Female of sex it seems—
That so bedeck'd, ornate, and gay,
Comes this way sailing?

MILTON.

NOT long after the incident of the Bible and the bank-notes, Fortune showed that she could surprise Mrs. Butler as well as her husband.   The minister, in order to accomplish the various pieces of business which his unwonted visit to Edinburgh rendered necessary, had been under the necessity of setting out from home in the latter end of the month of February, concluding justly that he would find the space betwixt his departure and the term of Whitsunday (24th May) short enough for the purpose of bringing forward those various debtors of old David Deans out of whose purses a considerable part of the price of his new purchase was to be made good.

Jeanie was thus in the unwonted situation of inhabiting a lonely house, and she felt yet more solitary from the death of the good old man, who used to divide her cares with her husband.   Her children were her principal resource, and to them she paid constant attention.

It happened, a day or two after Butler's departure, that, while she was engaged in some domestic duties, she heard a dispute among the young folks, which, being maintained with obstinacy, appeared to call for her interference.   All came to their natural umpire with their complaints.   Femie, not yet ten years old, charged Davie and Reubie with an attempt to take away her book by force; and David and Reuben replied—the elder, "That it was not a book for Femie to read," and Reuben, "That it was about a bad woman."

"Where did you get the book, ye little hempie?" said Mrs. Butler.   "How dare ye touch papa's books when he is away?"

But the little lady, holding fast a sheet of crumpled paper, declared, "It was nane o' papa's books, and May Hettly had taken it off the muckle cheese which came from Inverara;"

for, as was very natural to suppose, a friendly intercourse, with interchange of mutual civilities, was kept up from time to time between Mrs. Dolly Dutton, now Mrs. MacCorkindale, and her former friends.

Jeanie took the subject of contention out of the child's hand, to satisfy herself of the propriety of her studies ; but how much was she struck when she read upon the title of the broadside sheet, "The Last Speech, Confession, and Dying Words of Margaret MacCraw, or Murdockson, executed on Harabee Hill, near Carlisle, the—day of——, 1737." It was, indeed, one of those papers which Archibald had bought at Longtown, when he monopolized the pedler's stock, which Dolly had thrust into her trunk out of sheer economy. One or two copies, it seems, had remained in her repositories at Inverary, till she changed to need them in packing a cheese, which, as a very superior production, was sent in the way of civil challenge to the dairy at Knocktarlitie.

The title of this paper, so strangely fallen into the very hands from which, in well-meant respect to her feelings, it had been so long detained, was of itself sufficiently startling ; but the narrative itself was so interesting that Jeanie, shaking herself loose from the children, ran upstairs to her own apartment, and bolted the door, to peruse it without interruption.

The narrative, which appeared to have been drawn up, or at least corrected, by the clergyman who attended this unhappy woman, stated the crime for which she suffered to have been "her active part in that atrocious robbery and murder, committed near two years since near Haltwhistle, for which the notorious Frank Levitt was committed for trial at Lancaster assizes. It was supposed the evidence of the accomplice, Thomas Tuck, commonly called Tyburn Tom, upon which the woman had been convicted, would weigh equally heavy against him ; although many were inclined to think it was Tuck himself who had struck the fatal blow, according to the dying statement of Meg Murdockson."

After a circumstantial account of the crime for which she suffered, there was a brief sketch of Margaret's life. It was stated that she was a Scotchwoman by birth, and married a soldier in the Cameronian regiment ; that she long followed the camp, and had doubtless acquired in fields of battle, and similar scenes, that ferocity and love of plunder for which she had been afterwards distinguished ; that her husband, having obtained his discharge, became servant to a beneficed clergyman of high situation and character in Lincolnshire, and that she acquired the confidence and esteem of that honorable family. She had lost this many years after her husband's death, it was stated, in consequence of conniving, at the irregularities of her daughter with the heir of the family, added to the suspicious circumstances attending the birth of a child, which was strongly suspected to have met with foul play, in order to preserve, if possible, the girl's reputation. After this, she had led a wandering life both in England and Scotland, under color sometimes of telling fortunes, sometimes of driving a trade in smuggled wares, but, in fact, receiving stolen goods, and occasionally actively joining in the exploits by which they were obtained. Many of her crimes she had boasted of after conviction, and there was one circumstance for which she seemed to feel a mixture of joy and occasional compunction. When she was residing in the suburbs of Edinburgh during the preceding summer, a girl, who had been seduced by one of her confederates, was entrusted to her charge, and in her house delivered of a male infant. Her daughter, whose mind was in a state of derangement ever since she had lost her own child, according to the criminal's account, carried off the poor girl's infant, taking it for her own, of the reality of whose death she at times could not be persuaded.

Margaret Murdockson stated that she for some time believed her daughter had actually destroyed the infant in her mad fits, and that she gave the father to understand so, but afterwards learned that a female stroller had got it from her. She showed some compunction at having separated mother and child, especially as the mother had nearly suffered death, being condemned, on the Scottish law, for the supposed murder of her infant. When it was asked what possible interest she could have had in exposing the unfortunate girl to suffer for a crime she had not committed, she asked, if they thought she was going to put her own daughter into trouble to save another. She did not know what the Scottish law would have done to her for carrying the child away. This answer was by no means satisfactory to the clergyman, and he discovered, by close examination, that she had a deep and revengeful hatred against the young person whom she had thus injured. But the paper intimated that, whatever besides she had communicated upon this subject, was confided by her in private to the worthy and reverend archdeacon who had bestowed such particular pains in affording her

31

spiritual assistance.   The broadside went on to intimate that, after her execution, of which the particulars were given, her daughter, the insane person mentioned more than once, and who was generally known by the name of Madge Wildfire, had been very ill-used by the populace, under the belief that she was a sorceress, and an accomplice in her mother's crimes, and had been with difficulty rescued by the prompt interference of the police.

Such (for we omit moral reflections and all that may seem unnecessary to the explanation of our story) was the tenor of the broadside.   To Mrs. Butler it contained intelligence of the highest importance, since it seemed to afford the most unequivocal proof of her sister's innocence respecting the crime for which she had so nearly suffered.   It is true, neither she nor her husband, nor even her father, had ever believed her capable of touching her infant with an unkind hand when in possession of her reason ; but there was a darkness on the subject and what might have happened in a moment of insanity was dreadful to think upon. Besides whatever was their own conviction, they had no means of establishing Effie's innocence to the world, which, according to the tenor of this fugitive publication, was now at length completely manifested by the dying confession of the person chiefly interested in concealing it.

After thanking God for a discovery so dear to her feelings, Mrs. Butler began to consider what use she should make of it.   To have shown it to her husband would have been her first impulse ; but, besides that he was absent from home, and the matter too delicate to be the subject of correspondence by an indifferent penwoman, Mrs. Butler recollected that he was not possessed of the information necessary to form a judgment upon the occasion ; and that, adhering to the rule which she had considered as most advisable, she had best transmit the information immediately to her sister, and leave her to adjust with her husband the mode in which they should avail themselves of it.   Accordingly, she despatched a special messenger to Glasgow with a packet, inclosing the "Confession" of Margaret Murdockson, addressed, as usual, under cover to Mr. Whiterose of York.   She expected, with anxiety, an answer ; but none arrived in the usual course of post, and she was left to imagine how many various causes might account for Lady Staunton's silence. She began to be half sorry that she had parted with the printed paper, both for fear of its having fallen into bad hands, and from the desire of regaining the document, which might be essential to establish her sister's innocence. She was even doubting whether she had not better commit the whole matter to her husband's consideration, when other incidents occurred to divert her purpose.

Jeanie (she is a favorite, and we beg her pardon for still using the familiar title) had walked down to the seaside with her children one morning after breakfast, when the boys, whose sight was more discriminating than hers, exclaimed, that "the Captain's coach and six was coming right for the shore, with ladies in it." Jeanie instinctively bent her eyes on the approaching boat, and became soon sensible that there were two females in the stern, seated beside the gracious Duncan, who acted as pilot. It was a point of politeness to walk towards the landing-place, in order to receive them, especially as she saw that the Captain of Knockdhunder was upon honor and ceremony. His piper was in the bow of the boat, sending forth music, of which one half sounded the better that the other was drowned by the waves and the breeze. Moreover, he himself had his brigadier wig newly frizzed, his bonnet (he had abjured the cocked hat) decorated with St. George's red cross, his uniform mounted as a captain of militia, the Duke's flag with the boar's head displayed,—all intimated parade and gala.

As Mrs. Butler approached the landing-place, she observed the Captain hand the ladies ashore with marks of great attention, and the parties advanced towards her, the Captain a few steps before the two ladies, of whom the taller and elder leaned on the shoulder of the other, who seemed to be an attendant or servant.

As they met, Duncan, in his best, most important, and deepest tone of Highland civility, "pegged leave to introduce to Mrs. Putler, Lady—eh—eh—I hae forgotten your leddyship's name!"

"Never mind my name, sir," said the lady; "I trust Mrs. Butler will be at no loss. The Duke's letter——" And, as she observed Mrs. Butler look confused, she said again to Duncan, something sharply, "Did you not send the letter last night, sir?"

"In troth and I didna, and I crave your leddyship's pardon; but you see, matam, I thought it would do as weel to-day, pecause Mrs. Putler is never taen out o' sorts—never; and the coach was out fishing; and the gig was gane to Greenock for a cag of prandy; and—— Put here's his Grace's letter."

"Give it me, sir," said the lady, taking it out of his hand ; "since you have not found it convenient to do me the favor to send it before me, I will deliver it mysel."

Mrs. Butler looked with great attention, and a certain dubious feeling of deep interest, on the lady who thus expressed herself with authority over the man of authority, and to whose mandates he seemed to submit, resigning the letter with a "Just as your leddyship is pleased to order it."

The lady was rather above the middle size, beautifully made, though something *embonpoint,* with a hand and arm exquisitely formed. Her manner was easy, dignified, and commanding, and seemed to evince high birth and the habits of elevated society. She wore a traveling dress, a gray beaver hat, and a veil of Flanders lace. Two footmen, in rich liveries, who got out of the barge, and lifted out a trunk and portmanteau, appeared to belong to her suite.

"As you did not receive the letter, madam, which should have served for my introduction—for I presume you are Mrs. Butler—I will not present it to you till you are so good as to admit me into your house without it."

"To pe sure, matam," said Knockdunder, "ye canna doubt Mrs. Putler will do that. Mrs. Putler, this is Lady—Lady—these tamn'd Southern names rin out o' my head like a stane trowling downhill—put I believe she is a Scottish woman porn—the mair our credit ; and I presume her leddyship is of the house of——"

"The Duke of Argyle knows my family very well, sir," said the lady, in a tone which seemed designed to silence Duncan, or, at any rate, which had that effect completely.

There was something about the whole of this stranger's address, and tone, and manner which acted upon Jeanie's feelings like the illusions of a dream, that teaze us with a puzzling approach to reality. Something there was of her sister in the gait and manner of the stranger, as well as in the sound of her voice, and something also, when, lifting her veil, she showed features to which, changed as they were in expression and complexion, she could not but attach many remembrances.

The stranger was turned of thirty certainly ; but so well were her personal charms assisted by the power of dress and arrangement of ornament, that she might well have passed for one-and-twenty. And her behavior was so steady and so composed, that as often as Mrs. Butler perceived anew some point of resemblance to her unfortunate sister, so often the sustained self-command and absolute composure of the stranger destroyed the ideas which began to arise in her imagination. She led the way silently towards the manse, lost in a confusion of reflections, and trusting the letter with which she was to be there entrusted would afford her satisfactory explanation of what was a most puzzling and embarrassing scene.

The lady maintained in the mean while the manners of a stranger of rank. She admired the various points of view like one who has studied nature and the best representations of art. At length she took notice of the children.

"These are two fine young mountaineers. Yours, madam, I presume ? "

Jeanie replied in the affirmative. The stranger sighed, and sighed once more as they were presented to her by name.

"Come here, Femie," said Mrs. Butler, "and hold your head up."

"What is your daughter's name, madam ? " said the lady.

"Euphemia, madam," answered Mrs. Butler.

"I thought the ordinary Scottish contraction of the name had been Effie," replied the stranger, in a tone which went to Jeanie's heart ; for in that single word there was more of her sister—more of *lang syne* ideas—than in all the reminiscences which her own heart had anticipated, or the features and manner of the stranger had suggested.

When they reached the manse, the lady gave Mrs. Butler the letter which she had taken out of the hands of Knockdunder ; and as she gave it she pressed her hand, adding aloud, "Perhaps, madam, you will have the goodness to get me a little milk."

"And me a drap of the gray-peard, if you please, Mrs. Putler," added Duncan.

Mrs. Butler withdrew ; but deputing to May Hettley and to David the supply of the strangers' wants, she hastened into her own room to read the letter. The envelope was addressed in the Duke of Argyle's hand, and requested Mrs. Butler's attentions and civility to a lady of rank, a particular friend of his late brother, Lady Staunton of Willingham, who, being recommended to drink goats' whey by the physicians, was to honor the Lodge at Roseneath with her residence, while her husband made a short tour in Scotland. But within the same cover, which had been given to Lady Staunton unsealed, was a letter from that lady, intended to prepare her sister for meeting her, and which, but for the

Captain's negligence, she ought to have received on the preceding evening. It stated that the news in Jeanie's last letter had been so interesting to her husband that he was determined to inquire farther into the confession made at Carlisle, and the fate of that poor innocent, and that, as he had been in some degree successful, she had, by the most earnest entreaties, extorted rather than obtained his permission, under promise of observing the most strict incognito, to spend a week or two with her sister, or in her neighborhood, while he was prosecuting researches, to which (though it appeared to her very vainly) he seemed to attach some hopes of success.

There was a postscript, desiring that Jeanie would trust to Lady S. the management of their intercourse, and be content with assenting to what she should propose. After reading and again reading the letter, Mrs. Butler hurried downstairs, divided betwixt the fear of betraying her secret and the desire to throw herself upon her sister's neck. Effie received her with a glance at once affectionate and cautionary, and immediately proceeded to speak.

"I have been telling Mr.——, Captain——, this gentleman, Mrs. Butler, that if you could accommodate me with an apartment in your house, and a place for Ellis to sleep, and for the two men, it would suit me better than the Lodge, which his Grace has so kindly placed at my disposal. I am advised I should reside as near where the goats feed as possible."

"I have peen assuring my leddy, Mrs. Putler," said Duncan, "that, though it could not discommode you to receive any of his Grace's visitors or mine, yet she had mooch petter stay at the Lodge; and for the gaits, the creatures can be fetched there, in respect it is mair fitting they suld wait upon her leddyship, than she upon the like of them."

"By no means derange the goats for me" said Lady Staunton; "I am certain the milk must be much better here." And this she said with languid negligence, as one whose slightest intimation of humor is to bear down all argument.

Mrs. Butler hastened to intimate that her house, such as it was, was heartily at the disposal of Lady Staunton : but the Captain continued to remonstrate.

"The Duke" he said, "had written——"

"I will settle all that with his Grace——"

"And there were the things had been sent down frae Glasco——"

"Anything necessary might be sent over to the parsonage. She would beg the favor of Mrs. Butler to show her an apartment, and of the Captain to have her trunks, etc., sent over from Roseneath."

So she courtesied off poor Duncan, who departed, saying in his secret soul, "Cot tamn her English impudence! She takes possession of the minister's house as an it were her ain; and speaks to shentlemens as if they were pounden servants, an' pe tamn'd to her! And there's the deer that was shot too; but we will send it ower to the manse, whilk will pe put civil, seeing I hae prought worthy Mrs. Putler sic a fliskmahoy." And with these kind intentions, he went to the shore to give his orders accordingly.

In the mean time, the meeting of the sisters was as affectionate as it was extraordinary, and each evinced her feelings in the way proper to her character. Jeanie was so much overcome by wonder, and even by awe, that her feelings were deep, stunning and almost overpowering. Effie, on the other hand, wept, laughed, sobbed, screamed, and clapped her hands for joy, all in the space of five minutes, giving way at once, and without reserve, to a natural excessive vivacity of temper, which no one, however, knew better how to restrain under the rules of artificial breeding.

After an hour had passed like a moment in their expressions of mutual affection, Lady Staunton observed the Captain walking with impatient steps below the window. "That tiresome Highland fool has returned upon our hands," she said. "I will pray him to grace us with his absence."

"Hout no! hout no!" said Mrs. Butler, in a tone of entreaty; "ye maunna affront the Captain."

"Affront!" said Lady Staunton; "nobody is ever affronted at what I do or say, my dear. However, I will endure him, since you think it proper."

The Captain was accordingly graciously requested by Lady Staunton to remain during dinner. During this visit his studious and punctilious complaisance towards the lady of rank was happily contrasted by the cavalier air of civil familiarity in which he indulged towards the minister's wife.

"I have not been able to persuade Mrs. Butler," said Lady Staunton to the Captain, during the interval when Jeanie had left the parlor, "to let me talk of making any recompense for storming her house and garrisoning it in the way I have done."

"Doubtless, matam," said the Captain, "it wad ill pecome

Mrs. Putler, wha is a very decent pody, to make any such sharge to a lady who comes from my house, or his Grace's, which is the same thing. And, speaking of garrisons, in the year forty-five I was poot with a garrison of twenty of my lads in the house of Invergarry, whilk had near been unhappily, for——"

"I beg your pardon, sir. But I wish I could think of some way of imdemnifying this good lady."

"O, no need of intemnifying at all ; no trouble for her—nothing at all. So, peing in the house of Invergarry, and the people about it being uncanny, I doubted the warst, and——"

"Do you happen to know, sir," said Lady Staunton, "if any of these two lads—these young Butlers, I mean—show any turn for the army ?"

"Could not say, indeed my leddy," replied Knockdunder, "So, I knowing the people to pe unchancy, and not to lippen to, and hearing a pibroch in the wood, I pegan to pid my lads look to their flints, and then——"

"For," said Lady Staunton, with the most ruthless disregard to the narrative which she mangled by these interruptions, "if that should be the case, it should cost Sir George but the asking a pair of colors for one of them at the War Office, since we have always supported government, and never had occasion to trouble ministers."

"And if you please, my leddy," said Duncan, who began to find some savor in this proposal, " as I hae a braw weel-grown lad of a nevoy, ca'd Duncan MacGilligan, that is as pig as paith the Putler pairns putten thegither, Sir George could ask a pair for him at the same time, and it wad pe put ae asking for a'."

Lady Staunton only answered this hint with a well-bred stare, which gave no sort of encouragement.

Jeanie, who now returned, was lost in amazement at the wonderful difference betwixt the helpless and despairing girl whom she had seen stretched on a flock-bed in a dungeon, expecting a violent and disgraceful death, and last as a forlorn exile upon the midnight beach, with the elegant, well-bred, beautiful woman before her. The features, now that her sister's veil was laid aside, did not appear so extremely different as the whole manner, expression, look, and bearing. In outside show, Lady Staunton seemed completely a creature too soft and fair for sorrow to have touched ; so much accustomed to have all her whims complied with by those around her, that she seemed to expect she should even be saved the trouble of forming them; and so totally unacquainted with contradiction, that she did not even use the tone of self-will, since to breathe a wish was to have it fulfilled. She made no ceremony of ridding herself of Duncan as soon as the evening approached; but complimented him out of the house, under pretext of fatigue, with the utmost nonchalance.

When they were alone, her sister could not help expressing her wonder at the self-possession with which Lady Staunton sustained her part.

"I daresay you are surprised at it," said Lady Staunton, composedly; "for you, my dear Jeanie, have been truth itself from your cradle upwards; but you must remember that I am a liar of fifteen years' standing, and therefore must by this time be used to my character."

In fact, during the feverish tumult of feelings excited during the two or three first days, Mrs. Butler thought her sister's manner was completely contradictory of the desponding tone which pervaded her correspondence. She was moved to tears, indeed, by the sight of her father's grave, marked by a modest stone, recording his piety and integrity; but lighter impressions and associations had also power over her. She amused herself with visiting the dairy, in which she had so long been assistant, and was so near discovering herself to May Hettly, by betraying her acquaintance with the celebrated receipt for Dunlop cheese, that she compared herself to Bedredden Hassan, whom the vizier, his father-in-law, discovered by his superlative skill in composing cream-tarts with pepper in them. But when the novelty of such avocations ceased to amuse her, she showed to her sister but too plainly that the gaudy coloring with which she veiled her unhappiness afforded as little real comfort as the gay uniform of the soldier when it is drawn over his mortal wound. There were moods and moments in which her despondence seemed to exceed even that which she herself had described in her letters, and which too well convinced Mrs. Butler how little her sister's lot which in appearance was so brilliant, was in reality to be envied.

There was one source, however, from which Lady Staunton derived a pure degree of pleasure. Gifted in every particular with a higher degree of imagination than that of her sister, she was an admirer of the beauties of nature, a taste which compensates many evils to those who happen to enjoy it. Here her character of a fine lady stopped short, where she ought to have

Scream'd at ilk cleugh, and screech'd at ilka **how**,
As loud as she had seen the worriecow.

On the contrary, with the two boys for her guides, **she**
undertook long and fatiguing walks among the neighboring
mountains, to visits glens, lakes, waterfalls, or whatever
scenes of natural wonder or beauty lay concealed among
their recesses.　It is Wordsworth, I think, who, talking of
an old man under difficulties, remarks, with a singular attention to nature,

Whether it was care that spurred him,
God only knows; but to the very last,
He had the lighest foot in Ennerdale.

In the same manner, languid, listless, and unhappy within
doors, at times even indicating something which approached
near to contempt of the homely accommodations of her
sister's house, although she instantly endeavored, by a
thousand kindnesses, to atone for such ebullitions of spleen,
Lady Staunton appeared to feel interest and energy while in
the open air, and traversing the mountain landscapes in
society with the two boys, whose ears she delighted with
stories of what she had seen in other countries, and what
she had to show them at Willingham Manor.　And they, on
the other hand, exerted themselves in doing the honors of
Dunbartonshire to the lady who seemed so kind, insomuch
that there was scarce a glen in the neighboring hills to which
they did not introduce her.

Upon one of these excursions, while Reuben was otherwise
employed, David alone acted as Lady Staunton's guide, and
promised to show her a cascade in the hills, grander and
higher than any they had yet visited.　It was a walk of five
long miles, and over rough ground, varied, however, and
cheered, by mountain views, and peeps now of the firth and
its islands, now of distant lakes, now of rocks and precipices.　The scene itself, too, when they reached it, amply
rewarded the labor of the walk.　A single shoot carried a
considerable stream over the face of a black rock, which
contrasted strongly in color with the white foam of the
cascade, and, at the depth of about twenty feet, another
rock intercepted the view of the bottom of the fall.　The
water, wheeling out far beneath, swept round the crag,
which thus bounded their view, and tumbled down the
rocky glen in a torrent of foam.　Those who love nature
always desire to penetrate into its utmost recesses, and Lady
Staunton asked David whether there was not some mode of

gaining a view of the abyss at the foot of the fall. He said that he knew a station on a shelf on the further side of the intercepting rock, from which the whole waterfall was visible, but that the road to it was steep and slippery and dangerous. Bent, however, on gratifying her curiosity, she desired him to lead the way ; and accordingly he did so over crag and stone, anxiously pointing out to her the resting-places where she ought to step, for their mode of advancing soon ceased to be walking, and became scrambling.

In this manner, clinging like sea-birds to the face of the rock, they were enabled at length to turn round it, and came full in front of the fall, which here had a most tremendous aspect, boiling, roaring, and thundering with unceasing din into a black cauldron, a hundred feet at least below them, which resembled the crater of a volcano. The noise, the dashing of the waters, which gave an unsteady appearance to all around them, the trembling even of the huge crag on which they stood, the precariousness of their footing, for there was scarce room for them to stand on the shelf of rock which they had thus attained, had so powerful an effect on the senses and imagination of Lady Staunton, that she called out to David she was falling, and would in fact have dropped from the crag had he not caught hold of her. The boy was bold and stout of his age ; still he was but fourteen years old, and as his assistance gave no confidence to Lady Staunton, she felt her situation become really perilous. The chance was that, in the appalling novelty of the circumstances, he might have caught the infection of her panic, in which case it is likely that both must have perished. She now screamed with terror, though without hope of calling any one to her assistance. To her amazement, the scream was answered by a whistle from above, of a tone so clear and shrill that it was heard even amid the noise of the waterfall.

In this moment of terror and perplexity, a human face, black, and having grizzled hair hanging down over the forehead and cheeks, and mixing with mustaches and a beard of the same color, and as much matted and tangled, looked down on them from a broken part of the rock above.

"It is The Enemy!" said the boy, who had very nearly become incapable of supporting Lady Staunton.

"No, no," she exclaimed, inaccessible to supernatural terrors, and restored to the presence of mind of which she had been deprived by the danger of her situation, "it is a man. For God's sake, my friend, help us!"

The face glared at them, but made no answer; in a second or two afterwards, another, that of a young lad appeared beside the first, equally swart and begrimed, but having tangled black hair, descending in elf locks, which gave an air of wildness and ferocity to the whole expression of the countenance. Lady Staunton repeated her entreaties, clinging to the rock with more energy, as she found that, from the superstitions terror of her guide, he became incapable of supporting her. Her words were probably drowned in the roar of the falling stream, for, though she observed the lips of the younger being whom she supplicated move as he spoke in reply, not a word reached her ear.

A moment afterwards it appeared he had not mistaken the nature of her supplication, which, indeed was easy to be understood from her situation and gestures. The younger apparition disappeared, and immediately after lowered a ladder of twisted osiers, about eight feet in length, and made signs to David to hold it fast while the lady ascended. Despair gives courage, and finding herself in this fearful predicament Lady Staunton did not hesitate to risk the ascent by the precarious means which this accommodation afforded; and, carefully assisted by the person who had thus providentially come to her aid, she reached the summit in safety. She did not, however, even look around her until she saw her nephew lightly and actively follow her example, although there was now no one to hold the ladder fast. When she saw him safe she looked round, and could not help shuddering at the place and company in which she found herself.

They were on a sort of platform of rock, surrounded on every side by precipices, or overhanging cliffs, and which it would have been scarce possible for any research to have discovered, as it did not seem to be commanded by any accessible position. It was partly covered by a huge fragment of stone, which, having fallen from the cliffs above, had been intercepted by others in its descent, and jammed so as to serve for a sloping roof to the further part of the broad shelf or platform on which they stood. A quantity of withered moss and leaves, strewed beneath this rude and wretched shelter, showed the lairs—they could not be termed the beds—of those who dwelt in this eyrie, for it deserved no other name. Of these, two were before Lady Staunton. One, the same who had afforded such timely assistance, stood upright before them, a tall, lathy, young savage; his dress a tattered plaid and philabeg, no shoes, no stockings, no hat or bonnet, the place of the last being supplied by his hair, twisted and matted like the *glibb* of the ancient wild Irish, and, like theirs, forming a natural thicket, stout enough to bear off the cut of a sword. Yet the eyes of the lad were keen and sparkling; his gesture free and noble, like that of all savages. He took little notice of David Butler, but gazed with wonder on Lady Staunton, as a being different probably in dress, and superior in beauty, to anything he had ever beheld. The old man whose face they had first seen remained recumbent in the same posture as when he had first looked down on them, only his face was turned towards them as he lay and looked up with a lazy and listless apathy, which belied the general expression of his dark and rugged features. He seemed a very tall man, but was scarce better clad than the younger. He had on a loose Lowland greatcoat, and ragged tartan trews or pantaloons.

All around looked singularly wild and unpropitious. Beneath the brow of the incumbent rock was a charcoal fire, on which there was a still working, with bellows, pincers, hammers, a movable anvil, and other smiths' tools; three guns, with two or three sacks and barrels, were disposed against the wall of rock, under shelter of the superincumbent crag; a dirk and two swords, and a Lochaber ax, lay scattered around the fire, of which the red glare cast a ruddy tinge on the precipitous foam and midst of the cascade. The lad, when he had satisfied his curiosity with staring at Lady Staunton, fetched an earthen jar and a horn cup, into which he poured some spirits, apparently hot from the still, and offered them successively to the lady and to the boy. Both declined, and the young savage quaffed off the draught, which could not amount to less than three ordinary glasses. He then fetched another ladder from the corner of the cavern, if it could be termed so, adjusted it against the transverse rock, which served as a roof, and made signs for the lady to ascend it, while he held it fast below. She did so, and found herself on the top of a broad rock, near the brink of the chasm into which the brook precipitates itself. She could see the crest of the torrent flung loose down the rock, like the mane of a wild horse, but without having any view of the lower platform from which she had ascended.

David was not suffered to mount so easily; the lad, from sport or love of mischief, shook the ladder a good deal as he ascended, and seemed to enjoy the terror of young Butler; so that, when they had both come up, they looked on each other with no friendly eyes. Neither, however, spoke. The young caird, or tinker, or gipsy, with a good deal of attention, assisted Lady Staunton up a very perilous ascent which she had still to encounter, and they were followed by David Butler, until all three stood clear of the ravine on the side of a mountain, whose sides were covered with heather and sheets of loose shingle. So narrow was the chasm out of which they ascended, that, unless when they were on the very verge, the eye passed to the other side without perceiving the existence of a rent so fearful, and nothing was seen of the cataract, though its deep hoarse voice was still heard.

Lady Staunton, freed from the danger of rock and river, had now a new subject of anxiety. Her two guides confronted each other with angry countenances; for David, though younger by two years at least, and much shorter, was a stout, well-set, and very bold boy.

"You are the blackcoat's son of Knocktarlitie," said the young caird; "if you come here again, I'll pitch you down the linn like a foot-ball."

"Ay, lad, ye are very short to be sae lang," retorted young Butler, undauntedly, and measuring his opponent's height with an undismayed eye. "I am thinking you are a gillie of Black Donacha; if you come down the glen, we'll shoot you like a wild buck."

"You may tell your father," said the lad, "that the leaf on the timber is the last he shall see; we will hae amends for the mischief he has done to us."

"I hope he will live to see mony simmers, and do ye muckle mair," answered David.

More might have passed, but Lady Staunton stepped between them with her purse in her hand, and, taking out a guinea, of which it contained several visible through the network, as well as some silver in the opposite end, offered it to the caird.

"The white siller, lady—the white siller," said the young savage, to whom the value of gold was probably unknown.

Lady Staunton poured what silver she had into his hand, and the juvenile savage snatched it greedily, and made a sort of half inclination of acknowledgment and adieu.

"Let us make haste now, Lady Staunton," said David, "for there will be little peace with them since they hae seen your purse."

They hurried on as fast as they could ; but they had not descended the hill a hundred yards or two before they heard a halloo behind them, and looking back, saw both the old man and the young one pursuing them with great speed, the former with a gun on his shoulder. Very fortunately, at this moment, a sportsman, a gamekeeper of the Duke, who was engaged in stalking deer, appeared on the face of the hill. The bandits stopped on seeing him, and Lady Staunton hastened to put herself under his protection. He readily gave them his escort home, and it required his athletic form and loaded rifle to restore to the lady her usual confidence and courage.

Donald listened with much gravity to the account of their adventure ; and answered with great composure to David's repeated inquiries, whether he could have suspected that the cairds had been lurking there—"Inteed, Master Tavie, I might hae had some guess that they were there, or thereabout, though maybe I had nane. But I am aften on the hill ; and they are like wasps ; they stang only them that fashes them ; sae, for my part, I make a point not to see them, unless I were ordered out on the preceese errand by MacCallummore or Knockdunder, whilk is a clean different case."

They reached the manse late ; and Lady Staunton, who had suffered much both from fright and fatigue, never again permitted her love of the picturesque to carry her so far among the mountains without a stronger escort than David, though she acknowledged he had won the stand of colors by the intrepidity he had displayed, so soon as assured he had to do with an earthly antagonist. "I couldna maybe hae made muckle o' a bargain wi' yon lang callant," said David, when thus complimented on his valor ; "but when ye deal wi' thae folk, it's tyne heart tyne a'."

CHAPTER LI

What see you there,
That hath so cowarded and chased your blood
Out of appearance !

Henry V.

WE are under the necessity of returning to Edinburgh,
where the General Assembly was now sitting. It is well
known that some Scottish nobleman is usually deputed as
High Commissioner, to represent the person of the king in
this convocation ; that he has allowances for the purpose of
maintaining a certain outward show and solemnity, and supporting the hospitality of the representative of Majesty.
Whoever is distinguished by rank or office in or near the
capital usually attends the morning levees of the Lord Commissioner, and walks with him in procession to the place
where the Assembly meets.

The nobleman who held this office chanced to be particularly connected with Sir George Staunton, and it was in his
train that he ventured to tread the High Street of Edinburgh for the first time since the fatal night of Porteous's
execution. Walking at the right hand of the representative
of Sovereignty, covered with lace and embroidery, and with
all the paraphernalia of wealth and rank, the handsome
though wasted form of the English stranger attracted all
eyes. Who could have recognized in a form so aristocratic
the plebeian convict that, disguised in the rags of Madge
Wildfire, had led the formidable rioters to their destined
revenge ? There was no possibility that this could happen,
even if any of his ancient acquaintances, a race of men
whose lives are so brief, had happened to survive the span
commonly allotted to evil-doers. Besides, the whole affair
had long fallen asleep, with the angry passions in which it
originated. Nothing is more certain than that persons
known to have had a share in that formidable riot, and to
have fled from Scotland on that account, had made money
abroad, returned to enjoy it in their native country, and
lived and died undisturbed by the law.* The forbearance
of the magistrate was in these instances wise, certainly, and

* See Arnot's *Criminal Trials*, 4to ed., p. 235.

just ; for what good impression could be made on the public mind by punishment, when the memory of the offense was obliterated, and all that was remembered was the recent inoffensive, or perhaps exemplary, conduct of the offender ?

Sir George Staunton might, therefore, tread the scene of his former audacious exploits free from the apprehension of the law, or even of discovery or suspicion. But with what feelings his heart that day throbbed must be left to those of the reader to imagine. It was an object of no common interest which had brought him to encounter so many painful remembrances.

In consequence of Jeanie's letter to Lady Staunton, transmitting the confession, he had visited the town of Carlisle, and had found Archdeacon Fleming still alive, by whom that confession had been received. This reverend gentleman, whose character stood deservedly very high, he so far admitted into his confidence as to own himself the father of the unfortunate infant which had been spirited away by Madge Wildfire, representing the intrigue as a matter of juvenile extravagance on his own part, for which he was now anxious to atone, by tracing, if possible, what had become of the child. After some recollection of the circumstances, the clergyman was able to call to memory that the unhappy woman had written a letter to " George Staunton, Esq., younger, Rectory, Willingham, by Grantham " ; that he had forwarded it to the address accordingly, and that it had been returned, with a note from the Reverend Mr. Staunton, Rector of Willingham, saying, he knew no such person as him to whom the letter was addressed. As this had happened just at the time when George had, for the last time, absconded from his father's house to carry off Effie, he was at no loss to account for the cause of the resentment under the influence of which his father had disowned him. This was another instance in which his ungovernable temper had occasioned his misfortune ; had he remained at Willingham but a few days longer, he would have received Margaret Murdockson's letter, in which was exactly described the person and haunts of the woman, Annaple Bailzou, to whom she [Madge Wildfire] had parted with the infant. It appeared that Meg Murdockson had been induced to make this confession, less from any feelings of contrition, than from the desire of obtaining, through George Staunton or his father's means, protection and support for her daughter Madge. Her letter to George Staunton said, " That while the writer lived, her daughter would have needed nought

32

from anybody, and that she would never have meddled in these affairs, except to pay back the ill that George had done to her and hers.   But she was to die, and her daughter would be destitute, and without reason to guide her.   She had lived in the world long enough to know that people did nothing for nothing ; so she had told George Staunton all he could wish to know about his wean, in hopes he would not see the demented young creature he had ruined perish for want.   As for her motives for not telling them sooner, she had a long account to reckon for in the next world, and she would reckon for that too."

The clergyman said that Meg had died in the same desperate state of mind, occasionally expressing some regret about the child which was lost, but oftener sorrow that the mother had not been hanged—her mind at once a chaos of guilt, rage, and apprehension for her daughter's future safety ; that instinctive feeling of parental anxiety which she had in common with the she-wolf and lioness being the last shade of kindly affection that occupied a breast equally savage.

The melancholy catastrophe of Madge Wildfire was occasioned by her taking the confusion of her mother's execution as affording an opportunity of leaving the workhouse to which the clergyman had sent her, and presenting herself to the mob in their fury, to perish in the way we have already seen.   When Dr. Fleming found the convict's letter was returned from Lincolnshire, he wrote to a friend in Edinburgh, to inquire into the fate of the unfortunate girl whose child had been stolen, and was informed by his correspondent that she had been pardoned, and that, with all her family, she had retired to some distant part of Scotland, or left the kingdom entirely.   And here the matter rested, until, at Sir George Staunton's application, the clergyman looked out and produced Margaret Murdockson's returned letter, and the other memoranda which he had kept concerning the affair.

Whatever might be Sir George Staunton's feelings in ripping up this miserable history, and listening to the tragical fate of the unhappy girl whom he had ruined, he had so much of his ancient wilfulness of disposition left as to shut his eyes on everything save the prospect which seemed to open itself of recovering his son.   It was true, it would be difficult to produce him without telling much more of the history of his birth and the misfortunes of his parents than it was prudent to make known.   But let him once be found, let him but prove worthy of his father's protection, and many ways might be fallen upon to avoid such risk. Sir George Staunton was at liberty to adopt him as his heir, if he pleased, without communicating the secret of his birth ; or an Act of Parliament might be obtained, declaring him legitimate, and allowing him the name and arms of his father. He was, indeed, already a legitimate child according to the law of Scotland, by the subsequent marriage of his parents. Wilful in everything, Sir George's sole desire now was to see this son, even should his recovery bring with it a new series of misfortunes as dreadful as those which followed on his being lost.

But where was the youth who might eventually be called to the honors and estates of this ancient family ? On what heath was he wandering, and shrouded by what mean disguise ? Did he gain his precarious bread by some petty trade, by menial toil, by violence, or by theft ? These were questions on which Sir George's anxious investigations could obtain no light. Many remembered that Annaple Bailzou wandered through the country as a beggar and fortune-teller, or spae-wife ; some remembered that she had been seen with an infant in 1737 or 1738, but for more than ten years she had not traveled that district, and that she had been heard to say she was going to a distant part of Scotland, of which country she was a native. To Scotland, therefore, came Sir George Staunton, having parted with his lady at Glasgow ; and his arrival at Edinburgh happening to coincide with the sitting of the General Assembly of the Kirk, his acquaintance with the nobleman who held the office of Lord High Commissioner forced him more into public than suited either his views or inclinations.

At the public table of this nobleman, Sir George Staunton was placed next to a clergyman of respectable appearance, and well-bred though plain demeanor, whose name he discovered to be Butler. It had been no part of Sir George's plan to take his brother-in-law into his confidence, and he had rejoiced exceedingly in the assurances he received from his wife that Mrs. Butler, the very soul of integrity and honor, had never suffered the account he had given of himself at Willingham Rectory to transpire, even to her husband. But he was not sorry to have an opportunity to converse with so near a connection, without being known to him, and to form a judgment of his character and understanding. He saw much, and heard more, to raise Butler very high in his opinion. He found he was generally respected by those of

his own profession, as well as by the laity who had seats in
the Assembly.   He had made several public appearances in
the Assembly, distinguished by good sense, candor, and
ability ; and he was followed and admired as a sound, and
at the same time an eloquent, preacher.

This was all very satisfactory to Sir George Staunton's
pride, which had revolted at the idea of his wife's sister being obscurely married.   He now began, on the contrary, to
think the connection so much better than he expected, that
if it should be necessary to acknowledge it, in consequence
of the recovery of his son, it would sound well enough that
Lady Staunton had a sister who, in the decayed state of the
family, had married a Scottish clergyman, high in the opinion
of his countrymen, and a leader in the church.

It was with these feelings that, when the Lord High Commissioner's company broke up, Sir George Staunton, under
pretence of prolonging some inquiries concerning the constitution of the Church of Scotland, requested Butler to go
home to his lodgings in the Lawnmarket, and drink a cup
of coffee.   Butler agreed to wait upon him, providing Sir
George would permit him, in passing, to call at a friend's
house where he resided, and make his apology for not coming to partake her tea.   They proceeded up the High
Street, entered the Krames, and passed the begging-box,
placed to remind those at liberty of the distresses of the
poor prisoners.   Sir George paused there one instant, and
next day a £20 note was found in that receptacle for public
charity.

When he came up to Butler again, he found him with his
eyes fixed on the entrance of the tolbooth, and apparently
in deep thought.

"That seems a very strong door," said Sir George, by way
of saying something.

"It is so, sir," said Butler, turning off and beginning to
walk forward, "but it was my misfortune at one time to see
it prove greatly too weak."

At this moment, looking at his companion, he asked him
whether he felt himself ill ; and Sir George Staunton admitted that he had been so foolish as to eat ice, which sometimes disagreed with him.   With kind officiousness, that
would not be gainsaid, and ere he could find out where he was
going, Butler hurried Sir George into the friend's house, near
to the prison, in which he himself had lived since he came
to town, being, indeed, no other than that of our old friend
Bartoline Saddletree, in which Lady Staunton had served a

short noviciate as a shop-maid. This recollection rushed on
her husband's mind, and the blush of shame which it excited overpowered the sensation of fear which had produced
his former paleness. Good Mrs. Saddletree, however, bustled about to receive the rich English baronet as the friend
of Mr. Butler, and requested an elderly female in a black
gown to sit still, in a way which seemed to imply a wish
that she would clear the way for her betters. In the mean
while, understanding the state of the case, she ran to get
some cordial waters, sovereign, of course, in all cases of
faintishness whatsoever. During her absence, her visitor,
the female in black, made some progress out of the room, and
might have left it altogether without particular observation,
had she not stumbled at the threshold, so near Sir George
Staunton that he, in point of civility, raised her and assisted
her to the door.

"Mrs. Porteous is turned very doited now, puir body,"
said Mrs. Saddletree, as she returned with her bottle in
her hand. "She is no sae auld, but she got a sair back-
cast wi' the slaughter o' her husband. Ye had some trouble
about that job, Mr. Butler. I think, sir (to Sir George),
ye had better drink out the haill glass, for to my een ye
look waur than when ye came in."

And, indeed, he grew as pale as a corpse on recollecting
who it was that his arm had so lately supported—the widow
whom he had so large a share in making such.

"It is a prescribed job that case of Porteous now," said
old Saddletree, who was confined to his chair by the gout
—"clean prescribed and out of date."

"I am not clear of that, neighbor," said Plumdamas,
"for I have heard them say twenty years should rin, and
this is but the fifty-ane; Porteous's mob was in thretty-
seven."

"Ye'll no teach me law, I think, neighbor—me that has
four gaun pleas, and might hae had fourteen, an it hadna
been the gudewife? I tell ye, if the foremost of the Porteous mob were standing there where that gentleman stands,
the King's Advocate wadna meddle wi' him : it fa's under
the negative prescription."

"Haud your din, carles," said Mrs Saddletree, "and let
the gentleman sit down and get a dish of comfortable tea."

But Sir George had had quite enough of their conversation ; and Butler, at his request, made an apology to Mrs.
Saddletree, and accompanied him to his lodgings. Here
they found another guest waiting Sir George Staunton's

return. This was no other than our reader's old acquaintance, Ratcliffe.

This man had exercised the office of turnkey with so much vigilance, acuteness, and fidelity, that he gradually rose to be governor or captain of the tolbooth. And it is yet remembered in tradition, that young men who rather sought amusing than select society in their merry-meetings used sometimes to request Ratcliffe's company, in order that he might regale them with legends of his extraordinary feats in the way of robbery and escape.* But he lived and died without resuming his original vocation, otherwise than in his narratives over a bottle.

Under these circumstances, he had been recommended to Sir George Staunton by a man of the law in Edinburgh, as a person likely to answer any questions he might have to ask about Annaple Bailzou, who, according to the color which Sir George Staunton gave to his cause of inquiry, was supposed to have stolen a child in the west of England, belonging to a family in which he was interested. The gentleman had not mentioned his name, but only his official title ; so that Sir George Staunton, when told that the captain of the tolbooth was waiting for him in his parlor, had no idea of meeting his former acquaintance, Jem Ratcliffe.

This, therefore, was another new and most unpleasant surprise, for he had no difficulty in recollecting this man's remarkable features. The change, however, from George Robertson to Sir George Staunton baffled even the penetration of Ratcliffe, and he bowed very low to the baronet and his guest, hoping Mr. Butler would excuse his recollecting that he was an old acquaintance.

"And once rendered my wife a piece of great service," said Mr. Butler, "for which she sent you a token of grateful acknowledgment, which I hope came safe and was welcome."

"Deil a doubt on't," said Ratcliffe, with a knowing nod; "but ye are muckle changed for the better since I saw ye, Maister Butler."

"So much so, that I wonder you knew me."

"Aha, then ! Deil a face I see I ever forget," said Ratcliffe ; while Sir George Staunton, tied to the stake and incapable of escaping, internally cursed the accuracy of his memory. "And yet, sometimes," continued Ratcliffe, "the sharpest hand will be taen in. There is a face in this

---

* See Ratcliffe. Note 37.

very room, if I might presume to be sae bauld, that if I didna ken the honorable person it belangs to, I might think it had some cast of an auld acquaintance."

"I should not be much flattered," answered the Baronet, sternly, and roused by the risk in which he saw himself placed, "if it is to me you mean to apply that compliment."

"By no manner of means, sir," said Ratcliffe, bowing very low; "I am come to receive your honor's commands, and no to trouble your honor wi' my poor observations."

"Well, sir, " said Sir George, "I am told you understand police matters; so do I; to convince you of which, here are ten guineas of retaining fee; I make them fifty when you can find me certain notice of a person, living or dead, whom you will find described in that paper. I shall leave town presently; you may send your written answer to me to the care of Mr. —— (naming his highly respectable agent), or of his Grace the Lord High Commissioner."

Ratcliffe bowed and withdrew.

"I have angered the proud peat now," he said to himself, "by finding out a likeness; but if George Robertson's father had lived within a mile of his mother, d—n me if I should not know what to think, for as high as he carries his head."

When he was left alone with Butler, Sir George Staunton ordered tea and coffee, which were brought by his valet, and then, after considering with himself for a minute, asked his guest whether he had lately heard from his wife and family.

Butler, with some surprise at the question, replied, "That he had received no letter for some time; his wife was a poor penwoman."

"Then," said Sir George Staunton, "I am the first to inform you there has been an invasion of your quiet premises since you left home. My wife, whom the Duke of Argyle had the goodness to permit to use Roseneath Lodge, while she was spending some weeks in your country, has sallied across and taken up her quarters in the manse, as she says, to be nearer the goats, whose milk she is using; but I believe, in reality, because she prefers Mrs. Butler's company to that of the respectable gentleman who acts as seneschal on the Duke's domains."

Mr. Butler said, "He had often heard the late Duke and the present speak with high respect of Lady Staunton, and was happy if his house could accommodate any friend of theirs; it would be but a very slight acknowledgment of the many favors he owed them."

"That does not make Lady Staunton and myself the less

obliged to your hospitality, sir," said Sir George.   "May I inquire if you think of returning home soon?"

"In the course of two days," Mr. Butler answered, "his duty in the Assembly would be ended; and the other matters he had in town being all finished, he was desirous of returning to Dunbartonshire as soon as he could; but he was under the necessity of transporting a considerable sum in bills and money with him, and therefore wished to travel in company with one or two of his brethren of the clergy."

"My escort will be more safe," said Sir George Staunton, "and I think of setting off to-morrow or next day.   If you will give me the pleasure of your company, I will undertake to deliver you and your charge safe at the manse, provided you will admit me along with you."

Mr. Butler gratefully accepted of this proposal; the appointment was made accordingly, and by despatches with one of Sir George's servants, who was sent forward for the purpose, the inhabitants of the manse of Knocktarlitie were made acquainted with the intended journey; and the news rung through the whole vicinity, "that the minister was coming back wi' a braw English gentleman, and a' the siller that was to pay for the estate of Craigsture."

This sudden resolution of going to Knocktarlitie had been adopted by Sir George Staunton in consequence of the incidents of the evening.   In spite of his present consequence, he felt he had presumed too far in venturing so near the scene of his former audacious acts of violence, and he knew too well from past experience the acuteness of a man like Ratcliffe again to encounter him.   The next two days he kept his lodgings, under pretense of indisposition, and took leave, by writing, of his noble friend, the High Commissioner, alleging the opportunity of Mr. Butler's company as a reason for leaving Edinburgh sooner than he had proposed.   He had a long conference with his agent on the subject of Annaple Bailzou; and the professional gentleman, who was the agent also of the Argyle family, had directions to collect all the information which Ratcliffe or others might be able to obtain concerning the fate of that woman and the unfortunate child, and, so soon as anything transpired which had the least appearance of being important, that he should send an express with it instantly to Knocktarlitie.   These instructions were backed with a deposit of money, and a request that no expense might be spared; so that Sir George Staunton had little reason to apprehend negligence on the part of the persons entrusted with the commission.

The journey which the brothers made in company was attended with more pleasure, even to Sir George Staunton, than he had ventured to expect. His heart lightened in spite of himself when they lost sight of Edinburgh ; and the easy, sensible conversation of Butler was well calculated to withdraw his thoughts from painful reflections. He even began to think whether there could be much difficulty in removing his wife's connections to the rectory of Willingham ; it was only on his part procuring some still better preferment for the present incumbent, and on Butler's, that he should take orders according to the English Church, to which he could not conceive a possibility of his making objection, and then he had them residing under his wing. No doubt, there was pain in seeing Mrs. Butler, acquainted, as he knew her to be, with the full truth of his evil history. But then her silence, though he had no reason to complain of her indiscretion hitherto, was still more absolutely ensured. It would keep his lady, also, both in good temper and in more subjection ; for she was sometimes troublesome to him, by insisting on remaining in town when he desired to retire to the country, alleging the total want of society at Willingham. " Madam, your sister is there," would, he thought, be a sufficient answer to this ready argument.

He sounded Butler on this subject, asking what he would think of an English living of twelve hundred pounds yearly, with the burden of affording his company now and then to a neighbor whose health was not strong, or his spirits equal. " He might meet," he said, " occasionally, a very learned and accomplished gentleman, who was in orders as a Catholic priest, but he hoped that would be no insurmountable objection to a man of his liberality of sentiment. What," he said, " would Mr. Butler think of as an answer, if the offer should be made to him ? "

" Simply, that I could not accept of it," said Mr. Butler. " I have no mind to enter into the various debates between the churches ; but I was brought up in mine own, have received her ordination, am satisfied of the truth of her doctrines, and will die under the banner I have enlisted to."

" What may be the value of your preferment ? " said Sir George Staunton, " unless I am asking an indiscreet question."

" Probably one hundred a-year, one year with another, besides my glebe and pasture-ground."

" And you scruple to exchange that for twelve hundred

a-year, without alleging any damning difference of doctrine betwixt the two churches of England and Scotland ? "

" On that, sir, I have reserved my judgment ; there may be much good, and there are certainly saving means, in both, but every man must act according fo his own lights. I hope I have done, and am in the course of doing, my Master's work in this Highland parish ; and it would ill become me, for the sake of lucre, to leave my sheep in the wilderness. But, even in the temporal view which you have taken of the matter, Sir George, this hundred pounds a-year of stipend hath fed and clothed us, and left us nothing to wish for ; my father-in-law's succession, and other circumstances, have added a small estate of about twice as much more, and how we are to dispose of it I do not know. So I leave it to you, sir, to think if I were wise, not having the wish or opportunity of spending three hundred a year, to covet the possession of four times that sum."

" This is philosophy," said Sir George ; " I have heard of it, but I never saw it before."

" It is common sense," replied Butler, " which accords with philosophy and religion more frequently than pedants or zealots are apt to admit."

Sir George turned the subject, and did not again resume it. Although they travelled in Sir George's chariot, he seemed so much fatigued with the motion, that it was necessary for him to remain for a day at a small town called Mid-Calder, which was their first stage from Edinburgh. Glasgow occupied another day, so slow were their motions.

They travelled on to Dunbarton, where they had resolved to leave the equipage, and to hire a boat to take them to the shores near the manse, as the Gare Loch lay betwixt them and that point, besides the impossibility of traveling in that district with wheel-carriages. Sir George's valet, a man of trust, accompanied them, as also a footman ; the grooms were left with the carriage. Just as this arrangement was completed, which was about four o'clock in the afternoon, an express arrived from Sir George's agent in Edinburgh, with a packet, which he opened and read with great attention, appearing much interested and agitated by the contents. The packet had been despatched very soon after their leaving Edinburgh, but the messenger had missed the travelers by passing through Mid-Calder in the night, and overshot his errand by getting to Roseneath before them. He was now on his return, after having waited more

than four-and-twenty hours.   Sir George Staunton instantly
wrote back an answer, and, rewarding the messenger liberally, desired him not to sleep till he placed it in his agent's
hands.

At length they embarked in the boat, which had waited
for them some time.   During their voyage, which was slow,
for they were obliged to row the whole way, and often against
the tide, Sir George Staunton's inquiries ran chiefly on the
subject of the Highland banditti who had infested that
country since the year 1745.   Butler informed him that many
of them were not native Highlanders, but gipsies, tinkers, and
other men of desperate fortunes, who had taken advantage
of the confusion introduced by the civil war, the general
discontent of the mountaineers, and the unsettled state of
police, to practise their plundering trade with more audacity.
Sir George next inquired into their lives, their habits,
whether the violences which they committed were not sometimes atoned for by acts of generosity, and whether they
did not possess the virtues, as well as the vices, of savage
tribes.

Butler answered, that certainly they did sometimes show
sparks of generosity, of which even the worst class of malefactors are seldom utterly divested ; but that their evil propensities were certain and regular principles of action, while
any occasional burst of virtuous feeling was only a transient
impulse not to be reckoned upon, and excited probably by
some singular and unusual concatenation of circumstances.
In discussing these inquiries, which Sir George pursued with
an apparent eagerness that rather surprised Butler, the
latter chanced to mention the name of Donacha Dhu na
Dunaigh, with which the reader is already acquainted.   Sir
George caught the sound up eagerly, and as if it conveyed
particular interest to his ear.   He made the most minute inquiries concerning the man whom he mentioned, the number
of his gang, and even the appearance of those who belonged
to it.   Upon these points Butler could give little answer.
The man had a name among the lower class, but his exploits
were considerably exaggerated ; he had always one or two
fellows with him, but never aspired to the command of above
three or four.   In short, he knew little about him, and the
small acquaintance he had, had by no means inclined him to
desire more.

"Nevertheless, I should like to see him some of these
days."

"That would be a dangerous meeting, Sir George, unless

you mean we are to see him receive his deserts from the law, and then it were a melancholy one."

"Use every man according to his deserts, Mr. Butler, and who shall escape whipping ? But I am talking riddles to you. I will explain them more fully to you when I have spoken over the subject with Lady Staunton. Pull away, my lads," he added, addressing himself to the rowers; "the clouds threaten us with a storm."

In fact, the dead and heavy closeness of the air, the huge piles of clouds which assembled in the western horizon, and glowed like a furnace under the influence of the setting sun, that awful stillness in which nature seems to expect the thunderburst, as a condemned soldier waits for the platoon-fire which is to stretch him on the earth—all betokened a speedy storm. Large broad drops fell from time to time, and induced the gentlemen to assume the boat-cloaks; but the rain again ceased, and the oppressive heat, so unusual in Scotland in the end of May, inclined them to throw them aside. "There is something solemn in this delay of the storm," said Sir George; "it seems as if it suspended its peal till it solemnized some important event in the world below."

"Alas !" replied Butler, "what are we, that the laws of nature should correspond in their march with our ephemeral deeds or sufferings ? The clouds will burst when surcharged with the electric fluid, whether a goat is falling at that instant from the cliffs of Arran or a hero expiring on the field of battle he has won."

"The mind delights to deem it otherwise," said Sir George Staunton; "and to dwell on the fate of humanity as on that which is the prime central movement of the mighty machine. We love not to think that we shall mix with the ages that have gone before us, as these broad black raindrops mingle with the waste of waters, making a trifling and momentary eddy, and are then lost forever."

"*Forever !* We are not—we cannot be lost forever," said Butler, looking upward; "death is to us change, not consummation, and the commencement of a new existence, corresponding in character to the deeds which we have done in the body."

While they agitated these grave subjects, to which the solemnity of the approaching storm naturally led them, their voyage threatened to be more tedious than they expected, for gusts of wind, which rose and fell with sudden impetuosity, swept the bosom of the firth, and impeded the efforts of the rowers. They had now only to double a small headland in order to get to the proper landing-place in the mouth of the little river ; but in the state of the weather, and the boat being heavy, this was like to be a work of time, and in the mean while they must necessarily be exposed to the storm.

" Could we not land on this side of the headland," asked Sir George, " and so gain some shelter ? "

Butler knew of no landing-place, at least none affording a convenient or even practicable passage up the rocks which surrounded the shore.

" Think again," said Sir George Staunton ; " the storm will soon be violent."

" Hout, ay," said one of the boatmen, " there's the Caird's Cove ; but we dinna tell the minister about it, and I am no sure if I can steer the boat to it, the bay is sae fu' o' shoals and sunk rocks."

" Try," said Sir George, " and I will give you half-a-guinea."

The old fellow took the helm, and observed, " That if they could get in, there was a steep path up from the beach, and half an hour's walk from thence to the manse."

" Are you sure you know the way ? " said Butler to the old man.

" I maybe kenn'd it a wee better fifteen years syne, when Dandie Wilson was in the firth wi' his clean-ganging lugger. I mind Dandie had a wild young Englisher wi' him, that they ca'd——"

" If you chatter so much," said Sir George Staunton, " you will have the boat on the Grindstone ; bring that white rock in a line with the steeple."

" By G——," said the venteran, staring, " I think your honor kens the bay as weel as me. Your honor's nose has been on the Grindstane ere now, I'm thinking."

As they spoke thus, they approached the little cove, which, concealed behind crags, and defended on every point by shallows and sunken rocks, could scarce be discovered or approached, except by those intimate with the navigation. An old shattered boat was already drawn up on the beach within the cove, close beneath the trees, and with precautions for concealment.

Upon observing this vessel, Butler remarked to his companion, " It is impossible for you to conceive, Sir George, the difficulty I have had with my poor people, in teaching them the guilt and the danger of this contraband trade ; yet they have perpetually before their eyes all its dangerous consequences. I do not know anything that more effectually depraves and ruins their moral and religious principles."

Sir George forced himself to say something in a low voice, about the spirit of adventure natural to youth, and that unquestionably many would become wiser as they grew older.

"Too seldom, sir," replied Butler. "If they have been deeply engaged, and especially if they have mingled in the scenes of violence and blood to which their occupation naturally leads, I have observed that, sooner or later, they come to an evil end. Experience, as well as Scripture, teaches us, Sir George, that mischief shall hunt the violent man, and that the blood-thirsty man shall not live half his days. But take my arm to help you ashore."

Sir George needed assistance, for he was contrasting in his altered thought the different feelings of mind and frame with which he had formerly frequented the same place. As they landed, a low growl of thunder was heard at a distance.

"That is ominous, Mr. Butler," said Sir George.

"*Intonuit lævum:* it is ominous of good, then," answered Butler, smiling.

The boatmen were ordered to make the best of their way round the headland to the ordinary landing-place ; the two gentlemen, followed by their servant, sought their way by a blind and tangled path, through a close copsewood, to the manse of Knocktarlitie, where their arrival was anxiously expected.

The sisters in vain had expected their husbands' return on the preceding day, which was that appointed by Sir George's letter. The delay of the travelers at Calder had occasioned this breach of appointment. The inhabitants of the manse began even to doubt whether they would arrive on the present day. Lady Staunton felt this hope of delay as a brief reprieve ; for she dreaded the pangs which her husband's pride must undergo at meeting with a sister-in-law to whom the whole of his unhappy and dishonorable history was too well known. She knew, whatever force or constraint he might put upon his feelings in public, that she herself must be doomed to see them display themselves in full vehemence in secret—consume his health, destroy his temper, and render him at once an object of dread and compassion. Again and again she cautioned Jeanie to display no tokens of recognition, but to receive him as a perfect stranger, and again and again Jeanie renewed her promise to comply with her wishes.

Jeanie herself could not fail to bestow an anxious thought on the awkwardness of the approaching meeting ; but her conscience was ungalled, and then she was cumbered with many household cares of an unusual nature, which, joined to the anxious wish once more to see Butler, after an absence of unusual length, made her extremely desirous that the travelers should arrive as soon as possible.   And—why should I disguise the truth ?—ever and anon a thought stole across her mind that her gala dinner had now been postponed for two days ; and how few of the dishes, after every art of her simple *cuisine* had been exerted to dress them, could with any credit or propriety appear again upon the third ; and what was she to do with the rest ?   Upon this last subject she was saved the trouble of farther deliberation, by the sudden appearance of the Captain at the head of half a dozen stout fellows, dressed and armed in the Highland fashion.

" Goot-morrow morning to ye, Leddy Staunton, and I hope I hae the pleasure to see ye weel ?   And goot-morrow to you, goot Mrs. Putler ; I do peg you will order some victuals and ale and prandy for the lads, for we hae peen out on firth and moor since afore daylight, and a' to no purpose neither—Cot tam ! "

So saying, he sate down, pushed back his brigadier wig, and wiped his head with an air of easy importance, totally regardless of the look of well-bred astonishment by which Lady Staunton endeavored to make him comprehend that he was assuming too great a liberty.

" It is some comfort, when one has had a sair tussle," continued the Captain, addressing Lady Staunton, with an air of gallantry, " that it is in a fair leddy's service, or in the service of a gentleman whilk has a fair leddy, whilk is the same thing, since serving the husband is serving the wife, as Mrs. Putler does very weel know."

" Really, sir," said Lady Staunton, " as you seem to intend this compliment for me, I am at a loss to know what interest Sir George or I can have in your movements this morning."

" O Cot tam ! this is too cruel, my leddy ; as if it was not py special express from his Grace's honorable agent and commissioner at Edinburgh, with a warrant conform, that I was to seek for and apprehend Donacha Dhu na Dunaigh, and pring him pefore myself and Sir George Staunton, that he may have his deserts, that is to say, the gallows, whilk he has doubtless deserved, py peing the means of frightening your leddyship, as weel as for something of less importance."

"Frightening me!" said her ladyship. "Why, I never wrote to Sir George about my alarm at the waterfall."

"Then he must have heard it otherwise; for what else can give him sic an earnest tesire to see this rapscallion, that I maun rip the haill mosses and muirs in the country for him, as if I were to get something for finding him, when the pest o't might pe a pall through my prains?"

"Can it be really true that it is on Sir George's account that you have been attempting to apprehend this fellow?"

"Py Cot, it is for no other cause that I know than his honor's pleasure; for the creature might hae gone on in a decent quiet way for me, sae lang as he respectit the Duke's pounds; put reason goot he suld be taen, and hangit to poot, if it may pleasure ony honorable shentleman that is the Duke's friend. Sae I got the express over night, and I caused warn half a score of pretty lads and was up in the morning pefore the sun, an' I garr'd the lads take their kilts and short coats."

"I wonder you did that, Captain," said Mrs. Butler, "when you know the Act of Parliament against wearing the Highland dress."

"Hout, tout, ne'er fash your thumb, Mrs. Putler. The law is put twa-three years auld yet, and is ower young to hae come our length; and besides, how is the lads to climb the praes wi' thae tamn'd breekens on them? It makes me sick to see them. Put ony how, I thought I kenn'd Donacha's haunts gay and weel, and I was at the place where he had rested yestreen; for I saw the leaves the limmers had lain on, and the ashes of them; by the same token, there was a pit greeshoch purning yet. I am thinking they got some word out o' the island what was intended. I sought every glen and cleuch, as if I had been deer-stalking, but teil a wauff of his coat-tail could I see—Cot tam!"

"He'll be away down the firth to Cowall," said David; and Reuben, who had been out early that morning a-nutting, observed, "That he had seen a boat making for the Caird's Cove"; a place well known to the boys, though their less adventurous father was ignorant of its existence.

"Py Cot," said Duncan, "then I will stay here no longer than to trink this very horn of prandy and water, for it is very possible they will pe in the wood. Donacha's a clever fellow, and maype thinks it pest to sit next the chimley when the lum reeks. He thought naebody would look for him sae near hand! I peg your leddyship will excuse my aprupt departure, as I will return forthwith, and I will either pring you Donacha in life or else his head, whilk I dare to say will be as satisfactory. And I hope to pass a pleasant evening with your leddyship ; and I hope to have mine revenges on Mr. Putler at packgammon, for the four pennies whilk he won, for he will be surely at home soon, or else he will have a wet journey, seeing it is apout to pe a scud."

Thus saying, with many scrapes and bows, and apologies for leaving them, which were very readily received, and reiterated assurances of his speedy return, of the sincerity whereof Mrs. Butler entertained no doubt, so long as her best graybeard of brandy was upon duty, Duncan left the manse, collected his followers, and began to scour the close and entangled wood which lay between the little glen and the Caird's Cove. David, who was a favorite with the Captain, on account of his spirit and courage, took the opportunity of escaping to attend the investigation of that great man.

33

CHAPTER LII

I did send for thee,

That Talbot's name might be in thee revived,
When sapless age and weak unable limbs
Should bring thy father to his drooping chair.
But—O malignant and ill-boding stars !—
Henry VI. Part I.

DUNCAN and his party had not proceeded very far in the
direction of the Caird's Cove before they heard a shot, which
was quickly followed by one or two others. "Some tamn'd
villains among the roe-deer," said Duncan; "look sharp
out, lads."

The clash of swords was next heard, and Duncan and his
myrmidons, hastening to the spot, found Butler and Sir
George Staunton's servant in the hands of four ruffians.
Sir George himself lay stretched on the ground, with his
drawn sword in his hand. Duncan, who was as brave as a
lion, instantly fired his pistol at the leader of the band,
unsheathed his sword, cried out to his men, "Claymore !"
and run his weapon through the body of the fellow whom
he had previously wounded, who was no other than Donacha Dhu na Dunaigh himself. The other banditti were
speedily overpowered, excepting one young lad, who made
wonderful resistance for his years, and was at length secured
with difficulty.

Butler, so soon as he was liberated from the ruffians, ran
to raise Sir George Staunton; but life had wholly left him.

"A great misfortune," said Duncan; "I think it will
pe pest that I go forward to intimate it to the coot leddy.
Tavie, my dear, you hae smelled pouther for the first time
this day. Take my sword and hack off Donacha's head,
whilk will pe coot practise for you against the time you
may wish to do the same kindness to a living shentleman ;
or hould, as your father does not approve, you may leave
it alone, as he will pe a greater object of satisfaction to
Leddy Staunton to see him entire ; and I hope she will do
me the credit to pelieve that I can afenge a shentleman's
plood fery speedily and well."

Such was the observation of a man too much accustomed

514

to the ancient state of manners in the Highlands to look upon the issue of such a skirmish as anything worthy of wonder or emotion.

We will not attempt to describe the very contrary effect which the unexpected disaster produced upon Lady Staunton, when the bloody corpse of her husband was brought to the house, where she expected to meet him alive and well. All was forgotten but that he was the lover of her youth ; and, whatever were his faults to the world, that he had towards her exhibited only those that arose from the inequality of spirits and temper incident to a situation of unparalleled difficulty. In the vivacity of her grief she gave way to all the natural irritability of her temper ; shriek followed shriek, and swoon succeeded to swoon. It required all Jeanie's watchful affection to prevent her from making known, in these paroxysms of affliction, much which it was of the highest importance that she should keep secret.

At length silence and exhaustion succeeded to frenzy, and Jeanie stole out to take counsel with her husband, and to exhort him to anticipate the Captain's interference by taking possession in Lady Staunton's name of the private papers of her deceased husband. To the utter astonishment of Butler, she now for the first time explained the relation betwixt herself and Lady Staunton, which authorized, nay, demanded, that he should prevent any stranger from being unnecessarily made acquainted with her family affairs. It was in such a crisis that Jeanie's active and undaunted habits of virtuous exertion were most conspicuous. While the Captain's attention was still engaged by a prolonged refreshment, and a very tedious examination, in Gaelic and English, of all the prisoners, and every other witness of the fatal transaction, she had the body of her brother-in-law undressed and properly disposed. It then appeared, from the crucifix, the beads, and the shirt of hair which he wore next his person, that his sense of guilt had induced him to receive the dogmata of a religion which pretends, by the maceration of the body, to expiate the crimes of the soul. In the packet of papers which the express had brought to Sir George Staunton from Edinburgh, and which Butler, authorized by his connection with the deceased, did not scruple to examine, he found new and astonishing intelligence, which gave him reason to thank God he had taken that measure.

Ratcliffe, to whom all sorts of misdeeds and misdoers were familiar, instigated by the promised reward, soon

found himself in a condition to trace the infant of these unhappy parents. The woman to whom Meg Murdockson had sold that most unfortunate child had made it the companion of her wanderings and her beggary until he was about seven or eight years old, when, as Ratcliffe learned from a companion of hers, then in the correction-house of Edinburgh, she sold him in her turn to Donacha Dhu na Dunaigh. This man, to whom no act of mischief was unknown, was occasionally an agent in a horrible trade then carried on betwixt Scotland and America, for supplying the plantations with servants, by means of kidnapping, as it was termed, both men and women, but especially children under age. Here Ratcliffe lost sight of the boy, but had no doubt but Donacha Dhu could give an account of him. The gentleman of the law, so often mentioned, despatched therefore an express with a letter to Sir George Staunton, and another covering a warrant for apprehension of Donacha, with instructions to the Captain of Knockdunder to exert his utmost energy for that purpose.

Possessed of this information, and with a mind agitated by the most gloomy apprehensions, Butler now joined the Captain, and obtained from him with some difficulty a sight of the examinations. These, with a few questions to the elder of the prisoners, soon confirmed the most dreadful of Butler's anticipations. We give the heads of the information, without descending into minute details.

Donacha Dhu had indeed purchased Effie's unhappy child, with the purpose of selling it to the American traders, whom he had been in the habit of supplying with human flesh. But no opportunity occurred for some time; and the boy, who was known by the name of "The Whistler," made some impression on the heart and affections even of this rude savage, perhaps because he saw in him flashes of a spirit as fierce and vindictive as his own. When Donacha struck or threatened him—a very common occurrence—he did not answer with complaints and entreaties like other children, but with oaths and efforts at revenge; he had all the wild merit, too, by which Woggarwolfe's arrow-bearing page won the hard heart of his master:

> Like a wild cub, rear'd at the ruffian's feet,
> He could say biting jests, bold ditties sing,
> And quaff his foaming bumper at the board,
> With all the mockery of a little man.*

---

* *Ethwald.*

The death of Sir George Staunton.

In short, as Donacha Dhu said, the Whistler was a born imp of Satan, and *therefore* he should never leave him. Accordingly, from his eleventh year forward, he was one of the band, and often engaged in acts of violence. The last of these was more immediately occasioned by the researches which the Whistler's real father made after him whom he had been taught to consider as such. Donacha Dhu's fears had been for some time excited by the strength of the means which began now to be employed against persons of his description. He was sensible he existed only by the precarious indulgence of his namesake, Duncan of Knock-dunder, who was used to boast that he could put him down or string him up when he had a mind. He resolved to leave the kingdom by means of one of those sloops which were engaged in the traffic of his old kidnapping friends, and which was about to sail for America; but he was desirous first to strike a bold stroke.

The ruffian's cupidity was excited by the intelligence that a wealthy Englishman was coming to the manse. He had neither forgotten the Whistler's report of the gold he had seen in Lady Staunton's purse, nor his old vow of revenge against the minister; and, to bring the whole to a point, he conceived the hope of appropriating the money which, according to the general report of the country, the minister was to bring from Edinburgh to pay for his new purchase. While he was considering how he might best accomplish his purpose, he received the intelligence from one quarter that the vessel in which he proposed to sail was to sail immediately from Greenock; from another, that the minister and a rich English lord, with a great many thousand pounds, were expected the next evening at the manse; and from a third, that he must consult his safety by leaving his ordinary haunts as soon as possible, for that the Captain had ordered out a party to scour the glens for him at break of day. Donacha laid his plans with promptitude and decision. He embarked with the Whistler and two others of his band (whom, by the by, he meant to sell to the kidnappers), and set sail for the Caird's Cove. He intended to lurk till nightfall in the wood adjoining to this place, which he thought was too near the habitation of men to excite the suspicion of Duncan Knock, then break into Butler's peaceful habitation, and flesh at once his appetite for plunder and revenge. When his villainy was accomplished, his boat was to convey him to the vessel, which, according to previous agreement with the master, was instantly to set sail.

This desperate design would probably have suceeeded, but for the ruffians being discovered in their lurking-place by Sir George Staunton and **Butler, in** their accidental walk from the Caird's Cove **towards the** manse. Finding himself detected, and at the **same time** observing that the servant carried a casket, or strong-box, Donacha conceived that both his prize and his victims were within his power, and attacked the travelers without hesitation. Shots were fired and swords drawn on both sides ; Sir George Staunton offered the bravest resistance, till he fell, as there was too much reason to believe, by the hand of a son so long sought, and now at length so unhappily met.

While Butler was half-stunned with this intelligence, the hoarse voice of Knockdunder added to his consternation— "I will take the liperty to take down the pell-ropes, Mr. Putler, as I must pe taking order to hang these idle people up to-morrow morning, to teach them more consideration in their doings in future."

Butler entreated him to remember the act abolishing the heritable jurisdictions, and that he ought to send them to Glasgow or Inverary, to be tried by the circuit.

Duncan scorned the proposal.

"The Jurisdiction Act," he said, "had nothing to do put with the rebels, and specially not with Argyle's country ; and he would hang the men up all three in one row before coot Leddy Staunton's windows, which would be a creat comfort to her in the morning to see that the coot gentleman, her husband, had been suitably afenged."

And the utmost length that Butler's most earnest entreaties could prevail was, that he would reserve "the twa pig carles for the circuit, but as for him they ca'd the Fustler, he should try how he could fustle in a swinging tow. for it suldna be said that a shentleman, friend to the Duke. was killed in his country, and his people didna take at least twa lives for ane."

Butler entreated him to spare the victim for his soul's sake. But Knockdunder answered, "That the soul of such a scum had been long the tefil's property, and that, Cot tam ! he was determined to gif the tefil his due."

All persuasion was in vain, and Duncan issued his mandate for execution on the succeeding morning. The child of guilt and misery was separated from his companions, strongly pinioned, and committed to a separate room, of which the Captain kept the key.

In the silence of the night, however, Mrs. Butler arose,

resolved, if possible, to avert, at least to delay, the fate which hung over her nephew, especially if, upon conversing with him, she should see any hope of his being brought to better temper. She had a master-key that opened every lock in the house ; and at midnight, when all was still, she stood before the eyes of the astonished young savage, as, hard bound with cords, he lay, like a sheep designed for slaughter, upon a quantity of the refuse of flax which filled a corner in the apartment. Amid features sun-burned, tawny, grimed with dirt, and obscured by his shaggy hair of a rusted black color, Jeanie tried in vain to trace the likeness of either of his very handsome parents. Yet how could she refuse compassion to a creature so young and so wretched— so much more wretched than even he himself could be aware of, since the murder he had too probably committed with his own hand, but in which he had at any rate participated, was in fact a parricide. She placed food on a table near him, raised him, and slacked the cords on his arms, so as to permit him to feed himself. He stretched out his hands, still smeared with blood, perhaps that of his father, and he ate voraciously and in silence.

"What is your first name ?" said Jeanie, by way of opening the conversation.

"The Whistler."

"But your Christian name, by which you were baptized ?"

"I never was baptized that I know of. I have no other name than the Whistler."

"Poor unhappy abandoned lad !" said Jeanie. "What would ye do if you could escape from this place, and the death you are to die to-morrow morning ?"

"Join wi' Rob Roy, or wi' Sergeant More Cameron (noted freebooters at that time), and revenge Donacha's death on all and sundry."

"O, ye unhappy boy," said Jeanie, "do ye ken what will come o' ye when ye die ?"

"I shall neither feel cauld nor hunger more," said the youth, doggedly.

"To let him be executed in this dreadful state of mind would be to destroy baith body and soul, and to let him gang I dare not ; what will be done ? But he is my sister's son— my own nephew—our flesh and blood ; and his hands and feet are yerked as tight as cords can be drawn. Whistler, do the cords hurt you ?"

"Very much."

"But, if I were to slacken them, you would harm me ?"

"No, I would not; you never harmed me or mine."

"There may be good in him yet," thought Jeanie; "I will try fair play with him."

She cut his bonds. He stood upright, looked round with a laugh of wild exultation, clapped his hands together, and sprung from the ground, as if in transport on finding himself at liberty. He looked so wild that Jeanie trembled at what she had done.

"Let me out," said the young savage.

"I wunna, unless you promise——"

"Then I'll make you glad to let us both out."

He seized the lighted candle and threw it among the flax, which was instantly in a flame. Jeanie screamed, and ran out of the room; the prisoner rushed past her, threw open a window in the passage, jumped into the garden, sprung over its enclosure, bounded through the woods like a deer, and gained the seashore. Meantime, the fire was extinguished; but the prisoner was sought in vain. As Jeanie kept her own secret, the share she had in his escape was not discovered; but they learned his fate some time afterwards; it was as wild as his life had hitherto been.

The anxious inquiries of Butler at length learned that the youth had gained the ship in which his master, Donacha, had designed to embark. But the avaricious shipmaster, enured by his evil trade to every species of treachery, and disappointed of the rich booty which Donacha had proposed to bring aboard, secured the person of the fugitive, and having transported him to America, sold him as a slave, or indented servant, to a Virginian planter far up the country. When these tidings reached Butler, he sent over to America a sufficient sum to redeem the lad from slavery, with instructions that measures should be taken for improving his mind, restraining his evil propensities, and encouraging whatever good might appear in his character. But this aid came too late. The young man had headed a conspiracy in which his inhuman master was put to death, and had then fled to the next tribe of wild Indians. He was never more heard of; and it may therefore be presumed that he lived and died after the manner of that savage people, with whom his previous habits had well fitted him to associate.

All hopes of the young man's reformation being now ended, Mr. and Mrs. Butler thought it could serve no purpose to explain to Lady Staunton a history so full of horror. She remained their guest more than a year, during the greater part of which period her grief was excessive. In the latter months, it assumed the appearance of listlessness and low spirits, which the monotony of her sister's quiet establishment afforded no means of dissipating. Effie, from her earliest youth, was never formed for a quiet low content. Far different from her sister, she required the dissipation of society to divert her sorrow or enhance her joy. She left the seclusion of Knocktarlitie with tears of sincere affection, and after heaping its inmates with all she could think of that might be valuable in their eyes. But she *did* leave it; and when the anguish of the parting was over her departure was relief to both sisters.

The family at the manse of Knocktarlitie, in their own quiet happiness, heard of the well-dowered and beautiful Lady Staunton resuming her place in the fashionable world. They learned it by more substantial proof, for David received a commission; and as the military spirit of Bible Butler seemed to have revived in him, his good behavior qualified the envy of five hundred young Highland cadets, "come of good houses," who were astonished at the rapidity of his promotion. Reuben followed the law, and rose more slowly, yet surely. Euphemia Butler, whose fortune, augmented by her aunt's generosity, and added to her own beauty, rendered her no small prize, married a Highland laird, who never asked the name of her grandfather, and was loaded on the occasion with presents from Lady Staunton, which made her the envy of all the beauties of Dunbarton and Argyleshires.

After blazing nearly ten years in the fashionable world, and hiding, like many of her compeers, an aching heart with a gay demeanor, after declining repeated offers of the most respectable kind for a second matrimonial engagement, Lady Staunton betrayed the inward wound by retiring to the Continent and taking up her abode in the convent where she had received her education. She never took the veil, but lived and died in severe seclusion, and in the practise of the Roman Catholic religion, in all its formal observances, vigils, and austerities.

Jeanie had so much of her father's spirit as to sorrow bitterly for this apostacy, and Butler joined in the regret. "Yet any religion, however imperfect," he said, "was better than cold scepticism, or the hurrying din of dissipation, which fills the ears of the worldlings, until they care for none of these things."

Meanwhile, happy in each other, in the prosperity of their

family, and the love and honor of all who knew them, this simple pair lived beloved and died lamented.

READER—This tale will not be told in vain, if it shall be found to illustrate the great truth that guilt, though it may attain temporal splendor, can never confer real happiness; that the evil consequences of our crimes long survive their commission, and, like the ghosts of the murdered, forever haunt the steps of the malefactor; and that the paths of virtue, though seldom those of worldly greatness, are always those of pleasantness and peace.

L'Envoy, by JEDEDIAH CLEISHBOTHAM

THUS concludeth the Tale of *The Heart of Midlothian,* which hath filled more pages than I opined. The Heart of Midlothian is now no more, or rather it is transferred to the extreme side of the city, even as the Sieur Jean Baptiste hath it, in his pleasant comedy called *Le Medecin Malgre lui,* where the simulated doctor wittily replieth to a charge, Poquelin that he had placed the heart on the right side instead of the left, " *Cela étoit autrefois ainsi, mais nous avons changé tout cela.* " Of which witty speech, if any reader shall demand the purport, I have only to respond, that I teach the French as well as the classical tongues, at the easy rate of five shillings per quarter, as my advertisements are periodically making known to the public.

NOTES TO THE HEART OF MIDLOTHIAN.

NOTE 1.—TOMBSTONE TO HELEN WALKER, p. XI.

On Helen Walker's tombstone in Irongray churchyard, Dumfriesshire, there is engraved the following epitaph, written by Sir Walter Scott:—

THIS STONE WAS ERECTED

BY THE AUTHOR OF WAVERLEY

TO THE MEMORY

OF

HELEN WALKER,

WHO DIED IN THE YEAR OF GOD 1791.

THIS HUMBLE INDIVIDUAL PRACTISED IN REAL LIFE

THE VIRTUES

WITH WHICH FICTION HAS INVESTED

THE IMAGINARY CHARACTER OF

JEANIE DEANS;

REFUSING THE SLIGHTEST DEPARTURE

FROM VERACITY,

EVEN TO SAVE THE LIFE OF A SISTER,

SHE NEVERTHELESS SHOWED HER

KINDNESS AND FORTITUDE,

IN RESCUING HER FROM THE SEVERITY OF THE LAW

AT THE EXPENSE OF PERSONAL EXERTIONS

WHICH THE TIME RENDERED AS DIFFICULT

AS THE MOTIVE WAS LAUDABLE.

RESPECT THE GRAVE OF POVERTY

WHEN COMBINED WITH LOVE OF TRUTH

AND DEAR AFFECTION.

Erected October 1831.   (Laing.)

NOTE 2.—SIR WALTER SCOTT'S RELATIONS WITH THE QUAKERS, p. XVII.

It is an old proverb that 'many a true word is spoken in jest.' The existence of Walter Scott, third son of Sir William Scott of Harden, is instructed, as it is called, by a charter under the great seal, 'Domino Willielmo Scott de Harden militi, et Waltero Scott suo filio

legitimo tertio genito, terarum de Roberton.'* The munificent old
gentleman left all this four sons considerable estates, and settled those
of Eildrig and Raeburn, together with valuable possessions around
Lessudden, upon Walter, his third son, who is ancestor of the Scots
of Raeburn, and of the Author of Waverley. He appears to have
become a convert to the doctrine of the Quakers, or Friends, and a
great assertor of their peculiar tenets. This was probably at the time
when George Fox, the celebrated apostle of the sect, made an expedition into the south of Scotland about 1657. on which occasion he boasts
that 'as he first set his horse's feet upon Scottish ground he felt the
seed of grace to sparkle about him like innumerable sparks of fire.'
Upon the same occasion, probably, Sir Gideon Scott of Highchesters,
second son of Sir William, immediate elder brother of Walter, and
ancestor of the Author's friend and kinsman, the present representative of the family of Harden, also embraced the tenets of Quakerism.
This last convert, Gideon, entered into a controversy with the Rev.
James Kirkton, author of the Secret and True History of the Church
of Scotland, which is noticed by my ingenious friend, Mr. Charles
Kirkpatrick Sharpe, in his valuable and curious edition of that work,
4to, 1817. Sir William Scott, eldest of the brothers, remained, amid
the defection of his two younger brethren, an orthodox member of the
Presbyterian Church, and used such means for reclaiming Walter of
Raeburn from his heresy as savoured far more of persecution than
persuasion. In this he was assisted by MacDougal of Makerston,
brother to Isabella MacDougal, the wife of the said Walter, and who,
like her husband, had conformed to the Quaker tenets.

The interest possessed by Sir William Scott and Makerston was
powerful enough to procure the two following acts of the Privy Council of Scotland, directed against Walter of Raeburn as an heretic and
convert to Quakerism, appointing him to be imprisoned first in Edinburgh jail, and then in that of Jedburgh; and his children to be taken
by force from the society and direction of their parents, and educated
at a distance from them, besides the assignment of a sum for their
maintenance sufficient in those times to be burdensome to a moderate
Scottish estate:—

'Apud Edin, vigesimo Junii 1665.

'The Lords of his Maj. Privy Councill having received information that Scott of Raeburn, and Isobel Mackdougall, his wife, being
infected with the error of Quakerism, doe endeavour to breid and
traine up William, Walter, and Isobel Scotts, their children, in the
same profession, doe yrfore give order and command to Sir William
Scott of Ha den, the sd Raeburn's brother, to seperat and take away
the sds children from the custody and society of the sds parents, and
to cause educat and bring them up in his owne house, or any other
convenient place, and ordaines letters to be direct at the sd Sir William's instance against Raeburn, for a maintenance to the sds children, and that the sd. Sir Wm. gave ane account of his diligence with
all conveniency.'

'Edinburgh, 5th July 1666.

'Anent a petition presented by Sir Wm. Scott of Harden, for himself and in name and behalf of the three children of Walter Scott of
Raeburn, his brother, showing that the Lords of Councll, by ane act
of the 22d (20th) day of Junii 1665, did grant power and warrand to the
petitioner to separat and take away Raeburn's children from his family and education, and to breed them in some convenient place, where
they might be free from all infection in yr younger years from the
princepalls of Quakerism, and, for maintenance of the sds children,
did ordain letters to be direct against Raeburn; and, seeing the petitioner, in obedience to the sd order, did take away the sds children,
being two sonnes and a daughter, and after some paines taken upon
them in his owne family, hes sent them to the city of Glasgow, to be
bread at schooles, and there to be principled with the knowledge of
the true religion, and that it is necessary the Councill determine what
shall be the maintenance for qch Raeburn's three children may be
charged, as likewayes that Raeburn himself, being now prisoner in

---

*See Douglas's Baronage, p. 215.

the Tolbuith of Edin., where he dayley converses with all the Quakers who are prisoners there, and others who dayly resort to them,
whereby he is hardened in his pernitious opinions and principles,
without all hope of recovery, unlesse he be seperate from such pernitious company, humbly therefore, desyring that the Councill might
determine upon the soume of money to be payed be Raeburn, for the
education of his children, to the petitioner, who will be countable
yrfore; and yt, in order to his conversion, the place of his imprisonment may be changed. The Lords of his Maj. Privy Councill, having
at length heard and considered the forsd petition, doe modifie the
soume of two thousand pounds Scots, to be payed yearly at the terme
of Whitsunday be the said Walter Scott of Raeburn, furth of his
estate, to the petitioner, for the entertainment and education of the
sd children, beginning the first termes payment yrof at Whitsunday
last for the half year preceding, and so furth yearly, at the sd terme
of Whitsunday in tyme coming till further orders; and ordaines the
sd Walter Scott of Raeburn to be transported from the Tolbuith of
Edr to the prison of Jedburgh, where his friends and oyrs may
have occasion to convert him. And to the effect he may be secured
from the practice of oyr Quakers, the sds Lords doe hereby discharge
the magistrates of Jedburgh to suffer any percons suspect of these
principlls to have access to him; and in case any contraveen, that
they secure yr persons till they be yrfore puneist; and ordaines letters to be direct heirupon in form, as effeirs.'

Both the sons thus harshly separated from their father proved
good scholars. The eldest, William, who carried on the line of Raeburn, was, like his father, a deep Orientalist; the younger, Walter,
became a good classical scholar, a great friend and correspondent
of the celebrated Dr. Pitcairn, and a Jacobite so distinguished for
zeal that he made a vow never to shave his beard till the restoration
of the exiled family. This last Walter Scott was the Author's great-
grandfather.

There is yet another link betwixt the Author and the simple-
minded and excellent Society of Friends, through a proselyte of much
more importance than Walter Scott of Raeburn. The celebrated John
Swinton of Swinton, nineteenth baron in descent of that ancient and
once powerful family, was, with Sir William Lockhart of Lee, the
person whom Cromwell chiefly trusted in the management of the
Scottish affairs during his usurpation. After the Restoration, Swinton was devoted as a victim to the new order of things, and was
brought down in the same vessel which conveyed the Marquis of
Argyle to Edinburgh, where that nobleman was tried and executed.
Swinton was destined to the same fate. He had assumed the habit
and entered into the society of the Quakers, and appeared as one of
their number before the Parliament of Scotland. He renounced all
legal defence, though several pleas were open to him and answered,
in conformity to the principles of his sect, that at the time these
crimes were imputed to him he was in the gall of bitterness and bond
of iniquity; but that God Almighty having since called him to the
light, he saw and acknowledged these errors, and did not refuse to
pay the forfeit of them, even though, in the judgment of the Parliament, it should extend to life itself.

Respect to fallen greatness, and to the patience and calm resignation with which a man once in high power expressed himself under
such a change of fortune, found Swinton friends; family connexions
and some interested considerations of Middleton, the Commissioner,
joined to procure his safety, and he was dismissed, but after a long
imprisonment and much dilapidation of his estates. It is said that
Swinton's admonitions while confined in the Castle of Edinburgh had
a considerable share in converting to the tenets of the Friends Colonel
David Barclay, then lying there in garrison. This was the father of
Robert Barclay, author of the celebrated Apology for the Quakers.
It may be observed among the inconsistencies of human nature, that
Kirkton, Wodrow, and other Presbyterian authors, who have detailed
the sufferings of their own sect for non-conformity with the established church, censure the government of the time for not exerting
the civil power against the peaceful enthusiasts we have treated of,
and some express particular chagrin at the escape of Swinton. Whatever might be his motives for assuming the tenets of the Friends, the
old man retained them faithfully till the close of his life.

Jean Swinton, grand-daughter of Sir John Swinton, son of Judge
Swinton, as the Quaker was usually termed, was the mother of Anne
Rutherford, the Author's mother.

And thus, as in the play of the Anti-Jacobin, the ghost of the
Author's grandmother having arisen to speak the Epilogue, it is full
time to conlude, lest the reader should remonstrate that his desire to
know the author of Waverley never included a wish to be acquainted with his whole ancestry.

NOTE 3.—EDINBURGH CITY GUARD, p. 24

The Lord Provost was ex-officio commander and colonel of the
corps, which might be increased to three hundred men when the times
required it. No other drum but theirs was allowed to sound on the
High Street between the Luckenbooths and the Netherbow.

NOTE 4.—LAST MARCH OF THE CITY GUARD, p. 26.

This ancient corps is now entirely disbanded. Their last march to
do duty at Hallow Fair had something in it affecting. Their drums
and fifes had been wont on better days to play, on this joyous occasion, the lively tune of

'Jockey to the fair;'

but on this final occasion the afflicted veterans moved slowly to the
dirge of

'The last time I came ower the muir.'

NOTE 5.—THE KELPIE'S VOICE, p. 29

There is a tradition that, while a little stream was swollen into a
torrent by recent showers, the discontented voice of the Water Spirit
was heard to pronounce these words. At the same moment a man,
urged on by his fate, or in Scottish language, 'fey,' arrived at a gallop
and prepared to cross the water. No remonstrance from the bystanders was of power to stop him; he plunged into the stream and per·
ished.

NOTE 6.—BESS WYND, p. 35

Maitland calls it Best's Wynd, and later writers Beth's Wynd.
As the name implies, it was an open thoroughfare or alley leading
from the Lawnmarket, and extended in a direct line between the old
tolbooth to near the head of the Cowgate. It was partly destroyed
by fire in 1786, and was totally removed in 1809, preparatory to the
building of the new libraries of the Faculty of Advocates and Writers
to the Signet (Laing).

NOTE 7.—LAW RELATING TO CHILD-MURDER, p. 45

The Scottish Statute Book, anno 1690, chapter 21, in consequence
of the great increase of the crime of child-murder, both from the
temptations to commit the offence and the difficulty of discovery,
enacted a certain set of presumptions, which, in the absence of direct proof, the jury were directed to receive as evidence of the crime
having actually been committed. The circumstances selected for
this purpose were, that the woman should have concealed her situation during the whole period of pregnancy; that she should not have
called for help at her delivery; and that, combined with these grounds
of suspicion, the child should be either found dead or be altogether
missing. Many persons suffered death during the last century under
this severe act. But during the Author's memory a more lenient
course was followed, and the female accused under the act, and conscious of no competent defence, usually lodged a petition to the
Court of Justiciary, denying, for form's sake, the tenor of the indictment, but stating that, as her good name had been destroyed by the

charge, she was willing to submit to sentence of banishment, to which the crown counsel usually consented. This lenity in practice, and the comparative infrequency of the crime since the doom of public ecclesiastical penance has been generally dispensed with, have led to the abolition of the Statute of William and Mary, which is now replaced by another, imposing banishment in those circumstances in which the crime was formerly capital. This alteration took place in 1803.

NOTE 8.—ENGLISH TRANSLATION OF 'PORTA,' etc. p. 47.

> Wide is the fronting gate, and, raised on high,
> With adamantine columns threats the sky;
> Vain is the force of man, and Heaven's as vain,
> To crush the pillars which the pile sustain,
> Sublime on these a tower of steel is rear'd.
> DRYDEN'S Virgil, BOOK **VI.**

NOTE 9.—JOURNEYMEN MECHANICS, p. 53.

A near relation of the Author's used to tell of having been stopped by the rioters and escorted home in the manner described. On reaching her own home, one of her attendants, in appearance a 'baxter,' i. e. a baker's lad, handed her out of her chair, and took leave with a bow, which, in the lady's opinion, argued breeding that could hardly be learned beside the oven.

NOTE 10.—THE OLD TOLBOOTH, p. 55.

The **ancient** tolbooth of Edinburgh, situated and described as in chapter vi., was built by the citizens in 1561, and destined for the accommodation of Parliament, as well as of the High Courts of Justice, and at the same time for the confinement of prisoners for debt or on criminal charges. Since the year 1640, when the present Parliament House was erected, the tolbooth was occupied as a prison only. Gloomy and dismal as it was, the situation in the centre of the High Street rendered it so particularly well-aired, that when the plague laid waste the city, in 1645, it affected none within these melancholy precincts. The tolbooth was removed, with the mass of buildings in which it was incorporated, in the Autumn of the year 1817. At that time the kindness of his old schoolfellow and friend, Robert Johnstone, Esquire, then Dean of Guild of the city, with the liberal acquiescence of the persons who had contracted for the work, procured for the Author of Waverley the stones which composed the gateway, together with the door, and its ponderous fastenings, which he employed in decorating the entrance of his kitchen-court at Abbotsford. 'To such base offices may we return!' The application of these relics of the Heart of Midlothian to serve as the postern gate to a court of modern offices may be justly ridiculed as whimsical; but yet it is not without interest that we see the gateway through which so much of the stormy politics of a rude age, and the vice and misery of later times, had found their passage, now occupied in the service of rural economy. Last year, to complete the change, a tomtit was pleased to built her nest within the lock of the tolbooth, a strong temptation to have committed a sonnet, had the Author, like Tony Lumpkin, been in a concatenation accordingly.

It is worth mentioning that an act of beneficence celebrated the demolition of the Heart of Midlothian. A subscription, raised and applied by the worthy magistrate above-mentioned, procured the manumission of most of the unfortunate debtors confined in the old jail, so that there were few or none transferred to the new place of confiement.—

Few persons now living are likely to remember the interior of the Old Tolbooth, with narrow staircase, thick walls, and small apartments, nor to imagine that it could ever have been used for these purposes. Robert Chambers, in his Minor Antiquities of Edinburgh, has preserved ground-plans, or sections, which clearly show this. The largest hall was on the second floor, and measured 27 feet by 20,

and 12 feet high. It may have been intended for the meetings of the
Town Council, while the Parliament assembled, after 1560, in what
was called the Upper Tolbooth, that is, the south-west portion of the
Collegiate Church of St. Giles, until the year 1640, when the present
Parliament House was completed. Being no longer required for such
a purpose, it was set apart by the Town Council on the 24th December 1641 as a distinct church, with the name of the Tolbooth parish.
and therefore could not have derived the name from its vicinity to
the tolbooth, as usually stated. The figure of a heart upon the pavement between St. Giles's Church and the Edinburgh County Hall
now marks the site of the Old Tolbooth (Laing.)

NOTE 11.—THE MURDER OF CAPTAIN PORTEUS, p. 64.

The following interesting and authentic account of the inquiries
made by Crown Counsel into the affair of the Porteous Mob seems
to have been drawn up by the Solicitor-General. The office was held
in 1737 by Charles Erskine, Esq. I owe this curious illustration to the
kindness of a professional friend. It throws, indeed, little light on
the origin of the tumult; but shows how profound the darkness must
have been, which so much investigation could not dispel.

'Upon the 7th of September last, when the unhappy, wicked murder of Captain Porteus was committed, his Majesties Advocate and
Solicitor were out of town, the first beyond Inverness and the other
in Annandale, not far from Carlyle; neither of them knew anything
of the reprieve, nor did they in the least suspect that any disorder
was to happen.

'When the disorder happened, the magistrates and other persons
concerned in the management of the town, seemed to be all struck
of a heap; and whether, from the great terror that had seized all the
inhabitants, they thought ane immediate enquiry would be fruitless, or
whether being a direct insult upon the prerogative of the crown,
they did not care rashly to intermeddle—but no proceedings was had
by them. Only, soon after, ane express was sent to his Majesties
Solicitor, who came to town as soon as was possible for him; but, in
the meantime, the persons who had been most guilty had either run
off, or, at least, kept themselves upon the wing until they should see
what steps were taken by the Government.

'When the Solicitor arrived, he perceived the whole inhabitants
under a consternation. He had no materials furnished him; nay, the
inhabitants were so much afraid of being reputed informers, that
very few people had so much as the courage to speak with him on the
streets. However, having received her Majesties orders, by a letter
from the Duke of Newcastle, he resolved to sett about the matter in
earnest, and entered upon ane enquiry, gropeing in the dark. He
had no assistance from the magistrates worth mentioning, but called
witness after witness in the privatest manner before himself in his
own house, and for six weeks time, from morning to evening, went on
in the enquiry without taking the least diversion, or turning his
thoughts to any other business.

'He tried at first what he could do by declarations, by engaging
secresy, so that those who told the truth should never be discovered;
made use of no clerk, but wrote all the declarations with his own
hand, to encourage them to speak out. After all, for some time, he
could get nothing but ends of stories, which, when pursued, broke off;
and those who appeared and knew anything of the matter were under
the utmost terror lest it should take air that they had mentioned any
one man as guilty.

'During the course of the inquiry, the run of the town, which was
strong for the villanous actors, begun to alter a little, and when they
saw the King's servants in earnest to do their best, the generality,
who before had spoke very warmly in defence of the wickedness,
begun to be silent, and at that period more of the criminals begun to
abscond.

'At length the enquiry began to open a little, and the Sollicitor
was under some difficulty how to proceed. He very well saw that the
first warrand that was issued out would start the whole gang, and as
he had not come at any one of the most notorious offenders, he was
unwilling, upon the slight evidence he had, to begin. However, upon
notice given him by Generall Moyle that one King, a butcher in the
Canongate, had boasted in presence of Bridget Kneil, a soldier's wife,

the morning after Captain Porteus was hanged that he had a very active hand in the mob, a warrand was issued out, and King was apprehended and imprisoned in the Canongate tolbooth.

'This obliged the Sollic.tor immediately to proceed to take up those against whom he had any information. By a signed declaration, William Stirling, apprentice to James Stirling, merchant in Edinburgh, was charged as haveing been at the Nether-Bow, after the gates were shutt, with a Lochaber ax, or halbert, in his hand, and haveing begun a huzza, marched upon the head of the mob towards the Guard.

'James Braidwood, son to a candlemaker in town, was, by a signed declaration, charged as haveing been at the Tolbooth door, giveing directions to the mob about setting fire to the door, and that the mob named him by his name, and asked his advice

'By another declaration, one Stoddart, a journeyman smith, was charged of haveing boasted publickly, in a smith's shop at Leith that he had assisted in breaking open the Tolbooth door.

'Peter Traill, a journeyman wright, by one of the declarations, was also accused of haveing lockt the Nether-Bow Port when it was shutt by the mob.

'His Majesties Sollicitor having these nformations, imployed privately such persons as he could best rely on, and the truth was, there were very few in whom he could repose confidence. But he was, indeed, faithfully served by one Webster, a soldier in the Welsh fuzileers, recommended to him by Lieutenant Alshton, who, with very great address, informed himself, and really run some risque in getting his information, concerning the places where the persons informed against used to haunt, and how they might be seized. In consequence of which, a party of the Guard from the Canongate was agreed on to march up at a certain hour, when a message should be sent. The Sollicitor wrote a letter and gave it to one of the town officers, ordered to attend Captain Maitland, one of the town Captains, promoted to that command since the unhappy accident, who, indeed, was extremely diligent and active throughout the whole; and haveing got Stirling and Braidwood apprehended, dispatched the officers with the letter to the military in Canongate, who immediately begun their march, and by the time the Sollicitor had half examined the said two persons in the Burrow-room, where the magistrates were present, a party of fifty men, drums beating, marched into the Parliament closs, and drew up, which was the first thing that struck a terror, and from that time forward the insolence was succeeded by fear.

'Stirling and Braidwood were immediately sent to the Castle and imprisoned. That same night, Stoddart, the smith, was seized, and he was committed to the Castle also, as was likewise Traill, the journeyman wright, who were all severally examined, and denied the least accession.

'In the meantime the enquiry was going on, and it haveing cast up in one of the declarations, that a hump'd-backed creature marched with a gun as one of the guards to Porteus when he went up to the Lawn Markett, the person who emitted this declaration was employed to walk the streets to see if he could find him out; at last he came to the Sollicitor and told him he had found him, and that he was in a certain house. Whereupon a warrand was issued out against him, and he was apprehended and sent to the Castle, and he proved to be one Birnie, a helper to the Countess of Weemy's coachman.

'Thereafter, ane information was given in against William M'Lauchlan, ffootman to the said Countess, as haveing been very active in the mob; ffor some time he kept himself out of the way, but at last he was apprehended and likewise committed to the Castle.

'And these were all the prisoners who were putt under confinement in that place.

'There were other persons imprisoned in the Tolbooth at Edinburgh, and severalls against whom warrands were issued, but could not be apprehended, whose names and cases shall afterwards be more particularly taken notice of.

'The ffriends of Stirling made ane application to the Earl of Islay, Lord Justice-Generall, setting furth, that he was seized with a bloody fflux; that his life was in danger; and that upon ane examination of witnesses whose names were given in, it would appear to conviction that he had not the least access to any of the riotous proceedings of that wicked mob.

'This petition was by his Lordship putt in the hands of his Majesties Sollicitor, who examined the witnesses; and by their testimonies it appeared that the young man, who was not above eighteen years of age, was that night in company with about half a dozen companions, in a public house in Stephen Law's closs, near the back of the Guard, where they all remained untill the noise came to the house that the mob had shut the gates and seized the Guard, upon which the company broke up, and he and one of his companions went towards his master's house; and, in the course of the after examination, there was a witness who declared, nay, indeed swore—for the Sollicitor, by this time, saw it necessary to put those he examined upon oath—that he met him [Stirling] after he entered into the alley where his master lives, going towards his house; and another witness, fellow-prentice with Stirling, declares that after the mob had seized the Guard, he went home, where he found Stirling before him; and that his master lockt the door, and kept them both at home till after twelve at night: upon weighing of which testimonies, and upon consideration had, that he was charged by the declaration only of one person, who really did not appear to be a witness of the greatest weight, and that his life was in danger from the imprisonment, he was admitted to baill by the Lord Justice-Generall, by whose warrand he was committed.

'Braidwood's friends applyed in the same manner; but as he stood charged by more than one witness, he was not released—tho', indeed, the witnesses adduced for him say somewhat in his exculpation—that he does not seem to have been upon any original concert; and one of the witnesses says he was along with him at the Tolbooth door, and refuses what is said against him, with regard to his having advised the burning of the Tolbooth door. But he remains still in prison.

'As to Traill, the journeyman wright, he is charged by the same witness who declared against Stirling, and there is none concurrs with him; and to say the truth concerning him, he seemed to be the most ingenious of any of them whom the Sollicitor examined, and pointed out a witness by whom one of the first accomplices was discovered, and who escaped when the warrand was to be putt in execution against them. He positively denys his having shutt the gate, and 'tis thought Traill ought to be admitted to baill.

'As for Birnie, he is charged only by one witness, who had never seen him before, nor knew his name; so, tho' I dare say the witness honestly mentioned him, 'tis possible he may be mistaken; and in the examination of above 200 witnesses, there is no body concurrs with him, and he is ane insignificant little creature.

'With regard to M'Lauchlan, the proof is strong against him by one witness, that he acted as a serjeant or sort of commander, for some time, of a Guard that stood cross between the upper end of the Luckenbooths and the north side of the street, to stop all but friends from going towards the Tolbooth; and by other witnesses, that he was at the Tolbooth door with a link in his hand, while the operation of beating and burning it was going on; that he went along with the mob, with a halbert in his hand, until he came to the gallows-stone in the Grassmarket, and that he stuck the halbert into the hole of the gallows-stone; that afterwards he went in amongst the mob when Captain Porteus was carried to the dyer's tree; so that the proof seems very heavy against him.

'To sum up this matter with regard to the prisoners in the Castle, 'tis believed there is strong proof against M'Lauchlan; there is also proof against Braidwood. But as it consists only in emission of words said to have been had by him while at the Tolbooth door, and that he is an insignificant, pitiful creature, and will find people to swear heartily in his favours, 'tis at best doubtful whether a jury will be got to condemn him.

'As to those in the Tolbooth of Edinburgh, John Crawford, who had for some time been employed to ring the bells in the steeple of the new Church of Edinburgh, being in company with a soldier accidentally, the discourse falling in concerning Captain Porteus and his murder, as he appears to be a lightheaded fellow, he said that he knew people that were more guilty than any that were putt in prison. Upon this information Crawford was seized, and being examined, it appeared that, when the mob begun, as he was comeing down from the steeple, the mob took the keys from him: that he was that night in several corners, and did indeed delate severall persons whom he saw there, and immediately warrands were dispatched, and it was found they had absconded and fled. But there was no evidence against him of any kind. Nay, on the contrary, it appeared that he had been with the Magistrates in Clerk's, the vintner's, relating to them what he had seen in the streets. Therefore, after haveing detained him in prison ffor a very considerable time, his Majestie's Advocate and Sollicitor signed a warand for his liberation.

'There was also one James Wilson incarcerated in the said Tolbooth, upon the declaration of one witness, who said he saw him on the streets with a gun; and there he remained for some time in order to try if a concurring witness could be found, or that he acted any part in the tragedy and wickedness. But nothing further appeared against him; and being seized with a severe sickness, he is, by a warrand signed by his Majestie's Advocate and Sollicitor, liberated upon giveing sufficient baill.

'As to King, enquiry was made, and the ffact comes out beyond all exception, that he was in the lodge of the Nether-Bow, with Lindsay the waiter, and several other people, not at all concerned in the mob. But after the affair was over he went up towards the guard, and having met with Sandie the Turk and his wife, who escaped out of prison, they returned to his house at the Abbey, and then 'tis very possible he may have thought fitt in his beer to boast of villany, in which he could not possibly have any share; for that reason he was desired to find baill and he should be set at liberty. But he is a stranger and a fellow of very indifferent character, and 'tis believed it won't be easy for him to find baill. Wherefore, it's thought he must be sett at liberty without it. Because he is a burden upon the Government while kept in confinement, not being able to maintain himself.

'What is above is all that relates to persons in custody. But there are warrands out against a great many other persons who are fled, particularly against one William White, a journeyman baxter, who, by the evidence, appears to have been at the beginning of the mob, and to have gone along with the drum, from the West-Port, to the Nether-Bow, and is said to have been one of those who attacked the guard, and probably was as deep as any one there.

'Information was given that he was lurking at Falkirk, where he was born. Whereupon directions were sent to the Sheriff of the county, and a warrand from his Excellency Generall Wade to the commanding officers at Stirling and Linlithgow, to assist, and all possible endeavours were used to catch hold of him, and 'tis said he escaped very narrowly, having lyen concealed in some outhouse; and the misfortune was, that those who were employed in the search did not know him personally. Nor, indeed, was it easy to trust any of the acquaintances of so low, obscure a fellow with the secret of the warrand to be putt into execution.

'There was also strong evidence found against Robert Taylor, servant to William and Charles Thomsons, periwig-makers, that he acted as ane officer among the mob, and he is traced from the guard to the well at the head of Forrester's Wynd, where he stood and had the appellation of Captain from the mob, and from that walking down the Bow before Captain Porteus, with his Lochaber axe; and by the description given of one who had hawl'd the rope by which Captain Porteus was pulled up, 'tis believed Taylor was the person; and 'tis further probable that the witness who delated Stirling had mistaken Taylor for him, their stature and age (so far as can be gathered from the description) being much the same.

'A great deal of pains were taken, and no charge was saved, in order to have catched hold of this Taylor, and warrands were sent to the country where he was born; but it appears he had shipt himself off for Holland, where it is said he now is.

'There is strong evidence also against Thomas Burns, butcher, that he was ane active person from the beginning of the mob to the end of it. He lurkt for some time amongst those of his trade; and artfully enough a train was laid to catch him, under pretence of a message that had come from his father in Ireland, so that he came to a blind ale-house in the Flesh-market closs, and a party being ready, was by Webster the soldier, who was upon this exploit, advertised to come down. However, Burns escaped out at a back window, and hid

himself in some of the houses which are heaped together upon one
another in that place, so that it was not possible to catch him. 'Tis
now said he is gone to Ireland to his father, who lives there.

'There is evidence also against one Robert Anderson, journeyman
and servant to Colin Alison, wright, and against Thomas Linnen
[Linning] and James Maxwell, both servants also to the said Colin
Alison, who all seem to have been deeply concerned in the matter.
Anderson is one of those who putt the rope upon Captain Porteus's
neck. Linnen seems also to have been very active; and Maxwell—
which is pretty remarkable—is proven to have come to a shop upon
the Friday before, and charged the journeymen and prentices there
to attend in the Parliament close on Tuesday night, to assist to hang
Captain Porteus. These three did early abscond, and though warrands had been issued out against them, and all endeavours used to
apprehend them, could not be found.

'The like warrands had been issued with regard to ships from
Leith. But whether they had been scard, or whether the information had been groundless, they had no effect.

'This is a summary of the enquiry, ffrom which it appears there
is no prooff on which one can rely, but against M'Lauchlan. There
is a prooff also against Braidwood, but more exceptionable.

'One Waldie, a servant to George Campbell, wright, has also absconded, and many others, and 'tis informed that numbers of them
have shipt themselves off ffor the Plantations; and upon ane information that a ship was going off ffrom Glasgow, in which severall of
the rogues were to transport themselves beyond seas, proper warrands were obtained, and persons dispatched to search the said ship,
and seize any that can be found.

'His Majesties Advocate, since he came to town, has join'd with
the Solicitor, and has done his utmost to gett at the bottom of this
matter, but hitherto it stands as is above represented. They are resolved to have their eyes and their ears open and to do what they can.
But they labour'd exceedingly against the stream; and it may truly
be said that nothing was wanting on their part. Nor have they declined any labour to answer the commands laid upon them to search
the matter to the bottom.'

THE PORTEOUS MOB

In chapters ii.-vii., the circumstances of that extraordinary riot
and conspiracy, called the Porteous Mob, are given with as much accuracy as the Author was able to collect them. The order, regularity,
and determined resolution with which such a violent action was devised and executed were only equalled by the secrecy which was observed concerning the principal actors.

Although the fact was performed by torch-light, and in presence
of a great multitude, to some of whom, at least, the individual actors
must have been known, yet no discovery was ever made concerning
any of the perpetrators of the slaughter.

Two men only were brought to trial for an offence which the government were so anxious to detect and punish. William M'Lauchlan,
footman to the Countess of Wemyss, who is mentioned in the report
of the Solicitor-General (page 530), against whom strong evidence had
been obtained, was brought to trial in March, 1737, charged as having
been accessory to the riot, armed with a Lochaber axe. But this man,
who was at all times a silly creature, proved that he was in a state
of mortal intoxication during the time he was present with the rabble, incapable of giving them either advice or assistance, or indeed of
knowing what he or they were doing. He was also able to prove that
he was forced into the riot, and upheld while there by two bakers,
who put a Lochaber axe into his hand. The jury, wisely judging this
poor creature could be no proper subject of punishment, found the
panel 'Not guilty.' The same verdict was given in the case of Thomas
Linning, also mentioned in the Solicitor's memorial, who was tried in
1738. In short, neither then, nor for a long period afterwards, was
anything discovered relating to the organisation of the Porteous Plot.

The imagination of the people of Edinburgh was long irritated,
and their curiosity kept awake, by the mystery attending this extraordinary conspiracy. It was generally reported of such natives of
Edinburgh as, having left the city in youth, returned with a fortune

amassed in foreign countries, that they had originally fled on account of their share in the Porteous Mob. But little credit can be attached to these surmises, as in most of the cases they are contradicted by dates, and in none supported by anything but vague rumours, grounded on the ordinary wish of the vulgar to impute the success of prosperous men to some unpleasant source. The secret history of the Porteous Mob has been till this day unravelled; and it has always been quoted as a close, daring, and calculated act of violence of a nature peculiarly characteristic of the Scottish people.

Nevertheless, the Author, for a considerable time, nourished hopes to have found himself enabled to throw some light on this mysterious story. An old man, who died about twenty years ago, at the advanced age of ninety-three, was said to have made a communication to the clergyman who attended upon his death-bed, respecting the origin of the Porteous Mob. This person followed the trade of a carpenter, and had been employed as such on the estate of a family of opulence and condition. His character, in his line of life and amongst his neighbours, was excellent, and never underwent the slightest suspicion. His confession was said to have been to the following purpose:—That he was one of twelve young men belonging to the village of Pathhead, whose animosity against Porteous, on account of the execution of Wilson, was so extreme that they resolved to execute vengeance on him with their own hands rather than he should escape punishment. With this resolution they crossed the Forth at different ferries and rendezvoused at the suburb called Portsburgh, where their appearance in a body soon called numbers around them. The public mind was in such a state of irritation that it only wanted a single spark to create an explosion; and this was afforded by the exertions of the small and determined band of associates. The appearance of premeditation and order which distinguished the riot, according to his account, had its origin, not in any previous plan or conspiracy, but in the character of those who were engaged in it. The story also serves to show why nothing of the origin of the riot has ever been discovered, since, though in itself a great conflagration, its source, according to this account, was from an obscure and apparently inadequate cause.

I have been disappointed, however, in obtaining the evidence on which this story rests. The present proprietor of the estate on which the old man died (a particular friend of the Author) undertook to question the son of the deceased on the subject. This person follows his father's trade, and holds the employment of carpenter to the same family. He admits that his father's going abroad at the time of the Porteous Mob was popularly attributed to his having been concerned in that affair; but adds that, so far as is known to him, the old man had never made any confession to that effect, and, on the contrary, had uniformly denied being present. My kind friend, therefore, had recourse to a person from whom he had formerly heard the story; but who, either from respect to an old friend's memory or from failure of his own, happened to have forgotten that ever such a communication was made. So my obliging correspondent (who is a fox-hunter) wrote to me that he was completely planted; and that all that can be said with respect to the tradition is, that it certainly once existed and was generally believed.—

The Rev. Dr. Carlyle, minister of Inveresk, in his Autobiography, gives some interesting particulars relating to the Porteous Mob, from personal recollections. He happened to be present in the Tolbooth Church when Robertson made his escape, and also at the execution of Wilson in the Grassmarket, when Captain Porteous fired upon the mob and several persons were killed. Edinburgh, 1860, 8vo, pp. 33-42 (Laing).

NOTE 12.—DUMBIEDIKES, p. 69

Dumbiedikes, selected as descriptive of the taciturn character of the imaginary owner, is really the name of a house bordering on the King's Park, so called because the late Mr. Braidwood, an instructor of the deaf and dumb, resided there with his pupils. The situation of the real house is different from that assigned to the ideal mansion.

NOTE 13.—COLLEGE STUDENTS, p. 71

Immediately previous to the Revolution, the students at the Edinburgh College were violent anti-Catholics. They were strongly suspected of burning the house of Priestfield, belonging to the Lord Provost; and certainly were guilty of creating considerable riots in 1688-89.

NOTE 14.—RECOMMENDATION TO ARBORICULTURE, p. 71

The Author has been flattered by the assurance that this naive mode of recommending arboriculture—which was actually delivered in these very words by a Highland laird, while on his death-bed, to his son—had so much weight with a Scottish earl as to lead to his planting a large tract of country.

NOTE 15.—CARSPHARN JOHN, p. 84

John Semple, called Carspharn John, because minister of the parish in Galloway so called, was a Presbyterian clergyman of singular piety and great zeal, of whom Patrick Walker records the following passage: 'That night after his wife died, he spent the whole ensuing night in prayer and meditation in his garden. The next morning, one of his elders coming to see him, and lamenting his great loss and want of rest, he replied, "I declare I have not, all night, had one thought of the death of my wife I have been so taken up in meditating on Heavenly things. I have been this night on the banks of the Ulai, plucking an apple here and there." '—Walker's Remarkable Passages of the Life and Death of Mr. John Semple.

NOTE 16.—PATRICK WALKER, p. 94

This personage, whom it would be base ingratitude in the Author to pass over without some notice, was by far the most zealous and faithful collector and recorder of the actions and opinions of the Cameronians. He resided, while stationary, at the Bristo Port of Edinburgh, but was by trade an itinerant merchant or pedlar, which profession he seems to have exercised in Ireland as well as Britain. He composed biographical notices of Alexander Peden, John Semple, John Welwood, and Richard Cameron, all ministers of the Cameronian persuasion, to which the last-mentioned member gave the name.

It is from such tracts as these, written in the sense, feeling, and spirit of the sect, and not from the sophisticated narrative of a later period, that the real character of the persecuted class is to be gathered. Walker writes with a simplicity which sometimes slides into the burlesque, and sometimes attains a tone of simple pathos, but always expressing the most daring cofidence in his own correctness of creed and sentiments, sometimes with narrow-minded and disgusting bigotry. His turn for the marvellous was that of his time and sect; but there is little room to doubt his veracity concerning whatever he quotes on his own knowledge. His small tracts now bring a very high price, especially the earlier and authentic editions.

The tirade against dancing pronounced by David Deans is, as intimated in the text, partly borrowed from Peter [Patrick] Walker. He notices, as a foul reproach upon the name of Richard Cameron, that his memory was vituperated 'by pipers and fiddlers playing the Cameronian march—carnal vain springs, which too many professors of religion dance to; a practice unbecoming the professors of Christianity to dance to any spring, but somewhat more to this. Whatever," he proceeds, "be the many foul blots recorded of the saints in Scripture, none of them is charged with this regular fit of distraction. We find it has been practised by the wicked and profane, as the dancing at that brutish, base action of the calf-making; and it had been good for that unhappy lass who danced off the head of John the Baptist, that she had been born a cripple and never drawn a limb to her. Historians say that her sin was written upon her judgment, who some time thereafter was dancing upon the ice and it broke and snapt the head off her; her head danced above and her feet beneath. There is ground to think and conclude that, when the world's wickedness was great, dancing at their marriages was practised; but when the heavens above and the earth beneath were let loose upon them with that overflowing flood, their mirth was soon staid; and when the Lord in his holy justice rained fire and brimstone from heaven upon that wicked people and city Sodom, enjoying fulness of bread and idleness, their fiddle-strings and hands went all in a flame; and the whole people in thirty miles of length and ten of breadth, as historians say, were all made to fry in their skins; and at the end, whoever are giving in marriages and dancing when all will go in a flame, they will quickly change their note.

'I have often wondered thorow my life, how any, that ever knew what it was to bow a knee in earnest to pray, durst crook a hough to fyke and fling at a piper's and fiddler's springs. I bless the Lord that ordered my lot so in my dancing days, that made the fear of the bloody rope and bullets to my neck and head, the pain of boots, thumbikins, and irons, cold and hunger, wetness and weariness, to stop the lightness of my head and the wantonness of my feet. What the never-to-be-forgotten Man of God, John Knox, said to Queen Mary, when she gave him that sharp challenge, which would strike our mean-spirited, tongue-tacked ministers dumb, for his giving public faithful warning of the danger of church and nation, through her marrying the Dauphine of France, when he left her bubbling and greeting, and came to an outer court, where her Lady Maries were fyking and dancing, he said, "O brave ladies, a brave world, if it would last, and Heaven at the hinder end! But fye upon the knave Death, that will seize upon these bodies of yours; and where will all your fiddling and flinging be then?" Dancing being such a common evil, especially amongst young professors, that all the lovers of the Lord should hate, has caused me to insist the more upon it, especially that foolish spring the Cameronian march!'—Life and Death of three Famous Worthies, etc., by Peter [Patrick] Walker, 12mo, p. 59.

It may be here observed, that some of the milder class of Cameronians made a distinction between the two sexes dancing separately, and allowed of it as a healthy and not unlawful exercise; but when men and women mingled in sport, it was then called promiscuous dancing, and considered as a scandalous enormity.

NOTE 17.—MUSCHAT'S CAIRN, p. 107

Nicol Muschat, a debauched and profligate wretch, having conceived a hatred against his wife, entered into a conspiracy with another brutal libertine and gambler, named Campbell of Burnbank (repeatedly mentioned in Pennecuick's satirical poems of the times), by which Campbell undertook to destroy the woman's character, so as to enable Muschat, on false pretences, to obtain a divorce from her. The brutal devices to which these worthy accomplices resorted for that purpose having failed, they endeavored to destroy her by administering medicine of a dangerous kind, and in extraordinary quantities. This purpose also failing, Nicol Muschat, or Muschet, did finally, on the 17th October, 1720, carry his wife under cloud of night to the King's Park, adjacent to what is called the Duke's Walk, near Holyrood Palace, and there took her life by cutting her throat almost quite through, and inflicting other wounds. He pleaded guilty to the indictment, for which he suffered death. His associate, Campbell, was sentenced to transportation for his share in the previous conspiracy. See MacLaurin's Criminal Cases, pp. 64 and 738.

In memory, and at the same time execration, of the deed, a cairn, or pile of stones, long marked the spot. It is now almost totally removed, in consequence of an alteration on the road in that place.

NOTE 18.—HANGMAN OR LOCKMAN, p. 132

Lockman, so called from the small quantity of meal (Scottice, lock) which he was entitled to take out of every boll exposed to market in the city. In Edinburgh the duty has been very long commuted; but in Dumfries the finisher of the law still exercises, or did lately exercise, his privilege, the quantity taken being regulated by a small iron ladle, which he uses as the measure of his perquisite. The expression lock, for a small quantity of any readily divisible dry substance, as corn, meal, flax, or the like, is still preserved, not only popularly, but in a legal description, as the lock and gowpen, or small quantity and handful, payable in thirlage cases, as in town multure.

NOTE 19.—THE FAIRY BOY OF LEITH, p. 144

This legend was in former editions inaccurately said to exist in Baxter's World of Spirits; but is, in fact, to be found in Pandemonium, or the Devil's Cloyster; being a further blow to Modern Sadduceism, by Richard Bovet, Gentleman, 12mo, 1684 (p. 172, etc.) The work is inscribed to Dr. Henry More. The story is entitled, 'A remarkable passage of one named the Fairy Boy of Leith, in Scotland, given me by my worthy friend, Captain George Burton, and attested under his own hand,' and is as follows:—

'About fifteen years since, having business that detained me for some time in Leith, which is near Edenborough, in the Kingdom of Scotland, I often met some of my acquaintances at a certain house there, where we used to drink a glass of wine for our refection. The woman which kept the house was of honest reputation amongst the neighbours, which made me give the more attention to what she told me one day about a Fairy Boy (as they called him) who lived about that town. She had given me so strange an account of him that I desired her I might see him the first opportunity, which she promised; and not long after, passing that way, she told me there was the Fairy Boy but a little before I came by; and casting her eye into the street, said, "Look you, sir, yonder he is at play with those other boys," and designing him to me, I went, and by smooth words, and a piece of money, got him to come into the house with me; where, in the presence of divers people, I demanded of him several astrological questions, which he answered with great subtility, and through all his discourse carryed it with a cunning much above his years, which seemed not to exceed ten or eleven. He seemed to make a motion like drumming upon the table with his fingers, upon which I asked him, whether he could beat a drum, to which he replied, "Yes, sir, as well as any man in Scotland; for every Thursday night I beat all points to a sort of people that used to meet under yonder hill" (pointing to the great hill between Edenborough and Leith. "How, boy," quoth I; "what company have you there?" "There are, sir," said he, "a great company both of men and women, and they are entertained with many sorts of musick besides my drum; they have, besides, plenty of variety of meats and wine; and many times we are carried into France or Holland in a night, and return again; and whilst we are there, we enjoy all the pleasures the country doth afford." I demanded of him, how they got under that hill. To which he replied, "That there were a great pair of gates that opened to them, though they were invisible to others, and that within there were brave large rooms, as well accommodated as most in Scotland." I then asked him how I should know what he said to be true? Upon which he told me, he would read my fortune, saying I should have two wives, and that he saw the forms of them sitting on my shoulders; that both would be very handsome women. As he was thus speaking a woman of the neighbourhood, coming into the room, demanded of him what her fortune should be? He told her that she had had two bastards before she was married; which put her in such a rage that she desired not to hear the rest. The woman of the house told me that all the people in Scotland could not keep him from the rendesvous on Thursday night, upon which, by promising him some more money, I got a promise of him to meet me at the same place, in the afternoon the Thursday following, and so dismist him at that time. The boy came again at the place and time appointed, and I had prevailed with some friends to continue with me if possible to prevent his moving that night; he was placed between us, and answered many questions, without offering to go from us, until about eleven of the clock he was got away unperceived of the company; but I suddenly missing him, hasted to the door and took hold of him, and so returned him into the same room; we all watched him, and on a sudden he was again got out of the doors. I followed him close, and he made a noise in the street as if he had been set upon; but from that time I could never see him. GEORGE BURTON.

NOTE 20.—INTERCOURSE OF THE COVENANTERS WITH THE INVISIBLE

WORLD, p. 145

The gloomy, dangerous and constant wanderings of the persecuted sect of Cameronians naturally led to their entertaining with peculiar credulity the belief that they were sometimes persecuted, not only by the wrath of men, but by the secret wiles and open terrors of Satan. In fact, a flood could not happen, a horse cast a shoe, or any other the most ordinary interruption thwart a minister's wish to perform service at a particular spot, than the accident was imputed to the immediate agency of fiends. The encounter of Alexander Peden with the devil in the cave, and that of John Semple with the demon in the ford, are given by Peter [Patrick] Walker, almost in the language of the text.

NOTE 21.—JOCK DALGLEISH, p. 155

Among the flying leaves of the period there is one called 'Sutherland's Lament for the loss of his post,—with his advice to John Daglees, his successor.' He was whipped and banished, 25th July, 1722.

There is another, called 'The Speech and Dying Words of John Dalgleish, Lockman, alias Hangman, of Edinburgh,' containing these lines:—

> Death, I've a favour for to beg,
> That ye wad only gie a fleg,
>   And spare my life;
> As I did to ill-hanged Megg,
>
> (Laing.)

NOTE 22.—CALUMNIATOR OF THE FAIR SEX, p. 176

The journal of Graves, a Bow Street officer, despatched to Holland to obtain the surrender of the unfortunate William Brodie, bears a reflection on the ladies somewhat like that put in the mouth of the police officer Sharpitlaw. It had been found difficult to identify the unhappy criminal; and when a Scotch gentleman of respectability had seemed disposed to give evidence on the point required, his son-in-law, a clergyman in Amsterdam, and his daughter, were suspected by Graves to have used arguments with the witness to dissuade him from giving his testimony; on which subject the journal of the Bow Street officer proceeds thus:

'Saw then a manifest reluctance in Mr. ——, and had no doubt the daughter and parson would endeavour to persuade him to decline troubling himself in the matter, but judged he could not go back from what he had said to Mr. Rich.—NOTA BENE. No mischief but a woman or a priest in it—here both.'

NOTE 23.—THE MAGISTRATES AND THE PORTEOUS MOB, p. 185

The Magistrates were closely interrogated before the House of Peers, concerning the particulars of the Mob, and the patois in which these functionaries made their answers sounded strange in the ears of the Southern nobles. The Duke of Newcastle having demanded to know with what kind of shot the guard which Porteous commanded had loaded their muskets, was answered naively, 'Ow, just sic as ane shoots dukes and fools with.' This reply was considered as a contempt of the House of Lords, and the Provost would have suffered accordingly, but that the Duke of Argyle explained that the expression, properly rendered in English, means ducks and waterfowl.

NOTE 24.—SIR WILLIAM DICK OF BRAID, p. 186

This gentleman formed a striking example of the instability of
human prosperity. He was once the wealthiest man of his time in
Scotland, a merchant in an extensive line of commerce, and a farmer
of the public revenue; insomuch that, about 1640, he estimated his fortune at £200,000 sterling. Sir William Dick was a zealous Covenanter,
and in the memorable year 1641 he lent the Scottish Convention of
Estates one hundred thousand merks at once, and thereby enabled
them to support and pay their army, which must otherwise have
broken to pieces. He afterwards advanced £20,000 for the service of
King Charles, during the usurpation; and having, by owning the royal
cause, provoked the displeasure of the ruling party, he was fleeced of
more money, amounting in all to £65,000 sterling.

Being in this manner reduced to indigence, he went to London to
try to recover some part of the sums which had been lent on government security. Instead of receiving any satisfaction, the Scottish
Croesus was thrown into prison, in which he died 19th December, 1655.
It is said his death was hastened by the want of common necessaries.
But this statement is somewhat exaggerated, if it be true, as is commonly said, that, though he was not supplied with bread, he had
plenty of pie-crust, thence called "Sir William Dick's necessity."

The changes of fortune are commemorated in a folio pamphlet,
entitled The Lamentable Estate and Distressed Case of Sir William
Dick [1656.] It contains several copperplates, one representing Sir
William on horseback, and attended with guards as Lord Provost of
Edinburgh, superintending the unloading of one of his rich argosies;
a second exhibiting him as arrested and in the hands of the baliffs; a
third presents him dead in prison. The tract is esteemed highly valuable by collectors of prints. The only copy I ever saw upon sale was
rated at £30.

NOTE 25.—MEETING AT TALLA LINNS, p. 190

This remarkable convocation took place upon 15th June, 1682, and
an account of its confused and divisive proceedings may be found in
Michael Shields's Faithful Contendings Displayed. Glasgow, 1780, p.
21. It affords a singular and melancholy example how much a metaphysical and polemical spirit had crept in amongst these unhappy sufferers, since, amid so many real injuries which they had to sustain,
they were disposed to add disagreement and disunion concerning the
character and extent of such as were only imaginary.

NOTE 26.—DOOMSTER OR DEMPSTER OF COURT, p. 236

The name of this officer is equivalent to the pronouncer of doom
or sentence. In this comprehensive sense, the judges of the Isle of
Man were called Dempsters. But in Scotland the word was long restricted to the designation of an official person, whose duty is was to
recite the sentence after it had been pronounced by the Court, and
recorded by the clerk; on which occasion the Dempster legalized it
the words of form, 'And this I pronounce for doom.' For a length
of years, the office, as mentioned in the text, was held in commendam
with that of the executioner; for when this odious but necessary officer of justice received his appointment he petitioned the Court of
Justiciary to be received as their dempster, which was granted as a
matter of course.

The production of the executioner in open court, and in presence
of the wretched criminal, had something in it hideous and disgusting
to the more refined feelings of later times. But if an old tradition of
the Parliament House of Edinburgh may be trusted, it was the following anecdote which occasioned the disuse of the dempster's
office:—

It chanced at one time that the office of public executioner was
vacant. There was occasion for some one to act as dempster, and,
considering the party who generally held the office, it is not wonderful that a locum tenens was hard to be found. At length one Hume,
who had been sentenced to transportation for an attempt to burn his

own house, was induced to consent that he would pronounce the doom on this occasion. But when brought forth to officiate, instead of repeating the doom to the criminal, Mr. Hume addressed himself to their lordships in a bitter complaint of the injustice of his own sentence. It was in vain that he was interrupted, and reminded of the purpose for which he had come hither. 'I ken what ye want of me weel enough,' said the fellow, 'ye want me to be your dempster; but I am come to be none of your dempster; I am come to summon you, Lord T——, and you, Lord E——, to answer at the bar of another world for the injustice you have done me in this.' In short, Hume had only made a pretext of complying with the proposal, in order to have an opportunity of reviling the Judges to their faces, or giving them, in the phrase of his country, 'a sloan.' He was hurried off amid the laughter of the audience, but the indecorous scene which had taken place contributed to the abolition of the office of dempster. The sentence is now read over by the clerk of the court, and the formality of pronouncing doom is altogether omitted.—

The usage of calling the dempster into court by the ringing of a hand bell, to repeat the sentence on a criminal, is said to have been abrogated in March, 1773 (Laing).

NOTE 27.—JOHN DUKE OF ARGYLE AND GREENWICH, p. 239

This nobleman was very dear to his countrymen, who were justly proud of his military and political talents, and grateful for the ready zeal with which he asserted the rights of his native country. This was never more conspicuous than in the matter of the Porteous Mob, when the Ministers brought in a violent and vindictive bill for declaring the Lord Provost of Edinburgh incapable of bearing any public office in future for not foreseeing a disorder which no one foresaw, or interrupting the course of a riot too formidable to endure opposition. The same bill made provision for pulling down the city gates and abolishing the city guard,—rather a Hibernian mode of enabling them better to keep the peace within burgh in future.

The Duke of Argyle opposed this bill as a cruel, unjust and fanatical proceeding, and an encroachment upon the privileges of the royal burghs of Scotland, secured to them by the treaty of Union. 'In all the proceedings of that time,' said his Grace, 'the nation of Scotland treated with the English as a free and independent people; and as that treaty, my lords, had no further guarantee for the due performance of its articles but the faith and honour of a British Parliament, it would be both unjust and ungenerous should this House agree to any proceedings that have a tendency to injure it.'

Lord Hardwicke, in reply to the Duke of Argyle, seemed to insinuate that his Grace had taken up the affair in a party point of view, to which the nobleman replied in the spirited language quoted in the text. Lord Hardwicke apologized. The bill was much modified, and the clauses concerning the dismantling the city and disbanding the guard were departed from.

A fine of £2,000 was imposed on the city for the benefit of Porteus's widow. She was contented to accept three-fourths of the sum, the payment of which closed the transaction. It is remarkable that in our day the magistrates of Edinburgh have had recourse to both those measures, held in such horror by their predecessors, as necessary steps for the improvement of the city.

It may be here noticed, in explanation of another circumstance mentioned in the text, that there is a tradition in Scotland that George II., whose irascible temper is said sometimes to have hurried him into expressing his displeasure par voie du fait, offered to the Duke of Argyle, in angry audience, some menace of this nature, on which he left the presence in high disdain, and with little ceremony. Sir Robert Walpole, having met the Duke as he retired and learning the cause of his resentment and discomposure, endeavored to reconcile him to what had happened by saying, Such was his Majesty's way, and that he often took such liberties with himself without meaning any harm.' This did not mend matters in MacCallummore's eyes, who replied, in great disdain, 'You will please to remember, Sir Robert, the infinite distance there is betwixt

you and me.' Another frequent expression of passion on the part of
the same monarch is alluded to in the old Jacobite song:

> The fire shall get both hat and wig,
> As oft times they've got a' that.

NOTE 28.—MURDER OF THE TWO SHAWS, p. 242

In 1828, the Author presented to the Roxburgh Club a curious volume containing the Proceedings in the Court-Martial held upon John, Master of Sinclair . . . for the Murder of Ensign Schaw . . . and Captain Schaw . . . 17th October 1708 (Laing).

NOTE 29.—BORROWING DAYS, p. 275

The three last days of March, old style, are called the Borrowing Days; for, as they are remarked to be unusually stormy, it is feigned that March had borrowed them from April, to extend the sphere of his rougher sway. The rhyme on the subject is quoted in Leyden's edition of the Complaynt of Scotland.—

> March said to Aperill
> I see three hogs upon a hill:
>
> . . . .
>
> But when the borrowed days were gane,
> The three silly hogs came hirplin' hame.
>
> (Laing.)

NOTE 30.—BUCKHOLMSIDE CHEESE, p. 379

The hilly pastures of Buckholm, which the Author now surveys,

> Not in the frenzy of a dreamer's eye,

are famed for producing the best ewe-milk cheese in the south of Scotland.

NOTE 31.—EXPULSION OF THE BISHOPS FROM THE SCOTTISH CONVENTION, p. 391

For some time after the Scottish Convention had commenced its sittings, the Scottish prelates retained their seats, and said prayers by rotation to the meeting, until the character of the Convention became, through the secession of Dundee, decidedly Presbyterian. Occasion was then taken on the Bishop of Ross mentioning King James in his prayer, as him for whom they watered their couch with tears—on this the Convention exclaimed, they had no occasion for spiritual lords, and commanded the bishops to depart and return no more, Montgomery of Skelmorley breaking at the same time a coarse jest upon the scriptural expression used by the prelate. Davie Deans's oracle, Patrick Walker, gives this account of their dismission:—'When they came out, some of the Convention said they wished that the honest lads knew that they were put out, for then they would not win away with hael [whole] gowns. All the fourteen gathered together with pale faces and stood in a cloud in the Parliament Close. James Wilson, Robert Neilson, Francis Hislop, and myself were standing close by them. Francis Hislop with force thrust Robert Neilson upon them; their heads went hard upon one another. But there being so many enemies in the city fretting and gnashing their teeth, waiting for an occasion to raise a mob, where undoubtedly blood would have been shed, and we having laid down conclusions among ourselves to guard against giving the least occasion to all mobs, kept us from tearing of their gowns.

'Their graceless Graces went quickly off, and neither bishop nor curate was seen in the streets; this was a surprising sudden change not to be forgotten. Some of us would have rejoiced more than in great sums to have seen these bishops sent legally down the Bow, that they might have found the weight of their tails in a tow to dry their hose-soles; that they might know what hanging was, they having been active for themselves, and the main instigators to all the mischiefs, cruelties, and bloodshed of that time, wherein the streets of Edinburgh and other places of the land did run with the innocent, precious dear blood of the Lord's people.'—Life and Death of three famous Worthies (Semple, etc.), by Patrick Walker, Edin 1727, pp. 72, 73.

NOTE 32.—HALF-HANGED MAGGIE DICKSON, p. 399

In the Statistical Account of the Parish of Inveresk (vol. xvi. p. 34), Dr. Carlyle says, 'No person has been convicted of a capital felony since the year 1728, when the famous Maggy Dickson was condemned and executed for child-murder in the Grassmarket of Edinburgh, and was restored to life in a cart on her way to Musselburgh to be buried . . . She kept an ale-house in a neighboring parish for many years after she came to life again, which was much resorted to from curiosity.' After the body was cut down and handed over to her relatives, her revival is attributed to the jolting of the cart, and according to Robert Chambers—taking a retired road to Musselburgh, 'they stopped near Peffer-mill to get a dram; and when they came out from the house to resume their journey, Maggie was sitting up in the cart.' Among the poems of Alexander Pennecuick, who died in 1730 (1722), is one entitled 'The Merry Wives of Musselburgh's Welcome to Meg Dickson;' while another broadside, without any date or author's name, is called 'Margaret Dickson's Penitential Confession,' containing these lines referring to her conviction:

> Who found me guilty of that barbarous crime,
> And did, by law, end this wretched life of mine;
> But God . . . did me preserve, etc.

In another of these ephemeral productions hawked about the streets, called 'A Ballad by J—n B——s,' are the following lines:

> Please peruse the speech
>
> Of ill-hanged Maggy Dickson.
> Ere she was strung, the wicked wife
> Was sainted by the flamen (priest),
> But now, since she's return'd to life,
> Some say she's the old samen.

In his reference to Maggie's calling 'salt' after her recovery, the Author would appear to be alluding to another character, who went by the name of 'saut Maggie,' and is represented in one or more old etchings about 1790 (Laing).

NOTE 33.—MADGE WILDFIRE, p. 403

In taking leave of the poor maniac, the Author may observe that the first conception of the character, though afterwards greatly altered, was taken from that of a person calling herself, and called by others Feckless Fannie [weak or feeble Fannie], who always travelled with a small flock of sheep. The following account, furnished by the persevering kindness of Mr. Train, contains probably all that can now be known of her history, though many, among whom is the Author, may remember having heard of Feckless Fannie in the days of their youth.

'My leisure hours,' says Mr. Train, 'for some time past have been mostly spent in searching for particulars relating to the maniac called Feckless Fannie, who travelled over all Scotland and England, between the years 1767 and 1775, and whose history is altogether so like a romance, that I have been at all possible pains to collect every particular that can be found relative to her in Galloway or in Ayrshire.

'When Feckless Fannie appeared in Ayrshire, for the first time, in the summer of 1769, she attracted much notice from being attended by twelve or thirteen sheep, who seemed all endued with faculties so much superior to the ordinary race of animals of the same species as to excite universal astonishment. She had for each a different name, to which it answered when called by its mistress, and would likewise obey in the most surprising manner any command she thought proper to give. When travelling, she always walked in front of her flock, and they followed her closely behind. When she lay down at night in the fields, for she would never enter into a house, they always disputed who should lie next to her, by which means she was kept warm, while she lay in the midst of them; when she attempted to rise from the ground, an old ram, whose name was Charlie, always claimed the sole right of assisting her; pushing any that stood in his way aside, until he arrived right before his mistress; he then bowed his head nearly to the ground that she might lay her hands on his horns, which were very large; he then lifted her gently from the ground by raising his head. If she chanced to leave her flock feeding, as soon as they discovered she was gone, they all began to bleat most piteously, and would continue to do so until she returned; they would then testify their joy by rubbing their sides against her petticoat, and frisking about.

'Feckless Fannie was not, like most other demented creatures, fond of fine dress; on her head she wore an old slouched hat, over her shoulders an old plaid, and carried always in her hand a shepard's crook; with any of these articles she invariably declared she would not part for any consideration whatever. When she was interrogated why she set so much value on things seemingly so insignificant, she would sometimes relate the history of her misfortune, which was briefly as follows:—

' "I am the only daughter of a wealthy squire in the north of England, but I loved my father's shepard, and that has been my ruin; for my father, fearing his family would be disgraced by such an alliance, in a passion mortally wounded my lover with a shot from a pistol. I arrived just in time to receive the last blessing of the dying man, and to close his eyes in death. He bequeathed me his little all, but I only accepted these sheep to be my sole companions through life, and this hat, this plaid, and this crook, all of which I will carry until I descend into the grave."

'This is the substance of a ballad, eighty-four lines of which I copied down lately from the recitation of an old woman in this place, who says she has seen it in print, with a plate on the title page representing Fannie with her sheep behind her. As this ballad is said to have been written by Lowe, the author of "Mary's Dream," I am surprised that it has not been noticed by Cromek in his Remains of Nithsdale and Galloway Song; but he perhaps thought it unworthy of a place in his collection, as there is very little merit in the composition; which want of room prevents me from transcribing at present. But if I thought you had never seen it, I would take an early opportunity of doing so.

'After having made the tour of Galloway in 1769, as Fannie was wandering in the neighborhood of Moffat, on her way to Edinburgh, where, I am informed, she was likewise well known, Old Charlie, her favorite ram, chanced to break into a kale-yard, which the proprietor observing, let loose a mastiff, that hunted the poor sheep to death. This was a sad misfortune; it seemed to renew all the pangs which she formerly felt on the death of her lover. She would not part from the side of her old friend for several days, and it was with much difficulty she consented to allow him to be buried; but, still wishing to pay a tribute to his memory, she covered his grave with moss, and fenced it round with osiers, and annually returned to the same spot, and pulled the weeds from the grave and repaired the fence. This is altogether like a romance; but I believe that it is really true that she did so. The grave of Charlie is still held sacred even by the schoolboys of the present day in that quarter. It is now, perhaps, the only instance of the law of Kenneth being attended to, which says, "The grave where anie that is slaine lieth buried, leave untilled for seven years. Repute every grave hollie so as thou be well advised, that in no wise with thy feet thou tread upon it."

'Through the storms of winter, as well as in the milder season of the year, she continued her wandering course, nor could she be prevented from doing so, either by entreaty or promise of reward. The late Dr. Fullarton of Rosemount, in the neighbourhood of Ayr, being well acquainted with her father when in England, endeavoured, in a severe season, by every means in his power, to detain her at Rosemount for a few days until the weather should become more mild; but when she found herself rested a little, and saw her sheep fed, she raised her crook, which was the signal she always gave for the sheep to follow her, and off they all marched together.

'But the hour of poor Fannie's dissolution was now at hand, and she seemed anxious to arrive at the spot where she was to terminate her mortal career. She proceeded to Glasgow, and, while passing through that city, a crowd of idle boys, attracted by her singular appearance, together with the novelty of seeing so many sheep obeying her command, began to torment her with their pranks, till she became so irritated that she pelted them with bricks and stones, which they returned in such a manner that she was actually stoned to death between Glasgow and Anderston.

'To the real history of this singular individual, credulity has attached several superstitious appendages. It is said that the farmer who was the cause of Charlie's death shortly afterwards drowned himself in a peat-hag; and that the hand with which a butcher in Kilmarnock struck one of the other sheep became powerless, and withered to the very bone. In the summer of 1769, when she was passing by New Cumnock, a young man, whose name was William Forsyth, son of a farmer in the same parish, plagued her so much that she wished he might never see the morn; upon which he went home and hanged himself in his father's barn. And I doubt not many such stories may yet be remembered in other parts where she had been.'

So far Mr. Train. The Author can only add to this narrative, that Feckless Fannie and her little flock were well known in the pastoral districts.

In attempting to introduce such a character into fiction, the Author felt the risk of encountering a comparison with the Maria of Sterne; and, besides, the mechanism of the story would have been as much retarded by Feckless Fannie's flock as the night march of Don Quixote was delayed by Sancho's tale of the sheep that were ferried over the river.

The Author has only to add that, notwithstanding the preciseness of his friend Mr. Train's statement, there may be some hopes that the outrage on Feckless Fannie and her little flock was not carried to extremity. There is no mention of any trial on account of it, which, had it occurred in the manner stated, would have certainly taken place; and the Author has understood that it was on the Border she was last seen, about the skirts of the Cheviot Hills, but without her little flock.

NOTE 34.—SHAWFIELD'S MOB, p. 407

In 1725 there was a great riot in Glasgow on account of the malt tax. Among the troops brought in to restore order was one of the independent companies of Highlanders levied in Argyleshire, and distinguished in a lampoon of the period as 'Campbell of Carrick and his Highland thieves.' It was called Shawfield's Mob, because much of the popular violence was directed against Daniel Campbell, Esq., of Shawfield, M. P., provost of the town.

NOTE 35.—DEATH OF FRANCIS GORDON, p. 428

This exploit seems to have been one in which Patrick Walker prided himself not a little; and there is reason to fear that that excellent person would have highly resented the attempt to associate another with him in the slaughter of a King's Life Guardsman. Indeed, he would have had the more right to be offended at losing any share of the glory, since the party against Gordon was already three to one, besides having the advantage of firearms. The manner in which he vindicates his claim to the exploit, without committing himself by a direct statement of it, is not a little amusing. It is as follows:—

'I shall give a brief and true account of that man's death, which I did not design to do while I was upon the stage. I resolve, indeed (if the Lord will), to leave a more full account of that and many other remarkable steps of the Lord's dispensations towards me thorow my life. It was then commonly said that Francis Gordon was a volunteer out of wickedness of principles, and could not stay with the troop, but was still raging and ranging to catch hiding suffering people. Meldrum and Airly's troops lying at Lanark upon the first day of March, 1682, Mr. Gordon and another wicked comrade, with their two servants and four horses, came to Kilcaigow, two miles from Lanark, searching for William Caigow and others under hiding. Mr. Gordon, rambling throw the town, offered to abuse the women. At night, they came a mile further to the easter seat, to Robert Muir's, he being also under hiding. Gordon's comrade and the two servants went to bed, but he could sleep none, roaring all night for women. When day came, he took only his sword in his hand, and came to Moss-platt, and some men [who had been in the fields all night] seeing him, they fled, and he pursued. James Wilson, Thomas Young, and myself, having been in a meeting all night, were lyen down in the morning. We were alarmed, thinking there were many mo than one; he pursued hard, and overtook us. Thomas Young said, "Sir, what do ye pursue us for?" He said, "He was come to send us to hell." James Wilson said, "That shall not be, for we will defend ourselves." He said, "That either he or we should go to it now." He run his sword furiously thorow James Wilson's coat. James fired upon him, but missed him. All the time he cried, "Damn his soul!" He got a shot in his head out of a pocket pistol, rather fit for diverting a boy than killing such a furious, mad, brisk man, which, notwithstanding, killed him dead. The foresaid William Caigow and Robert Muir came to us. We searched him for papers, and found a long scroll of sufferers' names, either to kill or take. I tore it all in pieces. He had also some Popish books and bonds of money, with one dollar, which a poor man took off the ground; all which we put in his pocket again. Thus, he was four miles from Lanark, and near a mile from his comrade, seeking his own death, and got it. And for as much as we have been condemned for this, I could never see how any one could condemn us that allows of self-defence, which the laws both of God and nature allow to every creature. For my own part, my heart never smote me for this. When I saw his blood run, I wished that all the blood of the Lord's stated and avowed enemies in Scotland had been in his veins. Having such a clear call and opportunity, I would have rejoiced to have seen it all gone out with a gush. I have many times wondered at the greater part of the indulged, lukewarm ministers and professors in that time, who made more noise of murder when one of these enemies has been killed, even in our own defence, than of twenty of us being murdered by them. None of these men present was challenged for this but myself. Thomas Young thereafter suffered at Machline, but was not challenged for this; Robert Muir was banished; James Wilson outlived the persecution; William Caigow died in the Canongate tolbooth, in the beginning of 1685. Mr. Wodrow is misinformed, who says that he suffered unto death' (pp. 165-167).

NOTE 36.—TOLLING TO SERVICE IN SCOTLAND, p. 445.

In the old days of Scotland, when persons of property, unless they happened to be nonjurors, were as regular as their inferiors in attendance on parochial worship, there was a kind of etiquette in waiting till the patron or acknowledged great man of the parish should make his appearance. This ceremonial was so sacred in the eyes of a parish beadle in the Isle of Bute, that the kirk bell being out of order, he is said to have mounted the steeple every Sunday, to imitate with his voice the successive summonses which its mouth of metal used to send forth. The first part of this imitative harmony was simply the repetition of the words 'Bell bell, bell bell,' two or three times, in a manner as much resembling the sound as throat of flesh could imitate throat of iron. 'Bellum! bellum!' was sounded forth in a more urgent manner; but he never sent forth the third and conclusive peal, the varied tone of which is called in Scotland the 'ringing-in,' until the two principal heritors of the parish approached, when the chimes ran thus:—

Bellum Bellellum,
Bernera and Knockdow's coming!
Bellum Bellellum,
Bernera and Knockdow's coming!

Thereby intimating that service was instantly to proceed.—

Mr. Macinlay of Borrowstounness, a native of Bute, states that Sir Walter Scott had this story from Sir Adam Ferguson; but that the gallant knight had not given the lairds' titles correctly—the bellman's great men being Craich, Drumbuie, and Barnernie.—1842 (Laing).

NOTE 37.—RATCLIFFE, p. 502

There seems an anachronism in the history of this person. Ratcliffe, among other escapes from justice, was released by the Porteous mob when under sentence of death; and he was again under the same predicament when the Highlanders made a similar jail-delivery in 1745. He was too sincere a Whig to embrace liberation at the hands of the Jacobites, and in reward was made one of the keepers of the tolbooth. So at least runs a constant tradition.

GLOSSARY

OF

WORDS, PHRASES, AND ALLUSIONS.

ABUNE, ABOON. above

ACQUENT, acquainted

AD AVISANDUM, reserved for consideration

ADJOURNAL, BOOKS OF See Books of Adjournal

ADMINICLE, a collateral proof

AGAIN, in time for, before

AIN, own

AIR, early

AIRD'S MOSS, the scene of a skirmish in Ayrshire, on 20th July 1680

AIRN, iron

AIRT, to direct, point out the way

AITH, oath

AITS, oats

ALLENARLY, solely

A-LOW, on fire

ALTRINGHAM, THE MAYOR OF (p. 439), a well-known Cheshire proverb

AMAIST, almost

ANCE, ANES, once

ANDRO FERRARA, a Highland broadsword

ANKER, 10 wine gallons

ANSARS, helpers; particularly those inhabitants of Medina who he ped Moha'mmed when he fled from Mecca

ANTI-JACOBIN, George Canning, the statesman, in whose burlesque play, The Rovers: or, Double Arrangement, printed in The Anti-Jacobin, the ghost of Prologue's, not the Author's, grandmother appears

AQUA MIRABILIS, the wonderful water, a cordial made of spirits of wine and spices

ARGYLE, EARL OF, HIS ATTEMPT OF 1686, his rising in Scotland in

suport cf Monmouth in 1685

ARNISTON CHIELD. Robert Dundas of Arniston, the elder, succeeded Duncan Forbes of Culloden as Lord President in 1748

ARRIAGE AND CARRIAGE, a pɔrase in old Scotch leases, but bearing no precise meaning

ASSEMBLY OF DIVINES, the Westminster Confession of Faith, which, with the Longer and Shorter Catechisms, constitute the s andards of doctrine of the Presbyterians

ARTES PERDITAE, lost arts

AUGHT, eight; AUGHTY-NINE, the year 1689

AUGHT, possession

AULD, old; AULD SORROW, old wretch

AVA, at all

AWMOUS, alms

AWMRIE, the cupboard

BACK-CAST, a reverse, misfortune

BACK-FRIEND, a supporter, abettor

BALFOUR'S PRACTIQUES; OR A SYSTEM OF THE MORE ANCIENT LAW OF SCOTLAND (1754), by Sir James Balfour, Pre ident of the Court of Session in 1567

BAND, bond

BARK, BAWTIE. Compare Sir D. Lindsay's Complaynt of Bagsche . . . to Bawtie, the King's Best Belovit Dog

BARKENED, tanned

BARON BAILIE, the baron's deputy in a

burgh of barony

BATHER, to fatigue by ceaseless prating

BAULD, brave, hardy

BAUSON-FACED, having a white spot on the forehead

BAWBEE, a halfpenny

BAXTER, a baker

BEAN-HOOL, bean-hull, pod

BECHOUNCHED, be-flounced, decked out in ridiculous fashion

BEDRAL, beadle, sexton

BEDREDDIN HASSAN. See Arabian Nights: 'Noureddin and his Son'

BEEVER, Belvoir, the seat of the Duke of Rutland, on the border of Leicestershire

BELYVE, directly

BEND-LEATHER, thick sole-leather

BENEFIT OF CLERGY, the right to claim, 1 ke the clergy, exemption from the civil courts

BEN THE HOUSE, inside, into the inner room

BESS OF BEDLAM, a female lunatic.

BESTIAL, horned cat le.

BICKER, a wooden vessel.

BIDE, wait, stay; bear, rest under; BIDE A WEE, wait a minute.

BIEN, comfortable

BIGGONETS, a lady's headdress

BIKE, a hive, swarm

BINK, a wall plate-rack

BIRKIE, a lively fellow, young spark

BIRTHNIGHT, the court festival held on the evening of a royal birthday

BITTOCK, a little bit, proverbially a considerable distance

BLACK, DR DAVID, a zealous Scottish Presbyterian in the reign of James VI.

BLAIR, ROBERT, a prominent Presbyterian minister, of Bangor in Ireland

BLINK, a glance

BLUE PLUMS, bullets

BLUIDY MACKENZIE, Sir George, Lord Advocate, and an active prosecutor of the Cameronians in the reign of Charles II.

BOODLE, 1-6 of a penny

BOBIE, the lowest scholar on the form, a dunce

BOOKS OF ADJOURNAL, containing the minutes and orders, especially of adjournal, of the Court of Judiciary of Scotland, it being a peremptory court

BOOT-HOSE, coarse blue worsted hose worn in place of boots

BOUKING-WASHING, the annual washing of the family linen in a pecular ley (bouk)

BOUNTITH, a perquisite

BOUROCK, a mound, hillock

BOW, a boll (measure)

BOW-HEAD, leading from the High Street to the Grassmarket in Edinburgh

BOWIE, a milk-pail

BRAW, brave, fine, good; BRAWS, fine clothes

BRECHAM, collar of a cart-horse

BROCKIT (COW), with a speckled face

BROGUE, a highland shoe

BROO, taste for, opinion of

BROSE, oatmeal over which boiling water has been poured

BRUCE, ROBERT, of Edinburgh, a champion of spiritual authority in the reign of James VI.

BRUGH AND LAND, town and country

BRUILZIE, a scuffle, tumult

BRUNSTANE, brimstone, sulphur

BUCKHOLMSIDE, a village of Roxburghshire close to Galashiels

BULLER, to bellow

BULL OF PHALARIS, an invention for roasting people alive, devised by Phalaris, ruler of Agrigentum in ancient Sicily—so tradition

BULLSEGG, a gelded bull

BUSK, to dress up, arrange

BYE, besides; past

BYRE, cow-house, cowshed

CA', to call

CAESAREAN PROCESS, a surgical operation to secure delivery (as in the case of Caesar)

CAG, a small cask

CAIRD, a strolling tinker

CALENDAR WANTING AN EYE See Arabian Nights: 'Story of the First Calendar'

CALLANT, a lad

CALLER, fresh

CALLIVER-MEN, men armed with muskets

CAMBRIAN ANTIQUARY, Thomas Pennant, the traveller

CAMPVERE SKIPPER, a trader to Holland, Compvere or Camphire, on the Island of Walcheren, was the seat of a privileged Scottish trading factory from 1444 to 1795

CANNY, propitious, auspicous

CANTY, mirthful, jolly

CAPTION, a writ to imprison a debtor

CARCAKE, or CARECAKE, a small cake baked with eggs and eaten on Shrove Tuesday in Scotland

CARLE, a fellow

CARLINE, a beldam, old woman

CAROLINE PARK. See Roystoun

CARRIED, the mind wavering, wandering

CARRITCH, the Catechism

CAST, lot fate; a throw; a lift, ride

CAST-BYE, a castaway

CA'-THROW, an ado, a row

CATO'S DAUGHTER, Porcia, wife of Brutus, who stabbed Caesar

CATO THE CENSOR, the celebrated Roman, wrote a book about rural affairs

CAULD, cold

CAULDRIFE, chilly

CAUTELOUS, cautious, careful

CELA ETOIT AUTREFOIS, etc. (p. 538), it used to be so, but we have changed all that now

CESSIO BONORUM, surrender of effects

CHAFTS, jaws

CHALDERS, an old dry measure—nearly 16 qrs. of corn

CHAMBER OF DEAS, the best bedroom

CHANCE-MEDLEY, an undesigned occurrence not purely accidental

CHANGE-HOUSE, a small inn

CHAPPIT, struck (of a clock)

CHAPIT BACK, beaten, deterred, daunted

CHEVERONS, gloves

CHIELD, a young fellow

CHOP, a shop

CLACHAN, a Highland hamlet

CLAISE, CLAES, CLAITHS, clothes

CLARISSIMUS ICTUS, one who is a famous lawyer

CLAT, a hoard of money

CLAVERS, foolish gossip

CLAW UP MITTENS, to rebuke severely, tell home truths

CLECKIT, hatched

CLEEK, to catch, seize

CLEUGH, a ravine

CLOSE-HEAD, the entrance of a blind alley, a favorite rendezvous for gossips

CLUBBED (of hair), gathered into a club-shaped knot at the back of the head

CLUTE, a hoof, single beast

COCCEIAN, a follower of John Coccelus of Leyden (d. 1669), who held that the Old Testament shadowed forth the history of the Christian Church

COCKERNONIE, a lady's topknot

COD, a pillow, cushion

COGNOSCE, to examine judicially for insanity

COLUMELLA, a Roman writer on agriculture and similar topics

COMMENTARIES ON SCOTTISH CRIMINAL JURISPRUDENCE, 1797, by David Hume, Baron of the Exchequer in Scotland

COMUS, by Milton

CONDESCENDENCE, an enumeration of particulars, a Scots law term

CONFESSIO EXTRAJUDICIALIS, etc (p. 242), an unofficial confession is a nullity, and cannot be quoted in evidence

COUCH A HOGSHEAD, to lie down to sleep

COUP, to overturn, to barter

COUTHY, agreeable, pleasing

COWLEY'S COMPLAINT, his poem with that title, stanza 4

COWT, a colt
CRACK, gossip, talk
CRAFT, a croft, small farm
CRAIGMILLAR, a castle near Edinburgh, a residence of Queen Mary
CREAGH, stolen cattle; a foray
CREPE, to curl, crimp
CREWELS, CRUELS, scrofulous swellings on the neck
CRIFFEL, a mountain on the Scottish side of the Solway. When Skiddaw is capped with clouds, rain falls soon after oa Criffel
CRINING, pining
CROOK A HOUGH, to bend a joint, especially the knee-joint
CRUPPEN, crept
CUFFIN, QUEER, a justice of peace
CUIVIS EX POPULO, one of the people
CULL, a fool
CUMMER, a comrade, gossip
CUMRAYS, or CUMBRAES, in the Firth of Clyde
CURCH, a woman's cap
CU'ROSS, Culross, a village on the Firth of Forth
CURPEL, crupper
CUTTER'S LAW, thieves' rogues' law
CUTTY QUEAN, a worthless young woman

DAFFING, frolicsome jesting
DAFT, crazy, beside oneself
DAIDLING, trifling; loitering
DAIKER, to saunter, jog along
DALKEITH, one of the seats of the Duke of Buccleuch
DALLAS ON STILES: OR, SYSTEM OF STILES AS NOW PRACTICABLE WITHIN THE KINGDOM OF SCOTLAND, 1697, by George Dallas, sometime deputy-keeper of the privy seal of Scotland
DARG, a day's work
DEAS, CHAMBER OF, the best bedroom
DEAVE, to deafen
DEBITO TEMPORE, at the proper time
DE DIE IN DIEM, from day to day
DEEVIL'S BUCKIE, a limb of Satan
DEIL HAET, the devil a bit

DEMENS, QUI NIMBOS, etc. (p. 1), the madman, who sought to rival the rainclouds and the inimitable thunder, with brazen din and the tread of horny-hoofed steeds
DEMI-PIQUE SADDLE, one with low peaks or points
DING, to knock
DINNLE, a thrilling blow
DIRL, a thrilling knock
DIT, to stop, close up (the mouth)
DITTAY, indictment
DIVOT, a thin flat turf; DIVOT-CAST, a turf-pit
DOCH AN' DORROCH, a stirrup-cup, parting-cup
DOER, an agent, factor
DOITED, stupid, confused
DONNARD, stupid
DONNOT, or DONAUGHT, a good-for-nothing person
DOO, a dove
DOOKIT, ducked
DOOMS, utterly
DOOR-CHEEK, the door-post
DOUBLE CARRITCH, the Larger Catechism of the Church of Scotland
DOUCE, quiet, respectable
DOUGHT, was able to
DOUR, stubborn, obstinate
DOW, to be able; DOWNA, do not like to
DREICH, slow, leisurely
DROW, a qualm
DRY MULTURE, a duty of corn paid to a miller
DUDS, ragged clothes; DUDDY, ragged
DULCIS AMARYLLIDIS IRAE, the anger of gentle woman
DUNCH, to jog or punch
D'UNE GRANDE DAME, of a great lady, lady of fashion
DUNLOP (CHEESE), in Ayrshire
DURK, or DIRK, a Highlander's dagger
DYESTER, a dyer

ECLAIRCISSEMENT, an explanation
EDICT NAUTAE, etc., in ancient Rome, imposed thoughtless person liability for loss or damage to property committed to carriers, innkeepers, and stable-keepers
EE, eye; EEN, eyes
EFFECTUAL CALLING. See The Shorter Catechism, Qu. 31

EFFEIR OF, equivalent to
EIK, to add
ELSHIN, an awl
EME, uncle
EMERY, JOHN, actor who excelled in rustic parts, and played Dandie Dinmont, Ratcliffe, and similar characters of Scott's novels
ENEUCH, ENEUGH, ENOW, enough
ENLEVEMENT, the abduction of the heroine
ETHWALD, one of Joanna Baillie's Plays on the Passions, this one turning on Ambition. The passage is from Part I. Act iii. Sc. 5
EXAUCTORATE, to dismiss from service
EX JURE SANGUINIS, by blood, heredity

FAMA CLAMOSA, notoriety
FARINACEUS, or FARINACIUS, Prosper Farinaci, a celebrated Roman writer on criminal jurisprudence, lived 1544-1618
FASH, trouble; to trouble; FASHIOUS, troublesome
FASHERIE, trouble
FATHERS CONSCRIPT, the senators of ancient Rome; here the chosen fathers (of the town)
FATUUS, FURIOSUS, NATURALITER IDIOTA, foolish, mad, born idiot
FAULD, to fold
FAUSE MONTEATH, the reputed betrayer of Wallace
FAUT, fault
FECKLESS, insignificant, feeble
FEND, to provide
FERGUSON, or FERGUSSON, ROBERT, Scottish poet, born 1750, died 1774
FILE, to foul, disorder
FIT, foot
FLATS AND SHARPS, sword, using the sword
FLEE, a fly
FLEG, a fright
FLISKMAHOY, a giddy, thoughtless person
FLOW-MOSS, a morass See Note 9 to Bride of Lammermoor
FORANENT, directly opposite to
FORBEAR, forefather
FORBES, DUNCAN, appointed Lord President of the Court of Session in 1737. See footnote, p. 403
FORBYE, besides

FORE-HAMMER, sledge-hammer

FORGATHER, to come together, become intimate

FORPIT, ¼th of a peck

FOU, full, drunk correctly Figgate Whins, a tract of sand hillocks and whin bushes between Portobello

FRIGATE WHINS, more and Leith

FUGIT, etc. (p. 185), time

GAIT-MILK, goat-milk

GAITTS, or GYTES, or GETTS, brats, urchins Pilgrim's Progress

GALLIO. See Acts xviii.

GAIUS (LINCOLN-SHIRE), the Host in 12-27

GAME ARM, a crooked, lame arm

GANG, to go

gardez l'eau, an Edinburgh cry when dirty water was thrown out a

GARE-BRAINED, giddy, thoughtless

GATE, GAIT, way, direction, manner; NAE GATE, nowhere

GAUN, going

GAUN PLEAS, pending lawsuits

GAUNT, to yawn

GAWSIE, grand, fine

GAY SURE, pretty sure; GAY AND WELL, pretty well

GEE, TO TAKE THE, to take the pet, turn petty

GEAR, property

GIE, give; GIEN, given

GIF-GAF, mutual giving

GILPY, GILPIE, a lively young girl

GIRDLE, a circular iron plate for baking scones, cakes

GIRN, to grin, grimace

GLAIKS, TO FLING THE, GARDYLOO, from French IN ONE'S EEN, to dodge flying beyond recall

FYKE, to move restlessly in the same place window

GLEDE, GLED, the kite

GLEG, active, keen; GLEG AS A GLED, hungry as a hawk

GLIFF, an instant

GLIM, a light, hence anything at all

GLOWER, to stare hard

BORBALS, a suburb on

GORBALS, a suburb on the south side of Glasgow

GOUSTY, dreary, haunted

GOUTTE, a drop

GOWAN, a dog daisy

GOWDEN, golden

GOWPEN, a double handful of meal, the per-

quisite of a miller's servant

GRAITH, apparatus of any kind, harness

GRANTHAM GRUEL, a Lincolnshire proverb, ridiculing exaggerations of speech

GRAT, wept

GREE, to agree

GREE, pre-eminence

GREESHOCH, a turf fire without flame, smouldering embers

GREET, to cry, weep

GREY-PEARD, or GREY-BEARD, a stone jug for holding ale or liquor

GUDEMAN, the husband, head of the house

GUDESIRE, grandfather

GUDEWIFE, the wife, head of the household

GUIDE, to treat, direct; GUIDING, treatment

GULLEY, a large knife

GUSES GRASS, the area of grass a goose grazes during the summer

GUTTER-BLOOD, one meanly born

GYBE, a pass

GYTE, a young boy; CLEAN GYTE, quite crazy

HADDEN, held

HADDO'S HOLE, a portion of the nave of the ancient collegiate church, now incorporated with St. Giles' Cathedral, Edinburgh

HAFFETS, temples

HAFFLINS, young, entering the teens

HAFT, custody; to establish, fix

HAGBUTS OF FOUND, firearms made of cast metal (found)

HALE, or HILL, whole entire

HALLAN, a partition in a Scotch cottage

HAND-WALED, remarkable, notorious

FOOTMAN, RUNNING.

HARLE, to trail, drag

HAUD, hold

HAVINGS, behaviour, manners

HAWKIT, white-faced, having white spots or streaks

HEAL, healthy, felicity; HEALSOME, wholesome

HELLICAT, wild, desperate

HEMPIE, a rogue

HERITORS, the landowners in a Scotch parish

HERSE, hoarse

HERSHIP, plundering by armed force

HET, hot

HIGHLAND HOST. See Highlandmen in 1677,

in glossary to Old Mortality

HINNY, honey, a term of affection

HIRPLIN', limping

HIT (at backgammon), a game, a move in the game

HOG, a sheep older than a lamb that has not been shorn

HOLBORN HILL BACKWARD, the position of criminals on their way to execution at Tyburn

HOLLAND, FENS OF, the southern division of Lincolnshire, adjoining the Wash

HOMOLOGATE, to approve, ratify, sanction

HOW, a hollow

HOWDIE, a midwife

HOWFF, a haunt

HUSSY, a housewife case, needlecase

ILK, ILKA, each; ILK, the same name; ILKA-DAY, every-day

IMPOSTHUMES, abscesses, collections of pus

IN BYE, inside the house

IN COMMENDAM, in conjunction with

IN CONFITENIEM, etc. (p. 242), the judge's function ceases when there is confession of the crime

INGAN, an onion

INGINE, ingenuity, talent

IN HOC STATU, in this case

INIMICITIAM CONTRA, etc. (p. 264), enmity against all mankind

IN INITIALIBUS, to begin with

IN LOCO PARENTIS, in place of the parent

INPUT, contribution

IN REM VERSAM, chargeable against the estate

INTER APICES JURIS, on high points of law

INTER PARIETES, within doors

INTER RUSTICOS, a mere rustic

INTONUIT LAEVUM, the thunder is heard on the left

INTROMIT WITH, to interfere with

JAGG, a prick

JAMES'S PLACE OF REFUGE, in 1595

JARK, a seal

JAUD, a jade

JINK, a dodge, lively trick

JO, a sweetheart

JOW, to toll

JUS DIVINUM, divine right

KAIL, or KALE, cabbage, broth made of greens, dinner; KAIL-WORM, caterpillar; KALE-YARD, vegetable garden

KAIN, or CANE, a rent paid in kind

KAME, to comb

KAY'S CARICATURES, in A Series of Portraits and Caricature Etchings of Old Edinburgh characters, by John Kay, 1837-38; new ed., 1877

KEELYVINE, a lead pencil

KENSPECKLE, conspicuous, odd

KILLING TIME, the Covenanters' name for the period of Claverhouse's persecutions in the West of Scotland

KITTLE, ticklish, slippery

KNAVESHIP, a small due in meal paid to the under-miller

KYE, cows

KYTHE, to seem or appear

LAIKING, sporting, larking

LAMOUR, amber

LANDWARD, i n l a n d, country-bred

LANE, alone; THEIR LANE, themselves

LAUCH, law

LAVROCK, a lark

LAWING, the account, bill

LAWYERS FROM HOLLAND. Many of the Scottish lawyers and doctors were educated at Leyden and Utrecht in the 17th and 18th centuries

LAY, ON THE, on the lookout

L E A P, LAURENCE. Y O U ' R E L O N G ENOUGH. An adaptation or extension of the proverbial Lazy Lawrence or Long Lawrence

LEASING-MAKING, high treason

LEE, a lie

LEICESTER BEANS, extensively grown in Leicestershire; hence the proverb, 'Shake a Leicestershire man by the collar, and you shall hear the beans rattle in his belly

LENNOX, THE, a former county of Scotland, embracing Dumbartonshire and parts of Stirlingshire, Perthshire, and Renfrewshire

LESE-MAJESTY, treason

LIFT, the sky

LIMMER, a jade, scoundrel

LINCOLNSHIRE GAIUS. See Gaius

LINN, a cascade, waterfall

LIPPEN, to rely upon, trust to

LIVINGSTONE, JOHN, an influential Presbyterian during the Commonwealth, minister at Stranraer and Ancrum

LIVINGSTONE, J O H N, SAILOR IN BORROW-STOUNNESS. See Patrick Walker's Life of Peden, p. 107

LOCK, the perquisite of a servant in a mill, usually a handful (lock) or two of meal

LOCKERMACHUS, the local pronunciation in Scott's day of Longformacus, a village in Berwickshire

LOCKINGTON WAKE, a Leicestershire yearly merrymaking or festival

LOCO TUTORIS, in the place of a guardian

LOOF, the palm of the hand

LOOT, let, permitted

LORD OF SEAT, a judge

LORD OF STATE, a nobleman

LOUND, quiet, tranquil

LOUNDER, to thump, beat

LOW, a flame

LOWE, JOHN, author of 'Mary's Dream,' died 1798. See biography in Cromek, Remains of Galloway Song (1810)

LUCKIE, a title given to old women

LUCKIE DAD, grandfather

LUG, the ear

LUM, a chimney

LYING-DOG, a kind of setter

MACHEATH, a highwayman, the hero of Gay's Beggar's Opera

MAGG (COALS), to give short quantity, purloining the difference

MAGGOT, a whim, crochet

MAGNA EST VERITAS, &c. (p. 11), truth is great, and prevail it will

MAIL, to stain

MAIL-DUTIES, r e n t; MAILING, or MAIL, a farm rent

MAIR BY TOKEN, especially as

MAISTRY, mastery, power

MAN-SWORN, perjured

MANTY, mantle

MANU...NON BELLE, &c. (p. 488), it is not becoming to lift one's hand in jest and over the wine. See Catullus, xii.

MARITORNES, a coarse serving - wench whom Don Quixote mistook for a lady of noble birth

MARK OF BELLGRAVE. See 'Same again,' etc

MASHACKERED, clumsily cut, hacked

MASS JOHN, a parson

MATHEUS, or MATTHAEUS, ANTON, one of a family of celebrated German writers on jurisprudence, the 'second' Anton professor at Utrecht from 1636 to 1654

MAUKIN, a hare

MAUN, must

MAUNDER, to talk incoherently, nonsense

MAUT, malt

MAW, to mow

MEAL-ARK, meal-chest

MEAR, a mare

MELL, to meddle

MEN OF MARSHAM, etc., a Lincolnshire proverb, signifying disunion is the cause of ill-success

M E N S E F U', becoming, mannerly

MERK—1s. 1 1-3d.

MERSE, Berwickshire

MESSAN, a lapdog, cur

M E X I C A N MONARCH. Guatemozin, the Aztec emperor who, when put to the torture by Cortes, reproached a fellowsufferer, groaning with anguish, by asking, 'Do you think then I am enjoying my bed (lit. bath) of flowers?'

MIDDEN, a dunghill

MILE, SCOTTISH, about nine furlongs

MILLED, robbed

MINNIE, mamma

MISCA', to abuse, malign

MISGUGGLE, to disfigure

MISSET, displeased, out of humour

MISS KATIES, mosquitoes

MISTER, want

MIXEN, a dunghill

MOE, or Mo, more

MONSON, SIR WILLIAM, admiral, fought against the Spaniards and Dutch in the reigns of Elizabeth and James I.

MONTEATH, FAUSE, the reputed betrayer of Wallace to the English

MORISON'S DECISIONS, with fuller title, Decisions of the Court of Session [Edinburgh].....in the form of a Dictionary, by W. M. Morison, 40 vols., 1801-11

MOSS-HAG, a pit in a peat moor

MOTTY, full of motes

'MUCH HAVE I FEAR'D,' etc. (p. 10), from Crabbe's Borough, Letter xx.

MUCKLE, much

MUIR-ILL, a disease amongst black cattle

MUIR - POOTS, y o u n g grouse

MULL, a snuff-box

MULTURE, DRY. See Dry Multure

MUTCH, a woman's cap

MUTCHKIN, a liquid measure, containing ¾ pint

NAUTAE, CAUPONES, &c. See Edict Nautae

NEGER, nigger

NEMO ME IMPUNE LACESSIT, no one wounds me with impunity—the motto that accompanies the thistle, the badge of the crown of Scotland

NICK MOLL BLOOD, to cheat the gallows

NIFFERING, haggling; NIFFER, an exchange; PUT HIS LIFE IN A NIFFER, put his life at stake, in jeopardy

NIHIL INTEREST DE POSSESSIONE, the question of possession is immaterial

NOITED, rapped, struck smartly

NON CONSTAT, it is not certain

NON CUIVIS, etc. (p. 44), it is not every one that can gain admittance to the (select) society of Corinth

NOOP, the bone at the elbow-joint

NOR' LOCH, a swamp in Edinburgh, now Princes Street Gardens

NOWTE, cattle

OE, a grandchild

ON-DING, a heavy fall (of snow)

OPTAT EPHIPPIA, etc. (p. 45), the sluggish ox wishes for the horse's trappings

ORDINAR, AFTER HER, as is usual with her

ORMOND, James Butler, first Duke of, was for seven years in disfavour through the intrigues of enemies

ORRERY, a mechanism representing the motions of the planets

OUT-BYE, out of doors; beyond, without

OUTGATE, ostentatious display

OUTSIGHT AND INSIGHT PLENISHING, goods belonging to the outside and inside of the house respectively

OWER-BYE, over the way

OWRELAY, a cravat

PADDER, a highwayman; ON THE PAD, a highwayman on the look-out for victims

PAIK, a blow

PAIP, the Pope

PAITRICK, a partridge

PALMER, JOHN, of Bath, greatly improved the mail-coaches in the end of the 18th century

PAROCHINE, parish

PARSONAGE, a contribution for the support of a parson

PAR VOIE DU FAIT, by assault, act of violence

PASSEMENTS, gold, silver, or silk lace; PASSEMENTED, laced

PAUVRE HONTEUX, poor and humble-minded man

PAVE, the road, highway

PEARLIN-LACE, bone lace, made of thread or silk

PEAT, PROUD, a person of intolerable pride

PEAT-HAG, a pit in a peat moor

PEDEN, ALEXANDER, a celebrated Covenanting leader. See Old Mortality, Note 38

PEEBLE, to pelt with stones

PEN-GUN, CRACKING LIKE A, gabbling like a penguin

PENNANT, THOMAS, a keenly observant naturalist and traveller of the 18th century

PENNECUICK, ALEXANDER, M. D., of Newhall, near Edinburgh, author of Historical Account of the Blue Blanket; died in 1722

PENNY, SCOTS—1-12th of a penny English

PENNYSTANE, a stone quoit

PENNY WEDDING, one at which the expenses are met by the guests' contributions. See Burt's Letters from the North of Scotland, Letter xi.

PENTLAND, or RULLION GREEN, where Dalziel routed the Galloway Whigs in 1666

PEREGRINE (BERTIE), LORD WILLOUGHBY, one of Elizabeth's captains. The lines quoted are from 'The Brave Lord Willoughby' in Percy's Reliques

PERFERVIDUM, etc. (p. 12), the fiery nature of the Scots

PER VIGILIAS ET INSIDIAS, by snares and ambush

PESSIMI EXEMPLI, the worst of precedents, examples

PETTLE, to indulge, pamper

PIBROCH, a bagpipe tune, usually for the gathering of a clan

PICKLE IN THINE AIN POKENOOK, depend on thy own exertions

PICQUEERINGS, bickerings, disputes

PICTURESQUE. See Price

PIGG, an earthenware vessel, pitcher

PIKE, to pick

PILLION MAIL, baggage carried on a pillion

PIRN, a reel

PIT, put

PITCAIRN, DR., a well-known Edinburgh physician, died in 1713, who showed skill in writing Latin verse

PLACED MINISTER, one holding an ecclesiastical charge

PLACK, one-third of a penny

PLAGUE, trouble, annoyance

PLANKED A CHURY, concealed a knife

PLEASAUNTS, or PLEASANCE, a part of Edinburgh between the Cowgate and Salisbury Crags

PLENISHING, furniture

PLOUGH-GATE, as much land as can be tilled by one plough

PLOY, a spree, game

POCK, a poke, bag

POCOCURANTE, an easygoing, indifferent person

POENA ORDINARIA, usual punishment

POET OF GRASMERE, Wordsworth

POFFLE, a small farm, piece of land

POINT DEVISE, in or with the greatest exactitude, propriety

POLLRUMPTIOUS, unruly, restive

PONTAGES, bridge-tolls

POORFU', powerful

POPPLING, purling, rippling

POQUELIN, the real name of Moliere

PORTEOUS MOB. The actual order of events was—Robertson's escape, 11th April, 1736; Wilson's execution, 14th April; Queen's pardon for Porteous reached Edinburgh 2d September; riot took place 7th September; Porteous's execution was fixed for 8th September

POW, the head

PRICE'S APPROPRIATE PHRASE, PICTURESQUE—an allusion to Sir Uvedale Price's Essay on the Picturesque, 1796

PRIGG, to entreat, beg for
PROKITOR, a procurator, solicitor
PROPINE, a gift
PUND SCOTS—1s. 8d.
PURN, a burn, stream
PYKIT, picked, pilfered

QUADRELLE TABLE, a game at cards, not unlike ombre with a fourth player
QUARRY HOLES, where duels were frequently fought and female criminals sometimes drowned, at the foot of Calton Hill, not far from Holyrood Palace, Edinburgh
QUEAN, a young woman
QUEER CUFFIN, a justice of peace
QUEERING, quizzing, making fun
QUEER THE NOOSE, THE STIFLER, escape the gallows
QUEY, a young cow
QUILLET, a quibble, subtlety
QUIVIS EX POPULO, any ordinary citzen
QUODAMMODO, in a manner, certain measure
QUOS DILIGIT CASTEGAT, whom He loveth He chasteneth
QUOTHA, forsooth

RABBLE, to mob
RANNEL-TREES, a beam across the fireplace for suspending a pot on
RAPPING, swearing falsely
RARI APPARENT NANTES, etc. (p. 4), they appear swimming, widely scattered, in the vast deep
RATT-RHYME, doggerel verses, repeated by rote
RAX, to stretch
RECKAN, pining, miserable
RED, to counsel, advise
REDDING UP, clearing up
REEK, smoke
REMEDIUM MISERABILE, sad remedy for misfortune
RENWICK, MR. JAMES, the last of the 'martyrs' of the Covenant, executed at Edinburgh on 17th February, 1688
RIDING OF PARLIAMENT, the procession of dignitaries on their way to open a new session
RIN, to run
RINTHEREOUT, a houseless vagrant

RIPE, to search
RIVE, to tear
ROKELAY, a short cloak
ROOMS, portions of land, to own or occupy
ROSA SOLIS, a cordial, formerly in great repute, made of spirits flavored with cinnamon, orange-flower, etc.
ROUPIT, hoarse
ROVING, raving
ROUPING, selling off, auctioning
ROWING, rolling, revolving
ROYSTOUN, a mansion belonging to the Duke of Argyle at Cramond, near Edinburgh; it stood in Caroline Park
RUBBIT, robbed
RUE, TAEN THE, repented of
RUFFLER, a bullying beggar or thief
RUNNING FOOTMAN. See Note 9 to Bride of Lammermoor

SACKLESS, innocent, guileless
SAIN, to bless
ST. NICHOLAS'S CLERKS, highwaymen
SAIR, sore, much
SALMONEOUS, a mythical king who,, arrogantly imitating Zeus, was slain by his own thunderbolt. See Demons, etc.
'SAME AGAIN, QUOTH MARK OF BELGRAVE,' a Leicestershire proverb. The story goes that a militia officer, exercising his men before the lord-lieutenant, became confused, and continued to order 'The same again'
SAMEN, THE OLD, the same as before
SARK, a shirt
SARK FOOT, the lower portion of the boundary stream between England and Scotland
SASSENACH, Saxon, that is, English
SAUNT, saint
SAUT, salt
SCAITH, SCATHE, harm
SCART, a scratch
SCLATE, slate
SCOMFISH, to suffocate
SCOUPING, skipping
SCOUR, to thrust (a knife)
SCRAUGIN', screeching, screaming
SCREED, a mass, string
SCRIMGEOUR, JOHN, minister of Kinghorn, resisted the authority of his bishop to depose him, in 1620

SCUD, a sudden shower
SED TRANSEAT, etc. (p. 218), but let it pass with other blunders
SEIL, to sile, strain
SHIP, to ooze
SELL O' YE, yourself
SET, to suit, become
SHANKIT, handled
SHOON, shoes
SIC, SICCAN, such
SIGHT FOR SAIR EEN, a most welcome sight
SIGNET, WRITER TO. See Writer
SILLY HEALTH, poorly
SIMMER, summer
SINDERED, separated, sundered
SINDRY, sundry, different
SINGLE CARRITCH, the Shorter Catechism of the Church of Scotland
SINGULI IN SOLIDUM, singly responsible for the whole
SIT DOUN WITH, endure, take quietly
SKAITH, harm, injury
SKAITHLESS, free from harm
SKEEL, skill, knowledge; SKEELY, skilful, knowing
SKELP, to slap, beat
SKIDDAW. See criffel
SKIN AND BIRN, wholly, in entirety
SKIRL, to screech, scream
SKULDUDDERY, breach of chastity, indecency
SLAKE, a smear
SLOAN, abuse, rating
SMACKED CALF-SKIN, kissed the Testament, taken a false oath
SNACK, a snatch of food
SNAP, a snack, hurried meal
SNAPPER, stumble, scrape, moral error
SNOG AND SNOD, neat and tidy
'SOMETHING THERE WAS,' etc. (p. 102). From Crabbe's The Borough. Letter xv.
SONSY, comfortable-looking, plump
SORTED, looked after, attended to
SOUGH, to sigh; a sigh, rumor
SOUP, a sup
SOUTHER, to solder
SOWENS, a sort of gruel made from the soured siftings of oatmeal
SPAEING, telling fortunes
SPEER, to inquire, ask
SPIEL, to climb
SPLEUCHAN, a Highland tobacco pouch

SPORRAN, a Highland purse of goatskin

STAIG, an unbroken horse

STAIR'S INSTITUTES, OR, INSTITUTIONS OF THE LAW OF SCOTLAND, by James Dalrymple, First Viscount Stair, President of the Court of Session, 1609-95, a celebrated Scotch law-book

STED, to place, fix

STERN, a star

STIRK, a steer

STOIT, to stagger

STOUP, a wooden drinking vessel

STOW, to crop, cut off

STRAUGHTED, stretched

STREIGHT, strait, trouble

STURE, rough, hardy

SUI GENERIS, of its own kind, special

SUMMUM BONUM, the chief, good, prime consideration

SUNKETS, victuals

SURFLEET ON THE WASH. The Three Tuns Inn on the marsh (inclosed in 1777) beside the Welland at Surfleet was a resort of smugglers

SWITHER, suspense, hesitation

SYND, to wash, rinse

SYNE, since, ago

SYNE AS SUNE, late as soon

TAILZIE, entail

TAIT, a lock (of wool)

TAM CARUM CAPUT, a person so dear

TAP, a top

TAPE OUT, to eke out, make a little go a long way

TAP IN MY LAP (take up) my baggage and be off

TAWPIE, an awkward girl, foolish wench

TAWSE, a strap cut into narrow thongs for whipping boys

TEIND, tithe

TEMPUS NEMINI, time (waits for) no man

TENDER, in delicate health

TEN-MARK COURT, former Scotch small debt court for sums not exceeding ten merks (11s. 2d.) and servants' wages

TENT, care; TAK TENT, to take care

THATCH GROBY POOL WI' PANCAKES, a Leicestershire proverb, indicating an impossible promise or undertaking

THIRLAGE, the obligation to grind corn at a cer-

tain mill, and pay certain dues for its maintenance, etc.

THOLE, to suffer, endure

THRAWART, THRAWN, crabbed, ill-tempered

THRESHIE-COAT, a rough weather coat

THROUGH OTHER, confusedly, all together

THUMKINS, or THUMBIKINS, the thumb-screws

TIGHT, trim, neat

TINT, lost

TITTIE, a little pet, generally a sister

TOCHER, dowry

TOD, a fox

TOM OF LINCOLN, the large bell of Lincoln Cathedral

TONY LUMPKIN, a country clown in Goldsmith's She Stoops to Conquer

TOOM, empty; to empty, pour

TOUK, TOOK, tuck, beat (of a drum)

TOW, a rope

TOWN, a farm-house, with the outbuildings

TOY, a woman's cap

TRAIK, to dangle after

TREVISS, a bar or partition between two stalls in a stable

TRINQUET, or TRINKET, to correspond clandestinely, intrigue

TRIP TO THE JUBILEE, a comedy by G. Farquhar

TROW, to believe

TROWLING, rolling

TULLY, Marcus Tullius Cicero, the Roman orator

TURNPIKE STAIR, a winding or spiral stair

TUTOR DATIVE, a guardian appointed by a court or magistrate

TWAL, twelve

TWOMONT, a twelvemonth, year

TYNE, to lose; TYNE HEART TYNE A', to lose heart is to lose everything

ULAI. See Dan. viii. 2, 16

ULTRONEOUS, voluntary

UNCANNY, mischievous, not safe

UNCHANCY, dangerous, not safe to meddle with

UNCO, uncommon, strange, serious

UNSCYTHED CAR, the war-chariots of the ancient Britons and Gauls bore scythes affixed to their wheels

UPGANG, ascent

UPSIDES WI', quits with

USQUEBAUGH, whisky

UT FLOS IN SEPTIS, etc. (p. 487), as a flower springs up unseen in a walled garden

VALEAT QUANTUM, whatever it may be worth

VICARAGE, tithes

VIVAT REX, etc. (p. 276), long live the king, let the law takes its course

WA', a wall

WAD, a pledge, bet; to wager, bet

WAD, would

WADSET, a mortgage

WAE, woe; sorry; WAE-SOME, sorrowful, sad

WAFF, whisk, sudden puff

WAGGING, dangling by a piece of skin

WALE, to select, choose

WALLY-DRAIGLE, a poor weak creature, drone

WAMPISHING, brandishing, flourishing

WAN OUT, got out

WAN-THRIVEN, in a state of decline

WARE, to spend

WARSLE, WARSTLE, to wrestle

WASTRIFE, waste; WASTER, wasteful

WAT FINGER, TO BRING AFF WI' A. manage a thing very easily

WATNA, wot not

WAUFF, a passing glance, glimpse

WAUR, worse

WEAN, a young child, infant

WEBSTER, a weaver

WEIRD, destiny

WELL-TO-PASS, well-to-do

WHAUP IN THE RAPE, something wrong or rotten

WHEEN, a few, a parcel of

WHILES, sometimes

WHILLYWHA, to wheedle

WHIRRYING, hurrrying

WHISTER-POOP, a backhanded blow

WHISTLE ON HIS THUMB, completely disappointed

WHITTLE, a large knife

WHORN, a horn

WIGHT, WICHT, powerful, valiant

WILLYARD, wild, wilful, obstinate

WIMPLE, a wile, piece of craft, wrinkle

WINNA, will not

WOGGARWOLFE. See Ethwald

WOODIE, the halter

WORRIECOW, a hobgoblin
WORSET, worsted
WRITER TO THE SIG-
NET, a class of Scottish
law-agents, enjoying cer-
tain privileges
WUD, mad, violent
WULL-CAT, a wild cat
WUN, WON, WIN, to win,
get, gain
WUN OWER WI', to deal
with, get through with

WUSS, to wish
WUZZENT, wizened, with-
ered
WYND, a narrow pasage
or cul-de-sac
WYTE, blame

YEALD (COW), one whose
milk has dried up;
YEALD BEASTS, drapes

YEALDON, elding, fuel
YEARN, to cause to coagu-
late, make (cheese)
YERK, to bind tightly
YERL, an earl
YILL, ale
YILL-CAUP, a wooden
drinking-vessel

ZONE, a money-belt

INDEX

 INDEX